Louisa May Alcott Unmasked

Louisa May Alcott Unmasked

Collected Thrillers

Louisa May Alcott

Edited, and with an introduction, by Madeleine Stern

Northeastern University Press
BOSTON

Northeastern University Press

Library of Congress Cataloging in Publication Data
Alcott, Louisa May, 1832–1888.
Louisa May Alcott unmasked : collected thrillers / edited by
Madeleine Stern.
p.   cm.
Includes bibliographical references.
ISBN 1-55553-225-X (alk. paper)—ISBN 1-55553-226-8 (pbk. : alk. paper)
1. Detective and mystery stories, American.   2. Women—Social life
and customs—Fiction.   3. Man-woman relationships—Fiction.   4. Sex
role—Fiction.   I. Stern, Madeleine B., 1912–   .   II. Title.
PS1016.S73   1995
813'.4—dc20   95-1501

Designed by Dolly Carr

Composed in Perpetua by Coghill Composition, Richmond, Virginia.
Printed and bound by Edwards Brothers, Inc., Ann Arbor, Michigan.
The paper is Glatfelter Offset, an acid-free sheet.

MANUFACTURED IN THE UNITED STATES OF AMERICA
99   98   5   4

For Leona Rostenberg,
who began the unmasking

❧ Contents

❧ Acknowledgments

I WISH to express first of all my gratitude to the libraries that have supplied from their holdings of nineteenth-century story papers the original texts of Alcott's anonymous and pseudonymous narratives: the American Antiquarian Society Library, the Boston Public Library, Brown University Library, the Library of Congress, Houghton Library at Harvard University, the University of Michigan Library, the New-York Historical Society Library, the New York Public Library, Atkins Library at the University of North Carolina at Charlotte, the University of South Carolina Library, and Alderman Library at the University of Virginia.

The original discovery of the Alcott pseudonym and her clandestine relations with a Boston publishing house was made by my partner and lifelong friend, Dr. Leona Rostenberg. Since my gratitude to her is immeasurable, my acknowledgment of it must remain inadequate. To the literary detective Victor A. Berch of Marlborough, Mass., who located some of the anonymous Alcott stories, I also express my warm appreciation. To my co-workers, editors of the Alcott journals and letters, Prof. Joel Myerson of the University of South Carolina and Prof. Daniel Shealy of the University of North Carolina at Charlotte, I am deeply indebted. They have enriched the field of Alcott scholarship, and Dr. Shealy has also unearthed previously unknown Alcott thrillers and prepared their bibliography. Finally, to my editor, John Weingartner, I wish to express my appreciation of his perception and encouragement.

ᐧ Introduction

LOUISA MAY ALCOTT, America's best-loved author of juvenile fiction, led a double literary life. Proof of that extraordinary fact was announced more than fifty years ago.[1] Thirty years later, tangible evidence, in the form of the actual sensational narratives traced to Alcott's pen, was set before an avid reading public. In 1975 publication of *Behind a Mask: The Unknown Thrillers of Louisa May Alcott* disclosed to the world that, before the overwhelming success of *Little Women,* its author had written a succession of spellbinders that dealt in darkness and seemed to have little in common with the wholesome domesticity of her masterpiece.[2]

At intervals over the next twenty years, four additional volumes of Alcott thrillers appeared—tales of intrigue and suspense, violence and evil, jealousy and revenge, especially of woman's power and woman's passion. All those narratives had been written by the future author of *Little Women, Little Men,* and *Jo's Boys,* written for monetary reward as well as for psychological release, penned in secret out of the fabric of her own life and imaginings, and published anonymously or pseudonymously.[3]

Having a low regard for her sensational output, Alcott concealed her authorship of cliffhangers emblazoned in weekly story papers that yielded her anywhere from $25 to $100 apiece. Nonetheless, without divulging their authorship, she could not resist leaving intriguing clues that eventually tied the name of Louisa May Alcott to such narratives as "Pauline's Passion and Punishment," "A Marble Woman: or, The Mysterious Model," "Behind a Mask: or, A Woman's Power," "Taming a Tartar."

What and where were the clues that tantalized the scholar, quickened the pursuit, and led at last to the triumph of certain identification and the unveiling of a new literary image?

Once *Little Women* was published, the clues to the reality of Alcott's secret literary life were available for all to see. *Little Women* is not only a domestic novel and a classic of juvenile fiction, but autobiography. In it a Louisa May Alcott recast as Jo March relived much of her early life. In several remarkable chapters of that book she recounted her life as creator of sensational fiction and scattered clues to her career behind a mask.

In the chapter entitled "Secrets" in Part I of *Little Women,* published in October 1868, Jo whispers to her confidant, Laurie, that she has "left two stories with a newspaperman, and he's to give his answer next week." In due course the postman brings to the March door a copy of the *Spread Eagle* in which has been published a tale, "The Rival Painters," by Miss Josephine March. The author was indulging in fairly accurate recall, for her narrative "The Rival Painters. A Tale of Rome" had appeared on 8 May 1852 in the *Olive Branch.*

She was a bit more circumspect when, in Part II of *Little Women,* published in April 1869, she dredged up her more violent forays into sensationalism and transferred their authorship to Jo March. The chapter "Literary Lessons" describes the newspaper (the *Blarneystone Banner*) for which Jo March wove her gaudy stories as a "pictorial sheet" with the "melodramatic illustration of an Indian in full war costume, tumbling over a precipice with a wolf at his throat, while two infuriated young gentlemen . . . were stabbing each other close by, and a disheveled female was flying away in the background with her mouth wide open." Alcott describes too the type of story favored by that periodical: it "belonged to that class of light literature in which the passions have a holiday, and when the author's invention fails, a grand catastrophe clears the stage of one half the dramatis personae, leaving the other half to exult over their downfall." Moreover, mention is made of a "hundred-dollar prize offered in its columns for a sensational story," and here Alcott was remembering a "hundred-dollar prize" she herself had won for a narrative published anonymously in *Frank Leslie's Illustrated Newspaper* in 1863.[4]

The chapter "Literary Lessons" also contains the interesting statement that Jo March "began to feel herself a power in the house, for by the magic of a pen, her 'rubbish' turned into comforts for them all. *The Duke's Daughter* paid the butcher's bill, *A Phantom Hand* put down a new carpet, and the *Curse of the Coventrys* proved the blessing of the Marches in the way of groceries and gowns." Alcott is citing titles, but the citations are sly ones. Neither "The Duke's Daughter" nor the "Curse of the Coventrys" has ever surfaced. As for "A Phantom Hand," there is indeed a reference in the Alcott journals—not to "A Phantom Hand" but to "A Phantom Face," for which she earned $10 in 1859.[5] But neither the "Phantom Hand" nor the "Phantom Face" has been tracked down.

Finally, *Little Women* contains in the chapter "A Friend" the detailed description of the publication office and personnel of a newspaper called the *Weekly Volcano,* a periodical specializing in thrilling tales and sensation stories. Jo March's interview with editor Dashwood is recorded, along with her subsequent "plunge into the frothy sea of sensational literature": "Like most young scribblers, she went abroad for her characters and scenery; and banditti, counts, gypsies, nuns, and duchesses appeared upon her stage, and played their parts with as much accuracy and spirit as could be expected." It is then that Alcott proceeds to interject into her "plunge" into sensationalism the moral commentary doubtless expected from the author of *Little Women,* and she enlists the authoritative Professor Bhaer to lure Jo March away from the poisons of sub-literature.

Since the publication of *Little Women* some 125 years ago, generation after generation of readers has been aware that its heroine wrote sensation stories for money and abandoned them at the instigation of her future husband. Scholars, studying the pages of that novel, have deduced that, since it is largely autobiographical, both the *Weekly Volcano* and the *Blarneystone Banner* must have existed in some form, their pages electrified with such stories as "A Phantom Hand" and "The Duke's Daughter." But the actual newspapers for which Jo March's prototype had written, the titles of her stories, their precise nature, her pseudonym if she used one—all were mysteries, and despite the semi-revelations of *Little Women,* the products indeed of a phantom hand.

The clues to Alcott's double literary life were scattered not only in published but in unpublished sources. Researchers trailing her career could find, among the Alcott papers at Harvard's Houghton Library, a titillating letter she had written in 1862 to her young friend Alf Whitman, whom she would later weave into her portrait of Laurie. On June 22 she informed him:

> "*I intend to illuminate the Ledger with a blood & thunder tale as they are easy to 'compoze' & are better paid than moral & elaborate works of Shakespeare, so dont be shocked if I send you a paper containing a picture of Indians, pirates wolves, bears & distressed damsels in a grand tableau over a title like this 'The Maniac Bride' or 'The Bath of Blood. A thrilling tale of passion.' *"[6]

Such a clue served only to reinforce the suspicion that Alcott had produced blood-and-thunder stories, but it provided no specifics. Indeed, the picture described strongly resembles the melodramatic illustration she would assign in *Little Women* to the *Blarneystone Banner.*

Suspicion was further fired by a careful reading of the Alcott journals edited after her death for the author's admirers by the circumspect Ednah Dow Cheney.[7] Cheney, in accord with accepted nineteenth-century scholarship, did not hesitate to "improve" upon the original by altering punctuation, deleting personal names, and disregarding dates. She favored the use of ellipses for passages omitted, and, like Alcott herself in certain instances, the substitution of initials for names she believed might better be concealed. Hence, the clues discernible in the Cheney edition of Alcott's *Life, Letters, and Journals,* published in 1889, are as exasperating as they are titillating. There Alcott's 1862 journal announces that she "wrote two tales for L. I enjoy romancing to suit myself; and though my tales are silly, they are not bad; and my sinners always have a good spot somewhere. I hope it is good drill for fancy and language, for I can do it fast; and Mr. L. says my tales are so 'dramatic, vivid, and full of plot,' they are just what he wants." And a few months later she reports that "L. . . . wants more than I can send him." Mr. L. was not identified.

In 1865, the Cheney Alcott journals record: "Fell back on rubbishy tales, for they pay best, and I can't afford to starve on praise, when sensation stories are written in half the time and keep the family cosey." Again it is an enigmatic "L." who asks the tireless author "to be a regular contributor to his new paper," and bespeaks "two tales at once, $50 each." "Alcott brains seem in demand," the author writes, "whereat I sing 'Hallyluyer' and fill up my inkstand." Just how that inkstand was emptied is not explained. A year or more later, after a journey abroad as companion to an invalid, Alcott writes: "Fell to work on some stories, for things were, as I expected, behind-hand when the money-maker was away. Found plenty to do, as orders from E. . . . and several other offers waited for me." The Cheney-edited journals assure the researcher that Alcott did indeed write sensation stories, and that her publishers bore the initials L. and E. Such clues, however, offer up no proof but merely intensify suspicion.

Interviewed later in life by the author of *Across My Path: Memories of People I Have Known,* Alcott freely confessed her addiction to sensationalism but again failed to provide supporting facts:[8] "I think my natural ambition is for the lurid style," she declared. "I indulge in gorgeous fancies and wish that I dared inscribe them upon my pages and set them before the public." All such evidence, from letters, journals, and interview, confirms the strong belief that Louisa May Alcott not only indulged her "gorgeous fancies" but also "set them before the public." Confirmed suspicion is not proof. At that stage the pursuit had not yet yielded actual titles or bylines and had not named periodicals or publishers, and the flamboyant narratives that had flowed from a well-filled inkstand were still the work of a phantom hand.

The proof, the facts that turned suspicion to conviction, was provided not by letters *from* Louisa Alcott, but by letters *to* her. Why, insisting upon secrecy, she nonetheless kept such letters remains an enigma. They were written to her by her publishers, and perhaps she regarded them as business contracts. At all events, those are the letters that provided the facts of Alcott's double literary life. They were unearthed some fifty years ago by my partner, Dr. Leona Rostenberg, and it was her discovery that unmasked Louisa May Alcott and changed her image for all time.[9]

During the 1940s, when I was researching my biography of Louisa May Alcott,[10] Dr. Leona Rostenberg and I paid a visit to the Alcott collector Carroll Atwood Wilson, who, having shown us his treasures, advised me to complete my work on a Guggenheim Fellowship, and suggested to Leona that, since she was so immersed in the history of printing, she track down the printing history of the Alcott thrillers. "We all suspect she wrote them under some name or other. Now, Miss Rostenberg, you find out her pseudonym."

Not long after, we were both seated at a desk in Harvard's Houghton Library, examining the Alcott family papers and letters. Suddenly, the silence of that sedate room was pierced with a barbaric yawp. Miss Rostenberg had indeed found, in Box II of the Louisa May Alcott Manuscripts, the long-sought Alcott pseudonym, as well as the titles of three of Alcott's tales and the name of a periodical that had carried them. Among the manuscripts that had passed through Leona's hands were five letters written in 1865 and 1866 by James R. Elliott of the Boston publishing house of Elliott, Thomes & Talbot to Alcott, agreeing to publish her story "V.V." in the *Flag of Our Union,* declaring that her "Marble Woman" was "just splendid," accepting "Behind a Mask," and referring in passing to her nom de plume of "A. M. Barnard."[11]

All the necessary facts were there—they needed only to be verified. During World War II, however, most United States libraries placed their treasures in "safe keeping for the duration," and the best run of the *Flag of Our Union,* deposited in the Library of Congress, was therefore not available for examination. Leona Rostenberg was forced to content herself by announcing her discovery in the form of an article, "Some Anonymous and Pseudonymous Thrillers of Louisa M. Alcott," published in 1943 in the *Papers* of the Bibliographical Society of America.

The secret was out, though the stories had not yet been republished. Additional letters from the New York publishing house of Frank Leslie addressed to Alcott suggested that the author's immersion in sensationalism had been perhaps more prolonged and productive than had been surmised. A letter found in the Orchard House, where the Alcotts had lived, had been written in December 1862 by a Leslie editor informing Alcott that her story "Pauline" had been awarded a hundred-dollar prize.[12] Five years later another Leslie editor, in a letter now deposited at the University of Virginia, reported to Alcott: "Your favor of the 10th inst acknowledging the receipt of $72 for 'Taming a Tartar' came to hand this morning."[13] In between, other Leslie editors indicated in their letters to the author that she had become a fairly regular contributor to Leslie newspapers and that the publishing titan Frank Leslie would be glad to receive from her a sensational story every month at $50 each. As far as concealment of identity was concerned, the editors agreed that "if it woul[d be det]rimental to your [reputa]tion as a writer [for ch]ildren to have [your n]ame used on sensational stories Mr. Leslie would not desire any such sacrifice."[14]

The skeleton in Louisa Alcott's closet had been discovered. It was clothed in flesh and blood when, during the 1980s, a trio of editors (Myerson, Shealy, and Stern) reissued the Alcott journals, using original manuscripts wherever available, supplying full names for the initials employed by Alcott or by her editor Cheney, and publishing the "Notes and Memoranda" that recorded the titles of her stories and her earnings from them.

Now the missing pieces of the jigsaw materialized and fitted neatly into place. The elusive E. of the Cheney journals appeared clearly as the letter writer Elliott, who had accepted stories of A. M. Barnard. "Sold my Novelle to Elliot for $50," Alcott recorded in December 1864. "He offered 25 more if I'd let him put my *name to it,* but I wouldn't." A few months later she added, "Wrote a new Novelette for Elliott 'A Marble Woman' & got $75 for it."[15]

As for the "L." that represented Frank Leslie, allusions to his repeated requests and acceptances punctuate Alcott's journals of the 1860s. In August 1863 she wrote, "Leslie sent $40 for 'A Whisper in the Dark.' & wanted another—Sent 'A Pair of Eyes.' " The transaction proved successful, for in November Alcott noted: "Recieved $39 from Leslie for 'A Pair of Eyes,' not enough, but I'm glad to get even that. . . . Paid debts with it as usual." The productivity continued, along with the recording of it. In June 1864 the author "Wrote 'The Fate Of The Forrests' for Leslie who sent for a tale," and in March 1865 she agreed to be "a regular contributor" to his new paper, now identified as the *Chimney Corner,* "if he'd pay before hand." The prototype of Jo March wasted no time. The next month she "Sewed, cleaned house & wrote a story for Leslie, 'A Double Tragedy.' " In May, "after I'd done the scrubbing up I went to my pen & wrote Leslie's second tale [for the *Chimney Corner*] 'Ariel. A Legend of the Lighthouse.' " In December 1866 she added to her output for Leslie "a wild Russian story 'Taming a Tartar.' "[16]

Details not included in Alcott's journals are often found in her memoranda of earnings. In a ledger bound in half-leather she entered the titles of her stories and the payments for them. Throughout the 1860s the accounts were kept—the long list of melodramatic titles, from "A Pair of Eyes" and "Whisper In The Dark" to "Mrs. Vane's Charade" and "Honor's Fortune." In between there is an array of intriguing entries: "Pauline's Punishment," "Fate of the Forrests," "V.V.," "A Marble Woman," "Freaks of a Genius," "Behind a Mask," "Fatal Follies," "Perilous Play," with earnings that range from $25 to $100—earnings that would turn into comforts not for the March family, but for the Alcotts.

And so, in time, the jigsaw was completed and the clues led to identifications not only of story titles but of the periodicals where they were published. Just as Jo March's "necessity stories" had been traced, so too had her outlets, the *Weekly Volcano* and the *Blarneystone Banner*. The *Flag of Our Union,* published by a colorful trio who plied their trade on Boston's Washington Street, bears a close resemblance to both those fictional story papers. The mainstay of Elliott, Thomes & Talbot, it was a miscellaneous weekly designed for the home circle, and it specialized in riveting and violent narratives frequently concerned with convicts and opium addicts. Although editor James R. Elliott assured Alcott that it was "a literary paper that none need to blush for,"[17] she seems to have disagreed, since it was for the *Flag of Our Union* that she adopted her pseudonym of A. M. Barnard, using it in "A Marble Woman: or, The Mysterious Model," "Behind a Mask: or, A Woman's Power," and "The Abbot's Ghost: or, Maurice Treherne's Temptation."

Instead of using a pseudonym, Frank Leslie's periodicals issued nearly all Alcott's contributions anonymously. Moreover, her narratives for Leslie magazines far outnumber her writings for the *Flag of Our Union.* The New York publishing magnate could seldom resist launching a new periodical, with the result that in time his firm on Pearl Street distributed a fleet of weeklies and monthlies that catered to popular taste. In days when neither television nor cinema was available, the story paper provided escape and outlet. For the effusions of Louisa May Alcott it provided a steady market.[18]

The three Leslie papers for which Alcott wrote were designed for a mass readership, although they were geared to somewhat differing tastes. The flagship of the Leslie line was *Frank Leslie's Illustrated Newspaper,* launched in 1855. That weekly reported every cause célèbre from murders to executions, from revolutions to prizefights, from assassinations to scandals. And it did so graphically, running woodcuts or huge double-page engravings depicting the bloody battle scenes of the Civil War, volcanoes, earthquakes, and disasters domestic and foreign. The *Illustrated Newspaper* also offered serial stories that spiced domestic tranquillity with a touch of violence. For these it availed itself, from time to time, of the services of an anonymous writer from Concord, Massachusetts, who combined a strong imagination with a tireless pen. Alcott's anonymous contributions to the weekly began with her prizewinner, "Pauline's Passion and Punishment," and included a sequence of such page-turners as "A Whisper in the Dark" and "The Fate of the Forrests," "A Pair of Eyes" and "Taming a Tartar."

Frank Leslie's Chimney Corner was added to the Leslie list in 1865, and it was conceived and edited by Leslie's mistress and future wife, Miriam Squier. The *Chimney Corner* was touted as an illustrated fireside friend that would supply mothers with domestic tales, daughters with romances, sons with dramatic escapades, and youngsters with adventures and fairy tales. Where the *Illustrated Newspaper* concentrated upon national events, the *Chimney Corner* was almost exclusively a story paper. For the anonymous Louisa May Alcott it was a receptive outlet, and she contributed to its pages both serials and single-issue narratives, beginning with the periodical's first number, to which she contributed "A Double Tragedy. An Actor's Story." Between 1865 and 1869 the *Chimney Corner* carried several of her stories, including "Ariel. A Legend of the Lighthouse" and "A Nurse's Story," ending in 1869 with a short, unforgettable shocker entitled "Perilous Play."

For yet another Leslie periodical Alcott supplied nearly a dozen anonymous short tales. *Frank Leslie's Lady's Magazine,* under another name (*Frank Leslie's Ladies Gazette of Fashion*), had been the first of Leslie's periodical ventures. In 1863 Miriam Squier took over its editorship and molded it into a vehicle for women. Fashion news was highlighted—the attractions of Mexican mantelets and Ristori corselets, coiffures Creole and coiffures Josephine. Besides discoursing on "What Should be Worn and What Should Not," the *Lady's Magazine* found space not only to debate the question "Is Marriage A Lottery?" but to feature in each issue a short story that might have feminist undertones but must have feminine overtones. Here was a field for an author who could dilate upon the role of women in situations marked by conflict and passion, and offer against brilliant foreign backgrounds a modified and acceptable sensationalism. Between 1868 and 1870, the *Lady's Magazine* published anonymously a succession of short contributions by Alcott: "Doctor Dorn's Revenge," "Countess Varazoff," "Fatal Follies," "Fate in a Fan," "Which Wins?" "Honor's Fortune," "My Mysterious Mademoiselle," "Betrayed by a Buckle," "La Belle Bayadère."

All of Alcott's contributions to the *Flag of Our Union* and Leslie papers were published between 1863 and 1870. It is quite likely that earlier, during the 1850s, she had contributed sensation stories to yet another periodical—the *American Union*—and so served an apprenticeship in the genre. One of the letters discovered by Leona Rostenberg at Harvard's Houghton Library suggested this possibility. On 7 January 1865 James R. Elliott of the *Flag of Our Union* wrote to Alcott that his rate for payment would be "fully equal to $16.00 for a first page story in the 'American Union' which paper I think you have contributed to while it was under the management of Messrs. Graves & Weston."[19] Except for a few scattered issues preserved in libraries, the *American Union* seems to have been thumbed out of existence. One Alcott story can, however, be traced with certainty to its pages in 1858: "Marion Earle; or, Only An Actress!" Thanks to scholar-researcher Victor Berch, that narrative was found in the *New York Atlas,* where it was described as "From the American Union." In Alcott's memoranda of earnings for 1858, "Only An Actress" was listed as having brought in $6.[20] "Marion Earle; or, Only An Actress!" apparently set a pattern that was followed with numerous variations during the 1860s. Out of her experiences and her readings, her imagination and her observations, Louisa Alcott shaped a large corpus of sensational narratives for specialist papers.

By the mid-1970s enough of those narratives had been traced to warrant publication of a volume, *Behind a Mask: The Unknown Thrillers of Louisa May Alcott.* A year later a sequel was issued: *Plots and Counterplots: More Unknown Thrillers of Louisa May Alcott.* Not until 1988, when the Alcott manuscript journals were being edited, was the third volume of Alcott sensation stories presented to the public: *A Double Life: Newly Discovered Thrillers of Louisa May Alcott.* Three years later, after editor Daniel Shealy had discovered six additional narratives, *Freaks of Genius: Unknown Thrillers of Louisa May Alcott* appeared. Most recently, Northeastern University Press issued the fifth thriller anthology: *From Jo March's Attic: Stories of Intrigue and Suspense.*[21] The stories in that volume were located by Victor Berch from the elusive titles listed in the Alcott journals and brought to his attention.

Now at last the roster of Alcott thrillers has been brought together in one volume where the writer's backgrounds can be explored, her characters analyzed, and—most significantly—her themes investigated. In this omnibus publication readers can penetrate the mind behind the mask and savor the output of one writer's indefatigable double life.

What was the nature of the stories written in secret by the author of *Flower Fables, Hospital Sketches,* and *The Rose Family,* and published anonymously or pseudonymously in the weeklies of the 1860s? Their backgrounds and some of their characters reflect perhaps more of her imagining than of her observation. Alcott reveled in foreign backgrounds and set many of her narratives overseas. A haunted English abbey boasted, besides the "Abbot's Ghost" of the title, a thick-walled gallery and an arched stone roof, armored figures and screaming peacocks. An altogether different backdrop was painted for "Pauline's Passion and Punishment," the sequence of passion and punishment being enacted in an exotic paradise, a green wilderness with tamarind and almond trees, a Cuban *cafetal* with a tropical orchard of plantain and palm, not to mention a mansion surrounded by brilliant shrubs and flowers.

Europe provided the author with a multitude of romantic backgrounds—with few of which she was familiar. She had driven along the Promenade des Anglais in Nice in 1865 when she served as companion to a young invalid, Anna Weld.[22] A few years later, when Alcott sought a background for her story "Countess Varazoff," she summoned up that very promenade at the height of the season. For the most part, however, Alcott's settings stemmed from fancy bolstered by her readings and were often the result of purely imaginary voyages. Sybil Varna, the tamer of "Taming a Tartar," is taken to an estate in Volnoi, Russia. Details of Hindu background are scattered through several Alcott thrillers, "La Belle Bayadère" and especially "The Fate of the Forrests," a narrative based upon the horror of Hindu Thuggism. To the author and doubtless to her readers, exotic appurtenances and surroundings heightened the dramatic lives of fervid characters.

Those characters were drawn by a writer who could turn her imaginings and the episodes of her life into fiction. Her portrait of Kate Snow, the nurse-narrator in "A Nurse's Story," is in part a self-portrait, for Kate was "quick at reading faces" and "liked to study character, and fancied that [she] had some skill in understanding both faces and the natures of which they are the index." Alcott read faces, studied characters, understood natures, and portrayed them fairly realistically for readers of *Hospital Sketches* and *Little Women,* romantically for devourers of her thrillers. No matter how wild the plots she concocted, Alcott was more deeply concerned and more meticulous with character depiction, and her narratives were often carefully woven about problems of identity. She used broad brushstrokes to paint her dramatis personae, endowing an alluring heroine with magnificent Southern eyes, olive cheeks, and lips like pomegranate flowers, but such a heroine was usually more than a mere beauty. The luxuriant siren might combine a Spanish with a Saxon background; in her complex nature passion was coupled with conviction.

And so the gallery of femmes fatales who people so many Alcott shockers is studded with portraits of women strong-willed and imperious, experienced in sorrow, proud—women like Pauline of "Pauline's Passion and Punishment," the manipulating V.V., the three-dimensional Jean Muir of "Behind a Mask," the Sybil Varna of "Taming a Tartar."

Alcott experimented with a variety of male characters, often enigmatic, mysterious, intriguing. Paul, alias Paolo of "The Mysterious Key," shows traces of the Italian patriot Giuseppe Mazzini as well as of the author's young friends Alf Whitman and Ladislas Wisniewski, upon whom she modeled Laurie of *Little Women*. His background as a hero in the Italian Revolution enriches his persona as a charming young Italianate Englishman. Like Paul, Felix Stahl of "The Fate of the Forrests" is a man of mystery, "beardless, thin lipped, sharply featured," with "eyes of the intensest black" and face "colorless as ivory." Stahl is a seeming magician who foretells dire events and swiftly engages the sometimes perplexed attention of the reader. Many of Alcott's male characters are, in varying degree, foils to her strong-minded women. The black-bearded artist Max Erdmann of "A Pair of Eyes," who paints his wife as Lady Macbeth, is mesmerized and subdued by her in the end. Often the most macho male is pinpointed for a woman's mastery, notably in the case of the hero of "Taming a Tartar." Prince Alexis, "swarthy, black-eyed, scarlet-lipped," a man of "fearful temper" and impetuous moods, a tyrant born and bred, becomes a woman's willing victim, humbled, subdued, and conquered.

In the hands of such characters the inventive author places fascinating props that propel the action onward and are integral to plots of varying complexity. A seal ring, a satin slipper, a bit of lace, a poisoned fan are deftly introduced to spin a narrative of murder or revenge, to heighten and sustain suspense. Yet increasingly, as she gained experience and professionalism, Alcott painted and endowed with flesh and blood characters who dominated even her most intricate and outlandish plots.

In her narratives Alcott used a succession of themes that are frequently far more beguiling than any of her plots. For her immediate readership they provided titillation, excitement, escape. For a twentieth-century public those themes have often raised eyebrows. Some may be traced to the author's own experience, some to her reading, still others to her inner convictions. An analysis of the themes in this omnibus of thrillers helps to unmask the complex Alcott identity.

An abiding passion throughout Alcott's life was the theater. From the age of ten, when she assumed the post of author-director of the "Louy Alcott troupe," until late in life, when she dramatized *Michael Strogoff* and attended a performance of Emma Nevada, Alcott was stagestruck. In her teens she co-authored with her older sister Anna a succession of wild melodramas whose props would reappear in her blood-and-thunder stories. In drawing-room charades, in the Amateur Dramatic Company of Walpole and the Concord Dramatic Union, in charitable performances, she was an enthusiastic participant. In 1860 her farce, *Nat Bachelor's Pleasure Trip,* was staged in Boston's Howard Athenaeum. Her rendition of the Dickensian Mrs. Jarley of the famous Waxworks was memorable. She was familiar, as her character V.V. was, with disguises, "artifices of costume, cosmetics, and consummate acting."

This familiarity is reflected in the Alcott thrillers. Jean Muir, wielder of a woman's power, is indeed a consummate actress who hides her true character "behind a mask." The stage and the nature of the actor recur as themes in several of the sensation stories. "A Double Tragedy" is, as its subtitle indicates, "An Actor's Story." *Macbeth* pervades much of "A Pair of Eyes," a tale that opens in the theater during a performance of the tragedy. *The Tempest* is interwoven in "Ariel. A Legend of the Lighthouse," which is set on an enchanted island. As for "Taming a Tartar," that narrative is an overt reversal of *The Taming of the Shrew*. The plays that Alcott attended, the performances she herself gave, her absorption in Shakespeare, her addiction to private theatricals—all are threaded through the narratives she dispatched to popular story papers.

Another of Alcott's favorite themes also had its source in her own life. Vicariously, through the career of her younger sister May, the artist's life occupied the writer almost as much as the performer's. May, an enthusiastic art student, studied at the Boston School of Design, taught drawing in Syracuse, New York, and took anatomical drawing lessons under the distinguished Dr. William Rimmer. Later in life she would go abroad to continue her art studies, and after her premature death at age thirty-nine, her box of paintings would be sent home to Concord. Sister Louisa was deeply involved in May's pursuit of art and often helped to subsidize it. The results of that involvement punctuate several of the Alcott sensation stories.

The serial "Ariel. A Legend of the Lighthouse" reflects the author's preoccupation not only with the stage but with the art world. In it the poet-artist Philip Southesk sketches the nymph Ariel, producing a "likeness perfect with a happy stroke or two." The brushwork is far more detailed in "A Pair of Eyes." There Max Erdmann, artist incarnate, is utterly consumed by his devotion to a muse that was to him "wife, child, friend, food and fire." His portrait of Lady Macbeth, for which his wife serves as model, is described in minute detail—"the ghostly figure with wan face framed in hair, that streamed shadowy and long against white draperies," and it is that portrait that sets the sinister tone of the tale.

In an intriguing variation of the art motif, Alcott borrows a hint from the technique of the sculptor and shapes a Pygmalion-Galatea relationship between her characters. In "The Freak of a Genius" the relationship develops between two men as the forty-year-old Kent seeks to mold the nature of a young Apollo, the twenty-year-old St. George. The most overt example of Alcott's use of the Pygmalion-Galatea theme appears in "A Marble Woman: or, The Mysterious Model." In that shocker, the genius sculptor Bazil Yorke confuses flesh and blood with clay and attempts to metamorphose young Cecilia (called Cecil) into a marble goddess in an experiment that almost succeeds.

Alcott saw the Pygmalion-Galatea relationship as a form of mind control—a theme to which she would often return. The manifest vagaries of the human mind continued to fascinate her, and she used such knowledge of them as she had to intensify and explain her characters and enrich her plots. Insanity was especially interesting to her, and she seems to have had some actual experience with it.

Alcott's first biographer, Ednah Dow Cheney, states without elucidation or elaboration that during the summer of 1860 Alcott took care of a young friend suffering from a temporary fit of insanity. Such an experience must indeed have been both devastating and illuminating for an impressionable writer beginning her career. A few years later, during a trip abroad, Alcott served as companion to the young invalid Anna Weld, who from all indications suffered from some nervous disorder. She described her charge as "a very hard case to manage & needs the patience & wisdom of an angel."[23] In addition to these personal experiences, Alcott, as confidante of her sisters May and Anna, certainly heard reports of their work at Dr. Hervey B. Wilbur's Asylum in Syracuse, New York. Insanity was no stranger to Louisa Alcott.

When she came to use the subject as a theme in her thrillers, she did so with variations. Attempts to manipulate insanity in an elaborate plot to madden a heroine and the curse of inherited insanity became threads for the fabric of her stories. "A Whisper in the Dark," published in *Frank Leslie's Illustrated Newspaper* in 1863, describes an attempt on the part of a guardian to unhinge the mind of his eighteen-year-old ward, Sybil, so that her inheritance will be denied her. The horrors he manufactures provide fodder for a complex plot and introduce the reader to the disorders of the mind.

In "The Skeleton in the Closet," Reinhold Arnheim, suffering from a weakened brain, embodies the wreck of manhood. He is the victim of a "fearful malady," "a hereditary curse," and he affords the reader a case history in mental derangement. Hereditary madness is also pursued in "A Nurse's Story," wherein Elinor Carruth's "frantic paroxysms" are its manifestations. Like her creator, Elinor's nurse, Kate Snow, has had "some experience in the care of the insane" and knows "the power of a sane eye over a mad one." The "surest way of calming maniacs," she believes, is "to appear unconscious of their madness." The popular "solitude" treatment for insanity she shuns. The Carruth mother's insistence upon hiding the family curse from the world moves a heavy plot forward.

Elinor Carruth's frenzy yields only to powerful opiates. The evil guardian of "A Whisper in the Dark" uses the device of drugged sleep to aid him in his malevolent purpose. Drug addiction and experimentation are pivotal in many Alcott sensation stories and, like insanity, the nature of drugs was not unfamiliar to the writer.

The short period of Alcott's service as a Civil War nurse from December 1862 to January 1863 had long-term effects. During those few weeks at the Union Hotel Hospital in Georgetown, D.C., when she was "doing painful duties all day long, . . . surrounded by 3 or 4 hundred men in all stages of suffering, disease & death,"[24] she was stricken with a severe illness labeled typhoid-pneumonia and was forced to return home. There is little doubt that at some stage of her illness she was administered the derivative of the opium poppy known as tincture of opium or laudanum. Laudanum was part of the nineteenth-century physician's pharmacopoeia. As for *Cannabis sativa,* the source of hashish and marijuana, that was one of the oldest drugs known, and hashish was available at six cents a stick. Louisa Alcott was familiar with such "comfits" and joy-givers.

In "A Marble Woman," published in the *Flag of Our Union* in 1865, the ruthless sculptor Bazil Yorke gives young Cecil a bitter, dark liquid to induce a deep and dreamless sleep. Following their unconsummated marriage, Cecil develops strange symptoms and appears "dreamy, yet intense, blissfully calm, yet full of a mysterious brightness." Unnatural excitement is followed by "unconquerable drowsiness," until "restless sleep" turns into "deathlike immobility." A physician recognizes that Cecil has taken an overdose of laudanum and has survived the overdose because she is addicted. As he puts it to Yorke: "Your wife eats opium, I suspect." The role of the "dangerous comforter" is focal to the plot of "A Marble Woman."

The opium habit is skillfully applied in that narrative. But in a shorter and later sensation story, hashish experimentation *is* the plot. "Perilous Play," carried in 1869 in *Frank Leslie's Chimney Corner,* is a dramatic shocker. The narrative is simple enough. To while away a long afternoon for the sensuous heroine, Rose St. Just, and the rest of the party, Dr. Meredith produces a "little box of tortoiseshell and gold" containing the "Indian stuff which brings one fantastic visions." The doctor describes his own experiments with hashish and its effects: "A heavenly dreaminess comes over one, in which they move as if on air." When the trance comes on, the "pulse will rise, heart beat quickly, eyes darken and dilate, and an uplifted sensation will pervade you generally. Then these symptoms change, and the bliss begins." As for an overdose, that may result in "phantoms, frenzies, and a touch of nightmare, which seems to last a thousand years." Rose St. Just and her lover, Mark Done, experiment with the "taste of Elysium" and are caught up simultaneously in a storm at sea and the storm produced by *Cannabis sativa*. "Every nerve was overstrained, every pulse beating like a triphammer, and everything . . . was intensified and exaggerated with awful power. The thundershower seemed a wild hurricane." The author ingeniously gives the hashish experiment a happy ending with the protagonists exclaiming, "Heaven bless hashish, if its dreams end like this!" Alcott earned $75 for her four-part serial "A Marble Woman," and $25 for the short shocker "Perilous Play," welcome compensation for turning her knowledge of opiates into a narrative device.

One result of drug experimentation was described sometimes as "cerebral excitation." But it was not drugs alone that induced such an effect. There were many means of influencing or controlling the human mind, and Louisa Alcott was interested in all of them. As late as 1875, on a visit to New York, she would submit to a phrenological examination in the Cabinet of Fowler and Wells,[25] and toward the end of her life she would try a treatment known as mind cure to rid herself of various ills. She described her sensations after that treatment in a report to the *Woman's Journal*: "No effect was felt except sleepiness for the first few times; then mesmeric sensations occasionally came, sunshine in the head, a sense of walking on the air, and slight trances, when it was impossible to stir for a few moments."[26] Alcott seems to have been as familiar with "mesmeric sensations" as with the effects of hashish.

The eighteenth-century Austrian physician Franz Anton Mesmer had developed a theory of hypnotism based upon the activity of a magnetic force or fluid that permeated the universe and was called animal magnetism. When his theory reached Boston it roused a furor, and a stream of practitioners—clairvoyants, etherologists, psychometrists, and mesmerists—enjoyed a profitable practice. Alcott's venerated Concord neighbor Ralph Waldo Emerson wrote of mesmerism that it "broke into the inmost shrines, attempted the explanation of miracle and prophecy. . . . It was human, it was genial, it affirmed unity and connection between remote points." As for Hawthorne, he sensed that the penetrating intrusions of mesmerism might violate a human soul.[27] To Alcott such views were productive when she adapted the theme of mesmerism to sensational narrative.

In one thriller especially she displayed her knowledge of mesmerism and her awareness that it could become an exercise in power. "A Pair of Eyes," published in *Frank Leslie's Illustrated Newspaper* in 1863, is aptly titled, for the eyes—"two dark wells"—are the eyes of the mesmerist-heroine Agatha Eure. Her first exercise in mesmerism is practiced upon the artist Max Erdmann, and it is practiced without his knowledge or acquiescence. Thus it is indeed the violation of a human soul. The writer describes its effects almost clinically, as she would describe her own reactions to mind cure. Max Erdmann reports: "My eyelids began to be weighed down by a delicious drowsiness. . . . Everything grew misty. . . . A sensation of wonderful airiness came over me, and I felt as if I could float away like a thistledown. Presently every sense seemed to fall asleep. . . . I drifted away into a sea of blissful repose."

As for the practitioner Agatha Eure, who continues to mesmerize Max Erdmann, she is caught by Alcott in a striking pose: "she sat erect and motionless as an inanimate figure of intense thought; her eyes were fixed, face colorless, with an expression of iron determination, as if every energy of mind and body were wrought up to the achievement of a single purpose."

Soon that "single purpose" becomes clear to the reader. Agatha practices mesmerism upon her artist-husband, Max Erdmann, solely to conquer his will. If this results in the exploitation of a human soul, Hawthorne's unpardonable sin, so be it. The heroine must control Max Erdmann's mind to achieve the power she seeks—power of persona, power of gender.

Whether the exercise in mind control is practiced by a Pygmalion, as in "A Marble Woman," or by a mesmerist, as in "A Pair of Eyes," its goal is manifest: dominance in the sexual struggle for power. This struggle is a theme that runs consistently through most of the Alcott thrillers. Her fascination with the theme stems from both autobiographical and societal roots. Alcott's seven-week humiliation in Dedham, Massachusetts, when at age nineteen she served as a domestic for the Hon. James Richardson, was a contributory episode. She found Richardson's maudlin attentions intolerable, and her family found her $4 reward for service outrageous. The love-hate relationship between the young Louisa and her philosopher father Bronson Alcott may also have played a part in drawing her to the power struggle theme. In addition to her experiences, there was her own character. In her very genes resided the obligation to rebel against injustice: both her mother and her father were strong supporters of the anti-slavery movement and of the rights of women. The climate of the mid-nineteenth century gave her cause enough for revolt against the sexual inequality that flourished in the economic, political, and legal worlds as well as in marriage and domestic life.

In her thrillers Alcott's feminism took the form of a power struggle between the sexes. The conflict between master and slave, she found, could be applied productively and lucratively to sensation fiction. Upon some occasions she assigned the role of master to her male protagonist, but in her most effective stories the hero is reduced to submission by a woman's power. In her variations on the theme, she created a succession of colorful heroines who run the gamut from the thwarted and abused young woman to the triumphant female conqueror.

A child bride could be the perfect target for a Bazil Yorke, the Pygmalion sculptor of "A Marble Woman." "Be what I would have you," he enjoins her, seeking for power to mold her to his desires. Yorke, however, does not succeed in transforming young Cecil into a snow image; instead, she takes to drugs, and there is no victory either for would-be master or for slave.

Even Alcott's extensive gallery of manipulating women contains portraits of ultimate failures in the power struggle. Pauline Valary of the prize story, "Pauline's Passion and Punishment," is a femme fatale with a mysterious past and an electrifying present. Having lost both love and fortune, she is left with fury and a desire for revenge, ingredients stirred in a suspenseful plot. But in that "tournament so often held between man and woman," Pauline resorts to machinations that fail in the end. The result is the same in a later story, "Mrs. Vane's Charade." Celeste Vane engages in an unsuccessful power struggle with her former lover, Douglas, pretending submission when she feels none. "Ah, the art of the woman!" Alcott comments, "appealing to the love of power sure to be strong in such a man, . . . offering him a tender bond-slave in the woman who had ruled him like a queen." In their seesaw conflict Douglas is not fooled, and another manipulating heroine is unable to assert mastery.

In three major thrillers of the mid-1860s, however, Alcott portrayed feminist heroines who achieve complete mastery in the sexual power struggle. Nurse Kate Snow, the narrator of "A Nurse's Story," engages in a sparring match with the "fiery," masterful Robert Steele, who condescendingly informs her: "I'm not used to giving up my own will, but I admire your courage so much, that I am tempted to yield for the sake of enjoying a novel experience." To Steele's announcement "I am master in this house," independent, clear-eyed Kate Snow retorts, "Not my master," and when he declares, "I never permit myself to be conquered," she neatly replies, "except by a woman."

The ultimate in woman's mastery is reached in "Taming a Tartar," and in that serial the power struggle is most explicit. It is engaged in between a Tartar tyrant and an English teacher; the entire plot revolves about their contest; in the end there is no doubt about who is victorious. As Sybil Varna puts it, "Once conquer his will, . . . and I had gained a power possessed by no other person." Her desire to see her "haughty lover thoroughly subdued" is achieved; the Tartar eventually humbles himself; the heroine promises "to love, honor, and—*Not* obey" him. Having conquered her tyrannical Tartar, Sybil Varna achieves the ultimate in the power struggle between the sexes.

While less explicit than "Taming a Tartar," "Behind a Mask: or, A Woman's Power" is perhaps even more interesting since it offers a subtler approach to a similar theme. Like Pauline Valary, Jean Muir is bent upon revenge; like Celeste Vane, she resorts to subterfuges; and like Kate Snow and Sybil Varna, there is no mistaking her feminism. She is also an actress who assumes the role of a young governess at an ancestral English estate, and she proceeds to conquer every male member of the household until, in the end, she wins the head of the house of Coventry, a title, and the estate.

The spinster from Concord, Massachusetts, who would captivate the reading world with her domestic novel *Little Women,* delved into her impressions and her observations to find her themes. When she wrote her melodramatic serials they served her well: the theater and the art world, inherited insanity and drug addiction, mesmerism and mind control, feminist fury and the power struggle between the sexes. In 1869, after the success of *Little Women* was assured, she all but abandoned the secret writing of sensational narratives. Once or twice, however, she returned to the genre, no longer because she needed the money but because she found in that so-called sub-literature a psychological outlet and a professional satisfaction.

There is no doubt that when, in 1877, tired of providing "moral pap for the young," she wrote her anonymous and experimental novel, *A Modern Mephistopheles,* for Roberts Brothers' No Name Series, she thought back to a serial she had contributed to *Frank Leslie's Illustrated Newspaper* some ten years before. In both stories a Faustian pact is pivotal to the plot, and in both cases the pact is made by a young man ambitious for literary fame who yields up his liberty to an older man. St. George of "The Freak of a Genius" was an understudy for Felix Canaris of *A Modern Mephistopheles,* and the interest of both narratives is heightened by the sexual entanglements of what has been called a "psychologic quadrilateral."[28] Along with Goethe's *Faust* itself, and an as yet unpublished Alcott novel entitled "A Modern Mephistopheles or The Fatal Love Chase," "The Freak of a Genius" was a rich source for Alcott's anonymous novel of 1877.

Even more interesting was the use that Alcott made of yet another of her sensation stories. Between 1861 and 1873, when it was finally published, Alcott worked intermittently upon her autobiographical fiction, *Work.* Its chapters are patently based upon episodes of the author's life: "Servant," "Actress," "Governess," "Companion," "Seamstress." It is the chapter "Companion" that clearly recalls the thriller "A Nurse's Story" and suggests to the critic that perhaps a good part of that tale was less fictional than factual. In *Work,* the heroine Christie Devon follows the path of Kate Snow of "A Nurse's Story," becoming "companion to an invalid girl" who is afflicted with inherited insanity. There is every reason to believe that Alcott shaped both the chapter "Companion" and the tale "A Nurse's Story" around the nucleus of an actual experience. It is obvious, too, that the thriller adumbrated the chapter in *Work.*

Although she claimed to disdain her plunge into sensational literature and cloaked it in secrecy, she remembered it, and, to serve her professional purpose, she returned to the genre and recast it. The scholarly world first learned of her sensational output in 1943 but it was not until 1975 that the first volume of Alcott thrillers was made available to the public. Readers in search of page-turners were enthralled by the swift sequences of plot, the array of proud and powerful characters, the exotic backdrops. Scholars were enthralled by something else: the revelation of a new Louisa May Alcott. As one critic succinctly put it, "Never again will you have quite the same image of this particular 'little woman.' "[29]

The image projected in the first full-length biography that followed the appearance of the first volume of thrillers (*Behind a Mask: The Unknown Thrillers of Louisa May Alcott*) was arresting but in some respects devastating. Martha Saxton, in her *Louisa May: A Modern Biography of Louisa May Alcott* (1977), characterized the writer as a "depressed and sullen . . . withdrawn, hostile introvert" who alternated between "resentment" and "self-inflicted spite," whose "sexuality remained a mystery" to her and whose "devils of guilt" vied with her "deep fear of men." The biographer confessed that she had "chosen to present only those facts that seemed important in shaping Louisa's emotional and intellectual life." Most of those "facts" seem to have been culled from the sensation stories. Saxton concluded that Alcott "identified with Pauline [of "Pauline's Passion and Punishment"] and believed that passionate, sexual women like herself were wicked and grotesque members of her sex." Her "modern biography" of Alcott derived substantially—perhaps too substantially—from the thrillers Alcott had written and the characters she had imagined.[30]

Some critics warmly welcomed the Saxton interpretation. Ann Douglas, writing in 1978 under the heading "Mysteries of Louisa May Alcott" in the *New York Review of Books,* stated that Saxton's modern biography was "a major step in the process of reassessment. Her book follows logically upon Madeleine Stern's critical . . . republication of Alcott's lost 'thrillers.' . . . Saxton offers a psychological and cultural study of

Alcott and her milieu, emphasizing the darker sides of her life and career . . . [and]
has powerfully delineated what has too long been ignored: the compulsions and fears
that both inspired and limited the 'children's friend.' " Most interestingly, Douglas,
seeking connections, noted that "the little girls of Alcott's later work have something
in common with the *femmes fatales* of her early books: they too undergo metamorphosis,
not growth. In a sense, murder pervades the worlds of both."[31]

There is no doubt that publication of the anonymous and pseudonymous thrillers, with their strong feminist heroines, triggered a battery of revisionist criticism.
That criticism has been applied not only to the Alcott persona but to the entire Alcott
oeuvre, which is now viewed in light of the newly discovered narratives.

Judith Fetterley, in *"Little Women:* Alcott's Civil War," affirmed that "the work
of Stern in . . . recovering Alcott's sensation fiction provides an important context for
the reading of *Little Women.*" The "sensation fiction," she continued, "provides an
important gloss on the sexual politics involved in Jo's renunciation of the writing of
such fiction and on the sexual politics of Jo's relation with Professor Bhaer under
whose influence she gives it up."[32] The feminist critic Sarah Elbert perceives the
themes of Alcott's sensation fiction in much of her nonsensation work, writing that
"Murder, divorce, child abandonment, nervous disorders degenerating into madness—all these figure in Louisa's novels, and even creep into the *Little Women* trilogy.
. . . Without a rational, sexually egalitarian society, Alcott felt these abuses would
invade daylight reality as well as midnight fantasies."[33]

Both Alcott's "daylight reality" and her "midnight fantasies" have engaged close
attention as the reappraisals have continued. In one of the most recent, *"Whispers in
the Dark": The Fiction of Louisa May Alcott* (1994), Elizabeth Lennox Keyser clearly states
that "the current interest in Alcott, especially among feminist scholars . . . has been
kindled largely by the discovery of Alcott's anonymous and pseudonymous sensation
fiction." The author of that fiction, she concludes, was "not simply versatile but
complex"; "Beneath the placid surface [of the domestic fiction] . . . the passions,
antagonisms, and power struggles that complicate gender relations in the sensation
fiction continue unabated."[34]

Publication of Alcott's sensation fiction has revealed the hitherto unsuspected
dimensions of her work. It has also enriched Alcott's stature as a writer in the American Renaissance. Since the mid-1970s, The Children's Friend has been the subject not
only of biographical re-viewing and critical re-evaluation but of a variety of scholarly
investigations that would not have been pursued had her sensation stories never been
recovered. *Little Women* has been compared with *Pride and Prejudice;* Alcott's connections
with Henry James have been traced; the "Transatlantic Translations" of Alcott and
Charlotte Brontë have been studied; " 'Gorgeous Fancies': Louisa May Alcott, the
Female Gothic, and Nineteenth-Century Women Readers" is the title of a thesis.[35]

Alcott is now recognized as a many-faceted professional writer who had significant things to say and said them with the same power and passion that characterized
her sensational heroines. Thanks to this recognition, the sources of her life and work
have been made available in scholarly editions, and this too is a by-product of the
unearthing of her thrillers. Under the aegis of a trio of scholars, *The Selected Letters of
Louisa May Alcott* appeared in 1987, followed in 1989 by *The Journals of Louisa May
Alcott.*[36] At the end of each year of *The Journals* were added those telling "Notes and

Memoranda" from Alcott's ledger that provided clues to the identity of many of her anonymous blood-and-thunder stories. Anthologies of Alcott's work must now perforce include one or more of those thrillers. In the cleverly entitled *Alternative Alcott* compiled by Elaine Showalter, for example, "Behind a Mask" is reprinted as an example of Alcott's expertise in the sensational genre.[37]

The critics are rewriting Louisa Alcott. Some of that rewriting may result in distortion, but much of it is perceptive and valid. The author of "Behind a Mask," *Hospital Sketches, Moods, Little Women, Work,* and *A Modern Mephistopheles* is now viewed as a creative artist adept at the sensational and the sentimental, the realistic, the gothic, the domestic. She was not only a complex human being but a more adventurous writer than had once been supposed. Basically, she was both a professional and an experimenter in literary genres that took her from fairy tales to war sketches, from thrillers to a domestic saga.

The critical revision of Alcott is clearly due to the discovery and subsequent reprinting of her sensation tales. From behind her mask she has emerged as a rich and varied writer whose works are susceptible of productive analysis. Her image has been altered, her reputation extended, her stature increased. The springboard for this metamorphosis lies in the corpus of sensation stories that remained hidden for more than a century. Now they have been gathered together, in the order of their original appearance, in an omnibus volume that parades Alcott's vivid characters, unravels her complex plots, reflects her psychological insights and her feminist convictions. *Louisa May Alcott Unmasked* provides the scholar with a compendium for continued critical analysis. More importantly, it offers the reader a succession of suspenseful page-turners whose characters still beguile, whose themes are still relevant.

NOTES

1. Leona Rostenberg, "Some Anonymous and Pseudonymous Thrillers of Louisa M. Alcott," *Papers* of the Bibliographical Society of America (2d Quarter 1943).

2. Madeleine B. Stern, ed., *Behind a Mask: The Unknown Thrillers of Louisa May Alcott* (New York: William Morrow, 1975).

3. Madeleine B. Stern, ed., *Plots and Counterplots: More Unknown Thrillers of Louisa May Alcott* (New York: William Morrow, 1976); Madeleine B. Stern, Joel Myerson, and Daniel Shealy, eds., *A Double Life: Newly Discovered Thrillers of Louisa May Alcott* (Boston: Little, Brown, 1988); Daniel Shealy, Madeleine B. Stern, and Joel Myerson, eds., *Freaks of Genius: Unknown Thrillers of Louisa May Alcott* (Westport: Greenwood, 1991); Madeleine B. Stern and Daniel Shealy, eds., *From Jo March's Attic: Stories of Intrigue and Suspense* (Boston: Northeastern University Press, 1993).

4. "Pauline's Passion and Punishment," *Frank Leslie's Illustrated Newspaper* (3 and 10 January 1863).

5. Joel Myerson, Daniel Shealy, and Madeleine B. Stern, eds., *The Journals of Louisa May Alcott* (Boston: Little, Brown, 1989), p. 96 [hereinafter *Journals*].

6. Joel Myerson, Daniel Shealy, and Madeleine B. Stern, eds., *The Selected Letters of Louisa May Alcott* (Boston: Little, Brown, 1987), p. 79.

7. Ednah Dow Cheney, *Louisa May Alcott: Her Life, Letters, and Journals* (Boston: Roberts Brothers, 1889).

8. L. C. Pickett, *Across My Path: Memories of People I Have Known* (New York, 1916).

9. Rostenberg, "Some Anonymous and Pseudonymous Thrillers."

10. Madeleine B. Stern, *Louisa May Alcott* (Norman: University of Oklahoma Press, 1950, 1971, 1985).

11. James R. Elliott to Louisa May Alcott, 5, 7, 21 January, 15 June 1865, August 1866, Louisa May Alcott Manuscripts, Box II (Houghton Library, Harvard University). The letters were first published in Rostenberg, "Some Anonymous and Pseudonymous Thrillers."

12. E. G. Squier to Louisa May Alcott, ca. 18 December 1862 (formerly in Orchard House, Concord, Massachusetts, now in Houghton Library, Harvard University).

13. Benj. G. Smith for Frank Leslie to Louisa May Alcott, 13 June 1867 (Louisa May Alcott Collection [# 6255], Manuscripts Dept., University of Virginia Library).

14. Miriam Squier to Louisa May Alcott, 5 January [1864?] (Houghton Library, Harvard University).

15. *Journals*, pp. 134, 139.

16. Ibid., pp. 120, 121, 130, 139, 140, 154.

17. James R. Elliott to Louisa May Alcott, 5 January 1865 (Houghton Library, Harvard University).

18. For Frank Leslie, his publishing house, and his periodicals, see Madeleine B. Stern, *Purple Passage: The Life of Mrs. Frank Leslie* (Norman: University of Oklahoma Press, 1953, 1970).

19. Elliott to Alcott, 7 January 1865.

20. *Journals*, p. 92.

21. See notes 2 and 3.

22. For this and biographical details throughout, see Stern, *Louisa May Alcott.*

23. *Journals*, p. 142.

24. Ibid., p. 113.

25. Madeleine B. Stern and Kent Bicknell, "Louisa May Alcott Had Her Head Examined," *Studies in the American Renaissance 1995* (forthcoming).

26. "Miss Alcott on Mind-Cure," *Woman's Journal* (April 1885), p. 121.

27. Taylor Stoehr, "Hawthorne and Mesmerism," *Huntington Library Quarterly* (November 1969), p. 35, quoting from Emerson's "Historic Notes on Life and Letters in New England," and pp. 54–55, discussing Hawthorne and the unpardonable sin.

28. Edward R. Burlingane, review of *A Modern Mephistopheles*, *North American Review* (September 1877), pp. 316–318, reprinted in Madeleine B. Stern, *Critical Essays on Louisa May Alcott* (Boston: G. K. Hall, 1984), pp. 204–205.

29. Unsigned review of Stern, *Behind a Mask: The Unknown Thrillers of Louisa May Alcott,* in *Publishers Weekly* (5 May 1975), p. 89.

30. Martha Saxton, *Louisa May: A Modern Biography of Louisa May Alcott* (Boston: Houghton Mifflin, 1977), pp. 7, 9, 15, 154, 261, 388.

31. Ann Douglas, "Mysteries of Louisa May Alcott," *New York Review of Books* (28 September 1978), pp. 60–63; reprinted in Stern, *Critical Essays on Louisa May Alcott,* pp. 231–240.

32. Judith Fetterley, "*Little Women*: Alcott's Civil War," *Feminist Studies* (Summer 1979), pp. 369–370, 381–383; reprinted in Stern, *Critical Essays on Louisa May Alcott,* pp. 140–143.

33. Sarah Elbert, *A Hunger for Home: Louisa May Alcott and "Little Women"* (Philadelphia: Temple University Press, 1984), p. 130.

34. Elizabeth Lennox Keyser, *"Whispers in the Dark": The Fiction of Louisa May Alcott* (Knoxville: University of Tennessee Press, 1994), pp. xii, xiv.

35. Nina Auerbach, "*Little Women* [and *Pride and Prejudice*]," in *Communities of Women: An Idea in Fiction* (Cambridge: Harvard University Press, 1978), reprinted in Stern, *Critical Essays on Louisa May Alcott,* pp. 129–140; Adeline R. Tintner, "A Literary Youth and a Little Woman: Henry James Reviews Louisa Alcott," in Stern, *Critical Essays on Louisa May Alcott,* pp. 265–269; Charlotte Doyle Francis, "Transatlantic Translations: Louisa May Alcott and Charlotte Brontë," dissertation prospectus, University of Connecticut, 1993; Elizabeth Young, " 'Gorgeous Fancies': Louisa May Alcott, the

Female Gothic, and Nineteenth-Century Women Readers," honors thesis, Harvard and Radcliffe Colleges, 1985.

36. See notes 5 and 6.

37. Elaine Showalter, ed., *Alternative Alcott: Louisa May Alcott* (New Brunswick: Rutgers University Press, 1988).

Louisa May Alcott Unmasked

‌ Pauline's Passion and Punishment

Chapter I

To and fro, like a wild creature in its cage, paced that handsome woman, with bent head, locked hands, and restless steps. Some mental storm, swift and sudden as a tempest of the tropics, had swept over her and left its marks behind. As if in anger at the beauty now proved powerless, all ornaments had been flung away, yet still it shone undimmed, and filled her with a passionate regret. A jewel glittered at her feet, leaving the lace rent to shreds on the indignant bosom that had worn it; the wreaths of hair that had crowned her with a woman's most womanly adornment fell disordered upon shoulders that gleamed the fairer for the scarlet of the pomegranate flowers clinging to the bright meshes that had imprisoned them an hour ago; and over the face, once so affluent in youthful bloom, a stern pallor had fallen like a blight, for pride was slowly conquering passion, and despair had murdered hope.

Pausing in her troubled march, she swept away the curtain swaying in the wind and looked out, as if imploring help from Nature, the great mother of us all. A summer moon rode high in a cloudless heaven, and far as eye could reach stretched the green wilderness of a Cuban *cafetal*. No forest, but a tropical orchard, rich in lime, banana, plantain, palm, and orange trees, under whose protective shade grew the evergreen coffee plant, whose dark-red berries are the fortune of their possessor, and the luxury of one-half the world. Wide avenues diverging from the mansion, with its belt of brilliant shrubs and flowers, formed shadowy vistas, along which, on the wings of the wind, came a breath of far-off music, like a wooing voice; for the magic of night and distance lulled the cadence of a Spanish *contradanza* to a trance of sound, soft, subdued, and infinitely sweet. It was a southern scene, but not a southern face that looked out upon it with such unerring glance; there was no southern languor in the figure, stately and erect; no southern swarthiness on fairest cheek and arm; no southern darkness in the shadowy gold of the neglected hair; the light frost of northern snows lurked in the features, delicately cut, yet vividly alive, betraying a temperament ardent, dominant, and subtle. For passion burned in the deep eyes, changing their violet to black. Pride sat on the forehead, with its dark brows; all a woman's sweetest spells touched the lips, whose shape was a smile; and in the spirited carriage of the head appeared the freedom of an intellect ripened under colder skies, the energy of a nature that could wring strength from suffering, and dare to act where feebler souls would only dare desire.

Standing thus, conscious only of the wound that bled in that high heart of hers, and the longing that gradually took shape and deepened to a purpose, an alien presence changed the tragic atmosphere of that still room and woke her from her dangerous mood. A wonderfully winning guise this apparition wore, for youth, hope, and love endowed it with the charm that gives beauty to the plainest, while their reign endures. A boy in any other climate, in this his nineteen years had given him the stature of a man; and Spain, the land of romance, seemed embodied in this figure, full of the lithe slenderness of the whispering palms overhead, the warm coloring of the deep-toned flowers sleeping in the room, the native grace of the tame antelope lifting its human eyes to his as he lingered on the threshold in an attitude eager yet timid, watching that other figure as it looked into the night and found no solace there.

"Pauline!"

She turned as if her thought had taken voice and answered her, regarded him a moment, as if hesitating to receive the granted wish, then beckoned with the one word.

"Come!"

Instantly the fear vanished, the ardor deepened, and with an imperious "Lie down!" to his docile attendant, the young man obeyed with equal docility, looking as wistfully toward his mistress as the brute toward her master, while he waited proudly humble for her commands.

"Manuel, why are you here?"

"Forgive me! I saw Dolores bring a letter; you vanished, an hour passed, I could wait no longer, and I came."

"I am glad, I needed my one friend. Read that."

She offered a letter, and with her steady eyes upon him, her purpose strengthening as she looked, stood watching the changes of that expressive countenance. This was the letter:

Pauline—

Six months ago I left you, promising to return and take you home my wife; I loved you, but I deceived you; for though my heart was wholly yours, my hand was not mine to give. This it was that haunted me through all that blissful summer, this that marred my happiness when you owned you loved me, and this drove me from you, hoping I could break the tie with which I had rashly bound myself. I could not, I am married, and there all ends. Hate me, forget me, solace your pride with the memory that none knew your wrong, assure your peace with the knowledge that mine is destroyed forever, and leave my punishment to remorse and time.

Gilbert

With a gesture of wrathful contempt, Manuel flung the paper from him as he flashed a look at his companion, muttering through his teeth, "Traitor! Shall I kill him?"

Pauline laughed low to herself, a dreary sound, but answered with a slow darkening of the face that gave her words an ominous significance. "Why should you?

Such revenge is brief and paltry, fit only for mock tragedies or poor souls who have neither the will to devise nor the will to execute a better. There are fates more terrible than death; weapons more keen than poniards, more noiseless than pistols. Women use such, and work out a subtler vengeance than men can conceive. Leave Gilbert to remorse—and me."

She paused an instant, and by some strong effort banished the black frown from her brow, quenched the baleful fire of her eyes, and left nothing visible but the pale determination that made her beautiful face more eloquent than her words.

"Manuel, in a week I leave the island."

"Alone, Pauline?"

"No, not alone."

A moment they looked into each other's eyes, each endeavoring to read the other. Manuel saw some indomitable purpose, bent on conquering all obstacles. Pauline saw doubt, desire, and hope; knew that a word would bring the ally she needed; and, with a courage as native to her as her pride, resolved to utter it.

Seating herself, she beckoned her companion to assume the place beside her, but for the first time he hesitated. Something in the unnatural calmness of her manner troubled him, for his southern temperament was alive to influences whose presence would have been unfelt by one less sensitive. He took the cushion at her feet, saying, half tenderly, half reproachfully, "Let me keep my old place till I know in what character I am to fill the new. The man you trusted has deserted you; the boy you pitied will prove loyal. Try him, Pauline."

"I will."

And with the bitter smile unchanged upon her lips, the low voice unshaken in its tones, the deep eyes unwavering in their gaze, Pauline went on:

"You know my past, happy as a dream till eighteen. Then all was swept away, home, fortune, friends, and I was left, like an unfledged bird, without even the shelter of a cage. For five years I have made my life what I could, humble, honest, but never happy, till I came here, for here I saw Gilbert. In the poor companion of your guardian's daughter he seemed to see the heiress I had been, and treated me as such. This flattered my pride and touched my heart. He was kind, I grateful; then he loved me, and God knows how utterly I loved him! A few months of happiness the purest, then he went to make home ready for me, and I believed him; for where I wholly love I wholly trust. While my own peace was undisturbed, I learned to read the language of your eyes, Manuel, to find the boy grown into the man, the friend warmed into a lover. Your youth had kept me blind too long. Your society had grown dear to me, and I loved you like a sister for your unvarying kindness to the solitary woman who earned her bread and found it bitter. I told you my secret to prevent the utterance of your own. You remember the promise you made me then, keep it still, and bury the knowledge of my lost happiness deep in your pitying heart, as I shall in my proud one. Now the storm is over, and I am ready for my work again, but it must be a new task in a new scene. I hate this house, this room, the faces I must meet, the duties I must perform, for the memory of that traitor haunts them all. I see a future full of interest, a stage whereon I could play a stirring part. I long for it intensely, yet cannot make it mine alone. Manuel, do you love me still?"

Bending suddenly, she brushed back the dark hair that streaked his forehead and searched the face that in an instant answered her. Like a swift rising light, the eloquent blood rushed over swarthy cheek and brow, the slumberous softness of the eyes kindled with a flash, and the lips, sensitive as any woman's, trembled yet broke into a rapturous smile as he cried, with fervent brevity, "I would die for you!"

A look of triumph swept across her face, for with this boy, as chivalrous as ardent, she knew that words were not mere breath. Still, with her stern purpose uppermost, she changed the bitter smile into one half-timid, half-tender, as she bent still nearer, "Manuel, in a week I leave the island. Shall I go alone?"

"No, Pauline."

He understood her now. She saw it in the sudden paleness that fell on him, heard it in the rapid beating of his heart, felt it in the strong grasp that fastened on her hand, and knew that the first step was won. A regretful pang smote her, but the dark mood which had taken possession of her stifled the generous warnings of her better self and drove her on.

"Listen, Manuel. A strange spirit rules me tonight, but I will have no reserves from you, all shall be told; then, if you will come, be it so; if not, I shall go my way as solitary as I came. If you think that this loss has broken my heart, undeceive yourself, for such as I live years in an hour and show no sign. I have shed no tears, uttered no cry, asked no comfort; yet, since I read that letter, I have suffered more than many suffer in a lifetime. I am not one to lament long over any hopeless sorrow. A single paroxysm, sharp and short, and it is over. Contempt has killed my love, I have buried it, and no power can make it live again, except as a pale ghost that will not rest till Gilbert shall pass through an hour as bitter as the last."

"Is that the task you give yourself, Pauline?"

The savage element that lurks in southern blood leaped up in the boy's heart as he listened, glittered in his eye, and involuntarily found expression in the nervous grip of the hands that folded a fairer one between them. Alas for Pauline that she had roused the sleeping devil, and was glad to see it!

"Yes, it is weak, wicked, and unwomanly; yet I persist as relentlessly as any Indian on a war trail. See me as I am, not the gay girl you have known, but a revengeful woman with but one tender spot now left in her heart, the place you fill. I have been wronged, and I long to right myself at once. Time is too slow; I cannot wait, for that man must be taught that two can play at the game of hearts, taught soon and sharply. I can do this, can wound as I have been wounded, can sting him with contempt, and prove that I too can forget."

"Go on, Pauline. Show me how I am to help you."

"Manuel, I want fortune, rank, splendor, and power; you can give me all these, and a faithful friend beside. I desire to show Gilbert the creature he deserted no longer poor, unknown, unloved, but lifted higher than himself, cherished, honored, applauded, her life one of royal pleasure, herself a happy queen. Beauty, grace, and talent you tell me I possess; wealth gives them luster, rank exalts them, power makes them irresistible. Place these worldly gifts in my hand and that hand is yours. See, I offer it."

She did so, but it was not taken. Manuel had left his seat and now stood before her, awed by the undertone of strong emotion in her calmly spoken words, bewildered by the proposal so abruptly made, longing to ask the natural question hovering on his lips, yet too generous to utter it. Pauline read his thought, and answered it with no touch of pain or pride in the magical voice that seldom spoke in vain.

"I know your wish; it is as just as your silence is generous, and I reply to it in all sincerity. You would ask, 'When I have given all that I possess, what do I receive in return?' This—a wife whose friendship is as warm as many a woman's love; a wife who will give you all the heart still left her, and cherish the hope that time may bring a harvest of real affection to repay you for the faithfulness of years; who, though she takes the retribution of a wrong into her hands and executes it in the face of heaven, never will forget the honorable name you give into her keeping or blemish it by any act of hers. I can promise no more. Will this content you, Manuel?"

Before she ended his face was hidden in his hands, and tears streamed through them as he listened, for like a true child of the south each emotion found free vent and spent itself as swiftly as it rose. The reaction was more than he could bear, for in a moment his life was changed, months of hopeless longing were banished with a word, a blissful yes canceled the hard no that had been accepted as inexorable, and Happiness, lifting her full cup to his lips, bade him drink. A moment he yielded to the natural relief, then dashed his tears away and threw himself at Pauline's feet in that attitude fit only for a race as graceful as impassioned.

"Forgive me! Take all I have—fortune, name, and my poor self; use us as you will, we are proud and happy to be spent for you! No service will be too hard, no trial too long if in the end you learn to love me with one tithe of the affection I have made my life. Do you mean it? Am I to go with you? To be near you always, to call you wife, and know we are each other's until death? What have I ever done to earn a fate like this?"

Fast and fervently he spoke, and very winsome was the glad abandonment of this young lover, half boy, half man, possessing the simplicity of the one, the fervor of the other. Pauline looked and listened with a soothing sense of consolation in the knowledge that this loyal heart was all her own, a sweet foretaste of the devotion which henceforth was to shelter her from poverty, neglect, and wrong, and turn life's sunniest side to one who had so long seen only its most bleak and barren. Still at her feet, his arms about her waist, his face flushed and proud, lifted to hers, Manuel saw the cold mask soften, the stern eyes melt with a sudden dew as Pauline watched him, saying, "Dear Manuel, love me less; I am not worth such ardent and entire faith. Pause and reflect before you take this step. I will not bind you to my fate too soon lest you repent too late. We both stand alone in the world, free to make or mar our future as we will. I have chosen my lot. Recall all it may cost you to share it and be sure the price is not too high a one. Remember I am poor, you the possessor of one princely fortune, the sole heir to another."

"The knowledge of this burdened me before; now I glory in it because I have the more for you."

"Remember, I am older than yourself, and may early lose the beauty you love so well, leaving an old wife to burden your youth."

"What are a few years to me? Women like you grow lovelier with age, and you shall have a strong young husband to lean on all your life."

"Remember, I am not of your faith, and the priests will shut me out from your heaven."

"Let them prate as they will. Where you go I will go; Santa Paula shall be my madonna!"

"Remember, I am a deserted woman, and in the world we are going to my name may become the sport of that man's cruel tongue. Could you bear that patiently, and curb your fiery pride if I desired it?"

"Anything for you, Pauline!"

"One thing more. I give you my liberty; for a time give me forbearance in return, and though wed in haste woo me slowly, lest this sore heart of mine find even your light yoke heavy. Can you promise this, and wait till time has healed my wound, and taught me to be meek?"

"I swear to obey you in all things; make me what you will, for soul and body I am wholly yours henceforth."

"Faithful and true! I knew you would not fail me. Now go, Manuel. Tomorrow do your part resolutely as I shall do mine, and in a week we will begin the new life together. Ours is a strange betrothal, but it shall not lack some touch of tenderness from me. Love, good night."

Pauline bent till her bright hair mingled with the dark, kissed the boy on lips and forehead as a fond sister might have done, then put him gently from her; and like one in a blessed dream he went away to pace all night beneath her window, longing for the day.

As the echo of his steps died along the corridor, Pauline's eye fell on the paper lying where her lover flung it. At this sight all the softness vanished, the stern woman reappeared, and, crushing it in her hand with slow significance, she said low to herself, "This is an old, old story, but it shall have a new ending."

CHAPTER II

"WHAT JEWELS will the señora wear tonight?"

"None, Dolores. Manuel has gone for flowers—he likes them best. You may go."

"But the señora's toilette is not finished; the sandals, the gloves, the garland yet remain."

"Leave them all; I shall not go down. I am tired of this endless folly. Give me that book and go."

The pretty Creole obeyed; and careless of Dolores' work, Pauline sank into the deep chair with a listless mien, turned the pages for a little, then lost herself in thoughts that seemed to bring no rest.

Silently the young husband entered and, pausing, regarded his wife with mingled pain and pleasure—pain to see her so spiritless, pleasure to see her so fair. She seemed unconscious of his presence till the fragrance of his floral burden betrayed him, and looking up to smile a welcome she met a glance that changed the sad dreamer into an excited actor, for it told her that the object of her search was found. Springing erect, she asked eagerly, "Manuel, is he here?"

"Yes."

"Alone?"

"His wife is with him."

"Is she beautiful?"

"Pretty, petite, and petulant."

"And he?"

"Unchanged: the same imposing figure and treacherous face, the same restless eye and satanic mouth. Pauline, let me insult him!"

"Not yet. Were they together?"

"Yes. He seemed anxious to leave her, but she called him back imperiously, and he came like one who dared not disobey."

"Did he see you?"

"The crowd was too dense, and I kept in the shadow."

"The wife's name? Did you learn it?"

"Barbara St. Just."

"Ah! I knew her once and will again. Manuel, am I beautiful tonight?"

"How can you be otherwise to me?"

"That is not enough. I must look my fairest to others, brilliant and blithe, a happy-hearted bride whose honeymoon is not yet over."

"For his sake, Pauline?"

"For yours. I want him to envy you your youth, your comeliness, your content; to see the man he once sneered at the husband of the woman he once loved; to recall impotent regret. I know his nature, and can stir him to his heart's core with a look, revenge myself with a word, and read the secrets of his life with a skill he cannot fathom."

"And when you have done all this, shall you be happier, Pauline?"

"Infinitely; our three weeks' search is ended, and the real interest of the plot begins. I have played the lover for your sake, now play the man of the world for mine. This is the moment we have waited for. Help me to make it successful. Come! Crown me with your garland, give me the bracelets that were your wedding gift—none can be too brilliant for tonight. Now the gloves and fan. Stay, my sandals—you shall play Dolores and tie them on."

With an air of smiling coquetry he had never seen before, Pauline stretched out a truly Spanish foot and offered him its dainty covering. Won by the animation of her manner, Manuel forgot his misgivings and played his part with boyish spirit, hovering about his stately wife as no assiduous maid had ever done; for every flower was fastened with a word sweeter than itself, the white arms kissed as the ornaments went on, and when the silken knots were deftly accomplished, the lighthearted bridegroom performed a little dance of triumph about his idol, till she arrested him, beckoning as she spoke.

"Manuel, I am waiting to assume the last best ornament you have given me, my handsome husband." Then, as he came to her laughing with frank pleasure at her praise, she added, "You, too, must look your best and bravest now, and remember you must enact the man tonight. Before Gilbert wear your stateliest aspect, your tenderest to me, your courtliest to his wife. You possess dramatic skill. Use it for my sake, and come for your reward when this night's work is done."

The great hotel was swarming with life, ablaze with light, resonant with the tread of feet, the hum of voices, the musical din of the band, and full of the sights and sounds which fill such human hives at a fashionable watering place in the height of the season. As Manuel led his wife along the grand hall thronged with promenaders, his quick ear caught the whispered comments of the passers-by, and the fragmentary rumors concerning themselves amused him infinitely.

"*Mon ami!* There are five bridal couples here tonight, and there is the hand-somest, richest, and most enchanting of them all. The groom is not yet twenty, they tell me, and the bride still younger. Behold them!"

Manuel looked down at Pauline with a mirthful glance, but she had not heard.

"See, Belle! Cubans; own half the island between them. Splendid, aren't they? Look at the diamonds on her lovely arms, and his ravishing moustache. Isn't he your ideal of Prince Djalma, in *The Wandering Jew?*"

A pretty girl, forgetting propriety in interest, pointed as they passed. Manuel half-bowed to the audible compliment, and the blushing damsel vanished, but Pauline had not seen.

"Jack, there's the owner of the black span you fell into raptures over. My lord and lady look as highbred as their stud. We'll patronize them!"

Manuel muttered a disdainful *"Impertinente!"* between his teeth as he surveyed a brace of dandies with an air that augured ill for the patronage of Young America, but Pauline was unconscious of both criticism and reproof. A countercurrent held them stationary for a moment, and close behind them sounded a voice saying, confidentially, to some silent listener, "The Redmonds are here tonight, and I am curious to see how he bears his disappointment. You know he married for money, and was outwitted in the bargain; for his wife's fortune not only proves to be much less than he was led to believe, but is so tied up that he is entirely dependent upon her, and the bachelor debts he sold himself to liquidate still harass him, with a wife's reproaches to augment the affliction. To be ruled by a spoiled child's whims is a fit punishment for a man whom neither pride nor principle could curb before. Let us go and look at the unfortunate."

Pauline heard now. Manuel felt her start, saw her flush and pale, then her eye lit, and the dark expression he dreaded to see settled on her face as she whispered, like a satanic echo, "Let us also go and look at this unfortunate."

A jealous pang smote the young man's heart as he recalled the past.

"You pity him, Pauline, and pity is akin to love."

"I only pity what I respect. Rest content, my husband."

Steadily her eyes met his, and the hand whose only ornament was a wedding ring went to meet the one folded on his arm with a confiding gesture that made the action a caress.

"I will try to be, yet mine is a hard part," Manuel answered with a sigh, then silently they both paced on.

Gilbert Redmond lounged behind his wife's chair, looking intensely bored.

"Have you had enough of this folly, Babie?"

"No, we have but just come. Let us dance."

"Too late; they have begun."

"Then go about with me. It's very tiresome sitting here."

"It is too warm to walk in all that crowd, child."

"You are so indolent! Tell me who people are as they pass. I know no one here."

"Nor I."

But his act belied the words, for as they passed his lips he rose erect, with a smothered exclamation and startled face, as if a ghost had suddenly confronted him. The throng had thinned, and as his wife followed the direction of his glance, she saw no uncanny apparition to cause such evident dismay, but a woman fair-haired, violet-eyed, blooming and serene, sweeping down the long hall with noiseless grace. An air of sumptuous life pervaded her, the shimmer of bridal snow surrounded her, bridal gifts shone on neck and arms, and bridal happiness seemed to touch her with its tender charm as she looked up at her companion, as if there were but one human being in the world to her. This companion, a man slender and tall, with a face delicately dark as a fine bronze, looked back at her with eyes as eloquent as her own, while both spoke rapidly and low in the melodious language which seems made for lover's lips.

"Gilbert, who are they?"

There was no answer, and before she could repeat the question the approaching pair paused before her, and the beautiful woman offered her hand, saying, with inquiring smiles, "Barbara, have you forgotten your early friend, Pauline?"

Recognition came with the familiar name, and Mrs. Redmond welcomed the newcomer with a delight as unrestrained as if she were still the schoolgirl, Babie. Then, recovering herself, she said, with a pretty attempt at dignity, "Let me present my husband. Gilbert, come and welcome my friend Pauline Valary."

Scarlet with shame, dumb with conflicting emotions, and utterly deserted by self-possession, Redmond stood with downcast eyes and agitated mien, suffering a year's remorse condensed into a moment. A mute gesture was all the greeting he could offer. Pauline slightly bent her haughty head as she answered, in a voice frostily sweet, "Your wife mistakes. Pauline Valary died three weeks ago, and Pauline Laroche rose from her ashes. Manuel, my schoolmate, Mrs. Redmond; Gilbert you already know."

With the manly presence he could easily assume and which was henceforth to be his role in public, Manuel bowed courteously to the lady, coldly to the gentleman, and looked only at his wife. Mrs. Redmond, though childish, was observant; she glanced from face to face, divined a mystery, and spoke out at once.

"Then you have met before? Gilbert, you have never told me this."

"It was long ago—in Cuba. I believed they had forgotten me."

"I never forget." And Pauline's eye turned on him with a look he dared not meet.

Unsilenced by her husband's frown, Mrs. Redmond, intent on pleasing herself, drew her friend to the seat beside her as she said petulantly, "Gilbert tells me nothing, and I am constantly discovering things which might have given me pleasure had he only chosen to be frank. I've spoken of you often, yet he never betrayed the least knowledge of you, and I take it very ill of him, because I am sure he has not forgotten you. Sit here, Pauline, and let me tease you with questions, as I used to do so long ago. You were always patient with me, and though far more beautiful, your face is still the same kind one that comforted the little child at school. Gilbert, enjoy your friend, and leave us to ourselves until the dance is over."

Pauline obeyed; but as she chatted, skillfully leading the young wife's conversation to her own affairs, she listened to the two voices behind her, watched the two figures reflected in the mirror before her, and felt a secret pride in Manuel's address, for it was evident that the former positions were renewed.

The timid boy who had feared the sarcastic tongue of his guardian's guest, and shrunk from his presence to conceal the jealousy that was his jest, now stood beside his formal rival, serene and self-possessed, by far the manliest man of the two, for no shame daunted him, no fear oppressed him, no dishonorable deed left him at the mercy of another's tongue.

Gilbert Redmond felt this keenly, and cursed the falsehood which had placed him in such an unenviable position. It was vain to assume the old superiority that was forfeited; but too much a man of the world to be long discomforted by any contretemps like this, he rapidly regained his habitual ease of manner, and avoiding the perilous past clung to the safer present, hoping, by some unguarded look or word, to fathom the purpose of his adversary, for such he knew the husband of Pauline must be at heart. But Manuel schooled his features, curbed his tongue, and when his hot blood tempted him to point his smooth speech with a taunt, or offer a silent insult with the eye, he remembered Pauline, looked down on the graceful head below, and forgot all other passions in that of love.

"Gilbert, my shawl. The sea air chills me."

"I forgot it, Babie."

"Allow me to supply the want."

Mindful of his wife's commands, Manuel seized this opportunity to win a glance of commendation from her. And taking the downy mantle that hung upon his arm, he wrapped the frail girl in it with a care that made the act as cordial as courteous. Mrs. Redmond felt the charm of his manner with the quickness of a woman, and sent a reproachful glance at Gilbert as she said plaintively, "Ah! It is evident that my honeymoon is over, and the assiduous lover replaced by the negligent husband. Enjoy your midsummer night's dream while you may, Pauline, and be ready for the awakening that must come."

"Not to her, madame, for our honeymoon shall last till the golden wedding day comes round. Shall it not, *cariña?*"

"There is no sign of waning yet, Manuel," and Pauline looked up into her husband's face with a genuine affection which made her own more beautiful and filled his with a visible content. Gilbert read the glance, and in that instant suffered the first pang of regret that Pauline had foretold. He spoke abruptly, longing to be away.

"Babie, we may dance now, if you will."

"I am going, but not with you—so give me my fan, and entertain Pauline till my return."

He unclosed his hand, but the delicately carved fan fell at his feet in a shower of ivory shreds—he had crushed it as he watched his first love with the bitter thought "It might have been!"

"Forgive me, Babie, it was too frail for use; you should choose a stronger."

"I will next time, and a gentler hand to hold it. Now, Monsieur Laroche, I am ready."

Mrs. Redmond rose in a small bustle of satisfaction, shook out her flounces, glanced at the mirror, then Manuel led her away; and the other pair were left alone.

Both felt a secret agitation quicken their breath and thrill along their nerves, but the woman concealed it best. Gilbert's eye wandered restlessly to and fro, while Pauline fixed her own on his as quietly as if he were the statue in the niche behind him. For a moment he tried to seem unconscious of it, then essayed to meet and conquer it, but failed signally and, driven to his last resources by that steady gaze, resolved to speak out and have all over before his wife's return. Assuming the seat beside her, he said, impetuously, "Pauline, take off your mask as I do mine—we are alone now, and may see each other as we are."

Leaning deep into the crimson curve of the couch, with the indolent grace habitual to her, yet in strong contrast to the vigilant gleam of her eye, she swept her hand across her face as if obeying him, yet no change followed, as she said with a cold smile, "It is off; what next?"

"Let me understand you. Did my letter reach your hands?"

"A week before my marriage."

He drew a long breath of relief, yet a frown gathered as he asked, like one loath and eager to be satisfied, "Your love died a natural death, then, and its murder does not lie at my door?"

Pointing to the shattered toy upon the ground, she only echoed his own words. "It was too frail for use—I chose a stronger."

It wounded, as she meant it should; and the evil spirit to whose guidance she had yielded herself exulted to see his self-love bleed, and pride vainly struggle to conceal the stab. He caught the expression in her averted glance, bent suddenly a fixed and scrutinizing gaze upon her, asking, below his breath, "Then why are you here to tempt me with the face that tempted me a year ago?"

"I came to see the woman to whom you sold yourself. I have seen her, and am satisfied."

Such quiet contempt iced her tones, such pitiless satisfaction shone through the long lashes that swept slowly down, after her eye had met and caused his own to fall again, that Gilbert's cheek burned as if the words had been a blow, and mingled shame and anger trembled in his voice.

"Ah, you are quick to read our secret, for you possess the key. Have you no fear that I may read your own, and tell the world you sold your beauty for a name and fortune? Your bargain is a better one than mine, but I know you too well, though your fetters are diamonds and your master a fond boy."

She had been prepared for this, and knew she had a shield in the real regard she bore her husband, for though sisterly, it was sincere. She felt its value now, for it gave her courage to confront the spirit of retaliation she had roused, and calmness to answer the whispered taunt with an unruffled mien, as lifting her white arm she let its single decoration drop glittering to her lap.

"You see my 'fetters' are as loose as they are light, and nothing binds me but my will. Read my heart, if you can. You will find there contempt for a love so poor that it feared poverty; pity for a man who dared not face the world and conquer it, as a girl had done before him, and gratitude that I have found my 'master' in a true-hearted boy, not a falsehearted man. If I am a slave, I never know it. Can you say as much?"

Her woman's tongue avenged her, and Gilbert owned his defeat. Pain quenched the ire of his glance, remorse subdued his pride, self-condemnation compelled him to ask, imploringly, "Pauline, when may I hope for pardon?"

"Never."

The stern utterance of the word dismayed him, and, like one shut out from hope, he rose, as if to leave her, but paused irresolutely, looked back, then sank down again, as if constrained against his will by a longing past control. If she had doubted her power this action set the doubt at rest, as the haughtiest nature she had known confessed it by a bittersweet complaint. Eyeing her wistfully, tenderly, Gilbert murmured, in the voice of long ago, "Why do I stay to wound and to be wounded by the hand that once caressed me? Why do I find more pleasure in your contempt than in another woman's praise, and feel myself transported into the delights of that irrecoverable past, now grown the sweetest, saddest memory of my life? Send me away, Pauline, before the old charm asserts its power, and I forget that I am not the happy lover of a year ago."

"Leave me then, Gilbert. Good night."

Half unconsciously, the former softness stole into her voice as it lingered on his name. The familiar gesture accompanied the words, the old charm did assert itself, and for an instant changed the cold woman into the ardent girl again. Gilbert did not go but, with a hasty glance down the deserted hall behind him, captured and kissed the hand he had lost, passionately whispering, "Pauline, I love you still, and that look assures me that you have forgiven, forgotten, and kept a place for me in that deep heart of yours. It is too late to deny it. I have seen the tender eyes again, and the sight has made me the proudest, happiest man that walks the world tonight, slave though I am."

Over cheek and forehead rushed the treacherous blood as the violet eyes filled and fell before his own, and in the glow of mingled pain and fear that stirred her blood, Pauline, for the first time, owned the peril of the task she had set herself, saw the dangerous power she possessed, and felt the buried passion faintly moving in its grave. Indignant at her own weakness, she took refuge in the memory of her wrong, controlled the rebel color, steeled the front she showed him, and with feminine skill mutely conveyed the rebuke she would not trust herself to utter, by stripping the glove from the hand he had touched and dropping it disdainfully as if unworthy of its place. Gilbert had not looked for such an answer, and while it baffled him it excited his man's spirit to rebel against her silent denial. With a bitter laugh he snatched up the glove.

"I read a defiance in your eye as you flung this down. I accept the challenge, and will keep gage until I prove myself the victor. I have asked for pardon. You refuse it. I have confessed my love. You scorn it. I have possessed myself of your secret, yet you deny it. Now we will try our strength together, and leave those children to their play."

"We are the children, and we play with edge tools. There has been enough of this, there must be no more." Pauline rose with her haughtiest mien, and the brief command, "Take me to Manuel."

Silently Gilbert offered his arm, and silently she rejected it.

"Will you accept nothing from me?"

"Nothing."

Side by side they passed through the returning throng till Mrs. Redmond joined them, looking blithe and bland with the exhilaration of gallantry and motion. Manuel's first glance was at Pauline, his second at her companion; there was a shadow upon the face of each, which seemed instantly to fall upon his own as he claimed his wife with a masterful satisfaction as novel as becoming, and which prompted her to whisper, "You enact your role to the life, and shall enjoy a foretaste of your reward at once. I want excitement; let us show these graceless, frozen people the true art of dancing, and electrify them with the life and fire of a Cuban valse."

Manuel kindled at once, and Pauline smiled stealthily as she glanced over her shoulder from the threshold of the dancing hall, for her slightest act, look, and word had their part to play in that night's drama.

"Gilbert, if you are tired I will go now."

"Thank you, I begin to find it interesting. Let us watch the dancers."

Mrs. Redmond accepted the tardy favor, wondering at his unwonted animation, for never had she seen such eagerness in his countenance, such energy in his manner as he pressed through the crowd and won a place where they could freely witness one of those exhibitions of fashionable figurante which are nightly to be seen at such resorts. Many couples were whirling around the white hall, but among them one pair circled with slowly increasing speed, in perfect time to the inspiring melody of trumpet, flute, and horn, that seemed to sound for them alone. Many paused to watch them, for they gave to the graceful pastime the enchantment which few have skill enough to lend it, and made it a spectacle of life-enjoying youth, to be remembered long after the music ceased and the agile feet were still.

Gilbert's arm was about his little wife to shield her from the pressure of the crowd, and as they stood his hold unconsciously tightened, till, marveling at this unwonted care, she looked up to thank him with a happy glance and discovered that his eye rested on a single pair, kindling as they approached, keenly scanning every gesture as they floated by, following them with untiring vigilance through the many-colored mazes they threaded with such winged steps, while his breath quickened, his hand kept time, and every sense seemed to own the intoxication of the scene. Sorrowfully she too watched this pair, saw their grace, admired their beauty, envied their happiness; for, short as her wedded life had been, the thorns already pierced her through the roses, and with each airy revolution of those figures, dark and bright, her discontent increased, her wonder deepened, her scrutiny grew keener, for she knew no common interest held her husband there, fascinated, flushed, and excited as if his heart beat responsive to the rhythmic rise and fall of that booted foot and satin slipper. The music ended with a crash, the crowd surged across the floor, and the spell was broken. Like one but half disenchanted, Gilbert stood a moment, then remembered his wife, and looking down met brown eyes, full of tears, fastened on his face.

"Tired so soon, Babie? Or in a pet because I cannot change myself into a thistledown and float about with you, like Manuel and Pauline?"

"Neither; I was only wishing that you loved me as he loves her, and hoping he would never tire of her, they are so fond and charming now. How long have you known them—and where?"

"I shall have no peace until I tell you. I passed a single summer with them in a tropical paradise, where we swung half the day in hammocks, under tamarind and almond trees; danced half the night to music, of which this seems but a faint echo; and led a life of luxurious delight in an enchanted climate, where all is so beautiful and brilliant that its memory haunts a life as pressed flowers sweeten the leaves of a dull book."

"Why did you leave it then?"

"To marry you, child."

"That was a regretful sigh, as if I were not worth the sacrifice. Let us go back and enjoy it together."

"If you were dying for it, I would not take you to Cuba. It would be purgatory, not paradise, now."

"How stern you look, how strangely you speak. Would you not go to save your own life, Gilbert?"

"I would not cross the room to do that much, less the sea."

"Why do you both love and dread it? Don't frown, but tell me. I have a right to know."

"Because the bitterest blunder of my life was committed there—a blunder that I never can repair in this world, and may be damned for in the next. Rest satisfied with this, Babie, lest you prove like Bluebeard's wife, and make another skeleton in my closet, which has enough already."

Strange regret was in his voice, strange gloom fell upon his face; but though rendered doubly curious by the change, Mrs. Redmond dared not question further and, standing silent, furtively scanned the troubled countenance beside her. Gilbert spoke first, waking out of his sorrowful reverie with a start.

"Pauline is coming. Say adieu, not au revoir, for tomorrow we must leave this place."

His words were a command, his aspect one of stern resolve, though the intensest longing mingled with the dark look he cast on the approaching pair. The tone, the glance displeased his willful wife, who loved to use her power and exact obedience where she had failed to win affection, often ruling imperiously when a tender word would have made her happy to submit.

"Gilbert, you take no thought for my pleasures though you pursue your own at my expense. Your neglect forces me to find solace and satisfaction where I can, and you have forfeited your right to command or complain. I love Pauline, I am happy with her, therefore I shall stay until we tire of one another. I am a burden to you; go if you will."

"You know I cannot without you, Babie. I ask it as a favor. For my sake, for your own, I implore you to come away."

"Gilbert, do you love her?"

She seized his arm and forced an answer by the energy of her sharply whispered question. He saw that it was vain to dissemble, yet replied with averted head, "I did and still remember it."

"And she? Did she return your love?"

"I believed so; but she forgot me when I went. She married Manuel and is happy. Babie, let me go!"

"No! you shall stay and feel a little of the pain I feel when I look into your heart and find I have no place there. It is this which has stood between us and made all my efforts vain. I see it now and despise you for the falsehood you have shown me, vowing you loved no one but me until I married you, then letting me so soon discover that I was only an encumbrance to your enjoyment of the fortune I possessed. You treat me like a child, but I suffer like a woman, and you shall share my suffering, because you might have spared me, and you did not. Gilbert, you shall stay."

"Be it so, but remember I have warned you."

An exultant expression broke through the gloom of her husband's face as he answered with the grim satisfaction of one who gave restraint to the mind, and stood ready to follow whatever impulse should sway him next. His wife trembled inwardly at what she had done, but was too proud to recall her words and felt a certain bitter pleasure in the excitement of the new position she had taken, the new interest given to her listless life.

Pauline and Manuel found them standing silently together, for a moment had done the work of years and raised a barrier between them never to be swept away.

Mrs. Redmond spoke first, and with an air half resentful, half triumphant:

"Pauline, this morose husband of mine says we must leave tomorrow. But in some things I rule; this is one of them. Therefore we remain and go with you to the mountains when we are tired of the gay life here. So smile and submit, Gilbert, else these friends will count your society no favor. Would you not fancy, from the aspect he thinks proper to assume, that I had sentenced him to a punishment, not a pleasure?"

"Perhaps you have unwittingly, Babie. Marriage is said to cancel the follies of the past, but not those of the future, I believe; and, as there are many temptations to an idle man in a place like this, doubtless your husband is wise enough to own that he dares not stay but finds discretion the better part of valor."

Nothing could be softer than the tone in which these words were uttered, nothing sharper than the hidden taunt conveyed, but Gilbert only laughed a scornful laugh as he fixed his keen eyes full upon her and took her bouquet with the air of one assuming former rights.

"My dear Pauline, discretion is the last virtue I should expect to be accused of by you; but if valor consists in daring all things, I may lay claim to it without its 'better part,' for temptation is my delight—the stronger the better. Have no fears for me, my friend. I gladly accept Babie's decree and, ignoring the last ten years, intend to begin life anew, having discovered a *sauce piquante* which will give the stalest pleasures a redoubled zest. I am unfortunate tonight, and here is a second wreck; this I can rebuild happily. Allow me to do so, for I remember you once praised my skill in floral architecture."

With an air of eager gallantry in strange contrast to the malign expression of his countenance, Gilbert knelt to regather the flowers which a careless gesture of his own had scattered from their jeweled holder. His wife turned to speak to Manuel, and, yielding to the unconquerable anxiety his reckless manner awoke, Pauline whispered below her breath as she bent as if to watch the work, "Gilbert, follow your first impulse, and go tomorrow."

"Nothing shall induce me to."

"I warn you harm will come of it."

"Let it come; I am past fear now."

"Shun me for Babie's sake, if not for your own."

"Too late for that; she is headstrong—let her suffer."

"Have you no power, Gilbert?"

"None over her, much over you."

"We will prove that!"

"We will!"

Rapidly as words could shape them, these questions and answers fell, and with their utterance the last generous feeling died in Pauline's breast; for as she received the flowers, now changed from a love token to a battle gage, she saw the torn glove still crushed in Gilbert's hand, and silently accepted his challenge to the tournament so often held between man and woman—a tournament where the keen tongue is the lance, pride the shield, passion the fiery steed, and the hardest heart the winner of the prize, which seldom fails to prove a barren honor, ending in remorse.

CHAPTER III

FOR SEVERAL DAYS the Cubans were almost invisible, appearing only for a daily drive, a twilight saunter on the beach, or a brief visit to the ballroom, there to enjoy the excitement of the pastime in which they both excelled. Their apartments were in the quietest wing of the hotel, and from the moment of their occupancy seemed to acquire all the charms of home. The few guests admitted felt the atmosphere of poetry and peace that pervaded the nest which Love, the worker of miracles, had built himself even under that tumultuous roof. Strollers in the halls or along the breezy verandas often paused to listen to the music of instrument or voice which came floating out from these sequestered rooms. Frequent laughter and the murmur of conversation proved that ennui was unknown, and a touch of romance inevitably enhanced the interest wakened by the beautiful young pair, always together, always happy, never weary of the *dolce far niente* of this summer life.

In a balcony like a hanging garden, sheltered from the sun by blossoming shrubs and vines that curtained the green nook with odorous shade, Pauline lay indolently swinging in a gaily fringed hammock as she had been wont to do in Cuba, then finding only pleasure in the luxury of motion which now failed to quiet her unrest. Manuel had put down the book to which she no longer listened and, leaning his head upon his hand, sat watching her as she swayed to and fro with thoughtful eyes intent upon the sea, whose murmurous voice possessed a charm more powerful than his own. Suddenly he spoke:

"Pauline, I cannot understand you! For three weeks we hurried east and west to find this man, yet when found you shun him and seem content to make my life a heaven upon earth. I sometimes fancy that you have resolved to let the past sleep, but the hope dies as soon as born, for in moments like this I see that, though you devote yourself to me, the old purpose is unchanged, and I marvel why you pause."

Her eyes came back from their long gaze and settled on him full of an intelligence which deepened his perplexity. "You have not learned to know me yet; death is not more inexorable or time more tireless than I. This week has seemed one of indolent delight to you. To me it has been one of constant vigilance and labor, for scarcely a look, act, or word of mine has been without effect. At first I secluded myself that Gilbert might contrast our life with his and, believing us all and all to one another, find impotent regret his daily portion. Three days ago accident placed an unexpected weapon in my hand which I have used in silence, lest in spite of promises you should rebel and end his trial too soon. Have you no suspicion of my meaning?"

"None. You are more mysterious than ever, and I shall, in truth, believe you are the enchantress I have so often called you if your spells work invisibly."

"They do not, and I use no supernatural arts, as I will prove to you. Take my lorgnette that lies behind you, part the leaves where the green grapes hang thickest, look up at the little window in the shadowy angle of the low roof opposite, and tell me what you see."

"Nothing but a half-drawn curtain."

"Ah! I must try the ruse that first convinced me. Do not show yourself, but watch, and if you speak, let it be in Spanish."

Leaving her airy cradle, Pauline bent over the balcony as if to gather the climbing roses that waved their ruddy clusters in the wind. Before the third stem was broken Manuel whispered, "I see the curtain move; now comes the outline of a head, and now a hand, with some bright object in it. Santo Pablo! It is a man staring at you as coolly as if you were a lady in a balcony. What prying rascal is it?"

"Gilbert."

"Impossible! He is a gentleman."

"If gentlemen play the traitor and the spy, then he is one. I am not mistaken; for since the glitter of his glass first arrested me I have watched covertly, and several trials as successful as the present have confirmed the suspicion which Babie's innocent complaints of his long absences aroused. Now do you comprehend why I remained in these rooms with the curtains seldom drawn? Why I swung the hammock here and let you sing and read to me while I played with your hair or leaned upon your shoulder? Why I have been all devotion and made this balcony a little stage for the performance of our version of the honeymoon for one spectator?"

Still mindful of the eager eyes upon her, Pauline had been fastening the roses in her bosom as she spoke, and ended with a silvery laugh that made the silence musical with its heartsome sound. As she paused, Manuel flung down the lorgnette and was striding past her with ireful impetuosity, but the white arms took him captive, adding another figure to the picture framed by the green arch as she whispered decisively, "No farther! There must be no violence. You promised obedience and I exact it. Do you think detection to a man so lost to honor would wound as deeply as the sights which make his daily watch a torment? Or that a blow would be as hard to bear as the knowledge that his own act has placed you where you are and made him what he is? Silent contempt is the law now, so let this insult pass, unclench your hand and turn that defiant face to me, while I console you for submission with a kiss."

He yielded to the command enforced by the caress but drew her jealously from sight, and still glanced rebelliously through the leaves, asking with a frown, "Why show me this if I may not resent it? How long must I bear with this man? Tell me your design, else I shall mar it in some moment when hatred of him conquers love of you."

"I will, for it is time, because though I have taken the first step you must take the second. I showed you this that you might find action pleasanter than rest, and you must bear with this man a little longer for my sake, but I will give you an amusement to beguile the time. Long ago you told me that Gilbert was a gambler. I would not believe it then, now I can believe anything, and you can convince the world of this vice of his as speedily as you will."

"Do you wish me to become a gambler that I may prove him one? I also told you that he was suspected of dishonorable play—shall I load the dice and mark the cards to catch him in his own snares?"

Manuel spoke bitterly, for his high spirit chafed at the task assigned him; womanly wiles seemed more degrading than the masculine method of retaliation, in which strength replaces subtlety and speedier vengeance brings speedier satisfaction. But Pauline, fast learning to play upon that mysterious instrument, the human heart, knew when to stimulate and when to soothe.

"Do not reproach me that I point out a safer mode of operation than your own. You would go to Gilbert and by a hot word, a rash act, put your life and my happiness into his hands, for though dueling is forbidden here, he would not hesitate to break all laws, human or divine, if by so doing he could separate us. What would you gain by it? If you kill him he is beyond our reach forever, and a crime remains to be atoned for. If he kill you your blood will be upon my head, and where should I find consolation for the loss of the one heart always true and tender?"

With the inexplicable prescience which sometimes foreshadows coming ills, she clung to him as if a vision of the future dimly swept before her, but he only saw the solicitude it was a sweet surprise to find he had awakened, and in present pleasure forgot past pain.

"You shall not suffer from this man any grief that I can shield you from, rest assured of that, my heart. I will be patient, though your ways are not mine, for the wrong was yours, and the retribution shall be such as you decree."

"Then hear your task and see the shape into which circumstances have molded my design. I would have you exercise a self-restraint that shall leave Gilbert no hold upon you, accept all invitations like that which you refused when we passed him on the threshold of the billiard room an hour ago, and seem to find in such amusements the same fascination as himself. Your skill in games of chance excels his, as you proved at home where these pastimes lose their disreputable aspect by being openly enjoyed. Therefore I would have you whet this appetite of his by losing freely at first—he will take a grim delight in lessening the fortune he covets—then exert all your skill till he is deeply in your debt. He has nothing but what is doled out to him by Babie's father, I find; he dare not ask help there for such a purpose; other resources have failed else he would not have married; and if the sum be large enough, it lays him under an obligation which will be a thorn in his flesh, the sharper for your knowledge of his impotence to draw it out. When this is done, or even while it is in progress, I would have you add the pain of a new jealousy to the old. He neglects this young wife of his, and she is eager to recover the affections she believes she once possessed. Help her, and teach Gilbert the value of what he now despises. You are young, comely, accomplished, and possessed of many graces more attractive than you are conscious of; your southern birth and breeding gift you with a winning warmth of manners in strong contrast to the colder natures around you; and your love for me lends an almost tender deference to your intercourse with all womankind. Amuse, console this poor girl, and show her husband what he should be; I have no fear of losing your heart nor need you fear for hers; she is one of those spaniel-like creatures who love the hand that strikes them and fawn upon the foot that spurns them."

"Am I to be the sole actor in the drama of deceit? While I woo Babie, what will you do, Pauline?"

"Let Gilbert woo me—have patience till you understand my meaning; he still loves me and believes I still return that love. I shall not undeceive him yet, but let silence seem to confess what I do not own in words. He fed me with false promises, let me build my life's happiness on baseless hopes, and rudely woke me when he could delude no longer, leaving me to find I had pursued a shadow. I will do the same. He shall follow me undaunted, undeterred by all obstacles, all ties; shall stake his last throw and lose it, for when the crowning moment comes I shall show him that through me he is made bankrupt in love, honor, liberty, and hope, tell him I am yours entirely and forever, then vanish like an *ignis-fatuus,* leaving him to the darkness of despair and defeat. Is not this a better retribution than the bullet that would give him peace at once?"

Boy, lover, husband though he was, Manuel saw and stood aghast at the baleful spirit which had enslaved this woman, crushing all generous impulses, withering all gentle charities, and making her the saddest spectacle this world can show—one human soul rebelling against Providence, to become the nemesis of another. Involuntarily he recoiled from her, exclaiming, "Pauline! Are you possessed of a devil?"

"Yes! One that will not be cast out till every sin, shame, and sorrow mental ingenuity can conceive and inflict has been heaped on that man's head. I thought I should be satisfied with one accusing look, one bitter word; I am not, for the evil genii once let loose cannot be recaptured. Once I ruled it, now it rules me, and there is no turning back. I have come under the law of fate, and henceforth the powers I possess will ban, not bless, for I am driven to whet and wield them as weapons which may win me success at the price of my salvation. It is not yet too late for you to shun the spiritual contagion I bear about me. Choose now, and abide by that choice without a shadow of turning, as I abide by mine. Take me as I am; help me willingly and unwillingly; and in the end receive the promised gift—years like the days you have called heaven upon earth. Or retract the vows you plighted, receive again the heart and name you gave me, and live unvexed by the stormy nature time alone can tame. Here is the ring. Shall I restore or keep it, Manuel?"

Never had she looked more beautiful as she stood there, an image of will, daring, defiant, and indomitable, with eyes darkened by intensity of emotion, voice half sad, half stern, and outstretched hand on which the wedding ring no longer shone. She felt her power, yet was wary enough to assure it by one bold appeal to the strongest element of her husband's character: passions, not principles, were the allies she desired, and before the answer came she knew that she had gained them at the cost of innocence and self-respect.

As Manuel listened, an expression like a dark reflection of her own settled on his face; a year of youth seemed to drop away; and with the air of one who puts fear behind him, he took the hand, replaced the ring, resolutely accepted the hard conditions, and gave all to love, only saying as he had said before, "Soul and body, I belong to you; do with me as you will."

A fortnight later Pauline sat alone, waiting for her husband. Under the pretext of visiting a friend, she had absented herself a week, that Manuel might give himself entirely to the distasteful task she set him. He submitted to the separation, wrote daily, but sent no tidings of his progress, told her nothing when they met that night, and had left her an hour before asking her to have patience till he could show his finished work. Now, with her eye upon the door, her ear alert to catch the coming step, her mind disturbed by contending hopes and fears, she sat waiting with the vigilant immobility of an Indian on the watch. She had not long to look and listen. Manuel entered hastily, locked the door, closed the windows, dropped the curtains, then paused in the middle of the room and broke into a low, triumphant laugh as he eyed his wife with an expression she had never seen in those dear eyes before. It startled her, and, scarcely knowing what to desire or dread, she asked eagerly, "You are come to tell me you have prospered."

"Beyond your hopes, for the powers of darkness seem to help us, and lead the man to his destruction faster than any wiles of ours can do. I am tired, let me lie here and rest. I have earned it, so when I have told all say, 'Love, you have done well,' and I am satisfied."

He threw himself along the couch where she still sat and laid his head in her silken lap, her cool hand on his hot forehead, and continued in a muffled voice.

"You know how eagerly Gilbert took advantage of my willingness to play, and soon how recklessly he pursued it, seeming to find the satisfaction you foretold, till, obeying your commands, I ceased losing and won sums which surprised me. Then you went, but I was not idle, and in the effort to extricate himself, Gilbert plunged deeper into debt; for my desire to please you seemed to gift me with redoubled skill. Two days ago I refused to continue the unequal conflict, telling him to give himself no uneasiness, for I could wait. You were right in thinking it would oppress him to be under any obligation to me, but wrong in believing he would endure, and will hardly be prepared for the desperate step he took to free himself. That night he played falsely, was detected, and though his opponent generously promised silence for Babie's sake, the affair stole out—he is shunned and this resource has failed. I thought he had no other, but yesterday he came to me with a strange expression of relief, discharged the debt to the last farthing, then hinted that my friendship with his wife was not approved by him and must cease. This proves that I have obeyed you in all things, though the comforting of Babie was an easy task, for, both loving you, our bond of sympathy and constant theme has been Pauline and her perfections."

"Hush! No praise—it is a mockery. I am what one man's perfidy has made; I may yet learn to be worthy of another man's devotion. What more, Manuel?"

"I thought I should have only a defeat to show you, but today has given me a strange success. At noon a gentleman arrived and asked for Gilbert. He was absent, but upon offering information relative to the time of his return, which proved my intimacy with him, this Seguin entered into conversation with me. His evident desire to avoid Mrs. Redmond and waylay her husband interested me, and when he questioned me somewhat closely concerning Gilbert's habits and movements of late, my suspicions were roused; and on mentioning the debt so promptly discharged, I received a confidence that startled me. In a moment of despair Gilbert had forged the name of his former friend, whom he believed abroad, had drawn the money and freed himself from my power, but not for long. The good fortune which has led him safely through many crooked ways seems to have deserted him in this strait. For the forgery was badly executed, inspection raised doubts, and Seguin, just returned, was at his banker's an hour after Gilbert, to prove the fraud; he came hither at once to accuse him of it and made me his confidant. What would you have had me do, Pauline? Time was short, and I could not wait for you."

"How can I tell at once? Why pause to ask? What did you do?"

"Took a leaf from your book and kept accusation, punishment, and power in my own hands, to be used in your behalf. I returned the money, secured the forged check, and prevailed on Seguin to leave the matter in my hands, while he departed as quietly as he had come. Babie's presence when we met tonight prevented my taking you into my counsels. I had prepared this surprise for you and felt a secret pride in working it out alone. An hour ago I went to watch for Gilbert. He came, I took him to his rooms, told him what I had done, added that compassion for his wife had actuated me. I left him saying the possession of the check was a full equivalent for the money, which I now declined to receive from such dishonorable hands. Are you satisfied, Pauline?"

With countenance and gestures full of exultation she sprang up to pace the room, exclaiming, as she seized the forged paper, "Yes, that stroke was superb! How strangely the plot thickens. Surely the powers of darkness are working with us and have put this weapon in our hands when that I forged proved useless. By means of this we have a hold upon him which nothing can destroy unless he escape by death. Will he, Manuel?"

"No; there was more wrath than shame in his demeanor when I accused him. He hates me too much to die yet, and had I been the only possessor of this fatal fact, I fancy it might have gone hard with me; for if ever there was murder in a man's heart it was in his when I showed him that paper and then replaced it next the little poniard you smile at me for wearing. This is over. What next, my queen?"

There was energy in the speaker's tone but none in attitude or aspect, as, still lying where she had left him, he pillowed his head upon his arm and turned toward her a face already worn and haggard with the feverish weariness that had usurped the blithe serenity which had been his chiefest charm a month ago. Pausing in her rapid walk, as if arrested by the change that seemed to strike her suddenly, she recalled her thoughts from the dominant idea of her life and, remembering the youth she was robbing of its innocent delights, answered the wistful look which betrayed the hunger of a heart she had never truly fed, as she knelt beside her husband and, laying her soft cheek to his, whispered in her tenderest accents, "I am not wholly selfish or ungrateful, Manuel. You shall rest now while I sing to you, and tomorrow we will go away among the hills and leave behind us for a time the dark temptation which harms you through me."

"No! Finish what you have begun. I will have all or nothing, for if we pause now you will bring me a divided mind, and I shall possess only the shadow of a wife. Take Gilbert and Babie with us, and end this devil's work without delay. Hark! What is that?"

Steps came flying down the long hall, a hand tried the lock, then beat impetuously upon the door, and a low voice whispered with shrill importunity, "Let me in! Oh, let me in!"

Manuel obeyed the urgent summons, and Mrs. Redmond, half dressed, with streaming hair and terror-stricken face, fled into Pauline's arms, crying incoherently, "Save me! Keep me! I never can go back to him; he said I was a burden and a curse, and wished I never had been born!"

"What has happened, Babie? We are your friends. Tell us, and let us comfort and protect you if we can."

But for a time speech was impossible, and the poor girl wept with a despairing vehemence sad to see, till their gentle efforts soothed her; and, sitting by Pauline, she told her trouble, looking oftenest at Manuel, who stood before them, as if sure of redress from him.

"When I left here an hour or more ago I found my rooms still empty, and, though I had not seen my husband since morning, I knew he would be displeased to find me waiting, so I cried myself to sleep and dreamed of the happy time when he was kind, till the sound of voices woke me. I heard Gilbert say, 'Babie is with your wife, her maid tells me; therefore we are alone here. What is this mysterious affair, Laroche?' That tempted me to listen, and then, Manuel, I learned all the shame and misery you so generously tried to spare me. How can I ever repay you, ever love and honor you enough for such care of one so helpless and forlorn as I?"

"I am repaid already. Let that pass, and tell what brings you here with such an air of fright and fear?"

"When you were gone he came straight to the inner room in search of something, saw me, and knew I must have heard all he had concealed from me so carefully. If you have ever seen him when that fierce temper of his grows ungovernable, you can guess what I endured. He said such cruel things I could not bear it, and cried out that I would come to you, for I was quite wild with terror, grief, and shame, that seemed like oil to fire. He swore I should not, and oh, Pauline, he struck me! See, if I do not tell the living truth!"

Trembling with excitement, Mrs. Redmond pushed back the wide sleeve of her wrapper and showed the red outline of a heavy hand. Manuel set his teeth and stamped his foot into the carpet with an indignant exclamation and the brief question, "Then you left him, Babie?"

"Yes, although he locked me in my room, saying the law gave him the right to teach obedience. I flung on these clothes, crept noiselessly along the balcony till the hall window let me in, and then I ran to you. He will come for me. Can he take me away? Must I go back to suffer any more?"

In the very act of uttering the words, Mrs. Redmond clung to Manuel with a cry of fear, for on the threshold stood her husband. A comprehensive glance seemed to stimulate his wrath and lend the hardihood wherewith to confront the three, saying sternly as he beckoned, "Babie, I am waiting for you."

She did not speak, but still clung to Manuel as if he were her only hope. A glance from Pauline checked the fiery words trembling on his lips, and he too stood silent while she answered with a calmness that amazed him:

"Your wife has chosen us her guardians, and I think you will scarcely venture to use force again with two such witnesses as these to prove that you have forfeited your right to her obedience and justify the step she has taken."

With one hand she uncovered the discolored arm, with the other held the forgery before him. For a moment Gilbert stood daunted by these mute accusations, but just then his ire burned hottest against Manuel; and believing that he could deal a double blow by wounding Pauline through her husband, he ignored her presence and, turning to the young man, asked significantly, "Am I to understand that you refuse me my wife, and prefer to abide by the consequences of such an act?"

Calmed by Pauline's calmness, Manuel only drew the trembling creature closer, and answered with his haughtiest mien, "I do; spare yourself the labor of insulting me, for having placed yourself beyond the reach of a gentleman's weapon, I shall accept no challenge from a——"

A soft hand at his lips checked the opprobrious word, as Babie, true woman through it all, whispered with a broken sob, "Spare him, for I loved him once."

Gilbert Redmond had a heart, and, sinful though it was, this generous forbearance wrung it with a momentary pang of genuine remorse, too swiftly followed by a selfish hope that all was not lost if through his wife he could retain a hold upon the pair which now possessed for him the strong attraction of both love and hate. In that brief pause this thought came, was accepted and obeyed, for, as if yielding to an uncontrollable impulse of penitent despair, he stretched his arms to his wife, saying humbly, imploringly, "Babie, come back to me, and teach me how I may retrieve the past. I freely confess I bitterly repent my manifold transgressions, and submit to your decree alone; but in executing justice, oh, remember mercy! Remember that I was too early left fatherless, motherless, and went astray for want of some kind heart to guide and cherish me. There is still time. Be compassionate and save me from myself. Am I not punished enough? Must death be my only comforter? Babie, when all others cast me off, will you too forsake me?"

"No, I will not! Only love me, and I can forgive, forget, and still be happy!"

Pauline was right. The spaniel-like nature still loved the hand that struck it, and Mrs. Redmond joyfully returned to the arms from which she had so lately fled. The tenderest welcome she had ever received from him welcomed the loving soul whose faith was not yet dead, for Gilbert felt the value this once neglected possession had suddenly acquired, and he held it close; yet as he soothed with gentle touch and tone, could not forbear a glance of triumph at the spectators of the scene.

Pauline met it with that inscrutable smile of hers, and a look of intelligence toward her husband, as she said, "Did I not prophesy truly, Manuel? Be kind to her, Gilbert, and when next we meet show us a happier wife than the one now sobbing on your shoulder. Babie, good night and farewell, for we are off to the mountains in the morning."

"Oh, let us go with you as you promised! You know our secret, you pity me and will help Gilbert to be what he should. I cannot live at home, and places like this will seem so desolate when you and Manuel are gone. May we, can we be with you a little longer?"

"If Gilbert wishes it and Manuel consents, we will bear and forbear much for your sake, my poor child."

Pauline's eye said, "Dare you go?" and Gilbert's answered, "Yes," as the two met with a somber fire in each; but his lips replied, "Anywhere with you, Babie," and Manuel took Mrs. Redmond's hand with a graceful warmth that touched her deeper than his words.

"Your example teaches me the beauty of compassion, and Pauline's friends are mine."

"Always so kind to me! Dear Manuel, I never can forget it, though I have nothing to return but this," and, like a grateful child, she lifted up her innocent face so wistfully he could only bend his tall head to receive the kiss she offered.

Gilbert's black brows lowered ominously at the sight, but he never spoke; and, when her good-nights were over, bowed silently and carried his little wife away, nestling to him as if all griefs and pains were banished by returning love.

"Poor little heart! She should have a smoother path to tread. Heaven grant she may hereafter; and this sudden penitence prove no sham." Manuel paused suddenly, for as if obeying an unconquerable impulse, Pauline laid a hand on either shoulder and searched his face with an expression which baffled his comprehension, though he bore it steadily till her eyes fell before his own, when he asked smilingly:

"Is the doubt destroyed, *cariña?*"

"No; it is laid asleep."

Then as he drew her nearer, as if to make his peace for his unknown offense, she turned her cheek away and left him silently. Did she fear to find Babie's kiss upon his lips?

CHAPTER IV

THE WORK OF WEEKS is soon recorded, and when another month was gone these were the changes it had wrought. The four so strangely bound together by ties of suffering and sin went on their way, to the world's eye, blessed with every gracious gift, but below the tranquil surface rolled that undercurrent whose mysterious tides ebb and flow in human hearts unfettered by race or rank or time. Gilbert was a good actor, but, though he curbed his fitful temper, smoothed his mien, and sweetened his manner, his wife soon felt the vanity of hoping to recover that which never had been hers. Silently she accepted the fact and, uttering no complaint, turned to others for the fostering warmth without which she could not live. Conscious of a hunger like her own, Manuel could offer her sincerest sympathy, and soon learned to find a troubled pleasure in the knowledge that she loved him and her husband knew it, for his life of the emotions was rapidly maturing the boy into the man, as the fierce ardors of his native skies quicken the growth of wondrous plants that blossom in a night. Mrs. Redmond, as young in character as in years, felt the attraction of a nature generous and sweet, and yielded to it as involuntarily as an unsupported vine yields to the wind that blows it to the strong arms of a tree, still unconscious that a warmer sentiment than gratitude made his companionship the sunshine of her life. Pauline saw this, and sometimes owned within herself that she had evoked spirits which she could not rule, but her purpose drove her on, and in it she found a charm more perilously potent than before. Gilbert watched the three with a smile darker than a frown, yet no reproach warned his wife of the danger which she did not see; no jealous demonstration roused Manuel to rebel against the oppression of a presence so distasteful to him;

no rash act or word gave Pauline power to banish him, though the one desire of his soul became the discovery of the key to the inscrutable expression of her eyes as they followed the young pair, whose growing friendship left their mates alone. Slowly her manner softened toward him, pity seemed to bridge across the gulf that lay between them, and in rare moments time appeared to have retraced its steps, leaving the tender woman of a year ago. Nourished by such unexpected hope, the early passion throve and strengthened until it became the mastering ambition of his life, and, only pausing to make assurance doubly sure, he waited the advent of the hour when he could "put his fortune to the touch and win or lose it all."

"Manuel, are you coming?"

He was lying on the sward at Mrs. Redmond's feet, and, waking from the reverie that held him, while his companion sang the love lay he was teaching her, he looked up to see his wife standing on the green slope before him. A black lace scarf lay over her blonde hair as Spanish women wear their veils, below it the violet eyes shone clear, the cheek glowed with the color fresh winds had blown upon their paleness, the lips parted with a wistful smile, and a knot of bright-hued leaves upon her bosom made a mingling of snow and fire in the dress, whose white folds swept the grass. Against a background of hoary cliffs and somber pines, this figure stood out like a picture of blooming womanhood, but Manuel saw three blemishes upon it—Gilbert had sketched her with that shadowy veil upon her head, Gilbert had swung himself across a precipice to reach the scarlet nosegay for her breast, Gilbert stood beside her with her hand upon his arm; and troubled by the fear that often haunted him since Pauline's manner to himself had grown so shy and sad, Manuel leaned and looked forgetful of reply, but Mrs. Redmond answered blithely:

"He is coming, but with me. You are too grave for us, so go your ways, talking wisely of heaven and earth, while we come after, enjoying both as we gather lichens, chase the goats, and meet you at the waterfall. Now señor, put away guitar and book, for I have learned my lesson; so help me with this unruly hair of mine and leave the Spanish for today."

They looked a pair of lovers as Manuel held back the long locks blowing in the wind, while Babie tied her hat, still chanting the burthen of the tender song she had caught so soon. A voiceless sigh stirred the ruddy leaves on Pauline's bosom as she turned away, but Gilbert embodied it in words, "They are happier without us. Let us go."

Neither spoke till they reached the appointed tryst. The others were not there, and, waiting for them, Pauline sat on a mossy stone, Gilbert leaned against the granite boulder beside her, and both silently surveyed a scene that made the heart glow, the eye kindle with delight as it swept down from that airy height, across valleys dappled with shadow and dark with untrodden forests, up ranges of majestic mountains, through gap after gap, each hazier than the last, far out into that sea of blue which rolls around all the world. Behind them roared the waterfall swollen with autumn rains and hurrying to pour itself into the rocky basin that lay boiling below, there to leave its legacy of shattered trees, then to dash itself into a deeper chasm, soon to be haunted by a tragic legend and go glittering away through forest, field, and intervale to join the river rolling slowly to the sea. Won by the beauty and the grandeur of the scene, Pauline forgot she was not alone, till turning, she suddenly became aware that while she scanned the face of nature her companion had been scanning hers. What he saw there she could not tell, but all restraint had vanished from his manner, all reticence from his speech, for with the old ardor in his eye, the old impetuosity in his voice, he said, leaning down as if to read her heart, "This is the moment I have waited for so long. For now you see what I see, that both have made a bitter blunder, and may yet repair it. Those children love each other; let them love, youth mates them, fortune makes them equals, fate brings them together that we may be free. Accept this freedom as I do, and come out into the world with me to lead the life you were born to enjoy."

With the first words he uttered Pauline felt that the time had come, and in the drawing of a breath was ready for it, with every sense alert, every power under full control, every feature obedient to the art which had become a second nature. Gilbert had seized her hand, and she did not draw it back; the sudden advent of the instant which must end her work sent an unwonted color to her cheek, and she did avert it; the exultation which flashed into her eyes made it unsafe to meet his own, and they drooped before him as if in shame or fear, her whole face woke and brightened with the excitement that stirred her blood. She did not seek to conceal it, but let him cheat himself with the belief that love touched it with such light and warmth, as she softly answered in a voice whose accents seemed to assure his hope.

"You ask me to relinquish much. What do you offer in return, Gilbert, that I may not for a second time find love's labor lost?"

It was a wily speech, though sweetly spoken, for it reminded him how much he had thrown away, how little now remained to give, but her mien inspired him, and nothing daunted, he replied more ardently than ever:

"I can offer you a heart always faithful in truth though not in seeming, for I never loved that child. I would give years of happy life to undo that act and be again the man you trusted. I can offer you a name which shall yet be an honorable one, despite the stain an hour's madness cast upon it. You once taunted me with cowardice because I dared not face the world and conquer it. I dare do that now; I long to escape from this disgraceful servitude, to throw myself into the press, to struggle and achieve for your dear sake. I can offer you strength, energy, devotion—three gifts worthy any woman's acceptance who possesses power to direct, reward, and enjoy them as you do, Pauline. Because with your presence for my inspiration, I feel that I can retrieve my faultful past, and with time become God's noblest work—an honest man. Babie never could exert this influence over me. You can, you will, for now my earthly hope is in your hands, my soul's salvation in your love."

If that love had not died a sudden death, it would have risen up to answer him as the one sincere desire of an erring life cried out to her for help, and this man, as proud as sinful, knelt down before her with a passionate humility never paid at any other shrine, human or divine. It seemed to melt and win her, for he saw the color ebb and flow, heard the rapid beating of her heart, felt the hand tremble in his own, and received no denial but a lingering doubt, whose removal was a keen satisfaction to himself.

"Tell me, before I answer, are you sure that Manuel loves Babie?"

"I am; for every day convinces me that he has outlived the brief delusion, and longs for liberty, but dares not ask it. Ah! that pricks pride! But it is so. I have watched with jealous vigilance and let no sign escape me; because in his infidelity to you lay my chief hope. Has he not grown melancholy, cold, and silent? Does he not seek Babie and, of late, shun you? Will he not always yield his place to me without a token of displeasure or regret? Has he ever uttered reproach, warning, or command to you, although he knows I was and am your lover? Can you deny these proofs, or pause to ask if he will refuse to break the tie that binds him to a woman, whose superiority in all things keeps him a subject where he would be a king? You do not know the heart of man if you believe he will not bless you for his freedom."

Like the cloud which just then swept across the valley, blotting out its sunshine with a gloomy shadow, a troubled look flitted over Pauline's face. But if the words woke any sleeping fear she cherished, it was peremptorily banished, for scarcely had the watcher seen it than it was gone. Her eyes still shone upon the ground, and still she prolonged the bittersweet delight at seeing this humiliation of both soul and body by asking the one question whose reply would complete her sad success.

"Gilbert, do you believe I love you still?"

"I know it! Can I not read the signs that proved it to me once? Can I forget that, though you followed me to pity and despise, you have remained to pardon and befriend? Am I not sure that no other power could work the change you have wrought in me? I was learning to be content with slavery, and slowly sinking into that indolence of will which makes submission easy. I was learning to forget you, and be resigned to hold the shadow when the substance was gone, but you came, and with a look undid my work, with a word destroyed my hard-won peace, with a touch roused the passion which was not dead but sleeping, and have made this month of growing certainty to be the sweetest in my life—for I believed all lost, and you showed me that all was won. Surely that smile is propitious! and I may hope to hear the happy confirmation of my faith from lips that were formed to say 'I love!' "

She looked up then, and her eyes burned on him, with an expression which made his heart leap with expectant joy, as over cheek and forehead spread a glow of womanly emotion too genuine to be feigned, and her voice thrilled with the fervor of that sentiment which blesses life and outlives death.

"Yes, I love; not as of old, with a girl's blind infatuation, but with the warmth and wisdom of heart, mind, and soul—love made up of honor, penitence and trust, nourished in secret by the better self which lingers in the most tried and tempted of us, and now ready to blossom and bear fruit, if God so wills. I have been once deceived, but faith still endures, and I believe that I may yet earn this crowning gift of a woman's life for the man who shall make my happiness as I make his—who shall find me the prouder for past coldness, the humbler for past pride—whose life shall pass serenely loving. And that beloved is—my husband."

If she had lifted her white hand and stabbed him, with that smile upon her face, it would not have shocked him with a more pale dismay than did those two words as Pauline shook him off and rose up, beautiful and stern as an avenging angel. Dumb with an amazement too fathomless for words, he knelt there motionless and aghast. She did not speak. And, passing his hand across his eyes as if he felt himself the prey to some delusion, he rose slowly, asking, half incredulously, half imploringly, "Pauline, this is a jest?"

"To me it is; to you—a bitter earnest."

A dim foreboding of the truth fell on him then, and with it a strange sense of fear; for in this apparition of human judgment he seemed to receive a premonition of the divine. With a sudden gesture of something like entreaty, he cried out, as if his fate lay in her hands, "How will it end? how will it end?"

"As it began—in sorrow, shame and loss."

Then, in words that fell hot and heavy on the sore heart made desolate, she poured out the dark history of the wrong and the atonement wrung from him with such pitiless patience and inexorable will. No hard fact remained unrecorded, no subtle act unveiled, no hint of her bright future unspared to deepen the gloom of his. And when the final word of doom died upon the lips that should have awarded pardon, not punishment, Pauline tore away the last gift he had given, and dropping it to the rocky path, set her foot upon it, as if it were the scarlet badge of her subjection to the evil spirit which had haunted her so long, now cast out and crushed forever.

Gilbert had listened with a slowly gathering despair, which deepened to the blind recklessness that comes to those whose passions are their masters, when some blow smites but cannot subdue. Pale to his very lips, with the still white wrath, so much more terrible to witness than the fiercest ebullition of the ire that flames and feeds like a sudden fire, he waited till she ended, then used the one retaliation she had left him. His hand went to his breast, a tattered glove flashed white against the cliff as he held it up before her, saying, in a voice that rose gradually till the last words sounded clear above the waterfall's wild song:

"It was well and womanly done, Pauline, and I could wish Manuel a happy life with such a tender, frank, and noble wife; but the future which you paint so well never shall be his. For, by the Lord that hears me! I swear I will end this jest of yours in a more bitter earnest than you prophesied. Look; I have worn this since the night you began the conflict, which has ended in defeat to me, as it shall to you. I do not war with women, but you shall have one man's blood upon your soul, for I will goad that tame boy to rebellion by flinging this in his face and taunting him with a perfidy blacker than my own. Will that rouse him to forget your commands and answer like a man?"

"Yes!"

The word rang through the air sharp and short as a pistol shot, a slender brown hand wrenched the glove away, and Manuel came between them. Wild with fear, Mrs. Redmond clung to him. Pauline sprang before him, and for a moment the two faced each other, with a year's smoldering jealousy and hate blazing in fiery eyes, trembling in clenched hands, and surging through set teeth in defiant speech.

"This is the gentleman who gambles his friend to desperation, and skulks behind a woman, like the coward he is," sneered Gilbert.

"Traitor and swindler, you lie!" shouted Manuel, and, flinging his wife behind him, he sent the glove, with a stinging blow, full in his opponent's face.

Then the wild beast that lurks in every strong man's blood leaped up in Gilbert Redmond's, as, with a single gesture of his sinewy right arm he swept Manuel to the verge of the narrow ledge, saw him hang poised there one awful instant, struggling to save the living weight that weighed him down, heard a heavy plunge into the black pool below, and felt that thrill of horrible delight which comes to murderers alone.

So swift and sure had been the act it left no time for help. A rush, a plunge, a pause, and then two figures stood where four had been—a man and woman staring dumbly at each other, appalled at the dread silence that made high noon more ghostly than the deepest night. And with that moment of impotent horror, remorse, and woe, Pauline's long punishment began.

❧ A Whisper in the Dark

As we rolled along, I scanned my companion covertly, and saw much to interest a girl of seventeen. My uncle was a handsome man, with all the polish of foreign life fresh upon him; yet it was neither comeliness nor graceful ease which most attracted me; for even my inexperienced eye caught glimpses of something stern and somber below these external charms, and my long scrutiny showed me the keenest eye, the hardest mouth, the subtlest smile I ever saw—a face which in repose wore the look that comes to those who have led lives of pleasure and learned their emptiness. He seemed intent on some thought that absorbed him, and for a time rendered him forgetful of my presence, as he sat with folded arms, fixed eyes, and restless lips. While I looked, my own mind was full of deeper thought than it had ever been before; for I was recalling, word for word, a paragraph in that half-read letter:

> At eighteen Sybil is to marry her cousin, the compact having been made between my brother and myself in their childhood. My son is with me now, and I wish them to be together during the next few months, therefore my niece must leave you sooner than I at first intended. Oblige me by preparing her for an immediate and final separation, but leave all disclosures to me, as I prefer the girl to remain ignorant of the matter for the present.

That displeased me. Why was I to remain ignorant of so important an affair? Then I smiled to myself, remembering that I did know, thanks to the willful curiosity that prompted me to steal a peep into the letter that Mme. Bernard had pored over with such an anxious face. I saw only a single paragraph, for my own name arrested my eye; and, though wild to read all, I had scarcely time to whisk the paper back into the reticule the forgetful old soul had left hanging on the arm of her chair. It was enough, however, to set my girlish brain in a ferment, and keep me gazing wistfully at my uncle, conscious that my future now lay in his hands; for I was an orphan and he my guardian, though I had seen him but seldom since I was confided to Madame a six years' child.

Presently my uncle became cognizant of my steady stare, and returned it with one as steady for a moment, then said, in a low, smooth tone, that ill accorded with the satirical smile that touched his lips, "I am a dull companion for my little niece. How shall I provide her with pleasanter amusement than counting my wrinkles or guessing my thoughts?"

I was a frank, fearless creature, quick to feel, speak, and act, so I answered readily, "Tell me about my cousin Guy. Is he as handsome, brave, and clever as Madame says his father was when a boy?"

My uncle laughed a short laugh, touched with scorn, whether for Madame, himself, or me I could not tell, for his countenance was hard to read.

"A girl's question and artfully put; nevertheless I shall not answer it, but let you judge for yourself."

"But, sir, it will amuse me and beguile the way. I feel a little strange and forlorn at leaving Madame, and talking of my new home and friends will help me to know and love them sooner. Please tell me, for I've had my own way all my life, and can't bear to be crossed."

My petulance seemed to amuse him, and I became aware that he was observing me with a scrutiny as keen as my own had been; but I smilingly sustained it, for my vanity was pleased by the approbation his eye betrayed. The evident interest he now took in all I said and did was sufficient flattery for a young thing, who felt her charms and longed to try their power.

"I, too, have had my own way all my life; and as the life is double the length, the will is double the strength of yours, and again I say no. What next, mademoiselle?"

He was blander than ever as he spoke, but I was piqued, and resolved to try coaxing, eager to gain my point, lest a too early submission now should mar my freedom in the future.

"But that is ungallant, Uncle, and I still have hopes of a kinder answer, both because you are too generous to refuse so small a favor to your 'little niece,' and because she can be charmingly wheedlesome when she likes. Won't you say yes now, Uncle?" And pleased with the daring of the thing, I put my arm about his neck, kissed him daintily, and perched myself upon his knee with most audacious ease.

He regarded me mutely for an instant, then, holding me fast, deliberately returned my salute on lips, cheeks, and forehead, with such warmth that I turned scarlet and struggled to free myself, while he laughed that mirthless laugh of his till my shame turned to anger, and I imperiously commanded him to let me go.

"Not yet, young lady. You came here for your own pleasure, but shall stay for mine, till I tame you as I see you must be tamed. It is a short process with me, and I possess experience in the work; for Guy, though by nature as wild as a hawk, has learned to come at my call as meekly as a dove. Chut! What a little fury it is!"

I was just then; for exasperated at his coolness, and quite beside myself, I had suddenly stooped and bitten the shapely white hand that held both my own. I had better have submitted; for slight as the foolish action was, it had an influence on my afterlife as many another such has had. My uncle stopped laughing, his hand tightened its grasp, for a moment his cold eye glittered and a grim look settled round the mouth, giving to his whole face a ruthless expression that entirely altered it. I felt perfectly powerless. All my little arts had failed, and for the first time I was mastered. Yet only physically; my spirit was rebellious still. He saw it in the glance that met his own, as I sat erect and pale, with something more than childish anger. I think it pleased him, for swiftly as it had come the dark look passed, and quietly, as if we were the best of friends, he began to relate certain exciting adventures he had known abroad, lending to the picturesque narration the charm of that peculiarly melodious voice, which soothed and won me in spite of myself, holding me intent till I forgot the past; and when he paused I found that I was leaning confidentially on his shoulder, asking for more, yet conscious of an instinctive distrust of this man whom I had so soon learned to fear yet fancy.

As I was recalled to myself, I endeavored to leave him; but he still detained me, and, with a curious expression, produced a case so quaintly fashioned that I cried out in admiration, while he selected two cigarettes, mildly aromatic with the herbs they were composed of, lit them, offered me one, dropped the window, and leaning back surveyed me with an air of extreme enjoyment, as I sat meekly puffing and wondering what prank I should play a part in next. Slowly the narcotic influence of the herbs diffused itself like a pleasant haze over all my senses; sleep, the most grateful, fell upon my eyelids, and the last thing I remember was my uncle's face dreamily regarding me through a cloud of fragrant smoke. Twilight wrapped us in its shadows when I woke, with the night wind blowing on my forehead, the muffled roll of wheels sounding in my ear, and my cheek pillowed upon my uncle's arm. He was humming a French *chanson* about "love and wine, and the Seine tomorrow!" I listened till I caught the air, and presently joined him, mingling my girlish treble with his flutelike tenor. He stopped at once and, in the coolly courteous tone I had always heard in our few interviews, asked if I was ready for lights and home.

"Are we there?" I cried; and looking out saw that we were ascending an avenue which swept up to a pile of buildings that rose tall and dark against the sky, with here and there a gleam along its gray front.

"Home at last, thank heaven!" And springing out with the agility of a young man, my uncle led me over a terrace into a long hall, light and warm, and odorous with the breath of flowers blossoming here and there in graceful groups. A civil, middle-aged maid received and took me to my room, a bijou of a place, which increased my wonder when told that my uncle had chosen all its decorations and superintended their arrangement. "He understands women," I thought, handling the toilet ornaments, trying luxurious chair and lounge, and ending by slipping my feet into the scarlet-and-white Turkish slippers, coquettishly turning up their toes before the fire. A few moments I gave to examination, and, having expressed my satisfaction, was asked by my maid if I would be pleased to dress, as "the master" never allowed dinner to wait for anyone. This recalled to me the fact that I was doubtless to meet my future husband at that meal, and in a moment every faculty was intent upon achieving a grand toilette for this first interview. The maid possessed skill and taste, and I a wardrobe lately embellished with Parisian gifts from my uncle which I was eager to display in his honor.

When ready, I surveyed myself in the long mirror as I had never done before, and saw there a little figure, slender, yet stately, in a dress of foreign fashion, ornamented with lace and carnation ribbons which enhanced the fairness of neck and arms, while blond hair, wavy and golden, was gathered into an antique knot of curls behind, with a carnation fillet, and below a blooming dark-eyed face, just then radiant with girlish vanity and eagerness and hope.

"I'm glad I'm pretty!"

"So am I, Sybil."

I had unconsciously spoken aloud, and the echo came from the doorway where stood my uncle, carefully dressed, looking comelier and cooler than ever. The disagreeable smile flitted over his lips as he spoke, and I started, then stood abashed, till beckoning, he added in his most courtly manner, "You were so absorbed in the contemplation of your charming self that Janet answered my tap and took herself away unheard. You are mistress of my table now. It waits; will you come down?"

With a last touch to that unruly hair of mine, a last, comprehensive glance and shake, I took the offered arm and rustled down the wide staircase, feeling that the romance of my life was about to begin. Three covers were laid, three chairs set, but only two were occupied, for no Guy appeared. I asked no questions, showed no surprise, but tried to devour my chagrin with my dinner, and exerted myself to charm my uncle into the belief that I had forgotten my cousin. It was a failure, however, for that empty seat had an irresistible fascination for me, and more than once, as my eye returned from its furtive scrutiny of napkin, plate, and trio of colored glasses, it met my uncle's and fell before his penetrative glance. When I gladly rose to leave him to his wine—for he did not ask me to remain—he also rose, and, as he held the door for me, he said, "You asked me to describe your cousin. You have seen one trait of his character tonight; does it please you?"

I knew he was as much vexed as I at Guy's absence, so quoting his own words, I answered saucily, "Yes, for I'd rather see the hawk free than coming tamely at your call, Uncle."

He frowned slightly, as if unused to such liberty of speech, yet bowed when I swept him a stately little curtsy and sailed away to the drawing room, wondering if my uncle was as angry with me as I was with my cousin. In solitary grandeur I amused myself by strolling through the suite of handsome rooms henceforth to be my realm, looked at myself in the long mirrors, as every woman is apt to do when alone and in costume, danced over the mossy carpets, touched the grand piano, smelled the flowers, fingered the ornaments on étagère and table, and was just giving my handkerchief a second drench of some refreshing perfume from a filigree flask that had captivated me when the hall door was flung wide, a quick step went running upstairs, boots tramped overhead, drawers seemed hastily opened and shut, and a bold, blithe voice broke out into a hunting song in a tone so like my uncle's that I involuntarily flew to the door, crying, "Guy is come!"

Fortunately for my dignity, no one heard me, and hurrying back I stood ready to skim into a chair and assume propriety at a minute's notice, conscious, meanwhile, of the new influence which seemed suddenly to gift the silent house with vitality, and add the one charm it needed—that of cheerful companionship. "How will he meet me? And how shall I meet him?" I thought, looking up at the bright-faced boy, whose portrait looked back at me with a mirthful light in the painted eyes and a trace of his father's disdainful smile in the curves of the firm-set lips. Presently the quick steps came flying down again, past the door, straight to the dining room opposite, and, as I stood listening with a strange flutter at my heart, I heard an imperious young voice say rapidly, "Beg pardon, sir, unavoidably detained. Has she come? Is she bearable?"

"I find her so. Dinner is over, and I can offer you nothing but a glass of wine."

My uncle's voice was frostily polite, making a curious contrast to the other, so impetuous and frank, as if used to command or win all but one.

"Never mind the dinner! I'm glad to be rid of it; so I'll drink your health, Father, and then inspect our new ornament."

"Impertinent boy!" I muttered, yet at the same moment resolved to deserve his appellation, and immediately grouped myself as effectively as possible, laughing at my folly as I did so. I possessed a pretty foot, therefore one little slipper appeared quite naturally below the last flounce of my dress; a bracelet glittered on my arm as it emerged from among the lace and carnation knots; that arm supported my head. My profile was well cut, my eyelashes long, therefore I read with face half averted from the door. The light showered down, turning my hair to gold; so I smoothed my curls, retied my snood, and, after a satisfied survey, composed myself with an absorbed aspect and a quickened pulse to await the arrival of the gentlemen.

Soon they came. I knew they paused on the threshold, but never stirred till an irrepressible "You are right, sir!" escaped the younger.

Then I rose prepared to give him the coldest greeting, yet I did not. I had almost expected to meet the boyish face and figure of the picture; I saw instead a man comely and tall. A dark moustache half hid the proud mouth; the vivacious eyes were far kinder, though quite as keen as his father's; and the freshness of unspoiled youth lent a charm which the older man had lost forever. Guy's glance of pleased surprise was flatteringly frank, his smile so cordial, his "Welcome, cousin!" such a hearty sound that my coldness melted in a breath, my dignity was all forgotten, and before I could restrain myself I had offered both hands with the impulsive exclamation "Cousin Guy, I know I shall be very happy here! Are you glad I have come?"

"Glad as I am to see the sun after a November fog."

And bending his tall head, he kissed my hand in the graceful foreign fashion he had learned abroad. It pleased me mightily, for it was both affectionate and respectful. Involuntarily I contrasted it with my uncle's manner, and flashed a significant glance at him as I did so. He understood it, but only nodded with the satirical look I hated, shook out his paper, and began to read. I sat down again, careless of myself now; and Guy stood on the rug, surveying me with an expression of surprise that rather nettled my pride.

"He is only a boy, after all; so I need not be daunted by his inches or his airs. I wonder if he knows I am to be his wife, and likes it."

The thought sent the color to my forehead, my eyes fell, and despite my valiant resolution I sat like any bashful child before my handsome cousin. Guy laughed a boyish laugh as he sat down on his father's footstool, saying, while he warmed his slender brown hands, "I beg your pardon, Sybil. (We won't be formal, will we?) But I haven't seen a lady for a month, so I stare like a boor at sight of a silk gown and highbred face. Are those people coming, sir?"

"If Sybil likes, ask her."

"Shall we have a flock of people here to make it gay for you, Cousin, or do you prefer our quiet style better; just riding, driving, lounging, and enjoying life, each in his own way? Henceforth it is to be as you command in such matters."

"Let things go on as they have done then. I don't care for society, and strangers wouldn't make it gay to me, for I like freedom; so do you, I think."

"Ah, don't I!"

A cloud flitted over his smiling face, and he punched the fire, as if some vent were necessary for the sudden gust of petulance that knit his black brows into a frown, and caused his father to tap him on the shoulder with the bland request, as he rose to leave the room, "Bring the portfolios and entertain your cousin; I have letters to write, and Sybil is too tired to care for music tonight."

Guy obeyed with a shrug of the shoulder his father touched, but lingered in the recess till my uncle, having made his apologies to me, had left the room; then my cousin rejoined me, wearing the same cordial aspect I first beheld. Some restraint was evidently removed, and his natural self appeared. A very winsome self it was, courteous, gay, and frank, with an undertone of deeper feeling than I thought to find. I watched him covertly, and soon owned to myself that he was all I most admired in the ideal hero every girl creates in her romantic fancy; for I no longer looked upon this young man as my cousin, but my lover, and through all our future intercourse this thought was always uppermost, full of a charm that never lost its power.

Before the evening ended Guy was kneeling on the rug beside me, our two heads close together, while he turned the contents of the great portfolio spread before us, looking each other freely in the face, as I listened and he described, both breaking into frequent peals of laughter at some odd adventure or comical mishap in his own travels, suggested by the pictured scenes before us. Guy was very charming, I my blithest, sweetest self, and when we parted late, my cousin watched me up the stairs with still another "Good night, Sybil," as if both sight and sound were pleasant to him.

"Is that your horse Sultan?" I called from my window next morning, as I looked down upon my cousin, who was coming up the drive from an early gallop on the moors.

"Yes, bonny Sybil; come and admire him," he called back, hat in hand, and a quick smile rippling over his face.

I went, and standing on the terrace, caressed the handsome creature, while Guy said, glancing up at his father's undrawn curtains, "If your saddle had come, we would take a turn before 'my lord' is ready for breakfast. This autumn air is the wine you women need."

I yearned to go, and when I willed the way soon appeared; so careless of bonnetless head and cambric gown, I stretched my hands to him, saying boldly, "Play young Lochinvar, Guy; I am little and light; take me up before you and show me the sea."

He liked the daring feat, held out his hand, I stepped on his boot toe, sprang up, and away we went over the wide moor, where the sun shone in a cloudless heaven, the lark soared singing from the green grass at our feet, and the September wind blew freshly from the sea. As we paused on the upland slope, that gave us a free view of the country for miles, Guy dismounted, and standing with his arm about the saddle to steady me in my precarious seat, began to talk.

"Do you like your new home, Cousin?"

"More than I can tell you!"

"And my father, Sybil?"

"Both yes and no to that question, Guy; I hardly know him yet."

"True, but you must not expect to find him as indulgent and fond as many guardians would be to such as you. It's not his nature. Yet you can win his heart by obedience, and soon grow quite at ease with him."

"Bless you! I'm that already, for I fear no one. Why, I sat on his knee yesterday and smoked a cigarette of his own offering, though Madame would have fainted if she had seen me; then I slept on his arm an hour, and he was fatherly kind, though I teased him like a gnat."

"The deuce he was!"

With which energetic expression Guy frowned at the landscape and harshly checked Sultan's attempt to browse, while I wondered what was amiss between father and son, and resolved to discover; but finding the conversation at an end, started it afresh by asking, "Is any of my property in this part of the country, Guy? Do you know I am as ignorant as a baby about my own affairs; for, as long as every whim was gratified and my purse full, I left the rest to Madame and Uncle, though the first hadn't a bit of judgment, and the last I scarcely knew. I never cared to ask questions before, but now I am intensely curious to know how matters stand."

"All you see is yours, Sybil" was the brief answer.

"What, that great house, the lovely gardens, these moors, and the forest stretching to the sea? I'm glad! I'm glad! But where, then, is your home, Guy?"

"Nowhere."

At this I looked so amazed that his gloom vanished in a laugh, as he explained, but briefly, as if this subject were no pleasanter than the first, "By your father's will you were desired to take possession of the old place at eighteen. You will be that soon; therefore, as your guardian, my father has prepared things for you, and is to share your home until you marry."

"When will that be, I wonder?" And I stole a glance from under my lashes, wild to discover if Guy knew of the compact and was a willing party to it.

His face was half averted, but over his dark cheek I saw a deep flush rise, as he answered, stooping to pull a bit of heather, "Soon, I hope, or the gentleman sleeping there below will be tempted to remain a fixture with you on his knee as 'Madame my wife.' He is not your own uncle, you know."

I smiled at the idea, but Guy did not see it; and seized with a whim to try my skill with the hawk that seemed inclined to peck at its master, I said demurely, "Well, why not? I might be very happy if I learned to love him, as I should, if he were always in that kindest mood of his. Would you like me for a little mamma, Guy?"

"No!" short and sharp as a pistol shot.

"Then you must marry and have a home of your own, my son."

"Don't, Sybil! I'd rather you didn't see me in a rage, for I'm not a pleasant sight, I assure you; and I'm afraid I shall be in one if you go on. I early lost my mother, but I love her tenderly, because my father is not much to me, and I know if she had lived I should not be what I am."

Bitter was his voice, moody his mien, and all the sunshine gone at once. I looked down and touched his black hair with a shy caress, feeling both penitent and pitiful.

"Dear Guy, forgive me if I pained you. I'm a thoughtless creature, but I'm not malicious, and a word will restrain me if kindly spoken. My home is always yours, and when my fortune is mine you shall never want, if you are not too proud to accept help from your own kin. You are a little proud, aren't you?"

"As Lucifer, to most people. I think I should not be to you, for you understand me, Sybil, and with you I hope to grow a better man."

He turned then, and through the lineaments his father had bequeathed him I saw a look that must have been his mother's, for it was womanly, sweet, and soft, and lent new beauty to the dark eyes, always kind, and just then very tender. He had checked his words suddenly, like one who has gone too far, and with that hasty look into my face had bent his own upon the ground, as if to hide the unwonted feeling that had mastered him. It lasted but a moment, then his old manner returned, as he said gaily, "There drops your slipper. I've been wondering what kept it on. Pretty thing! They say it is a foot like this that oftenest tramples on men's hearts. Are you cruel to your lovers, Sybil?"

"I never had one, for Madame guarded me like a dragon, and I led the life of a nun; but when I do find one I shall try his mettle well before I give up my liberty."

"Poets say it is sweet to give up liberty for love, and they ought to know," answered Guy, with a sidelong glance.

I liked that little speech, and recollecting the wistful look he had given me, the significant words that had escaped him, and the variations of tone and manner constantly succeeding one another, I felt assured that my cousin was cognizant of the family league, and accepted it, yet with the shyness of a young lover, knew not how to woo. This pleased me, and quite satisfied with my morning's work, I mentally resolved to charm my cousin slowly, and enjoy the romance of a genuine wooing, without which no woman's life seems complete—in her own eyes at least. He had gathered me a knot of purple heather, and as he gave it I smiled my sweetest on him, saying, "I commission you to supply me with nosegays, for you have taste, and I love wild flowers. I shall wear this at dinner in honor of its giver. Now take me home; for my moors, though beautiful, are chilly, and I have no wrapper but this microscopic handkerchief."

Off went his riding jacket, and I was half smothered in it. The hat followed next, and as he sprang up behind I took the reins, and felt a thrill of delight in sweeping down the slope with that mettlesome creature tugging at the bit, that strong arm around me, and the happy hope that the heart I leaned on might yet learn to love me.

The day so began passed pleasantly, spent in roving over house and grounds with my cousin, setting my possessions in order, and writing to dear old Madame. Twilight found me in my bravest attire, with Guy's heather in my hair, listening for his step, and longing to run and meet him when he came. Punctual to the instant he appeared, and this dinner was a far different one from that of yesterday, for both father and son seemed in their gayest and most gallant mood, and I enjoyed the hour heartily. The world seemed all in tune now, and when I went to the drawing room I was moved to play my most stirring marches, sing my blithest songs, hoping to bring one at least of the gentlemen to join me. It brought both, and my first glance showed me a curious change in each. My uncle looked harassed and yet amused; Guy looked sullen and eyed his father with covert glances.

The morning's chat flashed into my mind, and I asked myself, "Is Guy jealous so soon?" It looked a little like it, for he threw himself upon a couch and lay there silent and morose; while my uncle paced to and fro, thinking deeply, while apparently listening to the song he bade me finish. I did so, then followed the whim that now possessed me, for I wanted to try my power over them both, to see if I could restore that gentler mood of my uncle's, and assure myself that Guy cared whether I was friendliest with him or not.

"Uncle, come and sing with me; I like that voice of yours."

"Tut, I am too old for that; take this indolent lad instead. His voice is fresh and young, and will chord well with yours."

"Do you know that pretty *chanson* about 'love and wine, and the Seine tomorrow,' cousin Guy?" I asked, stealing a sly glance at my uncle.

"Who taught you that?" And Guy eyed me over the top of the couch with an astonished expression which greatly amused me.

"No one; Uncle sang a bit of it in the carriage yesterday. I like the air, so come and teach me the rest."

"It is no song for you, Sybil. You choose strange entertainment for a lady, sir."

A look of unmistakable contempt was in the son's eye, of momentary annoyance in the father's, yet his voice betrayed none as he answered, still pacing placidly along the room, "I thought she was asleep, and unconsciously began it to beguile a silent drive. Sing on Sybil; that Bacchanalian snatch will do you no harm."

But I was tired of music now they had come, so I went to him, and passing my arm through his, walked beside him, saying with my most persuasive aspect, "Tell me about Paris, Uncle; I intend to go there as soon as I'm of age, if you will let me. Does your guardianship extend beyond that time?"

"Only till you marry."

"I shall be in no haste, then, for I begin to feel quite homelike and happy here with you, and shall be content without other society; only you'll soon tire of me, and leave me to some dismal governess, while you and Guy go pleasuring."

"No fear of that, Sybil; I shall hold you fast till some younger guardian comes to rob me of my merry ward."

As he spoke, he took the hand that lay upon his arm into a grasp so firm, and turned on me a look so keen, that I involuntarily dropped my eyes lest he should read my secret there. Eager to turn the conversation, I asked, pointing to a little miniature hanging underneath the portrait of his son, before which he had paused, "Was that Guy's mother, sir?"

"No, your own."

I looked again, and saw a face delicate yet spirited, with dark eyes, a passionate mouth, and a head crowned with hair as plenteous and golden as my own; but the whole seemed dimmed by age, the ivory was stained, the glass cracked, and a faded ribbon fastened it. My eyes filled as I looked, and a strong desire seized me to know what had defaced this little picture of the mother whom I never knew.

"Tell me about her, Uncle; I know so little, and often long for her so much. Am I like her, sir?"

Why did my uncle avert his eyes as he answered, "You are a youthful image of her, Sybil"?

"Go on, please, tell me more; tell me why this is so stained and worn; you know all, and surely I am old enough now to hear any history of pain and loss."

Something caused my uncle to knit his brows, but his bland voice never varied a tone as he placed the picture in my hand and gave me this brief explanation:

"Just before your birth your father was obliged to cross the Channel, to receive the last wishes of a dying friend. There was an accident; the vessel foundered, and many lives were lost. He escaped, but by some mistake his name appeared in the list of missing passengers; your mother saw it, the shock destroyed her, and when your father returned he found only a motherless little daughter to welcome him. This miniature, which he always carried with him, was saved with his papers at the last moment; but though the seawater ruined it he would never have it copied or retouched, and gave it to me when he died in memory of the woman I had loved for his sake. It is yours now, my child; keep it, and never feel that you are fatherless or motherless while I remain."

Kind as was both act and speech, neither touched me, for something seemed wanting. I felt yet could not define it, for then I believed in the sincerity of all I met.

"Where was she buried, Uncle? It may be foolish, but I should like to see my mother's grave."

"You shall someday, Sybil," and a curious change came over my uncle's face as he averted it.

"I have made him melancholy, talking of Guy's mother and my own; now I'll make him gay again if possible, and pique that negligent boy," I thought, and drew my uncle to a lounging chair, established myself on the arm thereof, and kept him laughing with my merriest gossip, both of us apparently unconscious of the long dark figure stretched just opposite, feigning sleep, but watching us through half-closed lids, and never stirring except to bow silently to my careless "Good night."

As I reached the stairhead, I remembered that my letter to Madame, full of the frankest criticisms upon people and things, was lying unsealed on the table in the little room my uncle had set apart for my boudoir; fearing servants' eyes and tongues, I slipped down again to get it. The room adjoined the parlors, and just then was lit only by a ray from the hall lamp.

I had secured the letter, and was turning to retreat, when I heard Guy say petulantly, as if thwarted yet submissive, "I *am* civil when you leave me alone; I *do* agree to marry her, but I won't be hurried or go a-wooing except in my own way. You know I never liked the bargain, for it's nothing else; yet I can reconcile myself to being sold, if it relieves you and gives us both a home. But, Father, mind this, if you tie me to that girl's sash too tightly I shall break away entirely, and then where are we?"

"I should be in prison and you a houseless vagabond. Trust me, my boy, and take the good fortune which I secured for you in your cradle. Look in pretty Sybil's face, and resignation will grow easy; but remember time presses, that this is our forlorn hope, and for God's sake be cautious, for she is a headstrong creature, and may refuse to fulfill her part if she learns that the contract is not binding against her will."

"I think she'll not refuse, sir; she likes me already. I see it in her eyes; she has never had a lover, she says, and according to your account a girl's first sweetheart is apt to fare the best. Besides, she likes the place, for I told her it was hers, as you bade me, and she said she could be very happy here, if my father was always kind."

"She said that, did she? Little hypocrite! For your father, read yourself, and tell me what else she babbled about in that early *tête-à-tête* of yours."

"You are as curious as a woman, sir, and always make me tell you all I do and say, yet never tell me anything in return, except this business, which I hate, because my liberty is the price, and my poor little cousin is kept in the dark. I'll tell her all, before I marry her, Father."

"As you please, hothead. I am waiting for an account of the first love passage, so leave blushing to Sybil and begin."

I knew what was coming and stayed no longer, but caught one glimpse of the pair. Guy in his favorite place, erect upon the rug, half laughing, half frowning as he delayed to speak, my uncle serenely smoking on the couch; then I sped away to my own room, thinking, as I sat down in a towering passion, "So he does know of the baby betrothal and hates it, yet submits to please his father, who covets my fortune—mercenary creatures! I can annul the contract, can I? I'm glad to know that, for it makes me mistress of them both. I like you already, do I, and you see it in my eyes? Coxcomb! I'll be the thornier for that. Yet I do like him; I do wish he cared for me, I'm so lonely in the world, and he can be so kind."

So I cried a little, brushed my hair a good deal, and went to bed, resolving to learn all I could when, where, and how I pleased, to render myself as charming and valuable as possible, to make Guy love me in spite of himself, and then say yes or no, as my heart prompted me.

That day was a sample of those that followed, for my cousin was by turns attracted or repelled by the capricious moods that ruled me. Though conscious of a secret distrust of my uncle, I could not resist the fascination of his manner when he chose to exert its influence over me; this made my little plot easier of execution, for jealousy seemed the most effectual means to bring my wayward cousin to subjection. Full of this fancy, I seemed to tire of his society, grew thorny as a brier rose to him, affectionate as a daughter to my uncle, who surveyed us both with that inscrutable glance of his, and slowly yielded to my dominion as if he had divined my purpose and desired to aid it. Guy turned cold and gloomy, yet still lingered near me as if ready for a relenting look or word. I liked that, and took a wanton pleasure in prolonging the humiliation of the warm heart I had learned to love, yet not to value as I ought, until it was too late.

One dull November evening as I went wandering up and down the hall, pretending to enjoy the flowers, yet in reality waiting for Guy, who had left me alone all day, my uncle came from his room, where he had sat for many hours with the harassed and anxious look he always wore when certain foreign letters came.

"Sybil, I have something to show and tell you," he said, as I garnished his buttonhole with a spray of heliotrope, meant for the laggard, who would understand its significance, I hoped. Leading me to the drawing room, my uncle put a paper into my hands, with the request "This is a copy of your father's will; oblige me by reading it."

He stood watching my face as I read, no doubt wondering at my composure while I waded through the dry details of the will, curbing my impatience to reach the one important passage. There it was, but no word concerning my power to dissolve the engagement if I pleased; and, as I realized the fact, a sudden bewilderment and sense of helplessness came over me, for the strange law terms seemed to make inexorable the paternal decree which I had not seen before. I forgot my studied calmness, and asked several questions eagerly.

"Uncle, did my father really command that I should marry Guy, whether we loved each other or not?"

"You see what he there set down as his desire; and I have taken measures that you *should* love one another, knowing that few cousins, young, comely, and congenial, could live three months together without finding themselves ready to mate for their own sakes, if not for the sake of the dead and living fathers to whom they owe obedience."

"You said I need not, if I didn't choose; why is it not here?"

"I said that? Never, Sybil!" and I met a look of such entire surprise and incredulity it staggered my belief in my own senses, yet also roused my spirit, and, careless of consequences, I spoke out at once.

"I heard you say it myself the night after I came, when you told Guy to be cautious, because I could refuse to fulfill the engagement, if I knew that it was not binding against my will."

This discovery evidently destroyed some plan, and for a moment threw him off his guard; for, crumpling the paper in his hand, he sternly demanded, "You turned eavesdropper early; how often since?"

"Never, Uncle; I did not mean it then, but going for a letter in the dark, I heard your voices, and listened for an instant. It was dishonorable, but irresistible; and if you force Guy's confidence, why should not I steal yours? All is fair in war, sir, and I forgive as I hope to be forgiven."

"You have a quick wit and a reticence I did not expect to find under that frank manner. So you have known your future destiny all these months then, and have a purpose in your treatment of your cousin and myself?"

"Yes, Uncle."

"May I ask what?"

I was ashamed to tell; and in the little pause before my answer came, my pique at Guy's desertion was augmented by anger at my uncle's denial of his own words the ungenerous hopes he cherished, and a strong desire to perplex and thwart him took possession of me, for I saw his anxiety concerning the success of this interview, though he endeavored to repress and conceal it. Assuming my coldest mien, I said, "No, sir, I think not; only I can assure you that my little plot has succeeded better than your own."

"But you intend to obey your father's wish, I hope, and fulfill your part of the compact, Sybil?"

"Why should I? It is not binding, you know, and I'm too young to lose my liberty just yet; besides, such compacts are unjust, unwise. What right had my father to mate me in my cradle? How did he know what I should become, or Guy? How could he tell that I should not love someone else better? No! I'll not be bargained away like a piece of merchandise, but love and marry when I please!"

At this declaration of independence my uncle's face darkened ominously, some new suspicion lurked in his eye, some new anxiety beset him; but his manner was calm, his voice blander than ever as he asked, "Is there then someone whom you love? Confide in me, my girl."

"And if there were, what then?"

"All would be changed at once, Sybil. But who is it? Some young lover left behind at Madame's?"

"No, sir."

"Who, then? You have led a recluse life here. Guy has no friends who visit him, and mine are all old, yet you say you love."

"With all my heart, Uncle."

"Is this affection returned, Sybil?"

"I think so."

"And it is not Guy?"

I was wicked enough to enjoy the bitter disappointment he could not conceal at my decided words, for I thought he deserved that momentary pang; but I could not as decidedly answer that last question, for I would not lie, neither would I confess just yet; so, with a little gesture of impatience, I silently turned away, lest he should see the telltale color in my cheeks. My uncle stood an instant in deep thought, a slow smile crept to his lips, content returned to his mien, and something like a flash of triumph glittered for a moment in his eye, then vanished, leaving his countenance earnestly expectant. Much as this change surprised me, his words did more, for, taking both my hands in his, he gravely said, "Do you know that I am your uncle by adoption and not blood, Sybil?"

"Yes, sir; I heard so, but forgot about it," and I looked up at him, my anger quite lost in astonishment.

"Let me tell you then. Your grandfather was childless for many years, my mother was an early friend, and when her death left me an orphan, he took me for his son and heir. But two years from that time your father was born. I was too young to realize the entire change this might make in my life. The old man was too just and generous to let me feel it, and the two lads grew up together like brothers. Both married young, and when you were born a few years later than my son, your father said to me, 'Your boy shall have my girl, and the fortune I have innocently robbed you of shall make us happy in our children.' Then the family league was made, renewed at his death, and now destroyed by his daughter, unless—Sybil, I am forty-five, you not eighteen, yet you once said you could be very happy with me, if I were always kind to you. I can promise that I will be, for I love you. My darling, you reject the son, will you accept the father?"

If he had struck me, it would scarcely have dismayed me more. I started up, and snatching away my hands, hid my face in them, for after the first tingle of surprise an almost irresistible desire to laugh came over me, but I dared not, and gravely, gently he went on.

"I am a bold man to say this, yet I mean it most sincerely. I never meant to betray the affection I believed you never could return, and would only laugh at as a weakness; but your past acts, your present words, give me courage to confess that I desire to keep my ward mine forever. Shall it be so?"

He evidently mistook my surprise for maidenly emotion, and the suddenness of this unforeseen catastrophe seemed to deprive me of words. All thought of merriment or ridicule was forgotten in a sense of guilt, for if he feigned the love he offered it was well done, and I believed it then. I saw at once the natural impression conveyed by my conduct; my half confession and the folly of it all oppressed me with a regret and shame I could not master. My mind was in dire confusion, yet a decided "No" was rapidly emerging from the chaos, but was not uttered; for just at this crisis, as I stood with my uncle's arm about me, my hand again in his, and his head bent down to catch my answer, Guy swung himself gaily into the room.

A glance seemed to explain all, and in an instant his face assumed that expression of pale wrath so much more terrible to witness than the fiercest outbreak; his eye grew fiery, his voice bitterly sarcastic, as he said, "Ah, I see; the play goes on, but the actors change parts. I congratulate you, sir, on your success, and Sybil on her choice. Henceforth I am *de trop,* but before I go allow me to offer my wedding gift. You have taken the bride, let me supply the ring."

He threw a jewel box upon the table, adding, in that unnaturally calm tone that made my heart stand still:

"A little candor would have spared me much pain, Sybil; yet I hope you will enjoy your bonds as heartily as I shall my escape from them. A little confidence would have made me your ally, not your rival, Father. I have not your address; therefore I lose, you win. Let it be so. I had rather be the vagabond this makes me than sell myself, that you may gamble away that girl's fortune as you have your own and mine. You need not ask me to the wedding, I will not come. Oh, Sybil, I so loved, so trusted you!"

And with that broken exclamation he was gone.

The stormy scene had passed so rapidly, been so strange and sudden, Guy's anger so scornful and abrupt, I could not understand it, and felt like a puppet in the grasp of some power I could not resist; but as my lover left the room I broke out of the bewilderment that held me, imploring him to stay and hear me.

It was too late, he was gone, and Sultan's tramp was already tearing down the avenue. I listened till the sound died, then my hot temper rose past control, and womanlike asserted itself in vehement and voluble speech. I was angry with my uncle, my cousin, and myself, and for several minutes poured forth a torrent of explanations, reproaches, and regrets, such as only a passionate girl could utter.

My uncle stood where I had left him when I flew to the door with my vain cry; he now looked baffled, yet sternly resolved, and as I paused for breath his only answer was "Sybil, you ask me to bring back that headstrong boy; I cannot; he will never come. This marriage was distasteful to him, yet he submitted for my sake, because I have been unfortunate, and we are poor. Let him go, forget the past, and be to me what I desire, for I loved your father and will be a faithful guardian to his daughter all my life. Child, it must be—come, I implore, I command you."

He beckoned imperiously as if to awe me, and held up the glittering betrothal ring as if to tempt me. The tone, the act, the look put me quite beside myself. I did go to him, did take the ring, but said as resolutely as himself, "Guy rejects me, and I have done with love. Uncle, you would have deceived me, used me as a means to your own selfish ends. I will accept neither yourself nor your gifts, for now I despise both

you and your commands." And as the most energetic emphasis I could give to my
defiance, I flung the ring, case and all, across the room; it struck the great mirror,
shivered it just in the middle, and sent several loosened fragments crashing to the
floor.

"Great heavens! Is the young lady mad?" exclaimed a voice behind us. Both
turned and saw Dr. Karnac, a stealthy, sallow-faced Spaniard, for whom I had an
invincible aversion. He was my uncle's physician, had been visiting a sick servant in
the upper regions, and my adverse fate sent him to the door just at that moment with
that unfortunate exclamation on his lips.

"What do you say?"

My uncle wheeled about and eyed the newcomer intently as he repeated his
words. I have no doubt I looked like one demented, for I was desperately angry, pale
and trembling with excitement, and as they fronted me with a curious expression of
alarm on their faces, a sudden sense of the absurdity of the spectacle came over me; I
laughed hysterically a moment, then broke into a passion of regretful tears, remembering that Guy was gone. As I sobbed behind my hands, I knew the gentlemen were
whispering together and of me, but I never heeded them, for as I wept myself calmer
a comforting thought occurred to me. Guy could not have gone far, for Sultan had
been out all day, and though reckless of himself he was not of his horse, which he
loved like a human being; therefore he was doubtless at the house of a humble friend
nearby. If I could slip away unseen, I might undo my miserable work, or at least see
him again before he went away into the world, perhaps never to return. This hope
gave me courage for anything, and dashing away my tears, I took a covert survey. Dr.
Karnac and my uncle still stood before the fire, deep in their low-toned conversation;
their backs were toward me; and hushing the rustle of my dress, I stole away with
noiseless steps into the hall, seized Guy's plaid, and, opening the great door unseen,
darted down the avenue.

Not far, however; the wind buffeted me to and fro, the rain blinded me, the
mud clogged my feet and soon robbed me of a slipper; groping for it in despair, I saw
a light flash into the outer darkness; heard voices calling, and soon the swift tramp of
steps behind me. Feeling like a hunted doe, I ran on, but before I had gained a dozen
yards my shoeless foot struck a sharp stone, and I fell half stunned upon the wet grass
of the wayside bank. Dr. Karnac reached me first, took me up as if I were a naughty
child, and carried me back through a group of staring servants to the drawing room,
my uncle following with breathless entreaties that I would be calm, and a most unchar-
acteristic display of bustle.

I was horribly ashamed; my head ached with the shock of the fall, my foot bled,
my heart fluttered, and when the doctor put me down the crisis came, for as my uncle
bent over me with the strange question "My poor girl, do you know me?" an irresistible impulse impelled me to push him from me, crying passionately, "Yes, I know and
hate you; let me go! Let me go, or it will be too late!" Then, quite spent with the
varying emotions of the last hour, for the first time in my life I swooned away.

Coming to myself, I found I was in my own room, with my uncle, the doctor,
Janet, and Mrs. Best, the housekeeper, gathered about me, the latter saying, as she

bathed my temples, "She's a sad sight, poor thing, so young, so bonny, and so unfortunate. Did you ever see her so before, Janet?"

"Bless you, no, ma'am; there was no signs of such a tantrum when I dressed her for dinner."

"What do they mean? Did they never see anyone angry before?" I dimly wondered, and presently, through the fast disappearing stupor that had held me, Dr. Karnac's deep voice came distinctly, saying, "If it continues, you are perfectly justified in doing so."

"Doing what?" I demanded sharply, for the sound both roused and irritated me, I disliked the man so intensely.

"Nothing, my dear, nothing," purred Mrs. Best, supporting me as I sat up, feeling weak and dazed, yet resolved to know what was going on. I was "a sad sight" indeed: my drenched hair hung about my shoulders, my dress was streaked with mud, one shoeless foot was red with blood, the other splashed and stained, and a white, wild-eyed face completed the ruinous image the opposite mirror showed me. Everything looked blurred and strange, and a feverish unrest possessed me, for I was not one to subside easily after such a mental storm. Leaning on my arm, I scanned the room and its occupants with all the composure I could collect. The two women eyed me curiously yet pitifully; Dr. Karnac stood glancing at me furtively as he listened to my uncle, who spoke rapidly in Spanish as he showed the little scar upon his hand.

That sight did more to restore me than the cordial just administered, and I rose erect, saying abruptly, "Please, everybody, go away; my head aches, and I want to be alone."

"Let Janet stay and help you, dear; you are not fit," began Mrs. Best; but I peremptorily stopped her.

"No, go yourself, and take her with you; I'm tired of so much stir about such foolish things as a broken glass and a girl in a pet."

"You will be good enough to take this quieting draft before I go, Miss Sybil."

"I shall do nothing of the sort, for I need only solitude and sleep to be perfectly well," and I emptied the glass the doctor offered into the fire.

He shrugged his shoulders with a disagreeable smile, and quietly began to prepare another draft, saying, "You are mistaken, my dear young lady; you need much care, and should obey, that your uncle may be spared further apprehension and anxiety."

My patience gave out at this assumption of authority; and I determined to carry matters with a high hand, for they all stood watching me in a way which seemed the height of impertinent curiosity.

"He is not my uncle! Never has been, and deserves neither respect nor obedience from me! I am the best judge of my own health, and you are not bettering it by contradiction and unnecessary fuss. This is my house, and you will oblige me by leaving it, Dr. Karnac; this is my room, and I insist on being left in peace immediately."

I pointed to the door as I spoke; the women hurried out with scared faces; the doctor bowed and followed, but paused on the threshold, while my uncle approached me, asking in a tone inaudible to those still hovering round the door, "Do you still persist in your refusal, Sybil?"

"How dare you ask me that again? I tell you I had rather die than marry you!"

"The Lord be merciful to us! Just hear how she's going on now about marrying Master. Ain't it awful, Jane?" ejaculated Mrs. Best, bobbing her head in for a last look.

"Hold your tongue, you impertinent creature!" I called out; and the fat old soul bundled away in such comical haste I laughed, in spite of languor and vexation.

My uncle left me, and I heard him say as he passed the doctor, "You see how it is."

"Nothing uncommon; but that virulence is a bad symptom," answered the Spaniard, and closing the door locked it, having dexterously removed the key from within.

I had never been subjected to restraint of any kind; it made me reckless at once, for this last indignity was not to be endured.

"Open this instantly!" I commanded, shaking the door. No one answered, and after a few ineffectual attempts to break the lock I left it, threw up the window and looked out; the ground was too far off for a leap, but the trellis where summer vines had clung was strong and high, a step would place me on it, a moment's agility bring me to the terrace below. I was now in just the state to attempt any rash exploit, for the cordial had both strengthened and excited me; my foot was bandaged, my clothes still wet; I could suffer no new damage, and have my own way at small cost. Out I crept, climbed safely down, and made my way to the lodge as I had at first intended. But Guy was not there; and returning, I boldly went in at the great door, straight to the room where my uncle and the doctor were still talking.

"I wish the key of my room" was my brief command.

Both started as if I had been a ghost, and my uncle exclaimed, "You here! How in heaven's name came you out?"

"By the window. I am no child to be confined for a fit of anger. I will not submit to it; tomorrow I shall go to Madame; till then I will be mistress in my own house. Give me the key, sir."

"Shall I?" asked the doctor of my uncle, who nodded with a whispered "Yes, yes; don't excite her again."

It was restored, and without another word I went loftily up to my room, locked myself in, and spent a restless, miserable night. When morning came, I breakfasted abovestairs, and then busied myself packing trunks, burning papers, and collecting every trifle Guy had ever given me. No one annoyed me, and I saw only Janet, who had evidently received some order that kept her silent and respectful, though her face still betrayed the same curiosity and pitiful interest as the night before. Lunch was brought up, but I could not eat, and began to feel that the exposure, the fall, and excitement of the evening had left me weak and nervous, so I gave up the idea of going to Madame till the morrow; and as the afternoon waned, tried to sleep, yet could not, for I had sent a note to several of Guy's haunts, imploring him to see me; but my messenger brought word that he was not to be found, and my heart was too heavy to rest.

When summoned to dinner, I still refused to go down; for I heard Dr. Karnac's voice, and would not meet him, so I sent word that I wished the carriage early the following morning, and to be left alone till then. In a few minutes, back came Janet, with a glass of wine set forth on a silver salver, and a card with these words: "Forgive, forget, for your father's sake, and drink with me, 'Oblivion to the past.' "

It touched and softened me. I knew my uncle's pride, and saw in this an entire relinquishment of the hopes I had so thoughtlessly fostered in his mind. I was passionate, but not vindictive. He had been kind, I very willful. His mistake was natural, my resentment ungenerous. Though my resolution to go remained unchanged, I was sorry for my part in the affair; and remembering that through me his son was lost to him, I accepted his apology, drank his toast, and sent him back a dutiful "Good night."

I was unused to wine. The draft I had taken was powerful with age, and, though warm and racy to the palate, proved too potent for me. Still sitting before my fire, I slowly fell into a restless drowse, haunted by a dim dream that I was seeking Guy in a ship, whose motion gradually lulled me into perfect unconsciousness.

Waking at length, I was surprised to find myself in bed, with a shimmer of daylight peeping through the curtains. Recollecting that I was to leave early, I sprang up, took one step, and remained transfixed with dismay, for the room was not my own! Utterly unfamiliar was every object on which my eyes fell. The place was small, plainly furnished, and close, as if long unused. My trunks stood against the wall, my clothes lay on a chair, and on the bed I had left trailed a fur-lined cloak I had often seen on my uncle's shoulders. A moment I stared about me bewildered, then hurried to the window. It was grated!

A lawn, sere and sodden, lay without, and a line of somber firs hid the landscape beyond the high wall which encompassed the dreary plot. More and more alarmed, I flew to the door and found it locked. No bell was visible, no sound audible, no human presence near me, and an ominous foreboding thrilled cold through nerves and blood, as, for the first time, I felt the paralyzing touch of fear. Not long, however. My native courage soon returned, indignation took the place of terror, and excitement gave me strength. My temples throbbed with a dull pain, my eyes were heavy, my limbs weighed down by an unwonted lassitude, and my memory seemed strangely confused; but one thing was clear to me: I must see somebody, ask questions, demand explanations, and get away to Madame without delay.

With trembling hands I dressed, stopping suddenly with a cry; for lifting my hands to my head, I discovered that my hair, my beautiful, abundant hair, was gone! There was no mirror in the room, but I could feel that it had been shorn away close about face and neck. This outrage was more than I could bear, and the first tears I shed fell for my lost charm. It was weak, perhaps, but I felt better for it, clearer in mind and readier to confront whatever lay before me. I knocked and called. Then, losing patience, shook and screamed; but no one came or answered me; and wearied out at last, I sat down and cried again in impotent despair.

An hour passed, then a step approached, the key turned, and a hard-faced woman entered with a tray in her hand. I had resolved to be patient, if possible, and controlled myself to ask quietly, though my eyes kindled, and my voice trembled with resentment, "Where am I, and why am I here against my will?"

"This is your breakfast, miss; you must be sadly hungry" was the only reply I got.

"I will never eat till you tell me what I ask."

"Will you be quiet, and mind me if I do, miss?"

"You have no right to exact obedience from me, but I'll try."

"That's right. Now all I know is that you are twenty miles from the Moors, and came because you are ill. Do you like sugar in your coffee?"

"When did I come? I don't remember it."

"Early this morning; you don't remember because you were put to sleep before being fetched, to save trouble."

"Ah, that wine! Who brought me here?"

"Dr. Karnac, miss."

"Alone?"

"Yes, miss; you were easier to manage asleep than awake, he said."

I shook with anger, yet still restrained myself, hoping to fathom the mystery of this nocturnal journey.

"What is your name, please?" I meekly asked.

"You can call me Hannah."

"Well, Hannah, there is a strange mistake somewhere. I am not ill—you see I am not—and I wish to go away at once to the friend I was to meet today. Get me a carriage and have my baggage taken out."

"It can't be done, miss. We are a mile from town, and have no carriages here; besides, you couldn't go if I had a dozen. I have my orders, and shall obey 'em."

"But Dr. Karnac has no right to bring or keep me here."

"Your uncle sent you. The doctor has the care of you, and that is all I know about it. Now I have kept my promise, do you keep yours, miss, and eat your breakfast, else I can't trust you again."

"But what is the matter with me? How can I be ill and not know or feel it?" I demanded, more and more bewildered.

"You look it, and that's enough for them as is wise in such matters. You'd have had a fever, if it hadn't been seen to in time."

"Who cut my hair off?"

"I did; the doctor ordered it."

"How dared he? I hate that man, and never will obey him."

"Hush, miss, don't clench your hands and look in that way, for I shall have to report everything you say and do to him, and it won't be pleasant to tell that sort of thing."

The woman was civil, but grim and cool. Her eye was unsympathetic, her manner businesslike, her tone such as one uses to a refractory child, half soothing, half commanding. I conceived a dislike to her at once, and resolved to escape at all hazards, for my uncle's inexplicable movements filled me with alarm. Hannah had left my door open, a quick glance showed me another door also ajar at the end of a wide hall, a glimpse of green, and a gate. My plan was desperately simple, and I executed it without delay. Affecting to eat, I presently asked the woman for my handkerchief from the bed. She crossed the room to get it. I darted out, down the passage, along the walk, and tugged vigorously at the great bolt of the gate, but it was also locked. In despair I flew into the garden, but a high wall enclosed it on every side; and as I ran round and round vainly looking for some outlet, I saw Hannah, accompanied by a man as gray and grim as herself, coming leisurely toward me, with no appearance of excitement or displeasure. Back I would not go; and inspired with a sudden hope, swung myself into one of the firs that grew close against the wall. The branches snapped under me, the slender tree swayed perilously, but up I struggled, till the wide coping of the wall was gained. There I paused and looked back. The woman was hurrying through the gate to intercept my descent on the other side, and close behind me the man, sternly calling me to stop. I looked down, a stony ditch was below, but I would rather risk my life than tamely lose my liberty, and with a flying leap tried to reach the bank; failed, fell heavily among the stones, felt an awful crash, and then came an utter blank.

For many weeks I lay burning in a fever, fitfully conscious of Dr. Karnac and the woman's presence; once I fancied I saw my uncle, but was never sure, and rose at last a shadow of my former self, feeling pitifully broken, both mentally and physically. I was in a better room now, wintry winds howled without, but a generous fire glowed behind the high closed fender, and books lay on my table.

I saw no one but Hannah, yet could wring no intelligence from her beyond what she had already told, and no sign of interest reached me from the outer world. I seemed utterly deserted and forlorn, my spirit was crushed, my strength gone, my freedom lost, and for a time I succumbed to despair, letting one day follow another without energy or hope. It is hard to live with no object to give zest to life, especially for those still blessed with youth, and even in my prison house I soon found one quite in keeping with the mystery that surrounded me.

As I sat reading by day or lay awake at night, I became aware that the room above my own was occupied by some inmate whom I never saw. A peculiar person it seemed to be; for I heard steps going to and fro, hour after hour, in a tireless march that wore upon my nerves, as many a harsher sound would not have done. I could neither tease nor surprise Hannah into any explanation of the thing, and day after day I listened to it, till I longed to cover up my ears and implore the unknown walker to stop, for heaven's sake. Other sounds I heard and fretted over: a low monotonous murmur, as of someone singing a lullaby; a fitful tapping, like a cradle rocked on a carpetless floor; and at rare intervals cries of suffering, sharp but brief, as if forcibly suppressed. These sounds, combined with the solitude, the confinement, and the books I read, a collection of ghostly tales and weird fancies, soon wrought my nerves to a state of terrible irritability, and wore upon my health so visibly that I was allowed at last to leave my room.

The house was so well guarded that I soon relinquished all hope of escape, and listlessly amused myself by roaming through the unfurnished rooms and echoing halls, seldom venturing into Hannah's domain; for there her husband sat, surrounded by chemical apparatus, poring over crucibles and retorts. He never spoke to me, and I dreaded the glance of his cold eye, for it looked unsoftened by a ray of pity at the little figure that sometimes paused a moment on his threshold, wan and wasted as the ghost of departed hope.

The chief interest of these dreary walks centered in the door of the room above my own, for a great hound lay before it, eyeing me savagely as he rejected all advances, and uttering his deep bay if I approached too near. To me this room possessed an irresistible fascination. I could not keep away from it by day, I dreamed of it by night, it haunted me continually, and soon became a sort of monomania, which I con-demned, yet could not control, till at length I found myself pacing to and fro as those invisible feet paced overhead. Hannah came and stopped me, and a few hours later Dr. Karnac appeared. I was so changed that I feared him with a deadly fear. He seemed to enjoy it; for in the pride of youth and beauty I had shown him contempt and defiance at my uncle's, and he took an ungenerous satisfaction in annoying me by a display of power. He never answered my questions or entreaties, regarded me as being without sense or will, insisted on my trying various mixtures and experiments in diet, gave me strange books to read, and weekly received Hannah's report of all that passed. That day he came, looked at me, said, "Let her walk," and went away, smiling that hateful smile of his.

Soon after this I took to walking in my sleep, and more than once woke to find myself roving lampless through that haunted house in the dead of night. I concealed these unconscious wanderings for a time, but an ominous event broke them up at last and betrayed them to Hannah.

I had followed the steps one day for several hours, walking below as they walked above; had peopled that mysterious room with every mournful shape my disordered fancy could conjure up; had woven tragical romances about it, and brooded over the one subject of interest my unnatural life possessed with the intensity of a mind upon which its uncanny influence was telling with perilous rapidity. At midnight I woke to find myself standing in a streak of moonlight, opposite the door whose threshold I had never crossed. The April night was warm, a single pane of glass high up in that closed door was drawn aside, as if for air; and as I stood dreamily collecting my sleep-drunken senses, I saw a ghostly hand emerge and beckon, as if to me. It startled me broad awake, with a faint exclamation and a shudder from head to foot. A cloud swept over the moon, and when it passed the hand was gone, but shrill through the keyhole came a whisper that chilled me to the marrow of my bones, so terribly distinct and imploring was it.

"Find it! For God's sake find it before it is too late!"

The hound sprang up with an angry growl; I heard Hannah leave her bed nearby; and with an inspiration strange as the moment, I paced slowly on with open eyes and lips apart, as I had seen *Amina* in the happy days when kind old Madame took me to the theater, whose mimic horrors I had never thought to equal with such veritable ones. Hannah appeared at her door with a light, but on I went in a trance of fear; for I was only kept from dropping in a swoon by the blind longing to fly from that spectral voice and hand. Past Hannah I went, she following; and as I slowly laid myself in bed, I heard her say to her husband, who just then came up, "Sleepwalking, John; it's getting worse and worse, as the doctor foretold; she'll settle down like the other presently, but she must be locked up at night, else the dog will do her a mischief."

The man yawned and grumbled; then they went, leaving me to spend hours of unspeakable suffering, which aged me more than years. What was I to find? Where was I to look? And when would it be too late? These questions tormented me; for I could find no answers to them, divine no meaning, see no course to pursue. Why was I here? What motive induced my uncle to commit such an act? And when should I be liberated? were equally unanswerable, equally tormenting, and they haunted me like ghosts. I had no power to exorcise or forget. After that I walked no more, because I slept no more; sleep seemed scared away, and waking dreams harassed me with their terrors. Night after night I paced my room in utter darkness—for I was allowed no lamp—night after night I wept bitter tears wrung from me by anguish, for which I had no name; and night after night the steps kept time to mine, and the faint lullaby came down to me as if to soothe and comfort my distress. I felt that my health was going, my mind growing confused and weak; my thoughts wandered vaguely, memory began to fail, and idiocy or madness seemed my inevitable fate; but through it all my heart clung to Guy, yearning for him with a hunger that would not be appeased.

At rare intervals I was allowed to walk in the neglected garden, where no flowers bloomed, no birds sang, no companion came to me but surly John, who followed with his book or pipe, stopping when I stopped, walking when I walked, keeping a vigilant eye upon me, yet seldom speaking except to decline answering my questions. These walks did me no good, for the air was damp and heavy with vapors from the marsh; for the house stood near a half-dried lake, and hills shut it in on every side. No fresh winds from upland moor or distant ocean ever blew across the narrow valley; no human creature visited the place, and nothing but a vague hope that my birthday might bring some change, some help, sustained me. It did bring help, but of such an unexpected sort that its effects remained through all my afterlife. My birthday came, and with it my uncle. I was in my room, walking restlessly—for the habit was a confirmed one now—when the door opened, and Hannah, Dr. Karnac, my uncle, and a gentleman whom I knew to be his lawyer entered, and surveyed me as if I were a spectacle. I saw my uncle start and turn pale; I had never seen myself since I came, but if I had not suspected that I was a melancholy wreck of my former self, I should have known it then, such sudden pain and pity softened his ruthless countenance for a single instant. Dr. Karnac's eye had a magnetic power over me; I had always felt it, but in my present feeble state I dreaded, yet submitted to it with a helpless fear that should have touched his heart—it was on me then, I could not resist it, and paused fixed and fascinated by that repellent yet potent glance.

Hannah pointed to the carpet worn to shreds by my weary march, to the walls which I had covered with weird, grotesque, or tragic figures to while away the heavy hours, lastly to myself, mute, motionless, and scared, saying, as if in confirmation of some previous assertion, "You see, gentlemen, she is, as I said, quiet, but quite hopeless."

I thought she was interceding for me; and breaking from the bewilderment and fear that held me, I stretched my hands to them, crying with an imploring cry, "Yes, I *am* quiet! I *am* hopeless! Oh, have pity on me before this dreadful life kills me or drives me mad!"

Dr. Karnac came to me at once with a black frown, which I alone could see; I evaded him, and clung to Hannah, still crying frantically—for this seemed my last hope—"Uncle, let me go! I will give you all I have, will never ask for Guy, will be obedient and meek if I may only go to Madame and never hear the feet again, or see the sights that terrify me in this dreadful room. Take me out! For God's sake take me out!"

My uncle did not answer me, but covered up his face with a despairing gesture, and hurried from the room; the lawyer followed, muttering pitifully, "Poor thing! Poor thing!" and Dr. Karnac laughed the first laugh I had ever heard him utter as he wrenched Hannah from my grasp and locked me in alone. My one hope died then, and I resolved to kill myself rather than endure this life another month; for now it grew clear to me that they believed me mad, and death of the body was far more preferable than that of the mind. I think I *was* a little mad just then, but remember well the sense of peace that came to me as I tore strips from my clothing, braided them into a cord, hid it beneath my mattress, and serenely waited for the night. Sitting in the last twilight I thought to see in this unhappy world, I recollected that I had not heard the feet all day, and fell to pondering over the unusual omission. But if the steps had been silent in that room, voices had not, for I heard a continuous murmur at one time: the tones of one voice were abrupt and broken, the other low, yet resonant, and that, I felt assured, belonged to my uncle. Who was he speaking to? What were they saying? Should I ever know? And even then, with death before me, the intense desire to possess the secret filled me with its old unrest.

Night came at last; I heard the clock strike one, and listening to discover if John still lingered up, I heard through the deep hush a soft grating in the room above, a stealthy sound that would have escaped ears less preternaturally alert than mine. Like a flash came the thought, "Someone is filing bars or picking locks: will the unknown remember me and let me share her flight?" The fatal noose hung ready, but I no longer cared to use it, for hope had come to nerve me with the strength and courage I had lost. Breathlessly I listened; the sound went on, stopped; a dead silence reigned; then something brushed against my door, and with a suddenness that made me tingle from head to foot like an electric shock, through the keyhole came again that whisper, urgent, imploring, and mysterious, "Find it! For God's sake find it before it is too late!" Then fainter, as if breath failed, came the broken words, "The dog—a lock of hair—there is yet time."

Eagerness rendered me forgetful of the secrecy I should preserve, and I cried aloud, "What shall I find? Where shall I look?" My voice, sharpened by fear, rang shrilly through the house; Hannah's quick tread rushed down the hall; something fell; then loud and long rose a cry that made my heart stand still, so helpless, so hopeless was its wild lament. I had betrayed and I could not save or comfort the kind soul who had lost liberty through me. I was frantic to get out, and beat upon my door in a paroxysm of impatience, but no one came; and all night long those awful cries went on above, cries of mortal anguish, as if soul and body were being torn asunder. Till dawn I listened, pent in that room which now possessed an added terror; till dawn I called, wept, and prayed, with mingled pity, fear, and penitence; and till dawn the agony of that unknown sufferer continued unabated. I heard John hurry to and fro, heard Hannah issue orders with an accent of human sympathy in her hard voice; heard Dr. Karnac pass and repass my door; and all the sounds of confusion and alarm in that once quiet house. With daylight all was still, a stillness more terrible than the stir; for it fell so suddenly, remained so utterly unbroken, that there seemed no explanation of it but the dread word death.

At noon Hannah, a shade paler but grim as ever, brought me some food, saying she forgot my breakfast, and when I refused to eat, yet asked no questions, she bade me go into the garden and not fret myself over last night's flurry. I went, and passing down the corridor, glanced furtively at the door I never saw without a thrill; but I experienced a new sensation then, for the hound was gone, the door was open, and with an impulse past control, I crept in and looked about me. It was a room like mine, the carpet worn like mine, the windows barred like mine; there the resemblance ended, for an empty cradle stood beside the bed, and on that bed, below a sweeping cover, stark and still a lifeless body lay. I was inured to fear now, and an unwholesome craving for new terrors seemed to have grown by what it fed on: an irresistible desire led me close, nerved me to lift the cover and look below—a single glance—then with a cry as panic-stricken as that which rent the silence of the night, I fled away, for the face I saw was a pale image of my own. Sharpened by suffering, pallid with death, the features were familiar as those I used to see; the hair, beautiful and blond as mine had been, streamed long over the pulseless breast, and on the hand, still clenched in that last struggle, shone the likeness of a ring I wore, a ring bequeathed me by my father. An awesome fancy that it was myself assailed me; I had plotted death, and with the waywardness of a shattered mind, I recalled legends of spirits returning to behold the bodies they had left.

Glad now to seek the garden, I hurried down, but on the threshold of the great hall door was arrested by the sharp crack of a pistol; and as a little cloud of smoke dispersed, I saw John drop the weapon and approach the hound, who lay writhing on the bloody grass. Moved by compassion for the faithful brute whose long vigilance was so cruelly repaid, I went to him, and kneeling there, caressed the great head that never yielded to my touch before. John assumed his watch at once, and leaning against a tree, cleaned the pistol, content that I should amuse myself with the dying creature, who looked into my face with eyes of almost human pathos and reproach. The brass collar seemed to choke him as he gasped for breath, and leaning nearer to undo it, I saw, half hidden in his own black hair, a golden lock wound tightly round the collar, and so near its color as to be unobservable, except upon a close inspection. No accident could have placed it there; no head but mine in that house wore hair of that sunny hue—yes, one other, and my heart gave a sudden leap as I remembered the shining locks just seen on that still bosom.

"Find it—the dog—the lock of hair," rang in my ears, and swift as light came the conviction that the unknown help was found at last. The little band was woven close. I had no knife, delay was fatal. I bent my head as if lamenting over the poor beast and bit the knot apart, drew out a folded paper, hid it in my hand, and rising, strolled leisurely back to my own room, saying I did not care to walk till it was warmer. With eager eyes I examined my strange treasure trove. It consisted of two strips of thinnest paper, without address or signature, one almost illegible, worn at the edges and stained with the green rust of the collar; the other fresher, yet more feebly written, both abrupt and disjointed, but terribly significant to me. This was the first:

> I have never seen you, never heard your name, yet I know that you are young, that you are suffering, and I try to help you in my poor way. I think you are not crazed yet, as I often am; for your voice is sane, your plaintive singing not like mine, your walking only caught from me, I hope. I sing to lull the baby whom I never saw; I walk to lessen the long journey that will bring me to the husband I have lost—stop! I must not think of those things or I shall forget. If you are not already mad, you will be; I suspect you were sent here to be made so; for the air is poison, the solitude is fatal, and Karnac remorseless in his mania for prying into the mysteries of human minds. What devil sent you I may never know, but I long to warn you. I can devise no way but this; the dog comes into my

room sometimes, you sometimes pause at my door and talk to him; you may find the paper I shall hide about his collar. Read, destroy, but obey it. I implore you to leave this house before it is too late.

The other paper was as follows:

I have watched you, tried to tell you where to look, for you have not found my warning yet, though I often tie it there and hope. You fear the dog, perhaps, and my plot fails; yet I know by your altered step and voice that you are fast reaching my unhappy state; for I am fitfully mad, and shall be till I die. Today I have seen a familiar face; it seems to have calmed and strengthened me, and though he would not help you, I shall make one desperate attempt. I may not find you, so leave my warning to the hound, yet hope to breathe a word into your sleepless ear that shall send you back into the world the happy thing you should be. Child! Woman! Whatever you are, leave this accursed house while you have power to do it.

That was all. I did not destroy the papers, but I obeyed them, and for a week watched and waited till the propitious instant came. I saw my uncle, the doctor, and two others follow the poor body to its grave beside the lake, saw all depart but Dr. Karnac, and felt redoubled hatred and contempt for the men who could repay my girlish slights with such a horrible revenge. On the seventh day, as I went down for my daily walk, I saw John and Dr. Karnac so deep in some uncanny experiment that I passed out unguarded. Hoping to profit by this unexpected chance, I sprang down the steps, but the next moment dropped half stunned upon the grass; for behind me rose a crash, a shriek, a sudden blaze that flashed up and spread, sending a noisome vapor rolling out with clouds of smoke and flame.

Aghast, I was just gathering myself up when Hannah fled out of the house, dragging her husband senseless and bleeding, while her own face was ashy with affright. She dropped her burden beside me, saying, with white lips and a vain look for help where help was not, "Something they were at has burst, killed the doctor, and fired the house! Watch John till I get help, and leave him at your peril." Then flinging open the gate she sped away.

"Now is my time," I thought, and only waiting till she vanished, I boldly followed her example, running rapidly along the road in an opposite direction, careless of bonnetless head and trembling limbs, intent only upon leaving that prison house far behind me. For several hours, I hurried along that solitary road; the spring sun shone, birds sang in the blooming hedges, green nooks invited me to pause and rest; but I heeded none of them, steadily continuing my flight, till spent and footsore I was forced to stop a moment by a wayside spring. As I stooped to drink, I saw my face for the first time in many months, and started to see how like that dead one it had grown, in all but the eternal peace which made that beautiful in spite of suffering and age. Standing thus and wondering if Guy would know me, should we ever meet, the sound of wheels disturbed me. Believing them to be coming from the place I had left, I ran desperately down the hill, turned a sharp corner, and before I could check myself passed a carriage slowly ascending. A face sprang to the window, a voice cried "Stop!" but on I flew, hoping the traveler would let me go unpursued. Not so, however; soon I heard fleet steps following, gaining rapidly, then a hand seized me, a voice rang in my ears, and with a vain struggle I lay panting in my captor's hold, fearing to look up and meet a brutal glance. But the hand that had seized me tenderly drew me close, the voice that had alarmed cried joyfully, "Sybil, it is Guy: Lie still, poor child, you are safe at last."

Then I knew that my surest refuge was gained, and too weak for words, clung to him in an agony of happiness, which brought to his kind eyes the tears I could not shed.

The carriage returned; Guy took me in, and for a time cared only to soothe and sustain my worn soul and body with the cordial of his presence, as we rolled homeward through a blooming world, whose beauty I had never truly felt before. When the first tumult of emotion had subsided, I told the story of my captivity and my escape, ending with a passionate entreaty not to be returned to my uncle's keeping, for henceforth there could be neither affection nor respect between us.

"Fear nothing, Sybil; Madame is waiting for you at the Moors, and my father's unfaithful guardianship has ended with his life."

Then with averted face and broken voice Guy went on to tell his father's purposes, and what had caused this unexpected meeting. The facts were briefly these: The knowledge that my father had come between him and a princely fortune had always rankled in my uncle's heart, chilling the ambitious hopes he cherished even in his boyhood, and making life an eager search for pleasure in which to drown his vain regrets. This secret was suspected by my father, and the household league was formed as some atonement for the innocent offense. It seemed to soothe my uncle's resentful nature, and as years went on he lived freely, assured that ample means would be his through his son. Luxurious, self-indulgent, fond of all excitements, and reckless in their pursuit, he took no thought for the morrow till a few months before his return. A gay winter in Paris reduced him to those straits of which women know so little; creditors were oppressive, summer friends failed him, gambling debts harassed him, his son reproached him, and but one resource remained—Guy's speedy marriage with the half-forgotten heiress. The boy had been educated to regard this fate as a fixed fact, and submitted, believing the time to be far distant; but the sudden summons came, and he rebelled against it, preferring liberty to love. My uncle pacified the claimants by promises to be fulfilled at my expense, and hurried home to press on the marriage, which now seemed imperative. I was taken to my future home, approved by my uncle, beloved by my cousin, and, but for my own folly, might have been a happy wife on that May morning when I listened to the unveiling of the past. My mother had been melancholy mad since that unhappy rumor of my father's death; this affliction had been well concealed from me, lest the knowledge should prey upon my excitable nature and perhaps induce a like misfortune. I believed her dead, yet I had seen her, knew where her solitary grave was made, and still carried in my bosom the warning she had sent me, prompted by the unerring instinct of a mother's heart. In my father's will a clause was added just below the one confirming my betrothal, a clause decreeing that, if it should appear that I inherited my mother's malady, the fortune should revert to my cousin, with myself a mournful legacy, to be cherished by him whether his wife or not. This passage, and that relating to my freedom of choice, had been omitted in the copy shown me on the night when my seeming refusal of Guy had induced his father to believe that I loved him, to make a last attempt to keep the prize by offering himself, and, when that failed, to harbor a design that changed my little comedy into the tragical experience I have told.

Dr. Karnac's exclamation had caused the recollection of that clause respecting my insanity to flash into my uncle's mind—a mind as quick to conceive as fearless to execute. I unconsciously abetted the stratagem, and Dr. Karnac was an unscrupulous ally, for love of gain was as strong as love of science; both were amply gratified, and I, poor victim, was given up to be experimented upon, till by subtle means I was driven to the insanity which would give my uncle full control of my fortune and my fate. How the black plot prospered has been told; but retribution speedily overtook them both, for Dr. Karnac paid his penalty by the sudden death that left his ashes among the blackened ruins of that house of horrors, and my uncle had preceded him. For before the change of heirs could be effected my mother died, and the hours spent in that unhealthful spot insinuated the subtle poison of the marsh into his blood; years of pleasure left little vigor to withstand the fever, and a week of suffering ended a life of generous impulses perverted, fine endowments wasted, and opportunities forever lost. When death drew near, he sent for Guy (who, through the hard discipline of poverty and honest labor, was becoming a manlier man), confessed all, and implored him to save me before it was too late. He did, and when all was told, when each saw the other by the light of this strange and sad experience—Guy poor again, I free, the old bond still existing, the barrier of misunderstanding gone—it was easy to see our way, easy to submit, to forgive, forget, and begin anew the life these clouds had darkened for a time.

Home received me, kind Madame welcomed me, Guy married me, and I was happy; but over all these years, serenely prosperous, still hangs for me the shadow of the past, still rises that dead image of my mother, still echoes that spectral whisper in the dark.

❧ A Pair of Eyes; or, Modern Magic

Part I

I WAS DISAPPOINTED—the great actress had not given me what I wanted, and my picture must still remain unfinished for want of a pair of eyes. I knew what they should be, saw them clearly in my fancy, but though they haunted me by night and day I could not paint them, could not find a model who would represent the aspect I desired, could not describe it to any one, and though I looked into every face I met, and visited afflicted humanity in many shapes, I could find no eyes that visibly presented the vacant yet not unmeaning stare of Lady Macbeth in her haunted sleep. It fretted me almost beyond endurance to be delayed in my work so near its completion, for months of thought and labor had been bestowed upon it; the few who had seen it in its imperfect state had elated me with commendation, whose critical sincerity I knew the worth of; and the many not admitted were impatient for a sight of that which others praised, and to which the memory of former successes lent an interest beyond mere curiosity. All was done, and well done, except the eyes; the dimly lighted chamber, the listening attendants, the ghostly figure with wan face framed in hair, that streamed shadowy and long against white draperies, and whiter arms, whose gesture told that the parted lips were uttering that mournful cry —

> "Here's the smell of blood still!
> All the perfumes of Arabia will not
> Sweeten this little hand — "

The eyes alone baffled me, and for want of these my work waited, and my last success was yet unwon.

I was in a curious mood that night, weary yet restless, eager yet impotent to seize the object of my search, and full of haunting images that would not stay to be reproduced. My friend was absorbed in the play, which no longer possessed any charm for me, and leaning back in my seat I fell into a listless reverie, still harping on the one idea of my life; for impetuous and resolute in all things, I had given myself body and soul to the profession I had chosen and followed through many vicissitudes for fifteen years. Art was wife, child, friend, food and fire to me; the pursuit of fame as a reward for my long labor was the object for which I lived, the hope which gave me courage to press on over every obstacle, sacrifice and suffering, for the word "defeat" was not in my vocabulary. Sitting thus, alone, though in a crowd, I slowly became aware of a disturbing influence whose power invaded my momentary isolation, and soon took shape in the uncomfortable conviction that some one was looking at me. Every one has felt this, and at another time I should have cared little for it, but just then I was laboring under a sense of injury, for of all the myriad eyes about me none would give me the expression I longed for; and unreasonable as it was, the thought that I was watched annoyed me like a silent insult. I sent a searching look through the boxes on either hand, swept the remoter groups with a powerful glass, and scanned the sea of heads below, but met no answering glance; all faces were turned stageward, all minds seemed intent upon the tragic scenes enacting there.

Failing to discover any visible cause for my fancy, I tried to amuse myself with the play, but having seen it many times and being in an ill-humor with the heroine of the hour, my thoughts soon wandered, and though still apparently an interested auditor, I heard nothing, saw nothing, for the instant my mind became abstracted the same uncanny sensation returned. A vague consciousness that some stronger nature was covertly exerting its power upon my own; I smiled as this whim first suggested itself, but it rapidly grew upon me, and a curious feeling of impotent resistance took possession of me, for I was indignant without knowing why, and longed to rebel against—I knew not what. Again I looked far and wide, met several inquiring glances from near neighbors, but none that answered my demand by any betrayal of especial interest or malicious pleasure. Baffled, yet not satisfied, I turned to myself, thinking to find the cause of my disgust there, but did not succeed. I seldom drank wine, had not worked intently that day, and except the picture had no anxiety to harass me; yet without any physical or mental cause that I could discover, every nerve seemed jangled out of tune, my temples beat, my breath came short, and the air seemed feverishly close, though I had not perceived it until then. I did not understand this mood and with an impatient gesture took the playbill from my friend's knee, gathered it into my hand and fanned myself like a petulant woman, I suspect, for Louis turned and surveyed me with surprise as he asked:

"What is it, Max; you seem annoyed?"

"I am, but absurd as it is, I don't know why, except a foolish fancy that someone whom I do not see is looking at me and wishes me to look at him."

Louis laughed—"Of course there is, aren't you used to it yet? And are you so modest as not to know that many eyes take stolen glances at the rising artist, whose ghosts and goblins make their hair stand on end so charmingly? I had the mortification to discover some time ago that, young and comely as I take the liberty of thinking myself, the upturned lorgnettes are not levelled at me, but at the stern-faced, black-bearded gentleman beside me, for he looks particularly moody and interesting to-night."

"Bah! I just wish I could inspire some of those starers with gratitude enough to set them walking in their sleep for my benefit and their own future glory. Your suggestion has proved a dead failure, the woman there cannot give me what I want, the picture will never get done, and the whole affair will go to the deuce for want of a pair of eyes."

I rose to go as I spoke, and there they were behind me!

What sort of expression my face assumed I cannot tell, for I forgot time and place, and might have committed some absurdity if Louis had not pulled me down with a look that made me aware that I was staring with an utter disregard of common courtesy.

"Who are those people? Do you know them?" I demanded in a vehement whisper.

"Yes, but put down that glass and sit still or I'll call an usher to put you out," he answered, scandalized at my energetic demonstrations.

"Good! then introduce me—now at once—Come on," and I rose again, to be again arrested.

"Are you possessed to-night? You have visited so many fever wards and mad-houses in your search that you've unsettled your own wits, Max. What whim has got into your brain now? And why do you want to know those people in such haste?"

"Your suggestion has not proved failure, a woman can give me what I want, the picture will be finished, and nothing will go to the deuce, for I've found the eyes—now be obliging and help me to secure them."

Louis stared at me as if he seriously began to think me a little mad, but restrained the explosive remark that rose to his lips and answered hastily, as several persons looked round as if our whispering annoyed them.

"I'll take you in there after the play if you must go, so for heaven's sake behave like a gentleman till then, and let me enjoy myself in peace."

I nodded composedly, he returned to his tragedy and shading my eyes with my hand, I took a critical survey, feeling more and more assured that my long search was at last ended. Three persons occupied the box, a well-dressed elderly lady dozing behind her fan, a lad leaning over the front absorbed in the play, and a young lady looking straight before her with the aspect I had waited for with such impatience. This figure I scrutinized with the eye of an artist which took in every accessory of outline, ornament and hue.

Framed in darkest hair, rose a face delicately cut, but cold and colorless as that of any statue in the vestibule without. The lips were slightly parted with the long slow breaths that came and went, the forehead was femininely broad and low, the brows straight and black, and underneath them the mysterious eyes fixed on vacancy, full of that weird regard so hard to counterfeit, so impossible to describe; for though absent, it was not expressionless, and through its steadfast shine a troubled meaning wandered, as if soul and body could not be utterly divorced by any effort of the will. She seemed unconscious of the scene about her, for the fixture of her glance never changed, and nothing about her stirred but the jewel on her bosom, whose changeful glitter seemed to vary as it rose and fell. Emboldened by this apparent absorption, I prolonged my scrutiny and scanned this countenance as I had never done a woman's face before. During this examination I had forgotten myself in her, feeling only a strong desire to draw nearer and dive deeper into those two dark wells that seemed so tranquil yet so fathomless, and in the act of trying to fix shape, color and expression in my memory, I lost them all; for a storm of applause broke the attentive hush as the curtain fell, and like one startled from sleep a flash of intelligence lit up the eyes, then a white hand was passed across them, and long downcast lashes hid them from my sight.

Louis stood up, gave himself a comprehensive survey, and walked out, saying, with a nod,

"Now, Max, put on your gloves, shake the hair out of your eyes, assume your best 'deportment,' and come and take an observation which may immortalize your name."

Knocking over a chair in my haste, I followed close upon his heels, as he tapped at the next door; the lad opened it, bowed to my conductor, glanced at me and strolled away, while we passed in. The elderly lady was awake, now, and received us graciously; the younger was leaning on her hand, the plumy fan held between her and the glare of the great chandelier as she watched the moving throng below.

"Agatha, here is Mr. Yorke and a friend whom he wishes to present to you," said the old lady, with a shade of deference in her manner which betrayed the companion, not the friend.

Agatha turned, gave Louis her hand, with a slow smile dawning on her lip, and looked up at me as if the fact of my advent had no particular interest for her, and my appearance promised no great pleasure.

"Miss Eure, my friend Max Erdmann yearned to be made happy by a five minutes audience, and I ventured to bring him without sending an *avant courier* to prepare the way. Am I forgiven?" with which half daring, half apologetic introduction, Louis turned to the chaperone and began to rattle.

Miss Eure bowed, swept the waves of silk from the chair beside her, and I sat down with a bold request waiting at my lips till an auspicious moment came, having resolved not to exert myself for nothing. As we discussed the usual topics suggested by the time and place, I looked often into the face before me and soon found it difficult to look away again, for it was a constant surprise to me. The absent mood had passed and with it the frost seemed to have melted from mien and manner, leaving a living woman in the statue's place. I had thought her melancholy, but her lips were dressed in smiles, and frequent peals of low-toned laughter parted them like pleasant music; I had thought her pale, but in either cheek now bloomed a color deep and clear as any tint my palette could have given; I had thought her shy and proud at first, but with each moment her manner warmed, her speech grew franker and her whole figure seemed to glow and brighten as if a brilliant lamp were lit behind the pale shade she had worn before. But the eyes were the greatest surprise of all—I had fancied them dark, and found them the light, sensitive gray belonging to highly nervous temperaments. They were remarkable eyes; for though softly fringed with shadowy lashes they were not mild, but fiery and keen, with many lights and shadows in them as the pupils dilated, and the irids shone with a transparent lustre which varied with her varying words, and proved the existence of an ardent, imperious nature underneath the seeming snow.

They exercised a curious fascination over me and kept my own obedient to their will, although scarce conscious of it at the time and believing mine to be the controlling power. Wherein the charm lay I cannot tell; it was not the influence of a womanly presence alone, for fairer faces had smiled at me in vain; yet as I sat there I felt a pleasant quietude creep over me, I knew my voice had fallen to a lower key, my eye softened from its wonted cold indifference, my manner grown smooth and my demeanor changed to one almost as courtly as my friend's, who well deserved his soubriquet of "Louis the Debonnair."

"It is because my long fret is over," I thought, and having something to gain, exerted myself to please so successfully that, soon emboldened by her gracious mood and the flattering compliments bestowed upon my earlier works, I ventured to tell my present strait and the daring hope I had conceived that she would help me through it. How I made this blunt request I cannot tell, but remember that it slipped over my tongue as smoothly as if I had meditated upon it for a week. I glanced over my shoulder as I spoke, fearing Louis might mar all with apology or reproof; but he was absorbed in the comely duenna, who was blushing like a girl at the half playful, half serious devotion he paid all womankind; and reassured, I waited, wondering how Miss Eure would receive my request. Very quietly; for with no change but a peculiar dropping of the lids, as if her eyes sometimes played the traitor to her will, she answered, smilingly,

"It is I who receive the honor, sir, not you, for genius possesses the privileges of royalty, and may claim subjects everywhere, sure that its choice ennobles and its power extends beyond the narrow bounds of custom, time and place. When shall I serve you, Mr. Erdmann?"

At any other time I should have felt surprised both at her and at myself; but just then, in the ardor of the propitious moment, I thought only of my work, and with many thanks for her great kindness left the day to her, secretly hoping she would name an early one. She sat silent an instant, then seemed to come to some determination, for when she spoke a shadow of mingled pain and patience swept across her face as if her resolve had cost her some sacrifice of pride or feeling.

"It is but right to tell you that I may not always have it in my power to give you the expression you desire to catch, for the eyes you honor by wishing to perpetuate are not strong and often fail me for a time. I have been utterly blind once and may be again, yet have no present cause to fear it, and if you can come to me on such days as they will serve your purpose, I shall be most glad to do my best for you. Another reason makes me bold to ask this favor of you, I cannot always summon this absent mood, and should certainly fail in a strange place; but in my own home, with all familiar things about me, I can more easily fall into one of my deep reveries and forget time by the hour together. Will this arrangement cause much inconvenience or delay? A room shall be prepared for you—kept inviolate as long as you desire it—and every facility my house affords is at your service, for I feel much interest in the work which is to add another success to your life."

She spoke regretfully at first, but ended with a cordial glance as if she had forgotten herself in giving pleasure to another. I felt that it must have cost her an effort to confess that such a dire affliction had ever darkened her youth and might still return to sadden her prime; this pity mingled with my expressions of gratitude for the unexpected interest she bestowed upon my work, and in a few words the arrangement was made, the day and hour fixed, and a great load off my mind. What the afterpiece was I never knew; Miss Eure stayed to please her young companion, Louis stayed to please himself, and I remained because I had not energy enough to go away. For, leaning where I first sat down, I still looked and listened with a dreamy sort of satisfaction to Miss Eure's low voice, as with downcast eyes, still shaded by her fan, she spoke enthusiastically and well of art (the one interesting theme to me) in a manner which proved that she had read and studied more than her modesty allowed her to acknowledge.

We parted like old friends at her carriage door, and as I walked away with Louis in the cool night air I felt like one who had been asleep in a close room, for I was both languid and drowsy, though a curious undercurrent of excitement still stirred my blood and tingled along my nerves. "A theatre is no place for me," I decided, and anxious to forget myself said aloud:

"Tell me all you know about that woman."

"What woman, Max?"

"Miss Agatha Eure, the owner of the eyes."

"Aha! smitten at last! That ever I should live to see our Benedict the victim of love at first sight!"

"Have done with your nonsense, and answer my question. I don't ask from mere curiosity, but that I may have some idea how to bear myself at these promised sittings; for it will never do to ask after her papa if she has none, to pay my respects to the old lady as her mother if she is only the duenna, or joke with the lad if he is the heir apparent."

"Do you mean to say that you asked her to sit to you?" cried Louis, falling back a step and staring at me with undisguised astonishment.

"Yes, why not?"

"Why, man, Agatha Eure is the haughtiest piece of humanity ever concocted; and I, with all my daring, never ventured to ask more than an occasional dance with her, and feel myself especially favored that she deigns to bow to me, and lets me pick up her gloves or carry her bouquet as a mark of supreme condescension. What witchcraft did you bring to bear upon her? and how did she grant your audacious request?"

"Agreed to it at once."

"Like an empress conferring knighthood, I fancy."

"Not at all. More like a pretty woman receiving a compliment to her beauty— though she is not pretty, by the way."

Louis indulged himself in the long, low whistle, which seems the only adequate expression for masculine surprise. I enjoyed his amazement, it was my turn to laugh now, and I did so, as I said:

"You are always railing at me for my avoidance of all womankind, but you see I have not lost the art of pleasing, for I won your haughty Agatha to my will in fifteen minutes, and am not only to paint her handsome eyes, but to do it at her own house, by her own request. I am beginning to find that, after years of effort, I have mounted a few more rounds of the social ladder than I was aware of, and may now confer as well as receive favors; for she seemed to think me the benefactor, and I rather enjoyed the novelty of the thing. Now tell your story of 'the haughtiest piece of humanity' ever known. I like her the better for that trait."

Louis nodded his head, and regarded the moon with an aspect of immense wisdom, as he replied:

"I understand it now; it all comes back to me, and my accusation holds good, only the love at first sight is on the other side. You shall have your story, but it may leave the picture in the lurch if it causes you to fly off, as you usually see fit to do when a woman's name is linked with your own. You never saw Miss Eure before; but what you say reminds me that she has seen you, for one day last autumn, as I was driving with her and old madame—a mark of uncommon favor, mind you—we saw you striding along, with your hat over your eyes, looking very much like a comet streaming down the street. It was crowded, and as you waited at the crossing you spoke to Jack Mellot, and while talking pulled off your hat and tumbled your hair about, in your usual fashion, when very earnest. We were blockaded by cars and coaches for a moment, so Miss Eure had a fine opportunity to feast her eyes upon you, 'though you are not pretty, by the way.' She asked your name, and when I told her she gushed out into a charming little stream of interest in your daubs, and her delight at seeing their creator; all of which was not agreeable to me, for I considered myself much the finer work of art of the two. Just then you caught up a shabby child with a big basket, took them across, under our horses' noses, with never a word for me, though I called to you, and, diving into the crowd, disappeared. 'I like that,' said Miss Eure; and as we drove on she asked questions, which I answered in a truly Christian manner, doing you no harm, old lad; for I told all you had fought through, with the courage of a stout-hearted man, all you had borne with the patience of a woman, and what a grand future lay open to you, if you chose to accept and use it, making quite a fascinating little romance of it, I assure you. There the matter dropped. I forgot it till this minute, but it accounts for the ease with which you gained your first suit, and is prophetic of like success in a second and more serious one. She is young, well-born, lovely to those who love her, and has a fortune and position which will lift you at once to the topmost round of the long ladder you've been climbing all these years. I wish you joy, Max."

"Thank you. I've no time for lovemaking, and want no fortune but that which I earn for myself. I am already married to a fairer wife than Miss Eure, so you may win and wear the lofty lady yourself."

Louis gave a comical groan.

"I've tried that, and failed; for she is too cold to be warmed by any flame of mine, though she is wonderfully attractive when she likes, and I hover about her even now like an infatuated moth, who beats his head against the glass and never reaches the light within. No; you must thankfully accept the good the gods bestow. Let Art be your Leah, but Agatha your Rachel. And so, good-night!"

"Stay and tell me one thing—is she an orphan?"

"Yes; the last of a fine old race, with few relatives and few friends, for death has deprived her of the first, and her own choice of the last. The lady you saw with her plays propriety in her establishment; the lad is Mrs. Snow's son, and fills the role of *cavaliere-servente;* for Miss Eure is a Diana toward men in general, and leads a quietly luxurious life among her books, pencils and music, reading and studying all manner of things few women of two-and-twenty care to know. But she has the wit to see that a woman's mission is to be charming, and when she has sufficient motive for the exertion she fulfils that mission most successfully, as I know to my sorrow. Now let me off, and be for ever grateful for the good turn I have done you to-night, both in urging you to go to the theatre and helping you to your wish when you got there."

We parted merrily, but his words lingered in my memory, and half unconsciously exerted a new influence over me, for they flattered the three ruling passions
that make or mar the fortunes of us all—pride, ambition and self-love. I wanted
power, fame and ease, and all seemed waiting for me, not in the dim future but the
actual present, if my friend's belief was as to be relied upon; and remembering all I
had seen and heard that night, I felt that it was not utterly without foundation. I
pleased myself for an idle hour in dreaming dreams of what might be; finding that
amusement began to grow dangerously attractive, I demolished my castles in the air
with the last whiff of my meerschaum, and fell asleep, echoing my own words:

"Art is my wife, I will have no other!"

Punctual to the moment I went to my appointment, and while waiting an
answer to my ring took an exterior survey of Miss Eure's house. One of an imposing
granite block, it stood in a West End square, with every sign of unostentatious opu-
lence about it. I was very susceptible to all influences, either painful or pleasant, and
as I stood there the bland atmosphere that surrounded me seemed most attractive; for
my solitary life had been plain and poor, with little time for ease, and few ornaments to
give it grace. Now I seemed to have won the right to enjoy both if I would; I no longer
felt out of place there, and with this feeling came the wish to try the sunny side of
life, and see if its genial gifts would prove more inspiring than the sterner masters I
had been serving so long.

The door opened in the middle of my reverie, and I was led through an ante-
room, lined with warmhued pictures, to a large apartment, which had been converted
into an impromptu studio by some one who understood all the requisites for such a
place. The picture, my easel and other necessaries had preceded me, and I thought to
have spent a good hour in arranging matters. All was done, however, with a skill that
surprised me; the shaded windows, the carefully-arranged brushes, the proper colors
already on the palette, the easel and picture placed as they should be, and a deep
curtain hung behind a small dais, where I fancied my model was to sit. The room was
empty as I entered, and with the brief message, "Miss Eure will be down directly,"
the man noiselessly departed.

I stood and looked about me with great satisfaction, thinking, "I cannot fail to
work well surrounded by such agreeable sights and sounds." The house was very still,
for the turmoil of the city was subdued to a murmur, like the far-off music of the sea;
a soft gloom filled the room, divided by one strong ray that fell athwart my picture,
gifting it with warmth and light. Through a half-open door I saw the green vista of a
conservatory, full of fine blendings of color, and wafts of many odors blown to me by
the west wind rustling through orange trees and slender palms; while the only sound
that broke the silence was the voice of a flame-colored foreign bird, singing a plaintive
little strain like a sorrowful lament. I liked this scene, and, standing in the doorway,
was content to look, listen and enjoy, forgetful of time, till a slight stir made me turn
and for a moment look straight before me with a startled aspect. It seemed as if my
picture had left its frame; for, standing on the narrow dais, clearly defined against the
dark background, stood the living likeness of the figure I had painted, the same white
folds falling from neck to ankle, the same shadowy hair, and slender hands locked
together, as if wrung in slow despair; and fixed full upon my own the weird, unseeing

eyes, which made the face a pale mask, through which the haunted spirit spoke eloquently, with its sleepless anguish and remorse.

"Good morning, Miss Eure; how shall I thank you?" I began, but stopped abruptly, for without speaking she waved me towards the easel with a gesture which seemed to say, "Prove your gratitude by industry."

"Very good," thought I, "if she likes the theatrical style she shall have it. It is evident she has studied her part and will play it well, I will do the same, and as Louis recommends, take the good the gods send me while I may."

Without more ado I took my place and fell to work; but, though never more eager to get on, with each moment that I passed I found my interest in the picture grow less and less intent, and with every glance at my model found that it was more and more difficult to look away. Beautiful she was not, but the wild and woful figure seemed to attract me as no Hebe, Venus or sweet-faced Psyche had ever done. My hand moved slower and slower, the painted face grew dimmer and dimmer, my glances lingered longer and longer, and presently palette and brushes rested on my knee, as I leaned back in the deep chair and gave myself up to an uninterrupted stare. I knew that it was rude, knew that it was as a trespass on Miss Eure's kindness as well as a breach of good manners, but I could not help it, for my eyes seemed beyond my control, and though I momentarily expected to see her color rise and hear some warning of the lapse of time, I never looked away, and soon forgot to imagine her feelings in the mysterious confusion of my own.

I was first conscious of a terrible fear that I ought to speak or move, which seemed impossible, for my eyelids began to be weighed down by a delicious drowsiness in spite of all my efforts to keep them open. Everything grew misty, and the beating of my heart sounded like the rapid, irregular roll of a muffled drum; then a strange weight seemed to oppress and cause me to sigh long and deeply. But soon the act of breathing appeared to grow unnecessary, for a sensation of wonderful airiness came over me, and I felt as if I could float away like a thistledown. Presently every sense seemed to fall asleep, and in the act of dropping both palette and brush I drifted away into a sea of blissful repose, where nothing disturbed me but a fragmentary dream that came and went like a lingering gleam of consciousness through the new experience which had befallen me.

I seemed to be still in the quiet room, still leaning in the deep chair with half-closed eyes, still watching the white figure before me, but that had changed. I saw a smile break over the lips, something like triumph flash into the eyes, sudden color flush the cheeks, and the rigid hands lifted to gather up and put the long hair back; then with noiseless steps it came nearer and nearer till it stood beside me. For awhile it paused there mute and intent, I felt the eager gaze searching my face, but it caused no displeasure; for I seemed to be looking down at myself, as if soul and body had parted company and I was gifted with a double life. Suddenly the vision laid a light hand on my wrist and touched my temples, while a shade of anxiety seemed to flit across its face as it turned and vanished. A dreamy wonder regarding its return woke within me, then my sleep deepened into utter oblivion, for how long I cannot tell. A pungent odor seemed to recall me to the same half wakeful state. I dimly saw a woman's arm holding a glittering object before me, when the fragrance came; an unseen hand stirred my hair with the grateful drip of water, and once there came a touch like the pressure of lips upon my forehead, soft and warm, but gone in an instant. These new sensations grew rapidly more and more defined; I clearly saw a bracelet on the arm and read the Arabic characters engraved upon the golden coins that formed it; I heard the rustle of garments, the hurried breathing of some near presence, and felt the cool sweep of a hand passing to and fro across my forehead. At this point my thoughts began to shape themselves into words, which came slowly and seemed strange to me as I searched for and connected them, then a heavy sigh rose and broke at my lips, and the sound of my own voice woke me, drowsily echoing the last words I had spoken:

"Good morning, Miss Eure; how shall I thank you?"

To my great surprise the well-remembered voice answered quietly:

"Good morning, Mr. Erdmann; will you have some lunch before you begin?"

How I opened my eyes and got upon my feet was never clear to me, but the first object I saw was Miss Eure coming towards me with a glass in her hand. My expression must have been dazed and imbecile in the extreme, for to add to my bewilderment the tragic robes had disappeared, the dishevelled hair was gathered in shining coils under a Venetian net of silk and gold, a white embroidered wrapper replaced the muslins Lady Macbeth had worn, and a countenance half playful, half anxious, now smiled where I had last seen so sorrowful an aspect. The fear of having committed some great absurdity and endangered my success brought me right with a little shock of returning thought. I collected myself, gave a look about the room, a dizzy bow to her, and put my hand to my head with a vague idea that something was wrong there. In doing this I discovered that my hair was wet, which slight fact caused me to exclaim abruptly:

"Miss Eure, what have I been doing? Have I had a fit? been asleep? or do you deal in magic and rock your guests off into oblivion without a moment's warning?"

Standing before me with uplifted eyes, she answered, smiling:

"No, none of these have happened to you; the air from the Indian plants in the conservatory was too powerful, I think; you were a little faint, but closing the door and opening a window has restored you, and a glass of wine will perfect the cure, I hope."

She was offering the glass as she spoke. I took it but forgot to thank her, for on the arm extended to me was the bracelet never seen so near by my waking eyes, yet as familiar as if my vision had come again. Something struck me disagreeably, and I spoke out with my usual bluntness.

"I never fainted in my life, and have an impression that people do not dream when they swoon. Now I did, and so vivid was it that I still remember the characters engraved on the trinket you wear, for that played a prominent part in my vision. Shall I describe them as proof of it, Miss Eure?"

Her arm dropped at her side and her eyes fell for a moment as I spoke; then she glanced up unchanged, saying as she seated herself and motioned me to do the same:

"No, rather tell the dream, and taste these grapes while you amuse me."

I sat down and obeyed her. She listened attentively, and when I ended explained the mystery in the simplest manner.

"You are right in the first part of your story. I did yield to a whim which seized me when I saw your picture, and came down *en costume,* hoping to help you by keeping up the illusion. You began, as canvas and brushes prove; I stood motionless till you turned pale and regarded me with a strange expression; at first I thought it might be inspiration, as your friend Yorke would say, but presently you dropped everything out of your hands and fell back in your chair. I took the liberty of treating you like a woman, for I bathed your temples and wielded my vinaigrette most energetically till you revived and began to talk of 'Rachel, art, castles in the air, and your wife Lady Macbeth'; then I slipped away and modernized myself, ordered some refreshments for you, and waited till you wished me 'Good-morning.' "

She was laughing so infectiously that I could not resist joining her and accepting her belief, for curious as the whole affair seemed to me I could account for it in no other way. She was winningly kind, and urged me not to resume my task, but I was secretly disgusted with myself for such a display of weakness, and finding her hesitation caused solely by fears for me, I persisted, and seating her, painted as I had never done before. Every sense seemed unwontedly acute, and hand and eye obeyed me with a docility they seldom showed. Miss Eure sat where I placed her, silent and intent, but her face did not wear the tragic aspect it had worn before, though she tried to recall it. This no longer troubled me, for the memory of the vanished face was more clearly before me than her own, and with but few and hasty glances at my model, I reproduced it with a speed and skill that filled me with delight. The striking of a clock reminded me that I had far exceeded the specified time, and that even a woman's patience has limits; so concealing my regret at losing so auspicious a mood, I laid down my brush, leaving my work unfinished, yet glad to know I had the right to come again, and complete it in a place and presence which proved so inspiring.

Miss Eure would not look at it till it was all done, saying in reply to my thanks for the pleasant studio she had given me—"I was not quite unselfish in that, and owe you an apology for venturing to meddle with your property; but it gave me real satisfaction to arrange these things, and restore this room to the aspect it wore three years ago. I, too, was an artist then, and dreamed aspiring dreams here, but was arrested on the threshold of my career by loss of sight; and hard as it seemed then to give up all my longings, I see now that it was better so, for a few years later it would have killed me. I have learned to desire for others what I can never hope for myself, and try to find pleasure in their success, unembittered by regrets for my own defeat. Let this explain my readiness to help you, my interest in your work and my best wishes for your present happiness and future fame."

The look of resignation, which accompanied her words, touched me more than a flood of complaints, and the thought of all she had lost woke such sympathy and pity in my frosty heart, that I involuntarily pressed the hand that could never wield a brush again. Then for the first time I saw those keen eyes soften and grow dim with unshed tears; this gave them the one charm they needed to be beautiful as well as penetrating, and as they met my own, so womanly sweet and grateful, I felt that one might love her while that mood remained. But it passed as rapidly as it came, and when we parted in the anteroom the cold, quiet lady bowed me out, and the tender-faced girl was gone.

I never told Louis all the incidents of that first sitting, but began my story where the real interest ended; and Miss Eure was equally silent, through forgetfulness or for some good reason of her own. I went several times again, yet though the conservatory door stood open I felt no ill effects from the Indian plants that still bloomed there, dreamed no more dreams, and Miss Eure no more enacted the somnambulist. I found an indefinable charm in that pleasant room, a curious interest in studying its mistress, who always met me with a smile, and parted with a look of unfeigned regret. Louis rallied me upon my absorption, but it caused me no uneasiness, for it was not love that led me there, and Miss Eure knew it. I never had forgotten our conversation on that first night, and with every interview the truth of my friend's suspicions grew more and more apparent to me. Agatha Eure was a strong-willed, imperious woman, used to command all about her and see her last wish gratified; but now she was conscious of a presence she could not command, a wish she dare not utter, and, though her womanly pride sealed her lips, her eyes often traitorously betrayed the longing of her heart. She was sincere in her love for art, and behind that interest in that concealed, even from herself, her love for the artist; but the most indomitable passion given humanity cannot long be hidden. Agatha soon felt her weakness, and vainly struggled to subdue it. I soon knew my power, and owned its subtle charm, though I disdained to use it.

The picture was finished, exhibited and won me all, and more than I had dared to hope; for rumor served me a good turn, and whispers of Miss Eure's part in my success added zest to public curiosity and warmth to public praise. I enjoyed the little stir it caused, found admiration a sweet draught after a laborious year, and felt real gratitude to the woman who had helped me win it. If my work had proved a failure I should have forgotten her, and been an humbler, happier man; it did not, and she became a part of my success. Her name was often spoken in the same breath with mine, her image was kept before me by no exertion of my own, till the memories it brought with it grew familiar as old friends, and slowly ripened into a purpose which, being born of ambition and not love, bore bitter fruit, and wrought out its own retribution for a sin against myself and her.

The more I won the more I demanded, the higher I climbed the more eager I became; and, at last, seeing how much I could gain by a single step, resolved to take it, even though I knew it to be a false one. Other men married for the furtherance of their ambitions, why should not I? Years ago I had given up love of home for love of fame, and the woman who might have made me what I should be had meekly yielded all, wished me a happy future, and faded from my world, leaving me only a bitter memory, a veiled picture and a quiet grave my feet never visited but once. Miss Eure loved me, sympathised in my aims, understood my tastes; she could give all I asked to complete the purpose of my life, and lift me at once and for ever from the hard lot I had struggled with for thirty years. One word would win the miracle, why should I hesitate to utter it?

I did not long—for three months from the day I first entered that shadowy room I stood there intent on asking her to be my wife. As I waited I lived again the strange hour once passed there, and felt as if it had been the beginning of another dream whose awakening was yet to come. I asked myself if the hard healthful reality was not better than such feverish visions, however brilliant, and the voice that is never silent when we interrogate it with sincerity answered, "Yes." "No matter, I choose to dream, so let the phantom of a wife come to me here as the phantom of a lover came to me so long ago." As I uttered these defiant words aloud, like a visible reply, Agatha appeared upon the threshold of the door. I knew she had heard me—for again I saw the soft-eyed, tender girl, and opened my arms to her without a word. She came at once, and clinging to me with unwonted tears upon her cheek, unwonted fervor in her voice, touched my forehead, as she had done in that earlier dream, whispering like one still doubtful of her happiness—

"Oh, Max! be kind to me, for in all the world I have only you to love."

I promised, and broke that promise in less than a year.

PART II

WE WERE MARRIED QUIETLY, went away till the nine days gossip was over, spent our honeymoon as that absurd month is usually spent, and came back to town with the first autumnal frosts; Agatha regretting that I was no longer entirely her own, I secretly thanking heaven that I might drop the lover, and begin my work again, for I was as an imprisoned creature in that atmosphere of "love in idleness," though my bonds were only a pair of loving arms. Madame Snow and son departed, we settled ourselves in the fine house and then endowed with every worldly blessing, I looked about me, believing myself master of my fate, but found I was its slave.

If Agatha could have joined me in my work we might have been happy; if she could have solaced herself with other pleasures and left me to my own, we might have been content; if she had loved me less, we might have gone our separate ways, and yet been friends like many another pair; but I soon found that her affection was of that exacting nature which promises but little peace unless met by one as warm. I had nothing but regard to give her, for it was not in her power to stir a deeper passion in me; I told her this before our marriage, told her I was a cold, hard man, rapt in a single purpose; but what woman believes such confessions while her heart still beats fast with the memory of her betrothal? She said everything was possible to love, and prophesied a speedy change; I knew it would not come, but having given my warning left the rest to time. I hoped to lead a quiet life and prove that adverse circumstances, not the want of power, had kept me from excelling in the profession I had chosen; but to my infinite discomfort Agatha turned jealous of my art, for finding the mistress dearer than the wife, she tried to wean me from it, and seemed to feel that having given me love, wealth and ease, I should ask no more, but play the obedient subject to a generous queen. I rebelled against this, told her that one-half my time should be hers, the other belonged to me, and I would so employ it that it should bring honor to the name I had given her. But, Agatha was not used to seeing her will thwarted or her pleasure sacrificed to another, and soon felt that though I scrupulously fulfilled my promise, the one task was irksome, the other all absorbing; that though she had her husband at her side his heart was in his studio, and the hours spent with her were often the most listless in his day. Then began that sorrowful experience old as Adam's reproaches to Eve; we both did wrong, and neither repented; both were self-willed, sharp tongued and proud, and before six months of wedded life had passed we had known many of those scenes which so belittle character and lessen self-respect.

Agatha's love lived through all, and had I answered its appeals by patience, self-denial and genial friendship, if no warmer tie could exist, I might have spared her an early death, and myself from years of bitterest remorse; but I did not. Then her forbearance ended and my subtle punishment began.

"Away again to-night, Max? You have been shut up all day, and I hoped to have you to myself this evening. Hear how the storm rages without, see how cheery I have made all within for you, so put your hat away and stay, for this hour belongs to me, and I claim it."

Agatha took me prisoner as she spoke, and pointed to the cosy nest she had prepared for me. The room was bright and still; the lamp shone clear; the fire glowed; warm-hued curtains muffled the war of gust and sleet without; books, music, a wide-armed seat and a woman's wistful face invited me; but none of these things could satisfy me just then, and though I drew my wife nearer, smoothed her shining hair, and kissed the reproachful lips, I did not yield.

"You must let me go, Agatha, for the great German artist is here, I had rather give a year of life than miss this meeting with him. I have devoted many evenings to you, and though this hour is yours I shall venture to take it, and offer you a morning call instead. Here are novels, new songs, an instrument, embroidery and a dog, who can never offend by moody silence or unpalatable conversation—what more can a contented woman ask, surely not an absentminded husband?"

"Yes, just that and nothing more, for she loves him, and he can supply a want that none of these things can. See how pretty I have tried to make myself for you alone; stay, Max, and make me happy."

"Dear, I shall find my pretty wife to-morrow, but the great painter will be gone; let me go, Agatha, and make me happy."

She drew herself from my arm, saying with a flash of the eye—"Max, you are a tyrant!"

"Am I? then you made me so with too much devotion."

"Ah, if you loved me as I loved there would be no selfishness on your part, no reproaches on mine. What shall I do to make myself dearer, Max?"

"Give me more liberty."

"Then I should lose you entirely, and lead the life of a widow. Oh, Max, this is hard, this is bitter, to give all and receive nothing in return."

She spoke passionately, and the truth of her reproach stung me, for I answered with that coldness that always wounded her:

"Do you count an honest name, sincere regard and much gratitude as nothing? I have given you these, and ask only peace and freedom in return. I desire to do justice to you and to myself, but I am not like you, never can be, and you must not hope it. You say love is all-powerful, prove it upon me, I am willing to be the fondest of husbands if I can; teach me, win me in spite of myself, and make me what you will; but leave me a little time to live and labor for that which is dearer to me than your faulty lord and master can ever be to you."

"Shall I do this?" and her face kindled as she put the question.

"Yes, here is an amusement for you, use what arts you will, make your love irresistible, soften my hard nature, convert me into your shadow, subdue me till I come at your call like a pet dog, and when you make your presence more powerful than painting I will own that you have won your will and made your theory good."

I was smiling as I spoke, for the twelve labors of Hercules seemed less impossible than this, but Agatha watched me with her glittering eyes; and answered slowly—

"I will do it. Now go, and enjoy your liberty while you may, but remember when I have conquered that you dared me to it, and keep your part of the compact. Promise this." She offered me her hand with a strange expression—I took it, said good-night, and hurried away, still smiling at the curious challenge given and accepted.

Agatha told me to enjoy my liberty, and I tried to do so that very night, but failed most signally, for I had not been an hour in the brilliant company gathered to meet the celebrated guest before I found it impossible to banish the thought of my solitary wife. I had left her often, yet never felt disturbed by more than a passing twinge of that uncomfortable bosom friend called conscience; but now the interest of the hour seemed lessened by regret, for through varying conversation held with those about me, mingling with the fine music that I heard, looking at me from every woman's face, and thrusting itself into my mind at every turn, came a vague, disturbing self-reproach, which slowly deepened to a strong anxiety. My attention wandered, words seemed to desert me, fancy to be frostbound, and even in the presence of the great man I had so ardently desired to see I could neither enjoy his society nor play my own part well. More than once I found myself listening for Agatha's voice; more than once I looked behind me expecting to see her figure, and more than once I resolved to go, with no desire to meet her.

"It is an acute fit of what women call nervousness; I will not yield to it," I thought, and plunged into the gayest group I saw, supped, talked, sang a song, and broke down; told a witty story, and spoiled it; laughed and tried to bear myself like the lightest-hearted guest in the rooms; but it would not do, for stronger and stronger grew the strange longing to go home, and soon it became uncontrollable. A foreboding fear that something had happened oppressed me, and suddenly leaving the festival at its height I drove home as if life and death depended on the saving of a second. Like one pursuing or pursued I rode, eager only to be there; yet when I stood on my own threshold I asked myself wonderingly, "Why such haste?" and stole in ashamed at my early return. The storm beat without, but within all was serene and still, and with noiseless steps I went up to the room where I had left my wife, pausing a moment at the half open door to collect myself, lest she should see the disorder of both mind and mien. Looking in I saw her sitting with neither book nor work beside her, and after a momentary glance began to think my anxiety had not been causeless, for she sat erect and motionless as an inanimate figure of intense thought; her eyes were fixed, face colorless, with an expression of iron determination, as if every energy of mind and body were wrought up to the achievement of a single purpose. There was something in the rigid attitude and stern aspect of this familiar shape that filled me with dismay, and found vent in the abrupt exclamation,

"Agatha, what is it?"

She sprang up like a steel spring when the pressure is removed, saw me, and struck her hands together with a wild gesture of surprise, alarm or pleasure, which I could not tell, for in the act she dropped into her seat white and breathless as if smitten with sudden death. Unspeakably shocked, I bestirred myself till she recovered, and though pale and spent, as if with some past exertion, soon seemed quite herself again.

"Agatha, what were you thinking of when I came in?" I asked, as she sat leaning against me with half closed eyes and a faint smile on her lips, as if the unwonted caresses I bestowed upon her were more soothing than any cordial I could give. Without stirring she replied,

"Of you, Max. I was longing for you, with heart and soul and will. You told me to win you in spite of yourself; and I was sending my love to find and bring you home. Did it reach you? did it lead you back and make you glad to come?"

A peculiar chill ran through me as I listened, though her voice was quieter, her manner gentler than usual as she spoke. She seemed to have such faith in her tender fancy, such assurance of its efficacy, and such a near approach to certain knowledge of its success, that I disliked the thought of continuing the topic, and answered cheerfully,

"My own conscience brought me home, dear; for, discovering that I had left my peace of mind behind me, I came back to find it. If your task is to cost a scene like this it will do more harm than good to both of us, so keep your love from such uncanny wanderings through time and space, and win me with less dangerous arts."

She smiled her strange smile, folded my hand in her own, and answered with soft exultation in her voice,

"It will not happen so again, Max; but I am glad, most glad you came, for it proves I have some power over this wayward heart of yours, where I shall knock until it opens wide and takes me in."

The events of that night made a deep impression on me, for from that night my life was changed. Agatha left me entirely free, never asked my presence, never up-braided me for long absences or silences when together. She seemed to find happiness in her belief that she should yet subdue me, and though I smiled at this in my indifference, there was something half pleasant, half pathetic in the thought of this proud woman leaving all warmer affections for my negligent friendship, the sight of this young wife laboring to win her husband's heart. At first I tried to be all she asked, but soon relapsed into my former life, and finding no reproaches followed, believed I should enjoy it as never before—but I did not. As weeks passed I slowly became conscious that some new power had taken possession of me, swaying my whole nature to its will; a power alien yet sovereign. Fitfully it worked, coming upon me when least desired, enforcing its commands regardless of time, place or mood; mysterious yet irresistible in its strength, this mental tyrant led me at all hours, in all stages of anxiety, repugnance and rebellion, from all pleasures or employments, straight to Agatha. If I sat at my easel the sudden summons came, and wondering at myself I obeyed it, to find her busied in some cheerful occupation, with apparently no thought or wish for me. If I left home I often paused abruptly in my walk or drive, turned and hurried back, simply because I could not resist the impulse that controlled me. If she went away I seldom failed to follow, and found no peace till I was at her side again. I grew moody and restless, slept ill, dreamed wild dreams, and often woke and wandered aimlessly, as if sent upon an unknown errand. I could not fix my mind upon my work; a spell seemed to have benumbed imagination and robbed both brain and hand of power to conceive and skill to execute.

At first I fancied this was only the reaction of entire freedom after long captivity, but I soon found I was bound to a more exacting mistress than my wife had ever been. Then I suspected that it was only the perversity of human nature, and that having gained my wish it grew valueless, and I longed for that which I had lost; but it was not this, for distasteful as my present life had become, the other seemed still more so when I recalled it. For a time I believed that Agatha might be right, that I was really learning to love her, and this unquiet mood was the awakening of that passion which comes swift and strong when it comes to such as I. If I had never loved I might have clung to this belief, but the memory of that earlier affection, so genial, entire and sweet, proved that the present fancy was only a delusion; for searching deeply into myself to discover the truth of this, I found that Agatha was no dearer, and to my own dismay detected a covert dread lurking there, harmless and vague, but threatening to deepen into aversion or resentment for some unknown offence; and while I accused myself of an unjust and ungenerous weakness, I shrank from the thought of her, even while I sought her with the assiduity but not the ardor of a lover.

Long I pondered over this inexplicable state of mind, but found no solution of it; for I would not own, either to myself or Agatha, that the shadow of her prophecy had come to pass, though its substance was still wanting. She sometimes looked inquiringly into my face with those strange eyes of hers, sometimes chid me with a mocking smile when she found me sitting idly before my easel without a line or tint given though hours had passed; and often, when driven by that blind impulse I sought her anxiously among her friends, she would glance at those about her, saying, with a touch of triumph in her mien, "Am I not an enviable wife to have inspired such devotion in this grave husband?" Once, remembering her former words, I asked her playfully if she still "sent her love to find and bring me home?" but she only shook her head and answered, sadly,

"Oh, no; my love was burdensome to you, so I have rocked it to sleep and laid it where it will not trouble you again."

At last I decided that some undetected physical infirmity caused my disquiet, for years of labor and privation might well have worn the delicate machinery of heart or brain, and this warning suggested the wisdom of consulting medical skill in time. This thought grew as month after month increased my mental malady and began to tell upon my hitherto unbroken health. I wondered if Agatha knew how listless, hollow-eyed and wan I had grown; but she never spoke of it, and an unconquerable reserve kept me from uttering a complaint to her.

One day I resolved to bear it no longer, and hurried away to an old friend in whose skill and discretion I had entire faith. He was out, and while I waited I took up a book that lay among the medical works upon his table. I read a page, then a chapter, turning leaf after leaf with a rapid hand, devouring paragraph after paragraph with an eager eye. An hour passed, still I read on. Dr. L—did not come, but I did not think of that, and when I laid down the book I no longer needed him, for in that hour I had discovered a new world, had seen the diagnosis of my symptoms set forth in unmistakable terms, and found the key to the mystery in the one word—Magnetism. This was years ago, before spirits had begun their labors for good or ill, before ether and hashish had gifted humanity with eternities of bliss in a second, and while Mesmer's mystical discoveries were studied only by the scientific or philosophical few. I knew nothing of these things, for my whole life had led another way, and no child could be more ignorant of the workings or extent of this wonderful power. There was Indian blood in my veins, and superstition lurked there still; consequently the knowledge that I was a victim of this occult magic came upon me like an awful revelation, and filled me with a storm of wrath, disgust and dread.

Like an enchanted spirit who has found the incantation that will free it from subjection, I rejoiced with a grim satisfaction even while I cursed myself for my long blindness, and with no thought for anything but instant accusation on my part, instant confession and atonement on hers, I went straight home, straight into Agatha's presence, and there, in words as brief as bitter, told her that her reign was over. All that was sternest, hottest and most unforgiving ruled me then, and like fire to fire roused a spirit equally strong and high. I might have subdued her by juster and more generous words, but remembering the humiliation of my secret slavery I forgot my own offence in hers, and set no curb on tongue or temper, letting the storm she had raised fall upon her with the suddenness of an unwonted, unexpected outburst.

As I spoke her face changed from its first dismay to a defiant calmness that made it hard as rock and cold as ice, while all expression seemed concentrated in her eye, which burned on me with an unwavering light. There was no excitement in her manner, no sign of fear, or shame, or grief in her mien, and when she answered me her voice was untremulous and clear as when I heard it first.

"Have you done? Then hear me: I knew you long before you dreamed that such a woman as Agatha Eure existed. I was solitary, and longed to be sincerely loved. I was rich, yet I could not buy what is unpurchasable; I was young, yet I could not make my youth sweet with affection; for nowhere did I see the friend whose nature was akin to mine until you passed before me, and I felt at once, 'There is the one I seek!' I never yet desired that I did not possess the coveted object, and believed I should not fail now. Years ago I learned the mysterious gift I was endowed with, and fostered it; for, unblessed with beauty, I hoped its silent magic might draw others near enough to see, under this cold exterior, the woman's nature waiting there. The first night you saw me I yielded to an irresistible longing to attract your eye, and for a moment see the face I had learned to love looking into mine. You know how well I succeeded—you know your own lips asked the favor I was so glad to give, and your own will led you to me. That day I made another trial of my skill and succeeded beyond my hopes, but dared not repeat it, for your strong nature was not easily subdued, it was too perilous a game for me to play, and I resolved that no delusion should make you mine. I would have a free gift or none. You offered me your hand, and believing that it held a loving heart, I took it, to find that heart barred against me, and another woman's name engraved upon its door. Was this a glad discovery for a wife to make? Do you wonder she reproached you when she saw her hopes turn to ashes, and could no longer conceal from herself that she was only a stepping-stone to lift an ambitious man to a position which she could not share? You think me weak and wicked; look back upon the year nearly done and ask yourself if many young wives have such a record of neglect, despised love, unavailing sacrifices, long suffering patience and deepening despair? I had been reading the tear-stained pages of this record when you bid me win you if I could; and with a bitter sense of the fitness of such a punishment, I resolved to do it, still cherishing a hope that some spark of affection might be found. I soon saw the vanity of such a hope, and this hard truth goaded me to redouble my efforts till I had entirely subjugated that arrogant spirit of yours, and made myself master where I would so gladly have been a loving subject. Do you think I have not suffered? have not wept bitter tears in secret, and been wrung by sharper anguish than you have ever known? If you had given any sign of affection, shown any wish to return to me, any shadow of regret for the wrong you had done me, I would have broken my wand like Prospero, and used no magic but the pardon of a faithful heart. You did not, and it has come to this. Before you condemn me, remember that you dared me to do it—that you bid me make my presence more powerful than Art—bid me convert you to my shadow, and subdue you till you came like a pet dog at my call. Have I not obeyed you? Have I not kept my part of the compact? Now keep yours."

There was something terrible in hearing words whose truth wounded while they fell, uttered in a voice whose concentrated passion made its tones distinct and deep, as if an accusing spirit read them from that book whose dread records never are effaced. My hot blood cooled, my harsh mood softened, and though it still burned, my resentment sank lower, for, remembering the little life to be, I wrestled with myself, and won humility enough to say, with regretful energy:

"Forgive me, Agatha, and let this sad past sleep. I have wronged you, but I believed I sinned no more than many another man who, finding love dead, hoped to feed his hunger with friendship and ambition. I never thought of such an act till I saw affection in your face; that tempted me, and I tried to repay all you gave me by the offer of the hand you mutely asked. It was a bargain often made in this strange world of ours, often repented as we repent now. Shall we abide by it, and by mutual forbearance recover mutual peace? or shall I leave you free, to make life sweeter with a better man, and find myself poor and honest as when we met?"

Something in my words stung her; and regarding me with the same baleful aspect, she lifted her slender hand, so wasted since I made it mine, that the single ornament it wore dropped into her palm, and holding it up, she said, as if prompted by the evil genius that lies hidden in every heart:

"I will do neither. I have outlived my love, but pride still remains; and I will not do as you have done, take cold friendship or selfish ambition to fill an empty heart; I will not be pitied as an injured woman, or pointed at as one who staked all on a man's faith and lost; I will have atonement for my long-suffering—you owe me this, and I claim it. Henceforth you are the slave of the ring, and when I command you must obey, for I possess a charm you cannot defy. It is too late to ask for pity, pardon, liberty or happier life; law and gospel joined us, and as yet law and gospel cannot put us asunder. You have brought this fate upon yourself, accept it, submit to it, for I have bought you with my wealth, I hold you with my mystic art, and body and soul, Max Erdmann, you are mine!"

I knew it was all over then, for a woman never flings such taunts in her husband's teeth till patience, hope and love are gone. A desperate purpose sprung up within me as I listened, yet I delayed a moment before I uttered it, with a last desire to spare us both.

"Agatha, do you mean that I am to lead the life I have been leading for three months—a life of spiritual slavery worse than any torment of the flesh?"

"I do."

"Are you implacable? and will you rob me of all self-control, all peace, all energy, all hope of gaining that for which I have paid so costly a price?"

"I will."

"Take back all you have given me, take my good name, my few friends, my hard-earned success; leave me stripped of every earthly blessing, but free me from this unnatural subjection, which is more terrible to me than death!"

"I will not!"

"Then your own harsh decree drives me from you, for I will break the bond that holds me, I will go out of this house and never cross its threshold while I live—never look into the face which has wrought me all this ill. There is no law, human or divine, that can give you a right to usurp the mastery of another will, and if it costs life and reason I will not submit to it."

"Go when and where you choose, put land and sea between us, break what ties you may, there is one you cannot dissolve, and when I summon you, in spite of all resistance, you must come."

"I swear I will not!"

I spoke out of a blind and bitter passion, but I kept my oath. How her eyes glittered as she lifted up that small pale hand of hers, pointed with an ominous gesture to the ring, and answered:

"Try it."

As she spoke like a sullen echo came the crash of the heavy picture that hung before us. It bore Lady Macbeth's name, but it was a painted image of my wife. I shuddered as I saw it fall, for to my superstitious fancy it seemed a fateful incident; but Agatha laughed a low metallic laugh that made me cold to hear, and whispered like a sibyl:

"Accept the omen; that is a symbol of the Art you worship so idolatrously that a woman's heart was sacrificed for its sake. See where it lies in ruins at your feet, never to bring you honor, happiness or peace; for I speak the living truth when I tell you that your ambitious hopes will vanish the cloud now rising like a veil between us, and the memory of this year will haunt you day and night, till the remorse you painted shall be written upon heart, and face, and life. Now go!"

Her swift words and forceful gesture seemed to banish me for ever, and, like one walking in his sleep, I left her there, a stern, still figure, with its shattered image at its feet.

That instant I departed, but not far—for as yet I could not clearly see which way duty led me. I made no confidante, asked no sympathy or help, told no one of my purpose, but resolving to take no decisive step rashly, I went away to a country house of Agatha's, just beyond the city, as I had once done before when busied on a work that needed solitude and quiet, so that if gossip rose it might be harmless to us both. Then I sat down and thought. Submit I would not, desert her utterly I could not, but I dared defy her, and I did; for as if some viewless spirit whispered the suggestion in my ear, I determined to oppose my will to hers, to use her weapons if I could, and teach her to be merciful through suffering like my own. She had confessed my power to draw her to me, in spite of coldness, poverty and all lack of the attractive graces women love; that clue inspired me with hope. I got books and pored over them till their meaning grew clear to me; I sought out learned men and gathered help from their wisdom; I gave myself to the task with indomitable zeal, for I was struggling for the liberty that alone made life worth possessing. The world believed me painting mimic woes, but I was living through a fearfully real one; friends fancied me busied with the mechanism of material bodies, but I was prying into the mysteries of human souls; and many envied my luxurious leisure in that leafy nest, while I was leading the life of a doomed convict, for as I kept my sinful vow so Agatha kept hers.

She never wrote, or sent, or came, but day and night she called me—day and night I resisted, saved only by the desperate means I used—means that made my own servant think me mad. I bid him lock me in my chamber; I dashed out at all hours to walk fast and far away into the lonely forest; I drowned consciousness in wine; I drugged myself with opiates, and when the crisis had passed, woke spent but victorious. All arts I tried, and slowly found that in this conflict of opposing wills my own grew stronger with each success, the other lost power with each defeat. I never wished to harm my wife, never called her, never sent a baneful thought or desire along that mental telegraph which stretched and thrilled between us; I only longed to free myself, and in this struggle weeks passed, yet neither won a signal victory, for neither proud heart knew the beauty of self-conquest and the power of submission.

One night I went up to the lonely tower that crowned the house, to watch the equinoctial storm that made a Pandemonium of the elements without. Rain streamed as if a second deluge was at hand; whirlwinds tore down the valley; the river chafed and foamed with an angry dash, and the city lights shone dimly through the flying mist as I watched them from my lofty room. The tumult suited me, for my own mood was stormy, dark and bitter, and when the cheerful fire invited me to bask before it I sat there wrapped in reveries as gloomy as the night. Presently the well-known premonition came with its sudden thrill through blood and nerves, and with a revengeful strength never felt before I gathered up my energies for the trial, as I waited some more urgent summons. None came, but in its place a sense of power flashed over me, a swift exultation dilated within me, time seemed to pause, the present rolled away, and nothing but an isolated memory remained, for fixing my thoughts on Agatha, I gave myself up to the dominant spirit that possessed me. I sat motionless, yet I willed to see her. Vivid as the flames that framed it, a picture started from the red embers, and clearly as if my bodily eye rested on it, I saw the well-known room, I saw my wife lying in a deep chair, wan and wasted as if with suffering of soul and body, I saw her grope with outstretched hands, and turn her head with eyes whose long lashes never lifted from the cheek where they lay so dark and still, and through the veil that seemed to wrap my senses I heard my own voice, strange and broken, whispering:

"God forgive me, she is blind!"

For a moment, the vision wandered mistily before me, then grew steady, and I saw her steal like a wraith across the lighted room, so dark to her; saw her bend over a little white nest my own hands placed there, and lift some precious burden in her feeble arms; saw her grope painfully back again, and sitting by that other fire—not solitary like my own—lay her pale cheek to that baby cheek and seem to murmur some lullaby that mother-love had taught her. Over my heart strong and sudden gushed a warmth never known before, and again, strange and broken through the veil that wrapped my senses, came my own voice whispering:

"God be thanked, she is not utterly alone!"

As if my breath dissolved it, the picture faded; but I willed again and another rose—my studio, dim with dust, damp with long disuse, dark with evening gloom—for one flickering lamp made the white shapes ghostly, and the pictured faces smile or frown with fitful vividness. There was no semblance of my old self there, but in the heart of the desolation and the darkness Agatha stood alone, with outstretched arms and an imploring face, full of a love and longing so intense that with a welcoming gesture and a cry that echoed through the room, I answered that mute appeal:

"Come to me! come to me!"

A gust thundered at the window, and rain fell like stormy tears, but nothing else replied; as the bright brands dropped the flames died out, and with it that sad picture of my deserted home. I longed to stir but could not, for I had called up a power I could not lay, the servant ruled the master now, and like one fastened by a spell I still sat leaning forward intent upon a single thought. Slowly from the gray embers smouldering on the hearth a third scene rose behind the smoke wreaths, changeful, dim and strange. Again my former home, again my wife, but this time standing on the threshold of the door I had sworn never to cross again. I saw the wafture of the cloak gathered about her, saw the rain beat on her shelterless head, and followed that slight figure through the deserted streets, over the long bridge where the lamps flickered in the wind, along the leafy road, up the wide steps and in at the door whose closing echo startled me to consciousness that my pulses were beating with a mad rapidity, that a cold dew stood upon my forehead, that every sense was supernaturally alert, and that all were fixed upon one point with a breathless intensity that made that little span of time as fearful as the moment when one hangs poised in air above a chasm in the grasp of nightmare. Suddenly I sprang erect, for through the uproar of the elements without, the awesome hush within, I heard steps ascending, and stood waiting in a speechless agony to see what shape would enter there.

One by one the steady footfalls echoed on my ear, one by one they seemed to bring the climax of some blind conflict nearer, one by one they knelled a human life away, for as the door swung open Agatha fell down before me, storm-beaten, haggard, spent, but loving still, for with a faint attempt to fold her hands submissively, she whispered:

"You have conquered, I am here!" and with that act grew still for ever, as with a great shock I woke to see what I had done.

Ten years have passed since then. I sit on that same hearth a feeble, white-haired man, and beside me, the one companion I shall ever know, my little son—dumb, blind and imbecile. I lavish tender names upon him, but receive no sweet sound in reply; I gather him close to my desolate heart, but meet no answering caress; I look with yearning glance, but see only those haunting eyes, with no gleam of recognition to warm them, no ray of intellect to inspire them, no change to deepen their sightless beauty; and this fair body moulded with the Divine sculptor's gentlest grace is always here before me, an embodied grief that wrings my heart with its pathetic innocence, its dumb reproach. This is the visible punishment for my sin, but there is an unseen retribution heavier than human judgment could inflict, subtler than human malice could conceive, for with a power made more omnipotent by death Agatha still calls me. God knows I am willing now, that I long with all the passion of desire, the anguish of despair to go to her, and He knows that the one tie that holds me is this aimless little life, this duty that I dare not neglect, this long atonement that I make. Day and night I listen to the voice that whispers to me through the silence of these years; day and night I answer with a yearning cry from the depths of a contrite spirit; day and night I cherish the one sustaining hope that Death, the great consoler, will soon free both father and son from the inevitable doom a broken law has laid upon them; for then I know that somewhere in the long hereafter my remorseful soul will find her, and with its poor offering of penitence and love fall down before her, humbly saying:

"You have conquered, I am here!"

❧ V. V.: or, Plots and Counterplots

Chapter I. Won and Lost

IN THE GREENROOM of a Parisian theater a young man was pacing to and fro, evidently waiting with impatience for some expected arrival.

The room was empty, for the last performance of a Grand Spectacle was going on, and the entire strength of the company in demand. Frequent bursts of barbaric music had filled the air; but now a brief lull had fallen, broken only by the soft melody of flutes and horns. Standing motionless, the young man listened with a sudden smile, an involuntary motion of the head, as if in fancy he saw and followed some object of delight. A storm of applause broke in on the last notes of the air. Again and again was it repeated, and when at length it died away, trumpet, clarion, and drum resumed their martial din, and the enchanting episode seemed over.

Suddenly, framed in the dark doorway, upon which the young man's eyes were fixed, appeared an apparition well worth waiting for. A sylph she seemed, costumed in fleecy white and gold; the star that glittered on her forehead was less brilliant than her eyes; the flowers that filled her graceful arms were outrivaled by the blooming face that smiled above them; the ornaments she wore were forgotten in admiration of the long blond tresses that crowned her spirited little head; and when the young man welcomed her she crossed the room as if borne by the shining wings upon her shoulders.

"My Virginie, how long they kept you," began the lover, as this beautiful girl leaned against him, flushed and panting, but radiant with the triumphs of the hour.

"Yes, for they recalled me many times; and see—not one bouquet without a billet-doux or gift attached!"

"I have much to say, Virginie, and you give me no time but this. Where is Victor?"

"Safe for many minutes; he is in the 'Pas des Enfers,' and then we are together in the 'Pas des Déesses.' Behold! Another offer from the viscount. Shall I accept?"

While speaking she had been rifling the flowers of their attractive burdens, and now held up a delicately scented note with an air half serious, half gay. Her lover crushed the paper in his hand and answered hotly, "You will refuse, or I shall make the viscount a different sort of offer. His devotion is an insult, for you are mine!"

"Not yet, monsieur. Victor has the first claim. And see, he has set his mark upon me."

Pushing up a bracelet, she showed two dark letters stamped or tattooed on the white flesh.

"And you permitted him to disfigure you? When, Virginie, and why?"

"Ah, that was years ago when I cared nothing for beauty, and clung to Victor as my only friend, letting him do what he would, quite content to please him, for he was very kind, and I, poor child, was nothing but a burden. A year ago we were betrothed, and next year he hopes to marry—for we do well now, and I shall then be eighteen."

"You will not marry him. Then why deceive him, Virginie?"

"Yes, but I may if no one else will offer me a name as he does. I do not love him, but he is useful; he guards me like a dragon, works for me, cherishes me, and keeps me right when from mere youth and gaiety of heart I might go astray. What then? I care nothing for lovers; they are false and vain, they annoy me, waste my time, keep Victor savage, and but for the éclat it gives me, I would banish all but—" She finished the sentence with a caress more eloquent than any words and, before he could speak, added half tenderly, half reproachfully, while the flowers strayed down upon the ground, "Not one of all these came from you. I thought you would remember me on this last night."

Passionately kissing the red lips so near his own, the lover answered, "I did remember you, but kept my gift to offer when we were alone."

"That is so like you! A thousand thanks. Now give it to me."

With a pretty gesture of entreaty she held out her little hand, and the young man put his own into it, saying earnestly, "I offer this in all sincerity, and ask you to be my wife."

A brilliant smile flashed over her face, and something like triumph shone in her eyes as she clasped the hand in both her own, exclaiming with mingled delight and incredulity, "You ask that of me, the *danseuse,* friendless, poor and humble? Do you mean it, Allan? Shall I go with you to Scotland, be 'my lady' by-and-by? *Ciel!* It is incredible."

"Yes, I mean it. Passion has conquered pride, and for love's sake I can forgive, forget anything but degradation. That you shall never know; and I thank Victor that his jealous vigilance has kept you innocent through all the temptation of a life like yours. The viscount offers you an establishment and infamy; I offer you an honorable name and a home with my whole heart. Which shall it be, Virginie?"

She looked at him keenly—saw a young and comely face, now flushed and kindled with the ardor of a first love. She had seen many such waiting for her smile; but beyond this she saw truth in the honest eyes, read a pride on the forehead that no dishonor could stain, and knew that she might trust one whose promises were never broken. With a little cry of joy and gratitude she laid her face down on the generous hand that gave so much, and thanked heaven that the desire of her life was won. Gathering her close, Allan whispered, with a soft cheek against his own, "My darling, we must be married at once, or Victor will discover and betray us. All is arranged, and this very night we may quit Paris for a happy honeymoon in Italy. Say yes, and leave the rest to me."

"It is impossible! I cannot leave my possessions behind me; I must prepare a little. Wait till tomorrow, and give me time to think."

She spoke resolutely; the young man saw that his project would fail unless he yielded the point, and controlling his impatience, he modified his plan and won her by the ease of that concession.

"I will not hurry you, but, Virginie, we must be married tonight, because all is prepared, and delay may ruin us. Once mine, Victor has no control over you, and my friends will have no power to part us. Grant me this boon, and you shall leave Paris when you will."

She smiled and agreed to it, but did not confess that the chief reason of her reluctance to depart so suddenly was a desire to secure the salary which on the morrow would be paid her for a most successful but laborious season. Mercenary, vain, and hollow-hearted as she was, there was something so genuine in the perfect confidence, the ardent affection of her lover, that it won her respect and seemed to gift the rank which she aspired to attain with a redoubled charm.

"Now tell me your plan, and tell me rapidly, lest Victor should divine that we are plotting and disturb us," she said, with the look of exultation still gleaming in her eyes.

"It is this. Your engagement ends tonight, and you have made no new one. You have spoken of going into the country to rest, and when you vanish people will believe that you have gone suddenly to rusticate. Victor is too proud to complain, and we will leave a penitent confession behind us to appease him."

"He will be terrible, Allan."

"You have a right to choose, I to protect you. Have no fear; we shall be far beyond his reach when he discovers his mistake. I asked you of him honorably once, and he refused with anger."

"He never told me that. We are requited, so let him rave. What next?"

"When your last dance is over, change your dress quickly, and instead of waiting here for your cousin, as usual, slip out by the private door. I shall be there with a carriage, and while Victor is detained searching for you, we will be married, and I shall take you home to gather up those precious possessions of yours. You will do this, Virginie?"

"Yes."

"Your courage will not fail when I am gone, and some fear of Victor keep you?"

"Bah! I fear nothing now."

"Then I am sure of you, and I swear you never shall regret your confidence; for as soon as my peace is made at home, you shall be received there as my honored wife."

"Are you very sure that you *will* be forgiven?" she asked anxiously, as if weighing possibilities even then.

"I *am* sure of pardon after the first anger is over, for they love me too much to disinherit or banish me, and they need only see you to be won at once."

"This marriage, Allan—it will be a true one? You will not deceive me; for if I leave Victor I shall have no friend in the wide world but you."

The most disloyal lover could not have withstood the pleading look, the gesture of appeal which accompanied her words, and this one, who harbored no treachery, assured her with solemn protestations and the most binding vows.

A few moments were spent in maturing their plan, and Virginie was just leaving him with the word "Tomorrow" on her lips when an animated flame of fire seemed to dart into the room. It was a youth whose scarlet-and-silver costume glowed and glittered in the light, as with one marvelous bound he crossed the room and stood before them. Supple, sinewy, and slight was the threatening figure which they saw; dark and defiant the face, with fierce black eyes, frowning brows, and the gleam of set teeth between lips parted by a muttered malediction. Lovely as the other apparition had been, this was far more striking, for it seemed full of the strong grace and beauty of the fallen angel whom it represented. The pose was magnificent; a flaming crown shone in the dark hair, and filmy pinions of scarlet flecked with silver drooped from shoulder to heel. So fiery and fierce he looked, it was little wonder that one lover drew back and the other uttered an exclamation of surprise. Instantly recovering herself, however, Virginie broke into a blithe laugh, and airily twirled away beyond the reach of Victor's outstretched hand.

"It is late; you are not dressed—you will be disgraced by a failure. Go!" he said, with an air of command.

"Au revoir, monsieur; I leave Paris with you." And as she uttered the words with a glance that pointed their double meaning, Virginie vanished.

Turning to the long mirror behind him, the young gentleman replaced his hat, resettled in his buttonhole the flower just given him, tranquilly drew on his gloves, saying, as he strolled toward the door, "I shall return to my box to witness this famous 'Pas des Déesses.' Virginie, Lucille, and Clotilde, upon my word, Paris, you will find it difficult to decide upon which of the three goddesses to bestow the golden apple."

Not a word spoke Victor, till the sounds of steps died away. Then he departed to his dressing room, moodily muttering as he went, "Tomorrow, she said. They intend to meet somewhere. Good! I will prevent *that.* There has been enough of this—it must end and Virginie shall keep her promise. I will stand guard tonight and watch them well tomorrow."

Three hours later, breathless and pale with fatigue and rage, Victor sprang up the steps leading to his cousin's chamber in the old house by the Seine. A lamp burned in a niche beside her door; a glass of wine and a plate of fruit stood there also, waiting as usual for him. As his eye fell upon these objects a long sigh of relief escaped him.

"Thank heaven, she has come home then. Yet hold! It may be but a ruse to prevent my discovering her absence. Virginie! Cousin! Are you there?"

He struck upon the door, lightly at first, then vehemently, and to his great joy a soft, sleepy voice replied, "Who calls?"

"It is Victor. I missed you, searched for you, and grew anxious when I found you gone. Why did you not wait, as usual?"

"Mlle. Clotilde offered me a seat in her carriage, and I gladly accepted it. She was set down first, and it is a long distance there and back, you know. Now let me rest; I am very tired."

"Good night, my heart," answered Victor, adding, in a tone of pain and tenderness, as he turned away, *"mon Dieu!* How I love that girl, and how she tortures me! Rest well, my cousin; I shall guard your sleep."

Hour after hour passed, and still a solitary figure paced to and fro with noiseless feet along the narrow terrace that lay between the ancient house and the neglected garden sloping to the river. Dawn was slowly breaking in the east when the window of Virginie's chamber opened cautiously, and her charming head appeared. The light was very dim, and shadows still lay dark upon the house; but Victor, coming from the water gate whither he had been drawn by the sound of a passing boat, heard the soft movement, glided behind a group of shrubs, and eyed the window keenly, remembering that now it was "tomorrow." For a moment the lovely face leaned out, looking anxiously across terrace, street, and garden. The morning air seemed to strike cold on her uncovered shoulders, and with a shiver she was drawing back when a man's hand laid a light cloak about her, and a man's head appeared beside her own.

"Imprudent! Go quickly, or Victor will be stirring. At noon I shall be ready," she said half aloud, and as she withdrew the curtain fell.

With the bound of a wounded tiger, Victor reached the terrace, and reckless of life or limb, took the short road to his revenge. The barred shutters of a lower window, the carved ornaments upon the wall, and the balcony that hung above, all offered foot-and handhold for an agile climber like himself, as, creeping upward like a stealthy shadow, he peered in with a face that would have appalled the lovers had they seen it. They did not, for standing near the half-opened door, they were parting as Romeo and Juliet parted, heart to heart, cheek to cheek, and neither saw nor heard the impending doom until the swift stroke fell. So sure, so sudden was it that Virginie knew nothing, till, with a stifled cry, her lover started, swayed backward from her arms, and dyeing her garments with his blood, fell at her feet stabbed through the heart.

An awful silence followed, for Virginie uttered no cry of alarm, made no gesture of flight, showed no sign of guilt; but stood white and motionless as if turned to stone.

Soon Victor grasped her arm and hissed into her ear, "Traitress! I could find it in my heart to lay you there beside him. But no, you shall live to atone for your falsehood to me and mourn your lover."

Something in the words or tone seemed to recall her scattered senses and rouse her to a passionate abhorrence of him and of his deed. She wrenched herself from his hold, saying vehemently, though instinctively below her breath, "No; it is you who shall atone! He was my husband, not my lover. Look if I lie!"

He did look as a trembling hand was stretched toward him over that dead form. On it he saw a wedding ring, and in it the record of the marriage which in a single night had made her wife and widow. With an ejaculation of despair he snatched the paper as if to tear and scatter it; but some sudden thought flashed into his mind, and putting the record in his bosom, he turned to Virginie with an expression that chilled her by its ominous resolve.

"Listen," he said, "and save yourself while you may; for I swear, if you raise your voice, lift your hand against me, or refuse to obey me now, that I will denounce you as the murderer of that man. You were last seen with him, were missed by others besides me last night. There lies his purse; here is the only proof of your accursed marriage; and if I call in witnesses, which of us looks most like an assassin, you or I?"

She listened with a terror-stricken face, glanced at her bloody garments, knew that she was in the power of a relentless man, and clasped her hands with a gesture of mute supplication and submission.

"You are wise," he said. "Apart, we are both in danger; together we may be strong and safe. I have a plan—hear it and help me to execute it, for time is life now. You have spoken to many of going into the country; it shall be so, but we will give our departure the appearance of a sudden thought, a lover's flight. Leave everything behind you but money and jewels. That purse will more than pay you the sum you cannot claim. While I go to fling this body into the river, to tell no tales till we are safe, destroy all traces of the deed, prepare yourself for traveling, and guard the room in silence until I come. Remember! One sign of treachery, one cry for help, and I denounce you where my word will have much weight and yours none."

She gave him her hand upon the dark bargain, and covering up her face to hide the tragic spectacle, she heard Victor leave the room with his awful burden.

When he returned, she was nearly ready, for though moving like one in a ghastly dream, bewildered by the sudden loss of the long coveted, just won prize, and daunted by the crime whose retribution a word might bring upon herself, she still clung to life and its delights with the tenacity of a selfish nature, a shallow heart. While she finished her hasty preparations, Victor set the room in order, saw that the red witnesses of the crime were burnt, and dashed off a gay note to a friend, enclosing money for all obligations, explaining their sudden flight as an innocent ruse to escape congratulations on their hasty marriage, and promising to send soon for such possessions as were left behind. Then, leaving the quiet room to be forever haunted by the memory of a night of love, and sin, and death, like two pale ghosts they vanished in the dimness of the dawn.

Chapter II. Earl's Mystery

FOUR LADIES SAT in the luxurious privacy of Lady Lennox's boudoir, whiling away the listless hour before dinner with social chat. Dusk was deepening, but firelight filled the room with its warm glow, flickering on mirrors, marbles, rich hues, and graceful forms, and bathing the four faces with unwonted bloom.

Stately Diana Stuart leaned on the high back of the chair in which sat her aunt and chaperon, the Honorable Mrs. Berkeley. On the opposite side of the wide hearth a slender figure lounged in the deep corner of a couch, with a graceful abandon which no Englishwoman could hope to imitate. The face was hidden by a hand-screen, but a pair of ravishing feet were visible, and a shower of golden hair shone against the velvet pillow. Directly before the fire sat Lady Lennox, a comely, hospitable matron who was never so content as when she could gather her female guests about her and refresh herself with a little good-natured gossip. She had evidently been discussing some subject which interested her hearers, for all were intently listening, and all looked eager for more, when she said, with a significant nod:

"Yes, I assure you there is a mystery in that family. Lady Carrick has known them all her life, and from what she has dropped from time to time, I quite agree with her in believing that something has gone wrong."

"Dear Lady Lennox, pray go on! There is nothing so charming as a family mystery when the narrator can give a clue to her audience, as I am sure you can," exclaimed the lady on the couch, in a persuasive voice which had a curious ring to it despite its melody.

"That is just what I cannot do, Mrs. Vane. However, I will gladly tell you all I know. This is in strict confidence, you understand."

"Certainly!" "Upon my honor!" "Not a word shall pass my lips!" murmured the three listeners, drawing nearer, as Lady Lennox fixed her eyes upon the fire and lowered her voice.

"It is the custom in ancient Scottish families for the piper of the house, when dying, to put the pipes into the hand of the heir to name or title. Well, when old Dougal lay on his deathbed, he called for Earl, the fourth son—"

"What a peculiar name!" interrupted Mrs. Berkeley.

"It was not his proper name, but they called him so because of his strong resemblance to the pictures of the great earl, Black Douglass. They continued to call him so to this day, and I really don't know whether his name is Allan, Archie, or Alex, for they are all family names, and one cannot remember which belongs to whom. Now the eldest son was Robert, and Dougal should have called for him, because the title and the fortune always go to the eldest son of the eldest son. But no, Earl must come; and into his hands the pipes were put, with a strange prophecy that no heir would enjoy the title but a year until it came to him."

"Was the prediction fulfilled?" asked Diana.

"To the letter. This was five or six years ago, and not one year has passed without a death, till now a single feeble life is all that stands between Earl and the title. Nor was this all. When his father died, though he had lain insensible for days, he rose up in his bed at the last and put upon Earl's hand the iron ring which is their most precious heirloom, because it belonged to the ancient earl. This, too, should have gone to Robert; but the same gift of second sight seemed given to the father as to the servant, and these strange things made a deep impression upon the family, as you may suppose."

"That is the mystery, then?" said Mrs. Vane, with an accent of disappointment in her voice.

"Only a part of it. I am not superstitious, so the prediction and all the rest of it don't trouble me much, but what occurred afterward does. When Earl was one-and-twenty he went abroad, was gone a year, and came home so utterly and strangely changed that everyone was amazed at the alteration. The death of a cousin just then drew people's attention from him, and when that stir was over the family seemed to be reconciled to the sad change in him. Nothing was said, nothing ever transpired to clear up the matter; and to this day he has remained a cold, grave, peculiar man, instead of the frank, gay fellow he once was."

"He met with some loss in an affair of the heart, doubtless. Such little tragedies often mar a young man's peace for years—perhaps for life."

As Mrs. Vane spoke she lowered her screen, showing a pair of wonderfully keen and brilliant eyes fixed full upon Diana. The young lady was unconscious of this searching glance as she intently regarded Lady Lennox, who said:

"That is my opinion, though Lady Carrick never would confirm it, being hampered by some promise to the family, I suspect, for they are almost as high and haughty now as in the olden time. There was a vague rumor of some serious entanglement at

Paris, but it was hushed up at once, and few gave it credence. Still, as year after year passed, and Earl remains unmarried, I really begin to fear there was some truth in what I fancied an idle report."

Something in this speech seemed to ruffle Mrs. Berkeley; a look of intelligence passed between her and her niece as she drew herself up, and before Diana could speak, the elder lady exclaimed, with an air of mystery, "Your ladyship does Mr. Douglas great injustice, and a few months, weeks, perhaps, will quite change your opinion. We saw a good deal of him last season before my poor brother's death took us from town, and I assure you that he is free to address any lady in England. More I am not at liberty to say at present."

Lady Lennox looked politely incredulous, but Diana's eyes fell and a sudden color bathed her face in a still deeper bloom than that which the firelight shed over it. A slight frown contracted Mrs. Vane's beautiful brows as she watched the proud girl's efforts to conceal the secret of her heart. But the frown faded to a smile of intelligent compassion as she said, with a significant glance that stung Diana like an insult, "Dear Miss Stuart, pray take my screen. This glowing fire is ruining your complexion."

"Thank you, I need no screens of any sort."

There was a slight emphasis upon the "I," and a smile of equal significance curled her lips. If any taunt was intended it missed its mark, for Mrs. Vane only assumed a more graceful pose, saying with a provoking little air of superior wisdom, "There you are wrong, for our faces are such traitors, that unless we have learned the art of self-control, it is not best for us to scorn such harmless aids as fans, screens, and veils. Emotions are not well-bred, and their demonstrations are often as embarrassing to others as to ourselves."

"That, doubtless, is the reason why you half conceal your face behind a cloud of curls. It certainly is a most effectual mask at times," replied Diana, pushing back her own smooth bands of hair.

"Thanks for the suggestion. I wonder it never occurred to me before," sweetly answered Mrs. Vane, adding, as she gathered up the disheveled locks, "my poor hair is called a great ornament, but indeed it is a trial both to Gabrielle and to myself."

Lady Lennox touched a long tress that rolled down the pillow, saying with motherly admiration, "My dear, I promised Mrs. Berkeley she should see this wonderful hair of yours, for she could not believe my account of it. The dressing bell will ring directly, so you may gratify us without making more work for Gabrielle."

"Willingly, dear Lady Lennox; anything for you!"

As she spoke with affectionate goodwill, Mrs. Vane rose, drew out a comb or two, and a stream of golden hair rippled far below her knee. Mrs. Berkeley exclaimed, and Diana praised, while watching with a very natural touch of envy the charming picture the firelight showed her. In its full glow stood Mrs. Vane; against the deep purple of her dress glittered the golden mass, and a pair of lovely hands parted the shining veil from a face whose beauty was as peculiar and alluring as the mingled spirit and sweetness of her smile.

"A thousand pardons! I thought your ladyship was alone." A deep voice broke the momentary silence, and a tall figure paused upon the threshold of the softly opened door. All started, and with a little cry of pleasure and surprise, Lady Lennox hurried forward to greet her guest.

"My dear Earl, this is a most inhospitable welcome. George should have apprised me of your arrival."

"He is a lazy fellow, as he bade me find you here. I tapped, but receiving no reply, fancied the room empty and peeped to make sure. Pray accept my apologies, and put me out if I intrude."

The voice of Mr. Douglas was remarkably calm, his manner stately yet cordial, and his dark eyes went rapidly from face to face with a glance that seemed to comprehend the scene at once.

"Not in the least," said Lady Lennox heartily. "Let me present you to Mrs. Berkeley, Miss Stuart, and—why, where is she? The poor little woman has run away in confusion, and must receive your apologies by-and-by."

"We must run away also, for it is quite time to dress." And with a most gracious smile Mrs. Berkeley led her niece away before the gentleman should have time to note her flushed face and telltale eyes.

"You did not mention the presence of those ladies in your ladyship's letter," began Douglas, as his hostess sat down and motioned him to do likewise.

"They came unexpectedly, and you have met before, it seems. You never mentioned that fact, Earl," said Lady Lennox, with a sharp glance.

"Why should I? We only met a few times last winter, and I quite forgot that you knew them. But pray tell me who was the fair one with golden locks, whom I frightened away?"

"The widow of Colonel Vane."

"My dear lady, do you mean to tell me that child is a widow?"

"Yes; and a very lovely one, I assure you. I invited you here expressly to fall in love with her, for George and Harry are too young."

"Thank you. Now be so kind as to tell me all about her, for I knew Vane before he went to India."

"I can only tell you that he married this lady when she was very young, took her to India, and in a year she returned a widow."

"I remember hearing something of an engagement, but fancied it was broken off. Who was the wife?"

"A Montmorenci; noble but poor, you know. The family lost everything in the revolution, and never regained their former grandeur. But one can see at a glance that she is of high birth—high enough to suit even a Douglas."

"Ah, you know our weakness, and I must acknowledge that the best blood in France is not to be despised by the best blood in Scotland. How long have you known her?"

"Only a few months; that charming Countess Camareena brought her from Paris, and left her when she returned. Mrs. Vane seemed lonely for so young a thing; her family are all gone, and she made herself so agreeable, seemed so grateful for any friendship, that I asked her here. She went into very little society in London, and was really suffering for change and care."

"Poor young lady! I will do my best to aid your friendly purpose—for Vane's sake, if not for her own," said Douglas, evidently continuing the subject, lest her ladyship should revert to the former one.

"That reminds me to give you one warning: Never speak to her or before her of the colonel. He died three or four years ago; but when I mentioned him, she implored me to spare her all allusion to that unhappy past, and I have done so. It is my belief that he was not all she believed him to be, and she may have suffered what she is too generous to complain of or confess."

"I doubt that; for when I knew him, though weak on some points, Vane was an excellent fellow. She wears no weeds, I observe."

"You have a quick eye, to discover that in such an instant," replied Lady Lennox, smiling.

"I could scarcely help looking longest at the most striking figure of the group."

"I forgive you for it. She left off her weeds by my advice, for the somber colors seemed to oppress and sadden her. Three or four years are long enough to mourn one whom she did not wholly love, and she is too young to shroud herself in sables for a lifetime."

"Has she fortune?"

"The colonel left her something handsome, I suspect, for she keeps both man and maid, and lives as becomes her rank. I ask no questions, but I feel deeply for the poor child, and do my best for her. Now tell me about home, and your dear mother."

Earl obeyed, and entertained his hostess till the dressing bell rang.

Chapter III. The Iron Ring

When Douglas entered the drawing rooms, he was instantly seized upon by Major Mansfield, and while he stood listening with apparent interest to that gentleman's communications, he took a survey of the party before him. The elder ladies were not yet down; Harry Lennox was worshiping Diana with all the frank admiration of a lad of eighteen, and Mrs. Vane was pacing up and down the rooms on the arm of George Lennox, the young master of the house. Few little women would have appeared to advantage beside the tall guardsman; but Mrs. Vane moved with a dignity that seemed to add many inches to her almost fairylike stature, and make her a fit companion for her martial escort. Everything about her was peculiar and piquant. Her dress was of that vivid silvery green which is so ruinous to any but the purest complexion, so ravishing when worn by one whose bloom defies all hues. The skirt swept long behind her, and the Pompadour waist, with its flowing sleeves, displayed a neck and arms of dazzling fairness, half concealed by a film of costly lace. No jewels but an antique opal ring, attached by a slender chain to a singular bracelet, or wide band of enchased gold. A single deep-hued flower glowed on her bosom, and in that wonderful hair of hers a chaplet of delicate ferns seemed to gather back the cloud of curls, and encircle coil upon coil of glossy hair, that looked as if it burdened her small head.

The young man watched her so intently that the major soon observed his preoccupation, and paused in the middle of his account of a review to ask good-naturedly, "Well, what do you think of the bewitching widow?"

"She reminds me of a little green viper," replied Douglas coolly.

"The deuce she does! What put such an odd fancy into your head?" asked the major.

"The color of her gown, her gliding gait, her brilliant eyes, and poor George's evident fascination."

"Faith! I see the resemblance, and you've expressed my feeling exactly. Do you know I've tried to fall in love with that woman, and, upon my soul, I can't do it!"

"She does not care to fascinate you, perhaps."

"Neither does she care to charm George, as I happen to know; yet you see what a deuce of a state he's getting into."

"His youth prevents his seeing the danger before it is too late; and there you have the advantage, Major."

"We shall see how you will prosper, Douglas; for you are not a lad of twenty, like George, or an old fellow of forty, like me, and, if rumor does not lie, you have had 'experiences,' and understand womankind."

Though he spoke in a tone of raillery, the major fixed a curious eye upon his companion's countenance. But the dark handsome face remained inscrutably calm, and the only answer he received was a low—

"Hush! they are coming. Present me, and I'll see what I can make of her."

Now Douglas was undoubtedly the best *parti* of the season, and he knew it. He was not a vain man, but an intensely proud one—proud of his ancient name, his honorable race, his ancestral home, his princely fortune; and he received the homage of both men and women as his due. Great, therefore, was his surprise at the little scene which presently occurred, and very visible was his haughty displeasure.

Lennox and his fair companion approached, the one bending his tall head to listen ardently, the other looking up with a most tempting face, as she talked rapidly, after softening a hard English phrase by an entrancing accent. The major presented his friend with much *empressement,* and Douglas was prepared to receive the gracious greeting which women seldom failed to give him. But scarcely pausing in her progress, Mrs. Vane merely glanced at him, as his name was mentioned, returned his bow with a slight inclination, and rustled on as if quite oblivious that a direct descendant of the great Scotch earl had been presented to her.

The major stifled an irrepressible laugh at this unexpected rebuff, and took a malicious pleasure in watching his friend's eye kindle, his attitude become more stately as he talked on, and deigned to take no notice of an act which evidently much annoyed and amazed him. Just then Lady Lennox entered, and dinner was announced. George beckoned, and Douglas reluctantly joined him.

"As host, I am obliged to take Mrs. Berkeley down; Harry has monopolized Miss Stuart, and the major belongs to my mother—so I must reluctantly relinquish Mrs. Vane to you."

Being a well-bred man, Douglas could only bow, and offer his arm. Mrs. Vane made George happy by a smile, as he left her, then turned to Douglas with a "May I trouble you?" as she gave him her fan and handkerchief to hold, while she gathered up her train and took his arm, as unconcernedly as if he had been a footman. Though rather piqued by her nonchalance, Douglas found something half amusing, half captivating in her demeanor; for, much as he had been courted and admired, few women were quite at ease with the highborn gentleman, whose manners were so coldly charming, whose heart seemed so invulnerable. It was a new sensation to be treated like other men, and set to serve an imperious lady, who leaned upon his arm as if she needed its support, and tranquilly expected the small courtesies which hitherto had been left to his own goodwill and pleasure to offer.

Whatever the secret of his past might be, and however well he might conceal his real self behind a grave demeanor, Douglas had not yet lost his passion for beautiful women, and though no word was spoken during the short transit from drawing room to dinner table, the power of loveliness and womanhood made itself felt beyond a doubt. The touch of a fair hand upon his arm, the dazzle of white shoulders at his side, the soft scent of violets shaken from the folds of lace and cambric which he held, the glimpse of a dainty foot, and the glance of a vivacious eye, all made the little journey memorable. When they took their places, the hauteur had melted from his manner, the coldness from his face, and with his courtliest air he began a conversation which soon became absorbing—for Mrs. Vane talked with the grace of a French woman, and the intelligence of an English woman.

When the gentlemen rejoined the ladies, they were found examining some antique jewels, which Lady Lennox had been prevailed upon to show.

"How well those diamonds look in Diana's dark hair. Ah, my dear, a coronet becomes you vastly. Does it not?" said Mrs. Berkeley, appealing to Douglas, who was approaching.

"So well that I hope you will soon see one rightfully there, madam," he answered, with a glance that made Diana's eyes fall, and Mrs. Berkeley look radiant.

Mrs. Vane saw the look, divined its meaning, and smiled a strange smile, as she looked down upon the jewels that strewed her lap.

Mrs. Berkeley mistook her attitude for one of admiration and envy, and said, "You wear no ornaments but flowers, I observe; from choice, doubtless, for, as you are the last of your race, you must possess many of the family relics."

Mrs. Vane looked up, and answered with an indescribable mixture of simplicity and dignity, "I wear flowers because I have no other ornaments. My family paid the price of loyalty with both life and fortune; but I possess one jewel which I value above all these—a noble name."

A banished princess might have so looked, so spoken, as, gathering up the glittering mass in her white hands, she let it fall again, with an air of gentle pride. Douglas gave her a glance of genuine admiration, and Diana took the diamonds from her hair, as if they burdened her. Mrs. Berkeley saw that her shot had failed, but tried again, only to be more decidedly defeated.

"Very prettily done, my dear; but I really thought you were going to say that your most valuable jewel was the peculiar bracelet you wear. Is there any charming legend or mystery concerning it? I fancied so, because you never take it off, however out of taste it may be; and otherwise your dress is always perfect."

"I wear it in fulfillment of a vow, and the beauty of the ring atones for the ugliness of the bracelet. Does it not?"

As she spoke, Mrs. Vane extended an exquisitely molded arm and hand to Douglas, who answered with most unusual gallantry, "The beauty of the arm would render any fetter an ornament."

He bent to examine the jewel as he spoke, and Mrs. Vane whispered, below her breath, "You have offended Diana; pray make your peace. I should be desolated to think my poor arm had estranged you, even for an hour."

So entirely was he thrown off his guard by this abrupt address, that he whispered eagerly, "Do my actions interest her? Have I any cause for hope? Does she—"

There he paused, recovered his self-possession, but not his countenance—for an angry flush stained his dark cheek, and he fixed a look upon Mrs. Vane that would have daunted any other woman. She did not seem to see it, for her head drooped till her face was hidden, and she sat absently playing with the little chain that shone against her hand. George Lennox looked fiercely jealous; Diana turned pale; Mrs. Berkeley frowned; and good, unconscious Lady Lennox said blandly, "Apropos to heirlooms and relics, I was telling these ladies about your famous iron ring, Earl. I wish you had it here to show them."

"I am happy to be able to gratify your ladyship's wish. I never leave without it, for I use it as my seal. I will ring for it."

Mrs. Vane lifted her head with an air of interest as Douglas gave an order, and his servant presently put a small steel-bound case into his hand. Opening this with a key that hung upon his watch guard, he displayed the famous relic. Antique, rusty, and massive it was, and on its shield the boar's head and the motto of the house.

"You say you use this as a signet ring; why do you not have your arms cut on some jewel, and set in a more graceful setting? This device is almost effaced, and the great ring anything but ornamental to one's hand or chatelaine," said Mrs. Vane, curiously examining the ring as it was passed to her.

"Because I am superstitious and believe that an especial virtue lies in this ancient bit of iron. The legend goes that no harm can befall its possessor, and as I have gone scatheless so far, I hold fast to the old faith."

As Douglas turned to hear and answer Mrs. Vane's question, Harry Lennox, with the freedom of a boy, had thrown back the lid of the case, which had been opened with peculiar care, and, lifting several worn papers, disclosed two objects that drew exclamations of surprise from several of the party. A satin slipper, of fairylike proportions, with a dull red stain upon its sole, and what looked like a ring of massive gold, till the lad lifted it, when coil after coil unwound, till a long curl of human hair touched the ground.

"My faith! That is the souvenir of the beautiful *danseuse* Virginie Varens, about whom you bored me with questions when you showed me that several years ago," said the major, staring with all his eyes.

Mrs. Vane had exclaimed with the rest, but her color faded perceptibly, her eye grew troubled, and when Harry leaned toward her to compare the long tress with her own, she shrank back with a shudder. Diana caught a muttered ejaculation from Douglas, saw Mrs. Vane's discomposure, and fixed a scrutinizing gaze upon her. But in a moment those obedient features resumed their former calm, and, with a little gesture of contrition, Mrs. Vane laid the long curl beside one of her own, saying tranquilly:

"Pardon, that I betrayed an instinctive shrinking from anything plebeian. The hair of the dancer is lighter than mine, you see; for this is pure gold, and mine is fast deepening to brown. Let me atone for my rudeness thus; and believe me, I can sympathize, for I, too, have loved and lost."

While speaking, she had refolded the lock, and, tying it together with a little knot of ribbon from her dress, she laid it back into its owner's hand, with a soft glance and a delicate dropping of the voice at the last words.

If it was a bit of acting, it was marvelously well done, and all believed it to be a genuine touch of nature. Diana looked consumed with curiosity, and Douglas answered hastily, "Thanks for the pity, but I need none. I never saw this girl, and as for love——"

He paused there, as if words unfit for time and place were about to pass his lips. His eye grew fierce, and his black brows lowered heavily, leaving no doubt on the mind of any observer that hate, not love, was the sentiment with which he now regarded the mysterious *danseuse*. An uncomfortable pause followed as Douglas relocked the case and put it in his pocket, forgetting, in his haste, the ring he had slipped upon his finger.

Feeling that some unpleasant theme had been touched upon, Lady Lennox asked for music. Diana coldly declined, but Mrs. Vane readily turned to the piano. The two elder ladies and the major went to chat by the fire; Lennox took his brother aside to administer a reproof; and Douglas, after a moment of moody thoughtfulness, placed himself beside Diana on the couch which stood just behind Mrs. Vane. She had begun with a brilliant overture, but suddenly passed to a softer movement, and filled the room with the whispering melody of a Venetian barcarole. This seeming caprice was caused by an intense desire to overhear the words of the pair behind her. But though she strained her keen ear to the utmost, she caught only broken fragments of their low-toned conversation, and these fragments filled her with disquiet.

"Why so cold, Miss Stuart? One would think you had forgotten me."

"I fancied the forgetfulness was yours."

"I never shall forget the happiest hours of my life. May I hope that you recall those days with pleasure?"

There was no answer, and a backward glance showed Mrs. Vane Diana's head bent low, and Douglas watching the deepening color on her half-averted cheek with an eager, ardent glance. More softly murmured the boat song, and scarcely audible was the whispered entreaty:

"I have much to say; you will hear me tomorrow, early, in the park?"

A mute assent was given, and, with the air of a happy lover, Douglas left her, as if fearing to say more, lest their faces should betray them. Then the barcarole ended as suddenly as it had begun, and Mrs. Vane resumed the stormy overture, playing as if inspired by a musical frenzy. So pale was she when she left the instrument that no one doubted the fact of her needing rest, as, pleading weariness, she sank into a deep chair, and leaning her head upon her hand, sat silent for an hour.

As they separated for the night, and Douglas stood listening to his young host's arrangements for the morrow, a singular-looking man appeared at the door of an anteroom and, seeing them, paused where he stood, as if waiting for them to precede him.

"Who is that, George? What does he want?" said Douglas, drawing his friend's attention to the dark figure, whose gleaming eyes belied his almost servile posture of humility and respect.

"Oh, that is Mrs. Vane's man, Jitomar. He was one of the colonel's Indian servants, I believe. Deaf and dumb, but harmless, devoted, and invaluable—*she* says. A treacherous-looking devil, to my mind," replied Lennox.

"He looks more like an Italian than an Indian, in spite of his Eastern costume and long hair. What is he after now?" asked Earl.

"Going to receive the orders of his mistress. I would gladly change places with him, heathen as he is, for the privilege of serving her. Good night."

As George spoke, they parted, and while the dark servant watched Douglas going up the wide oaken stairs, he shook his clenched hand after the retreating figure, and his lips moved as if he muttered something low between his teeth.

A few moments afterward, as Earl sat musing over his fire, there came a tap at his door. Having vainly bidden the knocker to enter, he answered the summons, and saw Jitomar obsequiously offering a handkerchief. Douglas examined it, found the major's name, and, pointing out that gentleman's room, farther down the corridor, he returned the lost article with a nod of thanks and dismissal. While he had been turning the square of cambric in his hands, the man's keen eyes had explored every corner of the room. Nothing seemed to escape them, from the ashes on the hearth, to a flower which Diana had worn, now carefully preserved in water; and once a gleam of satisfaction glittered in them, as if some desired object had met their gaze. Making a low obeisance, he retired, and Douglas went to bed, to dream waking dreams till far into the night.

The great hall clock had just struck one, and sleep was beginning to conquer love, when something startled him wide awake. What it was he could not tell, but every sense warned him of impending danger. Sitting up in his bed, he pushed back the curtains and looked out. The night lamp burned low, the fire had faded, and the room was full of dusky shadows. There were three doors: one led to the dressing room, one to the corridor, and the third was locked on the outside. He knew that it opened upon a flight of narrow stairs that communicated with the library, having been built for the convenience of a studious Lennox long ago.

As he gazed about him, to his great amazement the door was seen to move. Slowly, noiselessly it opened, with no click of lock, no creak of hinge. Almost sure of seeing some ghostly visitant enter, he waited mute and motionless. A muffled hand and arm appeared and, stretching to their utmost, seemed to take something from the writing table that stood near this door. It was a human hand, and with a single leap Douglas was halfway across the room. But the door closed rapidly, and as he laid his hand upon it, the key turned in the lock. He demanded who was there, but not a sound replied; he shook the door, but the lock held fast; he examined the table, but nothing seemed gone, till, with an ominous thrill, he missed the iron ring. On reaching his chamber, he had taken it off, meaning to restore it to its place; had laid it down, to put Diana's rose in water; had forgotten it, and now it was gone!

Flinging on dressing gown and slippers, and taking a pistol from his traveling case, he left his room. The house was quiet as a tomb, the library empty, and no sign of intruders visible, till, coming to the door itself, he found that the rusty lock had been newly oiled, for the rusty key turned noiselessly, and the hinges worked smoothly, though the dust that lay thickly everywhere showed that this passage was still unused. Stepping into his room, Douglas gave a searching glance about him, and in an instant an expression of utter bewilderment fell upon his face, for there, on the exact spot which had been empty five minutes ago, there lay the iron ring!

Chapter IV. A Shred of Lace

Long before any of the other guests were down, Diana stole into the garden on her way to the park. Hope shone in her eyes, smiles sat on her lips, and her heart sang for joy. She had long loved in secret; had believed and despaired alternately; and now her desire was about to be fulfilled, her happiness assured by a lover's voice. Hurrying through the wilderness of autumn flowers, she reached the shrubbery that divided park and garden. Pausing an instant to see if anyone awaited her beyond, she gave a great start, and looked as if she had encountered a ghost.

It was only Mrs. Vane; she often took early strolls in the park, followed by her man; Diana knew this, but had forgotten it in her new bliss. She was alone now, and as she seemed unconscious of her presence, Diana would have noiselessly withdrawn, if a glimpse of Mrs. Vane's face had not arrested and detained her. As if she had thrown herself down in a paroxysm of distress, sat Mrs. Vane, with both hands tightly clasped; her white lips were compressed, and in her eyes was a look of mingled pain, grief, and despair. The most careless observer would have detected the presence of some great anxiety or sorrow, and Diana, made generous by the assurance of her own happiness, for the first time felt a touch of pity for the woman of whom she had been both envious and jealous. Forgetting herself, she hastened forward, saying kindly, "Are you suffering, Mrs. Vane? What can I do for you?"

Mrs. Vane started as if she had been shot, sprang to her feet, and putting out her hands as if to keep the other off, cried, almost incoherently, "Go back! Go back, and save yourself! For me you can do nothing—it is too late!"

"Indeed, I hope not. Tell me your trouble, and let me help you if I can," urged Diana, shocked yet not alarmed by the wildness of Mrs. Vane's look and manner.

But she only clasped her hands before her face, saying despairingly, "You can help both of us—but at what a price!"

"No price will be too costly, if I can honorably pay it. I have been unjust, unkind; forgive it, and confide in me; for indeed, I pity you."

"Ah, if I dared!" sighed Mrs. Vane. "It seems impossible, and yet I ought—for you, not I, will suffer most from my enforced silence."

She paused an instant, seemed to calm herself by strong effort, and, fixing her mournful eyes upon Diana, she said, in a strangely solemn and impressive manner, "Miss Stuart, if ever a woman needed help and pity, it is I. You have misjudged, distrusted, and disliked me; I freely forgive this, and long to save you, as I alone can do. But a sacred promise fetters me—I dare not break it; yet if you will pledge your word to keep this interview secret, I will venture to give you one hint, one warning, which may save you from destroying your peace forever. Will you give me this assurance?"

Diana shrank back, disturbed and dismayed by the appeal and the requirement. Mrs. Vane saw her hesitation, and wrung her hands together in an agony of impotent regret.

"I knew it—I feared it. You will not trust me—you will not let me ease my conscience by trying to save another woman from the fate that darkens all my life. Go your way, then, and when the bitter hour comes, remember that I tried to save you from it, and you would not hear me."

"Stay, Mrs. Vane! I do trust you—I will listen; and I give you my word that I will conceal this interview. Speak quickly—I must go," cried Diana, won to compliance even against her wishes.

"Stoop to me—not even the air must hear what I breathe. Ask Allan Douglas the mystery of his life before you marry him, else you will rue the hour that you became his wife."

"Allan Douglas! You know his name? You know the secret of his past?" exclaimed Diana, lost in wonder.

"My husband knew him, and I—Hush! Someone is coming. Quick! Escape into the park, or your face will betray you. I can command myself; I will meet and accost whoever comes."

Before the rapid whisper ended, Diana was gone, and when Douglas came hastening to his tryst, he too found Mrs. Vane alone—and he too paused a moment, surprised to see her there. But the picture he saw was a very different one from that which arrested Diana. Great indeed must have been Mrs. Vane's command of countenance, for no trace of agitation was visible, and never had she looked more lovely than now, as she stood with a handful of flowers in the white skirt of her dress, her bright hair blowing in the wind, her soft eyes fixed on vacancy, while a tranquil smile proved that her thoughts were happy ones.

So young, so innocent, so blithe she looked that Douglas involuntarily thought, with a touch of self-reproach: "Pretty creature! What injustice my ungallant smile did her last night! I ask her pardon." Then aloud, as he approached, "Good morning, Mrs. Vane. I am off for an early stroll."

With the shy grace, the artless glance of a child, she looked up at him, offering a flower, and saying, as she smilingly moved on, "May it be a pleasant one."

It was not a pleasant one, however; and perhaps Mrs. Vane's wish had been sweetly ironical. Diana greeted her lover coldly, listened to his avowal with an air of proud reserve, that contrasted strangely with the involuntary betrayals of love and joy that escaped her. Entirely laying aside the chilly gravity, the lofty manner, which was habitual to him, Douglas proved that he could woo ardently, and forget the pride of the man in the passion of the lover. But when he sued for a verbal answer to his prayer, although he thought he read the assent in the crimson cheek half turned away, the downcast eyes, that would not meet his own, and the quick flutter of the heart that beat under his hand, he was thunderstruck at the change which passed over Diana. She suddenly grew colorless and calm as any statue, and freeing herself from his hold, fixed a searching look upon him, while she said slowly and distinctly, "When you have told me the mystery of your life, I will give my answer to your love—not before."

"The mystery of my life!" he echoed, falling back a step or two, with such violent discomposure in face and manner that Diana's heart sank within her, though she answered steadily:

"Yes; I must know it, before I link my fate with yours."

"Who told you that I had one?" he demanded.

"Lady Lennox. I had heard the rumor before, but never gave it thought till she confirmed it. Now I wait for your explanation."

"It is impossible to give it; but I swear to you, Diana, that I am innocent of any act that could dishonor my name, or mar your peace, if it were known. The secret is not mine to tell; I have promised to keep it, and I cannot forfeit my word, even for your sake. Be generous; do not let mere curiosity or pique destroy my hopes, and make you cruel when you should be kind."

So earnestly he spoke, so tenderly he pleaded, that Diana's purpose wavered, and would have failed her, had not the memory of Mrs. Vane's strange warning returned to her, bringing with it other memories of other mysterious looks, hints, and acts which had transpired since Douglas came. These recollections hardened her heart, confirmed her resolution, and gave her power to appear inexorable to the last.

"You mistake my motive, sir. Neither curiosity nor pique influenced me, but a just and natural desire to assure myself that in trusting my happiness to your keeping, I am not entailing regret upon myself, remorse upon you. I must know all your past, before I endanger my future; clear yourself from the suspicions which have long clung to you, and I am yours; remain silent, and we are nothing to each other from this day forth."

Her coldness chilled his passion, her distrust irritated his pride; all the old hauteur returned fourfold, his eye grew hard, his voice bitter, and his whole manner showed that his will was as inflexible as hers.

"Are you resolved on making this unjust, ungenerous test of my affection, Miss Stuart?"

"I am."

"You have no faith in my honor, then? No consideration for the hard strait in which my promise places me? No compassion for the loss I must sustain in losing the love, respect, and confidence of the woman dearest to me?"

"Assure me that you are worthy of love, respect, confidence, and I gladly accord them to you."

"I cannot, in the way you demand. Will nothing else satisfy you?"

"Nothing!"

"Then, in your words, we are nothing to one another from this day forth. Farewell, Diana!"

With an involuntary impulse, she put out her hand to detain him as he turned away. He took it, and bending, kissed it, with a lingering fondness that nearly conquered her. The act, the look that accompanied it, the tremor of the lips that performed it, touched the poor girl's heart, and words of free acceptance were rising to her lips, when, as he bent, a miniature, suspended by a chain of mingled hair and gold, swung forward from its hiding place in his breast, and though she saw no face, the haste with which he replaced it roused all her suspicions again, and redoubled all her doubts. Scorning herself for her momentary weakness, the gesture of recall was changed to one of dismissal, as she withdrew her hand, and turned from him, with a quiet "Farewell, then, forever!"

"One moment," he pleaded. "Do not let us destroy the peace of both our lives by an unhappy secret which in no way but this can do us harm. Bear with me for a few days, Diana; think over this interview, remember my great love for you, let your own generous nature appeal to your pride, and perhaps time may show you that it is possible to love, trust, and pardon me."

Glad of any delay which should spare her the pain of an immediate separation, she hesitated a moment, and then, with feigned reluctance, answered, "My visit was to have ended with the coming week; I will not shorten it, but give you till then to reconsider your decision, and by a full confession secure your happiness and my own."

Then they parted—not with the lingering adieus of happy lovers, but coldly, silently, like estranged friends—and each took a different way back, instead of walking blissfully together, as they had thought to do.

"Why so *triste,* Diana? One would think you had seen a ghost in the night, you look so pale and solemn. And, upon my word, Mr. Douglas looks as if he had seen one also," said Mrs. Berkeley, as they all gathered about the breakfast table two hours later.

"I did see one," answered Douglas, generously distracting general attention from Diana, who could ill sustain it.

"Last night?" exclaimed Mrs. Berkeley, full of interest at once.

"Yes, madam—at one o'clock last night."

"How charming! Tell us all about it; I dote upon ghosts, yet never saw one," said Mrs. Vane.

Douglas narrated his adventure. The elder ladies looked disturbed, Diana incredulous; and Mrs. Vane filled the room with her silvery laughter, as Harry protested that no ghost belonged to the house, and George explained the mystery as being the nightmare.

"I never have it; neither do I walk in my sleep, and seldom dream," replied Douglas. "I perfectly remember rising, partially dressing, and going down to the library, up the private stairs, and examining the door. This may be proved by the key, now changed to my side of the lock, and the train of wax which dropped from my candle as I hurried along."

"What woke you?" asked Mrs. Vane.

"I cannot tell; some slight sound, probably, although I do not remember hearing any, and fancy it was an instinctive sense of danger."

"That door could not have been opened without much noise, for the key was rusted in the lock. We tried to turn it the other day, and could not, so were forced to go round by the great gallery to reach that room."

Diana spoke, and for the first time since they parted in the park, Douglas looked at and addressed her.

"You have explored the private passage then, and tried the door? May I ask when?"

"Harry was showing us the house; anything mysterious pleased us, so we went up, tried the rusty key, and finding it immovable, we came down again."

"Of whom was the party composed?"

"My aunt, Mrs. Vane, and myself, accompanied by Harry."

"Then I must accuse Harry of the prank, for both key and lock have been newly oiled, and the door opens easily and noiselessly, as you may prove if you like. He must have had an accomplice among the housemaids, for it was a woman's hand that took the ring. She doubtless passed it to him, and while I was preparing to sally forth, both ran away—one to hide, the other to wait till I left my room, when he slipped in and restored the ring. Was that it, Hal?"

As Douglas spoke, all looked at Harry; but the boy shook his head, and triumphantly replied to his brother:

"George will tell you that your accusation is entirely unjust; and as he sat up till dawn, writing poetry, I could not have left him without his knowledge."

"True, Hal—you had nothing to do with it, I know. Did you distinctly see the hand that purloined your ring, Earl?" asked Lennox, anxious to divert attention from the revelation of his poetical amusements.

"No; the room was dusky, and the hand muffled in something dark. But it was no ghostly hand, for as it was hastily withdrawn when I sprang up, the wrapper slipped aside, and I saw white human flesh, and the outlines of a woman's arm."

"Was it a beautiful arm?" asked Lennox, with his eyes upon Mrs. Vane's, which lay like a piece of sculptured marble against the red velvet cushion of her chair.

"Very beautiful, I should say; for in that hasty glimpse it looked too fair to belong to any servant, and when I found this hanging to the lock, I felt assured that my spirit was a lady, for housemaids do not wear anything like this, I fancy," and Douglas produced a shred of black lace, evidently torn from some costly flounce or scarf.

The ladies put their heads together over the scrap, and all pronounced it quite impossible for any dressing maid to have come honestly by such expensive trimming as this must have been.

"It looks as if it had belonged to a deeply scalloped flounce," said Mrs. Vane. "Who of us wears such? Miss Stuart, you are in black; have I not seen you with a trimming like this?"

"You forget—I wear no trimming but crepe. This never was a part of a flounce. It is the corner of a shawl. You see how unequally rounded the two sides are; and no flounce was ever scalloped so deeply as this," returned Diana.

"How acute you are, Di! It is so, I really believe. See how exactly this bit compares with the corner of my breakfast shawl, made to imitate lace. Who wears a black lace shawl? Neither Di nor myself," said Mrs. Berkeley.

"Mrs. Vane often wears one."

Diana uttered the name with significance, and Douglas stirred a little, as if she put into words some vague idea of his own. Mrs. Vane shrugged her shoulders, sipped her coffee, and answered tranquilly, "So does Lady Lennox; but I will bear all the suspicions of phantom folly, and when I dress for dinner will put on every rag of lace I possess, so that you may compare this bit, and prove me guilty if it gives you pleasure. Though what object I could have in running about in the dark, oiling door locks, stealing rings, and frightening gentlemen is not as clear to me as it appears to be to you—probably because I am not as much interested in the sufferer."

Diana looked embarrassed, Lady Lennox grave, and, as if weary of the subject, Douglas thrust the shred of lace into his waistcoat pocket, and proposed a riding party. Miss Stuart preferred driving her aunt in the pony carriage, but Mrs. Vane accepted the invitation, and made George Lennox wretched by accepting the loan of one of Earl's horses in preference to his own, which she had ridden the day before.

When she appeared, ready for the expedition, glances of admiration shone in the eyes of all the gentlemen, even the gloomy Douglas, as he watched her, wondering if the piquant figure before him could be the same that he had seen in the garden, looking like a lovely, dreaming child. Her black habit, with its velvet facings, set off her little lithe figure to a charm; her hair shone like imprisoned sunshine through the scarlet net that held it, and her face looked bewilderingly brilliant and arch in the shadow of a cavalier hat, with its graceful plume.

As Douglas bent to offer his hand in mounting her, she uttered an exclamation of pain, and caught at his arm to keep herself from falling. Involuntarily he sustained her, and for an instant she leaned upon him, with her face hidden in his breast, as if to conceal some convulsion of suffering.

"My dear Mrs. Vane, what is it? Let me take you in—shall I call for help?" began Douglas, much alarmed.

But she interrupted him and, looking up with a faint smile, answered quietly, as she attempted to stand alone, "It is nothing but the cramp in my foot. It will be over in a moment; Gabrielle fastened my boot too tightly—let me sit down, and I will loosen it."

"Allow me; lean on my shoulder; it's but a moment."

Down knelt Douglas; and, with one hand lightly touching his shoulder to steady herself, the other still closely folded, as if not yet out of pain, Mrs. Vane stood glancing from under her long lashes at Diana, who was waiting in the hall for her aunt, and observing the scene in the avenue with ill-concealed anxiety. The string was in a knot, and Douglas set about his little service very leisurely, for the foot and ankle before him were the most perfect he had ever seen. While so employed, Jitomar, Mrs. Vane's man, appeared, and, tossing him the gloves she had taken off, she signed to him to bid her maid bring her another pair, as some slight blemish in these had offended her fastidious taste. He comprehended with difficulty, it seemed, for words were useless to a deaf-mute, and the motions of his mistress's hands appeared at first without meaning to him. The idea came with a flash, and bowing, he bounded into the house, with his white robes streaming, and his scarlet slippers taking him along as if enchanted, while the grooms wondered, and Mrs. Vane laughed.

Jitomar hurried to his lady's room, delivered his message, and while Gabrielle went down with a fresh pair of gloves, he enacted a curious little scene in the deserted chamber. Carefully unfolding the discarded gloves, he took from the inside of one of them the shred of lace that Douglas had put into his waistcoat pocket at the breakfast table. He examined it with a peculiar smile; then going to a tiger-skin rug that lay beside the bed, he lifted it and produced a black lace shawl, which seemed to have been hastily hidden there. One corner was gone; but laying the torn bit in its place, it fitted exactly, and, as if satisfied, Jitomar refolded both, put them in his pocket, glided to his own room, prepared himself for going out, and, unobserved by anyone, took the next train to London. Mrs. Vane meanwhile had effaced the memory of her first failure by mounting her horse alone, with an elasticity and grace that filled her escort with astonishment and admiration. Laughing her enchanting laugh, she settled herself in the saddle, touched her hat to Lady Lennox, and cantered away with Douglas, while Harry followed far behind, for George had suddenly remembered that an engagement would prevent his joining them, having no mind to see Mrs. Vane absorbed by another.

As they climbed a long hill, Mrs. Vane suddenly paused in her witty badinage, and after a thoughtful moment, and a backward glance at Harry, who followed apparently out of earshot, she said, earnestly yet timidly, "Mr. Douglas, I desire to ask a favor of you—not for myself, but for the sake of one who is dear to both of us."

"Mrs. Vane can ask no favor that I shall not be both proud and happy to grant for her own sake," returned Earl, eyeing her with much surprise.

"Well, then, I shall be most grateful if you will shun me for a few days; ignore my presence as far as possible, and so heal the breach which I fear I may unconsciously have caused between Miss Stuart and yourself."

"I assure you that you are mistaken regarding the cause of the slight coolness between us, and it is impossible to ignore the existence of Mrs. Vane, having once had the happiness of seeing her."

"Ah, you take refuge in evasion and compliments, as I feared you would; but it is my nature to be frank, and I shall compass my end by leaving you no subterfuge and no power to deny me. I met you both this morning, and read a happy secret in your faces; I hoped when next I saw you to find your mutual happiness secured. But no—I found you grave and cold; saw trouble in your eyes, jealousy and pain in Diana's. I have seen the latter sentiment in her eyes before, and could not but think that I was the unhappy cause of this estrangement. She is peculiar; she does not like me, will not let me love her, and wounds me in many ways. I easily forgive her, for she is not happy, and I long to help her, even against her will—therefore I speak to you."

"Again I assure you that you are wrong. Diana is jealous, but not of you alone, and she has placed me in a cruel strait. I, too, will be frank, and confess that she will not listen to me, unless I betray a secret that is not my own."

"You will not do this, having sworn to keep it?"

"Never! A Douglas cannot break his word."

"I comprehend now," said Mrs. Vane. "Diana wishes to test her power, and you rebel. It is not natural in both; yet I beseech you not to try her too much, because at a certain point she will become unmanageable. She comes of an unhappy race, and desperate things have been done in her family. Guard your secret, for honor demands it, but take my warning and shun me, that you may add nothing to the trouble she has brought upon herself."

"I have no wish to do so; but she also must beware of testing her power too severely, for I am neither a patient nor a humble man, and my will is inflexible when once I am resolved. She should see this, should trust me, and let us both be happy."

"Ah, if she truly loved, she would; for then one believes blindly, can think no ill, fear no wrong, desire no confidence that is not freely given. She does not know the bliss of loving with one's whole heart and soul, and asking no happier fate than to live for a man whose affection makes a heaven anywhere."

They had paused on the brow of the hill to wait for Harry, and as she spoke, Mrs. Vane's face kindled with a glow that made it doubly beautiful; for voice, eyes, lips, and gestures all betrayed how well *she* could love. Douglas regarded her with a curious consciousness of attraction and repulsion, feeling that had he met her before he saw and loved Diana, he never should have given his peace into the keeping of that exacting girl. An involuntary sigh escaped him; Mrs. Vane brightened instantly, saying:

"Nay, do not fall back into your gloomy mood again, or I shall think that I have increased, not lessened, your anxiety. I came to cheer you if I could, for though I have done with love myself, it gives me sincerest satisfaction to serve those who are just beginning to know its pleasant pain."

She was smiling as she spoke, but the lovely eyes lifted to her companion's face were full of tears. Remembering her loneliness, her loss, and with a grateful sense of all she desired to do for him, Douglas ungloved and offered her his hand, with an impulsive gesture, saying warmly, "You are very kind; I thank you, and feel already comforted by the thought that though I may have lost a lover, I have gained a friend."

Here Harry came up brimful of curiosity, for he had seen and heard more than they knew. After this they all rode on together, and when Douglas dismounted Mrs. Vane she whispered, "Remember, you are to shun me, no matter how pointedly. I shall forgive you, and she will be happier for our little ruse."

This speech, as well as the first uttered by Mrs. Vane when their serious conversation began, was overheard by Harry, and when Diana carelessly asked him if he had enjoyed his ride, he repeated the two remarks, hoping to gain some explanation of them before he told his brother, whose cause he heartily espoused. He knew nothing of Miss Stuart's love, and made her his confidante without a suspicion of the pang he was inflicting. She bade him forget what he had heard, but could not do so herself, and all that day those two sentences rang through her mind unceasingly.

Pausing that evening in the hall to examine one of the ancient portraits hanging there, Douglas heard a soft rustle, and turning, saw Mrs. Vane entering, as if from a moonlight stroll on the balcony. The night was cool, and over her head was drawn a corner of the black lace shawl that drooped from her shoulders. Her dress of violet silk was trimmed with a profusion of black lace, and wonderingly becoming to white skin and golden hair was the delicate tint and its rich decoration. Douglas went to her, saying, as he offered his hand, "You see how well I keep my word; now let me reward myself by taking you in. But, first, pray tell me if this is a picture of Sir Lionel."

He led her to the portrait that had excited his curiosity, and while she told him some little legend of it, he still lingered, held as much by the charm of the living voice as by the exploits of the dead knight. Standing thus, arm in arm, alone and engrossed in one another, neither, apparently, saw Diana pausing on the threshold of the library with an expression of deep displeasure in her face. Douglas did not see her; Mrs. Vane did, though not a sign betrayed it, except that in an instant her whole expression changed. As Douglas looked up at the picture, she looked up at him with love, grief, pain, and pity visibly contending in her beautiful face; then suddenly withdrawing her arm, she said, "I forgot, we are strangers now. Let me enter alone." And gliding from him with bent head, she passed into the drawing room.

Much amazed at her abrupt flight, Earl looked after her, saw Diana watching him, and inexpressibly annoyed by the contretemps, he started, colored, bowed coldly, and followed Mrs. Vane without a word. For a moment, Diana lingered with her head in her hands, thinking disconsolately: "What secret lies between them? She leaned and looked as if she had a right there. He is already more at ease with her than me, although they met but yesterday. Have they not met before? She asked some favor 'for the sake of one dear to both.' Who is it? He must shun her that someone may be happy, though deceived. Is that me? She knows his mystery, has a part in it, and I am to be kept blind. Wait a little! I too can plot, and watch, and wait. I can read faces, fathom actions, and play a part, though my heart breaks in doing it."

All that evening she watched them; saw that Douglas did not shun Mrs. Vane; also that he feigned unconsciousness of her own keen scrutiny, and seemed endeavoring to chase from her mind the memory of the morning's interview, or the evening's discovery. She saw Mrs. Vane act surprise, pique, and displeasure at his seeming desertion, and console herself by making her peace with Lennox. To others, Diana appeared unusually animated and carefree, but never had an evening seemed so interminable, and never had she so gladly hailed the hour of separation.

She was standing by Lady Lennox when Mrs. Vane came up to say good night. Her ladyship did not like Diana, and did both love and pity the lonely little widow, who had endeared herself in so many ways. As she swept a curtsy, with the old-fashioned reverence that her hostess liked, Lady Lennox drew her nearer and kissed her with motherly affection, saying playfully as she did so, "No pranks tonight among the spirits, my dear, else these friends will think you and I are witches in good earnest."

"That reminds me, I have kept my promise, and Mr. Douglas can compare his telltale bit with my mother's, and, as you see, very precious in every respect."

Gravely exploring one pocket after another, Earl presently announced, with some chagrin, that the bit was lost, blown away while riding, probably. So nothing could be done, and Mrs. Vane was acquitted of lending her laces to the household ghost. Diana looked disappointed, and taking up a corner of the shawl, said, as she examined it narrowly, "As I remember the shred, it matched this pattern exactly. It is a peculiar one, and I observed it well. I wish the bit was not lost, for if people play such games with your clothes, they may take equal liberties with mine."

Seeing suspicion in her eyes, Mrs. Vane gathered the four corners of the shawl together, and with great care spread each over her violet skirt before Diana. Not a fracture appeared, and when she had done the same with every atom of trimming on her dress, she drew her slender figure up with an air of proud dignity, asking almost sternly, "Am I acquitted of this absurd charge, Miss Stuart?"

Entirely disconcerted by the quickness with which her distrust had been seen and exposed, Diana could only look guilty, apologize, and find herself convicted of an unjust suspicion. Mrs. Vane received her atonement graciously, and wrapping her shawl about her, went away to bed, with a mischievous smile shining in her eyes as she bowed to Douglas, whose glance followed her till the last glimpse of the violet dress disappeared.

Chapter V. Treason

THE WEEK PASSED gaily enough, externally, but to several of the party it was a very dreary and very memorable week. George Lennox basked in the light of Mrs. Vane's smiles, and his mother began to hope that Douglas would not take her at her word, but leave her son to woo and win the bonny widow, if he could. Earl watched and waited for Diana to relent, pleading with his eyes, though never a word of submission or appeal passed his lips. And poor Diana, hoping to conquer him, silenced the promptings of her reason, and stood firm, when a yielding look, a tender word, would have overcome his pride, and healed the breach. She suffered much, but told no one her pain till the last day came. Then, driven by the thought that a few hours would seal her fate, she resolved to appeal to Mrs. Vane. She knew the mystery; she professed to pity her. She was a woman, and to her this humiliation would not be so hard, this confession so impossible.

Diana haunted the hall and drawing rooms all that morning, hoping to find Mrs. Vane alone. At last, just before lunch, she caught her playing with Earl's spaniel, while she waited for Lennox to bring her hat from the garden seat where she had left it.

"Be so kind as to take a turn with me on the balcony, Mrs. Vane. I wish much to say a few words to you," began Diana, with varying color and anxious eyes, as she met her at the great hall door.

"With pleasure. Give me your arm, and let us have our little chat quite comfortably together. Can I do anything for you, my dear Miss Stuart? Pray speak freely, and, believe me, I desire to be your friend."

So kind, so cordial was the tone, the look, that poor Diana felt comforted at once; and bending her stately head to the bright one at her side, she said, with a sad humility, which proved how entirely her love had subdued her pride, "I hope so, Mrs. Vane, for I need a friend. You, and you alone, can help me. I humble myself to you; I forget not my own misgivings. I endeavor to see in you only a woman younger, yet wiser than myself, who, knowing my sore necessity, will help me by confessing the share she bears in the secret that is destroying my peace."

"I wish I could! I wish I dared! I have thought of it often; have longed to do it at all costs; and then remembering my vow, I have held my peace!"

"Assure me of one thing and I will submit. I will ask Allan to forgive me, and I will be happy in my ignorance, if I can. He told me that this mystery would not stain his honor, or mar my peace if it were known. Mrs. Vane, is this true?" asked Diana solemnly.

"No; a man's honor is not tarnished in his eyes by treachery to a woman, and he believes that a woman's peace will not be marred by the knowledge that in God's sight she is not his wife, although she may be in the eyes of the world."

"Mrs. Vane, I conjure you to tell me what you mean! I have a right to know; it is your duty to save me from sin and sorrow if you can, and I will make any promise you exact to keep eternally secret whatever you may tell me. If you fear Douglas, he shall never know that you have broken your vow, whether I marry or discard him. Have pity upon me, I implore you, for this day must make or mar my life!"

Few women could have withstood the desperate urgency of Diana's prayer; Mrs. Vane did not. A moment she stood, growing paler as some purpose took shape in her mind, then drew her companion onward, saying hurriedly, as George Lennox appeared in the avenue, "Invite me to drive out alone with you after lunch, and then you shall know all. But, O Miss Stuart, remember that you bring the sorrow upon yourself if you urge this disclosure. I cannot think it right to see you give yourself to this man without a protest; but you may curse me for destroying your faith in him, while powerless to kill your love. Go now, and if you retract your wish, be silent; I shall know."

They parted, and when Lennox came up, the balcony was deserted.

"My love, you get so pale and spiritless that I am quite reconciled to our departure; for the air here does not suit you, and we must try the seashore," said Mrs. Berkeley, as they rose from the table after lunch.

"I shall be myself again soon, Aunt. I need more exercise, and if Mrs. Vane will allow me, I should enjoy a long drive with her this afternoon," returned Diana, growing still paler as she spoke.

Mrs. Vane bowed her acceptance, and as she left the room a curious shiver seemed to shake her from head to foot as she pressed her hands together and hurried to her chamber.

The two ladies drove in silence, till Diana said abruptly, "I am ready, Mrs. Vane; tell me all, and spare nothing."

"Your solemn oath first, that living or dying, you will never reveal to any human soul what I shall tell you." And as she spoke, Mrs. Vane extended her hand.

Diana gave her own, and took the oath which the other well knew she would keep inviolate.

"I shall not torture you by suspense," Mrs. Vane began, "but show you at once why I would save you from a greater suffering than the loss of love. Miss Stuart, read that, and learn the mystery of your lover's life."

With a sudden gesture, she took from her bosom a worn paper, and unfolding it, held before the other's eyes the marriage record of Allan Douglas and Virginie Varens.

Not a word passed Diana's lips, but with the moan of a broken heart she covered up her face, and slowly, tremulously, the voice at her side went on, "You see here the date of that mysterious journey to Paris, from which he returned an altered man. There, too, is his private seal. That long lock of hair, that stained slipper, belonged to Virginie; and though he said he had never seen her, the lie cost him an effort, and well it might, for I sat there before him, and I am Virginie."

Diana's hands dropped from her pallid face, as she shrank away from her companion, yet gazed at her like one fascinated by an awful spell.

"Hear my story, and then judge between us," the voice continued, so melancholy, yet so sweet that tears came to the listener's eyes, as the sad story was unfolded. "I am of a noble family, but was left so poor, so friendless, that but for a generous boy I should have perished in the streets of Paris. He was a dancer, his poor earnings could not support us both. I discovered this, and in my innocence, thought no labor degrading that lessened my great debt to him. I, too, had become a dancer. I had youth, beauty, health, and a grateful heart to help me on. I made money. I had many lovers, but Victor kept me safe, for he, too, loved, but in secret, till he was sure I could give him love, not gratitude. Then Allan came, and I forgot the world about me; for I loved as only a girl of seventeen can love the first man who has touched her heart. He offered me his hand and honorable name, for I was as wellborn as himself, and even in my seeming degradation, he respected me. We were married, and for a year I was as happy as an angel. Then my boy was born, and for a time I lost my beauty. That cooled Allan's waning passion. Some fear of consequences, some later regret for his rash act, came over him, and made him very bitter to me when I most needed tenderness. He told me that our marriage had been without witnesses, that our faith was different, and that vows pronounced before a Catholic priest alone were not binding upon him. That he was weary of me, and having been recalled to Scotland, he desired to return as free as he went. If I would promise solemnly to conceal the truth, he would support the boy and me abroad, until I chose to marry; that I must destroy the record of the deed, and never claim him, or he would denounce me as an impostor, and take away the boy. Miss Stuart, I was very ignorant and young; my heart was broken, and I believed myself dying. For the child's sake, I promised all things, and he left me; but remorse haunted him, and his peace was poisoned from that hour."

"And you? You married Colonel Vane?" whispered Diana, holding her breath to listen.

"No, I have never married, for in my eyes that ceremony made me Allan's wife, and I shall be so till I die. When I was most forlorn, Colonel Vane found me. He was Allan's friend; he had seen me with him, and when we met again, he pitied me; and finding that I longed to hide myself from the world, he took me to India under an assumed name, as the widow of a friend. My boy went with me, and for a time I was as happy as a desolate creature could be. Colonel Vane desired to marry me; for, though I kept my promise, he suspected that I had been deceived and cruelly deserted, and longed to atone for his friend's perfidy by his own devotion. I would not marry him; but when he was dying, he begged me to take his name as a shield against a curious world, to take his fortune, and give my son the memory of a father when his own had cast him off. I did so; and no one knew me there except under my false name. It was believed that I had married him too soon after my husband's death to care to own it at once, and when I came to England, no one denied me the place I chose to fill."

"Oh, why did you come?" cried Diana, with a tearless sob.

"I came because I longed to know if Allan had forgotten me, if he had married, and left his poor boy fatherless. I saw him last winter, saw that you loved him, feared that he would love you, and when I learned that both were coming here, I resolved to follow. It was evident that Allan had not forgotten me, that he had suffered as well as I; and perhaps if he could bring himself to brave the pity, curiosity, and criticism of the world, he might yet atone for his deceit, and make me happy. We had met in London; he had told me to remember my vow; had confessed that he still loved me, but dared not displease his haughty family by owning me; had seen his boy, and reiterated his promise to provide for us as long as we were silent. I saw him no more till we met here, and this explains all that has seemed so strange to you. It was I who entered his room, but not to juggle with the ring. He invented that tale to account for the oiled lock, and whatever stir might have been overheard. I went to implore him to pause before he pledged himself to you. He would not yield, having gone too far to retract with honor, he said. Then I was in despair; for well I knew that if ever the knowledge of this passage in his life should come to you, you would feel as I feel, and regard that first marriage as sacred in God's eye, whatever the world might say. I gave him one more opportunity to spare you by the warning I whispered in the park. That has delayed the wrong, but you would have yielded had not other things roused suspicion of me. I had decided to say no more, but let you two tangle your fates as you would. Your appeal this morning conquered me, and I have broken every vow, dared every danger, to serve and save you. Have I done all this in vain?"

"No; let me think, let me understand—then I will act."

For many minutes they rolled on silently, two pale, stern-faced women, sitting side by side looking out before them, with fixed eyes that saw nothing but a hard task performed, a still harder one yet to be done. Diana spoke first, asking, "Do you intend to proclaim your wrong, and force your husband to do you justice?"

"No, I shall not ask that of him again, but I shall do my best to prevent any other woman from blindly sacrificing her happiness by marrying him, unconscious of my claim. For the boy's sake I have a right to do this."

"You have. I thank you for sparing me the affliction of discovering that man's perfidy too late. Where is your boy, Mrs. Douglas?"

Steadily she spoke; and when her lips pronounced the name she had hoped to make her own, a stern smile passed across her white face, and left a darker shadow behind. Mrs. Vane touched her lips with a warning gesture, saying pitifully, yet commandingly: "Never call me that until he gives me the right to bear it openly. You ask for my boy; will you come and see him? He is close by; I cannot be parted from him long, yet must conceal him, for the likeness to his father would betray him at once, if we were seen together."

Turning down a grassy lane, Mrs. Vane drove on till the way became too narrow for the carriage. Here they alighted, and climbing a wooded path, came to a lonely cottage in a dell.

"My faithful Jitomar found this safe nook for me, and brings me tidings of my darling every day," whispered Mrs. Vane, as she stole along the path that wound round the house.

Turning a sharp corner, a green, lawnlike bit of ground appeared. On a vine-covered seat sat an old French *bonne,* knitting as she nodded in the sun. But Diana saw nothing but a little figure tossing buttercups into the air, and catching them as they fell with peals of childish laughter. A three-year-old boy it was, with black curls blowing round a bold bright face, where a healthful color glowed through the dark skin, and brilliant eyes sparkled under a brow so like that other that she could not doubt that this was Allan's son. Just then the boy spied his mother, and with a cry of joy ran to her, to be gathered close, and covered with caresses.

There was no acting here, for genuine mother love transformed Mrs. Vane from her usual inexplicable self into a simple woman, whose heart was bound up in the little creature whom she loved with the passionate fondness of an otherwise cold and superficial nature.

Waving off the old *bonne* when she would have approached, Mrs. Vane turned to Diana, asking, "Are you satisfied?"

"Heaven help me, yes!"

"Is he not like his father? See, the very shape of his small hands, the same curve to his baby mouth. Stay, you shall hear him speak. Darling, who am I?"

"Mamma, my dear mamma," replied the little voice.

"And who is this?" asked Mrs. Vane, showing a miniature of Douglas.

"Oh, Papa! When will he come again?"

"God only knows, my poor baby. Now kiss Mamma, and go and make a pretty daisy chain against I come next time. See, love, here are bonbons and new toys; show them to Babette. Quick, let us slip away, Miss Stuart."

As the boy ran to his nurse the ladies vanished, and in silence regained the carriage. Only one question and answer passed between them, as they drove rapidly homeward.

"Diana, what will you do?"

"Go tomorrow, and in silence. It is all over between us, forever. Mrs. Vane, I envy you, I thank you, and I could almost *hate* you for the kind yet cruel deed you have done this day."

A gloomy darkness settled down on her altered face; despair sat in her eyes, and death itself could not have stricken hope, energy, and vitality out of it more utterly than the bitter truth which she had wrung from her companion.

George Lennox and Douglas were waiting at the door, and both ran down to help them alight. Diana dragged her veil over her face, while Mrs. Vane assumed an anxious, troubled air as the carriage stopped, and both gentlemen offered a hand to Miss Stuart. Putting Earl's aside with what seemed almost rude repugnance, she took George's arm, hurried up the steps, and as her foot touched the threshold of the door, she fell heavily forward in a swoon.

Douglas was springing toward her, when a strong grasp detained him, and Mrs. Vane whispered, as she clung to his arm tremblingly, "Do not touch her; she must not see you; it will kill her."

"Good heavens! What is the cause of this?" he asked, as Lennox carried Diana in, and help came flocking at his call.

"O Mr. Douglas, I have had an awful drive! She terrified me so by her wild conversation, her fierce threats of taking her own life, that I drove home in agony. You saw how she repulsed you, and rushed away to drop exhausted in the hall; imagine what it all means, and spare me the pain of telling you."

She spoke breathlessly, and glanced nervously about her, as if still in fear. Earl listened, half bewilderingly at first, then, as her meaning broke upon him, his dark cheek whitened, and he looked aghast.

"You do not mean that she is mad?" he whispered, recalling her fierce gesture, and the moody silence she had preserved for days.

"No, oh, no, I dare not say that *yet;* but I fear that her mind is unsettled by long brooding over one unhappy thought, and that the hereditary taint may be upon the point of showing itself. Poor girl!"

"Am I the cause of this outbreak? Is our disagreement the unhappy thought that has warped her reason? What shall I, what ought I to do?" Earl asked in great distress, as Diana's senseless body was carried up the stairs, and her aunt stood wringing her hands, while Lady Lennox dispatched a servant for medical help.

"Do nothing but avoid her, for she says your presence tortures her. She will go tomorrow. Let her leave quietly, and when absence has restored her, take any steps toward a reconciliation that you think best. Now I must go to her; do not repeat what I have said. It escaped me in my agitation, and may do her harm if she learns that her strange behavior is known."

Pressing his hand with a sympathizing glance, Mrs. Vane hurried in, and for an hour busied herself about Diana so skillfully that the physician sent all the rest away and gave directions to her alone. When recovered from her faint, Diana lay like one dead, refusing to speak or move, yet taking obediently whatever Mrs. Vane offered her, as if a mutual sorrow linked them together with a secret bond. At dusk she seemed to fall asleep, and leaving Gabrielle to watch beside her, Mrs. Vane went down to join the others at a quiet meal.

Chapter VI. A Dark Death

The party separated early. Diana was still sleeping, and leaving her own maid to watch in the dressing room between their chambers, Mrs. Berkeley went to bed. As he passed them down the gallery to his apartment, Earl heard Mrs. Vane say to the maid, "If anything happens in the night, call me." The words made him anxious, and instead of going to bed, he sat up writing letters till very late. It was past midnight when the sound of a closing door broke the long silence that had filled the house. Stepping into the gallery, he listened. All was still, and nothing stirred but the heavy curtain before the long window at the end of the upper hall; this swayed to and fro in the strong current of air that swept in. Fearing that the draft might slam other doors and disturb Diana, he went to close it.

Pausing a moment to view the gloomy scene without, Douglas was startled by an arm flung violently about his neck, lips pressed passionately to his own, and a momentary glimpse of a woman's figure dimly defined on the dark curtain that floated backward from his hand. Silently and suddenly as it came, the phantom went, leaving Douglas so amazed that for an instant he could only stare dumbly before him, half breathless, and wholly bewildered by the ardor of that mysterious embrace. Then he sprang forward to discover who the woman was and whither she had gone. But, as if blown outward by some counterdraft, the heavy curtain wrapped him in its fold, and when he had freed himself, neither ghost nor woman was visible.

Earl was superstitious, and for a moment he fancied the spirit of Diana had appeared to him, foretelling her death. But a second thought assured him that it was a human creature, and no wraith, for the soft arms had no deathly chill in them, the lips were warm, living breath had passed across his face, and on his cheek he felt a tear that must have fallen from human eyes. The light had been too dim to reveal the partially shrouded countenance, or more than a tall and shadowy outline, but with a thrill of fear he thought, "It was Diana, and she is mad!"

Taking his candle, he hurried to the door of the dressing room, tapped softly, and when the sleepy maid appeared, inquired if Miss Stuart still slept.

"Yes, sir, like a child, it does one's heart good to see her."

"You are quite sure she is asleep?"

"Bless me, yes, sir, I've just looked at her, and she hasn't stirred since I looked an hour ago."

"Does she ever walk in her sleep, Mrs. Mason?"

"Dear, no, sir."

"I thought I saw her just now in the upper gallery. I went to shut the great window, lest the wind should disturb her, and someone very like her certainly stood for a moment at my side."

"Lord, sir! You make my blood run cold. It couldn't have been her, for she never left her bed, much less her room."

"Perhaps so; never mind; just look again, and tell me if you see her, then I shall be at ease."

Mrs. Mason knew that her young lady loved the gentleman before her, and never doubted that he loved her, and so considering his anxiety quite natural and proper, she nodded, crept away, and soon returned, saying, with a satisfied air, "She's all right, sir, sleeping beautifully. I didn't speak, for once when I looked at her, she said, quite fierce, 'Go away, and let me be until I call you.' So I've only peeped through the curtain since. I see her lying with her face to the wall, and the coverlet drawn comfortably round her."

"Thank God! She is safe. Excuse my disturbing you, Mrs. Mason, but I was very anxious. Be patient and faithful in your care of her; I shall remember it. Good night."

"Handsome creeter; how fond he is of her, and well he may be, for she dotes on him, and they'll make a splendid couple. Now I'll finish my nap, and then have a cup of tea."

With a knowing look and a chilly shiver, Mrs. Mason resettled herself in a luxurious chair, and was soon dozing.

Douglas meanwhile returned to his room, after a survey of the house, and went to bed, thinking with a smile and frown that if all spirits came in such an amicable fashion, the fate of a ghost seer was not a hard one.

In the dark hour just before the dawn, a long shrill cry rent the silence, and brought every sleeper under that roof out of his bed, trembling and with fright. The cry came from Diana's room, and in a moment the gallery, dressing room, and chamber were filled with pale faces and half-dressed figures, as ladies and gentlemen, men and maids came flocking in, asking breathlessly, "What is it? Oh, what is it?"

Mrs. Berkeley lay on the floor in strong hysterics, and Mrs. Mason, instead of attending to her, was beating her hands distractedly together, and running wildly about the room, as if searching for something she had lost. Diana's bed was empty, with the clothes flung one way and the pillows another, and every sign of strange disorder, but its occupant was nowhere to be seen.

"Where is she?" "What has happened?" "Why don't you speak?" cried the terrified beholders.

A sudden lull fell upon the excited group, as Mrs. Vane, white, resolute, and calm, made her way through the crowd, and laying her hand on Mrs. Mason's shoulder, commanded her to stand still and explain the mystery. The poor soul endeavored to obey, but burst into tears, and dropping on her knees, poured out her story in a passion of penitent despair.

"You left her sleeping, ma'am, and I sat as my lady bid me, going now and then to look at Miss. The last time I drew the curtain, she looked up and said, sharp and short, 'Let me be in peace, and don't disturb me till I call you.' After that, I just peeped through the crack, and she seemed quiet. You know I told you so, sir, when you came to ask, and oh, my goodness me, it wasn't her at all, sir, and she's gone! She's gone!"

"Hush! Stop sobbing, and tell me how you missed her. Gabrielle and Justine, attend to Mrs. Berkeley; Harry, go at once and search the house. Now, Mrs. Mason."

Mrs. Vane's clear, calm voice seemed to act like a spell on the agitation of all about her, and the maids obeyed; Harry, with the menservants, hurried away, and Mrs. Mason more coherently went on:

"Well, ma'am, when Mr. Douglas came to the door asking if Miss was here, thinking he saw her in the hall, I looked again, and thought she lay as I'd left her an hour before. But oh, ma'am, it wasn't her, it was the pillow that she'd fixed like herself, with the coverlet pulled round it, like she'd pulled it round her own head and shoulders when she spoke last. It looked all right, the night lamp being low, and me so sleepy, and I went back to my place, after setting Mr. Douglas's mind at rest. I fell asleep, and when I woke, I ran in here to make sure she was safe, for I'd had a horrid dream about seeing her laid out, dead and dripping, with weeds in her hair, and her poor feet all covered with red clay, as if she'd fallen into one of them pits over yonder. I ran in here, pulled up the curtain, and was just going to say, 'Thank the Lord,' when, as I stooped down to listen if she slept easy, I saw she wasn't there. The start took my wits away, and I don't know what I did, till my lady came running in, as I was tossing the pillows here and there to find her, and when I told what had happened, my lady gave one dreadful scream, and went off in a fit."

There was a dead silence for a moment, as Mrs. Mason relapsed into convulsive sobbing, and everyone looked into each other's frightened face. Douglas leaned on Lennox, as if all the strength had gone out of him, and George stood aghast. Mrs. Vane alone seemed self-possessed, though an awful anxiety blanched her face, and looked out at her haggard eyes.

"What did you see in the hall?" she asked of Douglas. Briefly he told the incident, and Lady Lennox clasped her hands in despair, exclaiming, "She has destroyed herself, and that was her farewell."

"Your ladyship is mistaken, I hope, for among the wild things she said this afternoon was a longing to go home at once, as every hour here was torture to her. She may have attempted this in her delirium. Look in her wardrobe, Mrs. Mason, and see what clothes are gone. That will help us in our search. Be calm, I beg of you, my lady; I am sure we shall find the poor girl soon."

"It's no use looking, ma'am; she's gone in the clothes she had on, for she wouldn't let me take 'em off her. It was a black silk with crepe trimmings, and her black mantle's gone, and the close crepe bonnet. Here's her gloves just where they dropped when we laid her down in her faint."

"Is her purse gone?" asked Mrs. Vane.

"It's always in her pocket, ma'am; when she drives out, she likes to toss a bit of money to the little lads that open gates, or hold the ponies while she gets flowers, and such like. She was so generous, so kind, poor dear!"

Here Harry came in, saying that no trace of the lost girl was visible in the house. But as he spoke, Jitomar's dark face and glittering eyes looked over his shoulder with an intelligent motion, which his mistress understood, and put into words.

"He says that one of the long windows in the little breakfast room is unfastened and ajar. Go, gentlemen, at once, and take him with you; he is as keen as a hound, and will do good service. It is just possible that she may have remembered the one o'clock mail train, and taken it. Inquire, and if you find any trace of her, let us know without delay."

In an instant they were gone, and the anxious watchers left behind traced their progress by the glimmer of the lantern, which Jitomar carried low, that he might follow the print her flying feet had left here and there in the damp earth.

A long hour passed, then Harry and the Indian returned, bringing the good news that a tall lady in black had been seen at the station alone, had not been recognized, being veiled, and had taken the mail train to London. Douglas and Lennox had at once ordered horses, and gone with all speed to catch an early train that left a neighboring town in an hour or two. They would trace and discover the lost girl, if she was in London.

"There can be no doubt that it was she, no lady would be traveling alone at such an hour, and the station people say that she seemed in great haste. Now let us compose ourselves, hope for the best, and comfort her poor aunt."

As Mrs. Vane spoke, Harry frankly looked his admiration of the cheerful, courageous little woman, and his mother took her arm, saying affectionately, "My dear, what should we do without you? For you have the nerves of a man, the quick wit of a woman, and presence of mind enough for us all."

The dreary day dawned, and slowly wore away. A dull rain fell, and a melancholy wind sighed among the yellowing leaves. All occupations flagged, all failed, except the one absorbing hope. The servants loitered, unreproved, and gossiped freely among themselves about the sad event. The ladies sat in Mrs. Berkeley's room, consoling her distress, while Harry haunted the station, waiting for an arrival or a telegram. At noon the letter came.

"The lady in black not Diana. On another scent now. If that fails, home at night."

No one knew how much they leaned upon this hope, until it failed and all was uncertainty again. Harry searched house, garden, park, and riverside, but found no trace of the lost girl beyond the point where her footprints ended on the hard gravel of the road. So the long afternoon wore on, and at dusk the gentlemen returned, haggard, wet, and weary, bringing no tidings of good cheer. The lady in black proved to be a handsome young governess, called suddenly to town by her father's dangerous illness. The second search was equally fruitless, and nowhere had Diana been seen.

Their despondent story was scarcely ended when the bell rang. Every servant in the house sprang to answer it, and every occupant of the drawing room listened breathlessly. A short parley followed the ring; then an astonished footman showed in a little farmer lad, with a bundle under his arm.

"He wants to see my lady, and would come in," said the man, lingering, as all eyes were fixed on the newcomer.

The boy looked important, excited, and frightened, but when Lady Lennox bade him to do his errand without fear, he spoke up briskly, though his voice shook a little, and he now and then gave a nervous clutch at the bundle under his arm.

"Please, my lady, Mother told me to come up as soon as ever I got home, so I ran off right away, knowing you'd be glad to hear something, even if it weren't good."

"Something about Miss Stuart, you mean?"

"Yes, my lady, I know where she is."

"Where? Speak quickly, you shall be paid for your tidings."

"In that pit, my lady," and the boy began to cry.

"No!"

Douglas spoke, and turned on the lad a face that stopped his crying, and sent the words to his lips faster than he could utter them, so full of mute entreaty was its glance of anguish.

"You see, sir, I was here this noon, and heard about it. Mrs. Mason's dream scared me, because my brother was drowned in the pit. I couldn't help thinking of it all the afternoon, and when work was done, I went home that way. The first thing I saw were tracks in the red clay, coming from the lodge way. The pit has overflowed and made a big pool, but just where it's deepest, the tracks stopped, and there I found these."

With a sudden gesture of the arm, he shook out the bundle; a torn mantle, heavily trimmed, and a crushed crepe bonnet dropped upon the floor. Lady Lennox sank back in her chair, and George covered up his face with a groan; but Earl stood motionless, and Mrs. Vane looked as if the sight of these relics had confirmed some wordless fear.

"Perhaps she is not there, however," she said below her breath. "She may have wandered on and lost herself. Oh, let us look!"

"She *is* there, ma'am, I see her sperrit," and the boy's eyes dilated as they glanced fearfully about him while he spoke. "I was awful scared when I see them things, but she was good to me, and I loved her, so I took 'em up and went on round the pool, meaning to strike off by the great ditch. Just as I got to the bit of brush that grows down by the old clay pits, something flew right up before me, something like a woman, all black but a white face and arms. It gave a strange screech, and seemed to go out of sight all in a minute, like as if it vanished in the pits. I know it warn't a real woman, it flew so, and looked so awful when it wailed, as Granny says the sperrits do."

The boy paused, till Douglas beckoned solemnly, and left the room with the one word "Come."

The brothers went, the lad followed, Mrs. Vane hid her face in Lady Lennox's lap, and neither stirred nor spoke for one long dreadful hour.

"They are coming," whispered Mrs. Vane, when at length her quick ear caught the sound of many approaching feet. Slowly, steadily they came on, across the lawn, up the steps through the hall; then there was a pause.

"Go and see if she is found, I cannot," implored Lady Lennox, spent and trembling with the long suspense.

There was no need to go, for as she spoke, the wail of women's voices filled the air, and Lennox stood in the doorway with a face that made all question needless.

He beckoned, and Mrs. Vane went to him as if her feet could hardly bear her, while her face might have been that of a dead woman, so white and stony had it grown. Drawing her outside, he said, "My mother must not see her yet. Mrs. Mason can do all that is necessary, if you will give her orders, and spare my mother the first sad duties. Douglas bade me come for you, for you are always ready."

"I will come; where is she?"

"In the library. Send the servants away, in pity to poor Earl. Harry can't bear it, and it kills me to see her look so."

"You found her there?"

"Yes, quite underneath the deepest water of the pool. That dream was surely sent by heaven. Are you faint? Can you bear it?"

"I can bear anything. Go on."

Poor Diana! There she lay, a piteous sight, with stained and dripping garments, slimy weeds entangled in her long hair, a look of mortal woe stamped on her dead face, for the blue lips were parted, as if by the passage of the last painful breath, and the glassy eyes seemed fixed imploringly upon some stern specter, darker and more dreadful even than the most desperate death she had sought and found.

A group of awestricken men and sobbing women stood about her. Harry leaned upon the high arm of the couch where they had laid her, with his head down upon his arm, struggling to control himself, for he had loved her with a boy's first love, and the horror of her end unmanned him. Douglas sat at the head of the couch, holding the dead hand, and looking at her with a white tearless anguish, which made his face old and haggard, as with the passage of long and heavy years.

With an air of quiet command, and eyes that never once fell on the dead girl, Mrs. Vane gave a few necessary orders, which cleared the room of all but the gentlemen and herself. Laying her hand softly on Earl's shoulder, she said, in a tone of tenderest compassion, "Come with me, and let me try to comfort you, while George and Harry take the poor girl to her room, that these sad tokens of her end may be removed, and she made beautiful for the eyes of those who loved her."

He heard, but did not answer in words, for waving off the brothers, Earl took his dead love in his arms, and carrying her to her own room, laid her down tenderly, kissed her pale forehead with one lingering kiss, and then without a word shut himself into his own apartment.

Mrs. Vane watched him go with a dark glance, followed him upstairs, and when his door closed, muttered low to herself, "He loved her better than I knew, but she has made my task easier than I dared to hope it would be, and now I can soon teach him to forget."

A strange smile passed across her face as she spoke, and still, without a glance at the dead face, left the chamber for her own, whither Jitomar was soon summoned, and where he long remained.

Chapter VII. The Footprint by the Pool

THREE SAD AND SOLEMN DAYS had passed, and now the house was still again. Mr. Berkeley had removed his wife, and the remains of his niece, and Lennox had gone with him. Mrs. Vane devoted herself to her hostess, who had been much affected by the shock, and to Harry, who was almost ill with the excitement and the sorrow. Douglas had hardly been seen except by his own servant, who reported that he was very quiet, but in a stern and bitter mood, which made solitude his best comforter. Only twice had he emerged during those troubled days. Once, when Mrs. Vane's sweet voice came up from below singing a sacred melody in the twilight, he came out and paced to and fro in the long gallery, with a softer expression than his face had worn since the night of Diana's passionate farewell. The second time was in answer to a tap at his door, on opening which he saw Jitomar, who with the graceful reverence of his race, bent on one knee, as with dark eyes full of sympathy, he delivered a lovely bouquet of the flowers Diana most loved, and oftenest wore. The first tears that had been seen there softened Earl's melancholy eyes, as he took the odorous gift, and with a grateful impulse stretched his hand to the giver. But Jitomar drew back with a gesture which signified that his mistress sent the offering, and glided away. Douglas went straight to the drawing room, found Mrs. Vane alone, and inexpressibly touched by her tender thought of him, he thanked her warmly, let her detain him for an hour with her soothing conversation, and left her, feeling that comfort was possible when such an angel administered it.

On the third day, impelled by an unconquerable wish to revisit the lonely spot hereafter, and forever to be haunted by the memory of that tragic death, he stole out, unperceived, and took his way to the pool. It lay there dark and still under a gloomy sky, its banks trampled by many hasty feet; and in one spot the red clay still bore the impress of the pale shape drawn from the water on that memorable night. As he stood there, he remembered the lad's story of the spirit which he believed he had seen. With a dreary smile at the superstition of the boy, he followed his tracks along the bank as they branched off toward the old pits, now half-filled with water by recent rains. Pausing where the boy had passed when the woman's figure sprang up before him with its old-witch cry, Douglas looked keenly all about, wondering if it were possible for any human being to vanish as the lad related. Several yards from the clump of bushes and coarse grass at his feet lay the wide pit; between it and the spot where he stood stretched a smooth bed of clay, unmarked by the impress of any step, as he first thought. A second and more scrutinizing glance showed him the print of a human foot on the very edge of the pit. Stepping lightly forward, he examined it. Not the boy's track, for he had not passed the bushes, but turned and fled in terror, when the phantom seemed to vanish. It was a child's footprint, apparently, or that of a very small woman; probably the latter, for it was a slender, shapely print, cut deep into the yielding clay, as if by the impetus of a desperate spring. But whither had she sprung? Not across the pit, for that was impossible to any but a very active man, or a professional gymnast of either sex. Douglas took the leap, and barely reached the other side, though a tall agile man. Nor did he find any trace of the other leaper, though the grass that grew to the very edge of that side might have concealed a lighter, surer tread than his own.

With a thrill of suspicion and dread, he looked down into the turbid water of the pit, asking himself if it were possible that two women had found their death so near together on that night. The footprint was not Diana's; hers was larger, and utterly unlike; whose was it, then? With a sudden impulse he cut a long, forked pole, and searched the depths of the pit. Nothing was found; again and again he plunged in the pole and drew it carefully up, after sweeping the bottom in all directions. A dead branch, a fallen rod, a heavy stone were all he found.

As he stood pondering over the mysterious mark, having recrossed the pit, some sudden peculiarity in it seemed to give it a familiar aspect. Kneeling down, he examined it minutely, and as he looked, an expression of perplexity came into his face, while he groped for some recollection in the dimness of the past, the gloom of the present.

"Where have I seen a foot like this, so dainty, so slender, yet so strong, for the tread was firm here, the muscles wonderfully elastic to carry this unknown woman over that wide gap? Stay! It was not a foot, but a shoe that makes this mark so familiar. Who wears a shoe with a coquettish heel like this stamped here in the clay? A narrow sole, a fairylike shape, a slight pressure downward at the top, as if the wearer walked well and lightly, yet danced better than she walked? Good heavens! Can it be? That word 'danced' makes it clear to me—but it is impossible—unless—can she have discovered me, followed me, wrought me fresh harm, and again escaped me? I will be satisfied at all hazards, and if I find her, Virginie shall meet a double vengeance for a double wrong."

Up he sprang, as these thoughts swept through his mind, and like someone bent on some all-absorbing purpose, he dashed homeward through bush and brake, park and garden, till, coming to the lawn, he restrained his impetuosity, but held on his way, turning neither to the right nor the left, till he stood in his own room. Without pausing for breath, he snatched the satin slipper from the case, put it in his breast, and hurried back to the pool. Making sure that no one followed him, he cautiously advanced, and bending, laid the slipper in the mold of that mysterious foot. It fitted exactly! Outline, length, width, even the downward pressure at the toe corresponded, and the sole difference was to the depth of heel, as if the walking boot or shoe had been thicker than the slipper.

Bent on assuring himself, Douglas pressed the slipper carefully into the smooth clay beside the other print, and every slight peculiarity was repeated with wonderful accuracy.

"I am satisfied," he muttered, adding, as he carefully effaced both the little tracks, "no one must follow this out but myself. I have sworn to find her and her accomplice, and henceforth it shall be my life business to keep my vow."

A few moments he stood buried in dark thoughts and memories, then putting up the slipper, he bent his steps toward the home of little Wat, the farmer's lad. He was watering horses at the spring, his mother said, and Douglas strolled that way, saying he desired to give the boy something for the intelligence he brought three days before. Wat lounged against the wall, while the tired horses slowly drank their fill, but when he saw the gentleman approaching, he looked troubled, for his young brain had been sadly perplexed by the late events.

"I want to ask you a few questions, Wat; answer me truly, and I will thank you in a way you will like better than words," began Douglas, as the boy pulled off his hat and stood staring.

"I'm ready; what will I say, sir?" he asked.

"Tell me just what sort of a thing or person the spirit looked like when you saw it by the pit."

"A woman, sir, all black but her face and arms."

"Did she resemble the person we were searching for?"

"No, sir; leastways, I never saw Miss looking so; of course she wouldn't when she was alive, you know."

"Did the spirit look like the lady afterward? When we found her, I mean?"

The boy pondered a minute, seemed perplexed, but answered slowly, as he grew a little pale, "No, sir, then she looked awful, but the spirit seemed scared like, and screamed as any woman would if frightened."

"And she vanished in the pit, you say?"

"She couldn't go nowhere else, sir, 'cause she didn't turn."

"Did you see her go down into the water, Wat?"

"No, sir, I only see her fly up out of the bushes, looking at me over her shoulder, and giving a great leap, as light and easy as if she hadn't no body. But it started me, so that I fell over backward, and when I got up, she was gone."

"I thought so. Now tell me, was the spirit large or small?"

"I didn't mind, but I guess it wasn't very big, or them few bushes wouldn't have hid it from me."

"Was its hair black or light?"

"Don't know, sir, a hood was all over its head, and I only see the face."

"Did you mind the eyes?"

"They looked big and dark, and scared me horridly."

"You said the face was handsome but white, I think?"

"I didn't say anything about handsome, sir; it was too dark to make out much, but it was white, and when she threw up her arms, they looked like snow. I never see any live lady with such white ones."

"You did not go down to the edge of the pit to leap after her, did you?"

"Lord, no, sir. I just scud the other way, and never looked back till I see the lodge."

"Is there any strange lady down at the inn, or staying anywhere in the village?"

"Not as I know, sir. I'm down there every day, and guess I'd hear of it if there was. Do you want to find anyone, sir?"

"No, I thought your spirit might have been some live woman, whom you frightened as much as she did you. Are you quite sure it was not?"

"I shouldn't be sure, if she hadn't flown away so strange, for no woman could go over the pit, and if she'd fell in, I'd have heard the splash."

"So you would. Well, let the spirit go, and keep away from the pit and the pool, lest you see it again. Here is a golden thank-you, my boy, so good-bye."

"Oh, sir, that's a deal too much! I'm heartily obliged. Be you going to leave these parts, please, sir?"

"Not yet; I've much to do before I go."

Satisfied with his inquiries, Douglas went on, and Wat, pulling on his torn hat as the gentleman disappeared, fell to examining the bit of gold that had been dropped into his brown palm.

"Do you want another, my lad?" said a soft voice behind him, and turning quickly, he saw a man leaning over the wall, just below the place where he had lounged a moment before.

The man was evidently a gypsy; long brown hair hung about a brown face with black eyes, a crafty mouth, and glittering teeth. His costume was picturesquely ragged and neglected, and in his hand he held a stout staff. Bending farther over, he eyed the boy with a nod, repeating his words in a smooth low tone, as he held up a second half-sovereign between his thumb and finger.

"Yes, I do," answered Wat sturdily, as he sent his horses trotting homeward with a chirrup and a cut of his long whip.

"Tell me what the gentleman said, and you shall have it," whispered the gypsy.

"You might have heard for yourself, if you'd been where you are a little sooner," returned Wat, edging toward the road—for there was something about the swarthy-faced fellow that he did not like, in spite of his golden offer.

"I was there," said the man with a laugh, "but you spoke so low I couldn't catch it all."

"What do you want to know for?" demanded Wat.

"Why, perhaps I know something about that spirit woman he seemed to be asking about, and if I do, he'd be glad to hear it, wouldn't he? Now I don't want to go and tell him myself, for fear of getting into trouble, but I might tell you, and you could do it. Only I must know what he said, first; perhaps he has found out for himself what I could tell him."

"What are you going to give me that for, then?" asked Wat, much reassured.

"Because you are a clever little chap, and were good to some of my people here once upon a time. I'm rich, though I don't look it, and I'd like to pay for the news you give me. Out with it, and then here's another yellow boy for you."

Wat was entirely conquered by the grateful allusion to a friendly act of his own on the previous day, and willingly related his conversation with Douglas, explaining as he went on. The gypsy questioned and cross-questioned, and finished the interview by saying, with a warning glance, "He's right; you'd better not tell anyone you saw the spirit—it's a bad sign, and if it's known, you'll find it hard to get on in the world. Now here's your money; catch it, and then I'll tell you my story."

The coin came ringing through the air, and fell into the road not far from Wat's feet. He ran to pick it up, and when he turned to thank the man, he was gone as silently and suddenly as he had come. The lad stared in amaze, listened, searched, but no gypsy was heard or seen, and poor bewildered Wat scampered home as fast as his legs could carry him, believing that he was bewitched.

That afternoon Douglas wrote a long letter, directed it to "M. Antoine Duprès, Rue Saint Honoré, Paris," and was about to seal it when a servant came to tell him that Mrs. Vane desired her adieus, as she was leaving for town by the next train. Anxious to atone for his seeming negligence, not having seen her that day, and there-fore being in ignorance of her intended departure, he hastily dropped a splash of wax on his important letter, and leaving it upon his table hurried down to see her off. She was already in the hall, having bidden Lady Lennox farewell in her boudoir—for her ladyship was too poorly to come down. Harry was giving directions about the baggage, and Gabrielle chattering her adieus in the housekeeper's room.

"My dear Mrs. Vane, forgive my selfish sorrow; when you are settled in town let me come to thank you for the great kindness you have shown me through these dark days."

Douglas spoke warmly; he pressed the hand she gave him in both his own, and gratitude flushed his pale face with a glow that restored all its lost comeliness.

Mrs. Vane dropped her beautiful eyes, and answered, with a slight quiver of the lips that tried to smile, "I have suffered for you, if not with you, and I need no thanks for the sympathy that was involuntary. Here is my address; come to me when you will, and be assured that you will always find a welcome."

He led her to the carriage, assiduously arranging all things for her comfort, and when she waved a last adieu, he seized the little hand, regardless of Harry, who accompanied her, and kissed it warmly as he said, "I shall not forget, and shall see you soon."

The carriage rolled away, and Douglas watched it, saying to the groom, who was just turning stableward, "Does not Jitomar go with his mistress?"

"No, sir; he's to take some plants my lady gave Mrs. Vane, so he's to go in a later train—and good riddance to the sly devil, I say," added the man, under his breath, as he walked off.

Had he turned his head a moment afterward, he would have been amazed at the strange behavior of the gentleman he had left behind him. Happening to glance downward, Douglas gave a start, stooped suddenly, examining something on the ground, and as he rose, struck his hands together like one in great perplexity or exultation, while his face assumed a singular expression of mingled wonder, pain, and triumph. Well it might, for there, clearly defined in the moist earth, was an exact counterpart of the footprint by the pool.

Chapter VIII. On the Trail

THE PACKET from Havre was just in. It had been a stormy trip, and all the passengers hurried ashore, as if glad to touch English soil. Two gentlemen lingered a moment, before they separated to different quarters of the city. One was a stout, gray-haired Frenchman, perfectly dressed, blandly courteous, and vivaciously grateful, as he held the other's hand, and poured out a stream of compliments, invitations, and thanks. The younger man was evidently a Spaniard, slight, dark, and dignified, with melancholy eyes, a bronzed, bearded face, and a mien as cool and composed as if he had just emerged from some elegant retreat, instead of the cabin of an overcrowded packet, whence he had been tossing about all day.

"It is a thousand pities we do not go on together; but remember I am under many obligations to Señor Arguelles, and I implore that I may be allowed to return them during my stay. I believe you have my card; now *au revoir,* and my respectful compliments to Madame your friend."

"Adieu, Monsieur Dupont—we shall meet again."

The Frenchman waved his hand, the Spaniard raised his hat, and they separated.

Antoine Duprès, for it was he, drove at once to a certain hotel, asked for M. Douglas, sent up his name, and was at once heartily welcomed by his friend, with whom he sat in deep consultation till very late.

Arguelles was set down at the door of a lodging house in a quiet street, and admitting himself by means of a latchkey, he went noiselessly upstairs and looked about him. The scene was certainly a charming one, though somewhat peculiar. A bright fire filled the room with its ruddy light; several lamps added their milder shine; and the chamber was a flush of color, for carpet, chairs, and tables were strewn with brilliant costumes. Wreaths of artificial flowers strewed the floor; mock jewels glittered here and there; a lyre, a silver bow and arrow, a slender wand of many colors, a pair of ebony castanets; a gaily decorated tambourine lay on the couch; little hats, caps, bodices, jackets, skirts, boots, slippers, and clouds of rosy, blue, white, and green tulle were heaped, hung, and scattered everywhere. In the midst of this gay confusion stood a figure in perfect keeping with it. A slight blooming girl of eighteen she looked, evidently an actress—for though busily sorting the contents of two chests that stood before her, she was *en costume,* as if she had been reviewing her wardrobe, and had forgotten to take off the various parts of different suits which she had tried on. A jaunty hat of black velvet, turned up with a white plume, was stuck askew on her blond head; scarlet boots with brass heels adorned her feet; a short white satin skirt was oddly contrasted with a blue-and-silver hussar jacket; and a flame-colored silk domino completed her piquant array.

A smile of tenderest joy and admiration lighted up the man's dark features, as he leaned in, watching the pretty creature purse up her lips and bend her brows, in deep consideration, over a faded pink-and-black Spanish dress, just unfolded.

"Madame, it is I."

He closed the door behind him, as he spoke, and advanced with open arms.

The girl dropped the garment she held, turned sharply, and surveyed the newcomer with little surprise but much amazement, for suddenly clapping her hands, she broke into a peal of laughter, exclaiming, as she examined him, "My faith! You are superb. I admire you thus; the melancholy is becoming, the beard ravishing, and the *tout ensemble* beyond my hopes. I salute you, Señor Arguelles."

"Come, then, and embrace me. So long away, and no tenderer welcome than this, my heart?"

She shrugged her white shoulders, and submitted to be drawn close, kissed, and caressed with ardor, by her husband or lover, asking a multitude of questions the while, and smoothing the petals of a crumpled camellia, quite unmoved by the tender names showered upon her, the almost fierce affection that glowed in her companion's face, and lavished itself in demonstrations of delight at regaining her.

"But tell me, darling, why do I find you at such work? Is it wise or needful?"

"It is pleasant, and I please myself now. I have almost lived here since you have been gone. At my aunt's in the country, they say, at the other place. The rooms there were dull; no one came, and at last I ran away. Once here, the old mania returned; I was mad for the gay life I love, and while I waited, I played at carnival."

"Were you anxious for my return? Did you miss me, *carina?*"

"That I did, for I needed you, my Juan," she answered, with a laugh. "Do you know we must have money? I am deciding which of my properties I will sell, though it breaks my heart to part with them. Mother Ursule will dispose of them, and as I shall never want them again, they must go."

"Why will you never need them again? There may be no course but that in the end."

"My husband will never let me dance, except for my own pleasure," she answered, dropping a half-humble, half-mocking curtsy, and glancing at him with a searching look.

Juan eyed her gloomily, as she waltzed away clinking her brass heels together, and humming a gay measure in time to her graceful steps. He shook his head, threw himself wearily into a chair, and leaned his forehead upon his hand. The girl watched him over her shoulder, paused, shook off her jaunty hat, dropped the red domino, and stealing toward him, perched herself upon his knee, peering under his hand with a captivating air of penitence, as she laid her arm about his neck and whispered in his ear, "I meant you, *mon ami,* and I will keep my promise by-and-by when all is as we would have it. Believe me, and be gay again, because I do not love you when you are grim and grave, like an Englishman."

"Do you ever love me, my—"

She stopped his mouth with a kiss, and answered, as she smoothed the crisp black curls off his forehead, "You shall see how well I love you, by-and-by."

"Ah, it is always 'by-and-by,' never now. I have a feeling that I never shall possess you, even if my long service ends this year. You are so cold, so treacherous, I have no faith in you, though I adore you, and shall until I die."

"Have I ever broken the promise made so long ago?"

"You dare not; you know the penalty of treason is death."

"Death for you, not for me. I am wiser now; I do not fear you, but I need you, and at last I think—I love you."

As she added the last words, the black frown that had darkened the man's face lifted suddenly, and the expression of intense devotion returned to make it beautiful. He turned that other face upward, scanned it with those magnificent eyes of his, now soft and tender, and answered with a sigh, "It would be death to me to find that after all I have suffered, done, and desired for you, there was no reward but falsehood and base ingratitude. It must not be so; and in that thought I will find patience to work on for one whom I try to love for your sake."

A momentary expression of infinite love and longing touched the girl's face, and filled her eyes with tenderness. But it passed, and settling herself more comfortably, she asked, "How have you prospered since you wrote? Well, I know, else I should have read it at the first glance."

"Beyond my hopes. We crossed together; we are friends already, and shall meet as such. It was an inspiration of yours, and has worked like a charm. Monsieur from the country has not yet appeared, has he?"

"He called when I was out. I did not regret it, for I feel safer when you are by, and it is as well to whet his appetite by absence."

"How is this to end? As we last planned?"

"Yes; but not yet. We must be sure, and that we only can be through himself. Leave it to me. I know him well, and he is willing to be led, I fancy. Now I shall feed you, for it occurs to me that you are fasting. See, I am ready for you."

She left him and ran to and fro, preparing a dainty little supper, but on her lips still lay a smile of conscious power, and in the eyes that followed her still lurked a glance of disquiet and distrust.

Mrs. Vane was driving in the park—not in her own carriage, for she kept none—but having won the hearts of several amiable dowagers, their equipages were always at her command. In one of the most elegant of these she was reclining, apparently unconscious of the many glances of curiosity and admiration fixed upon the lovely face enshrined in the little black tulle bonnet, with its frill of transparent lace to heighten her blond beauty.

Two gentlemen were entering the great gate as she passed by for another turn; one of them pronounced her name, and sprang forward. She recognized the voice, ordered the carriage to stop, and when Douglas came up, held out her hand to him, with a smile of welcome. He touched it, expressed his pleasure of meeting her, and added, seeing her glance at his companion, "Permit me to present my friend, M. Dupont, just from Paris, and happy in so soon meeting a countrywoman."

Duprès executed a superb bow, and made his compliments in his mother tongue.

Mrs. Vane listened with an air of pretty perplexity, and answered, in English, while she gave him her most beaming look, "Monsieur must pardon me that I have forgotten my native language so sadly that I dare not venture to use it in his presence. My youth was spent in Spain, and since then England or India has been my home; but to this dear country I must cordially welcome any friend of M. Douglas."

As she turned to Earl, and listened to his tidings of Lady Lennox, Duprès fixed a searching glance upon her. His keen eyes ran over her from head to foot, and nothing seemed to escape his scrutiny. Her figure was concealed by a great mantle of black velvet; her hair waved plainly away under her bonnet; the heavy folds of her dress flowed over her feet; and her delicately gloved hands lay half buried in the deep lace of her handkerchief. She was very pale, her eyes were languid, her lips sad even in smiling, and her voice had lost its lightsome ring. She looked older, graver, more pensive and dignified than when Douglas last saw her.

"You have been ill, I fear?" he said, regarding her with visible solicitude, while his friend looked down, yet marked every word she uttered.

"Yes, quite ill; I have been through so much in the last month that I can hardly help betraying it in my countenance. A heavy cold, with fever, has kept me a prisoner till these few days past, when I have driven out, being still too feeble to walk."

Earl was about to express his sorrow when Duprès cried, "Behold! It is he—the friend who so assuaged the tortures of that tempestuous passage. Let me reward him by a word from M. Douglas, and a smile from Madame. Is it permitted?"

Scarcely waiting for an assent, the vivacious gentleman darted forward and arrested the progress of a gentleman who was bending at the moment to adjust his stirrup. A few hasty words and emphatic gestures prepared the stranger for the interview, and with the courtesy of a Spaniard, he dismounted and advanced bareheaded, to be presented to Madame. It was Arguelles; and even Douglas was struck with his peculiar beauty, and the native pride that was but half veiled by the Southern softness of his manners. He spoke English well, but when Mrs. Vane addressed him in Spanish, he answered with a flash of pleasure that proved how grateful to him was the sound of his own melodious tongue.

Too well-bred to continue the conversation in a language which excluded the others, Mrs. Vane soon broke up the party by inviting Douglas and his friend to call upon her that evening, adding, with a glance toward the Spaniard, "It will gratify me to extend the hospitalities of an English home to Señor Arguelles, if he is a stranger here, and to enjoy again the familiar sound of the language which is dearer to me than my own."

Three hats were lifted, and three grateful gentlemen expressed their thanks with smiles of satisfaction; then the carriage rolled on, the *señor* galloped off, looking very like some knightly figure from a romance, and Douglas turned to his companion with an eager "Tell me, is it she?"

"No; Virginie would be but one-and-twenty, and this woman must be thirty if she is a day, ungallant that I am to say so of the charming creature."

"You have not seen her to advantage, Antoine. Wait till you meet her again tonight in full toilet, and then pronounce. She has been ill; even I perceive the great change this short time has wrought, for we parted only ten days ago," said Douglas, disappointed, yet not convinced.

"It is well; we will go; I will study her, and if it be that lovely devil, we will cast her out, and so avenge the past."

At nine o'clock, a cab left Douglas at the door of a handsome house in a West End square. A servant in livery admitted him, and passing up one flight of stairs, richly carpeted, softly lighted, and decorated with flowers, he entered a wide doorway, hung with curtains of blue damask, and found himself in a charming room. Directly opposite hung a portrait of Colonel Vane, a handsome, soldierly man, with such a smile upon his painted lips that his friend involuntarily smiled in answer and advanced as if to greet him.

"Would that he were here to welcome you."

The voice was at his side, and there stood Mrs. Vane. But not the woman whom he met in Lady Lennox's drawing room; that was a young and blooming creature, festally arrayed—this a pale, sad-eyed widow, in her weeds. Never, surely, had weeds been more becoming, for the black dress, in spite of its nunlike simplicity, had an air of elegance that many a balldress lacks, and the widow's cap was a mere froth of tulle, encircling the fair face, and concealing all the hair but two plain bands upon the forehead. Not an ornament was visible but a tiny pearl brooch which Douglas himself had given his friend long ago, and a wedding ring upon the hand that once had worn the opal also. She, too, was looking upward toward the picture, and for an instant a curious pause fell between them.

The apartment was an entire contrast to the gay and brilliant drawing rooms he had been accustomed to see. Softly lighted by the pale flame of antique lamps, the eye was relieved from the glare of gas, while the graceful blending of blue and silver, in furniture, hangings, and decorations, pleased one as a change from the more garish colors so much in vogue. A few rare pictures leaned from the walls; several statues stood cool and still in remote recesses; from the curtained entrance of another door was blown the odorous breath of flowers; and the rustle of leaves, the drip of falling water, betrayed the existence of a conservatory close at hand.

"No wonder you were glad to leave the country, for a home like this," said Douglas, as she paused.

"Yes, it is pleasant to be here; but I should tell you that it is not my own. My kind friend Lady Leigh is in Rome for the winter, and knowing that I was a homeless little creature, she begged me to stay here, and keep both servants and house in order till she came again. I was very grateful, for I dread the loneliness of lodgings, and having arranged matters to suit my taste, I shall nestle here till spring tempts me to the hills again."

She spoke quite simply, and seemed as thankful for kindness as a solitary child. Despite his suspicions, and all the causes for distrust—nay, even hatred, if his belief was true—Douglas could not resist the wish that she might be proved innocent, and somewhere find the safe home her youth and beauty needed. So potent was the fascination of her presence that when with her his doubts seemed unfounded, and so great was the confusion into which his mind was thrown by these conflicting impressions that his native composure quite deserted him at times.

It did so then, for, leaning nearer, as they sat together on the couch, he asked almost abruptly, "Why do I find you so changed, in all respects, that I scarcely recognize my friend just now?"

"You mean this?" and she touched her dress. "As you have honored me with the name of friend, I will speak frankly, and explain my seeming caprice. At the desire of Lady Lennox, I laid aside my weeds, and found that I could be a gay young girl again. But with that discovery came another, which made me regret the change, and resolve to return to my sad garb."

"You mean that you found that the change made you too beautiful for George's peace? Poor lad—I knew his secret, and now I understand your sacrifice," Earl said, as she paused, too delicate to betray her young lover, who had asked and been denied.

She colored beautifully, and sat silent; but Douglas was possessed by an irresistible desire to probe her heart as deeply as he dared, and quite unconscious that interest lent his voice and manner an unusual warmth, he asked, thinking only of poor George, "Was it not possible to spare both yourself and him? You see I use a friend's privilege to the utmost."

She still looked down, and the color deepened visibly in her smooth cheek as she replied, "It was not possible, nor will it ever be, for him."

"You have not vowed yourself to an eternal widowhood, I trust?"

She looked up suddenly, as if to rebuke the persistent questioner, but something in his eager face changed her own expression of displeasure into one of half-concealed confusion.

"No, it is so sweet to be beloved that I have not the courage to relinquish the hope of retasting the happiness so quickly snatched from me before."

Douglas rose suddenly, and paced down the room, as if attracted by a balmy gust that just then came floating in. But in truth he fled from the siren by his side, for despite the bitter past, the late loss, the present distrust, something softer than pity, warmer than regard, seemed creeping into his heart, and the sight of the beautiful blushing face made his own cheek burn with a glow such as his love for Diana had never kindled. Indignant at his own weakness, he paused halfway down the long room, wheeled about, and came back, saying, with his accustomed tone of command disguised by a touch of pity, "Come and do the honors of your little paradise. I am restless tonight, and the splash of that fountain has a soothing sound that tempts me to draw nearer."

She went with him, and standing by the fountain's brim talked tranquilly of many things, till the sound of voices caused them to look toward the drawing room. Two gentlemen were evidently coming to join them, and Earl said with a smile, "You have not asked why I came alone; yet your invitation included Arguelles and Dupont."

Again the blush rose to her cheek, and she answered hastily, as she advanced to meet her guests, "I forgot them, now I must atone for my rudeness."

Down the green vista came the gentlemen—the stout Frenchman tripping on before, the dark Spaniard walking behind, with a dignity of bearing that made his companion's gait more ludicrous by comparison. Compliments were exchanged, and then, as the guests expressed a desire to linger in the charming spot, Mrs. Vane led them on, doing the honors with her accustomed grace.

Busied in translating the names of remarkable plants into Spanish for Arguelles, they were somewhat in advance of the other pair; and after a sharp glance or two at Douglas, Duprès paused behind a young orange tree, saying, in a low whisper, "You are going fast, Earl. Finish this business soon, or it will be too late for anything but flight."

"No fear; but what can *I* do? I protest I never was so bewildered in my life. Help me, for heaven's sake, and do it at once!" replied Douglas, with a troubled and excited air.

"Chut! You English have no idea of *finesse;* you bungle sadly. See, now, how smoothly I will discover all I wish to know." Then aloud, as he moved on, "I assure you, *mon ami,* it is an orange, not a lemon tree. Madame shall decide the point, and award me yonder fine flower if I am right."

"Monsieur is correct, and here is the prize."

As she spoke, Mrs. Vane lifted her hand to break the flower which grew just above her. As she stretched her arm upward, her sleeve slipped back, and on her white wrist shone the wide bracelet once attached to the opal ring. As if annoyed by its exposure, she shook down her sleeve with a quick gesture, and before either gentleman could assist her, she stepped on a low seat, gathered the azalea, and turned to descend. Her motion was sudden, the seat frail; it broke as she turned, and she would have fallen, had not Arguelles sprung forward and caught her hands. She recovered herself instantly, and apologizing for her awkwardness, presented the flower with a playful speech. To Earl's great surprise, Duprès received it without his usual flow of compliments, and bowing, silently settled it in his buttonhole, with such a curious expression that his friend fancied he had made some unexpected discovery. He had—but not what Douglas imagined, as he lifted his brows inquiringly when Mrs. Vane and her escort walked on.

"Hush!" breathed Duprès in answer. "Ask her where Jitomar is, in some careless way."

"Why?" asked Earl, recollecting the man for the first time.

But his question received no reply, and the entrance of a servant with refreshments offered the desired pretext for the inquiry.

"Where is your handsome Jitomar? His Oriental face and costume would give the finishing touch to this Eastern garden of palms and lotus flowers," said Douglas, as he offered his hostess a glass of wine, when they paused at a rustic table by the fountain.

"Poor Jitomar—I have lost him!" she replied.

"Dead?" exclaimed Earl.

"Oh, no; and I should have said happy Jitomar, for he is on his way home to his own palms and lotus flowers. He dreaded another winter here so much that when a good opportunity offered for his return, I let him go, and have missed him sadly ever since—for he was a faithful servant to me."

"Let us drink the health of the good and faithful servant, and wish him a prosperous voyage to the torrid land where he belongs," cried Duprès, as he touched his glass to that of Arguelles, who looked somewhat bewildered both by the odd name and the new ceremony.

By some mishap, as Duprès turned to replace his glass upon the table, it slipped from his hand and fell into the fountain, with a splash that caused a little wave to break over the basin's edge, and wet Mrs. Vane's foot with an unexpected bath.

"Great heavens—what carelessness! A thousand pardons! Madame, permit me to repair the damage, although it is too great an honor for me, *maladroit* that I am," exclaimed the Frenchman, with a gesture of despair.

Mrs. Vane shook her dress and assured him that no harm was done; but nothing could prevent the distressed gentleman from going down upon his knees, and with his perfumed handkerchief removing several drops of water from the foot of his hostess—during which process he discovered that, being still an invalid, she wore quilted black silk boots, with down about the tops; also that though her foot was a very pretty one, it was by no means as small as that of Virginie Varens.

When this small stir was over, Mrs. Vane led the way back to the saloon, and here Douglas was more than ever mystified by Duprès's behavior. Entirely ignoring Madame's presence, he devoted himself to Arguelles, besetting him with questions regarding Spain, his own family, pursuits, and tastes; on all of which points the Spaniard satisfied him, and accepted his various invitations for the coming days, looking much at their fair hostess the while, who was much engrossed with Douglas, and seemed quite content.

Arguelles was the first to leave, and his departure broke up the party. As Earl and Duprès drove off together, the former exclaimed, in a fever of curiosity, "Are you satisfied?"

"Entirely."

"She is not Virginie, then?"

"On the contrary, she *is* Virginie, I suspect."

"You suspect? I thought you were entirely satisfied."

"On another point, I am. She baffles me somewhat, I confess, with her woman's art in dress. But I shall discover her yet, if you let me conduct the affair in my own way. I adore mystery; to fathom a secret, trace a lie, discover a disguise, is my delight. I should make a superb detective. Apropos to that, promise me that you will not call in the help of your blundering constabulary, police, or whatever you name them, until I give the word. They will destroy the éclat of the *dénouement,* and annoy me by their stupidity."

"I leave all to you, and regret that the absence of this Jitomar should complicate the affair. What deviltry is he engaged in now, do you think? Not traveling to India, of course, though she told it very charmingly."

His companion whispered three words in his ear.

Earl fell back and stared at him, exclaiming presently, "It is impossible!"

"Nothing is impossible to me," returned the other, with an air of conviction. "That point is clear to my mind; one other remains, and being more difficult, I must consider it. But have no fear; this brain of mine is fertile in inventions, and by morning will have been inspired with a design which will enchant you by its daring, its acuteness, its romance."

CHAPTER IX. MIDNIGHT

FOR A WEEK the three gentlemen haunted the house of the widow, and were much together elsewhere. Duprès was still enthusiastic in praise of his new-made friend, but Douglas was far less cordial, and merely courteous when they met. To outside observers this seemed but natural, for the world knew nothing of his relations to Diana, nor the sad secret that existed between himself and Mrs. Vane. And when it was apparent that the Spaniard was desperately in love with that lady, Douglas could not but look coldly upon him as a rival, for according to rumor the latter gentleman was also paying court to the bewitching widow. It was soon evident which was the favored lover, for despite the dark glances and jealous surveillance of Arguelles, Mrs. Vane betrayed, by unmistakable signs, that Douglas possessed a power over her which no other man had ever attained. It was impossible to conceal it, for when the great passion for the first time possessed her heart, all her art was powerless against this touch of nature, and no timid girl could have been more harassed by the alternations of hope and fear, and the effort to hide her passion.

Going to their usual rendezvous somewhat earlier than usual one evening, Duprès stopped a moment in an anteroom to exchange a word with Gabrielle, the coquettish maid, who was apt to be in the way when the Frenchman appeared. Douglas went on to the drawing room, expecting to find Mrs. Vane alone. The apartment was empty, but the murmur of voices was audible in the conservatory, and going to the curtained arch, he was about to lift the drapery that had fallen from its fastening, when through a little crevice in the middle he saw two figures that arrested him, and, in spite of certain honorable scruples, held him motionless where he stood.

Mrs. Vane and the Spaniard were beside the fountain; both looked excited. Arguelles talked vehemently; she listened with a hard, scornful expression, and made brief answers that seemed to chafe and goad him bitterly. Both spoke Spanish, and even if they had not, so low and rapid were their tones that nothing was audible but the varied murmur rising or falling as the voices alternated. From his gestures, the gentleman seemed by turns to reproach, entreat, command; the lady to recriminate, refuse, and defy. Once she evidently announced some determination that filled her companion with despair; then she laughed, and in a paroxysm of speechless wrath he broke from her, hurrying to the farthest limits of the room, as if unconscious whither he went, and marking with scattered leaves and flowers the passage of his reckless steps.

As he turned from her, Mrs. Vane dipped her hands in the basin and laid them on her forehead, as if to cool some fever of the brain, while such a weight of utter weariness came over her that in an instant ten years seemed to be added to her age. Her eyes roved restlessly to and fro, as if longing to discover some method of escape from the danger or the doubt that oppressed her.

A book from which Douglas had read to her lay on the rustic table at her side, and as her eye fell on it, all her face changed beautifully, hope, bloom, and youth returned, as she touched the volume with a lingering touch, and smiled a smile in which love and exultation blended. A rapid step announced the Spaniard's return; she caught her hand away, mused a moment, and when he came back to her, she spoke in a softer tone, while her eyes betrayed that now she pleaded for some boon, and did not plead in vain. Seizing both her hands in a grasp more firm than tender, Arguelles seemed to extort some promise from her with sternest aspect. She gave it reluctantly; he looked but half satisfied, even though she drew his tall head down and sealed her promise with a kiss; and when she bade him go, he left her with a gloomy air, and some dark purpose stamped upon his face.

So rapidly had this scene passed, so suddenly was it ended, that Douglas had barely time to draw a few paces back before the curtain was pushed aside and Arguelles stood in the arch. Unused to the dishonorable practices to which he had lent himself for the completion of a just work, Earl's face betrayed him.

The Spaniard saw that the late interview had not been without a witness, and forgetting that they had spoken in an unknown tongue, for a moment he looked perfectly livid with fear and fury. Some recollection suddenly seemed to reassure him, but the covert purpose just formed appeared to culminate in action, for, with ungovernable hatred flaming up in his eyes, he said, in a suppressed voice that scarcely parted his white lips, "Eavesdropper and spy! I spit upon you!" And advancing one step struck Douglas full in the face.

It had nearly been his last act, for, burning with scorn and detestation, Earl took him by the throat, and was about to execute swift retribution for both the old wrong and the new when Duprès came between them, whispering, as he wrenched Earl's arm away, "Hold! Remember where you are. Come away, señor, I am your friend in this affair. It shall be arranged. Douglas, remain here, I entreat you."

As he spoke, Duprès gave Earl a warning glance, and drew Arguelles swiftly from the house. Controlling a desperate desire to follow, Douglas remembered his promise to let his friend conduct the affair in his own way, and by a strong effort composed himself, though his cheek still tingled with the blow, and his blood burned within him. The whole encounter had passed noiselessly, and when after a brief pause Douglas entered the conservatory, Mrs. Vane still lingered by the fountain, unconscious of the scene which had just transpired. She turned to greet the newcomer with extended hand, and it was with difficulty that he restrained the rash impulse to strike it from him. The very effort to control this desire made the pressure of his own hand almost painful as he took that other, and the strong grasp sent a thrill of joy to Mrs. Vane's heart, as she smiled and glowed under his glance like a flower at the coming of the sun. The inward excitement, which it was impossible to wholly subdue, manifested itself in Earl's countenance and manner more plainly than he knew, and would have excited some of ill in his companion's mind had not love blinded her, and left none but prophecies of good. A little tremble of delight agitated her, and the eyes that once were so coldly bright and penetrating now were seldom lifted to the face that she had studied so carefully, not long ago. After the first greetings, she waited for him to speak, for words would not come at her will when with him; but he stood thoughtfully, dipping his hand into the fountain as she had done, and laying the wet palm against his cheek, lest its indignant color should betray the insult he had just received.

"Did you meet Señor Arguelles as you came in?" she asked presently, as the pause was unbroken.

"He passed me, and went out."

"You do not fancy him, I suspect."

"I confess it, Mrs. Vane."

"And why?"

"Need I tell *you?*"

The words escaped him involuntarily, and had she seen his face just then, her own would have blanched with fear. But she was looking down, and as he spoke the traitorous color rose to her forehead, though she ignored the betrayal by saying, with an accent of indifference, "He will not annoy you long. Tomorrow he fulfills some engagement with a friend in the country, and in the evening will take leave of me."

"He is about to return to Spain, then?"

"I believe so. I did not question him."

"You will not bid him adieu without regret?"

"With the greatest satisfaction, I assure you, for underneath that Spanish dignity of manner lurks fire, and I have no desire to be consumed." And the sigh of relief that accompanied her words was the most sincere expression of feeling that had escaped her for weeks.

Anxious to test his power to the utmost, Douglas pursued the subject, though it was evidently distasteful to her. Assuming an air of loverlike anxiety, he half timidly, half eagerly inquired, "Then when he comes again to say farewell, you will not consent to go with him to occupy the 'castle in Spain' which he has built up for himself during this short week?"

He thought to see some demonstration of pleasure at the jealous fear his words implied, but her color faded suddenly, and she shivered as if a chilly gust had blown over her, while she answered briefly, with a little gesture of the hand as she set the topic decidedly aside, "No, he will go alone."

There was a momentary pause, and in it something like pity knocked at the door of Earl's heart, for with all his faults he was a generous man, and as he saw this woman sitting there, so unconscious of impending danger, so changed and beautiful by one true sentiment, his purpose wavered, a warning word rose to his lips, and with an impetuous gesture he took her hand, and turned away with an abrupt "Pardon me—it is too soon—I will explain hereafter."

The entrance of a servant with coffee seemed to rouse him into sudden spirits and activity, for begging Mrs. Vane to sit and rest, he served her with assiduous care.

"Here is your own cup of violet and gold; you see I know your fancy even in trifles. Is it right? I took such pains to have it as you like it," he said, as he presented the cup with an air of tender solicitude.

"It does not matter, but one thing you have forgotten, I take no sugar," she answered, smiling as she tasted.

"I knew it, yet the line 'Sweets to the sweet' was running in my head, and so I unconsciously spoiled your draft. Let me retrieve the error?"

"By no means. I drink to you." And lifting the tiny cup to her lips, she emptied it with a look which proved that his words had already retrieved the error.

He received the cup with a peculiar smile, looked at his watch, and exclaimed, "It is late, and I should go, yet—"

"No, not yet; stay and finish the lines you began yesterday. I find less beauty in them when I read them to myself," she answered, detaining him.

Glad of an excuse to prolong his stay, Earl brought the book, and sitting near her, lent to the poem the sonorous music of his voice.

The last words came all too soon, and when Douglas rose, Mrs. Vane bade him good night with a dreamy softness in her eyes which caused a gleam of satisfaction to kindle in his own. As he passed through the anteroom, Gabrielle met him with a look of anxious though mute inquiry in her face. He answered it with a significant nod, a warning gesture, and she let him out, wearing an aspect of the deepest mystery.

Douglas hurried to his rooms, and there found Duprès with Major Mansfield, who had been put in possession of the secret, and the part he was expected to play in its unraveling.

"What in heaven's name did you mean by taking the wrong side of the quarrel, and forcing me to submit quietly to such an indignity?" demanded Earl, giving vent to the impatience which had only been curbed till now, that he might perform the portion of the plot allotted to him.

"Tell me first, have you succeeded?" said Duprès.

"I have."

"You are sure?"

"Beyond a doubt."

"It is well; I applaud your dexterity. Behold the major, he knows all, he is perfect in his role. Now hear yours. You will immediately write a challenge."

"It is impossible! Antoine, you are a daft to ask me to meet that man."

"Bah! I ask you to meet, but not to honor him by blowing his brains out. He is a dead shot, and thirsts for your blood, but look you, he will be disappointed. We might arrest him this instant, but he will confess nothing, and that clever creature will escape us. No, my little arrangement suits me better."

"Time flies, Duprès, and so perhaps may this crafty hind that you are about to snare," said the major, whose slow British wits were somewhat confused by the Frenchman's *finesse.*

"It is true; see then, my Earl. In order that our other little affair may come smoothly off without interference from our friend, I propose to return to the *señor,* whom I have lately left writing letters, and amuse myself by keeping him at home to receive your challenge, which the major will bring about twelve. Then we shall arrange the affair to take place at sunrise, in some secluded spot out of town. You will be back here by that time, you will agree to our plans, and present yourself at the appointed time, when the grand *dénouement* will take place with much *éclat.*"

"Am I not to know more?" asked Douglas.

"It would be well to leave all to me, for you will act your part better if you do not know the exact program, because you do not perform so well with Monsieur as with Madame. But if you must know, the major will tell you, while you wait for Hyde and the hour. I have seen him, he has no scruples; I have ensured his safety, and he will not fail us. Now the charming *billet* to the *señor,* and I go to my post."

Douglas wrote the challenge; Duprès departed in buoyant spirits; and while Earl waited for the stranger, Hyde, the major enlightened him upon the grand finale.

The city clocks were striking twelve as two men, masked and cloaked, passed up the steps of Mrs. Vane's house and entered noiselessly. No light beamed in the hall, but scarcely had they closed the door behind them when a glimmer shone from above, and at the stairhead appeared a woman beckoning. Up they stole, as if shod with velvet, and the woman flitted like a shadow before them, till they reached a door to the second story. Opening this, she motioned them to enter, and as they passed in, she glided up another flight, as if to stand guard over her sleeping fellow servants.

One of the men was tall and evidently young, the other a bent and withered little man, whose hands trembled slightly as he adjusted his mask, and peered about him. It was a large still room, lighted by a night lamp, burning behind its shade, richly furnished, and decorated with warm hues, that produced the effect of mingled snow and fire. A luxurious nest it seemed, and a fit inmate of it looked the beautiful woman asleep in the shadow of the crimson-curtained bed. One white arm pillowed her head; from the little cap that should have confined it flowed a mass of golden hair over neck and shoulders; the long lashes lay dark against her cheek; the breath slept upon her lips; and perfect unconsciousness lent its reposeful charm to both face and figure.

Noiselessly advancing, the taller man looked and listened for a moment, as if to assure himself that this deep slumber was not feigned; then he beckoned the other to bring the lamp. It flickered as the old man took it up, but he trimmed the wick, removed the shade, and a clear light shone across the room. Joining his companion, he too looked at the sleeping beauty, shook his gray head, and seemed to deplore some fact that marred the pretty picture in his sight.

"Is there no danger of her waking, sir?" he whispered, as the light fell on her face.

"It is impossible for an hour yet. The bracelet is on that wrist; we must move her, or you cannot reach it," returned the other; and with a gentle touch drew the left arm from underneath her head.

She sighed in her sleep, knit her brows, as if a dream disturbed her, and turning on her pillow, all the bright hair fell about her face, but could not hide the glitter of the chain about her neck. Drawing it forth, the taller man started, uttered an exclamation, dragged from his own bosom a duplicate of the miniature hanging from that chain, and compared the two with trembling intentness. Very like they were, those two young faces, handsome, frank and full of boyish health, courage, and blithesomeness. One might have been taken a year after the other, for the brow was bolder, the mouth graver, the eye more steadfast, but the same charm of expression appeared in both, making the ivory oval more attractive even to a stranger's eye than the costly setting, or the initial letters *A. D.* done in pearls upon the back. A small silver key hung on the chain the woman wore, and as if glad to tear his thoughts from some bitter reminiscence, the man detached this key, and glanced about the room, as if to discover what lock it would be.

His action seemed to remind the other of his own task, for setting down the lamp on the little table where lay a prayer book, a bell, and a rosary, he produced a case of delicate instruments and a bunch of tiny keys, and bending over the bracelet, examined the golden padlock that fastened it. While he carefully tried key after key upon that miniature lock, the chief of this mysterious inspection went to and fro with the silver key, attempting larger locks. Nowhere did it fit, till in passing the toilet table his foot brushed its draperies aside, disclosing a quaint foreign-looking casket of ebony and silver. Quick as thought it was drawn out and opened, for here the key did its work. In the upper tray lay the opal ring in its curiously thick setting, beside it a seal, rudely made from an impression in wax of his own iron ring, and a paper bearing its stamp. The marriage record was in hand, and he longed to keep or destroy it, but restrained the impulse; and lifting the tray, found below two or three relics of his friend Vane, and some childish toys, soiled and broken, but precious still.

"A child! Good God! What have I done?" he said to himself, as the lid fell from his hand.

"Hush, come and look, it is off," whispered the old man, and hastily restoring all things to their former order, the other relocked and replaced the casket, and obeyed the call.

For a moment a mysterious and striking picture might have been seen in that quiet room. Under the crimson canopy lay the fair figure of the sleeping woman, her face half hidden by the golden shadow of her hair, her white arm laid out on the warm-hued coverlet, and bending over it, the two masked men, one holding the lamp nearer, the other pointing to something just above the delicate wrist, now freed from the bracelet, which lay open beside it. Two distinctly traced letters were seen, V. V., and underneath a tiny true-lover's knot, in the same dark lines.

The man who held the lamp examined the brand with minutest care, then making a gesture of satisfaction, he said, "It is enough, I am sure now. Put on the bracelet, and come away; there is nothing more to be done tonight."

The old man skillfully replaced the hand, while the other put back locket and key, placed the lamp where they found it; and with a last look at the sleeper, whose unconscious helplessness appealed to them for mercy, both stole away as noiselessly as they had come. The woman reappeared the instant they left the room, lighted them to the hall door, received some reward that glittered as it passed from hand to hand, and made all fast behind them, pausing a moment in a listening attitude, till the distant roll of a carriage assured her that the maskers were safely gone.

CHAPTER X. IN THE SNARE

THE FIRST RAYS of the sun fell on a group of five men, standing together on a waste bit of ground in the environs of London. Major Mansfield and Duprès were busily loading pistols, marking off the distance, and conferring together with a great display of interest. Douglas conversed tranquilly with the surgeon in attendance, a quiet, unassuming man, who stood with his hand in his pocket, as if ready to produce his case of instruments at a moment's notice. The Spaniard was alone, and a curious change seemed to have passed over him. The stately calmness of his demeanor was gone, and he paced to and fro with restless steps, like a panther in his cage. A look of almost savage hatred lowered on his swarthy face; desperation and despair alternately glowed and gloomed in his fierce eye; and the whole man wore a look of one who after long restraint yields himself utterly to the dominion of some passion, dauntless and indomitable as death.

Once he paused, drew from his pocket an ill-spelled, rudely written letter, which had been put into his hand by a countryman as he left his hotel, reread the few lines it contained, and thrust it back into his bosom, muttering, "All things favor me; this was the last tie that bound her; now we must stand or fall together."

"Señor, we are prepared," called Duprès, advancing, pistol in hand, to place his principal, adding, as Arguelles dropped hat and cloak, "our custom may be different from yours, but give heed, and at the word 'Three,' fire."

"I comprehend, monsieur," and a dark smile passed across the Spaniard's face as he took his place and stretched his hand to receive the weapon.

But Duprès drew back a step—and with a sharp metallic click, around that extended wrist snapped a handcuff. A glance showed Arguelles that he was lost, for on his right stood the counterfeit surgeon, with the well-known badge now visible on his blue coat, behind him Major Mansfield, armed, before him Douglas, guarding the nearest outlet of escape, and on his left Duprès, radiant with satisfaction, exclaiming, as he bowed with grace, "A thousand pardons, Monsieur Victor Varens, but this little ruse was inevitable."

Quick as a flash that freed left hand snatched the pistol from Duprès, aimed it at Douglas, and it would have accomplished its work had not the Frenchman struck up the weapon. But the ball was sped, and as the pistol turned in his hand, the bullet lodged in Victor's breast, sparing him the fate he dreaded more than death. In an instant all trace of passion vanished, and with a melancholy dignity that nothing could destroy, he offered his hand to receive the fetter, saying calmly, while his lips whitened, and a red stain dyed the linen on his breast, "I am tired of my life; take it."

They laid him down, for as he spoke, consciousness ebbed away. A glance assured the major that the wound was mortal, and carefully conveying the senseless body to the nearest house, Douglas and the detective remained to tend and guard the prisoner, while the other gentlemen posted to town to bring a genuine surgeon and necessary help, hoping to keep life in the man till his confession had been made.

At nightfall, Mrs. Vane, or Virginie, as we may now call her, grew anxious for the return of Victor, who was to bring her tidings of the child, because she dared not visit him just now herself.

When dressed for the evening, she dismissed Gabrielle, opened the antique casket, and put on the opal ring, carefully attaching the little chain that fastened it securely to her bracelet, for the ring was too large for the delicate hand that wore it. Then with steady feet she went down to the drawing room to meet her lover and her victim.

But some reproachful memory seemed to start up and haunt the present with a vision of the past. She passed her hand across her eyes, as if she saw again the little room, where in the gray dawn she had left her husband lying dead, and she sank into a seat, groaning half aloud, "Oh, if I could forget!"

A bell rang from below, but she did not hear it; steps came through the drawing room, yet she did not heed them; and Douglas stood before her, but she did not see him till he spoke. So great was her surprise, that with all her power of dissimulation she would have found difficulty in concealing it, had not the pale gravity of the newcomer's face afforded a pretext for alarm.

"You startled me at first, and now you look as if you brought ill news," she said, with a vain effort to assume her usual gaiety.

"I do" was the brief reply.

"The señor? Is he with you? I am waiting for him."

"Wait no longer, he will never come."

"Where is he?"

"Quiet in his shroud."

He thought to see her shrink and pale before the blow, but she did neither; she grasped his arm, searched his face, and whispered, with a look of relief, not terror, in her own, "You have killed him?"

"No, his blood is not upon my head; he killed himself."

She covered up her face, and from behind her hands he heard her murmur, "Thank God, he did not come! I am spared that."

While he pondered over the words, vainly trying to comprehend them, she recovered herself, and turning to him said, quite steadily though very pale, "This is awfully sudden; tell me how it came to pass. I am not afraid to hear."

"I will tell you, for you have a right to know. Sit, Mrs. Vane; it is a long tale, and one that will try your courage to the utmost.

"Six years ago I went abroad to meet my cousin Allan," Douglas began, speaking slowly, almost sternly. "He was my senior by a year, but we so closely resembled each other that we were often taken for twin brothers. Alike in person, character, temper, and tastes, we were never so happy as when together, and we loved one another as tenderly as women love. For nearly a year we roamed east and west, then our holiday was over, for we had promised to return. One month more remained; I desired to revisit Switzerland, Allan to remain in Paris, so we parted for a time, each to our own pleasures, appointing to meet on a certain day at a certain place. I never saw him again, for when I reached the spot where he should have met me, I found only a letter, saying that he had been called from Paris suddenly, but that I should receive further intelligence before many days. I waited, but not long. Visiting the Morgue that very week, I found my poor Allan waiting for me there. His body had been taken from the river, and the deep wound in his breast showed that foul play was at the bottom of the mystery. Night and day I labored to clear up the mystery, but labored secretly, lest publicity should warn the culprits, or bring dishonor upon our name, for I soon found that Allan had led a wild life in my absence, and I feared to make some worse discoveries than a young man's follies. I did so; for it appeared that he had been captivated by a singularly beautiful girl, a *danseuse,* had privately married her, and both had disappeared with a young cousin of her own. Her apartments were searched, but all her possessions had been removed, and nothing remained but a plausible letter, which would have turned suspicion from the girl to the cousin, had not the marriage been discovered, and in her room two witnesses against them. The handle of a stiletto, half consumed in the ashes, which fitted the broken blade entangled in the dead man's clothes, and, hidden by the hangings of the bed, a woman's slipper, with a bloodstain on the sole. Ah, you may well shudder, Mrs. Vane; it is an awful tale."

"Horrible! Why tell it?" she asked, pressing her hand upon her eyes, as if to shut out some image too terrible to look upon.

"Because it concerns our friend Arguelles, and explains his death," replied Earl, in the same slow stern voice. She did not look up, but he saw that she listened breathlessly, and grew paler still behind her hand.

"Nothing more was discovered then. My cousin's body was sent home, and none but our two families ever knew the truth. It was believed by the world that he died suddenly of an affection of the heart—poor lad! it was the bitter truth—and whatever rumors were about regarding his death, and the change it wrought in me, were speedily silenced at the time, and have since died away. Over the dead body of my dearest friend, I vowed a solemn vow to find his murderer and avenge his death. I have done both."

"Where? How?"

Her hand dropped, and she looked at him with a face that was positively awful in its unnatural calmness.

"Arguelles was Victor Varens. I suspected, watched, ensnared him, and would have let the law avenge Allan's death, but the murderer escaped by his own hand."

"Well for him it was so. May his sins be forgiven. Now let us go elsewhere, and forget this dark story and its darker end."

She rose as she spoke, and a load seemed lifted off her heart; but it fell again, as Douglas stretched his hand to detain her, saying, "Stay, the end is not yet told. You forget the girl."

"She was innocent—why should she suffer?" returned the other, still standing as if defying both fear and fate.

"She was *not* innocent—for she lured that generous boy to marry her, because she coveted his rank and fortune, not his heart, and, when he lay dead, left him to the mercies of wind and wave, while she fled away to save herself. But that cruel cowardice availed her nothing, for though I have watched and waited long, at length I have found her, and at this moment her life lies in my hand—for you and Virginie are one!"

Like a hunted creature driven to bay, she turned on him with an air of desperate audacity, saying haughtily, "Prove it!"

"I will."

For a moment they looked at one another. In his face she saw pitiless resolve; in hers he read passionate defiance.

"Sit down, Virginie, and hear the story through. Escape is impossible—the house is guarded, Duprès waits in yonder room, and Victor can no longer help you with quick wit or daring hand. Submit quietly, and do not force me to forget that you are my cousin's—wife."

She obeyed him, and as the last words fell from his lips a new hope sprang up within her, the danger seemed less imminent, and she took heart again, remembering the child, who might yet plead for her, if her own eloquence should fail.

"You ask me to prove that fact, and evidently doubt my power to do it; but well as you have laid your plots, carefully as you have erased all traces of your former self, and skillfully as you have played your new part, the truth has come to light, and through many winding ways I have followed you, till my labors end here. When you fled from Paris, Victor, whose mother was a Spaniard, took you to Spain, and there, among his kindred, your boy was born."

"Do you know that, too?" she cried, lost in wonder at the quiet statement of what she believed to be known only to herself, her dead cousin, and those far-distant kindred who had succored her in her need.

"I know everything," Earl answered, with an expression that made her quail; then a daring spirit rose up in her, as she remembered more than one secret, which she now felt to be hers alone.

"Not everything, my cousin; you are keen and subtle, but I excel you, though you win this victory, it seems."

So cool, so calm she seemed, so beautifully audacious she looked, that Earl could only resent the bold speech with a glance, and proceed to prove the truth of his second assertion with the first.

"You suffered the sharpest poverty, but Victor respected your helplessness, forgave your treachery, supplied your wants as far as possible, and when all other means failed, left you there, while he went to earn bread for you and your boy. Virginie, I never can forgive him my cousin's death, but for his faithful, long-suffering devotion to you, I honor him, sinner though he was."

She shrugged her shoulders, with an air of indifference or displeasure, took off the widow's cap, no longer needed for a disguise, and letting loose the cloud of curls that seemed to cluster round her charming face, she lay back in her chair with all her former graceful ease, saying, as she fixed her lustrous eyes upon the man she meant to conquer yet, "I let him love me, and he was content. What more could I do, for I never loved *him?*"

"Better for him that you did not, and better for poor Allan that he never lived to know it was impossible for you to love."

Earl spoke bitterly, but Virginie bent her head till her face was hidden, as she murmured, "Ah, if it were impossible, this hour would be less terrible, the future far less dark."

He heard the soft lament, divined its meaning, but abruptly continued his story, as if he ignored the sorrowful fact which made her punishment heavier from his hand than from any other.

"While Victor was away, you wearied of waiting, you longed for the old life of gaiety and excitement, and, hoping to free yourself from him, you stole away, and for a year were lost to him. Your plan was to reach France, and under another name dance yourself into some other man's heart and home, making him your shield against all danger. You did reach France, but weary, ill, poor, and burdened with the child, you failed to find help, till some evil fortune threw Vane in your way. You had heard of him from Allan, knew his chivalrous nature, his passion for relieving pain or sorrow, at any cost to himself, and you appealed to him for charity. A piteous story of a cruel husband, desertion, suffering, and destitution you told him; he believed it, and being on the point of sailing for India, offered you the place of companion to a lady sailing with him. Your tale was plausible, your youth made it pathetic, your beauty lent it power, and the skill with which you played the part of a sad gentlewoman won all hearts, and served your end successfully. Vane loved you, wished to marry you, and would have done so had not death prevented. He died suddenly; you were with him, and though his last act was to make generous provision for you and the boy, some devil prompted you to proclaim yourself his wife, as soon as he was past denying it. His love for you was well-known among those with whom you lived, and your statement was believed."

"You are a magician," she said suddenly. "I have thought so before; now I am sure of it, for you must have transported yourself to India, to make these discoveries."

"No—India came to me in the person of a Hindoo, and from him I learned these facts," replied Douglas, slow to tell her of Victor's perfidy, lest he should put her on her guard, and perhaps lose some revelation which in her ignorance she might make. Fresh bewilderment seemed to fall upon her, and with intensest interest she listened, as that ruthless voice went on.

"Your plan was this: From Vane you had learned much of Allan's family, and the old desire to be 'my lady' returned more strongly than before. Once in England, you hoped to make your way as Colonel Vane's widow, and if no safe, sure opportunity appeared of claiming your boy's right, you resolved to gain your end by wooing and winning another Douglas. You were on the point of starting with poor Vane's fortune in your power (for he left no will, and you were prepared to produce forged papers, if your possession was questioned in England), when Victor found you. He had traced you with the instinct of a faithful dog, though his heart was nearly broken by your cruel desertion. You saw that he could not serve you; you appeased his anger and silenced his reproaches by renewed promises to be his when the boy was acknowledged, if he would aid you in that project. At the risk of his life, this devoted slave consented, and disguised as an Indian servant came with you to England. On the way, you met and won the good graces of the Countess Camareena; she introduced you to the London world, and you began your career as a lady under the best auspices. Money, beauty, art served you well, and as an unfortunate descendant of the noble house of Montmorenci, you were received by those who would have shrunk from you as you once did from the lock of hair of the plebeian French *danseuse,* found in Allan's bosom."

"I *am* noble," she cried, with an air that proved it, "for though my mother was a peasant, my father was a prince, and better blood than that of the Montmorencis flows in my veins."

He only answered with a slight bow, which might be intended as a mocking obeisance in honor of her questionable nobility, or a grave dismissal of the topic.

"From this point the tale is unavoidably egotistical," he said, "for through Lady Lennox you heard of me, learned that I was the next heir to the title, and began at once to weave the web in which I was to be caught. You easily understood what was the mystery of my life, as it was called among the gossips, and that knowledge was a weapon in your hands, which you did not fail to use. You saw that Diana loved me, soon learned my passion for her, and set yourself to separate us, without one thought of the anguish it would bring us, one fear of the consequences of such wrong to yourself. You bade her ask of me a confession that I could not make, having given my word to Allan's mother that her son's name should not be tarnished by the betrayal of the rash act that cost his life. That parted us; then you told her a tale of skillfully mingled truth and falsehood, showed her the marriage record on which a name and date appeared to convict me, took her to the boy whose likeness to his father, and therefore to myself, completed the cruel deception, and drove that high-hearted girl to madness and to death."

"I did not kill her! On my soul, I never meant it! I was terror-stricken when we missed her, and knew no peace or rest till she was found. Of that deed I am innocent—I swear it to you on my knees."

The haunting horror of that night seemed again to overwhelm her; she fell down upon her knees before him, enforcing her denial with clasped hands, imploring eyes, and trembling voice. But Douglas drew back with a gesture of repugnance that wounded her more deeply than his sharpest word, and from that moment all traces of compassion vanished from his countenance, which wore the relentless aspect of a judge who resolves within himself no longer to temper justice with mercy.

"Stand up," he said. "I will listen to no appeal, believe no oath, let no touch of pity soften my heart, for your treachery, your craft, your sin deserve nothing but the heavy retribution you have brought upon yourself. Diana's death lies at your door, as much as if you had stabbed her with the same dagger that took Allan's life. It may yet be proved that you beguiled her to that fatal pool, for you were seen there, going to remove all traces of her, perhaps. But in your hasty flight you left traces of yourself behind you, as you sprang away with an agility that first suggested to me the suspicion of Virginie's presence. I tried your slipper to the footprint, and it fitted too exactly to leave me in much doubt of the truth of my wild conjecture. I had never seen you. Antoine Duprès knew both Victor and yourself. I sent for him, but before the letter went, Jitomar, your spy, read the address, feared that some peril menaced you both, and took counsel with you how to delude the newcomer, if any secret purpose lurked behind our seeming friendliness. You devised a scheme that would have baffled us, had not accident betrayed Victor. In the guise of Arguelles he met Duprès in Paris, returned with him, and played his part so well that the Frenchman was entirely deceived, never dreaming of being sought by the very man who would most desire to shun him. You, too, disguised yourself, with an art that staggered my own senses, and perplexed Duprès, for our masculine eye could not fathom the artifices of costume, cosmetics, and consummate acting. We feared to alarm you by any open step, and resolved to oppose craft to craft, treachery to treachery. Duprès revels in such intricate affairs, and I yielded, against my will, till the charm of success drew me on with increasing eagerness and spirit. The day we first met here, in gathering a flower you would have fallen, had not the Spaniard sprung forward to save you; that involuntary act betrayed him, for the momentary attitude he assumed recalled to Duprès the memory of a certain pose which the dancer Victor often assumed. It was too peculiar to be accidental, too striking to be easily forgotten, and the entire unconsciousness of its actor was a proof that it was so familiar as to be quite natural. From that instant Duprès devoted himself to the Spaniard; this first genuine delusion put Victor off his guard with Antoine; and Antoine's feigned friendship was so adroitly assumed that no suspicion woke in Victor's mind till the moment when, instead of offering him a weapon with which to take my life, he took him prisoner."

"He is not dead, then? You lie to me; you drive me wild with your horrible recitals of the past, and force me to confess against my will. Who told you these things? The dead alone could tell you what passed between Diana and myself."

Still on the ground, as if forgetful of everything but the bewilderment of seeing plot after plot unfolded before her, she had looked up and listened with dilated eyes, lips apart, and both hands holding back the locks that could no longer hide her from his piercing glance. As she spoke, she paled and trembled with a sudden fear that clutched her heart, that Diana was not dead, for even now she clung to her love with a desperate hope that it might save her.

Calm and cold as a man of marble, Douglas looked down upon her, so beautiful in all her abasement, and answered steadily, "You forget Victor. To him all your acts, words, and many of your secret thoughts were told. Did you think his love would endure forever, his patience never tire, his outraged heart never rebel, his wild spirit never turn and rend you? All day I have sat beside him, listening to his painful confessions, painfully but truthfully made, and with his last breath he cursed you as the cause of a wasted life, and ignominious death. Virginie, this night your long punishment begins, and that curse is a part of it."

"Oh, no, no! You will have mercy, remembering how young, how friendless I am? For Allan's sake you will pity me; for his boy's sake you will save me; for your own sake you will hide me from the world's contempt?"

"What mercy did you show poor Diana? What love for Allan? What penitence for your child's sake? What pity for my grief? I tell you, if a word would save you, my lips should not utter it!"

He spoke passionately now, and passionately she replied, clinging to him, though he strove to tear his hands away.

"You have heard Victor's confession, now hear mine. I *have* longed to repent; I did hope to make my life better, for my baby's sake; and oh, I did pity you, till my cold heart softened and grew warm. I should have given up my purpose, repaid Victor's fidelity, and gone away to grow an honest, happy, humble woman, if I had not loved *you*. That made me blind, when I should have been more keen-sighted than ever; that kept me here to be deceived, betrayed, and that should save me now."

"It will not; and the knowledge that I detest and despise you is to add bitterness to your threefold punishment; the memory of Allan, Victor, and Diana is another part of it; and here is the heaviest blow which heaven inflicts as a retribution that will come home to you."

As he spoke, Douglas held to her a crumpled paper, stained with a red stain, and torn with the passage of a bullet that ended Victor's life. She knew the writing, sprang up to seize it, read the few lines, and when the paper fluttered to the ground, the white anguish of her face betrayed that the last blow *had* crushed her as no other could have done. She dropped into a seat, with the wail of tearless woe that breaks from a bereaved mother's heart as she looks on the dead face of the child who has been her idol, and finds no loving answer.

"My baby gone—and I not there to say good-bye! Oh, my darling, I could have borne anything but this!"

So utterly broken did she seem, so wild and woeful did she look, that Douglas had not the heart to add another pang to her sharp grief by any word of explanation or compassion. Silently he poured out a glass of wine and placed it nearer, then resumed his seat and waited till she spoke. Soon she lifted up her head, and showed him the swift and subtle blight that an hour had brought upon her. Life, light, and beauty seemed to have passed away, and a pale shadow of her former self alone remained. Some hope or some resolve had brought her an unnatural calmness, for her eyes were tearless, her face expressionless, her voice tranquil, as if she had done with life, and neither pain nor passion could afflict her now.

"What next?" she said, and laid her hand upon the glass, but did not lift it to her lips, as if the former were too tremulous, or the latter incapable of receiving the draft.

"Only this," he answered, with a touch of pity in his voice. "I will not have my name handed from mouth to mouth, in connection with an infamous history like this. For Allan's sake, and for Diana's, I shall keep it secret, and take your punishment into my hands. Victor I leave to a wiser judge than any human one; the innocent child is safe from shame and sorrow; but you must atone for the past with the loss of liberty and your whole future. It is a more merciful penalty than the law would exact, were the truth known, for you are spared public contempt, allowed time for repentance, and deprived of nothing but the liberty which you have so cruelly abused."

"I thank you. Where is my prison to be?"

She took the glass into her hand, yet still held it suspended, as she waited for his answer, with an aspect of stony immobility which troubled him.

"Far away in Scotland I own a gray old tower, all that now remains of an ancient stronghold. It is built on the barren rock, where it stands like a solitary eagle's eyrie, with no life near it but the sound of the wind, the scream of the gulls, the roll of the sea that foams about it. There with my faithful old servants you shall live, cut off from all the world, but not from God, and when death comes to you, may it find you ready and glad to go, a humble penitent, more fit to meet your little child than now."

A long slow tremor shook her from head to foot, as word by word her merciful yet miserable doom was pronounced, leaving no hope, no help but the submission and repentance which it was not in her nature to give. For a moment she bowed her head, while her pale lips moved, and her hands, folded above the glass, were seen to tremble as if some fear mingled even in her prayers. Then she sat erect, and fixing on him a glance in which love, despair, and defiance mingled, she said, with all her former pride and spirit, as she slowly drank the wine, "Death cannot come too soon; I go to meet it."

Her look, her tone, awed Douglas, and for a moment he regarded her in silence, as she sat there, leaning her bright head against the dark velvet of the cushioned chair. Her eyes were on him still brilliant and brave, in spite of all that had just passed; a disdainful smile curved her lips, and one fair arm lay half extended on the table, as it fell when she put the glass away. On this arm the bracelet shone; he pointed to it, saying, with a meaning glance, "I know that secret, as I know all the rest."

"Not all; there is one more you have not discovered—yet."

She spoke very slowly, and her lips seemed to move reluctantly, while a strange pallor fell on her face, and the fire began to die out of her eyes, leaving them dim, but tender.

"You mean the mystery of the iron ring; but I learned that last night, when, with an expert companion, I entered your room, where you lay buried in the deep sleep produced by the drugged coffee which I gave you. I saw my portrait on your neck, as I wear Allan's, ever since we gave them to each other, long ago, and beside the miniature, the silver key that opened your quaint treasure casket. I found the wax impression of my signet, taken, doubtless, on the night when, as a ghost, you haunted my room; I found the marriage record, stamped with that counterfeit seal, to impose upon Diana; I found relics of Vane, and of your child; and when Hyde called me, I saw and examined the two letters on your arm, which he had uncovered by removing the bracelet from it."

He paused there, expecting some demonstration. None appeared; she leaned and listened, with the same utter stillness of face and figure, the same fixed look and deathly pallor. He thought her faint and spent with the excitement of the hour, and hastened to close the interview, which had been so full of contending emotions to them both.

"Go now, and rest," he said. "I shall make all necessary arrangements here, all proper explanations to Lady Leigh. Gabrielle will prepare for your departure in the morning; but let me warn you not to attempt to bribe her, or to deceive me by any new ruse, for now escape is impossible."

"I have escaped!"

The words were scarcely audible, but a glance of exultation flashed from her eyes, then faded, and the white lids fell, as if sleep weighed them down. A slight motion of the nerveless hand that lay upon the table drew Earl's attention, and with a single look those last words were explained. The opal ring was turned inward on her finger, and some unsuspected spring had been touched when she laid her hands together; for now in the deep setting appeared a tiny cavity, which had evidently contained some deadly poison. The quick and painless death that was to have been Victor's had fallen to herself, and, unable to endure the fate prepared for her, she had escaped, when the net seemed most securely drawn about her. Horror-stricken, Douglas called for help; but all human aid was useless, and nothing of the fair, false Virginie remained but a beautiful, pale image of repose.

❧ The Fate of the Forrests

PART I

A GROUP OF FOUR, two ladies and two gentlemen, leaned or lounged together in the soft brilliance of mingled moonlight and lamplight, that filled the luxurious room. Through the open windows came balmy gusts of ocean air, up from below rose the murmurous plash of waves, breaking on a quiet shore, and frequent bursts of music lent another charm to place and hour. A pause in the gay conversation was broken by the younger lady's vivacious voice:

"Now if the day of witches and wizards, astrologers and fortunetellers was not over, how I should enjoy looking into a magic mirror, having my horoscope cast, or hearing my fate read by a charming black-eyed gipsy."

"The age of enchantment is not yet past, as all who are permitted to enter this magic circle confess; and one need not go far for 'a charming black-eyed gipsy' to decide one's destiny."

And with a half-serious, half-playful gesture the gentleman offered his hand to the fair-faced girl, who shook her head and answered, smilingly:

"No, I'll not tell your fortune, Captain Hay; and all your compliments cannot comfort me for the loss of the delightful *diablerie* I love to read about and long to experience. Modern gipsies are commonplace. I want a genuine Cagliostro, supernaturally elegant, gifted and mysterious. I wish the fable of his eternal youth were true, so that he might visit us, for where would he find a fitter company? You gentlemen are perfect sceptics, and I am a firm believer, while Ursula would inspire the dullest wizard, because she looks like one born to live a romance."

She did indeed. The beautiful woman, sitting where the light showered down upon her, till every charm seemed doubled. The freshest bloom of early womanhood glowed in a face both sweet and spirited, eloquent eyes shone lustrous and large, the lips smiled as if blissful visions fed the fancy, and above the white forehead dark, abundant hair made a graceful crown for a head which bore itself with a certain gentle pride, as if the power of beauty, grace and intellect lent an unconscious queenliness to their possessor. In the personal atmosphere of strength, brilliancy and tenderness that surrounded her, an acute observer would detect the presence of a daring spirit, a rich nature, a deep heart; and, looking closer, might also discover, in the curves of that sensitive mouth, the depths of those thoughtful eyes, traces of some hidden care, some haunting memory, or, perhaps, only that vague yet melancholy prescience which often marks those fore-doomed to tragic lives. As her companions chatted this fleeting expression touched her face like a passing shadow, and the gentleman who had not yet spoken leaned nearer, as if eager to catch that evanescent gloom. She met his wistful glance with one of perfect serenity, saying, as an enchanting smile broke over her whole face:

"Yes, my life has been a romance thus far; may it have a happy ending. Evan, you were born in a land of charms and spells, can you not play the part of a Hindoo conjuror, and satisfy Kate's longing?"

"I can only play the part of a Hindoo devotee, and exhaust myself with strivings after the unattainable, like this poor little fireworshipper," replied the young man, watching, with suspicious interest, a moth circling round the globe of light above his head, as if he dared not look at the fair speaker, lest his traitorous eyes should say too much.

"You are both sadly unromantic and ungallant men not to make an effort in our favor," exclaimed the lively lady. "I am in just the mood for a ghostly tale, a scene of mystery, a startling revelation, and where shall I look for an obliging magician to gratify me?"

"Here!"

The voice, though scarcely lifted above a whisper, startled the group as much as if a spirit spoke, and all eyes were turned towards the window, where white draperies were swaying in the wind. No uncanny apparition appeared behind the tentlike aperture, but the composed figure of a small, fragile-looking man, reclining in a lounging-chair. Nothing could have been more unimpressive at first glance, but at a second the eye was arrested, the attention roused, for an indefinable influence held one captive against one's will. Beardless, thin lipped, sharply featured and colorless as ivory was the face. A few locks of blonde hair streaked the forehead, and underneath it shone the controlling feature of this singular countenance. The eyes, that should have been a steely blue to match the fair surroundings, were of the intensest black, varying in expression with a startling rapidity, unless mastered by an art stronger than nature; by turns stealthily soft, keenly piercing, fiercely fiery or utterly expressionless, these mysterious eyes both attracted and repelled, with a subtle magnetism which few wills could resist, and which gave to this otherwise insignificant man a weird charm, which native grace and the possession of rare accomplishments made alluring, even to those who understood the fateful laws of temperament and race.

Languidly leaning in his luxurious chair, while one pale hand gathered back the curtain from before him, the new comer eyed the group with a swift glance, which in an instant had caught the meaning of each face and transferred it to the keeping of a memory which nothing could escape. Annoyance was the record set down against Ursula Forrest's name; mingled joy and shame against the other lady's; for, with the perfect breeding which was one of the man's chief attractions, he gave the precedence to women even in this rapid mental process. Aversion was emphatically marked against Evan Forrest's name, simple amusement fell to his companion's share. Captain Hay was the first to break the sudden silence which followed that one softly spoken word:

"Beg pardon, but upon my life I forgot you, Stähl. I thought you went half an hour ago, in your usual noiseless style, for who would dream of your choosing to lounge in the strong draught of a seabreeze?"

"It is I who should beg pardon for forgetting myself in such society, and indulging in the reveries that will come unbidden to such poor shadows as I."

The voice that answered, though low-toned, was singularly persuasive, and the words were uttered with an expression more engaging than a smile.

"Magician, you bade me look to you. I take you at your word. I dare you to show your skill, and prove that yours is no empty boast," said Kate Heath, with evident satisfaction at the offer and interest in its maker.

Rising slowly, Felix Stähl advanced towards her, and, despite his want of stature and vigor, which are the manliest attributes of manhood, no one felt the lack of them, because an instantaneous impression of vitality and power was made in defiance of external seeming. With both hands loosely folded behind him, he paused before Miss Heath, asking, tranquilly:

"Which wish shall I grant? Will you permit me to read your palm? Shall I show you the image of your lover in yonder glass? or shall I whisper in your ear the most secret hope, fear or regret, which you cherish? Honor me by choosing, and any one of these feats I will perform."

Kate stole a covert glance at the tall mirror, saw that it reflected no figure but that of the speaker, and with an irrepressible smile she snatched her eyes away, content, saying hastily:

"As the hardest feat of the three, you shall tell me what I most ardently desire, if the rest will submit to a like test. Can you read their hearts as well as mine?"

His eye went slowly round the little circle, and from each face the smile faded, as that searching gaze explored it. Constrained by its fascination, more than by curiosity or inclination, each person bowed their acquiescence to Kate's desire, and as Stähl's eye came back to her, he answered briefly, like one well assured of his own power:

"I can read their hearts. Shall I begin with you?"

For a moment she fluttered like a bird caught in a fowler's net, then with an effort composed both attitude and aspect, and looked up half-proudly, half-pleadingly, into the colorless countenance that bent till the lips were at her ear. Only three words, and the observers saw the conscious blood flush scarlet to her forehead, burning hotter and deeper as eyes fell, lips quivered and head sank in her hands, leaving a shame-stricken culprit where but an instant ago a bright, happy-hearted woman sat.

Before Ursula could reach her friend, or either gentleman exclaim, Stähl's uplifted hand imposed passive silence and obtained it, for already the magnetism of his presence made itself felt, filling the room with a supernatural atmosphere, which touched the commonplace with mystery, and woke fantastic fears or fancies like a spell. Without a look, a word for the weeping girl before him, he turned sharply round on Evan Forrest, signified by an imperious gesture that he should bend his tall head nearer, and when he did so, seemed to stab him with a breath. Pale with indignation and surprise, the young man sprang erect, demanding in a smothered voice:

"Who will prevent me?"

"I will."

As the words left Stähl's lips, Evan stirred as if to take him by the throat, but that thin, womanish hand closed like a steel spring round his wrist and held the strong arm powerless, as, with a disdainful smile, and warning "Remember where you are!" the other moved on undisturbed. Evan flung himself into a seat, vainly attempting self-control, while Stähl passed to Captain Hay, who sat regarding him with undisguised interest and amazement, which latter sentiment reached its climax as the magic whisper came.

"How in Heaven's name did you know that?" he cried, starting like one stupefied; then overturning his chair in his haste, he dashed out of the room with every mark of uncontrollable excitement and alarm.

"Dare you let me try my power on you, Miss Forrest?" asked Stähl, pausing at her side, with the first trace of emotion visible in his inscrutable face.

"I dare everything!" and as she spoke, Ursula's proud head rose erect, Ursula's dauntless eyes looked full into his own.

"In truth you do dare everything," he murmured below his breath, with a glance of passionate admiration. But the soft ardor that made his eyes wonderfully lovely for an instant flamed as suddenly into a flash of anger, for there was a perceptible recoil of the white shoulder as his breath touched it in bending, and when he breathed a single word into her ear, his face wore the stealthy ferocity of a tiger in the act of springing upon his unsuspecting prey. Had she been actually confronted with the veritable beast, it could scarcely have wrought a swifter panic than that one word. Fixed in the same half-shrinking, half-haughty attitude, she sat as if changed suddenly to stone. Her eyes, dark and dilated with some unconquerable horror, never left his face while light, color, life itself seemed to ebb slowly from her own, leaving it as beautiful yet woful to look upon as some marble Medusa's countenance. So sudden, so entire was the change in that blooming face, that Kate forgot her own dismay, and cried:

"Ursula, what is it?" while Evan, turning on the worker of the miracle, demanded hotly:

"What right have you to terrify women and insult men by hissing in their ears secret information dishonorably obtained?"

Neither question received an answer, for Ursula and Stähl seemed unconscious of any presence but their own, as each silently regarded the other with a gaze full of mutual intelligence, yet opposing emotions of triumph and despair. At the sound of Evan's voice, a shudder shook Ursula from head to foot, but her eye never wavered, and the icy fixture of her features remained unchanged as she asked in a sharp, shrill whisper—

"Is it true?"

"Behold the sign!" and with a gesture, too swift and unsuspected for any but herself to see or understand the revelation made, Stähl bared his left arm, held it before her eyes, and dropped it in the drawing of a breath. Whatever Ursula saw confirmed her dread; she uttered neither cry nor exclamation, but wrung her hands together in dumb anguish, while her lips moved without uttering a sound.

Kate Heath's over-wrought nerves gave way, and weeping hysterically, she clung to Evan, imploring him to take her home. Instantly assuming his usual languid courtesy of mien and manners, Stähl murmured regretful apologies, rang the bell for Miss Heath's carriage, and bringing her veil and mantle from the ante-room, implored the privilege of shawling her with a penitent devotion wonderfully winning, yet which did not prevent her shrinking from him and accepting no services but such as Evan half-unconsciously bestowed.

"You are coming with me? You promised mama to bring me safely back. Mr. Forrest, take pity on me, for I dare not go alone."

She spoke tearfully, still agitated by the secret wound inflicted by a whisper.

"Hay will gladly protect you, Kate; I cannot leave Ursula," began Evan, but a smooth, imperious voice took the word from his lips.

"Hay is gone, I shall remain with Ursula, and you, Forrest, will not desert Miss Heath in the distress which I have unhappily caused by granting her wish. Forgive me, and good-night."

As Stähl spoke, he kissed the hand that trembled in his own, with a glance that lingered long in poor Kate's memory, and led her towards her friend. But Evan's dark face kindled with the passion that he had vainly striven to suppress, and though he tried to curb his tongue, his eye looked a defiance as he placed himself beside his cousin, saying doggedly:

"I shall not leave Ursula to the tender mercies of a charlatan unless she bids me go. Kate, stay with us and lend your carriage to this gentleman, as his own is not yet here."

Bowing with a face of imperturbable composure, Stähl answered in his softest tones, bending an inquiring glance on Ursula:

"Many thanks, but I prefer to receive my dismissal from the lady of the house, not from its would-be master. Miss Forrest, shall I leave you to begin the work marked out for me? or shall I remain to unfold certain matters which nearly concern yourself, and which, if neglected, may result in misfortune to more than one of us?"

As if not only the words but the emphasis with which they were pronounced recalled some forgotten fact, woke some new fear, Ursula started from her stupor of surprise and mental suffering into sudden action. All that had passed while she sat dumb seemed to return to her, and a quick glance from face to face appeared to decide her in the course she must pursue.

Rising, she went to Kate, touched her wet cheek with lips that chilled it, and turning to her companions regarded them with an eye that seemed to pierce to the heart's core of each. What she read there none knew, but some purpose strong enough to steady and support her with a marvellous composure seemed born of that long scrutiny, for motioning her cousin from her she said:

"Go, Evan, I desire it."

"Go! and leave you with that man? I cannot, Ursula!"

"You must, you will, if I command it. I wish to be alone with him; I fear nothing, not even this magician, who in an instant has changed my life by a single word. See! I trust myself to his protection; I throw myself upon his mercy, and implore you to have faith in me."

With an air of almost pathetic dignity, a gesture of infinite grace, she stretched a hand to either man, and as each grasped the soft prize a defiant glance was exchanged between them, a daring one was fixed upon the beautiful woman for whom, like spirits of good and ill, they were henceforth to contend.

"I shall obey you, but may I come to-morrow?" Evan whispered, as he pressed the hand that in his own was tremulous and warm.

"Yes, come to me early, I shall need you then—if ever."

And as the words left her lips that other hand in Felix Stähl's firm hold grew white and cold as if carved in marble.

With Kate still trembling on his arm, Evan left them; his last glance showing him his rival regarding his departure with an air of tranquil triumph, and Ursula, his proud, high-hearted cousin, sinking slowly on her knees before this man, who in an hour seemed to have won the right to make or mar her happiness for ever.

How the night passed Evan Forrest never knew. He took Kate home, and then till day dawned haunted beach and cliff like a restless ghost, thinking only of Ursula, remembering only that she bade him come early, and chiding the tardy sun until it rose upon a day that darkened all his life. As the city bells chimed seven from the spires that shone across the little bay, Evan re-entered his cousin's door; but before he could pronounce her name the lady who for years had filled a mother's place to the motherless girl came hurrying to meet him, with every mark of sleepless agitation in her weary yet restless face and figure.

"Thank heaven, you are come!" she ejaculated, drawing him aside into the ante-room. "Oh, Mr. Forrest, such a night as I have passed, so strange, so unaccountable, I am half distracted."

"Where is Ursula?" demanded Evan.

"Just where you left her, sir; she has not stirred since that dreadful Mr. Stähl went away."

"When was that?"

"Past midnight. At eleven I went down to give him a hint, but the door was fast, and for another hour the same steady sound of voices came up to me as had been going on since you left. When he did go at last it was so quietly I only knew it by the glimpse I caught of him gliding down the walk, and vanishing like a spirit in the shadow of the great gate."

"Then you went to Ursula?"

"I did, sir; I did, and found her sitting as I saw her when I left the room in the evening."

"What did she say? what did she do?"

"She said nothing, and she looked like death itself, so white, so cold, so still; not a sigh, a tear, a motion; and when I implored her to speak she only broke my heart with the look she gave me, as she whispered, 'Leave me in peace till Evan comes.' "

With one stride he stood before the closed door, but when he tapped no voice bade him enter, and opening he noiselessly glided in. She was there, sitting as Mrs. Yorke described her, and looking more like a pale ghost than a living woman. Evan's eye wandered round the room, hungry to discover some clue to the mystery, but nothing was changed. The lamps burned dimly in the glare of early sunshine streaming through the room; the curtains were still wafted to and fro by balmy breezes; the seats still stood scattered here and there as they were quitted; Captain Hay's chair still lay overthrown; Kate's gloves had been trodden under foot, and round the deep chair in the window still glowed the scattered petals of the rose with which Felix Stähl had regaled himself while lying there.

"Ursula!"

No answer came to his low call, and drawing nearer, Evan whispered tenderly:

"My darling, speak to me! It breaks my heart to see you so, and have no power to help you."

The dark eyes fixed on vacancy relaxed in their strained gaze, the cold hands locked together in her lap loosened their painful pressure, and with a long sigh Ursula turned towards him, saying, like one wakened from a heavy dream:

"I am glad you are come;" then as if some fear stung her, added with startling abruptness, "Evan! what did he whisper in your ear last night?"

Amazed at such a question, yet not ill pleased to answer it even then, for his full heart was yearning to unburden itself, the young man instantly replied, while his face glowed with hope, and his voice grew tender with the untold love that had long hovered on his lips:

"He said, 'You will never win your cousin;' but, Ursula, he lied, for I will win you even if he bring the powers of darkness to confound me. He read in my face what you must have read there long ago, and did not rebuke by one cold look, one forbidding word. Let me tell my love now; let me give you the shelter of my heart if you need it, and whatever grief or shame or fear has come to you let me help you bear it if I cannot banish it."

She did not speak, till kneeling before her he said imploringly:

"Ursula, you bade me trust you; I do entirely. Can you not place a like confidence in me?"

"No, Evan."

"Then you do not love as I love," he cried, with a foreboding fear heavy at his heart.

"No, I do not love as you love." The answer came like a soft echo, and her whole frame trembled for an instant as if some captive emotion struggled for escape and an iron hand restrained it. Her cousin saw it, and seizing both her hands, looked deep into her eyes, demanding, sternly:

"Do you love this man?"

"I shall marry him."

Evan stared aghast at the hard, white resolution stamped upon her face, as she looked straight before her with a blank yet steady gaze, seeming to see and own allegiance to a master invisible to him. A moment he struggled with a chaos of conflicting passions, then fought his way to a brief calmness, intent on fathoming the mystery that had wrought such a sudden change in both their lives.

"Ursula, as the one living relative whom you possess, I have a right to question you. Answer me truly, I conjure you, and deal honestly with the heart that is entirely your own. I can forget myself, can put away my own love and longing, can devote my whole time, strength, life to your service, if you need me. Something has happened that affects you deeply, let me know it. No common event would move you so, for lovers do not woo in this strange fashion, nor betrothed brides wear their happiness with such a face as you now wear."

"Few women have such lovers as mine, or such betrothals to tell. Ask me nothing, Evan, I have told you all I may; go now, and let me rest, if any rest remains for me."

"Not yet," he answered, with as indomitable a purpose in his face as that which seemed to have fixed and frozen hers. "I must know more of this man before I give you up. Who and what is he?"

"Study, question, watch and analyse him. You will find him what he seems—no more, no less. I leave you free to do what you will, and claim an equal liberty for myself," she said.

"I thought he was a stranger to you as to me and others. You must have known him elsewhere, Ursula?"

"I never saw or knew him till a month ago."

Evan struck his hands together with a gesture of despair, as he sprang up, saying:

"Ah! I see it now. A month ago I left you, and in that little time you learned to love."

"Yes, in that little time I did learn to love."

Again the soft echo came, again the sadder tremor shook her, but she neither smiled, nor wept, nor turned her steady eyes away from the unseen but controlling presence that for her still seemed to haunt the room.

Evan Forrest was no blind lover, and despite his own bitter loss he was keen-eyed enough to see that some emotion deeper than caprice, stronger than pity, sharper than regret, now held possession of his cousin's heart. He felt that some tie less tender than that which bound him to her bound her to this man, who exercised such power over her proud spirit and strong will. Bent on reading the riddle, he rapidly glanced through the happy past, so shared with Ursula that he believed no event in the life of either was unknown to the other; yet here was a secret lying dark between them, and only one little month of absence had sowed the seed that brought such a harvest of distrust and pain. Suddenly he spoke:

"Ursula, has this man acquired power over you through any weakness of your own?"

A haughty flash kindled in her eyes, and for an instant her white face glowed with womanly humiliation at the doubt implied.

"I am as innocent of any sin or shame, any weakness or wrong, as when I lay a baby in my mother's arms. Would to God I lay there now as tranquilly asleep as she!"

The words broke from her with a tearless sob, and spreading her hands before her face he heard her murmur like a broken-hearted child:

"How could he, oh, how could he wound me with a thought like that?"

"I will not! I do not! Hear me, Ursula, and forgive me, if I cannot submit to see you leave me for a man like this without one effort to fathom the inexplicable change I find in you. Only tell me that he is worthy of you, that you love him and are happy, and I will be dumb. Can you do this to ease my heart and conscience, Ursula?"

"Yes, I can do more than that. Rest tranquil, dearest Evan. I know what I do; I do it freely, and in time you will acknowledge that I did well in marrying Felix Stähl."

"You are betrothed to him?"

"I am; his kiss is on my cheek, his ring is on my hand; I accept both."

With a look and gesture which he never could forget she touched the cheek where one deep spot of color burned as if branded there, and held up the hand whose only ornament beside its beauty was a slender ring formed of two twisted serpents, whose diamond eyes glittered with an uncanny resemblance of life.

"And you will marry him?" repeated Evan, finding the hard fact impossible to accept.

"I will."

"Soon, Ursula?"

"Very soon."

"You wish it so?"

"I wish what he wishes."

"You will go away with him?"

"To the end of the earth if he desires it."

"My God! is this witchcraft or infatuation?"

"Neither, it is woman's love, which is quick and strong to dare and suffer all things for those who are dearer to her than her life."

He could not see her face, for she had turned it from him, but in her voice trembled a tender fervor which could not be mistaken, and with a pang that wrung his man's heart sorely he relinquished all hope, and bade farewell to love, believing that no mystery existed but that which is inexplicable, the workings of a woman's heart.

"I am going, Ursula," he said; "you no longer have any need of me, and I must fight out my fight alone. God bless you, and remember whatever befalls, while life lasts you have one unalterable friend and lover in me."

As he spoke with full eyes, broken voice and face eloquent with love, regret and pity, Ursula rose suddenly and fell upon his bosom, clinging there with passionate despair that deepened his ever growing wonder.

"God help you, Evan! love me, trust me, pity me, and so goodbye! good-bye!" she cried, in that strange paroxysm of emotion, as tearless, breathless, trembling and wearied, yet still self-controlled, she kissed and blessed and led him to the door. No pause upon the threshold; as he lingered she put him from her, closed and bolted it: then as if with him the sustaining power of her darkened life departed, she fell down upon the spot where he had stood, and lay there, beautiful and pale and still as some fair image of eternal sleep.

PART II

THE NINE DAYS' WONDER at the sudden wedding which followed that strange betrothal had died away, the honeymoon was over, and the bridal pair were alone together in their new home. Ursula stood at the window looking out, with eyes as wistful as a caged bird's, upon the fading leaves that fluttered in the autumn wind. Her husband lay on his couch, apparently absorbed in a vellum-covered volume, the cabalistic characters of which were far easier to decipher than the sweet, wan face he was studying covertly. The silence which filled the room was broken by a long sigh of pain as the book fell from Stähl's hand, and his head leaned wearily upon the pillow. Ursula heard the sigh, and, like a softly moving shadow, glided to his side, poured wine from an antique flask, and kneeling, held it to his lips. He drank thirstily, but the cordial seemed to impart neither strength nor comfort, for he drew his wife's head down beside him, saying:

"Kiss me, Ursula; I am so faint and cold, nothing seems to warm my blood, and my body freezes, while my heart burns with a never-dying fire."

With a meek obedience that robbed the act of all tenderness, she touched her ruddy lips to the paler ones that ardently returned the pressure, yet found no satisfaction there. Leaning upon his arm, he held her to him with a fierce fondness, in strange contrast to his feeble frame, saying earnestly:

"Ursula, before I married you I found such strength and solace, such warmth and happiness in your presence, that I coveted you as a precious healing for my broken health. Then I loved you, forgetful of self—loved you as you never will be loved again, and thanked heaven that my fate was so interwoven with your own that the utterance of a word secured my life's desire. But now, when I have made you wholly mine, and hope to bask in the sunshine of your beauty, youth and womanhood, I find a cold, still creature in my arms, and no spark of the fire that consumes me ever warms the image of my love. Must it be so? Can I never see you what you were again?"

"Never!" she answered, leaning there as pale and passive as if she were in truth a marble woman. "I vowed obedience at the altar, nothing more. I did not love you; I could not honor you, but I felt that I might learn to obey. I have done so, be content."

"Not I! Colder women have been taught love as well as obedience; you, too, shall be a docile pupil, and one day give freely what I sue for now. Other men woo before they wed, my wooing and my winning will come later—if I live long enough."

He turned her face towards him as he spoke and scanned it closely; but no grateful sign of softness, pity or regret appeared, and, with a broken exclamation, he put her from him, locked both hands across his eyes and lay silent, till some uncontrollable paroxysm of emotion had passed by. Presently he spoke, and the words betrayed what the pain had been.

"My mother—heaven bless her for her tenderness!—used to pray that her boy's life might be a long and happy one; it is a bitter thing to feel that the only woman now left me to love prays for the shortening of that same life, and can bestow no look or word to make its failing hours happy."

The unwonted tone of filial affection, the keen sorrow and the mournful acknowledgment of an inevitable doom touched Ursula as no ardent demonstration or passionate reproach had ever done. She softly lifted up the folded hands, saw that those deep eyes were wet with tears, and in that pallid countenance read the melancholy record of a life burdened with a sad heritage of pain, thwarted by unhappy love and darkened by allegiance to a superstitious vow. Great as her sacrifice had been, deep as the wound still was, and heavily as her captivity weighed on her proud heart, it was still womanly, generous and gentle; and, despite all wrongs, all blemishes, all bitter memories, she felt the fascination of this wild and wayward nature, as she had never done before, and yielded to its persuasive potency. Laying her cool hand on his hot forehead, she leaned over him, saying, with an accent of compassion sweeter to his ear than her most perfect song:

"No, Felix, I pray no prayers that heaven would refuse to grant. I only ask patience for myself, a serener spirit for you, and God's blessing upon Evan, wherever he may be."

Before the words of tender satisfaction which rose to Stähl's lips could be uttered, a noiseless servant brought a black-edged card. Ursula read and handed it to her husband.

"Mrs. Heath. Shall we see her, love?" he asked.

"As you please," was the docile answer, though an expression of mingled pain and sorrow passed across her face in speaking.

He half frowned at her meekness, then smiled and bade the man deny them, adding, as he left the room,

"I am too well content with this first glimpse of the coming happiness to be saddened by the lamentations of that poor lady over her wilful daughter, who had the bad taste to drown herself upon our wedding-day."

"Felix, may I ask you a question?"

"Anything of me, Ursula."

"Tell me what you whispered in Kate's ear on the evening which both of us remember well."

Questions were so rare, and proving a sign of interest, that Stähl made haste to answer, with a curious blending of disdain and pity,

"She bade me tell her the most ardent desire of her life, and I dared to answer truly, 'To win my heart.' "

"A true answer, but a cruel one," Ursula said.

"That cruel truthfulness is one of the savage attributes which two generations of civilization cannot entirely subdue in my race. Those who tamely submit to me I despise, but those who oppose me I first conquer and then faithfully love."

"Had you made poor Kate happy, you would not now regret the possession of a cold, untender wife."

"Who would gather a gay tulip when they can reach a royal rose, though thorns tear the hand that seizes it? For even when it fades its perfume lingers, gifting it with an enduring charm. Love, I have found my rose, so let the tulip fade—"

There he paused abruptly in his flowery speech, for with the swift instinct of a temperament like his, he was instantly conscious of the fact when her thoughts wandered, and a glance showed him that, though her attitude was unaltered, she was listening intently. A far-off bell had rung, the tones of a man's voice sounded from below, and the footsteps of an approaching servant grew audible. Stähl recognised the voice, fancied that Ursula did also, and assured himself of it by an unsuspected test that took the form of a caress. Passing his arm about her waist, his hand lay lightly above her heart, and as her cousin's name was announced he felt the sudden bound that glad heart gave, and counted the rapid throbs that sent the color to her cheeks and made her lips tremble. A black frown lowered on his forehead, and his eyes glittered ominously for an instant, but both betrayals were unseen, and nothing marred the gracious sweetness of his voice.

"Of course you will see your cousin, Ursula. I shall greet him in passing, and return when you have enjoyed each other alone."

"Alone!" she echoed, with a distrustful look at him, an anxious one about the room, as if no place seemed safe or sacred in that house where she was both mistress and slave.

He understood the glance, and answered with one so reproachful that she blushed for the ungenerous suspicion, as he said, with haughty emphasis:

"Yes, Ursula, alone. Whatever evil names I may deserve, those of spy and eavesdropper cannot be applied to me; and though my wife can neither love nor honor me, I will prove that she may trust me."

With that he left her, and meeting Evan just without, offered his hand frankly, and gave his welcome with a cordial grace that was irresistible. Evan could not refuse the hand, for on it shone a little ring which Ursula once wore, and yielding to the impulse awakened by that mute reminder of her, he betrayed exactly what his host desired to know, for instantaneous as was both recognition and submission, Stähl's quick eye divined the cause.

"Come often to us, Evan; forget the past, and remember only that through Ursula we are kindred now. She is waiting for you; go to her and remain as long as you incline, sure of a hearty welcome from both host and hostess."

Then he passed on, and Evan hurried to his cousin; eager, yet reluctant to meet her, lest in her face he should read some deeper mystery or greater change than he last saw there. She came to meet him smiling and serene, for whatever gust of joy or sorrow had swept over her, no trace of it remained; yet, when he took her in his arms, there broke from him the involuntary exclamation:

"Is this my cousin Ursula?"

"Yes, truly. Am I then so altered?"

"This is a reflection of what you were; that of what you are. Look, and tell me if I have not cause for wonder."

She did look as he drew a miniature from his bosom and led her to the mirror. The contrast was startling even to herself, for the painted face glowed with rosy bloom, hope shone in the eyes, happiness smiled from the lips, while youthful purity and peace crowned the fair forehead with enchanting grace. The living face was already wan and thin, many tears had robbed the cheeks of color, sleepless nights had dimmed the lustre of the eyes, much secret suffering and strife had hardened the soft curves of the mouth and deepened the lines upon the brow. Even among the dark waves of her hair silver threads shone here and there, unbidden, perhaps unknown; and over the whole woman a subtle blight had fallen, more tragical than death. Silently she compared the two reflections, for the first time realising all that she had lost, yet as she returned the miniature she only said, with pathetic patience:

"I am not what I was, but my heart remains unchanged, believe that, Evan."

"I do. Tell me, Ursula, are you happy now?"

Her eyes rose to his, and over her whole face there shone the sudden magic of a glow warmer and brighter than a smile.

"I am supremely happy now."

It was impossible to doubt her truth, however past facts or present appearances might seem to belie it, and Evan was forced to believe, despite his disappointment.

"He is kind to you, Ursula? You suffer no neglect, no tyranny nor wrong from this strange man?" he asked, still haunted by vague doubts.

She waved her hand about the lovely room, delicately dainty as a bride's bower should be, and answered, with real feeling:

"Does this look as if I suffered any neglect or wrong? Every want and whim is seen and gratified before expressed; I go and come unwatched, unquestioned; the winds of heaven are not allowed to visit me too roughly, and as for kindness, look there and see a proof of it."

She pointed to the garden where her husband walked alone, never quitting the wide terrace just below her window, though the sunshine that he loved had faded from the spot, and the autumn winds he dreaded blew gustily about him. He never lifted up his eyes, nor paused, nor changed his thoughtful attitude, but patiently paced to and fro, a mute reproach for Ursula's unjust suspicion.

"How frail he looks; if life with you cannot revive him he must be past hope."

Evan spoke involuntarily, and Ursula's hand half checked the words upon his lips; but neither looked the other in the face, and neither owned, even to themselves, how strong a hidden wish had grown.

"He will live because he resolves to live, for that frail body holds the most indomitable spirit I have ever known. But let me tell you why he lingers where every breath brings pain," said Ursula, and having told him, she added:

"Is not that both a generous and a gentle rebuke for an unkind doubt?"

"It is either a most exquisite piece of loverlike devotion or of consummate art. I think it is the latter, for he knows you well, and repays great sacrifices by graceful small ones, which touch and charm your woman's heart."

"You wrong him, Evan, and aversion blinds you to the better traits I have learned to see. An all absorbing love ennobles the most sinful man, and makes it possible for some woman to forgive and cling to him."

"I have no right to ask, but the strange spirit that has taken possession of you baffles and disquiets me past endurance. Tell me, Ursula, what you would not tell before, do you truly, tenderly love this man whom you have married?"

The question was uttered with an earnestness so solemn that it forced a truthful answer, and she looked up at him with the old frankness unobscured by any cloud, as she replied:

"But for one thing I should long ago have learned to love him. I know this, because even now I cannot wholly close my heart against the ardent affection that patiently appeals to it."

"And that one thing, that cursed mystery which has wrecked two lives, when am I to know it, Ursula?"

"Never till I lie on my deathbed, and not even then, unless——"

She caught back the words hovering on her lips, but her eye glanced furtively upon the solitary figure pacing there below, and Evan impetuously finished the broken sentence:

"Unless he is already dead—let it be so; I shall wait and yet prove his prophecy a false one by winning and wearing you when his baleful love is powerless."

"He is my husband, Evan, remember that. Now come with me, I am going to him, for he must not shiver there when I can give him the warmth his tropical nature loves."

But Evan would not go, and soon left her plunged in a new sea of anxious conjectures, doubts and dreads. Stähl awaited his wife's approach, saying within himself as he watched her coming under the gold and scarlet arches of the leafy walk, with unwonted elasticity in her step, color on her cheeks and smiles upon her lips:

"Good! I have found the spell that turns my snow image into flesh and blood; I will use it and enjoy the summer of her presence while I may."

He did use it, but so warily and well that though Ursula and Evan were dimly conscious of some unseen yet controlling hand that ruled their intercourse and shaped events, they found it hard to believe that studious invalid possessed and used such power. Evan came daily, and daily Ursula regained some of her lost energy and bloom, till an almost preternatural beauty replaced the pale loveliness her face had worn, and she seemed to glow and brighten with an inward fire, like some brilliant flower that held the fervor of a summer in its heart and gave it out again in one fair, fragrant hour.

Like a watchful shadow Evan haunted his cousin, conscious that they were drifting down a troubled stream without a pilot, yet feeling powerless to guide or govern his own life, so inextricably was it bound up in Ursula's. He saw that the vigor and vitality his presence gave her was absorbed by her husband, to whom she was a more potent stimulant than rare winds, balmy airs or costly drugs. He knew that the stronger nature subdued the weaker, and the failing life sustained itself by draining the essence of that other life, which, but for some sinister cross of fate, would have been an ever springing fountain of joy to a more generous and healthful heart.

The blind world applauded Felix Stähl's success, and envied him the splendid wife in whose affluent gifts of fortune, mind and person he seemed to revel with luxurious delight. It could not see the secret bitterness that poisoned peace; could not guess the unavailing effort, unappeased desire and fading hope that each day brought him; nor fathom the despair that filled his soul as he saw and felt the unmistakable tokens of his coming fate in hollow temples, wasting flesh and a mortal weariness that knew no rest; a despair rendered doubly bitter by the knowledge of his impotence to prevent another from reaping what he had sown with painful care.

Ursula's hard won submission deserted her when Evan came, for in reanimating the statue Stähl soon felt that he had lost his slave and found a master. The heart which had seemed slowly yielding to his efforts closed against him in the very hour of fancied conquest. No more meek services, no more pity shown in spite of pride, no more docile obedience to commands that wore the guise of entreaties. The captive spirit woke and beat against its bars, passionately striving to be free, though not a cry escaped its lips. Very soon her recovered gaiety departed, and her life became a vain effort to forget, for like all impetuous natures she sought oblivion in excitement and hurried from one scene of pleasure to another, finding rest and happiness in none. Her husband went with her everywhere, recklessly squandering the strength she gave him in a like fruitless quest, till sharply checked by warnings which could no longer be neglected.

One night in early spring when winter gaieties were drawing to a close, Ursula came down to him shining in festival array, with the evening fever already burning in her cheeks, the expectant glitter already kindling in her eyes, and every charm heightened with that skill which in womanly women is second nature. Not for his pride or pleasure had she made herself so fair, he knew that well, and the thought lent its melancholy to the tone in which he said:

"Ursula, I am ready, but so unutterably weak and weary that I cannot go."

"I can go without you. Be so good," and quite unmoved by the suffering that rarely found expression, she held her hand to him that he might clasp her glove. He rose to perform the little service with that courtesy which never failed him, asking, as he bent above the hand with trembling fingers and painful breath,

"Does Evan go with you?"

"Yes, he never fails me, he has neither weakness nor weariness to mar my pleasure or to thwart my will."

"Truly a tender and a wifely answer."

"I am not tender nor wifely; why assume the virtues which I never shall possess? They were not set down in the bond; that I fulfilled to the letter when I married you, and beyond the wearing of your name and ring I owe you nothing. Do I?"

"Yes, a little gratitude for the sincerity that placed a doomed life in your keeping; a little respect for the faith I have kept unbroken through all temptations; a little compassion for a malady that but for you would make my life a burden I would gladly lay down."

Time was when words like these would have touched and softened her, but not now, for she had reached the climax of her suffering, the extent of her endurance, and turning on him she gave vent to the passionate emotion which could no longer be restrained:

"I should have given you much gratitude if in helping me to save one life you had not doomed another. I should honestly respect the faith you boast of if such costly sacrifices were not demanded for its keeping. I should deeply pity that mortal malady if you had bravely borne it alone instead of seeking a selfish solace in bequeathing it to another. I tell you, Felix, you are killing me swiftly and surely by this dreadful life. Better end me at once than drive me mad, or leave me a strong soul prisoned in a feeble body like yourself."

For the first time in his life Stähl felt the touch of fear, not for himself but for her, lest that terrible affliction which so baffles human skill and science should fall upon the woman whom he loved with a selfish intensity which had tangled two lives and brought them to this pass.

"Hush, Ursula," he said, soothingly, "have patience, I shall soon be gone, and then—what will you do then?"

The question leaped to his lips, for at the word "gone" he saw the gloom lift from her face, leaving an expression of relief that unmistakably betrayed how heavily her burden had oppressed her. Undaunted by the almost fierce inquiry she fixed her eyes upon him, and answered steadily:

"I shall put off my bridal white, wear widow's weeds for a single year, and then"—there she, too, paused abruptly; but words were needless, for as Evan's step sounded on the stair she turned and hurried towards him, as if love, liberty and life all lay waiting for her there. Stähl watched them with a jealous pang that pierced the deeper as, remembering Ursula's taunt, he compared the young man with himself; the one rich in the stature, vigor, comeliness that make a manly man; the other, in sad truth, a strong spirit imprisoned in a ruined body. As he looked he clenched his pale hand hard, and muttered low between his set teeth:

"He shall not have her, if I sell my soul to thwart him!"

To Ursula's intense surprise and Evan's annoyance Stähl followed them into the carriage, with a brief apology for his seeming caprice. No one spoke during the short drive, but as they came into the brilliant rooms Ursula's surprise deepened to alarm, for in the utter change of mien and manner which had befallen her husband she divined the presence of some newborn purpose, and trembled for the issue. Usually he played the distasteful part of invalid with a grace and skill which made the undisguisable fact a passport to the sympathy and admiration of both men and women. But that night no vigorous young man bore himself more debonnairly, danced more indefatigably, or devoted himself more charmingly to the service of matron, maid and grateful hostess. Lost in amazement, Ursula and Evan watched him, gliding to and fro, vivacious, blithe and bland, leaving a trail of witty, wise or honied words behind him, and causing many glances of approval to follow that singular countenance, for now its accustomed pallor was replaced by a color no art could counterfeit, and the mysterious eyes burned with a fire that fixed and fascinated other eyes.

"What does it mean, Evan?" whispered Ursula, standing apart with her faithful shadow.

"Mischief, if I read it rightly," was the anxious answer, and at that moment, just before them, the object of their thoughts was accosted by a jovial gentleman, who exclaimed:

"God bless me, Stähl! Rumor said you were dying, like a liar as she is, and here I find you looking more like a bridegroom than when I left you at the altar six months ago."

"For once rumor tells the truth, Coventry. I am dying, but one may make their exit gracefully and end their tragedy or comedy with a grateful bow! I have had a generous share of pleasure; I thank the world for it; I make my adieu to-night, and tranquilly go home to rest."

Spoken with an untroubled smile the words were both touching and impressive, and the friendly Coventry was obliged to clear his voice before he could answer with an assumption of cheery unbelief:

"Not yet, my dear fellow, not yet; we cannot spare you this forty years, and with such a wife what right have you to talk of ending the happy drama which all predict your life will be?" then glad to change the subject, he added: "Apropos of predictions, do take pity on my curiosity and tell me if it is true that you entertained a party with some very remarkable prophecies, or something of that sort, just before your marriage with Miss Forrest. Hay once spoke mysteriously of it, but he went to the bad so soon after that I never made him satisfy me."

"I did comply with a lady's wish, but entertainment was not the result. I told Hay, what all the world knew, the next day, that certain dishonorable transactions of his were discovered, and warrants out for his arrest, and they hurried home to find my warning true."

"Yes, no one dreamed of such an end for the gay captain. I don't ask how your discovery was made, but I do venture to inquire if Miss Heath's tragical death was foretold that night?"

"That which indirectly caused her death was made known to her that night, but for her sake you will pardon me that I keep the secret."

"A thousand pardons for asking, and yet I am tempted to put one more question. You look propitious, so pray tell me if your other predictions were fulfilled with equal success?"

"Yes; sooner or later they always are."

"Upon my life, that's very singular! Just for the amusement of the thing make one now, and let me see if your skill remains undiminished. Nothing personal, you know, but some general prediction that any one may know and verify."

Stähl paused a moment, bending his eyes on Ursula, who stood unseen by his companion, then answered slowly with a memorable tone and aspect:

"I prophesy that before the month is out the city will be startled by a murder, and the culprit will elude justice by death."

Coventry's florid countenance paled visibly, and hastily returning thanks for the undesirable favor so complacently granted, he took himself away to whisper the evil portent in the ears of all he met. As he disappeared Stähl advanced to his wife, asking with an air of soft solicitude:

"Are you weary, love? or will you dance? Your cousin is negligent to-night."

"Oh, no, I have not wished to dance. Let us go now, and Evan, come to me to-morrow evening, when you will find a few friends and much music," she answered, with an unquiet glance at her husband, a significant one at her cousin, who obeyed it by leaving them with a silent bow.

The homeward drive was as quiet as the other had been, and when they alighted Stähl followed his wife into the drawing-room; there, dropping wearily into a seat, he removed the handkerchief which had been pressed to his lips, and she saw that it was steeped in blood.

"Pardon me—it was unavoidable. Please ring for Marjory," he said, feebly.

Ursula neither spoke nor stirred, but stood regarding him with an expression which alarmed him, it was so full of a strange, stern triumph. It gave him strength to touch the bell, and when the faithful old woman who had nursed him from his babyhood came hurrying in, to say quietly:

"Take that ugly thing away, and bring my drops; also your mistress's vinaigrette, she needs it."

"Not she, the icicle," muttered Marjory, who adored her master, and heartily disliked her mistress because she did not do likewise.

When the momentary faintness had cleared away Stähl's quick eye at once took in the scene before him. Marjory was carefully preparing the draught, and Ursula stood watching her with curious intentness.

"What is that?" she asked, as the old woman put down the tiny vial, containing a colorless and scentless liquid.

"Poison, madam, one drop of which will restore life, while a dozen will bring a sure and sudden death."

Ursula took up the little vial, read the label containing both the medicine and its maker's name, and laid it back again with a slight motion of head and lips, as if she gave a mute assent to some secret suggestion. Marjory's lamentations as she moved about him drew the wife's eyes to her husband, and meeting his she asked coldly:

"Can I help you?"

"Thanks, Marjory will tend me. Good-night, you'll not be troubled with me long."

"No, I shall not; I have borne enough."

She spoke low to herself, but both listeners heard her, and the old woman sternly answered:

"May the Lord forgive you for that speech, madam."

"He will, for He sees the innocent and the guilty, and He knows my sore temptation."

Then without another look or word she left them with the aspect of one walking in an evil dream.

All night Marjory hovered about her master, and early in the morning his physician came. A few words assured Stähl that his hour was drawing very near, and that whatever work remained to be done must be accomplished speedily. He listened calmly to the truth which he had forced from the reluctant doctor, and when he paused made no lament, but said, with more than his accustomed gentleness:

"You will oblige me by concealing this fact from my wife. It is best to let it break upon her by merciful degrees."

"I understand, sir, I will be dumb; but I must caution you not to exert or agitate yourself in the least, for any undue exertion or excitement would be fatal in your weak state."

The worthy doctor spoke earnestly, but to his infinite amazement and alarm his patient rose suddenly from the couch on which he lay half dressed, and standing erect before him, said forcibly, while his hollow cheeks burned crimson, and his commanding eye almost enforced belief in his assertion:

"You are mistaken; I am not weak, for I have done with fear as well as hope, and if I choose to barter my month of life for one hour, one moment of exertion or excitement, I have the right to do it."

He paused, took breath and added:

"My wife intended to receive her friends tonight; she must not be disappointed, therefore you will not only tell her I am in no danger, but add that an unexpected crisis in my malady has come, and that with care and a season at the South I shall yet be a hale and hearty man. Grant me this favor, I shall not forget it."

The doctor was both a poor and a timid man; his generous but eccentric patient was a fortune to him; the falsehood seemed a kind one; the hint of a rich remembrance was irresistible, and bowing his acquiescence, he departed to obey directions to the letter.

All that day Ursula sat in her room writing steadily, and all that day her husband watched and waited for her coming, but sent no invitation and received no message. At dusk she went out alone. Her departure was unheard and unseen by any but the invalid, whose every sense was alert; his quick ear caught the soft rustle of her dress as she passed his door, and dragging himself to the window he saw her glide away, wrapped in a shrouding cloak. At that sight Stähl's hand was lifted to the bell, but he dropped it, saying to himself:

"No, if she did not mean to return she would have taken care to tell me she was coming back; women always betray themselves by too much art. I have it! she has been writing, Marjory says; the letter is to Evan; she fears he may not come to-night, and trusts no one but herself to post it. I must assure myself of this."

Nerved with new strength, he went down into the dainty room so happily prepared and dedicated to Ursula's sole use. It was empty, but the charm of her presence lingered there, and every graceful object spoke of her. Lights burned upon the writing-table; the ink was still wet in the pen, and scattered papers confirmed the report of her day's employment; but no written word was visible, no note or packet anywhere appeared. A brief survey satisfied her husband, and assured him of the truth of his suspicion.

"Oh, for an hour of my old strength to end this entanglement like a man, instead of being forced to wait for time and chance to aid me like a timorous woman," he sighed, looking out into the wild March night, tormented by an impotent desire to follow his truant wife, yet conscious that it was impossible unless he left a greater work undone, for hourly he felt his power decline, and one dark purpose made him tenacious of the life fast slipping from his hold.

For many moments he stood thinking deeply, so deeply that the approach of a light, rapid step roused him too late for escape. It was his wife's step; why was she returning so soon? had her heart failed her? had some unforeseen occurrence thwarted her? She had not been absent long enough to post a letter to reach Evan's lodgings, or the house of any friend, then where had she been? An uncontrollable impulse caused Stähl to step noiselessly into the shadow of a curtained recess as these thoughts flashed through his mind, and hardly had he done so when Ursula hurried in wet, wild-eyed and breathless, but wearing a look of pale determination which gave place to an expression of keen anxiety as she glanced about the room as if in search of something. Presently she murmured half aloud, "He shall never say again that I do not trust his honor. Lie there in safety till I need you, little friend," and lifting the cover of a carved ivory casket that ornamented the low chimneypiece, she gave some treasure to its keeping, saying, as she turned away with an air of feverish excitement, "Now for Evan and—my liberty!"

Nothing stirred in the room but the flicker of the fire and the softly moving pendulum of the clock that pointed to the hour of seven, till the door of Ursula's distant dressing-room closed behind her and a bell had summoned her maid. Then, from the recess, Stähl went straight to the ivory ornament and laid his hand upon its lid, yet paused long before he lifted it. The simple fact of her entire trust in him at any other time would have been the earnest safeguard of her secret; even now it restrained him by appealing to that inconsistent code of honor which governs many a man who would shoot his dearest friend for a hot word, and yet shrink with punctilious pride from breaking the seal of any letter that did not bear his name. Stähl hesitated till her last words stung his memory, making his own perfidy seem slight compared to hers. "I have a right to know," he said, "for when she forgets her honor I must preserve mine at any cost." A rapid gesture uncovered the casket, and showed him nothing but a small, sealed bottle, lying alone upon the velvet lining. A harmless little thing it looked, yet Stähl's face whitened terribly, and he staggered to a seat, as if the glance he gave had shown him his own death-warrant. He believed it had, for in size, shape, label and colorless contents the little vial was the counterpart of another last seen in Ursula's hand, one difference only in the two—that had been nearly empty, this was full to the lip.

In an instant her look, tone, gesture of the preceding night returned to him, and with the vivid recollection came the firm conviction that Ursula had yielded to a black temptation, and in her husband's name had purchased her husband's death. Till now no feeling but the intensest love had filled his heart towards her; Evan he had learned to hate, himself to despise, but of his wife he had made an idol and worshipped her with a blind passion that would not see defects, own disloyalty or suspect deceit.

From any other human being the treachery would not have been so base, but from her it was doubly bitter, for she knew and owned her knowledge of his exceeding love. "Am I not dying fast enough for her impatience? Could she not wait a little, and let me go happy in my ignorance?" he cried within himself, forgetting in the anguish of that moment the falsehood told her at his bidding, for the furtherance of another purpose as sinful but less secret than her own. How time passed he no longer knew nor cared, as leaning his head upon his hands, he took counsel with his own unquiet heart, for all the evil passions, the savage impulses of his nature were aroused, and raged rebelliously in utter defiance of the feeble prison that confined them. Like all strong yet selfish souls, the wrongs he had committed looked to him very light compared with this, and seeing only his own devotion, faith and patience, no vengeance seemed too heavy for a crime that would defraud him of his poor remnant of unhappy life. Suddenly he lifted up his head, and on his face was stamped a ruthless, reckless purpose, which no earthly power could change or stay. An awesome smile touched his white lips, and the ominous fierceness glittered in his eye—for he was listening to a devil that sat whispering in his heart.

"I shall have my hour of excitement sooner than I thought," he said low to himself, as he left the room, carrying the vial with him. "My last prediction will be verified, although the victim and the culprit are one, and Evan shall live to wish that Ursula had died before me."

An hour later Ursula came to him as he sat gloomily before his chamber fire, while Marjory stood tempting him to taste the cordial she had brought. As if some impassable and unseen abyss already yawned between them, she gave him neither wifely caress nor evening greeting, but pausing opposite, said, with an inclination of her handsome head, which would have seemed a haughty courtesy but for the gentle coldness of her tone:

"I have obeyed the request you sent me, and made ready to receive the friends whose coming would else have been delayed. Is it your pleasure that I excuse you to them, or will you join us as you have often done when other invalids would fear to leave their beds?"

Her husband looked at her as she spoke, wondering what woman's whim had led her to assume a dress rich in itself, but lustreless and sombre as a mourning garb; its silken darkness relieved only by the gleam of fair arms through folds of costly lace, and a knot of roses, scarcely whiter than the bosom they adorned.

"Thanks for your compliance, Ursula. I will come down later in the evening for a moment to receive congratulations on the restoration promised me. Shall I receive yours then?"

"No, now, for now I can wish you a long and happy life, can rejoice that time is given you to learn a truer faith, and ask you to forgive me if in thought, or word, or deed I have wronged or wounded you."

Strangely sweet and solemn was her voice, and for the first time in many months her old smile shed its serenest sunshine on her face, touching it with a meeker beauty than that which it had lost. Her husband shot one glance at her as the last words left her lips, then veiled the eyes that blazed with sudden scorn and detestation. His voice was always under his control, and tranquilly it answered her, while his heart cried out within him:

"I forgive as I would be forgiven, and trust that the coming years will be to you all that I desire to have them. Go to your pleasures, Ursula, and let me hear you singing, whether I am there or here."

"Can I do nothing else for you, Felix, before I go?" she asked, pausing, as she turned away, as if some involuntary impulse ruled her.

Stähl smiled a strange smile as he said, pointing to the goblet and the minute bottle Marjory had just placed on the table at his side:

"You shall sweeten a bitter draught for me by mixing it, and I will drink to you when I take it by-and-by."

His eye was on her now, keen, cold and steadfast, as she drew near to serve him. He saw the troubled look she fixed upon the cup, he saw her hand tremble as she poured the one safe drop, and heard a double meaning in her words:

"This is the first, I hope it may be the last time that I shall need to pour this dangerous draught for you."

She laid down the nearly emptied vial, replaced the cup and turned to go. But, as if bent on trying her to the utmost, though each test tortured him, Stähl arrested her by saying, with an unwonted tremor in his voice, a rebellious tenderness in his eyes:

"Stay, Ursula, I may fall asleep and so not see you until—morning. Bid me good-night, my wife."

She went to him, as if drawn against her will, and for a moment they stood face to face, looking their last on one another in this life. Then Stähl snatched her to him with an embrace almost savage in its passionate fervor, and Ursula kissed him once with the cold lips, that said, without a smile, "Good-night, my husband, sleep in peace!"

"Judas!" he muttered, as she vanished, leaving him spent with the controlled emotions of that brief interview. Old Marjory heard the word, and from that involuntary betrayal seemed to gather courage for a secret which had burned upon her tongue for two mortal hours. As Stähl sunk again into his cushioned seat, and seemed about to relapse into his moody reverie, she leaned towards him, saying in a whisper:

"May I tell you something, sir?"

"Concerning what or whom, my old gossip?" he answered, listlessly, yet with even more than usual kindliness, for now this humble, faithful creature seemed his only friend.

"My mistress, sir," she said, nodding significantly.

His face woke then, he sat erect, and with an eager gesture bade her speak.

"I've long mistrusted her; for ever since her cousin came she has not been the woman or the wife she was at first. It's not for me to meddle, but it's clear to see that if you were gone there'd be a wedding soon."

Stähl frowned, eyed her keenly, seemed to catch some helpful hint from her indignant countenance, and answered, with a pensive smile:

"I know it, I forgive it; and am sure that, for my sake, you will be less frank to others. Is this what you wished to tell me, Marjory?"

"Bless your unsuspecting heart, I wish it was, sir. I heard her words last night, I watched her all to-day, and when she went out at dusk I followed her, and saw her buy it."

Stähl started, as if about to give vent to some sudden passion, but repressed it, and with a look of well-feigned wonder asked:

"Buy what?"

Marjory pointed silently to the table, upon which lay three objects, the cup, the little vial and a rose that had fallen from Ursula's bosom as she bent to render her husband the small service he had asked of her. There was no time to feign horror, grief or doubt, for a paroxysm of real pain seized him in its gripe, and served him better than any counterfeit of mental suffering could have done. He conquered it by the power of an inflexible spirit that would not yield yet, and laying his thin hand on Marjory's arm, he whispered, hastily:

"Hush! Never hint that again, I charge you. I bade her get it, my store was nearly gone, and I feared I should need it in the night."

The old woman read his answer as he meant she should, and laid her withered cheek down on his hand, saying, with the tearless grief of age:

"Always so loving, generous and faithful! You may forgive her, but I never can."

Neither spoke for several minutes, then Stähl said:

"I will lie down and try to rest a little before I go—"

The sentence remained unfinished, as, with a weary yet wistful air, he glanced about the shadowy room, asking, dumbly, "Where?" Then he shook off the sudden influence of some deeper sentiment than fear that for an instant thrilled and startled him.

"Leave me, Marjory, set the door ajar, and let me be alone until I ring."

She went, and for an hour he lay listening to the steps of gathering guests, the sound of music, the soft murmur of conversation, and the pleasant stir of life that filled the house with its social charm. making his solitude doubly deep, his mood doubly bitter. Once Ursula stole in, and finding him apparently asleep, paused for a moment studying the wan face, with its stirless lids, its damp forehead and its pale lips, scarcely parted by the fitful breath, then, like a sombre shadow, flitted from the room again, unconscious that the closed eyes flashed wide to watch her go.

Presently there came a sudden hush, and borne on the wings of an entrancing air Ursula's voice came floating up to him, like the sweet, soft whisper of some better angel, imploring him to make a sad life noble by one just and generous action at its close. No look, no tone, no deed of patience, tenderness or self-sacrifice of hers but rose before him now, and pleaded for her with the magic of that unconscious lay. No ardent hope, no fair ambition, no high purpose of his youth, but came again to show the utter failure of his manhood, and in the hour darkened by a last temptation his benighted soul groped blindly for a firmer faith than that which superstition had defrauded of its virtue. Like many another man, for one short hour Felix Stähl wavered between good and evil, and like so many a man in whom passion outweighs principle, evil won. As the magical music ceased, a man's voice took up the strain, a voice mellow, strong and clear, singing as if the exultant song were but the outpouring of a hopeful, happy heart. Like some wild creature wounded suddenly, Stähl leaped from his couch and stood listening with an aspect which would have appalled the fair musician and struck the singer dumb.

"She might have spared me that!" he panted, as through the heavy beating of his heart he heard the voice he hated lending music to the song he loved, a song of lovers parting in the summer night, whose dawn would break upon their wedding-day. Whatever hope of merciful relenting might have been kindled by one redeeming power was for ever quenched by that ill-timed air, for with a gesture of defiant daring, Stähl drew the full vial from his breast, dashed its contents into the cup, and drained it to the dregs.

A long shudder crept over him as he set it down, then a pale peace dawned upon his face, as, laying his weary head upon the pillow it would never find sleepless any more, he pressed the rose against his lips, saying, with a bitter smile that never left his face again:

"I won my rose, and her thorns have pierced me to the heart; but my blight is on her, and no other man will wear her in his bosom when I am gone."

PART III

STAY, EVAN, when the others go; I have much to say to you, and a packet of valuable papers to entrust to you. Do not forget."

"You regard me with a strange look, Ursula, you speak in a strange tone. What has happened?"

"They tell me that Felix will live, with care and a journey to the South."

"I catch your meaning now. You will go with him."

"No, my journey will be made alone."

She looked beyond him as she spoke, with a rapt yet tranquil glance, and such a sudden brightness shone upon her face that her cousin watched her half bewildered for a moment; then caught at a hope that filled him with a troubled joy, and whispered with beating heart and lowered voice:

"Shall I not follow you, Ursula?"

Her eye came back to him, clear and calm, yet very tender in its wistfulness, and though her words sounded propitious his hope died suddenly.

"I think you will follow soon, and I shall wait for you in the safe refuge I am seeking."

They stood silent for many minutes, thinking thoughts for which they had no words, then as a pause fell after music, Ursula said:

"Now I must sing again. Give me a draught of water, my throat is parched."

Her cousin served her, but before the water touched her lips the glass fell shattered at her feet, for a wild, shrill cry rang through the house silencing the gay sounds below, and rudely breaking the long hush that had reigned above. For one breathless instant all stood like living images of wonder, fear and fright, all waited for what should follow that dread cry. An agitated servant appeared upon the threshold seeking his mistress. She saw him, yet stood as if incapable of motion, as he made his way to her through a crowd of pale, expectant faces.

"What is it?" she asked, with lips that could hardly syllable the words.

"My master, madam—dead in his bed—old Marjory has just found him. I've sent for Doctor Keen," began the man, but Ursula only seemed to hear and understand one word:

"Dead!" she echoed—"so suddenly, so soon—it cannot be true. Evan, take me to him."

She stretched out her hands as if she had gone blind, and led by her cousin, left the room, followed by several guests, in whom curiosity or sympathy was stronger than etiquette or fear. Up they went, a strange procession, and entering the dusky room, lighted only by a single shaded lamp, found Marjory lamenting over her dead master in a paroxysm of the wildest grief. Evan passed in before his cousin, bent hastily and listened at the breathless lips, touched the chill forehead, and bared the wrist to feel if any flutter lingered in the pulse. But as he pushed back the loose sleeve of the wrapper, upon the wasted arm appeared a strange device. Two slender serpents twined together like the ring, and in the circle several Hindoo characters traced in the same deep red lines. At that sight the arm dropped from his hold, and he fell back daunted by a nameless fear which he could neither master nor divine.

As Ursula appeared the old woman's grief changed to an almost fierce excitement, for rising she pointed from the dead husband to the living wife, crying shrilly:

"Come; come and see your work, fair-faced devil that you are! Here he lies, safe in the deadly sleep you gave him. Look at him and deny it if you dare!"

Ursula did look, and through the horror that blanched her face many eyes saw the shadow of remorse, the semblance of guilt. Stähl lay as she left him, his head pillowed on his arm with the easy grace habitual to him, but the pallor of that sleeping face was now changed to the awful grayness that living countenances never wear. A bitter smile still lingered on the white lips, and those mysterious eyes were wide open, full of a gloomy intelligence that appalled the beholder with the scornful triumph which still lurked there unconquered even by death. These defiant eyes appeared fixed on Ursula alone; she could not look away, nor break the spell that held her own, and through the hurried scene that followed she seemed to address her dead husband, not her living accuser.

"My work? the sleep I gave? what dare I not deny?" she said, below her breath, like one bewildered.

"See her feign innocence with guilt stamped on her face!" cried Marjory, in a passion of indignant sorrow. "You killed him, that is your work. You drugged that cup with the poison I saw you buy to-day—that is the sleep you gave him—and you dare not deny that you hated him, wished him dead, and said last night you'd not be troubled long, for you had borne enough."

"I did not kill him! You saw me prepare his evening draught, and what proof have you that he did not pass away in sleep?" demanded Ursula, more firmly, yet with an awestruck gaze still fixed upon her husband's face.

"This is my proof!" and Marjory held up the empty counterpart of the little vial that lay on the table.

"That here! I left it in my—"

A hand at Ursula's lips cut short the perilous admission, as Evan whispered:

"Hush! for God's sake, own nothing yet."

"Too late for that," screamed Marjory, more and more excited by each word.

"I found it in the ashes where she flung it in her haste, believing it was destroyed. I saw it glitter when I went to mend the fire before I woke my master. I knew it by the freshness of the label, and in a moment felt that my poor master was past all waking of mine, and found it so. I saw her buy it, I told him of it, but he loved her still and tried to deceive me with the kind lie that he bade her do it. I showed him that I knew the truth, and he only said, 'I know it, I forgive her, keep the secret for my sake,' and trusting her to the last, paid for his blind faith with his life."

"No, no, I never murdered him! I found him sleeping like a child an hour ago, and in that sleep he died," said Ursula, wringing her hands like one well nigh distraught.

"An hour ago! hear that and mark it all of you," cried Marjory. "Two hours ago she bade him good night before me, and he called her 'Judas,' as she kissed him and went. Now she owns that she returned and found him safely sleeping—God forgive me that I ever left him! for then she must have remixed the draught in which he drank his death. Oh, madam! could you have no pity, could you not remember how he loved you? see your rose fast shut in his poor dead hand—could you not leave him the one little month of life he had to live before you were set free?"

"One month!" said Ursula, with a startled look. "They told me he would live to be a hale, old man. Why was I so deceived?"

"Because he would not mar your pleasure even for a single night. He meant to tell you the sad truth gently, for he thought you had a woman's heart, and would mourn him a little though you could not love."

Paler Ursula could not become, but as mesh after mesh of the net in which she had unconsciously helped to snare herself appeared, her husband's purpose flashed upon her, yet seemed too horrible for belief, till the discovery of that last deceit was made; then like one crushed by an overwhelming blow, she covered up her face and sunk down at Evan's feet. He did not raise her up, and though a gust of eager, agitated voices went whispering through the room, no one spoke to her, no one offered comfort to the widow, counsel to the woman, pity to the culprit. They listened only to old Marjory, who poured forth her story with such genuine grief, such perfect sincerity, that all felt its pathos and few doubted its entire truth. Evan alone believed in Ursula's denial, even while to himself he owned that she had borne enough to make any means of liberation tempting. He saw more clearly than the rest how every act, look and word of hers condemned her; and felt with a bitter pang that such an accusation, even if proved false, must cast a shadow on her name and darken all her life.

Suddenly, when the stir was at its height, Ursula rose, calm, cold and steady; yet few who saw her then ever forgot the desolate despair which made that beautiful face a far more piteous sight than the dead one. Turning with all her wonted dignity, she confronted the excited group, and without a tear in her eye, a falter in her voice, a trace of shame, guilt or fear in mien or manner, she said clearly, solemnly,

"I am guilty of murder in my heart, for I did wish that man dead; but I did not kill him. The words I spoke that night were the expression of a resolve made in a moment of despair, a resolve to end my own life, when I could bear no more. To-day I was told that he would live; then my time seemed come, and believing this to be my last night on earth, I bade my husband farewell as we parted, and in a few hours hoped to lay down the burden he had made heavier than I could bear. That poison was purchased for myself, not him; he discovered it, believed I meant his death, and with a black art, which none can fathom but myself, so distorted my acts and words, before a witness, that the deed committed by himself should doom me to ignominy and avenge his wrong. I have no hope that any one will credit so wild a tale, and therein his safety lies; but God knows I speak the truth, and He will judge between us at a more righteous bar than any I can stand at here. Now do with me as you will, I am done."

Through all the bitter scenes of public accusation, trial and condemnation Ursula preserved the same mournful composure, as if having relinquished both hope and fear, no emotion remained to disturb the spirit of entire self-abnegation which had taken possession of her. All her cousin's entreaties, commands and prayers failed to draw from her the key to the mystery of her strange marriage; even when, after many merciful delays, sentence was at length pronounced upon her, and captivity for life was known to be her doom, she still refused to confess, saying:

"This fate is worse than death; but till I lie on my deathbed I will prove faithful to the promise made that man, traitorous as he was to me. I have done with the world, so leave me to such peace as I can know, and go your way, dear Evan, to forget that such a mournful creature lives."

But when all others fell away, when so-called friends proved timid, when enemies grew insolent and the whole world seemed to cast her off, one man was true to her, one man still loved, believed and honored her, still labored to save her when all others gave her up as lost, still stood between her and the curious, sharp-tongued, heavy-handed world, earning a great compassion for himself, and, in time, a juster, gentler sentiment in favor of the woman whose sin and shame he had so nobly helped to bear.

Weeks and months went heavily by, the city wearied itself with excited conjectures, conflicting rumors, varying opinions, and slowly came to look with more lenient eyes upon the beautiful culprit, whose tragic fate, with its unexplained mystery, began to plead for her more eloquently than the most gifted advocate. Few doubted her guilt, and, as she feared, few believed the accusations she brought against her dead husband; but the plea of temporary insanity had been made by her counsel, and though she strenuously denied its truth, there were daily growing hopes of pardon for an offense which, thanks to Evan's tireless appeals, now wore a far less heinous aspect than at first.

All the long summer days Ursula sat alone in her guarded room, tranquilly enjoying the sunshine that flickered through the leaves with which Evan had tried to mask the bars that shut out liberty but not heaven's light. All the balmy summer nights she lay on her narrow bed, haunted by dreams that made sleep a penance and not a pleasure, or watched, with wakeful eyes, the black shadow of a cross the moon cast upon her breast as it peered through the barred window like a ghostly face. To no one did she reveal the thoughts that burdened her, whitening her hair, furrowing her face and leaving on her forehead the impress of a great grief which no human joy could ever efface.

One autumn day Evan came hastening in full of a glad excitement, which for the moment seemed to give him back the cheery youthfulness he was fast losing. He found his cousin lying on the couch he had provided for her, for even the prison officers respected that faithful love, and granted every favor in their power. She, too, seemed to be blessed with a happy mood, for the gloom had left her eyes, a peaceful smile sat on her lips, and when she spoke her voice was musical, with an undertone of deep emotion.

"Bless your tranquil face, Ursula! One would think you guessed my tidings without telling. Yes, it is almost certain that the pardon will be granted, in answer to my prayers. One more touch will win the men who hold your fate in their hands, and that touch you can give by clearing up the mystery of Stähl's strange power over you. For your own sake and for mine do not deny me now."

"I will not."

The joy, surprise and satisfaction of the moment caused Evan to forget the sad condition upon which this confidence could be accorded. He thought only of all they had suffered, all they might yet enjoy if the pardon could be gained, and holding that thin hand fast in both his own, he listened, with absorbing interest, to the beloved voice that unfolded to him the romance within a romance, which had made a tragedy of three lives.

"I must take you far back into the past, Evan, for my secret is but the sequel of one begun long before our birth. Our grandfather, as you know, was made governor of an Indian province while still a young and comely man. One of the native princes, though a conquered subject, remained his friend, and the sole daughter of this prince loved the handsome Englishman with the despotic fervor of her race. The prince offered the hand of the fair Naya to his friend, but being already betrothed to an English girl, he courteously declined the alliance. That insult, as she thought it, never was forgiven or forgotten by the haughty princess; but, with the subtle craft of her half-savage nature, she devised a vengeance which should not only fall upon the offender, but pursue his descendants to the very last. No apparent breach was made in the friendship of the prince and governor, even when the latter brought his young wife to the residence. But from that hour Naya's curse was on his house, unsuspected and unsleeping, and as years went by the Fate of the Forrests became a tragical story throughout British India, for the brothers, nephews and sons of Roger Forrest all died violent or sudden deaths, and the old man himself was found murdered in the jungle when at the height of fame and favor.

"Two twin lads alone remained of all who had borne the name, and for a time the fatal doom seemed averted, as they grew to manhood, married and seemed born to know all the blessings which virtue and valor could deserve. But though the princess and her father were dead, the curse was still relentlessly executed by some of her kindred, for in the year of your birth your father vanished suddenly, utterly, in broad day, yet left no trace behind, and from that hour to this no clue to the lost man was ever found beyond a strong suspicion, which was never confirmed. In that same year a horrible discovery was made, which shocked and dismayed all Christian India, and was found hard of belief across the sea. Among the tribes that infested certain provinces, intent on mischief and difficult to subdue, was one class of assassins unknown even to the native governments of the country, and entirely unsuspected by the English. This society was as widely spread and carefully organized as it was secret, powerful and fanatical. Its members worshipped a gloomy divinity called Bohwanie, who, according to their heathen belief, was best propitiated by human sacrifices. The name of these devotees was Phansegars, or Brothers of the Good Work; and he who offered up the greatest number of victims was most favored by the goddess, and received a high place in the Hindoo heaven. All India was filled with amazement and affright at this discovery, and mysteries, till then deemed unfathomable, became as clear as day. Among others the Fate of the Forrests was revealed; for by the confession of the one traitor who betrayed the society, it appeared that the old prince and his sons had been members of the brotherhood, which had its higher and its lower grades, and when the young governor drew down upon himself the wrath of Naya, her kindred avenged her by propitiating Bohwanie with victim after victim from our fated family, always working so secretly that no trace of their art remained but the seal of death.

"This terrible discovery so dismayed my father that, taking you, an orphan then, and my mother, he fled to England, hoping to banish the dreadful past from his mind. But he never could, and it preyed upon him night and day. No male Forrest had escaped the doom since the curse was spoken, and an unconquerable foreboding haunted him that sooner or later he too should be sacrificed, though continents and oceans lay between him and the avengers. The fact that the black brotherhood was discovered and destroyed weighed little with him, for still a fear pursued him that Naya's kindred would hand down the curse from generation to generation, and execute with that tenacity of purpose which in that climate of the passions makes the humblest foe worthy of fear. He doubted all men, confided his secret to none, not even to his wife, and led a wandering life with us until my mother died. You remember, Evan, that the same malady that destroyed her fell likewise upon you, and that my father was forced to leave us in Paris, that he might comply with my mother's last desire and lay her in English ground. Before he went he took me apart and told me the dark history of our unfortunate family, that I might be duly impressed with the necessity of guarding you with a sleepless vigilance; for even then he could not free himself from that ominous foreboding, soon, alas! to be confirmed. It was a strange confidence to place in a girl of seventeen, but he had no friend at hand, and knowing how wholly I loved you, how safe I was from the Fate of the Forrests, he gave you to my charge and left us for a week. You know he never came again, but found his ghostly fear a sad reality in England, and on the day that was to give my mother's body to the earth he was discovered dead in his bed, with the marks of fingers at his throat, yet no other trace of his murderer ever appeared, and another dark secret was buried in the grave. You remember the horror and the grief that nearly killed me when the tidings came, and how from that hour there was a little cloud between us, a cloud I could not lift because I had solemnly promised my father that I would watch over you, yet conceal the fate that menaced you, lest it should mar your peace as it had done his own. Evan, I have kept my word till the danger is for ever past."

She paused there, but for a moment her cousin could only gaze at her, bewildered by the sudden light let in by the gloomy past. Presently he said, impetuously:

"You have, my faithful Ursula, and I will prove that I am grateful by watching over you with a vigilance as sleepless and devoted as your own. But tell me, was there nowhere in the world justice, power or wit enough to stay that savage curse? Why did not my father, or yours, appeal to the laws of either country and obtain redress?"

"They did, and, like others, appealed in vain; for, till the Phansegars were discovered, they knew not whom to accuse. After that, as Naya's kindred were all gone but a few newly-converted women and harmless children, no magistrate in India would condemn the innocent for the crimes of their race, and my father had no proofs to bring against them. Few in England believed the seemingly incredible story when it was related to them in the Indian reports. No, Evan, the wily princess entrusted her revenge to able hands, and well they did the work to the very last, as we have bitter cause to know. Every member of the brotherhood, and every helper of the curse, bore on his left arm the word 'Bohwanie!' in Hindoo characters. You saw the sign on that dead arm. Do you understand the secret now?"

"Great heavens, Ursula! Do you mean that Stähl, a Christian man, belonged to this heathen league? Surely you wrong him there."

"You will not think so when I have told all. It seemed as horrible, as incredible to me as now to you, when I first saw and comprehended on the night that changed both our lives. Stähl suspected, from many unconscious betrayals of mine (my dislike of India, my anxiety for you, then absent, and a hundred indications unseen by other eyes) that I knew the secret of the curse; he proved it by whispering the hated name of Bohwanie in my ear, and showing me the fatal sign—I knew it, for my father had told me that also. Need I tell you what recollections rushed upon me when I saw it, what visions of blood rose red before my panic-stricken eyes, how instantly I felt the truth of my instinctive aversion to him, despite his charms of mind and manner, and, above all, how utterly I was overpowered by a sense of your peril in the presence of your unknown enemy? A single thought, hope, purpose ruled me, to save you at any cost, and guard the secret still; for I felt that I possessed some power over that dread man, and resolved to use it to the uttermost. You left us, and then I learned at what a costly price I could purchase the life so dear to me. Stähl briefly told me that his mother and one old woman were the last of Naya's race, and when his grandfather, who belonged to the brotherhood, suffered death with them, he charged her to per-petuate the curse, as all the members of the family had pledged themselves to do. She promised, and when my father left India she followed, but could not discover his hiding-place, and with a blind faith in destiny, as native to her as her superstition, she left time to bring her victim to her. While resting from her quest in Germany she met and married Felix Stähl, the elder, a learned man, fond of the mysticism and wisdom of the East, who found an irresistible charm in the dark-eyed woman, who, for his sake, became a Christian in name, though she still clung to her Pagan gods in secret. With such parents what wonder that the son was the man we found him? for his father bequeathed him his features, feeble health, rare learning and accomplishments; his mother those Indian eyes that I never can forget, his fiery yet subtle nature, the superstitious temperament and the fatal vow.

"While the father lived she kept her secret hidden; when he died, Felix, then a man, was told it, and having been carefully prepared by every art, every appeal to the pride and passion of his race, every shadow years of hatred could bring to blacken the memory of the first Forrest and the wrong he was believed to have done their ances-tors, Felix was induced to take upon himself the fulfilment of the family vow. Yet living in a Christian community, and having been bred up by a virtuous father, it was a hard task to assume, and only the commands of the mother whom he adored would have won compliance. He was told that but two Forrests now remained, one a girl who was to go scatheless, the other a boy, who, sooner or later, was to fall by his hand, for he was now the last male of his race as you our ours. How his mother discovered these facts he never knew, unless from the old woman who came to them from England to die near her kin. I suspect that she was the cause of my poor father's death, though Stähl swore that he never knew of it until I told him.

"After much urging, many commands, he gave the promise, asking only freedom to do the work as he would, for though the savage spirit of his Hindoo ancestors lived again in him, the influence of civilization made the savage modes of vengeance abhorrent to him. His mother soon followed the good professor, then leaving our meeting still to chance, Felix went roaming up and down the world a solitary, studious man, for ever haunted by the sinful deed he had promised to perform, and which grew ever more and more repugnant to him.

"In an evil hour we met; my name first arrested him; my beauty (I may speak of it now for it is gone) attracted him; my evident aversion piqued his pride and roused his will to overcome it; and then the knowledge of my love for you fanned his smouldering passion to a blaze and confirmed his wavering purpose. You asked on that sad night if I had learned to love while you were gone? I spoke truly when I answered yes, for absence proved how dear you had become to me, and I only waited your return to gratefully accept the love with which I knew your heart was overflowing. You came, and seeing Stähl's devotion, doubted the affection I never had confessed. He saw it plainly, he divined your passion, and in an hour decided upon gratifying his own desire, keeping the promise he made his mother, yet sparing himself the crime of murder, well knowing that for you life without me would be a fate more dark than any death he could devise. I pleaded, prayed and wept, but he was inexorable. To tell you was to destroy you, for he feared nothing; to keep the secret was to forfeit your love and sacrifice myself. One hope alone remained to me, a sinful yet a pardonable one in such a strait as mine; Felix could not live long; I might support life for a time by the thought that I had saved you, by the hope that I might soon undeceive and recompense you for the loss you had sustained. Evan, it was a natural yet unrighteous act, for I did evil that good might come of it, and such deeds never prosper. Better have left you in God's hand, better even have seen you dead and at peace than have condemned you to the life you have led and still must lead for years perhaps. I was a weak, loving, terror-stricken woman, and in that dreadful hour one fear overwhelmed all other passions, principles and thoughts. I could save you, and to accomplish that I would so gladly have suffered death in any shape. Believe that, dearest Evan, and forgive me for the fate to which I have condemned the man I love, truly, tenderly even to the end."

Her voice died in a broken sob as Evan gathered her close to his sore heart, and she clung there spent and speechless, as if the pain of parting were for ever over and her refuge found at last. Evan spoke first, happily and hopefully, for the future opened clearly, and the long twilight seemed about to break into a blissful dawn.

"You shall be repaid for your exceeding love, Ursula, with a devotion such as man never gave to woman until now. There is no longer any cloud between us, nor shall there be between you and the world. Justice shall be done, and then we will leave this city of bitter memories behind us, and go away together to begin the new life that lies before us."

"We shall begin a new life, but not together, Evan," was the low answer, as she tenderly laid her pale cheek to his, as if to soften the hard truth.

"But, love, you will be free at once; there can be no doubt of the pardon now."

"Yes, I shall soon be free, but human hands will not open my prison doors, and I humbly trust that I may receive pardon, but not from human lips. Evan, I told you I would never tell my secret till I lay on my deathbed; I lie there now."

If she had stabbed him with the hand folded about his neck, the act would not have shocked and startled him like those last words. They pierced him to the heart, and as if in truth he had received a mortal wound, he could only gaze at her in dumb dismay, with eyes full of anguish, incredulity and grief.

"Let me seem cruel that I may be merciful, and end both suspense and fear by telling all at once. There is no hope for me. I have prayed to live, but it cannot be, for slowly yet surely Felix has killed me. I said I would gladly die for you, God takes me at my word, and now I am content. Let me make my sacrifice cheerfully, and let the suffering I have known be my atonement for the wrong I did myself and you."

As she spoke so tranquilly, so tenderly, a veil seemed to fall from before her cousin's eyes. He looked into the face that smiled at him, saw there the shadow which no human love can banish, read perfect peace in its pale serenity, felt that life was a poor boon to ask for her, and with a pang that rent that faithful heart of his, silently relinquished the one sustaining hope which had upheld him through that gloomy year. Calm with a grief too deep for tears, he drew the wan and wasted creature who had given herself for him closer to the shelter of his arms, and changed her last fear to loving pride by saying, with a manful courage, a meek resignation that ennobled him by its sincerity:

"Rest here in peace, my Ursula. No selfish grief shall cloud your sunset or rob you of one hour of happy love. I can bear the parting, for I shall follow soon; and thank God that after the long bewilderment of this sad world we may enjoy together the new life which has no end."

ᔰ A Marble Woman: or, The Mysterious Model

CHAPTER I. LITTLE CECIL

"WHAT DO YOU MEAN by pulling the bell fit to bring the house down?" demanded gruff old Anthony, as he flung the door open and found himself confronted with a large trunk and a small girl holding a letter in her hand.

"It was the coachman, please, sir" was the composed answer.

"Well, what do you want, child?"

"I wish to come in. This is my luggage; I'll help you with it."

The small personage laid hold of one handle with such perfect good faith in her own strength that it produced a chuckle from the old servant as he drew the trunk in with one hand, the child with the other, and shut the door, saying more respectfully, "Now, ma'am, what next?"

Smoothing her disordered dress with dignity, the little girl replied, as if repeating a carefully learned lesson, "You are to give this letter to Mr. Bazil Yorke, and say Miss Stein has come. Then I am to wait till he tells me what to do."

"Are you Miss Stein?" asked Anthony, bewildered by the appearance of a child in that lonely house.

"Yes, sir; and I've come to live here if Mr. Yorke will keep me," said the little girl, glancing wistfully about her as if waiting for a welcome.

"Are you a relation of Master's?" questioned Anthony, still more mystified.

"No, sir. He knew my papa and mamma, but he never saw me. That's all I know about it."

The old man shook his head with an air of resignation as he muttered to himself, "Some whim of Master's; it's just like him." Then aloud, "I'll take up the letter, but you'd better play out here till you're wanted; for when Master gets busy up aloft, it's no use trying to fetch him down before the time."

Leading her through the hall, he opened a glass door and ushered her into a city garden, where a few pale shrubs and vines rustled in the wind. The child glanced listlessly about her as she walked, for nothing was in bloom, and the place had a neglected air. Suddenly a splendid, full-blown rose softly brushed her cheek and fell at her feet. With an exclamation of pleasure she caught it up and looked skyward to see what friendly fairy had divined her wish and granted it.

"Here I am," called a laughing voice, and turning about she saw a boy leaning on the low wall that divided Mr. Yorke's garden from an adjoining one. A rosy, bright-eyed boy about her own age he seemed, full of the pleasant audacity which makes boyhood so charming, and in a neighborly mood just then; for as she looked up wondering, he nodded, smiled, and said merrily, "How are you? Do you like the rose?"

"Oh, yes! Did you mean it for me?"

"I thought you looked as if you needed one, so I tossed it over. It's very dismal down there. Suppose you come up here, and then you can see my garden while we talk a bit. Don't be afraid of me; just give me your hand and there you are."

There was something so winning in voice, face, and gesture that little Miss Stein could not resist the invitation. She gave her hand, and soon sat on the wide coping of the wall, regarding her new friend with a shy yet confiding look as he did the honors of the place with well-bred eagerness. Neither asked the other's name, but making the rose their master of ceremonies, introduced themselves through that pretty medium, and soon forgot that they had been entire strangers five minutes before.

"Do you like my garden?" asked the boy, as the girl smelled her flower and smiled down upon the blooming plot below her.

"Very much; I wish Mr. Yorke would have one like it."

"He don't care for such things; he's odd and busy, and a genius, you know."

"I hope that's nothing bad, because I'm going to live with him. Tell me all about him, for I never saw him in my life."

"He's a sculptor and makes splendid statues up in that tower where nothing but the sun and sparrows can see him. He never shows them, and no one would ever see them if they didn't beg and tease and give him no peace till they do."

"Is he kind and pleasant?" asked the girl.

"He looks precious grim with his long hair and beard, but he's got kind eyes, though his face is dark and strange."

"Has he got a wife and any little children?"

"Oh, dear, no! He lives here with old Tony and Mrs. Hester, the maid. I heard my mother tell a lady that Mr. Yorke had a love trouble and can't bear women, so none dare go near him. He's got a splendid great dog, but he's as fierce as a wolf to everyone but his master and Tony."

"I wish I hadn't come. I don't like odd people, and I'm afraid of dogs," sighed Miss Stein.

"Mr. Yorke will be kind to such a little thing as you, and make old Judas like you, I dare say. Perhaps you won't have to stay long if you don't like it. Is your home far away?"

"I've got no home now. Oh, Mamma! Mamma!" And covering her face with her little black frock, the child broke into such sudden, bitter sobs that the boy was stricken with remorse. Finding words vain, he sprang impetuously off the wall, and filling his hands with his choicest flowers, heaped them into the child's lap with such demonstrations of penitence and goodwill that she could not refuse to be comforted.

Just then Anthony called her, and with a hasty good-bye she turned to obey, but the boy detained her for a moment to say, "Don't forget to ask Mr. Yorke if you may play with me, because you'll be very dull all by yourself, and I should like you for my little sweetheart."

"Alfred! Alfred! It is rather too soon for that," called a smiling lady from a window of the adjoining house, whereat the boy sprang down, laughing at the unexpected publicity of his declaration, and Miss Stein walked away, looking much disturbed by Anthony's chuckles.

"The master will be down to his tea directly, so you can look out a winder and not meddle till he comes," said the old man as he left her.

The memory of the pretty lad warmed the child's heart and seemed to shed a ray of cheerfulness over the somber room. A table was spread with care, and beside one plate lay a book, as if "the master" was in the habit of enlivening his solitary meals with such society as the full shelves about afforded him. The furniture was ancient, the window hangings dark, the pictures weird or gloomy, and the deep silence that reigned through the house oppressed the lonely child. Approaching the table she ventured to examine the book. It proved intelligible and picturesque; so establishing herself in the armchair, she spread the volume before her, and soon became happily forgetful of orphanage and solitude.

So intent was she that a man came to the door unobserved, and pausing there, scrutinized her from head to foot. Had she looked up she would have seen a tall, athletic figure and a singularly attractive face, though it was neither beautiful nor gentle. The dark, neglected hair was streaked with gray at thirty; the forehead was marked with deep lines, and under the black brows were magnificent yet melancholy eyes, that just then looked as if some strong emotion had kindled an unwonted fire in their depths. The lower part of the face gave flat contradiction to the upper, for the nose was disdainful, the chin square and grim, the whole contour of the mouth relentless, in spite of the softening effect of a becoming beard. Dressed in velvet cap and paletot, and framed in the dark doorway, he looked like a striking picture of some austere scholar aged with care or study, not with years; yet searching closer, one would have seen traces of deep suffering, latent passion, and a strange wistfulness, as if lonely eyes were forever seeking something they had lost.

For many minutes Bazil Yorke watched the unconscious child, as if there was some strong attraction for him in the studious little figure poring over the book with serious eyes, one hand turning the pictured pages, the other pushing back the wavy hair from a blooming cheek and a forehead possessing delicate brows and the harmonious lines about the temples which artists so love. The man's eyes softened as he looked, for the child's patient trust made her friendlessness the more pathetic. He put out his hand as if to draw her to him, then checked the impulse, and the hard mouth grew grimmer as he swept off the cap, saying coldly, "Miss Stein, I am ready now."

His guest started, shut the book, slipped down, and went to meet her host, offering her hand as if anxious to atone for the offense of meddling.

Like one unused to such acts, Mr. Yorke took the small hand, gave it a scarcely perceptible pressure, and dropped it without a word. The action grieved the child, yet nothing betrayed the pang of disappointment it gave her except a slight tremor in the voice that timidly asked, "Did you get the letter, sir?"

"I did. Your mother wished me to keep you till you were eighteen, when you were to choose a guardian for yourself. Her family will not receive you, and your father's family is far away; but your mother and myself were old friends many years ago, and she hoped I would take you for a time."

"Will you, sir? I'll try not to be a trouble."

"No, I cannot. This is no place for a child; nor am I a fit guardian if it was. I will find some better home for you tomorrow. But as you will remain here tonight, you may take off your hat and cloak, or whatever it is."

Half pityingly, half impatiently he spoke, and eyed the child as if he longed to yet dared not keep her. The little hat was taken off, but the ribbons of the mantle were in a knot, and after pulling at it for a moment, she turned to her companion for help. As he stooped to give it with a curious reluctance in his manner, she scanned the face so near her own with innocent freedom, and presently murmured, as if to herself, "Yes, the boy was right; his eyes *are* kind."

With a wrench that tore the silk, and caused the child to start, Mr. Yorke broke the knot, and turning away, rang the bell with vehemence.

"What is your name?" he asked, carefully averting his eyes as the little girl sat down.

"Cecilia Bazil Stein."

"What an ominous conjunction!"

She did not understand the scornful exclamation and proceeded to explain.

"Mamma's name was Cecilia, yours is Bazil, and Papa's was Stein. You can call me Celia as Mamma did, if you please, sir."

"No, I shall call you Cecil. I dislike the other name."

Quick tears sprang to the child's eyes, but none fell, and lowering her voice she said, with trembling lips, "Mamma wished me to tell you that she sent her love, and the one precious thing she had as a keepsake, and hoped you'd take it in memory of the happy days when you and she were friends."

Mr. Yorke turned his back upon her for several minutes, then asked abruptly, "Where have you been this last year?"

"Here in America. We were in England before that, because Mamma did not like Germany since Papa died, and we were tired of going about."

"Your father died when you were a baby, I think. Have you been with your mother ever since?" asked Mr. Yorke with a half-smile, as the little creature spoke of these countries as composedly as if they were neighboring towns.

"Yes, I was always with her, and we were very happy staying in all sorts of new and pleasant places. But Mamma wished to save up some money for me, so we came here and lived very plainly in the country till she—"

The child stopped there, for her lips trembled and she did not wish to disgrace herself by crying twice in one hour. He saw that she controlled herself, and the little trait of character pleased him as did the pretty mixture of innocent frankness and good breeding betrayed by her manner and appearance.

"When did she leave you?" he ventured to ask, carefully avoiding the hard word "die."

"Three weeks ago."

"How old are you, Cecil?" he said presently, in order to change the current of her thoughts, although the question was an unnecessary one.

"Nearly twelve, sir."

"Twelve years, twelve long years since I saw her last, and then gave up the world."

He spoke low to himself, and his thoughts seemed to wander from the present to the past, as, bending his head upon his breast, he stood mute and motionless till Anthony announced, "Tea is ready, master."

Looking up with the melancholy shadow gloomier than ever in his eyes, Yorke led the child to the table, filled her cup, put everything within her reach, and opening a book, read more than he ate. Twilight was deepening in the room; the oppressive silence made the meal unsocial, and Cecil's heart was heavy, for she felt doubly forlorn, bereft of the protection she had hoped to find and the familiar name her mother's voice had endeared to her. She ate a few morsels, then leaned back in her chair, looking drearily about and wondering what would happen next. She did not wait long before a somewhat startling incident occurred.

As her eye roved to and fro it was arrested by the sudden appearance of a face at one of the windows. A strange, uncanny face, half concealed by a black beard that made the pallor of the upper part more striking. It was gone again instantly, but Cecil had only time to catch her breath and experience a thrill of alarm, when the long curtains that hung before the other half-open window stirred as if a hand grasped them, and through the narrow aperture between the folds the glitter of an eye was plainly visible. Fascinated by fear, the child sat motionless, longing to cry out, yet restrained by timidity and the hope that her companion would look up and see the intruder for himself.

He seemed absorbed in his book, and utterly unconscious of the hidden watcher, till an involuntary gesture caused another movement of the curtains, as if the hand loosened its grasp, for the eye vanished and Cecil covered her face with a long sigh of relief. Mr. Yorke glanced up, mistook the gesture for one of weariness, and evidently glad of an excuse to dispose of the child, he said abruptly, "You have come a long way today, and must be tired. Will you go to bed?"

"Oh, yes, I shall be glad to go," cried Cecil, eager to leave what to her was now a haunted room.

Taking a lamp, he led her along dimly lighted halls, up wide stair cases, into a chamber that seemed immense to its small occupant, while the darkly curtained bed was so like a hearse she instantly decided that it would be impossible to sleep in it. Mr. Yorke glanced about as if desirous of making her comfortable, but quite ignorant how to set about it.

"The old woman who would have attended you is sick, but if you want anything, ring for Anthony. Good night."

Cecil was on the point of lifting her face for the good-night kiss she had been accustomed to receive from other lips, but remembering the careless pressure of his hand, the cold welcome he had given her, she restrained the impulse, and let him leave her with no answer but a quiet echo of his own "Good night."

The moment his steps died away, she opened the door again and watched the light mount higher and higher as he wound his way up a spiral flight of stairs that evidently led to the tower. Cecil longed to follow, for she was sleepless with the excitement of novelty and a lingering touch of fear (for the face still haunted her), and she now reproached herself for not having spoken to Mr. Yorke. She was about to make this an excuse for following him, when the sound of noises from above made her hesitate.

"I'll wait till he comes down, or till the person goes, for he ought to know about the man I saw, because it might be a thief," she thought.

After lingering on the threshold till she was tired, Cecil seated herself in an easy chair beside the door, and amused herself by examining the pictures on the wall. But she was more weary than she knew; the chair was luxuriously cushioned, the steady murmur of voices very soothing, and she soon lapsed away into a drowse.

The certainty that someone had touched her suddenly startled her wide awake. An instant's thought recalled her purpose, and fearing to be up too late, she ran into the upper hall, hoping to find Mr. Yorke descending. No one was in sight, however, yet so sure was she that a hand had touched her and a footstep sounded in the room that she looked over the balustrade, intending to call. Not a word left her lips, however, for neither Mr. Yorke nor Anthony appeared; but a man was going slowly down, wrapped in a cloak, with a shadowy hat drawn low over his brows. A slender hand shone white against the dark cloak, and as he reached the hall below he glanced over his shoulder, showing Cecil the same colorless face with its black beard and glittering eyes that had frightened her before, though he evidently did not see her now.

It alarmed her again, for it was a singularly sinister face in spite of its beauty. Never pausing to see what became of him, and conscious of nothing but an uncontrollable longing to be near Mr. Yorke, Cecil climbed the winding stairs without a pause till she reached an arched doorway, and seemed to see a gathering of ghosts beyond. The long, large room was filled with busts, statues, uncut blocks, tools, dust, and disorder, in the midst of which stood Mr. Yorke, dressed in a suit of gray linen, and intent on modeling something from a handful of clay. Many children would have been more alarmed at these inanimate figures than at the other, but Cecil found so much that was inviting, she forgot fear in delight, and boldly entered. A smiling woman seemed to beckon to her, a winged child to offer flowers, and all about the room pale gods and goddesses looked down upon her from their pedestals with what to her beauty-loving eye seemed varying expressions of welcome. Judas, the great dog, lay like a black statue on a tawny tiger skin, and the strong glow from a chandelier shone on his master as he worked with a swift dexterity that charmed Cecil.

Eager to ask questions, she began her explanations with a sudden "Bazil, I came up to—"

But got no further, for with a start that sent the model crumbling to the floor, he turned upon her almost angrily, demanding, "Who calls me by that name?"

"It's me; Mamma always said Bazil, and so I got used to it. What can I call you, sir?"

"Simply *Yorke,* as others do. I forbid that hateful name. Why are you here?"

"Indeed, I could not help it. I was so lonely and so frightened down there. I saw a face at the window, and wanted to tell you, but heard someone talking up here and I waited. But when I waked I saw the same face going down the stairs, and so I ran to you."

Yorke listened with curious intentness to her story, asked a question or two, mused a moment, then said, pointing to a half-finished athlete, "The man is my model for that. He is a strange person, and does odd things, but you need not fear him."

A quick-witted woman would have seen at a glance that dust lay thick on the clay figure, and have known that the slender hand grasping the cloak could never have belonged to the arm that served as a model for the brawny athlete. But Cecil's childish eyes saw no discrepancy between the two. and she believed the explanation at once. With a sigh of mingled satisfaction and relief, she looked about her, and said beseechingly, "Please let me stop and see your work. I like it so much, so very much!"

"What do you know about it, child?" Yorke answered, wondering at her interest and sudden animation.

"Why, I used to do it; Mamma taught me as you taught her, with wax first, then pretty brown clay like this; and I was very happy doing it, because I liked it best of all my plays."

"Your mother taught you! Why, Cecil?" And Yorke's grave face kindled with an expression that won the child to franker speech at once.

"She liked it as well as I, and always called me little Bazil when I made pretty things. She was fond of it because she used to be very happy doing it a long time ago. She often told me about you when you lived in her father's house; how you hated lessons, and loved to make splendid things in wax and wood and clay; how you didn't care to eat or sleep when you were busy, and how you made an image of her, but broke it when she was unkind to you. She didn't tell me what she did, but I wish you would, so that I may be careful not to do it while I'm here."

He laughed such a bitter laugh, it both touched and troubled her, as he answered harshly, "No fear of that; I never can be hurt again as she hurt me thirteen years ago." Then with a sudden change in countenance and manner, he sat down on a block of marble with a half-finished angel's head looking out of it, drew Cecil toward him, and looked at her with hungry eyes as he said eagerly, "Tell me more. Did she talk of me? Did she teach you to care for me? Child, speak fast—I vowed I would ask no questions, but I must!"

His voice rose, his glance searched her face, his stern mouth grew tremulous, and the whole man seemed to wake and glow with an unconquerable desire. Reassured by this sudden thaw in the frosty aspect of her guardian, Cecil leaned confidingly against his knee and softly answered, with her hand upon his shoulder, "Yes, Mamma often spoke of you; she wished me to love you dearly—and the last thing she said was that about the keepsake. I think she will be sorry if you send me away, because she thought you'd care for me as you once did for her."

Some strange emotion rushed warm and tender over Bazil Yorke, and as if the words, the gentle touch, had broken down some barrier set up by pride or will, he took the child into his arms with an impetuous gesture, saying brokenly, "She remembered me—and she sent me her all. Surely I may keep the gift and put one drop of sweetness into this bitter life of mine."

Bewildered, yet glad, Cecil clung to him, drawn by an attraction that she could not understand. For a moment Yorke hid his face in her long hair, then put her away as abruptly as he had embraced her, and returned to his work as if unused to such betrayals of feeling and ashamed of them. He merely said, as he took up his tools, "Amuse yourself as you please; I must work."

Quite contented, Cecil roved about the room till curiosity was satisfied; made timid advances toward the great dog, which were graciously received; and at length gathering up the crumbled clay that fell from Yorke's hand, she sat down beside Judas and began to mold as busily as the master.

Presently a little voice broke the silence, humming a song that Yorke remembered well. Softly as it was sung, Judas pricked up his ears, his master paused in his work, and leaning with folded arms, listened till the long hush recalled the singer from her happy reverie. She stopped instantly, but seeing no displeasure in the altered face above her, she held out her work, asking shyly, "Is it very bad, sir?"

It was a bunch of grapes deftly fashioned by small fingers that needed no other tool than their own skill, and though swiftly done, it was as graceful as if the gray cluster had just been broken from a vine. Yorke examined it critically, lifted the child's face and studied it intently for a moment, kissed it gravely on the forehead so like his own, and said, with an air of decision, "It is well done; I shall keep both it and you. Will you stay and work with me, Cecil, and be content with no friend but myself, no playmate but old Judas?"

Cecil read the yearning of the man's heart in his eyes with the quick instinct of a child, and answered it by exclaiming heartily, "Yes, I will; and be very happy here, for I like this place, I like Judas, and I love you already, because you make these lovely things, and are so kind to me now."

"Are you a discreet girl, Cecil? Can you see and hear things, and yet not ask questions or tell tales?" asked Yorke, somewhat anxiously.

"I think I am."

"So do I. Now I have a mind to keep you, for you are one of my sort; but I wish you to understand that nothing which goes on in my house is to be talked about outside of it. I let the world alone, and desire the world to do the same by me; so remember if you forget your promise, you march at once."

"I always keep my promises. But may I ask two questions now before I promise? Then I'll never do it anymore."

"Well, my inquisitive little person, what is it?"

"I want to know if I can sometimes see the pleasant boy who gave me this rose."

"And kissed you on the wall," added Yorke, with such a satirical look that Cecil colored high and involuntarily exclaimed, "Did you see us? I thought you couldn't from this high place."

"I see everything that happens on my premises. If you do not gossip you may see the boy occasionally. What is the other question?"

"Will that disagreeable man come here often—the model, I mean? He frightens me, and I don't want to see him unless you wish me to."

"You will not see him anymore. I shall not work at this figure for the present, so there will be no need of him. Make yourself easy; I shall never wish you to see or speak to him."

"You are very kind. I'll try to please you and not peep or ask questions. Can I wash my hands and look at this pretty book? I'll go quietly away to bed when I get sleepy."

With very much the air of a man who had undertaken the care of a butterfly, Yorke established her with the coveted portfolio on her lap, and soon entirely forgot her.

Accustomed to the deep reveries of a solitary life, hour after hour passed unheeded, and the city clocks tolled their warnings to deaf ears. After glancing once at the little chair and finding the child gone, he thought no more of her, till rising to rest his cramped limbs he saw her lying fast asleep on the tiger skin. One arm embraced the dog's shaggy neck, her long hair swept the dusty floor, and the rosy warmth of slumber made the childish face blooming and beautiful.

"Truly I am a fit guardian for a little creature like this," Yorke muttered, as he watched her a moment; then he covered her with a cloak and began to pace the room, busied with some absorbing thought. Once he paused and looked at the sleeper with an expression of grim determination, saying to himself as he eyed the group, "If I had power to kill the savage beast, skill to subdue the fierce dog, surely I can mold the child as I will, and make the daughter pay the mother's debt."

His face darkened as he spoke, the ruthless look deepened, and the sudden clenching of the hand boded ill for the young life he had taken into his keeping.

All night the child lay dreaming of her mother, all night the man sat pondering over an early wrong that had embittered a once noble nature, and dawn found them unchanged, except that Cecil had ceased to smile in her sleep, and Bazil Yorke had shaped a fugitive emotion into a relentless purpose.

Chapter II. The Broken Cupid

Five years later, a new statue stood in the studio; we might have said two new statues, though one was a living creature. The marble figure was a lovely, Psyche-bending form, and with her graceful hand above her eyes, as if she watched her sleeping lover. Of all Bazil Yorke's works this was the best, and he knew it, for, surrounded by new influences, he had wrought at it with much of his youthful ardor— had found much of the old happiness while so busied, and was so proud of his success that no offer could tempt him to part with it—no certainty of fame persuade him to exhibit it, except to a chosen few.

The human figure was Cecil, changed from a rosy child into a slender, deep-eyed girl. Colorless, like a plant deprived of sunshine, strangely unyouthful in the quiet grace of her motions, the sweet seriousness of her expression, but as beautiful as the Psyche and almost as cold. Her dress heightened the resemblance, for the white folds draped her from neck to ankle; not an ornament marred its severe simplicity, and the wavy masses of her dark hair were gathered up with a fillet, giving her the head of a young Hebe. It was a fancy of Yorke's, and as few eyes but his beheld her, she dressed for him alone, unconscious that she served as a model for his fairest work. Standing in the one ray of sunshine that shot athwart the subdued light of the studio, she seemed intent upon a little Cupid exquisitely carved in the purest marble. She was not working now, for the design was finished, but seemed to be regarding it with mingled satisfaction and regret—satisfaction that it was done so well, regret that it was done so soon. The little god was just drawing an arrow from his quiver with an arch smile, and the girl watched him with one almost as gay. A rare sight upon her lips, but some happy fancy seemed to bring it, and more than once she gave the graceful figure a caressing touch, as if she had learned to love it.

"Don't fire again, little Cupid, I surrender," suddenly exclaimed a blithe voice behind her, and, turning, Cecil saw her friend and neighbor, Alfred, now a tall young man, though much of the boyish frankness and impetuosity still remained.

"Do you like it, Alf?" she asked, with a quiet smile of welcome, and a repose of manner contrasting strongly with the eagerness of the newcomer's.

"You know I do, Cecil, for it has been my delight ever since you began it. The little god is perfect, and I must have him at any cost. Name your price, and let it be a high one."

"Yorke would not like that, neither should I. You have more than paid for it by friendly acts and words through these five years, so let me give it to you with all my heart."

She spoke tranquilly, and offered her hand as if transferring to him the lovely figure it had wrought. He took the white hand in both his own, and with a sudden glow on his cheek, a sudden ardor in his eye, said, in an impulsive voice, "With all your heart, Cecil? Let me take you at your word, let me claim, not only the image of love, but the reality, and keep this hand as mine."

A soft tinge of color touched the girl's cheek as she drew her hand away, but the quiet smile remained unchanged, and she still looked up at him with eyes as innocent and frank as any child's.

"I did not mean that, Alf; we are too young for such things yet, and I know nothing of love except in marble."

"Let me teach you then; we never are too young to learn that lesson," he urged eagerly. "I meant to wait another year before I spoke, for then I shall be my own master, and have a home to give you. But you grow so lovely and so dear, I must speak out and know my fate. Dear Cecil, what is it to be?"

"I cannot tell; this is so new and strange to me, I have no answer ready."

She looked troubled now, but more by his earnestness than by any maidenly doubts or fears of her own, and leaning her head upon her hand seemed to search for an answer, and search in vain. Alfred watched her a moment, then broke out indignantly, "No wonder it seems new and strange, for you have led a nun's life all these years, and know nothing of the world outside these walls. Yorke lets you read neither romance nor poetry, gives you no companions but marble men and women, no change but a twilight walk each day, or a new design to work out in this gloomy place. You never have been told you have a heart and a right to love like other women. Let me help you to know it, and find an answer for myself."

"Am I so different from other girls? Is my life strange and solitary? I've sometimes thought so, but I never felt quite sure. What *is* love, Alfred?"

"This!" And opening his arms her young lover would have answered her wistful question eloquently, but Cecil shrank a little, and put up her hand to check his impulse.

"Not so, tell me in words, Alf, how one feels when one truly loves."

"I only know how *I* feel, Cecil. I long for you day and night; think of you wherever I am; see no one half so beautiful, half so good as you; care for nothing but being here, and have no wish to live unless you will make life happy for me."

"And that is love?" She spoke low, to herself, for as he answered her face had slowly been averted, a soft trouble had dawned in her eyes, and a deeper color risen to her cheek, as if the quiet heart was waking suddenly.

"Yes: and you do love me, Cecil? Now I know it—now you will not deny it."

She looked up, pale but steady, for the child's expression was quite gone, and in her countenance was all a woman's pain and pity, as she said decidedly, "No, Alf, I do not love you. I know myself now, and feel that it is impossible."

But Alfred would not accept the hard word "impossible," and pleaded passionately, in spite of the quiet determination to end the matter, which made Cecil listen almost as coldly as if she did not hear. Anger succeeded surprise and hope, as the young man bitterly exclaimed, "You might make it possible, but you will not try!"

"No, I will not, and it is unkind of you to urge me. Let me be in peace—I'm happy with my work, and my nun's life was pleasant till you came to trouble it with foolish things."

She spoke impatiently, and the first glimpse of passion ever seen upon her face now disturbed its quietude, yet made it lovelier than ever.

"Well said, Cecil; my pupil does honor to her master."

Both started as the deep voice sounded behind them, and both turned to see Bazil Yorke leaning in the doorway with a satirical smile on his lips. Cecil made an involuntary motion to go to him, but checked herself as Alfred said hotly, "It is not well said! And but for the artful training you have given her, she would be glad to change this unnatural life, though she dare not say so, for you are a tyrant, in spite of your seeming kindness!"

"Do you fear me too much to tell the truth, Cecil?" asked Yorke, quite unmoved.

"No, master."

"Then decide between us two, now and forever, because I will not have your life or mine disturbed by such scenes as this. If you love Alfred, say so freely, and when my guardianship ends I will give you to his. If you prefer to stop with me, happy in the work you are wonderfully fitted to perform, content with the quiet life I deem best for you, and willing to be the friend and fellow laborer of the old master, then come to him and let us hear no more of lovers or of tyrants."

As he spoke Cecil had listened breathlessly, and when he paused, she went to him with such a glad and grateful face, such instant and entire willingness, that it touched him deeply, though he showed no sign of it except to draw her nearer, with a caressing gesture which he had not used since she ceased to be a child.

The words, the act, wounded the young lover to the heart, and he broke out, in a voice trembling with anger, sorrow, and reproach, "I might have known how it would be; I should have known if my own love had not blinded me. You have taught her something beside your art—have made too sure of her to fear any rival, and when the time comes you will change the guardian to a husband, and become her master in earnest."

"Not I! My day for such folly is long since past. Cecil will never be anything to me but my ward and pupil, unless some more successful lover than yourself should take her from me."

Yorke laughed scornfully at the young man's accusation, but looked down at the girl with an involuntary pressure of the arm that held her, for despite his careless manner, she was dearer to him than he knew.

"I will never leave you for any other—never, my dear master."

Alfred heard her soft whisper, saw her cling to Yorke, knew that there was no hope for him, and with a broken "Good-bye, Cecil, I shall not trouble you again," he was gone.

"Poor lad, he takes it hardly, but he'll soon forget. I should have warned him, had I not been sure it would have hastened what I desired to prevent. It is over at last, thank heaven, so look up, foolish child; there are no lovers here to frighten you now."

But Cecil did not look up, she hid her face and wept quietly, for Alfred had been her only young friend since the day he gave the rose and made the new home pleasant by his welcome.

Yorke let her tears flow unreproved for a few moments, then his patience seemed exhausted, and placing her in a seat, he turned away to examine the Cupid which Alfred had not accepted. As he looked at it he smiled, then frowned, as if some unwelcome fancy had been conjured up by it, and asked abruptly, "What suggested the idea of this, Cecil?"

"You did!" was the half-audible answer.

"I did? Never to my knowledge."

"Your making Psyche suggested Cupid, for though you did not tell me the pretty fable, Alf did, and told me how my image should be made. I could not do a large one, so I pleased myself with trying a little winged child with the bandage and the bow."

"Why would you not let me see it till it was done?"

"At first because I hoped to make it good enough to give you, then I thought it too full of faults to offer, so I gave it to Alf; but he would not have it without me, and now I don't care for it anymore."

Yorke smiled, as if well pleased at this proof of her indifference to the youth, then with a keen glance at the drooping face before him, he asked, "Are you quite sure that you do not care for Alfred?"

"Very sure, master."

"Then what has changed you so within a week or two? You sang yesterday like an uncaged bird, a thing you seldom do. You smile to yourself as you work, and when I wished to use your face as a model not an hour ago, you could not fix your eyes on me as I bade you, and cried when I chid you. What is it, Cecil? If you have anything upon your mind, tell me, and let nothing disturb us again if possible."

If the girl had been trained to repress all natural emotions and preserve an unvarying calmness of face, voice, and manner, she had also been taught to tell the truth, promptly and fearlessly. Now it was evident that she longed to escape the keen eye and searching questions of her master, as she loved to call him, but she dared not hesitate, and answered slowly, "I should have told you something before, only I did not like to, and I thought perhaps you knew it."

"Well, well, stop blushing and speak out; I know nothing but this boy's love and the change in you." Yorke spoke impatiently, and wore an anxious look, as if he dreaded more tender confessions, for Cecil never lifted her eyes as she rapidly went on:

"A week ago, as we came in from our evening walk, you stopped at the corner to call Judas, and I went on to open the door for you. Just as I put the key into the latch, a hand took mine, as if to slip something into it, but I was so startled I let the paper drop, and should have called to you if someone had not wrapped me in a cloak so closely that I could not speak, though I was kissed more than once and called 'my darling' in a very tender voice. It all happened in a minute, and before I knew what to do, the man was gone, and I ran in, too frightened to wait for you."

As she paused, Cecil looked up, and was amazed to see no wonder on Yorke's face, but an expression of pain and indignation that she could not understand. "Back again and I not know it," he muttered to himself, then aloud, almost sternly, "why did you not tell me this before?"

"You were busy that night, and when I'd thought of it a little I did not like to speak of it, because I remembered that you called me silly when I told you that people made me uncomfortable by looking at me as I walked in the day. I thought I'd wait, but it troubled me and made me seem unlike myself, I suppose."

"Are you sure it was not Alfred, playing some foolish prank in the twilight?" asked Yorke.

"I know it was not Alf; he wears no beard, and is not tall like this strange man."

"It could not have been Anthony?"

"Oh, no, that is impossible. Old Tony's hands are rough; these were soft though very strong, and the voice was too low and kind for his."

"Have you no suspicion who it might have been?" asked Yorke, searching her thoughtful face intently.

She blushed deeper than before, but answered steadily, "I did think of you, master, for you are tall and strong, you wear a beard and cloak, and your hand is soft. But your voice never is like that voice, and you never say 'my darling' in that tender way."

Yorke knit his brows, saying, a little bitterly, "You seem to have forgiven this insolent stranger already because of that, and to reproach me that I never use such sentimental phrases, or embrace my ward upon my doorstep. Shall I tell you who this interesting phantom probably was? The model, whom you disliked so much that I dismissed him when you came."

Cecil turned pale, for her childish terror had remained as fresh in her memory as the events that wakened it; and though she had merely caught glimpses of the man as he occasionally glided into Yorke's private room during the past five years, she still felt a curious mixture of interest and fear, and often longed to break her promise and ask questions concerning him and his peculiar ways.

"Why do you let him come?" she said, forgetting everything but surprise, as Yorke spoke as he had never done before.

"I wish I could prevent it!" he answered, eyeing her half sadly, half jealously. "I've bidden him to go, but he *will* come back to harass me. Now I'll end it at any cost."

"But why does he care for me?" asked Cecil, finding that her first question had received an answer.

"Because you are beautiful and—" There Yorke caught back the coming words, and after a pause said coldly, "Remember your promise—no more of this."

For several minutes he went to and fro, busied with anxious thoughts, while Cecil mused over the mystery, and grieved for Alfred's disappointment. Suddenly Yorke paused before her.

"Do you understand to what you pledge yourself when you say you will never leave me, Cecil?"

"I think I do" was the ready answer.

"Nothing is to be changed, you know."

"I hope not."

"No romances—no poetry to be allowed."

"I do not want them."

"No frivolities and follies like other women."

"I can be happy without."

"No more Cupids of any sort."

"Shall I break this one?"

"No, leave it as a warning, or send it to poor Alf."

"What else, master?" she asked wistfully.

"Only this: Can you be content year after year with study, solitude, steady progress, and in time fame for yourself, but never any knowledge of love as Alfred paints it?"

"*Never, Yorke?*"

"*Never, Cecil!*"

She shivered, as if the words fell cold upon her heart, all the glad light and color faded from her face, and she looked about her with longing eyes, as if the sunshine had gone out of her life forever. Yorke saw the change, and a momentary expression of pity softened the stern determination of his face.

"This never would have happened but for that romantic boy," he thought. "There shall be no more of it, and a little pain now shall spare us all misunderstanding hereafter."

"Cecil," he said aloud, "love makes half the misery of the world; it has been the bane of my life—it has made me what I am, a man without ambition, hope, or happiness—and out of my own bitter experience I warn you to beware of it. You know nothing of it yet, and if you are to stay with me you never will, unless this boy's folly has done more harm than I suspect. Carving Cupid has filled your head with fancies that will do you no good; banish them and be what I would have you."

"A marble woman like your Psyche, with no heart to love you, only grace and beauty to please your eye and bring you honor; is that what you would have me?"

He started, as if she had put some hidden purpose into words; his eye went from the gleaming statue to the pale girl, and saw that he had worked out his design in stone, but not yet in that finer material given him to mold well or ill. He did not see the pain and passion throbbing in her heart; he only saw her steady eyes; he only heard her low spoken question, and answered it, believing that he served her better than she knew.

"Yes, I would have you beautiful and passionless as Psyche, a creature to admire with no fear of disturbing its quiet heart, no fear of endangering one's own. I am kinder than I seem in saying this, for I desire to save you from the pain I have known. Stay with me always, if you can, but remember, Cecil, I am done with love."

"I shall remember, sir."

Yorke left her, glad to have the task over, for it had not been as easy as he fancied. Cecil listened and answered with her usual submission, stood motionless till the sound of a closing door assured her that he was gone, then a look of sharp anguish banished the composure of her face, and a woman's passionate pride trembled in her voice as she echoed his last words.

"I am done with love!" And lifting the little Cupid let it drop broken at her feet.

Chapter III. Germain

For a week Cecil saw little of Yorke, as, contrary to his custom, he was out a greater part of each day, and when at home was so taciturn and absorbed that he was scarcely more than a shadow in the house. She asked no questions, appeared unconscious of any change, and worked busily upon a new design, thinking bitter thoughts the while. Alfred never came, and Cecil missed him; but Yorke was well satisfied, for the purpose formed so long ago had never changed; and though the young man's love endangered its fulfillment, that cloud had passed by, leaving the girl all his own again. She too seemed to cherish some purpose, that soon showed its influence over her; for her face daily grew more cold and colorless, her manner quieter, her smiles fewer, her words briefer, her life more nunlike than ever, till unexpected events changed the current of her thoughts, and gave her new mysteries to brood over.

One evening, as Cecil sat drawing, while Yorke paced restlessly up and down, he said suddenly, after watching her for several minutes, "Cecil, will you do me a great favor?"

"With pleasure, if I can and ought," she answered, without pausing in her work.

"I am sure you can, I think you ought, yet I cannot explain why I ask it, although it will annoy and perplex you. Will you have faith in me, and believe that what I do is done for the best?"

"I trust you, sir; you have taught me to bear in silence many things that perplex and annoy me, so I think I can promise to bear one more."

Something in her meek answer seemed to touch him like a reproach, for his voice softened, as he said regretfully, "I know I am not all I might be to you, but the day may come when you will see that I have spared you greater troubles, and made my dull home a safer shelter than it seems."

He took a turn or two, then stopped again, asking abruptly, "A gentleman is to dine with me tomorrow; will you do the honors of the house?"

It was impossible to conceal the surprise which this unusual request produced, for during all the years they had been together, few strangers had been admitted, and Cecil, being shy, had gladly absented herself on these rare occasions. Now she laid down her pencil and looked up at him, with mingled reluctance and astonishment in her face.

"How can I, when I know nothing of such things? Hester has always suited you till now."

"I have neglected many womanly accomplishments which you should have acquired, this among them; now you shall learn to be the little mistress of the house, and leave Hester in her proper place. Will you oblige me, Cecil?"

Yorke spoke as if discharging a painful duty which had been imposed upon him;

Cecil was quick to see this, and any pleasure she might have felt in the proposal was destroyed by his uneasy manner.

"As you please, sir" was all her answer.

"Thank you; now one thing more. Haven't you a plain gray gown?"

"Yes."

"Be kind enough to wear it tomorrow, instead of that white one, which is more becoming, but too peculiar to appear in before strangers. This, also, I want altered; let me show you how."

He untied the band that held her hair, and as it fell upon her shoulders, he gathered the dark locks plainly back into a knot behind, smoothing away the ripples on her forehead, and the curls that kept breaking from his hold.

"Wear it so tomorrow. Look in the glass, and see how I mean," he said, as he surveyed the change he had effected.

She looked, and smiled involuntarily, though a vainer girl would have frowned, for the alteration added years to her age, apparently; destroyed the beautiful outline of her face, and robbed her head of its most graceful ornament.

"You wish me to look old and plain, I see. If you like it, I am satisfied."

He looked annoyed at her quickness in divining his purpose, and shook out the curls again, as he said hastily, "I do wish it, for my guest worships beauty, and I have no desire for more love passages at present."

"No fear of that till poor Alf's forgotten."

She spoke proudly, and took up her pencil as if weary of the subject. Yorke stood for a moment, wondering if she found it hard to forget "poor Alf," but he said no more, and sat down as if a load were off his mind. Opening a book, he seemed to read, but Cecil heard no leaves turned, and a covert glance showed him regarding the page with absent eyes and a melancholy expression that troubled her. There had been a time when she would have gone to him with affectionate solicitude, but not now; and though her heart was full of sympathy, she dared not show it, so sat silent till the clock struck ten, then with a quiet "Good night" she was gone.

"We shall dine at six; I'll ring for you when Germain comes," said Yorke, as they came in from their walk the following day.

"I shall be ready, sir."

Cecil watched and waited for the stranger's arrival, in a flutter of expectation, which proved that in spite of Yorke's severe training, feminine curiosity was not yet dead. She heard Anthony admit the guest, heard Yorke receive him, and heard the old woman who came to help Hester on such occasions ejaculate from behind a door, "Bless me, what a handsome man!" But minute after minute passed, and no bell rang, no summons came for her. The clock was on the stroke of six, and she was thinking, sorrowfully, that he had forgotten her, when Yorke's voice was heard at the door, saying with unusual gentleness, "Come, Cecil; it is time."

"I thought you were to ring for me," she said, as they went down together.

"And I thought it more respectful to come and wait upon the little mistress, than to call her like a servant. How your heart beats! You need fear nothing. I shall be near you, child."

He took her by the hand with a protecting gesture that surprised her, but a moment later she understood both speech and action. A gentleman was standing at the far end of the room, and as they noiselessly approached, Cecil had time to mark the grace and strength of his tall figure, the ease of his attitude, the beauty of the hands loosely locked together behind him, before Yorke spoke.

"Germain, my ward, Miss Stein."

He turned quickly, and the eyes that Cecil was shyly averting, dilated with undisguised astonishment, for a single glance assured her that Germain was the mysterious model. Her hand closed over Yorke's, trembling visibly, as the stranger, in a singularly musical voice and with an unmistakably highbred air, paid his compliments to Miss Stein.

"Control yourself, and bear with this man for my sake, Cecil," whispered Yorke, as he led her to a seat, and placed himself so as to screen her for a moment.

She did control herself, for that had been her earliest lesson, and she had learned it well. She did bear with this man, for whom she felt such an aversion, and when he offered his arm to lead her in to dinner, she took it, though her eyes never met his, and she spoke not a word. It was long before she ventured to steal a look at him, and when she did so, it was long before she looked away again. The old woman was right, he *was* a handsome man; younger apparently than his host, and dressed with an elegance that Yorke had never attempted. Black hair and beard, carefully arranged, brilliant dark eyes, fine features, and that persuasive voice, all helped to make a most attractive person, for now the sinister expression was replaced by one of the serenest suavity, the stealthy gait and gestures exchanged for a graceful carriage, and some agreeable change seemed to have befallen both the man and his fortunes, as there was no longer any appearance of mystery or poverty about him. Cecil observed these things with a woman's quickness, and smiled to think she had ever feared the gay and gallant gentleman. Then she turned to examine Yorke, and saw that the accustomed gravity of his face was often disturbed by varying emotions; for sometimes it was sad, then stern, then tender, and more than once his eye met hers with a grateful look, as if he thanked her for granting him a greater favor than she knew.

Cecil performed her duties gracefully and well, but said little, and listened attentively to the conversation, which never strayed from general subjects. Though interested, she was not sorry when Yorke gave her the signal to withdraw, and went away into the drawing room. Here, leaning in an easy chair before the fire, she hoped to enjoy a quiet half hour at least, but was disappointed. Happening to lift her eyes to the mirror over the low chimneypiece, to study the effect of the plain bands of hair, she saw another face beside her own, and became aware that Mr. Germain was intently watching her in the glass, as he leaned upon the high back of her chair. Meeting her eyes, he came and stood upon the rug, which Judas yielded to him with a surly growl. Cecil arrested the dog, feeling a sense of security while he was by, for the childish dread was not yet quite gone, and despite his promise, Yorke did not appear. Germain seemed to understand the meaning of her hasty glance about the room, and answered it.

"Your guardian will follow presently, and sent me on to chat with you, meantime. Permit me."

As he spoke, Anthony entered, bringing coffee, but Germain brought Cecil's cup himself, and served her with an air of devotion that both confused and pleased her by its novelty. Drawing a chair to the other side of the tiny table between them, he sat down, and before she knew it, Cecil found herself talking to this dreaded person, shyly at first, then frankly and with pleasure.

"How was the great Rachel last night, Miss Stein?"

"I did not see her, sir."

"Ah, you prefer the opera, as I do, perhaps?"

"I never went."

"Then Yorke should take you, if you love music."

"I do next to my art, but I seldom hear any."

"Your art—then you are to be a sculptor?"

"I hope to be in time, but I have much to learn."

"You will go to Italy before long, I fancy? That's part of every artist's education."

"No, sir, I shall not go. Yorke has been, and can teach me all I need."

"You have no desire for it, then? Or do you wait till some younger guardian appears, who has not seen Italy, and can show it to you as it should be shown?"

"I shall never have any guardian but Yorke, we have already settled that—"

Here Cecil paused, for Germain looked at her keenly, smiled, and said significantly, "Pardon me, I had not learned that he intended to end his romance in the good old fashion, by making his fair ward his wife. I am an early friend, and have a right to take an interest in his future, so I offer my best wishes."

"You mistake me, sir; I should not have said that. Yorke is my guardian, nothing more, nor will he ever be. I have no father, and he tries to be one to me."

Cecil spoke with a bashful eagerness, burning cheeks, and downcast eyes, unconscious of the look of relief that passed over her companion's face as she explained.

"A thousand pardons; my mistake was natural, and may prove a prophecy. Now let me atone for it by asking how the Psyche prospers. Is it worthy of its maker and its model?"

"It is done, and very beautiful; everyone who sees it thinks it worthy of its maker, except me. I know he will do nobler things than that. He had no model but his own design; you have seen that, perhaps?"

"I see it now," he answered, bowing.

"Indeed, I am not; he never makes a model of me now, except for a moment. He has had none since you left."

A curious expression swept over Germain's face, and he exclaimed, with ill-disguised satisfaction, "You recognize me then? I was not sure that you had ever seen me, though I used to haunt the house like a restless spirit, as I am."

"Yes, I knew you at once, because I never could forget the fright you gave me years ago, peeping in, the night I came. Since then I've seen you several times, but never heard your name until yesterday."

"That is like Yorke. He hides his good deeds, and when I was most unfortunate, he befriended me, and more than once has kept me from what fate seems bent on making me, a solitary vagabond. The world goes better with me now, and one day I hope to take my proper place again; till then, I must wait to pay the debt I owe him."

This impulsive speech went straight to Cecil's heart, and banished the last trace of distrust. In the little pause that followed, she found time to wonder why Yorke did not come, and thinking of him, she asked if he would approve all she had been saying.

A moment's recollection showed her that she had unconsciously given her companion many hints of the purpose, pursuits, and prospects of her life, during that seemingly careless conversation. She felt uncomfortable, and hoping Yorke had not heard her, sat silent until Germain spoke again.

"I see an instrument yonder. Let me lead you to it, for having owned that you love music, you cannot deny me the pleasure of listening to it."

Fearing to commit herself again, if she continued to talk, Cecil complied, but as they crossed the room together, she saw Yorke standing in the shadow of a curtained window. He made a warning sign, that caused her to hesitate an instant, trying to understand it; Germain's quick eye followed hers like a flash, and kindled with sudden fire; but before either could speak, Yorke advanced, saying gravely, "Will you venture, Cecil? Germain is a connoisseur in music."

"Then I dare not try; please let me refuse," she answered, drawing back, for now she comprehended that she was not to sing.

But Germain led her on, saying, with his most persuasive air, "You will not refuse me presently, when I have given you courage by doing my part first."

He sat down as he spoke, and began to sing; Cecil was stealing back to her seat, but paused in the act to listen; for a moment stood undecided, then turned, and slowly, step by step, drew nearer, like a fascinated bird, till she was again beside him, forgetful now of everything but the wonderful voice that filled the room with its mellow music. As it ceased, she gave a long sigh of pleasure, and exclaimed like a delighted child, "Oh! Sing again; it is so beautiful!"

Germain flashed a meaning glance over his shoulder at Yorke, who stood apart, gloomily watching them.

"Sit then, and let me do my best to earn a song from you." And placing a chair for her, he gave her music such as she had never dreamed of, as song after song poured from his lips, stirring her with varying emotions, as the airs were plaintive, passionate, or gay.

"Now may I claim my reward?" he said at length, and Cecil, without a thought of Yorke, gladly obeyed him.

Why she chose a little song her mother used to sing she could not tell; it came to her, and she sang it with all her heart, giving the tender words with unwonted spirit and sweetness. Sitting in his seat, Germain leaned his arm upon the instrument and watched her with absorbing interest. Unconsciously, she had pushed away the heavy bands that annoyed her, and now showed again the fair forehead with the delicate brow; her cheeks were rosy with excitement, her eyes shone, her lips smiled as she sang, and in spite of the gray gown with no ornament but a little knot of pansies, Cecil had never looked more beautiful than now. When she ended, she was surprised to see that this strange man's eyes were full of tears, and instead of compliments, he only pressed her hand, saying with lowered voice, "I cannot thank you as I would for this."

Yorke called the girl to him, and Germain slowly followed. At dinner he had led the conversation, now he left it to his host, saying little, but sitting with his eyes on Cecil, who, to her own surprise and Yorke's visible disquiet, did not feel abashed or offended by the pertinacious gaze. He lingered long, and went with evident reluctance, bidding Cecil good night in a tone so like the mysterious "my darling" that she retreated hastily, convinced that it must have been uttered by himself alone.

"How do you like this gentleman?" asked Yorke, returning from a somewhat protracted farewell in the hall.

"Very much. But why didn't you tell me who I was to see?"

"I had a fancy to test your powers of self-control, and I was satisfied."

"I will take care that you shall be, sir," she answered, with set lips and a flash of the eye.

"You seem to have quite outlived your old dislike, and quite forgotten his last offense," continued Yorke, as if ill pleased.

"I am no longer a silly child, and I have not forgotten his offense; but as you overlooked the insult, I could not refuse to meet your guest when you bade me to bear with him for your sake."

There was an air of dignity about her, and a touch of sarcasm in her tone, that was both new and becoming, yet it ruffled Yorke, though he disdained to show it.

"Of one thing I am satisfied. Seclude a woman as you may; when an opportunity comes, she will find her tongue. I did not know my silent girl tonight."

"You heard me, then? I am sorry, but I did not know what I was doing till it was done. You gave me a part to play, and I am no actress, as you see. Is the masquerade over now?"

"Yes, and it has not proved as successful as I hoped, yet I am glad it was no worse."

"So am I," and Cecil shook down her hair with an aspect of relief.

"Where are your pansies?" Yorke asked suddenly.

"They fell out as I was singing, they must have dropped just here," and she looked all about, but no pansies were visible.

"I thought so," muttered Yorke. "I shall repent this night's experiment, I fear, but God knows I did it for the best."

Cecil stood, thoughtfully coiling a dark lock around her finger for a moment, then she asked wistfully, "Will Mr. Germain come again? He said he hoped to do so, when he went."

"He will not, rest assured of that," answered Yorke grimly, adding, as if against his will, "he is a treacherous and dangerous man, in spite of his handsome face and charming manners. Beware of him, child, and shun him, if you would preserve your peace; mine is already lost."

"Then why do you—" There she checked herself, remembering that she was not to ask questions.

"Why do I bring him here? you would ask. That I shall never tell you, and it will never happen again, for the old spell is as strong as ever, I find."

He spoke bitterly, because in the girl's face he saw the first sign of distrust, and it wounded him deeply. It had been a hard evening for him, and he had hoped for a different result, but his failure was made manifest, as Cecil bowed her mute good-night, and went away more perplexed than ever.

Chapter IV. In the Dark

DAYS PASSED and Germain did not reappear, though Cecil strongly suspected that he had endeavored to do so more than once; for now the door was always locked.

Anthony often mounted guard in the hall; Yorke seldom went out, and when they walked together chose a new route each day, while his face wore a vigilant expression as if he were perpetually on the watch. These changes kept the subject continually before the girl's mind, though not a word was spoken. More than once she caught glimpses of a familiar figure haunting the street, more than once she heard the mellow voice singing underneath her window, and more than once she longed to see this strange Germain again.

Standing at the window one somber afternoon, she thought of these things as she watched her guardian giving orders to Anthony, who was working in the garden. As Yorke turned to enter the house, she remembered that the studio was not lighted as he liked to find it, and hurried away to have it ready for his coming. Halfway up the first flight she stopped a moment, for a gust of fresh air blew up from below as if from some newly opened door or window. The hall was dusky with early twilight, and looking downward she saw nothing.

"Is that you, Yorke?" she asked, but no one answered, and she went on her way. At the top of the second flight she paused again, fancying that she heard steps behind her. The sound ceased as she stopped, and thinking to herself, "It's Judas," she ran up the spiral stairs leading to the tower. These were uncarpeted, and in a moment the sound of steps was distinctly audible behind her; neither the slow tread of Yorke, nor the quick patter of the dog, but soft and stealthy footfalls as of someone anxious to follow unsuspected. She paused, and the steps paused also; she went on and the quick sound began again; she peered downward through the gloom, but the stairs wound abruptly round and round, and nothing could be seen. She called to Yorke and the dog again, but there was no reply except the rustle of garments brushing against the wall, and the rapid breathing of a human creature. A nervous thrill passed over her; the thought of Germain flashed into her mind, and the early terror woke again, for time and place suggested the forbidding figure she had seen lurking there so long ago. Fearing to descend and meet him, she sprang on, hoping to reach the studio in time to call Yorke from the window and lock the door. As she darted upward, the quick tread of a man's foot was plainly heard, and when she flung the door behind her, a strong hand prevented it from closing, a tall figure entered, the key was turned, and Germain's well-remembered voice exclaimed:

"Do not cry out. I have risked my life by entering at a window, for I must speak to you, and Yorke guards you like a dragon."

"Why do you come if he forbids it, following and frightening me in the dark?" cried Cecil, grasping vainly for a lamp as Germain placed himself between her and the window.

"Because he keeps you from me, and he has no right to do it. I love you as he never can, yet though I plead day and night, and promise anything, he will not let me see you, even for an hour. Do not fear or shun me, but come to me, little Cecil, come to me, and let me feel that you are mine."

With voice and gesture of intensest love and longing, he advanced as if to claim her, but Cecil, terrified by this impetuous wooing, fled before him to an inner room, bolted the door, and rang the bell until it broke. Vainly Germain shook the door and implored her to hear him; she neither answered nor listened, but called for help till the room rang again.

Soon, very soon, Yorke's familiar step came leaping up the stairs, and his voice demanded, in tones of wonder and alarm, "Cecil, where are you? Speak to me, and open instantly."

"I cannot come—it is Germain—"

More she could not say, for with the arrival of help her strength deserted her, and she dropped down upon the floor, faint but not unconscious. Lying thus, she heard the outer door give way, heard a wrathful exclamation from Yorke, an exultant laugh from Germain, then hurried conversation too low for her to catch a word, till suddenly both voices rose, one defiant, the other determined.

"I tell you, Bazil, I *will* see her!"

"Not if I can prevent it."

"Then I swear I will use force!"

"I swear you shall not!"

A quick movement followed, and the terrified listener heard unmistakable sounds of a fierce but brief struggle in the darkened room, the stamp of feet, the hard breathing of men wrestling near at hand, the crash of a falling statue and a human body, a low groan, then sudden silence. In that silence Cecil lost her consciousness, for her quiet life had ill prepared her for such scenes. Only for a moment, however; the sound of retreating footsteps recalled her, and trying to control the frightened flutter of her heart, she listened breathlessly. What had happened? Where was Yorke? These questions roused her, and the longing to answer them gave her courage to venture from her refuge.

Softly drawing the bolt, she looked out. Nothing could be seen but the pale glimmer of stars through the western window; all near at hand was hidden by the deep shadow of a tall screen that divided the studio. A moment she stood trembling with apprehension lest Germain had not gone, then stole a few steps forward, whispering, "Yorke, are you here?"

There was no answer, but as the words left her lips she stumbled over something at her feet, something that stirred and faintly sighed. Losing fear in an all-absorbing anxiety, Cecil sprang boldly forward, groped for a match, lighted the lamp with trembling hands, and looked about her. The beautiful Psyche lay headless on the ground, but the girl scarcely saw it, for half underneath it lay Yorke, pale and senseless. How she dragged him out she never knew; superhuman strength seemed given her, and self-possession to think and do her best for him. Throwing up the window, she called to Anthony still busy in the garden, then bathed the white face, fanned the breathless lips, chafed the cold hands, and soon had the joy of seeing Yorke's eyes open with a conscious look.

"It is I. Where are you hurt? What shall I do for you, dear master?"

"Tell them the Psyche fell, nothing more," he answered, painfully, but with a clear mind and a commanding glance.

She understood and obeyed him when the old man arrived. With many exclamations of concern and much wonderment as to how the accident could have occurred, Anthony laid his master on the couch, gave him such restoratives as were at hand, and then went to fetch a surgeon and find Hester, who was gossiping in a neighbor's kitchen, according to her wont.

"Tell me what happened, my poor child," whispered Yorke when they were alone, and Cecil sat beside him with a face almost as pallid as his own.

"Not now, you are not fit. Wait awhile," she began.

But he interrupted her, saying with a look she dared not disobey, "No, tell me now—I must know it!"

She told him, but he seemed too weak for indignation, and looked up at her with a faint glimmer of his old sarcastic smile.

"Another lover, Cecil, and a strange one; but you need not fear him, for though as rash and headstrong as a boy, he will not harm you." Then Yorke's face changed and darkened as he said, earnestly, "Promise me that you will never listen to him, never meet him, or countenance his mad pursuit of you. No good can come of it to you, and only the bitterest disappointment to me. Promise me this, I implore you, Cecil."

She hesitated, but his face grew haggard with suspense, and something in her own heart pleaded for him more persuasively than his anxious eyes or urgent words.

"I promise this. Now rest and let me fan you, for your lips are white with pain."

He did not speak again till steps and voices were heard approaching; then he drew her down to him, whispering, "Not a word of Germain to anyone; keep near me till I am up again, then I will take measures to prevent the recurrence of a scene like this."

For several days Yorke saw no one but the doctor and his servants, for the fall and the heavy weight upon his chest had seriously injured him. He rebelled against the order to be still, finding a single week's confinement very irksome with no society but Hester, no occupation but a book or his own thoughts. Cecil did not come to nurse him as she used to do when slighter indispositions kept him in his rooms. She sent no little gifts to tempt his appetite or enliven his solitude; she made daily inquiries for his health, but nothing more. He missed his familiar spirit and her gentle ministrations, but would not send for her, thinking, with a mixture of satisfaction and regret, "She takes me at my word, and perhaps it's better so, for absence will soon cure any girlish pique my frankness may have caused her."

But though he would not call her, he left his room sooner than was wise, and went to find her in the studio. Everything was in its accustomed order, Cecil at her place, and his first exclamation one of pleasant surprise.

"Why, here's my Psyche mended and mounted again! Many thanks. my little girl."

She went to take the hand he offered, saying very quietly, "I am glad to see you, master, and to find you like what I have done."

"I never thought my Psyche would cause me so much suffering, but I forgive her for her beauty's sake," answered Yorke, laughing, for an unusual cheerfulness possessed him, and it was pleasant to be back in his old haunt again. "Well, what do you see in it?" he asked, observing that the girl stood with her eyes fixed on the statue.

"I see my model."

He remembered his own words, and was glad to change the conversation by a question or two.

"How have you got on through these days that have been so wearisome to me? Have you missed the old master?"

"I have been busily at work, and I have missed you, for I often want help, and Tony cannot always walk with me."

Yorke felt slightly disappointed both at the answer and her welcome, but showed no sign of it as he said, "Nothing has been seen of Germain since his last freak, I fancy?"

"He has been here."

"The deuce he has!" ejaculated Yorke, looking amazed. "Did you see him, Cecil?"

"Yes; I could not help it. I was watching for the doctor one day, and hearing a ring, I opened the door, for Tony and Hester were with you. Germain stepped quickly in and asked, 'Is Yorke alive?' I said yes. 'I thank God for that!' he cried. 'Tell him to get well in peace; I'll not disturb him if I can keep away—' Then Anthony appeared and he was gone as quickly as he came."

"That was like him, reckless and generous, fierce and gentle by turns. Pity that so fine a nature should be so early wrecked."

Yorke mused a moment, and Cecil, as if anxiety or pity made her forget her promise, asked suddenly, "Shall you let him go unmolested after such an outrage as this?"

"Yes, even if he had half murdered me or maimed me for life, I would not lift a finger against him. God knows I have my faults, and plenty of them, but I can forgive blows like his easier than some that gentler hands have dealt me."

Cecil made no answer, but seemed lost in wonderment, till Yorke, observing how pale and heavy-eyed she looked, said kindly, "Have you, too, been ill? I asked for you every day, and Hester always gave a good report. Is anything amiss? Tell me, child."

"I am not ill, and nothing is amiss except that I do not sleep, owing to want of exercise, perhaps."

"This must be mended; I'll give you sleep tonight, and tomorrow we will have a long drive together."

Going to an ancient cabinet, he took from it a quaint flask, poured a few drops of some dark liquid into a tiny glass, and mingling it with water, brought it to her.

"It is bitter, but it will bring you deep and dreamless sleep. Drink, little wakeful spirit, drink and rest."

Without offering to take the glass, she bent and drank, not the first bitter draft his hand had given her.

"I think you would drink hemlock without a question if I gave it to you," he said, smiling at her mute obedience.

"I think I should. But I asked no questions now because I knew that this was laudanum. Mamma used it when in pain, and I have often tasted it, playing that I made it sweet for her."

Yorke turned hastily away as if to replace the flask and cup, and when he spoke again he was his gravest self. "Go now, and sleep, Cecil. Tomorrow the old quiet life shall begin again."

It did begin again, and week after week, month after month passed in the same monotonous seclusion. They went nowhere, saw scarcely anyone; Yorke's genius was almost unknown, Cecil's beauty blooming unseen; and so the year rolled slowly by.

CHAPTER V. GOSSIP

PUTTING HIS HEAD into the studio where Cecil was at work as usual, and Yorke lounged on the sofa in a most unwonted fit of indolence, "Mrs. Norton's compliments, and can she see the master for a few minutes?" said Anthony.

"Alfred's mother! What next? I'll come, Tony," answered the master, turning to observe the effect of this announcement upon the girl.

But she scarcely seemed to have heard the question or answer, and went on smoothing the rounded limbs of a slender Faun, with an aspect of entire absorption.

"What an artist I have made of her, if a lump of clay is more interesting than the news of her first lover," thought her guardian, as he left the room with a satisfied smile.

Since Alfred's disappointment, there had been a breach between the neighbors, and his mother discontinued the friendly calls she had been wont to make since Cecil came. She was a gray-haired, gracious lady, with much of her son's frankness and warmth of manner. After a few moments spent in general inquiries, she said, with some embarrassment but with her usual directness, "Mr. Yorke, I have felt it my duty to come and tell you certain things, of which I think you should be informed without delay. You lead such a secluded life that you are not likely to hear any of the injurious rumors that are rife concerning Cecil and yourself. They are but natural, for any appearance of mystery or peculiarity always excites curiosity and gossip, and as a woman and a neighbor, I venture to warn you of them, because I take a deep interest in the girl, both for her own sake and my son's."

"I thank you, Mrs. Norton, and I beg you will speak freely. I am entirely ignorant of these rumors, though I know that tattling tongues find food for scandal in the simplest affairs."

The guest saw that the subject was distasteful to her host, but steadily continued, "While she was a child, the relationship of guardian and ward was all sufficient; but now that she is a woman, and so beautiful a woman, it strikes outside observers that you are too young a man to be her sole companion. It is known that you live here together with no society, few friends, and those chiefly gentlemen; that you have neither governess nor housekeeper, only an old female servant. Cecil goes nowhere, and never walks without yourself or Anthony; while her beauty attracts so much attention that interest and curiosity are unavoidably aroused and increased by the peculiarity of her life. It would be a trying task to repeat the reports and remarks that have come to me; you can imagine them, and feel how much pain they cause me, although I know them to be utterly groundless and unjust."

Intense annoyance was visible in Yorke's face, as he listened and answered haughtily, "Those who know me will need no denial of these absurd rumors. I care nothing for the idle gossip of strangers, nor does Cecil, being too innocent to dream that such things exist."

"But you know it, sir, and you know that a man may defy public opinion, and pass scatheless, a woman must submit and walk warily, if she would keep her name unsullied by the breath of slander. A time may come when she will learn this, and reproach you with unfaithfulness to your charge, if you neglect to surround her with the safeguards which she is, as yet, too innocent to know that she needs."

Mrs. Norton spoke earnestly, and her maternal solicitude for the motherless girl touched Yorke's heart, for he *had* one, though he had done his best to starve and freeze it. His manner softened, his eye grew anxious, and he asked, with the air of one convinced in spite of himself, "What would you have me do? I sincerely desire to be faithful to my duty, but I begin to fear that I have undertaken more than I can perform."

"May I suggest that the presence of a respectable gentlewoman in your house would most effectually silence busy tongues, and might be a great advantage to Miss Stein, who must suffer for the want of female society?"

"I have tried that plan and it failed too entirely to make me willing to repeat the experiment."

A slight flush on Yorke's dark cheek and a disdainful curl of the lips told the keen-eyed lady as plainly as words that the cause of the dismissal of a former governess had been too much devotion to the guardian, too little to the ward. Mrs. Norton was silent a moment, and then said, with some hesitation. "May I ask you a very frank question, Mr. Yorke?"

"Your interest in Cecil gives you a right to ask anything, madam," he replied, bowing with the grace of manner which he could assume at will.

"Then let me inquire if you intend to make this girl your wife, at some future time?"

"Nothing can be further from my intentions" was the brief but decided reply.

"Pardon me; Alfred received an impression that you were educating her for that purpose, and I hoped it might be so. I can suggest nothing else, unless some other gentleman is permitted to give the protection of his name and home. My poor boy still loves her, in spite of absence, time, and efforts to forget; he is still eager to win her, and I would gladly be a mother to the sweet girl. Is there no hope for him?"

"None, I assure you. She loves nothing but her art, as I just had an excellent proof; for when you were announced, and your son's name mentioned, she seemed to hear nothing, remember nothing, but worked on, undisturbed."

Mrs. Norton rose, disappointed and disheartened by the failure of her mission.

"I have ventured too far, perhaps, but it seemed a duty, and I have performed it as best I could. I shall not intrude again, but I earnestly entreat you to think of this, for the girl's sake, and take immediate steps to contradict these injurious rumors. Call upon me freely, if I can aid you in any way, and assure Cecil that I am still her friend, although I may have seemed estranged since Alfred's rejection."

Yorke thanked her warmly, promised to give the matter his serious consideration, and bade her adieu, with a grateful respect that won her heart, in spite of sundry prejudices against him.

As the door closed behind her, he struck his hands impatiently together, saying to himself, "I might have known it would be so! Why did I keep the child until I cannot do without her, forgetting that she would become a woman, and bring trouble as inevitably as before? I'll not have another companion to beset me with the romantic folly I've forsworn; neither will I marry Cecil to silence these malicious gossips; I'll take her away from here, and in some quiet place we will find the old peace, if possible."

In pursuance of this purpose, he announced that he was going away upon business that might detain him several days, and after many directions, warnings, and misgivings, he went. He was gone a week, for the quiet place was not easily found, and while he looked, he saw and heard enough to convince him that Mrs. Norton was right. He took pains to gather, from various sources, the reports to which she had alluded, and was soon in a fever of indignation and disgust. Her words haunted him; he soon saw clearly the wrong he had been doing Cecil, felt that his present plan would but increase it, and was assured that one of two things must be done without delay, either provide her with a chaperon or marry her himself, for he rebelled against the idea of giving her to any other. The chaperon was the wisest but most disagreeable expedient, for well he knew that a third person, however discreet and excellent, would destroy the seclusion and freedom which he loved so well, and had enjoyed so long. It was in every respect repugnant to him, and he believed it would be to Cecil also. The other plan to his own surprise did not seem so impossible or distasteful, and the more he thought of it, the more attractive it became. Nothing need be changed except her name, slander would be silenced, and her society secured to him for life. But would she consent to such a marriage? He recalled with pleasure the expression of her face when she went to him, saying, "I will never leave you, my dear master, never"; and half regretted that he had checked the growth of the softer sentiment, which seemed about to take the place of her childish affection. He did not love her as a husband should, but he felt how sweet it was to be beloved, knew that she was happy with him, and longed to keep his little ward, at any cost, to himself.

Still undecided, but full of new and not unpleasurable fancies, he hurried home, feeling a strong curiosity to know how Cecil would regard this proposition should he make it. No one ran to meet him, as he entered, no one called out a glad welcome, and the young face that used to brighten when he came was nowhere visible.

"Where is Miss Cecil?" he asked of Hester.

"In the garden, master," she answered, with a significant nod, that sent him to the nearest window that opened on the garden.

Cecil was walking here with Alfred, and Yorke's face darkened ominously, as a jealous fear assailed him that she was about to solve the question for herself. He eyed her keenly, but her face was half averted, and he could see that she listened intently to her companion, who talked rapidly, and with an expression that made his handsome face more eloquent than his ardent voice.

"Cecil!" called Yorke sharply, unwilling to prolong a scene that angered him, more than he would confess even to himself.

Alfred looked up, bowed with a haughty, half-defiant air, said a few words to Cecil, and leaped the wall again. But she, after one glance upward, went in so slowly that her guardian chafed at the delay, and when at length she came to him with a cold handclasp, and a tranquil "Home so soon?" he answered, almost harshly, "Too soon, perhaps. Why do I find that boy here? I thought he was away again."

"He is going soon, and came because he could not keep away, he said. Poor Alf, I wish he did not care for me so much."

While she was speaking, Yorke examined her with a troubled look, for that brief absence made him quick to see the changes a year had wrought, unobserved till now. Something was gone that once made her beauty a delight to heart as well as eye; some nameless but potent charm that gave warmth, grace, and tenderness to her dawning womanhood. He felt it, and for the first time found a flaw in what he had thought faultless until now. There was no time to analyze the feeling, for drawing away the hand he had detained, she brought him from her desk three letters, directed to herself, in a man's bold writing.

"Germain!" exclaimed Yorke, as his eye fell on them. "Has he dared to write, when he swore he would not? Have you read them?"

She turned them in his hand, and showed the seals unbroken. A flash of pleasure banished the disquiet from his face, and there was no harshness in his voice as he asked, "How did they come? I forbade Tony to receive any communication he might venture to make."

"Tony knows nothing of them. One came in a bouquet, which was tossed over the wall the very day you went; one was brought by a carrier dove soon afterward; the bird came pecking at my window, and thinking it was hurt, I took it in; the third was thrust into my hand by someone whom I did not see, as I was walking with Hester yesterday. I suspected who they were from, and did not open them, because I promised not to listen to this man."

"Rare obedience in a woman! Have you no wish to see them? Will you give me leave to look at them before I burn them?"

"Do what you like, I care nothing for them now."

She spoke so confidingly, and smiled so contentedly, as she stood folding up his gloves, that Yorke felt his purpose strengthening every instant. The letters confirmed it, for as he flung the last into the fire, he said to himself, "There is no way but this; there will be peace for neither of us while Alfred and Germain have hopes of her. Once mine, and I shall have a legal right to defy and banish both."

Turning with decision, he drew her down to a seat beside him, saying, in a tone he had not used since the Cupid was broken, "Sit here and listen, for I've many things to tell you, my little girl. You are eighteen tomorrow, and according to your mother's desire may choose what guardian you will. I leave you free, having no right to influence you, but while I have a home it always will be yours, if you are happy here."

She turned her face away, and for an instant some inward agitation marred its habitual repose, but she answered steadily, though there was an undertone of pain in her voice, "I know it, Yorke, and you are very kind. I am happy here, but I cannot stay, because hard things are said of us, things that wrong you and wound me, more than tongue can tell."

"Who told you this?" he demanded, angrily.

"Alfred; he said I ought to know it, and if you would not follow his mother's advice, I should choose another guardian."

"And will you, Cecil?"

"Yes, for your sake as well as my own."

The tone of resolution made her soft voice jar upon his ear, and convinced him that she would keep her word.

"Whom will you choose?" he gravely asked.

"It is hard to tell; I have made no friends in all these years, and now I have nowhere to go, unless I turn to Mrs. Norton. She will be a mother to me, Alfred a very gentle guardian, and in time I may learn to love him."

Yorke felt both reproached and satisfied; reproached, because it was his fault that the girl had made no friends, and satisfied because there was as much regret as resolution in her voice, and his task grew easier as he thought of Alfred, whom she should never learn to love.

"But you promised to stay with me, and I want you, Cecil."

"I did promise, but then I knew nothing of all this. I want to stay, but now I cannot, unless you do something to make it safe and best."

"Something shall be done. Will you have another governess or an elderly companion?" he asked, wishing to assure himself of her real feeling before he spoke more plainly.

She sighed, and looked all the repugnance that she felt, but answered sorrowfully, "I dread it more than you do, but there is no other way."

"One other way. Shall I name it?"

"Oh, yes, anything is better than another Miss Ulster."

"If my ward becomes my wife, gossip will be silenced, and we may still keep together all our lives."

He spoke very quietly, lest he should startle her, but his voice was eager, and his glance wistful in spite of himself. The eager eyes that had been lifted to his own fell slowly, a faint color came up to her cheek and she answered with a slight shake of the head, as if more perplexed than startled, "How can I, when we don't care for one another?"

"But we do care for one another. I love you as if you were a child of my own, and I think if nothing had disturbed us that you would have chosen me to be your guardian for another year, at least, would you not?"

"Yes, you are my one friend, and this is home."

"Then stay, Cecil, and keep both. Nothing need be changed between us; to the world we can be husband and wife, here guardian and ward, as we have been for six pleasant years. No one can reproach or misjudge us then; I shall have the right to protect my little pupil, she to cling to her teacher and her friend. We are both solitary in the world. Why can we not go on together in the old way, with the work we love and live for?"

"It sounds very pleasant, but I am so ignorant I cannot tell if it is best. Perhaps you will regret it if I stay, perhaps I shall become a burden when it is too late to put me away, and you may tire of the old life, with no one but a girl to share it with you."

Her face was downcast, and he did not see her eyes fill, her lips tremble, or the folded hands, pressed tight together, as she listened to the proposition which gave her a husband's name, but not a husband's heart. He saw that she thought only of him, forgetful of herself—knew that he offered very little in exchange for the liberty of this young life, and began to think that he had been mistaken in supposing that she loved him, because she showed so little emotion now; but in spite of all this, the purpose formed so long ago was still indomitable, and though forced by circumstances to modify it, he would not relinquish his design. The relentless look replaced all others, as he rose to leave her, though he said, "Do not answer yet, think well of this, be assured that I desire it, shall be happy in it, and see no other course open, unless you choose to leave me. Decide for yourself, my child, and when we meet tomorrow morning, tell me which guardian you have chosen."

"I will."

Cecil was usually earliest down, but when the morrow came, Yorke waited for her with an impatience that he could not control, and when she entered, he went to meet her, with an inquiring eye, an extended hand. She put her own into it without a word, and he grasped the little hand with a thrill of joy that surprised him as much as did the sudden impulse which caused him to stoop and kiss the beautiful, uplifted face that made the sunshine of his life.

Ashamed of this betrayal of his satisfaction, he controlled himself, and said, with as much of his usual composure as he could assume, "Thank you, Cecil; now all is decided, and you never shall regret this step, if I can help it. We will be married privately, and at once, then let the gossips tattle as they please."

"Are you quite satisfied with me for choosing as I have done?" she asked, as he led her to her place.

"Quite satisfied, quite proud and happy that my ward is to be mine forever. Is she content?"

"Yes, I chose what was pleasantest, and will do my best to be all you would have me, to thank you for giving me so much."

No more was said, and very soon all trace of any unusual emotion had vanished from Cecil's face; not so with Yorke. A secret unrest possessed him, and did not pass away. He thought it was doubt, anxiety, remorse, perhaps, for what he was about to do, but try as he would, the inward excitement kept him from his usual pursuits, and made him long to have all over without delay. Feeling that he owed Mrs. Norton some explanation of his seeming caprice, he went to her, frankly stated his reasons for the change, and took counsel with her upon many matters. With the readiness of a generous nature, she put aside her own disappointment, and freely did her best for her peculiar neighbor, glad that she had served the girl so well.

She soon convinced him that it would be better not to have a private wedding, but openly to marry and give the young wife a gay welcome home, that nothing mysterious or hasty should give fresh food for remark. He yielded, for Cecil's sake, and the good lady, with a true woman's love of such affairs, soon had everything her own way, much to Yorke's annoyance, and Cecil's bewilderment. Alfred was gone, and his mother wisely left him in ignorance of the approaching marriage, and stifled many a sigh, as she gave her orders and prepared the little bride.

Great was the stir and intense the surprise among the sculptor's few friends when it was known what was afloat, and Yorke was driven half wild with questions, congratulations, and praises of his betrothed. So much interest and goodwill pleased even while it fretted him; and bent on righting both himself and Cecil, in a manner that should preclude all further misconception, he asked friends and neighbors from far and near to his wedding, thinking, with a half-sad, half-scornful smile, "Let them come, they will see that she is lovely, will think that I am happy, and never guess what a mockery it is to me."

They did come, did think the bride beautiful, the bridegroom happy; and would have had no suspicion of the mockery, but for one little incident that had undue effect upon the eager-eyed observers. Among the guests was one whom none of the others

knew; a singularly handsome man, who glided in unannounced, just before the ceremony, and placed himself in the shadow of the draperies that hung before a deep
window in the drawing room. Two or three of the neighbors whispered together, and
nodded their heads significantly, as if they had suspicions; but the entrance of the
bridal pair hushed the whispers, and suspended the nods for a time at least. As they
took their places, Cecil was seen to start and change color when her eye fell on the
stranger, leaning in the purple gloom of the recess; Yorke did the same, then he
frowned; she drew her veil about her, and stern bridegroom and pale bride appeared
to compose themselves for the task before them.

The instant the ceremony was over, one gossip whispered to another, "I told
you so, it is the same person who used to sing under her window, and watch the
house for hours. A lover, without doubt, and why she preferred this gloomy Mr. Yorke
to that devoted creature passes my comprehension."

"It's my opinion that she didn't prefer him, but was persuaded into it. He's far
too old and grave for such a young thing, and I suspect she agrees with me. Did you
see her turn as pale as her dress when she saw that fine-looking man in the recess?
Poor thing, it's plain to see that she is marrying from gratitude, or fear, or something
of that sort."

This romantic fancy soon took wing, and flew from ear to ear, although the
stranger vanished as suddenly as he came. Yorke caught a hint of it, but only smiled
disdainfully, and watched Cecil with a keen sense of satisfaction, in the knowledge
that she was all his own. Not only was his eye gratified by her beauty that day, but his
pride also, for the admiration she excited would have satisfied the most enamored
bridegroom. She seemed to have grown a woman suddenly, for gentle dignity replaced
her former shyness, and she bore herself like a queen; pale as the flowers in her
bosom, calm as the marble Psyche that adorned an alcove, and so like it that more
than one enthusiastic gentleman begged Yorke to part with the statue, now that he
possessed the beautiful model. All this flattered his pride as man and artist, enhanced
his pleasure in the events of the day, roused his ambition that had slept so long, and
banished his last doubt regarding the step he had so hastily taken.

When all was over, and the house quiet again, he roamed through the empty
rooms, still odorous and bright with bridal decorations, looking for his wife, and
smiling, as he spoke the word low to himself, for the pleasant excitement of the day
was not yet gone. But nowhere did he see the slender white figure in the misty veil;
her little glove lay where she dropped it when the ring was put on, her bouquet of
roses and orange flowers was fading in the seat she left, and an array of glittering gifts
still stood unexamined by their new mistress. Thinking she was worn out and had
gone to rest, he went slowly toward the studio, wondering if he should not feel more
like his old self in that familiar place. Passing Cecil's room, he saw that the door was
open, and no one within but the newly hired maid, who was busy folding up the
silvery gown.

"Where is Miss Cecil?" he asked.

"Mrs. Yorke is in the tower, sir," answered the woman, with a simper at his
mistake.

He bit his lip, and went on; but as he climbed the winding stairs, he passed his
hand across his eyes, remembering a happy time, nineteen years ago, when that name

had almost been another and a dearer woman's. Dressed in the plain gray gown, and with no change about her but the ring on the hand that caressed the dog's shaggy head, Cecil sat reading as if nothing had disturbed the usual quiet routine of her day. If she had looked up with a word of welcome or a smile of pleasure, it would have pleased him well, for his heart was very tender just then, and she was very like her mother. But she seemed unconscious of his presence till he stood before her, regarding her with the expression that was so attractive and so rare.

"Are you worn out with the bustle of the day, and so come here to rest and find yourself, as I do?" he asked, stroking the soft waves of her hair.

"Yes, I am tired, but I was never more myself than I have been today," she answered, turning a leaf, as if waiting to read on.

"What did it all seem like, Cecil?"

"A pretty play, but I was glad to have it over."

"It was a pretty play, though Germain might have spoiled it if I had not warned him away. But it is not quite over, as I was reminded on my way up. We must remember that before others I am your husband, and you my little wife, else I shall call you 'Miss Cecil' again, and you say 'master,' as you did half an hour ago."

"What would you have me do? I know I shall forget, for there is nothing to remind me but this," and she turned the ring to and fro upon her finger, adding, as he thought, regretfully, "It begins to make a difference already, and you said nothing would be changed."

"Nothing shall be changed, except that," he answered, chilled by her coldness, and turning sharply round, he seized chisel and mallet, and fell to work, regardless of bridal broadcloth and fine linen.

Chapter VI. Cecil's Secret

It was easy to say that nothing should be changed, but they soon found it very hard to prevent decided alterations in the lives of both. Yorke's friends, rejoicing in the new tie that seemed about to give him back to the world he had shunned so long, did everything in their power to help on the restoration by all manner of festivities after the wedding. Having yielded once or twice by Mrs. Norton's advice, Yorke found it both difficult and irksome to seclude himself again, for it seemed as if a taste of the social pleasures neglected for so many years had effectually roused him from his gloom and given him back his youth again. But the chief cause of the change was Cecil. Wherever she went she won such admiration that his pride was fostered by the praise it fed on, and regarding her as his best work, he could not deny himself the satisfaction of beholding the homage paid his beautiful young wife. She submitted with her usual docility, yet expressed so little interest in anything but her art that he soon grew jealous of it, and often urged her to go pleasuring lest she should grow old and gray before her time, as he had done.

"Look your loveliest tonight, Cecil, for there will be many strangers at Coventry's, and I have promised him that my handsome wife would come," he said, as he came into the drawing room one tempestuous afternoon and found her looking out into the deserted street where the rain fell in torrents and the wind blew gustily.

"It is so stormy, need we go?"

"We must. The wind will fall at dark, and one does not mind rain in a closed carriage. You wonder at me, I dare say, and so do I at myself; but I think I'm waking up and growing young again. Now I shall be old Yorke and read studiously for an hour."

He laughed as he spoke and laid himself on the couch, book in hand. But he read little, for Cecil's unusual restlessness distracted his attention, and he had fallen into a way of observing her lately while she worked or studied and he sat idle. She too opened a book, but soon put it down; she made a sketch, but seemed ill pleased with it, and threw it in the fire; she worked half a flower at her embroidery frame, turned over two or three portfolios with a listless air, then began to wander up and down the room so noiselessly that it would not have disturbed him had he been as absorbed as he seemed. Watching her covertly, he saw her steps grow rapid, her eyes wistful, her whole face and figure betray impatience and an intense desire for something beyond her reach. Several times she seemed about to follow an almost uncontrollable impulse, but checked herself on the way to the door and resumed her restless march, pausing with each turn to look out into the storm.

"What is it, Cecil? You want something. Can I get it for you?" he said at last, unable to restrain the question.

"I do want something, but you cannot get it for me," she answered, pausing with an expression of mingled doubt and desire infinitely more becoming than her usual immobility.

"Come here and tell me what it is; you so seldom ask anything of me I am curious to know what this may be."

Drawing her down upon the couch where he still lay, he waited for her request with an amused smile, expecting some girlish demand. But she delayed so long that he turned her face to his, saying, as he studied its new aspect, "Is it to stay at home tonight, little girl?"

"No, it is to go out now, and alone."

"Alone, and in this raging storm? You are crazy, child."

"I like the storm; I'm tired of the house. Please let me go for just half an hour."

"Why do you wish to be alone, and where are you so eager to go?"

"I cannot tell you. Be kind and don't ask me, Yorke."

"A secret from me! That's something new. When shall I know it?"

"Never, if I can help it."

He lay looking at her with a curious feeling of wonder and admiration, for this sudden earnestness made her very charming, and he found it extremely pleasant to while away an idle hour discovering the cause of this new waywardness in Cecil.

"I think you will tell me like an obedient little wife, and ask me prettily to go with or for you."

"I cannot tell you, and you must not come with me. Dear Yorke, let me go, please let me go!"

She folded her hands, dropped on her knees before him, and pleaded so earnestly with voice, and eyes, and outstretched hands, that he sat up amazed.

"What does it mean, Cecil? You have no right to keep a secret from me, and I cannot let you go out in such a storm on such a mysterious errand as this. A month ago you promised to obey me. Will you rebel so soon, and risk your health if nothing else by this strange freak?"

There was a sudden kindling of the eye as she rose and turned away with a resolute, white face, saying, in a tone that startled him, "I have the same right to my secret as you have to yours, and I shall keep it as carefully. A month ago I did promise to love, honor, and obey; but the promises meant nothing, and your will is not my law, because though my husband before the world, you are only my guardian here. I harm no one but myself in doing this, and I *must* go."

"Will you go if I forbid it?" he asked, rising in real perplexity and astonishment.

"Yes," she answered, steadily.

"How if I follow you?"

"I shall do something desperate, I'm afraid."

She looked as if she might, and he dared not insist. Entreaties and commands had failed; perhaps submission might succeed, and he tried it.

"Go, then; I shall not follow. I trust you in this, as you have trusted me more than once, and hope you will be as worthy of confidence as I try to be."

He thought he had conquered, for as he spoke, gravely yet kindly, she covered up her face as if subdued, and expecting a few tears, an explanation, and penitence, he stood waiting and recalling scenes of childish waywardness which had always ended so. No, not so; for to his unspeakable surprise Cecil left the room without a word. Five minutes later the hall door closed, and he saw her fighting her way against wind and rain with the same intense longing, the same fixed resolution in her face.

For an hour he watched and waited, racking his brain to discover some clue to this mysterious outbreak. Several trifling events now returned to his memory and deepened his perplexity. Just before they were married he brought her home a pretty bonbonnière to hold the comfits for which she still had a childish fancy. Having filled it for her, he was about to drop it into one of the ornamented pockets of the little apron she wore, but as he touched it a paper rustled, and as if the sound recalled some forgotten secret, she had clutched the pocket in a sudden panic and begged him to stop. He had accused her of having love letters from Alfred hidden there, and she had indignantly denied it, but hurried away as if to put her secret under lock and key. Later she had ventured out alone once or twice, always asking pardon when reproved for these short flights, but repeating them till strictly forbidden. Since then she had grown more taciturn than ever, and often went away to her own room to read or rest, she said. How she did spend the long hours passed there, Yorke was too proud to ask either mistress or maid, though he had felt much curiosity to know. The present mystery recalled these lesser ones, but gave no help in explaining anything, and he could only roam about the room and watch the storm more restlessly than Cecil.

Another hour passed and he began to feel anxious, for twilight gathered fast and still she did not come. A third hour rolled slowly by; the streetlamps glimmered through the mist, but among the passing figures no familiar one appeared, and he was fast reaching that state of excitement which makes passive waiting impossible when, as he stood peering out into the wild, wet night, a slight rustle was heard behind him, and a soft voice broke the long silence.

"I am ready, Yorke."

Turning with a start, he saw that all his fears had been in vain, for no storm-beaten figure stood before him, but Cecil shining in festival array.

"Thank heaven you are safe! I've been watching for you, but I did not see you come," he said, eyeing her with renewed wonder.

"No, I took care that you should not, and have been busy for an hour making myself pretty, as you bade me. Are you satisfied?"

He would have been hard to please if he was not satisfied with the fair apparition standing in the light of the newly kindled chandelier. A rosy cloud seemed to envelop her, bridal pearls gathered up the dark hair, shone on graceful neck and arms, and glimmered here and there among the soft-hued drapery. A plumy fan stirred in her hand, and a white down-trimmed cloak half covered shoulders almost as fair, for Yorke adorned his living statue with a prodigal hand. He could not but smile delightedly and forgive her, though she asked no pardon, for he was too glad to have her back to think of questions or reproaches.

"I am more than satisfied. Now come and let me play hostess among the teapots, for you are too splendid for anything but to be looked at, and you must need refreshment after your wild walk."

"No, I want nothing; let Hester fill my place. I'll wait for you here, and enjoy the pleasant fire you have made for me."

She knelt down before it, and he went slowly away, looking backward at the pretty picture the firelight showed him. When he rejoined her after tea and toilet, she was lying in a deep chair looking straight before her with a singular expression, dreamy, yet intense, blissfully calm, yet full of a mysterious brightness that made her face strangely beautiful. He examined her keenly, but she did not see him, he spoke, but she did not hear him, and not until he touched her did she seem conscious of his presence. Then the rapt look passed away, and she roused herself with an effort.

But Yorke could not forget it, and later in the evening when Coventry's rooms were full of friends and strangers, he stepped aside into a corner to observe Cecil from a distance and receive the compliments that now were so welcome to him. Two gentlemen paused nearby and, unconscious who was overhearing them, spoke freely of his ward.

"Where is Yorke's statue as they call her? A dozen people are waiting for my opinion, and I must not disappoint them," said the elder of the two, with the air of an experienced connoisseur.

"She is sitting yonder. Do you see her, Dent? The dark-haired angel with the splendid eyes," returned the younger, speaking with artistic enthusiasm.

Dent took a survey, and Yorke waited for his opinion, feeling sure that it would be one of entire and flattering approval.

"As a work of art she is exquisite, but as a woman she is a dead failure. Why in heaven's name didn't Yorke marry one of his marble goddesses and be done with it?"

"They say he has," laughed Ascot, as Dent put down his glass with a shake of the head. "He fell in love with her beauty, and is as proud of it as if he had carved the fine curves of her figure and cut the clear outline of her face. If it were not for color and costume, she might be mounted on a pedestal as a mate for that serenely classical Pallas just behind her."

"Now to my eye," said Dent, "that rosy, sweet-faced little woman sitting near her is far lovelier than this expressionless, heartless-looking beauty. See how young Mrs. Vivian kindles and glows with every passing emotion; look at her smile, hear her laugh, see her meet her husband's eye with a world of love in her own, and then contrast her with your statuesque Mrs. Yorke."

"Every man to his taste. I admire the sculptor's, but I don't envy him his handsome wife unless he possesses the art of warming and waking his Galatea. I doubt it, however, for he hasn't the look of a Pygmalion, though a very personable man. Come and introduce me to charming Mrs. Vivian: I've looked at the snow image till I'm positively chilled."

They passed on, and Yorke sent a glance after them that might have hastened their going had they met it. He had heard nothing but praise before, and this was quite a revelation to him. He was hurt and angry, yet ashamed of being so, and drawing back into his corner, began to contrast Cecil with her neighbor. The gentlemen were right; that indefinable something which she had once possessed was gone now, and her beauty had lost its magic. The woman near her was all they had said, young, blooming, blithe, and tender, with her new happiness shining in her face, and making her far more winsome than her fairer neighbor. He watched her look up at her husband with her heart in her eyes, and felt a sense of wrong because he had never met a glance like that in the dark eyes he knew so well. He saw the young pair dance together, and as they floated by, forgetful of everything but one another, he sighed involuntarily, remembering that he had done with love. He looked long at Cecil, and began to wonder if he did possess the power to animate his statue. For the first time he forgot his purpose, and yielding to the impulse of the moment, crossed the room, bent over her, and asked, "Cecil, can you waltz?"

"Yes; poor Alf taught me."

The tone in which the name was uttered roused the old jealous feeling, for she never spoke *his* name in that softened voice.

"Come, then, and waltz with me," he said, with a masterful air as novel as the request.

"With you? I thought you never danced."

"I will show you that I do. Lean on my arm, and let me see if I can bring some color into those white cheeks of yours."

She glanced up at him with a curious smile, for he looked both melancholy and excited; the next minute she forgot his face to wonder at his skill, for with a strong arm and steady foot he bore her round and round with a delightsome sense of ease and motion as the music rose and fell and their flying feet kept time. Yorke often looked down to mark the effect of this on Cecil, and was satisfied, for soon she glowed with the soft excitement of exercise and pleasure; the mysterious brightness returned to her eyes again and shone upon her face. Once he paused purposely before Dent and Ascot, and as he waited as if to catch the time, he heard the young man whisper, "Look at her now and own that she is beautiful."

"That she is, for this is nature and not art. The man *can* animate his statue and I envy him," returned the other, drawing nearer to watch the brilliant creature swaying on her husband's arm as Yorke swept her away, wearing an expression that caused more than one friend to smile and rejoice.

"Rest a little, then we will dance again," he said, when he seated her, and leaning on her chair began to ply the fan, still bent on trying his power, for the test interested him.

"Do you see Mrs. Vivian yonder, Cecil? Tell me what you think of her."

"I think she is very pretty, and that her husband loves her very much."

"Don't you envy her?"

"No."

"Now that you have seen something of the world, and tasted many of its pleasures, do you never regret that you tied yourself to me so young, never reproach me for asking you to do it?" He leaned nearer as he spoke and looked deep into her eyes; they looked back at him as if they read his heart, and something in their lustrous depths stirred him strangely; but he saw no love there, and she answered in that undemonstrative voice of hers, "I am contented, Yorke."

"Call me Bazil; I am tired of the other, and it is too ugly for your lips."

She smiled to herself, remembering a time when Bazil was forbidden, and asked a question in her turn.

"Who are the gentlemen just passing?"

"Dent and Ascot, artists, I believe. Why do you ask?"

"I thought they were friends of yours, they seem to take so much interest in us."

"They are no friends of mine. Shall I tell you what they say of us?"

"Yes, Bazil, if you like."

He did not answer for a moment, because the long unused name came very sweetly from her lips, and he paused to enjoy it. Then he told her; but she only smoothed the ruffled plumage of the fan he had been using, and looked about her undisturbed.

"Mrs. Vivian tries to please her husband by being fond and gay; I try to please mine by being calm and cool. If both are satisfied, why care for what people say?"

"But I do care, and it displeases me to have you criticized in that way. Be what you like at home, but in public try to look as if you cared for me a little, because I will not have it said that I married you for your beauty alone."

"Shall I imitate Mrs. Vivian? You are hard to please, but I can try."

He laughed a sudden and irrepressible laugh, partly at her suggestion, partly at his own request, and she smiled for sympathy, so blithe and pleasant was the sound.

"What a capricious fool I am becoming," he said. "I no longer know myself, and shall begin to think my gray hairs have come too soon if this goes on. *Am* I very old and grave, Cecil?"

"Eight-and-thirty is not old, Bazil, and if you always dressed as carefully as tonight, and looked as happy, no one would call you my old husband, as a lady did just now."

Yorke glanced at a mirror opposite and fancied she was right; then his face clouded over, and he shook his head as if reproaching himself for a young man's folly. But the reflection he saw was that of a stately-looking man, with fine eyes and a thoughtful countenance which just then wore a smile that made it singularly attractive. Here their host was seen approaching with the strangers, and Yorke whispered suddenly, "Imitate Mrs. Vivian if you can; I want to try the effect upon these gentlemen."

She bowed and held the fan above her eyes a moment, as if to screen them from the light. When it dropped, as the newcomers were presented, they saw a blooming, blushing face, with smiles on the lips, light in the eyes, and happiness in every tone of the youthful voice. Amazed at the rapidity of the change, yet touched by her obedience and charmed with her address, her husband could only look and listen for the first few minutes, wondering what spirit possessed the girl. So well did she act her part that he soon entered heartily into his own, and taking young Vivian for his model, played the devoted husband so successfully that Dent and Ascot lingered long, and went away at last to report that Mrs. Yorke was the most charming woman in the room, and the sculptor the happiest man.

"Was my imitation a good one? Is that what you wish me to be in public?" asked Cecil, dropping back into her accustomed manner the instant they were alone, though her face still wore its newly acquired charm.

"It was done to the life, and you quite took my breath away with your 'loves' and 'dears,' and all manner of small fascinations. Where did you learn them? What possesses you tonight, Cecil?"

"An evil spirit. I have called it up, and now I cannot lay it."

She laid her hands against her cheeks, where a color like the deep heart of a rose burned steadily, while her eyes glittered and the flowers on her bosom trembled with the rapid beating of her heart, and some inward excitement seemed to kindle her into a life and loveliness that startled Yorke and half frightened herself. She saw that her words bewildered him still more than her actions, and, as if anxious to make him forget both, she rose, saying with an imperious little gesture, "We have sat apart in this nook too long; it is ill-bred. Come and dance with me."

He obeyed as if they had changed places, and for an hour Cecil danced like a devotee, delighting and surprising those about by the gaiety and grace with which she bore her part in the brilliant scene. When not with her, Yorke lingered nearby, longing to take her home, for her spirits seemed unnatural to him, and a half-painful, half-pleasurable sentiment of tender anxiety replaced his former pride in her. She had blossomed so suddenly he scarcely knew his quiet pupil, and while her secret perplexed him, this new change both charmed and troubled him, and kept him hovering about her till she came to him flushed and breathless, saying in the same excited manner as before, "Take me home, Bazil, or I shall dance myself to death. I want to be quiet now, for my head aches and burns, and I'm so tired I shall fall asleep before I know it."

Making their adieus, he took her to a quiet anteroom and left her to rest while he went to find his carriage. He was absent many minutes, being detained by the way, and when he returned it was to find Cecil fast asleep. Her fan and gloves had fallen from her hands, and she lay with her disordered hair scattered on the pillow, her white arms folded under her head, looking as if an unconquerable drowsiness had overpowered her. Wrapping her in her cloak Yorke took her away half awake, let her sleep undisturbed on his shoulder during the drive, and reluctantly gave her into the hands of her maid when they reached home.

Very little sleep did he get that night, for Cecil's figure was continually dancing before his eyes, sometimes as he first saw it that evening in the firelight, then as it looked when she played Mrs. Vivian with such spirit, or when she answered with that strange expression, "An evil spirit. I have called it up, and now I cannot lay it." But oftenest as he watched it by the light of the streetlamps, with a soft cheek against his own, and recollections of that other Cecil curiously blended with thoughts of the one sleeping on his shoulder. Calling himself a fool, with various adjectives attached, and resolutely fixing his mind on other things, having failed to bring repose, he lighted both lamp and meerschaum and read till dawn.

His first question when he met Victorine in the morning was "How is Mrs. Yorke?"

"Still asleep, sir, and I haven't called her, for the only thing she said last night was to bid me let her rest all day unless she woke."

"Very well, let her be quiet, and tell me when she rises."

He went to his studio, but could settle to nothing, and found the day wearisomely long, for Cecil did not rise. He asked for her at dinner, but she was still asleep, and hoping for a long evening with her, he resigned himself to a solitary afternoon. The clock was on the stroke of six when Victorine came in, looking frightened.

"I think Mrs. Yorke is ill, sir."

"Is she awake?" he asked, starting up.

"I've tried to wake her, but I can't. Perhaps you could, sir, for something must be amiss—she looks so strangely and hasn't stirred since morning."

Before the last sentence was out of her mouth Yorke was halfway upstairs, and in another minute at Cecil's bedside. A great change had come over her since he saw her last, a change that alarmed him terribly. The restless sleep had deepened into a deathlike immobility; the feverish flush was gone, and violet shadows gave her closed eyes a sunken look; through her pale lips slow breaths came and went; and when he felt her pulse her hand dropped heavily as he relinquished it. Stooping, he whispered gently yet urgently, "Cecil, wake up, it is time."

But there was no sign of waking, and nothing stirred but the faint flutter of her breath. He raised her, brushed the damp hair from her forehead, and cried in a voice tremulous with fear, "My darling, speak to me!"

But she lay mute and motionless. With a desperate sort of energy he flung up the window, rolled the bed where a fresh wind blew in, laid her high on the pillows, bathed her head and face, held pungent salts to her nostrils, and chafed her hands. Still all in vain; not a sound or motion answered him, and all his appeals, now tender, now commanding, could not break the trance that held her. Desisting suddenly from his fruitless efforts, he sent Victorine for a physician, and till he came suffered the most terrible suspense. Before Dr. Home could open his lips Yorke explained hurriedly, and bade him do something for heaven's sake.

The old gentleman took a long survey, touched pulse and temples, listened to her breathing, and then asked, though his own medicine case was in his hand, "Do you keep laudanum in the house?"

"I have some that I've had a long time. I'll get it for you." And Yorke was gone in spite of Victorine's offer of assistance. But he returned with a fresh anxiety, for the little flask was empty.

"It was half full two days ago; no one goes to that cabinet but myself. I don't understand it," he began.

"I do."

And there was something in the doctor's tone that caused the bottle to drop from Yorke's hand as he whispered, with a look of incredulity and dismay, "Do you think she has taken it?"

"I have no doubt of it."

Yorke seized the old man's arm with a painful grip, asking in a terror-stricken tone, "Do you mean she tried to destroy herself?"

"Nothing of the sort; she has only taken an overdose and must sleep it off."

"Doctor, you deceive me! I know enough of this perilous stuff to know that the bottle under my feet contained enough to kill a man."

"Perhaps so, but not your wife; and the fact that she is still alive proves that I am right."

Terror changed to intense relief as Yorke asked with an appeasing gesture, "Can you do nothing for her? Will she not sleep herself to death?"

"I assure you there is no danger; she will wake in a few hours, weak and languid, but all the better for the lesson she has unintentionally given herself. It's a dangerous habit, and I advise you to put a stop to it."

"To what? I don't understand you, sir."

The doctor looked up from the powder he was preparing, saw Yorke's perplexity, and answered with a significant nod, "I see you don't, but you shall, for she is too young for such things yet. Your wife eats opium, I suspect."

For a moment Yorke stared at him blankly, then said impetuously, "I'll not believe it!"

"Ask the maid," returned the doctor, but Victorine spoke for herself.

"Upon my word, sir, I know nothing of it. Mrs. Yorke sleeps a deal some days and is very quiet, but I never saw her take anything but the little comfits."

"Hum! She is more careful than I suspected. I'm sure of it, however, and perhaps you can satisfy yourself if you choose to look."

The doctor cast a suggestive glance about the room. Yorke understood it, and taking Cecil's keys began his search, saying sternly, "I have a right to satisfy myself and save her from further danger if it is so."

He did not look long, for in a corner of the drawer where certain treasures were kept he found a paper which had evidently been a wrapper for something that left a faintly acrid odor behind. A few grayish crumbs were shaken from the folds, and Dr. Home tasted them with a satisfied "I thought so."

Yorke crushed the paper in his hand, asking in a tone of mingled pain and perplexity, "Why should she do it?"

"A whim, perhaps, ennui, wakefulness; a woman's reasons for such freaks are many. You must ask her and put a stop to it, though I think this may break up the habit."

"What led you to suspect her of it?" asked Yorke, trying to find his way out of the mystery.

"I detected laudanum in her breath; that explained the unnatural sleep. The fact that it had not already killed her assured me that she was used to it, for, as you said, a dose like that would kill a man, but not a woman who had been taking opium for months. I can do nothing now; keep the room cool, let her wake naturally, then give her this, and if she is not comfortable tomorrow, let me know."

With that the doctor left him, Victorine began her watch beside the pale sleeper, and Yorke went away to wander through the silent house haunted by thoughts that would not let him rest.

Chapter VII. Heart For Heart

Dr. Home was right; Cecil's heavy sleep gradually passed into a natural one, and in the morning she woke, wan and nerveless, but entirely ignorant that she had lost a day. A misty recollection of some past excitement remained, but brought no explanation of her present lassitude, except a suspicion that she had taken more opium than was prudent. Finding herself alone when she woke, she did not ring for Victorine, but made her toilet hastily, rubbed a transient color into her pale cheeks, drew her hair low on her temples to conceal her heavy eyes, and went down fearing that it was very late.

Yorke sat in his place with a newspaper in his hand, but he was not reading, and there was something in his face that made Cecil pause involuntarily to examine it. It seemed as if years had been added to his age since she saw him last; his mouth was grave, his eye sad; a weary yet resolute expression was visible, but also the traces of some past suffering that touched the girl and caused her to lay her hand upon his shoulder, saying in her gentlest tone, "Good morning, Bazil; forgive me for being so wilful yesterday. I am punished for my fault by finding you so grave and tired now."

"I am only tired of waiting for my breakfast" was all the answer she got, but she felt him start and saw the paper rustle in his hand as she spoke, though whether surprise or displeasure caused these demonstrations she could not tell, and fancying him in one of his moody fits, took her place in silence. His coffee stood untouched till it was cold before he looked up and said, with a keen glance which made her eyes falter and fall, "Are you quite rested, Cecil?"

"Not quite; I danced too much last night."

"The night before last, you mean."

"We were at Coventry's last evening, Bazil."

"No, on Monday evening."

"Yes, and today is Tuesday."

He turned the paper toward her and Wednesday stared her full in the face. She looked incredulous, then bewildered, and putting her hand to her forehead seemed trying to recollect, while a foreboding fear came over her.

"Then what became of yesterday? I remember nothing of it," she asked with a troubled look.

"You slept it away."

"What! All day?"

"For six-and-thirty hours, without a word, almost without a motion." His eye was still upon her, his voice was ominously quiet, and as he spoke her wandering glance fell on an open book that lay beside him. She read its title—*Confessions of an Opium-Eater*—and overcome by a painful blending of shame and fear, she covered up her face without a word.

"Is it true, Cecil?"

"Yes, Bazil."

"How long has it been?"

"A year."

"What tempted you to try such a dangerous cure, or pleasure?"

"Yourself."

"I! How? When?"

"You gave me laudanum when I could not sleep. I liked its influence, and after that I tried it whenever I was sad or tired."

"Was this the secret I nearly discovered once, the cause of your solitary walks, the evil spirit that possessed you at Coventry's?"

"Yes; I had opium in my pocket that day, and was so frightened when I thought you would discover it, because I knew you would be angry. I went out those times to get it, for I dared not trust anyone. Last night, no, Monday night, I had none, and I longed for it so intensely I could not wait. I disobeyed you, but the storm was too much for me, and I was just turning back in despair, when I remembered the little flask. You seldom go to the cabinet, never use the laudanum, and I thought I could replace it by-and-by."

"But, child, had you no fear of consequences when playing such perilous pranks with yourself? You might have killed yourself, as you came near doing just now."

"I was used to it because Mamma often had it, and at first I was very careful; but the habit grew upon me unconsciously, and became so fascinating I could not resist it. In my hurry I took too much, and was frightened afterward, for everything seemed strange. I don't know what I did, but nothing seemed impossible to me, and it was a splendid hour; I wish it had been my last."

Tears fell between her fingers, and for a moment she was shaken by some uncontrollable emotion. Yorke half rose as if to go to her, but checked the impulse and sat down again with the air of a man bent on subduing himself at any cost. Cecil was herself again almost immediately, and wiping away her tears, seemed to await his reproof with her accustomed meekness.

But none came, for very gently he said, "Was this kind to yourself or me?"

"No; forgive me, Bazil. I will amend my fault."

"And promise never to repeat it?"

"I promise, but you cannot know how hard a thing it is to give up when I need it so much."

"Why, Cecil?"

"Because—" she stopped an instant, as if to restrain some impetuous word, and added, in an altered tone, "because I find it hard to tame myself to the quiet, lonely life you wish me to lead. I am so young, so full of foolish hopes and fancies, that it will take time to change me entirely, and what I have seen of the world lately makes it still more difficult. Have patience with me, and I shall be wiser and more contented soon."

He had left the table as if to throw up a window, and lingered for a moment to enjoy the balmy air, perhaps to conceal or conquer some pang of self-reproach, some late regret for what he had done. When he returned, it was to say, with an undertone of satisfaction in his grave voice, "Yes, it is too soon to ask so much of you, and if you give up this dangerous comforter, surely I can give up a little of the seclusion that I love. It is hard to break off such a habit. I will help you, and for a time we will forget

these troubles in new scenes and employments. Will you go to the seashore for a
month, Cecil, and so make home pleasanter by absence?"

"Oh, so gladly! I love the sea, and it will do me good. You are very kind to
think of it, and I thank you so much, Bazil!"

She did thank him, with eyes as well as lips, for her face brightened like a
prisoner's when the key turns in the lock and sunshine streams into his cell. Yorke
saw the joy, heard the tone of gratitude, and stifled a sigh, for they showed him what
a captive he had made of her, and betrayed how much she had suffered silently.

"Shall I go with you?" he asked, in a curiously unauthoritative tone, but with a
longing look that might have changed her reply had she seen it.

"If you care to, I shall feel safer; but do not unless it is pleasant to you."

"It is pleasant. We will go tomorrow," he said decidedly. "Rest and prepare
today; take Victorine with you, and leave your troubles all behind, and in a month we
will come back our happy selves again."

"I hope so" was all her answer, and the change was settled without more words.

"The charm does not work," sighed Yorke within himself, as he looked down
at Cecil leaning on his arm while they went pacing along the smooth beach seven days
later, with the great waves rolling up before them, a fresh wind blowing inward from
the sea, and summer sunshine brooding over the green islands of the bay. The week
had brought no change to Cecil; air and bathing, exercise and change of scene,
thoughtful care and daily devotion on her husband's part, all seemed to have failed,
and she walked beside him with the old quietude and coldness intensified instead of
lightened.

"What shall I do with you, Cecil? You don't get strong and rosy as I hoped you
would, and you often have a longing look as if you wanted your opium again; but you
know I dare not give it to you."

"I shall learn to do without it in time, or find something else to take its place.
Hark!"

As the words left her lips, her hand arrested him, her eyes kindled, a smile
broke over her face, and her whole figure seemed to start into life. He stood still
wondering, but instantly he learned what magic had wrought the spell, for on the
wings of the wind came the fitful music of a song from a solitary boatman whose skiff
lay rocking far out in the bay. Both recognized the voice, both watched the white sail
gliding nearer, and both faces altered rapidly; Cecil's warmed and brightened as she
listened with head erect and detaining hand, but Yorke's darkened with the blackest
frown it had ever worn as he drew her away with an impatient gesture and peremptory
"Come in; it is too warm to linger here for a fisherman's song!"

The smile broke into a laugh as she said, following with evident reluctance, "Do
fishermen sing Italian and go fishing in costumes like that?"

"Your ears and eyes must be keener than mine if you can discover what I neither
hear nor see," he answered almost petulantly. But still smiling, she looked backward
as she began to sing like a soft echo of the stranger's voice, and let him lead her where
he would. Till sunset he kept her in their rooms, busy with pencil, book, or needle,
blind to the wistful glances she often sent seaward, and deaf to hints that they were
losing the hours best suited for sketching. Victorine came in at last, bringing Cecil's

hat and mantle, and, as if the nod she gave him was a preconcerted signal, Yorke rose at once, saying promptly, "Yes, now we can go, without fear of sun or—"

"Fishermen," added Cecil, with a slightly scornful smile.

"Exactly." And Yorke put on her mantle without a sign of displeasure at her interruption. She seemed upon the point of refusing the stroll that now had no charm for her, but yielded, and they went out together, leaving Victorine to lift her hands and wonder afresh at the strange behavior of her master and mistress.

"I have a fancy to walk upon the rocks; can I, Bazil?" were the first words Cecil uttered, as they came into the splendor of the evening hour that bathed sea and sky within its ruddy glow.

A single sail was skimming down the bay, and not a figure sat or stood among the rocks. Yorke saw this, and answered with a gracious smile, "Walk where you will; I leave the path to you."

She climbed the cliffs and stood watching the lonely boat until it vanished round the rocky point where the lighthouse tower showed its newly kindled spark. Then she turned and said wearily, "Let us go home. I find it chilly here."

He led her down another path than that by which they came, but stopped suddenly, and she felt his hand tighten its hold as he exclaimed, "Go back; it is not safe. Go, I beg of you!"

It was too late, for she had seen a figure lying on a smooth ledge of the cliff, had recognized it, and glided on with a willful look, a smile of satisfaction. He set his teeth and sprang after her, but neither spoke, for Germain lay asleep, and the entire repose of his fine face not only restrained their tongues, but riveted their beauty-loving eyes. Cecil was touched to see how changed he was; for all the red glow shining over him, his face was very pale; the wind blew back the hair from his temples, showing how hollow they had grown; and stooping to brush an insect from his forehead, she saw many gray hairs among the dark locks scattered on the stone. His mouth was half hidden by the black beard, but the lips smiled as if some happy dream haunted his sleep, and in the hands folded on his broad chest, she saw a little knot of ribbon that had dropped from her dress that morning as she listened to his song.

Yorke saw it also, and made an involuntary gesture to pluck it from the sleeper's hold, but Cecil caught his arm, whispering sharply, "Let him keep it! You care nothing for it, and he needs something to comfort him, if I read his face aright."

Yorke stood motionless an instant, then seemed to take some sudden resolution, for drawing her gently aside, he said with a mildness that was as new as winning, "You are right; he does need comfort, and he shall have it. Go on alone, Cecil; I will follow soon."

She obeyed him, but glancing backward as she went, she saw him turn his face to the cliff behind him, and lay his head down on his arm in an attitude of deep dejection or of doubt. He stood so till the last sound of her light step died away, then he stopped and touched the sleeper, with a low-spoken "August, it is I."

Germain leaped to his feet as if the slight touch had been a blow, the quiet call a pistol shot, and his hand went to his breast with an instinctive motion that half revealed a hidden weapon. A single glance seemed to reassure him, for though his heart beat audibly, and his very lips were white, he laughed and offered the hand that had just been ready to deal death to some imaginary captor. Yorke did not take it, and, as if the discourtesy reminded him of something, Germain drew back, bowed with the grace that was habitual to him, and said coolly, "Pardon me; your sudden waking makes me forgetful. I was dreaming of you, and in the dream we were friends as of old."

"Never again, August; it is impossible. But I will do my best for you now, as before, if I may trust you."

"Have I not kept my word this time? Have I not left you in peace for nearly a year? Did I not obey you today when you bade me shun you, though the merest accident betrayed your presence to me?"

"You have done well for one so tempted and so impetuous; but you forget the letters written to Cecil in my absence, and lying down to sleep in our very path is not putting the bay between us as I bade you."

"Forgive the letters; they did no harm, for she never read them, I suspect. Ah, you smile! Then I am right. As for finding me here, it was no plot of mine. I thought you always walked on the beach, so I crept up to catch one glimpse of her unseen, before I went away for another year, perhaps. Be generous, Bazil. You have made her all your own; do not deny me this poor boon."

"I will not. Promise me to keep our secret sacredly, and you shall see her when you will. But you must control yourself, eye, tongue, voice, and manner, else I must banish you again. Remember your life is in my hands, and I will give you up rather than let harm come to her."

"I swear it, Bazil. You may safely indulge me now, for I shall not haunt you long; my wanderings are almost over, and you may hear Death knocking at my heart."

Real solicitude appeared in Yorke's face as the other spoke with a melancholy smile, and obeying a kindly impulse, he laid his hand on Germain's shoulder.

"I hope not, for it is a very tender heart, in spite of all its waywardness and past offenses. But if it be so, you shall not be denied the one happiness that I can give you. Come home with me, and for an hour sun yourself in Cecil's presence. I do not fear you in this mood, and there is no danger of disturbing her; I wish there was!"

"God bless you, Bazil! Trust me freely. The wild devil is cast out, and all I ask is a quiet time in which to repent before I die. Take me to her; I will not mar her peace or yours. May I keep this? It is my only relic."

He showed the ribbon with a beseeching look, and remembering Cecil's words, Yorke bowed a mute assent as he led the way down the rude path and along the beach where slender footprints were still visible in the damp sand.

She was waiting in the softly lighted room, with no sign of impatience as she sat singing at the instrument. It was the air Germain had sung, and pausing behind her, he blended the music of his voice with hers in the last strains of the song. She turned then, and put out her hand, but caught it back and glanced at Yorke, for the recollection of the struggle in the dark returned to check the impulse that prompted her to welcome this man whom she could not dislike, in spite of mystery, violence, and unmistakable traces of a turbulent life. Yorke saw her doubt and answered it instantly.

"Give him your hand, Cecil, and forgive the past; there is no ill will between us now, and he will not forget himself again."

Germain bowed low over the little hand, saying in the tone that always won its way, "Rest assured of that, Mrs. Yorke, and permit me to offer my best wishes, now that my prophecy has been fulfilled."

In half an hour Yorke saw the desired change, for Germain worked the miracle, and Cecil began to look as she had done a year ago. Sitting a little apart, he watched them intently, as if longing to learn the secret, for he had failed to animate his statue since the night when for a time he believed he had some power over her, but soon learned that it was to opium, not to love, that he owed his brief success. Cecil paid no heed to him, but seemed forgetful of his presence, as Germain entertained her with an animation that increased the fascination of his manner. An irresistible mingling of interest, curiosity, and compassion attracted her to him. Yorke's assurance, as well as his own altered demeanor, soon removed all misgivings from her mind, and the indescribable charm of his presence made the interview delightful, for he was both gay and gentle, devoted and respectful. The moment the hour struck, he rose and went, with a grateful glance at Yorke, a regretful one at Cecil. She did not ask now as before, "Will he come again?" but her eyes looked the question.

"Yes, he will come tomorrow, if you like. He is ill and lonely, and not long for this world; so do your best for him while you may."

"I will, with all my heart, for indeed I pity him. It is very generous of you to forget his wrongdoing, and give me this pleasure."

"Then come and thank me for it a la Mrs. Vivian."

He spoke impulsively and held his hands to her, but she drew back, swept him a stately little curtsy, and answered with her coolest air, "We are not in public now, so, thank you, guardian, and good night."

She smiled as she spoke, but he turned as if he had been struck, and springing out of the low window, paced the sands until the young moon set.

They had come to the seaside before the season had begun, but now the great hotel was filling fast, and solitude was at an end. Cecil regretted this, and so did Yorke, for the admiration which she always excited no longer pleased but pained him, because pride had changed to a jealous longing to keep her to himself. In public she was the brilliant, winning wife, in private, the cold, quiet ward, and nothing but Germain's presence had power to warm her then. He came daily, seeming to grow calmer and better in the friendly atmosphere about him. Cecil enjoyed his society with unabated pleasure, and Yorke left them free after being absent for hours and apparently intent upon some purpose of his own. Of course, there were many eyes to watch, many tongues to comment upon the actions of the peculiar sculptor and his lovely wife. Germain was known to be a friend; it was evident that he was an invalid, and no longer young; but flirting young ladies and gossiping old ones would make romances, while the idle gentlemen listened and looked on. Cecil soon felt that something was amiss, for though her secluded life had made her singularly childlike in some things, she was fast learning to know herself, and understand her relations to the world. She wondered if Yorke heard what was said, and hoped he would speak if anything displeased him; but till he did, she went on her way as if untroubled, walking, sailing, singing, and driving with Germain, who never forgot his promise, and who daily won from her fresh confidence and regard. So the days passed till the month was gone, and with a heavy heart Cecil heard her husband give orders to prepare for home.

"Are you ready?" he asked, coming in as she stood recalling the pleasant hours spent with Germain, and wondering if he would come to say farewell.

"Yes, Bazil, I am ready."

"But not glad to go?"

"No, for I have been very happy here."

"And home is not made pleasanter by absence?"

"I shall try to think it is pleasanter."

"And I shall try to make it so. Here is the carriage. Shall we go?"

As they rolled away, Cecil looked back, half suspecting to see some signal of adieu from window, cliff, or shore, but there was none, and Yorke said, interpreting the look aright, "It is in vain to look for him; he has already gone."

"It is much better so. I am glad of it," she said decidedly, as she drew down her veil, and leaning back, seemed to decline all further conversation. Her companion consoled himself with Judas, but something evidently filled him with a pleasant excitement, for often he smiled unconsciously, and several times sang softly to himself, as if well pleased at some fancy of his own. Cecil thought her disappointment amused him, and much offended, sat with her eyes closed behind her veil, careless of all about her, till the sudden stopping of the carriage roused her, and looking up, she saw Yorke waiting to hand her out.

"Why stop here? This is not home," she said, looking at the lovely scene about with wondering eyes.

"Yes, this is home," he answered, as leading her between blooming parterres and up the wide steps, he brought her into a place so beautiful that she stood like one bewildered. A long, lofty hall, softly lighted by the sunshine that crept in through screens of flowers and vines. A carpet, green and thick as forest moss, lay underfoot; warm-hued pictures leaned from the walls, and all about in graceful alcoves stood Yorke's fairest statues, like fit inhabitants of this artist's home. Before three wide windows airy draperies swayed in the wind, showing glimpses of a balcony that overhung the sea, whose ever-varying loveliness was a perpetual joy, and on this balcony a man sat, singing.

"Does it please you, Cecil? I have done my best to make home more attractive by bringing to it all that you most love."

Yorke spoke with repressed eagerness, for his heart was full, and try as he might, he could not quite conceal it. Cecil saw this, and a little tremor of delight went through her; but she only took his hand in both her own, exclaiming gratefully, "It is too beautiful for me! How shall I thank you? This is the work you have been doing secretly, and this is why you sent Germain before us to give me a sweet welcome. How thoughtful, and how beautiful it was of you."

He looked pleased but not satisfied, and led her up and down, showing all the wonders of the little summer palace by the sea. Everywhere she found her tastes remembered, her comfort consulted, her least whim gratified, and sometimes felt as if she had found something dearer than all these. Still no words passed her lips warmer than gratitude, and when they returned to the hall of statues, she only pressed the generous hand that gave so much, and said again, "It is too beautiful for me. How can I thank you for such kindness to your little ward?"

"Say wife, Cecil, and I am satisfied."

"Pardon me, I forgot that, and like the other best because it is truer. Now let me go and thank Germain."

She went on before him, and coming out into the wide balcony, saw nothing for a moment but the scene before her. Below, the waves broke musically on the shore, the green islands slept in the sunshine, the bay was white with sails, the city spires glittered in the distance, and beyond, the blue sea rolled to meet the far horizon.

"Has he not done well? Is it not a charming home to live and die in?" said Germain, as she turned to greet him, with both hands extended, and something more than gratitude in her face. That look, so confiding and affectionate, was too much for Germain; he took the hands and bent to give her a tenderer greeting, remembering his promise just in time, and with a half-audible apology, hurried away, as if fearing to trust himself.

Cecil looked after him sorrowfully, but when Yorke approached, asking in some surprise, "Where is Germain?" she answered reproachfully, "He is gone, and he must not come again."

"Why not?"

"Because he cannot forget, and others see it as well as I. You might have spared him this, and for my sake have remembered that it is not always wise to be kind."

"Ah, they gossip again, do they? Let them; I've done one rash and foolish thing to appease Mrs. Grundy, and now I shall trouble myself no further about her or her tongue."

Leaning on the balustrade, he did not look at her, though he held his breath to catch her reply, but seemed intent on watching leaf after leaf float downward to the sea. His careless tone, his negligent attitude wounded Cecil as deeply as his words; her eyes kindled, and real resentment trembled in her voice.

"Who should care, if not you? Do you know what is said of us?"

"Only what is said of every pretty woman at a watering place." And he leaned over to watch the last leaf fall.

"You do not care, then? It gives you no pain to have it said that I am happier with Germain than with you?"

He clenched the hand she could not see, but shrugged his shoulders and looked far off at sea, as if watching a distant sail.

"For once, rumor tells the truth, and why should I deny it? My pride may be a little hurt, but I'm not jealous of poor Germain."

If he had seen her hold her lips together with almost as grim a look as his own often wore, and heard her say within herself, "I will prove that," he would have carried his experiment no further. But he never turned his head, and Cecil asked, with a touch of contempt in her voice that made him wince, "Do you wish this mysterious friend of yours to go and come as freely as he has done of late?"

"Why not, if he is happy? He has not long to enjoy either life or love."

"And I am to receive him as before, am I?"

"As you please. If his society is agreeable to you, I have no desire to deprive you of it, since mine is burdensome and Alfred away."

Something in the emphasis unconsciously put upon the last name caused a smile to flit over Cecil's face, but it was gone instantly, and her voice was cold as ice.

"Thank you; and you have no fear of the consequences of this unparalleled generosity of yours?"

"None for myself or my snow image. Has she for herself?"

"I fear nothing for myself; I have no heart, you know."

She laughed a sudden laugh that made him start, and as she vanished behind the floating curtains, he struck his hand on the iron bar before him with a force that brought blood, saying, in an accent of despair, "And she will never know that I have one, till she has broken it!"

Chapter VIII. Masks

"Cecil, the world begins to wonder why Mrs. Yorke does not admit it to a glimpse of her new home."

"Mrs. Yorke is supremely indifferent to the world's wonder or its wishes."

She certainly looked so, as she sat in the couch corner singing to herself, and playing with a useless fan—for the room was breezy with sea airs, though an August sun blazed without. Yorke was strolling from alcove to alcove, as if studying the effects among his statues, and Germain lounged on the wide step of the balcony window, with a guitar across his knee, for he still came daily, as neither master nor mistress had forbidden him.

"I think I have proved my indifference, but people annoy me with questions, and I suspect we shall have no peace till we give some sort of an entertainment, and purchase freedom hereafter by the sacrifice of one evening now."

"You are right, Yorke; I, too, have been beset by curious inquirers, and I suggest that you end their suspense at once. Why not have a masquerade? These rooms are admirably fitted for it, there has been none this season, and the moon is at the full next week. What does 'my lady' say?"

Germain spoke in his persuasive voice, and Cecil looked interested now.

"If we must have anything let it be that. I like such things, and it is pleasant to forget oneself sometimes. Does the fancy suit you, Basil?"

"Anything you please, or nothing at all. I only spoke of it, thinking you might find some pleasure in pleasing others," he returned, still busy with the piping Faun that had a place among the finer works of his own hands.

"I used to do so, and tried very hard to please, but no good came of it, so now I enjoy myself, and leave others to do likewise. What characters shall we assume, Germain?"

As she asked the question, her voice changed as abruptly as her manner, and languid indifference was replaced by lively interest.

"I shall assume none, I have not spirits enough for it, but in a domino can glide about and collect compliments for you. Your husband must take the brilliant part, as a host should."

"He had better personate Othello; the costume would be becoming, and the character an easy one for him to play, he is such a jealous soul."

She spoke ironically, and he answered in the same tone.

"No, thank you, I prefer Hamlet, but you would succeed well as the princess in the fairy tale, who turned to stone whenever her husband approached her, though a very charming woman to all others. Perhaps, however, you would prefer to personate some goddess; I can recommend Diana, as a cool character for a sultry summer evening."

"I hate goddesses, having lived with them all my life. Everyone will expect me to be some classical creature or other, so I shall disappoint them, and enjoy myself like a mortal woman. I'll imitate the French marquise whom we saw last winter at the theater; she was very charming, and the dress is easily prepared, if one has jewels enough."

Germain laughed involuntarily at the idea of Cecil in such a character, and she laughed also, a lighthearted laugh, pleasant to hear.

"You think I cannot do it? Wait and see. I am a better actress than you think; I've had daily practice since I was married, and Bazil will testify that I do my part well."

"So well that sometimes it is impossible not to mistake art for nature. When shall this fete take place, Madame la Marquise?"

"Next week; four days are enough for preparation, and if we wait longer, I shall get tired of the fancy, and give it up."

"Next week it shall be then."

Yorke stood looking down the long room at the pretty tableau at the end, for Germain was leaning on the back of the couch now, dropping odorous English violets into the white hands lifted to catch them, and Cecil looked as if she was already enjoying herself as a mortal woman. Standing apart among the statues, he wondered if she remembered the time when his will was law, and it was herself who obeyed with a weakness he had not yet learned. Now this was changed, and he called himself a fool for losing his old power, yet gaining no new hold upon her. She ruled him, but seemed not to know it, and keeping her smiles for others, showed her darkest side to him, being as lovely and as thorny as any brier rose. Presently she sprang up, saying with unusual animation, "I will go and consult with Victorine, and then we will drive to town and give our orders. You must come with me, Germain. I want your taste in my selection; Bazil has none, except in stones."

"One cannot doubt that, with such proofs all about one," answered Germain, as he followed her toward the door. "When shall we have another statue, Yorke? You have been idle of late."

"Never busier in my life; I have a new design in my mind, but it takes time to work it out. Wait a few weeks longer, and I will show you something that shall surpass all these."

"Unless you have lost your skill."

Yorke's face had kindled as he spoke, but it fell again when Cecil whispered these words in passing, with a glance that seemed to prophesy a failure for the new design, whatever it might be. A flush of passionate pain passed across his face, and he lifted his arms as if to hurl poor Psyche down again, but the sight of the bruised hand seemed to recall some purpose, and calm him by its spell.

For four days there was much driving to and fro between the city and the beach; the great hotel was all astir, and the villas along the shore were full of busy tongues and needles, for summer is the time for pleasure, and the Yorkes' masquerade was the event of the season. On the appointed evening all things were propitious, the night was balmy, the sky cloudless, the moon lent her enchantment to the scene, and the lonely home beside the sea wore its most inviting aspect, for the hall of statues was brilliant with lights, blooming with flowers, and haunted by the fitful music of a band concealed among the shrubbery without. Yorke, looking stately and somber as the melancholy Dane, and Germain in a plain black silk domino, stood waiting for Cecil, mask in hand. Presently she came rustling down, in a costume both becoming and piquant, for the powdered hair made her fair skin dazzling, and the sweeping brocades of violet and silver set off her slender figure. She wore no ornaments, but a profusion of rich lace upon the dress, white plumes in her hair, and a cluster of roses on her bosom. With the costume she seemed to have assumed the coquetry of the French marquise, and greeted her companions in broken English, spoken with a charming accent and sprightly grace that caused Germain to compliment her on her skill, and Yorke to survey her with undisguised pride, as he said, with a significant smile, "Let me put the last touch to this ravishing toilet of yours, and prove that you were right in saying I had some taste in stones."

Cecil bent her beautiful neck to let him clasp a diamond necklace about it, and held out a pair of lovely arms to receive their glittering fetters, with a little cry of pleasure, and a characteristic *"Merci, monsieur!* You are too gallant in so revenging yourself upon me for my idle words. These are superb, I kiss your munificent hands," and as he essayed to fasten in the brooch, she touched his hand with her lips. The pin dropped, Germain took it up, and turning to him, she said, in her own voice, "Put it in my hair just here, there is no room for it below; diamonds are best on the head, and roses on the heart."

As he deftly fastened it above her white forehead, she drew out a flower broken by Yorke's unskillful hand, and tying it to the ribbon of Germain's domino, she said, "Wear this, else among so many black dominoes I shall not know my friend, and make my confidences to wrong ears."

"Now I am prouder of my rose than you of your jewels, madame, and thank you for it heartily," he replied, surveying it with delight.

"Shall I wear not your favor, also?" asked Yorke, with extended hand.

"Oh, yes, but not that one, because it does not suit you. There's rue for you; and here's some for me, but we may wear our rue with a difference."

As she quoted poor Ophelia's words, from a vase nearby she gathered a flowerless sprig, and gave it to him with a glance that cut him to the heart. He took it silently, and instantly resuming her gay manner, she exclaimed, as the roll of a carriage was heard, "It is the Coventrys, they come early, because I asked them to play the host and hostess for an hour to increase the bewilderment of our guests, and give us greater freedom. She is to be Juno, and while she is masked, no one will suspect that it is not I. Come, Germain, let us slip away, and return later."

The rooms filled rapidly, and the mock host and hostess did the honors so well that the guests had no doubt of their identity, while the real master of the house moved among them unsuspected, watching impatiently for the arrival of the marquise and her friend. He waited long, but at last the white plumes were seen approaching, and many eyes followed the brilliant figure that entered, not on the arm of a black domino, but a young courtier in the picturesque costume of Elizabeth's time. Yorke saw at a glance that this was not Germain; who was it then? Alfred flashed into his mind, but he was across the water, and not expected to return for months. No new-made acquaintance of Cecil's carried himself with such a gay and gallant air; for the disguise seemed to sit easily upon him, and he wore doublet and hose, velvet cloak and lovelocks, ruff and sword with none of the awkwardness that most men exhibit when in costume. Nor was this all he saw to disturb him; the charming marquise leaned upon the arm of this debonair Sir Walter Raleigh, talking with an animation that attracted attention, while the devotion of her escort, and the grace of both, roused much curiosity concerning this striking young couple. Hamlet followed them like a shadow, but their conversation was in whispers, and they went their way as if unconscious of anything but themselves. Yorke soon met the black domino with the white rose dangling on his breast, and drew him apart to ask eagerly, "Who is that with Cecil?"

"I have no idea."

"Where did she meet him?"

"I cannot tell you."

"But you went away together, and were to return together. When and how did you part?"

"We went to the music room to wait a little, but soon she sent me for her fan, which had been forgotten. I was gone some time, for the maid was busy with the ladies; when I returned Madame had disappeared, and I saw no more of her till she came in with Sir Walter."

"Rude to you, that is not like her!"

"I was to blame, if anyone; she grew tired of waiting, doubtless, and finding some friend, left me to follow her. I am glad she did, for he is a fitter escort for youth and beauty than I. They look like a prince and princess out of a fairy tale, and it does one's heart good to watch them."

Yorke made no reply, but stood motionless beside Germain, looking where *he* looked, for the dancing had begun, and the young pair were slowly circling round the room to the sound of music, inspiring enough to stir the coldest blood. Twice the marquise floated by, with a glance over her shoulder as she passed; but the third time she looked in vain, for the two dark figures were gone, and a splendid Cleopatra held her court in the deserted recess.

"I am out of breath; let us stroll about and hear people's comments on me and mine; that will be amusing," she said, pausing, and her escort obeyed.

It was amusing, and something more, for as they passed through the glittering throng, or mingled with the groups gathered about each statue-haunted alcove, Cecil saw and heard the wonder, admiration, and reverence her husband's genius inspired. This was the first time his works had been exhibited, and there was something so romantic in the fact that these fine statues had stood unknown, unseen, till they were brought to decorate his wife's home, as if love alone could make him care for fame, that their beauty seemed increased fourfold in the spectators' eyes; and so warm were the commendations bestowed upon the marbles, so varied and beautiful the tributes paid the man, that Cecil glowed behind the mask, and was glad of that screen to hide her smiles and tears. From many lips she heard the same story, sorrow, love, and fame, with endless embellishments, but always the same contrast between romance and reality for her. If he loved her, why so careless about Germain? What was the mystery that bound the two so closely together, with such a strange mingling of dislike and gratitude, forbearance and submission? Had she not a right to solve the secret if she could, now that her happiness depended on it? These thoughts saddened and silenced her so visibly that her companion soon perceived it.

"Where are all your spirits gone? Have I really offended you by coming? Or do these chattering people weary you? Tell me, Cecil, and let me do my best to make you gay again," he whispered, bending till his curling locks touched her shoulder.

"Neither, Sir Walter; the heat oppresses me, so take me out into the garden, and leave me to rest, while you play the cavalier to some other lady, lest your devotion to one should give offense."

"If I submit now, I may join you when I've done penance in a single dance, may I not? Remember how short my time is, and how much I have to say."

"You may come if you will forget the past, and think only of the future."

"I can safely promise that, for it is now the desire of my heart," and with a curious blending of joy and regret in his voice, Sir Walter left the marquise on the broad steps that led down into the garden. Moonlight flooded the terrace, grove, and flowery paths where changing figures wandered to and fro, or sat in the green nooks, each group making a graceful picture in that magic light. Here a troubadour sang to his guitar, as knights and ladies listened to his lay; there glided a monk or nun, somber and silent, as if blind and deaf to the gaiety about them; elves glittered in the grove; Mephistopheles followed a blond Margaret; Louis Fourteenth and Marie Stuart promenaded with stately pace along the terrace; and Rebecca the Jewess was flirting violently with Cardinal Wolsey on the steps. Enjoying the mirth and mystery with a divided mind, Cecil wandered on, declining all courteous offers of companionship from fellow wanderers, and came at last to a retired nook, where a rustic seat stood under a leafy arch before the little fountain that sparkled in the moonlight. Scarcely was she seated, however, before a long shadow fell across the path, and turning, she saw a black domino behind her.

"Does Madame recognize me?"

The voice was feigned, nothing but the outline of the figure was visible, and no badge distinguished this domino from a dozen others, but after a moment's pause and a brief scrutiny, Cecil seemed satisfied, and removing her mask, exclaimed with an air of perfect confidence, "It is Germain; you cannot hide yourself from me."

"Is Madame sure?"

"Yes, I know you by the rapid beating of your heart. You forget that, *mon ami*."

"Does no other heart beat fast when it approaches you, lovely marquise?"

"None but yours, I fancy. You have been dancing, and I bade you not, it is dangerous. Come now, and rest with me; the music is delicious from this distance, and the night too beautiful to waste in crowded rooms."

With an inviting gesture she swept her silken train aside, that he might share the little seat, and as he took it, put up her hand to remove his mask, with the smile still shining on her face, the friendly tone still softening her voice.

"Take off that ugly thing, it impedes your breathing, and is bad for you."

But he caught the hand, and imprisoned it in both his own, while the heartbeats grew more audible, and some inward agitation evidently made it difficult to speak quietly.

"No, permit me to keep it on; I cannot show as calm a face as you tonight, so let me hide it."

Something in the touch and tone caused Cecil to look closer at the mask, which showed nothing but glittering eyes and glimpses of a black beard.

"Where is the sign that will assure me you are Germain?" she demanded.

"Here," and turning to a fold of the black domino she saw the rose still hanging as she had tied it.

"No wonder you did not care to show your badge, it is so faded. Break a fresh one from the trellis yonder, and I will place it better for you."

"Give me one from your bouquet, that is fresher and sweeter to me than any other in the garden or the world."

"Moonlight and masquerading make you romantic; I feel so too, and will make a little bargain with you, since you prize my rose so highly. You shall take your choice of these I wear, if you will answer a few questions."

"Ask anything—" he began eagerly, but caught back the words, adding, "put your questions, and if I can answer them without forfeiting my word, I will, truly and gladly."

"Ah, I thought that would follow. If I forfeit my word in asking, surely you may do the same in answering. I promised Bazil to control my curiosity; I have kept my promise till he broke his, now I am free to satisfy myself."

"What promise has he broken?"

"I will answer that when you have earned the rose. Come, grant my wish, and then you may question in return."

"Speak, I will do my best."

"Tell me then what tie binds you to Yorke?"

"The closest, yet most inexplicable."

"You are his brother?"

"No."

"He cannot be your father, that is impossible?"

"Decidedly, as there are but a few years difference between our ages."

She heard a short laugh as this answer came, and smiled at her own foolish question.

"Then you must be akin to me, and so bound to him in some way. Is that it?"

"I am not akin to you, yet I am bound to you both, and thank God for it."

"What is the mystery? Why do you haunt me? Why does Yorke let you come? And why do I trust you in spite of everything?"

"The only key I can give you to all this is the one word, love."

She drew back, as he bent to whisper it, and put up her hand as if to forbid the continuance of the subject, but Germain said warmly, "It is because I love you that I haunt you. Yorke permits it, because he cannot prevent it, and you trust me, because your heart is empty and you long to fill it. Is not this true? I have answered your questions, now answer mine, I beg of you."

"No, it is not true."

"Then you do love?"

"Yes."

"Whom, Cecil, whom?"

"Not you, Germain, believe that, and ask no more."

"Is it a younger, comelier man than I?"

"Yes."

"And you have loved him long?"

"For years."

"He is here tonight?"

"He is. Now let us go in, I am tired of this."

"Not yet, stay and answer me once more. You shall not go till I am satisfied. Tell me, have you no love for Yorke?"

His sudden violence terrified her, for, as she endeavored to rise, he held her firmly, speaking vehemently, and waiting her reply, with eyes that flashed behind the mask. Remembering his wild nature, and fearing some harm to Bazil, she dared not answer truly, and hoping to soothe him, she laid her hand upon his arm, saying, with well-feigned coldness, "How can I love him, when I have been taught for years only to respect and obey him? He has been a stern master, and I never can forget my lesson. Now release me, Germain, and never let this happen again. It was my fault, so I forgive you, but there must be no more of it."

There was no need to bid him release her, for as the words left her lips, like one in a paroxysm of speechless repentance, grief, or tenderness, he covered her hands with passionate tears and kisses, and was gone as suddenly as he had come. Cecil lingered a moment to recover herself and readjust her mask, and hardly had she done so when down the path came Hamlet, as if in search of her. The difference between the two had never been more strongly marked than now, for Germain had been in his most impetuous mood, and Yorke seemed unusually mild and calm, as Cecil hurried toward him, with a pleasant sense of safety as she took his arm, and listened to his quiet question.

"What has frightened you, my child?"

"Germain, he is so violent, so strange, that I can neither control nor understand him, and he must be banished, though it is hard to do it."

"Poor Germain, he suffers for the sins of others as well as for his own. But if he makes you unhappy, he shall go, and go at once. Why did you not tell me so before?"

"I did, but you said, let him stay. Have you forgotten that so soon?"

Yorke laughed low to himself.

"It seems that I have forgotten. It was kind of me, however, to let him stay where he was the happiest; did you not think so, Cecil?"

"No, I thought it very unwise. I was hurt at your indifference, and tried to show you your mistake; but I have done harm to Germain, and he must go, although in him I lose my dearest friend, my pleasantest companion. I am very proud, but I humble myself to ask this favor of you, Bazil."

"Gentle heart, how can he ever thank you for your compassion and affection? Be easy, he shall go; but as a last boon, give him one more happy day, and I will make sure that he shall not offend again, as he seems to have done tonight. I, too, am proud, but I humble myself, Cecil, to ask this favor of you."

So gently he spoke, so entirely changed he seemed, that Cecil's eyes filled, for her heart felt very tender, and before she could restrain it, an impulsive exclamation escaped her.

"Ah, Bazil, if you were always as kind as now, how different my life would be."

"So would mine, if I dared be kind." The answer was impulsive as the exclamation, and he made a gesture as if to take her to himself; but something restrained him, and with a heavy sigh he walked in silence.

"Dared to be kind?" she echoed, in a grieved and wondering tone. "Are you afraid to show that you care for me a little?"

"Mortally afraid, because I cannot tell you all. But, thank heaven, there will come a time when I may speak, and for that hour I long, though it will be my last."

"O Bazil, what do you mean by such strange words?"

"I mean that when I lie dying, I can tell my miserable mystery, and you will pity and pardon me at last."

"But you once said you would never tell me."

"Did I? Well, then Germain shall tell you when he dies. You'll not have long to wait."

Cecil shivered at the ominous words, and started with a faint cry, for they seemed confirmed, as her eye fell on a dark figure lying with hidden face among the grass, not far from the solitary path they had unconsciously chosen. There was something so pathetic about the prostrate figure, flung down as if in the abandonment of despair, that Cecil was on the point of going to offer comfort, when her companion detained her, whispering earnestly, "Leave him to me, and go on alone. It is time for the unmasking, and we shall be missed. I'll follow soon, and bring him with me."

She obeyed, and went on, more heavyhearted than when she came. Within, the gaiety was at its height, and as she entered, Sir Walter was instantly at her side, leading her away for the last dance before the masks were removed. Presently silence fell upon the motley throng, and all stood ready to reveal themselves, when a signal came. A single horn sounded a mellow blast, and in a moment the room brightened with smiling faces, as the black masks fell, while a general peal of laughter filled the air. Cecil glanced about her for her husband and Germain. They were standing together near the door, both unmasked now, and both more mysterious to her than ever. Neither looked as she expected to see them; Yorke was grim and pale, with smileless lips and gloomy eyes; Germain leaned near him, smiling his enchanting smile, and wearing the indescribable air of romance which always attached to him, and even now, rendered him a more striking figure than many of the gayer ones about him.

"Shall I ever understand them?" she sighed to herself, as her eyes turned from them to Sir Walter, standing beside her, one hand on his sword hilt, the other still holding the half-mask before his face, as if anxious to preserve his incognito as long as possible. Yorke's eye was upon him, also, as he waited with intense impatience to see his suspicion confirmed; but in the confusion of the moment, he lost sight of the marquise and her attendant before this desire was gratified. Making his way through the crowd as fast as frequent salutations, compliments, and jests permitted, he came at last to the balcony. A single glance assured him that his search was ended, and stepping into the deep shadow of the projecting wall, he eyed the group before him with an eye that boded ill to the unconscious pair.

Cecil's face was toward him, and it wore a look of happiness that had long been a stranger to it, as she spoke earnestly but in so low a tone that not a word was audible. Her companion listened intently, and made brief replies; he was unmasked now, but the long plume of his hat drooping between his face and the observer still prolonged his suspense. Only a few moments did they stand so, for, as if bidding him adieu, Cecil waved her hand to him, and reentered the hall through the nearest window. Sir Walter seated himself on the wide railing of the balcony, flung his hat at his feet, and turned his face full to the light, as if enjoying the coolness of the sea breeze. One instant he sat humming a blithe cavalier song to himself, the next, a strong hand clutched and swung him over the low balustrade, as a face pale with passion came between him and the moon, and Yorke's voice demanded fiercely, "What brings you here? Answer me truly, or I will let go my hold, and nothing but my hand keeps you from instant death."

It was true, for though Alfred's feet still clung to the bars, his only support was the arm, inflexible as iron, that held him over the rocky precipice, below which rolled the sea. But he was brave, and though his face whitened, his eye was steady, his voice firm, as he replied unhesitatingly, "I came to see Cecil."

"I thought so! Are you satisfied?"

"Fully satisfied."

"That she loves you as you would have her love?"

"Yes, as I would have her love."

"You dare say this to me!" and Yorke's grip tightened, as a savage light shot into his black eyes, and his voice shook with fury.

"I dare anything. If you doubt it, try me."

Alfred's blood was up now, and he forgot himself in the satisfaction it gave him to inflict a pang of jealousy as sharp as his own had been.

"What was she saying to you as she left?" demanded Yorke, under his breath.

"I shall answer no questions, and destroy no confidences" was the brief reply.

"Then I swear I will let go my hold!"

"Do it, and tell Cecil I was true to the end."

With a defiant smile, Alfred took his hands from the other's arm, and hung there only by that desperate clutch. The smile, the words, drove Yorke beyond himself; a mad devil seemed to possess him, and in the drawing of a breath, the young man would have been dashed upon the jagged cliffs below, had not Germain saved them both. Where he came from, neither saw, nor what he did, for with inconceivable rapidity Yorke was flung back, Alfred drawn over the balustrade, and planted firmly on his feet again. Then the three looked at one another: Yorke was speechless with the mingled rage, shame, and grief warring within him; Alfred still smiling disdainfully; Germain pale and panting with the shock of surprise at such a sight, and the sudden exertion which had spared the gay evening a tragic close. He spoke first, and as one having authority, drawing the young man with him, as he slowly retreated toward the steep steps that wound from the balcony to the cliff that partially supported it.

"Go, Bazil, and keep this from Cecil; I have a right to ask it, for half the debt to you is canceled by saving you from this act, that would have made your life as sad a failure as my own. I shall return tomorrow for the last time; till then I shall guard this boy, for you are beside yourself."

With that they left him, and he let them go without a word, feeling that indeed he was beside himself. How long he stood there, he did not know; a stir within recalled him to the necessity of assuming composure, and fighting down the agitation that must be controlled, he went in to play the courteous host at his own table, and answer to the toasts drunk to the health and happiness of himself and his fair wife. He went through with his duties with a desperate sort of gaiety that deceived careless observers, but not Cecil. She too was feverishly restless for Alfred did not appear, and Germain was gone also; but she hid her disquiet better than Yorke, and the effort made her so brilliantly beautiful and blithe that the old fancy of "Yorke's statue" was forgotten, and "Yorke's wife" became "the star of the goodly companie."

The evening came to an end at last, and Yorke's long torment was over. Early birds were beginning to twitter, and the short summer night was nearly past, as the latest guest departed, leaving the weary host and hostess alone. Cecil's first act was to unclasp the diamonds, and offer to restore them to the giver, saying gratefully, yet with gravity, "I thank you for your generous thought of me, and have tried to do honor to your gift, but please take them back now, they are too costly ornaments for me."

"Too heavy chains, you mean," and with a sudden gesture, he sent the glittering handful to the ground, adding, in a tone that made her start, "Did you bring that boy here?"

"Do you mean the gallant Sir Walter?"

"I mean Alfred Norton."

"No, I did not ask him."

"You knew he was coming?"

"I only hoped so."

The dark veins rose on Yorke's forehead, he locked his hands tightly together behind him, and fixed on her a look that she never could forget, as he said slowly, as if every word was wrung from him, "You must see him no more. I warn you, harm will come of it if you persist."

A smile broke over her face, and with a shrug of her white shoulders, and an accent of merry malice that almost drove him frantic, she answered nonchalantly, "Why mind him more than poor Germain? If he comes, I cannot shun him, unless my lord and master has turned jealous, and forbids it; does he?"

"Yes."

Yorke left the room, as he uttered the one word that was both an answer and a confession; had he looked backward, he would have seen Cecil down upon her knees gathering up the scattered diamonds, with that inexplicable smile quenched in tears, and on her face that tender expression he so longed to see.

CHAPTER IX. ON THE RACK

THE HOUSE was not astir till very late next day, for master and mistress breakfasted in their own rooms at noon, and seemed in no haste to meet. A more miserable man than Yorke the sun did not shine on. Oppressed with remorse for last night's violence, shame at last night's betrayal of jealousy, and bitter sorrow for last night's defeat, he longed yet dreaded to see Cecil, feeling that all hope of winning her heart was lost, and nothing but the resignation of despair remained for him.

Fearing that Alfred might venture back, he haunted house and garden like a restless ghost, despising himself the while, yet utterly unable to resist the power that controlled him. No one came, however; not even Germain, and the afternoon was half over before Cecil appeared. He knew the instant she left her room, for not a sound escaped him; he saw her come down into her boudoir looking so fresh and fair he found it hard to feign unconsciousness of her presence, till he was composed enough to meet her as he would. The windows of her room opened on the shady terrace where he had been walking for an hour. After passing and repassing several times, in hopes that she would speak to him, he pulled his hat low over his brows, and looking in, bade her "Good morning." She answered with unusual animation, but her eye did not meet his, and she bent assiduously over her work as if to hide her varying color. Yorke was quick to see these signs of disquiet, but the thought of Alfred made him interpret them in his own way, and find fresh cause of suffering in them.

Both seemed glad to ignore last night, for neither spoke of it, though conversation flagged, and long pauses were frequent, till Yorke, in sheer desperation, took up a book, offering to read aloud to her. She thanked him, and leaning on the window ledge he opened at random and began to read. Of late, poems and romances had found their way into the house, apparently introduced by Germain, and to her surprise Yorke allowed Cecil to read them, which she did with diligence, but no visible effect as yet. In five minutes Yorke wished she had refused his offer, for the lines he had unwittingly chosen were of the tenderest sort, and he found it very hard to read the tuneful raptures of a happy lover, when his own heart was heaviest. He hurried through it as best he could, and not till the closing line was safely delivered did he venture to look at Cecil. For the first time she seemed affected by the magic of poetry; her hands lay idle, her head was averted, and her quickened breath stirred the long curls that half hid her face.

"She thinks of Alfred," groaned Yorke, within himself, and throwing down the book, he abruptly left her for another aimless saunter through the garden and the grove. He did not trust himself near her again, but lying in the grass where he could see her window, he watched her unobserved. Still seated at her embroidery frame, she worked at intervals, but often dropped her needle to look out as if longing for someone who did not come. "She waits for Alfred," sighed Yorke, and laying his head down on his arm, he fell to imagining how different all might have been had he not marred his own happiness by blindly trying to atone for one wrong with another. The air was sultry, the soft chirp of insects very soothing; the weariness of a wakeful night weighed down his eyelids, and before he was aware of its approach, a deep sleep fell upon him, bringing happier dreams to comfort him than any his waking thoughts could fashion.

A peal of thunder startled him wide awake, and glancing at his watch, he found he had lost an hour. Springing up, he went to look for Cecil, as he no longer saw her at her window. But nowhere did he find her, and after a vain search he returned to the boudoir, thinking some clue to her whereabouts might be discovered there. He did discover a clue, but one that drove him half mad with suspense and fear. Turning over the papers on her writing table, hoping to find some little message such as she often left for him, he came upon a card bearing Alfred's name, and below it a single line in French.

"At five, on the beach. Do not fail."

Yorke's face was terrible as he read the words that to his eyes seemed a sentence of lifelong desolation, for, glancing despairingly about the room, he saw that Cecil's hat was gone, and understood her absence now. A moment he stood staring at the line like one suddenly gone blind; then all the pain and passion passed into an unnatural calmness as he thrust the card into his pocket and rang like a man who has work to do that will not brook delay.

"Where is Mrs. Yorke?" was the brief question that greeted Anthony when he appeared.

"Gone to the beach, I think, sir."

"How long ago?"

"Nearly an hour, I should say. It was half past four when I came home; she was here then, for I gave her the note; but she went out soon after, and now it's half past five."

"What note was that?"

"An answer to one I carried to the hotel, sir."

"To Mr. Alfred, was it not?"

"Yes, sir."

"Did you see him, Anthony?"

"Gave it into his own hand, sir, as Mistress bade me, for it was important, she said."

"Very important! He answered it, you say?"

"Yes, sir. I met him on the lawn, and when he'd read the note, he just wrote something outlandish on his card and told me to hurry back. Is anything wrong, master?"

"Mrs. Yorke has gone boating with him, I believe, and I am anxious about her, for a storm is blowing up and Mr. Alfred is no sailor. Are you sure she went that way?"

"Very sure, sir; she had her boat cloak with her, and went down the beach path. I thought she spoke to you lying under the pine, but I suppose you were asleep, so she didn't wake you."

"She stopped, did she?"

"Yes, sir, several minutes, and stooped down as if speaking to you."

"You were watching her, it seems. Why was that?"

"Beg pardon, sir, but I couldn't help it; she looked so gay and pretty it did my old eyes good to look at her."

"You may go."

The instant he was alone, Yorke caught up a delicate lace handkerchief that lay on a chair, and calling Judas, showed it to him with a commanding "Find her." The dog eyed his master intelligently, smelled the bit of cambric, and with nose to the ground, dashed out of the house, while Yorke followed, wearing the vigilant, restless look of an Indian on the war trail. Under the pine Judas paused, snuffed here and there, hurried down the path, and set off across the beach, till coming to a little cove, he seemed at fault, ran to and fro a minute, then turned his face seaward and gave a long howl as if disappointed that he could not follow his mistress by water as by land. Yorke came up breathless, looked keenly all about him, and discovered several proofs of the dog's sagacity. Cecil's veil lay on a rocky seat, large and small footprints were visible in the damp sand, and a boat had been lately drawn up in the cove, for the receding tide had not washed the mark of the keel away.

"She could not be so treacherous—she has gone with Germain—I will not doubt her yet." But as the just and generous emotion rose, his eye fell on an object which plainly proved that Alfred *had* been there. A gold sleeve button lay shining at his feet; he seized it, saw the initials *A. N.* upon it, and doubted no longer, as the hand that held it closed with a gesture full of ominous significance, and turning sharply, he went back more rapidly than he came. Straight home he hurried, and calling Anthony, alarmed the old man as much by his appearance as by the singular orders he gave.

"If Germain comes, tell him to wait here for me; if young Norton comes, do not admit him; if Mrs. Yorke comes, put a light in the little turret window. I am going to look for her, and shall not return till I find her, unless the light recalls me."

"Lord bless us, sir! If you're scared about Mistress, let someone go with you. I'll be ready in a jiffy."

"No; I shall go alone. Get me the key of the boathouse, and do as I tell you."

"But, master, they'll put in somewhere when they see the squall coming on. Better send down to the hotel, or ride round to the Point. It's going to be a wild night, and you don't look fit to face it."

But Yorke was deaf to warnings or suggestions, and hastily preparing himself for the expedition, he repeated his orders, and left Anthony shaking his head over "Master's recklessness."

As he unmoored the boat, Judas leaped in, and standing in the bow, looked into the dim distance with an alert, intent expression, as if he shared the excitement of his companion. Up went the sail, and away flew the *Sea Gull,* leaving a track of foam behind, and carrying with it a heart more unquiet than stormy sea or sky. Across the bay skimmed the boat, and landing on the now deserted beach, Yorke went up to the hotel, so calm externally that few would have suspected the fire that raged within.

"Is young Norton here?" he asked of a clerk lounging in the office.

"Left this afternoon, sir."

"Rather sudden, wasn't it? Are you sure he's gone?"

"Don't know about the suddenness, Mr. Yorke, but I do know that he paid his bill, sent his baggage by the four-thirty train, and said he should follow in the next."

"Did he say anything about coming over to the Cliffs? I expected him today."

"I heard nothing of it, and the last I saw of him he was going toward the beach to bid the ladies good-bye, I supposed."

"Thank you, Gay. I had a message for him, but I can send it by mail." And Yorke sauntered away as if his disappointment was a very trifling one. But the instant he was out of sight his pace quickened to a stride, and he made straight for the depot, cursing his ill-timed sleep as he went. Another official was soon found and questioned, but no young gentleman answering to Alfred's description had purchased a ticket; of this the man was quite sure, as very few persons had left by either of the last trains.

"Well planned for so young a head, but Judas and his master will outwit him yet," muttered Yorke between his teeth, concentrating all his wrath on Alfred, for he dared not think of Cecil.

Stopping at Germain's lodging, he was told that his friend had gone to town at noon, and had not yet returned. This intelligence settled one point in his mind and confirmed his worst fear. Regardless of the gathering storm, he put off again, shaping his course for the city, led by a conviction that the lovers would endeavor to conceal themselves there for a time at least. A strange pair of voyagers went scudding down the harbor that afternoon: the great black hound, erect and motionless at the bow, though the spray dashed over him, and the boat dipped and bounded as it drove before the wind; the man erect and motionless at the helm, one hand on the rudder and one on the sail, his mouth grimly set, and his fiery eye fixed on the desired haven with an expression which proved that an indomitable will defied both danger and defeat. Craft of all sorts were hurrying into port, and more than one belated pleasure boat crossed Yorke's track. The occupants of each were scanned with a scrutinizing glance, and once or twice he shouted an inquiry as they passed. But in none appeared the faces he sought, no answer brought either contradiction or confirmation of his fear, and no backward look showed him the welcome light burning in the little turret window. Coming at last to the wharf where they always landed, he questioned the waterman to whose care he gave his boat.

"Aye, aye, sir; this squall line sent more than one philandering young couple home in a hurry. The last came in twenty minutes ago, just in time to save the crew from more water than they bargained for."

"Did you observe them? Was the lady beautiful? The gentleman young? Did you catch the name of either? Where—"

"Drop anchor there, sir, till I overhaul the first cargo of questions," broke in the man, for Yorke was hurrying one inquiry upon the heels of another without waiting for an answer to any. "Did I observe 'em? No, I didn't, particularly. Was the lady pretty? Don't know; she was wrapped up and scared. Was the gentleman young? Not more than three-and-twenty, I should say. Did I catch their names? Not a name, being busy with the boats."

"Did they seem fond of one another? Were they in a hurry? Which way did they go?"

"Uncommon fond, and in a devil of a hurry. Which way they went I can't tell; it was no business of mine, so I didn't look. Anything more, sir?" said the man good-humoredly.

"Yes; take this for your trouble, and show me the boat they came in."

"Thanky, sir; that's it over yonder. The lad must have been half-seas over with love or liquor, to bring his sweetheart all the way from the Point in a cockleshell like that."

"From the Point? It is a hotel boat, then?"

"Aye, sir; I know 'em all, and the *Water Witch* is the worst of the lot, but her smart rigging gives her a rakish look to them that don't know a mud scow from a wherry."

"Did the young man give you any orders about the boat?"

"Only to keep her till she was called for."

"And you have no idea which way they went?"

"No, sir; they steered straight ahead as far as the corners, but what course they took then I can't say."

Yorke was gone before the man had finished his sentence, and with Judas at his heels, turned toward his old home, feeling little doubt but he should find the fugitives at Mrs. Norton's close by; for though she was absent for the summer, her house was accessible to her son. Admitting himself without noise, he searched his own premises, and from the garden reconnoitered the adjoining ones. Every window was closely shuttered; no light anywhere appeared, and the house was evidently unoccupied. Hester, when called, had heard and seen nothing of Mr. Alfred for months, and was much surprised at her master's sudden appearance, though he fabricated a plausible excuse for it. Out he went again into the storm that now raged furiously, and for several hours searched every place where there was the least possibility of finding those he sought. He looked also for Germain, hoping he might lend some help; but he was in none of his usual haunts, and no clue to the lost wife was found.

Drenched, despairing, and exhausted with his fruitless quest, he stepped into a lighted doorway for shelter, while he took a moment's thought what course to pursue next. As he stood there, Ascot, the young artist, came from the billiard room within; he had been Yorke's guest the night before, and recognizing his host in the haggard, weatherbeaten man standing in the light, he greeted him gaily.

"Good evening, ancient mariner; you look as if your last voyage had not been a prosperous one. I can sympathize with you, for thanks to that confounded *Water Witch,* we nearly went to the bottom in the squall this afternoon."

"The *Water Witch?*" cried Yorke, checking himself in the act of abruptly quitting Ascot, whose gaiety was unbearable just then.

"Yes, I warn you against her. We came over from the Point in her, and had a narrow escape of being made 'demd, damp, moist, unpleasant bodies,' as Manteline says."

"This afternoon, Ascot? At what time?"

"Between five and six."

"Did you leave the boat at the lower wharf where we usually land?"

"Yes; and there she may stay till doomsday, though we ought to be grateful to her, after all."

"We? Then you were not alone?"

"No, my Grace was with me—" There Ascot stopped, looking half embarrassed, half relieved, but added, with a frank laugh, "I never could keep a secret, and as I have betrayed myself, I may as well confess that I took advantage of the storm and danger to make myself a very happy man. Give me joy, Yorke; Grace Coventry is mine."

"Joy! Your torment has but just begun," with which gloomy answer Yorke left the astonished young gentleman to console himself with love dreams and a cigar.

"Have I lost my senses as well as my heart, that I go chasing shadows, and deluding myself with jealous fears and fancies, when perhaps there is no mystery or wrong but what I conjure up?" mused Yorke, as he crossed the deserted park, intent upon a new and hopeful thought. Having made one mistake, he began to believe that he had made another, and wasted time and strength in looking for what never had been lost. Weariness calmed him now, the rain beating on his uncovered head cooled the fever of his blood, and the new hope seemed to brighten as he cherished it.

"I'll go back and wait; perhaps she has already come, or tidings of her. Anything is better than this terrible suspense," he said, and set about executing his design in spite of all obstacles.

It was nearly midnight now, too dark and wild to attempt returning by water, and the last train had left; but only a few miles lay between him and home, and neither weariness nor tempest could deter him. Soon mounted on a powerful horse, he was riding swiftly through the night, recalling legends of the Wild Huntsman to the few belated travelers who saw the dark horseman dash by them, with the dark hound following noiselessly behind. The storm was in accordance with his mood, and he liked it better than a summer night, though the gusts buffeted him and the rain poured down with unabated violence. At the first point where the Cliffs were visible, he reined up and strained his eyes to catch a glimpse of the light that should assure him of Cecil's safety. But a thick mist obscured land and sea, and no cheering ray could pierce the darkness. A mile nearer his eye was gladdened by the sight of a pale gleam high above the lower lights that glimmered along the shore. Brighter and brighter it grew as he approached, and soon, with a thrill of joy that made his heart leap, he saw that it shone clear and strong from the little turret window. An irrepressible shout broke from his lips as he galloped up the steep road, leaped the gate, and burst into the hall before man or maid could open for him.

"Where is she?" he cried, in a voice that would have assured the wanderer of a tender welcome had she been there to hear and answer it.

Anthony started from a restless doze in his chair, and shook his gray head as he eyed his master pitifully.

"She ain't here, sir, but we've had news of her; so I lit the lamp to bring you home."

Yorke dropped into a seat as if he had been shot, for with the loss of his one hope, all strength seemed to desert him, and he could only look at Anthony with such imploring yet despairing eyes that the old man's hard face began to work as he said below his breath, "After you'd gone, sir, I went down to the Point and stayed round there till dark. Just as I was coming away, old Joe came in bringing a sail he'd picked up halfway down the harbor. There were several of us standing about the pier, and naturally we asked questions. Then it come out from one and another that the sail belonged to the boat Mr. Alfred took this afternoon. He left there alone, but one of the men saw him with a lady afterward, and by his description I knew it was Mistress."

Yorke covered up his face as if he knew what was coming and had not courage to meet it; but soon he said, brokenly, "Go on," and Anthony obeyed.

"The man wasn't quite sure about Mr. Alfred, as he don't know him, and didn't mind him much; but he was sure of Mistress, and could swear to the boat and sail, for he helped rig it, and his sweetheart made the streamer. I'd like to think he was wrong, but as Mr. Alfred hired the boat, and the dear lady was seen in it, I'm awfully afraid they were wrecked in the squall."

How still the house seemed as the words dropped slowly from Anthony's lips. Nothing stirred but poor Judas panting on his mat, and nothing broke the silence but the soft tick of a clock and the sobbing of the wind without. Yorke had laid down his head as if he never cared to lift it up again, and sat motionless in an attitude of utter despair, while the old servant stood respectfully silent, with tears rolling down his withered cheeks, for his gentle mistress had won his heart, and he mourned for her as for a child of his own.

Suddenly Yorke looked up and spoke.

"Have you sent anyone to look for them?"

"Yes, master, long ago, and—"

"What is it? You keep something back. Out with it, man; I can bear anything but suspense."

"They found the boat, and it was empty, master."

"Where was it? Tell me all, Anthony."

"Just outside the little bay, where the gale would blow hardest and the tide run strongest. The mast was broken short off, the boat half full of water, and one broken oar still hung in the rowlock, but there was no signs of anyone except this."

Turning his face away, Anthony offered a little silken scarf, wet, torn, and stained, but too familiar to be mistaken. Yorke took it, looked at it with eyes out of which light and life seemed to have died, then put it in his breast, and turning to the faithful hound, said in a tone the more pathetic for its calmness: "Come, Judas; we went together to look for her alive, now let us go together and look for her dead."

Before Anthony could detain him he had flung himself into the saddle and was gone. All that night he haunted the shores, looking long after others had relinquished the vain search, and morning found him back in the city, inquiring along the wharves for tidings of the lost.

Taking his own boat, he turned homeward at last, feeling that he could do no more, for the reaction had begun, and he was utterly spent. The storm had passed, and dawn was breaking beautifully in the east; the sea was calm, the sky cloudless; the wind blew balmily, and the sea gull floated along a path of gold as the sun sent its first shaft of light over the blue waste. A strange sense of peace came to the lonely man after that wild night of tempest and despair. The thought of Cecil quiet underneath the sea was more bearable than the thought of Cecil happy with another, for in spite of repentance and remorse, he could not accept his punishment from Alfred's hand, and clung to the belief that she was dead, trying to find some poor consolation for his loss in the thought that life was made desolate by death, not by treachery. So sailing slowly through the rosy splendor of a summer dawn, he came among the cluster of small islands that lay midway between the city and the little bay. Some were green and fair, some were piles of barren rocks; none were inhabited, but on one still stood a rude hut, used as a temporary shelter for pleasure parties or such fishermen as frequented the neighborhood. Yorke saw nothing of the beauty all about him; his eyes were fixed upon the white villa that once was home; his mind was busy with memories of the past, and he was conscious of nothing but the love that had gone down into that shining sea. Judas was more alert, for, though sitting with his head on his master's knee, as if trying to comfort him by demonstrations of mute affection, he caught sight of a little white flag fluttering from the low roof of the hut, and leaped up with a bound that nearly took him overboard. The motion roused Yorke, and following the direction of the dog's keen eye, he saw the signal—saw, also, a woman wrapped in a dark cloak sitting in the doorway, with her head upon her knees, as if asleep.

In an instant both dog and man were trembling with excitement, for there was something strangely familiar about the cloak, the bent head with its falling hair, the slender hands folded one upon another. Like one inspired with sudden life, Yorke plied his oars with such energy that a few vigorous strokes sent the boat high upon the pebbly shore, and leaping up the bank, while Judas followed baying with delight, he saw the figure start to its feet, and found himself face to face with Cecil.

Chapter X. At Last

WHILE YORKE SLEPT, on the previous afternoon, Cecil met Alfred on the beach, talked with him for half an hour, and when he left her, hastily, she stood waving her hand till he was out of sight; then she looked about her, as if in search of someone, and her face brightened as she saw Germain approaching.

"I am glad you are come," she said, "for I was just trying to find a man to take this boat home, and here I find a gentleman. Alfred came in it, but delayed so long that he had only time to run across the cliffs and catch the train. Will you ferry me over to the Point, and add another favor to the many I already owe you?"

"Nothing would please me better, but instead of landing so soon, let me take you down below the lighthouse, as I promised you I would. This will be my only opportunity, for I go away tomorrow, and you know you said I should have one more happy day."

"Did Bazil tell you that?" asked Cecil, looking disturbed, as his words recalled last night's adventure.

"No, but I am well aware that I trouble you—that you wish me gone, and I shall obey; but give me this last pleasure, for I may never come again."

The smile he gave her was both melancholy and submissive; she longed to bid him stay but dared not, yet remembering Bazil's wish that she should bear with him a little longer, she was glad to grant it, for she felt her power over this man, and feared nothing for herself. A moment's hesitation, then she went toward the boat, saying, in her friendliest tone, "I trust you, and you shall have your pleasure; but, believe me, if I wish you gone it is for your own sake, not mine."

"I know it—I am grateful for your pity, and I will not disturb your confidence by any violence. Indeed, I think I'm done with my old self, and grow quieter as the end approaches."

Cecil doubted that, as she remembered the scene before the fountain, but Germain was certainly his gentlest self now, and as they sailed across the bay before the freshening wind she found the hour full of real rest and enjoyment despite her care. Absorbed in animated conversation, and unconscious of the lapse of time, they glided past the Point, the pleasant islands, the city with its cloud of smoke, the lighthouse on its lonely rock, and were floating far down the harbor, when the growling of distant thunder recalled them from the delights of a musical discussion to the dangers of an impending storm. A bank of black clouds was piled up in the west, the wind came in strong gusts, the waves rolled in long swells, and sea and sky portended a summer squall.

"How careless I have been," exclaimed Germain, looking anxiously about him. "But I fancy we need fear nothing except a drenching, for it will take some time to return in the teeth of this gale. Wrap your cloak about you, and enjoy the fine sight, while I do my best to atone for my forgetfulness."

Cecil had no fear, for Germain was a skillful boatman, and she loved to watch the grand effects of light and shade as the thunderous clouds swept across the sky, blotting out the blue and making the water somber with their shadows. An occasional flash seemed to rend the dark wall, but no rain fell, and by frequent tacking Germain was rapidly decreasing the distance between them and home. Safely past the city they went, for Cecil would not land there lest Yorke should be alarmed at her long absence, and as the storm still delayed, she hoped to reach shelter before it broke.

"Once past the islands and we are quite safe, for the little bay is quiet, and we can land at any point if the rain begins. A few minutes more of this rough work, and we can laugh at the gale. Bend your head, please, I must tack again else—"

The rest of the sentence was lost in a crash of thunder like the report of cannon, as a fierce gust swept down upon them, snapping the slender mast like a bulrush, and carrying Germain overboard wrapped in the falling sail. With a cry of horror Cecil sprang up, eager yet impotent to save either herself or him; but in a moment he appeared, swimming strongly, cleared away the wreck of the sail, righted the boat, and climbed in, dripping but unhurt.

"Only another of my narrow escapes. I'm surely born to die quietly in my bed, for nothing kills me," he said coolly, as he brushed the wet hair from his eyes and took breath.

"Thank heaven! You are safe. Land anywhere, for now the sail is gone we must not think of reaching home," cried Cecil, looking about her for the nearest shore.

"We will make for the lower island; the storm will not last long, and we can find shelter there. Unfortunate that I am, to make my last day one of danger and discomfort for you."

"I like it, and shall enjoy relating my adventures when we are at home. Let me row, it is too violent exercise for you," she said, as he drew out the oars and took off his coat.

"It will not hurt me—or if it does what matter? I would gladly give my life to see you safe."

"No, no, you must not do it. Let the boat drift, or give me an oar; I am strong; I fear nothing; let me help you, Germain."

"Take the rudder then and steer for the island; that will help me, and the sight of you will give me strength for a short tussle with the elements."

Cecil changed her seat, and with her hand upon the helm, her steady eyes upon the green spot before them, sat smiling at the storm, so fair and fearless that the sight would have put power into any arm, courage into any heart. For a time it seemed to inspire Germain, and he pulled stoutly against wind and tide; but soon, to his dismay, he felt his strength deserting him, each stroke cost a greater effort, each heartbeat was a pang of pain. Cecil watched the drops gather on his forehead, heard his labored breathing, and saw him loosen the ribbon at his throat, and more than once dash water over his face, alternately deeply flushed and deadly pale. Again and again she implored him to desist, to let her take his place, or trust to chance for help, rather than harm himself by such dangerous exertion. But to all entreaties, suggestions, and commands, he answered with a gentle but inflexible denial, an utter disregard of self, and looks of silent love that Cecil never could forget.

The rain fell now in torrents, the gale steadily increased, and the waves were white with foam as they dashed high against the rocky shore of the island which the little boat was struggling to reach. Nearer and nearer it crept, as Germain urged it on with the strength of desperation, till, taking advantage of a coming billow, they were carried up and left upon the sand, with a violence that nearly threw them on their faces. Cecil sprang out at once; Germain leaned over the broken oars panting heavily, as if conscious of nothing but the suffering that racked him. Her voice roused him, but only to fresh exertion, for seizing her hand he staggered up the bank, flung open the door of the hut, and dropped down at her feet as if in truth he had given his life to save her. For a moment she was in despair; she ran out into the storm, called, waved her handkerchief, and looked far and near, hoping some passing boat might bring help. But nothing human was in sight; the nearest point of land was inaccessible, for an ebbing wave had washed the boat away, and she was utterly alone with the unconscious man upon the barren island. She had a brave spirit, a quick wit, and these were her supporters now, as, forgetting her own fears, she devoted herself to her suffering comrade. Fortunately, her vinaigrette was in her pocket, and water plentiful; using these simple remedies with skill, the deathlike swoon yielded at last, and Germain revived.

With the return of consciousness he seemed to remember her situation before his own, and exert himself to lighten its discomforts by feeble efforts to resume his place as protector. As soon as he had breath enough to speak, he whispered, with a reassuring glance, "Do not be afraid, I will take care of you. The pain has gone for this time, and I shall be better soon."

"Think of yourself, not me. If I only had a fire to dry and warm you I should be quite happy and content," answered Cecil, looking round the gloomy place that darkened momentarily.

With the courtesy as native to him as his impetuosity, Germain tried to rise as he took out a little case and pointed toward a corner of the hut.

"You need fire more than I; here are matches, there is wood; help me a little and you shall be 'quite happy and content.' "

But as he spoke the case dropped from his hand, and he fell back with a sharp pang that warned him to submit.

"Lie still and let me care for you; I like to do it, and the exercise will keep me warm. Here is wood enough to last all night, and with light and heat we shall be very comfortable till morning and help comes."

With the heartiness of a true woman when compassion stirs her, Cecil fell to work, and soon the dark hut glowed with a cheery blaze, the wooden shutter was closed, excluding wind and rain, the straw scattered here and there was gathered into a bed for Germain, and with her cloak over him, he lay regarding her with an expression that both touched and troubled her, so humble, grateful, and tender was it. When all was done, she stepped to the door, thinking she heard the sound of passing oars; nothing appeared, however, but as she listened on the threshold Germain's voice called her with an accent of the intensest longing.

"Do not leave me! Come back to me, my darling, and let nothing part us anymore."

She thought he was wandering, and gave no answer but a soothing "Hush, rest now, poor Germain."

"Never that again; call me Father, and let me die happy in my daughter's arms."

"Father?" echoed Cecil, as a thrill of wonder, joy, and blind belief shook her from head to foot.

"Yes, I may claim you at last, for I am dying. Let our hearts speak; come to me, my little Cecil, for as God lives I am your father."

He struggled up, spread wide his arms, and called her in a tone of tenderness that would have carried conviction to the most careless listener. Cecil's heart did speak; instinct was quicker than memory or reason. In an instant she understood the attraction that led her to him, owned the tender tie that bound them, and was gathered to her father's bosom, untroubled by a doubt or fear. For a time there were only broken exclamations, happy tears, and demonstrations of delight, as father and daughter forgot everything but the reunion that gave them back to one another. Soon Cecil calmed herself for his sake, made him lie down again, and while she dried his hair and warmed his cold hands in her own, she began to question eagerly.

"Why was I never told of this before?" she sorrowfully said, regretting the long years of ignorance that had deferred the happiness which made that hour so bright, in spite of darkness and danger.

"My life depended upon secrecy, and this knowledge would have been no joy, but a shame and sorrow to you, my poor child."

"Mamma always told me that you died when I was a baby; did she believe it?"

"No, she knew I was alive, but in one sense I did die to her, and all the world, for a convict has no country, home, or friends."

"A convict!" And Cecil shrank involuntarily.

He saw it, but clung to her, saying imploringly, "Hear me before you cast me off. Try to pity and forgive me, for with all his sins your father loves you better than his life."

"I do not cast you off—I will love, pity, and forgive; believe this, and trust your daughter, now that she is yours again."

Cecil spoke tenderly, and tried to reassure him with every affectionate demonstration she could devise, for the one word "father" had unlocked her heart, and all its pent-up passion flowed freely now that a natural vent was found. Lying with her hand in his, August Stein told the story of the past, and Cecil learned the secret of her father's and her husband's life.

"Dear, nineteen years ago Bazil and your mother were betrothed. The gifted young man was a fit mate for the beautiful girl, and but for me they might have been a happy pair this day. In an evil hour I saw her, loved her, and resolved to win her in spite of every obstacle, for my passions ruled me, and opposition only made me the more resolute and reckless. I used every art to dazzle, captivate, and win her, even against her will, and I succeeded; but the brief infatuation was not love, and though she fled with me, she soon discovered that her heart still clung to Bazil. Well it might, for though we had wronged him deeply he took no revenge, and would have helped us in our sorest strait. We were not happy, for I led a wild life, and your mother longed for home. Her father disowned her, when our secret marriage was discovered, her friends deserted her, and for a year we wandered from place to place, growing poorer and more wretched as hope after hope failed. I had squandered my own fortune, and had no means of earning a livelihood except my voice. That had won me my wife, and I tried to sing my way to competence for her sake. To do this, I was obliged to leave her; I always did so reluctantly, for the birth of my little daughter made the mother dearer than before. Cecil, always remember that I loved you both with all the fervor of an undisciplined nature, and let that fact lighten your condemnation of what follows."

"I shall remember, Father."

"Coming home unexpectedly one day, I found Bazil there. He had discovered us and, seeing our poverty, generously offered help. I should have thanked and honored him for that, but knowing that he did it for Cecilia's sake I hated and distrusted him, refused his kindness, and forbade him the house. He bore with me, promised your mother that he would befriend her, and went away, hoping I would relent when I was calmer. His nobleness made my own conduct seem more base; the knowledge that my wife reproached me for destroying her happiness wounded me deeply; and the thought that Bazil saw my failure and pitied me rankled in my heart and made me miserable. I had been brooding darkly over these things as I returned from my distasteful work a night or two later, and was in a desperate mood. As I entered quietly, I saw a man bending over the cradle where my baby lay; I thought it was Bazil, my wrath rose hot against him, some devil goaded me to it, and I felled him with a single blow. But when the light shone on his dead face I saw that it was not Bazil but the young surgeon who had saved both wife and child for me."

There was a long pause, broken only by Stein's fluttering breath and Cecil's whisper.

"Do not go on; be quiet and forget."

"I cannot forget or be quiet till I tell you everything. I was tried, sentenced to imprisonment for life, and for ten years was as dead to the world as if I had lain in my grave. I raged and pined like a savage creature in my prison, made many desperate attempts to escape, and at last succeeded. I left Australia, and after wandering east and west, a homeless vagabond for two weary years, I ventured back to England, hoping to learn something of my wife, as no tidings of her had reached me all those years. I could not find her, and dared not openly inquire; Yorke tells me she concealed herself from everyone, accepted nothing even from him, but devoted herself to you, and waited patiently till it pleased heaven to release her."

"Poor Mamma! Now I know how heavy her burden must have been, and why she longed to lay it down."

"Child, she did not find it half so heavy as I found mine, nor long to lay it down as bitterly as I have longed for eighteen years. If she had loved me it would have saved us both, for affection can win and hold me as nothing else has power to do. It has done much for me already, because, since I knew you, my darling, I have learned to repent and, for your sake, to atone, as far as may be, for my wasted life."

"It is very sweet to hear you say that, Father, and to feel that I have helped you, even unconsciously. Now leave the sorrowful past, and tell me how you found Bazil and myself."

"Growing bold, after two years of safety, I ventured to inquire for Yorke, thinking that he could tell me something of your mother. He had left Germany, where we first met, and had gone home to America. I followed, and found him leading the solitary life you know so well. He was so changed I hardly recognized him; I was still more altered, and trusting to the disguise which had baffled keener eyes than his, I offered myself as a model, feeling curiously drawn to him as the one link between Cecilia and myself. He accepted my services, and paid me well, for I was very poor; he pitied me, knowing only that I was a lonely creature like himself, and so generously befriended me that I could not harden my heart against him; but overpowered by remorse and gratitude I betrayed myself, and put my life into his hands, only asking to see or hear of my wife. He knew nothing of her then, but with a magnanimity that bound me to him forever, he kept my secret, and endeavored to forgive the wrong which he never could entirely forget."

"O Bazil, so generous, so gentle, why did I not know this sooner, and thank you as I ought?"

The tender words were drowned in sudden tears, as Cecil hid her face, weeping with mingled self-reproach and joy over each revelation that showed her something more to love and honor in her husband. But she soon dried her tears to listen, for her father hurried on as if anxious to be done.

"I saw you, my child, the night you came, and was sure you were mine, you were so like your mother. I implored Bazil to let me have you, when I knew that she was gone, but he would not, having promised to guard you from me, and never let your life be saddened by the knowledge of your convict father. He has kept that promise sacredly, and bound me to an equal silence, under penalty of betrayal if I break it, except as I do now, when I have nothing more to fear. He let me see you secretly, when you slept, or walked, or were busy at your work, for he had not the heart to deny me that. Ah, Cecil, you never knew how near I often was to you—never guessed what right I had to love you, or how much I longed to tell you who I was. More than once I forgot myself, and would have broken my word at any cost, but something always checked me in time, and Bazil's patience was long-suffering. The night he let me see and sing to you did me more good than years of prison life, for you unconsciously touched all that was best in me, and by the innocent affection that you could not control made that hour more beautiful and precious than I can tell you. Since then, whether near or absent, gloomy or gay, I have regarded you as my saving angel, and tried in my poor way to be more worthy of you, and earn a place in your memory when I am gone."

Such love and gratitude shone in his altered face that Cecil could only lay her head upon his shoulder, praying that he might be spared for a longer, better life, and a calmer death at last. Soon her father spoke again, smiling the old sweet smile, as he caressed the beautiful head that leaned against him as if its place were there.

"Did my little girl think me a desperate lover, with my strange devices to attract and win her? Bazil told me that I frightened you, and I tried to control myself; but it was so hard to stand aside and see my own child pass me like a stranger, that I continually forgot your ignorance and betrayed how dear you were to me. What did you think of that mysterious Germain?"

"What could I think but that he loved me? How could I dream that you were my father when all my life I had believed you dead? Even now I almost doubt it, you are so young, so charming and lighthearted when you please."

"I am past forty, Cecil, and what I am is only the shadow of what I was, a man endowed with many good gifts; but all have been wasted or misused, owing to a neglected education, a wayward will, an impetuous nature, and a sanguine spirit, which has outlived disgrace and desolation, suffering and time."

"And this is the mystery that has perplexed me for so long. I think you might have told me as well as Bazil, and let me do my part to make you happy, Father."

"I longed to do so, and assured him that we might trust you; but he would not break his promise to your mother. It was wise, though very hard to bear. I was not a fit guardian for a beautiful young girl like mine, and I knew it, yet I wanted you, and made his life a burden to him by my importunity. Love him, Cecil, love him faithfully, for he has spared you much sorrow, and through you has saved your father."

She did not answer, but looking into her face, he was satisfied. Thus opening their hearts to one another, the night wore on, yet neither found it long, and when at last Stein slept, exhausted, Cecil sat beside him, thinking happy thoughts, while the wind raved without, the rain beat on the low roof, the sea thundered round the island, and Yorke went searching for her far and wide.

Morning dawned at last, and as her father still slept, she opened the little window that the balmy air might refresh him, put up her signal of distress, and sat down to watch and wait. The sound of hurrying feet roused her from her reverie, and looking up, she saw her husband coming toward her, so changed and haggard that her joy turned to fear. Dreading to excite her father, she instantly glanced over her shoulder, and barred the entrance with her extended arm. Her gesture, her expression, instantly arrested Yorke, and while Judas fawned delightedly about her feet, he stood apart, with the sad certainty that she was not alone, to mar his joy at finding her.

"Is he there?" was his first question, sternly put.

"Yes; he is ill and sleeping; you must not disturb him. Blame me if you will, but he shall be left in peace."

She spoke resolutely, and closed the door between them and the sleeper, keeping her place upon the threshold, as if ready to defend him, for Yorke's manner alarmed her even more than his wild appearance. The action seemed to affect him like an insult; he seized her arm, and holding it in a painful grasp, eyed her almost fiercely, as he said, with a glance that made her tremble, "Then you did leave me sleeping, and go away with this man, to be wrecked here, and so be discovered?"

"Yes; why should I deny it?"

"And you love him, Cecil?"

"With all my heart and soul, and you can never part us anymore."

As she answered, with a brave, bright smile, and a glad voice, she felt Yorke quiver as if he had received a blow, saw his face whiten, and heard an accent of despair in his voice, when he said slowly, "You will leave him, if I command it?"

"No—he has borne enough. I can make him happy, and I shall cling to him through everything, for you have no right to take me from him."

"No right?" ejaculated Yorke, loosening his hold, with a bewildered look.

"None that I will submit to, if it parts us. You let me know him, let me learn to love him, and now, when he needs me most, you would take me from him. Bazil, you have been very generous, very kind to both of us, and I am truly grateful, but while he lives, I must stay with him, because I have promised."

He looked at her with a strange expression, at first as if he felt his senses going, then he seemed to find a clue to her persistency. A bitter laugh escaped him, but his voice betrayed wounded pride and poignant sorrow.

"I understand now; you intend to hold me to my bond, and see in me nothing but your guardian. You are as ignorant as headstrong, if you think this possible. I gave up that foolish delusion long ago, and tried to show you a truer, happier tie. But you were blind and would not see, deaf and would not hear, hardhearted and would not relent."

"You bade me be a marble woman, with no heart to love you, only grace and beauty, to please your eye and do you honor. Have I not obeyed you to the letter?"

Coldly and quietly she spoke, yet kept her eyes on the ground, her hand on her breast, as if to hold some rebellious emotion in check. As the soft voice reechoed the words spoken long ago, all that scene came back to Yorke, and made the present moment doubly hard to bear.

"You have, you have! God forgive me for the wrong I did you. I tried to atone for it, but I have failed, and this is my punishment."

He spoke humbly, despairingly, and his proud eyes filled as he turned his face to hide the grief he was ashamed to show. Cecil stood with bent head, and face half hidden by her falling hair, but though she trembled, she compelled voice and features to obey her with the ease which long practice had made second nature.

"If you had cared to teach me a gentler lesson, I would have gladly learned it; but you did not, and having done your best to kill love in my heart, you should not reproach me if you are disappointed now, or wonder that I turn to others for the affection without which none of us can live."

"I will not reproach; I do not wonder, but I cannot give you up. Cecil, there is still time to relent, and to return; let me tell you how hard I have tried to make you love me, in spite of my own decree, and perhaps my patience, my penitence, may touch your heart. I will not urge my right as husband, but plead as lover. Will you listen?"

"Yes."

Cecil stole a glance at him as she spoke, and a curious smile touched her lips, though she listened with beating heart to words poured out with the rapidity of strong emotion.

"When you came to me, I kept you because you were like your mother, whom I loved, and who deserted me. That loss embittered my whole nature, and I resolved to make your life as loveless as my own. It seemed a small atonement for a great wrong, and believing that it was just to visit the sins of the parents upon the children, I carried out my purpose with a blind persistency that looks like madness to me now. But the sentiment I had forsworn revenged itself upon me, and while trying to cheat you of love, it crept into my own heart, and ruled me like a tyrant. Unconsciously, I loved you long before I knew it; that was why I disliked Alfred, why I was so willing to marry you, and why I was so disappointed when others found in you the same want that I felt yet would not own. The night I watched beside you, fearing you would never wake, I found the key to my own actions, saw my delusion, and resolved to conquer it."

He paused for breath, but Cecil did not speak, though the hidden face brightened, and the heart fluttered like a caged bird.

"I could not conquer it, for it was my master. You can never know how hard I tried, how rebellious my pride was, or how firm my purpose, but all failed, and I was forced to own that my happiness, my peace, depended upon you. Then I determined to undo my six years' work, to teach you how to love, and make my wife mine in heart as in name. I gave myself wholly to the task of winning you; I studied your tastes, gratified your whims, and tried every art that can attract a woman. You were tired of the old home, and I gave you a new one; you enjoyed Germain's society, and I let him come, in defiance of my better judgment; you had some pride in my talent, for your sake I displayed it; you loved pleasure, and I labored to supply it freely; I even tried to lure you with splendor and bribe you with diamonds. But I had lost my skill, and all my efforts were in vain, for no veritable marble woman could have received my gifts more coldly, or ignored my unspoken love more utterly than you. One smile like those you daily gave Germain would have repaid me, but you never shed it over me; one frank word or affectionate look would have brought me to your feet; but all the compassion, confidence, and tenderness were given to others—for me you had only indifference, gratitude, and respect. Cecil, I have suffered one long torment since I married you, longing for my true place, yet not daring to claim it, lest I should rouse aversion and not love."

Still with her head bent, her face hidden, and her hand upon her heart, she stood, and Yorke went on, more passionately than before.

"I know that I have forfeited my right to expect affection or demand obedience, but I implore you to forget this infatuation, and retrieve this rash step. You do not know what you are doing, for this will mar your whole life, and make mine worthless. Cecil, come back to me, and let me try again to win you! I will work and wait for years, will be your servant, not your master, will bear and suffer anything if I may hope to touch your heart at last. Is this impossible? Do you love Alfred more than reputation, home, or husband?"

"I never have loved Alfred."

"Then who, in God's name, is this man to whom you will cling through everything?"

"My father."

She looked up now, and turned on him a face so full of hope and joy, that he stood dumb with astonishment as she drew nearer and nearer, with outstretched hands, beaming eyes, and tender voice.

"O Bazil! I know all; the past is forgiven, your long labor and atonement are over, and there is no need for you to work or wait, because my heart always has been yours."

If the dead Cecilia had come to him in the youthful guise she used to wear, it would not have more amazed and startled him than did these words from his wife's lips, and not till he felt her clinging to him so trustfully, so tenderly, did he fully realize his happiness.

"What does it mean? Why keep this from me so long? Did you not see I loved you, Cecil?"

"It means that I, too, tried to conquer myself, and failed. Till very lately, I was not sure you loved me, and I could not bear to be repulsed again."

"Ah, there is the thorn that has vexed you! You are a true woman, in spite of all my training, and you could not forget that hour, so I had to suffer till you were appeased. Is it possible that my innocent, artless girl could lay such plots, and wear a mask so long, that she might subdue her guardian's proud heart?"

"Everything is possible to a woman when she loves, and you were only conquered with your own weapons, Bazil. Let me make my confession now, and you shall see that you have not suffered, worked, and waited all alone. When you bade me renounce love, I found it very hard to kill the affection that had grown warmer than you chose to have it. But I did my best to seem what you desired me to be, and your lessons of self-control stood me in good stead. I chilled and hardened myself rigorously; I forced myself to be meek, cold, and undemonstrative to you, whatever I might be to others; I took opium, that I might forget my pain, and feign the quietude I could not feel, and I succeeded beyond my hopes. When you asked me to marry you, I was half prepared for it, because Alfred insisted that you loved me. I wished to believe it; I wanted to stay, and would have frankly owned how dear you were to me, if you had not insisted upon offering me protection, but no love. That night I resolved to show you your mistake, to prove to you that you had a heart, and teach you a better lesson than any you had taught your pupil."

"You have done so, little dearest, and I am your scholar henceforth. Teach me gently, and I will study all my days. What more, Cecil?"

"I found it very hard to resist when you grew so kind, and should have been sure you loved me, but for Germain. Why you let him come, and showed no displeasure at my delight in his society, was so inexplicable to me that I would not yield till I was satisfied. Last night my father told me all, and if anything could make you dearer, it would be the knowledge of the great debt we owe you. My generous, patient husband, how can I thank you as I ought?"

He showed her how, and for several minutes they stood in the sunshine, very silent, very happy, while the waves broke softly on the shore, as if all storms had passed away forever. Yorke spoke first.

"One thing more, Cecil, lest I forget it, for this sudden happiness has turned my brain, I think, and nothing is clear to me but that you are mine. What does this mean?" And drawing out the card, he held it before her eyes, with some anxiety dimming the brightness of his own.

She took it, tore it up, and as the white shreds went flying away on the wind, she said smiling, "Let all your jealous fears go with them, never to come back again. What a miserable night you must have had, if you believed that I had left you for Alf."

"An awful night, Cecil," and he told her all the wanderings and his fears.

"I will not say that you deserved it for harboring such a thought, because you have suffered enough, and it is so much sweeter to forgive than to reproach. But you must promise never to be jealous anymore, not even of 'poor Alf.'"

The happy-hearted laugh he had so longed to hear gladdened his ear, as she looked up at him with the arch expression that made her charming.

"I'll try," he answered meekly, "but keep him away till I am very sure you love me, else I shall surely fling him into the sea, as I nearly did the night Sir Walter and the marquise tormented me. Why did he come? And why did you meet him yesterday?"

"He came to tell me that he had replaced my image with a more gracious one, for when he heard that I was married, he cast me off, and found consolation in his pretty cousin's smiles. His was a boyish love, ardent but short-lived, and he is happy now, with one who loves him as I never could have loved. Hearing of our masque, he planned to come in disguise, and tell his story as a stranger, that he might the better watch its effect on me. But I knew him instantly, and we enjoyed mystifying those about us, till I forgot him in my own mystification. You did not wish him to come again, so I wrote to him, saying good-bye, and begging him to go at once. The disobedient boy had more to tell me, and sent word he should be on the beach at five. I knew he would come to the house unless I met him, and fearing a scene—for you have grown very tragic, dear—I went. He delayed so long that he had only time to hurry across to the lower depot for the last train, leaving his boat to Father and myself."

"What misery the knowledge of this would have spared me! Why did you not tell me, when we were together yesterday, that Alfred had forgotten you?"

"I meant to do so, but you gave me no opportunity, for you were so restless and strange I was half afraid of you. Besides, since you had confessed jealousy, I hoped you would confess love also, and I waited, thinking it would come."

"How could I own it, when *you* had confessed you loved a younger man than I, and my eyes were blinded by Alfred's silence and your own?"

"I did not tell you that it was my father. Did he betray me?"

She looked perplexed, and Yorke half ashamed, as he confessed another proof of his affection.

"It was I, Cecil, who came to you in the garden, who questioned you, and was stabbed to the heart by your answers. Good heavens, how blind I've been!"

"Never reproach me with treachery, after that. Why did you change dresses? To try me?"

"Yes; and as you sat there so near me, so gentle, frank, and beautiful, I found it almost impossible to sustain my character; but I knew if I revealed myself, you would freeze again, and all the charm be gone. Heaven knows I was a miserable man that night, for you disappointed me, and Alfred drove me half mad; but your father saw my folly, and saved me from myself. God bless him for that!"

"Yes, God bless him for that, and for saving me to be your happy wife. Come now and wake him; he has been very ill, and needs care."

They went, and kneeling by him, Cecil called him gently, but he did not answer; and taking her into his arms, her husband whispered tenderly, "Dear, he will never wake again."

Never again in this world, for the restless heart was still at last, and the sunshine fell upon a face of such reposeful beauty that it was evident the long sleep had painlessly deepened into death.

ঞ A Double Tragedy.
An Actor's Story

CHAPTER I

CLOTILDE WAS in her element that night, for it was a Spanish play, requiring force
and fire in its delineation, and she threw herself into her part with an *abandon* that
made her seem a beautiful embodiment of power and passion. As for me I could not
play ill, for when with her my acting was not art but nature, and I *was* the lover that I
seemed. Before she came I made a business, not a pleasure, of my profession, and was
content to fill my place, with no higher ambition than to earn my salary with as little
effort as possible, to resign myself to the distasteful labor to which my poverty condemned me. She changed all that; for she saw the talent I neglected, she understood
the want of motive that made me indifferent, she pitied me for the reverse of fortune
that placed me where I was; by her influence and example she roused a manlier spirit
in me, kindled every spark of talent I possessed, and incited me to win a success I had
not cared to labor for till then.

She was the rage that season, for she came unheralded and almost unknown.
Such was the power of beauty, genius, and character, that she made her way at once
into public favor, and before the season was half over had become the reigning favorite.
My position in the theatre threw us much together, and I had not played the lover to
this beautiful woman many weeks before I found I was one in earnest. She soon knew
it, and confessed that she returned my love; but when I spoke of marriage, she answered with a look and tone that haunted me long afterward.

"Not yet, Paul; something that concerns me alone must be settled first. I cannot
marry till I have received the answer for which I am waiting; have faith in me till then,
and be patient for my sake."

I did have faith and patience; but while I waited I wondered much and studied
her carefully. Frank, generous, and deephearted, she won all who approached her; but
I, being nearest and dearest, learned to know her best, and soon discovered that some
past loss, some present anxiety or hidden care, oppressed and haunted her. A bitter
spirit at times possessed her, followed by a heavy melancholy, or an almost fierce
unrest, which nothing could dispel but some stormy drama, where she could vent her
pent-up gloom or desperation in words and acts which seemed to have a double

significance to her. I had vainly tried to find some cause or explanation of this one blemish in the nature which, to a lover's eyes, seemed almost perfect, but never had succeeded till the night of which I write.

The play was nearly over, the interest was at its height, and Clotilde's best scene was drawing to a close. She had just indignantly refused to betray a state secret which would endanger the life of her lover; and the Duke had just wrathfully vowed to denounce her to the Inquisition if she did not yield, when I her lover, disguised as a monk, saw a strange and sudden change come over her. She should have trembled at a threat so full of terror, and have made one last appeal to the stern old man before she turned to defy and dare all things for her lover. But she seemed to have forgotten time, place, and character, for she stood gazing straight before her as if turned to stone. At first I thought it was some new presentiment of fear, for she seldom played a part twice alike, and left much to the inspiration of the moment. But an instant's scrutiny convinced me that this was not acting, for her face paled visibly, her eyes dilated as they looked beyond the Duke, her lips fell apart, and she looked like one suddenly confronted by a ghost. An inquiring glance from my companion showed me that he, too, was disturbed by her appearance, and fearing that she had over-exerted herself, I struck into the dialogue as if she had made her appeal. The sound of my voice seemed to recall her; she passed her hand across her eyes, drew a long breath, and looked about her. I thought she had recovered herself and was about to resume her part, but, to my great surprise, she only clung to me, saying in a shrill whisper, so full of despair, it chilled my blood—

"The answer, Paul, the answer: it has come!"

The words were inaudible to all but myself; but the look, the gesture were eloquent with terror, grief, and love; and taking it for a fine piece of acting, the audience applauded loud and long. The accustomed sound roused Clotilde, and during that noisy moment a hurried dialogue passed between us.

"What is it? Are you ill?" I whispered.

"He is here, Paul, alive; I saw him. Heaven help us both!"

"Who is here?"

"Hush! not now; there is no time to tell you."

"You are right; compose yourself; you must speak in a moment."

"What do I say? Help me, Paul; I have forgotten every thing but that man."

She looked as if bewildered; and I saw that some sudden shock had entirely unnerved her. But actors must have neither hearts nor nerves while on the stage. The applause was subsiding, and she must speak. Fortunately I remembered enough of her part to prompt her as she struggled through the little that remained; for, seeing her condition, Denon and I cut the scene remorselessly, and brought it to a close as soon as possible. The instant the curtain fell we were assailed with questions, but Clotilde answered none; and though hidden from her sight, still seemed to see the object that had wrought such an alarming change in her. I told them she was ill, took her to her dressing-room, and gave her into the hands of her maid, for I must appear again, and delay was impossible.

How I got through my part I cannot tell, for my thoughts were with Clotilde; but an actor learns to live a double life, so while Paul Lamar suffered torments of anxiety Don Felix fought a duel, killed his adversary, and was dragged to judgment.

Involuntarily my eyes often wandered toward the spot where Clotilde's had seemed fixed. It was one of the stage-boxes, and at first I thought it empty, but presently I caught the glitter of a glass turned apparently on myself. As soon as possible I crossed the stage, and as I leaned haughtily upon my sword while the seconds adjusted the preliminaries, I searched the box with a keen glance. Nothing was visible, however, but a hand lying easily on the red cushion; a man's hand, white and shapely; on one finger shone a ring, evidently a woman's ornament, for it was a slender circlet of diamonds that flashed with every gesture.

"Some fop, doubtless; a man like that could never daunt Clotilde," I thought. And eager to discover if there was not another occupant in the box, I took a step nearer, and stared boldly into the soft gloom that filled it. A low derisive laugh came from behind the curtain as the hand gathered back as if to permit me to satisfy myself. The act showed me that a single person occupied the box, but also effectually con-cealed that person from my sight; and as I was recalled to my duty by a warning whisper from one of my comrades, the hand appeared to wave me a mocking adieu. Baffled and angry, I devoted myself to the affairs of Don Felix, wondering the while if Clotilde would be able to reappear, how she would bear herself, if that hidden man was the cause of her terror, and why? Even when immured in a dungeon, after my arrest, I beguiled the tedium of a long soliloquy with these questions, and executed a better stage-start than any I had ever practised, when at last she came to me, bringing liberty and love as my reward.

I had left her haggard, speechless, overwhelmed with some mysterious woe, she reappeared beautiful and brilliant, with a joy that seemed too lovely to be feigned. Never had she played so well; for some spirit, stronger than her own, seemed to possess and rule her royally. If I had ever doubted her love for me, I should have been assured of it that night, for she breathed into the fond words of her part a tenderness and grace that filled my heart to overflowing, and inspired me to play the grateful lover to the life. The last words came all too soon for me, and as she threw herself into my arms she turned her head as if to glance triumphantly at the defeated Duke, but I saw that again she looked beyond him, and with an indescribable expression of mingled pride, contempt, and defiance. A soft sound of applause from the mysterious occupant of that box answered the look, and the white hand sent a superb bouquet flying to her feet. I was about to lift and present it to her, but she checked me and crushed it under foot with an air of the haughtiest disdain. A laugh from behind the curtain greeted this demonstration, but it was scarcely observed by others; for that first bouquet seemed a signal for a rain of flowers, and these latter offerings she permitted me to gather up, receiving them with her most gracious smiles, her most graceful obeisances, as if to mark, for one observer at least, the difference of her regard for the givers. As I laid the last floral tribute in her arms I took a parting glance at the box, hoping to catch a glimpse of the unknown face. The curtains were thrown back and the door stood open, admitting a strong light from the vestibule, but the box was empty.

Then the green curtain fell, and Clotilde whispered, as she glanced from her full hands to the rejected bouquet—

"Bring that to my room; I must have it."

I obeyed, eager to be enlightened; but when we were alone she flung down her fragrant burden, snatched the stranger's gift, tore it apart, drew out a slip of paper, read it, dropped it, and walked to and fro, wringing her hands, like one in a paroxysm of despair. I seized the note and looked at it, but found no key to her distress in the enigmatical words—

"I shall be there. Come and bring your lover with you, else—"

There it abruptly ended; but the unfinished threat seemed the more menacing for its obscurity, and I indignantly demanded,

"Clotilde, who dares address you so? Where will this man be? You surely will not obey such a command? Tell me; I have a right to know."

"I cannot tell you, now; I dare not refuse him; he will be at Keen's; we *must* go. How will it end! How will it end!"

I remembered then that we were all to sup *en costume,* with a brother actor, who did not play that night. I was about to speak yet more urgently, when the entrance of her maid checked me. Clotilde composed herself by a strong effort—

"Go and prepare," she whispered; "have faith in me a little longer, and soon you shall know all."

There was something almost solemn in her tone; her eye met mine, imploringly, and her lips trembled as if her heart were full. That assured me at once; and with a reassuring word I hurried away to give a few touches to my costume, which just then was fitter for a dungeon than a feast. When I rejoined her there was no trace of past emotion; a soft color bloomed upon her cheek, her eyes were tearless and brilliant, her lips were dressed in smiles. Jewels shone on her white forehead, neck, and arms, flowers glowed in her bosom; and no charm that art or skill could lend to the rich dress or its lovely wearer, had been forgotten.

"What an actress!" I involuntarily exclaimed, as she came to meet me, looking almost as beautiful and gay as ever.

"It is well that I am one, else I should yield to my hard fate without a struggle. Paul, hitherto I have played for money, now I play for love; help me by being a calm spectator to-night, and whatever happens promise me that there shall be no violence."

I promised, for I was wax in her hands; and, more bewildered than ever, followed to the carriage, where a companion was impatiently awaiting us.

CHAPTER II

WE WERE LATE; and on arriving found all the other guests assembled. Three strangers appeared; and my attention was instantly fixed upon them, for the mysterious "he" was to be there. All three seemed gay, gallant, handsome men; all three turned admiring eyes upon Clotilde, all three were gloved. Therefore, as I had seen no face, my one clue, the ring, was lost. From Clotilde's face and manner I could learn nothing, for a smile seemed carved upon her lips, her drooping lashes half concealed her eyes, and her voice was too well trained to betray her by a traitorous tone. She received the greetings, compliments, and admiration of all alike, and I vainly looked and listened till supper was announced.

As I took my place beside her, I saw her shrink and shiver slightly, as if a chilly wind had blown over her, but before I could ask if she were cold a bland voice said,

"Will Mademoiselle Varian permit me to drink her health?"

It was one of the strangers; mechanically I offered her glass; but the next instant my hold tightened till the slender stem snapped, and the rosy bowl fell broken to the table, for on the handsome hand extended to fill it shone the ring.

"A bad omen, Mr. Lamar. I hope my attempt will succeed better," said St. John, as he filled another glass and handed it to Clotilde, who merely lifted it to her lips, and turned to enter into an animated conversation with the gentleman who sat on the other side. Some one addressed St. John, and I was glad of it; for now all my interest and attention was centered in him. Keenly, but covertly, I examined him, and soon felt that in spite of that foppish ornament he *was* a man to daunt a woman like Clotilde. Pride and passion, courage and indomitable will met and mingled in his face, though the obedient features wore whatever expression he imposed upon them. He was the handsomest, most elegant, but least attractive of the three, yet it was hard to say why. The others gave themselves freely to the enjoyment of a scene which evidently possessed the charm of novelty to them; but St. John unconsciously wore the half sad, half weary look that comes to those who have led lives of pleasure and found their emptiness. Although the wittiest, and most brilliant talker at the table, his gaiety seemed fitful, his manner absent at times. More than once I saw him knit his black brows as he met my eye, and more than once I caught a long look fixed on Clotilde,—a look full of the lordly admiration and pride which a master bestows upon a handsome slave. It made my blood boil, but I controlled myself, and was apparently absorbed in Miss Damareau, my neighbor.

We seemed as gay and care-free a company as ever made midnight merry; songs were sung, stories told, theatrical phrases added sparkle to the conversation, and the varied costumes gave an air of romance to the revel. The Grand Inquisitor still in his ghostly garb, and the stern old Duke were now the jolliest of the group; the page flirted violently with the princess; the rivals of the play were bosom-friends again, and the fair Donna Olivia had apparently forgotten her knightly lover, to listen to a modern gentleman.

Clotilde sat leaning back in a deep chair, eating nothing, but using her fan with the indescribable grace of a Spanish woman. She was very lovely, for the dress became her, and the black lace mantilla falling from her head to her shoulders, heightened her charms by half concealing them; and nothing could have been more genial and gracious than the air with which she listened and replied to the compliments of the youngest stranger, who sat beside her and was all devotion.

I forgot myself in observing her till something said by our opposite neighbors arrested both of us. Some one seemed to have been joking St. John about his ring, which was too brilliant an ornament to pass unobserved.

"Bad taste, I grant you," he said, laughing, "but it is a *gage d'amour,* and I wear it for a purpose."

"I fancied it was the latest Paris fashion," returned Keen. "And apropos to Paris, what is the latest gossip from the gay city?"

A slow smile rose to St. John's lips as he answered, after a moment's thought and a quick glance across the room.

"A little romance; shall I tell it to you? It is a love story, ladies, and not long."

A unanimous assent was given; and he began with a curious glitter in his eyes, a stealthy smile coming and going on his face as the words dropped slowly from his lips.

"It begins in the old way. A foolish young man fell in love with a Spanish girl much his inferior in rank, but beautiful enough to excuse his folly, for he married her. Then came a few months of bliss; but Madame grew jealous. Monsieur wearied of domestic tempests, and, after vain efforts to appease his fiery angel, he proposed a separation. Madame was obdurate, Monsieur rebelled; and in order to try the soothing effects of absence upon both, after settling her in a charming chateau, he slipped away, leaving no trace by which his route might be discovered."

"Well, how did the experiment succeed?" asked Keen. St. John shrugged his shoulders, emptied his glass, and answered tranquilly.

"Like most experiments that have women for their subjects, for the amiable creatures always devise some way of turning the tables, and defeating the best laid plans. Madame waited for her truant spouse till rumors of his death reached Paris, for he had met with mishaps, and sickness detained him long in an obscure place, so the rumors seemed confirmed by his silence, and Madame believed him dead. But instead of dutifully mourning him, this inexplicable woman shook the dust of the chateau off her feet and disappeared, leaving everything, even to her wedding ring, behind her."

"Bless me, how odd! what became of her?" exclaimed Miss Damareau, forgetting the dignity of the Princess in the curiosity of the woman.

"The very question her repentant husband asked when, returning from his long holiday, he found her gone. He searched the continent for her, but in vain; and for two years she left him to suffer the torments of suspense."

"As he had left her to suffer them while he went pleasuring. It was a light punishment for his offence."

Clotilde spoke; and the sarcastic tone, for all its softness, made St. John wince, though no eye but mine observed the faint flush of shame or anger that passed across his face.

"Mademoiselle espouses the lady's cause, of course, and as a gallant man I should do likewise, but unfortunately my sympathies are strongly enlisted on the other side."

"Then you know the parties?" I said, impulsively, for my inward excitement was increasing rapidly, and I began to feel rather than to see the end of this mystery.

"I have seen them, and cannot blame the man for claiming his beautiful wife, when he found her," he answered, briefly.

"Then he did find her at last? Pray tell us how and when," cried Miss Damareau.

"She betrayed herself. It seems that Madame had returned to her old profession, and fallen in love with an actor; but being as virtuous as she was fair, she would not marry till she was assured beyond a doubt of her husband's death. Her engagements would not allow her to enquire in person, so she sent letters to various places asking for proofs of his demise; and as ill, or good fortune would have it, one of these letters fell into Monsieur's hands, giving him an excellent clue to her whereabouts, which he followed indefatigably till he found her."

"Poor little woman, I pity her! How did she receive Monsieur De Trop?" asked Keen.

"You shall know in good time. He found her in London playing at one of the great theatres, for she had talent, and had become a star. He saw her act for a night or two, made secret inquiries concerning her, and fell more in love with her than ever. Having tried almost every novelty under the sun he had a fancy to attempt something of the dramatic sort, so presented himself to Madame at a party."

"Heavens! what a scene there must have been," ejaculated Miss Damareau.

"On the contrary, there was no scene at all, for the man was not a Frenchman, and Madame was a fine actress. Much as he had admired her on the stage he was doubly charmed with her performance in private, for it was superb. They were among strangers, and she received him like one, playing her part with the utmost grace and self-control, for with a woman's quickness of perception, she divined his purpose, and knowing that her fate was in his hands, endeavored to propitiate him by complying with his caprice. Mademoiselle, allow me to send you some of these grapes, they are delicious."

As he leaned forward to present them he shot a glance at her that caused me to start up with a violence that nearly betrayed me. Fortunately the room was close, and saying something about the heat, I threw open a window, and let in a balmy gust of spring air that refreshed us all.

"How did they settle it, by duels and despair, or by repentance and reconciliation all round, in the regular French fashion?"

"I regret that I'm unable to tell you, for I left before the affair was arranged. I only know that Monsieur was more captivated than before, and quite ready to forgive and forget, and I suspect that Madame, seeing the folly of resistance, will submit with a good grace, and leave the stage to play 'The Honey Moon' for a second time in private with a husband who adores her. What is the Mademoiselle's opinion?"

She had listened, without either question or comment, her fan at rest, her hands motionless, her eyes downcast; so still it seemed as if she had hushed the breath upon her lips, so pale despite her rouge, that I wondered no one observed it, so intent and resolute that every feature seemed under control,—every look and gesture guarded. When St. John addressed her, she looked up with a smile as bland as his own, but fixed her eyes on him with an expression of undismayed defiance and supreme contempt that caused him to bite his lips with ill-concealed annoyance.

"My opinion?" she said, in her clear, cold voice, "I think that Madame, being a woman of spirit, would *not* endeavor to propitiate that man in any way except for her lover's sake, and having been once deserted would not subject herself to a second indignity of that sort while there was a law to protect her."

"Unfortunately there is no law for her, having once refused a separation. Even if there were, Monsieur is rich and powerful, she is poor and friendless; he loves her, and is a man who never permits himself to be thwarted by any obstacle; therefore, I am convinced it would be best for this adorable woman to submit without defiance or delay—and I do think she will," he added, significantly.

"They seem to forget the poor lover; what is to become of him?" asked Keen.

"*I* do not forget him;" and the hand that wore the ring closed with an ominous gesture, which I well understood. "Monsieur merely claims his own, and the other, being a man of sense and honor, will doubtless withdraw at once; and though 'desolated,' as the French say, will soon console himself with a new *inamorata*. If he is so unwise as to oppose Monsieur, who by the by is a dead shot, there is but one way in which both can receive satisfaction."

A significant emphasis on the last word pointed his meaning, and the smile that accompanied it almost goaded me to draw the sword I wore, and offer him that satisfaction on the spot. I felt the color rise to my forehead, and dared not look up, but leaning on the back of Clotilde's chair, I bent as if to speak to her.

"Bear it a little longer for my sake, Paul," she murmured, with a look of love and despair, that wrung my heart. Here some one spoke of a long rehearsal in the morning, and the lateness of the hour.

"A farewell toast before we part," said Keen. "Come, Lamar, give us a sentiment, after that whisper you ought to be inspired."

"I am. Let me give you—The love of liberty and the liberty of love."

"Good! That would suit the hero and heroine of St. John's story, for Monsieur wished much for his liberty, and, no doubt, Madame will for her love," said Denon, while the glasses were filled.

Then the toast was drunk with much merriment and the party broke up. While detained by one of the strangers, I saw St. John approach Clotilde, who stood alone by the window, and speak rapidly for several minutes. She listened with half-averted head, answered briefly, and wrapping the mantilla closely about her, swept away from him with her haughtiest mien. He watched for a moment, then followed, and before I could reach her, offered his arm to lead her to the carriage. She seemed about to refuse it, but something in the expression of his face restrained her; and accepting it, they went down together. The hall and little ante-room were dimly lighted, but as I slowly followed, I saw her snatch her hand away, when she thought they were alone; saw him draw her to him with an embrace as fond as it was irresistible; and turning her indignant face to his, kiss it ardently, as he said in a tone, both tender and imperious—

"Good night, my darling. I give you one more day, and then I claim you."

"Never!" she answered, almost fiercely, as he released her. And wishing me pleasant dreams, as he passed, went out into the night, gaily humming the burden of a song Clotilde had often sung to me.

The moment we were in the carriage all her self-control deserted her, and a tempest of despairing grief came over her. For a time, both words and caresses were unavailing, and I let her weep herself calm before I asked the hard question—

"Is all this true, Clotilde?"

"Yes, Paul, all true, except that he said nothing of the neglect, the cruelty, the insult that I bore before he left me. I was so young, so lonely, I was glad to be loved and cared for, and I believed that he would never change. I cannot tell you all I suffered, but I rejoiced when I thought death had freed me; I would keep nothing that reminded me of the bitter past, and went away to begin again, as if it had never been."

"Why delay telling me this? Why let me learn it in such a strange and sudden way?"

"Ah, forgive me! I am so proud I could not bear to tell you that any man had wearied of me and deserted me. I meant to tell you before our marriage, but the fear that St. John was alive haunted me, and till it was set at rest I would not speak. To-night there was no time, and I was forced to leave all to chance. He found pleasure in tormenting me through you, but would not speak out, because he is as proud as I, and does not wish to hear our story bandied from tongue to tongue."

"What did he say to you, Clotilde?"

"He begged me to submit and return to him, in spite of all that has passed; he warned me that if we attempted to escape it would be at the peril of your life, for he would most assuredly follow and find us, to whatever corner of the earth we might fly; and he will, for he is as relentless as death."

"What did he mean by giving you one day more?" I asked, grinding my teeth with impatient rage as I listened.

"He gave me one day to recover from my surprise, to prepare for my departure with him, and to bid you farewell."

"And will you, Clotilde?"

"No!" she replied, clenching her hands with a gesture of dogged resolution, while her eyes glittered in the darkness. "I never will submit; there must be some way of escape; I shall find it, and if I do not—I can die."

"Not yet, dearest; we will appeal to the law first; I have a friend whom I will consult to-morrow, and he may help us."

"I have no faith in law," she said, despairingly, "money and influence so often outweigh justice and mercy. I have no witnesses, no friends, no wealth to help me; he has all, and we shall only be defeated. I must devise some surer way. Let me think a little; a woman's wit is quick when her heart prompts it."

I let the poor soul flatter herself with vague hopes; but I saw no help for us except in flight, and that she would not consent to, lest it should endanger me. More than once I said savagely within myself, "I will kill him," and then shuddered at the counsels of the devil, so suddenly roused in my own breast. As if she divined my thought by instinct, Clotilde broke the heavy silence that followed her last words, by clinging to me with the imploring cry,

"Oh, Paul, shun him, else your fiery spirit will destroy you. He promised me he would not harm you unless we drove him to it. Be careful, for my sake, and if any one must suffer let it be miserable me."

I soothed her as I best could, and when our long, sad drive ended, bade her rest while I worked, for she would need all her strength on the morrow. Then I left her, to haunt the street all night long, guarding her door, and while I paced to and fro without, I watched her shadow come and go before the lighted window as she paced within, each racking our brains for some means of help till day broke.

CHAPTER III

EARLY on the following morning I consulted my friend, but when I laid the case before him he gave me little hope of a happy issue should the attempt be made. A divorce was hardly possible, when an unscrupulous man like St. John was bent on opposing it; and though no decision could force her to remain with him, we should not be safe from his vengeance, even if we chose to dare everything and fly together. Long and earnestly we talked, but to little purpose, and I went to rehearsal with a heavy heart.

Clotilde was to have a benefit that night, and what a happy day I had fancied this would be; how carefully I had prepared for it; what delight I had anticipated in playing Romeo to her Juliet; and how eagerly I had longed for the time which now seemed to approach with such terrible rapidity, for each hour brought our parting nearer! On the stage I found Keen and his new friend amusing themselves with fencing, while waiting the arrival of some of the company. I was too miserable to be dangerous just then, and when St. John bowed to me with his most courteous air, I returned the greeting, though I could not speak to him. I think he saw my suffering, and enjoyed it with the satisfaction of a cruel nature, but he treated me with the courtesy of an equal, which new demonstration surprised me, till, through Denon, I discovered that having inquired much about me he had learned that I was a gentleman by birth and education, which fact accounted for the change in his demeanor. I roamed restlessly about the gloomy green room and stage, till Keen, dropping his foil, confessed himself outfenced and called to me.

"Come here, Lamar, and try a bout with St. John. You are the best fencer among us, so, for the honor of the company, come and do your best instead of playing Romeo before the time."

A sudden impulse prompted me to comply, and a few passes proved that I was the better swordsman of the two. This annoyed St. John, and though he complimented me with the rest, he would not own himself outdone, and we kept it up till both grew warm and excited. In the midst of an animated match between us, I observed that the button was off his foil, and a glance at his face assured me that he was aware of it, and almost at the instant he made a skilful thrust, and the point pierced my flesh. As I caught the foil from his hand and drew it out with an exclamation of pain, I saw a gleam of exultation pass across his face, and knew that his promise to Clotilde was but idle breath. My comrades surrounded me with anxious inquiries, and no one was more surprised and solicitous than St. John. The wound was trifling, for a picture of Clotilde had turned the thrust aside, else the force with which it was given might have rendered it fatal. I made light of it, but hated him with a redoubled hatred for the cold-blooded treachery that would have given to revenge the screen of accident.

The appearance of the ladies caused us to immediately ignore the mishap, and address ourselves to business. Clotilde came last, looking so pale it was not necessary for her to plead illness; but she went through her part with her usual fidelity, while her husband watched her with the masterful expression that nearly drove me wild. He haunted her like a shadow, and she listened to him with the desperate look of a hunted creature driven to bay. He might have softened her just resentment by a touch of generosity or compassion, and won a little gratitude, even though love was impossible; but he was blind, relentless, and goaded her beyond endurance, rousing in her fiery Spanish heart a dangerous spirit he could not control. The rehearsal was over at last, and I approached Clotilde with a look that mutely asked if I should leave her. St. John said something in a low voice, but she answered sternly, as she took my arm with a decided gesture.

"This day is mine; I will not be defrauded of an hour," and we went away together for our accustomed stroll in the sunny park.

A sad and memorable walk was that, for neither had any hope with which to cheer the other, and Clotilde grew gloomier as we talked. I told her of my fruitless consultation, also of the fencing match; at that her face darkened, and she said, below her breath, "I shall remember that."

We walked long together, and I proposed plan after plan, all either unsafe or impracticable. She seemed to listen, but when I paused she answered with averted eyes—

"Leave it to me; I have a project; let me perfect it before I tell you. Now I must go and rest, for I have had no sleep, and I shall need all my strength for the tragedy to-night."

All that afternoon I roamed about the city, too restless for anything but constant motion, and evening found me ill prepared for my now doubly arduous duties. It was late when I reached the theatre, and I dressed hastily. My costume was new for the occasion, and not till it was on did I remember that I had neglected to try it since the finishing touches were given. A stitch or two would remedy the defects, and, hurrying up to the wardrobe room, a skilful pair of hands soon set me right. As I came down the winding-stairs that led from the lofty chamber to a dimly-lighted gallery below, St. John's voice arrested me, and pausing I saw that Keen was doing the honors of the theatre in defiance of all rules. Just as they reached the stair-foot some one called to them, and throwing open a narrow door, he said to his companion—

"From here you get a fine view of the stage; steady yourself by the rope and look down. I'll be with you in a moment."

He ran into the dressing-room from whence the voice proceeded, and St. John stepped out upon a little platform, hastily built for the launching of an aeriel-car in some grand spectacle. Glad to escape meeting him, I was about to go on, when, from an obscure corner, a dark figure glided noiselessly to the door and leaned in. I caught a momentary glimpse of a white extended arm and the glitter of steel, then came a cry of mortal fear, a heavy fall; and flying swiftly down the gallery the figure disappeared. With one leap I reached the door, and looked in; the raft hung broken, the platform was empty. At that instant Keen rushed out, demanding what had happened, and scarcely knowing what I said, I answered hurriedly,

"The rope broke and he fell."

Keen gave me a strange look, and dashed down stairs. I followed, to find myself in a horror-stricken crowd, gathered about the piteous object which a moment ago had been a living man. There was no need to call a surgeon, for that headlong fall had dashed out life in the drawing of a breath, and nothing remained to do but to take the poor body tenderly away to such friends as the newly-arrived stranger possessed. The contrast between the gay crowd rustling before the curtain and the dreadful scene transpiring behind it, was terrible; but the house was filling fast; there was no time for the indulgence of pity or curiosity, and soon no trace of the accident remained but the broken rope above, and an ominous damp spot on the newly-washed boards below. At a word of command from our energetic manager, actors and actresses were sent away to retouch their pale faces with carmine, to restoring their startled nerves with any stimulant at hand, and to forget, if possible, the awesome sight just witnessed.

I returned to my dressing-room hoping Clotilde had heard nothing of this sad, and yet for us most fortunate accident, though all the while a vague dread haunted me, and I feared to see her. Mechanically completing my costume, I looked about me for the dagger with which poor Juliet was to stab herself, and found that it was gone.

Trying to recollect where I put it, I remembered having it in my hand just before I went up to have my sword-belt altered; and fancying that I must have inadvertently taken it with me, I reluctantly retraced my steps. At the top of the stairs leading to that upper gallery a little white object caught my eye, and, taking it up, I found it to be a flower. If it had been a burning coal I should not have dropped it more hastily than I did when I recognized it was one of a cluster I had left in Clotilde's room because she loved them. They were a rare and delicate kind, no one but herself was likely to possess them in that place, nor was she likely to have given one away, for my gifts were kept with jealous care; yet how came it there? And as I asked myself the question, like an answer returned the remembrance of her face when she said, "I shall remember this." The darkly-shrouded form was a female figure, the white arm a woman's, and horrible as was the act, who but that sorely-tried and tempted creature would have committed it. For a moment my heart stood still, then I indignantly rejected the black thought, and thrusting the flower into my breast went on my way, trying to convince myself that the foreboding fear which oppressed me was caused by the agitating events of the last half hour. My weapon was not in the wardrobe-room; and as I returned, wondering what I had done with it, I saw Keen standing in the little doorway with a candle in his hand. He turned and asked what I was looking for. I told him, and explained why I was searching for it there.

"Here it is; I found it at the foot of these stairs. It is too sharp for a stage-dagger, and will do mischief unless you dull it," he said, adding, as he pointed to the broken rope, "Lamar, that was cut; I have examined it."

The light shone full in my face, and I knew that it changed, as did my voice, for I thought of Clotilde, and till that fear was at rest resolved to be dumb concerning what I had seen, but I could not repress a shudder as I said, hastily,

"Don't suspect me of any deviltry, for heaven's sake. I've got to go on in fifteen minutes, and how can I play unless you let me forget this horrible business."

"Forget it then, if you can; I'll remind you of it to-morrow." And, with a significant nod, he walked away, leaving behind him a new trial to distract me. I ran to Clotilde's room, bent on relieving myself, if possible, of the suspicion that would return with redoubled pertinacity since the discovery of the dagger, which I was sure I had not dropped where it was found. When I tapped at her door, her voice, clear and sweet as ever, answered "Come!" and entering, I found her ready, but alone. Before I could open my lips she put up her hand as if to arrest the utterance of some dreadful intelligence.

"Don't speak of it; I have heard, and cannot bear a repetition of the horror. I must forget it till to-morrow, then——." There she stopped abruptly, for I produced the flower, asking as naturally as I could—

"Did you give this to any one?"

"No; why ask me that?" and she shrunk a little, as I bent to count the blossoms in the cluster on her breast. I gave her seven; now there were but six, and I fixed on her a look that betrayed my fear, and mutely demanded its confirmation or denial. Other eyes she might have evaded or defied, not mine; the traitorous blood dyed her face, then fading, left it colorless; her eyes wandered and fell, she clasped her hands imploringly, and threw herself at my feet, crying in a stifled voice,

"Paul, be merciful; that was our only hope, and the guilt is mine alone!"

But I started from her, exclaiming with mingled incredulity and horror—

"Was this the tragedy you meant? What devil devised and helped you execute a crime like this?"

"Hear me! I did not plan it, yet I longed to kill him, and all day the thought would haunt me. I have borne so much, I could bear no more, and he drove me to it. To-night the thought still clung to me, till I was half mad. I went to find you, hoping to escape it; you were gone, but on your table lay the dagger. As I took it in my hand I heard his voice, and forgot every thing except my wrongs and the great happiness one blow could bring us. I followed then, meaning to stab him in the dark; but when I saw him leaning where a safer stroke would destroy him, I gave it, and we are safe."

"Safe!" I echoed. "Do you know you left my dagger behind you? Keen found it; he suspects me, for I was near; and St. John has told him something of the cause I have to wish you free."

She sprung up, and seemed about to rush away to proclaim her guilt, but I restrained her desperate purpose, saying sternly—

"Control yourself and be cautious. I may be mistaken; but if either must suffer, let it be me. I can bear it best, even if it comes to the worst, for my life is worthless now."

"And I have made it so? Oh, Paul, can you never forgive me and forget my sin?"

"Never, Clotilde; it is too horrible."

I broke from her trembling hold, and covered up my face, for suddenly the woman whom I once loved had grown abhorrent to me. For many minutes neither spoke or stirred; my heart seemed dead within me, and what went on in that stormy soul I shall never know. Suddenly I was called, and as I turned to leave her, she seized both my hands in a despairing grasp, covered them with tender kisses, wet them with repentant tears, and clung to them in a paroxysm of love, remorse, and grief, till I was forced to go, leaving her alone with the memory of her sin.

That night I was like one in a terrible dream; every thing looked unreal, and like an automaton I played my part, for always before me I seemed to see that shattered body and to hear again that beloved voice confessing a black crime. Rumors of the accident had crept out, and damped the spirits of the audience, yet it was as well, perhaps, for it made them lenient to the short-comings of the actors, and lent another shadow to the mimic tragedy that slowly darkened to its close. Clotilde's unnatural composure would have been a marvel to me had I not been past surprise at any demonstration on her part. A wide gulf now lay between us, and it seemed impossible for me to cross it. The generous, tender woman whom I first loved, was still as beautiful and dear to me as ever, but as much lost as if death had parted us. The desperate, despairing creature I had learned to know within an hour, seemed like an embodiment of the murderous spirit which had haunted me that day, and though by heaven's mercy it had not conquered me, yet I now hated it with remorseful intensity. So strangely were the two images blended in my troubled mind that I could not separate them, and they exerted a mysterious influence over me. When with Clotilde she seemed all she had ever been, and I enacted the lover with a power I had never known before, feeling the while that it might be for the last time. When away from her the darker impression returned, and the wildest of the poet's words were not too strong to embody my own sorrow and despair. They told me long afterwards that never had the tragedy been better played, and I could believe it, for the hapless Italian lovers never found better representatives than in us that night.

Worn out with suffering and excitement, I longed for solitude and silence with a desperate longing, and when Romeo murmured, "With a kiss I die," I fell beside the bier, wishing that I too was done with life. Lying there, I watched Clotilde, through the little that remained, and so truly, tenderly, did she render the pathetic scene that my heart softened; all the early love returned strong, and warm as ever, and I felt that I *could* forgive. As she knelt to draw my dagger, I whispered, warningly,

"Be careful, dear, it is very sharp."

"I know it," she answered with a shudder, then cried aloud,

"Oh happy dagger! this is thy sheath; there rust, and let me die."

Again I saw the white arm raised, the flash of steel as Juliet struck the blow that was to free her, and sinking down beside her lover, seemed to breathe her life away.

"I thank God it's over," I ejaculated, a few minutes later, as the curtain slowly fell. Clotilde did not answer, and feeling how cold the cheek that touched my own had grown, I thought she had given way at last.

"She has fainted; lift her, Denon, and let me rise," I cried, as Count Paris sprang up with a joke.

"Good God, she has hurt herself with that cursed dagger!" he exclaimed, as raising her he saw a red stain on the white draperies she wore.

I staggered to my feet, and laid her on the bier she had just left, but no mortal skill could heal that hurt, and Juliet's grave-clothes were her own. Deaf to the enthusiastic clamor that demanded our re-appearance, blind to the confusion and dismay about me, I leaned over her passionately, conjuring her to give me one word of pardon and farewell. As if my voice had power to detain her, even when death called, the dark eyes, full of remorseful love, met mine again, and feebly drawing from her breast a paper, she motioned Keen to take it, murmuring in a tone that changed from solemn affirmation to the tenderest penitence,

"Lamar is innocent—I did it. This will prove it. Paul, I have tried to atone—oh, forgive me, and remember me for my love's sake."

I did forgive her; and she died, smiling on my breast. I did remember her through a long, lonely life, and never played again since the night of that DOUBLE TRAGEDY.

ᐒ Ariel. A Legend of the Lighthouse

PART I

"Good morning, Mr. Southesk. Aren't you for the sea, today?"

"Good morning, Miss Lawrence. I am only waiting for my boat to be off."

As he answered her blithe greeting, the young man looked up from the rock where he was lounging, and a most charming object rewarded him for the exertion of lifting his dreamy eyes. Some women have the skill to make even a bathing costume graceful and picturesque; and Miss Lawrence knew that she looked well in her blue suit, with loosened hair blowing about her handsome face, glimpses of white ankles through the net-work of her bathing-sandals, and a general breeziness of aspect that became her better than the most elaborate toilet she could make. A shade of disappointment was visible on receiving the answer to her question, and her voice was slightly imperious, for all its sweetness, as she said, pausing beside the indolent figure that lay basking in the sunshine.

"I meant bathing, not boating, when I spoke of the sea. Will you not join our party and give us another exhibition of your skill in aquatic gymnastics?"

"No, thank you; the beach is too tame for me; I prefer deep water, heavy surf and a spice of danger, to give zest to my pastime."

The languid voice was curiously at variance with the words; and Miss Lawrence almost involuntarily exclaimed—

"You are the strangest mixture of indolence and energy I ever knew! To see you now, one would find it difficult to believe the stories told of your feats by land and sea; yet I know that you deserve your soubriquet of 'Bayard,' as well as the other they give you of '*Dolce far niente.*' You are as changeable as the ocean which you love so well; but we never see the moon that rules your ebb and flow."

Ignoring the first part of her speech, Southesk replied to the last sentence with sudden animation.

"I *am* fond of the sea, and well I may be, for I was born on it, both my parents lie buried in it, and out of it my fate is yet to come."

"Your fate?" echoed Miss Lawrence, full of the keenest interest, for he seldom spoke of himself, and seemed anxious to forget the past in the successful present, and the promising future. Some passing mood made him unusually frank, for he answered, as his fine eyes roved far across the glittering expanse before them—

"Yes, I once had my fortune told by a famous wizard, and it has haunted me ever since. I am not superstitious, but I cannot help attaching some importance to her prediction:

> 'Watch by the sea-shore early and late,
> For out of its depths will rise your fate,
> Both love and life will be darkly crossed,
> And a single hour see all won or lost.'

"That was the prophecy; and though I have little faith in it, yet I am irresistibly drawn towards the sea, and continually find myself watching and waiting for the fate it is to bring me."

"May it be a happy one."

All the imperiousness was gone from the woman's voice, and her eyes turned as wistfully as her companion's, to the mysterious ocean which had already brought *her* fate. Neither spoke for a moment. Southesk, busied with some fancy of his own, continued to scan the blue waves that rolled to meet the horizon, and Helen scanned his face with an expression which many men would have given much to have awakened, for the world said that Miss Lawrence was as proud and cold as she was beautiful. Love and longing met and mingled in the glance she fixed on that unconscious countenance; and once, with an involuntary impulse, her small hand was raised to smooth away the wind-tossed hair that streaked his forehead, as he sat with uncovered head, smiling to himself—forgetful of her presence. She caught back her hand in time and turned away to hide the sudden color that dyed her cheeks at the momentary impulse which would have betrayed her to a less absorbed companion. Before she could break the silence, there came a call from a group gathered on the smoother beach beyond, and, glad of another chance to gain her wish, she said, in a tone that would have won compliance from any man except Southesk:

"They are waiting for us; can I not tempt you to join the mermaids yonder, and let the boat wait till it's cooler?"

But he shook his head with a wilful little gesture, and looked about him for his hat, as if eager to escape, yet answered smiling—

"I've a prior engagement with the mermaid of the island, and, as a gallant man, must keep it, or expect shipwreck on my next voyage. Are you ready, Jack?" he added, as Miss Lawrence moved away, and he strolled towards an old boatman, busy with his wherry.

"In a jiffy, sir. So you've seen her, have you?" said the man, pausing in his work.

"Seen whom?"

"The mermaid at the island."

"No; I only fabricated that excuse to rid myself of the amiable young ladies who bore me to death. You look as if you had a yarn to spin; so spin away while you work, for I want to be off."

"Well, sir, I jest thought you'd like to know that there *is* a marmaid down there, as you're fond of odd and pretty things. No one has seen her but me, or I should a heard of it, and I've told no one but my wife, being afraid of Rough Ralph, as we call the lighthouse-keeper. He don't like folks comin' round his place; and if I said a word about the marmaid, every one would go swarmin' to the island to hunt up the pretty creeter, and drive Ralph into a rage."

"Never mind Ralph; tell me how and where you saw the mermaid; asleep in your boat, I fancy."

"No, sir; wide awake and sober. I had a notion one day to row round the island, and take a look at the chasm, as they call a great split in the rock that stands up most as high as the lighthouse. It goes from top to bottom of the Gull's Perch, and the sea flows through it, foamin' and ragin' like mad, when the tide rises. The waves have worn holes in the rocks on both sides of the chasm, and in one of these basins I see the marmaid, as plain as I see you."

"What was she doing, Jack?"

"Singin' and combin' her hair; so I knew she was gennywine."

"Her hair was green or blue, of course," said Southesk, with such visible incredulity that old Jack was nettled and answered gruffly.

"It was darker and curlier than the lady's that's jest gone; so was her face handsomer, her voice sweeter, and her arms whiter; believe it or not as you please."

"How about the fins and scales, Jack?"

"Not a sign of 'em, sir. She was half in the water, and had on some sort of white gown, so I couldn't see whether there were feet or a tail. But I'll swear I saw her; and I've got her comb to prove it."

"Her comb! let me see it, and I shall find it easier to believe the story," said the young man, with a lazy sort of curiosity.

Old Jack produced a dainty little comb, apparently made of a pearly shell, cut and carved with much skill, and bearing two letters on its back.

"Faith! it *is* a pretty thing, and none but a mermaid could have owned it. How did you get it?" asked Southesk, carefully examining the delicate lines and letters, and wishing that the tale could be true, for the vision of the fair-faced mermaiden pleased his romantic fancy.

"It was this way, sir," replied Jack. "I was so took aback that I sung out before I'd had a good look at her. She see me, give a little screech, and dived out of sight. I waited to see her come up, but she didn't; so I rowed as nigh as I dared, and got the comb she'd dropped; then I went home and told my wife. She advised me to hold my tongue and not go agin, as I wanted to; so I give it up; but I'm dreadful eager to have another look at the little thing, and I guess you'd find it worth while to try for a sight of her."

"I can see women bathing without that long row, and don't believe Ralph's daughter would care to be disturbed again."

"He ain't got any, sir—neither wife nor child; and no one on the island but him and his mate—a gruff chap that never comes ashore, and don't care for nothin' but keepin' the lantern tidy."

Southesk stood a moment measuring the distance between the main land and the island, with his eye, for Jack's last speech gave an air of mystery to what before had seemed a very simple matter.

"You say Ralph is not fond of having visitors, and rarely leaves the lighthouse; what else do you know about him?" he asked.

"Nothing, sir, only he's a sober, brave, faithful man that does his duty well, and seems to like that bleak, lonesome lighthouse more than most folks would. He's seen better days, I guess, for there's something of the gentleman about him in spite of his rough ways. Now she's ready, sir, and you're just in time to find the little marmaid doin' up her hair."

"I want to visit the light-house, and am fond of adventures, so I think I'll follow your advice. What will you take for this comb, Jack?" asked Southesk, as the old man left his work, and the wherry danced invitingly upon the water.

"Nothing from you, sir; you're welcome to it, for my wife's fretted ever since I had it, and I'm glad to be rid of it. It ain't every one I give it to, or tell about what I saw; but you've done me more'n one good turn, and I'm eager to give you a bit of pleasure to pay for 'em. On the further side of the island you'll find the chasm. It's a dangerous place, but you're a reg'lar fish; so I'll risk you. Good luck, and let me know how you get on."

"What do you suppose the letters stand for?" asked Southesk, as he put the comb in his pocket, and trimmed his boat.

"Why, A. M. stands for a Mermaid; don't it?" answered Jack, soberly.

"I'll find another meaning for them before I come back. Keep your secret, and I'll do the same, for I want the mermaid all to myself."

With a laugh the young man skimmed away, deaf to the voices of the fashionable syrens, who vainly endeavored to detain him, and blind to the wistful glances following the energetic figure that bent to the oars with a strength and skill which soon left the beach and its gay groups far behind.

The light-house was built on the tallest cliff of the island, and the only safe landing place appeared to be at the foot of the rock, whence a precipitous path and an iron ladder led to the main entrance of the tower. Barren and forbidding it looked, even in the glow of the summer sun, and remembering Ralph's dislike of visitors, Southesk resolved to explore the chasm alone, and ask leave of no one. Rowing along the craggy shore he came to the enormous rift that cleft the rocks from top to bottom. Bold and skillful as he was he dared not venture very near, for the tide was coming in, and each advancing billow threatened to sweep the boat into the chasm, where angry waves chafed and foamed, filling the dark hollow with a cloud of spray and reverberating echoes that made a mellow din.

Intent on watching the splendid spectacle he forgot to look for the mermaid, till something white flashed by, and turning with a start he saw a human face rise from the sea, followed by a pair of white arms, that beckoned as the lips smiled and the bright eyes watched him while he sat motionless, till, with a sound of musical laughter, the phantom vanished.

Uttering an exclamation, he was about to follow, when a violent shock made him reel in his seat, and a glance showed him the peril he was in, for the boat had drifted between two rocks; the next wave would shatter it.

The instinct of self-preservation being stronger than curiosity, he pulled for his life and escaped just in time.

Steering into calmer water he took an observation, and decided to land if possible, and search the chasm where the watery sprite or bathing-girl had seemed to take refuge. It was some time, however, before he found any safe harbor, and with much difficulty he at last gained the shore, breathless, wet and weary.

Guided by the noise of the waves he came at length to the brink of the precipice and looked down. There were ledges and crannies enough to afford foothold for a fearless climber, and full of the pleasurable excitement of danger and adventures, Southesk swung himself down with a steady head, strong hand and agile foot. Not many steps were taken when he paused suddenly, for the sound of a voice arrested him. Fitfully it rose and fell through the dash of advancing and retreating billows, but he heard it distinctly, and with redoubled eagerness looked and listened.

Half-way down the chasm lay a mass of rock, firmly wedged between the two sides by some convulsion of nature which had hurled it there. Years had evidently passed since it fell, for a tree had taken root and shot up, fed by a little patch of earth, and sheltered from wind and storm in that secluded spot. Wild vines, led by their instinct for the light, climbed along either wall and draped the cliff with green. Some careful hand had been at work, however, for a few hardy plants blossomed in the almost sunless nook; every niche held a delicate fern, every tiny basin was full of some rare old weed, and here and there a suspended shell contained a tuft of greenish moss, or a bird's eggs, or some curious treasure gathered from the deep. The sombre verdure of the little pine concealed a part of this airy nest, but from the hidden nook the sweet voice rose singing a song well suited to the scene—

"Oh, come unto the yellow sands."

Feeling as if he had stepped into a fairy tale, the young man paused with suspended breath till the last soft note and its softer echo had died away, then he noiselessly crept on. Soon his quick eye discovered a rope ladder, half hidden by the vines and evidently used as a path to the marine bower below. Availing himself of it he descended a few steps, but not far, for a strong gust blew up the rift, and swaying aside the leafy screen disclosed the object of his search. No mermaid but a young girl, sitting and singing like a bird in her green nest.

As the pine waved to and fro, Southesk saw that the unknown sat in a thoughtful attitude, looking out through the wide rift into the sunny blue beyond. He saw, too, that a pair of small, bare feet shone white against the dark bottom of a rocky basin, full of newly fallen rain; that a plain grey gown defined the lithe outlines of a girlish figure, and that the damp dark rings of hair were fastened back with a pretty band of shells.

So intent on looking was he that he leaned nearer and nearer, till a sudden gesture caused the comb to slip from his pocket and fall into the basin with a splash that roused the girl from her reverie. She started, seized it eagerly, and looking upward exclaimed with a joyful accent,

"Why, Stern, where did you find my comb?"

There was no answer to her question, and the smile died on her lips, for instead of Stern's rough, brown countenance she saw, framed in green leaves, a young and comely face.

Blonde and blue-eyed, flushed and eager, the pleasant apparition smiled down upon her with an aspect which brought no fear, but woke wonder and won confidence by the magic of a look. Only a moment did she see it; then the pine boughs came between them. The girl sprang up, and Southesk, forgetting safety in curiosity, leaped down.

He had not measured the distance; his foot slipped and he fell, striking his head with a force that stunned him for a moment. The cool drip of water on his forehead roused him, and he soon collected himself, although somewhat shaken by his fall. Half-opening his eyes he looked into a dark yet brilliant face, of such peculiar beauty that it struck and charmed him at a single glance. Pity, anxiety and alarm were visible in it, and glad of a pretext for prolonging the episode, he resolved to feign the suffering he did not feel. With a sigh he closed his eyes again, and for a moment lay enjoying the soft touch of hands about his head, the sound of a quickly-beating heart near him, and the pleasant consciousness that he was an object of interest to this sweet-voiced unknown. Too generous to keep her long in suspense, he soon raised his head and looked about him, asking faintly,

"Where am I?"

"In the chasm, but quite safe with me," replied a fresh young voice.

"Who is this gentle 'me' whom I mistook for a mermaid, and whose pardon I ask for this rude intrusion?"

"I'm Ariel, and I forgive you willingly."

"Pretty name—is it really yours?" asked Southesk, feeling that his simplest manner was the surest to win her confidence, for the girl spoke with the innocent freedom of a child.

"I have no other, except March, and that is not pretty."

"Then, 'A. M.' on the comb does not mean 'A mermaid,' as old Jack thought when he gave it to me?"

A silvery laugh followed his involuntary smile, as, still kneeling by him, Ariel regarded him with much interest, and a very frank expression of admiration in her beautiful eyes.

"Did you come to bring it back to me?" she asked, turning the recovered treasure in her hand.

"Yes; Jack told me about the pretty water-sprite he saw, so I came to find her, and am not yet sure that you're not a Lorelei, for you nearly wrecked me, and vanished in a most unearthly manner."

"Ah!" she said, with the blithe laugh again, "I lead the life of a mermaid though I'm not one, and when I'm disturbed I play pranks, for I know every cranny of the rocks, and learned swimming and diving from the gulls."

"Flying also, I should think, by the speed with which you reached this nook, for I made all haste, and nearly killed myself, as you see."

As he spoke, Southesk tried to rise, but a sharp twinge in his arm made him pause, with an exclamation of pain.

"Are you much hurt? Can I do anything more for you?" and the voice was womanly pitiful, as the girl watched him.

"I've cut my arm, I think, and lamed my foot; but a little rest will set them right. May I wait here a few minutes, and enjoy your lovely nest; though it's no place for a clumsy mortal like me?"

"Oh, yes; stay as long as you please, and let me bind up your wound. See how it bleeds."

"You are not afraid of me then?"

"No; why should I be?" and the dark eyes looked fearlessly into his as Ariel bent to examine the cut. It was a deep one, and he fancied she would cry out or turn pale; but she did neither, and having skilfully bound a wet handkerchief about it, she glanced from the strong arm and shapely hand to their owner's face, and said, naively,

"What a pity there will be a scar."

Southesk laughed outright, in spite of the smart, and, leaning on the uninjured arm, prepared to enjoy himself, for the lame foot was a fiction.

"Never mind the scar. Men consider them no blemish, and I shall be prouder of this than half a dozen others I have, because by means of it I get a glimpse into fairy land. Do you live here on foam and sunshine, Ariel?"

"No; the lighthouse is my home now."

There was evident reluctance in her manner. She seemed to weigh her words, yet longed to speak out, and it was plain to see that the newcomer was very welcome to her solitude. With all his boldness, Southesk unconsciously tempered his manner with respect, and neither by look nor tone caused any touch of fear to disturb the innocent creature whose retreat he had discovered.

"Then you are Ralph's daughter, as I fancied?" he went on, putting his questions with an engaging air that was hard to resist.

"Yes."

Again she hesitated, and again seemed eager to confide even in a stranger, but controlled the impulse, and gave brief replies to all home questions.

"No one knows you are here, and you seem to lead a hidden life like some enchanted princess. It only needs a Miranda to make a modern version of the Tempest." He spoke half aloud, as if to himself, but the girl answered readily—

"Perhaps I am to lead you to her as the real Ariel led Ferdinand to Miranda, if you've not already found her."

"Why, what do you know of Shakespeare? and how came you by your pretty name?" asked Southesk, wondering at the look and tone which suddenly gave the girl's face an expression of elfish intelligence.

"I know and love Shakespeare better than any of my other books, and can sing every song he wrote. How beautiful they are! See, I have worn out my dear book with much reading."

As she spoke, from a dry nook in the rock she drew a dilapidated volume, and turned its pages with a loving hand, while all the innocent sweetness returned to her young face, lending it new beauty.

"What a charming little sprite it is," thought Southesk, adding aloud, with an irresistible curiosity that banished politeness,

"And the name, how came that?"

"Father gave it to me." There she paused, adding hastily, "He loves Shakespeare as well as I do, and taught me to understand him."

"Here's a romantic pair, and a mystery of some sort, which I'll amuse myself by unraveling, if possible," he thought, and put another question—"Have you been here long?"

"No; I only spend the hot hours here."

"Another evasion. I shall certainly be driven into asking her, point blank, who and what she is," said Southesk to himself, and, to avoid temptation, returned to the comb which Ariel still held.

"Who carved that so daintily? I should like to bespeak one for myself it is so pretty."

"I carved it, and was very happy at my work. It's hard to find amusement on this barren island, so I invent all sorts of things to while away the time."

"Did you invent this hanging garden and make this wilderness blossom?" asked Southesk, trying the while to understand the lights and shadows that made her face as changeful as an April sky.

"Yes; I did it, and spend half my time here, for here I escape seeing people on the beach, and so forget them."

A little sigh followed, and her eyes turned wistfully to the dark rift, that gave her but a glimpse of the outer world.

"You can scarcely see the beach, much less the people on it, I should think," said Southesk, wondering what she meant.

"I can see well with the telescope from the tower, and often watch the people on the shore—they look so gay and pretty."

"Then, why wish to forget them?"

"Because since they came it is more lonely than before."

"Do you never visit the mainland? Have you no friends or companions to enliven your solitude?"

"No."

Something in the tone in which the monosyllable was uttered checked further inquiries, and prompted him to say smilingly:

"Now it is your turn; ask what you will."

But Ariel drew back, answering with an air of demure propriety that surprised him more than her self-possession or her rebuke.

"No, thank you, it is ill-bred to question strangers."

Southesk colored at the satirical glance she gave him, and rising, he made his most courtly bow, saying, with a pleasant mixture of candor and contrition:

"Again I beg pardon for my rudeness. Coming so suddenly upon a spirit singing to itself between sea and sky, I forgot myself, and fancied the world's ways out of place. Now I see my mistake, and though it spoils the romance, I will call you Miss March, and respectfully take my leave."

The silvery laugh broke in on the last sentence, and in her simplest manner Ariel replied:

"No, don't call me that nor go away, unless you are quite out of pain. I like your rudeness better than your politeness, for it made you seem like a pleasant boy, and now you are nothing but a fine gentleman."

Both amused and relieved by her reply, he answered, half in jest, half in earnest,

"Then, I'll be a boy again, and tell you who I am, as you are too well bred to ask, and it is but proper to introduce myself. Philip Southesk by name, gentleman by birth, poet by profession; but I don't deserve the title, though certain friendly persons do me the honor to praise a few verses I once wrote. Stay, I forgot two things that ladies usually take an interest in. Fortune ample—age four-and-twenty."

"You did not ask me either of these two questions," said Ariel, with a flicker of merriment in her eyes, as she glanced up rather shyly at the would-be boy, who now stood straight and tall before her.

"No; even in the midst of my delusion I remembered that one never ventures to put the last of those questions to a woman—the first I cared nothing about."

"I like that," said the girl in her quick way, adding frankly, "I am poor, and seventeen."

She half rose as she spoke, but hastily sat down again, recollecting her bare feet. The change of color, and an anxious look toward a pair of little shoes that lay near by, suggested to Southesk a speedy withdrawal, and, turning toward the half-hidden ladder, he said, lingering in the act of going:

"Good-by; may I come again, if I come properly, and do not stay too long? Poets are privileged persons, you know, and this is a poet's paradise."

She looked pleased, yet troubled, and answered reluctantly:

"You are very kind to say so, but I cannot ask you to come again, for father would be displeased, and it is best for me to go on as before."

"But why hide yourself here? Why not enjoy the pleasures fitting for your age, instead of watching them afar off, and vainly longing for them?" exclaimed Southesk, impetuously, for the eloquent eyes betrayed what the tongue would not confess.

"I cannot tell you."

As she spoke her head was bowed upon her hands, her abundant hair veiled her face, and as it fell the little chaplet of shells dropped at Southesk's feet.

"Forgive me; I have no right to question you, and will not disturb your solitude again, unless your father is willing. But give me some token to prove that I have really visited an enchanted island, and heard Ariel sing. I returned the comb, may I have this in exchange?"

He spoke playfully, hoping to win a smile of pardon for his last trespass. She looked up quite calm again, and freely gave him the chain of shells for which he asked. Then he sprang up the precipitous path, and went his way, but his parting glance showed him the fair face still wistfully watching him from the green gloom of Ariel's nest.

PART II

IN THE LOWER ROOM of the lighthouse sat three persons, each apparently busy with his own thoughts, yet each covertly watching the others. Ralph March, a stern, dark-browed, melancholy-looking man, leaned back in his chair, with one hand above his eyes, which were fixed on Ariel, who sat near the narrow window cut in the thick wall, often gazing out upon the sea, glowing with the gold and purple of a sunset sky, but oftener stealing a glance toward her father, as if she longed to speak yet dared not. The third occupant of the room was a rough, sturdy-looking man, whose age it was hard to discover, for an unsightly hump disfigured his broad shoulders, and a massive head was set upon a stunted body. Shaggy-haired, tawny-bearded and bronzed by wind and weather he was a striking, not a pitiful figure, for his herculean strength was visible at a glance, and a somewhat defiant expression seemed to repel compassion and command respect. Sitting in the doorway, he appeared to be intent on mending a torn net, but his keen eye went stealthily from father to daughter, as if trying to read their faces. The long silence that had filled the room was broken by March's deep voice, saying suddenly, as he dropped his hand and turned to Ariel:

"Are you sick or sad, child, that you sigh so heavily?"

"I'm lonely, father."

Something in the plaintive tone and drooping figure touched March's heart, and, drawing the girl to his knee, he looked into her face with a tender anxiety that softened and beautified his own.

"What can I do for you, dear? Where shall I take you to make you forget your loneliness? —or whom shall I bring here to enliven you?"

Her eyes woke and her lips parted eagerly, as if a wish was ready, but some fear restrained its utterance, and, half averting her face, she answered meekly:

"I ought to be contented with you, and I try to be, but sometimes I long to do as others do, and enjoy my youth while it lasts. If you liked to mingle with people I should love to try it; as you do not, I'll endeavor to be happy where I am."

"Poor child, it is but natural, and I am selfish to make a recluse of you, because I hate the world. Shall we leave the island and begin our wandering life again?"

"Oh, no; I like the island now, and could be quite contented if I had a young companion. I never have had, and did not know how pleasant it was until two days ago."

Her eyes turned toward the open door, through which the Gull's Perch was visible, with the chasm yawning near it, and again she sighed. March saw where she looked; a frown began to gather, but some gentler emotion checked his anger, and with a sudden smile he said, stroking her smooth cheek:

"Now I know the wish you would not tell, the cause of your daily watch from the tower, and the secret of these frequent sighs. Silly child, you want young Southesk to return, yet dare not ask me to permit it."

Ariel turned her face freely to his, and leaning confidingly upon his shoulder, answered with the frankness he had taught her.

"I do wish he'd come again, and I think I deserve some reward for telling you all that happened, for bidding him go away, and for being so careful what I said."

"Hard tasks, I know, especially the last, for such an open creature as my girl. Well, you shall be rewarded, and if he come again you may see him, and so will I."

"Oh, thank you, father, that is so kind. But you look as if you thought he would not come."

"I am afraid he has already forgotten all about the lonely island and the little bare-footed maiden he saw on it. Young men's memories are treacherous things, and curiosity once gratified, soon dies."

But Ariel shook her head, as if refusing to accept the ungracious thought, and surprised her father by the knowledge of human nature which she seemed to have learned by instinct, for she answered gravely, yet hopefully:

"I think he *will* come, simply because I forbade it. He is a poet, and cares for things that have no charm for other men. He liked my nest, he liked to hear me sing, and his curiosity was not gratified, because I only told enough to make him eager for more. I have a feeling that he will come again, to find that the island is not always lonely, nor the girl always barefooted."

Her old blithe laugh broke out again as she glanced from the little mirror that reflected the glossy waves of her hair, bound with a band of rosy coral, to the well-shod feet that peeped from below the white hem of her gown. Her father watched her fondly, as she swept him a stately curtsey, looking so gay and lovely that he could not but smile and hope her wish might be granted.

"Little vanity," he said, "who taught you to make yourself so bonny, and where did you learn these airs and graces? Not from Stern or me, I fancy."

"Ah, I have not looked through the telescope and watched the fine ladies in vain, it seems, since you observe the change. I study fashion and manners at a disadvantage, but I am an apt scholar, I find. Now I'm going up to watch and wait for my reward."

As she ran up the winding-stairs that led to the great lantern, and the circular balcony that hung outside, Stern said, with the freedom of one privileged to speak his mind:

"The girl is right; the boy will come again, and mischief will grow out of it."

"What mischief?" demanded March.

"Do you suppose he can see her often and not love her?" returned Stern, almost angrily.

"Let him love her."

"Do you mean it? After hiding her so carefully, will you let her be won by this romantic boy, if his fancy last? You are making a false step, and you'll repent of it."

"I have already made a false step, and I do repent of it; but it's not this one. I have tried to keep Ariel a child, and she was happy until she became a woman. Now the old simple life is not enough for her, and her heart craves its right. I live only for her, and if her happiness demands the sacrifice of the seclusion I love, I shall make it—shall welcome anyone who can give her pleasure, and promote any scheme that spares her from the melancholy that curses me."

"Then you are resolved to let this young man come if he choose, and allow her to love him, as she most assuredly will?"

"Yes, chance brought him here at first, and if inclination brings him again let it be so. I have made inquiries concerning him, and am satisfied. He is Ariel's equal in birth, is fitted to make her happy, and has already wakened an unusual interest in her mind. Sooner or later I must leave her; she is alone in the world, and to whom can I confide her so safely as to a husband."

A dark flush had passed over Stern's face as he listened, and more than once impetuous words seemed to have risen to his lips, to be restrained by set teeth and an emotion of despair.

March saw this, and it seemed to confirm his purpose, though he made no comment on it, and abruptly closed the conversation; for, as Stern began—

"I warn you, sir—" he interrupted him, saying with decision:

"No more of this; I have had other warnings than yours, and must listen to them, for the time is not far distant when I must leave the child alone, unless I give her a guardian soon. Wild as my plan may seem, it is far safer than to take her into the world, for here I can observe this young man, and shape her future as I will. You mean kindly, Stern, but you cannot judge for me nor understand my girl as I do. Now, leave me, I must go and rest."

Stern's black eyes glowed with an ireful spark, and he clenched his strong hands as if to force himself to silence, as he went without a word, while March passed into an inner room, with the melancholy expression deeper than ever on his face.

For a few moments the deserted room was silent and solitary, but presently a long shadow fell athwart the sunny floor, and Southesk stood in the open doorway, with a portfolio and a carefully folded parcel underneath his arm. Pausing to look about him for someone to address, the sound of Ariel's voice reached his ear, and, as if no other welcome were needed, he followed it as eagerly as before. Stealing up the steep stairs, he came into the many-windowed tower, and on the balcony saw Ariel straining her eyes through a telescope, which was pointed toward the beach he had left an hour ago. As he lingered, uncertain how to accost her, she dropped the glass, exclaiming with a sigh of weariness and disappointment:

"No, he is not there!" In the act she turned, saw him, and uttered a little cry of delight, while her face brightened beautifully as she sprang forward, offering her hand with a gesture as graceful as impulsive, saying joyfully—

"I knew you would come again!"

Well pleased at such a cordial welcome, he took the hand, and still holding it, asked in that persuasive voice of his—

"For whom were you looking, Ariel?"

She colored, and turned her traitorous eyes away, yet answered with an expression of merry mischief that was very charming—

"I looked for Ferdinand!"

"And here he is," replied Southesk, laughing at her girlish evasion. "Though you forbade my return, I was obliged to break my promise, because I unconsciously incurred a debt which I wish to discharge. When I asked you for those pretty shells I did not observe that they were strung on a little gold chain, and afterward it troubled me to think I had taken a gift of value. Much as I want to keep it, I shall not like to do so unless you will let me make some return for that, and for the hospitality you showed me. May I offer you this, with many thanks?"

While speaking rapidly, he had undone the parcel, and put into her hands a beautiful volume of Shakespeare, daintily bound, richly illustrated, and bearing on the fly-leaf a graceful little poem to herself. So touched and delighted was she that she stood silent, reading the musical lines, glancing at the pictured pages, and trying to summon words expressive enough to convey her thanks. None came that suited her, but her eyes filled, and she exclaimed with a grateful warmth that well repaid the giver:

"It is too beautiful for me, and you are too kind! How did you know I wanted a new book, and would have chosen one like this?"

"I am glad I guessed so well, and now consider the mermaid's rosary my own. But tell me, did you ask if I might come again, or did you leave it to me?"

"I tell my father everything, and when I spoke of you again today, much to my surprise, he said you might come if you chose. But he added that you'd probably forgotten all about the island by this time."

"And you knew I had not—thank you for that. No; so far from forgetting, I've dreamed about it ever since, and should have returned before had not my arm been too lame for rowing, and I would not bring any intruder but myself. I want to sketch your nest, for some day it will get into verse, and I wish to keep it fresh before me. May I?"

"I shall be very proud to see it drawn, and to read the poem if it is as sweet as this. I think I like your songs better than Shakespeare's."

"What a compliment! It is I who am proud now. How beautiful it is up here; one feels like a bird on this airy perch. Tell me what those places are that look so like celestial cities in this magical light?"

Willingly she obeyed, and standing at her side he listened, feeling the old enchantment creep over him as he watched the girl, who seemed to glow and brighten like a flower at the coming of the sun. Nor did the charm lie in her beauty alone; language, mien, and manner betrayed the native refinement which comes from birth and breeding, and, despite her simple dress, her frank ways, and the mystery that surrounded her, Southesk felt that this lighthouse-keeper's daughter was a gentlewoman, and every moment grew more interested in her.

Presently he professed a desire to sketch a picturesque promontory not far distant; and, seated on the step of the narrow door, he drew industriously, glancing up now and then at Ariel, who leaned on the balustrade turning the pages of her book with her loveliest expression, as she read a line here and there, sung snatches of the airs she loved so well, and paused to talk, for her companion wasted little time in silence. Place, hour, and society suited him to a charm, and he luxuriated in the romance and the freedom, both being much enhanced by the strong contrast between this hour and those he had been spending among the frivolous crowds at the great hotel. He took no thought for the future but heartily enjoyed the present, and was in his gayest, most engaging mood as he feasted his eyes on the beauty all about him while endeavoring to copy the graceful figure and spirited face before him.

Quite unconscious of his purpose she pored over the book, and presently exclaimed, as she opened on a fine illustration of the Tempest—

"Here we all are! Prospero is not unlike my father, but Ferdinand is much plainer than you. Here's Ariel swinging in a vine, as I've often done, and Caliban watching her as Stern watches me. He is horrible here, however, and my Caliban has a fine face, if one can get a sight of it when he is in good humor."

"You mean the deformed man who glowered at me as I landed? I want much to know who he is, but I dare not ask, lest I get another lesson in good manners," said Southesk, with an air of timidity belied by his bold, bright eyes.

"I'll tell you without asking. He is the lighthouse-keeper, for my father only helps him a little, because he likes the wild life. People call him the master, as he goes to the mainland for all we need instead of Stern, who hates to be seen, poor soul."

"Thank you," returned Southesk, longing to ask more questions, and on the alert for any hint that might enlighten him regarding this peculiar pair.

Ariel went back to her book, smiling to herself, as she said, after a long look at one figure in the pictured group—

"This Miranda is very charming, but not so queenly as yours."

"Mine!" ejaculated Southesk, with as much amusement as surprise. "How do you know I have one?"

"She came here to look for you," stealing a glance at him from under her long lashes.

"The deuce, she did! When—how? Tell me about it, for, upon my honor, I don't know who you mean," and Southesk put down his pencil to listen.

"Yesterday a boatman rowed a lady down here, and though the steep path and the ladder rather daunted her at first, she climbed up, and asked to see the lighthouse. Stern showed it, but she was not soon satisfied, and peered about as if bent on searching every corner. She asked many questions, and examined the book for visitors' names, which hangs below. Yours was not there, but she seemed to suspect that you had been here, and Stern told her that it was so. It was not like him, but he was unusually gracious, though he said nothing about father and myself, and when she had roamed up and down for a long time, the lady went away."

"Was she tall and dark, with fine eyes and a proud air?" asked Southesk, with a frown.

"Yes; but I thought she could be very sweet and gentle when she chose, she changed so as she spoke of you."

"Did she see you, Ariel?"

"No; I ran away and hid, as I always do when strangers come; but I saw her, and longed to know her name, for she would not give it, so I called her your Miranda."

"Not she! Her name is Helen Lawrence, and I wish she was—" He checked himself, looking much annoyed, yet ashamed of his petulant tone, and added, with a somewhat disdainful smile—"less inquisitive. She must have come while I was in the city searching for your book, but she never breathed a word of it to me. I shall feel like a fly in a cobweb if she keeps such close watch over me."

"Why did she think you had been here? Did you tell her?" asked Ariel, looking as if she quite understood Miss Lawrence's motive in coming, and rather enjoyed her disappointment.

"That puppy, Dr. Haye, who dressed my arm, and found your handkerchief on it, made a story out of nothing, and set the gossips chattering. The women over yonder have nothing else to do, so a fine romance was built up, founded on the wounded arm, the little handkerchief, and the pretty chain, of which Haye caught a glimpse. Miss Lawrence must have bribed old Jack to tell her where I'd been, for I told no one, and stole off to-day so carefully that I defy them to track me here."

"Thank you for remembering that we did not wish to be disturbed; but I am sorry that you have been annoyed, and hope this handsome Helen will not come again. You think her handsome, don't you?" asked the girl, in the demure tone that she sometimes used with much effect.

"Yes; but she is not to my taste. I like spirit, character, and variety of expression in a face more than mere beauty of coloring or outline. One doesn't see faces like hers in one's dreams, or imagine it at one's fireside; it is a fine picture—not the image of the woman one would live and die for."

A soft color had risen to Ariel's cheek as she listened, wondering why those few words sounded so sweet to her. Southesk caught the fleeting emotion, and made the likeness perfect with a happy stroke or two. Pausing to survey his work with pleasure, he said low to himself—

"What more does it need?"

"Nothing—it is excellent."

The paper fluttered from his hand as a man's voice answered, and turning quickly, he saw March standing behind him. He knew who it was at once, for several times he had passed on the beach this roughly-dressed, stern-faced man, who came and went as if blind to the gaiety all about him. Now, the change in him would have greatly surprised his guest had not his interviews with Ariel prepared him for the discovery, and when March greeted him with the air and manner of a gentleman, he betrayed no astonishment, but, giving his name, repeated his desire to sketch the beauties of the island, and asked permission to do so. A satirical smile passed over March's grave face, as he glanced from the paper he had picked up to the bare cliffs below, but his tone was very courteous as he replied—

"I have no right to forbid any one to visit the island, though its solitude was the attraction that brought me here. But poets and painters are privileged; so come freely, and if your pen and pencil make it too famous for us we can emigrate to a more secluded spot, for we are only birds of passage."

"There shall be no need of that, I assure you, sir. Its solitude is as attractive to me as to yourself, and no word or act of mine shall destroy the charm." Southesk spoke eagerly, adding, with a longing glance at the paper which March still held: "I ventured to begin with the island's mistress, and, with your permission, I will finish it as you pronounce it good."

"It is excellent, and I shall be glad to bespeak a copy, for I've often tried to sketch my will-o'-the-wisp, but never succeeded. What magic did you use to keep her still so long?"

"This, father," and Ariel showed her gift, as she came to look over his shoulder, and smile and blush to see herself so carefully portrayed.

Southesk explained, and the conversation turning upon poetry, glided smoothly on till the deepening twilight warned the guest to go, and more than ever charmed and interested, he floated homeward to find Miss Lawrence waiting for him on the beach, and to pass her with his coolest salutation.

From that day he led a double life—one gay and frivolous for all the world to see, the other sweet and secret as a lover's first romance. Hiring a room at a fisherman's cottage that stood in a lonely nook, and giving out that he was seized with a fit of inspiration, he secluded himself whenever he chose, without exciting comment or curiosity. Having purchased the old couple's silence regarding his movements, he came and went with perfect freedom, and passers-by surveyed with respectful interest the drawn curtains behind which the young poet was believed to be intent on songs and sonnets, while, in reality, he was living a sweeter poem than any he could write far away on the lighthouse tower, or hidden in the shadowy depths of Ariel's nest. Even Helen was deceived, for, knowing that hers were the keenest eyes upon him, he effectually blinded them for the time by slowly changing his former indifference to the gallant devotion which may mean much or little, yet which is always flattering to a woman, and doubly so to one who loves and waits for a return. Her society was more agreeable to him than that of the giddy girls and *blasé* men about him, and believing that the belle of several seasons could easily guard the heart that many had besieged, he freely enjoyed the intercourse which their summer sojourn facilitated, all unconscious of the hopes and fears that made those days the most eventful of her life.

Stern was right; the young man could not see Ariel without loving her. For years, he had roamed about the world, heart-free; but his time came at last, and he surrendered without a struggle. For a few weeks he lived in an enchanted world, too happy to weigh consequences or dread disappointment. There was no cause for doubt or fear—no need to plead for love—because the artless girl gave him her heart as freely as a little child, and reading the language of his eyes, answered eloquently with her own. It was a poet's wooing; summer, romance, beauty, innocence and youth—all lent their charms, and nothing marred its delight. March watched and waited hopefully, well pleased at the success of his desire; and seeing in the young man the future guardian of his child, soon learned to love him for his own sake as well as hers. Stern was the only cloud in all this sunshine; he preserved a grim silence, and seemed to take no heed of what went on about him; but, could the cliffs have spoken, they might have told pathetic secrets of the lonely man who haunted them by night, like a despairing ghost; and the sea might have betrayed how many tears, bitter as its own billows, had been wrung from a strong heart that loved, yet knew that the passion never could be returned.

The mystery that seemed at first to surround them no longer troubled him, for a few words from March satisfied him that sorrow and misfortune made them seek solitude, and shun the scenes where they had suffered most. A prudent man would have asked more, but Southesk cared nothing for wealth or rank, and with the delicacy of a generous nature, feared to wound by questioning too closely. Ariel loved him; he had enough for all, and the present was too blissful to permit any doubt of the past—any fears for the future.

So the summer days rolled on, sunny and serene, as if tempests were unknown, and brought, at last, the hour when Southesk longed to claim Ariel for his own, and show the world the treasure he had found.

Full of this purpose, he went to his tryst one golden August afternoon, intent on seeing March first, that he might go to Ariel armed with her father's consent. But March was out upon the sea, where he often floated aimlessly for hours, and Southesk found no one but Stern, busily burnishing the great reflectors until they shone again.

"Where is Ariel?" was the young man's second question, though usually it was the first.

"Why ask me, when you know better than I where to find her," Stern answered harshly, as he frowned over the bright mirror that reflected both his own and the happy lover's face; and too lighthearted to resent a rude speech, Southesk went smiling away to find the girl, waiting for him in the chasm.

"What pretty piece of work is in hand, to-day, busy creature?" he said, as he threw himself down beside her with an air of supreme content.

"I'm stringing these for you, because you carry the others so constantly they will soon be worn out," she answered, busying herself with a redoubled assiduity, for something in his manner made her heart beat fast and her color vary. He saw it, and fearing to agitate her by abruptly uttering the ardent words that trembled on his lips, he said nothing for a moment, but leaning on his arm, looked at her with lover's eyes, till Ariel, finding silence more dangerous than speech, said hastily, as she glanced at a ring on the hand that was idly playing with the many-colored shells that strewed her lap:

"This is a curious old jewel; are those your initials on it?"

"No, my father's;" and he held it up for her to see.

"R. M., where is the S. for Southesk?" she asked, examining it with girlish curiosity.

"I shall have to tell you a little story all about myself in order to explain that. Do you care to hear it?"

"Yes, your stories are always pleasant; tell it, please."

"Then, you must know that I was born on the long voyage to India, and nearly died immediately after. The ship was wrecked, and my father and mother were lost; but, by some miracle, my faithful nurse and I were saved. Having no near relatives in the world, an old friend of my father's adopted me, reared me tenderly, and dying, left me his name and fortune."

"Philip Southesk is not your true name, then?"

"No; I took it at my good old friend's desire. But you shall choose which name you will bear, when you let me put a more precious ring than this on the dear little hand I came to ask you for. Will you marry Philip Southesk or Richard Marston, my Ariel?"

If she had leaped down into the chasm the act would not have amazed him more than the demonstration which followed these playful, yet tender words. A stifled exclamation broke from her, all the color died out of her face, in her eyes grief deepened to despair, and when he approached her she shrunk from him with a gesture of repulsion that cut him to the heart.

"What is it? Are you ill? How have I offended you? Tell me, my darling, and let me make my peace at any cost," he cried, bewildered by the sudden and entire change that had passed over her.

"No, no; it is impossible. You must not call me that. I must not listen to you. Go—go at once, and never come again. Oh, why did I not know this sooner?" and, covering up her face, she burst into a passion of tears.

"How could you help knowing that I loved you when I showed it so plainly—it seemed hardly necessary to put it into words. Why do you shrink from me with such abhorrence? Explain this strange change, Ariel. I have a right to ask it," he demanded distressfully.

"I can explain nothing till I have seen my father. Forgive me. This is harder for me to hear than it ever can be for you," she answered through her grief, and in her voice there was the tenderest regret, as well as the firmest resolution.

"You do not need your father to help you. Answer whether you love me, and that is all I ask. Speak, I conjure you." He took her hands and made her look at him. There was no room for doubt; one look assured him, for her heart spoke in her eyes before she answered, fervently as a woman, simply as a child:

"I love you more than I can ever tell."

"Then, why this grief and terror? What have I said to trouble you? Tell me that, also, and I am content."

He had drawn her toward him as the sweet confession left her lips, and was already smiling with the happiness it gave him; but Ariel banished both smile and joy by breaking from his hold, pale and steady as if tears had calmed and strengthened her, saying, in a tone that made his heart sink with an ominous foreboding of some unknown ill:

"I must not answer you without my father's permission. I have made a bitter mistake in loving you, and I must amend it if I can. Go now, and come again to-morrow; then I can speak and make all clear to you. No, do not tempt me with caresses; do not break my heart with reproaches, but obey me, and whatever comes between us, oh, remember that I shall love you while I live."

Vain were all his prayers and pleadings, questions and commands: some power more potent than love kept her firm through the suffering and sorrow of that hour. At last he yielded to her demand, and winning from her a promise to set his heart at rest early on the morrow, he tore himself away, distracted by a thousand vague doubts and dreads.

PART III

A SLEEPLESS NIGHT, an hour or two of restless pacing to and fro upon the beach, then the impatient lover was away upon his fateful errand, careless of observation now, and rowing as he had never rowed before. The rosy flush of early day shone over the island, making the grim rocks beautiful, and Southesk saw in it a propitious omen; but when he reached the lighthouse a sudden fear dashed his sanguine hopes, for it was empty. The door stood open—no fire burned upon the hearth, no step sounded on the stairs, no voice answered when he called, and the dead silence daunted him.

Rapidly searching every chamber, shouting each name, and imploring a reply, he hurried up and down like one distraught, till but a single hope remained to comfort him. Ariel might be waiting at the chasm, though she had bid him see her father first. Bounding over the cliffs, he reached the dearest spot the earth held for him, and looking down saw only desolation. The ladder was gone, the vines torn from the walls, the little tree lay prostrate; every green and lovely thing was crushed under the enormous stones that some ruthless hand had hurled upon them, and all the beauty of the rock was utterly destroyed as if a hurricane had swept over it.

"Great heavens! who has done this?"

"I did."

Stern spoke, and standing on the opposite side of the chasm, regarded Southesk with an expression of mingled exultation, hatred, and defiance, as if the emotions which had been so long restrained had found a vent at last.

"But why destroy what Ariel loved?" demanded the young man, involuntarily retreating a step from the fierce figure that confronted him.

"Because she has done with it, and no other shall enjoy what she has lost."

"Done with it," echoed Southesk, forgetting everything but the fear that oppressed him. "What do you mean? Where is she? For God's sake end this horrible suspense."

"She is gone, never to return," and as he answered Stern smiled a smile of bitter satisfaction in the blow he was dealing the man he hated.

"Where is March?"

"Gone with her."

"Where are they gone?"

"I will never tell you."

"When did they go, and why? Oh! answer me!"

"At dawn, and to shun you."

"But why let me come for weeks and then fly me as if I brought a curse with me?"

"Because you are what you are."

Questions and answers had been too rapidly exchanged to leave time for anything but intense amazement and anxiety. Stern's last words arrested Southesk's impetuous inquiries and he stood a moment trying to comprehend that enigmatical reply. Suddenly he found a clue, for in recalling his last interview with Ariel, he remembered that for the first time he had told her his father's name. The mystery was there—that intelligence, and not the avowal of his love, was the cause of her strange agitation, and some unknown act of the father's was now darkening the son's life. These thoughts flashed through his mind in the drawing of a breath, and with them came the recollection of Ariel's promise to answer him.

Lifting the head that had sunk upon his breast, as if this stroke fell heavily, he stretched his hands imploringly to Stern, exclaiming:

"Did she leave no explanation for me, no word of comfort, no farewell? Oh! be generous, and pity me; give me her message and I will go away, never to disturb you any more."

"She bade me tell you that she obeyed her father, but her heart was yours forever, and she left you this."

With a strong effort at self-control, Stern gave the message, and slowly drew from his breast a little parcel, which he flung across the chasm. It fell at Southesk's feet, and tearing it open a long, dark lock of hair coiled about his fingers with a soft caressing touch, reminding him so tenderly of his lost love, that for a moment he forgot his manhood, and covering up his face, cried in a broken voice:

"Oh! Ariel, come back to me—come back to me!"

"She will never come back to you; so cast yourself down among the ruins yonder, and lament the ending of your love dream, like a romantic boy, as you are."

The taunting speech, and the scornful laugh that followed it calmed Southesk better than the gentlest pity. Dashing away the drops he turned on Stern with a look that showed it was fortunate the chasm parted the two men, and answered in a tone of indomitable resolve:

"No, I shall not lament, but find and claim her as my own, even if I search the world till I am grey, and a thousand obstacles be between us. I leave the ruins and the tears to you, for I am rich in hope and Ariel's love."

Then they parted, Southesk full of the energy of youth, and a lover's faith in friendly fortune, sprang down the cliffs, and shot away across the glittering bay on his long search, but Stern, with despair for his sole companion, flung himself on the hard bosom of the rocks, struggling to accept the double desolation which came upon his life.

"An early row and an early ride without a moment's rest between. Why, Mr. Southesk, we shall not dare to call you *dolce far niente* any more," began Miss Lawrence, as she came rustling out upon the wide piazza, fresh from her morning toilette, to find Southesk preparing to mount his fleetest horse; but as he turned to bow silently the smile vanished from her lips, and a keen anxiety banished the gracious sweetness from her face.

"Good heavens, what has happened?" she cried, forgetting her self-betrayal in alarm at the haggard countenance she saw.

"I have lost a very precious treasure, and I am going to find it. Adieu;" and he was gone without another word.

Miss Lawrence was alone, for the gong had emptied halls and promenades of all but herself, and she had lingered to caress the handsome horse till its master came. Her eye followed the reckless rider until he vanished, and as it came back to the spot where she had caught that one glimpse of his altered face, it fell upon a little case of curiously-carved and scented Indian wood. She took it up, wondering that she had not seen it fall from his pocket as he mounted, for she knew it to be his, and opening it, found the key to his variable moods and frequent absences of late. The string of shells appeared first, and, examining it with a woman's scrutiny, she found letters carved on the inside of each. Ten rosy shells—ten delicate letters, making the name Ariel March. A folded paper came next, evidently a design for a miniature to form a locket for the pretty chain, for in the small oval, drawn with all a lover's skill, was a young girl's face, and underneath, in Southesk's hand, as if written for his eye alone, the words, "My Ariel." A long, dark lock of hair, and a little knot of dead flowers were all the case held beside.

"This is the mermaid old Jack told me of, this is the muse Southesk has been wooing, and this is the lost treasure he has gone to find."

As she spoke low to herself, Helen made a passionate gesture as if she would tear and trample on the relics of this secret love, but some hope or purpose checked her, and concealing the case, she turned to hide her trouble in solitude, thinking as she went:

"He will return for this, till then I must wait."

But Southesk did not return, for the lesser loss was forgotten in the greater, and he was wandering over land and sea, intent upon a fruitless quest. Summer passed, and Helen returned to town still hoping and waiting with a woman's patience for some tidings of the absentee.

Rumor gossiped much about the young poet—the eccentricities of genius—and prophesied an immortal work as the fruit of such varied and incessant travel.

But Helen knew the secret of his restlessness, and while she pitied his perpetual disappointment she rejoiced over it, sustaining herself with the belief that a time would come when he would weary of this vain search, and let her comfort him. It did come; for, late in the season, when winter gaieties were nearly over, Southesk returned to his old haunts, so changed that curiosity went hand in hand with sympathy.

He gave no reason for it but past illness; yet it was plain to see the malady of his mind. Listless, taciturn, and cold, with no trace of his former energy except a curiously vigilant expression of the eye and a stern folding of the lips, as if he was perpetually looking for something and perpetually meeting with disappointment. This was the change which had befallen the once gay and *debonair* Philip Southesk.

Helen Lawrence was among the first to hear of his return, and to welcome him, for, much to her surprise, he came to see her on the second day, drawn by the tender recollections of a past with which she was associated.

Full of the deepest joy at beholding him again, and the gentlest pity for his dejection, Helen had never been more charming than during that interview.

Eager to assure herself of the failure which his face betrayed, she soon inquired, with an air and accent of the friendliest interest:

"Was your search successful, Mr. Southesk? You left so suddenly, and have been so long away I hoped the treasure had been found, and that you had been busy putting that happy summer into song for us."

The color rose to Southesk's forehead, and fading left him paler than before, as he answered with a vain attempt at calmness.

"I shall never find the thing I lost, and never put that summer into song, for it was the saddest of my life;" then, as if anxious to change the direction of her thoughts, he said abruptly, "I am on another quest now, looking for a little case which I think I dropped the day I left you, but whether at the hotel or on the road I cannot tell. Did you hear anything of such a trifle being found?"

"No. Was it of much value to you?"

"Of infinite value now, for it contains the relics of a dear friend lately lost."

Helen had meant to keep what she had found, but his last words changed her purpose, for a thrill of hope shot through her heart, and, turning to a cabinet behind her, she put the case into his hand, saying in her softest tone:

"I heard nothing of it because I found it, believed it to be yours, and kept it sacred until you came to claim it, for I did not know where to find you."

Then, with a woman's tact, she left him to examine his recovered treasure, and, gliding to an inner room, she busied herself among her flowers till he rejoined her.

Sooner than she had dared to hope he came, with signs of past emotion on his face, but much of his old impetuosity of manner, as he pressed her hand, saying warmly:

"How can I thank you for this? Let me atone for my past insincerity by confessing the cause of it; you have found a part of my secret, let me add the rest. I need a confidant, will you be mine?"

"Gladly, if it will help or comfort you."

So, sitting side by side under the passion flowers, he told his story, and she listened with an interest that insensibly drew him on to further confidences than he had intended.

When he had described the parting, briefly yet very eloquently, for voice, eye, and gesture lent their magic, he added, in an altered tone, and with an expression of pathetic patience:

"There is no need to tell you how I searched for them, how often I thought myself upon their track, how often they eluded me, and how each disappointment strengthened my purpose to look till I succeeded, though I gave years to the task. A month ago I received this, and knew that my long search was ended."

He put a worn letter into her hand, and with a beating heart Helen read:

> "*Ariel is dead. Let her rest in peace, and do not pursue me any longer, unless you would drive me into my grave as you have driven her.*
>
> *Ralph March.*"

A little paper, more worn and stained than the other, dropped from the letter as Helen unfolded it, and seeing a woman's writing, she asked no permission, but read it eagerly, while Southesk sat with hidden face, unaware that he had given her that sacred farewell.

"Good-by, good-by," it said, in hastily-written letters, blurred by tears that had fallen long ago. "I have obeyed my father to the last, but my heart is yours for ever. Believe this, and pray, as I do, that you may meet again your Ariel."

A long silence followed, for the simple little note had touched Helen deeply, and while she could not but rejoice in the hope which this discovery gave her, she was too womanly a woman not to pity the poor child who had loved and lost the heart she coveted. As she gently laid the letter back in Southesk's hand, she asked, turning her full eyes on his,

"Are you sure that this is true?"

"I cannot doubt it, for I recognise the writing of both, and I know that neither would lend themselves to a fraud like this. No; I must accept the hard truth, and bear it as I can. My own heart confirms it, for every hope dies when I try to revive it, and the sad belief remains unshaken" was the spiritless reply.

Helen turned her face away, to hide the passionate joy that glowed in it; then, veiling her emotion with the tenderest sympathy, she gave herself up to the sweet task of comforting the bereaved lover. So well did she perform her part, so soothing did he find her friendly society, that he came often and lingered long, for with her, and her alone, he could talk of Ariel. She never checked him, but listened to the distasteful theme with unwearied patience, till, by insensible degrees and unperceived allurements, she weaned him from these mournful reminiscences, and woke a healthier interest in the present. With feminine skill she concealed her steadily increasing love under an affectionate friendliness, which seemed a mute assurance that she cherished no hopes for herself, but knew that his heart was still Ariel's. This gave him confidence in her, while the new and gentle womanliness which now replaced her former pride, made her more attractive and more dangerous. Of course, the gossips gave them to one another, and Southesk felt aggrieved, fearing that he must relinquish the chief comfort of his solitary life. But Helen showed such supreme indifference to the clack of idle tongues, and met him with such unchanged composure, that he was reassured, and by remaining lost another point in this game of hearts.

With the summer came an unconquerable longing to revisit the island. Helen detected this wish before he uttered it, and, feeling that it would be vain to oppose it, quietly made her preparations for the sea-side, though otherwise she would have shunned it, fearing the old charm would revive and undo her work. Such visible satisfaction appeared in Southesk's face when she bade him goodby for a time, that she departed, sure that he would follow her to that summer haunt as to no other. He did follow, and resolving to have the trial over at once, during their first stroll upon the beach Helen said, in the tone of tranquil regard which she always used with him:

"I know you are longing to see your enchanted island again, yet, perhaps, dread to go alone. If it is so, let me go with you, for, much as I desire to see it, I shall never dare to trespass a second time."

Her voice trembled a little as she spoke—the first sign of emotion she had betrayed for a long time. Remembering that he had deceived her once, and recalling all he owed her since, Southesk felt that she had been very generous, very kind, and gratitude warmed his manner as he answered, turning toward the boats, which he had been eyeing wistfully:

"How well you understand me, Helen. Thank you for giving me courage to revisit the ruins of my little paradise. Come with me, for you are the only one who knows how much I have loved and lost. Shall we go now?"

"Blind and selfish, like a true man," thought Helen, with a pang, as she saw his eye kindle and the old elasticity return to his step as he went on before her. But she smiled and followed, as if glad to serve him, and a keen observer might have added, "patient and passionate, like a true woman."

Little was said between them as they made the breezy voyage. Once Southesk woke out of a long reverie, to say, pausing on his oars:

"A year to-day since I first saw Ariel."

"A year to-day since you told me that your fate was to come to you out of the sea," and Helen sighed involuntarily as she contrasted the man before her with the happy dreamer who smiled up at her that day.

"Yes, and it has come even to the hour when all was to be won or lost," he answered, little dreaming that the next hour was to verify the prophecy more perfectly than any in the past.

As they landed, he said, beseechingly:

"Wait for me at the lighthouse; I must visit the chasm alone, and I have no desire to encounter Stern, if I can help it."

"Why not?" asked Helen, wondering at his tone.

"Because he loved her, and could not forgive me that I was more beloved than he."

"I can pity him," she said, below her breath, adding, with unusual tenderness of manner—

"Go, Philip; I know how to wait."

"And I thank you for it."

The look he gave her made her heart leap, for he had never bent such a one on her before, yet she feared that the memory of his lost love stirred and warmed him, not a dawning passion for herself, and would have wrung her hands in despair could she have known how utterly she was forgotten, as Southesk strode across the cliffs, almost as eagerly as if he knew that Ariel waited for him in her nest. It was empty; but something of its former beauty had been restored to it, for the stones were gone, green things were struggling up again, and the ladder was replaced.

"Poor Stern, he has repented of his frantic act, and tried to make the nest beautiful again as a memorial of her," thought Southesk; and descending, he threw himself down upon the newly-piled moss to dream his happy dream again, and fancy Ariel was there.

Well for him that he did not see the wrathful face that presently peered over the chasm's edge, as Stern watched him with the air of a man driven to desperation. The old hatred seemed to possess him with redoubled violence, and some new cause for detestation appeared to goad him with a hidden fear. More than once he sprang up and glanced anxiously behind him, as if he was not alone; more than once he laid his sinewy hands on a ponderous stone near by, as if tempted to hurl it down the chasm; and more than once he ground his teeth, like some savage creature who sees a stronger enemy approaching to deprive him of his prey.

The tide was coming in, the sky was over-cast, and a gale was rising; but though Southesk saw, heard and heeded nothing about him, Stern found hope in the gathering storm; for some evil spirit seemed to have been born of the tempest that raged within him, and to teach him how to make the elements his friends.

"Mr. Southesk."

Philip leaped to his feet as if a pistol had been fired at his ear, and saw Stern standing beside him with an air of sad humility, that surprised him more than the sight of his grey hair and haggard face. Pity banished resentment, and offering his hand, he said, with a generous oblivion of their parting words—

"Thank you for the change you have wrought here, and forgive me that I come back to see it once before I go away for ever. We both loved her; let us comfort one another."

A sudden color passed over Stern's swarthy face, he drew a long breath as he listened, and clenched one hand behind him as he put the other into Southesk's, answering in the same suppressed tone and with averted eyes—

"You know it, then, and try to submit as I do?"

Philip's lips were parted to reply, but no words followed, for a faint, far-off sound was heard, a woman's voice singing—

"Oh, come unto the yellow sands!"

Southesk turned pale, believing for an instant that Ariel's spirit came to welcome him; but the change in Stern's face, and the look of baffled rage and despair that played up in his eyes, betrayed him. Clutching his arm, the young man cried out, trembling with a sudden conviction—

"You have lied to me; she is not dead!"

What passed in Stern's heart during the second in which the two stood face to face, it would be impossible to tell, but with an effort that shook his strong body, he wrenched himself away and controlled his desperate desire to send his rival down the gulf. Some thought seemed to flash across him, calming the turbulence of his nature like a spell; and assuming the air of one defeated, he said slowly—

"I have lost, and I confess, I did lie to you, for March never sent the letter. I forged it, knowing that you would believe it if I added the note Ariel left for you a year ago. I could not give it to you then, but kept it with half the lock of hair. You followed them, but I followed you, and more than once thwarted you when you had nearly found them. As time passed, your persistence and her suffering began to soften March; I saw this, and tried to check you by the story of her death."

"Thank God I came, else I should never have recovered her. Give her up, Stern; she is mine, and I claim her."

Southesk turned to spring up the ladder, with no thought now but to reach Ariel; Stern arrested him, by saying with grim reluctance—

"You'll not find her, for she will not come here any more, but sit below by the basin where you saw her first. You can reach her by climbing down the steps I have made. Nay, if you doubt me, listen."

He did listen, and as the wind swept over the chasm, clearer and sweeter came the sound of that beloved voice. Southesk hesitated no longer, but swung himself recklessly downward, followed by Stern, whose black eyes glittered with a baleful light as they watched the agile figure going on before him. When they reached the basin, full to overflowing with the rising tide, they found the book her lover gave her and the little comb he knew so well, but no Ariel.

"She has gone into the cave for the weeds and shells you used to like. I'll wait for you; there is no need of me now."

Again Southesk listened; again he heard the voice, and followed it without a thought of fear; while Stern, seating himself on one of the fragments of rock cleared from the nest, leaned his head despondently upon his hand, as if his work was done.

The cave, worn by the ceaseless action of the waves at high tide, wound tortuously through the cliff to a lesser opening on the other side. Glancing rapidly into the damp nooks on either hand, Southesk hurried through this winding passage, which grew lower, narrower and darker toward the end, yet Ariel did not appear, and, standing still, he called her. Echo after echo caught up the word, and sent it whispering to and fro, but no human voice replied, though still the song came fitfully on the wind that blew coldly through the cave.

"She has ventured on to watch the waves boil in the Kelpie's Cauldron. Imprudent child, I'll punish her with a kiss," thought Southesk, smiling to himself, as he bent his tall head and groped his way toward the opening. He reached it, and looked down upon a mass of jagged rocks, over and among which the great billows dashed turbulent and dark with the approaching storm. Still no Ariel; and as he stood, more clearly than ever sounded her voice, above him now.

"She has not been here, but has climbed the Gull's Perch to watch the sky as we used to do. I have wasted all this time. Curse Stern's stupidity!"

In a fever of impatience he retraced his steps, stopping suddenly as his feet encountered a pool which had not been there when he came.

"Ah! the tide is nearer in than I thought. Thank heaven, my darling is not here!" he said, and hurried round a sharp corner, expecting to see the entrance before him. It was not there! A ponderous stone had been rolled against it, effectually closing it, and permitting only a faint ray of light to penetrate this living tomb. At first he stood panic-stricken at the horrible death that confronted him; then he thought of Stern, and in a paroxysm of wrath dashed himself against the rock, hoping to force it outward. But Stern's immense strength had served him well; and while his victim struggled vainly, wave after wave broke against the stone, wedging it more firmly still, yet leaving crevices enough for the bitter waters to flow in, bringing sure death to the doomed man, unless help came speedily from without. Not till the rapidly advancing tide drove him back did Southesk desist; then drenched, breathless and bruised he retreated to the lesser opening, with a faint hope of escape that way. Leaning over the Cauldron, he saw that the cliff sunk sheer down, and well he knew that a leap there would be fatal. As far up as he could see, the face of the cliff offered foothold for nothing but a bird. He shouted till the cave rang, but no answer came, though Ariel's song began again, for the same wind that brought her voice to him bore his away from her. There was no hope unless Stern relented, and being human, he might have, had he seen the dumb despair that seized his rival as he lay waiting for death, while far above him the woman he loved unconsciously chanted a song he had taught her, little dreaming it would be his dirge.

Left alone, Helen entered the lighthouse, and looked about her with renewed interest. The room was empty, but through a half-open door she saw a man sitting at a table covered with papers. He seemed to have been writing, but the pen had dropped from his hand, and leaning back in his deep chair he appeared to be asleep. His face was turned from her; yet when she advanced, he did not hear her, and when she spoke, he neither stirred nor answered. Something in the attitude and silence of the unknown man alarmed her; involuntarily she stepped forward and laid her hand on his. It was icy cold, and the face she saw had no life in it. Tranquil and reposeful, as if death had brought neither pain nor fear, he lay there with his dead hand on the paper, which some irresistible impulse had prompted him to write. Helen's eye fell on it, and despite the shock of this discovery, a single name made her seize the letter and devour its contents, though she trembled at the act and the solemn witness of it.

> *"To Philip Southesk:*
>
> *"Feeling that my end is very near, and haunted by a presentiment that it will be sudden—perhaps solitary—I am prompted to write what I hope to say to you if time is given me to reach you. Thirty years ago your father was my dearest friend, but we loved the same beautiful woman and he won her, unfairly I believed and in the passionate disappointment of the moment I swore undying hatred to him and his. We parted and never met again, for the next tidings I received were of his death. I left the country and was an alien for years; thus I heard no rumor of your birth and never dreamed that you were Richard Marston's son till I learned it through Ariel. Her mother, like yours, died at her birth. I reared her with jealous care, for she was my all, and I loved her with the intensity of a lonely heart; you came; I found that you could make her happy. I knew that my life was drawing to a close; I trusted you and I gave her up. Then I learned your name, and at the cost of breaking my child's heart I kept my sinful oath. For a year you have followed me with unwearied patience; for a year Ariel's fading youth has pleaded silently, and for a year I have been struggling to harden myself against both. But love has conquered hate, and standing in the shadow of death I see the sin and folly of the past. I repent and retract my oath, I absolve Ariel from the promise I exacted, I freely give her to the man she loves, and may God deal with him as he deals with her.*
>
> *Ralph March, June—"*

There the pen had fallen, blotting the date; but Helen saw only the last two lines and her hand closed tighter on the paper as if she felt that it would be impossible to give it up. Forgetting everything but that she held her rival's fate in her grasp, she yielded to the terrible temptation, and thrusting the paper into her bosom glided away like a guilty creature to find Southesk and prevent him from discovering that the girl lived, if it was not too late. He was nowhere to be seen, and crossing the rude bridge that spanned the chasm she ventured to call him as she passed, round the base of the tall rock named the Gull's Perch. A soft voice answered her, and turning a sharp angle she came upon a woman who sat alone looking down into the Kelpie's Cauldron that foamed far below. She had half risen with a startled look at the sound of a familiar name, and as Helen paused to recover herself, Ariel asked half imploringly, half imperiously,

"Why do you call Philip? Tell me, is he here?" But for the paper in her breast Helen would have answered no, and trusted all to chance; now, feeling sure that the girl would keep her promise more faithfully than her father had kept his oath, unless he absolved her from it, she answered:

"Yes, but I implore you to shun him. He thinks you dead; he has learned to love me, and is happy. Do not destroy my hope, and rob me of my hard-won prize, for you cannot reward him unless you break the solemn promise you have given."

Ariel covered up her face, as if confessing the hard truth, but love clamored to be heard, and, stretching her hands to Helen, she cried:

"I will not come between you; I will keep my word; but let me see him once, and I will ask no more. Where is he? I can steal a look at him unseen; then you may take him away for ever, if it must be so."

Trying to silence the upbraidings of her conscience, and thinking only of her purpose, Helen could not refuse this passionate prayer, and, pointing toward the chasm, she said anxiously:

"He went to the place you made so dear to him, but I do not see him now, nor does he answer when I call. Can he have fallen down that precipice?"

Ariel did not answer, for she was at the chasm's brink, looking into its gloom with eyes that no darkness could deceive. No one was there, and no sound answered the soft call that broke from her lips, but the dash of water far below. Glancing toward the basin, with a sudden recollection of the precious book left there, she saw, with wonder, that the stone where she had sat was gone, and that the cavern's mouth was closed. Stern's hat lay near her, and as her eye fell on it, a sudden horror shook her, for he had left her, meaning to return, yet had not come, and was nowhere to be seen.

"Have you seen Stern?" she asked, grasping Helen's arm, with a face of pale dismay.

"I saw him climbing the ladder, as if he was going to bind up his hands, which were bleeding. He looked wet and wild, and, as he did not see me, I did not speak. Why do you ask?"

"Because I fear he has shut Philip in the cave, where the rising tide will drown him. It is too horrible to believe; I must be sure."

Back she flew to the seat she had left, and flinging herself down on the edge of the sloping cliff, she called his name till she was hoarse and trembling with the effort. Once a faint noise seemed to answer, but the wind swept the sound away, and Helen vainly strained her ear to catch some syllable of the reply. Suddenly Ariel sprung up, with a cry:

"He is there! I see the flutter of his handkerchief! Help me, and we will save him."

She was gone as she spoke, and before Helen could divine her purpose or steady her own nerves, Ariel was back again, dragging the rope ladder, which she threw down, and began to tear up the plaid on which she had been sitting.

"It is too short, and even these strips will not make it long enough. What can I give to help?" cried Helen, glancing at the frail silks and muslins which composed her dress.

"You can give nothing, and there is not time to go for help. I shall lengthen it in this way."

Tying back the hair that blew about her face, and gathering the rope on her arm, Ariel slid over the edge of the cliff, and unstartled by Helen's cry of alarm, climbed with wary feet along a perilous path, where one mis-step would be her last. Half way down a ledge appeared where a tree had once grown; the pine was blasted and shattered now, but the roots held fast, and to these Ariel hung the ladder, with a stone fastened to the lower end to keep the wind from blowing it beyond the opening. Straight as a plummet it fell, and for a moment neither woman breathed; then a cry broke from both, for the ropes tightened, as if a hand tried the strength of that frail road. Another pause of terrible suspense, and out from the dark cave below came a man, who climbed swiftly upward, regardless of the gale that nearly tore the ladder from his hold, the hungry sea that wet him with its spray, the yielding roots that hardly bore his weight, or the wounded hands that marked his way with blood, for his eyes were fixed on Ariel, and on his face, white with the approach of a cruel death, shone an expression brighter than a smile, as he neared the brave girl who lent all her strength to save him, with one arm about the tree, the other clutching the ladder as if she defied all danger to herself.

Kneeling on the cliff above, Helen saw all this, and when Southesk stood upon the ledge, with Ariel gathered to the shelter of his arms, her heart turned traitor to her will, remorse made justice possible, love longed to ennoble itself by sacrifice, and all that was true and tender in her nature pleaded for the rival who had earned happiness at such a cost. One sharp pang, one moment of utter despair, followed by utter self-forgetfulness, and Helen's temptation became a triumph that atoned for an hour's suffering and sin.

What went on below her she never knew, but when the lovers came to her, spent yet smiling, she gave the paper to Southesk, and laid her hand on Ariel's head with a gesture soft and solemn, as she said, wearing an expression that made her fine face strangely beautiful:

"You have won him and you deserve him; for you are nobler than I. Forgive me, Philip; and when you are happiest, remember that, though sorely tempted, I resisted, hoping to grow worthier to become your friend."

Even while she spoke he had caught the meaning of the paper, and Ariel guessed it from his face before she, too, read the words that set her free. But her tears of joy changed to tears of grief when Helen gently broke to her the sad fact of her father's death, trying to comfort her so tenderly that, by the blessed magic of sympathy, all bitterness was banished from her own sore heart. As they turned to leave that fateful cliff, Stern confronted them with an aspect that daunted even Southesk's courage. Calm with the desperate calmness of one who had staked his last throw and lost it, he eyed them steadily a moment; then with a gesture too sudden to be restrained, he snatched Ariel to him—kissed her passionately, put her from him, and springing to the edge of the cliff, turned on Southesk, saying in an accent of the intensest scorn, as he pointed downward to the whirlpool below—

"Coward! you dared not end your life when all seemed lost, but waited for a woman to save you. I will show you how a brave man dies." And as the last words left his lips he was gone.

Years have passed since then; Ariel has long been a happy wife; Philip's name has become a household word on many lips, and Helen's life has grown serenely cheerful, though still solitary. But so the legend runs: Stern yet haunts the island; for the light-house keepers tell of a wild and woeful phantom that wanders day and night among the cliffs and caverns by the sea. Sometimes they see it, in the strong glare of the lantern, leaning on the balcony, and looking out into the night, as if it watched and waited to see some ship come sailing by. Often those who visit the Kelpie's Cauldron are startled by glimpses of a dark, desperate face that seems to rise and mock them with weird scorn. But oftenest a shadowy shape is seen to flit into the chasm, wearing a look of human love and longing, as it vanishes in the soft gloom of Ariel's nest.

❧ A Nurse's Story

CHAPTER I. MY PATIENT

"MY DEAR MISS SNOW,—*Learning that my friend, Mrs. Carruth, is in want of a nurse for her invalid daughter, I hasten to suggest the place to you, as I think you peculiarly suited to it, unless the duties prove too arduous. Your letters of recommendation, and my hearty endorsement of them, will, I doubt not, secure the situation, if you desire it. We sail to-morrow, and I write in great haste, but with best wishes for your future success, and sincere thanks for past services.*

"*I am, very truly yours,*
"*L. S. Hamilton.*"

This friendly letter, from a former employer, was handed me as I came in, weary and disheartened, after a fruitless search for a place like the one now offered me. Being very much in earnest, I hurried away again, hoping no-one had forestalled me with the Carruths. One of an imposing granite block, the house stood in a quiet West End square, which possessed its own small park, where a little fountain played, and pretty children wandered, with their white-capped bonnets. Well-appointed carriages rolled in and out, ladies tripped up and down the wide steps with a silken rustle, and gentlemen, in irreproachable riding costumes, cantered by on their handsome horses. Even the men and maid servants looked as if "High Life Below Stairs" was enacted in this century as well as in the last, and everything partook of the air of luxury that pervaded the place, as pleasantly as the autumn sunshine. "The Carruths must be a happy family," I thought, sighing over the loneliness and poverty of my own lot, as I stood waiting an answer to my modest ring.

A supercilious servant admitted me, and, learning my errand, took me to an anteroom till his mistress was disengaged. Through the half-open door I could look into the drawing-room, where several ladies sat talking. Anxious to see what sort of a person I was to encounter, I examined the one bonnetless lady of the group with much interest. Mrs. Carruth was a handsome woman in spite of her fifty years, for her hair was still dark, her teeth still fine, her eyes brilliant, and she bore herself with a dignity that betrayed much native pride, as well as grace.

She was evidently entertaining her guests successfully, for their listless faces brightened, and frequent laughter followed her animated words.

"A fashionable, light-hearted woman, it seems, in spite of the invalid daughter," I said to myself as I watched her. Five minutes later, I changed my opinion, for, when she had smiled the last guest out, and was alone, she seemed another creature. All the animation faded from her face, leaving it pale and worn. Her stately bearing changed, and she dropped into a seat, like one spent, both soul and body. Only an instant did she sit so; the servant's approaching step caused her to start up and assume an air of the most perfect composure, as she listened to the man's announcement that "a young person waited to see her."

Briefly explaining my errand, I presented my credentials, and while she examined them I observed her with redoubled interest, for, having caught a glimpse of her without a mask, I could no longer be deceived by the cold calmness she now wore. I am quick at reading faces, and her's was the most tragical I ever saw. Such anxious eyes, such melancholy lines about the mouth, such a hopeless undertone in the steady voice, and an indescribable expression of unsubmissive sorrow!—all proved that life had brought some heavy cross, from which her wealth could purchase no release, for which her pride could find no effectual screen.

"You are an Englishwoman, it seems; have you friends in this country?"

Mrs. Carruth spoke suddenly, and fixed a keen look upon me. I met it with one as keen, and answered quietly:

"Not one, when Mrs. Hamilton is gone, and no near relatives across the water. I am an orphan, dependent on myself alone, and, though a gentleman's daughter, not too proud to earn my bread by any honest work."

Something in my look or speech seemed to please her; she drew a little nearer, and her tone was milder, as she said, returning my letters:

"These are quite satisfactory, Miss Snow; but, before going further, it is right that I should tell you what Mrs. Hamilton has delicately avoided mentioning in her note. My daughter's malady is not physical, but mental."

As the last sentence reluctantly left her lips, I saw the white hands that lay in her lap fold together with a slow, strong pressure, that betrayed how much it cost the mother to confide the affliction of her daughter to a stranger's keeping. The words, the gesture, the look that accompanied them, made my eyes fill, and my face involuntarily expressed the sympathy I knew not how to utter. Mrs. Carruth's glance softened still more, and grew almost wistful as she said:

"I learned from Mrs. Hamilton that you have had some experience in the care of the insane, and have peculiar power over them. You look young for such a sad profession; are you wise to continue this sort of nursing?"

"I am thirty, and though the profession *is* a sad one, I like it better than being a governess or a companion; and the very fact that I am fitted for it makes me glad to do my best for those who need all the help and tenderness their fellow-beings can bestow upon them."

A long sigh of relief escaped her lips, and, lowering her voice, she said, with an air of confidence that was very agreeable to me:

"Several persons have applied, but none suited me. I think you will, and hope the care will not be too much for you. I should yield this duty to no one could I perform it myself, but, as is often the case, my poor girl now dislikes most those who once were dearest to her, and will not allow me to approach her. Therefore I am forced to see my place filled by a stranger, though it breaks my heart to be shut out from her."

She paused a moment, then added hastily, as if she read my thought in my face:

"Perhaps you wonder why this unfortunate child is not sent from home? Simply because I will not trust her from my keeping, nor lose the sad pleasure of watching over her and doing the little that I can for her. Now, let me tell you about her. She has been ill for a year, but the violent attacks occur at intervals; between them she is almost herself again and needs only such care and amusement as any compassionate and intelligent person can give her. The old nurse, who has been with me for years, is worn out, and must rest; Elinor will allow none of the women I now have to come near her, and we have decided to try the experiment of a young companion. Experienced persons are at hand to care for her in her frantic paroxysms, and all I ask of you is to amuse and occupy her saner days. Will you do this?"

"Gladly, if I can," I answered heartily.

"Thank you. I have little doubt of your success, unless she takes a dislike to you. Mrs. Hamilton told me of your various accomplishments and skill in using them. I shall leave much to your judgment regarding the choice of amusements and occupations for Elinor. As much sleep as possible is desirable, unexciting conversation, and quiet employment. She is just recovering from one of these attacks, and is very moody, but no longer violent, and for several months will grow gradually better before another relapse occurs; therefore you need fear nothing at present."

"I never fear those whom I love, and I soon learn to love those whom I pity."

"Then you will love my poor child, for she will rouse your deepest pity. But do not let me forget one point that must be arranged to your satisfaction. Money cannot pay for such services, and any sum you may name I shall gladly agree to, and willingly increase if the duties are harder than you expect."

"I am not a mercenary person; I only want a home, and a little sum to make me independent of charity. Let me try a week before we settle this point. I can begin at once if you wish it, and will do my best."

I know my manner and my earnestness affected her pleasantly, she took my hand and pressed it with an impulsive gesture as she rose and led me to her chamber, saying:

"Come, then, and give Elinor a sight of your cheerful face. I only fear that you will find it a dull life, and so lose your bloom and spirits. My daughter cannot go out, and will not see any of her former friends, so you will be a prisoner much of the time. Can you bear it?"

"I think so, if I can have a run in the air once a day, and my nights undisturbed. I am very strong and well, and never know despondency, though I have good cause for it sometimes."

"Happy soul, I envy you!"

I was taking off my hat and cloak as I spoke, and she had watched me, till, with that exclamation, she turned and walked down the room with a quick step, as if some bitter memory or care were dogging her. She paused before a dressing-table strewn with elegant trifles, and tossing them over with a careless hand, she selected three keys, and approached me as I stood ready.

"These are the keys of the conservatory, which is her only place of exercise just now, of the library she used to enjoy, and the wardrobes that contain her clothes. During her ill turns she destroys and injures things sadly, but now is able to enjoy these sources of amusement freely. The conservatory is sacred to her; the books you can select as you think best; the ornaments and dresses she plays with, and seems to love for their associations with the past. The piano has been newly tuned, and is her greatest consolation, when she is well enough to use it."

Putting the keys into my hand, she led me up the stairways, and through rooms whose spacious elegance charmed my eye, and gave promise of luxurious quarters for the poor companion when she left her dingy little nook in a cheap boardinghouse. Opening a door that led into a remote wing, Mrs. Carruth showed me an apartment that looked a perfect nest of comfort, telling me it was mine. Passing on through a gallery and an anteroom, where two middle-aged, official-looking women sat at work, she paused upon the threshold of the door she dared not cross, and with a look I never shall forget, said solemnly:

"Miss Snow, in this house you will see much that will wring your heart, and demand your patience and your pity; I need not ask of you that silence which will add to the obligation we shall owe you, nor offer any bribe to faithfulness; let the appeal of an unhappy mother win your tenderest companion for a most unhappy daughter."

"You may trust me, madam, in my eyes such afflictions are sacred."

I said no more, but she was satisfied, and, with a tremor in her steady voice, a longing look on her proud face, she pointed to the door, whispering:

"I can go no farther. Treat her as if nothing was amiss, and humor any harmless whim. If she is quiet, amuse yourself till she speaks, and if you are perplexed or alarmed by anything, ring the bell, these women are here to answer it. Go, my good girl, but let me see you before you leave."

With a little flutter at my heart, not of fear but expectation, I went in and looked about me. At the first glance, the room seemed a daintily-furnished and most attractive boudoir for a rich man's daughter, but a second discovered many traces of the frantic scenes enacted there. The windows were draped with rich hangings, but iron bars cast their shadows on the sunny floor. A long mirror was defaced by cracks, unsightly stains marred the flowery carpet, broken toys lay about, and on rosewood and marble furniture appeared the marks of reckless hands. All the doors were locked, except that by which I entered, the fire was guarded by a wire screen, and several wardrobes were close shut. The piano alone stood open, and heaps of torn music strewed the ground about it. On a low couch, in the darkest corner, lay a more pathetic object than any in that beautiful yet mournful room. A tall, splendidly developed girl, so like her comely mother, it was little wonder the sight was a daily anguish to that mother. Very pale, but not wasted, by a year of suffering, and that fine physique only made the mental malady more sad and striking. On the strong white arms, folded underneath her head, appeared dark bruises—self-inflicted, doubtless—a quantity of curling, auburn hair streamed about her, tangled and neglected; her lips were closely shut, and wearily drooping lids half hid the strangest eyes I ever saw. Very light hazel, they seemed almost a tawny yellow, like a tiger's eyes; infinitely wild and woeful was the expression they wore, till a slight rustle of my dress, as I moved forward, disturbed her; instantly they flashed wide open, darkening and dilating till they grew black and fierce, as she fixed them on me with a glance that made me tremble for a moment, but she neither moved nor spoke, and remembering her mother's last words, I merely bowed, saying quietly:

"Good morning, Miss Carruth, I am come to sit with you a little while. I'll not disturb you if you are disposed to sleep," and passing by her I sat down beside the window, and began to turn over several books that lay there.

A long silence followed, during which I tranquilly turned my pages, and seemed absorbed in the story, not a word of which did I read, for the consciousness that those wild eyes were staring at me affected me curiously.

Presently, as if satisfied with her scrutiny of my face, and anxious to hear my voice again, she said, in the sharp, unmodulated tone of the insane:

"What is my new keeper's name?"

"The name of your new companion and friend, if you will allow her to be so, is Kate Snow."

Seeing that she wished to talk, I laid down the book, and turned towards her, as if ready to be questioned. She was leaning on her elbow and still looking at me, but the fierce expression was replaced by one of mingled doubt and curiosity. With the freedom of one for whom forms and ceremonies had ceased to exist, she looked and spoke, regardless of courtesy or self-control.

"Why did you come here? Was there nothing else in the world for you to do than to be shut up in prison with a miserable creature like me?"

"I could have done many other things, but I preferred this, for I like to nurse the sick, because I find I have the power of making them comfortable, and that is very pleasant, as you may suppose."

"I wish you could do it for me; but I'm past help—past help."

She rose suddenly, and paced the room with rapid steps, as if to escape from some desperate thought. To and fro she went, like a wild creature in its cage, still glancing furtively at me, and more than once half pausing before she turned sharply away for another restless march from wall to wall. Hoping to quiet her by drawing her attention to myself, I took up a bit of tapestry-work that lay in an overturned basket, and began to examine it. Elinor stopped at once, eyed me for a moment, then drew nearer, saying with a somewhat haughty air:

"Do not touch that, it is all in a tangle, and you'll make it worse."

"So I see; but I think I can smooth it out, and then you can finish it, for it is too pretty to be spoiled. By-and-bye, you may like to work on it, and let me read aloud to you. I fancy we shall have pleasant times together, Miss Carruth."

I spoke in a cheerful tone, exactly as if addressing a sane person, for I had learned by experience that the surest way of calming maniacs was to appear unconscious of their madness, and to take it for granted that they would behave with propriety. It helped them to gain self-control, and usually won obedience, by appealing to one of the strongest motives we possess—the desire for the good opinion of others. Elinor seemed surprised at first, then troubled, and said hastily:

"Do you know what is the matter with me? Haven't they told you what an awful life I've been leading for a year? You treat me as if I were a common invalid."

"I know all about the past, but that is over now, never to return, I hope. Forget it, and let us make the present happy, if we can."

"Forget it! how can I, when I know that this horror will come again and again, and haunt me till I die? How can I be happy with such a future in store for me, and these reminders of my misery constantly before me."

She cast a despairing look about the room, and stretched out her injured arms with a pathetic gesture of appeal, that went straight to my heart, and made my voice tremble as I took both of her hands in mine, and said tenderly:

"All things are possible with God; hope and wait, and wait, and He will help you in his own good time. Meanwhile let me do my best for you, and make your hard life happier if I can."

I think my face, my act, did more to touch her than my speech, for human sympathy finds more eloquent interpreters than words. She felt it, yielded to it, and dropping on her knees, clung about me with the close grasp of a despairing soul that had found support at last, crying passionately.

"Yes, help me, love me, save me if you can; no suffering creature in the world needs you as much as I."

I held her fast, and let my tears flow freely, hoping that she, too, would weep and cool the fever of her brain. She did not, but my tears comforted her poor heart, for they assured her of my sincerity, and soothed her with the balm of compassion. Presently she looked up, dry-eyed, but more calm, and with a sweet expression, drew my face down and kissed me.

"You are very kind, I thank you, and I'll try to prove my gratitude by being quiet and obedient. Don't cry for me, dear; I can't, and it troubles me to see you do it. I wish I could believe there was any hope; do you really think I may be well in time?"

She looked and spoke now like a little child, and watched me wistfully, still kneeling at my side, with my arm about her.

"I do, for you are young and have bodily health to help you. Much depends on yourself, and if you try to keep your mind cheerful and quiet, I believe you may yet be well, for I have seen worse cases than your own entirely cured."

She shook her head, and murmured loud, as if to herself, while the old gloom fell on her face again.

"What can be worse than mine, if all was known. The sins of the parents shall be visited upon the children, and they must pay the penalty."

The daughter's words recalled the mother's mournful countenance, and assured me that this luxurious home was darkened by the shadow of some domestic tragedy hidden from the world. I only pitied the poor girl the more, and was trying to devise some cheerful scheme for her amusement, when one of the women entered with a tray in her hand.

"Miss must eat something now, for she would not take her breakfast. Perhaps you can coax her to it. The doctor says she may have wine to-day, and the soup's extra nice."

The woman's manner was perfectly respectful but her voice was harsh, her eye cold, and as she spoke, she tasted the soup, with an appreciative smack of the lips, which would have effectually spoiled the appetite of a fastidious invalid. As the spoon was descending into the bowl again, I arrested it, saying gently:

"A clean one, please; Miss Carruth won't care to use that now."

"Bless me, how particular." And with a shrug Hannah went to bring another.

It was a very little thing, but it had its effect, for Elinor, who had sullenly thrown herself on the couch again, and watched the woman with a frown, turned to me with a sudden smile, though she said, plaintively:

"Ah, you treat me like a gentlewoman, though I am a poor, half crazy creature, they think it is no matter what they say and do, but I feel the difference, and I'll eat my dinner to please *you*, Miss Snow."

As if anxious to show that she had not forgotten the manners of a gentlewoman, she rose as she spoke, and began to gather up her hair and smooth the delicate white wrapper which she wore, making a hasty toilet for this lonely dinner, as she used to do for prayer feasts before her sad captivity began. Eager to encourage her, I set out the soup and wine upon the oval table, rolled an easy chair towards it, and, unlocking the conservatory door, gathered a handful of flowers to fill an empty vase which I stood before her face. Hannah stared when she returned, but made no comment, and merely asked in her dry tone:

"Will you have your lunch in the next room, Miss Snow, while I see to things here?"

"I will take it with Miss Elinor, if she will allow me; I think if her meals were more social she would enjoy them, and have a better appetite."

"I thank you; that will be pleasant. It is very dismal to eat alone day after day, and never see any one but those women and the doctor. You are a good nurse, Kate."

She looked quite sane and quiet as she stood waiting till my tray was brought, and it was touching to see how hard she tried to control her wandering thoughts and do the honors of the table.

I was hungry, and ate heartily as I talked on various cheerful subjects; my healthful appetite seemed to increase her's, and society gave a relish to the food which till now had been distasteful. She said little, but smiled several times, and laughed once at some mild joke of mine. The sound seemed an unusual one, for it brought Hannah to the door, looking surprised and anxious. Elinor knit her brows, and cried out sharply.

"Go away, and leave us in peace. Miss Snow can take care of me better than a dozen such as you and Jane."

With a nod the woman vanished. Elinor tried to conceal the irritation of her nerves under a tranquil air, and I chatted on, much elated at my success, till an unlucky word undid my work. As she ceased eating, I pushed back my chair, and said briskly:

"Now let us go and walk in the conservatory, exercise is good for you, and you are fond of being there, your mother says."

As the last words left my lips, Elinor sprung up with a violence that overturned the table, and made me start to my feet.

"My mother!" she fiercely echoed; "how dare you speak of her when I have forbidden it? I cannot hear the sound of her name, for she is the cause of all I suffer. Oh, why did you do it—why did you do it?" and dropping into her chair, she covered up her face, with a gesture more pitiful than tears.

Dismayed at the effect of my momentary forgetfulness, I dared not speak, but quietly gathering up the broken glass and china, I took it away, and lifting the table, laid books and work upon it hoping to efface the memory of my trespass by some pleasant occupation when she looked up. But she did not stir, and glancing about me for some safe means of rousing her, my eye fell on the piano. A fragment of Beethoven's "Sonata Pathetique" lay on the rack; I knew it all, and seating myself, played it softly, with frequent glances at the motionless figure in the great chair. It was the wisest thing I could have done, for soon her tears began to flow, hysterically at first, but presently the passionate sobbing grew still, and quiet showers fell, relieving the weary brain, and refreshing the sad heart as no spoken consolation could have done.

Glad to have wrought this favorable change, I played on and on till the tears were dry, and she seemed to sleep with head pillowed on the cushioned arm of the chair. Then I stopped, but the instant I moved, her eyes opened; not as before, however, but with a tranquil look which proved how beneficial the tears had been.

"I thought you were asleep; shall I go on?" I said, ignoring my slip of the tongue, and the outbreak that followed it.

"No, I seldom sleep; I wish I could. Can I go in there, it looks so cool and quiet?" She pointed to the conservatory, and, giving her my arm, I led her in.

It was a lonely place, shadowy and still, with the soft glimmer of sunshine on green leaves, the delicate breath of flowers, and the lulling murmur of a little fountain, in the midst of which a marble mermaid lay asleep.

As Elinor paused here, I sat down on the turf that encircled the basin, and drawing her beside me, laid her head in my lap while I bathed her hot forehead, and sung a dreamy little air that had soothed more than one restless spirit.

At first she glanced about as if glad to see her favorite haunt again, but her eyes always returned to me with a mute confidence that touched me very much.

At last she put up her hand and softly stroked my cheek, saying humbly, yet affectionately:

"This is such a kind and cheerful face that I cannot keep my eyes away from it. Does my rudeness trouble you?"

"Oh, no; but I wish you'd sleep. May I make you?"

"If you can; I long to forget, but when I try my thoughts torment me, and I get no rest. A long, deep sleep would do more for me than all the morphine in the world."

Without a word I laid my hands upon her forehead, fixed my eyes on hers, and gave myself up to the task of making her sleep. Sooner even than I thought, her lids drooped, the rapid throbbing in her temples quieted, the breath came softly from her parted lips, and with a sigh of dreamy satisfaction, she drifted away into a tranquil slumber. I had tried my powers before, but never with such entire success, and as I watched her, with that deep peace beautifying her young face, I thanked God for the good gift I possessed. Sitting thus, I was roused from a happy reverie by the soft descent of a flower, and looking up to see whence it fell, I saw Mrs. Carruth leaning from a little window, high up in the wall that separated the conservatory from the house. With an enquiring glance she pointed towards her daughter, and I answered in a whisper—

"Yes, she is asleep."

"Thank heaven for that! It is the first natural rest she has had for days. How did you work the miracle, Miss Snow?"

"I magnetized her, and she will sleep for hours, unless I awake her. I should have asked leave, perhaps, before I did it, but you were not here, and I knew it would not harm her," I said confidently.

"You were quite right, anything to quiet her. We have tried this before, but it failed. May her brothers come and look at her? I dare not."

"Yes, any one may come—she will not wake."

"Kiss her for me, and go on as you have begun."

Mrs. Carruth's voice trembled, and she hastily withdrew as if to hide the grief for which there was no cure. A few moments afterwards a cautious step made me turn my head to see a young man, in the dress of a Catholic priest, stealing towards me, with eyes fixed eagerly upon the sleeper. As if unconscious of my presence, he stood looking down at her, while his lips moved noiselessly, and his hands seemed involuntarily to search for a rosary, as if he prayed for this poor soul. The hasty entrance of another and a younger man disturbed his devotions, and with a glance, a grave bow, and a half audible greeting, he stepped back. The newcomer was as unlike his brother in appearance as in manner, and as they stood a moment side by side I scrutinized them covertly. The elder possessed a pale, ascetic face, with melancholy eyes, stern mouth, and the absorbed expression of one who led an inward life. His cold, shy air, plain costume, and devout expression recalled old pictures of monks and saints, and when I heard his name its fitness struck me. The younger's face was far more attractive, for though bearing marks of dissipation and a reckless spirit, it was both handsome and winning. The eyes were frank, the mouth sweet, the whole aspect betokened a generous, ardent nature, proud and willful, yet lovable in spite of all defects. His manner was impetuous as a boy's, for with a hasty nod to me, he knelt down by his sister, and taking her hand in his, kissed it gently, while his chest rose and fell with the emotion to which he would not yield.

"Look at her, Augustine, so beautiful, so quiet. What a comfort it is to see her like herself again," he whispered as he looked.

"Yes, and but for the sin of it, I could wish she might never wake again," returned the other gloomily.

"Don't say that, for while there's life there's hope, even for poor Nell. Do you find her very ill, Miss Snow?" asked Harry, glancing up at me with an imploring look.

"No; she is better than I thought to find her, and with care, will soon be quite herself again, I hope."

"That's brave news; thank you for it. You must be very tired; cannot we move her to the sofa? If she sleeps long you'll faint from weariness," he said, in a friendly tone, as if anxious to show his thanks by serving me.

"She had better be moved; it is damp here. Lift her carefully, and I will follow."

Augustine advanced, and together they bore the sleeping girl into the room, and laid her down. She sighed as her head touched the pillow, and her arm clung to Harry's neck as if she felt his nearness even in her sleep. He put his cheek to her's an instant, smoothed back her hair, and lingered over her with an affection of solicitude beautiful to see. Augustine stretched his hand above her as if in silent benediction, gave me another grave bow, and went away as noiselessly as he came. But Harry kissed her on lips and forehead, took my hand, and whispered with a falter in that impetuous voice of his:

"Be kind to this poor girl, Miss Snow, and in return ask anything of me."

He did not wait to hear my answer, but hurried from the room. A few minutes later Hannah brought me a little note from Mrs. Carruth.

"My son tells me that Elinor sleeps quietly, and may not wake for hours; that you look very weary, and must need some rest. Come down and leave her to Hannah; you have done enough today; let me thank you, and send you home for a quiet night before you begin your good work tomorrow.

E. C."

I went, and after a long interview with Mrs. Carruth, in which I described what had passed above, and received some hints for the future, Harry put me into the carriage, and I rolled away more than ever interested in my patient.

Chapter II. The First Link

EARLY NEXT MORNING I presented myself at my new place. The servant again informed me that his mistress was engaged, but added that Miss Elinor would see me whenever I was ready. Anxious to learn how she had passed the night, I was hastening up to take off my things, but was detained by my trunks, which were being carried up before me; and, while I waited at the foot of the second flight, the sound of eager voices came suddenly from a room close by. The conversation was in French, but I distinctly heard Mrs. Carruth speaking in an imploring tone, Augustine as if remonstrating with her, and Harry apparently defying one. His voice rose above the rest, and a few words reached my ear.

"You have no right to hold us to that promise, Steele."

"Perhaps not, but I have the power."

Anything more exasperating than the cool, sarcastic tones of this new voice I never heard. It arrested me, for it was peculiar, and as I paused with my foot on the first stair, I heard Harry exclaim passionately:

"Haven't you brought enough dishonor upon us without forcing us to treachery, like this? I swear I'll haunt you after you have driven me to shoot or hang myself."

"Don't be melodramatic, Hal."

A low laugh followed the words, and I sprung up stairs just in time to avoid Harry, who dashed out of the room and out of the house like one in a desperate mood. Much amazed and somewhat troubled, I went to my room, and as I prepared to meet Elinor, I tried to recall where I had heard that peculiar voice and laugh before. I was sure I had done so, but when or how had entirely escaped my memory, and after puzzling vainly over it, I gave it up, feeling that it was not worth wasting time upon. As I passed through the ante-room, Hannah said, in answer to my greeting:

"You'll find Miss Elinor dreadful fractious this morning. You'd better not try your magnetizing again; it don't suit her."

Fearing that I had done harm, I hurried in. Elinor was standing at the open window, with both hands grasping one of the iron bars, as if she longed to wrench it away and escape. She looked flushed and excited, but had evidently done her best to make ready for me. Her fine hair was smoothly fastened up, her dress carefully arranged, and the room set in order. So absorbed was she in some disturbing thought, that she neither saw nor heard me enter, and, sitting quietly down, I watched and waited. Presently I saw the frown disappear from her forehead, her eyes grow less intense in their gaze, and her hands relax their tight grasp, as she drew a long breath or two, as if some weight were lifted off. Suddenly she turned and saw me, uttered an exclamation of surprise, and came towards me with both hands extended.

"I might have known you were here; you bring peace with you, and I felt so even before I saw you," she said, with a smile of welcome.

"I did not try to make you feel me, for Hannah says you are not so well for my little experiment of yesterday," I began, rather surprised at my influence over her, but she cut me short by saying, with a scornful glance towards the door, and a darkening face:

"Hannah knows nothing about it. I am not worse; I slept deliciously all night, and woke feeling like myself. I longed to have you come and see how much good you'd done me. I got ready for you, and was very happy till something happened that would have driven a saner person than I am half distracted. Let me tell you about it."

She spoke excitedly, and hoping to soothe her, I said quietly, as I drew her towards the piano:

"Never mind telling me about it now. Come and sing a little, I quite long to hear you."

"Sing!" she cried, with a shudder; "you don't know what you ask. Could you sing when your heart was heavy with the knowledge of a sin about to be committed by those nearest to you? I must talk whether you listen or not; I shall go frantic if I don't tell some one; all the world will know it soon. Sit down, I'll not hurt you, but don't thwart me."

Speaking with a vehemence that left her breathless, she thrust me down upon the sofa, and holding me with a grasp I could not have resisted, had I tried, she went on with more coherency than I expected, while I, knowing the power of a sane eye over a mad one, looked steadily at her, and listened in passive silence.

"Harry told me; he comes to see me every morning before he goes out. To-day he was very angry, I saw it, and asked why. He can refuse me nothing, poor Hal, so he told me. Amy is to be married in a month, and no one will prevent it. Think how wicked when such a curse is on us all."

A question rose to my lips but did not pass them, yet my face must have betrayed me, for bending nearer she answered my unspoken inquiry in a shrill whisper, that made my blood tingle, so full of suppressed pain and passion was it.

"The curse of insanity I mean. We are all mad, or shall be; we come of a mad race, and for years they have gone recklessly on bequeathing this awful inheritance to their descendants. It should end with us, we are the last; none of us should marry, none of us dare think of it but Amy, and that proves that she is the maddest of all. She must be stopped, she must be kept from the agony of seeing her children become what I am and what Harry will be."

Here Elinor wrung her hands and paced the room in such a paroxysm of impotent despair and grief, that I sat bewildered, wondering if this could be only the wandering of a troubled brain. Mrs. Carruth's face, words and manner, returned to me, so did Augustine's gloomy expression and strange wish uttered over his sleeping sister; Harry's violence, just witnessed, confirmed the suspicion that this tragical assertion was true, and again, as if called up by the word "Amy," there returned to me a

strong impression that I had heard all the names before, and felt a passing interest in
their unknown possessors. There was no time to revive the vague fancy, for Elinor
paused abruptly before me.

"You wonder that I cannot bear to hear my mother's name, I'll tell you why.
Long ago, when she was beautiful and young, she married my father, though she knew
the sad history of his family. He was rich, she poor and proud; ambition made her
wicked, and she did it after being warned that, though he escaped, his children were
sure to inherit the curse, for when one generation goes free it falls more heavily upon
the next. I have her to thank for all I suffer, and I cannot love her. It may be wrong
to say these things, but they are true and I cannot help saying them, for I tell you
there always comes a time when children learn to criticize their parents as men and
women, and woe to those whose actions change affection and respect to hatred or
contempt."

The bitter grief, the solemn fervor of her manner both touched and awed me;
I dared not speak, feeling that words were powerless to comfort her or to control the
overflow of a long pent up sorrow, that now found vent when will was not strong
enough to restrain it. Almost sternly she went on.

"If ever a woman had cause to repent it is my mother, but she will not, and till
she does, God has forsaken us. Nothing can subdue her pride, not even an affliction
like mine. She hides it; she hides me, and tells the world I'm dying of consumption;
not a word about insanity; these women are paid to keep the secret, and you would
not have been allowed to come to me if she had not been sure of your discretion.
This is why I'm not sent away; no one knows anything about our past history here,
for we only came two years ago; I was well then, and oh, how happy!"

Clasping her hands above her head she stood like a beautiful pale image of
despair. Tearless and mute, but with such an expression of love and longing in the
eyes lifted to a picture hanging above us, that it needed no words to tell the story of
a lost love, a broken heart. It was the only picture in the room, a man's face, comely
and young, with a singularly strong and noble air about it, which had attracted me the
day before and made me long to speak of it, and nothing but the fear of another
outbreak like that which followed the utterance of her mother's name had restrained
me. Now I looked again with redoubled interest, for in the gaze the poor girl fixed
upon it, I read another chapter in the history of this unhappy family.

"How I loved him!" she said softly, while her whole face glowed with a tender
warmth and light, "and how he loved me! too well to let me burden my life with a
remorse which would come too late for an atonement. I thought him cruel then, now
I bless him for it, and had rather be the innocent sufferer I am, than a wretched
woman like my mother. I shall never see him any more, but I know he thinks of me
far away in India, and when I die one faithful heart will mourn for me."

Her voice faltered and failed, and for a moment the fire of her eyes was
quenched in tears. I thought the reaction had come, and rose, meaning to try and
comfort her. In an instant her hand was on my shoulder, and pressing me back into
my seat she said almost fiercely:

"I'm not done yet, you must hear the whole—no, not the whole, the worst I
keep to myself for my father's sake. Is that a noble, true, and tender face? I know you
think so, well, he was my lover a year ago. I knew nothing of the blight that hung over

us, that was carefully concealed till Augustine discovered it. He should have spoken sooner and saved me in time, but he was away till I was engaged, then he warned me of the fate that was in store for me. I could not believe it, mamma denied it, but my father confessed it. So Edward went away, although it broke his heart, and I became what I am. Do you see that mark?"

With a quick gesture she tore open her dress, and on her white bosom I saw a deep purple scar. Involuntarily I shuddered, and turned pale, guessing what was to follow.

"Yes, I tried to kill myself, but they would not let me die. And the old tragedy begins again. Augustine became a priest, hoping to hide his calamity and expiate his father's sin by endless prayers. Harry turned reckless, a short life and a gay one, he says, and when his turn comes he will spare himself long suffering, as I would have done. Amy is like mamma, she thinks only of herself, she will marry and perpetuate the curse. Her lover knows this, but he will not give up her fortune, and none of us dare to tell him another bitter secret which would part them, because we have promised Steele to keep it till the year is out."

"Who is Steele?"

The question broke from my lips before I could arrest it, but I got no farther, for Elinor laid her hand upon my lips, whispering with an apprehensive glance behind her.

"Hush, don't ask me; I'm afraid I shall tell in spite of my promise. He is the evil genius of our family, beware of him, or he will take possession of you as he has of us."

After this enigmatical reply, she stood silent a moment, then broke out more violently than at first.

"Now do you wonder that I'm wild! Now will you ask me to sing, and smile and sit quietly by while this deviltry goes on? You say I may recover, I tell you it is impossible, death is the only cure for a mad Carruth. I am so young and strong it will be long in coming unless I bring it."

She clenched her hands, set her teeth, and looked about her with a desperate expression, as if ready for any frantic act that should set her free from the dark and dreadful future that lay before her. Many women would have trembled and called for help, I should have done so had not pity conquered fear; I forgot myself, I only thought of this poor girl so hopeless, helpless, and afflicted; I went to her and put my arms about her as tenderly as if she had been my sister; I did not speak, but held her close, feeling that I could control her by gentleness alone. At first she seemed unconscious of my presence, as she stood rigid and motionless, with her wild eyes wandering to and fro, her teeth still set, her hands still clinched. Suddenly both strength and excitement seemed to leave her, and she would have fallen but for my arms. I laid her on the couch, wet her lips, fanned her and spoke soothingly, as I busied myself about her till she looked up at me quite herself again, but so wan and weak it made my heart ache to see her.

"It's over now," she whispered, wearily closing her eyes. "Don't let me talk, don't let me think, or I shall get desperate again. Read to me, I don't care what, anything to keep me quiet if you can."

I looked among the books in the room, but found nothing that suited me, till, down behind a pile of dull novels and weak poems, I discovered Dickens's "Christmas Carol." It was just what I wanted, and seating myself beside Elinor, I began to read as dramatically as I could, hoping to rouse my listener. For some time she lay with her hands over her eyes and no sign of interest, but when we came to the "Cratchits," I saw smiles touch her lips, a soft expression steal over her face, and "Tiny Tim" brought quiet tears into those sad eyes of hers, for the magic of the simple story won her from herself and proved the best medicine I could have administered. Happy in my success, I read for several hours from the liveliest books at hand; Elinor said little, but evidently enjoyed it, and lay listening while the rain fell heavily without, and melancholy winds complained. She ate a little dinner, and afterward seemed inclined to sleep, so I took up my work and entertained myself as best I could till twilight fell. Sitting in the dusk, I heard Hannah call me from the door-way, and going to her she said:

"Mrs. Carruth would like to see you, in her room, before she goes out. I'll attend to Miss."

Glad to escape from the gloomy influences of that chamber, I went down, enjoying the glimpses of luxury and beauty that I saw by the way. Mrs. Carruth was in full dinner toilet, and to most observers would have seemed a stately, smiling matron, blessed with every good gift that makes life happy, but to me she looked a sadder woman than her daughter, for pride had set its stamp upon her, and an indomitable will betrayed itself in the steady fire of her eye and the defiant curl of her lips.

With a gracious air she received me, made a few inquiries, hoped I was quite comfortable, and then said:

"As the rain prevents your going out for exercise, you may like to rest and amuse yourself by walking about the house. If you care to do so, I beg you will; you will disturb no one, as we are all going out. Another thing I wish to speak of; as there will necessarily be some irregularity in your meals, pray feel quite free to ring for them whenever it is most convenient and agreeable to yourself. The little breakfast room near the library is at your disposal, and Morris will see that you have all you wish. Tell Miss Amy I am ready Lizette. Good evening, Miss Snow."

With a slight bend she went rustling away leaving me to wonder where Mr. Carruth was. I had fancied he was dead, as I saw and heard nothing of him, but there were no signs of widowhood about his wife's dress, and I now remembered that Elinor had spoken of him as she would hardly have spoken had death dropped its veil between them.

While these thoughts were passing through my mind, I strolled along the wide hall, not yet lighted, except by the brilliant glow that streamed from Mrs. Carruth's room behind me, and another at the extreme end. The door of this apartment stood ajar, and as I approached a young lady stepped out, drawing on her gloves as she came. A slender, blonde girl, far less beautiful than Elinor, for in her face there was no trace of innate nobility, no warmth, no strength. A cold, shallow, selfish nature I saw at a glance; wandering blue eyes, a weak, yet wilful expression, and a half-nervous, half-coquetish manner, without either dignity or grace. She stopped on seeing me, stared an instant, then nodded, as if recognizing me.

"Miss Snow, I believe? How is poor dear Nell tonight? I should have run up to let her see me if there had been time. She likes to look at pretty things, and I'm glad to indulge her. Tell her I've some wedding presents to show her. Do you find her very poorly?"

While speaking in a careless tone, Amy had still been intent upon herself, fastening her gloves, setting her lace flounces, and shaking out a gosamer handkerchief. Hardly waiting to hear my reply, she prepared to move on, saying, as she threw the cashmere round her shoulders:

"Give her my love, please, and say I'll come and describe the dinner party to her to-morrow. Is she quiet, and quite safe, Miss Snow?"

"I think so, if one is careful to avoid exciting subjects," I began, but she interrupted me.

"Aren't you afraid to be alone with her?"

"Not at all."

"Dear, I should be. I never dare see her without Hannah or Jane is with me. You have done this sort of thing before, haven't you?"

"Yes, I was with a friend two years, and with Mrs. Hamilton's imbecile little son for the last six months."

"What a dreadful life it must be! I should think you'd turn gray with it; but you look as young and rosy as if you'd been enjoying yourself in the calmest manner. I'm quite—"

She stopped abruptly, and glided away without apology or adieu.

Turning to look after her, I saw a gentleman advancing down the hall, and, as she passed him, saw her gather back her dress, lest it should touch him, yet bow with the utmost deference in answer to his greeting.

"Out again, Amy?" he said, without pausing.

"Yes, Steele; do you mind?" she answered timidly.

"Not I; dance while you may," was the careless answer.

Amy hurried down stairs with a grateful "Thank you," and the gentleman came on behind me. I had turned to continue my walk, and now the passage was too dusky to permit me to see anything but a tall, dark figure that glided by me as noiseless as a shadow.

Being a woman, I was curious; and, being idle, I amused myself with all manner of queer and romantic fancies about this "evil genius of the family," as Elinor called him. But, as I mused, roamed here and there, admiring all I saw, till, feeling hungry, I went in search of the little breakfast-room and Morris. Opening the door, in my quiet way, I went in without disturbing two persons who, to my surprise, occupied the room. Of one I took no notice, for a single glance at the other gave me a clue I had been searching for, and I recalled a long-forgotten incident so vividly that I stood mute and motionless.

Augustine stood before the fire, his head bowed down upon the marble chimney-piece, and despondency in every line of his drooping figure. Lounging in a low, luxurious chair, was a man of thirty, slight and graceful, with a beardless, olive face, possessing sharply-cut features, brilliant black eyes, a scornful mouth, and a high, smooth forehead, from which dark hair was brushed straight back, in a fashion few faces could have borne. Though very simply dressed, there was an air of elegance about him, which even handsome Harry lacked; yet, in spite of this, and of unmistakable signs of good birth and breeding, a more repulsive man I never saw. A smile, both insolent and cruel, played over his face, and the malicious gleam in his eye was as irritating as a spoken insult.

"This life is killing both of us, for night after night I have to find and bring the poor boy home worse than dead," said Augustine.

"Keep to your prayers, and let him go," began the other, coldly, but got no farther, for the sound of voices startled me out of my maze, the handle at the door slipped from my hand with a sudden click, and both looked up.

What expression Augustine wore I cannot tell, my eyes remained fixed on his companion, who underwent an instantaneous and entire change, as rising with a bland and deferential air, he stood waiting to be addressed. Collecting myself, I murmured something about "Mrs. Carruth's orders, my tea, and regret at disturbing them."

"Not at all, allow me to ring for Morris," which he did with the most engaging alacrity, then, as Augustine still stood silent, he added smilingly, "I see I must introduce myself, I am Robert Steele, a friend of the family, and Miss Snow's humble servant."

I bowed and sat down, not knowing what else to do. There was no time to feel awkward for, assuming the part of host, Steele ordered tea, and while it was preparing, leaned on the high back of the chair opposite me, talking easily while his keen eyes searched my face till I colored indignantly, and addressed myself to Augustine, who still lingered, looking moodily into the fire.

"Your sister desired me to say, if I saw you, Mr. Carruth, that she hoped you would pass an hour with her tomorrow."

He turned towards me, and his worn face grew beautiful with real feeling, as he said, heartily:

"Thank you, both for bringing so pleasant a message, and for your interest in Elinor. My mother tells me that you have succeeded admirably with her so far, and I have strong hopes that she will improve under your friendly influence."

I had opened my lips to answer, when a flurried looking servant put his head in, saying, with a glance at Augustine:

"Please, sir, will you come to Mr. Harry, I can't do nothing with him, he's so far gone."

"Hush! I'll come, John."

The young priest spoke sternly, though the color burnt in his pale cheek, and both shame and grief trembled in his voice. The servant vanished, Augustine followed hastily, and Morris signified that my supper waited. Steele moved a chair to the table, and as I took it he said, in a bland tone, which was more disagreeable to me than his sarcastic one:

"You look lonely, supping all by yourself, and since the saint has deserted, will you accept the sinner's society, and give him a cup of tea, Miss Snow?"

I assented, of course; and, while I prepared it, I resolved to observe this man as closely as he did me, for a curious feeling of antagonism had sprung up within me. I liked to study character, and fancied that I had some skill in understanding both faces and the natures of which they are the index. Courage, patience, and tact would be necessary in this case, but I was not daunted by anything as yet; and while tranquilly eating bread and butter, I looked and listened with all my senses alert. Something in my manner evidently puzzled him, for I met his keen glances without changing color now, showed no signs of disquiet at his presence, and paid no tribute of admiration to his gifts of mind or person, such as he was in the habit of receiving from most women, I suspect. My coolness amused him at first, then surprised, and lastly, annoyed. A less acute observer than he would soon have set me down as a matter-of-fact, self-possessed young woman, intent on her supper and nothing else. I was flattered, in spite of my dislike, by the trouble he took to satisfy himself to the contrary, and the decision he evidently arrived at, namely, that I was an enigma worth finding out, for reasons best known to himself. I think he suspected that Elinor had given me some hints concerning him, and this idea made him uneasy, for he asked many questions, and received such brief replies, that his patience was severely tried.

"You find Elinor an interesting charge, I fancy?"

"Yes."

"This is not the first case you have treated, I believe?"

"No."

"As Amy says, you look too young and blooming for such a life."

This required no answer, and I gave none, as I put a steaming cup into the slender, brown hand extended to receive it. He had not taken a seat, but stood on the rug in an easy attitude, glancing often at me, sometimes openly, but more frequently sending side-long looks from under his drooping lids, as if desirous of reading my face, yet concealing the most tell-tale feature of his own. Softly stirring his tea, he asked in a tone of friendly interest.

"How has she been to-day, quiet or excited?"

"Both," I answered, apparently intent on helping myself to a neat slice of marmalade.

"Turbulent and talkative, I suppose?"

"Rather so."

"What seemed to be the cause of her excitement?"

"The unfortunate state of her mind."

He put down his cup with an impatient gesture, and asked, with his eyes fixed full upon me:

"I mean what particular whim or delusion possessed her to-day? In short, what did she talk about?"

I put down my cup also, and turning a little, looked straight at him, saying with an air of decision that evidently surprised him:

"Will you allow me to ask if you are Miss Carruth's physician?"

"No, I haven't that honor," and a curious smile passed over his face as he replied.

"Then you must permit me to decline repeating anything this unhappy young lady may say in my presence. Her misfortune makes her an object of compassion, not curiosity, and to her mother or her physician alone can I report her words and actions."

I knew he was angry, for his black eyes glittered, and he shot a quick glance at me that would have daunted a timid woman, but his voice was bland as ever, and his manner more respectful than before.

"Quite right, Miss Snow; I admire your discretion, and congratulate you upon standing so well the little test I ventured to apply for my own satisfaction. As your position in this family is of a peculiar and confidential nature, I may as well tell you that I occupy a place even more peculiar and confidential than your own. Nothing occurs without my knowledge, and all affairs are referred to me without reservation, for since Mr. Carruth's retirement from the world, I play the part of elder son, as Mrs. Carruth will tell you."

He paused there, evidently expecting that I should express interest, surprise, or curiosity; I felt all three, but concealed the fact under an indifferent expression, merely saying:

"May I trouble you for the cake-basket."

He passed it, and, drawing a chair to the table, sat down, helped himself to a delicate biscuit, and while affecting to enjoy it, turned the conversation abruptly to myself.

"Are the Snows of Leicestershire relatives of yours? I met a very charming family of that name when I was abroad."

"He wants to discover where I come from," I thought to myself, and finding the amusement of thwarting him agreeable, after my dull day, I answered in my most reserved tone:

"There are many Snowdons in Leicestershire, but no Snows, I believe; they are Lincolnshire folk."

"So they are, I recollect now; but one naturally confuses names so alike. Then Major Snow's pretty daughters are cousins of yours, or some relation, I imagine?"

"None at all; I have no connections in England."

He looked annoyed, but would not be rebuffed, and assuming an expression of surprise, said hastily:

"I beg pardon, I understood you were an Englishwoman, and flattered myself that I could speak to you of persons in whom we took a mutual interest."

"I am an Englishwoman, but without relatives now, except two old aunts in Scotland."

And having vouchsafed him this one bit of intelligence, I rose, bowed gravely, and walked out of the room.

I heard him push back his chair, and lay his hand on the door-handle, but he did not turn it, and I ran up to sing Elinor to sleep, before I went to my own chamber. Free at last, I sat myself down to think, for the events of this day became doubly interesting, since the discovery I had made.

To explain this, I must briefly relate an incident that occurred more than six months ago. Being at that time out of employment, I lodged at a second-class boarding-house, the table of which did not suit me, so I took my meals at a quiet restaurant near by. Seated in my curtained box one day, while waiting for my dinner, a few words spoken in the next alcove attracted me, or rather the voice that uttered them, for it was peculiar. Sharp, and yet sweet, it had a metallic ring, like the sound of a bronze bell, and the laugh that followed was as musical as it was mirthless.

"Augustine, Elinor, Harry, and Amy, you will remember, madame, ma mere?"

A woman's voice answered, but too low for me to catch what she said, and the murmur of conversation went on for several minutes before the clear tones rose again.

"We may have long to wait, but we shall not be safe till that old marplot goes, so we will be patient."

"Good; and, meantime, we enjoy ourselves."

There was an unmistakable French accent in the woman's voice, and the fizz of a champagne-cork followed her speech.

I heard no more, for just then the waiter came to me, and his energetic demonstrations among the knives and forks, effectually warned them of my proximity. Soon I heard them rise to go, and peeping out after they had passed, I saw a tall, elderly, well-dressed woman sweeping down the hall, accompanied by the man whom I now knew as Robert Steele. I watched them a moment, thinking them mother and son, for the woman's face bore traces of the beauty which the man possessed in an eminent degree, and as I ate my dinner, I amused myself by wondering who Augustine, Elinor, Harry, and Amy might be, for what this pair must wait, and who the "old marplot" was. Then I forgot all about it till the names were uttered again, but not till I saw Steele's face did I recall where I had heard them, as well as that singular voice and laugh. Now it came back to me, and as I thought of it, Elinor's manner haunted me as she whispered—"He is the evil genius of this family."

I was getting excited with all manner of conjectures upon the subject, so I went to bed, after a two hours' reverie, resolving to trust to my instinct, which never yet had deceived me, to watch this repulsive Steele, and to serve these unhappy Carruths if I could.

CHAPTER III. HARRY

FOR A WEEK or two I led a quiet, busy life, and was rewarded for my efforts by the daily improvement of poor Elinor. I was soon convinced that the treatment she had received hitherto was all wrong; solitude was the worst thing for her, yet owing to a mistaken belief in the necessity of entire seclusion and repose, she had been left to brood over her affliction with no pleasant occupation, and no society but that of an old servant and the two women, who were merely watchful keepers, not skillful nurses or cheerful companions. The success of the new experiment proved this, and her rapid restoration surprised and delighted her family, causing them to regard me with a respect and gratitude which I did not altogether deserve.

Elinor clung to me as if I was all in all to her, growing daily more docile, quiet and self-possessed. Augustine paid frequent visits, but I did not encourage them, for a never-dying remorse seemed to oppress him more heavily, than his native melancholy, as if he could not forget that his act, just as it was, had hastened the outbreak of their inherited malady in his sister. She forgave him, and endeavored to show an unchanged affection, but the memory of the past overshadowed both, and he could never be to her what the younger brother was.

Not a day passed without bringing Harry with some new or pleasant trifle to amuse and occupy Elinor. She was happiest when with him, for then she knew he was safe, and seeing her anxiety, I did all in my power to make these interviews agreeable, that he might come often and stay long, secure from the influences that surrounded him outside of that secluded room.

It was touching to see how these unfortunate young creatures clung to one another, she tenderly trying to keep him from the reckless life that was surely hastening the fate he might otherwise escape for years; he patiently bearing with all her moods, eager to soothe and cheer the sad captivity from which he could not save her. I soon learned to love them both like an elder sister, and they regarded me as a friend whom they could trust.

Amy seldom came, being absorbed in wedding finery, but when I met her, always excused her neglect by fears that she should disturb poor, dear Nell, or sent messages which meant nothing, and which were received in silence.

Mrs. Carruth went steadily on her way, always courteous and calm in public, watchful of Elinor's comfort, and graciously confidential to me; but I could see that some terrible anxiety wore upon her, for she aged fast, and at times her face had an almost desperate expression that betrayed how fierce a battle pride and will were waging with some strong and secret adversary.

Steele haunted the house, observing all that went on with a quiet vigilance that never tired. The servants liked him, and obeyed him as if he were the master, but the family obviously hated and dreaded him, though all but Harry treated him with scrupulous politeness. I followed their example in the latter particular, but feeling neither fear nor hatred, I showed none, and the difference seemed to gratify him. If there was a good side to his nature I think I touched it, for with me he seldom showed the sarcastic, cruel spirit that made him so repulsive to the others. For some reason, he appeared anxious to please me, and I soon came to the conclusion that fearing me as an enemy, he had set himself to secure me as a friend, though what harm I could do one who seemed all-powerful in this peculiar household, I could not conceive.

It was impossible to resist the charm of his manners and conversation, when he chose to exert their fascination; but while I enjoyed this, I guarded my own face and words, and studied him with daily increasing interest. Every evening I found him waiting in the little parlor, as if it were a part of my duty to give him his tea, though I accidentally discovered, from Morris, that this was a new arrangement.

He asked no questions about Elinor (I suspect Hannah supplied him with such information as she could gather), but devoted himself to making that half-hour agreeable to us both with such apparent carelessness, yet real skill, that I could not take offence, though Morris stared, and Lizette simpered when I mentioned the fact to Mrs. Carruth. She looked surprised, mused a moment, but answered in her stately way—

"It is quite right, Miss Snow. Steele is peculiar, and is allowed to do as he likes here; so if it is not disagreeable to you, you will oblige me by letting him share your tea-table, as he comes in too late for our dinner."

So Steele continued to come, though I shrewdly suspected Mrs. Carruth had nothing to do with it, and could not have prevented it had she tried. I had no objection, for his cheerful society was very pleasant after a long day spent in the performance of my painful duty, and the new books he brought, the lively chat he kept up refreshed my mind quite as much as the rest and food did my body. I often wished that nothing had ever occurred to prejudice me against him, for he seemed to desire my good opinion, and very engaging were the various means he employed to win it; but I could not conquer my instinctive distrust and dislike, although I concealed them under a tranquil demeanor which seemed both to please and pique him.

Matters stood thus till the end of the second week, when a new care came to disturb our brief quietude. On the Saturday morning Harry came in looking weary and despondent.

"Good day, Miss Snow. How goes it, Nell? I know you had a quiet night, because you meet me smiling; I wish I could do the same."

She did meet him with a smile, but it faded as she looked up at him with tender yet reproachful eyes, and brushing the curly brown hair from his hot forehead, said gently:

"Poor lad, yours is a harder life than mine, because you have no friend like Kate, always near to keep you from temptation. Did you forget your promise again, last night, and go all wrong, Hal?"

"Look in my face, and see if I did."

He turned it fully towards her, and she was satisfied, for, though pale and worn, it was evident that the sleepless night had not been spent in dissipation. She put her arm about his neck and kissed him with a look of gratitude and love, that made his proud eyes fill, his steady lips tremble.

"Good boy, now I'm truly happy, for the thought that I can do some good in the world makes it worth my while to live. What troubled you last night, dear, that you didn't sleep?"

"The old fret, Nell. I can't bear it much longer. Amy's to be married Christmas Day, and won't put it off till New Year's, because then we are free from our promise to Steele, curse him!"

"Hush, Hal, leave condemnation to God, and help me to plan some way to evade this rash promise while there is time. I've thought till my head aches, and I don't see any way, but you are so quick you'll think of something, and Kate will help us to carry it out, though we can't tell her all just yet."

I shook my head, but privately resolved to do all I dared to hinder this unwise and mercenary marriage. Arm-in-arm the brother and sister strolled up and down the long walk in the conservatory, where we had been found; I sat by the fountain busy with my work, catching snatches of their low-toned conversation, for they had begged me not to go away.

"It is fortunate I'm never alone with Carrol, for I know I should tell him, but at home here Amy mounts guard over me, and abroad Steele or some of his spies are always at hand to keep us apart."

Harry spoke dejectedly, as though the enforced silence weighed heavily upon his spirits, but Elinor answered, with a defiant air:

"I'd not be guarded and watched, I'd go to Carrol, tell the truth, and take the consequences like a man."

"I long to do it, Nell, but I can't, for I've given my word to Steele and it is dishonorable to break a promise."

"Not when it is given to a villain—no, I won't call him that, because he is what he is.

"Perhaps, it is only natural to feel as he does, and it's not for us to talk of honor. Oh, Hal, I wish we were all dead!"

"Better wish we never had been born," he answered, in a tone more bitter than her own, and for several minutes they walked in silence.

"If father would only exert his authority, only face the world bravely and end all this, I could bear the disgrace that's come upon us," burst from Harry, "but he is so pitiably weak, so entirely under Steele's control, so afraid to thwart Amy, and—" he stopped there, as if fearing to utter the forbidden name, which should have been the dearest and sweetest to their hearts and lips.

"Remorse makes cowards of the bravest, Augustine says, what wonder that it makes a timid man the broken creature our poor father is. When did you see him, Hal?"

"Last week, I went again yesterday, but Steele was there and wouldn't let me in. Said he was too feeble to talk, and for a time it would be better for no one but—you know who, to come. That means no one, but she shall come."

"What does this portend?" asked Elinor, pausing near me, as if a sudden sense of danger made her turn to the friend she trusted most.

"Some new torment I suppose. I think that man is possessed of a devil, and takes real pleasure in giving pain, else he would pity and not revenge himself upon us for the wrong we have innocently done him. Do you believe in Satan, Miss Snow?" and Harry sat down on the fountain's brim, listlessly turning over the bright stones that lined the basin.

"I think I do, though Mr. Steele is not exactly my ideal of that historical personage. He has got a conscience, I assure you, in spite of the evil spirit that possesses him."

"Thank you, mademoiselle!"

A clear voice uttered the words, and, looking up, I saw Steele coolly surveying us from the little window, at which Mrs. Carruth had appeared.

Elinor shrunk behind her brother, but he sprung to his feet, and sent a stone singing through the air, with an impetuous gesture that gave force, though not accuracy to his aim.

Bending his head to escape the blow, Steele only laughed, as he said, in that exasperating tone of his:

"Not a gentlemanly argument, Hal."

"I'll try a stronger one then!" and Harry was turning to dash out of the conservatory in a towering passion, but Elinor held him, and Steele said, as he vanished with a wave of the hand:

"Don't disturb yourself, I'll come down to join your pleasant little party."

"Oh, Kate, he must not come! I cannot bear it!" cried Elinor excitedly.

"I'll prevent it if I murder him in doing so; the dishonorable spy and eavesdropper!" returned Harry, trying to escape from her hold.

"Stay here both of you, I will attend to Mr. Steele," and, hurrying out, I closed the door behind me.

Not a moment too soon, for, as I turned the key in the lock, he entered, smiling still, but with a glitter in his black eyes that boded no good to those he came in search of.

"Steele is the countersign, so allow me to pass, fair and faithful sentinel," he said, advancing as near as possible without touching me.

"That is not the countersign, therefore you cannot pass, comrade," and, putting the key in my pocket, I leaned against the door regarding him with a much calmer and cooler face than his own.

"Really, Miss Snow, you carry matters with a high hand. Are you aware that it is somewhat dangerous to oppose me?" He knit his brows, and eyed me with an air of mingled anger and surprise.

"I see it is for others, but I know nothing of fear, and must obey orders at any cost."

"Whose orders?"

"Dr. Shirley's; he insists that Elinor be kept quiet, your appearance has already done her harm; you can go no further."

"But I have an equal right with that boy to visit her."

"Permit me to doubt that."

He seemed about to speak, but checked himself hastily, and folding his arms, looked at me with a strange expression. Soon, he spoke more quietly, but more imperatively:

"Mrs. Carruth allows me to come; I wish to see Elinor, and I am accustomed to be obeyed. Be kind enough to open the door."

"Pardon me if I refuse; Mrs. Carruth gave Elinor into my care, and this very morning begged I would use my own judgment about admitting her brothers and sister. I think it unwise and unsafe to allow you to intrude upon her, and I cannot permit it."

"Do you know that I am master in this house, Miss Snow?"

"Not my master, Mr. Steele, and I am mistress here till Mrs. Carruth dismisses me."

I was indignant at his persistence, and though I controlled my voice, my eyes kindled, and I confronted him with as resolute a mien as his own. He stepped back a step; the frown changed to a half smile, the look of haughty displeasure to one of frank admiration, and he said with a curious expression of mingled annoyance, submission, and friendliness:

"I'm not used to giving up my own will, but I admire your courage so much, that I am tempted to yield for the sake of enjoying a novel experience. What will you give me, Miss Snow, if I submit to this new mistress of ours?"

"My thanks, and much respect for a man who can control his temper, forgive a small injury, and pity a great affliction."

A wonderfully soft and sweet expression swept across his face, as I looked up at him with a confiding air, for I felt that I had won the victory this time.

"Will you shake hands, and not forget to come down at dusk as you did last night?"

He offered his hand, and I readily withdrew mine from my pocket where I had kept it; in doing so the key caught in my ring, and fell to the floor. I sprung to recover it, but he was quicker than I, and holding it fast, glanced at me with all the old malice in his eyes, the old sharpness in his voice, as he said, smiling:

"Now the tables are turned, it is you who must ask admittance, and I who may refuse it if I will. Shall I follow your stern example?"

"Yes, by doing what you know to be right, however disagreeable it may be."

"Was it disagreeable to deny me?"

"I rather liked it till you gave in."

He laughed at that, turned the key to and fro, and seemed debating some point in his own mind. I stood silent, still before the locked door, and bent on resisting to the last. I think he saw that, and found a new charm in encountering a will as strong as his own. The bad expression faded away, to be replaced by one I had never seen till now, and half sad, half wistful was the glance he gave me, as he said, thoughtfully eyeing me:

"You are a curious person; I think you could cast out my devil if you tried. Hal is right in saying I have one. Some day I'll tell you what it is. Won't you even ask me for the key?"

"No."

"Why not? I think you could plead eloquently if you chose."

"There is no need of it; I know you will be generous, and show that you value the good opinion of even so insignificant a person as myself."

I held out my hand as I spoke, he put the key into it, and left the room, with a quiet "Thank you."

Eager to know how my prisoners had fared, I opened the door and went in, to find Elinor still trembling, yet laughing, as she watched Harry, who had dragged a stout flower-stand to the wall, climbed in at the window, locked the little room door, and was in the act of descending, muttering vengeance as he came.

"There, you are safe in that direction, Nell, and I'll stand guard before your door if nothing else will keep him out. Well, Miss Snow, have you routed the enemy?"

"Yes, he has signed a truce and left the field. Now, Mr. Harry, promise me one thing, control yourself and avoid him for Elinor's sake, if not for your own," I said earnestly, as the sister leaned against me, and the brother stood before us still flushed and ireful.

"I'll promise, but I shall have to leave the house in order to keep it, or the first time he looks at me in that insulting way of his, I shall knock him down. Can you trust me away, Nell?"

"I must; but, dear, be careful; remember how much my happiness depends on you, and come home the same good lad you go. See father if you can, and be with Augustine as much as possible; you are safe there, though I know it's dull."

"He bores me desperately with his piety, but I'll do my best to stand it, and be back as soon as my wrath has subsided. It's useless to wait for Steele's to die out; he never forgets or forgives, and sooner or later I shall have to suffer for the pebble that went over his head. Good bye, Nell, keep up your spirits, dear. Take care of her Miss Snow, and don't let the enemy steal a march upon you while I'm gone."

Trying to speak cheerfully, Harry embraced his sister, shook me warmly by the hand, and went away to face temptation without that he might escape it within.

I kept my promise, and at dusk went down to the little parlor, wondering how Steele would meet me. A handful of winter roses lay beside my plate, but he was not there, and I missed him, for my meal seemed very lonely, very dull, without his dark, vivacious face opposite, and his familiar voice sounding in my ear. I was soon done, yet lingered musing over my flowers till he entered hastily, evidently expecting to find the room empty. He had looked gloomy, hard, and cold, but a glance of surprise and pleasure broke over his face as he saw me.

"Ah, you have waited; thank you."

"No, I am done, and must go directly. Will you have some tea?"

"I have just dined, but I will take one cup, as you are here to pour it out for me."

He took it, standing before the fire, and, having served him, I turned to go. A rose dropped from my bouquet. As I took it up he stooped for it, and in the act a small stone slipped from his vest pocket and went rolling across the rug. It was nearest to me. I took it up, recognizing it as the one Harry had flung, and a sudden fear came over me as his words returned to my memory. He looked somewhat annoyed, but stood idly playing with the flower, as my eye went from the stone to his face.

"There is an old saying that a revengeful man will keep a stone in his pocket seven years, turn it, keep it seven more years and then hurl it at his enemy. You are not one of that sort, I hope, Mr. Steele."

He shrugged his shoulders with a laugh, and answered, as he tossed the rose into the fire:

"I shall not touch the boy, neither shall I forget his insolence, though it is beneath me to take further notice of it. Do you like your flowers?"

"Yes, they are English roses, and brought me a dream of home, for which I thank you."

"Are you going so soon?"

"Elinor is waiting for me; good night," and I went away, carrying the offending pebble with me.

All that week Steele was unusually gay and amiable, and all that week we heard nothing of Harry. From Augustine we learned that he had not visited either his brother or his father, nor was he to be found in his old haunts; and, as day after day passed, we grew very anxious. I felt sure that Steele knew something of him, but he protested upon his honor that he had not seen him, and assured us that he would come back when the reckless fit was over.

Elinor grew restless, and I harbored thoughts that I dared not utter, but the rest of the family seemed to have grown used to his wayward habits, and waited, without much disquiet, for his return.

On Friday evening there was company, and I stayed with Elinor until she slept, for the sound of music reached us even in our remote apartment, and disturbed her by recalling the time when she was the gayest of the gay in scenes like these. She was still at last, and, slipping down into the little parlor, I refreshed myself, then taking a book, sat reading, and enjoying the pleasant stir that went on above. Suddenly some one tapped at the long window that opened on the rear of the house. I drew up the curtain, saw Harry, and, with an exclamation of joy, unfastened the sash and threw it wide. Without a word he staggered in, cast himself down upon the couch, and lay there breathing heavily. I approached him with some hesitation, the cause of which he seemed to understand, for, turning his haggard face towards me, he said hoarsely:

"I'm sober; don't be afraid of me. I'm wet, and cold, and sick. Let me lie here till I get my breath, then I'll creep away and trouble no one."

A second glance showed me that he spoke the truth, and I went to him full of sympathy. He was a sad sight as he lay there coughing a hollow cough, with feverish color, sunken eyes, and parched lips. His clothes were stained and wet, his hair neglected, his whole appearance that of one who had passed through wild scenes, and barely escaped alive.

"What has happened? Where have you been? Elinor has been very anxious and so have I," I said, stirring the fire and bringing a cushion for his head, as he leaned back, exhausted with his cough. He looked up at me with a piteous expression, and whispered with a shudder:

"Don't ask me; don't tell poor Nell, she'll be so disappointed. I couldn't help it. I tried to keep away, but they got me once, and then it was all over with me."

"Who got you, Harry?" I demanded indignantly, as he paused to wipe his damp forehead and drink the water I held to his lips.

"Steele's tools, they know where to find me, and how to tempt me, and they have no pity."

"But he protested that he knew nothing of you?"

"How could he know when they took me away and kept me beside myself for days? A word to them was enough, and all my promises, my resolutions were in vain. I told you he'd neither forgive nor forget, and he has not."

As the words left his lips, Steele entered, started on seeing the deplorable sight before him, shot a quick look at me, then, composing himself, advanced, with well feigned surprise.

"Why, Hal, what is it? Ah, I see; Miss Snow, this is no place for you; I will find John and see to the boy."

Before I could answer, Harry struggled to his feet, and, pointing to himself with a gesture, as full of pathetic significance as his broken voice, he said, with the saddest look I ever saw on a human face:

"Are you satisfied? Is a week of suffering and degradation punishment enough for a moment's anger?"

"What do you mean? I don't understand you," began Steele, whose face was now as impassive as that of the bronze bust above his head.

"You know that I am in your way, and you want me out of it. This is not the first time you've tried to rid yourself of me, though it would be more merciful to shoot me than to play this game, that kills soul as well as body. Augustine has renounced everything. Amy will soon be gone, poor Nell is harmless, and I shan't trouble you long; I've got my death at last, I think."

A paroxysm of coughing that shook him from head to foot, checked his passionate speech, and forced him to drop down again till it was over. Steele had turned pale to his lips, but commanded himself perfectly, for, with an accent of pity and regret, he exclaimed, as he approached to offer aid:

"I forgive these hard words, for you are not yourself tonight. Let me help you to your room, and make you comfortable if I can."

"Hands off!" cried Harry, starting up. "I'd rather creep on my hands and knees than owe you any favor, for I despise and hate you, though you are—"

"Stop!" and Steele's voice rung through the room with a tone that would have quelled a more rebellious spirit than poor Harry's. He did stop for the other's eye flashed ominously, and he pointed to the door with an aspect that compelled obedience from one party, but roused the other to open defiance.

"Go to your room, young man, and remember what you are before you insult a gentleman with such maudlin bravado. Remain, if you please, Miss Snow; I wish to speak to you."

"I refuse to listen. Come, Harry, lean on me, and let me fill your sister's place tonight."

How Steele received my answer I cannot tell, for, without turning my head, I drew Harry's arm through mine, and led him from the room. No one followed us, but I heard the hall door close as I helped the poor lad up the private staircase that shut us out from the gay confusion of the front part of the house, and hardly had I landed him in his own apartment, and called his man, when Dr. Shirley, who lived near by, came bustling in, sent by Mr. Steele, he said. There was no further need of me, and I was going away when Harry called me back, to whisper, as he pressed my hand with a grateful look:

"Don't tell Elinor; I may be well enough to see her in the morning."

I promised, and left him with a full heart, but in the morning he was tossing in a high fever, and for days there was but little hope that Elinor would ever see him in this world again.

Chapter IV. Thrice Baffled

"I HAVE DECIDED, and my last hope is in you, Kate."

I was startled from the reverie in which I was indulging, as I sewed, by Elinor's hand on my shoulder, and the sound of her voice abruptly breaking the long silence that had reigned between us.

"What have you decided on, and how can I help you, dear?" I asked as she sat down beside me, with a look of calm determination, and lowering her voice, said earnestly:

"To prevent this wedding, and you must carry out my plan, because I am a prisoner here. Listen, and don't disappoint me. Augustine will do nothing but lament and pray. Harry is ill, and feels bound in honor to keep this dreadful promise. That is a man's idea of honor, mine is different, and I will have the truth told at all costs. Steele has no right to force us to this new disgrace, and whatever the consequences of my act may be, I shall brave them. Will you help me, Kate?"

Her eyes pleaded more eloquently than her tongue; I knew she was perfectly sane now, and from various hints thought I had gathered readily: "I will."

"God bless you!" she said, with a face of the intensest gratitude. "I thought you would befriend me; with your wit and courage on my side, I am sure we will succeed. This is my plan, very simple and straightforward in itself, but, with Steele to watch us, it will need much skill to carry it out. I've written to Carrol, and you must give him the note unseen by any one. Can you?"

"Nothing easier," I began, but paused as the recollection came over me that, though I often caught glimpses of Amy's lover, he never was alone. His bethrothed, Mrs. Carruth, Steele, or some young companion was always with him, and, as I had hitherto avoided him, I could not change my manner suddenly without exciting suspicion. But, trusting to chance and my own wit, I had no doubt that some opportunity would appear, now that I was on the watch for it. Elinor did not observe my pause, so eager was she, and drawing a sealed note from her bosom, put it into my hand, whispering anxiously:

"Be careful; be sure you are alone with him before you give it, and watch Steele safely away, else he will surprise you. Go now for your evening stroll about the house; it's just the time that Carrol comes, they say; you cannot fail to meet him somewhere."

The excitement of the little venture pleased me, and, slipping the note into my pocket, I left her, with assurances that I would do my best. First I took a tour of all the lower rooms, and satisfied myself that Steele was not there; next I ran up and inquired for Harry, taking a comprehensive survey of the apartment as I stood at the door. No one but John, and the poor lad fast asleep, were to be seen. John and I were on good terms, and I ventured to ask, as I turned away, "Is Mr. Steele in, do you think?"

"No, miss; I'm quite sure he went out half an hour ago. Shall I see for you?"

"No, thank you, it's of no consequence."

Arming myself with a book of his, I did what I had never done before—went to his room, intending to return it if he was there, or to assure myself that he was out, if such was the case. There was no answer to my tap, and, after several repetitions of it, I opened the door and boldly looked in. The glow of a brilliant fire lighted every corner, and a single glance satisfied me of his absence. Well pleased with my success, so far, I was about to close the door, when something on the table caught my eye, and made me involuntarily advance a step or two nearer, to assure myself of what I saw. Nothing but a little nosegay of white and purple heath, that I had worn the day before, for Elinor took pleasure in seeing me wear the flowers she liked. I knew they were the same, for the bit of scarlet silk she tied about them still remained, as I plainly saw through the transparent glass of the slender vase that held them. I could not remember where I had lost them, but here they were, carefully preserved, and set apart as if beautiful or precious in their new possessor's sight. Forgetting everything else, I stood a moment, wondering if he loved Elinor, for no discovery or demonstration would have surprised me now, especially concerning him. Then I recollected that he did not know these were her flowers, and, recalling his looks and manner of late, I smiled a little scornfully, yet colored at the same time, as the thought would come that he had kept them for my sake.

Angry with him and with myself, I left the room and took up my quiet march again, through deserted halls and drawing-rooms, waiting and watching for young Carrol. This gentleman, though of good family, had not a character to match; and, having squandered his own fortune, was ready to sell himself for another. Amy had secured the prize, and seemed quite satisfied with her purchase, for competition added to its value. I particularly disliked him, for he belonged to that class of fashionable men who knew nothing of real manliness, and are a disgrace to society. A spice of feminine pride and pique mingled with my dislike, for Mr. Carrol did me what he considered the honor of admiring me, and took no pains to conceal his opinion, much to Amy's indignation. The first time I crossed his path, as he stood in the hall, with his fiancée, he said, without taking the trouble to lower his voice, as he looked after me:

"Who is that?"

"Only Nell's companion," the reply.

"I envy Nell, then; that's a deuced fine woman."

"Fred, be quiet, I'll allow you to admire no one but me."

"Of course not; but you'll allow me to look at a pretty woman, won't you? One amuses one's self with handsome governesses and companions, but one loves and admires angels, like yourself."

More of this charming dialogue I did not hear but walked away, resolving to show Mr. Carrol that it was impossible to amuse one's self with companions like Miss Snow.

Since then, no gray-haired duenna could have been more forbidding than myself when we occasionally met; and, learning from some one that I was a gentlewoman, Mr. Carrol soon contented himself by staring in a manner which strongly tempted me to ask Steele to effect an improvement in the gentleman's manners. Thinking of these things as I roamed up and down, I was in no humor to meet the expected guest; and but for Elinor's sake I would have refused the task.

Expecting to be warned of his approach by a ring, I was rather startled by suddenly hearing his voice in the hall, and, peeping out of the dusky room where I chanced to be, into the light beyond, I was still more disturbed to see Steele entering with him. Pausing a moment to put down their hats, they went into the library, apparently intent upon some business matter. The ladies were not at home, and I knew the gentlemen would not linger long. Steele would be with Carrol to the last, so my opportunity was lost. Anxious not to disappoint Elinor, I followed a sudden impulse, and, gliding down the hall, put the note into the pocket of the coat Carrol had thrown upon a chair. Hardly had I done so when a stir announced their coming; I darted back into the dim parlor, and, a moment after, would have given all I possessed to have had the note again.

"Much obliged for the use of it; I should have suffered with the cold if I hadn't had it; but it's so mild tonight, I'll wear my own home," said Carrol, pausing to cherish his newly-lighted cigar from the draft of the opening door.

"It's in my room; I'll get it for you; I don't allow the servants to meddle on my premises," answered Steele, as he threw the coat over his arm and ran up stairs.

Great was my dismay, and doubly trying was my failure, for there stood Carrol alone; but the note was gone, and gone into the hands of the person from whom I would most carefully have guarded it.

I wrung my hands in the darkness, and could have cried with vexation, while Carrol admired his blasé countenance in the long mirror, and enjoyed his cigar. There was little time for either of us to pursue our employments, for Steele, who always moved with noiseless rapidity, was back again before I could decide what to do; and, with a few words, they parted, Carrol leaving the house, the other going to wait for me below. Without stopping to think, I flew up stairs, straight to Steele's room again, and looked about me for the coat. It lay, folded, over the arm of the sofa, and, feeling like a thief, I plunged my hand into the pocket. Thank heaven! the note was there. I seized it, hurried to my own chamber, and sat down, trembling and breathless with the excitement of the adventure.

As soon as I was myself again, I returned to Elinor, and told my story. She was bitterly disappointed, but bore it well, and, saying we must try again, sent me away to my supper. With no appetite, but much secret exultation over the defeat he had unconsciously sustained, I took my place, and puzzled Steele by my unwonted spirits. Since Harry's return I had been cold and quiet when with "our enemy," as we called Steele; but his manner had never varied, except to grow more amiable and submissive. If he intended to express penitence, and solicit friendship or regard, he failed decidedly, for I had no faith in him, but looked upon him as an accomplished actor, and remained untouched by his most engaging demonstrations. This angered him; yet, though he had gone away in a calm, white rage more than once, he always came again, next night, as cheerful and serene as if nothing had been amiss. I could not understand him, but found a curious pleasure in watching him, for my secluded life allowed me no other companionship, and most women would have found it both charming and dangerous. I did not, for my love-dream had ended long ago, never to return again. I simply enjoyed his society, and regarded him as an agreeable enigma, the solution of which grew more exciting as I went on.

"You look wicked to-night, Miss Snow; what have you been doing?" he said, after observing me in his covert way a few minutes.

"I've been taking my usual exercise," I answered demurely, though my eyes still shone with excitement and secret mirth.

"Unusually lively exercise, I fancy, for your blooming cheeks belie your name."

"That is a better compliment than the other; but my nature does not belie my name though my cheeks may."

"Have you been dancing again to-night?"

"Yes," and I laughed involuntarily as I thought of my run upstairs and down. "How do you know I ever dance?" I added sharply.

"Last night I saw you performing a stately sort of minuet alone in the twilight, and was strongly tempted to applaud. I think I deserve a smile instead of a frown for my self-control."

He looked wicked now, but I was disturbed, for his words confirmed a vague fancy of my own and I felt sure that he had watched me more than once when I believed myself alone.

"I shall neither dance nor walk again, but leave the house to you, since you are fond of twilight strolls," I said in my coldest manner.

"I give you my word I'll never haunt your steps again if it displeases you. Will you allow me to atone for my misdemeanor by driving you out tomorrow in the sunshine?"

"No, thank you; I'm still too English for that. At home masters do not take their servants out to drive, however bright the sunshine or fine the roads."

"But you are not a servant, and no lady in the land is prouder than yourself. Neither am I your master, as you once informed me. I wish I were," he added under his breath.

That did not suit me, and I froze immediately, eating in silence, and leaving him the instant I had done.

Next morning Elinor met me with a new plan. I was to go out ostensibly to make purchases for her, as I had done several times before, but after doing an errand or two, I was to go to Mrs. Carrol's, inquire for her son, and boldly give him the note as if from Amy, who kept the servant pacing to and fro with endless messages concerning the bridal preparations. Steele never visited there, for there was a house full of romantic young ladies, who were his especial horror, as all six adored him in school-girl fashion.

"If you go early, Fred will not have gone out and the girls will be busy. Ask Amy if she has any commissions for you. She will probably give you a note or message as she did the other day and that will cover your real purpose. Will you try once more for me, Kate?"

I agreed, and, with many misgivings, set out upon my second adventure, often glancing behind me, sure that I should see Steele following on my trail. No one was visible, however, and I reached the Carrols undisturbed.

Amy had given me a note to her lover, and holding both in my muff, I rung the bell. A sleepy servant admitted me, looked somewhat surprised when I asked for his master, said he would see if he was up, and left me in a dining-room, evidently just vacated by the housemaid for dust still flew, and windows stood open. Near one of these I seated myself, and, while I waited, idly compared the difference in the two addresses of the letters I held. The words were the same, but the writing was as unlike as the characters of the sisters. Elinor's lay uppermost, and I was arranging a little speech which should secure Carrol's immediate attention for it, when a sudden im-pulse made me look up to see Steele at the window, with his eyes fixed upon the letter.

I felt as I imagine a fascinated bird feels when the serpent first arrests its eye; it was impossible to speak or move, and for a moment I sat looking at him as if he were a ghost.

His noiseless approach startled me, and I was conscious of a nervous conviction that I never should be alone again. He had evidently followed me, for he showed no surprise on seeing me, and some suspicion of my purpose must have brought him to that unwonted place at that unseasonable hour. The minute I stirred, his eye rose to mine; the smile that always roused me like an insult played about his mouth, and the tones of his voice betrayed at once that he foreboded mischief, and was on the alert.

"Good morning—it rains—you forgot your umbrella, and I came to bring you one."

The appearance of Carrol restored my self-possession, and turning my back upon Steele, I adroitly whisked Elinor's letter into my muff as I rose to offer Amy's to her yawning lover. With a nod to Steele, a gracious bow to me, and much wonder-ment at my appearance visible in his face, Carrol read his note, threw it on the table, and observed, with a most unlover-like expression:

"It was cruel of her to send you out at this absurd hour, and drag me up just to tell me Miss Somebody or other can't be bridesmaid. She wants an answer, so just tell her, Miss Snow, that I say, have none at all, and beg to be left in peace to prepare for my doom—I mean my bliss."

While he was speaking I had gained the door, hoping that in the hall I could give him the note; but Steele was there before me, and nothing left for me to do but to decline Carrol's urgent invitation to sit and rest, and leave the house, still followed by my unwished for escort. I was desperately angry, but my anger, like his, was of the quiet, undemonstrative sort, so I contented myself by silently refusing both the arm and the umbrella he offered, and walking rapidly away through the rain with a calm countenance and a very wrathful spirit. He kept beside me, with his eyes upon my muff, for he had evidently seen both notes, recognized Elinor's writing, and was bent on discovering what it contained. I was equally bent on disappointing him, and not knowing what his next move might be, I destroyed the note as I walked, intending to dispose of the fragments at the first opportunity. It soon came. I had unfastened my cloak as I sat, and forgotten to rearrange it in my flurry, on reaching the corner of the street, a strong gust blew it off my shoulders. It was impossible to tie it with one hand. Steele saw that, and said in his most courteous voice, from which he could not keep an undertone of eagerness, however:

"Let me hold your muff for you, Miss Snow."

With a little shake, that sent the fragments of the note flying away on the wind, I handed him the muff and fastened my cloak, with an irrepressible smile at the blank look he wore. Only for an instant, then, the expression of mingled anger, disappointment, and admiration, which I had seen when I put the key in my pocket, flashed over his face—his mouth grew grim, but his eyes smiled, and his voice was perfectly calm.

"Very well done, mademoiselle, I knew it was there and meant to have it, but you have outwitted me. I admire your skill and courage, but I never allow any one to thwart me with impunity, therefore you will atone for this by going home on my arm and under my umbrella."

As he spoke he drew my hand through his arm, and held it there so firmly that I could not liberate myself without a struggle, which I was too proud to attempt. Submitting in silence, I walked on till the ludicrous side of the affair struck me so strongly that I could not restrain a noiseless fit of merriment. I turned my head away, but he felt my hand tremble, thought I was crying, and, stooping, looked into my face with a troubled expression in his own. I never shall forget the astonished glance he gave me—it capped the climax, and I laughed aloud, for my spirits were not banished yet, in spite of the sombre life I had led.

"Well, of all the inexplicable, tantalizing, capricious women, you are the queen. Shall I never understand you, Kate?"

He spoke almost petulantly, but held my hand closer, and regarded me with something warmer than either anger or admiration in his eyes.

"Never, Mr. Steele; but I understand you better than you think, and henceforth I shall place implicit faith in my own instinct."

"Did your instinct warn you against me?" he asked, after studying my face a moment.

"Yes, decidedly."

"And mine as decidedly counseled me to respect and trust you. I heartily wish you could say the same."

"How can I after all I have seen and heard?"

"What have you seen? What have you heard?" and his voice grew imperious again.

"I have seen and heard how you treat poor Harry, and this is but another example of the dishonorable surveillance which you exercise over all the inmates of the Carruth's house. What right have you to do these things?"

"I will tell you on New Year's Day. Will you wait till then?"

"Not if I can satisfy myself before."

"Ah, you enter the lists against me, do you? Beware in time. You have a brave heart, a quick wit, and a face that would beguile a saint, but you will not succeed, for I never permit myself to be conquered."

"Except by a woman," and with a smile which, I suspect, would have tried the temper of the meekest man, I glanced significantly at several tiny fragments of the torn note that still clung to the trimming of my cloak.

But the more I defied and thwarted him the better he seemed to like me, and though he flushed to his hat brim, he eyed me with the look I did not like to meet, as he said, lowering his voice:

"My name expresses my nature better than yours does your own, cool as you are. I may be bent, but a woman's hand cannot break me, so be warned, for if I begin to fence in earnest you will be wounded to the heart, perhaps, Kate."

I shrugged my shoulders, a trick learned from him, and answered as we paused before the house:

"This is not a game of hearts, and I have no fears for my own. Have I your permission to go in?"

"Not till you thank me in your most charming manner for my care of you this rainy morning. You will not? Then I shall punish your ingratitude as I please;" and, under cover of the umbrella, he bent and kissed my hand as he released it.

"Don't be melo-dramatic, Mr. Steele."

My tongue was my only weapon of retaliation and I used it with effect when I echoed his own words, for, as I ran up stairs, I heard him fling his umbrella into one chair, his hat into another, and mutter something between his teeth which proved that his patience was exhausted at last.

Elinor was in despair when I told her of this second failure, for now but a single day remained before the wedding. The fact that Steele suspected us, and was on the watch seemed to rob her of both energy and hope; but I would not despond nor believe that wrong should conquer right, though how to prevent it in this case I failed to discover. Harry was mending, but still too feeble to be of any use; Augustine, when I appealed to him, answered, with the spiritless submission of a weak man entirely subjugated by fear of a strong one, that though he had done with pride, ambition, and the hope of happiness for himself, he had no right to judge for others; the family were at Steele's mercy, and if they choose to purchase safety at the cost of truth and honor, he dared not interfere. I thought of speaking to Mrs. Carruth, but she avoided me, and I felt that no appeal even from her daughter would have power to turn her from her purpose. Amy was equally inaccessible, and failing in all these directions, my last hope lay in Steele. Daring as the design was, I resolved to appeal to him, thereby testing whether the regard he had professed for me was genuine, or merely an attempt to blind my eyes, and secure my interest by flattering my vanity. Brief as the time had been, circumstances had thrown us much together in a manner which soon did away with ceremony and reserve; I now began to think he really loved me, for though he had not confessed in words his face betrayed it, and my first fancy that it was a consummate piece of acting, was fast yielding to that consciousness of power, which seldom fails to assure a woman when she is beloved. I was both grieved and glad at this, grieved because I could make no return, glad because it gave me a weapon, which

I determined to use for his own good and that of those in whom I felt as strong an interest as if I had been akin to them.

I said nothing to Elinor of my purpose, but on the night before the wedding, waited for Steele with an anxious heart. He came later, looking morose and tired, but his face brightened as it always did, when he found me there, and he was about to seat himself like one well pleased, when fearing interruptions, I arrested him.

"Can I speak to you a moment, Mr. Steele?"

"You know you can, and the longer the moment the better. What is amiss, Kate?"

He had begun playfully, but ended seriously for my face disturbed him; he was alert at once, his eyes grew vigilant, his voice commanding, and standing opposite me on the rug, he seemed to prepare himself for ill news. Looking up at him with a beseeching glance, I said earnestly:

"You once asked me to plead to you, then I would not, now I will with all the eloquence I can bring to my petition. Will you hear me?"

"Yes."

Only one word, but I took heart, for it was uttered quickly, and he looked away as if he feared that my eyes would plead better for me than my voice. Drawing a step nearer, I went straight to the point.

"I know you have a heart, I believe you have a conscience, and I appeal to both when I ask you to free this family from the dishonorable silence you have imposed upon them, or to tell Carrol the secret he should know before he marries Amy."

Steele drew a long breath, as if relieved from some hidden fear, and the frown vanished from his forehead, as he said gravely, with his keen eyes full upon me now:

"It appears that some of them have already freed themselves from the promise which all made willingly a few months ago, else how did you know there was a secret?"

"No one could live long in this house, without discovering that something was wrong," I said. "Elinor told me of the sad inheritance which oppresses them, but nothing more except that there is some obstacle to Amy's marriage, of which Carrol should be informed. You alone can do this without breaking a promise, and I conjure you to do it, for the sake of truth and justice, if not for the sake of the poor girl who sues to you through me."

"You are deceived, Miss Snow; Elinor's excited mind exaggerates the matter. The betrayal of this secret would not influence Carrol; he cares only for money; Mr. Carruth is a millionaire; Amy's portion a fortune in itself, and that being secured to her, Carrol would not give her up even if the obstacle were greater than it is."

"But Elinor says it would influence him, and though it may mar Amy's happiness, it should be told, for silence is treachery and dishonor."

"I assure you it is not so; will you believe a half-insane girl before me?"

"Yes."

"Have you no faith in me?"

"Not a whit."

His eyes flashed, the pale olive of his face darkened with a fiery glow, and, for the second time, I saw the fierce spirit that possessed him. Had I been a man I think he would have struck me; being a woman, he only set his teeth, walked fast through the room, and paused at the window to control himself. That instant gave me time to bethink myself, to remember that if I angered him my cause was lost, and to devise a safer way of winning it, I went to him, laid my hand upon his arm, and said, with genuine feeling in my voice:

"Forgive me if I judge you harshly, and prove me in the wrong. Be generous and just; if you have power use it magnanimously, and make these people friends, not enemies. I want to respect and trust you, show me that you deserve esteem, and you shall have it."

He did not speak, but, in his half-averted face, I saw no anger, and forgetting myself, I earnestly went on:

"Grant Elinor's desire, and earn real gratitude from both of us. She has little hope, but I have much, for, in spite of all I have seen and heard, I do believe that you possess a better nature than the hard one you show the world. Do not disappoint me, but give me the happiness of knowing that I can rouse and touch it, making you the man you should be."

"I will, on one condition."

He turned now, took both my hands, and bent on me the soft, bright look so rarely seen upon his face, so beautiful when there. I knew what was coming, longed to prevent it, but found no words, and in a tone I had never heard before, he rapidly went on:

"You are right; I have a better nature than the one I show the world, but it has been neglected all my life. No one has had the will or power to call it out but you, and in you I find my fate. I will do all you ask me, though it may cost me dear, if in return you will give me, not only the respect and confidence you promise, but love. Shall I receive it, Kate?"

There was no acting here; this was nature, not art; I felt that instantly, for there was real emotion in his voice, real passion in his eye, and his hands held mine as if I was indeed his fate, and he implored me to be kind. Had I loved him I should have confessed it then, and found a sweet satisfaction in the knowledge that I had the power to serve and save a fellow creature. I did not love him, and the self reproach that moment brought me was my punishment for so long believing that the one true affection of this man's life was all a lie. Much as I longed to help Elinor I could not deceive him now, though in denying him, I lost my cause. Steadying my voice, and letting my voice betray both penitence and pity, I looked up at him with a feeling at my heart which I never thought he could rouse, and said as gently as firmly:

"It is impossible, I have no love to give you, for happy as I seem, there is a memory in my heart which keeps it faithful to the past. I thank you, I will gladly be your friend, I can be nothing more."

"You must be, I am lost if you desert me! Wait a little and let me try to win you; I never failed in anything I set my heart upon, and never did I desire anything so ardently as I desire you."

No need to tell me that, for his face was all aglow with love and longing, and he drew me towards him as if to claim and keep me in defiance of all opposition. But I broke away and retreated to the door, feeling that the sooner we parted now the better for us both.

"I cannot change my answer, forgive me and forget me, it will be easy, for you have known me too short a time to nourish a very deep affection. Will not your reply be kinder than mine? May I tell Elinor, that you will grant her prayer, and so win many friends instead of one?"

Steele had grown very pale, a sure sign of strong excitement; the veins rose dark upon his forehead, the bitter, bad expression returned, and when he spoke his voice shook with suppressed wrath, though it never rose above its usual low tone.

"I never forgive nor forget, Miss Snow, and by another week, I think you will repent the answer you have given me to-night. Tell Elinor, that if a word from me could save them all from the disgrace in store for them, I would not utter it, though I confirmed my own damnation by the silence."

Trembling before the storm I had raised, I crept away to my own room to awake and watch and weep, for this fiery lover recalled the memory of another, who had wooed more gently and received a kinder answer. Death had parted us, but like Elinor's, mine was a widowed heart and would remain so all my life.

Chapter V. Behind a Veil

AMY WAS TO BE MARRIED in the morning, and sail on the same day, for her honeymoon was to be spent in Paris. She had set her heart on a splendid wedding, but her mother insisted on a very private one, feeling, doubtless, that she had neither strength nor courage for display. Still the house was in a stir on Christmas morning, and even stolid Hannah looked excited. The six Misses Carrol pervaded the premises, and a few intimate friends arrived at the appointed time.

Elinor seemed to have relinquished all hope, and I, having done my best, determined to stand aside and let this ill-fated family make or mar their fortunes as they would. But when the hour drew near, Elinor grew restless; all my efforts to amuse her failed. I got her into the conservatory, where not a sound could reach us, and was reading aloud, when, suddenly, she struck her hands together, and sprung up with unwonted energy. I looked at her, fearing some outbreak. She stood, with her eyes fixed on the little window, but no one was there, and it remained shut, as Harry left it.

"What is it?" I asked.

She did not answer for several minutes; then, as if my question had just reached her preoccupied mind, she replied, with a curious smile:

"I've thought of something that will amuse us both. You never saw my wedding dress. I'm going to put it on, and divert myself with playing bride, since I cannot see the real one to-day. Amy promised to let me see her, but she has forgotten. Sit still; I'll be back directly."

She went into her room, and I heard her moving hurriedly about, unlocking drawers, rustling silks, and singing to herself, in an undertone. All this disturbed me; but, hoping she would find some pleasure in her strange freak, I let her alone, and waited patiently. Sooner than I expected, she returned, so changed I scarcely knew her. All in white, with the silvery shimmer of silk under lace, a costly veil upon her head, pearls on her neck and arms, and a glow, a brightness, in her usually pale face, that made her very beautiful.

"See, Kate, I should have looked like this. I would have no orange blossoms; Edward liked white roses better. He was to bring them, but the day never came."

I had no words in which to answer her, for my lips trembled, and my eyes were full. She understood the sympathy, the grief that made my heart ache for her, and, laying her arm about my neck, she said, in the same quiet tone:

"Don't grieve for me, dear; those heavy times are over now. Yet all the bitterness comes back to-day, and it seems hard, very hard, that Amy may be happy, and not I. Ah! well, my turn will come hereafter, in a world where there is neither marrying nor giving in marriage."

She stood silent for a moment; then said, as if to herself:

"I wonder if it is over yet? How I should like to see them all!"

"I wish it were possible; but when I asked Dr. Shirley, you know he said, decidedly, that it was better not," I answered.

"He is right, I submit; but I do long to see my father; he is to come, Harry told me; but he will not visit me. He is afraid of me, no matter how well I may be, and so I never ask him to come. A strange, sad family we are; and the saddest thing to-day is, that I may not see my only sister married."

"You will hear about it, dear, and Amy will soon be up to say good-bye."

"She will forget me; no one will tell me anything, for Harry is not there, and Augustine never talks of worldly things. I wish you would go down and look for me, please, Kate; just one peep with your keen eyes, and then I shall be satisfied."

"It is impossible; I am not dressed; there is no place for me; I was not asked—"

There she interrupted me, with eagerness:

"No matter for all that; you can see without being seen. I heard Jane telling Hannah where she was going to peep. The little passage, at the foot of the back stairs, opens into the closet lined with books; there is only a curtain between it and the drawing-room, and you could stand there quite unobserved. Oh, Kate, be kind!—go quick; see all you can, and then come back and make me happy for the day."

So urgent was she, and so strong my own desire, that I soon yielded; and, with a word of caution to Hannah, I ran down to share Jane's hiding-place. Standing behind the half-drawn curtain, I looked out upon a brilliant scene beyond, for it was brilliant, though the great rooms were not full. The wintry sun streamed in upon the various groups, as brightly as if this were the gayest wedding ever seen; but on several faces I could see a shadow that made their smiles a mockery. Mrs. Carruth was her stateliest, blandest self, though the lines of suffering were deeply graven on her handsome face, and many gray threads showed among her dark hair. When her duties as hostess permitted, she always paused near a white-haired, feeble-looking man, who leaned back in a deep chair, as if anxious to conceal himself from observation. I observed him well, and, from his likeness to Augustine, I knew it must be Mr. Carruth. Harry's phrase, "pitiably weak," described him perfectly. He looked like a man out of whom circumstances had crushed hope, strength, and happiness. The power to fear seemed all that was left him, and as his restless eyes went furtively from face to face, he appeared to shrink and cower, as if contempt and condemnation met him everywhere. Few addressed him after the first greeting, and he sat, somewhat apart, more like an unwelcome guest than the master of the house. I had longed to know something of him, yet had never questioned the servants, and gleaned but little information from the family; now I ventured to ask Jane if that was he.

"Yes, miss, and dreadful poorly he's looking. He's always ill; his nerves are in a sad state, the doctor says, and nothing but rest and quiet will set him up. He can't bear the noise in town, nor the gay doings here, so he lives at the country house, a mile or so out. Mr. Augustine stays with him, being as fond of quiet as his father, and Mr. Steele sees to things for 'em at both places."

As she uttered his name, my roving eyes found Steele, and I heard no more of her gossip. I had not seen him since our last interview, and something in his face and manner arrested my attention. He was changed, though I found it difficult to define the alteration.

Usually he was vivacious and intent, now he looked listless. The fire seemed to have died out of him; even his old scornful air was gone, and he surveyed the scene before him with an absent eye, as if he took no interest in it. When I caught sight of him, the three youngest and most romantic of the Misses Carrol hemmed him in, all talking at once, and all begging him to select a flower for his button-hole from one of their bouquets. His face woke a little as he eyed the three blooming pyramids held up before him.

"Not an English rose among them all," I heard him say, for they stood near, and Steele's clear voice rose distinctly above the giggling chatter of the girls.

"Dear, no; but here's heliotrope, that's my pet; so sweet, you know, and such a pretty significance is given to it. Do choose that, Mr. Steele."

He shook his head, and the sarcastic smile touched his lips, as he replied:

"No, thank you; it fades too soon; I like an enduring flower. Neither the scent nor the significance of the heliotrope suit me, Miss Amelia."

"Roses are not enduring, and I'm sure the thorns quite destroy one's pleasure in their beauty."

"Not mine. I'll take this, if Fanny gives me leave."

"Why, Mr. Steele, that's nothing at all, just a sprig of white heath without a particle of odor."

"I find a very sweet perfume in it," and, declining the services of three white-gloved hands, he settled the flower to his liking; but hardly had he done so when he pulled it out, threw it from him, and left the room.

The three young ladies looked after him, interchanged confidential whispers, and sailed away to flirt with more devoted gentlemen. I fell to watching Augustine, who stood behind his father's chair, looking more monkish and melancholy than ever. Seeing one brother recalled the other, and I said, without moving my eyes:

"How is Mr. Harry today, Jane?"

She did not answer, and, half-turning, I saw that she was gone. A gentleman stood behind me, with a chair in his hand. The room was dark, but I knew the voice at once.

"Sit, Miss Snow; the service is long, and you will be tired before it is through."

The tone was very cold, but more polite than ever, and, much relieved by the pacific mood in which he seemed to be, I sat down, trying to say as easily as if nothing had occurred between us:

"I thank you—how did you know I was here, Mr. Steele?"

"I saw the skirt of your dress below the curtain."

There was no time for more; a stir in the room beyond silenced us, and both became intent upon the spectacle before our eyes. Remembering Elinor as I had last seen her, I could not think Amy a lovely bride, and with sad forebodings for her future, I listened to the words that bound her to a man who loved her fortune better than herself.

The ring was on, the mutual vows spoken, and the last words of the benediction on the minister's lips, when Carruth started from his chair with a cry, and stood pointing towards the hall, looking like one paralyzed with fear. Steele saw him first, for as the old man rose, the young one divined some danger, flung back the curtain, and stepped out to stand aghast at the sight of Elinor. She had taken off her veil, but still wore her bridal dress, and pausing on the threshold of the door, lifted her hand with a gesture of solemn warning, as her voice ran through the sudden hush.

"This must not go on. Before God I protest against it, and declare—"

"Hush! it is too late—they are married!"

Steele's hand was on her mouth, and his strong arm detained her, as she would have advanced.

"It never is too late for the truth. Father, for God's sake, tell them—"

But her appeal ended there, for Steele caught her in his arms, and carried her away, uttering cries that haunted many ears long afterward. A confused vision of Augustine, supporting his father, Mrs. Carruth sitting as if turned to stone, Amy clinging to her husband, and the six Misses Carroll in hysterics, flashed before my eyes as I flew upstairs to find Steele, with difficulty preventing Elinor from injuring herself and him, in the fit of frantic despair that had come over her.

Fortunately, Dr. Shirley was among the guests for I could do nothing with her, and was forced to leave her to his care, assisted by Jane and Hannah. Steele led me out of the room, and when he dropped into a chair, quite spent with the dreadful scene, he brought me a draught of water, with no sign of agitation, but quickened breath, and slight tremor of the hand that offered the glass.

"Slip away to your room and rest, you can do nothing here. I must go down, all is in confusion below."

He went, but I still lingered near the poor girl, useless as I was. For a time the house was in tumult, but gradually the excitement subsided, guests departed, the family composed themselves as best they could, and Elinor's frenzy yielded to the influence of a powerful opiate. Much to my surprise Amy came to bid me good-bye, left a tearful message for her sister, and drove away as sad a bride as she deserved to be.

When all was quiet, I learned from Hannah how Elinor had managed to escape. The woman had not left her post, but having looked in and found her charge reading quietly, had left her undisturbed. Both of us being disposed of, Elinor had drawn the empty flower-stand below the window as Harry had done, and climbing into the little room, had gone through the deserted chamber down to the front hall, without being seen. Her appearance and strange language were accounted for to the astonished guests, as I afterward learned, by Mrs. Carruth's confession of her daughter's real malady, and, as all were friends, the affair was hushed up as well as could be expected, when so many women were cognizant of it.

Elinor woke weak and wandering, and for several days was in a sad state. The doctor shook his head, as only a doctor can, Hannah predicted another attack, and Elinor seemed to struggle against it with all the strength her feeble mind possessed.

"The old horror is coming back; I feel it creeping over me; don't let it come, Kate, stay by me, help me, keep me sane, and if you cannot, pray God that I may die."

As she spoke she clung to me, as if I could save her, and heaven knows I did pray that she might be spared or taken from her misery. Soul and body, I devoted myself to her, and began to hope the haunting horror would go by, as quiet gloom succeeded wild excitement. I vibrated between her and Harry, quite unconscious at the moment how this life of intense anxiety was wearing upon her. Mrs. Carruth bore up wonderfully for a time, but the reaction came, and she turned to me as if I was what Harry called me, the good angel of the house. I liked the name and tried to deserve it, feeling that they needed some friendly spirit to oppose their evil genius.

Going to her room late one afternoon, I was startled by encountering the woman I had seen long ago with Steele. I had tapped as usual, a voice had bidden me enter, and obeying, I saw Mrs. Carruth lying on her bed as white and haggard as a ghost while this person, richly dressed and highly perfumed, sat surveying her with a face in which exultation and pity were curiously blended.

"It is your maid, madam, I leave you to her care. My compliments to your husband, and beg him not to forget our little party on New Year's Eve," and with much grace the lady gathered up her voluminous flounces and departed.

"Lizette, I want Miss Snow."

"I am here."

Mrs. Carruth turned her head, beckoned, and when I reached her head, laid a cold hand on mine, and her eyes searched my face with a wistfulness that was pathetic.

"You are ill, what shall I bring you?" I asked.

"Nothing, I am often ill, but this last week has been too much for me, and all my strength has left me when I most need it. Will you lend me yours?" she said.

"Gladly; how shall I serve you?"

"Is Elinor well enough for you to leave her for an hour or two?"

"Yes, she is asleep."

"That's well, Miss Snow, I have great confidence in you, and as Augustine is away and Harry ill, I wish to ask you to perform a somewhat delicate commission for me."

"Mr. Steele is at home, I believe, would not he do it better?"

Her hand closed over mine with a nervous clutch, and real terror looked out at her eyes, but she controlled her voice, though it sunk still lower as if she feared to be overheard.

"No, I prefer not to ask him, and I am sorry he is at home; Lizette said he was out."

"I heard him order his horse, and spoke of going to ride with Major Davenant, as I came up."

Mrs. Carruth thought intently for a moment, seemed to decide some point, and spoke more firmly.

"Twice a week I go out to oversee the other household, where my husband and son are, as you already know. Today I cannot go, I have tried to leave my bed, but faint upon attempting to sit up; yet, to-day, of all days in the year, it is important that

I should see Mr. Carruth, or get a message to him. The servants are not trustworthy, you are, and I venture to ask you to do me this favor."

"With pleasure. Shall I go at once?"

"Presently; I have more to say, for Mr. Steele's being in the house makes the matter difficult, simple as it seems. Miss Snow, you have, probably, learned, by this time, that he takes so strong an interest in our affairs that his interference is sometimes unnecessary. In Mr. Carruth's absence he assumes too much, and often annoys me by his conduct. If he knows that you go to the Larche instead of myself, I shall be obliged to enter into explanations which I prefer to avoid. I cannot wait till he goes out; his movements are so uncertain; time is precious. Will you put on my cloak and bonnet and personate me for an hour?"

The proposition was so peculiar, the whole affair so mysterious, that I hesitated. She drew much nearer, and her manner grew agitated, as she whispered, with white lips:

"In a few days a great trouble will fall upon this family; befriend us in our hour of need, and grant my strange request, as you would give charity to the forlornest creature whom you know."

"I will. Don't tremble, Mrs. Carruth. I will do anything; but Steele will recognize me if I meet him."

"We must run the risk of that. You are of my height, and in the dusk, with a veil down, few would see that you are slighter than I. You can imitate my manner, and if you meet, pass him silently, as I often do. The carriage was ordered half an hour ago, please ring, and tell John to have it brought round to the side door. I usually go out that way with my packages. There they are, not many; I've been too ill to think of anything."

Speaking with feverish eagerness, she had half risen, and, supporting her dizzy head, directed me where to find her cloak and hat.

A servant answered my ring, and, giving her order, she added:

"Tell Lizette I am going out, and shall not want her for several hours."

Rapidly assuming a rich silk skirt, to conceal my own, for Steele's eye would have detected it at once, I put on the velvet mantle, the costly furs, the fashionable bonnet, with its plumes, and, dropping a deeply-wrought veil over my face, presented, even to my own eyes, the figure of a second Mrs. Carruth.

"The disguise is better than I dared hope, dark is increasing rapidly, and once out of the house you are safe. Let me whisper the message. Tell Mr. Carruth or Augustine that madame has been here, and they must be prepared to meet her on New Year's Eve. Nothing more except the reason why I could not come. They will understand your masquerade, and no one will oppose you there, unless Steele follows. There is little fear of that; he has just come from the Larches, and will not return today. Hark, that's the carriage! Go, now, I shall lock the door until you return, and rest."

"But if any one asks for me and I am not found?" I said, pausing as I took up the little basket of delicacies for the invalid.

"They will think you are gone out for your walk."

"Mr. Steele will know I have not."

"Does he watch you so closely as that?"

I felt myself color, but the veil concealed it, and I answered composedly:

"Yes; he annoys me very much. However, as I have eluded him once or twice, he will fancy I have done so again, if he is on guard today."

"Kind creature, God bless you," and, to my great surprise, Mrs. Carruth, who had risen to lock the door behind me, took me in her arms and kissed me tenderly.

Much touched, I returned the embrace, for, with all her faults, she was a sister-woman, and I pitied her; then, fixing my mind upon the task before me, I glided down stairs, and reached the side door in safety.

As John shut me into the carriage, I heard Steele's voice saying to the man:

"Where is Miss Snow?"

"Gone out, sir, I believe, it's about her time."

I laughed to myself at the truth of John's answer, and leaned back enjoying the luxurious roll of the coupe, the soft warmth of the sables, and the excitement of my mysterious masquerade.

At first my eyes wandered over the wintry landscape, for I had not been out for several days, but twilight was gathering fast, and I soon fell to musing.

My suspicion was that Mr. Carruth had increased his wealth by some fraudulent transaction, that Steele had discovered it, and ruled the family through fear of disclosure and disgrace; but why the promise was exacted, and what madame's message covered I could not imagine. The rapid passage of a horseman roused me, and looking out, I found we had left the city far behind us. Presently the road wound along by what seemed to be a private park, and I began to fancy that my journey was at an end.

I was right; lights soon twinkled through the leafless trees, and, turning into an avenue, the carriage drew up before a house that rose tall and dark against the misty sky.

Wishing to reach Mr. Carruth as quietly as possible, I entered without ringing. A servant sat in the hall reading; a stout, sleek man, with an obsequious manner and a mean face.

"I wish to see Mr. Carruth."

"Very sorry, ma'am, he's out," replied the man, rising, with an inquisitive stare.

"Old Mr. Carruth, I mean."

"Exactly, he's out, ma'am."

"I thought he seldom left the house—never in the evening."

"Yes, ma'am, it's very rare for him to do it, but important business took him to town, and he's not home yet."

"Then I will see Mr. Augustine."

"He's with his father, ma'am; the old gentleman never goes away without him."

I was not prepared for this emergency, and paused to think. The man rubbed his hands, and, standing in an attitude of respectful attention, still peered at my face behind the veil.

"If I wait, shall I be likely to see them?" I asked, reluctant to leave my errand undone.

"I'm fearful they won't come tonight ma'am. It's so late now, the old gentleman won't like the drive; likewise it's cold, and he's but delicate, you know."

"I am very sorry, however, give him this from Mrs. Carruth, if you please."

"Any message with the basket, ma'am?" said the man as he took it.

"No," I answered, not daring to leave the one I had brought, for fear it should do harm. "Who shall I say called, ma'am?"

"No name is necessary."

Having been disappointed myself, I took comfort in disappointing him, for his manner displeased me, and, returning to the carriage, I drove away, strongly impressed with the belief that I heard a chuckle as the door closed behind me. We had not gone far when, as we slowly climbed a hill, the door of the coupe opened noiselessly, and some one took the seat beside me. "Steele!" flashed through my mind, but it was not a man, and, by the dim light, I saw a dark, foreign-looking girl, young and pretty, but wearing a determined look, that disturbed me more than her sudden appearance. Instantly she spoke, earnestly, but respectfully.

"Be quiet, Mrs. Carruth, I mean no harm. I've much to say, and can only reach you so, for I'm watched."

"Who are you?" I demanded, quite steady again after the first start, for I felt that I could cope with anything in female shape.

"I am Marie Grahn."

"And what have you to tell me?"

"That Mrs. Carruth is dead."

She breathed the words shrilly into my ear, with strong emphasis upon the word "is."

"What do you mean? You call me Mrs. Carruth, and then you tell me she is dead."

"I mean what I say. You think I don't know your secret, but I'll prove that I do. You believe that Robert's mother is alive, that Madame Duval is she, that you are not Mr. Carruth's lawful wife; he believes this also, but I know the truth, and I'm come to tell it."

My head spun round for a minute. This was such an entirely different solution of the mystery from what I expected that I was bewildered at first. But I speedily collected my wits, and, seeing the value of this discovery to the family, tried to make the most of it.

"How do you know the truth of what you assert, young woman?"

"I found it out. Let me tell you the story as fast as I can, for I've no time to waste. Did Mr. Carruth tell you of his early marriage before madame came?"

"No. "

"He'd not be likely to, nor to tell it truly when driven to confess. His mother made him promise that he would not marry, because there's madness in the family, but after she was dead he broke his word, and, when abroad, married Therese, madame's sister. She was handsome, but poor, and had a fiery temper—he tired of her soon, was sorry he had been rash enough to marry her, and went away. Therese vowed never to forgive him; she never did, and when she died, made her sister promise to tell him that the child died also. Mr. Carruth had never told his friends of his marriage, and few in the little French town knew that Steele was not his true name, so that when word came of Therese's and the baby's death, he thought he was quite free and safe. Madame kept Robert, but she hated his father, and never told him who he was, but taught him to hate as she did. About a year ago madame heard in some way that Mr. Carruth was married again, had children, and was very rich. She is a cunning, heartless woman, and cares for nothing but money and Robert. She thought he ought to have his name and rights, and she came to America to claim them. She loves plots, and she went slyly to work. She found that trouble had come upon Mr. Carruth's family, that he was ill and feeble in mind and body, and felt sure she could wring much from him through fear. If he owned Robert she would get less than if she tried another plan that entered her wicked head. Mr. Carruth had never seen madame, and did not know that Therese had a sister. They looked much alike when young, and in growing old Therese would have changed as madame has changed, so she boldly went to him and said she was his wife. She brought so many proofs that he believed her, was in despair, and offered anything to save you and his children from disgrace. Madame was wary, and though she would not give up what she called her rights, she would wait a little and be generous, she said. You know the rest."

"And Steele joined in this plot?"

"He knew nothing of it at first, for not until her grand stroke was made did she tell him that he was Mr. Carruth's son. He did not like it, but she knew how to work upon him; she has been kind to him and he is grateful; she taught him to hate his father; he is revengeful, and he agreed to help her to return wrong for wrong. The plan was well laid, and prospered for a time, but we came to ruin it. Therese died suddenly among strangers, and, after nearly thirty years, was forgotten, as madame thought, for she made inquiry, and no one in the place remembered anything of it, so she felt safe. My grandmother had not forgotten, however, she laid Therese out, and learned something of her from papers found upon her. When my parents died we came to my brother here, and six months ago, by mere chance, she met madame. She knew her, for madame was sent for to take the boy when Therese died. A few words satisfied madame that grandmère could betray her if she knew the plot, for though Mr. Carruth was only known to the old woman as Mr. Steele, the name in Therese's letters she would suspect if Robert called him father.

"They were much troubled, but grandmère was deaf, very old and failing fast, she could not trouble them long, so they waited and watched us well."

"Now I understand why the promise was exacted, why Steele was so vigilant, and why madame consented to be silent. Go on, go on, how came you to discover all this?" I asked breathlessly.

"Ah, that is hard to tell, but I will do it. I take a leaf from his own book, and will have some revenge for all he has made me suffer," she answered, with a passionate gesture, and eyes that glittered in the dusk.

"Whom do you mean?"

"Robert, do you think I could see so much of him and not love him? He was kind, I had no other friend, I thought he cared for me, and I was happy till that woman came."

"What woman?"

"He calls her Kate, she is your daughter's nurse or governess, he loves her, and I—I hate them both!"

It was not a pleasant position for me, and I blessed the disguise that protected me, for the girl spoke with southern vehemence, and looked as if she could avenge her wrongs with southern promptitude. Wishing to divert her thoughts and assure myself of my incognito, I said:

"How did you know me, we never met I think?"

"I saw him riding with you once, I knew he went often to the place you have just left, and watching him I've seen you more than once, so when I wanted you I knew where to come. I dared not go to your house in town, for since that woman came he is always there."

"You have not told me how you discovered madame's design," I said, feeling easy now.

"When Robert stayed away so long and was so changed, I grew anxious and questioned madame. She lives with us to watch us, but we thought her very kind, when she took us to a pretty house out of the city, and paid well for her rooms. She laughed at me, gave me no explanation, and so I, too, began to watch. Often when they thought me safe asleep, I listened at madame's door and heard much. They fancied me a silly child, but I was a jealous woman when I loved, and I deceived them. I heard about this Kate—tell me is she handsome?"

"Not very."

"Young?"

"Thirty."

"But charming, wise, good?"

"I do not think so."

"He does; oh, my God, how he talks of her! I could beat in the door as I listen, but for grandmère's sake, I dared not betray myself."

"It will be impossible to conceal what you have told me, but you need fear nothing, neither of you shall suffer."

"Grandmère is safe, and for myself, I do not care. Let me finish, I must go. Much that I overheard I could not understand, for I knew nothing of Steele's story; I went to grandmère for comfort, and when I told her she saw the game at once. She was dying slowly, but her mind was clear, she told me all, and made me swear to come and tell it. I would not till she was safe; for madame is furious in her rage, and the dear old soul should die in peace. They have watched and waited for her death many months; last night she died, and I came to-day."

"You should have come before, while she was alive to prove it."

"I dared not, and when she found me set on keeping her safe, she thought of that, and before she died màde me write down her story, and get two persons to witness it. This paper and my testimony will be enough to prove madame's treachery, and when all is known, I think the disgrace will keep that woman from marrying Robert, for he said she was as proud as she was lovely. Do you believe she will do it?"

"No, she does not love him I assure you. Now tell me what reward you ask for this discovery, it is worth much to me?"

"Money cannot buy me Robert's heart, I want nothing else," and with a sob the girl dropped her face upon her hand.

"It is not worth your tears, Marie, let it go and find an honest one that never will deceive you."

"His would have been honest, if madame had not spoilt it; she has neglected all the good in him and nourished all the bad, what wonder he is what he is. I thought I could save him by loving him, but that woman came between us; she will do the work and receive the reward. He will become anything for her. Only last night he asked madame to give up her plan, and let him provide for her, because he wanted to earn Kate's esteem by one just action if he could."

"And madame would not?"

"No, she said, she had risked everything for him, and having promised to keep the secret he must do it."

The girl stopped weeping, and intent upon my purpose, I asked anxiously:

"This paper, did you bring it?"

"I was afraid to trust it out of its hiding-place, till I was sure I could put it safely in your hands. I could not have got out to-night if madame were not away, and Steele haunting that woman. It's in the keeping of the persons who witnessed it, they are trusty people; and if you will come to the bridge at eight to-morrow night, I'll try to meet you there."

"Good, I will come. But, Marie, what becomes of you, now your grandmother is gone?"

"I neither know nor care. Madame promised to befriend me, but I cannot stay with her; Robert is taken from me, and I have no wish to live."

"You named no reward, leave it to me, keep up good heart, and to-morrow night you shall be taken into a safe home, my poor girl, till then—"

Before I could finish she was gone, for, looking up, she saw we were entering the city, and without a word, she sprung away into the darkness, as swiftly and silently as she had come, leaving me in a fever of excitement. I entered the house with a haste, Mrs. Carruth never showed, the sight of Steele reminded me of my assumed character, and I swept by him with a silent bend of the head. He was leaning in the doorway of the drawing-room, with an unusual color in his cheek and a general breeziness of aspect, which made me fancy that he, too, had just come in; I was speedily assured of this, for as I passed him I was greeted with a laughing

"Good evening, Miss Snow."

I was startled, but, preserving my dignity, moved on as if I had not appropriated his address.

"She is on her guard," I heard him say, then a light step sprung up the stairs, and planting himself before me, he threw back the veil, surveying me with an air of intense amusement. Now I understood the cause of his exhilaration, and felt sure that he was at the bottom of my repulse. The thought of the power I had so singularly gained made me indifferent to my failure, and when he asked, with a mocking smile:

"Had you a pleasant drive, Miss Snow?" I answered blandly:

"Charming, thank you."

"I wonder if anything can conquer your spirit—defeat cannot, it seems."

"Defeat!" I echoed, with a gayer laugh than his, "mine has been a splendid success."

I could not keep a touch of exultation out of my voice, and it was evident that both my words and manner puzzled him. The baffled, curious look he wore satisfied me that he knew nothing of the girl's strange freak, and anxious to know how he had discovered mine, I said, with my most engaging expression:

"What put you on the track, Mr. Steele? I thought I had succeeded well, for no eye but yours detected me."

"Your character was well carried out, and the costume quite perfect, with one exception. Mrs. Carruth does not own a foot like that, nor does she go out so shod."

He pointed to my feet. I looked, and saw that in my haste I had forgotten to change my slippers. I bit my lip with vexation as he added, enjoying my chagrin:

"The sweeping dress hid them when you walked, but in entering the carriage, I saw your foot, and knew it."

"And so followed me, to make my journey a fruitless one? That was like you!" I exclaimed, remembering the horseman that dashed by me in the dusk. He laughed again, and, stepping back that I might pass, ignored my question, as he said, with merry malice in his eyes and voice:

"Reluctant as I am to rob myself of your society, I think your double must be very tired of waiting for you, so pray go to her. I am not curious to learn the answer you bring, therefore, you can chat in peace; but allow me to suggest that the next time you go on secret service, you leave the coquettish little slippers at home."

Chapter VI. Snow Versus Steele

I FOUND MRS. CARRUTH waiting anxiously, and taking her into an inner room, where it was impossible that we should be overheard, I poured my story into her ear. She had suffered so much, despaired so utterly, that when hope came it unnerved her; all her pride, her self-control gave way, and for a time, she could only vent her emotions in tears and broken thanksgivings.

When quieter, we took counsel together, for now that chance had betrayed her hidden sorrow it was but natural that she should find comfort in confiding entirely in me.

"My burden has been a heavy one, and I deserved it," she said. "God knows my pride was great, and needed humbling, but I thank Him that I am spared this last affliction. The first I brought upon myself, and thought it bitter enough to atone for my early ambition, my wicked willfulness. Sorrow I could bear, but shame crushed me, and when I believed that I and my children were disgraced, I thought my punishment unjust, and I grew desperate. Do you wonder that my husband is a broken man, hiding from the world, and longing for death; that I was willing to save Amy from the coming storm at the cost of truth, and that I did anything to delay the hour that would make us all objects of pity or contempt."

"I only wonder that you bore up as you did and it is not for me to condemn till I have been as hardly tried," I answered gently, as I held her trembling hands in mine.

"No daughter could have been more faithful," she went on. "I seemed blind and cold, but I saw it all, and loved you for it; I dared not show my feeling for yours is such a strong, yet sympathetic nature, that I knew I should be tempted to forget my promise, and make a confidante of you."

It was very sweet to hear this from a woman whom I had thought so heartless, and, truly, I enjoyed my reward. But, eager to improve the good fortune that had befallen, I turned her thoughts from the past to the dangers and duties of the present.

"This paper must be secured without exciting Steele's suspicion. If I keep the appointment with Marie, he will follow and discover it; therefore, you must go, Mrs. Carruth, while I keep him safely here."

"How can you keep him? He submits to no one but that detestable Frenchwoman."

"I think he will submit to me."

A smile of conscious power rose involuntarily to my lips. She saw it, and said, with an expression of almost maternal solicitude:

"Miss Snow, Lizette's gossip, and my own observation, convinces me that Robert loves you. I hope, I earnestly hope that you are not interested in him."

"I am not, and I will prove it by doing all I can to defeat and punish him and his accomplice. I have more influence over him than that woman, I think, and for a day will feign what I do not feel, to accomplish my purpose. It is a distasteful task, but there is no other way of keeping him safe while this paper is secured. Strategy must be met by strategy, and for your sakes, I will stoop to a brief deceit."

"I know it will be forgiven, and I never can forget your kindness to me and mine. Tell me your plan, that I may not fail in my part. How will you detain him while I go, and how shall I be sure that he is safe?"

"For some time he has not come to join me in the little parlor, but, though he assumes a cool indifferent air, I know he longs to return, and word from me would bring him. Hitherto I have been glad of this, and would not recall him, now I will, and once there, I can keep him for hours, unless I much deceive myself. As eight o'clock approaches, listen; if you hear our voice go at once; if he leaves me, I'll come and warn you, but he will not."

"You speak with confidence, Miss Snow, and if I read your face aright, this task is not entirely without attractions. Has he made an enemy of you in spite of his love?"

"I will confess that I do take a womanish satisfaction in outwitting him, for he defied me to do it. He has thwarted me, angered me often, and with my whole soul I despise him for his unjust ungenerous conduct to you all. Mr. Carruth will be lenient with him, because he is his son, but he deserves a sharp lesson, and he shall have it."

"Yes; it is but just that he should suffer, and you will requite our wrongs better than we could ourselves. One thing more—madame came today to tell me that she could wait no longer; the death of the old woman explains this. She bade us all meet here on New Year's evening to learn her pleasure and prepare for the disgrace in store for us. I wished my husband to know this at once, lest a sudden summons at the last moment should entirely unfit him for the interview. I no longer care to warn him, joy cannot harm him, and his intelligence will be a welcome home after his sad exile. Let madame and Robert come to find defeat not victory, waiting for them, and let the new year begin for us with liberty and happiness."

Then we parted, each intent upon our part, each hopeful of success, and, after a quiet half hour in my room, I went down to begin the work of reconciliation with my discarded lover. He was roaming restlessly about the rooms, but saw me instantly, and approached with an air of nonchalance which could not conceal the real eagerness he felt. Pausing at the top of the stairs that led to the small parlor, I looked over my shoulder with a smile, and said half timidly, half wistfully:

"Shall I wait for you, or sup alone?"

He could not conceal the satisfaction the words gave him, but he shook his head, saying coldly:

"The draughts you give me are bitter. I shall never come again."

"But bitter draughts are wholesome, and only often finds sweetness at the bottom of the cup if one has courage to drink on."

I looked back at him invitingly as I descended; he took an impulsive step towards me, checked himself, turned sharply, and, catching up his hat, left the house as if he feared to stay. I was content, well knowing that having soothed his wounded pride by one refusal, a second invitation would be all the surer of acceptance.

Elinor was moody the next day, and wished to be alone, so I was free, and used my leisure to some purpose. The day was fine, and soon after breakfast I went out feeling sure that Steele would follow. He did so, but so skilfully that if I had not been upon the watch I never should have known it. Taking a malicious pleasure in exciting his curiosity and wearying his patience, I led him a long and intricate chase, and completed his discomfiture by waiting at a quiet corner till he came stealing round it, when I walked straight up to him, saying, with mingled anger and submission in my manner:

"Mr. Steele, I am not on secret service now, but if you must know where I go walk with me like a gentleman, and not dog me like a detective."

"Thank you, I will with pleasure," and, lifting his hat, he turned to accompany me. But coolly as he took it, I knew he was ashamed, for he condescended to apologize.

"As you are the soul of truth, Miss Snow, I must believe you, and try to soften your displeasure by explaining that the Carruths' and my own affairs are just now in a very critical state, and my anxiety makes me restless, suspicious, and discourteous. Soon, very soon, these perplexities will be over, and you will see me in my true colors."

"I heartily hope so."

I spoke with energy, but when he called me "the soul of truth," in that confident tone, my conscience pricked me, and I felt a guilty sense of treachery.

"You do take a little interest in me then? That gives me a pleasure. I confess it, for the anger you excite soon dies, and I shall covet your esteem if I can have no more."

"You are as proud as Lucifer, but having humbled yourself by a confession, I will do the same. Mr. Steele, I wish—"

There I paused to choose my words, and he exclaimed with suppressed eagerness in face and tone:

"Wish what? Speak freely, Kate; I am in a yielding humor to-day, improve it."

"Well, then, I wish sincerely that we might be friends again, at least while we inhabit the same house. I want to stay with Elinor—I am happy there, but I must go away unless this ends."

"What ends?"

"You know, need I tell you, that it troubles me to see you so changed, to feel that you never will forgive me, to find that I am watched, distrusted, and disliked by one who has been very kind to me, and to whom I am grateful, though I cannot show it."

"Is this your confession?"

"Yes, I'll even own that your craft, so far, has excelled mine, and that, after today, I will oppose you no more, for I am tired of mystery and intrigue."

"You own yourself defeated, then, and repent your defiance, do you?"

"Be generous, and spare me, else I shall be tempted to retract, and defy you again."

"I almost wish you would, for you are particularly captivating when your spirit is roused. I don't know in which of your many moods I like you best, all are so pleasant to me."

"I know which of yours I like best."

"Tell me, and I will always try to be in it when you are by."

"The yielding one, it becomes you, and I like to see the good side of your nature, for I've not quite lost my faith in it yet. Will you grant my wish, and be friendly for the little time we are together. Please say yes."

I looked up at him, with the confiding glance that pleased him most, because so few eyes shed it upon him, and he answered, as his face kindled and his voice grew mild:

"How can I say no to what I most desire? I shall be miserable, but I will have the courage to drink on, hoping that after the bitter I may find the sweet."

As he echoed my words significantly, my cheeks burned, my eyes fell, and I turned my head away, feeling that my task was harder than I thought. He saw the change, and laughed low to himself—not the sneering laugh, but a hopeful, happy sound, that would have touched any woman's heart.

"Why did you blush, and drop your veil, Kate? Did I offend again?"

"No; I am tired; I am going home."

"May I go with you?"

"You ask with humility, therefore you may go."

"It is slippery; will you take my arm? I claimed the act as a forfeit once; now I entreat it as a favor."

I took it, and, recovering from my momentary fit of self-reproach, exerted myself to be as charming as possible, with such success that my companion was soon in brilliant spirits. Slackening his already slow pace as we approached the house, he said:

"Having granted your wish, I am audacious enough to propose that you grant one of mine."

"Name it."

"Will you go and drive with me this afternoon, just by way of ratifying our peace treaty?"

"Elinor will want me."

"But if Elinor does not."

"Mrs. Carruth will object."

"Mrs. Carruth often objects, but does not interfere."

"The servants will gossip."

"Bah! what then?—we neither of us care."

"Your friends will laugh at you if they see an unfashionable bonnet in your fine carriage."

"Not if they see the face inside the bonnet."

"The six Misses Carroll will make your life a burden after it."

"Hang the Carrolls! they do that now. Please say yes, Kate: it is the sweetest word a woman utters."

"Pertinacious man, I'll think of it."

"Good!—that means you will go. At three I shall expect you."

At three I went, for Elinor did not need me, and Mrs. Carruth did not interfere. As he wrapped the furs about my feet, while the mettlesome horses pawed the ground, Steele said, with a meaning smile:

"Will you go to the Larches, Kate?"

"Not I; one repulse is enough; but you may appease me by confessing whether Mr. Carruth and his son went there last night."

"Must I tell the truth?"

"Always to me."

"I will; they went there."

"And you made the man deny it?"

"Yes."

"It was you, then, who passed me on the road?"

"Yes, and nearly spoilt my horse in doing it."

"I'm glad of that. Why did you do it?"

"I'd rather not tell you."

"You need not; drive on."

Where we went I never knew, for I was so intent on keeping the conversation in a safe channel, that I took no heed of earth or sky, but chatted volubly upon every subject, except love. To Steele the drive was full of delight, for some hope had sprung up within him, and every friendly look and word of mine strengthened it. This troubled me, yet I took a certain satisfaction in giving him a little pleasure, before much pain, for no woman can remain quite untouched when a man gives her all his heart, however faulty he may be. That hour showed me many good traits of character which I never had suspected; and the more I saw the more I pitied him, the guiltier I felt. Coming home, in the early twilight, he said, as we drew up before the door:

"Shall I see you again to-night?"

"Not unless you come down as usual."

"Do you miss me, Kate?"

I did not answer, and he laughed the hopeful, happy laugh again.

"Ah, I see; too honest to say no, too proud to say yes. May I come?"

"If you dare;" and with that I left him, sure of his appearance at the usual time.

After reading Elinor to sleep, I dressed myself with elaborate care, and, finding the parlors empty, sat down to the grand piano and played my best, feeling sure that I should soon have an auditor.

Steele loved music. I had sung to him once or twice before, and knew his taste now. Anxious to prolong the "yielding mood," I repeated all his favorites, and presently a sidelong glance at the great mirror showed me that my musical incantation had raised the spirit I desired. He stood behind me, listening intently, and as he listened, over his face crept the rare expression which made it singularly attractive. I gave no sign that I was conscious of his presence till I saw him lift his hand with an impulsive gesture, as if to touch my head with a caress. Then I said suddenly:

"Is my comb loose, Mr. Steele?"

His hand dropped, and coming round beside me, he exclaimed, looking well pleased:

"Did you feel that I was near as I do when you approach?"

"I saw you in the glass."

"I forgot that, and my flattering fancy proves a failure. I should say you had no sentiment if you did not put so much into your music that you would touch a heart of stone, and make even Augustine forget himself."

"Then I will sing no more to-night," and, turning from the instrument, I saw both our figures reflected in the mirror. Steele's eye followed mine, and after an instant's silence he asked with a sudden smile: "What do we look like?"

"Like a pair of friends, I hope."

"Like a pair of lovers, I think."

We did, and I scarcely knew myself as I looked. The excitement of the moment gave my eyes unusual brilliancy, my cheeks unusual color, my lips unusual smiles, my manner a sprightliness which contrasted strongly with my customary quietude, while the flower in my hair, the ornaments I wore, and the gayer dress which replaced my plain one, all made me look as I had looked years ago, when I rejoiced that I was beautiful. Steele was close beside me, and if I had never thought him handsome before I should have done so then, for all that was manliest in him was awake, and love touched his fine features with the magic glow which can beautify the plainest. This happy face reproached me, and I turned my eyes away with an unconscious sigh.

"That was a regretful sigh, Kate; are you sorry that you were cruel to me?" he softly said.

"I begin to think I shall be," I truly answered.

He walked through the long rooms, and, coming back to me, asked a question that would have seemed strange had I not possessed a key to his thoughts.

"Do you love ease and splendor, Kate?"

"What woman does not?"

"Would you not take pleasure in a home like this—in knowing that you never need feel the gloom of poverty, the weight of servitude, the chill of loneliness again—in the assurance that you would be cherished tenderly all your life, and become the salvation of a fellow-creature?"

I was spared an answer to this appeal by the appearance of a servant with the announcement:

"A gentleman for you, sir."

"Tell him I'm engaged."

"So I see," a strange voice spoke, and the new comer advanced with a knowing smile.

"My dear fellow, you must forgive me for interrupting so delightful a *tête-a-tête,* but it's a matter of importance, and I won't detain you five minutes."

With an impatient frown Steele submitted, and I left them, inwardly thanking the persistent gentleman for helping me out of one difficulty, and earnestly hoping that he would not plunge me into another, by remaining too long.

The little parlor looked warm and bright, and I bestirred myself to make it still more so, dropping the curtains, rolling two easy chairs to the hearth, settling my books and work on a little table, laying the evening papers ready, and poking the fire till it filled the room with a ruddy glow. All was prepared, but Steele did not come. I listened at the stair-foot, and a steady murmur of voices came down to me. It was past seven, and Mrs. Carruth would be getting anxious, but could not stir, with the parlor doors wide open, and those keen eyes on the watch. I began to fear that I had over-estimated my power, that he saw through my design, and had discovered our plan. More than once I was on the point of going up, but what could I do when there? Several times I was tempted to steal away to Marie alone, but having failed to baffle him so often, I would not risk discovery now. At last, as the half hour struck, I threw myself into a chair, and, leaning my head on my arms, tried to be patient. I was very tired. It had been a week of excitement, a day of effort—my nerves were worn, my spirits out of tune, and the fear of disappointment wrung a few tears from me as the clock ticked on, and no one came. I chid myself for such weakness, but could not restrain it, and soon was thankful I had yielded to it.

"At last that bore has gone. Well for him that he did; five minutes more and I should have turned him out."

As Steele came hastily in I started up, and relief from suspense made me exclaim impetuously:

"I thought you would never come!"

"Then you did want me? You've betrayed yourself, Kate; you were weeping when I came in."

"I was half asleep, I think, tired of waiting."

"Do you cry in your sleep, and start and blush with pleasure on being waked?"

"Come and have your tea, Mr. Steele."

"I don't want it; I've had something better; send it away and talk a little before I go out."

"Must you go out? It's cold and snowy now, and I thought—"

"That I would stay, perhaps? It is pleasant here, but I ought to go."

"Go then; I can spend the evening very comfortably alone."

"You are not wanted with Elinor?"

"No."

"How will you amuse yourself?"

"Read and work, and think, and sleep—"

"And cry again for me, Kate?"

"You flatter yourself, Mr. Steele."

"Now she is Miss Snow again, stately and cold as the Jungfrau."

"Snow melts," I said, with a smile.

"And steel bends," he answered, with a brighter one. "Own that you wish me to stay."

"Well, then, I do."

"Why?"

"I'd rather not tell."

"Where are all your pride and fire gone? You look shy; your eyes avoid mine, and you are entirely unlike yourself. What does it mean?"

I made no answer, but my face seemed to satisfy him, and silence served me better than words. He had gone towards the door; now he turned, held out his hand, and said, in a masterful tone, that would have angered me at any other time:

"Not long ago, I begged you to stay with me, and you would not; will you atone for that by asking me to remain now?"

"If you will still understand we are only friends."

He laughed.

"Your sort of friendship suits me excellently. Come, then, ask me to stay, and call me Robert. I only allow those who care for me to do that."

The quarter struck; I heard the roll of the carriage as it came round; a moment might mar all, and I had promised. With an inward protest, but outward submission, I went to him, and, taking his hand, said meekly, as I drew him to a seat:

"Robert, please stay."

He yielded at once, drew my chair nearer, and sat down, with an aspect of supreme content. I took up my work, conscious that my mingled repentance and resolve gave me the appearance of a woman agitated by secret emotions of love, or doubt, or shame. All three, he thought, and took heart, believing that I repented my refusal, yet was too proud to own it.

"Kate, I discover that you are a coquette," he said, leaning on the arm of my chair, and watching the movements of my fingers as I tried to sew.

"And I discover that you are a tyrant."

"I am, so I must have an answer to my question."

"Which?"

"The one I asked up stairs. Shall I repeat it?"

"No; I will answer it if you will tell me something first—something I'm curious about. Where were you going to-night?"

"To meet a lady."

"Handsome?"

"A fine woman, for her age."

"Not young, then."

"No."

"A friend?"

"Yes; the only one I have besides you."

"Do you care much for her?"

"Not as much as I used to do. You like that; no need to look scornful. I know why you ask and thank you for being jealous; it is a good sign."

"I beg you will go to this lady; she will be disappointed."

"Not much; she can wait; the little one will fret, but to-morrow will do as well for her."

"What little one?—the lady's child?"

"No, the young girl who stays with her. She is romantic, and fancies me a hero—sad delusion, you will say."

"I hope you will be kind to her, and make her happy in her delusion, by trying to be what she believes you."

"I thought I should marry her once, but that no longer pleases me; she is too simple, too meek, a child still; I am better suited elsewhere."

"You speak like a Sultan in a slave market. Will you hold this for me?"

I offered him a skein of silk, intent upon keeping him for an hour at least. He took it, and directly it was in an almost inextricable tangle, at which I labored diligently, without making much progress.

"A symbolical situation," he said, smiling. "You have taken me prisoner, and now you cannot undo the fetters which you put on. You tried to break them once, but that hurt both of us; now you are trying to slip them gently off, and that fails also. Shall I show you how to get out the snarl, Kate?"

"No, thank you; I can wind it sooner than you think."

"Pull away, then, and meantime, give me my answer."

I hoped he had forgotten it; finding he had not, I no longer tried to evade it, for the surest way to interest people, is to lead them to talk about themselves.

"All that you described would be very welcome, if I could have it honestly," I said slowly.

"What does that mean?" and I got a sharp glance over the scarlet tangle between us.

"It means that unless I was very sure I loved the giver of these good gifts, I should not dare to take them. By love I mean something more than the feeling that attracts and charms, and makes one enjoy the society of another—that is the beginning, but the end must be entire respect and confidence, if one would be happy."

He seemed to ponder over my words, and presently said, seriously:

"Is it impossible for a man, not wholly bad, to win a good woman's heart, if he waits, and works, and, through her, learns the beauty and the worth of virtue?"

Now I could be myself, now I could speak truly, and I did, hoping to help the better part of him, even while I betrayed the worse.

"Everything is possible to love, and whether hearts be won or not, no good woman would regret that she had inspired a desire for virtue in the soul of any man—for that, and that alone, makes life worth having. Believe this, strive for it, and you cannot fail of your reward."

I spoke earnestly, and for the first time saw his keen eyes fill, his firm lips tremble, and in his face a humility that ennobled it, as neither pride nor comeliness had ever done. Still in that altered tone he asked again:

"But if, in order to earn this reward, much must be sacrificed—friends, position, wealth, the good opinion of the world, perhaps the heart most coveted—how then, Kate?"

"Better be poor and honest than rich and base. The friends, if sincere, will but cling the closer; the position, in God's sight, will be higher; the fortune one that cannot pass away; the world's opinion one to sustain, if conscience commends, and integrity sustains. See, the tangle is out, and you are free."

"Not yet; it is worse than ever."

The silk was wound, and I took up my work again; but Steele, leaning back in his chair, fixed his eyes upon the fire, and seemed to forget me in an anxious reverie. I sat still, glad to rest, and while he knit his brows over some perplexing thought, I placidly sewed on, counting the minutes as they slipped away.

Long he sat so, deaf to the sound of the returning carriage, and blind to the sight of Lizette, who appeared at the door; but, comprehending the situation with the quickness of a Frenchwoman, would have vanished silently, if I had not asked her errand.

"My lady would be glad to see Miss Snow, if she is at leisure."

"I will come at once."

She went, and, with a long sigh of relief, I rose to follow. Steele roused then, glanced at the clock, and exclaimed, regretfully: "Nine so soon! Where has this hour gone?"

"I have spent it profitably, as my work will show," I said, gathering up my books and basket as I spoke.

"So have I, as you shall see, negligent and idle as I have seemed. It was so pleasant to sit here by you; feeling that you were my friend, I forgot that I must seem careless and ungrateful, but I will show that I am not. The last time we parted here, I said before the week was out you would repent your answer; was I not right?"

"I will tell you that to-morrow," I replied, eager to be gone.

"To-morrow!" he echoed with emphasis; "yes, I think you will, and make the answer a kind one, for then you will know me better. Good night, Kate; I wish you happy dreams."

"Good night, Robert; I wish you happier ones than mine will be."

I gave him my hand, feeling that he would never call me friend again, and left him, with no sense of triumph, for well I knew that on the morrow he would come to me as Mr. Carruth's son and heir, and, laying all his fortune at my feet, ask me to let him earn my love.

Wearily I went up to learn that the paper was safe, to read it, to promise to be present when it was produced, and then to bed, still haunted by Steele's altered face, as he sat near me in the pleasant little room.

CHAPTER VII. ELINOR'S NEW YEAR

ALL THE NEXT DAY I carefully avoided him, and devoted myself to Elinor, who had come out of her gloom and was unusually calm and sweet. We feared to tell her what had happened, lest it should excite her, but she seemed to feel the cheerful influence of our happiness, for when Augustine and Harry came to wish her a happy New Year each bringing a gift, she said to them:

"It will be happy, I am sure of that, and never mean to afflict you any more, for I think I shall get well. Kate predicted it, and she is always right."

So hopefully she spoke, so tranquilly she smiled, that we all rejoiced over her believing, that she might yet conquer her malady in spite of our forebodings. The brothers lingered long, and when they went with unusually affectionate adieux, she put her arms about them, saying tenderly:

"Kiss me, Harry, bless me, Augustine, and both pray for me, that my New Year may be calm and happy."

After they were gone she sat silent for an hour, with a placid look that quieted my own secret unrest. At last she spoke, suddenly, but composedly.

"Is my father here, to-day?"

"I think so, dear."

"I want to see him, do you believe he will come?"

"Yes, shall I go and ask him?"

"Please do; tell him I am the old Elinor now, and long for him very much."

"Is Mr. Steele in, Hannah?" I asked, as I passed through the room where she sat at her eternal stitching.

"No, miss, he said, he'd not be in till evening."

Much relieved I went upon my errand, hoping that it might not be a fruitless one. It was afternoon; dinner was over and a splendid sunset filled the great drawing-room with light; the doors stood open, and as I advanced I saw what I had never seen in that house before, the family together. Mr. Carruth had come home in a double sense, and sitting on his own hearth looked another man. His wife stood beside him, as if glad to take her place again; one hand was on his shoulder, the other smoothed his white hair, as she looked down at him with an expression that made her worn face beautiful. Harry lay on the couch wan and wasted, but his gay self again, for he was laughing at Augustine who tried to settle his pillows with brotherly solicitude, and laughed with him. It was a happy, home-like scene, only needing the presence of the daughters to be complete; they seemed to feel that, and to have done their best to supply the want, for the curtain was withdrawn from the picture of Elinor and Amy, and their childish beauty shone undimmed by the years that had so altered them. As I went in I was much surprised, and touched by the warm welcome I received from all; Mr. Carruth came to meet and led me to his wife, who greeted me with a maternal kiss, Harry held out both hands, and Augustine laid his upon my head, as if he blessed me. Before I could find words, Mrs. Carruth spoke in her benignest manner:

"A happy New Year, Kate, and will you let us make it happier by offering you these tokens of our gratitude, for services which we shall long remember?"

She drew me to a table, and there I saw costly presents from each member of the family, for they had forestalled Amy's thanks, and even poor Elinor had remembered me. Quite speechless with emotion I examined them, and when I opened the envelope which contained Mr. Carruth's gift, its munificence overcame me and I could only cry.

"No thanks, no thanks, my dear," he said, "It's but a trifle to make you comfortable, when you are tired of making others so. Money cannot pay for some things, but it lightens the obligation a little, so you will be generous and let us do it in this way till we can find a better."

I did let them, and after thanking them heartily gave my message, which was instantly complied with.

"I will see the poor child, of course I will; I can look her in the face now, and nothing would please me more than to pay my little girl a visit, if she can bear it."

I went up with him carrying my presents, for I thought it would amuse Elinor to talk them over with me. The meeting between father and daughter was very quiet, and for an hour they sat side by side talking cheerfully together, but neither mentioned Mrs. Carruth. I hoped Elinor would send for her, would forgive her, and begin the year with nothing to mar the union of the family. The poor woman had followed us with imploring eyes as we left her, and I had whispered that I would try to soften the girl's heart toward her.

"Is there no one else you would like to see, dear?" I asked, when her father had left her, with a tender good-bye, till to-morrow. She understood me, but answered gently as she turned her face away.

"Yes, Kate, but not now. To-day is a good day to forgive as we would be forgiven, and I mean to do it before I sleep. Let me rest now, and get ready to see mamma. Sing a little, some of the beautiful old hymns that make one feel devout and happy."

I sung to her with a glad heart, and when I ceased, she laid her cheek to mine, whispering:

"You have been to me what David was to Saul. I have no words warm enough to thank you, but I know it will give you a great pleasure to do one thing more for me, so you shall give mamma my love, and tell her that when I am quiet for the night, I wish she would come and get me to sleep with the old lullabies she used to sing when I was a happy little child. "

No gift bestowed that day was as precious to me as the privilege of carrying this loving message from daughter to mother. How Mrs. Carruth received it I need not tell. She would have gone at once, but I advised her to wait for Elinor's summons, and, meantime, prepared to meet madame and Steele. Gathered in the drawing-room, we waited, with the paper laid ready, and Marie where she could be produced if necessary. As the clock struck eight, Steele entered alone. His manner was calm and grave, but his eyes shone, and in his face there was a pale excitement, which he could not conceal. Pausing an instant on the threshold, he looked about the room, saw that all were there, smiled, as if well satisfied, and said, as he approached his father:

"A happy new year, friends, and many of them."

No one answered his greeting, and Mrs. Carruth, in her haughtiest tone, asked briefly:

"Where is madame?"

A look of pain passed over Steele's face; but still, in that new tone of mingled humility and happiness, he replied:

"Madame will trouble you no more, and I have lost my one friend in losing her."

"Lost her! by death, Robert?" cried Mrs. Carruth, with a startled air.

"No; by estrangement. For thirty years we have loved one another through many vicissitudes, but a single act of disobedience on my part has separated us for ever; and, heavy as my loss is, I must not regret it."

"What act has parted you?" demanded Mr. Carruth.

"I came to tell you, father."

The brave, sweet expression broke over Steele's face as he spoke; then, fixing his eyes on me, he stood up manfully, and confessed all the wrong he would have done them, generously sparing the woman who devised the plot, by assuming the sin and shame himself. How the rest received it I cannot tell; me it overwhelmed with astonishment, for I had not thought there was so much courage and virtue in the man, nor dreamed that his love was strong enough for such a sacrifice as this. Breathlessly I listened, held by the steady fire of the eyes fast fixed on mine, and stirred to the heart by the straightforward confession in which he dealt so sternly by himself, so mercifully by another. When all was told, he waited for no reply but mine, as, with a sudden change from bitter self-accusation to tender entreaty, he said, humbly, yet hopefully:

"Now, Kate, I am a little worthier the good woman's respect, for I am 'poor and honest, not rich and base.' This is your work; you will continue it, and help me to become what you would have me?"

What could I answer? Words deserted me, and I covered up my face, wishing the work of yesterday undone. For several minutes I heeded nothing that went on, though the sound of many voices filled my ears. Soon I calmed myself, to hear Mr. Carruth telling his son that the confession came too late, as everything was already known, and the old woman's testimony secured. A mild paternal rebuke was about to follow, when Steele broke in, demanding:

"Who discovered this?"

"Miss Snow."

"It is impossible!" he began, indignantly, but Mrs. Carruth took up the tale, and told the part I had played in it. She was a proud woman; he had made her suffer keenly, and she could not resist this opportunity of inflicting a wound as deep as her own had been.

As if eager to do me honor, she repeated briefly, but faithfully, every act of mine, making me the prominent figure in the plot which had ended in his defeat; and as I listened, though done from a just and generous motive, my double-dealing looked very base, after the frank confession which had cost so much. To him it must have seemed the blackest treachery, and as I watched the baleful spirit wake and stir within him, I felt that my power for good was lost for ever with this man. When Mrs. Carruth paused he turned to me, drew my hands from before my face, and, holding them in a painful grasp, asked, in the quiet tone of suppressed passion, more terrible to me than the fiercest denunciation:

"Is this true?"

"Yes."

"Was yesterday all a farce? Did your caprice, kindness, blushes, and tender smiles mean nothing? Were you deceiving me to the very last?"

I did not speak, and with a wrathful flush, and rising voice, a desperate look, he crushed both my hands in one of his, as, with the other, he lifted my bent head, searched my face, and said, in a commanding tone:

"Look at me, Kate; I will have the truth!"

His violence calmed my agitation; the consciousness that I had done my best to prevent a great wrong strengthened me; my eyes rose to his, clear and steady now, and my voice was both fearless and pitiful.

"You shall have the truth. I did deceive you for a day, that these injured people might obtain the means of righting themselves. Chance put this power into my hands, and I freely used it. Had you been kinder to poor Marie, she never would have betrayed you, and you only reap what you have sowed. You defied me to outwit you; gave me lessons in duplicity, and every inducement to defeat you with your own weapons. I despise them, but none other would serve, and I used them to some purpose, though I wounded my own self-respect in doing so. Are you satisfied?"

As I spoke, all the passion had passed from his face—grief, reproach, and hopeless love remained. The accent of despair was in his voice; the chill of separation in the hand that still held mine, and no lament could have made my heart ache like the bitter scorn and sorrow of his words.

"And this is the woman whose truth and virtue I so honored, who was my good angel, intent on saving me, and making repentance easy by love. A pretty delusion— pity that it ends so soon. Better have clung to my fellow sinner, carried our purpose bravely out, and so been happy, for money can buy everything, even Kate Snow's truth!"

With the last words he flung my hand from him, and turning away, leaned on the low chimney-piece, as if to hide some rebellious emotion which ruled him for the moment.

A long silence followed, each longing to speak, yet ignorant how to comfort or reprove. Harry, always generous, was the first to pardon the culprit, in spite of all he had suffered. Rising feebly, he went to the unhappy man, and laying a kind hand on his shoulder, said, with real feeling:

"Robert, I don't forget that we are brothers, and though that made it very hard to bear your unkindness once, it makes it easy to forgive you now. I do heartily, and, if I know him, Augustine will say the same."

He did not say it, for the old fear lingered still, but he drew near with a mild air, and conciliatory—

"Here's my hand, brother; do not let us be enemies."

Steele neither stirred nor spoke. Mrs. Carruth, touched by his mute misery, relented, and womanlike, tried to heal the wounds she had made.

"This confession does you honor, Mr. Carruth, and I will not be the last to thank you for it, much as you have wronged me and mine. We both have sinned and suffered through pride and ambition. Let mutual pardon and humility make our future better than our past. You would have taken away my husband, but I will not alienate your father from you."

Still no answer from the motionless figure with bent head, and the old man spoke more leniently even than I had expected.

"She is right; I will repair my long neglect, for you are my son, and as such I will own you, will forgive you, and keep silence for your sake. You shall suffer neither want nor reproach, Robert, but take your place among us, if you will, and though this young lady cannot love you, the ties that bind us together will make it possible for us to comfort you with the natural affection of parents, brothers and sisters. My son, forgive me, as I forgive you."

Now Steele looked up, untouched by any appeal, unsoftened by any emotion; for the devil that haunted him was in the ascendant, as his face at once betrayed. All the noble warmth and sweetness was gone; nothing but pride, bitterness, and indomitable will remained, giving his fine countenance the half-stern, half-scornful beauty of a fallen spirit as artists picture them.

Turning on the group that had drawn about him, he said, with a look that made them shrink away:

"I will accept nothing. You, sir, have never been a father to me—I will never be a son to you. Hide nothing for my sake and, in betraying me, betray yourself to the world, whose blame I defy. Your suffering, madam, has avenged my mother's wrongs, and I am satisfied. To my brothers I leave the name I have dishonored, the fortune I no longer covet, the horrible inheritance that is in store for them. To you—" here his voice broke, but he checked the tremor fiercely, and said, slowly, while his eye turned on me with a glance I could not meet:

"To you I leave the memory of the heartless treachery that not only robbed my hard confession of its worth, but my life of its one hope. You have destroyed my faith in truth, my desire for virtue, my power of loving nobly, and sent me out into the world a desperate man. God may forgive you—I never will!" and with these hard words upon his lips, he was gone.

A strange sense of relief fell on me as he vanished, yet it was mingled with disquiet, for though the evil genius of the house had departed, he had left his malign influence behind, and we all felt it. For a time we talked excitedly, wondering how he had conquered madame, and what would become of him in his reckless mood; then, glad to put away the foreboding fear that seemed to oppress us, we spoke of the peace that was in store for us, and tried to enjoy it.

Mrs. Carruth soon begged me to see if Elinor was ready, for time had slipped away unperceived, and she longed for the happy moment that should cancel a year of such sad separation.

I went up, feeling ill and spent, and found Elinor already in bed. She seemed asleep, and grieved at the thought of her mother's disappointment, I stood a moment, hoping she would rouse. She did not, and I was about to leave her, when, as I settled the clothes, something dropped at my feet—a little pearl-handled penknife of my own—but a thrill of fear went through me, for it was open, and when I took it up a red stain came off upon my hand. Elinor's face was turned from me, and, bending nearer, I shuddered to see how pale it looked in the gloom of the darkened room. I listened at her lips, only a fairy flutter of breath parted them. I turned her head and uttered a cry of horror, for on her neck appeared a little wound, from which the blood still flowed, though all the pillows were deeply dyed with that dreadful stain. Like a flash the meaning of the sudden change which had come over her grew clear to me—her tender parting with father and brothers, her wish to be at peace with every one, her longing for her mother, and the tragic death she had chosen rather than continue the tragic life that lay before her.

My strength had been tried to the utmost—the shock of this discovery was too much for me, and, in the act of calling Hannah, I fainted for the first time in my life.

When I recovered the room seemed full of people—terror-stricken faces passed before my eyes—broken voices whispered about me:

"No hope—it is too late to save her." "She is most gone." "It is better so, sad as it seems."

And as I sat up I saw a group about the bed that made me wish for unconsciousness again.

Elinor lay in her father's arms quietly breathing her life away, for though the deathful wound was staunched, and everything that love and skill could devise had been tried to save her, the little knife in that resolute hand had done its work, and this world held no more suffering for her. Harry was down upon his knees beside her trying to stifle his passionate grief. Augustine prayed audibly above her, and the devout fervor of his broken words calmed and comforted all hearts but one. At the bed's foot, half hidden in the dark hangings, lay the miserable mother, as if crushed by the blow, fearing to show herself lest her presence should mar the peace of her child's departing soul. Dr. Shirley stood near me, sobbing like a boy, for the kind old man had loved and served the poor girl as faithfully as if she had been his own.

"Cannot you save her?" I whispered, as the priest's faltering prayer ended, and a sound of weeping filled the room.

"No; she is sane and safe at last, thank God."

I could not but echo his thanksgiving, for the blessed tranquility of the girl's countenance was such as no joy of this life could bring her, and as I looked her eyes opened, beautifully clear and calm before the mist of death dimmed them for ever. They went from face to face, as if searching for some one, and her lips moved with vain endeavors to speak.

"She wants you—she asked for you once—go, my dear," said Dr. Shirley, and I went. She gave me a loving, grateful look as I kissed her cold forehead, but still those wide, wistful eyes searched the room as if unsatisfied, and with a longing that conquered the mortal weakness of the body, her heart sent forth one tender cry:

"My mother—I want my mother!"

There was no need to repeat the faint call. At the first word up from the ground sprung that poor mother, and gathering her daughter in her arms held her close long after death had set his seal upon the voiceless prayers for pardon which passed between those re-united hearts, leaving one to expiate a great sin by a great sorrow, the other to feel with its last throb the beauty of forgiveness.

Even when she was asleep, at last, Mrs. Carruth would let no one touch her darling but me, and together we made her ready for her grave, weeping as we worked with tender hands, and praying prayers that sanctified our grief.

So beautiful she looked when all was done that in the early dawn we called her father and her brothers, that they might not lose the memory of the indescribable sweetness which touched her peaceful face. Her favorite flowers were about her, poor Edward's white roses on her breast, and as the first rays of the sun stole in to bathe her in its ruddy glow, and kiss her smiling lips, we too smiled, feeling that Elinor's New Year was happily begun in heaven.

CHAPTER VIII. ATONEMENT

YEARS HAVE PASSED since that sad night, and many changes have come and gone. I am an old woman now, still single, but neither poor nor solitary, for the Carruths gave me both home and friends. The fact, that I had been so curiously connected with the secret afflictions of the family, became a sort of tie between us, and they claimed me as one belonging to them. I was glad to stay for I loved them all, and when Amy died, in the second year of her marriage, leaving no child to inherit the curse, I became the daughter of the house. For a few years Mrs. Carruth devoted herself to her husband, and when he went did not long survive him. But her great trouble had chastened her pride and ennobled her character; and I mourned for her as if she had been my mother. On her death-bed she charged me to be a sister to her sons, I promised, and through all these years have faithfully kept my word.

Elinor's death wrought a great change in Harry, and developed unexpected strength of character. He went abroad for several years, and when his parents died came home to comfort Augustine, who had been a dutiful son to the last. Much to my surprise Harry had laid out a plan of life, had already begun it and has never swerved from it. In spite of his wealth and the temptations to ease, pleasure and ambition, which it offered, he became a physician, studied patiently, worked energetically, and now in his prime has earned a reputation he may well be proud of. No sign of the hereditary madness ever appeared in him since he gave himself to an active and absorbing profession, but by the law of compensation he seems gifted with a wonderful insight into the mysteries of all mental maladies, possesses rare skill in the treatment of them, and Doctor Carruth is sought far and wide for experience, patience, and an almost womanly tenderness of heart, that make his ministrations doubly welcome.

His brave example woke a spirit of emulation in Augustine's weaker nature, and while the younger brother helped afflicted minds and bodies, he labored for lost or troubled souls with the devout zeal of a priest of old. Great he will never be, but much beloved, for many bless the meek man who so gently comforts sorrow, pities weakness, pardons sins, and so beautifully mingles human charities with divine beliefs, that Protestants respect his genuine piety, and Catholics will canonize him as a saint. Neither can ever marry, for Harry has taken a vow of celibacy as binding as his brother's but, though they renounced the dear delight of seeing wives and children of their own about their fireside, it is not solitary, for one woman so loves and honors them for this, that she devotes her life to making home happy. Surely, I have my reward, when they call me their sunshine, tell me all their plans and cares and joys, and come to me for comfort when their hearts clamor for the love that is the right of all, unless principle opposes passion. Remembering what had passed and what might be, many would have thought that our household must be a sad one, but three happier souls do not live than we; not that we are gay, but always cheerful, always busy, each in our different way, and no brothers could be more devoted than they, no sister prouder than I of the two earnest, useful, noble men, whose lives are passing side by side with mine.

Of Steele's fate we knew nothing for a long time. Madame returned to France unreconciled; Marie in time forgot her first love and made a humbler, better man happy, but Robert remained self-exiled. Harry saw him once abroad gambling recklessly, and winning large sums with the strange success, which often attends a careless player. Harry placed himself where it was impossible to escape notice, but Steele showed no sign of recognition; Harry addressed him by his true title, but Steele answered like a perfect stranger.

"Monsieur mistakes, my name is not Carruth." Harry called him brother, and would have added some friendly question but Steele cut him short by saying in a sternly significant tone, as he left him with a haughty bow:

"Monsieur mistakes again, I have no brothers."

Harry made inquiries concerning him, learned that he passed for a misanthropic Englishman, who played for pleasure, drove fine horses and never spoke to a woman. With this Harry was forced to be contented, for Steele disappeared and they met no more. Year after year went by, and his brothers began to believe that he was dead, but I never gave up hoping, for something told me that we should meet again, and ten years from the time he went we did meet again.

I often accompanied Harry when he visited patients in neighboring cities, for my skill as nurse had not deserted me, and we loved to work together. On one of these occasions, after doing our best for the poor lady to whom we had been called, we went to visit the private asylum of Dr. Maurice, a French physician of some celebrity. With the courtesy of his nation, the good doctor did the honors of his well-kept house, taking us into every room, and showing every patient but one. A single door he passed unopened, and without the least allusion to its occupant. This omission excited my curiosity, and as the two gentlemen paused to look down into the sunny garden, where several mild lunatics were walking, I stole a hasty peep through the half-opened wicket in that closed door. I saw nothing, except a wasted hand, watering a little pot of heath; but the sight of the flower recalled the past so vividly, that my face betrayed me.

"Why, Kate, what troubles you?" asked Harry, as I joined them.

"I saw something that reminded me of Steele," I answered.

"Poor Robert! I wish I knew where to look for him," said Harry, with a sigh.

Dr. Maurice glanced from one to the other, in a peculiar way that had struck me before, once when I was introduced as Miss Snow, and again when Harry called me Kate; now Steele's name brought back the same half-anxious, half-curious expression, and he repeated, as if to himself, the names:

"Robert Steele, Kate Snow, Harry Carruth."

Then, aloud, as if recollecting himself:

"Pardon me, and permit that I ask a question or two. You wish to find Monsieur Steele? and why?"

"He is my brother," Harry answered, eagerly, while I cried out, with a terrible foreboding at my heart:

"Oh, do not tell us he is here!"

Gently putting me aside, Dr. Maurice drew Harry to the door, pushed open the panel, and bade him look in. Harry obeyed, looked long, but turned away with a troubled, disappointed, yet grateful face.

"It is not Robert; thank God for that!"

"Let mademoiselle try; her eyes may be keener than yours. Approach, and examine this unhappy creature."

Trembling with hope and fear, I gazed into the sunny little room, which was a sadder prison than the darkest cell, for not only liberty, but the life of life was lost to the poor soul hidden there. No wonder Harry did not know the shadow of a man he saw; I doubted my own sight at first, but the flower, the eyes, the attitude, were all aids to memory; and the stir of sorrow and remorse that filled my heart, assured me that this was Steele. Bent and feeble as an old man, pallid and hollow-eyed, with one half his face concealed by a neglected beard, he sat, leaning his gray head on his wasted hand, brooding vacantly, unconscious of all about him. He looked like some strong, savage creature, broken by captivity; and as I watched him, the memory of his face and figure as he bravely made his hard confession ten years ago, came back to me so vividly that my eyes grew too dim for seeing, and I turned away, exclaiming:

"It *is* Robert; let me go to him!"

"Good! you shall go presently, mademoiselle; but now compose yourself, and let me relate what I know of this friend."

Leading us into an adjoining room, Dr. Maurice rapidly gave us the following facts:

"Seven years ago, Monsieur Steele came to me, asking to be received as a patient. He had been insane once, and felt that another attack would soon follow, for madness was in his family. He said he had no friends to care for him, and, placing a large sum of money in my hands, implored me to help him if I could. He had an intense dread of becoming an object of pity or curiosity to strangers, and desired me to conceal his presence here, and let him live unknown. I was much interested in him, for it was evident that he was in a dangerous way, and nothing but the force of a strong will restrained the mental suffering that tortured him. I received the unfortunate, and for seven years he has been a case of the most horrible and hopeless insanity. For a long time I expected friends would come to claim him, but till now none have appeared. I have done my duty honestly by him, have husbanded his means, and when they were exhausted, served him from pity, for a more desolate creature I never knew."

"Is there no hope for him?" asked Harry, as I let my tears flow freely at the thought of the bitter penance poor Robert had been doing all these years.

"Six months ago I should have answered no; now there is one chance in a hundred that he may recover, though I fear the restoration of his mind may be at the expense of his worn-out body. Of late a change has come over him; the violence of his malady has abated, and he broods instead of raving, sits motionless all day, instead of walking incessantly, like a caged panther, and talks coherently, though of persons and events unknown to those about him. Some pleasurable shock might rouse his mind, temporarily, if no more. I have tried many experiments, but all failed; you may help me if you will, for you possess the clue to his past."

"Does he speak of us?" I asked.

"Yes; the name Kate Snow was so familiar to me, that I started when Dr. Carruth called you by it. My patient sometimes speaks of Augustine, Harry, Elinor, and Amy; but talks constantly of Kate, implores her to come to him, then denounces her as a traitress, then defies her to make his heart ache; yet always returns to the same longing cry for you. Will mademoiselle answer it?"

"I will."

Then Harry told him all, feeling that the good man deserved entire confidence in return for his faithful care of the unhappy outcast, whom he had so long befriended.

"His recovery depends on you," said the doctor, with a glance at me. "Yours is the most vivid image in his mind, and your influence will be both soothing and strengthening. When you are quite calm go in to him, and see if he recognizes you. Dr. Carruth and I will be near, but you need fear nothing."

I put off my hat and cloak, and went at once, feeling that if any one could save poor Robert it was me. Entering noiselessly, I placed myself in the broad ray of sunshine that fell athwart the floor, and waited for him to see me. He still sat with his head propped upon his hand, his vacant eyes fixed on the sunshine, his lips moving rapidly, as he talked inaudibly with some phantom seen by him alone.

My shadow attracted him, and his eye rose to mine, but no change appeared in the pathetic patience of his face. He sighed, and looked away, saying, as if to himself:

"Back again so soon. I hoped she would give me a little rest before she came again!"

"Do you know me, Robert?" I gently asked.

"Can I help it, when you have haunted me for years? You say you are Kate, but I know that you are only a tormenting devil, as fair and false as she, and I'll not believe you."

"I am not spirit, but Kate herself. Is this a phantom's hand—a phantom's face?"

Intent on rousing him, I knelt down before him, took his hand in mine, and made him look at me. A slow light kindled in his mournful eyes, a faint smile rose to his lips, and presently he touched me as if to assure himself that I was real.

"This looks like Kate," he said. "This is her bonny hair, these are her soft hands, and that was her voice I heard just now."

"You shall hear it again, if you will, for I am come to comfort my poor friend."

He shrunk away from me, as if I had touched some jarring chord.

"She called me friend, and then betrayed me. I'll neither look nor listen; for, though this is a beautiful, consoling spirit, it will go like all the rest, and leave me to my misery!"

"It will never go, if you will let it stay. What shall I do to make you know and trust me?"

"Nothing. I can never trust again. Kate deceived me, and that broke my heart!"

"Forgive her. Let her prove that she can be true. Robert! dear Robert! it is really Kate—the old Kate who tried to help you once, and will again, for she loves and pities you, and longs for pardon more than she can tell."

"That sounds pleasant. Say it again—'she loves and pities you!' Ah! well, she is a woman, and can seem kindest when most cruel. I believed her once—I am wiser now."

He put me away, and began to wander aimlessly about the room, as if disturbed, yet not excited. I glanced towards the door where Harry and the doctor still stood.

"It is well; go on," whispered the latter, and anxious to try all my powers, I began to sing the song Robert best loved. He stopped at once, listened with an eager air, beat time, and watched me intently; but when I paused, he struck his hands together with a passionate gesture, and cried out fiercely:

"Be still! How dare you sing that here, and bring back the one happy day in which I thought she loved me. For God's sake let me forget, or I shall go mad again."

He cast himself down upon his narrow bed, and lay there with averted face, as if trying to shut out the phantom that haunted him. Excitement was better than apathy, and much encouraged, I laid my hands on his hot forehead, putting the whole force of my will into the effort to calm this troubled mind.

But the power had gone out of me, and when he looked up with those magnificent, yet melancholy eyes, in which love still shone through the darkness of that sad eclipse, I could only tremble, and turn away to weep remorseful tears over the ruin I had helped to make.

It was the wisest thing I could have done. My weakness seemed to give him strength, my sorrow to touch the heart I had won and wounded long ago. He rose, and came to me, smoothed my hair, and eyed me wistfully, yet still seemed slow to believe in my reality.

"She shed tears that night, and I thought they were for me. Now I do not delude myself, yet it is pleasant to have her here even if she makes me miserable. She says she is Kate, I wish I could believe her, but she will never come, never know how my sinful wish recoiled upon myself, and brought me here. Kate, if you are real, make me believe it; let me feel that you do love and pity me in blessed earnest."

As he spoke, he stretched his arms to me, with such mingled, longing, incredulity and tenderness in eye and voice, that I could not hesitate to free him from the sad delusion that kept me from serving him as I desired to do. Gladly I went to him, and drawing the haggard face to mine, kissed it with repentant lips. He clutched me to him for a moment, then held me off to look again with eager, ardent eyes, exclaiming breathlessly:

"She never did that before; the phantom only repeated her acts and words; this is new, this is real, this is my Kate! Oh, stay with me the little while I have to live; I need you very much."

"I shall never leave you, Robert."

Gathering me close, he laid his gray head on my shoulder, sobbing like a lost child who has found his mother, and through the momentary silence came Harry's glad ejaculation:

"Thank God, she has saved him!"

I had, but only for a little while. We took him home, and all three devoted our lives to him. Harry tried to save the shattered body, Augustine to uplift the sad soul, I to warm and cheer the desolate heart, which had cherished such a faithful love for me.

Dr. Maurice was right: as reason returned strength departed, and Robert only came back to us to die. Yet in those few months he redeemed his faultful past by patience, penitence, and an affection that bound us tenderly together. As the end drew nearer he grew nobler, and death did for him what life had failed to do, showing us glimpses of the fine nature which neglect, injustice and temptation had not entirely ruined. His long suffering atoned for his deceit, taught him that sin brings its own retribution, and that God tempers infinite justice with infinite mercy.

In the hush of a summer night his summons came, and he received it manfully, happily, for, with either hand held fast by a brother, his head pillowed on the bosom of the woman whom he loved, he went prayerfully down into the valley of the shadow, leaving three hearts to mourn for him, and one to remember him long after the grave had closed over the last of the Carruths.

ᴥ Behind a Mask: or, A Woman's Power

Chapter I. Jean Muir

"Has she come?"

"No, Mamma, not yet."

"I wish it were well over. The thought of it worries and excites me. A cushion for my back, Bella."

And poor, peevish Mrs. Coventry sank into an easy chair with a nervous sigh and the air of a martyr, while her pretty daughter hovered about her with affectionate solicitude.

"Who are they talking of, Lucia?" asked the languid young man lounging on a couch near his cousin, who bent over her tapestry work with a happy smile on her usually haughty face.

"The new governess, Miss Muir. Shall I tell you about her?"

"No, thank you. I have an inveterate aversion to the whole tribe. I've often thanked heaven that I had but one sister, and she a spoiled child, so that I have escaped the infliction of a governess so long."

"How will you bear it now?" asked Lucia.

"Leave the house while she is in it."

"No, you won't. You're too lazy, Gerald," called out a younger and more energetic man, from the recess where he stood teasing his dogs.

"I'll give her a three days' trial; if she proves endurable I shall not disturb myself; if, as I am sure, she is a bore, I'm off anywhere, anywhere out of her way."

"I beg you won't talk in that depressing manner, boys. I dread the coming of a stranger more than you possibly can, but Bella *must* not be neglected; so I have nerved myself to endure this woman, and Lucia is good enough to say she will attend to her after tonight."

"Don't be troubled, Mamma. She is a nice person, I dare say, and when once we are used to her, I've no doubt we shall be glad to have her, it's so dull here just now. Lady Sydney said she was a quiet, accomplished, amiable girl, who needed a home, and would be a help to poor stupid me, so try to like her for my sake."

"I will, dear, but isn't it getting late? I do hope nothing has happened. Did you tell them to send a carriage to the station for her, Gerald?"

"I forgot it. But it's not far, it won't hurt her to walk" was the languid reply.

"It was indolence, not forgetfulness, I know. I'm very sorry; she will think it so rude to leave her to find her way so late. Do go and see to it, Ned."

"Too late, Bella, the train was in some time ago. Give your orders to me next time Mother and I'll see that they are obeyed," said Edward.

"Ned is just at an age to make a fool of himself for any girl who comes in his way. Have a care of the governess, Lucia, or she will bewitch him."

Gerald spoke in a satirical whisper, but his brother heard him and answered with a good-humored laugh.

"I wish there was any hope of your making a fool of yourself in that way, old fellow. Set me a good example, and I promise to follow it. As for the governess, she is a woman, and should be treated with common civility. I should say a little extra kindness wouldn't be amiss, either, because she is poor, and a stranger."

"That is my dear, good-hearted Ned! We'll stand by poor little Muir, won't we?" And running to her brother, Bella stood on tiptoe to offer him a kiss which he could not refuse, for the rosy lips were pursed up invitingly, and the bright eyes full of sisterly affection.

"I do hope she has come, for, when I make an effort to see anyone, I hate to make it in vain. Punctuality is *such* a virtue, and I know this woman hasn't got it, for she promised to be here at seven, and now it is long after," began Mrs. Coventry, in an injured tone.

Before she could get breath for another complaint, the clock struck seven and the doorbell rang.

"There she is!" cried Bella, and turned toward the door as if to go and meet the newcomer.

But Lucia arrested her, saying authoritatively, "Stay here, child. It is her place to come to you, not yours to go to her."

"Miss Muir," announced a servant, and a little black-robed figure stood in the doorway. For an instant no one stirred, and the governess had time to see and be seen before a word was uttered. All looked at her, and she cast on the household group a keen glance that impressed them curiously; then her eyes fell, and bowing slightly she walked in. Edward came forward and received her with the frank cordiality which nothing could daunt or chill.

"Mother, this is the lady whom you expected. Miss Muir, allow me to apologize for our apparent neglect in not sending for you. There was a mistake about the carriage, or, rather, the lazy fellow to whom the order was given forgot it. Bella, come here."

"Thank you, no apology is needed. I did not expect to be sent for." And the governess meekly sat down without lifting her eyes.

"I am glad to see you. Let me take your things," said Bella, rather shyly, for Gerald, still lounging, watched the fireside group with languid interest, and Lucia never stirred. Mrs. Coventry took a second survey and began:

"You were punctual, Miss Muir, which pleases me. I'm a sad invalid, as Lady Sydney told you, I hope; so that Miss Coventry's lessons will be directed by my niece, and you will go to her for directions, as she knows what I wish. You will excuse me if

I ask you a few questions, for Lady Sydney's note was very brief, and I left everything to her judgment."

"Ask anything you like, madam," answered the soft, sad voice.

"You are Scotch, I believe."

"Yes, madam."

"Are your parents living?"

"I have not a relation in the world."

"Dear me, how sad! Do you mind telling me your age?"

"Nineteen." And a smile passed over Miss Muir's lips, as she folded her hands with an air of resignation, for the catechism was evidently to be a long one.

"So young! Lady Sydney mentioned five-and-twenty, I think, didn't she, Bella?"

"No, Mamma, she only said she thought so. Don't ask such questions. It's not pleasant before us all," whispered Bella.

A quick, grateful glance shone on her from the suddenly lifted eyes of Miss Muir, as she said quietly, "I wish I was thirty, but, as I am not, I do my best to look and seem old."

Of course, every one looked at her then, and all felt a touch of pity at the sight of the pale-faced girl in her plain black dress, with no ornament but a little silver cross at her throat. Small, thin, and colorless she was, with yellow hair, gray eyes, and sharply cut, irregular, but very expressive features. Poverty seemed to have set its bond stamp upon her, and life to have had for her more frost than sunshine. But something in the lines of the mouth betrayed strength, and the clear, low voice had a curious mixture of command and entreaty in its varying tones. Not an attractive woman, yet not an ordinary one; and, as she sat there with her delicate hands lying in her lap, her head bent, and a bitter look on her thin face, she was more interesting than many a blithe and blooming girl. Bella's heart warmed to her at once, and she drew her seat nearer, while Edward went back to his dogs that his presence might not embarrass her.

"You have been ill, I think," continued Mrs. Coventry, who considered this fact the most interesting of all she had heard concerning the governess.

"Yes, madam, I left the hospital only a week ago."

"Are you quite sure it is safe to begin teaching so soon?"

"I have no time to lose, and shall soon gain strength here in the country, if you care to keep me."

"And you are fitted to teach music, French, and drawing?"

"I shall endeavor to prove that I am."

"Be kind enough to go and play an air or two. I can judge by your touch; I used to play finely when a girl."

Miss Muir rose, looked about her for the instrument, and seeing it at the other end of the room went toward it, passing Gerald and Lucia as if she did not see them. Bella followed, and in a moment forgot everything in admiration. Miss Muir played like one who loved music and was perfect mistress of her art. She charmed them all by the magic of this spell; even indolent Gerald sat up to listen, and Lucia put down her needle, while Ned watched the slender white fingers as they flew, and wondered at the strength and skill which they possessed.

"Please sing," pleaded Bella, as a brilliant overture ended.

With the same meek obedience Miss Muir complied, and began a little Scotch melody, so sweet, so sad, that the girl's eyes filled, and Mrs. Coventry looked for one of her many pocket-handkerchiefs. But suddenly the music ceased, for, with a vain attempt to support herself, the singer slid from her seat and lay before the startled listeners, as white and rigid as if struck with death. Edward caught her up, and, ordering his brother off the couch, laid her there, while Bella chafed her hands, and her mother rang for her maid. Lucia bathed the poor girl's temples, and Gerald, with unwonted energy, brought a glass of wine. Soon Miss Muir's lips trembled, she sighed, then murmured, tenderly, with a pretty Scotch accent, as if wandering in the past, "Bide wi' me, Mither, I'm sae sick an sad here all alone."

"Take a sip of this, and it will do you good, my dear," said Mrs. Coventry, quite touched by the plaintive words.

The strange voice seemed to recall her. She sat up, looked about her, a little wildly, for a moment, then collected herself and said, with a pathetic look and tone, "Pardon me. I have been on my feet all day, and, in my eagerness to keep my appointment, I forgot to eat since morning. I'm better now; shall I finish the song?"

"By no means. Come and have some tea," said Bella, full of pity and remorse.

"Scene first, very well done," whispered Gerald to his cousin.

Miss Muir was just before them, apparently listening to Mrs. Coventry's remarks upon fainting fits; but she heard, and looked over her shoulders with a gesture like Rachel. Her eyes were gray, but at that instant they seemed black with some strong emotion of anger, pride, or defiance. A curious smile passed over her face as she bowed, and said in her penetrating voice, "Thanks. The last scene shall be still better."

Young Coventry was a cool, indolent man, seldom conscious of any emotion, any passion, pleasurable or otherwise; but at the look, the tone of the governess, he experienced a new sensation, indefinable, yet strong. He colored and, for the first time in his life, looked abashed. Lucia saw it, and hated Miss Muir with a sudden hatred; for, in all the years she had passed with her cousin, no look or word of hers had possessed such power. Coventry was himself again in an instant, with no trace of that passing change, but a look of interest in his usually dreamy eyes, and a touch of anger in his sarcastic voice.

"What a melodramatic young lady! I shall go tomorrow."

Lucia laughed, and was well pleased when he sauntered away to bring her a cup of tea from the table where a little scene was just taking place. Mrs. Coventry had sunk into her chair again, exhausted by the flurry of the fainting fit. Bella was busied about her; and Edward, eager to feed the pale governess, was awkwardly trying to make the tea, after a beseeching glance at his cousin which she did not choose to answer. As he upset the caddy and uttered a despairing exclamation, Miss Muir quietly took her place behind the urn, saying with a smile, and a shy glance at the young man, "Allow me to assume my duty at once, and serve you all. I understand the art of making people comfortable in this way. The scoop, please. I can gather this up quite well alone, if you will tell me how your mother likes her tea."

Edward pulled a chair to the table and made merry over his mishaps, while Miss Muir performed her little task with a skill and grace that made it pleasant to watch her. Coventry lingered a moment after she had given him a steaming cup, to observe her more nearly, while he asked a question or two of his brother. She took no more notice of him than if he had been a statue, and in the middle of the one remark he addressed to her, she rose to take the sugar basin to Mrs. Coventry, who was quite won by the modest, domestic graces of the new governess.

"Really, my dear, you are a treasure; I haven't tasted such tea since my poor maid Ellis died. Bella never makes it good, and Miss Lucia always forgets the cream. Whatever you do you seem to do well, and that is *such* a comfort."

"Let me always do this for you, then. It will be a pleasure, madam." And Miss Muir came back to her seat with a faint color in her cheek which improved her much.

"My brother asked if young Sydney was at home when you left," said Edward, for Gerald would not take the trouble to repeat the question.

Miss Muir fixed her eyes on Coventry, and answered with a slight tremor of the lips, "No, he left home some weeks ago."

The young man went back to his cousin, saying, as he threw himself down beside her, "I shall not go tomorrow, but wait till the three days are out."

"Why?" demanded Lucia.

Lowering his voice he said, with a significant nod toward the governess, "Because I have a fancy that she is at the bottom of Sydney's mystery. He's not been himself lately, and now he is gone without a word. I rather like romances in real life, if they are not too long, or difficult to read."

"Do you think her pretty?"

"Far from it, a most uncanny little specimen."

"Then why fancy Sydney loves her?"

"He is an oddity, and likes sensations and things of that sort."

"What do you mean, Gerald?"

"Get the Muir to look at you, as she did at me, and you will understand. Will you have another cup, Juno?"

"Yes, please." She liked to have him wait upon her, for he did it to no other woman except his mother.

Before he could slowly rise, Miss Muir glided to them with another cup on the salver; and, as Lucia took it with a cold nod, the girl said under her breath, "I think it honest to tell you that I possess a quick ear, and cannot help hearing what is said anywhere in the room. What you say of me is of no consequence, but you may speak of things which you prefer I should not hear; therefore, allow me to warn you." And she was gone again as noiselessly as she came.

"How do you like that?" whispered Coventry, as his cousin sat looking after the girl, with a disturbed expression.

"What an uncomfortable creature to have in the house! I am very sorry I urged her coming, for your mother has taken a fancy to her, and it will be hard to get rid of her," said Lucia, half angry, half amused.

"Hush, she hears every word you say. I know it by the expression of her face, for Ned is talking about horses, and she looks as haughty as ever you did, and that is saying much. Faith, this is getting interesting."

"Hark, she is speaking; I want to hear," and Lucia laid her hand on her cousin's lips. He kissed it, and then idly amused himself with turning the rings to and fro on the slender fingers.

"I have been in France several years, madam, but my friend died and I came back to be with Lady Sydney, till—" Muir paused an instant, then added, slowly, "till I fell ill. It was a contagious fever, so I went of my own accord to the hospital, not wishing to endanger her."

"Very right, but are you sure there is no danger of infection now?" asked Mrs. Coventry anxiously.

"None, I assure you. I have been well for some time, but did not leave because I preferred to stay there, than to return to Lady Sydney."

"No quarrel, I hope? No trouble of any kind?"

"No quarrel, but—well, why not? You have a right to know, and I will not make a foolish mystery out of a very simple thing. As your family, only, is present, I may tell the truth. I did not go back on the young gentleman's account. Please ask no more."

"Ah, I see. Quite prudent and proper, Miss Muir. I shall never allude to it again. Thank you for your frankness. Bella, you will be careful not to mention this to your young friends; girls gossip sadly, and it would annoy Lady Sydney beyond everything to have this talked of."

"Very neighborly of Lady S. to send the dangerous young lady here, where there are *two* young gentlemen to be captivated. I wonder why she didn't keep Sydney after she had caught him," murmured Coventry to his cousin.

"Because she had the utmost contempt for a titled fool." Miss Muir dropped the words almost into his ear, as she bent to take her shawl from the sofa corner.

"How the deuce did she get there?" ejaculated Coventry, looking as if he had received another sensation. "She has spirit, though, and upon my word I pity Sydney, if he did try to dazzle her, for he must have got a splendid dismissal."

"Come and play billiards. You promised, and I hold you to your word," said Lucia, rising with decision, for Gerald was showing too much interest in another to suit Miss Beaufort.

"I am, as ever, your most devoted. My mother is a charming woman, but I find our evening parties slightly dull, when only my own family are present. Good night, Mamma." He shook hands with his mother, whose pride and idol he was, and, with a comprehensive nod to the others, strolled after his cousin.

"Now they are gone we can be quite cozy, and talk over things, for I don't mind Ned any more than I do his dogs," said Bella, settling herself on her mother's footstool.

"I merely wish to say, Miss Muir, that my daughter has never had a governess and is sadly backward for a girl of sixteen. I want you to pass the mornings with her, and get her on as rapidly as possible. In the afternoon you will walk or drive with her, and in the evening sit with us here, if you like, or amuse yourself as you please. While in the country we are very quiet, for I cannot bear much company, and when my sons want gaiety, they go away for it. Miss Beaufort oversees the servants, and takes my place as far as possible. I am very delicate and keep my room till evening, except for an airing at noon. We will try each other for a month, and I hope we shall get on quite comfortably together."

"I shall do my best, madam."

One would not have believed that the meek, spiritless voice which uttered these words was the same that had startled Coventry a few minutes before, nor that the pale, patient face could ever have kindled with such sudden fire as that which looked over Miss Muir's shoulder when she answered her young host's speech.

Edward thought within himself, Poor little woman! She has had a hard life. We will try and make it easier while she is here; and began his charitable work by suggesting that she might be tired. She acknowledged she was, and Bella led her away to a bright, cozy room, where with a pretty little speech and a good-night kiss she left her.

When alone Miss Muir's conduct was decidedly peculiar. Her first act was to clench her hands and mutter between her teeth, with passionate force, "I'll not fail again if there is power in a woman's wit and will!" She stood a moment motionless, with an expression of almost fierce disdain on her face, then shook her clenched hand as if menacing some unseen enemy. Next she laughed, and shrugged her shoulders with a true French shrug, saying low to herself, "Yes, the last scene *shall* be better than the first. *Mon dieu,* how tired and hungry I am!"

Kneeling before the one small trunk which held her worldly possessions, she opened it, drew out a flask, and mixed a glass of some ardent cordial, which she seemed to enjoy extremely as she sat on the carpet, musing, while her quick eyes examined every corner of the room.

"Not bad! It will be a good field for me to work in, and the harder the task the better I shall like it. *Merci,* old friend. You put heart and courage into me when nothing else will. Come, the curtain is down, so I may be myself for a few hours, if actresses ever are themselves."

Still sitting on the floor she unbound and removed the long abundant braids from her head, wiped the pink from her face, took out several pearly teeth, and slipping off her dress appeared herself indeed, a haggard, worn, and moody woman of thirty at least. The metamorphosis was wonderful, but the disguise was more in the expression she assumed than in any art of costume or false adornment. Now she was alone, and her mobile features settled into their natural expression, weary, hard, bitter. She had been lovely once, happy, innocent, and tender; but nothing of all this remained to the gloomy woman who leaned there brooding over some wrong, or loss, or disappointment which had darkened all her life. For an hour she sat so, sometimes playing absently with the scanty locks that hung about her face, sometimes lifting the glass to her lips as if the fiery draught warmed her cold blood; and once she half uncovered her breast to eye with a terrible glance the scar of a newly healed wound. At last she rose and crept to bed, like one worn out with weariness and mental pain.

Chapter II. A Good Beginning

Only the housemaids were astir when Miss Muir left her room next morning and quietly found her way into the garden. As she walked, apparently intent upon the flowers, her quick eye scrutinized the fine old house and its picturesque surroundings.

"Not bad," she said to herself, adding, as she passed into the adjoining park, "but the other may be better, and I will have the best."

Walking rapidly, she came out at length upon the wide green lawn which lay before the ancient hall where Sir John Coventry lived in solitary splendor. A stately old place, rich in oaks, well-kept shrubberies, gay gardens, sunny terraces, carved gables, spacious rooms, liveried servants, and every luxury befitting the ancestral home of a rich and honorable race. Miss Muir's eyes brightened as she looked, her step grew firmer, her carriage prouder, and a smile broke over her face; the smile of one well pleased at the prospect of the success of some cherished hope. Suddenly her whole air changed, she pushed back her hat, clasped her hands loosely before her, and seemed absorbed in girlish admiration of the fair scene that could not fail to charm any beauty-loving eye. The cause of this rapid change soon appeared. A hale, handsome man, between fifty and sixty, came through the little gate leading to the park, and, seeing the young stranger, paused to examine her. He had only time for a glance, however; she seemed conscious of his presence in a moment, turned with a startled look, uttered an exclamation of surprise, and looked as if hesitating whether to speak or run away. Gallant Sir John took off his hat and said, with the old-fashioned courtesy which became him well, "I beg your pardon for disturbing you, young lady. Allow me to atone for it by inviting you to walk where you will, and gather what flowers you like. I see you love them, so pray make free with those about you."

With a charming air of maidenly timidity and artlessness, Miss Muir replied, "Oh, thank you, sir! But it is I who should ask pardon for trespassing. I never should have dared if I had not known that Sir John was absent. I always wanted to see this fine old place, and ran over the first thing, to satisfy myself."

"And *are* you satisfied?" he asked, with a smile.

"More than satisfied—I'm charmed; for it is the most beautiful spot I ever saw, and I've seen many famous seats, both at home and abroad," she answered enthusiastically.

"The Hall is much flattered, and so would its master be if he heard you," began the gentleman, with an odd expression.

"I should not praise it to him—at least, not as freely as I have to you, sir," said the girl, with eyes still turned away.

"Why not?" asked her companion, looking much amused.

"I should be afraid. Not that I dread Sir John; but I've heard so many beautiful and noble things about him, and respect him so highly, that I should not dare to say much, lest he should see how I admire and—"

"And what, young lady? Finish, if you please."

"I was going to say, love him. I will say it, for he is an old man, and one cannot help loving virtue and bravery."

Miss Muir looked very earnest and pretty as she spoke, standing there with the sunshine glinting on her yellow hair, delicate face, and downcast eyes. Sir John was not a vain man, but he found it pleasant to hear himself commended by this unknown girl, and felt redoubled curiosity to learn who she was. Too well-bred to ask, or to abash her by avowing what she seemed unconscious of, he left both discoveries to chance; and when she turned, as if to retrace her steps, he offered her the handful of hothouse flowers which he held, saying, with a gallant bow, "In Sir John's name let me give you my little nosegay, with thanks for your good opinion, which, I assure you, is not entirely deserved, for I know him well."

Miss Muir looked up quickly, eyed him an instant, then dropped her eyes, and, coloring deeply, stammered out, "I did not know—I beg your pardon—you are too kind, Sir John."

He laughed like a boy, asking, mischievously, "Why call me Sir John? How do you know that I am not the gardener or the butler?"

"I did not see your face before, and no one but yourself would say that any praise was undeserved," murmured Miss Muir, still overcome with girlish confusion.

"Well, well, we will let that pass, and the next time you come we will be properly introduced. Bella always brings her friends to the Hall, for I am fond of young people."

"I am not a friend. I am only Miss Coventry's governess." And Miss Muir dropped a meek curtsy. A slight change passed over Sir John's manner. Few would have perceived it, but Miss Muir felt it at once, and bit her lips with an angry feeling at her heart. With a curious air of pride, mingled with respect, she accepted the still offered bouquet, returned Sir John's parting bow, and tripped away, leaving the old gentleman to wonder where Mrs. Coventry found such a piquant little governess.

"That is done, and very well for a beginning," she said to herself as she approached the house.

In a green paddock close by fed a fine horse, who lifted up his head and eyed her inquiringly, like one who expected a greeting. Following a sudden impulse, she entered the paddock and, pulling a handful of clover, invited the creature to come and eat. This was evidently a new proceeding on the part of a lady, and the horse careered about as if bent on frightening the newcomer away.

"I see," she said aloud, laughing to herself. "I am not your master, and you rebel. Nevertheless, I'll conquer you, my fine brute."

Seating herself in the grass, she began to pull daisies, singing idly the while, as if unconscious of the spirited prancings of the horse. Presently he drew nearer, sniffing curiously and eyeing her with surprise. She took no notice, but plaited the daisies and sang on as if he was not there. This seemed to pique the petted creature, for, slowly approaching, he came at length so close that he could smell her little foot and nibble at her dress. Then she offered the clover, uttering caressing words and making soothing sounds, till by degrees and with much coquetting, the horse permitted her to stroke his glossy neck and smooth his mane.

It was a pretty sight—the slender figure in the grass, the high-spirited horse bending his proud head to her hand. Edward Coventry, who had watched the scene, found it impossible to restrain himself any longer and, leaping the wall, came to join the group, saying, with mingled admiration and wonder in countenance and voice, "Good morning, Miss Muir. If I had not seen your skill and courage proved before my eyes, I should be alarmed for your safety. Hector is a wild, wayward beast, and has damaged more than one groom who tried to conquer him."

"Good morning, Mr. Coventry. Don't tell tales of this noble creature, who has not deceived my faith in him. Your grooms did not know how to win his heart, and so subdue his spirit without breaking it."

Miss Muir rose as she spoke, and stood with her hand on Hector's neck while he ate the grass which she had gathered in the skirt of her dress.

"You have the secret, and Hector is your subject now, though heretofore he has rejected all friends but his master. Will you give him his morning feast? I always bring him bread and play with him before breakfast."

"Then you are not jealous?" And she looked up at him with eyes so bright and beautiful in expression that the young man wondered he had not observed them before.

"Not I. Pet him as much as you will; it will do him good. He is a solitary fellow, for he scorns his own kind and lives alone, like his master," he added, half to himself.

"Alone, with such a happy home, Mr. Coventry?" And a softly compassionate glance stole from the bright eyes.

"That was an ungrateful speech, and I retract it for Bella's sake. Younger sons have no position but such as they can make for themselves, you know, and I've had no chance yet."

"Younger sons! I thought—I beg pardon." And Miss Muir paused, as if remembering that she had no right to question.

Edward smiled and answered frankly, "Nay, don't mind me. You thought I was the heir, perhaps. Whom did you take my brother for last night?"

"For some guest who admired Miss Beaufort. I did not hear his name, nor observe him enough to discover who he was. I saw only your kind mother, your charming little sister, and—"

She stopped there, with a half-shy, half-grateful look at the young man which finished the sentence better than any words. He was still a boy, in spite of his one-and-twenty years, and a little color came into his brown cheek as the eloquent eyes met his and fell before them.

"Yes, Bella is a capital girl, and one can't help loving her. I know you'll get her on, for, really, she is the most delightful little dunce. My mother's ill health and Bella's devotion to her have prevented our attending to her education before. Next winter, when we go to town, she is to come out, and must be prepared for that great event, you know," he said, choosing a safe subject.

"I shall do my best. And that reminds me that I should report myself to her, instead of enjoying myself here. When one has been ill and shut up a long time, the country is so lovely one is apt to forget duty for pleasure. Please remind me if I am negligent, Mr. Coventry."

"That name belongs to Gerald. I'm only Mr. Ned here," he said as they walked toward the house, while Hector followed to the wall and sent a sonorous farewell after them.

Bella came running to meet them, and greeted Miss Muir as if she had made up her mind to like her heartily. "What a lovely bouquet you have got! I never can arrange flowers prettily, which vexes me, for Mamma is so fond of them and cannot go out herself. You have charming taste," she said, examining the graceful posy which Miss Muir had much improved by adding feathery grasses, delicate ferns, and fragrant wild flowers to Sir John's exotics.

Putting them into Bella's hand, she said, in a winning way, "Take them to your mother, then, and ask her if I may have the pleasure of making her a daily nosegay; for I should find real delight in doing it, if it would please her."

"How kind you are! Of course it would please her. I'll take them to her while the dew is still on them." And away flew Bella, eager to give both the flowers and the pretty message to the poor invalid.

Edward stopped to speak to the gardener, and Miss Muir went up the steps alone. The long hall was lined with portraits, and pacing slowly down it she examined them with interest. One caught her eye, and, pausing before it, she scrutinized it carefully. A young, beautiful, but very haughty female face. Miss Muir suspected at once who it was, and gave a decided nod, as if she saw and caught at some unexpected chance. A soft rustle behind her made her look around, and, seeing Lucia, she bowed, half turned, as if for another glance at the picture, and said, as if involuntarily, "How beautiful it is! May I ask if it is an ancestor, Miss Beaufort?"

"It is the likeness of my mother" was the reply, given with a softened voice and eyes that looked up tenderly.

"Ah, I might have known, from the resemblance, but I scarcely saw you last night. Excuse my freedom, but Lady Sydney treated me as a friend, and I forget my position. Allow me."

As she spoke, Miss Muir stooped to return the handkerchief which had fallen from Lucia's hand, and did so with a humble mien which touched the other's heart; for, though a proud, it was also a very generous one.

"Thank you. Are you better, this morning?" she said, graciously. And having received an affirmative reply, she added, as she walked on, "I will show you to the breakfast room, as Bella is not here. It is a very informal meal with us, for my aunt is never down and my cousins are very irregular in their hours. You can always have yours when you like, without waiting for us if you are an early riser."

Bella and Edward appeared before the others were seated, and Miss Muir quietly ate her breakfast, feeling well satisfied with her hour's work. Ned recounted her exploit with Hector, Bella delivered her mother's thanks for the flowers, and Lucia more than once recalled, with pardonable vanity, that the governess had compared her to her lovely mother, expressing by a look as much admiration for the living likeness as for the painted one. All kindly did their best to make the pale girl feel at home, and their cordial manner seemed to warm and draw her out; for soon she put off her sad, meek air and entertained them with gay anecdotes of her life in Paris, her travels in Russia when governess in Prince Jermadoff's family, and all manner of witty stories that kept them interested and merry long after the meal was over. In the middle of an absorbing adventure, Coventry came in, nodded lazily, lifted his brows, as if surprised at seeing the governess there, and began his breakfast as if the ennui of another day had already taken possession of him. Miss Muir stopped short, and no entreaties could induce her to go on.

"Another time I will finish it, if you like. Now Miss Bella and I should be at our books." And she left the room, followed by her pupil, taking no notice of the young master of the house, beyond a graceful bow in answer to his careless nod.

"Merciful creature! she goes when I come, and does not make life unendurable by moping about before my eyes. Does she belong to the moral, the melancholy, the romantic, or the dashing class, Ned?" said Gerald, lounging over his coffee as he did over everything he attempted.

"To none of them; she is a capital little woman. I wish you had seen her tame Hector this morning." And Edward repeated his story.

"Not a bad move on her part," said Coventry in reply. "She must be an observing as well as an energetic young person, to discover your chief weakness and attack it so soon. First tame the horse, and then the master. It will be amusing to watch the game, only I shall be under the painful necessity of checkmating you both, if it gets serious."

"You needn't exert yourself, old fellow, on my account. If I was not above thinking ill of an inoffensive girl, I should say you were the prize best worth winning, and advise you to take care of your own heart, if you've got one, which I rather doubt."

"I often doubt it, myself; but I fancy the little Scotchwoman will not be able to satisfy either of us upon that point. How does your highness like her?" asked Coventry of his cousin, who sat near him.

"Better than I thought I should. She is well-bred, unassuming, and very entertaining when she likes. She has told us some of the wittiest stories I've heard for a long time. Didn't our laughter wake you?" replied Lucia.

"Yes. Now atone for it by amusing me with a repetition of these witty tales."

"That is impossible; her accent and manner are half the charm," said Ned. "I wish you had kept away ten minutes longer, for your appearance spoilt the best story of all."

"Why didn't she go on?" asked Coventry, with a ray of curiosity.

"You forget that she overheard us last night, and must feel that you consider her a bore. She has pride, and no woman forgets speeches like those you made," answered Lucia.

"Or forgives them, either, I believe. Well, I must be resigned to languish under her displeasure then. On Sydney's account I take a slight interest in her; not that I expect to learn anything from her, for a woman with a mouth like that never confides or confesses anything. But I have a fancy to see what captivated him; for captivated he was, beyond a doubt, and by no lady whom he met in society. Did you ever hear anything of it, Ned?" asked Gerald.

"I'm not fond of scandal or gossip, and never listen to either." With which remark Edward left the room.

Lucia was called out by the housekeeper a moment after, and Coventry left to the society most wearisome to him, namely his own. As he entered, he had caught a part of the story which Miss Muir had been telling, and it had excited his curiosity so much that he found himself wondering what the end could be and wishing that he might hear it.

What the deuce did she run away for, when I came in? he thought. If she *is* amusing, she must make herself useful; for it's intensely dull, I own, here, in spite of Lucia. Hey, what's that?

It was a rich, sweet voice, singing a brilliant Italian air, and singing it with an expression that made the music doubly delicious. Stepping out of the French window, Coventry strolled along the sunny terrace, enjoying the song with the relish of a connoisseur. Others followed, and still he walked and listened, forgetful of weariness or time. As one exquisite air ended, he involuntarily applauded. Miss Muir's face appeared for an instant, then vanished, and no more music followed, though Coventry lingered, hoping to hear the voice again. For music was the one thing of which he never wearied, and neither Lucia nor Bella possessed skill enough to charm him. For an hour he loitered on the terrace or the lawn, basking in the sunshine, too indolent to seek occupation or society. At length Bella came out, hat in hand, and nearly stumbled over her brother, who lay on the grass.

"You lazy man, have you been dawdling here all this time?" she said, looking down at him.

"No, I've been very busy. Come and tell me how you've got on with the little dragon."

"Can't stop. She bade me take a run after my French, so that I might be ready for my drawing, and so I must."

"It's too warm to run. Sit down and amuse your deserted brother, who has had no society but bees and lizards for an hour."

He drew her down as he spoke, and Bella obeyed; for, in spite of his indolence, he was one to whom all submitted without dreaming of refusal.

"What have you been doing? Muddling your poor little brains with all manner of elegant rubbish?"

"No, I've been enjoying myself immensely. Jean is *so* interesting, so kind and clever. She didn't bore me with stupid grammar, but just talked to me in such pretty French that I got on capitally, and like it as I never expected to, after Lucia's dull way of teaching it."

"What did you talk about?"

"Oh, all manner of things. She asked questions, and I answered, and she corrected me."

"Questions about our affairs, I suppose?"

"Not one. She don't care two sous for us or our affairs. I thought she might like to know what sort of people we were, so I told her about Papa's sudden death, Uncle John, and you, and Ned; but in the midst of it she said, in her quiet way, 'You are getting too confidential, my dear. It is not best to talk too freely of one's affairs to strangers. Let us speak of something else.' "

"What were you talking of when she said that, Bell?"

"You."

"Ah, then no wonder she was bored."

"She was tired of my chatter, and didn't hear half I said; for she was busy sketching something for me to copy, and thinking of something more interesting than the Coventrys."

"How do you know?"

"By the expression of her face. Did you like her music, Gerald?"

"Yes. Was she angry when I clapped?"

"She looked surprised, then rather proud, and shut the piano at once, though I begged her to go on. Isn't Jean a pretty name?"

"Not bad; but why don't you call her Miss Muir?"

"She begged me not. She hates it, and loves to be called Jean, alone. I've imagined such a nice little romance about her, and someday I shall tell her, for I'm sure she has had a love trouble."

"Don't get such nonsense into your head, but follow Miss Muir's well-bred example and don't be curious about other people's affairs. Ask her to sing tonight; it amuses me."

"She won't come down, I think. We've planned to read and work in my boudoir, which is to be our study now. Mamma will stay in her room, so you and Lucia can have the drawing room all to yourselves."

"Thank you. What will Ned do?"

"He will amuse Mamma, he says. Dear old Ned! I wish you'd stir about and get him his commission. He is so impatient to be doing something and yet so proud he won't ask again, after you have neglected it so many times and refused Uncle's help."

"I'll attend to it very soon; don't worry me, child. He will do very well for a time, quietly here with us."

"You always say that, yet you know he chafes and is unhappy at being dependent on you. Mamma and I don't mind; but he is a man, and it frets him. He said he'd take matters into his own hands soon, and then you may be sorry you were so slow in helping him."

"Miss Muir is looking out of the window. You'd better go and take your run, else she will scold."

"Not she. I'm not a bit afraid of her, she's so gentle and sweet. I'm fond of her already. You'll get as brown as Ned, lying here in the sun. By the way, Miss Muir agrees with me in thinking him handsomer than you."

"I admire her taste and quite agree with her."

"She said he was manly, and that was more attractive than beauty in a man. She does express things so nicely. Now I'm off." And away danced Bella, humming the burden of Miss Muir's sweetest song.

" 'Energy is more attractive than beauty in a man.' She is right, but how the deuce *can* a man be energetic, with nothing to expend his energies upon?" mused Coventry, with his hat over his eyes.

A few moments later, the sweep of a dress caught his ear. Without stirring, a sidelong glance showed him Miss Muir coming across the terrace, as if to join Bella. Two stone steps led down to the lawn. He lay near them, and Miss Muir did not see him till close upon him. She started and slipped on the last step, recovered herself, and glided on, with a glance of unmistakable contempt as she passed the recumbent figure of the apparent sleeper. Several things in Bella's report had nettled him, but this look made him angry, though he would not own it, even to himself.

"Gerald, come here, quick!" presently called Bella, from the rustic seat where she stood beside her governess, who sat with her hand over her face as if in pain.

Gathering himself up, Coventry slowly obeyed, but involuntarily quickened his pace as he heard Miss Muir say, "Don't call him; *he* can do nothing"; for the emphasis on the word "he" was very significant.

"What is it, Bella?" he asked, looking rather wider awake than usual.

"You startled Miss Muir and made her turn her ankle. Now help her to the house, for she is in great pain; and don't lie there anymore to frighten people like a snake in the grass," said his sister petulantly.

"I beg your pardon. Will you allow me?" And Coventry offered his arm.

Miss Muir looked up with the expression which annoyed him and answered coldly, "Thank you, Miss Bella will do as well."

"Permit me to doubt that." And with a gesture too decided to be resisted, Coventry drew her arm through his and led her into the house. She submitted quietly, said the pain would soon be over, and when settled on the couch in Bella's room dismissed him with the briefest thanks. Considering the unwonted exertion he had made, he thought she might have been a little more grateful, and went away to Lucia, who always brightened when he came.

No more was seen of Miss Muir till teatime; for now, while the family were in retirement, they dined early and saw no company. The governess had excused herself at dinner, but came down in the evening a little paler than usual and with a slight limp in her gait. Sir John was there, talking with his nephew, and they merely acknowledged her presence by the sort of bow which gentlemen bestow on governesses. As she slowly made her way to her place behind the urn, Coventry said to his brother, "Take her a footstool, and ask her how she is, Ned." Then, as if necessary to account for his politeness to his uncle, he explained how he was the cause of the accident.

"Yes, yes. I understand. Rather a nice little person, I fancy. Not exactly a beauty, but accomplished and well-bred, which is better for one of her class."

"Some tea, Sir John?" said a soft voice at his elbow, and there was Miss Muir, offering cups to the gentlemen.

"Thank you, thank you," said Sir John, sincerely hoping she had overheard him.

As Coventry took his, he said graciously, "You are very forgiving, Miss Muir, to wait upon me, after I have caused you so much pain."

"It is my duty, sir" was her reply, in a tone which plainly said, "but not my pleasure." And she returned to her place, to smile, and chat, and be charming, with Bella and her brother.

Lucia, hovering near her uncle and Gerald, kept them to herself, but was disturbed to find that their eyes often wandered to the cheerful group about the table, and that their attention seemed distracted by the frequent bursts of laughter and fragments of animated conversation which reached them. In the midst of an account of a tragic affair which she endeavored to make as interesting and pathetic as possible, Sir John burst into a hearty laugh, which betrayed that he had been listening to a livelier story than her own. Much annoyed, she said hastily, "I knew it would be so! Bella has no idea of the proper manner in which to treat a governess. She and Ned will forget the difference of rank and spoil that person for her work. She is inclined to be presumptuous already, and if my aunt won't trouble herself to give Miss Muir a hint in time, I shall."

"Wait till she has finished that story, I beg of you," said Coventry, for Sir John was already off.

"If you find that nonsense so entertaining, why don't you follow Uncle's example? I don't need you."

"Thank you. I will." And Lucia was deserted.

But Miss Muir had ended and, beckoning to Bella, left the room, as if quite unconscious of the honor conferred upon her or the dullness she left behind her. Ned went up to his mother, Gerald returned to make his peace with Lucia, and, bidding them good-night, Sir John turned homeward. Strolling along the terrace, he came to the lighted window of Bella's study, and wishing to say a word to her, he half pushed aside the curtain and looked in. A pleasant little scene. Bella working busily, and near her in a low chair, with the light falling on her fair hair and delicate profile, sat Miss Muir, reading aloud. "Novels!" thought Sir John, and smiled at them for a pair of romantic girls. But pausing to listen a moment before he spoke, he found it was no novel, but history, read with a fluency which made every fact interesting, every sketch of character memorable, by the dramatic effect given to it. Sir John was fond of history, and failing eyesight often curtailed his favorite amusement. He had tried readers, but none suited him, and he had given up the plan. Now as he listened, he thought how pleasantly the smoothly flowing voice would wile away his evenings, and he envied Bella her new acquisition.

A bell rang, and Bella sprang up, saying, "Wait for me a minute. I must run to Mamma, and then we will go on with this charming prince."

Away she went, and Sir John was about to retire as quietly as he came, when Miss Muir's peculiar behavior arrested him for an instant. Dropping the book, she threw her arms across the table, laid her head down upon them, and broke into a passion of tears, like one who could bear restraint no longer. Shocked and amazed, Sir John stole away; but all that night the kindhearted gentleman puzzled his brains with conjectures about his niece's interesting young governess, quite unconscious that she intended he should do so.

CHAPTER III. PASSION AND PIQUE

FOR SEVERAL WEEKS the most monotonous tranquillity seemed to reign at Coventry House, and yet, unseen, unsuspected, a storm was gathering. The arrival of Miss Muir seemed to produce a change in everyone, though no one could have explained how or why. Nothing could be more unobtrusive and retiring than her manners. She was devoted to Bella, who soon adored her, and was only happy when in her society. She ministered in many ways to Mrs. Coventry's comfort, and that lady declared there never was such a nurse. She amused, interested and won Edward with her wit and womanly sympathy. She made Lucia respect and envy her for her accomplishments, and piqued indolent Gerald by her persistent avoidance of him, while Sir John was charmed with her respectful deference and the graceful little attentions she paid him in a frank and artless way, very winning to the lonely old man. The very servants liked her; and instead of being, what most governesses are, a forlorn creature hovering between superiors and inferiors, Jean Muir was the life of the house, and the friend of all but two.

Lucia disliked her, and Coventry distrusted her; neither could exactly say why, and neither owned the feeling, even to themselves. Both watched her covertly yet found no shortcoming anywhere. Meek, modest, faithful, and invariably sweet-tempered—they could complain of nothing and wondered at their own doubts, though they could not banish them.

It soon came to pass that the family was divided, or rather that two members were left very much to themselves. Pleading timidity, Jean Muir kept much in Bella's study and soon made it such a pleasant little nook that Ned and his mother, and often Sir John, came in to enjoy the music, reading, or cheerful chat which made the evenings so gay. Lucia at first was only too glad to have her cousin to herself, and he too lazy to care what went on about him. But presently he wearied of her society, for she was not a brilliant girl, and possessed few of those winning arts which charm a man and steal into his heart. Rumors of the merrymakings that went on reached him and made him curious to share them; echoes of fine music went sounding through the house, as he lounged about the empty drawing room; and peals of laughter reached him while listening to Lucia's grave discourse.

She soon discovered that her society had lost its charm, and the more eagerly she tried to please him, the more signally she failed. Before long Coventry fell into a habit of strolling out upon the terrace of an evening, and amusing himself by passing and repassing the window of Bella's room, catching glimpses of what was going on and reporting the result of his observations to Lucia, who was too proud to ask admission to the happy circle or to seem to desire it.

"I shall go to London tomorrow, Lucia," Gerald said one evening, as he came back from what he called "a survey," looking very much annoyed.

"To London?" exclaimed his cousin, surprised.

"Yes, I must bestir myself and get Ned his commission, or it will be all over with him."

"How do you mean?"

"He is falling in love as fast as it is possible for a boy to do it. That girl has bewitched him, and he will make a fool of himself very soon, unless I put a stop to it."

"I was afraid she would attempt a flirtation. These persons always do, they are such a mischief-making race."

"Ah, but there you are wrong, as far as little Muir is concerned. She does not flirt, and Ned has too much sense and spirit to be caught by a silly coquette. She treats him like an elder sister, and mingles the most attractive friendliness with a quiet dignity that captivates the boy. I've been watching them, and there he is, devouring her with his eyes, while she reads a fascinating novel in the most fascinating style. Bella and Mamma are absorbed in the tale, and see nothing; but Ned makes himself the hero, Miss Muir the heroine, and lives the love scene with all the ardor of a man whose heart has just waked up. Poor lad! Poor lad!"

Lucia looked at her cousin, amazed by the energy with which he spoke, the anxiety in his usually listless face. The change became him, for it showed what he might be, making one regret still more what he was. Before she could speak, he was gone again, to return presently, laughing, yet looking a little angry.

"What now?" she asked.

" 'Listeners never hear any good of themselves' is the truest of proverbs. I stopped a moment to look at Ned, and heard the following flattering remarks. Mamma is gone, and Ned was asking little Muir to sing that delicious barcarole she gave us the other evening.

" 'Not now, not here,' she said.

" 'Why not? You sang it in the drawing room readily enough,' said Ned, imploringly.

" 'That is a very different thing,' and she looked at him with a little shake of the head, for he was folding his hands and doing the passionate pathetic.

" 'Come and sing it there then,' said innocent Bella. 'Gerald likes your voice so much, and complains that you will never sing to him.'

" 'He never asks me,' said Muir, with an odd smile.

" 'He is too lazy, but he wants to hear you.'

" 'When he asks me, I will sing—if I feel like it.' And she shrugged her shoulders with a provoking gesture of indifference.

" 'But it amuses him, and he gets so bored down here,' began stupid little Bella. 'Don't be shy or proud, Jean, but come and entertain the poor old fellow.'

" 'No, thank you. I engaged to teach Miss Coventry, not to amuse Mr. Coventry' was all the answer she got.

" 'You amuse Ned, why not Gerald? Are you afraid of him?' asked Bella.

"Miss Muir laughed, such a scornful laugh, and said, in that peculiar tone of hers, 'I cannot fancy anyone being *afraid* of your elder brother.'

" 'I am, very often, and so would you be, if you ever saw him angry.' And Bella looked as if I'd beaten her.

" 'Does he ever wake up enough to be angry?' asked that girl, with an air of surprise. Here Ned broke into a fit of laughter, and they are at it now, I fancy, by the sound."

"Their foolish gossip is not worth getting excited about, but I certainly would send Ned away. It's no use trying to get rid of 'that girl,' as you say, for my aunt is as deluded about her as Ned and Bella, and she really does get the child along splendidly. Dispatch Ned, and then she can do no harm," said Lucia, watching Coventry's altered face as he stood in the moonlight, just outside the window where she sat.

"Have you no fears for me?" he asked smiling, as if ashamed of his momentary petulance.

"No, have you for yourself?" And a shade of anxiety passed over her face.

"I defy the Scotch witch to enchant me, except with her music," he added, moving down the terrace again, for Jean was singing like a nightingale.

As the song ended, he put aside the curtain, and said, abruptly, "Has anyone any commands for London? I am going there tomorrow."

"A pleasant trip to you," said Ned carelessly, though usually his brother's movements interested him extremely.

"I want quantities of things, but I must ask Mamma first." And Bella began to make a list.

"May I trouble you with a letter, Mr. Coventry?"

Jean Muir turned around on the music stool and looked at him with the cold keen glance which always puzzled him.

He bowed, saying, as if to them all, "I shall be off by the early train, so you must give me your orders tonight."

"Then come away, Ned, and leave Jean to write her letter."

And Bella took her reluctant brother from the room.

"I will give you the letter in the morning," said Miss Muir, with a curious quiver in her voice, and the look of one who forcibly suppressed some strong emotion.

"As you please." And Coventry went back to Lucia, wondering who Miss Muir was going to write to. He said nothing to his brother of the purpose which took him to town, lest a word should produce the catastrophe which he hoped to prevent; and Ned, who now lived in a sort of dream, seemed to forget Gerald's existence altogether.

With unwonted energy Coventry was astir at seven next morning. Lucia gave him his breakfast, and as he left the room to order the carriage, Miss Muir came gliding downstairs, very pale and heavy-eyed (with a sleepless, tearful night, he thought) and, putting a delicate little letter into his hand, said hurriedly, "Please leave this at Lady Sydney's, and if you see her, say 'I have remembered.' "

Her peculiar manner and peculiar message struck him. His eye involuntarily glanced at the address of the letter and read young Sydney's name. Then, conscious of his mistake, he thrust it into his pocket with a hasty "Good morning," and left Miss Muir standing with one hand pressed on her heart, the other half extended as if to recall the letter.

All the way to London, Coventry found it impossible to forget the almost tragical expression of the girl's face, and it haunted him through the bustle of two busy days. Ned's affair was put in the way of being speedily accomplished, Bella's commissions were executed, his mother's pet delicacies provided for her, and a gift for Lucia, whom the family had given him for his future mate, as he was too lazy to choose for himself.

Jean Muir's letter he had not delivered, for Lady Sydney was in the country and her townhouse closed. Curious to see how she would receive his tidings, he went quietly in on his arrival at home. Everyone had dispersed to dress for dinner except Miss Muir, who was in the garden, the servant said.

"Very well, I have a message for her"; and, turning, the "young master," as they called him, went to seek her. In a remote corner he saw her sitting alone, buried in thought. As his step roused her, a look of surprise, followed by one of satisfaction, passed over her face, and, rising, she beckoned to him with an almost eager gesture. Much amazed, he went to her and offered the letter, saying kindly, "I regret that I could not deliver it. Lady Sydney is in the country, and I did not like to post it without your leave. Did I do right?"

"Quite right, thank you very much—it is better so." And with an air of relief, she tore the letter to atoms, and scattered them to the wind.

More amazed than ever, the young man was about to leave her when she said, with a mixture of entreaty and command, "Please stay a moment. I want to speak to you."

He paused, eyeing her with visible surprise, for a sudden color dyed her cheeks, and her lips trembled. Only for a moment, then she was quite self-possessed again. Motioning him to the seat she had left, she remained standing while she said, in a low, rapid tone full of pain and of decision:

"Mr. Coventry, as the head of the house I want to speak to you, rather than to your mother, of a most unhappy affair which has occurred during your absence. My month of probation ends today; your mother wishes me to remain; I, too, wish it sincerely, for I am happy here, but I ought not. Read this, and you will see why."

She put a hastily written note into his hand and watched him intently while he read it. She saw him flush with anger, bite his lips, and knit his brows, then assume his haughtiest look, as he lifted his eyes and said in his most sarcastic tone, "Very well for a beginning. The boy has eloquence. Pity that it should be wasted. May I ask if you have replied to this rhapsody?"

"I have."

"And what follows? He begs you 'to fly with him, to share his fortunes, and be the good angel of his life.' Of course you consent?"

There was no answer, for, standing erect before him, Miss Muir regarded him with an expression of proud patience, like one who expected reproaches, yet was too generous to resent them. Her manner had its effect. Dropping his bitter tone, Coventry asked briefly, "Why do you show me this? What can I do?"

"I show it that you may see how much in earnest 'the boy' is, and how open I desire to be. You can control, advise, and comfort your brother, and help me to see what is my duty."

"You love him?" demanded Coventry bluntly.

"No!" was the quick, decided answer.

"Then why make him love you?"

"I never tried to do it. Your sister will testify that I have endeavored to avoid him as I—" And he finished the sentence with an unconscious tone of pique, "As you have avoided me."

She bowed silently, and he went on:

"I will do you the justice to say that nothing can be more blameless than your conduct toward myself; but why allow Ned to haunt you evening after evening? What could you expect of a romantic boy who had nothing to do but lose his heart to the first attractive woman he met?"

A momentary glisten shone in Jean Muir's steel-blue eyes as the last words left the young man's lips; but it was gone instantly, and her voice was full of reproach, as she said, steadily, impulsively, "If the 'romantic boy' had been allowed to lead the life of a man, as he longed to do, he would have had no time to lose his heart to the first sorrowful girl whom he pitied. Mr. Coventry, the fault is yours. Do not blame your brother, but generously own your mistake and retrieve it in the speediest, kindest manner."

For an instant Gerald sat dumb. Never since his father died had anyone reproved him; seldom in his life had he been blamed. It was a new experience, and the very novelty added to the effect. He saw his fault, regretted it, and admired the brave sincerity of the girl in telling him of it. But he did not know how to deal with the case, and was forced to confess not only past negligence but present incapacity. He was as honorable as he was proud, and with an effort he said frankly, "You are right, Miss Muir. I *am* to blame, yet as soon as I saw the danger, I tried to avert it. My visit to town was on Ned's account; he will have his commission very soon, and then he will be sent out of harm's way. Can I do more?"

"No, it is too late to send him away with a free and happy heart. He must bear his pain as he can, and it may help to make a man of him," she said sadly.

"He'll soon forget," began Coventry, who found the thought of gay Ned suffering an uncomfortable one.

"Yes, thank heaven, that is possible, for men."

Miss Muir pressed her hands together, with a dark expression on her half-averted face. Something in her tone, her manner, touched Coventry; he fancied that some old wound bled, some bitter memory awoke at the approach of a new lover. He was young, heart-whole, and romantic, under all his cool nonchalance of manner. This girl, who he fancied loved his friend and who was beloved by his brother, became an object of interest to him. He pitied her, desired to help her, and regretted his past distrust, as a chivalrous man always regrets injustice to a woman. She was happy here, poor, homeless soul, and she should stay. Bella loved her, his mother took comfort in her, and when Ned was gone, no one's peace would be endangered by her winning ways, her rich accomplishments. These thoughts swept through his mind during a brief pause, and when he spoke, it was to say gently:

"Miss Muir, I thank you for the frankness which must have been painful to you, and I will do my best to be worthy of the confidence which you repose in me. You were both discreet and kind to speak only to me. This thing would have troubled my mother extremely, and have done no good. I shall see Ned, and try and repair my long neglect as promptly as possible. I know you will help me, and in return let me beg of you to remain, for he will soon be gone."

She looked at him with eyes full of tears, and there was no coolness in the voice that answered softly, "You are too kind, but I had better go; it is not wise to stay."

"Why not?"

She colored beautifully, hesitated, then spoke out in the clear, steady voice which was her greatest charm, "If I had known there were sons in this family, I never should have come. Lady Sydney spoke only of your sister, and when I found two gentlemen, I was troubled, because—I am so unfortunate—or rather, people are so kind as to like me more than I deserve. I thought I could stay a month, at least, as your brother spoke of going away, and you were already affianced, but—"

"I am not affianced."

Why he said that, Coventry could not tell, but the words passed his lips hastily and could not be recalled. Jean Muir took the announcement oddly enough. She shrugged her shoulders with an air of extreme annoyance, and said almost rudely, "Then you should be; you will be soon. But that is nothing to me. Miss Beaufort wishes me gone, and I am too proud to remain and become the cause of disunion in a happy family. No, I will go, and go at once."

She turned away impetuously, but Edward's arm detained her, and Edward's voice demanded, tenderly, "Where will you go, my Jean?"

The tender touch and name seemed to rob her of her courage and calmness, for, leaning on her lover, she hid her face and sobbed audibly.

"Now don't make a scene, for heaven's sake," began Coventry impatiently, as his brother eyed him fiercely, divining at once what had passed, for his letter was still in Gerald's hand and Jean's last words had reached her lover's ear.

"Who gave you the right to read that, and to interfere in my affairs?" demanded Edward hotly.

"Miss Muir" was the reply, as Coventry threw away the paper.

"And you add to the insult by ordering her out of the house," cried Ned with increasing wrath.

"On the contrary, I beg her to remain."

"The deuce you do! And why?"

"Because she is useful and happy here, and I am unwilling that your folly should rob her of a home which she likes."

"You are very thoughtful and devoted all at once, but I beg you will not trouble yourself. Jean's happiness and home will be my care now."

"My dear boy, do be reasonable. The thing is impossible. Miss Muir sees it herself; she came to tell me, to ask how best to arrange matters without troubling my mother. I've been to town to attend to your affairs, and you may be off now very soon."

"I have no desire to go. Last month it was the wish of my heart. Now I'll accept nothing from you." And Edward turned moodily away from his brother.

"What folly! Ned, you *must* leave home. It is all arranged and cannot be given up now. A change is what you need, and it will make a man of you. We shall miss you, of course, but you will be where you'll see something of life, and that is better for you than getting into mischief here."

"Are you going away, Jean?" asked Edward, ignoring his brother entirely and bending over the girl, who still hid her face and wept. She did not speak, and Gerald answered for her.

"No, why should she if you are gone?"

"Do you mean to stay?" asked the lover eagerly of Jean.

"I wish to remain, but——" She paused and looked up. Her eyes went from one face to the other, and she added, decidedly, "Yes, I must go, it is not wise to stay even when you are gone."

Neither of the young men could have explained why that hurried glance affected them as it did, but each felt conscious of a willful desire to oppose the other. Edward suddenly felt that his brother loved Miss Muir, and was bent on removing her from his way. Gerald had a vague idea that Miss Muir feared to remain on his account, and he longed to show her that he was quite safe. Each felt angry, and each showed it in a different way, one being violent, the other satirical.

"You are right, Jean, this is not the place for you; and you must let me see you in a safer home before I go," said Ned, significantly.

"It strikes me that this will be a particularly safe home when your dangerous self is removed," began Coventry, with an aggravating smile of calm superiority.

"And *I* think that I leave a more dangerous person than myself behind me, as poor Lucia can testify."

"Be careful what you say, Ned, or I shall be forced to remind you that I am master here. Leave Lucia's name out of this disagreeable affair, if you please."

"You *are* master here, but not of me, or my actions, and you have no right to expect obedience or respect, for you inspire neither. Jean, I asked you to go with me secretly; now I ask you openly to share my fortune. In my brother's presence I ask, and *will* have an answer."

He caught her hand impetuously, with a defiant look at Coventry, who still smiled, as if at boy's play, though his eyes were kindling and his face changing with the still, white wrath which is more terrible than any sudden outburst. Miss Muir looked frightened; she shrank away from her passionate young lover, cast an appealing glance at Gerald, and seemed as if she longed to claim his protection yet dared not.

"Speak!" cried Edward, desperately. "Don't look to him, tell me truly, with your own lips, do you, can you love me, Jean?"

"I have told you once. Why pain me by forcing another hard reply," she said pitifully, still shrinking from his grasp and seeming to appeal to his brother.

"You wrote a few lines, but I'll not be satisfied with that. You shall answer; I've seen love in your eyes, heard it in your voice, and I know it is hidden in your heart. You fear to own it; do not hesitate, no one can part us—speak, Jean, and satisfy me."

Drawing her hand decidedly away, she went a step nearer Coventry, and answered, slowly, distinctly, though her lips trembled, and she evidently dreaded the effect of her words, "I will speak, and speak truly. You have seen love in my face; it is in my heart, and I do not hesitate to own it, cruel as it is to force the truth from me, but this love is not for you. Are you satisfied?"

He looked at her with a despairing glance and stretched his hand toward her beseechingly. She seemed to fear a blow, for suddenly she clung to Gerald with a faint cry. The act, the look of fear, the protecting gesture Coventry involuntarily made were too much for Edward, already excited by conflicting passions. In a paroxysm of blind wrath, he caught up a large pruning knife left there by the gardener, and would have dealt his brother a fatal blow had he not warded it off with his arm. The stroke fell, and another might have followed had not Miss Muir with unexpected courage and strength wrested the knife from Edward and flung it into the little pond near by. Coventry dropped down upon the seat, for the blood poured from a deep wound in his arm, showing by its rapid flow that an artery had been severed. Edward stood aghast, for with the blow his fury passed, leaving him overwhelmed with remorse and shame.

Gerald looked up at him, smiled faintly, and said, with no sign of reproach or anger, "Never mind, Ned. Forgive and forget. Lend me a hand to the house, and don't disturb anyone. It's not much, I dare say." But his lips whitened as he spoke, and his strength failed him. Edward sprang to support him, and Miss Muir, forgetting her terrors, proved herself a girl of uncommon skill and courage.

"Quick! Lay him down. Give me your handkerchief, and bring some water," she said, in a tone of quiet command. Poor Ned obeyed and watched her with breathless suspense while she tied the handkerchief tightly around the arm, thrust the handle of his riding whip underneath, and pressed it firmly above the severed artery to stop the dangerous flow of blood.

"Dr. Scott is with your mother, I think. Go and bring him here" was the next order; and Edward darted away, thankful to do anything to ease the terror which possessed him. He was gone some minutes, and while they waited Coventry watched the girl as she knelt beside him, bathing his face with one hand while with the other she held the bandage firmly in its place. She was pale, but quite steady and self-possessed, and her eyes shone with a strange brilliancy as she looked down at him. Once, meeting his look of grateful wonder, she smiled a reassuring smile that made her lovely, and said, in a soft, sweet tone never used to him before, "Be quiet. There is no danger. I will stay by you till help comes."

Help did come speedily, and the doctor's first words were "Who improvised that tourniquet?"

"She did," murmured Coventry.

"Then you may thank her for saving your life. By Jove! It was capitally done"; and the old doctor looked at the girl with as much admiration as curiosity in his face.

"Never mind that. See to the wound, please, while I run for bandages, and salts, and wine."

Miss Muir was gone as she spoke, so fleetly that it was in vain to call her back or catch her. During her brief absence, the story was told by repentant Ned and the wound examined.

"Fortunately I have my case of instruments with me," said the doctor, spreading on the bench a long array of tiny, glittering implements of torture. "Now, Mr. Ned, come here, and hold the arm in that way, while I tie the artery. Hey! That will never do. Don't tremble so, man, look away and hold it steadily."

"I can't!" And poor Ned turned faint and white, not at the sight but with the bitter thought that he had longed to kill his brother.

"I will hold it," and a slender white hand lifted the bare and bloody arm so firmly, steadily, that Coventry sighed a sigh of relief, and Dr. Scott fell to work with an emphatic nod of approval.

It was soon over, and while Edward ran in to bid the servants beware of alarming their mistress, Dr. Scott put up his instruments and Miss Muir used salts, water, and wine so skillfully that Gerald was able to walk to his room, leaning on the old man, while the girl supported the wounded arm, as no sling could be made on the spot. As he entered the chamber, Coventry turned, put out his left hand, and with much feeling in his fine eyes said simply, "Miss Muir, I thank you."

The color came up beautifully in her pale cheeks as she pressed the hand and without a word vanished from the room. Lucia and the housekeeper came bustling in, and there was no lack of attendance on the invalid. He soon wearied of it, and sent them all away but Ned, who remorsefully haunted the chamber, looking like a comely young Cain and feeling like an outcast.

"Come here, lad, and tell me all about it. I was wrong to be domineering. Forgive me, and believe that I care for your happiness more sincerely than for my own."

These frank and friendly words healed the breach between the two brothers and completely conquered Ned. Gladly did he relate his love passages, for no young lover ever tires of that amusement if he has a sympathizing auditor, and Gerald *was* sympathetic now. For an hour did he lie listening patiently to the history of the growth of his brother's passion. Emotion gave the narrator eloquence, and Jean Muir's character was painted in glowing colors. All her unsuspected kindness to those about her was dwelt upon; all her faithful care, her sisterly interest in Bella, her gentle attentions to their mother, her sweet forbearance with Lucia, who plainly showed her dislike, and most of all, her friendly counsel, sympathy, and regard for Ned himself.

"She would make a man of me. She puts strength and courage into me as no one else can. She is unlike any girl I ever saw; there's no sentimentality about her; she is wise, and kind, and sweet. She says what she means, looks you straight in the eye, and is as true as steel. I've tried her, I know her, and—ah, Gerald, I love her so!"

Here the poor lad leaned his face into his hands and sighed a sigh that made his brother's heart ache.

"Upon my soul, Ned, I feel for you; and if there was no obstacle on her part, I'd do my best for you. She loves Sydney, and so there is nothing for it but to bear your fate like a man."

"Are you sure about Sydney? May it not be some one else?" and Ned eyed his brother with a suspicious look.

Coventry told him all he knew and surmised concerning his friend, not forgetting the letter. Edward mused a moment, then seemed relieved, and said frankly, "I'm glad it's Sydney and not you. I can bear it better."

"Me!" ejaculated Gerald, with a laugh.

"Yes, you; I've been tormented lately with a fear that you cared for her, or rather, she for you."

"You jealous young fool! We never see or speak to one another scarcely, so how could we get up a tender interest?"

"What do you lounge about on that terrace for every evening? And why does she get fluttered when your shadow begins to come and go?" demanded Edward.

"I like the music and don't care for the society of the singer, that's why I walk there. The fluttering is all your imagination; Miss Muir isn't a woman to be fluttered by a man's shadow." And Coventry glanced at his useless arm.

"Thank you for that, and for not saying 'little Muir,' as you generally do. Perhaps it was my imagination. But she never makes fun of you now, and so I fancied she might have lost her heart to the 'young master.' Women often do, you know."

"She used to ridicule me, did she?" asked Coventry, taking no notice of the latter part of his brother's speech, which was quite true nevertheless.

"Not exactly, she was too well-bred for that. But sometimes when Bella and I joked about you, she'd say something so odd or witty that it was irresistible. You're used to being laughed at, so you don't mind, I know, just among ourselves."

"Not I. Laugh away as much as you like," said Gerald. But he did mind, and wanted exceedingly to know what Miss Muir had said, yet was too proud to ask. He turned restlessly and uttered a sigh of pain.

"I'm talking too much; it's bad for you. Dr. Scott said you must be quiet. Now go to sleep, if you can."

Edward left the bedside but not the room, for he would let no one take his place. Coventry tried to sleep, found it impossible, and after a restless hour called his brother back.

"If the bandage was loosened a bit, it would ease my arm and then I could sleep. Can you do it, Ned?"

"I dare not touch it. The doctor gave orders to leave it till he came in the morning, and I shall only do harm if I try."

"But I tell you it's too tight. My arm is swelling and the pain is intense. It can't be right to leave it so. Dr. Scott dressed it in a hurry and did it too tight. Common sense will tell you that," said Coventry impatiently.

"I'll call Mrs. Morris; she will understand what's best to be done." And Edward moved toward the door, looking anxious.

"Not she, she'll only make a stir and torment me with her chatter. I'll bear it as long as I can, and perhaps Dr. Scott will come tonight. He said he would if possible. Go to your dinner, Ned. I can ring for Neal if I need anything. I shall sleep if I'm alone, perhaps."

Edward reluctantly obeyed, and his brother was left to himself. Little rest did he find, however, for the pain of the wounded arm grew unbearable, and, taking a sudden resolution, he rang for his servant.

"Neal, go to Miss Coventry's study, and if Miss Muir is there, ask her to be kind enough to come to me. I'm in great pain, and she understands wounds better than anyone else in the house."

With much surprise in his face, the man departed and a few moments after the door noiselessly opened and Miss Muir came in. It had been a very warm day, and for the first time she had left off her plain black dress. All in white, with no ornament but her fair hair, and a fragrant posy of violets in her belt, she looked a different woman from the meek, nunlike creature one usually saw about the house. Her face was as altered as her dress, for now a soft color glowed in her cheeks, her eyes smiled shyly, and her lips no longer wore the firm look of one who forcibly repressed every emotion. A fresh, gentle, and charming woman she seemed, and Coventry found the dull room suddenly brightened by her presence. Going straight to him, she said simply, and with a happy, helpful look very comforting to see, "I'm glad you sent for me. What can I do for you?"

He told her, and before the complaint was ended, she began loosening the bandages with the decision of one who understood what was to be done and had faith in herself.

"Ah, that's relief, that's comfort!" ejaculated Coventry, as the last tight fold fell away. "Ned was afraid I should bleed to death if he touched me. What will the doctor say to us?"

"I neither know nor care. I shall say to him that he is a bad surgeon to bind it so closely, and not leave orders to have it untied if necessary. Now I shall make it easy and put you to sleep, for that is what you need. Shall I? May I?"

"I wish you would, if you can."

And while she deftly rearranged the bandages, the young man watched her curiously. Presently he asked, "How came you to know so much about these things?"

"In the hospital where I was ill, I saw much that interested me, and when I got better, I used to sing to the patients sometimes."

"Do you mean to sing to me?" he asked, in the submissive tone men unconsciously adopt when ill and in a woman's care.

"If you like it better than reading aloud in a dreamy tone," she answered, as she tied the last knot.

"I do, much better," he said decidedly.

"You are feverish. I shall wet your forehead, and then you will be quite comfortable." She moved about the room in the quiet way which made it a pleasure to watch her, and, having mingled a little cologne with water, bathed his face as unconcernedly as if he had been a child. Her proceedings not only comforted but amused Coventry, who mentally contrasted her with the stout, beer-drinking matron who had ruled over him in his last illness.

"A clever, kindly little woman," he thought, and felt quite at his ease, she was so perfectly easy herself.

"There, now you look more like yourself," she said with an approving nod as she finished, and smoothed the dark locks off his forehead with a cool, soft hand. Then seating herself in a large chair near by, she began to sing, while tidily rolling up the fresh bandages which had been left for the morning. Coventry lay watching her by the dim light that burned in the room, and she sang on as easily as a bird, a dreamy, low-toned lullaby, which soothed the listener like a spell. Presently, looking up to see the effect of her song, she found the young man wide awake, and regarding her with a curious mixture of pleasure, interest, and admiration.

"Shut your eyes, Mr. Coventry," she said, with a reproving shake of the head, and an odd little smile.

He laughed and obeyed, but could not resist an occasional covert glance from under his lashes at the slender white figure in the great velvet chair. She saw him and frowned.

"You are very disobedient; why won't you sleep?"

"I can't, I want to listen. I'm fond of nightingales."

"Then I shall sing no more, but try something that has never failed yet. Give me your hand, please."

Much amazed, he gave it, and, taking it in both her small ones, she sat down behind the curtain and remained as mute and motionless as a statue. Coventry smiled to himself at first, and wondered which would tire first. But soon a subtle warmth seemed to steal from the soft palms that enclosed his own, his heart beat quicker, his breath grew unequal, and a thousand fancies danced through his brain. He sighed, and said dreamily, as he turned his face toward her, "I like this." And in the act of speaking, seemed to sink into a soft cloud which encompassed him about with an atmosphere of perfect repose. More than this he could not remember, for sleep, deep and dreamless, fell upon him, and when he woke, daylight was shining in between the curtains, his hand lay alone on the coverlet, and his fair-haired enchantress was gone.

CHAPTER IV. A DISCOVERY

FOR SEVERAL DAYS Coventry was confined to his room, much against his will, though everyone did their best to lighten his irksome captivity. His mother petted him, Bella sang, Lucia read, Edward was devoted, and all the household, with one exception, were eager to serve the young master. Jean Muir never came near him, and Jean Muir alone seemed to possess the power of amusing him. He soon tired of the others, wanted something new; recalled the piquant character of the girl and took a fancy into his head that she would lighten his ennui. After some hesitation, he carelessly spoke of her to Bella, but nothing came of it, for Bella only said Jean was well, and very busy doing something lovely to surprise Mamma with. Edward complained that he never saw her, and Lucia ignored her existence altogether. The only intelligence the invalid received was from the gossip of two housemaids over their work in the next room. From them he learned that the governess had been "scolded" by Miss Beaufort for going to Mr. Coventry's room; that she had taken it very sweetly and kept herself carefully out of the way of both young gentlemen, though it was plain to see that Mr. Ned was dying for her.

Mr. Gerald amused himself by thinking over this gossip, and quite annoyed his sister by his absence of mind.

"Gerald, do you know Ned's commission has come?"

"Very interesting. Read on, Bella."

"You stupid boy! You don't know a word I say," and she put down the book to repeat her news.

"I'm glad of it; now we must get him off as soon as possible—that is, I suppose he will want to be off as soon as possible." And Coventry woke up from his reverie.

"You needn't check yourself, I know all about it. I think Ned was very foolish, and that Miss Muir has behaved beautifully. It's quite impossible, of course, but I wish it wasn't, I do so like to watch lovers. You and Lucia are so cold you are not a bit interesting."

"You'll do me a favor if you'll stop all that nonsense about Lucia and me. We are not lovers, and never shall be, I fancy. At all events, I'm tired of the thing, and wish you and Mamma would let it drop, for the present at least."

"Oh Gerald, you know Mamma has set her heart upon it, that Papa desired it, and poor Lucia loves you so much. How can you speak of dropping what will make us all so happy?"

"It won't make me happy, and I take the liberty of thinking that this is of some importance. I'm not bound in any way, and don't intend to be till I am ready. Now we'll talk about Ned."

Much grieved and surprised, Bella obeyed, and devoted herself to Edward, who very wisely submitted to his fate and prepared to leave home for some months. For a week the house was in a state of excitement about his departure, and everyone but Jean was busied for him. She was scarcely seen; every morning she gave Bella her lessons, every afternoon drove out with Mrs. Coventry, and nearly every evening went up to the Hall to read to Sir John, who found his wish granted without exactly knowing how it had been done.

The day Edward left, he came down from bidding his mother good-bye, looking very pale, for he had lingered in his sister's little room with Miss Muir as long as he dared.

"Good-bye, dear. Be kind to Jean," he whispered as he kissed his sister.

"I will, I will," returned Bella, with tearful eyes.

"Take care of Mamma, and remember Lucia," he said again, as he touched his cousin's beautiful cheek.

"Fear nothing. I will keep them apart," she whispered back, and Coventry heard it.

Edward offered his hand to his brother, saying, significantly, as he looked him in the eye, "I trust you, Gerald."

"You may, Ned."

Then he went, and Coventry tired himself with wondering what Lucia meant. A few days later he understood.

Now Ned is gone, little Muir will appear, I fancy, he said to himself; but "little Muir" did not appear, and seemed to shun him more carefully than she had done her lover. If he went to the drawing room in the evening hoping for music, Lucia alone was there. If he tapped at Bella's door, there was always a pause before she opened it, and no sign of Jean appeared though her voice had been audible when he knocked. If he went to the library, a hasty rustle and the sound of flying feet betrayed that the room was deserted at his approach. In the garden Miss Muir never failed to avoid him, and if by chance they met in hall or breakfast room, she passed him with downcast eyes and the briefest, coldest greeting. All this annoyed him intensely, and the more she eluded him, the more he desired to see her—from a spirit of opposition, he said, nothing more. It fretted and yet it entertained him, and he found a lazy sort of pleasure in thwarting the girl's little maneuvers. His patience gave out at last, and he resolved to know what was the meaning of this peculiar conduct. Having locked and taken away the key of one door in the library, he waited till Miss Muir went in to get a book for his uncle. He had heard her speak to Bella of it, knew that she believed him with his mother, and smiled to himself as he stole after her. She was standing in a chair, reaching up, and he had time to see a slender waist, a pretty foot, before he spoke.

"Can I help you, Miss Muir?"

She started, dropped several books, and turned scarlet, as she said hurriedly, "Thank you, no; I can get the steps."

"My long arm will be less trouble. I've got but one, and that is tired of being idle, so it is very much at your service. What will you have?"

"I—I—you startled me so I've forgotten." And Jean laughed, nervously, as she looked about her as if planning to escape.

"I beg your pardon, wait till you remember, and let me thank you for the enchanted sleep you gave me ten days ago. I've had no chance yet, you've shunned me so pertinaciously."

"Indeed I try not to be rude, but—" She checked herself, and turned her face away, adding, with an accent of pain in her voice, "It is not my fault, Mr. Coventry. I only obey orders."

"Whose orders?" he demanded, still standing so that she could not escape.

"Don't ask; it is one who has a right to command where you are concerned. Be sure that it is kindly meant, though it may seem folly to us. Nay, don't be angry, laugh at it, as I do, and let me run away, please."

She turned, and looked down at him with tears in her eyes, a smile on her lips, and an expression half sad, half arch, which was altogether charming. The frown passed from his face, but he still looked grave and said decidedly, "No one has a right to command in this house but my mother or myself. Was it she who bade you avoid me as if I was a madman or a pest?"

"Ah, don't ask. I promised not to tell, and you would not have me break my word, I know." And still smiling, she regarded him with a look of merry malice which made any other reply unnecessary. It was Lucia, he thought, and disliked his cousin intensely just then. Miss Muir moved as if to step down; he detained her, saying earnestly, yet with a smile, "Do you consider me the master here?"

"Yes," and to the word she gave a sweet, submissive intonation which made it expressive of the respect, regard, and confidence which men find pleasantest when women feel and show it. Unconsciously his face softened, and he looked up at her with a different glance from any he had ever given her before.

"Well, then, will you consent to obey me if I am not tyrannical or unreasonable in my demands?"

"I'll try."

"Good! Now frankly, I want to say that all this sort of thing is very disagreeable to me. It annoys me to be a restraint upon anyone's liberty or comfort, and I beg you will go and come as freely as you like, and not mind Lucia's absurdities. She means well, but hasn't a particle of penetration or tact. Will you promise this?"

"No."

"Why not?"

"It is better as it is, perhaps."

"But you called it folly just now."

"Yes, it seems so, and yet—" She paused, looking both confused and distressed.

Coventry lost patience, and said hastily, "You women are such enigmas I never expect to understand you! Well, I've done my best to make you comfortable, but if you prefer to lead this sort of life, I beg you will do so."

"I *don't* prefer it; it is hateful to me. I like to be myself, to have my liberty, and the confidence of those about me. But I cannot think it kind to disturb the peace of anyone, and so I try to obey. I've promised Bella to remain, but I will go rather than have another scene with Miss Beaufort or with you."

Miss Muir had burst out impetuously, and stood there with a sudden fire in her eyes, sudden warmth and spirit in her face and voice that amazed Coventry. She was angry, hurt, and haughty, and the change only made her more attractive, for not a trace of her former meek self remained. Coventry was electrified, and still more surprised when she added, imperiously, with a gesture as if to put him aside, "Hand me that book and move away. I wish to go."

He obeyed, even offered his hand, but she refused it, stepped lightly down, and went to the door. There she turned, and with the same indignant voice, the same kindling eyes and glowing cheeks, she said rapidly, "I know I have no right to speak in this way. I restrain myself as long as I can, but when I can bear no more, my true self breaks loose, and I defy everything. I am tired of being a cold, calm machine; it is impossible with an ardent nature like mine, and I shall try no longer. I cannot help it if people love me. I don't want their love. I only ask to be left in peace, and why I am tormented so I cannot see. I've neither beauty, money, nor rank, yet every foolish boy mistakes my frank interest for something warmer, and makes me miserable. It is my misfortune. Think of me what you will, but beware of me in time, for against my will I may do you harm."

Almost fiercely she had spoken, and with a warning gesture she hurried from the room, leaving the young man feeling as if a sudden thunder-gust had swept through the house. For several minutes he sat in the chair she left, thinking deeply. Suddenly he rose, went to his sister, and said, in his usual tone of indolent good nature, "Bella, didn't I hear Ned ask you to be kind to Miss Muir?"

"Yes, and I try to be, but she is so odd lately."

"Odd! How do you mean?"

"Why, she is either as calm and cold as a statue, or restless and queer; she cries at night, I know, and sighs sadly when she thinks I don't hear. Something is the matter."

"She frets for Ned perhaps," began Coventry.

"Oh dear, no; it's a great relief to her that he is gone. I'm afraid that she likes someone very much, and someone don't like her. Can it be Mr. Sydney?"

"She called him a 'titled fool' once, but perhaps that didn't mean anything. Did you ever ask her about him?" said Coventry, feeling rather ashamed of his curiosity, yet unable to resist the temptation of questioning unsuspecting Bella.

"Yes, but she only looked at me in her tragical way, and said, so pitifully, 'My little friend, I hope you will never have to pass through the scenes I've passed through, but keep your peace unbroken all your life.' After that I dared say no more. I'm very fond of her, I want to make her happy, but I don't know how. Can you propose anything?"

"I was going to propose that you make her come among us more, now Ned is gone. It must be dull for her, moping about alone. I'm sure it is for me. She is an entertaining little person, and I enjoy her music very much. It's good for Mamma to have gay evenings; so you bestir yourself, and see what you can do for the general good of the family."

"That's all very charming, and I've proposed it more than once, but Lucia spoils all my plans. She is afraid you'll follow Ned's example, and that is so silly."

"Lucia is a—no, I won't say fool, because she has sense enough when she chooses; but I wish you'd just settle things with Mamma, and then Lucia can do nothing but submit," said Gerald angrily.

"I'll try, but she goes up to read to Uncle, you know, and since he has had the gout, she stays later, so I see little of her in the evening. There she goes now. I think she will captivate the old one as well as the young one, she is so devoted."

Coventry looked after her slender black figure, just vanishing through the great gate, and an uncomfortable fancy took possession of him, born of Bella's careless words. He sauntered away, and after eluding his cousin, who seemed looking for him, he turned toward the Hall, saying to himself, I will see what is going on up here. Such things have happened. Uncle is the simplest soul alive, and if the girl is ambitious, she can do what she will with him.

Here a servant came running after him and gave him a letter, which he thrust into his pocket without examining it. When he reached the Hall, he went quietly to his uncle's study. The door was ajar, and looking in, he saw a scene of tranquil comfort, very pleasant to watch. Sir John leaned in his easy chair with one foot on a cushion. He was dressed with his usual care and, in spite of the gout, looked like a handsome, well-preserved old gentleman. He was smiling as he listened, and his eyes rested complacently on Jean Muir, who sat near him reading in her musical voice, while the sunshine glittered on her hair and the soft rose of her cheek. She read well, yet Coventry thought her heart was not in her task, for once when she paused, while Sir John spoke, her eyes had an absent expression, and she leaned her head upon her hand, with an air of patient weariness.

Poor girl! I did her great injustice; she has no thought of captivating the old man, but amuses him from simple kindness. She is tired. I'll put an end to her task; and Coventry entered without knocking.

Sir John received him with an air of polite resignation, Miss Muir with a perfectly expressionless face.

"Mother's love, and how are you today, sir?"

"Comfortable, but dull, so I want you to bring the girls over this evening, to amuse the old gentleman. Mrs. King has got out the antique costumes and trumpery, as I promised Bella she should have them, and tonight we are to have a merrymaking, as we used to do when Ned was here."

"Very well, sir, I'll bring them. We've all been out of sorts since the lad left, and a little jollity will do us good. Are you going back, Miss Muir?" asked Coventry.

"No, I shall keep her to give me my tea and get things ready. Don't read anymore, my dear, but go and amuse yourself with the pictures, or whatever you like," said Sir John; and like a dutiful daughter she obeyed, as if glad to get away.

"That's a very charming girl, Gerald," began Sir John as she left the room. "I'm much interested in her, both on her own account and on her mother's."

"Her mother's! What do you know of her mother?" asked Coventry, much surprised.

"Her mother was Lady Grace Howard, who ran away with a poor Scotch minister twenty years ago. The family cast her off, and she lived and died so obscurely that very little is known of her except that she left an orphan girl at some small French pension. This is the girl, and a fine girl, too. I'm surprised that you did not know this."

"So am I, but it is like her not to tell. She is a strange, proud creature. Lady Howard's daughter! Upon my word, that is a discovery," and Coventry felt his interest in his sister's governess much increased by this fact; for, like all wellborn Englishmen, he valued rank and gentle blood even more than he cared to own.

"She has had a hard life of it, this poor little girl, but she has a brave spirit, and will make her way anywhere," said Sir John admiringly.

"Did Ned know this?" asked Gerald suddenly.

"No, she only told me yesterday. I was looking in the *Peerage* and chanced to speak of the Howards. She forgot herself and called Lady Grace her mother. Then I got the whole story, for the lonely little thing was glad to make a confidant of someone."

"That accounts for her rejection of Sydney and Ned: she knows she is their equal and will not snatch at the rank which is hers by right. No, she's not mercenary or ambitious."

"What do you say?" asked Sir John, for Coventry had spoken more to himself than to his uncle.

"I wonder if Lady Sydney was aware of this?" was all Gerald's answer.

"No, Jean said she did not wish to be pitied, and so told nothing to the mother. I think the son knew, but that was a delicate point, and I asked no questions."

"I shall write to him as soon as I discover his address. We have been so intimate I can venture to make a few inquiries about Miss Muir, and prove the truth of her story."

"Do you mean to say that you doubt it?" demanded Sir John angrily.

"I beg your pardon, Uncle, but I must confess I have an instinctive distrust of that young person. It is unjust, I dare say, yet I cannot banish it."

"Don't annoy me by expressing it, if you please. I have some penetration and experience, and I respect and pity Miss Muir heartily. This dislike of yours may be the cause of her late melancholy, hey, Gerald?" And Sir John looked suspiciously at his nephew.

Anxious to avert the rising storm, Coventry said hastily as he turned away, "I've neither time nor inclination to discuss the matter now, sir, but will be careful not to offend again. I'll take your message to Bella, so good-bye for an hour, Uncle."

And Coventry went his way through the park, thinking within himself, The dear old gentleman is getting fascinated, like poor Ned. How the deuce does the girl do it? Lady Howard's daughter, yet never told us; I don't understand that.

CHAPTER V. HOW THE GIRL DID IT

AT HOME he found a party of young friends, who hailed with delight the prospect of a revel at the Hall. An hour later, the blithe company trooped into the great saloon, where preparations had already been made for a dramatic evening.

Good Sir John was in his element, for he was never so happy as when his house was full of young people. Several persons were chosen, and in a few moments the curtains were withdrawn from the first of these impromptu tableaux. A swarthy, darkly bearded man lay asleep on a tiger skin, in the shadow of a tent. Oriental arms and drapery surrounded him; an antique silver lamp burned dimly on a table where fruit lay heaped in costly dishes, and wine shone redly in half-emptied goblets. Bending over the sleeper was a woman robed with barbaric splendor. One hand turned back the embroidered sleeve from the arm which held a scimitar; one slender foot in a scarlet sandal was visible under the white tunic; her purple mantle swept down from snowy shoulders; fillets of gold bound her hair, and jewels shone on neck and arms. She was looking over her shoulder toward the entrance of the tent, with a steady yet stealthy look, so effective that for a moment the spectators held their breath, as if they also heard a passing footstep.

"Who is it?" whispered Lucia, for the face was new to her.

"Jean Muir," answered Coventry, with an absorbed look.

"Impossible! She is small and fair," began Lucia, but a hasty "Hush, let me look!" from her cousin silenced her.

Impossible as it seemed, he was right nevertheless; for Jean Muir it was. She had darkened her skin, painted her eyebrows, disposed some wild black locks over her fair hair, and thrown such an intensity of expression into her eyes that they darkened and dilated till they were as fierce as any southern eyes that ever flashed. Hatred, the deepest and bitterest, was written on her sternly beautiful face, courage glowed in her glance, power spoke in the nervous grip of the slender hand that held the weapon, and the indomitable will of the woman was expressed—even the firm pressure of the little foot half hidden in the tiger skin.

"Oh, isn't she splendid?" cried Bella under her breath.

"She looks as if she'd use her sword well when the time comes," said someone admiringly.

"Good night to Holofernes; his fate is certain," added another.

"He is the image of Sydney, with that beard on."

"Doesn't she look as if she really hated him?"

"Perhaps she does."

Coventry uttered the last exclamation, for the two which preceded it suggested an explanation of the marvelous change in Jean. It was not all art: the intense detestation mingled with a savage joy that the object of her hatred was in her power was too perfect to be feigned; and having the key to a part of her story, Coventry felt as if he caught a glimpse of the truth. It was but a glimpse, however, for the curtain dropped before he had half analyzed the significance of that strange face.

"Horrible! I'm glad it's over," said Lucia coldly.

"Magnificent! Encore! Encore!" cried Gerald enthusiastically.

But the scene was over, and no applause could recall the actress. Two or three graceful or gay pictures followed, but Jean was in none, and each lacked the charm which real talent lends to the simplest part.

"Coventry, you are wanted," called a voice. And to everyone's surprise, Coventry went, though heretofore he had always refused to exert himself when handsome actors were in demand.

"What part am I to spoil?" he asked, as he entered the green room, where several excited young gentlemen were costuming and attitudinizing.

"A fugitive cavalier. Put yourself into this suit, and lose no time asking questions. Miss Muir will tell you what to do. She is in the tableau, so no one will mind you," said the manager pro tem, throwing a rich old suit toward Coventry and resuming the painting of a moustache on his own boyish face.

A gallant cavalier was the result of Gerald's hasty toilet, and when he appeared before the ladies a general glance of admiration was bestowed upon him.

"Come along and be placed; Jean is ready on the stage." And Bella ran before him, exclaiming to her governess, "Here he is, quite splendid. Wasn't he good to do it?"

Miss Muir, in the charmingly prim and puritanical dress of a Roundhead damsel, was arranging some shrubs, but turned suddenly and dropped the green branch she held, as her eye met the glittering figure advancing toward her.

"You!" she said with a troubled look, adding low to Bella, "Why did you ask him? I begged you not."

"He is the only handsome man here, and the best actor if he likes. He won't play usually, so make the most of him." And Bella was off to finish powdering her hair for "The Marriage à la Mode."

"I was sent for and I came. Do you prefer some other person?" asked Coventry, at a loss to understand the half-anxious, half-eager expression of the face under the little cap.

It changed to one of mingled annoyance and resignation as she said, "It is too late. Please kneel here, half behind the shrubs; put down your hat, and—allow me— you are too elegant for a fugitive."

As he knelt before her, she disheveled his hair, pulled his lace collar awry, threw away his gloves and sword, and half untied the cloak that hung about his shoulders.

"That is better; your paleness is excellent—nay, don't spoil it. We are to represent the picture which hangs in the Hall. I need tell you no more. Now, Roundheads, place yourselves, and then ring up the curtain."

With a smile, Coventry obeyed her; for the picture was of two lovers, the young cavalier kneeling, with his arm around the waist of the girl, who tries to hide him with her little mantle, and presses his head to her bosom in an ecstasy of fear, as she glances back at the approaching pursuers. Jean hesitated an instant and shrank a little as his hand touched her; she blushed deeply, and her eyes fell before his. Then, as the bell rang, she threw herself into her part with sudden spirit. One arm half covered him with her cloak, the other pillowed his head on the muslin kerchief folded over her bosom, and she looked backward with such terror in her eyes that more than one chivalrous young spectator longed to hurry to the rescue. It lasted but a moment; yet in that moment Coventry experienced another new sensation. Many women had

smiled on him, but he had remained heart-whole, cool, and careless, quite unconscious of the power which a woman possesses and knows how to use, for the weal or
woe of man. Now, as he knelt there with a soft arm about him, a slender waist yielding
to his touch, and a maiden heart throbbing against his cheek, for the first time in his
life he felt the indescribable spell of womanhood, and looked the ardent lover to
perfection. Just as his face assumed this new and most becoming aspect, the curtain
dropped, and clamorous encores recalled him to the fact that Miss Muir was trying to
escape from his hold, which had grown painful in its unconscious pressure. He sprang
up, half bewildered, and looking as he had never looked before.

"Again! Again!" called Sir John. And the young men who played the Roundheads, eager to share in the applause begged for a repetition in new attitudes.

"A rustle has betrayed you, we have fired and shot the brave girl, and she lies
dying, you know. That will be effective; try it, Miss Muir," said one. And with a long
breath, Jean complied.

The curtain went up, showing the lover still on his knees, unmindful of the
captors who clutched him by the shoulder, for at his feet the girl lay dying. Her head
was on his breast, now, her eyes looked full into his, no longer wild with fear, but
eloquent with the love which even death could not conquer. The power of those
tender eyes thrilled Coventry with a strange delight, and set his heart beating as rapidly
as hers had done. She felt his hands tremble, saw the color flash into his cheek, knew
that she had touched him at last, and when she rose it was with a sense of triumph
which she found it hard to conceal. Others thought it fine acting; Coventry tried to
believe so; but Lucia set her teeth, and, as the curtain fell on that second picture, she
left her place to hurry behind the scenes, bent on putting an end to such dangerous
play. Several actors were complimenting the mimic lovers. Jean took it merrily, but
Coventry, in spite of himself, betrayed that he was excited by something deeper than
mere gratified vanity.

As Lucia appeared, his manner changed to its usual indifference; but he could
not quench the unwonted fire of his eyes, or keep all trace of emotion out of his face,
and she saw this with a sharp pang.

"I have come to offer my help. You must be tired, Miss Muir. Can I relieve
you?" said Lucia hastily.

"Yes, thank you. I shall be very glad to leave the rest to you, and enjoy them
from the front."

So with a sweet smile Jean tripped away, and to Lucia's dismay Coventry followed.

"I want you, Gerald; please stay," she cried.

"I've done my part—no more tragedy for me tonight." And he was gone before
she could entreat or command.

There was no help for it; she must stay and do her duty, or expose her jealousy
to the quick eyes about her. For a time she bore it; but the sight of her cousin leaning
over the chair she had left and chatting with the governess, who now filled it, grew
unbearable, and she dispatched a little girl with a message to Miss Muir.

"Please, Miss Beaufort wants you for Queen Bess, as you are the only lady with
red hair. Will you come?" whispered the child, quite unconscious of any hidden sting
in her words.

"Yes, dear, willingly though I'm not stately enough for Her Majesty, nor handsome enough," said Jean, rising with an untroubled face, though she resented the feminine insult.

"Do you want an Essex? I'm all dressed for it," said Coventry, following to the door with a wistful look.

"No, Miss Beaufort said *you* were not to come. She doesn't want you both together," said the child decidedly.

Jean gave him a significant look, shrugged her shoulders, and went away smiling her odd smile, while Coventry paced up and down the hall in a curious state of unrest, which made him forgetful of everything till the young people came gaily out to supper.

"Come, bonny Prince Charlie, take me down, and play the lover as charmingly as you did an hour ago. I never thought you had so much warmth in you," said Bella, taking his arm and drawing him on against his will.

"Don't be foolish, child. Where is—Lucia?"

Why he checked Jean's name on his lips and substituted another's, he could not tell; but a sudden shyness in speaking of her possessed him, and though he saw her nowhere, he would not ask for her. His cousin came down looking lovely in a classical costume; but Gerald scarcely saw her, and, when the merriment was at its height, he slipped away to discover what had become of Miss Muir.

Alone in the deserted drawing room he found her, and paused to watch her a moment before he spoke; for something in her attitude and face struck him. She was leaning wearily back in the great chair which had served for a throne. Her royal robes were still unchanged, though the crown was off and all her fair hair hung about her shoulders. Excitement and exertion made her brilliant, the rich dress became her wonderfully, and an air of luxurious indolence changed the meek governess into a charming woman. She leaned on the velvet cushions as if she were used to such support; she played with the jewels which had crowned her as carelessly as if she were born to wear them; her attitude was full of negligent grace, and the expression of her face half proud, half pensive, as if her thoughts were bittersweet.

One would know she was wellborn to see her now. Poor girl, what a burden a life of dependence must be to a spirit like hers! I wonder what she is thinking of so intently. And Coventry indulged in another look before he spoke.

"Shall I bring you some supper, Miss Muir?"

"Supper!" she ejaculated, with a start. "Who thinks of one's body when one's soul is—" She stopped there, knit her brows, and laughed faintly as she added, "No, thank you. I want nothing but advice, and that I dare not ask of anyone."

"Why not?"

"Because I have no right."

"Everyone has a right to ask help, especially the weak of the strong. Can I help you? Believe me, I most heartily offer my poor services."

"Ah, you forget! This dress, the borrowed splendor of these jewels, the freedom of this gay evening, the romance of the part you played, all blind you to the reality. For a moment I cease to be a servant, and for a moment you treat me as an equal."

It was true; he *had* forgotten. That soft, reproachful glance touched him, his distrust melted under the new charm, and he answered with real feeling in voice and face, "I treat you as an equal because you *are* one; and when I offer help, it is not to my sister's governess alone, but to Lady Howard's daughter."

"Who told you that?" she demanded, sitting erect.

"My uncle. Do not reproach him. It shall go no further, if you forbid it. Are you sorry that I know it?"

"Yes."

"Why?"

"Because I will not be pitied!" And her eyes flashed as she made a half-defiant gesture.

"Then, if I may not pity the hard fate which has befallen an innocent life, may I admire the courage which meets adverse fortune so bravely, and conquers the world by winning the respect and regard of all who see and honor it?"

Miss Muir averted her face, put up her hand, and answered hastily, "No, no, not that! Do not be kind; it destroys the only barrier now left between us. Be cold to me as before, forget what I am, and let me go on my way, unknown, unpitied, and unloved!"

Her voice faltered and failed as the last word was uttered, and she bent her face upon her hand. Something jarred upon Coventry in this speech, and moved him to say, almost rudely, "You need have no fears for me. Lucia will tell you what an iceberg I am."

"Then Lucia would tell me wrong. I have the fatal power of reading character; I know you better than she does, and I see—" There she stopped abruptly.

"What? Tell me and prove your skill," he said eagerly.

Turning, she fixed her eyes on him with a penetrating power that made him shrink as she said slowly, "Under the ice I see fire, and warn you to beware lest it prove a volcano."

For a moment he sat dumb, wondering at the insight of the girl; for she was the first to discover the hidden warmth of a nature too proud to confess its tender impulses, or the ambitions that slept till some potent voice awoke them. The blunt, almost stern manner in which she warned him away from her only made her more attractive; for there was no conceit or arrogance in it, only a foreboding fear emboldened by past suffering to be frank. Suddenly he spoke impetuously:

"You are right! I am not what I seem, and my indolent indifference is but the mask under which I conceal my real self. I could be as passionate, as energetic and aspiring as Ned, if I had any aim in life. I have none, and so I am what you once called me, a thing to pity and despise."

"I never said that!" cried Jean indignantly.

"Not in those words, perhaps; but you looked it and thought it, though you phrased it more mildly. I deserved it, but I shall deserve it no longer. I am beginning to wake from my disgraceful idleness, and long for some work that shall make a man of me. Why do you go? I annoy you with my confessions. Pardon me. They are the first I ever made; they shall be the last."

"No, oh no! I am too much honored by your confidence; but is it wise, is it loyal to tell *me* your hopes and aims? Has not Miss Beaufort the first right to be your confidante?"

Coventry drew back, looking intensely annoyed, for the name recalled much that he would gladly have forgotten in the novel excitement of the hour. Lucia's love, Edward's parting words, his own reserve so strangely thrown aside, so difficult to resume. What he would have said was checked by the sight of a half-open letter which fell from Jean's dress as she moved away. Mechanically he took it up to return it, and, as he did so, he recognized Sydney's handwriting. Jean snatched it from him, turning pale to the lips as she cried, "Did you read it? What did you see? Tell me, tell me, on your honor!"

"On my honor, I saw nothing but this single sentence, 'By the love I bear you, believe what I say.' No more, as I am a gentleman. I know the hand, I guess the purport of the letter, and as a friend of Sydney, I earnestly desire to help you, if I can. Is this the matter upon which you want advice?"

"Yes."

"Then let me give it?"

"You cannot, without knowing all, and it is so hard to tell!"

"Let me guess it, and spare you the pain of telling. May I?" And Coventry waited eagerly for her reply, for the spell was still upon him.

Holding the letter fast, she beckoned him to follow, and glided before him to a secluded little nook, half boudoir, half conservatory. There she paused, stood an instant as if in doubt, then looked up at him with confiding eyes and said decidedly, "I will do it; for, strange as it may seem, you are the only person to whom I *can* speak. You know Sydney, you have discovered that I am an equal, you have offered your help. I accept it; but oh, do not think me unwomanly! Remember how alone I am, how young, and how much I rely upon your sincerity, your sympathy!"

"Speak freely. I am indeed your friend." And Coventry sat down beside her, forgetful of everything but the soft-eyed girl who confided in him so entirely.

Speaking rapidly, Jean went on, "You know that Sydney loved me, that I refused him and went away. But you do not know that his importunities nearly drove me wild, that he threatened to rob me of my only treasure, my good name, and that, in desperation, I tried to kill myself. Yes, mad, wicked as it was, I did long to end the life which was, at best, a burden, and under his persecution had become a torment. You are shocked, yet what I say is the living truth. Lady Sydney will confirm it, the nurses at the hospital will confess that it was not a fever which brought me there; and here, though the external wound is healed, my heart still aches and burns with the shame and indignation which only a proud woman can feel."

She paused and sat with kindling eyes, glowing cheeks, and both hands pressed to her heaving bosom, as if the old insult roused her spirit anew. Coventry said not a word, for surprise, anger, incredulity, and admiration mingled so confusedly in his mind that he forgot to speak, and Jean went on, "That wild act of mine convinced him of my indomitable dislike. He went away, and I believed that this stormy love of his would be cured by absence. It is not, and I live in daily fear of fresh entreaties, renewed persecution. His mother promised not to betray where I had gone, but he found me out and wrote to me. The letter I asked you to take to Lady Sydney was a reply to his, imploring him to leave me in peace. You failed to deliver it, and I was glad, for I thought silence might quench hope. All in vain; this is a more passionate appeal than ever, and he vows he will never desist from his endeavors till I give another man the right to protect me. I *can* do this—I am sorely tempted to do it, but I rebel against the cruelty. I love my freedom, I have no wish to marry at this man's bidding. What can I do? How can I free myself? Be my friend, and help me!"

Tears streamed down her cheeks, sobs choked her words, and she clasped her hands imploringly as she turned toward the young man in all the abandonment of sorrow, fear, and supplication. Coventry found it hard to meet those eloquent eyes and answer calmly, for he had no experience in such scenes and knew not how to play his part. It is this absurd dress and that romantic nonsense which makes me feel so unlike myself, he thought, quite unconscious of the dangerous power which the dusky room, the midsummer warmth and fragrance, the memory of the "romantic nonsense," and, most of all, the presence of a beautiful, afflicted woman had over him. His usual self-possession deserted him, and he could only echo the words which had made the strongest impression upon him:

"You *can* do this, you are tempted to do it. Is Ned the man who can protect you?"

"No" was the soft reply.

"Who then?"

"Do not ask me. A good and honorable man; one who loves me well, and would devote his life to me; one whom once it would have been happiness to marry, but now—"

There her voice ended in a sigh, and all her fair hair fell down about her face, hiding it in a shining veil.

"Why not now? This is a sure and speedy way of ending your distress. Is it impossible?"

In spite of himself, Gerald leaned nearer, took one of the little hands in his, and pressed it as he spoke, urgently, compassionately, nay, almost tenderly. From behind the veil came a heavy sigh, and the brief answer, "It is impossible."

"Why, Jean?"

She flung her hair back with a sudden gesture, drew away her hand, and answered, almost fiercely, "Because I do not love him! Why do you torment me with such questions? I tell you I am in a sore strait and cannot see my way. Shall I deceive the good man, and secure peace at the price of liberty and truth? Or shall I defy Sydney and lead a life of dread? If he menaced my life, I should not fear; but he menaces that which is dearer than life—my good name. A look, a word can tarnish it; a scornful smile, a significant shrug can do me more harm than any blow; for I am a woman—friendless, poor, and at the mercy of his tongue. Ah, better to have died, and so have been saved the bitter pain that has come now!"

She sprang up, clasped her hands over her head, and paced despairingly through the little room, not weeping, but wearing an expression more tragical than tears. Still feeling as if he had suddenly stepped into a romance, yet finding a keen pleasure in the part assigned him, Coventry threw himself into it with spirit, and heartily did his best to console the poor girl who needed help so much. Going to her, he said as impetuously as Ned ever did, "Miss Muir—nay, I will say Jean, if that will comfort you—listen, and rest assured that no harm shall touch you if I can ward it off. You are needlessly alarmed. Indignant you may well be, but, upon my life, I think you wrong Sydney. He is violent, I know, but he is too honorable a man to injure you by a light word, an unjust act. He did but threaten, hoping to soften you. Let me see him, or write to him. He is my friend; he will listen to me. Of that I am sure."

"Be sure of nothing. When a man like Sydney loves and is thwarted in his love, nothing can control his headstrong will. Promise me you will not see or write to him. Much as I fear and despise him, I will submit, rather than any harm should befall you—or your brother. You promise me, Mr. Coventry?"

He hesitated. She clung to his arm with unfeigned solicitude in her eager, pleading face, and he could not resist it.

"I promise; but in return you must promise to let me give what help I can; and, Jean, never say again that you are friendless."

"You are so kind! God bless you for it. But I dare not accept your friendship; *she* will not permit it, and I have no right to mar her peace."

"Who will not permit it?" he demanded hotly.

"Miss Beaufort."

"Hang Miss Beaufort!" exclaimed Coventry, with such energy that Jean broke into a musical laugh, despite her trouble. He joined in it, and, for an instant they stood looking at one another as if the last barrier were down, and they were friends indeed. Jean paused suddenly, with the smile on her lips, the tears still on her cheek, and made a warning gesture. He listened: the sound of feet mingled with calls and laughter proved that they were missed and sought.

"That laugh betrayed us. Stay and meet them. I cannot." And Jean darted out upon the lawn. Coventry followed; for the thought of confronting so many eyes, so many questions, daunted him, and he fled like a coward. The sound of Jean's flying footsteps guided him, and he overtook her just as she paused behind a rose thicket to take breath.

"Fainthearted knight! You should have stayed and covered my retreat. Hark! they are coming! Hide! Hide!" she panted, half in fear, half in merriment, as the gay pursuers rapidly drew nearer.

"Kneel down; the moon is coming out and the glitter of your embroidery will betray you," whispered Jean, as they cowered behind the roses.

"Your arms and hair will betray you. 'Come under my plaiddie,' as the song says." And Coventry tried to make his velvet cloak cover the white shoulders and fair locks.

"We are acting our parts in reality now. How Bella will enjoy the thing when I tell her!" said Jean as the noises died away.

"Do not tell her," whispered Coventry.

"And why not?" she asked, looking up into the face so near her own, with an artless glance.

"Can you not guess why?"

"Ah, you are so proud you cannot bear to be laughed at."

"It is not that. It is because I do not want you to be annoyed by silly tongues; you have enough to pain you without that. I am your friend, now, and I do my best to prove it."

"So kind, so kind! How can I thank you?" murmured Jean. And she involuntarily nestled closer under the cloak that sheltered both.

Neither spoke for a moment, and in the silence the rapid beating of two hearts was heard. To drown the sound, Coventry said softly, "Are you frightened?"

"No, I like it," she answered, as softly, then added abruptly, "But why do we hide? There is nothing to fear. It is late. I must go. You are kneeling on my train. Please rise."

"Why in such haste? This flight and search only adds to the charm of the evening. I'll not get up yet. Will you have a rose, Jean?"

"No, I will not. Let me go, Mr. Coventry, I insist. There has been enough of this folly. You forget yourself."

She spoke imperiously, flung off the cloak, and put him from her. He rose at once, saying, like one waking suddenly from a pleasant dream, "I do indeed forget myself."

Here the sound of voices broke on them, nearer than before. Pointing to a covered walk that led to the house, he said, in his usually cool, calm tone, "Go in that way; I will cover your retreat." And turning, he went to meet the merry hunters.

Half an hour later, when the party broke up, Miss Muir joined them in her usual quiet dress, looking paler, meeker, and sadder than usual. Coventry saw this, though he neither looked at her nor addressed her. Lucia saw it also, and was glad that the dangerous girl had fallen back into her proper place again, for she had suffered much that night. She appropriated her cousin's arm as they went through the park, but he was in one of his taciturn moods, and all her attempts at conversation were in vain. Miss Muir walked alone, singing softly to herself as she followed in the dusk. Was Gerald so silent because he listened to that fitful song? Lucia thought so, and felt her dislike rapidly deepening to hatred.

When the young friends were gone, and the family were exchanging good-nights among themselves, Jean was surprised by Coventry's offering his hand, for he had never done it before, and whispering, as he held it, though Lucia watched him all the while, "I have not given my advice, yet."

"Thanks, I no longer need it. I have decided for myself."

"May I ask how?"

"To brave my enemy."

"Good! But what decided you so suddenly?"

"The finding of a friend." And with a grateful glance she was gone.

Chapter VI. On the Watch

"If you please, Mr. Coventry, did you get the letter last night?" were the first words that greeted the "young master" as he left his room next morning.

"What letter, Dean? I don't remember any," he answered, pausing, for something in the maid's manner struck him as peculiar.

"It came just as you left for the Hall, sir. Benson ran after you with it, as it was marked 'Haste.' Didn't you get it, sir?" asked the woman, anxiously.

"Yes, but upon my life, I forgot all about it till this minute. It's in my other coat, I suppose, if I've not lost it. That absurd masquerading put everything else out of my head." And speaking more to himself than to the maid, Coventry turned back to look for the missing letter.

Dean remained where she was, apparently busy about the arrangement of the curtains at the hall window, but furtively watching meanwhile with a most unwonted air of curiosity.

"Not there, I thought so!" she muttered, as Coventry impatiently thrust his hand into one pocket after another. But as she spoke, an expression of amazement appeared in her face, for suddenly the letter was discovered.

"I'd have sworn it wasn't there! I don't understand it, but she's a deep one, or I'm much deceived." And Dean shook her head like one perplexed. but not convinced.

Coventry uttered an exclamation of satisfaction on glancing at the address and, standing where he was, tore open the letter.

Dear C:

I'm off to Baden. Come and join me, then you'll be out of harm's way; for if you fall in love with J. M. (and you can't escape if you stay where she is), you will incur the trifling inconvenience of having your brains blown out by

Yours truly, F. R. Sydney

"The man is mad!" ejaculated Coventry, staring at the letter while an angry flush rose to his face. "What the deuce does he mean by writing to me in that style? Join him—not I! And as for the threat, I laugh at it. Poor Jean! This headstrong fool seems bent on tormenting her. Well, Dean, what are you waiting for?" he demanded, as if suddenly conscious of her presence.

"Nothing, sir; I only stopped to see if you found the letter. Beg pardon, sir."

And she was moving on when Coventry asked, with a suspicious look, "What made you think it was lost? You seem to take an uncommon interest in my affairs today."

"Oh dear, no, sir. I felt a bit anxious, Benson is so forgetful, and it was me who sent him after you, for I happened to see you go out, so I felt responsible. Being marked that way, I thought it might be important so I asked about it."

"Very well, you can go, Dean. It's all right, you see."

"I'm not so sure of that," muttered the woman, as she curtsied respectfully and went away, looking as if the letter had *not* been found.

Dean was Miss Beaufort's maid, a grave, middle-aged woman with keen eyes and a somewhat grim air. Having been long in the family, she enjoyed all the privileges of a faithful and favorite servant. She loved her young mistress with an almost jealous affection. She watched over her with the vigilant care of a mother and resented any attempt at interference on the part of others. At first she had pitied and liked Jean Muir, then distrusted her, and now heartily hated her, as the cause of the increased indifference of Coventry toward his cousin. Dean knew the depth of Lucia's love, and though no man, in her eyes, was worthy of her mistress, still, having honored him with her regard, Dean felt bound to like him, and the late change in his manner disturbed the maid almost as much as it did the mistress. She watched Jean narrowly, causing that amiable creature much amusement but little annoyance, as yet, for Dean's slow English wit was no match for the subtle mind of the governess. On the preceding night, Dean had been sent up to the Hall with costumes and had there seen something which much disturbed her. She began to speak of it while undressing her mistress, but Lucia, being in an unhappy mood, had so sternly ordered her not to gossip that the tale remained untold, and she was forced to bide her time.

Now I'll see how *she* looks after it; though there's not much to be got out of *her* face, the deceitful hussy, thought Dean, marching down the corridor and knitting her black brows as she went.

"Good morning, Mrs. Dean. I hope you are none the worse for last night's frolic. You had the work and we the play," said a blithe voice behind her; and turning sharply, she confronted Miss Muir. Fresh and smiling, the governess nodded with an air of cordiality which would have been irresistible with anyone but Dean.

"I'm quite well, thank you, miss," she returned coldly, as her keen eye fastened on the girl as if to watch the effect of her words. "I had a good rest when the young ladies and gentlemen were at supper, for while the maids cleared up, I sat in the 'little anteroom.' "

"Yes, I saw you, and feared you'd take cold. Very glad you didn't. How is Miss Beaufort? She seemed rather poorly last night" was the tranquil reply, as Jean settled the little frills about her delicate wrists. The cool question was a return shot for Dean's hint that she had been where she could oversee the interview between Coventry and Miss Muir.

"She is a bit tired, as any *lady* would be after such an evening. People who are *used* to *play-acting* wouldn't mind it, perhaps, but Miss Beaufort don't enjoy *romps* as much as *some* do."

The emphasis upon certain words made Dean's speech as impertinent as she desired. But Jean only laughed, and as Coventry's step was heard behind them, she ran downstairs, saying blandly, but with a wicked look, "I won't stop to thank you now, lest Mr. Coventry should bid me good-morning, and so increase Miss Beaufort's indisposition."

Dean's eyes flashed as she looked after the girl with a wrathful face, and went her way, saying grimly, "I'll bide my time, but I'll get the better of her yet."

Fancying himself quite removed from "last night's absurdity," yet curious to see how Jean would meet him, Coventry lounged into the breakfast room with his usual air of listless indifference. A languid nod and murmur was all the reply he vouchsafed to the greetings of cousin, sister, and governess as he sat down and took up his paper.

"Have you had a letter from Ned?" asked Bella, looking at the note which her brother still held.

"No" was the brief answer.

"Who then? You look as if you had received bad news."

There was no reply, and, peeping over his arm, Bella caught sight of the seal and exclaimed, in a disappointed tone, "It is the Sydney crest. I don't care about the note now. Men's letters to each other are not interesting."

Miss Muir had been quietly feeding one of Edward's dogs, but at the name she looked up and met Coventry's eyes, coloring so distressfully that he pitied her. Why he should take the trouble to cover her confusion, he did not stop to ask himself, but seeing the curl of Lucia's lip, he suddenly addressed her with an air of displeasure, "Do you know that Dean is getting impertinent? She presumes too much on her age and your indulgence, and forgets her place."

"What has she done?" asked Lucia coldly.

"She troubles herself about my affairs and takes it upon herself to keep Benson in order."

Here Coventry told about the letter and the woman's evident curiosity.

"Poor Dean, she gets no thanks for reminding you of what you had forgotten. Next time she will leave your letters to their fate, and perhaps it will be as well, if they have such a bad effect upon your temper, Gerald."

Lucia spoke calmly, but there was an angry color in her cheek as she rose and left the room. Coventry looked much annoyed, for on Jean's face he detected a faint smile, half pitiful, half satirical, which disturbed him more than his cousin's insinuation. Bella broke the awkward silence by saying, with a sigh, "Poor Ned! I do so long to hear again from him. I thought a letter had come for some of us. Dean said she saw one bearing his writing on the hall table yesterday."

"She seems to have a mania for inspecting letters. I won't allow it. Who was the letter for, Bella?" said Coventry, putting down his paper.

"She wouldn't or couldn't tell, but looked very cross and told me to ask you."

"Very odd! I've had none," began Coventry.

"But I had one several days ago. Will you please read it, and my reply?" And as she spoke, Jean laid two letters before him.

"Certainly not. It would be dishonorable to read what Ned intended for no eyes but your own. You are too scrupulous in one way, and not enough so in another, Miss Muir." And Coventry offered both the letters with an air of grave decision, which could not conceal the interest and surprise he felt.

"You are right. Mr. Edward's note *should* be kept sacred, for in it the poor boy has laid bare his heart to me. But mine I beg you will read, that you may see how well I try to keep my word to you. Oblige me in this, Mr. Coventry; I have a right to ask it of you."

So urgently she spoke, so wistfully she looked, that he could not refuse and, going to the window, read the letter. It was evidently an answer to a passionate appeal from the young lover, and was written with consummate skill. As he read, Gerald could not help thinking, If this girl writes in this way to a man whom she does *not* love, with what a world of power and passion would she write to one whom she *did* love. And this thought kept returning to him as his eye went over line after line of wise argument, gentle reproof, good counsel, and friendly regard. Here and there a word, a phrase, betrayed what she had already confessed, and Coventry forgot to return the letter, as he stood wondering who was the man whom Jean loved.

The sound of Bella's voice recalled him, for she was saying, half kindly, half petulantly, "Don't look so sad, Jean. Ned will outlive it, I dare say. You remember you said once men never died of love, though women might. In his one note to me, he spoke so beautifully of you, and begged me to be kind to you for his sake, that I try to be with all my heart, though if it was anyone but you, I really think I should hate them for making my dear boy so unhappy."

"You are too kind, Bella, and I often think I'll go away to relieve you of my presence; but unwise and dangerous as it is to stay, I haven't the courage to go. I've been so happy here." And as she spoke, Jean's head dropped lower over the dog as it nestled to her affectionately.

Before Bella could utter half the loving words that sprang to her lips, Coventry came to them with all languor gone from face and mien, and laying Jean's letter before her, he said, with an undertone of deep feeling in his usually emotionless voice, "A right womanly and eloquent letter, but I fear it will only increase the fire it was meant to quench. I pity my brother more than ever now."

"Shall I send it?" asked Jean, looking straight up at him, like one who had entire reliance on his judgment.

"Yes, I have not the heart to rob him of such a sweet sermon upon self-sacrifice. Shall I post it for you?"

"Thank you; in a moment." And with a grateful look, Jean dropped her eyes. Producing her little purse, she selected a penny, folded it in a bit of paper, and then offered both letter and coin to Coventry, with such a pretty air of business, that he could not control a laugh.

"So you won't be indebted to me for a penny? What a proud woman you are, Miss Muir."

"I am; it's a family failing." And she gave him a significant glance, which recalled to him the memory of who she was. He understood her feeling, and liked her the better for it, knowing that he would have done the same had he been in her place. It was a little thing, but if done for effect, it answered admirably, for it showed a quick insight into his character on her part, and betrayed to him the existence of a pride in which he sympathized heartily. He stood by Jean a moment, watching her as she burnt Edward's letter in the blaze of the spirit lamp under the urn.

"Why do you do that?" he asked involuntarily.

"Because it is my duty to forget" was all her answer.

"Can you always forget when it becomes a duty?"

"I wish I could! I wish I could!"

She spoke passionately, as if the words broke from her against her will, and, rising hastily, she went into the garden, as if afraid to stay.

"Poor, dear Jean is very unhappy about something, but I can't discover what it is. Last night I found her crying over a rose, and now she runs away, looking as if her heart was broken. I'm glad I've got no lessons."

"What kind of a rose?" asked Coventry from behind his paper as Bella paused.

"A lovely white one. It must have come from the Hall; we have none like it. I wonder if Jean was ever going to be married, and lost her lover, and felt sad because the flower reminded her of bridal roses."

Coventry made no reply, but felt himself change countenance as he recalled the little scene behind the rose hedge, where he gave Jean the flower which she had refused yet taken. Presently, to Bella's surprise, he flung down the paper, tore Sydney's note to atoms, and rang for his horse with an energy which amazed her.

"Why, Gerald, what has come over you? One would think Ned's restless spirit had suddenly taken possession of you. What are you going to do?"

"I'm going to work" was the unexpected answer, as Coventry turned toward her with an expression so rarely seen on his fine face.

"What has waked you up all at once?" asked Bella, looking more and more amazed.

"You did," he said, drawing her toward him.

"I! When? How?"

"Do you remember saying once that energy was better than beauty in a man, and that no one could respect an idler?"

"I never said anything half so sensible as that. Jean said something like it once, I believe, but I forgot. Are you tired of doing nothing, at last, Gerald?"

"Yes, I neglected my duty to Ned, till he got into trouble, and now I reproach myself for it. It's not too late to do other neglected tasks, so I'm going at them with a will. Don't say anything about it to anyone, and don't laugh at me, for I'm in earnest, Bell."

"I know you are, and I admire and love you for it, my dear old boy," cried Bella enthusiastically, as she threw her arms about his neck and kissed him heartily. "What will you do first?" she asked, as he stood thoughtfully smoothing the bright head that leaned upon his shoulder, with that new expression still clear and steady in his face.

"I'm going to ride over the whole estate, and attend to things as a master should; not leave it all to Bent, of whom I've heard many complaints, but have been too idle to inquire about them. I shall consult Uncle, and endeavor to be all that my father was in his time. Is that a worthy ambition, dear?"

"Oh, Gerald, let me tell Mamma. It will make her so happy. You are her idol, and to hear you say these things, to see you look so like dear Papa, would do more for her spirits than all the doctors in England."

"Wait till I prove what my resolution is worth. When I have really done something, then I'll surprise Mamma with a sample of my work."

"Of course you'll tell Lucia?"

"Not on any account. It is a little secret between us, so keep it till I give you leave to tell it."

"But Jean will see it at once; she knows everything that happens, she is so quick and wise. Do you mind her knowing?"

"I don't see that I can help it if she is so wonderfully gifted. Let her see what she can, I don't mind her. Now I'm off." And with a kiss to his sister, a sudden smile on his face, Coventry sprang upon his horse and rode away at a pace which caused the groom to stare after him in blank amazement.

Nothing more was seen of him till dinnertime, when he came in so exhilarated by his brisk ride and busy morning that he found some difficulty in assuming his customary manner, and more than once astonished the family by talking animatedly on various subjects which till now had always seemed utterly uninteresting to him. Lucia was amazed, his mother delighted, and Bella could hardly control her desire to explain the mystery; but Jean took it very calmly and regarded him with the air of one who said, "I understand, but you will soon tire of it." This nettled him more than he would confess, and he exerted himself to silently contradict that prophecy.

"Have you answered Mr. Sydney's letter?" asked Bella, when they were all scattered about the drawing room after dinner.

"No," answered her brother, who was pacing up and down with restless steps, instead of lounging near his beautiful cousin.

"I ask because I remembered that Ned sent a message for him in my last note, as he thought you would know Sydney's address. Here it is, something about a horse. Please put it in when you write," and Bella laid the note on the writing table nearby.

"I'll send it at once and have done with it," muttered Coventry and, seating himself, he dashed off a few lines, sealed and sent the letter, and then resumed his march, eyeing the three young ladies with three different expressions, as he passed and repassed. Lucia sat apart, feigning to be intent upon a book, and her handsome face looked almost stern in its haughty composure, for though her heart ached, she was too proud to own it. Bella now lay on the sofa, half asleep, a rosy little creature, as unconsciously pretty as a child. Miss Muir sat in the recess of a deep window, in a low lounging chair, working at an embroidery frame with a graceful industry pleasant to see. Of late she had worn colors, for Bella had been generous in gifts, and the pale blue muslin which flowed in soft waves about her was very becoming to her fair skin and golden hair. The close braids were gone, and loose curls dropped here and there from the heavy coil wound around her well-shaped head. The tip of one dainty foot was visible, and a petulant little gesture which now and then shook back the falling sleeve gave glimpses of a round white arm. Ned's great hound lay nearby, the sunshine flickered on her through the leaves, and as she sat smiling to herself, while the dexterous hands shaped leaf and flower, she made a charming picture of all that is most womanly and winning; a picture which few men's eyes would not have liked to rest upon.

Another chair stood near her, and as Coventry went up and down, a strong desire to take it possessed him. He was tired of his thoughts and wished to be amused by watching the changes of the girl's expressive face, listening to the varying tones of her voice, and trying to discover the spell which so strongly attracted him in spite of himself. More than once he swerved from his course to gratify his whim, but Lucia's presence always restrained him, and with a word to the dog, or a glance from the window, as pretext for a pause, he resumed his walk again. Something in his cousin's face reproached him, but her manner of late was so repellent that he felt no desire to resume their former familiarity, and, wishing to show that he did not consider himself bound, he kept aloof. It was a quiet test of the power of each woman over this man; they instinctively felt it, and both tried to conquer. Lucia spoke several times, and tried to speak frankly and affably; but her manner was constrained, and Coventry, having answered politely, relapsed into silence. Jean said nothing, but silently appealed to eye and ear by the pretty picture she made of herself, the snatches of song she softly sang, as if forgetting that she was not alone, and a shy glance now and then, half wistful, half merry, which was more alluring than graceful figure or sweet voice. When she had tormented Lucia and tempted Coventry long enough, she quietly asserted her supremacy in a way which astonished her rival, who knew nothing of the secret of her birth, which knowledge did much to attract and charm the young man. Letting a ball of silk escape from her lap, she watched it roll toward the promenader, who caught and returned it with an alacrity which added grace to the trifling service. As she took it, she said, in the frank way that never failed to win him, "I think you must be tired; but if exercise is necessary, employ your energies to some purpose and put your mother's basket of silks in order. They are in a tangle, and it will please her to know that you did it, as your brother used to do."

"Hercules at the distaff," said Coventry gaily, and down he sat in the long-desired seat. Jean put the basket on his knee, and as he surveyed it, as if daunted at his task, she leaned back, and indulged in a musical little peal of laughter charming to hear. Lucia sat dumb with surprise, to see her proud, indolent cousin obeying the commands of a governess, and looking as if he heartily enjoyed it. In ten minutes she was as entirely forgotten as if she had been miles away; for Jean seemed in her wittiest, gayest mood, and as she now treated the "young master" like an equal, there was none of the former meek timidity. Yet often her eyes fell, her color changed, and the piquant sallies faltered on her tongue, as Coventry involuntarily looked deep into the fine eyes which had once shone on him so tenderly in that mimic tragedy. He could not forget it, and though neither alluded to it, the memory of the previous evening seemed to haunt both and lend a secret charm to the present moment. Lucia bore this as long as she could, and then left the room with the air of an insulted princess; but Coventry did not, and Jean feigned not to see her go. Bella was fast asleep, and before he knew how it came to pass, the young man was listening to the story of his companion's life. A sad tale, told with wonderful skill, for soon he was absorbed in it. The basket slid unobserved from his knee, the dog was pushed away, and, leaning forward, he listened eagerly as the girl's low voice recounted all the hardships, loneliness, and grief of her short life. In the midst of a touching episode she started, stopped, and looked straight before her, with an intent expression which changed to one of intense contempt, and her eye turned to Coventry's, as she said, pointing to the window behind him, "We are watched."

"By whom?" he demanded, starting up angrily.

"Hush, say nothing, let it pass. I am used to it."

"But *I* am not, and I'll not submit to it. Who was it, Jean?" he answered hotly.

She smiled significantly at a knot of rose-colored ribbon, which a little gust was blowing toward them along the terrace. A black frown darkened the young man's face as he sprang out of the long window and went rapidly out of sight, scrutinizing each green nook as he passed. Jean laughed quietly as she watched him, and said softly to herself, with her eyes on the fluttering ribbon, "That was a fortunate accident, and a happy inspiration. Yes, my dear Mrs. Dean, you will find that playing the spy will only get your mistress as well as yourself into trouble. You would not be warned, and you must take the consequences, reluctant as I am to injure a worthy creature like yourself."

Soon Coventry was heard returning. Jean listened with suspended breath to catch his first words, for he was not alone.

"Since you insist that it was you and not your mistress, I let it pass, although I still have my suspicions. Tell Miss Beaufort I desire to see her for a few moments in the library. Now go, Dean, and be careful for the future, if you wish to stay in my house."

The maid retired, and the young man came in looking both ireful and stern.

"I wish I had said nothing, but I was startled, and spoke involuntarily. Now you are angry, and I have made fresh trouble for poor Miss Lucia. Forgive me as I forgive her, and let it pass. I have learned to bear this surveillance, and pity her causeless jealousy," said Jean, with a self-reproachful air.

"I will forgive the dishonorable act, but I cannot forget it, and I intend to put a stop to it. I am not betrothed to my cousin, as I told you once, but you, like all the rest, seem bent on believing that I am. Hitherto I have cared too little about the matter to settle it, but now I shall prove beyond all doubt that I am free."

As he uttered the last word, Coventry cast on Jean a look that affected her strangely. She grew pale, her work dropped on her lap, and her eyes rose to his, with an eager, questioning expression, which slowly changed to one of mingled pain and pity, as she turned her face away, murmuring in a tone of tender sorrow, "Poor Lucia, who will comfort her?"

For a moment Coventry stood silent, as if weighing some fateful purpose in his mind. As Jean's rapt sigh of compassion reached his ear, he had echoed it within himself, and half repented of his resolution; then his eye rested on the girl before him looking so lonely in her sweet sympathy for another that his heart yearned toward her. Sudden fire shot into his eye, sudden warmth replaced the cold sternness of his face, and his steady voice faltered suddenly, as he said, very low, yet very earnestly, "Jean, I have tried to love her, but I cannot. Ought I to deceive her, and make myself miserable to please my family?"

"She is beautiful and good, and loves you tenderly; is there no hope for her?" asked Jean, still pale, but very quiet, though she held one hand against her heart, as if to still or hide its rapid beating.

"None," answered Coventry.

"But can you not learn to love her? Your will is strong, and most men would not find it a hard task."

"I cannot, for something stronger than my own will controls me."

"What is that?" And Jean's dark eyes were fixed upon him, full of innocent wonder.

His fell, and he said hastily, "I dare not tell you yet."

"Pardon! I should not have asked. Do not consult me in this matter; I am not the person to advise you. I can only say that it seems to me as if any man with an empty heart would be glad to have so beautiful a woman as your cousin."

"My heart is not empty," began Coventry, drawing a step nearer, and speaking in a passionate voice. "Jean, I *must* speak; hear me. I cannot love my cousin, because I love you."

"Stop!" And Jean sprang up with a commanding gesture. "I will not hear you while any promise binds you to another. Remember your mother's wishes, Lucia's hopes, Edward's last words, your own pride, my humble lot. You forget yourself, Mr. Coventry. Think well before you speak, weigh the cost of this act, and recollect who I am before you insult me by any transient passion, any false vows."

"I have thought, I do weigh the cost, and I swear that I desire to woo you as humbly, honestly as I would any lady in the land. You speak of my pride. Do I stoop in loving my equal in rank? You speak of your lowly lot, but poverty is no disgrace, and the courage with which you bear it makes it beautiful. I should have broken with Lucia before I spoke, but I could not control myself. My mother loves you, and will be happy in my happiness. Edward must forgive me, for I have tried to do my best, but love is irresistible. Tell me, Jean, is there any hope for me?"

He had seized her hand and was speaking impetuously, with ardent face and tender tone, but no answer came, for as Jean turned her eloquent countenance toward him, full of maiden shame and timid love, Dean's prim figure appeared at the door, and her harsh voice broke the momentary silence, saying, sternly, "Miss Beaufort is waiting for you, sir."

"Go, go at once, and be kind, for my sake, Gerald," whispered Jean, for he stood as if deaf and blind to everything but her voice, her face.

As she drew his head down to whisper, her cheek touched his, and regardless of Dean, he kissed it, passionately, whispering back, "My little Jean! For your sake I can be anything."

"Miss Beaufort is waiting. Shall I say you will come, sir?" demanded Dean, pale and grim with indignation.

"Yes, yes, I'll come. Wait for me in the garden, Jean." And Coventry hurried away, in no mood for the interview but anxious to have it over.

As the door closed behind him, Dean walked up to Miss Muir, trembling with anger, and laying a heavy hand on her arm, she said below her breath, "I've been expecting this, you artful creature. I saw your game and did my best to spoil it, but you are too quick for me. You think you've got him. There you are mistaken; for as sure as my name is Hester Dean, I'll prevent it, or Sir John shall."

"Take your hand away and treat me with proper respect, or you will be dismissed from this house. Do you know who I am?" And Jean drew herself up with a haughty air, which impressed the woman more deeply than her words. "I am the daughter of Lady Howard and, if I choose it, can be the wife of Mr. Coventry."

Dean drew back amazed, yet not convinced. Being a well-trained servant, as well as a prudent woman, she feared to overstep the bounds of respect, to go too far, and get her mistress as well as herself into trouble. So, though she still doubted Jean, and hated her more than ever, she controlled herself. Dropping a curtsy, she assumed her usual air of deference, and said, meekly, "I beg pardon, miss. If I'd known, I should have conducted myself differently, of course, but ordinary governesses make so much mischief in a house, one can't help mistrusting them. I don't wish to meddle or be overbold, but being fond of my dear young lady, I naturally take her part, and must say that Mr. Coventry has not acted like a gentleman."

"Think what you please, Dean, but I advise you to say as little as possible if you wish to remain. I have not accepted Mr. Coventry yet, and if he chooses to set aside the engagement his family made for him, I think he has a right to do so. Miss Beaufort would hardly care to marry him against his will, because he pities her for her unhappy love," and with a tranquil smile, Miss Muir walked away.

Chapter VII. The Last Chance

"She will tell Sir John, will she? Then I must be before her, and hasten events. It will be as well to have all sure before there can be any danger. My poor Dean, you are no match for me, but you may prove annoying, nevertheless."

These thoughts passed through Miss Muir's mind as she went down the hall, pausing an instant at the library door, for the murmur of voices was heard. She caught no word, and had only time for an instant's pause as Dean's heavy step followed her. Turning, Jean drew a chair before the door, and, beckoning to the woman, she said, smiling still, "Sit here and play watchdog. I am going to Miss Bella, so you can nod if you will."

"Thank you, miss. I will wait for my young lady. She may need me when this hard time is over." And Dean seated herself with a resolute face.

Jean laughed and went on; but her eyes gleamed with sudden malice, and she glanced over her shoulder with an expression which boded ill for the faithful old servant.

"I've got a letter from Ned, and here is a tiny note for you," cried Bella as Jean entered the boudoir. "Mine is a very odd, hasty letter, with no news in it, but his meeting with Sydney. I hope yours is better, or it won't be very satisfactory."

As Sydney's name passed Bella's lips, all the color died out of Miss Muir's face, and the note shook with the tremor of her hand. Her very lips were white, but she said calmly, "Thank you. As you are busy, I'll go and read my letter on the lawn." And before Bella could speak, she was gone.

Hurrying to a quiet nook, Jean tore open the note and read the few blotted lines it contained.

> *I have seen Sydney; he has told me all; and, hard as I found it to believe, it was impossible to doubt, for he has discovered proofs which cannot be denied. I make no reproaches, shall demand no confession or atonement, for I cannot forget that I once loved you. I give you three days to find another home, before I return to tell the family who you are. Go at once, I beseech you, and spare me the pain of seeing your disgrace.*

Slowly, steadily she read it twice over, then sat motionless, knitting her brows in deep thought. Presently she drew a long breath, tore up the note, and rising, went slowly toward the Hall, saying to herself, "Three days, only three days! Can it be accomplished in so short a time? It shall be, if wit and will can do it, for it is my last chance. If this fails, I'll not go back to my old life, but end all at once."

Setting her teeth and clenching her hands, as if some memory stung her, she went on through the twilight, to find Sir John waiting to give her a hearty welcome.

"You look tired, my dear. Never mind the reading tonight; rest yourself, and let the book go," he said kindly, observing her worn look.

"Thank you, sir. I am tired, but I'd rather read, else the book will not be finished before I go."

"Go, child! Where are you going?" demanded Sir John, looking anxiously at her as she sat down.

"I will tell you by-and-by, sir." And opening the book, Jean read for a little while.

But the usual charm was gone; there was no spirit in the voice of the reader, no interest in the face of the listener, and soon he said, abruptly, "My dear, pray stop! I cannot listen with a divided mind. What troubles you? Tell your friend, and let him comfort you."

As if the kind words overcame her, Jean dropped the book, covered up her face, and wept so bitterly that Sir John was much alarmed; for such a demonstration was doubly touching in one who usually was all gaiety and smiles. As he tried to soothe her, his words grew tender, his solicitude full of a more than paternal anxiety, and his kind heart overflowed with pity and affection for the weeping girl. As she grew calmer, he urged her to be frank, promising to help and counsel her, whatever the affliction or fault might be.

"Ah, you are too kind, too generous! How can I go away and leave my one friend?" sighed Jean, wiping the tears away and looking up at him with grateful eyes.

"Then you do care a little for the old man?" said Sir John with an eager look, an involuntary pressure of the hand he held.

Jean turned her face away, and answered, very low, "No one ever was so kind to me as you have been. Can I help caring for you more than I can express?"

Sir John was a little deaf at times, but he heard that, and looked well pleased. He had been rather thoughtful of late, had dressed with unusual care, been particularly gallant and gay when the young ladies visited him, and more than once, when Jean paused in the reading to ask a question, he had been forced to confess that he had not been listening; though, as she well knew, his eyes had been fixed upon her. Since the discovery of her birth, his manner had been peculiarly benignant, and many little acts had proved his interest and goodwill. Now, when Jean spoke of going, a panic seized him, and desolation seemed about to fall upon the old Hall. Something in her unusual agitation struck him as peculiar and excited his curiosity. Never had she seemed so interesting as now, when she sat beside him with tearful eyes, and some soft trouble in her heart which she dared not confess.

"Tell me everything, child, and let your friend help you if he can." Formerly he said "father" or "the old man," but lately he always spoke of himself as her "friend."

"I will tell you, for I have no one else to turn to. I must go away because Mr. Coventry has been weak enough to love me."

"What, Gerald?" cried Sir John, amazed.

"Yes; today he told me this, and left me to break with Lucia; so I ran to you to help me prevent him from disappointing his mother's hopes and plans."

Sir John had started up and paced down the room, but as Jean paused he turned toward her, saying, with an altered face, "Then you do not love him? Is it possible?"

"No, I do not love him," she answered promptly.

"Yet he is all that women usually find attractive. How is it that you have escaped, Jean?"

"I love someone else" was the scarcely audible reply.

Sir John resumed his seat with the air of a man bent on getting at a mystery, if possible.

"It will be unjust to let you suffer for the folly of these boys, my little girl. Ned is gone, and I was sure that Gerald was safe; but now that his turn has come, I am perplexed, for he cannot be sent away."

"No, it is I who must go; but it seems so hard to leave this safe and happy home, and wander away into the wide, cold world again. You have all been too kind to me, and now separation breaks my heart."

A sob ended the speech, and Jean's head went down upon her hands again. Sir John looked at her a moment, and his fine old face was full of genuine emotion, as he said slowly, "Jean, will you stay and be a daughter to the solitary old man?"

"No, sir" was the unexpected answer.

"And why not?" asked Sir John, looking surprised, but rather pleased than angry.

"Because I could not be a daughter to you; and even if I could, it would not be wise, for the gossips would say you were not old enough to be the adopted father of a girl like me. Sir John, young as I am, I know much of the world, and am sure that this kind plan is impractical; but I thank you from the bottom of my heart."

"Where will you go, Jean?" asked Sir John, after a pause.

"To London, and try to find another situation where I can do no harm."

"Will it be difficult to find another home?"

"Yes. I cannot ask Mrs. Coventry to recommend me, when I have innocently brought so much trouble into her family; and Lady Sydney is gone, so I have no friend."

"Except John Coventry. I will arrange all that. When will you go, Jean?"

"Tomorrow."

"So soon!" And the old man's voice betrayed the trouble he was trying to conceal.

Jean had grown very calm, but it was the calmness of desperation. She had hoped that the first tears would produce the avowal for which she waited. It had not, and she began to fear that her last chance was slipping from her. Did the old man love her? If so, why did he not speak? Eager to profit by each moment, she was on the alert for any hopeful hint, any propitious word, look, or act, and every nerve was strung to the utmost.

"Jean, may I ask one question?" said Sir John.

"Anything of me, sir."

"This man whom you love—can he not help you?"

"He could if he knew, but he must not."

"If he knew what? Your present trouble?"

"No. My love."

"He does know this, then?"

"No, thank heaven! And he never will."

"Why not?"

"Because I am too proud to own it."

"He loves you, my child?"

"I do not know—I dare not hope it," murmured Jean.

"Can I not help you here? Believe me, I desire to see you safe and happy. Is there nothing I can do?"

"Nothing, nothing."

"May I know the name?"

"No! No! Let me go; I cannot bear this questioning!" And Jean's distressful face warned him to ask no more.

"Forgive me, and let me do what I may. Rest here quietly. I'll write a letter to a good friend of mine, who will find you a home, if you leave us."

As Sir John passed into his inner study, Jean watched him with despairing eyes and wrung her hands, saying to herself, Has all my skill deserted me when I need it most? How can I make him understand, yet not overstep the bounds of maiden modesty? He is so blind, so timid, or so dull he will not see, and time is going fast. What shall I do to open his eyes?

Her own eyes roved about the room, seeking for some aid from inanimate things, and soon she found it. Close behind the couch where she sat hung a fine miniature of Sir John. At first her eye rested on it as she contrasted its placid comeliness with the unusual pallor and disquiet of the living face seen through the open door, as the old man sat at his desk trying to write and casting covert glances at the girlish figure he had left behind him. Affecting unconsciousness of this, Jean gazed on as if forgetful of everything but the picture, and suddenly, as if obeying an irresistible impulse, she took it down, looked long and fondly at it, then, shaking her curls about her face, as if to hide the act, pressed it to her lips and seemed to weep over it in an uncontrollable paroxysm of tender grief. A sound startled her, and like a guilty thing, she turned to replace the picture; but it dropped from her hand as she uttered a faint cry and hid her face, for Sir John stood before her, with an expression which she could not mistake.

"Jean, why did you do that?" he asked, in an eager, agitated voice.

No answer, as the girl sank lower, like one overwhelmed with shame. Laying his hand on the bent head, and bending his own, he whispered, "Tell me, is the name John Coventry?"

Still no answer, but a stifled sound betrayed that his words had gone home.

"Jean, shall I go back and write the letter, or may I stay and tell you that the old man loves you better than a daughter?"

She did not speak, but a little hand stole out from under the falling hair, as if to keep him. With a broken exclamation he seized it, drew her up into his arms, and laid his gray head on her fair one, too happy for words. For a moment Jean Muir enjoyed her success; then, fearing lest some sudden mishap should destroy it, she hastened to make all secure. Looking up with well-feigned timidity and half-confessed affection, she said softly, "Forgive me that I could not hide this better. I meant to go away and never tell it, but you were so kind it made the parting doubly hard. Why did you ask such dangerous questions? Why did you look, when you should have been writing my dismissal?"

"How could I dream that you loved me, Jean, when you refused the only offer I dared make? Could I be presumptuous enough to fancy you would reject young lovers for an old man like me?" asked Sir John, caressing her.

"You are not old, to me, but everything I love and honor!" interrupted Jean, with a touch of genuine remorse, as this generous, honorable gentleman gave her both heart and home, unconscious of deceit. "It is I who am presumptuous, to dare to love one so far above me. But I did not know how dear you were to me till I felt that I must go. I ought not to accept this happiness. I am not worthy of it; and you will regret your kindness when the world blames you for giving a home to one so poor, and plain, and humble as I."

"Hush, my darling. I care nothing for the idle gossip of the world. If you are happy here, let tongues wag as they will. I shall be too busy enjoying the sunshine of your presence to heed anything that goes on about me. But, Jean, you are sure you love me? It seems incredible that I should win the heart that has been so cold to younger, better men than I."

"Dear Sir John, be sure of this, I love you truly. I will do my best to be a good wife to you, and prove that, in spite of my many faults, I possess the virtue of gratitude."

If he had known the strait she was in, he would have understood the cause of the sudden fervor of her words, the intense thankfulness that shone in her face, the real humility that made her stoop and kiss the generous hand that gave so much. For a few moments she enjoyed and let him enjoy the happy present, undisturbed. But the anxiety which devoured her, the danger which menaced her, soon recalled her, and forced her to wring yet more from the unsuspicious heart she had conquered.

"No need of letters now," said Sir John, as they sat side by side, with the summer moonlight glorifying all the room. "You have found a home for life; may it prove a happy one."

"It is not mine yet, and I have a strange foreboding that it never will be," she answered sadly.

"Why, my child?"

"Because I have an enemy who will try to destroy my peace, to poison your mind against me, and to drive me out from my paradise, to suffer again all I have suffered this last year."

"You mean that mad Sydney of whom you told me?"

"Yes. As soon as he hears of this good fortune to poor little Jean, he will hasten to mar it. He is my fate; I cannot escape him, and wherever he goes my friends desert me; for he has the power and uses it for my destruction. Let me go away and hide before he comes, for, having shared your confidence, it will break my heart to see you distrust and turn from me, instead of loving and protecting."

"My poor child, you are superstitious. Be easy. No one can harm you now, no one would dare attempt it. And as for my deserting you, that will soon be out of my power, if I have my way."

"How, dear Sir John?" asked Jean, with a flutter of intense relief at her heart, for the way seemed smoothing before her.

"I will make you my wife at once, if I may. This will free you from Gerald's love, protect you from Sydney's persecution, give you a safe home, and me the right to cherish and defend with heart and hand. Shall it be so, my child?"

"Yes; but oh, remember that I have no friend but you! Promise me to be faithful to the last—to believe in me, to trust me, protect and love me, in spite of all misfortunes, faults, and follies. I will be true as steel to you, and make your life as happy as it deserves to be. Let us promise these things now, and keep the promises unbroken to the end."

Her solemn air touched Sir John. Too honorable and upright himself to suspect falsehood in others, he saw only the natural impulse of a lovely girl in Jean's words, and, taking the hand she gave him in both of his, he promised all she asked, and kept that promise to the end. She paused an instant, with a pale, absent expression, as if she searched herself, then looked up clearly in the confiding face above her, and promised what she faithfully performed in afteryears.

"When shall it be, little sweetheart? I leave all to you, only let it be soon, else some gay young lover will appear, and take you from me," said Sir John, playfully, anxious to chase away the dark expression which had stolen over Jean's face.

"Can you keep a secret?" asked the girl, smiling up at him, all her charming self again.

"Try me."

"I will. Edward is coming home in three days. I must be gone before he comes. Tell no one of this; he wishes to surprise them. And if you love me, tell nobody of your approaching marriage. Do not betray that you care for me until I am really yours. There will be such a stir, such remonstrances, explanations, and reproaches that I shall be worn out, and run away from you all to escape the trial. If I could have my wish, I would go to some quiet place tomorrow and wait till you come for me. I know so little of such things, I cannot tell how soon we may be married; not for some weeks, I think."

"Tomorrow, if we like. A special license permits people to marry when and where they please. My plan is better than yours. Listen, and tell me if it can be carried out. I will go to town tomorrow, get the license, invite my friend, the Reverend Paul Fairfax, to return with me, and tomorrow evening you come at your usual time, and, in the presence of my discreet old servants, make me the happiest man in England. How does this suit you, my little Lady Coventry?"

The plan which seemed made to meet her ends, the name which was the height of her ambition, and the blessed sense of safety which came to her filled Jean Muir with such intense satisfaction that tears of real feeling stood in her eyes, and the glad assent she gave was the truest word that had passed her lips for months.

"We will go abroad or to Scotland for our honeymoon, till the storm blows over," said Sir John, well knowing that this hasty marriage would surprise or offend all his relations, and feeling as glad as Jean to escape the first excitement.

"To Scotland, please. I long to see my father's home," said Jean, who dreaded to meet Sydney on the continent.

They talked a little longer, arranging all things, Sir John so intent on hurrying the event that Jean had nothing to do but give a ready assent to all his suggestions. One fear alone disturbed her. If Sir John went to town, he might meet Edward, might hear and believe his statements. Then all would be lost. Yet this risk must be incurred, if the marriage was to be speedily and safely accomplished; and to guard against the meeting was Jean's sole care. As they went through the park—for Sir John insisted upon taking her home—she said, clinging to his arm:

"Dear friend, bear one thing in mind, else we shall be much annoyed, and all our plans disarranged. Avoid your nephews; you are so frank your face will betray you. They both love me, are both hot-tempered, and in the first excitement of the discovery might be violent. You must incur no danger, no disrespect for my sake; so shun them both till we are safe—particularly Edward. He will feel that his brother has wronged him, and that you have succeeded where he failed. This will irritate him, and I fear a stormy scene. Promise to avoid both for a day or two; do not listen to them, do not see them, do not write to or receive letters from them. It is foolish, I know; but you are all I have, and I am haunted by a strange foreboding that I am to lose you."

Touched and flattered by her tender solicitude, Sir John promised everything, even while he laughed at her fears. Love blinded the good gentleman to the peculiarity of the request; the novelty, romance, and secrecy of the affair rather bewildered though it charmed him; and the knowledge that he had outrivaled three young and ardent lovers gratified his vanity more than he would confess. Parting from the girl at the garden gate, he turned homeward, feeling like a boy again, and loitered back, humming a love lay, quite forgetful of evening damps, gout, and the five-and-fifty years which lay so lightly on his shoulders since Jean's arms had rested there. She hurried toward the house, anxious to escape Coventry; but he was waiting for her, and she was forced to meet him.

"How could you linger so long, and keep me in suspense?" he said reproachfully, as he took her hand and tried to catch a glimpse of her face in the shadow of her hat brim. "Come and rest in the grotto. I have so much to say, to hear and enjoy."

"Not now; I am too tired. Let me go in and sleep. Tomorrow we will talk. It is damp and chilly, and my head aches with all this worry." Jean spoke wearily, yet with a touch of petulance, and Coventry, fancying that she was piqued at his not coming for her, hastened to explain with eager tenderness.

"My poor little Jean, you do need rest. We wear you out, among us, and you never complain. I should have come to bring you home, but Lucia detained me, and when I got away I saw my uncle had forestalled me. I shall be jealous of the old gentleman, if he is so devoted. Jean, tell me one thing before we part; I am free as air, now, and have a right to speak. Do you love me? Am I the happy man who has won your heart? I dare to think so, to believe that this telltale face of yours has betrayed you, and to hope that I have gained what poor Ned and wild Sydney have lost."

"Before I answer, tell me of your interview with Lucia. I have a right to know," said Jean.

Coventry hesitated, for pity and remorse were busy at his heart when he recalled poor Lucia's grief. Jean was bent on hearing the humiliation of her rival. As the young man paused, she frowned, then lifted up her face wreathed in softest smiles, and laying her hand on his arm, she said, with most effective emphasis, half shy, half fond, upon his name, "Please tell me, Gerald!"

He could not resist the look, the touch, the tone, and taking the little hand in his, he said rapidly, as if the task was distasteful to him, "I told her that I did not, could not love her; that I had submitted to my mother's wish, and, for a time, had felt tacitly bound to her, though no words had passed between us. But now I demanded my liberty, regretting that the separation was not mutually desired."

"And she—what did she say? How did she bear it?" asked Jean, feeling in her own woman's heart how deeply Lucia's must have been wounded by that avowal.

"Poor girl! It was hard to bear, but her pride sustained her to the end. She owned that no pledge tied me, fully relinquished any claim my past behavior had seemed to have given her, and prayed that I might find another woman to love me as truly, tenderly as she had done. Jean, I felt like a villain; and yet I never plighted my word to her, never really loved her, and had a perfect right to leave her, if I would."

"Did she speak of me?"

"Yes."

"What did she say?"

"Must I tell you?"

"Yes, tell me everything. I know she hates me and I forgive her, knowing that I should hate any woman whom *you* loved."

"Are you jealous, dear?"

"Of you, Gerald?" And the fine eyes glanced up at him, full of a brilliancy that looked like the light of love.

"You make a slave of me already. How do you do it? I never obeyed a woman before. Jean, I think you are a witch. Scotland is the home of weird, uncanny creatures, who take lovely shapes for the bedevilment of poor weak souls. Are you one of those fair deceivers?"

"You are complimentary," laughed the girl. "I *am* a witch, and one day my disguise will drop away and you will see me as I am, old, ugly, bad and lost. Beware of me in time. I've warned you. Now love me at your peril."

Coventry had paused as he spoke, and eyed her with an unquiet look, conscious of some fascination which conquered yet brought no happiness. A feverish yet pleasurable excitement possessed him; a reckless mood, making him eager to obliterate the past by any rash act, any new experience which his passion brought. Jean regarded him with a wistful, almost woeful face, for one short moment; then a strange smile broke over it, as she spoke in a tone of malicious mockery, under which lurked the bitterness of a sad truth. Coventry looked half bewildered, and his eye went from the girl's mysterious face to a dimly lighted window, behind whose curtains poor Lucia hid her aching heart, praying for him the tender prayers that loving women give to those whose sins are all forgiven for love's sake. His heart smote him, and a momentary feeling of repulsion came over him, as he looked at Jean. She saw it, felt angry, yet conscious of a sense of relief; for now that her own safety was so nearly secured, she felt no wish to do mischief, but rather a desire to undo what was already done, and be at peace with all the world. To recall him to his allegiance, she sighed and walked on, saying gently yet coldly, "Will you tell me what I ask before I answer your question, Mr. Coventry?"

"What Lucia said of you? Well, it was this. 'Beware of Miss Muir. We instinctively distrusted her when we had no cause. I believe in instincts, and mine have never changed, for she has not tried to delude me. Her art is wonderful; I feel yet cannot explain or detect it, except in the working of events which her hand seems to guide. She has brought sorrow and dissension into this hitherto happy family. We are all changed, and this girl has done it. Me she can harm no further; you she will ruin, if she can. Beware of her in time, or you will bitterly repent your blind infatuation!' "

"And what answer did you make?" asked Jean, as the last words came reluctantly from Coventry's lips.

"I told her that I loved you in spite of myself, and would make you my wife in the face of all opposition. Now, Jean, your answer."

"Give me three days to think of it. Good night." And gliding from him, she vanished into the house, leaving him to roam about half the night, tormented with remorse, suspense, and the old distrust which would return when Jean was not there to banish it by her art.

CHAPTER VIII. SUSPENSE

ALL THE NEXT DAY, Jean was in a state of the most intense anxiety, as every hour brought the crisis nearer, and every hour might bring defeat, for the subtlest human skill is often thwarted by some unforeseen accident. She longed to assure herself that Sir John was gone, but no servants came or went that day, and she could devise no pretext for sending to glean intelligence. She dared not go herself, lest the unusual act should excite suspicion, for she never went till evening. Even had she determined to venture, there was no time, for Mrs. Coventry was in one of her nervous states, and no one but Miss Muir could amuse her; Lucia was ill, and Miss Muir must give orders; Bella had a studious fit, and Jean must help her. Coventry lingered about the house for several hours, but Jean dared not send him, lest some hint of the truth might reach him. He had ridden away to his new duties when Jean did not appear, and the day dragged on wearisomely. Night came at last, and as Jean dressed for the late dinner, she hardly knew herself when she stood before her mirror, excitement lent such color and brilliancy to her countenance. Remembering the wedding which was to take place that evening, she put on a simple white dress and added a cluster of white roses in bosom and hair. She often wore flowers, but in spite of her desire to look and seem as usual, Bella's first words as she entered the drawing room were "Why, Jean, how like a bride you look; a veil and gloves would make you quite complete!"

"You forget one other trifle, Bell," said Gerald, with eyes that brightened as they rested on Miss Muir.

"What is that?"asked his sister.

"A bridegroom."

Bella looked to see how Jean received this, but she seemed quite composed as she smiled one of her sudden smiles, and merely said, "That trifle will doubtless be found when the time comes. Is Miss Beaufort too ill for dinner?"

"She begs to be excused, and said you would be willing to take her place, she thought."

As innocent Bella delivered this message, Jean glanced at Coventry, who evaded her eye and looked ill at ease.

A little remorse will do him good, and prepare him for repentance after the grand coup, *she said to herself, and was particularly gay at dinnertime, though Coventry looked often at Lucia's empty seat, as if he missed her. As soon as they left the table, Miss Muir sent Bella to her mother; and, knowing that Coventry would not linger long at his wine, she hurried away to the Hall. A servant was lounging at the door, and of him she asked, in a tone which was eager in spite of all efforts to be calm, "Is Sir John at home?"

"No, miss, he's just gone to town."

"Just gone! When do you mean?" cried Jean, forgetting the relief she felt in hearing of his absence in surprise at his late departure.

"He went half an hour ago, in the last train, miss."

"I thought he was going early this morning; he told me he should be back this evening."

"I believe he did mean to go, but was delayed by company. The steward came up on business, and a load of gentlemen called, so Sir John could not get off till night, when he wasn't fit to go, being worn out, and far from well."

"Do you think he will be ill? Did he look so?" And as Jean spoke, a thrill of fear passed over her, lest death should rob her of her prize.

"Well, you know, miss, hurry of any kind is bad for elderly gentlemen inclined to apoplexy. Sir John was in a worry all day, and not like himself. I wanted him to take his man, but he wouldn't; and drove off looking flushed and excited like. I'm anxious about him, for I know something is amiss to hurry him off in this way."

"When will he be back, Ralph?"

"Tomorrow noon, if possible; at night certainly, he bid me tell anyone that called."

"Did he leave no note or message for Miss Coventry, or someone of the family?"

"No, miss, nothing."

"Thank you." And Jean walked back to spend a restless night and rise to meet renewed suspense.

The morning seemed endless, but noon came at last, and under the pretense of seeking coolness in the grotto, Jean stole away to a slope whence the gate to the Hall park was visible. For two long hours she watched, and no one came. She was just turning away when a horseman dashed through the gate and came galloping toward the Hall. Heedless of everything but the uncontrollable longing to gain some tidings, she ran to meet him, feeling assured that he brought ill news. It was a young man from the station, and as he caught sight of her, he drew bridle, looking agitated and undecided.

"Has anything happened?" she cried breathlessly.

"A dreadful accident on the railroad, just the other side of Croydon. News telegraphed half an hour ago," answered the man, wiping his hot face.

"The noon train? Was Sir John in it? Quick, tell me all!"

"It was that train, miss, but whether Sir John was in it or not, we don't know; for the guard is killed, and everything is in such confusion that nothing can be certain. They are at work getting out the dead and wounded. We heard that Sir John was expected, and I came up to tell Mr. Coventry, thinking he would wish to go down. A train leaves in fifteen minutes; where shall I find him? I was told he was at the Hall."

"Ride on, ride on! And find him if he is there. I'll run home and look for him. Lose no time. Ride! Ride!" And turning, Jean sped back like a deer, while the man tore up the avenue to rouse the Hall.

Coventry was there, and went off at once, leaving both Hall and house in dismay. Fearing to betray the horrible anxiety that possessed her, Jean shut herself up in her room and suffered untold agonies as the day wore on and no news came. At dark a sudden cry rang through the house, and Jean rushed down to learn the cause. Bella was standing in the hall, holding a letter, while a group of excited servants hovered near her.

"What is it?" demanded Miss Muir, pale and steady, though her heart died within her as she recognized Gerald's handwriting. Bella gave her the note, and hushed her sobbing to hear again the heavy tidings that had come.

> *Dear Bella:*
>
> *Uncle is safe; he did not go in the noon train. But several persons are sure that Ned was there. No trace of him as yet, but many bodies are in the river, under the ruins of the bridge, and I am doing my best to find the poor lad, if he is there. I have sent to all his haunts in town, and as he has not been seen, I hope it is a false report and he is safe with his regiment. Keep this from my mother till we are sure. I write you, because Lucia is ill. Miss Muir will comfort and sustain you. Hope for the best, dear.*
>
> *Yours, G. C.*

Those who watched Miss Muir as she read these words wondered at the strange expressions which passed over her face, for the joy which appeared there as Sir John's safety was made known did not change to grief or horror at poor Edward's possible fate. The smile died on her lips, but her voice did not falter, and in her downcast eyes shone an inexplicable look of something like triumph. No wonder, for if this was true, the danger which menaced her was averted for a time, and the marriage might be consummated without such desperate haste. This sad and sudden event seemed to her the mysterious fulfilment of a secret wish; and though startled she was not daunted but inspirited, for fate seemed to favor her designs. She did comfort Bella, control the excited household, and keep the rumors from Mrs. Coventry all that dreadful night.

At dawn Gerald came home exhausted, and bringing no tiding of the missing man. He had telegraphed to the headquarters of the regiment and received a reply, stating that Edward had left for London the previous day, meaning to go home before returning. The fact of his having been at the London station was also established, but whether he left by the train or not was still uncertain. The ruins were still being searched, and the body might yet appear.

"Is Sir John coming at noon?" asked Jean, as the three sat together in the rosy hush of dawn, trying to hope against hope.

"No, he had been ill, I learned from young Gower, who is just from town, and so had not completed his business. I sent him word to wait till night, for the bridge won't be passable till then. Now I must try and rest an hour; I've worked all night and have no strength left. Call me the instant any messenger arrives."

With that Coventry went to his room, Bella followed to wait on him, and Jean roamed through house and grounds, unable to rest. The morning was far spent when the messenger arrived. Jean went to receive his tidings, with the wicked hope still lurking at her heart.

"Is he found?" she asked calmly, as the man hesitated to speak.

"Yes, ma'am."

"You are sure?"

"I am certain, ma'am, though some won't say till Mr. Coventry comes to look."

"Is he alive?" And Jean's white lips trembled as she put the question.

"Oh no, ma'am, that warn't possible, under all them stones and water. The poor young gentleman is so wet, and crushed, and torn, no one would know him, except for the uniform, and the white hand with the ring on it."

Jean sat down, very pale, and the man described the finding of the poor shattered body. As he finished, Coventry appeared, and with one look of mingled remorse, shame, and sorrow, the elder brother went away, to find and bring the younger home. Jean crept into the garden like a guilty thing, trying to hide the satisfaction which struggled with a woman's natural pity, for so sad an end for this brave young life.

"Why waste tears or feign sorrow when I must be glad?" she muttered, as she paced to and fro along the terrace. "The poor boy is out of pain, and I am out of danger."

She got no further, for, turning as she spoke, she stood face to face with Edward! Bearing no mark of peril on dress or person, but stalwart and strong as ever, he stood there looking at her, with contempt and compassion struggling in his face. As if turned to stone, she remained motionless, with dilated eyes, arrested breath, and paling cheek. He did not speak but watched her silently till she put out a trembling hand, as if to assure herself by touch that it was really he. Then he drew back, and as if the act convinced as fully as words, she said slowly, "They told me you were dead."

"And you were glad to believe it. No, it was my comrade, young Courtney, who unconsciously deceived you all, and lost his life, as I should have done, if I had not gone to Ascot after seeing him off yesterday."

"To Ascot?" echoed Jean, shrinking back, for Edward's eye was on her, and his voice was stern and cold.

"Yes; you know the place. I went there to make inquiries concerning you and was well satisfied. Why are you still here?"

"The three days are not over yet. I hold you to your promise. Before night I shall be gone; till then you will be silent, if you have honor enough to keep your word."

"I have." Edward took out his watch and, as he put it back, said with cool precision, "It is now two, the train leaves for London at halfpast six; a carriage will wait for you at the side door. Allow me to advise you to go then, for the instant dinner is over I shall speak." And with a bow he went into the house, leaving Jean nearly suffocated with a throng of contending emotions.

For a few minutes she seemed paralyzed; but the native energy of the woman forbade utter despair, till the last hope was gone. Frail as that now was, she still clung to it tenaciously, resolving to win the game in defiance of everything. Springing up, she went to her room, packed her few valuables, dressed herself with care, and then sat down to wait. She heard a joyful stir below, saw Coventry come hurrying back, and from a garrulous maid learned that the body was that of young Courtney. The uniform being the same as Edward's and the ring, a gift from him, had caused the men to believe the disfigured corpse to be that of the younger Coventry. No one but the maid came near her; once Bella's voice called her, but some one checked the girl, and the call was not repeated. At five an envelope was brought her, directed in Edward's hand, and containing a check which more than paid a year's salary. No word accompanied the gift, yet the generosity of it touched her, for Jean Muir had the relics of a once honest nature, and despite her falsehood could still admire nobleness and respect virtue. A tear of genuine shame dropped on the paper, and real gratitude filled her heart, as she thought that even if all else failed, she was not thrust out penniless into the world, which had no pity for poverty.

As the clock struck six, she heard a carriage drive around and went down to meet it. A servant put on her trunk, gave the order, "To the station, James," and she drove away without meeting anyone, speaking to anyone, or apparently being seen by anyone. A sense of utter weariness came over her, and she longed to lie down and forget. But the last chance still remained, and till that failed, she would not give up. Dismissing the carriage, she seated herself to watch for the quarter-past-six train from London, for in that Sir John would come if he came at all that night. She was haunted by the fear that Edward had met and told him. The first glimpse of Sir John's frank face would betray the truth. If he knew all, there was no hope, and she would go her way alone. If he knew nothing, there was yet time for the marriage; and once his wife, she knew she was safe, because for the honor of his name he would screen and protect her.

Up rushed the train, out stepped Sir John, and Jean's heart died within her. Grave, and pale, and worn he looked, and leaned heavily on the arm of a portly gentleman in black. The Reverend Mr. Fairfax, why has he come, if the secret is out?

thought Jean, slowly advancing to meet them and fearing to read her fate in Sir John's face. He saw her, dropped his friend's arm, and hurried forward with the ardor of a young man, exclaiming, as he seized her hand with a beaming face, a glad voice, "My little girl! Did you think I would never come?"

She could not answer, the reaction was too strong, but she clung to him, regardless of time or place, and felt that her last hope had not failed. Mr. Fairfax proved himself equal to the occasion. Asking no questions, he hurried Sir John and Jean into a carriage and stepped in after them with a bland apology. Jean was soon herself again, and, having told her fears at his delay, listened eagerly while he related the various mishaps which had detained him.

"Have you seen Edward?" was her first question.

"Not yet, but I know he has come, and have heard of his narrow escape. I should have been in that train, if I had not been delayed by the indisposition which I then cursed, but now bless. Are you ready, Jean? Do you repent your choice, my child?"

"No, no! I am ready, I am only too happy to become your wife, dear, generous Sir John," cried Jean, with a glad alacrity, which touched the old man to the heart, and charmed the Reverend Mr. Fairfax, who concealed the romance of a boy under his clerical suit.

They reached the Hall. Sir John gave orders to admit no one and after a hasty dinner sent for his old housekeeper and his steward, told them of his purpose, and desired them to witness his marriage. Obedience had been the law of their lives, and Master could do nothing wrong in their eyes, so they played their parts willingly, for Jean was a favorite at the Hall. Pale as her gown, but calm and steady, she stood beside Sir John, uttering her vows in a clear tone and taking upon herself the vows of a wife with more than a bride's usual docility. When the ring was fairly on, a smile broke over her face. When Sir John kissed and called her his "little wife," she shed a tear or two of sincere happiness; and when Mr. Fairfax addressed her as "my lady," she laughed her musical laugh, and glanced up at a picture of Gerald with eyes full of exultation. As the servants left the room, a message was brought from Mrs. Coventry, begging Sir John to come to her at once.

"You will not go and leave me so soon?" pleaded Jean, well knowing why he was sent for.

"My darling, I must." And in spite of its tenderness, Sir John's manner was too decided to be withstood.

"Then I shall go with you," cried Jean, resolving that no earthly power should part them.

CHAPTER IX. LADY COVENTRY

WHEN THE FIRST EXCITEMENT of Edward's return had subsided, and before they could question him as to the cause of this unexpected visit, he told them that after dinner their curiosity should be gratified, and meantime he begged them to leave Miss Muir alone, for she had received bad news and must not be disturbed. The family with difficulty restrained their tongues and waited impatiently. Gerald confessed his love for Jean and asked his brother's pardon for betraying his trust. He had expected an outbreak, but Edward only looked at him with pitying eyes, and said sadly, "You too! I have no reproaches to make, for I know what you will suffer when the truth is known."

"What do you mean?" demanded Coventry.

"You will soon know, my poor Gerald, and we will comfort one another."

Nothing more could be drawn from Edward till dinner was over, the servants gone, and all the family alone together. Then pale and grave, but very self-possessed, for trouble had made a man of him, he produced a packet of letters, and said, addressing himself to his brother, "Jean Muir has deceived us all. I know her story; let me tell it before I read her letters."

"Stop! I'll not listen to any false tales against her. The poor girl has enemies who belie her!" cried Gerald, starting up.

"For the honor of the family, you must listen, and learn what fools she has made of us. I can prove what I say, and convince you that she has the art of a devil. Sit still ten minutes, then go, if you will."

Edward spoke with authority, and his brother obeyed him with a foreboding heart.

"I met Sydney, and he begged me to beware of her. Nay, listen, Gerald! I know she has told her story, and that you believe it; but her own letters convict her. She tried to charm Sydney as she did us, and nearly succeeded in inducing him to marry her. Rash and wild as he is, he is still a gentleman, and when an incautious word of hers roused his suspicions, he refused to make her his wife. A stormy scene ensued, and, hoping to intimidate him, she feigned to stab herself as if in despair. She did wound herself, but failed to gain her point and insisted upon going to a hospital to die. Lady Sydney, good, simple soul, believed the girl's version of the story, thought her son was in the wrong, and when he was gone, tried to atone for his fault by finding Jean Muir another home. She thought Gerald was soon to marry Lucia, and that I was away, so sent her here as a safe and comfortable retreat."

"But, Ned, are you sure of all this? Is Sydney to be believed?" began Coventry, still incredulous.

"To convince you, I'll read Jean's letters before I say more. They were written to an accomplice and were purchased by Sydney. There was a compact between the two women, that each should keep the other informed of all adventures, plots and plans, and share whatever good fortune fell to the lot of either. Thus Jean wrote freely, as you shall judge. The letters concern us alone. The first was written a few days after she came.

"*Dear Hortense:*

"*Another failure. Sydney was more wily than I thought. All was going well, when one day my old fault beset me, I took too much wine, and I carelessly owned that I had been an actress. He was shocked, and retreated. I got up a scene, and gave myself a safe little wound, to frighten him. The brute was not frightened, but coolly left me to my fate. I'd have died to spite him, if I dared, but as I didn't, I lived to torment him. As yet, I have had no chance, but I will not forget him. His mother is a poor, weak creature, whom I could use as I would, and through her I found an excellent place. A sick mother, silly daughter, and two eligible sons. One is engaged to a handsome iceberg, but that only renders him more interesting in my eyes, rivalry adds so much to the charm of one's conquests. Well, my dear, I went, got up in the meek style, intending to do the pathetic; but before I saw the family, I was so angry I could hardly control myself. Through the indolence of Monsieur the young master, no carriage was sent for me, and I intend he shall atone for that rudeness by-and-by. The younger son, the mother, and the girl received me patronizingly, and I understood the simple souls at once. Monsieur (as I shall call him, as names are unsafe) was unapproachable, and took no pains to conceal his dislike of governesses. The cousin was lovely, but detestable with her pride, her coldness, and her very visible adoration of Monsieur, who let her worship him, like an inanimate idol as he is. I hated them both, of course, and in return for their insolence shall torment her with jealousy, and teach him how to woo a woman by making his heart ache. They are an intensely proud family, but I can humble them all, I think, by captivating the sons, and when they have committed themselves, cast them off, and marry the old uncle, whose title takes my fancy."*

"She never wrote that! It is impossible. A woman could not do it," cried Lucia indignantly, while Bella sat bewildered and Mrs. Coventry supported herself with salts and fan. Coventry went to his brother, examined the writing, and returned to his seat, saying, in a tone of suppressed wrath, "She did write it. I posted some of those letters myself. Go on, Ned."

"I made myself useful and agreeable to the amiable ones, and overheard the chat of the lovers. It did not suit me, so I fainted away to stop it, and excite interest in the provoking pair. I thought I had succeeded, but Monsieur suspected me and showed me that he did. I forgot my meek role and gave him a stage look. It had a good effect, and I shall try it again. The man is well worth winning, but I prefer the title, and as the uncle is a hale, handsome gentleman, I can't wait for him to die, though Monsieur is very charming, with his elegant languor, and his heart so fast asleep no woman has had power to wake it yet. I told my story, and they believed it, though I had the audacity to say I was but nineteen, to talk Scotch, and bashfully confess that Sydney wished to marry me. Monsieur knows S. and evidently suspects something. I must watch him and keep the truth from him, if possible.

"I was very miserable that night when I got alone. Something in the atmosphere of this happy home made me wish I was anything but what I am. As I sat there trying to pluck up my spirits, I thought of the days when I was lovely and young, good and gay. My glass showed me an old woman of thirty, for my false locks were off, my paint gone, and my face was without its mask. Bah! how I hate sentiment! I drank your health from your own little flask, and went to bed to dream that I was playing Lady Tartuffe—as I am. Adieu, more soon."

No one spoke as Edward paused, and taking up another letter, he read on:

"My Dear Creature:

"All goes well. Next day I began my task, and having caught a hint of the character of each, tried my power over them. Early in the morning I ran over to see the Hall. Approved of it highly, and took the first step toward becoming its mistress, by piquing the curiosity and flattering the pride of its master. His estate is his idol; I praised it with a few artless compliments to himself, and he was charmed. The cadet of the family adores horses. I risked my neck to pet his beast, and he was charmed. The little girl is romantic about

flowers; I made a posy and was sentimental, and she *was charmed. The fair icicle loves her departed mamma, I had raptures over an old picture, and she thawed. Monsieur is used to being worshipped. I took no notice of him, and by the natural perversity of human nature, he began to take notice of me. He likes music; I sang, and stopped when he'd listened long enough to want more. He is lazily fond of being amused; I showed him my skill, but refused to exert it in his behalf. In short, I gave him no peace till he began to wake up. In order to get rid of the boy, I fascinated him, and he was sent away. Poor lad, I rather liked him, and if the title had been nearer would have married him.*

"Many thanks for the honor." And Edward's lip curled with intense scorn. But Gerald sat like a statue, his teeth set, his eyes fiery, his brows bent, waiting for the end.

"The passionate boy nearly killed his brother, but I turned the affair to good account, and bewitched Monsieur by playing nurse, till Vashti (the icicle) interfered. Then I enacted injured virtue, and kept out of his way, knowing that he would miss me. I mystified him about S. by sending a letter where S. would not get it, and got up all manner of soft scenes to win this proud creature. I get on well and meanwhile privately fascinate Sir J. by being daughterly and devoted. He is a worthy old man, simple as a child, honest as the day, and generous as a prince. I shall be a happy woman if I win him, and you shall share my good fortune; so wish me success.

"This is the third, and contains something which will surprise you," Edward said, as he lifted another paper.

"Hortense:

"I've done what I once planned to do on another occasion. You know my handsome, dissipated father married a lady of rank for his second wife. I never saw Lady H_____d but once, for I was kept out of the way. Finding that this good Sir J. knew something of her when a girl, and being sure that he did not know of the death of her little daughter, I boldly said I was the child, and told a pitiful tale of my early life. It worked like a charm; he told Monsieur, and both felt the most chivalrous compassion for Lady Howard's daughter, though before they had secretly looked down on me, and my real poverty and my lowliness. That boy pitied me with an honest warmth and never waited to learn my birth. I don't forget that and shall repay it if I can. Wishing to bring Monsieur's affair to a successful crisis, I got up a theatrical evening and was in my element. One little event I must tell you, because I committed an actionable offense and was nearly discovered. I did not go down to supper, knowing that the moth would return to flutter about the candle, and preferring that the fluttering should be done in private, as Vashti's jealousy is getting uncontrollable. Passing through the gentlemen's dressing room, my quick eye caught sight of a letter lying among the costumes. It was no stage affair, and an odd sensation of fear ran through me as I recognized the hand of S. I had feared this, but I believe in chance; and having found the letter, I examined it. You know I can imitate almost any hand. When I read in this paper the whole story of my affair with S., truly told, and also that he had made inquiries into my past life and discovered the truth, I was in a fury. To be so near success and fail was terrible, and I resolved to risk everything. I opened the letter by means of a heated knife blade under the seal, therefore the envelope was perfect; imitating S.'s hand, I penned a few lines in his hasty style, saying he was at Baden, so that if

Monsieur answered, the reply would not reach him, for he is in London, it seems. This letter I put into the pocket whence the other must have fallen, and was just congratulating myself on this narrow escape, when Dean, the maid of Vashti, appeared as if watching me. She had evidently seen the letter in my hand, and suspected something. I took no notice of her, but must be careful, for she is on the watch. After this the evening closed with strictly private theatricals, in which Monsieur and myself were the only actors. To make sure that he received my version of the story first, I told him a romantic story of S.'s persecution, and he believed it. This I followed up by a moonlight episode behind a rose hedge, and sent the young gentleman home in a half-dazed condition. What fools men are!"

"She is right!" muttered Coventry, who had flushed scarlet with shame and anger, as his folly became known and Lucia listened in astonished silence.

"Only one more, and my distasteful task will be nearly over," said Edward, unfolding the last of the papers. "This is not a letter, but a copy of one written three nights ago. Dean boldly ransacked Jean Muir's desk while she was at the Hall, and, fearing to betray the deed by keeping the letter, she made a hasty copy which she gave me today, begging me to save the family from disgrace. This makes the chain complete. Go now, if you will, Gerald. I would gladly spare you the pain of hearing this."

"I will not spare myself; I deserve it. Read on," replied Coventry, guessing what was to follow and nerving himself to hear it. Reluctantly his brother read these lines:

"The enemy has surrendered! Give me joy, Hortense; I can be the wife of this proud monsieur, if I will. Think what an honor for the divorced wife of a disreputable actor. I laugh at the farce and enjoy it, for I only wait till the prize I desire is fairly mine, to turn and reject this lover who has proved himself false to brother, mistress, and his own conscience. I resolved to be revenged on both, and I have kept my word. For my sake he cast off the beautiful woman who truly loved him; he forgot his promise to his brother, and put by his pride to beg of me the worn-out heart that is not worth a good man's love. Ah well, I am satisfied, for Vashti has suffered the sharpest pain a proud woman can endure, and will feel another pang when I tell her that I scorn her recreant lover, and give him back to her, to deal with as she will."

Coventry started from his seat with a fierce exclamation, but Lucia bowed her face upon her hands, weeping, as if the pang had been sharper than even Jean foresaw.

"Send for Sir John! I am mortally afraid of this creature. Take her away; do something to her. My poor Bella, what a companion for you! Send for Sir John at once!" cried Mrs. Coventry incoherently, and clasped her daughter in her arms, as if Jean Muir would burst in to annihilate the whole family. Edward alone was calm.

"I have already sent, and while we wait, let me finish this story. It is true that Jean is the daughter of Lady Howard's husband, the pretended clergyman, but really a worthless man who married her for her money. Her own child died, but this girl, having beauty, wit and a bold spirit, took her fate into her own hands, and became an actress. She married an actor, led a reckless life for some years; quarreled with her husband, was divorced, and went to Paris; left the stage, and tried to support herself as governess and companion. You know how she fared with the Sydneys, how she has duped us, and but for this discovery would have duped Sir John. I was in time to prevent this, thank heaven. She is gone; no one knows the truth but Sydney and ourselves; he will be silent, for his own sake; we will be for ours, and leave this dangerous woman to the fate which will surely overtake her."

"Thank you, it has overtaken her, and a very happy one she finds it."

A soft voice uttered the words, and an apparition appeared at the door, which made all start and recoil with amazement—Jean Muir leaning on the arm of Sir John.

"How dare you return?" began Edward, losing the self-control so long preserved. "How dare you insult us by coming back to enjoy the mischief you have done? Uncle, you do not know that woman!"

"Hush, boy, I will not listen to a word, unless you remember where you are," said Sir John, with a commanding gesture.

"Remember your promise: love me, forgive me, protect me, and do not listen to their accusations," whispered Jean, whose quick eye had discovered the letters.

"I will; have no fears, my child," he answered, drawing her nearer as he took his accustomed place before the fire, always lighted when Mrs. Coventry was down.

Gerald, who had been pacing the room excitedly, paused behind Lucia's chair as if to shield her from insult; Bella clung to her mother; and Edward, calming himself by a strong effort, handed his uncle the letters, saying briefly, "Look at those, sir, and let them speak."

"I will look at nothing, hear nothing, believe nothing which can in any way lessen my respect and affection for this young lady. She has prepared me for this. I know the enemy who is unmanly enough to belie and threaten her. I know that you both are unsuccessful lovers, and this explains your unjust, uncourteous treatment now. We all have committed faults and follies. I freely forgive Jean hers, and desire to know nothing of them from your lips. If she has innocently offended, pardon it for my sake, and forget the past."

"But, Uncle, we have proofs that this woman is not what she seems. Her own letters convict her. Read them, and do not blindly deceive yourself," cried Edward, indignant at his uncle's words.

A low laugh startled them all, and in an instant they saw the cause of it. While Sir John spoke, Jean had taken the letters from the hand which he had put behind him, a favorite gesture of his, and, unobserved, had dropped them on the fire. The mocking laugh, the sudden blaze, showed what had been done. Both young men sprang forward, but it was too late; the proofs were ashes, and Jean Muir's bold, bright eyes defied them, as she said, with a disdainful little gesture, "Hands off, gentlemen! You may degrade yourselves to the work of detectives, but I am not a prisoner yet. Poor Jean Muir you might harm, but Lady Coventry is beyond your reach."

"Lady Coventry!" echoed the dismayed family, in varying tones of incredulity, indignation, and amazement.

"Aye, my dear and honored wife," said Sir John, with a protecting arm about the slender figure at his side; and in the act, the words, there was a tender dignity that touched the listeners with pity and respect for the deceived man. "Receive her as such, and for my sake, forbear all further accusation," he continued steadily. "I know what I have done. I have no fear that I shall repent it. If I am blind, let me remain so till time opens my eyes. We are going away for a little while, and when we return, let the old life return again, unchanged, except that Jean makes sunshine for me as well as for you."

No one spoke, for no one knew what to say. Jean broke the silence, saying coolly, "May I ask how those letters came into your possession?"

"In tracing out your past life, Sydney found your friend Hortense. She was poor, money bribed her, and your letters were given up to him as soon as received. Traitors are always betrayed in the end," replied Edward sternly.

Jean shrugged her shoulders, and shot a glance at Gerald, saying with her significant smile, "Remember that, monsieur, and allow me to hope that in wedding you will be happier than in wooing. Receive my congratulations, Miss Beaufort, and let me beg of you to follow my example, if you would keep your lovers."

Here all the sarcasm passed from her voice, the defiance from her eye, and the one unspoiled attribute which still lingered in this woman's artful nature shone in her face, as she turned toward Edward and Bella at their mother's side.

"You have been kind to me," she said, with grateful warmth. "I thank you for it, and will repay it if I can. To you I will acknowledge that I am not worthy to be this good man's wife, and to you I will solemnly promise to devote my life to his happiness. For his sake forgive me, and let there be peace between us."

There was no reply, but Edward's indignant eyes fell before hers. Bella half put out her hand, and Mrs. Coventry sobbed as if some regret mingled with her resentment. Jean seemed to expect no friendly demonstration, and to understand that they forbore for Sir John's sake, not for hers, and to accept their contempt as her just punishment.

"Come home, love, and forget all this," said her husband, ringing the bell, and eager to be gone. "Lady Coventry's carriage."

And as he gave the order, a smile broke over her face, for the sound assured her that the game was won. Pausing an instant on the threshold before she vanished from their sight, she looked backward, and fixing on Gerald the strange glance he remembered well, she said in her penetrating voice, "Is not the last scene better than the first?"

ᐁ The Freak of a Genius

I. St. George and the Dragon

"St. George!"

"Kent."

"We are going out to-night."

"Very well."

"It is now ten. I'll give you half an hour to dress."

"Ten minutes will be quite enough."

"No, we are going among ladies, and you must look your best."

"To hear is to obey."

A pause followed the brief dialogue—a pause during which Kent continued to walk up and down the room and St. George to lie motionless on a couch. Nothing could have been more striking than the contrast between the two. Kent, a man past forty, was as ugly as it is possible for a person to be without any positive deformity. St. George, a youth of nineteen or twenty, was as beautiful as a Greek statue. Kent was very tall, with a student stoop of the broad shoulders; uncouth in figure and ungraceful in gesture. A massive head, covered with a growth of dark hair, already streaked with gray; the lower part of the face was hidden by a shaggy beard; the features were roughly hewn, the cheek bronzed, the high brow lined with marks of thought or care; in the keen, dark eyes lurked a latent fire; his voice was harsh, his laugh sardonic, his manner commanding and abrupt. St. George was of middle height, slender yet well knit, and every limb so perfectly proportioned that strength and beauty were harmoniously blended. His face was classically molded; a low, broad forehead, shaded by clustering rings of bright brown hair, with arched brows darker than the hair; large white lids hid the eyes, and long lashes rested on cheeks as smoothly rounded as a girl's. The nose, that rarely perfect feature, was without fault, yet not characterless, for the disdainful nostrils were full of spirit. A boyish mustache made the red lips look redder, and the graceful chin had the upward curve of the Antinous, giving the face that indefinable expression of power, pride and passion, which redeemed its beauty from effeminacy. Kent roamed to and fro with the restless step of some wild creature caged but not conquered. St. George lay on the low couch, with his handsome head pillowed on his arm, as tranquilly as a sleeping child. Till his friend spoke, nothing had marred the beautiful serenity of his face; now a slight frown contracted the brows, and a petulant motion was observable in one of the crossed feet. Kent paused and eyed him with an air of almost paternal admiration before he spoke again.

"Have you no curiosity to know where you are going?"

"Not a particle," returned the other, without troubling himself to open his eyes.

Kent smiled grimly as he resumed his march.

"Perhaps you will when I tell you more. Listen, if you please."

"I do," and the young man half turned his head.

"You are going to see two young girls to-night—sisters—lovely, accomplished, well-born, rich and beautiful. I intend you to marry one of them, if possible."

At this announcement, St. George opened wide a pair of brilliant dark eyes, full of mingled surprise, amazement and annoyance, as he exclaimed with a laugh:

"Rather soon for that, Kent; I'm not of age yet."

"No matter; geniuses are privileged, and any freak of this sort won't affect your inheritance if I am satisfied, you know."

"But why in such haste? Why must I give up my liberty so soon?" asked the youth, looking pleased.

"I'll tell you why, though giving reasons for my commands and acts was not in the bond. A year ago you became famous by a very successful book. You have enjoyed your laurels for a twelvemonth and are tired of them. The world has petted you, and now begins to expect something new. You must give it amusement in return for its praise, or it will forget you. As yet no second book is ready—"

"Whose fault is that?" interrupted St. George, with an odd smile.

Kent frowned, but took no heed, and rapidly continued:

"There was but one blemish in your first attempt, the critics said. The poet wrote of love, yet it was evident he had never felt it."

"I'm not so sure of that," murmured the boy, with a sidelong glance at his companion.

"Now, in the second book you must prove that you understand the passion of which you write, so make haste and fall in love."

"Upon my life that is the wildest plan I ever heard. How can it succeed when—"

"Leave that to me," broke in Kent. "I have my own motives for the step—nor is it as wild as it seems. You want fame; and, in the eyes of the world a marriage such as I plan for you would much increase that which you already possess. Nothing helps a poet more than living as well as weaving romances, for even those who merely watch these little love dramas are inspired, though they may not have the power to put their admiration into song. You have done well; now I wish you to do better. You are getting indifferent and lazy, you want excitement, and I mean to give it to you."

"Many thanks; but I doubt whether these young ladies will have the power to do so. Am I to adore both?"

"No; the younger is the best mate for you. She is but seventeen, and a very charming creature; the elder is your senior by a year or two, and a genius herself, so you must not think of her."

" 'Two of a trade never agree,' as the old proverb says. I dare say you are right, and resign myself to the charming lady, if you think best," replied St. George, with a yawn.

"You take so little interest in the affair that I will arrange it for you, and give you as little trouble as possible."

"You are very kind; I leave it entirely to you. It would facilitate your project immensely if you would relieve me of the wooing and wedding also."

"Me!"

St. George had spoken impatiently, and a significant smile had touched his lips as he glanced at the rugged figure before him, but as Kent fixed his melancholy eyes upon him with that one reproachful word, the young man sprang up, and laying his hand on the other's shoulder, said, impulsively:

"Forgive me—I forgot myself. Do with me what you will; I'll not rebel."

"Go, then, and dress," was the brief order.

"And you—won't you make yourself fine for the grand interview?" asked St. George, still lingering, as if anxious to atone for some offense.

"I am well enough; who will see me when you are by? I am but a foil to the famous young poet, whose beauty, wit and genius are on every tongue."

There was no bitterness in the tone, but an accent of sadness, which touched St. George, who drew nearer, and said, earnestly:

"Kent, do you repent of your bargain? If so, remember, I release you from it freely, and still remain your debtor."

A singular expression passed over Kent's dark face, ennobling ugliness by sudden benignity. With a paternal gesture he brushed the hair back from the handsome face looking into his own, and answered, cheerfully:

"No, my boy, I never have repented; I think I never shall, for as yet I do not find that I have paid too high a price for affection. Now, go, Apollo, and prepare to meet the Flowers."

"You are getting poetical; see what it is to live with a poet," said St. George, with the odd glance again.

"When you see May and Margaret Flower, you will understand my sudden flight of fancy," returned Kent.

"Pretty names. Are those the fair sisters?" asked St. George, pausing at the door.

"Yes."

"Have you seen them?"

"Yes."

"Spoken with them?"

"Yes."

"And they are handsome?"

"I thought them lovely."

"Are you a judge of beauty?"

"People told me so when I adopted you."

At this reply St. George colored, laughed, and vanished for, though vain, like all handsome men, he was rather shy of any demonstrations of admiration from his own sex.

He was soon back again, looking fresh, *debonnair* and graceful in that most ungraceful of costumes, a gentlemen's evening dress. Not an ornament appeared, but the fineness of his linen, and the exquisite fit of everything, from the perfectly shod feet to the delicately gloved hands, made him, in the truest sense of the word, elegant.

"Not a dandy, thank Heaven!" ejaculated Kent, as he surveyed him critically. "Not even a flower in the button-hole, yet that is permissible in a young poet. Shall I get you one, Saint?"

"No, thank you; I shall have one for every button-hole before I get back. Women are always boring me with bits of laurel and myrtle, and expecting me to wear the rubbish. What pretty fools they are!"

"You are getting spoilt; it is time to teach you to respect the 'pretty fools,' as you ungratefully and ungallantly call your most devoted admirers, by giving you a charming tyrant, who will rule you with a rod of iron. Come, Byron!"

And Kent led the way to the well-appointed brougham which waited at the door.

Half an hour later a sudden stir pervaded a group of young ladies gathered in one of the flowery nooks at Mrs. Dudley Russell's brilliant reception.

"They have come!" passed from lip to lip, in an eager whisper, and all the bright eyes turned in one direction.

"Who have come?" asked a girlish voice in the background.

"St. George and the Dragon."

"Beauty and the Beast."

"The poet and his shadow."

"Mr. St. George and his friend Kent."

Such were the various replies to the question.

"Oh, let me see! I've heard so much of him, I *must* get a sight of the great creature," cried the young voice as a very petite girl thrust her lovely head between the gauzy skirts of her tall companions, and looked intently at a group near the door.

St. George had just been presented to the hostess, and while that gratified lady was pouring forth her compliments, he stood before her with his eyes down, a slight smile on his lips, and an air of well-bred resignation, which caused several of the young ladies to advance to the rescue, and one of those who remained behind to say, compassionately:

"How can Mrs. Russell torment him in that way? He hates being complimented and lionized."

"Then why does he go where he is sure to suffer both inflictions?" said the only young lady who had not left her seat or shown any enthusiasm at the approach of the genius, yet who had, nevertheless, scrutinized the new comers more keenly than any of the others.

"He can't help himself; it is the doom of genius," said the first speaker, sentimentally. "Now they are dragging him away to be victimized by that dreadfully blue Miss Roland, whom he hates. I shall go after them, for though I'm afraid to speak to him, I like to gaze from a distance," and the worshiper departed, leaving the sisters alone.

"Isn't he beautiful?" said May, behind her fan, as St. George disappeared, Kent having vanished as soon as the introductions were over.

"He is too handsome for a man. If he would put on antique drapery and mount a pedestal, I'd admire the boy, but now I like his friend best."

"Oh, Greta, how can you fancy that ugly man? I could not look at him, he is so rough and big and dark. What is there to admire in the Dragon, as they call him?"

"He *is* ugly, but there is nothing repulsive in his ugliness. He has a finer head than the poet. There is a strong, self-reliant look about him that I like, and in his sarcastic voice an undertone of sadness that touches me. I hope he will come and speak to us to-night."

"You always fancy oddities, Greta. I don't, and I long to see St. George again. I shall be afraid to say anything, though he looks so like a boy, but I want to see him nearer. Isn't it wonderful that such a young man should know so much?"

"Yes, but poets learn without books, and comprehend without actual experience. This boy is but twenty, they say, and yet he has the wisdom of a man of fifty. It is one of the miracles which cannot be explained."

A long pause followed, for Margaret fell to musing and May to watching for the reappearance of the young lion. Sooner than she expected he came, with his hostess on his arm, and as they paused before the sisters, Kent joined them. With true breeding Mrs. Russell would have presented the elder gentleman first, but Kent drew back, signifying by a gesture, that St. George should take precedence of himself. Margaret's quick eye saw this; she liked it, and showed that she did, by the gracious reception she gave to Kent, while her greeting to the poet was simply polite. St. George, in obedience to the orders received, devoted himself to the younger sister. A single glance showed him that she was a lovely, shy, yet artless little creature; and anxious to put her at her ease, he assumed his gentlest air, picked up the bouquet she had dropped in her flutter, and taking the chair that stood before her, he said, as simply and naturally as a boy:

"I like hawthorn. What a pretty fancy it was of yours to wear your rosy name-sake."

May blushed and smiled, and quite forgot her fear of the genius when she saw him leaning over the chair-back and looking alternately at her and her flowers with quite the air of a mortal man.

"Greta chooses my bouquets, and never lets me wear hot-house flowers. She has charming taste, though she dresses so plainly herself."

May thought he would look at and admire the lovely sister thus alluded to, but he seemed absorbed in the hawthorn, and never turned his head.

"Are you making poetry?" she said, with a half respectful, half inquisitive expression in her childish face, which made St. George smile as he answered in a confidential tone:

"I never do that now—I'm too lazy."

"But you will some time, it is so beautiful."

"Do you like my verses?"

"Some of them very much, but I'm such a stupid little thing I can't understand all of them," she said, with a contrite air that was charming.

"Neither do I. They are great nonsense, I dare say."

"Oh, don't speak of them so slightingly! Greta says they are wonderful; she understands and admires them, and cries over them, and thinks they are perfect. She is such a talented creature nothing perplexes her, but I'm a dunce, and always shall be," and May shook her pretty head with a despairing sigh.

"I'll write you a song which won't perplex you if I may have a bit of this before I give it back," said St. George, with his hand on a ruddy cluster of the May-bloom.

"Will you really write it for me alone? How proud I shall be of such an honor! Take what you will; I wish it was fresher. Shall I break it for you?"

In her delight, May clapped her hands and tore the bouquet apart to find a pretty bit for the poet's button-hole. St. George glanced over his shoulder at Kent, who stood talking to Margaret. May caught the significant look which passed between the men, saw the smile on her sister's face change to a warning frown, and threw down the flowers, saying, petulantly:

"Now I know I've done something wrong. I am always forgetting myself and shocking people. I never shall learn to behave like other young ladies."

"I sincerely hope you won't," whispered St. George, as he restored the nosegay, and appropriated a portion to himself.

"Why not?" asked May, forgetting her pique in surprise.

"Because I like wild flowers best."

She looked at him an instant with her eyes wide open like a puzzled child, then, as his meaning grew clear to her, she smiled and said, artlessly:

"You mean you like natural, simple people better than prim, artificial ones? So do I, but it isn't the fashion to be oneself, and I am always getting out of order by forgetting the proprieties. Greta is never prim nor artificial, but she can be herself, and yet be charming also. I wish I could," and the bright little face clouded over with a sudden shadow.

"Do you like this sort of thing, Miss Flower?" asked St. George, with a glance about the room, hoping to divert her by a change in the conversation.

"At first I thought I didn't, but now I think I do," and the shadow lifted as suddenly as it fell. "I like dancing better than talking usually, but at these literary places they never dance, and every one is so wise I soon get quite sleepy."

St. George laughed outright, and May joined him, feeling entirely at her ease, for the "great creature" was so friendly and gay, she dared to talk and look as pretty as she liked.

"If you won't betray me, I'll confess that I, too, get so sleepy, particularly when Miss Roland talks to me, that I should disgrace myself by nodding if Kent didn't come and stir me up now and then."

"As Greta does me. But, Mr. St. George, you only say that to make me feel comfortable. You can enjoy all the wise and witty people here, and play your part with the best of them for you are a genius, and know everything they say."

"I wish I did! What do you call a genius?" and St. George, leaning his chin on the arm that lay along the chair back, fixed his handsome eyes on the girlish face opposite with a curious expression.

"I can't tell you. I have a very vague idea that it is something beautiful and splendid; something that everyone admires and wants; and that the few who possess it are very happy and very much beloved. Margaret can tell you better than I. Greta, what is a genius?" and glad to escape the question May turned to her sister, who had paused a moment in her own conversation with Kent to hear what the other pair were saying. Now St. George looked at her, and saw how fair and womanly she was; how sweet and spirited the face; how clear and candid the eyes; how rich in soft tints, smooth curves and graceful lines the tall figure in its simple dress; how full of something nobler than beauty the whole expression was, and how significant of a large, deep nature every hint of voice, countenance and manner were. Looking at him with a searching, straightforward glance that seemed to read him through, she said, in a peculiar tone:

"A genius is one who, possessing a rich gift, regards it with reverence, uses it nobly and lets neither ambition, indolence nor neglect degrade or lessen the worth of the beautiful power given them for their own and others' good."

As she paused St. George's eyes fell like a bashful girl's; he colored, and sat silent for a moment; then as Kent moved away he rose, turned the chair and sat down near Margaret with such an altered air that May shrunk back with sudden timidity, for the boy had vanished, and the man appeared. In five minutes the conversation was far beyond her depth, and finding it impossible to understand, she consoled herself by watching the poet and enjoying his beauty as only a romantic girl could do. Now she felt that he could have written the famous book, for wise and witty words fell from his lips, and the face which had been dreamily quiet while talking with her woke and kindled wonderfully as he spoke with Margaret. Fire, energy and passion passed into the languid youth, and he looked the poet to life. Most women would have caught some reflection of this mood, have been flattered by arousing it, and have shown admiration, if no more, for the eloquence, grace and power of this richly-gifted young man. But Margaret remained unchanged, except to grow more earnest in defense of the sanctity of genius, condemning all who failed in being true to themselves and the power given them. Kent stood a little apart, apparently intent on a portfolio of rare engravings, but May fancied he listened attentively as herself, for she detected an occasional flash of the eye, curl of the lip or involuntary gesture of the head, which betrayed him though he uttered not a word.

A sudden movement toward the supper-room broke up the group. A gentleman took Margaret away; Kent strolled out alone, and St. George turned toward May, who leaned in the sofa corner, looking flushed and uneasy.

"Shall we go?" he said, offering his arm.

"No, thank you; I'm too tired to bear the heat and noise, and the sight of so many people making themselves ill," she answered, adding reproachfully, "I've been trying to follow you and Greta, and have got a headache for my pains."

"Then you shall stay in this quiet corner, and let me take care of you. What shall I bring you?" and St. George assumed a devoted air which appeased the girl at once.

"Anything you like that is cool and sweet. I leave it to you," she said, smiling again as he brought her a foot-stool, drew back the curtain to admit a breath of the mild May air, and then departed with the most flattering alacrity. She felt both melancholy and excited; but before she could discover the cause of this unusual mood, St. George was back again, with a salver, bearing delicate ices, dainty conceits in frosted sugar, and a fine cluster of grapes on a mimic leaf. Drawing up a little table, he arranged the supper temptingly before her, surveyed it critically, and said with a regretful air:

"Neither honey nor dew could be found, so the Flower must accept the best substitutes I could get. Can I bring anything else?"

"Thanks—no—it is charming. I didn't mean for you to bring it yourself; it is too much honor," and May looked quite fluttered, yet pleased.

"Nay, that is for me to say. Have I guessed your taste?"

"Exactly, except the grapes; I never eat them, though I like to see them when they are beautiful, like these."

"Those are mine. May I sit here and enjoy myself if I don't disturb you?" asked St. George, persuasively.

The girl gave a ready assent, and quite glowed with pride as the poet sat down beside her, and, pulling off his gloves, ate grapes and chatted while he paid her the little attentions which women like most. She had her small vanities, and could not help thinking within herself how her companions would envy her could they witness that charming *tête-a-tête,* for St. George was the idol of the fashionable world just then, especially the female part of it. Presently a gentleman appeared, looking anxiously about him, as if seeking for something. His eye fell on the pair sitting in the flowery recess, and he came forward with an eager yet respectful air.

"Mr. St. George, I've been looking everywhere for you. Mrs. Russell begs you will honor her supper-table with your presence."

"Quite impossible, Mr. Albany. I was left to take care of this young lady, who is delicate, and I cannot desert my post, of course. Please make my excuses," was the cool reply.

"Allow me to fill your place here. Madame will be in despair if you fail her," began Albany.

"Go and comfort her despair—there is a good fellow. You should not have found me—it was quite a mistake."

"Kent told me where you were," and a smile came to the speaker's lips, as if called up by some mirthful memory.

"What did he say? Out with it," commanded St. George, with the air of one used to having his own way.

"When I asked where you were, he answered, 'I left the boy playing with a pretty little girl in the red drawing-room.' I beg your pardon, Miss Flower, for Kent's rudeness."

May blushed, but St. George laughed his little laugh, and said, like a spoilt child:

"Go and tell him the boy won't come, for he likes playing with the pretty little girl better than talking with a crowd of grown-up people who make him sleepy."

Much amused, Albany went away, and nestling more comfortably into his corner, St. George said merrily:

"Now they'll be shocked, and say all manner of hard things about me. Abusing the absent will be capital amusement for them—I don't mind, do you?"

"No; but I beg you'll go if you like to. It is very dull here, I know," said May, meekly.

"But I don't like to; I'm going to stop where I am till you are tired of me."

"Then you'll stay a long time," said the girl, innocently.

"Thank you," and he gave her a little bow which made her blush for her frank speech, and hastily add:

"I wonder that you refuse to go and be merry when so many people want you. I should think it would be delightful to be sought after, admired and petted. Don't you like it?" she asked, looking up at him wistfully.

"No, I don't," was the quick answer, as St. George knit his brows, and glanced scornfully about the room so lately filled with admirers. "Miss Flower, it is all humbug; I've done nothing to be proud of, yet a sort of delusion has taken possession of people, and they go on in this absurd manner till, upon my life, I feel like a fool."

"Ah, that is because you are so modest, Greta says true genius is always humble."

"I'm not a true genius then, for I'm as proud as Lucifer."

"I should think you would be of the wonderful poems you've written," began May, with a reverential look.

"They are just what I'm not proud of," was the abrupt reply.

"Why not?" she asked, with the pretty puzzled expression.

"Because I mean to do a great deal better soon."

"I wish I knew what you would write about."

"I'll tell you in confidence," and learning toward her, he said softly, "It will be a love story."

"So was the other."

"Ah, but then I didn't know much about the passion; now I do, and intend to charm you with my little romance. Will you read it?"

May was bewildered by the capricious mood of the young man, but each change attracted and fascinated her in spite of herself. She knew little of the world, and in her child-like simplicity believed that all people were what they seemed. Other men had paid her compliments, looked their admiration, and been devoted, but none had charmed her like St. George, peculiar as he was. "He is a genius, and they are always unlike other persons," she thought; and when he looked deep into her innocent eyes with that softly searching glance, she smiled back at him, and answered readily:

"Oh, yes, I'll gladly read it. Write it soon, and let it be as sweet and simple as the songs were in the other book. I love to sing those, and think them so lovely, I am never tired of hearing them."

"I'll not keep you waiting long. Now we must be firm, for here come some of the grown-up people," and St. George's free, frank manner changed to a cool, indolent air, as he surveyed a flock of young ladies who eyed the pair with various expressions of surprise, envy and curiosity.

"What a flirt that little thing is becoming," said one amiable creature to another, in an audible whisper, as they affected to admire the passion-flowers near by.

"It is really sad to see such art in one so young. Mrs. Russell will never forgive her for keeping him. Of course he couldn't leave her when she asked him to stay; so rude, so very improper," returned the other, with asperity.

"They are at it; isn't it amusing?" whispered St. George—for May looked distressed and angry.

"Not to me; let us talk of something else. Do you think them pretty—they are considered belles."

"I never admire belles. These girls are too large, and gay, and loud; they tire me; I like women to be womanly."

Very low was the whisper, but the listeners heard it, as their suddenly heightened color betrayed, and the indignant glances they cast upon the offender only showed them the look of approval which the poet gave the figure near him. That was womanly in every sense, for out of a cloud of soft white drapery rose dimpled shoulders, fair arms, a blue-eyed, delicately-featured face, and a graceful little head of sunny brown hair, with no ornament but its own luxuriant curls and the rosy hawthorn-flowers. A soft, sweet, tender little creature, half child still; full of pretty caprices, charms and graces, yet wholly unconscious of the artless loveliness which touched and won who-ever approached. Keenly alive to beauty in all its forms, and heartily tired of flattery, St. George found "the pretty little girl" very charming, and her naive expressions of admiration and respect more agreeable than the finest compliments ever showered upon him.

"I'm resigned to the baby," he whispered to Kent, as they followed the sisters to the cloakroom when they left.

What Kent would have answered remained unknown, for May's voice was heard saying within:

"Beauty and the Beast is a better name for them than the others; though it is very rude of me to call them so when Mr. Kent was so kind to me."

"Then don't do it, dear, and remember how, in the fairy tale, the rough disguise of the Beast concealed the heart of a prince," answered Margaret's clear voice.

Both men heard, but neither uttered a word.

II. UNDER THE LINDEN

"GRETA, DO PUT DOWN your brush and talk to me. I'm so tired of being quiet."

"Poor little thing! Did she want some one to play with her?"

"Yes, I do; I wish—" there May checked herself with a smile, for her sister's words suggested something which she did not care to tell.

Margaret looked up from the misty mountains she was painting with exquisite skill, and asked, with a smart mixture of sisterly and maternal fondness in her tone:

"What shall I do for you, dear? You are not well, I fear. You talk in your sleep, look pale, and seem to find pleasure in none of your usual amusements."

"What did I say in my sleep?" questioned May, hiding her face behind her curls.

"Something about liking wild flowers best and hoping somebody would not forget the poem. I spoke to you, and you kissed me and went to sleep again. Of what were you dreaming, child?"

"I don't quite remember. I think I'll take a book and sit in the garden, Greta. Call me if any one comes;" and full of remorse for her fib, May ran away to sit under the blossoming linden, with St. George's poems open on her knee.

It was a charming spot, for the house was one of the delightful little villas which lie just out of London; embosomed in trees, ivy-covered to the chimney-tops, and the garden a wilderness of flowers. Even the hedges that shut it from the highway were full of white and rosy hawthorn blossoms, and the delicate contrast of purple wisterias and golden laburnums. But the fairest object of all was the little figure under the linden. A childish white frock with a violet sash, and clustering curls loose about the shoulders, added to its youthful appearance; yet the charming face wore its most serious aspect, as May leaned her head upon her hand, in a pretty, studious attitude, knitting her brows with deep thought over the poems which she could not understand. So intent was she that a bell rang unheard, voices sounded in the drawing room, the long windows of which opened on the lawn, and figures passed and repassed without disturbing her.

"I never shall like it, and I won't try. 'Prometheus' *is* stupid with his 'strophes' and 'antistrophes,' his vultures and his sea-nymphs. I'll go play," cried the girl, suddenly shutting the book, with a petulant tone and gesture.

"So I would. Cut 'Prometheus' and come and play with me."

The laughing voice startled her to her feet, and the book dropped from her hand as she looked round, with blushing cheek and eager eyes, to meet St. George, who stood there, bare-headed, with a great bouquet of American May-flowers in one hand and a little basket in the other.

"Oh, I am so glad!" escaped from May's lips before she could bethink herself; then, with a comically demure air she offered her hand, saying primly:

"Good morning, sir. I beg pardon for not seeing you sooner."

"I am glad you didn't. I like surprises and pranks of all sorts. Now I must deliver my message before I forget. There are your country-cousins, sent by 'the boy,' who hopes you will give them a welcome;" and, with his most boyish air, he presented the flowers. "This little beast Kent begs you to accept in place of the lost Fanfan, with his compliments;" and, bowing gravely, he produced from a basket a tiny white dog, with a rose-colored ribbon round its neck.

May uttered an exclamation of delight and took the new pet into her arms with an enthusiastic welcome, but still held fast the bouquet, which she had received with a shy "Thank you," and a sudden dropping of the eyes very pretty to see. Resuming her seat, she continued to caress the dog, while St. George lounged upon the short turf at her feet, looking up at her with a half-merry, half-admiring glance which soon set her at her ease.

"Greta should have called me—I told her to," she said, eager to break the silence which fell between them after the first greetings were over.

"Did you expect us?"

"Oh, no, but I wonder I did not see or hear you come."

"You were too busy with that 'stupid "Prometheus";' " and St. George gave her a sly look as he tossed the book away.

"I beg you'll forget that. It is I who am stupid. Let us speak of something else, please," stammered poor May, with scarlet cheeks.

"With all my heart. I've got a question ready, for I am consumed with curiosity about the dog and all the rest of—perhaps I ought not to ask, but I always do as I like; and, as I can get nothing out of Kent, I must apply to you. I want to know where, when and how you met my dear old Dragon, as they call him?"

Much relieved, May answered readily:

"I'll tell you with pleasure, though it will betray what a naughty, disobedient thing I am. You must know that I lost my dog last week; he got out when the garden gate was open, and wandered away over the downs, unless some one stole him in the lane. I was in despair when I came in, and begged to be allowed to go and look for him. But it was late, going to rain, and Greta said, very sensibly, that one of the servants would do it better than I. They went, but didn't find poor Fanfan; and I cried and was very angry, and said I'd go myself, because I knew the man didn't half look. Greta and Mrs. Chandos forbade my going out, but I went, and ran away over the downs, calling my pet, till I came to some gipsies. It was nearly dark, the rain came on, and I was *so* tired; but the gipsy woman offered to show me where Fanfan was if I would give her a shilling. I was rather frightened at them, but I gave her one, and she led me a long way on. What would have come of it I don't know, if I had not met Mr. Kent riding over the common. He saw that something was wrong, for when he came up and looked at us, the woman ran away, and I was frightened to find how far from home I was, and that I didn't know the way back."

"Poor little thing! It was well for you that you did meet Kent," said St. George, sitting up with an interested face.

May half hid her own under pretense of smelling the arbutus and hurried on:

"Indeed, it was, for I was so tired I could hardly walk, and the rain began to pour. He was very kind; I felt at once that I could trust him, and having told my name and story, I just let him do as he liked."

"What did he do?" asked St. George, curiously.

"Put me on his horse, wrapped me in his overcoat, and took me home, talking so pleasantly that I was soon quite gay, and really enjoyed my adventure."

"I wish I'd gone with him that day. I was lazy, so I lost it all," said St. George, regretfully.

"Did he tell you nothing of it?" asked May surprised.

"Not a word. It's like him; he never lets his left hand know the good his right hand does. So this was the way he came to know you? I wondered, but could discover nothing till I saw you at Mrs. Russell's."

"He knew we were to be there, then? Greta asked him to come and see us, or rather Mr. Chandos, our guardian, did, and he promised, but never came till today. People say he is very peculiar—is that so?"

"Yes, but—" here Margaret came stepping lightly over the new-mown lawn, and St. George rose to meet her.

"Mr. Kent is busy in the library with Mr. Chandos, so I came to join you. Pray don't let me interrupt you," she said, with the gentle decision which seemed to be as habitual as the sweet graciousness of her manner.

In speaking, she seated herself by her sister, and the young man resumed his place on the sward before them.

"He was telling me about Mr. Kent. Greta will like to hear; please go on," said May.

And with a more serious air than before St. George obeyed:

"I was merely going to say that, though Kent is peculiar, there is nothing selfish, morose, or disagreeable in his oddities. A more generous, noble, true-hearted man I never knew. His life is full of beautiful charities, which he conceals as jealously as most men hide their sins. Let me tell you one of them. If any apology is needed for doing so, please find it in the fact that you have permitted us to know you, and my desire that you should know us for what we are."

He paused an instant, and Margaret said, with a glance at the book half hidden in the fragrant hay:

"We fancied that we did know you."

He gave her a singular look, and answered, slowly:

"No one knows me but Kent. I'll tell you a story."

And with a rapid change of manner he sat up, fixed his eyes upon the sisters, and giving to his little narrative the magical accompaniments of a fine voice, handsome face, and graceful gesture, he went on.

"Nearly five years ago, a boy of sixteen came up to London to seek his fortune, as many another ambitious lad has done. He was the son of a gentleman, but very poor, an orphan, and alone in the world. He fancied himself a poet and brought his first efforts to the great city where so many fail—so few succeed. Without friends, fortune, name or influence, the boy could scarcely hope to find a foothold in the crowd; but he did his best, fought against defeat, neglect, poverty, and despair, till his heart failed him, and having lived like poor Chatterton, at last prepared to die like him. In that dark hour chance—no, Providence—sent him a friend, a solitary man, who, having known something of like suffering in his youth, had not forgotten it in after years when fortune favored him. This man saved the boy, heard his story, saw his need, pitied his failure, and took the lonely lad into the shelter of his kind heart, his luxurious home, there to be cherished, helped and inspired till he won a most undeserved success. Miss Flower, do you understand my story?"

With his own face flushed and kindled with emotion, St. George looked up into the two lovely faces before him, and was satisfied. Tears stood in the eyes of both, for the little tale had been well told, and a generous deed possesses in itself the power to touch and win all hearts. Margaret silently offered him her hand as if to assure him that this confidence would be no bar to the friendship just begun. May turned a remorseful glance toward the house, remembering her dislike of the man who had served her. As she looked, Kent appeared with his host, going toward the greenhouse. Obeying the impulse of the moment, May dropped both dog and posy in her sister's lap, and ran across the lawn, exclaiming, with a grateful voice, and both hands eagerly extended:

"Oh, Mr. Kent, let me thank you again for your great kindness and your remembrance of my loss!"

Those left behind saw Kent's grave face brighten as he took the little hands in his and looked down at the pretty creature with an almost tender smile. What he said they could not hear, but as he went on, with May still beside him, looking up with eloquent eyes and grateful words, while he half bent to hear and answer her, still wearing that softened look, St. George and Margaret glanced at one another with one of those involuntary impulses which sometimes make strangers forget that they are strange when the same thought suddenly fills both minds at once. Neither spoke, yet both said within themselves: "Perhaps those two will love." St. George half smiled as his eye came back to Margaret, but she half frowned, and a deeper tinge of color came up in her cheek. With one of the inexplicable caprices of a woman she let the nosegay slip from her hold and roll down upon the grass, as she caressed the little creature nestling in her silken lap.

"I never knew there was such a charming nest as this so near London," began the young man, abruptly, as the others vanished and his companion did not speak.

"Mr. Chandos found it for us. We have been abroad for a year, and when we returned we could not bear to go back to the old home, empty now, so we came here."

Involuntarily St. George's eye rested on the sombre dress which Margaret wore, and an expression of sympathy passed into his face.

"I'll persuade Kent to find another for us. I'm going to work soon, and must be in the country. I fancy it will be difficult to discover another such wilderness of sweets so near town."

"No, there are several near by. Mr. Chandos can tell you all about them." Very cool and quiet was the reply, and St. George fancied that he detected a sudden expression of dissatisfaction in the young lady's half averted face, and was piqued to see it.

"I shall be of age in a few months, and then I can choose for myself, if Kent objects; but I don't think he will. He spoils me by indulging every whim."

"As I do May. My four-and-twenty years make me feel old enough to be her mother, she is such a child; and, mother-like, I spoil the little one."

"What did she say that for?" thought St. George, rather nettled at the speech, which seemed made for a purpose. "Why tell me she is four years older than I, and May a child? Does she wish to warn me from herself or her sister?" He eyed her with a covert glance, but could make no discovery except that the long curled lashes of her downcast eyes were very beautiful.

"I wish I had some one to spoil; it must be pleasant," he said, laughing. "I've tried dogs and horses, and tired of them. Kent won't stand petting, and I have no little sister. What shall I do, Miss Flower?"

"Pet your muse, as a poet should," was all the answer he received to his sentimental question, and before he could put another, Margaret asked, with one of her keen glances:

"Are the published poems your earliest ones, Mr. St. George?"

"No," was the reply, after an instant's hesitation.

"I thought not."

"May I ask why?"

"Because there was a power and depth of thought in them such as few boys possess, even when born poets."

"I'm only a boy now, you know."

"Not exactly; at least not always or with all people."

"Ah, you've found that out, have you?"

"Yes; I am quick at finding out things of all kinds."

"I wish there was anything interesting to find out about me, I'd like to try your powers; but I've told you all there is to tell," he said, with his charming laugh.

"Have you?"

The sudden question, which seemed to escape her lips involuntarily, as well as the quick glance she gave him, made St. George color and look daunted for an instant.

The whole thing was over in a moment—speech, look, blush and start, and Margaret was quietly settling the ribbon on Fanfan's neck, while the young man said, easily, as the others appeared:

"I've not seen the aloe Mr. Chandos spoke of; may I go and look at it while Kent enjoys a *tête-a-tête* under the linden?"

"Certainly; shall I not come and show it to you?"

"Thanks, but that would disappoint Kent. Perhaps your sister will be kind enough," and as the other pair approached he went to meet them. May readily offered to do the honors of the aloe, and Kent advanced alone, for Mr. Chandos had been called away. Why Margaret put down the dog and took up the bouquet it would be hard to say. Kent observed the change, and a sarcastic smile passed over his lips, though he said with unusual gentleness as his eye followed the young pair:

"There is a pretty picture for your brush. One seldom sees so much beauty so well matched. Pardon my admiration, but I'm very proud of the boy, as you may well be of your sister."

To St. George, Margaret had been frank and cordial; to Kent she seemed shy and cold, and a sense of disappointment came to him as she looked only at her flowers, and answered briefly:

"Yes; you have a right to be proud of your *protégé.*"

Then, as if desirous of turning the conversation, she asked:

"When are we to have a new book?"

"In autumn, I believe."

"Does he write much?"

"At times, like all authors, he is ruled by moods. You like his first attempt, your sister tells me."

"I admire it intensely, and find wonderful promise in it; almost too much, perhaps, for such genius reminds one of the old saying, 'Whom the gods love, die young.' "

"He'll not die young if care can keep him. Yet I am anxious sometimes lest the very gift meant to be a blessing should prove a curse."

"May I ask how?" and Margaret looked with surprise into Kent's peculiar face, now so melancholy with a sudden shadow.

"I will gladly tell you if you care to hear. Saint is young in heart, though old in mind, and our solitary life is bad for him. It seems a gay one to others, but we cannot always enjoy society, and our home is not what it should be for a sensitive nature like his. I intend that this shall be changed; the magic of a woman's presence is needed, and he shall have it."

"I understand—it will be wise," said Margaret, not quite knowing what to say, and thinking this a somewhat peculiar subject for conversation; but then Kent was a peculiar man, she remembered.

"I am glad you think so. I'll have no wasting of heart and life in frivolous flirtations or worse. Young as he is, he shall be kept safe and happy by a home and wife of his own."

"He! I thought you meant yourself," said Margaret, with irrepressible surprise.

"I marry!" and Kent laughed a sardonic laugh, which affected the girl more sadly than the most pathetic complaint, for it seemed to say, "Who could love *me*."

"I beg pardon, I never thought of one so young as he marrying; yet it may be well, as you say, for poets' hearts are often vagrants, and need anchoring more than others less richly freighted," she said, hastily.

"He has genius, youth, beauty and fortune; I think he will not ask in vain. If I could see him happy, I should feel as if I had done him no harm."

"Harm!" interrupted Margaret; "that is impossible. He has been telling us the good you have done him, and I consider you the greater poet of the two, for such acts outlive the finest verse."

Kent gave one look at the face which shone with a sudden glow of feeling, as the impetuous words sprang from her lips; then averting his eyes, he said impatiently:

"Foolish lad, why did he bore you with that old story when I forbade it? Do me the honor to forget it, and see in him only what the world sees. We are staying too long; where is he?" Kent rose as he spoke, and looked about him as if eager to be gone. Margaret rose also, saying earnestly, as they walked across the lawn:

"Forgive me that I spoke of this, and do not reproach St. George because gratitude outweighed discretion. I shall never speak of it, but I do not wish to forget. They are in the greenhouse. Shall we go to them?"

Smoothing his brow Kent followed her, and when he found the young people loitering among the roses, quite unconscious of the lapse of time, he smiled his benignant smile and looked well pleased.

"Adieu, little Paradise," said St. George, as he entered the drawing-room, with a backward glance at the blooming nook behind him. Then, as he touched May's hand, he said softly, "Look at 'Prometheus,' and see if you don't understand it now."

The instant they were gone the girl flew to the garden, caught up the book, and turning to the page, found between the leaves, worn by her long study, a paper bearing "Lines to a May-flower." Very musical were the smoothly flowing stanzas, and very sweet the sentiment they expressed, but as Margaret read them, over May's shoulder, she shook her head and said half aloud:

"The boy wrote those, not the author of the book. He suits his song to his reader. Poor little May, the peace of your Paradise is already disturbed."

But May did not hear; eyes, heart, and soul were all intent on the poem, which she understood only too well, yet pondered over half the morning under the linden.

III. A Chink in the Wall

Hyde Park was all alive with fine equipages, gay liveries, handsome women, magnificent horses, and accomplished equestrians. Rotten Row was crowded, for it was the fashionable hour. An exciting sight to lookers-on, as well as riders, for the fresh spring air was exhilarating, the animals were full of spirit, the riding costumes new, and every one bent on beginning the season with *eclat*. The Ladies' Mile was a succession of gorgeous footmen, coroneted carriages, and dashing vehicles of all sorts, driven by equally dashing exquisites, who, glass in eye, criticized the blonde beauties, languishing and chatting as they drove under the ancient oaks that cast their shadows everywhere. Two gentlemen came slowly up the row, both well mounted, both good riders, and both attracting much attention, one, apparently, by his extreme plainness, the other by his extreme beauty. The elder rode tranquilly on, briefly answering when spoken to, and seeming busy with his own thoughts; the younger was quite conscious of the glances which followed him, but seemed intent on finding some one, for his eye scrutinized every party of gay girls who cantered by and dived into every carriage which drew up outside the railing. His quest was vain, and abruptly turning his horse, he said, impatiently:

"Come and have a rousing gallop over the downs. I'm tired of this treadmill."

"Are you now?" asked Kent, with a significant glance before him.

"No!" and the young man's face brightened as he saw two ladies, followed by a gray-haired groom, coming toward them at full speed, vails flying, cheeks glowing, eyes sparkling, and slender figures erect, riding with the grace and skill which only English girls possess. With a laugh and a bow they dashed by, but, wheeling about, St. George and Kent gave chase, till all four drew bridle at the entrance of the row.

"Now let us walk back; May is not strong enough for more than one race a day," said Margaret, when they had exchanged half-breathless greetings, and brought the spirited horses into order.

Back they paced, the sisters side by side, with Kent next the elder and St. George next the younger.

"Have you been so busy all this week that you could not come and let me thank you for the lovely May flowers?" asked May, with a reproachful glance at the gallant figure next her.

"I wanted to come, but Kent wouldn't let me; he said it was too soon."

"I thought you always did as you liked?" said May, slyly.

"So I do with every one but the Dragon. My will has to bend to his sometimes."

"Isn't it hard? I hate to obey."

"Yes, it's very hard just now; for he orders me out of town, and I want to stay."

"Why, the season has just begun," and May's face fell.

"That is why he takes me away; too much gayety is bad for me."

"Are you to be gone all summer?"

"Yes; we are off to-morrow."

"A pleasant trip," was all the girl could say, for he was watching her, and no affected indifference could hide the disappointment she felt. With a man's pleasure in trying experiments with a woman's heart, St. George saw and was satisfied with this evidence of his power, for the ingenious little face betrayed every emotion as it rose.

"You remain at Linden Lodge till autumn, I believe?" he said, carelessly.

"Yes; and it will be very dull for two or three weeks. Greta is obliged to go down to the old place in Devonshire—some stupid business which she must attend to."

"Alone?" asked St. George, with sudden interest.

"No; Mr. Chandos goes with her. I shall be quite forlorn, with only madam and Fanfan."

"Don't you go into company without your sister?"

"No; I don't care for parties yet. I am not regularly out, you know, till next year. Greta takes me now and then, as a change, but it's dull work, I think."

"Wait till your first season begins, and then tell me your opinion. What shall you do to beguile your solitude while Miss Margaret is away?"

"Read novels, pet my dog, study Italian, and grub in the garden, because madam thinks it good for my health."

"May I send you the first chapter of my romance to amuse you?"

"Is it begun?"

"Yes; the first lines were written the night of Mrs. Russell's reception. Will you read it?"

"I shall be charmed to do so. When will it be finished?"

"In about a month, I think," and St. George gave her such a peculiar glance that she paused to wonder what it meant and why it made her heart beat quicker than before.

"You must promise to keep it secret, Miss Flower. No one is to see or know about it but yourself."

"Not even Greta?"

"By no means. I want your opinion only, and feel much honored by your consent. You'll promise?"

It was impossible to resist the persuasive tone, the half-pleading, half-command-ing eyes, and the flattering thought that she alone was to see the wonderful and new romance first.

"I promise—don't keep me waiting long," she said, like a child eager for some much-desired pleasure.

"You shall have it soon; but don't expect it by post or messenger. It will come in a mysterious way when you least look for it. I thought that would amaze you," and St. George's laughing eyes very plainly expressed that amazement became her well.

Meanwhile Margaret was getting bewildered by Kent. In chatting over the vari-ous topics of the day they touched upon a recent marriage which had caused much excitement by the discovery that the bridegroom was an imposter.

"But she forgave him, and they seem happy, I am told," said Kent, in his sarcastic tone.

"That is what surprises me. I cannot fancy the possibility of pardoning a fraud like that," replied Margaret, warmly.

"She thought, doubtless, that the humiliation of such a discovery was punish-ment enough, and as he really loved her, she generously forgave the wrong."

"She will repent of it, I am sure. I met the man once or twice, and felt an instinctive distrust of him. He had a false face, his manner was uneasy, and he never looked me full in the eye; I always judge a man by that."

"A hard test for a young man, Miss Flower."

"Nay, don't turn the subject by a compliment, Mr. Kent. An honest man, old or young, can look a woman in the face, and let her read his own."

In speaking Margaret always fixed her eyes upon the person addressed with a clear, candid gaze peculiar to herself. She had been looking so at Kent, when, to her surprise, she saw him suddenly flush to the hat-brim and droop his eyes. This change in him made her add involuntarily:

"Can you?"

Instantly, with an almost haughty gesture, he turned and fixed on her a glance so strong and steady that it bore down her own, and brought the color to her cheeks, as she said, hastily yet with dignity:

"Pardon me, I am very rude, but I have such an intense love of truth I almost unconsciously test every one who comes near me. I might have known that you would not be found wanting."

"Be not too sure of that; no man is without something which he would gladly conceal."

He spoke gravely, and for a moment both rode in silence. Then, more abruptly than usual, he asked:

"Don't you think there may be cases where a person should be forgiven for deceit if the motive be a generous one?"

"No; better die than look, utter or act a lie. Deceit is almost the only sin *I* cannot pardon."

She spoke forcibly, and eyed him keenly, seeing with pain that his dark cheek paled a shade as he said in a low voice:

"You are right; sooner or later comes discovery and humiliation."

"He thinks of some one who has deceived him and whom he has forgiven," said Margaret to herself, wondering at the changes of that usually impassive face. Here they reached the great gate, and turning to her sister, she said:

"We must go, dear; it is nearly six."

"Good-by as well as good-evening," returned St. George, lifting his hat.

"Are you going away?" asked Margaret, quickly.

"Yes—you, also, your sister tells me."

"And I am called to Paris for a week or two; what a scattering of—may I say friends?" and Kent looked at May with an earnest, troubled look, which puzzled Margaret more than all the rest.

For a moment they talked together, the two elders, but St. George sat silent, bare-headed and smiling, with his brown curls stirring in the wind and his delicate, ungloved hand playing with the mane of his fiery black horse. A comely figure touched with the spring sunshine, and of all the admiring eyes fixed on it, May's were most eloquent; but her face was rather tragical as she watched the friends ride away, and all the charm of time and place seemed to vanish with them.

"Now, Saint, remember, I trust you. Do nothing till I return. I'm not sure that it is wise to carry out my plan, so be prudent, and do not commit yourself yet," said Kent, next morning, as he was departing.

"You are getting as capricious as a woman. You order me to fall in love, and when I obey, then comes a counter order, and I'm expected to execute both. What has changed your mind?" demanded St. George. But, ignoring the question, Kent asked anxiously:

"Have you fallen in love?"

"I think I have," he answered, with averted eyes.

"A boy's fancy, soon forgotten, I dare say."

"No, I'm a boy in many things, but not in this. I'll not trifle with the girl, Kent: you bade me marry her, and I will, but in my own way. My happiness is at stake here, not yours; I obeyed for your sake; now I must go on for my own."

"I undertook too much when I began to shape your career; I see it now and doubt my power. Well, be careful while I am gone, and when I return the affair shall be settled. You agree to this?"

"Yes, if I must," returned the other, moodily.

"Good. You will find everything ready at the Larches, for that whim shall be gratified if the other cannot. Good-by, my boy; enjoy your freedom, but do not misuse it," and with an anxious mien Kent set out for Paris, whither business called him.

As he drove away, St. George muttered, with a resolute frown, which ended in a mischievous smile:

"I'll show him that the boy has a man's will, and take him at his word. I'll prove to Margaret that there are some things which she cannot discover, and I'll enjoy my holiday in my own fashion. Now for the Larches and the fascinating baby."

On the afternoon of this same day, May sat in the garden, listless and lonely, longing for something pleasant to happen, though what she desired that vague something should be she would not confess even to herself.

Suddenly, from the adjoining garden, came the sound of voices and the scent of a cigar. The house had long been vacant, and, prompted by girlish curiosity to discover who the new tenants were, May ran to a shady corner of the wall, softly put aside the thick curtain of ivy, and peeped through a wide chink made by a missing stone.

A hammock was slung between two trees, and luxuriously swaying and smoking in it was a young man. He was apparently taking his dessert on the lawn, for decanters, fruit and glasses stood on a rustic table near by, and a servant was just retiring with an empty tray. All this May saw before she caught a glimpse of the stranger's face. Half rising to lay a paper on the table, she saw, with a start of joyful surprise, that the new comer was St. George.

"This is the country, and here he means to stay all summer," was the thought that flashed through her mind as she crept away with all the listlessness gone from her face, the loneliness from her heart.

"What will he do? When will he discover himself? How shall I meet him?" and absorbed by these unanswerable questions, May sat blushing and smiling till a little white object, tied to a great bunch of roses, came flying over the wall. A mirthful "Thank you!" escaped her, as she took it up, and a moment after St. George's head appeared above the ivy-covered barrier.

"How did you know I was here?" he asked, with a laughing salutation and much surprise in his tone.

"I saw you," answered the girl, entering into the prank with all her heart.

"How? The windows of your house don't overlook my lawn, " he said, looking about him as if rather disappointed at the partial failure of his surprise.

"Ah, that you must discover for yourself. I have my secrets as well as you."

"You looked over the wall?"

"No."

"Through it, then?"

"How could I?"

"I'll tell you directly," and he vanished. Very soon she heard a satisfied, "Ah, ha, here it is!" and saw a hand beckoning through the chink. Going to it, she unconsciously made a charming little picture, by peeping under the ivy which framed her face with its green tendrils.

"This friendly hole was doubtless made by some modem Pyramus and Thisbe.

It is just what I want, a romantic post-office for my romantic dispatches. May I use it?" asked St. George, peeping back at her and making a picture of himself as well.

"If you like. But tell me how you came there? I thought you were going into the country."

"So I was, and here I am. Kent has shut me up to do my task; I'm to work hard all day and enjoy myself in the evening. Isn't that a hard fate? I hope you'll take pity on me and let me come for a visit now and then, if I'm good?" said the persuasive youth.

"If Mrs. Chandos is willing"—began May, with a cordial welcome in both voice and eyes.

"She is; I told her in confidence that we were going to take this house, and she was delightfully hospitable. How does the Italian and the gardening come on?"

"I've done neither. Greta only went this morning, and it takes me a day to get over the parting. Now I shall go and read the romance while you finish your dessert."

"Please put it in the office, with your comments and criticisms, when you are done. Postage is a shake of the hand. Let us pay it now, lest we forget."

May paid it graciously, and went back to read the beginning of a love story singularly like her own. From that hour an enchanted life began for her, and the little garden became in truth a paradise. Each day brought a new chapter to both written and living romance, each sweeter than the last, and the only comments made were smiles and blushes, timid praises, and sometimes tender tears over sorrows which she had never felt. She understood this poem perfectly; it needed no explanation, and its author found "the stupid little thing" wonderfully quick to see and feel the workings of the passions he portrayed. Often he came openly, and was soon a universal favorite in the house, but the pleasantest hours he spent were those passed under the linden or chatting in the twilight through the chink. May wrote but seldom to her sister; and having delayed at first to speak of the new neighbor, deterred by a playful request from him to let his arrival be a surprise, she made no allusion to the change in her life or the more marvelous change going on in her young heart. Both Margaret and Kent were delayed longer than they expected, neither dreamed of the dangerous play the young people were at, and so the weeks went on till the fourth brought them back to find the mischief done.

"Where are madam and my sister?" asked Margaret, finding none but servants to welcome her on her arrival.

"Mrs. Chandos is in the park. Miss May went last evening to Mrs. Russell's and remained to pass the day. She left a note for you, in case you came, miss," and the footman brought it.

Warm and weary with her journey, Margaret went out into the garden, cool with the long shadows of late afternoon, and, sitting on the rustic seat, opened May's note to find a single line:

"Look in the chink of the wall and take what you discover."

"Dear little girl, she has prepared some pretty surprise for me," said Margaret, smiling, as she went to the remembered spot. But the smile faded suddenly, for all she found was a letter, and a foreboding fear thrilled through her as she drew it out.

"Dearest Greta, forgive me," it began. "I fear I am doing very wrong, yet I know that no one but you will reproach me. I have deceived you for a little while, because *he* bade me. Now I'll tell you all, and beg you to pardon me, that nothing may mar my happiness. I've gone away to be married to St. George. He loves me so tenderly I could not refuse, and I, oh, Greta, I would die for him! We did not steal away through fear, but for the romance of the thing. We hated the stir and parade of a fashionable wedding, and, having a fancy to surprise you both, we planned this little flight. By the time you have recovered from it and want us back, we shall be with you. Our guardian and Mr. Kent will not object, and you, dear, will forgive me, though I shall then be no longer your   MAY FLOWER."

How Margaret bore the first shock of this discovery no one ever knew. Kent, coming hastily into the garden, with a face full of dismay, found her sitting, white and still, with the letter in her hand.

"Miss Flower, I swear to you I knew nothing of this," he said, in an indignant, agitated voice, which proved the truth of his assertion. "I did desire it, did speak of it to the boy, did ask your guardian if we might be permitted to come; but my last injunction to St. George was to do nothing till I returned, for even then he loved her."

"How do you know of their flight now?" demanded Margaret, sternly.

"A letter, purposely timed to prevent my interference, reached me in Paris this morning. I came at once, to find myself too late. Read it."

She obeyed, and, in St. George's peculiar handwriting, saw these words:

"DEAR KENT—*I have obeyed your first orders with an obedience which deserves praise. You told me to love and marry as soon as possible. I have done so for it was not 'a boy's fancy soon to be forgotten,' but a man's love, which no obstacle can oppose. We have settled our affairs more promptly than you do yours, and, for such young experimenters, I think we have done well. Mrs. Chandos favors my suit, though she, as yet, knows nothing of the charming* denouement. *In a week we shall return to go down upon our knees in the approved style and ask your blessing. You'll not refuse it, I know. My compliments to sister Margaret and please ask her* if there are not some things which she is not quick at finding out? *Your very happy and, if necessary, repentant son,*

St. George."

Without a word, Margaret gave it back, and, after a moment's hesitation, offered Kent her sister's letter. As he read it, his troubled face cleared, his angry eyes softened, and, when he spoke, his agitated voice was calm and cheerful.

"Pursuit is vain, reproach unavailing, resentment unkind. What can we do but give them pardon and a welcome when they come?"

"I must forgive the deceit for May's sake, but I never can forget it," and Margaret bent her face upon her hands to hide the grief she was too proud to show.

"I do not wonder that your anger falls heaviest on St. George. He deserves it; I make no excuse for him. The willful boy has had his way, and it shall be my care that no unhappiness arising from this hasty act shall reach your sister. She is but a child, easily led, and who can blame her that she yielded to the power which bends the strongest natures?"

"I do not wonder, I pity the weakness; and regret too deeply for words to express that I was not here to save her. They are not well mated; too wide a difference of character, temperament and tastes exists—nothing but misery can come of such a marriage, and I tremble for my little May."

As Margaret looked up with her usually cloudless eyes all wet with tears, Kent turned away with a heavy sigh, for she had expressed the secret fear that haunted him. He knew St. George was one of those of whom might be said, "Unstable as water, thou shalt not excel," and despite the success already his, this friend alone knew what the promise of his future was. Margaret heard the sigh, saw the keen anxiety that came into that rugged face, and the sight of another's trouble made her own seem less. Like all womanly women, the art of comforting was native to her, and generously putting by her grief, she tried to lighten his.

"You are right—regret and anger are useless. We will forgive them; and if any negligence of ours had part in this rash act, we will forgive each other, and atone for it by making those we love as happy as we may."

She tried to speak heartily, and offered him her hand with a half-doubting, half-confiding look, which touched him to the heart. Holding the soft hand in his own, he fixed his searching eyes upon her as he said, reproachfully:

"Do you distrust me? Do you believe that I was cognizant of the plot? that my distress was feigned, my part prepared?"

"I do not; I trust you now; I will never doubt again. It was not that—another thought was in my mind—"

There she paused, coloring faintly as she withdrew her hand.

"Tell me the thought. I have a right to know," and Kent's commanding voice constrained her to reply reluctantly, yet frankly:

"I did not think your distress feigned, but for a moment fancied it might spring from a deeper disappointment than the mere knowledge of St. George's disobedience to your will. I had a passing fear that May might be more to you than a grateful little friend."

Kent started, and the dark glow rose to his forehead as he glanced at Margaret, with the look of one who sees his own thoughts in another's face.

"Have no fears for me. I am not mad enough to dream love-dreams now. I have no right to look at such as May with any but friendly thoughts and hopes."

"Why not?"

The abrupt question passed Margaret's lips unawares, and startled her as much as it did Kent. An expression of sharp suffering crossed his face, and all the melancholy gloomed in his eyes again, as he said, with pathetic humility:

"Ten years ago I asked that question of a woman whom I loved, and she answered, pointing to a mirror which reflected all my ugliness, 'Because women are not blind.' "

"Cruel! It is such as she who *are* blind to that which is better than mere beauty," cried Margaret, with a flash of the eye, a curl of the lip that made her doubly lovely.

Kent smiled the rare smile that softened his whole face, and said, with the dignity of true manhood:

"It nearly broke my heart then, but I was the better for it, and have no right to complain, for others have been kinder to me than I deserve. Ambition was my besetting sin at thirty; a woman's frown killed it, and at forty I have none but to live cheerfully for others."

Warm and bright over Margaret's face shone a glow of genuine admiration and respect for one who bore so beautifully the cross which kept a deep heart solitary.

She said nothing, but that glance of approval was better than words, and an impulsive gesture welcomed him to a seat beside her. With a grateful look he took it, and for an hour they sat together, where the young lovers had so lately been, and talked freely of the future which lay before the truants, for a great surprise, like a great joy or sorrow, sweeps away artificial barriers, and makes strangers friends.

IV. A Little Cloud

THE YOUNG PAIR came home to receive a kinder welcome than they expected or deserved. Mr. and Mrs. Chandos, after the first surprise was over, were delighted at the brilliant match their ward had made, for Kent possessed a princely fortune, and St. George was known to be his heir. Margaret was deeply wounded, and full of sad forebodings, but for May's sake she hid her fears, and was motherly tender over the little bride. St. George she did not forgive, nor did she forget that he had taught her sister the first deceit that ever marred the confidence between them. A few words of reproach and a slight coldness of manner toward him were the only signs she showed of the displeasure and distrust she felt. To her surprise, the chief culprit betrayed no repentance, asked no pardon, and met all reproaches with a defiant gayety which nothing could destroy. From his first interview with Kent he returned with a half-sullen, half-exultant air, which puzzled Margaret almost as much as did the sad humility of Kent's demeanor, for he appeared to assume the burden of the fault and silently endeavor to atone for it. May was too blissfully happy to see or care for any one but her husband, of whom she made an idol, which she worshipped like a devotee. This homage he accepted graciously, and repaid by ruling her with the tender tyranny which brides think so charming for a time.

This hasty marriage produced the effect Kent had foretold. All the world talked of it, ran to see the young pair, re-read the poet's book with renewed admiration, demanded another, and *fêted* and flattered the St. Georges to its heart's content, for youth and beauty, genius and wealth added to the romance, and left nothing for the most critical to desire. The summer was a whirl of gayety; but when the season ended and domestic life began Margaret's forebodings proved true. May pleaded to remain with her sister, so a suite of apartments were fitted up for them in the house of her guardian, and Kent lived alone in the adjoining villa. A door was cut in the wall, and he came and went at will, which was but seldom, till September took the fashionable crowd away. Solitary he lived, yet not indolent, for often, when she went late to bed, Margaret saw his light still burning, and caught glimpses of his thoughtful face bent over books and papers, wearing an expression she never saw at any other time. When his holiday ended, St. George fell to work also in his own peculiar way, and then May's trials began. The butterfly life she had been leading just suited her, and when it ceased she missed it. Love made her selfish and exacting, as it does many a woman who lives in the affections only. Petted and indulged, she knew nothing of self-denial or the art of living for others. St. George had been devoted for three months, and when he left her for hours she was forlorn. She never cared for books, and when they took her husband from her, she hated them. His genius had been her pride while it was satisfied with the results already won; but when it began to long and labor for fresh laurels, she grew jealous of it, and, ignorant of the harm she was doing, wearied and irritated her husband by entreaties, reproaches and complaints. For a time he bore with her, trying to satisfy her by caresses, charming gifts, playful excuses, and every persuasive art in his power. But the girl's heart was awake, and hungry for that genuine love the absence of which she felt long before the hard truth broke upon her. She ceased to be a child, and childish things no longer satisfied her; yet, having taken a woman's duties upon her before she was fitted for them, they burdened and bewildered her, and the hand that should have helped her tenderly was busy painting ficticious woes in most melodious verse. Margaret saw all this, yet could do nothing, for May, with a certain wifely pride, kept the trouble to herself, till her full heart overflowed, and her sister became her *confidante*. One evening Margaret found her sobbing in the sofa corner, and, after some hesitation, received an answer to her anxious questions:

"I haven't seen Saint all day, and am so tried of waiting I must cry. Isn't it unkind of him, when he knows how dismal I am without him?"

"He is busy, dear, and forgets how time goes. He is not unkind but absorbed, and you must not reproach him; for by-and-by you will be proud of the work for which he seems to neglect you now."

"I dare say I shall; but I don't see why he need write so soon and so much. Everyone knows he can do splendid things if he tries; why can't he be satisfied with that for a year or two longer? Greta, I often wish he wasn't a genius, it is so hard to understand and suit him."

"I could have told you that, and prepared you to bear it, had you given me your confidence and waited wisely before you took this great responsibility upon yourself, my poor little girl," said Margaret, sorrowfully.

"I know it; I wish I had; but it is too late now, and I must do the best I can. It would all be easy and delightful if he would only put away that hateful pen, and stay with me all the time as he used to do. One would think he had to earn his bread, he works so hard," returned May, petulantly.

"But the hateful pen is his delight. A man with a gift like his cannot let it be idle; it asserts itself, and he must work as inevitably as the sun shines or birds sing. Do not blame him for that, but be patient now, that you may be proud of him hereafter. Give him entire freedom, and when the composing fever is over he will come back to you all the more fond and faithful for your uncomplaining forbearance."

"Ah, it is easy to advise when one merely looks on. You would be as angry as I am if you knew all. Let me tell you; I must tell some one, and if you won't hear me I shall go to Kent; he is always ready to help to please me."

"Am not I? Dear May, if I have seemed indifferent or cold, it was because I feared to speak. Things are changed now; Saint is more to you than I; he has the first right to your confidence, and I stand aside till you want me, glad and ready always, but not curious or anxious to come between you in any way."

"That is comfortable; now you shall be my Greta again, and let me tell you all my troubles, though I dare say you will only laugh at them."

"Will Saint like it, dear?"

"No, but I shall do as I please. When I go to him with anything that vexes or puzzles me, he only says, 'I'm busy now; another time, love,' and there it ends, for he always is busy, and 'another time' never comes. He is selfish and unkind, and I don't love him half as well as I did, and I told him so yesterday," cried the girl, passionately.

"What did he say?"

"He laughed, and said I spoke like a child who had got tired of her doll, and when I cried, he laughed again and asked if I would like him to go and marry that dreadful Miss Roland as punishment for his sins. He always behaves in that way when I complain, and he treats me as if I was a baby. Ought I to bear it, Greta?"

"Yes, May, bear it till you cure it by proving that you are a woman. Never complain or reproach; be cheerful, kind and gentle. Make happiness for yourself, and learn to get on alone. The wives of geniuses almost always have a high price to pay for the honor of bearing the famous name, the joy of being nearest and dearest to the famous man."

"But I'm not dearest and nearest; he likes that stupid new book much better than he does me, and the way he behaves proves it. You know we were going out to a charming party last night; I made myself as pretty as I could in the colors he likes best, and waited for him. He didn't come, so I went down to his study, and there he was in his house coat, his hair all in a toss, and great blots on the beautiful hands I was so proud of.

" 'Do I look nice, dear?' I asked very sweetly, though I was angry. Wasn't that good of me?

" 'Like an angel,' was all he said, with his pen in the inkstand, and a nod over his shoulder, hardly looking at me.

" 'Won't you come and get ready, please?'

" 'Not now; go with Mrs. Chandos; I'll come by-and-by.'

"I begged and coaxed, but he scribbled on till I took his pen away; then he just said, in the commanding way he's caught from Kent:

" 'You must not distract me now. Go and show the world what a charming little wife I've got,' and with that he led me to the door and bowed me out in his most elegant manner. Well, I went, but he never came, and when I got home he was locked up in the study. I kept awake as long as I could, and this morning found him fast asleep on the couch in his dressing-room. He had his breakfast sent up while we were in the garden, and then ran away to Kent's den, where he has been all day. Oh, Greta, it isn't right! it isn't right!" and the poor girl sobbed again on her sister's shoulder.

Margaret had smiled and frowned as she listened, and when the story ended she sat silent, tenderly caressing the afflicted creature in her arms, much troubled, yet uncertain how to act. May spoke first; looking up with wistful eyes and comically pathetic tone, she said:

"I can't go on so, for I cry and fret, and then I look ugly, and then Saint will hate me, and then I shall break my heart and die. If you were to speak to him in your quiet, wise way, I think it would set everything straight. He has such respect for your judgment and opinions, that he will take your advice and not be offended. He said once that you had the rare art of ruling people without their knowing it. Do try to rule him, and make me happy."

"I will, but you must seem to be the one who wins him out of his abstraction. I'll teach you how, and you must learn to work as well as wait for his life."

"I can't; I don't know how; I've been so petted and spoilt that I can do nothing but fold my hands and be taken care of. You do it, Greta; talk to him and don't be afraid. You are his sister now, and he is so much younger it is quite proper for you to scold him when he is bad. Come, now, I'm going to ask if he is coming home to-night. Kent is out, I know, for I've been watching all the afternoon."

Unable to resist the pleading voice, the eager eyes, Margaret yielded, and they went together through the dewy garden and the little door to the long window of a room on the ground floor at the Larches. A light was burning within, and pausing, they surveyed the scene before entering. St. George was alone; not working, but lying on a couch, looking so wan and weary that Margaret relented and felt a sudden anxiety lest the young man should wear himself out too fast. Two trays stood on a side-table, with dinner and supper both untouched, but among the manuscripts that littered the writing-table appeared a half empty decanter and the remains of a cluster of grapes.

"Worse and worse," thought Margaret, as her eye went from these objects to St. George's face. No inspiration shone there, nor the satisfaction which remains in spite of weariness after successful composition. A bitter, restless, moody expression sat on his face, marring its beauty with the gloom of a desperate melancholy. Neither book, pen, cigar nor glass occupied him, but he lay staring at the wall with bent brows, and the anxious, absent look of a man whose thoughts absorb and harass him.

"Something worries him; we will be kind, and perhaps he will let you comfort him," whispered Margaret. "Go in and pet him, May. Ask no questions, but talk in your pleasant way, and see how he takes it. I'll wait here."

Ready to forgive and forget his neglect and her own displeasure, May stepped in, went to him, knelt down, and with a kiss on his forehead, said softly:

"You are very tired, Saint; won't you come home and let me sing you to sleep as I used to do?"

Turning his head, he gave her a strange look, as if his thoughts were so far away he found it difficult to call them back.

"No, I want nothing," he said, with an effort, evidently having but half heard her question.

"But you must not write any more; it is bad for you; Kent said so, and he knows. Do stop and come away where it is cheerful; we all want you, and I'm so lonely when you are gone. Dear, do you know I have not seen you all day long?"

She laid her head down on the cushion beside his with a treacherous tremor in the voice she tried to make patient and persuasive. But he turned his face away impatiently, and answered with averted eyes, like one driven to say unkind things in spite of himself:

"You have got on alone for seventeen years; can't you live without me one day, you exacting child?"

It wounded May deeply, and froze up the love ready to flow freely forth and comfort him. She rose, grieved and angry, saying reproachfully:

"I shall soon live without you altogether, and learn not to miss you. Will that be pleasant?"

"Try it if you like, then I can tell you," he said with a mirthless laugh, that frightened her.

"Can I do anything for you?" she asked meekly.

"Leave me in peace, if you please."

She turned to creep away, but Margaret arrested her by stepping in with an indignant mien:

"St. George!"

He sprung to his feet as if the clear voice had been a trumpet in his ear, and stood regarding her with the bright, yet half bewildered look of one who starts suddenly from sleep to find his dream a fact. This glance came first, then shame sent a red flush to his forehead and made his kindling eyes falter and fall before her own. An instant he stood so, abashed, yet ghastly, but when she spoke he looked up with the most engaging aspect of penitence and waited smilingly for a reprimand. This sudden change surprised but did not soften Margaret.

"I came with May to find you, and could not help hearing your ungentle welcome; for her sake I speak, and for her sake you must forgive me."

"Say what you will, I'll hear it. But first, let me say that I own I am a surly brute. May is an angel, but she drives me half distracted and being a mortal man, I lose my temper. Is this a kinder welcome, little wife?"

He had spoken frankly, impulsively, and as he ended, turned to May with open arms, and an aspect of repentant tenderness that touched both girls, and conquered one. May clung to him, too happy for reproaches, and softly caressing the bright head leaning on his breast, St. George looked at Margaret, saying humbly, yet with an irrepressible gleam of defiance in his eyes:

"Now, speak; I'm ready for my sentence and my punishment."

"By confession and atonement you have lightened both. Do not offend again if you value May's love and my respect. Now, by way of punishment, I condemn you to a holiday to-morrow and the pain of eating your dinner at once."

"Merciful judge, I thank you. But I've had my dinner," began St. George, evidently relieved at the playful change in Margaret's grave tone. As he spoke, she pointed to the trays, and after a surprised stare at their untouched contents, he said, laughing:

"Upon my word I thought I'd eaten it. I remember some one's blundering in with it some time ago, and my saying, 'I'll come directly,' but I forgot."

"Ah, Saint, better remember the dinner and forget this."

There was an accent of sisterly solicitude in Margaret's voice as she touched the decanter and gave him a warning look.

"Indeed you need have no fears of that sort," he said, eagerly. "I don't love it, and only take it because it keeps me up for a time."

"Burgundy is a bad stimulant for a well man; put it by at once, and drink claret, if anything. You want some one to take care of you, else you will be ill. May I play elder sister in good earnest and attend to these things? for they must not be neglected, unromantic as they are."

"Will you—can you? Won't it be a burden? No, I don't deserve such kindness from you, Margaret!" and St. George's face showed how much he felt this thoughtful friendliness in one whose tastes and pleasures were as intellectual as his own.

"I will with all my heart; but don't thank me too much, for I am selfish in my offer. If you neglect rest and food and proper exercise, you get moody and—shall I say?—irritable. That afflicts May, and her trouble grieves me. If I quietly see that you go on properly, you will be kept in good temper and spirits; May will be happy, and then I am repaid."

A shadow passed over the young man's countenance as he said, with less animation than before, though with grateful eyes still fixed on Margaret's beautiful, benignant face:

"I know it is not for my sake, yet it is pleasant to be cared for by a woman. I never knew my mother, and have been a lonely boy all my life till I met you—and May."

The last words were added hastily, as his wife's little hand came stealing round his neck, a mute reminder that another woman longed to care for him. His tone and look touched Margaret as much as the words; and, seeing that she must take the lead if anything was to be accomplished, she began her work by selecting from the neglected meals such viands as were still eatable, and, arranging them invitingly, rolled up a chair and beckoned him. Putting May aside with a soft word, he obeyed, and ate his dinner with an appetite which he insisted was solely owing to the society of the two charming waiting-maids who served him. Margaret exerted herself to make it a merry meal, and May looked on, wondering at her skill.

"Follow my example another time, dear. Watch and see how I do it, and improve upon it by-and-by," she whispered as she passed her sister on her way to order coffee and send off the decanter.

"I never can. It's lovely to see you do it, but I've no power to imitate you. Go on, Greta—go on; I'll learn perhaps in time, if you are patient with me," sighed May, and then went back to annoy her husband by upsetting glasses, jingling silver, and talking persistently of what he most desired to forget—her entire forgiveness of his late unkindness.

With a warning glance Margaret silenced her, and, as St. George enjoyed the fragrant draught she brought him, she moved about the room, giving those touches by which some women know so well how to change disorder and discomfort into beauty and refreshment. Talking the while in her cheerful way, and soothing the tired nerves with the music of her voice, she shaded the flaring lamp, let in the cool night-air, laden with odors, from the garden, sent away the relics of the dinner, carefully laid the scattered papers straight, and in their midst set a lovely rose from her bosom in the empty wine-glass, as if gracefully hinting that it should henceforth be devoted to this harmless purpose. When all was to her mind, she came up to the young pair, and said, with the motherly smile which made her so womanly and winning:

"Now I shall go away and leave the children to enjoy a quiet hour together. Write no more tonight, Saint, but let May sing to you, and to-morrow we will plan our holiday."

"Stay, Margaret," cried St. George, rising to detain her. "Don't leave us; we shall be happier with you. Stop a little longer; it is so different when you are here. What can I do to bribe you?"

"Read me your new work," she answered, sure that this request would be denied, and so let her escape, for he never had permitted a look, a question, even from May, and was singularly sensitive about showing half-finished poems. But now, to her surprise, he looked gratified, and answered instantly:

"Nothing would please me more. I've longed to show it to you and to ask your opinion. It is done, but still in the rough, so you must pardon imperfections and help me to amend them. Sit here, and let me read, if I'm not too much overcome by this unexpected honor to do justice to myself."

Being really interested and eager to hear, Margaret readily complied, and, refusing the couch that May might sit beside her husband, she placed herself opposite, and soon forgot everything in wonder and delight. With May nestling against his shoulder, his manuscript spread out before him, and the mild light shining down upon his beautiful pale face, St. George read as only a poet can read his own words. At least one listener thought so, and, as the fine voice rolled on through the melodious pathos of the story, it seemed to endow the characters with life, and make an all-absorbing drama of their fictitious hopes and fears. Doubtless the reader received inspiration from the rapt face opposite, so eloquent with the varying emotions which proved his skill in touching the chords of that mysterious instrument, the human heart. May listened in silence, soon perceiving that this was a very different poem from the romance he had begun for her. Any talented and ardent youth could have written that, but only true genius, kindled and uplifted by the strongest passion of a man's life, could have conceived and executed this great poem. Its beauty, tenderness and melody charmed and touched her; but its power oppressed and bewildered her, for she could not comprehend it. St. George seemed to forget that he had two listeners, and addressed himself solely to Margaret, watching covertly the effect which he produced, and exulting in it with a secret joy that glowed and glittered in his face, despite his efforts to conceal it. When the last lines came, stately sweet and solemn, beautifully ending the history of a man whose heroism ennobled life and made death proud to take him, St. George paused and looked at Margaret, waiting for her verdict. Still leaning forward, with clasped hands, lips apart, eyes fixed, unconscious tears upon her cheeks, and over her whole face a radiant expression of admiration, wonder and delight too deep for words, she sat as if still listening to the lay that stirred her to the heart.

"Is it good?" he asked, simply.

She drew a long breath, lifted her hand to put away a braid of hair that had fallen unheeded, felt her wet cheek, and with a brilliant smile, said as her eyes shone into his, as never eyes had shone on him before:

"It is perfect! I have no words strong enough to express my satisfaction. Here is a proof of your power; see, you have won the tribute of tears from eyes that seldom weep."

St. George made no reply, but in his face Margaret saw something that troubled her, and made her add with a woman's tact:

"Ask May her opinion; her praise will be pleasanter than mine."

She turned toward her sister and uttered an exclamation; May was fast asleep. She never forgot the look St. George gave her, as he said, with a bitter smile:

"Is such praise pleasant? Is such appreciation flattering—such society attractive to a man like me? Do you wonder, now, that I prefer solitude? Do you blame me that I lose patience when my most precious hours are marred by foolish demands and peevish complaints? Am I not sufficiently punished for the rash act which binds me for life to a pretty child, when I long for the love, the help, and sympathy of a woman?"

"Hush! She will hear you," whispered Margaret, pale with dismay, for the passion of his last words daunted her by showing in a breath the fulfillment of her worst foreboding. St. George had dropped his head upon his arm, as if to hide the pain he could not control, and at that sight Margaret's womanly heart ached with pity, for well she knew the burden that must weigh down the young man's aspiring spirit. Laying her hand on the neglected curls, she said, softly:

"I do not blame nor wonder—I sympathize and hope. Do not despair, nor think that one act, however unwise, can utterly ruin your whole life. It was a mistake, but it can be retrieved in a measure by love and patience. May will not always be a child; she has a tender heart, a docile nature—you can teach and mold her as you will. Remember that you placed her where she is, and that your first duty is to fit her for the responsibilities you have thrust upon her. I will help you, but never let me hear again what I have heard tonight."

Here May stirred and woke, smiled, and looked about her, happily unconscious of all that had passed, and eager to excuse her rudeness.

"It was lovely, Saint, and I was very impolite to go to sleep; but I was awake so long last night, I really couldn't help it, your voice was so soothing, dear."

"No matter, it was as well perhaps," and St. George broke from her hold to conceal his agitation.

"Poor boy, his head aches, I know. Come home, and let me bathe it, and then go to sleep. Make him, Greta," and May went toward him as she spoke, with the evident intention of coaxing the wayward husband.

"Please go and rest—you need it," said Margaret.

"Come, then," and suddenly taking May's hand, he led her away through the garden, after a backward glance, and brief "Good-night" to her sister.

Left alone, Margaret stood a moment to recover her composure. As her eye roved about the room, trying to recall the scene just enacted there, it fell upon the manuscript and lingered, as if glad to seek comfort in the strong, sweet words she had so lately heard. Turning leaf after leaf, she read on, forgetful of time and place, and all unconscious of Kent's face fitfully appearing and disappearing at the window as he went to and fro with noiseless steps, wearing an expression of mingled remorse and regret, which would have startled her as much as the despairing echo of her own words that broke from Kent's lips, as he turned away from a long look at the figure bending over the book:

"Deceit is almost the only sin I cannot forgive."

V. A DOUBLE DANGER

"BIRDS SING SWEETEST after rain," said Margaret, thinking of the pretty Swedish proverb, as she looked up from her painting to watch May, who was sitting gayly in the garden as she played work. She had undertaken to pull all the dead leaves off the ivy that covered the low wall, and lightened her labors by frequent frolics with Fanfan, much lively chat with Kent, who had gone to help her, and occasional runs into the house to see how the others got on, for Margaret was painting St. George's portrait, by her desire. Matters had gone smoothly since Margaret had begun to take care of the self-forgetful poet. Nothing had been said to Kent, but he seemed to understand the case, and lent his aid unasked, amusing May so skillfully that soon she ceased to complain of her husband's long absences, and always met him when he reappeared with a cheerful face and merry reports of the pleasant adventures she had been having with "dear old Kent." Her prejudice was quite gone, for she had learned to respect and love him, and now thought the grave, plain face the kindest and the truest she had ever seen. Kent was fatherly, patient and tender with her, as if St. George's negligence was but a part of the wrong which he had undertaken to repair. Never too busy to walk, read, or amuse her; never too tired to go her errands; never harsh, sarcastic, or abrupt with little madam, but always the same devoted friend, gentle, wise and just. No wonder the girl loved him, and clung to this strong arm when her capricious mate forgot to offer his. No wonder the solitary man found it sweet to be so loved, and trusted, and conscious of the years that lay between them, saw no danger in the friendship which strengthened daily.

Meanwhile Margaret did her work faithfully, and St. George throve marvelously under her care. As he once said, she was a woman to rule others imperceptibly; he felt, but never saw her power, and soon learned to obey with a docility which surprised the lookers-on. To a young man the interest and influence of a beautiful woman older than himself is peculiarly flattering and powerful. Margaret, on the strength of her four years' seniority, assumed a maternal air, which was very charming, and treated St. George like a boy, thinking this the wisest course to pursue, though she saw that it annoyed him, and was forced to confess to herself that few boys resembled her gifted brother-in-law. With her St. George was always his best self, frank and friendly, grateful and gay, showing her the manliest part of his nature, telling her his hopes and plans, consulting her about his future, and giving her his entire confidence in a way which made it impossible for her to refuse to accept it. Many of their tastes were similar, and, through the medium of the poetry both loved so well they learned to know each other. When May begged for the portrait, her sister found it impossible to deny her, for to an artist a face like St. George's was a strong temptation. She consented, and the first hours of the bright October mornings were spent by her in studying the harmonious lines, soft tints, and varying expressions of that mysteriously beautiful countenance. A change had come to it of late, a tranquil, happy look replaced the former moodiness which often darkened it. He seemed like one who dreamed a pleasant dream and never wished to wake. Margaret did not understand it, but felt its charm, and reproduced it on her canvas with a skill which surprised herself. While she painted, St. George read aloud, or talked, or sat with his fine eyes fixed on her with an intentness that sometimes half abashed her. He was a model sitter, never tired or restless, never critical or imperious, singularly careless about the picture, yet very punctual in his daily appointment. Dangerous hours for these two, as for the other pair who came and went, the one all unconscious of the undercurrent which flowed fast and strong below these quiet lines, the other with eyes grown keen through suffering, watching anxiously the growth of the little cloud which threatened to obscure the sunny day for all.

"Yes, she is very happy now; long may she remain so," answered St. George, as Margaret spoke and his eyes followed hers. May, mounted on a garden chair, was peeping into a deserted bird's nest among the ivy, one hand rested for support on Kent's shoulder, and he stood looking at her with a smile on his lips, but a wistful expression in his eyes, plain to see for his hat was held up to shade the sun from little madam's face. Involuntarily Margaret glanced at St. George expecting to see some sign of annoyance, such as she had often seen there in the first month of his marriage, when admiration for young Mrs. St. George had been too visibly expressed by others. Now he met her glance with a meaning smile, an untroubled face and a careless—

"I'm not jealous; don't be anxious, Greta."

"No, there is no occasion for it. I was thinking of the time when you looked daggers at any one who showed May any kindness or paid her a compliment. You are wiser now, I am glad to see."

"Yes, the delusion is over, and I see things as they are. Pity that one ever wakes from the blissful infatuation of one's honeymoon."

"One should wake to find the reality fairer than the dream. Love changes, but is not lost."

"How do you know—you never tried?"

He put the question so abruptly that she paused an instant before she answered slowly, thoughtfully:

"I have observed and studied others, and am sure that where the love is true and deep, nothing can destroy or weaken it, not even death."

"And if there is neither truth nor depth, how then?"

"One of the two things happens. If there is any nobleness, self-sacrifice, and Christian patience in the pair, they see, acknowledge and repent of the rash act, waste no time in reproaches or regrets, but earnestly try to do their duty. If they are selfish, weak and reckless, then comes misery, and lookers-on despise instead of pitying and respecting them."

With her steady eyes fixed on his, Margaret had answered him, and as she paused, took up her brush as if the subject was ended. St. George leaned his head upon his hand, forgetting that he was a sitter, and unwilling to disturb him, the artist retouched the glossy rings of hair that half hid his forehead.

"We've filled the basket seven times, and I'm not tired yet," cried May, dancing in with Fanfan in her arm, and a bright, breezy aspect, which became her well. "How do you get on? That's lovely! But do make his eyelashes curly; it won't be good if you don't; and please have the mustache darker—it's becoming to his mouth. The eyes are perfect; just the way they look when he sees something dear or beautiful. What were you thinking of when Greta did them?"

She waited for no answer, but running to her husband, exclaimed, in a tone of despair:

"Oh, Saint, Saint, how can you rumple up your hair, when I took such pains to have it right? Your collar is all askew, and you'll be a fright if you don't let me put you in order. Lift your head, you sleepy, careless boy, and be made tidy. Margaret's waiting, and so am I."

Perching herself on his knee May smoothed the hair, retied the ribbon at his throat, settled the collar, and having taken a critical survey, bestowed an approving kiss on the lips that did not repay her even by a smile.

"Why do you look at me so tragically? Has Greta been giving you a lecture?" asked the child-wife. "You've been very good lately, but in spite of her care, you don't always do your duty, Saint."

"I try, May, I try."

As the words broke from him St. George drew her close, and laid his cheek to hers, as if to hide the sudden emotion which made his eyes fill, his lips tremble, and his heart ache with a pain she could never know. Too surprised for words May clung close to him, wondering what it meant. Margaret noiselessly left the room, and when St. George looked up they were alone.

"My little wife, I want to say now what I've felt for a long time but never saw so clearly as today. We are not suited to each other; we married too soon, and must pay for that willfulness by some trouble. But we'll be patient, May; we'll try to bear and forbear and so learn to be happy in spite of everything," he said seriously.

"Of course we will. Now don't be dismal, and fancy all sorts of dreadful things, and call us names. I'm very happy now, for we are all together every day. You and Greta are good friends, and get on pleasantly; you both pet me, and when you get too deep for me I can go to dear old Kent and be amused delightfully. Saint, it's a thousand pities he's a bachelor; he'd make a perfect husband."

"Can't I, if I try?" asked St. George, with a sad sort of smile.

"You are charming, and I adore you, and I wouldn't change you for any man in the world; but, Kent is so reliable; *he* never has moods and whims; he's always kind, and sweet, and ready to do anything for one. You are lazy, and just a tiny bit selfish, though I wouldn't own it to a soul but you."

"I want to be a good husband to you, May, but I don't know how. I'm too young. I forget the responsibility I've taken on myself and live as if nothing was changed in my life. Bear with me, dear, I'll do my best."

"Bless me, don't be so pathetic, or I shall think you are going to die, and I want you to take me to the theatre, like a model husband, as you are going to be," was May's laughing answer to his sorrowful confession and appeal. She was not heartless, but incapable of feeling very deeply, and just then, being gay herself, could not sympathize with melancholy.

"You shall go, sweetheart. Can I do anything else for you? Name your wishes, and I'll gratify them, if it is possible. You shall be happy, as far as I can make you."

"What a heavenly frame of mind you are in! Yes. I've got a wish all ready, and you must agree to it. I want to go to Paris for a little holiday when the picture is done. It's time I thought about my winter things, and I'd rather get them there than here; besides, Margaret needs change, and Kent is always ready to go and see that poor old friend whom he supports there. Can we go?"

"Anywhere you like," was the kind answer, and May danced away to tell Kent, who still was busily at work on the ivy leaves.

St. George got up and stood before the easel, thinking bitterly as he examined the comely likeness of himself.

"I dared not tell what dear and beautiful thing these eyes were looking at when she painted them; that's proof enough that there should be an end of this, unless—"

There he checked himself, put on his hat, ordered his horse, and rode away as if intent on escaping from some unfortunate fancy or desire. He was not seen again till dinner-time, when he came in late, looking pale and tired, but in his gentlest mood. The three were waiting for him, but going to his wife, he knelt down before her, and playfully spread out upon her lap four tickets for the theatre, a dainty fan, and a bouquet of her favorite flowers, which she received with delight and the rapturous exclamation:

"Saint, you are an angel! I only expressed one wish, and you have granted three. You certainly are the best and dearest husband in the world. But you were very ungallant not to bring Greta a posy, too. Why didn't you?"

"Margaret knows," was all he said, with a significant yet humble glance, as if he said: "I try to do my duty; am I right?" It touched Margaret, and she gave him a smile of approval as she warmly thanked him for the promised pleasure of the evening.

"My dear boy, you are very kind. I wanted to see 'Lear' again, and now we can all enjoy it together. It was like you to remember that I do not love to carry flowers where they die so soon."

"I shall be of age in a week; shall you call me a boy then?" asked St. George, laughing, yet with a half wistful, half proud expression.

"No, I'll say Sir, if you like it better. Now come to dinner, Mr. St. George."

He usually took her down, but today he drew May's hand through his arm and led her away trying to look unconscious of Kent's surprise or Margaret's smile. He drank his wife's health at table, and devoted himself to her as she sat beside him, for Mr. and Mrs. Chandos were away, and May left all domestic duties to Margaret. When the carriage came round he was assiduous in cloaking May, and when they reached the theatre he placed himself beside her, still wearing the air of lover-like devotion, which in him was peculiarly fascinating. Left to themselves, Margaret and Kent enjoyed the play and their own conversation with unusual zest, for the young people's happiness added to their own, at least they seemed to think so.

"I always wonder why Cordelia did not love faithful Kent instead of that stupid Edgar. She was a good daughter, but not a discerning woman, or she would have appreciated that excellent man," said Margaret, between two of the acts.

"He was so old," said the gentleman beside her.

"Eight and forty is not very old; his virtues outweighed his years; his beautiful devotion to the poor old king, who banished him, was truly noble, and any princess might have been proud to love him."

"You forgot to mention that he was an earl."

"I never care to remember that, because I think so little of titles. What I like in Kent is his honesty; it appears even in his description of himself—'I do profess to be no less, no more, than I seem; to serve him truly that doth put me in trust; to love him that is honest; to converse with him that is wise; to fear judgment; to keep honest counsel; deliver a plain message bluntly; and the best of me is diligence.' "

"Yet for all his honesty, he deceived Lear by serving him in the disguise of a servant;" and Kent, the modern, looked at her with a keen glance.

"Yes, but that was a kind fraud, and one cannot but pardon it, though one may not approve. He suffered for it, you see, and was ignominiously set in the stocks. I always feel so angry at that, though I admire the cheerful philosophy which enables him to bear it calmly, and fall asleep, saying, gayly: 'Fortune, good night; smile once more, and turn thy wheel.' "

"Cordelia did not blame him, you remember, but said gratefully that life would be too short to thank him. True, that was a different deceit from—" Here Kent checked himself as the curtain rose on the last act; yet, though he looked steadily at the stage, he saw but little, for his mind was busied with a question which he found it had to settle.

When the tragedy was over, May, being tired, said she would go, but begged her sister to stay for the afterpiece, in which a favorite comedian appeared. Glad to leave the young pair together, Margaret remained, and May went away, saying, as her husband led her carefully out:

"I hardly know you to-day, Saint, and feel as if our honeymoon had come again."

"It never can, May; don't expect it," was the decided answer.

Pondering over these words, Margaret sat silent till voices in the next box caught her ear. Curtains hid the speakers but the voices were quite audible above the hum that rose from below.

"That affair of St. George's will end exactly as I foretold. They are gone now, and we can speak safely. I always thought he'd regret that hasty marriage of his, and it's plain to see he does. He is another man since he burdened himself with that silly little wife."

"She is a charming girl, Hastings. Childish, perhaps, but that is a fault which every year will mend. She is rich and pretty, and desperately fond of him, as any woman would be of such an Adonis. What more would you have?"

"Ah, but she isn't fond of him, and there's the fault. Miss Roland, who passed a week there by invitation of Mrs. Chandos, who wants the blue-belle to captivate Kent, says she had no chance for Mrs. St. G—absorbed the old fellow entirely, and he was her most devoted."

"How did Adonis take it?"

"Very coolly, being absorbed himself. I used to think the talented sister just the mate for him, and told him so; but he lost his chance, and now he repents. There will be trouble between those four people before the year is out, if appearances may be trusted."

Here the orchestra pealed out in a grand march, and Margaret heard no more. But the words had startled and enlightened her with a sudden shock. Fears like these had haunted her of late, and she had resolutely put them away, but now a stranger's voice had given them utterance, and they seemed to stand before her sad, stern facts. She glanced at Kent; his carefully averted face, the red flush on his dark cheek, and a certain conscience-stricken look, assured her that he, too, had overheard. What the vaudeville was she never knew, and any observer would have fancied from the grave faces in that box that a tragedy was being enacted before them. By the time the curtain fell Margaret's resolution was taken. The drive was a long one, the carriage dusky, they were alone, and there would be time enough to say what she felt must be said. While she hesitated how to begin, Kent helped her by asking abruptly:

"What do you think of the Paris plan?"

"That it is an excellent one, if Saint and May go alone."

"Why alone, if you please?"

"Because the sooner they learn to be happy and contented together the better for us all."

"They'll not go without you."

"They must."

"May begs that I will go."

"And will you?"

"Why should I not?"

"Need you ask?"

"No, but I choose to ask."

"Let what we overheard just now be my answer."

"You believe that gossip, then?"

"No, I only fear that it may prove true unless we are wise in time. Kent, you once said you were our friend. Will you prove it now by letting me speak frankly, and forgive me if I seem to wrong you by a doubt?"

Margaret's voice trembled with its earnestness, and by the starlight Kent saw a beautiful beseeching face bent toward his own.

"I will," was all he said; but the words gave her courage and confidence to say, earnestly:

"Do not think me unwomanly or vain to speak of these things. I have no one to do it for me, and my nature is too frank to make anything but the plain truth possible to me. Half the sins and sorrows of the world would be averted or mitigated by entire sincerity. Believing this, I cannot let false shame of the fear of misconception deter me, and must say freely what disturbs me. You and I are better away from St. George and May. I am sure you see this. I know you are too honest to deny it, and I think you will listen to me when I ask you to spare my sister's peace, as I shall try to spare that of your son."

"You are right in one fear. Saint does love you, and struggles hard to hide it, but May's peace never can be marred by me; it is impossible," was the brief answer.

"I pray God it may be. As yet, I think there is no harm done, you—"

Margaret's voice failed here, and she did not finish.

"If she were free, and I did love her, would you give her to me?" was Kent's sudden question.

"Gladly—willingly—if her heart was yours."

A sign, almost a groan, escaped him, as he shrunk back into the darkness of his corner. The sound wrung Margaret's heart, and, forgetting everything but the sympathy of a generous nature, she laid her soft hand on the two strong ones locked together on Kent's knee, saying, in her tender voice:

"My poor friend, is it too late? I feared this, and should have spoken sooner had I dared. What can I do or say to comfort you?"

With an impulsive gesture he lifted the hand to his lips, saying, brokenly:

"Only trust me, I have conquered one love; I can another."

"I do—I do! May time be kind to you, and some good woman make you happy yet."

Tears were in Margaret's eyes, but none fell, and in a moment Kent was himself again. Gently putting her hand away, he said, with no token of emotion in voice or face, except an under-tone of manly submission, which made music of his words:

"Friendship is a beautiful and comfortable thing; you shall give me that, and I will be contented. Now tell me how to act, that I may do no more harm to these poor children."

"Why do you always speak as if all the fault was yours, and you alone must make atonement? Tell me, Kent."

"Because I first put the idea of marrying into St. George's mind. I wished him to marry soon, before he was spoiled. I saw May; thought her a sweet little mate for him, and bade him love her if he could. He obeyed me too well. Out of a perverse desire to thwart us both and have his own will, he married her before he had proved his love, and now he sees his mistake. Mine was the fault; I should have left him free, and let time teach him to love wisely. I arrogantly thought I had the right, the power, to mold his nature and plan his life as I would. I have failed in both attempts; I give up my hopes, I leave the future to a better builder than myself, and devote my heart and strength to repairing the mistakes of the past."

"Let me help you? Woman's wit is sometimes quicker at solving a difficulty than man's reason. The Paris plan is fortunate; it must be carried out, and I have little doubt that some months of absence will weaken the memory of us, and endear them to each other. We will not go, but stay at home and comfort one another."

"Do you need comfort, too?" asked Kent, quickly, as if he caught at some hint of a suspected truth.

"Yes; all human creatures need it in their lives."

"And can I give it to you?"

"If you will."

"Rely upon me now and always."

Then there came a long pause, broken only by the soft roll of the carriage through leafy roads, the audible beating of Margaret's heart, and one long, patient sigh from Kent. The woman spoke first, sorrowfully:

"I too, have fault to regret; I should not have left May so long. I hesitated even while I told myself it was foolish to fear any serious consequences from so slight an acquaintance, for she had seen St. George but three times then. At the first meeting I had a fancy that she would be charmed, and when he staid by her all the evening—a rare thing for him, I found—my fancy became a fear that he might be won by her innocence and simplicity. Each interview strengthened my fear, and I had almost decided not to go when I heard that he was going to leave town. I was relieved, and went; and so the harm was done."

"Were not you charmed on that first evening, as well as May?"

"Yes; but not as she was. I do not lose my heart so lightly," answered Margaret, with a sudden shyness in her manner.

"And afterward it was stolen from you?"

"By whom?" she asked, almost sharply.

"Adonis," and Kent laughed his sardonic laugh as he uttered the word.

"How dare you say that?" she cried, indignantly.

"You confessed it yourself."

"Never! How? When? You must not think it, Kent."

"You said you also needed comfort; you pity him; paint him; wait upon him in a way that leaves no doubt in my mind. Though neither by look or word would I confess it until now."

"Could you think this of me? Then you do not know me, and you wrong me deeply," she cried, passionately.

"Yet you thought a like thing of me, and I uttered no reproach."

"What do you say? I do not understand; explain, Kent."

"Not now; I can bear it, so let it pass, and pardon me if I venture to be as frank as yourself, and for the boy's sake I ask openly—do you love him?"

"No—a thousand times no! I do pity him, do serve him, and feel a sisterly affection for him—nothing more. I painted him at May's desire; and when I said I needed comfort, I meant only for my sister's loss, my own anxiety, and the unhappiness which seems to threaten us. Do you believe me?"

She made him look at her, showed him her grieved, proud face, full of maidenly shame and indignation at the doubt, and forced him to feel and see how deeply he had wounded her, how innocent she was of any disloyalty to friend or sister.

"I do believe you—forgive me. He is so beautiful, so full of all that makes a man dangerous to a woman's peace, I could not but think you love him against your will, in spite of every obstacle."

"Ah, how poorly you must think of me to imagine I had so little self-control! No! I shall never let love so conquer me that I can forget my duty and my truth."

"Wait till love comes, Margaret; it has conquered stronger wills and hearts as noble as your own. Wait till you are tried."

"I will."

And, as he handed her out, she gave him a glance which haunted him all night.

VI. Comforting One Another

"Done at last, and just in time. To-day is Saint's birthday, and in return for my miniature he gives me this," said May, a week later, as St. George's portrait stood ready for its frame.

"Are you satisfied, dear?" asked Margaret, anxiously, for to her quick ear there seemed a lack of warmth and heartiness in the young wife's expressions of delight.

"Quite satisfied and charmed, and so grateful for your kindness, Greta. I only wish I had Kent's likeness to hang opposite, then I could call them—"

"Beauty and the—"

A little hand on his mouth silenced Kent, as May cried, indignantly:

"You shall not say that; no one thinks it, and I could beat myself for ever repeating such a false and foolish sobriquet. I meant to say I'd call the two a pair of friends, as you are, and I'd show every one how much I respect and love and value my dear old Kent."

Much touched, Kent took the imperious little hand in his, saying playfully:

"If you really want this ugly face of mine by way of contrast to your handsome husband's, I'll try to find some artist with nerves strong enough to take it for you while you are gone."

"Gone where?" asked May, forgetting gratitude in surprise.

"To Paris, for your holiday."

"But why? Don't you want to go?"

"Decidedly not," was the unexpected answer.

"I thought you always liked to be with us?" and May looked at him with grieved wonder in her face.

"My dear little madam, don't think me unkind. I've been a recluse so long that solitude is sometimes as necessary to me as society is to you, and I like to go away and enjoy it. Now is an excellent time to do so, for among the gayeties of Paris neither of you will miss the Dragon."

"I shall, dreadfully, but I won't be selfish. If it was not for disappointing Greta I wouldn't go, for I shall not enjoy anything without you."

"It will be no disappointment to me, May; I'm not going, but you must," began Margaret, who meant to have quietly prepared her sister for the change before it was openly announced.

"Not going!" exclaimed St. George, throwing down the book in which he had seemed absorbed.

"No; you and May are better alone."

"Are you tired of taking care of me?"

"Yes."

This answer was received with such visible dismay that Margaret added kindly, yet gravely:

"You are a man now, and should learn to take care of yourself and your wife also."

"That is not your only reason," he said, suspiciously.

"It is a good one, so be satisfied with it."

"Do you really mean that you will not go?" and he came nearer, eyeing her as if bent on discovering true reason.

"I really mean it."

"Why not?" he asked, with a glance that angered her.

"Need I tell you!"

The sorrowful reproach in Margaret's steady eyes was more significant than the emphasis on that last word. St. George flushed scarlet, turned sharply round on Kent, and asked abruptly:

"What will you do with yourself during our exile?"

"I'll go down to Hurst for a little shooting," was the cool reply, as Kent brought a cushion for May, who had thrown herself disconsolately on the sofa.

"It will be the first time you ever did go down for a little shooting so early. I don't know as that will matter, though, for you'll be more likely to damage yourself than the birds," said St. George, utterly forgetting the respect he usually paid his friend and benefactor.

With the quiet dignity, habitual to him, Kent fixed a commanding look on the young man's excited face, and answered in a tone the other could not mistake:

"Thank you; have no fears for me; I have learned to keep myself out of danger; let me advise you to do likewise."

St. George's eyes flashed; he said not a word, and taking up his book, appeared to be absorbed in it as before, but it was evident that he no longer took a particle of interest or pleasure in the proposed journey. May bewailed herself pathetically for an hour, then Kent's lively pictures of Paris delights and Margaret's promises to write often consoled her, and she was soon happily intent on making ready. St. George preserved an almost sullen demeanor all that day. He uttered neither expostulations nor entreaties, but plainly showed that he obeyed under protest, and took his revenge at parting. When all was ready, while Kent and the servants were settling little madam and the luggage, St. George turned to Margaret, who stood in the hall, and said, with an expression which haunted her long afterward:

"You will be sorry for this. I shall do my best, but I know I shall fail; then I shall go to destruction, and it will be your fault. Margaret, will you come?"

"No."

"Then you must take the consequences!"

"I will."

"This is the first of them," and with sudden vehemence he gathered her close and kissed her lips and forehead; then drew his hat over his face, sprang into the carriage and was gone before she could recover herself.

Kent saw it, hurried in before the servants, and drawing her trembling hand through his own, led her away to the safe seclusion of the painting-room, where he would have left her with a silent pressure of the hand had hers not detained him. Unable to speak for a moment, Margaret hid her face and wept hot tears of shame and sorrow while her friend stood beside her longing, yet unable to offer any consolation. Unconsciously his presence calmed her; soon she looked up, and with an imploring glance said, as if unable to resist the impulse to confide everything to him:

"He said if he was lost it would be my fault. Oh, Kent, how will it end?"

"I cannot tell; we must do what seems to us right, and leave the rest in wiser hands than ours."

"But May, I fear for her. He does not love her; she will discover it, and then—. Will he dare leave her?" and Margaret's face grew pale at the fear which seized her.

"I'll disown him if he does, and make him rue it to the last day of his life," was the stern answer, as Kent's eye kindled with sudden fire, and his hand closed with an ominous gesture. "No," he added, after a moment's pause. "St. George is weak, but not wicked; the passionate, ambitious nature which first attracted me is hard to rule, but not without principle. He has made a fatal blunder, and rebels against the inevitable consequences of it. Time and patience will teach him to endure, unless—"

"Unless what?" demanded Margaret, as he stopped abruptly.

"Unless his love for you, being thwarted, proves too strong for him to conquer, and so wrecks his peace forever."

"What shall I do? How can I save him? Have I been to blame for this?" and Margaret wrung her hands, dismayed.

"No; rest assured of that. You could not suspect or guard against it, for it came so soon, so stealthily, there was no time. Now you act wisely. Keep up good heart and let us hope the best, for absence and pleasure can work wonders."

"I'll try. Never before did I feel so oppressed by fears and forebodings, for mine is a cheerful, hopeful nature; but now I am quite lost. Do you never feel despair, Kent?" she asked, turning to him with the womanly instinct of the weak toward the strong.

It gratified him deeply, for Margaret seldom lost the courage which was as native to her as her candor or her tenderness. The expression which ennobled his plain face came to it as he answered, with the confidence of a steadfast spirit, an indomitable will:

"Never. If I had not conquered despair, my life would have ended long ago. No man should dare to say there is no hope for him while there is a God, who out of the darkness can bring light, and turn the bitterest sorrow to the sweetest peace. Believe this, Margaret, and nothing in the world can daunt or defeat you."

As if uplifted by his words, she rose steady and serene again, and with a glance of reverential gratitude, said, earnestly:

"Thank you for this. I shall remember it, and prove that I do by trying heartily to cultivate the cheerful faith that makes your life so beautiful and happy."

A look of pain crossed Kent's face as he echoed her words:

" 'Beautiful and happy!' Does it seem so to others? Well, I should be glad of that if it gives comfort, in spite of the delusion. Good-by. I am going in the morning."

He spoke with more than his usual abruptness, and seemed in haste to get away. Margaret longed to keep him, but dared not own it, and with a hasty hand-shake he was gone.

"What is the matter, Mills, you look frightened?" were her first words next morning, as her maid came in, pale and flurried.

"I beg pardon, miss; but, really, I quite forgot, till Jane said you'd rung three times, which I didn't hear for the noise and talk below," was the hurried answer.

"What has happened? Why this unusual noise and talk?"

"Good gracious me, miss, don't you know? I'd just got down, an hour ago, when I heard a gun go off, close by, and directly afterward Baptiste, Mr. St. George's man, came flying in to get our James to fetch a doctor, as Mr. Kent had shot himself."

"What!" and Margaret caught the woman by the shoulder, with a cry that echoed through the room.

"Dear heart, miss, don't faint. It wasn't true; it's only his arm. There—there, sit down and smell the salts while I finish. I was a fool to tell it so sudden, seeing he's such a friend."

Margaret did sit down, for her limbs trembled under her, but she refused the salts, and said, with a composure belied by her pale lips:

"Go on, Mills; I'm quite well now. It startled me for a moment, but is nothing."

"Yes, miss, it happened in this way: Mr. Kent was looking over his guns, and one, being left loaded, went off unexpectedly, and hit him in the arm. The doctor has seen him, and says it's not dangerous. He can't use it for a while, but he won't suffer much, and can be about, as usual, by to-morrow."

"I'm glad to hear that. Now make haste, Mills."

Margaret hurried down to hear the maid's story corroborated by Mr. Chandos and his wife, and to envy that stout matron because she could go and satisfy herself regarding Kent's condition. The young lady could only send friendly messages and receive brief answers, which was very trying. The day seemed very long with all the younger members of the family gone, for, of late, Kent had been almost constantly with them. Next morning she was early astir, and received the welcome intelligence that the wounded man was up and doing well. Upon the strength of these good tidings she felt equal to a day of hard work in her studio, but found it very hard to keep her thoughts from wandering over the garden wall, and her fancy from painting Kent in his lonely sick room, instead of her fingers putting the last touches to the mountain sketch. During the day she sent him some fruit, a new book, and a little note of inquiry, in return for which came always the same answer: "Many thanks, very comfortable," and with that she was forced to content herself. Next day the invalid went out with his arm in a sling, but did not call at his neighbor's, which much surprised Margaret. In the afternoon, as she took Fanfan an airing in the garden, she heard steps in the adjoining one, and, planning to peep in with a friendly "good morrow," put her hand on the latch of the little door, which usually stood open. It was locked, and, though the falling latch made an audible noise, no one came to admit her.

"That's odd; it was never so before," she thought, and, surprised at this unwonted inhospitality, she repaired to the chink to satisfy herself that the walker was not Kent. It was Kent, and she at once forgot her wonder in concern, so pale and ill did he look, though he strode up and down with as firm a step as ever, and showed no sign of weakness except in his face, which was haggard and unquiet. As she looked he glanced often toward the windows of the lodge, and more than once turned as if about to open and enter at the low door; but each time he checked himself, frowned heavily, and returned to his former promenade with the air of a man who rebelled even while he restrained himself.

"Poor soul, he is lonely and in pain, but fancies it might annoy us if he came with his sling. I'll speak to him;" and as Kent came down the walk, a white hand was waved through the ivy, and a familiar voice called cheerily:

"How is our neighbor to-day? Won't he come and let me have a peep at him for old acquaintance sake?"

He came at once, in spite of his former hesitation, and stooping, smiled to see the bright face opposite, as he said, in an impatient tone which she had never heard before:

"As well as such a clumsy sportsman deserves to be. St. George was right, for, in spite of my boast, I can't keep myself out of danger, you see."

"Never mind, we'll not tell him that. What have you been doing to kill time all this day long?"

"Nothing, time has been killing me."

"Why don't you come in and let us amuse you?"

"I was afraid."

"Of what, pray?"

"Myself. I was not fit; I had no right—"

Here Margaret interrupted him with a laugh, as he lifted his face out of eye-shot, and seemed to be afflicted with sudden bashfulness.

"You foolish man! Did you think a loose sleeve and a sling unfitted you from seeing your nearest friends? Don't you know that a wound makes a man a hero in the eyes of women?"

"So much the worse for him!" she heard him say, grimly.

"It's evident that solitude is not good for you, in spite of your explanation to May. Wouldn't you like to come out of your den and be amused?" she asked, cordially.

"Yes, I should, but—"

"Let the buts go, and hear what I want you to do for me, if you feel able," and hoping to lighten his loneliness, Margaret designed her purpose in the form of a favor, thinking he would be more likely to grant it. "I feel like working, but have nothing to work on, so I am going to ask you to allow me to paint you, as a mate to my other portrait. It will surprise and please both the children, as you call them. May I?"

"No."

The blunt denial made Margaret start, and feel as if she had taken an unwarrantable liberty. She colored, though no one could see her, and said, hastily:

"As you please. I thought, perhaps, it would amuse you. I've long wanted a bold, striking head to try, but never dared to ask till now. It is chilly; you will take cold in your wounded arm. Good-by," and away she went to the shelter of her studio, half angry, half amused.

Hardly had she collected herself after this rebuff, when Kent walked in, sat down in the chair opposite, and in his mildest tone, said, with a gesture toward the easel:

"I'm ready."

"For what?" she asked, rather coldly, wishing, woman-like, to make him atone for his rudeness.

"To have my portrait taken, if you wish it," was the meek reply.

"Why did you refuse?"

"Because I was wise then, and now I am a fool."

"You mean you were foolish then and wise now. Well, I forgive you and will do my best."

Relenting with a cordial smile, Margaret set up a prepared drawing-paper, pointed her crayon, and began a rough sketch, talking gayly as she worked. But Kent answered so briefly that conversation flagged and long pauses followed short dialogues. She had never studied Kent's face before, fearing that it might displease him; now as an artist, it was necessary, and at first she made good use of the occasion. Soon she found it difficult to meet the fixed gaze of his eyes, for in them was a look which perplexed and agitated her as the glance of no human eye had ever done before. It touched her strangely, and as she tried to read it by furtive glances, she felt as if those mournful eyes silently reproached her; as if in the man's heart stirred some desire, or pain, or regret, which tried to break loose, but which he put down imperiously, and defied her to discover. His face seemed hardened by the stern effort, every feature was fixed in a grave, almost grim expression, so unlike that which they usually wore that it became impossible to catch a likeness of the real man.

"Does your arm pain you?" she asked, thinking some bodily discomfort might be the cause of this peculiar expression.

"Not at all."

"Perhaps that chair is not easy? If so, try the couch."

"I sit very well, thank you."

She worked in silence for several minutes, without looking up; when she did so, a look of patient endurance had come into his face, and made it so pathetic, that tears filled her eyes, as she exclaimed, suddenly:

"I can do nothing with you, Kent. You are not like yourself today. You look as if you sat in a surgeon's chair and had nerved yourself for some painful trial."

"I have."

"Is this such a trying operation, then?"

"Yes."

"But why consent, if you dislike it so much?"

"Because you asked me."

"Thank you very, very much—" began Margaret.

"Nay, it is I who should thank you. I love beauty too well myself not to feel keenly how hard it must be for beauty-loving eyes like yours to look so long on a face like mine. You can conceal the effort better than I; and for that I thank you, and do my best."

"You shall do no more! I'll not draw another line now; I can finish from memory. You are quite wrong about me, but let your effort end at once. Come, and let me sing to you."

Throwing down her crayon, Margaret made him follow her to the drawing-room, where, aided by Mrs. Chandos and Albany, now a frequent visitor, she entertained him for an hour, and sent him home with no trace of the melancholy shadow on his face.

The wound proved more serious than the doctor predicted, and kept Kent a prisoner for several weeks. Mrs. Chandos took possession of him, and made it quite impossible for him to lead the life of a recluse, as he persisted in trying to do for a time. The good lady had a motive for her devoted neighborliness, for though she knew very little of what had transpired between the four, she perceived that something was amiss, and fearing that St. George had, by offending his adopted father, endangered his inheritance, she endeavored to secure the fortune to the elder ward, lest the younger should lose it. Margaret had refused many fine offers, saying she loved her liberty too well to relinquish it for an establishment; but Margaret liked oddities, was more friendly with Kent than with any gentleman of her acquaintance, and Mrs. Chandos tried to improve this excellent opportunity by throwing the two as much together as English etiquette would permit. Kent was odder than ever during these weeks, sometimes genial and gentle, then, without apparent cause, suddenly becoming morose or melancholy, and now and then he vanished altogether, shutting himself "to romp about the house as if he was a raging sort of a ghost," as the housemaid said in confidence to Mills, who, of course, reported it to her mistress. At first Margaret laughed at his moods, and often rallied him out of them, but all at once, in a day, she changed entirely. A shy, deferential manner replaced her former free and frank demeanor. She met him now with averted eyes, yet often stole covert glances at him as if she found some new charm in that rugged face. She spoke of him to others with a certain proud humility which caused them to smile significantly as they went away. When he talked she listened intently and often a quick rising light and warmth flashed over her face as if she caught or recognized some hidden trait, some suspected fact intelligible to her alone. And sometimes when St. George's name was mentioned she looked up at his picture with a glance in which pity, pain and exultation were curiously blended. These changes in the two much perplexed Mrs. Chandos, but hoping for the best, she wisely held her peace, and was a model chaperon.

Meanwhile letters from Paris had brought many alternations of hope and fear to the anxious pair at home. On this subject Kent and Margaret never differed, and being in the secret, were obliged to hold private conferences from time to time. St. George wrote but once, and then only on business to Kent. May wrote often and freely, but soon the lively accounts of a gay visit were accompanied by complaints of St. George's reckless mode of life, entreaties for advice, and longings to see "Greta and dear Kent."

"How long must we stay?" she asked, though the month was barely gone. "I'm wearying to get back, and never want to come again. At first it was charming, and I enjoyed everything. Now I am heartily tired, for Saint gives me no rest. He is kind, but so unnaturally gay he frightens me sometimes, and I keep with him as much as possible, for if he is alone he goes and plays with some dashing young Frenchman whom I do not like. I scold him, and beg him not to do it, but he only laughs and proposes some new gayety, to which I assent to keep him safe. It is all glitter and noise and hurry here, and I am worn out. I long for you and Fanfan, the quiet garden, and my dear old Kent. Let me come soon or I shall be ill."

"What must we do?" asked Margaret, as she showed this letter to her friend.

"Wait a little, and if matters do not mend I will go and take her place, sending her home to you, while I carry Saint away to Switzerland to cool his fever among the Alps."

"Are you not anxious about the gambling?"

"Not yet; he will soon tire of it, and the money is well spent if it teaches him a lesson. Leave him to me, and do you write a wise, kind letter to poor little madam."

"Will you add a line?" and Margaret stole a look at him, wondering if he had begun to conquer his love yet.

"I have nothing to say, thank you. Give her my regards, and tell her to be patient."

The words were kind, but the manner calm and cool, and the absent expression of his face was most unloverlike.

"I never shall understand him," she said, petulantly to herself, as he left her; then she laughed, and added, with a tone of triumph. "Let him be as mysterious as he pleases, I shall find him out at last. No man can deceive a woman long, artful as he may be."

VII. THE RUSE

ANOTHER WEEK brought a letter which dismayed Margaret.

"I am so unhappy I *must* come home," it began. "I have begged Saint to go, but he will not; and when I proposed having you and Kent come over he was quite savage, and said, with a look that frightened me: 'When I am out of the way he may come and welcome; as for Margaret, she will not stir unless we are dying.' Oh, Greta! he is so strange, so unlike his former self, my heart is nearly broken. I begin to fear his mind is not right, for when he would not listen to my warnings against these bad Frenchmen, I lost my temper, and said I wished I'd never married him. Of course I didn't mean it, and he knew it, but he turned on me, looking so white and stern that I cried out as he said, in a way that haunts me now: 'I wish to God you never had!' Pray, pray, don't repeat this. I ought not to, but my heart is so full I must speak. It isn't the gambling or the hard things he says which trouble me most; it is the reckless life he leads. It will kill him if he does not stop, for he is not strong, you know. All day and night he hurries from one thing to another, without resting, till he is forced to stop against his will. He takes too much wine, to keep up his spirits, he says, and so it does for a time, but after being brilliantly gay he suddenly becomes so desperately melancholy, I'm almost afraid to leave him alone. He never loses his self-control or behaves like the young men after supper at our London parties; he's not foolish, nor dull, nor disagreeable, but really splendid, while the excitement lasts, and every one admires and seeks him and insists on having him at their dinners, balls and *fêtes*. He hates those things, yet he goes, and, when I beg him not, he says he *must*, and rushes off with La Mene and Senerin, to be gone till morning. Your dear letters help me very much, but something must be done soon or it will be too late. I depend on you and Kent."

"Something shall be done," cried Margaret, decidedly; but as she rose to send for Kent, he entered, with an anxious face and a paper in his hand. Margaret's heart sank, for she saw it was a telegram, and seizing it, read eagerly these words, under St. George's address at Paris:

"May is sick. Come at once and bring Margaret."

"How soon can we go?" was all she said, with a glance at the clock.

"Not to-night, for no train leaves till six in the morning. We will take that and reach them tomorrow evening. Have you had a letter? May I see it?"

Forgetting May's caution, Margaret gave it to him, and a moment afterward was startled by a wrathful exclamation, which made her look up to see Kent's face pale with anger and wearing the remorseful expression which always appeared when May's unhappiness was spoken of.

"Hush! Don't speak to me now. I cannot bear it. Go and rest. I'll come for you early in the morning. Good night." And, throwing down the letter, he went away, leaving Margaret oppressed with a new and nameless anxiety.

In the gray dawn of a dull November morning they started, and, through all the discomforts of that hurried journey, Margaret was cheered and supported by the watchful kindness, the calm self-reliance of her companion. In bustling stations, crowded trains, uncomfortable steamers and rattling cabs, the quick eye, helpful hand and cheery smile, were always ready for her service, and that hasty trip showed them, as it has many another pair, unsuspected traits of character and strengthened friendship by the trifling trials of a very unromantic day. The passage was tempestuous, and several delays belated them so that it was eleven instead of seven when they reached the Grand Hotel at Paris. Upon making inquiries of the superb *garcon,* who came bowing into the saloon, whether the St. Georges might have retired, they were surprised to learn that monsieur was out.

"And madame, could she see her?"

"Madame was also out."

"Impossible; she was ill."

The polite creature was desolated to contradict monsieur, but *en verite,* madame was at the Opera with her husband.

Margaret looked at Kent, bewildered, but he only shook his head, and ordered the man to conduct them to Mr. St. George's *appartement,* where they would wait. An elegant saloon was shown them, and while Kent ordered supper, Margaret passed into the adjoining room, hoping to find some note or message from her sister. May's maid was gadding in the lower regions, instead of arranging the chamber, which still showed all the disorder of a hasty evening toilet. Not only did sad confusion reign, but Margaret discovered various things that troubled her more than finding satin slippers on the table, lace handkerchiefs on the floor, or open wardrobes, drawers and jewel-boxes.

Empty bottles and cigar-ashes lay among the costly toys and rare engravings which littered the room; French novels peeped from under the sofa-cushions; play-bills, ball-books, notes of invitation and unpaid accounts covered the writing table; and, glancing into one of the latter, hoping to find a line for herself, Margaret was startled at its amount. Wax candles still flared unsnuffed on the toilet; rich dresses encumbered the chairs, all manner of gentleman's apparel was tossed about in the dressing-room; a dull fire smoldered on the hearth, and everything was untidily elegant, comfortlessly splendid. With a heavy heart Margaret went back, to find Kent frowning over the names he was reading on the cards which filled the little salver. As she entered she heard him mutter to himself:

"A bad set; it's worse than I thought."

"I find no signs of illness there; what can it mean?" she asked, anxiously.

His face cleared instantly, and assuming the grave yet cheerful air he had worn all day, he answered, as he rolled a chair to the table, where refreshment stood ready:

"It means that May has recovered, and, not expecting us so soon, they have gone out for the evening. Now come and eat; you need it, and must not forget yourself entirely. I've sent for the maid, and while we wait we can question her."

Margaret obeyed, for in Kent's manner there was a gentle authority which she could not resist. Presently a coquettish damsel appeared, full of apologies, compliments, and explanations, but from her they received little intelligence or comfort. Madame had been somewhat indisposed with a cold, nothing serious, and had gone out without leaving any message for monsieur or mademoiselle, whose arrival would be such a charming surprise.

They had not been expected, then? Had nothing been said of the telegram or their possible arrival?

"Nothing by madame; and if she had known, she would certainly have spoken of it when Hortense was arranging her ravishing toilet that evening."

Quite at a loss to understand the matter, Margaret dismissed the maid to set her mistress's room in order, and resigned herself to patient waiting, while Kent wandered about the room, and both paused in their fitful talk to listen whenever a carriage drove into the courtyard. The clock was on the stroke of twelve as St. George's voice was heard singing the drinking-song from "Lucretia," as he came along the passage. The door was impatiently flung open, and he came in with May leaning wearily on his arm. Both started and stopped short on the threshold when they saw those two familiar figures before them. In that brief pause Kent and Margaret had time to see how sadly the two young creatures had changed in those few weeks. May was pale and thin, and in her innocent eyes there was an anxious, frightened look, as if some dread, unseen but ever present, oppressed her. Her gay costume, in the height of the fashion, with all its costly and fanciful decorations, was a striking contrast to the former sweet simplicity which once made her doubly lovely and betrayed a perfect taste.

In St. George's handsome, haggard face the alteration was more marked. It was flushed with a hectic color, his eyes were feverishly bright, his hair disordered, as if by frequent pushing off his hot forehead; the voice which sung the bacchanalian song had lost its freshness, and, in spite of youth, beauty, and the grace which was too natural to be lost, he looked like a reckless weary, miserable man. He was the first to speak, and with a mocking laugh he advanced, saying coolly:

"I thought that message would bring you, though not quite so soon. You are very welcome."

He offered his hand to Margaret, looking at her half-tenderly, half-defiantly; but she took no heed of him, for, with a cry of joyful surprise May had run into her arms, and clung there, sobbing hysterically, as she cried:

"Oh, Greta, now I am safe! Did my letter make you come?"

"Yes, my darling; but the telegram hurried us off at once."

"What telegram?" asked May, looking bewildered.

"That which Saint sent, telling us you were ill."

"But I'm not ill! Why did you do it? Is it true?" and May turned toward her husband, who, with a nod to Kent, had withdrawn to the hearth, where he stood lounging against the low chimney-piece, with the defiant expression plainer than before.

"I said you were sick, and you are—homesick. I did it because I'm tired of being tormented about the matter, and it is as true as anything is about me."

The explanation was made in such a singular tone that no one answered for a moment; then May turned to Kent, like a child to its father, and said, as he pressed the little hand she gave him: "We can't get on without you, so you must take charge of us again, for we are nothing but a pair of children."

"I will certainly take charge of *you*, my child—"

Kent got no further, for St. George broke in with a haughty:

"Thank you; but you forget that I am a man now, and can take care of my wife as well as myself."

"Prove it, and I will resign my authority. This does not look like it," and he pointed to May, who leaned wearily against her sister with tears still shining on her cheeks.

"You sent us away to be merry and forget; we have done our best to do the impossible, so you must blame only yourself for the changes you see," was St. George's careless reply, though his eyes turned reproachfully on Margaret.

Anxious to end the scene for poor worn-out May, Kent begged Margaret to take her away to rest, leaving him to tell St. George the plan they had arranged.

Margaret gladly complied; and with a whispered entreaty not to be severe with Saint, and a timid "Good-night, dear," to her husband, May went into her room to pour out all her woes and cry like a broken-hearted child. As the door closed behind them, St. George lighted a cigar, seated himself astride of a chair, and leaning his arms on the back, looked at Kent with an expression of mingled shame and defiance, saying, as he nodded coolly:

"Now, then, I'm ready to hear what you have to say."

"Very little; but first, let me ask if you intend to continue this reckless course of life?" asked Kent, mildly.

"No; I'm tired of it, and it's a failure."

"What will you do then?"

"One of two things—blow my brains out, or get a divorce."

"Good God, boy! what do you mean?" ejaculated Kent, aghast at the desperate look and tone which accompanied the determined words.

"Exactly what I say. I am miserable, and so is May; it is useless to drag on in this wretched way, and I cannot bear it much longer. It must end somehow, I care little which way, so long as I am free. I've suffered enough for my folly; May will be happy if I'm out of the way, and Margaret—"

He stopped abruptly, and smoked in fierce silence, lest he should betray how much he felt. Deeply grieved and alarmed at the state in which he found him, Kent did his best to calm and cheer the unhappy young man, but all his efforts failed. St. George was by turns excited, reckless and morose; he rejected all plans, refused all counsel, renounced all hope of happiness, and begged to be left to go to ruin as he would.

For an hour they talked, and when Margaret appeared, saying that May slept at last, Kent whispered to her:

"I can do nothing with him; will you try?"

"Yes," was the unhesitating reply.

"Then I leave you while I go to order rooms, and will return presently."

With that Kent went away, and Margaret stood a moment looking at St. George. He still sat as he had placed himself when she left the room, but the cigar was out, the defiant face hidden on his arm, and not a word greeted the new comer. Something in his attitude, his silence, touched Margaret, and remembering May's tearful entreaty not to be severe, her heart softened, and pity replaced anger. Going to him, she softly laid her hand on his bent head, and said, in her gentlest tone:

"Dear Saint, what can I do for you?"

"You might have done everything—now it is too late," was the answer, in a half-stifled voice, for the speaker did not lift his head.

"It never is too late to do one's duty. It is mine to be a sister to you, and I shall try to do it faithfully. You once gave me leave to care for you: may I try again?"

"Why did you stop—tell me that?"

Here he looked up with all his love eloquently written in his face. The color rose to Margaret's forehead, but her eye met his, clear and steadfast, and her tone was full of dignity as well as pity.

"I stopped for May's sake; now I begin again for yours. You are my brother, your peace and happiness are dear to me as well as hers, and I long to help and comfort you."

"There is but one way, and that is impossible," began St. George, taking her hand with an ardent glance.

Still calm and kind, but colder in manner, and more resolute in tone, Margaret drew away her hand and answered, with her steady eyes looking full into those passionate ones of his:

"There are two ways—one wrong and impossible, the other right and easy. You will choose the last. Nay, I'll not hear you; I am the one to speak, you to listen and obey."

"I will listen; speak, Greta," he said, leaning his head on his arm with a weary sigh.

"In a few days I shall take May home to England for rest and quiet. You and

Kent will go to Switzerland for a little trip or to Italy if you prefer it. All of us are better apart just now; time and absence work great changes, and when we meet again we shall all be stronger, wiser, happier I hope. This is the best plan we can devise; Kent proposes it, I approve, May consents, and you will agree also, will you not?"

"No," was the brief, stern answer.

"What is to be done, then?"

"All go home and live together, as before, or else—"

"Why do you pause? What is the alternative?"

"Separation from May."

"Oh, Saint, you do not mean it! Not a year married, and yet part! It must not, cannot be. Have you no love for May, no respect for yourself, no pity for me?"

He rose, as she spoke with sudden pain and terror in her face, and stood looking at her gloomily. Suddenly he broke out impetuously.

"Margaret, I must be free, or I shall do something desperate. I do love May—not as my wife, but as a little sister. She wearies me intensely with her childishness; she is no companion, no help, no inspiration to me, and I long to break loose from the tie that binds me to her. I know it was my own folly, my own rash haste that forged the fetter; nevertheless, I will not wear it all my life, and if she will not consent, I'll end the matter with a pistol."

Pale as death, but calm, almost stern, Margaret confronted him, asking, with a look of contempt, that stung his pride and checked his passionate despair:

"And when you are free, what then?"

His suddenly kindling face, his quick step toward her, answered better than the three eager words he uttered:

"You know, Greta!"

"I know that an act so selfish, base and cruel, will win for you the scorn and detestation of every true man and woman. Leave the poor, loving child, if you will, my home is always hers; but never let me see you while you live, never let me hear your name, and never ask or expect anything from me but pity and contempt, for the cowardice that dare not face and bear the fate your own waywardness has brought upon you."

She would have turned and left him then, but he threw himself down before her, and clung to her with the entire *abandon* of a boy, exclaiming, imploringly:

"No, no, it shall never be so! I am weak and wicked, but you can save me. Don't cast me off, Margaret; think how young, how miserable, and undone I am. Save and help me; I'll be docile to you, only do not desert and scorn me, for in all the world you are the only creature whose respect and love I care for."

"You promise to obey me, Saint? to win my respect, keep my love, rouse my confidence and admiration by bravely doing your duty?" she asked as she looked down at the beautiful despairing face upturned to hers.

"Yes, I promise anything! I will be as wax in your hands, and become a hero for your sake. You have said 'Keep my love,' and that makes me strong and happy, though I know it is not love like mine," he cried, kissing with ardent lips the hands he held.

"The first command I give is, that you never speak of love to me, nor show it.

This insult to myself is also a wrong to May, and I forbid it. Stand up and bear yourself like a man, or I will go."

He rose at once and stood opposite, flushed and excited, but obedient to the one voice which could control him. Margaret felt a strong desire to relent and comfort the poor boy, weak and willful as he was, so beseeching were the eyes fixed on her own, so full of love and longing the face he showed her as he said humbly:

"What next, Greta?"

"Comply with Kent's desire, and go away with him for a time."

"If you bid me I will." There was a treacherous tremor in St. George's voice and he clinched his hands as if the words cost him a sharp pang.

A glad, approving smile shone on him as Margaret offered her hand with the gracious gesture which made the act in her doubly cordial.

"Thanks! now you are the man I thought you, now I feel that May's future is not wrecked and that I may still love and respect my brother. Go and rest; to-morrow we will arrange our plans. Dear Saint, good-night."

He answered not a word, but laid his face down on the beloved hand with an irrepressible sob, for with a poet's gift, he had also a poet's temperament, sensitive, impulsive and feminine. Deeply touched, Margaret smoothed the thick, disordered locks from his forehead with a caressing touch, and as he lifted his head as if disdaining to hide his grief, she said, with tears in her own soft eyes:

"Remember, even when this mood is past, that I have received your promise, and I am sure you will keep it faithfully!"

"I will forfeit my life if I break it," was the answer given in solemn earnest, as they parted.

VIII. Locked In and Found Out

Kent and Margaret were much surprised at the change in "the children," as they called the young pair, for when they met the next morning, though both looked pale and worn-out, both were very quiet, very docile and grateful. May's first words were:

"It is all arranged, Greta. Saint told me about it, and we both agree. I shall miss him dreadfully; but he needs a change, and I need rest, so we will go away in opposite directions with our kind guardians, like truants tired of having their own way. Won't we dear?"

"Yes, it shall be as Kent says," returned St. George, with all his former deference of manner, and a glance that mutely asked pardon for past disrespect.

Arrangements were soon made for the temporary separation, and after several hours of amicable discussion, St. George and May drove out to pay parting calls, Kent went to the banker's, and Margaret, taking a book, strolled away into the garden of the Tuileries. By noon the sun shone warmly, the gay place was full of pretty children, coquettish maids, and loungers of all kinds. Choosing a quiet, sunny nook, Margaret read the book which never failed to charm and absorb her with an ever new delight, and was sitting quite unconscious of time or place, when a shadow falling on the page made her look up, to see Kent standing before her.

"What author has the happy power of engrossing you so entirely, and calling up such a smile?" he asked, as he lifted his hat with his own peculiarly charming smile.

Silently returning his salutation, she turned the book so that he could see its title, and looked up at him with the moved expression still in her face. He glanced at it, said, "Fortunate St. George," and abruptly changed the subject by asking, as he pointed to the towers of Notre Dame, visible through the leafless trees:

"Have you ever seen the wonders of that place?"

"No; I have often longed to do so; for when we were here last year, Mr. Chandos said the towers were not worth seeing, so I let them go."

"It is too cool for you to sit here long; shall we go and hunt up Quasimodo's haunts among the roofs of Notre Dame?" he asked, persuasively.

"With pleasure," and rising, Margaret walked away beside him, looking as if his presence brought her rest and peace.

At the church they fortunately found a party just going up, and joining it, followed the guide up the winding stairs, through mysterious little doors, along dizzy galleries, and out upon airy balconies, from whence they looked down upon the great city and its environs. Coming to the highest tower of all, they lingered to examine the quaintly carved saints that adorn the pinnacles, and to watch the flocks of doves sunning themselves in the niches and along the roof. The party went on, but these two forgot to follow at the time, and when at length they prepared to descend, the door was locked. In vain Kent knocked and called; no one was within hearing, and mocking echoes alone answered.

"What shall we do?" asked Margaret, looking anxious.

"We must wait till we are missed by the guide, or till another party comes up. It is just the time for sightseers, and we shall soon be released. Meanwhile, let us enjoy ourselves over this wonderful view."

His quiet way of taking it reassured Margaret, and for half an hour an interesting and animating chat was easily sustained. An unfortunate look destroyed the calm of the *tête-a-tête.* Margaret was standing in an angle of the tower, looking far away with the bright, rapt look which one often wears when gazing on some limitless scene. Her bonnet was off, and her hair, a little loosened by the wind, was blown back from her face, showing all its delicate, decided outlines, and enhancing its soft tints; Kent, standing near, looked not at the landscape, but at her, with an expression betraying something warmer and deeper than mere admiration. A sudden consciousness of his fixed regard made Margaret turn quickly to see and wonder at the look. She averted her eyes at once, and Kent colored with the deep flush she had seen before. Neither spoke for an instant; then Margaret, with a woman's tact, opened the book still in her hand, and said, simply:

"Please read the beautiful passage which describes a scene something like this. I never fully appreciated its power before."

She gave the book, and when he fumbled over the leaves, turned at once to the page, with a peculiar glance, half-mischievous, half-timid. He obeyed her, and she listened still with that odd look, but when he paused, she said, laughing:

"You don't read as well as Saint, and poets seldom read their own poems well, which makes his skill more remarkable."

"One would think they would read their own things better than another. Which is your favorite bit here?" answered Kent, slowly turning the pages, without looking up.

"I like them all; the book has but one fault in my eyes."

"Ah, and what is that, pray?"

She looked at him an instant with a curious mixture of daring and hesitation in her face, then gently retook the book, drew out a pencil, wrote two words on the title-page, and handed it back, saying, significantly:

"Now it is as true as it is beautiful, and perfect in all respects."

He looked, started, turned pale and stood dumb, though all he saw was his own name written over St. George's, which was crossed out with a decided stroke. Margaret watched him with increasing certainty as she saw his discomposure. Not a word did he speak, and, laying her finger on the words, she made him look at her and answer her question instantly:

"There must be truth between us two, for May's sake, if no more. Tell me, am I not right?"

"Yes."

She clapped her hands with a delighted gesture, and laughed out like a girl, as she said, gayly:

"I knew it! Oh, Kent, how could you deceive us all? How could you let another claim your honors, wear your laurels, and usurp your place in people's hearts? Confess it all now. I've guessed so much you cannot hide the rest, and I will promise to keep the secret, if you say so."

Relieved and yet distressed, Kent flung the book away, and walked hastily round the tower before he answered. Coming back, he resumed his place, saying, frankly, though he still wore the look of a detected school-boy:

"I will confess, for you must not blame Saint. But first tell me why you suspected this, and how, in heaven's name, you discovered it?"

"I can hardly say how the suspicion came; something in your face suggested it vaguely the first time I saw you, and I thought to myself: 'He looks more like the writer of that strong book than the boy.' It was only a passing fancy, but it returned again and again after I knew you both, for Saint, though poetical, is not a poet. He has talent, but no genius. The night he read me his—no, *your* last book, I felt sure it was not his, or, if he wrote it, that you had retouched and refined it as you only could. In it, as in Saint's conversation, I detected your modes of expression, your style of thought, your depth and power of feeling, and sundry little tests convinced me that you were the author. A week ago Fanfan came frisking in with a bit of paper in her mouth. She often steals and destroys notes, so I took it away to see if it was of any value. It proved to be a bit from one of Saint's letters to you, and was something like this:

" 'On looking over the MS., I am disgusted with the passages which you made me put in that I might have some claim to it. I've taken them out, and you must restore the original that it may be perfect, at least as perfect as it can be while our compact lasts.' "

"Hang the dog; why couldn't she choose some safer scrap from my waste paper-basket, or take it to any one but you!" exclaimed Kent, angrily, yet laughing in spite of himself at the odd fashion of the betrayal.

"Bless the dog! it was a splendid bit of instinct, and I have petted the little heart half to death by way of proving my gratitude. Don't frown, Kent; it was to be; you may hide your true self from all the world, but not from me."

"Yes, I begin to think so, and you must pay the penalty of your acuteness by learning what a hypocrite and coward I am. I'll tell the tale as briefly as I can. Five or six years ago I came home from weary wanderings over the face of the earth; I wanted a home, but had none; I longed for a friend, yet not one who called himself so could be to me as near and dear as the companion I desired. I could not marry, having vowed never to be repulsed again, and only a woman whom I respect can I love, so no tie was possible to me but the wedlock I had renounced. Just then I found Saint, and my heart was drawn to him at once, for when a boy I hoped and suffered as he did, but fortune came to me, and I was spared his last desperation. I saw his talent; enjoyed his beauty; pitied his friendlessness, and loved him like a son, for he was grateful and affectionate. I said, 'Why not live again in this boy? my wealth, experience and power give me no happiness; for I ask more, and fate denies it to me. Lend my good gifts to the boy, and let his life be what I would have had my own. He has youth, beauty, ambition and some power; help him up, and in return for all I give he will love me as I would be loved.' "

"And you did it?" said Margaret, with beaming eyes and glow of admiration on her face.

"Yes; I tried not to be selfish, but when the boy was so docile, fond and dear to me, I felt as if I did not give enough. At first I had no thought of the literary deceit; it came about in the simplest way. Saint wrote poems, and had tried to publish them; they were sweet, but weak, and failed. As a boy I wrote also, and once in rummaging an old chest of papers I came upon my verses and tossed them to Saint to laugh over. Since my last love I had given up all ambitious hopes, and wrote no more. But in those boyish ditties Saint found much to envy and admire, and begged me to publish them. I refused, of course; 'Then I shall,' said he, in his willful way.

"Put your own name to them if you do," was my answer, thinking the whole thing a joke. 'May I?' he asked. 'You don't care for fame, and you throw these away as worthless, but I long for it; I see more power in these than any I can ever write; why not let me arrange and try them in my name, taking the consequences, whatever they may be.' I assented, fancying he would soon tire of the freak; but he did not; the book came out, and to my utter amazement Saint was famous. The deceit troubled me then; not that I cared for the fame; to that he was heartily welcome; but I felt guilty of double-dealing, yet could not confess without harming the boy."

"You were right," began Margaret, eagerly.

"Is this a deceit which you can forgive?" asked Kent, with a touch of malice in his tone.

She remembered her own words and blushed, but said, honestly:

"Yes, I can; though I think it will yet bring you into trouble, and you will have to atone for it, generous as it is."

"I have already," he said, very low, adding, in his former tone, "Saint was so delighted with his success, and enjoyed it so intensely, I made up my mind to say nothing. It was my own affair, and I alone had a right to complain. He more than repaid any loss of reputation as a poet by making me happy as a man. He hungered and thirsted after praise, I cared nothing for it, and having promised to make his fortune, I would keep my word. For a year he reveled in the position he had longed for, yet never hoped to win so soon, and I endeavored to cultivate and strengthen his powers for a genuine work. But success spoiled him; the talent which poverty might have forced into real genius is weakened by wealth, and I find he is content with this cheap victory. It is my fault; I made him what he is, and I must endeavor to repair my mistake."

For several minutes both stood busied with many thoughts, sweet as well as bitter; Margaret broke the silence:

"And the new book which you wrote while we played, and which Saint copied that it might seem his, will that appear in his name also?"

"I cannot tell; I did my best to have at least a part of it his own, but he rejects that and will have all mine. When the first one came out, we made a mutual promise that neither would betray the other, and if I own this book I shall betray Saint, for the style is the same. I have begged him to put it by and write one himself, but he reminded me that by allowing the first fraud I had committed myself and could not recede without breaking my word. He is so miserable just now, and the fault is mine, so I leave him to do as he will, for if it give him any comfort, or May any pleasure, I am content to bear the blame."

"But do you really care nothing for fame? Does it give you no pleasure to hear your work commended, and to see respect and admiration in the faces of those whose opinion you value?"

"I care very little for the world's praise; it does please me to *know* that my work is liked, and sometimes I do desire to take a small share of the respect of some whose commendation is very dear to me."

As he spoke regretfully and turned to her with that look again visible in his face, Margaret felt her heart beat fast and said within herself, "Can it be that Kent loves me?" Abruptly as before he walked round the tower, tried the door, and came back again to be led into another unexpected confession.

"At what hour do we start to-morrow?" asked Margaret, feeling that the last was not a safe subject to dwell upon.

"At noon, so that you may reach home the day after. The Winthrops go there, and they will devote themselves to you."

"Is everything ready? I have fallen into an indolent habit of leaving my affairs to you. Is there nothing for me to do before we part?"

"Yes, one thing, and this is perhaps as good a time as any for me to speak of it." Kent looked ill at ease, but being a man to face disagreeables manfully, he dashed into the subject at once. "Just before we left home Albany gave me a commission which the sudden journey prevented my executing. It was not to my taste, but I felt for him, and thinking I might spare him pain or you annoyance, I undertook it. He desired me to ask you if there was any hope for him."

"None," was the prompt reply.

"I feared so;" and Kent sighed.

"Why say fear?" she asked, sharply.

"Because I saw his love and know how hard it is to find it hopeless."

Angry with herself because her eyes filled and her voice shook, Margaret said, hastily:

"He does me much honor, I thank him, but it is impossible to make any return; I have no heart to give him. Please tell him so."

"No heart to give him—is it lost?" and Kent looked at her with a searching glance, as if eager to learn whether the words were merely a form of speech or a truth. Margaret's cheeks burned and her eyes fell, but she answered truly at any cost:

"Yes;" then added rather haughtily, "Tell Mr. Albany also, the next time he woos a woman, not to do it by proxy!"

"He was timid, poor fellow, humble in his own conceit, and fearful of seeing her with that keen glance."

"A man should not be timid nor humble at such a time, if his love is true and deep, it is an honor to bestow it, and a woman respects courage at all times. If he love, say so manfully, and bear the answer bravely."

"I will. Margaret, I love you—will you be my wife?"

As Kent spoke out with sudden fire and force and offered her his hand, Margaret was so surprised at his promptitude in taking her at her word, that she stood speechless and half-bewildered, though her heart leaped within her at the words he uttered. Straight and strong he stood before her, steadily he looked into her eyes, and softly, slowly, he repeated:

"Margaret, I love you—will you be my wife?"

"With all my heart!" and as the answer broke from her lips, Margaret put one hand into his, and with the other hid her face, for tears broke forth against her will. Very few fell, for Kent drew her to him and turning the shy face to his, asked eagerly with such intense joy, gratitude and love in his own, that she could not hesitate to answer:

"Greta, is it true? I never dared to hope, never thought of speaking till you made me forget everything but the desire of my life. Do you really mean it? is it possible that you can love me, old, ugly, odd and faulty as I am?"

She turned on him a face full of a happiness, a humility he could not doubt and answered with the perfect frankness which was her chief charm to him:

"I do love you true, tenderly, Kent. To me you are not ugly, old, faulty nor odd, but all that I respect, admire and value in a man. I loved you long before I knew it, and only lately have I guessed why I was happiest with you. I did not dream that you could care for me, though I have learned to see that you did not love May, as I once thought. Believe me, it is not the discovery I made which won me; it was your patience, generosity and excellence; of these and many other virtues I am far prouder than a dozen books like that. Oh Kent, what have I done that I should be so blessed?"

No need to tell how he answered that question, how patiently the lovers waited till the guide returned to free them, nor how blissfully they went away together, carrying with them an enduring memory of the towers of Notre Dame.

"Owen," and Margaret made the ugly name sweet by the tender tone in which she uttered it.

"Greta," and Kent pressed the hand that lay confidingly upon his arm as they went slowly homeward through the gardens, brighter to them at sunset than at noon.

"We must not tell this to St. George for a long while yet—he cannot bear it."

Kent stopped short, with a sudden shadow on his happy face, as he exclaimed, regretfully:

"I forgot that dreadful parting. When I proposed it, I thought it would be best for me as for him, as both had something to forget. Now the exile will be doubly hard. Love makes one very selfish, and I want to stay."

"Not more than I want you to; but I know you will not let our happiness add to the misery of these poor children. Go, for a time, and cheer your absence with the memory that I shall love you better for it, and give you a heartier welcome when you come."

It was well for the lovers that the St. Georges had not returned when they reached the hotel, and after a delicious little *tête-a-tête,* they separated to dress for dinner.

Margaret was first down, and found the *salon* still empty, at which she rejoiced, for on the table lay the book with Kent's name still on the title-page. Hastily erasing it, she congratulated herself upon her escape, for had St. George caught a glimpse of it, he would have known that the secret was out. Happily she could not see him pacing to and fro in his dressing room, saying to himself in a tone of desperate despair—for he had opened the book by chance:

"She knows, she knows, and I cannot bear her contempt."

It was a quiet meal, and they parted early, for the next day was to be a busy one. Kent and Margaret had done their best to hide their newborn happiness. May suspected nothing, but as they separated, St. George held a hand of each, saying earnestly, and with a wistful, loving look:

"Good-night, God bless you both."

"He sees it, and bears it nobly," whispered Kent, as he led Margaret to her room. He tried to speak hopefully, but both waited for the morning with anxiety.

May was alone when they met at breakfast, and in answer to their inquiries regarding her husband, she said:

"He sat up writing till after I was asleep, and was up before I woke. He often goes for an early walk; I'm such a lazy creature, I tell him not to wait for me, so he breakfasts when he likes, and sometimes I don't see him till noon."

Margaret looked at Kent, who smiled at her unexpressed fear, but went out immediately after breakfast. From the porter he learned that Monsieur St. George left late in the night, and had not yet returned. Still refusing to acknowledge the foreboding which haunted him, Kent hurried from place to place, searching for his ward; but nowhere did he find him nor glean any tidings of him. Back to the hotel he went; monsieur had not returned, and fearing to alarm the sisters, Kent set out upon another and more careful search. Still vain; and sending word that they were unavoidably detained and would not leave till evening, he drove to and fro like a restless ghost all that dreadful day. Pausing at last to take counsel with himself, a terrible thought rose suddenly before him, and following the impulse, he dismissed the carriage, crossed the bridge, dived into a narrow street behind Notre Dame and entered a low, small building on the river-side. A moment after he came staggering out ghastly pale, and with the air of a man overwhelmed by a sudden shock. Well might he look so; for the little building by the river-side, with a crowd flowing in and out at its open doors, was the *Morgue,* and on one of the stone tables behind the grating he had seen St. George.

Cold and pale as a beautiful statue he lay under the scanty covering allowed the dead in that sad place. A stream of water flowed continually over the rounded limbs, pale face, and drenched hair, and above him hung the plain suit he had worn. Before the grating stood a curious throng, admiring, criticising, pitying "the young man, so charming, so romantic, so pathetic," and at the door, surrounded by sympathizing men and women, leaned Kent, bowed down with a speechless, tearless sorrow, which left its traces on him all his life.

In the dusk he took the poor boy home and broke the heavy truth to the sisters. The young widow gave way at once, and Margaret spent that night of grief in watching over her, while Kent searched for some last wish or word left by St. George.

In his desk appeared a letter for Kent, a parcel for Margaret, his ring, a lock of his hair, and a little note for May.

"I know all," said Kent's letter. "You love each other, and Greta has discovered the truth. I am so tired of my life, it only needed this to make me gladly end it. Take no blame to yourself; it is my fault that your generous scheme fails. I have neither genius, patience nor courage to work, wait, or fight; I throw up the game, and leave you to enjoy the fame rightfully yours, the love you deserve, the happiness in store for you, when I relieve you of the presence which should have been a comfort but is a burden." Then followed thanks, last wishes, and the hope that he would befriend May for her sister's sake.

Margaret's packet contained the manuscript of Kent's poem, and on the title page, where his own name had been, now appeared, fairly written, "Owen Kent, author of 'Early Lays.'" This was his legacy to Margaret, and such it remained, for the world never saw that book or knew the tragedy in which it bore a part.

Long after, when the young poet was forgotten by all but the faithful three, when Kent was a happy man with children on his knee and a noble wife beside him, when May had put off her widow's weeds and found comfort in Albany's affection, another and an entirely different book appeared, to take the public by storm, give the author a late-won but enduring fame, and stamp his long silence as "THE FREAK OF A GENIUS."

🐦 The Mysterious Key, and What It Opened

Chapter I. The Prophecy

Trevlyn lands and Trevlyn gold,
Heir nor heiress e'er shall hold,
Undisturbed, till, spite of rust,
Truth is found in Trevlyn dust.

"This is the third time I've found you poring over that old rhyme. What is the charm, Richard? Not its poetry I fancy."

And the young wife laid a slender hand on the yellow, time-worn page where, in Old English text, appeared the lines she laughed at.

Richard Trevlyn looked up with a smile and threw by the book, as if annoyed at being discovered reading it. Drawing his wife's hand through his own, he led her back to her couch, folded the soft shawls about her, and, sitting in a low chair beside her, said in a cheerful tone, though his eyes betrayed some hidden care, "My love, that book is a history of our family for centuries, and that old prophecy has never yet been fulfilled, except the 'heir and heiress' line. I am the last Trevlyn, and as the time draws near when my child shall be born, I naturally think of his future, and hope he will enjoy his heritage in peace."

"God grant it!" softly echoed Lady Trevlyn, adding, with a look askance at the old book, "I read that history once, and fancied it must be a romance, such dreadful things are recorded in it. Is it all true, Richard?"

"Yes, dear. I wish it was not. Ours has been a wild, unhappy race till the last generation or two. The stormy nature came in with old Sir Ralph, the fierce Norman knight, who killed his only son in a fit of wrath, by a blow with his steel gauntlet, because the boy's strong will would not yield to his."

"Yes, I remember, and his daughter Clotilde held the castle during a siege, and married her cousin, Count Hugo. 'Tis a warlike race, and I like it in spite of the mad deeds."

"Married her cousin! That has been the bane of our family in times past. Being too proud to mate elsewhere, we have kept to ourselves till idiots and lunatics began to appear. My father was the first who broke the law among us, and I followed his example: choosing the freshest, sturdiest flower I could find to transplant into our exhausted soil."

"I hope it will do you honor by blossoming bravely. I never forget that you took me from a very humble home, and have made me the happiest wife in England."

"And I never forget that you, a girl of eighteen, consented to leave your hills and come to cheer the long-deserted house of an old man like me," returned her husband fondly.

"Nay, don't call yourself old, Richard; you are only forty-five, the boldest, handsomest man in Warwickshire. But lately you look worried; what is it? Tell me, and let me advise or comfort you."

"It is nothing, Alice, except my natural anxiety for you—Well, Kingston, what do you want?"

Trevlyn's tender tones grew sharp as he addressed the entering servant, and the smile on his lips vanished, leaving them dry and white as he glanced at the card he handed him. An instant he stood staring at it, then asked, "Is the man here?"

"In the library, sir."

"I'll come."

Flinging the card into the fire, he watched it turn to ashes before he spoke, with averted eyes: "Only some annoying business, love; I shall soon be with you again. Lie and rest till I come."

With a hasty caress he left her, but as he passed a mirror, his wife saw an expression of intense excitement in his face. She said nothing, and lay motionless for several minutes evidently struggling with some strong impulse.

"He is ill and anxious, but hides it from me; I have a right to know, and he'll forgive me when I prove that it does no harm."

As she spoke to herself she rose, glided noiselessly through the hall, entered a small closet built in the thickness of the wall, and, bending to the keyhole of a narrow door, listened with a half-smile on her lips at the trespass she was committing. A murmur of voices met her ear. Her husband spoke oftenest, and suddenly some word of his dashed the smile from her face as if with a blow. She started, shrank, and shivered, bending lower with set teeth, white cheeks, and panic-stricken heart. Paler and paler grew her lips, wilder and wilder her eyes, fainter and fainter her breath, till, with a long sigh, a vain effort to save herself, she sank prone upon the threshold of the door, as if struck down by death.

"Mercy on us, my lady, are you ill?" cried Hester, the maid, as her mistress glided into the room looking like a ghost, half an hour later.

"I am faint and cold. Help me to my bed, but do not disturb Sir Richard."

A shiver crept over her as she spoke, and, casting a wild, woeful look about her, she laid her head upon the pillow like one who never cared to lift it up again. Hester, a sharp-eyed, middle-aged woman, watched the pale creature for a moment, then left the room muttering, "Something is wrong, and Sir Richard must know it. That black-bearded man came for no good, I'll warrant."

At the door of the library she paused. No sound of voices came from within; a stifled groan was all she heard; and without waiting to knock she went in, fearing she knew not what. Sir Richard sat at his writing table pen in hand, but his face was hidden on his arm, and his whole attitude betrayed the presence of some overwhelming despair.

"Please, sir, my lady is ill. Shall I send for anyone?"

No answer. Hester repeated her words, but Sir Richard never stirred. Much alarmed, the woman raised his head, saw that he was unconscious, and rang for help. But Richard Trevlyn was past help, though he lingered for some hours. He spoke but once, murmuring faintly, "Will Alice come to say good-bye?"

"Bring her if she can come," said the physician.

Hester went, found her mistress lying as she left her, like a figure carved in stone. When she gave the message, Lady Trevlyn answered sternly, "Tell him I will not come," and turned her face to the wall, with an expression which daunted the woman too much for another word.

Hester whispered the hard answer to the physician, fearing to utter it aloud, but Sir Richard heard it, and died with a despairing prayer for pardon on his lips.

When day dawned Sir Richard lay in his shroud and his little daughter in her cradle, the one unwept, the other unwelcomed by the wife and mother, who, twelve hours before, had called herself the happiest woman in England. They thought her dying, and at her own command gave her the sealed letter bearing her address which her husband left behind him. She read it, laid it in her bosom, and, waking from the trance which seemed to have so strongly chilled and changed her, besought those about her with passionate earnestness to save her life.

For two days she hovered on the brink of the grave, and nothing but the indomitable will to live saved her, the doctors said. On the third day she rallied wonderfully, and some purpose seemed to gift her with unnatural strength. Evening came, and the house was very still, for all the sad bustle of preparation for Sir Richard's funeral was over, and he lay for the last night under his own roof. Hester sat in the darkened chamber of her mistress, and no sound broke the hush but the low lullaby the nurse was singing to the fatherless baby in the adjoining room. Lady Trevlyn seemed to sleep, but suddenly put back the curtain, saying abruptly, "Where does he lie?"

"In the state chamber, my lady," replied Hester, anxiously watching the feverish glitter of her mistress's eye, the flush on her cheek, and the unnatural calmness of her manner.

"Help me to go there; I must see him."

"It would be your death, my lady. I beseech you, don't think of it," began the woman; but Lady Trevlyn seemed not to hear her, and something in the stern pallor of her face awed the woman into submission.

Wrapping the slight form of her mistress in a warm cloak, Hester half-led, half-carried her to the state room, and left her on the threshold.

"I must go in alone; fear nothing, but wait for me here," she said, and closed the door behind her.

Five minutes had not elapsed when she reappeared with no sign of grief on her rigid face.

"Take me to my bed and bring my jewel box," she said, with a shuddering sigh, as the faithful servant received her with an exclamation of thankfulness.

When her orders had been obeyed, she drew from her bosom the portrait of

Sir Richard which she always wore, and, removing the ivory oval from the gold case, she locked the former in a tiny drawer of the casket, replaced the empty locket in her breast, and bade Hester give the jewels to Watson, her lawyer, who would see them put in a safe place till the child was grown.

"Dear heart, my lady, you'll wear them yet, for you're too young to grieve all your days, even for so good a man as my blessed master. Take comfort, and cheer up, for the dear child's sake if no more."

"I shall never wear them again" was all the answer as Lady Trevlyn drew the curtains, as if to shut out hope.

Sir Richard was buried and, the nine days' gossip over, the mystery of his death died for want of food, for the only person who could have explained it was in a state which forbade all allusion to that tragic day.

For a year Lady Trevlyn's reason was in danger. A long fever left her so weak in mind and body that there was little hope of recovery, and her days were passed in a state of apathy sad to witness. She seemed to have forgotten everything, even the shock which had so sorely stricken her. The sight of her child failed to rouse her, and month after month slipped by, leaving no trace of their passage on her mind, and but slightly renovating her feeble body.

Who the stranger was, what his aim in coming, or why he never reappeared, no one discovered. The contents of the letter left by Sir Richard were unknown, for the paper had been destroyed by Lady Trevlyn and no clue could be got from her. Sir Richard had died of heart disease, the physicians said, though he might have lived years had no sudden shock assailed him. There were few relatives to make investigations, and friends soon forgot the sad young widow; so the years rolled on, and Lillian the heiress grew from infancy to childhood in the shadow of this mystery.

CHAPTER II. PAUL

"COME, CHILD, the dew is falling, and it is time we went in."

"No, no, Mamma is not rested yet, so I may run down to the spring if I like." And Lillian, as willful as winsome, vanished among the tall ferns where deer couched and rabbits hid.

Hester leisurely followed, looking as unchanged as if a day instead of twelve years had passed since her arms received the little mistress, who now ruled her like a tyrant. She had taken but a few steps when the child came flying back, exclaiming in an excited tone, "Oh, come quick! There's a man there, a dead man. I saw him and I'm frightened!"

"Nonsense, child, it's one of the keepers asleep, or some stroller who has no business here. Take my hand and we'll see who it is."

Somewhat reassured, Lillian led her nurse to one of the old oaks beside the path, and pointed to a figure lying half hidden in the fern. A slender, swarthy boy of sixteen, with curly black hair, dark brows, and thick lashes, a singularly stern mouth, and a general expression of strength and pride, which added character to his boyish face and dignified his poverty. His dress betrayed that, being dusty and threadbare, his shoes much worn, and his possessions contained in the little bundle on which he pillowed his head. He was sleeping like one quite spent with weariness, and never stirred, though Hester bent away the ferns and examined him closely.

"He's not dead, my deary; he's asleep, poor lad, worn out with his day's tramp, I dare say."

"I'm glad he's alive, and I wish he'd wake up. He's a pretty boy, isn't he? See what nice hands he's got, and his hair is more curly than mine. Make him open his eyes, Hester," commanded the little lady, whose fear had given place to interest.

"Hush, he's stirring. I wonder how he got in, and what he wants," whispered Hester.

"I'll ask him," and before her nurse could arrest her, Lillian drew a tall fern softly over the sleeper's face, laughing aloud as she did so.

The boy woke at the sound, and without stirring lay looking up at the lovely little face bent over him, as if still in a dream.

"Bella cara," he said, in a musical voice. Then, as the child drew back abashed at the glance of his large, bright eyes, he seemed to wake entirely and, springing to his feet, looked at Hester with a quick, searching glance. Something in his face and air caused the woman to soften her tone a little, as she said gravely, "Did you wish to see any one at the Hall?"

"Yes. Is Lady Trevlyn here?" was the boy's answer, as he stood cap in hand, with the smile fading already from his face.

"She is, but unless your business is very urgent you had better see Parks, the keeper; we don't trouble my lady with trifles."

"I've a note for her from Colonel Daventry; and as it is *not* a trifle, I'll deliver it myself, if you please."

Hester hesitated an instant, but Lillian cried out, "Mamma is close by, come and see her," and led the way, beckoning as she ran.

The lad followed with a composed air, and Hester brought up the rear, taking notes as she went with a woman's keen eye.

Lady Trevlyn, a beautiful, pale woman, delicate in health and melancholy in spirit, sat on a rustic seat with a book in her hand; not reading, but musing with an absent mind. As the child approached, she held out her hand to welcome her, but neither smiled nor spoke.

"Mamma, here is a—a person to see you," cried Lillian, rather at a loss how to designate the stranger, whose height and gravity now awed her.

"A note from Colonel Daventry, my lady," and with a bow the boy delivered the missive.

Scarcely glancing at him, she opened it and read:

My Dear Friend,

The bearer of this, Paul Jex, has been with me some months and has served me well. I brought him from Paris, but he is English born, and, though friendless, prefers to remain here, even after we leave, as we do in a week. When I last saw you you mentioned wanting a lad to help in the garden; Paul is accustomed to that employment, though my wife used him as a sort of page in the house. Hoping you may be able to give him shelter, I venture to send him. He is honest, capable, and trustworthy in all respects. Pray try him, and oblige,

Yours sincerely,
J. R. Daventry

"The place is still vacant, and I shall be very glad to give it to you, if you incline to take it," said Lady Trevlyn, lifting her eyes from the note and scanning the boy's face.

"I do, madam," he answered respectfully.

"The colonel says you are English," added the lady, in a tone of surprise.

The boy smiled, showing a faultless set of teeth, as he replied, "I am, my lady, though just now I may not look it, being much tanned and very dusty. My father was an Englishman, but I've lived abroad a good deal since he died, and got foreign ways, perhaps."

As he spoke without any accent, and looked full in her face with a pair of honest blue eyes under the dark lashes, Lady Trevlyn's momentary doubt vanished.

"Your age, Paul?"

"Sixteen, my lady."

"You understand gardening?"

"Yes, my lady."

"And what else?"

"I can break horses, serve at table, do errands, read aloud, ride after a young lady as groom, illuminate on parchment, train flowers, and make myself useful in any way."

The tone, half modest, half eager, in which the boy spoke, as well as the odd list of his accomplishments, brought a smile to Lady Trevlyn's lips, and the general air of the lad prepossessed her.

"I want Lillian to ride soon, and Roger is rather old for an escort to such a little horsewoman. Don't you think we might try Paul?" she said, turning to Hester.

The woman gravely eyed the lad from head to foot, and shook her head, but an imploring little gesture and a glance of the handsome eyes softened her heart in spite of herself.

"Yes, my lady, if he does well about the place, and Parks thinks he's steady enough, we might try it by-and-by."

Lillian clapped her hands and, drawing nearer, exclaimed confidingly, as she looked up at her new groom, "I know he'll do, Mamma. I like him very much, and I hope you'll let him train my pony for me. Will you, Paul?"

"Yes."

As he spoke very low and hastily, the boy looked away from the eager little face before him, and a sudden flush of color crossed his dark cheek.

Hester saw it and said within herself, "That boy has good blood in his veins. He's no clodhopper's son, I can tell by his hands and feet, his air and walk. Poor lad, it's hard for him, I'll warrant, but he's not too proud for honest work, and I like that."

"You may stay, Paul, and we will try you for a month. Hester, take him to Parks and see that he is made comfortable. Tomorrow we will see what he can do. Come, darling, I am rested now."

As she spoke, Lady Trevlyn dismissed the boy with a gracious gesture and led her little daughter away. Paul stood watching her, as if forgetful of his companion, till she said, rather tartly, "Young man, you'd better have thanked my lady while she was here than stare after her now it's too late. If you want to see Parks, you'd best come, for I'm going."

"Is that the family tomb yonder, where you found me asleep?" was the unexpected reply to her speech, as the boy quietly followed her, not at all daunted by her manner.

"Yes, and that reminds me to ask how you got in, and why you were napping there, instead of doing your errand properly?"

"I leaped the fence and stopped to rest before presenting myself, Miss Hester" was the cool answer, accompanied by a short laugh as he confessed his trespass.

"You look as if you'd had a long walk; where are you from?"

"London."

"Bless the boy! It's fifty miles away."

"So my shoes show; but it's a pleasant trip in summer time."

"But why did you walk, child! Had you no money?"

"Plenty, but not for wasting on coaches, when my own stout legs could carry me. I took a two days' holiday and saved my money for better things."

"I like that," said Hester, with an approving nod. "You'll get on, my lad, if that's your way, and I'll lend a hand, for laziness is my abomination, and one sees plenty nowadays."

"Thank you. That's friendly, and I'll prove that I am grateful. Please tell me, is my lady ill?"

"Always delicate since Sir Richard died."

"How long ago was that?"

"Ten years or more."

"Are there no young gentlemen in the family?"

"No, Miss Lillian is an only child, and a sweet one, bless her!"

"A proud little lady, I should say."

"And well she may be, for there's no better blood in England than the Trevlyns, and she's heiress to a noble fortune."

"Is that the Trevlyn coat of arms?" asked the boy abruptly, pointing to a stone falcon with the motto ME AND MINE carved over the gate through which they were passing.

"Yes. Why do you ask?"

"Mere curiosity; I know something of heraldry and often paint these things for my own pleasure. One learns odd amusements abroad," he added, seeing an expression of surprise on the woman's face.

"You'll have little time for such matters here. Come in and report yourself to the keeper, and if you'll take my advice ask no questions of him, for you'll get no answers."

"I seldom ask questions of men, as *they* are not fond of gossip." And the boy nodded with a smile of mischievous significance as he entered the keeper's lodge.

A sharp lad and a saucy, if he likes. I'll keep my eye on him, for my lady takes no more thought of such things than a child, and Lillian cares for nothing but her own will. He has a taking way with him, though, and knows how to flatter. It's well he does, poor lad, for life's a hard matter to a friendless soul like him.

As she thought these thoughts Hester went on to the house, leaving Paul to win the good graces of the keeper, which he speedily did by assuming an utterly different manner from that he had worn with the woman.

That night, when the boy was alone in his own room, he wrote a long letter in Italian describing the events of the day, enclosed a sketch of the falcon and motto, directed it to "Father Cosmo Carmela, Genoa," and lay down to sleep, muttering, with a grim look and a heavy sigh, "So far so well; I'll not let my heart be softened by pity, or my purpose change till my promise is kept. Pretty child, I wish I had never seen her!"

Chapter III. Secret Service

In a week Paul was a favorite with the household; even prudent Hester felt the charm of his presence, and owned that Lillian was happier for a young companion in her walks. Hitherto the child had led a solitary life, with no playmates of her own age, such being the will of my lady; therefore she welcomed Paul as a new and delightful amusement, considering him her private property and soon transferring his duties from the garden to the house. Satisfied of his merits, my lady yielded to Lillian's demands, and Paul was installed as page to the young lady. Always respectful and obedient, he never forgot his place, yet seemed unconsciously to influence all who approached him, and win the goodwill of everyone.

My lady showed unusual interest in the lad, and Lillian openly displayed her admiration for his accomplishments and her affection for her devoted young servitor. Hester was much flattered by the confidence he reposed in her, for to her alone did he tell his story, and of her alone asked advice and comfort in his various small straits. It was as she suspected: Paul was a gentleman's son, but misfortune had robbed him of home, friends, and parents, and thrown him upon the world to shift for himself. This sad story touched the woman's heart, and the boy's manly spirit won respect. She had lost a son years ago, and her empty heart yearned over the motherless lad. Ashamed to confess the tender feeling, she wore her usual severe manner to him in public, but in private softened wonderfully and enjoyed the boy's regard heartily.

"Paul, come in. I want to speak with you a moment," said my lady, from the long window of the library to the boy who was training vines outside.

Dropping his tools and pulling off his hat, Paul obeyed, looking a little anxious, for the month of trial expired that day. Lady Trevlyn saw and answered the look with a gracious smile.

"Have no fears. You are to stay if you will, for Lillian is happy and I am satisfied with you."

"Thank you, my lady." And an odd glance of mingled pride and pain shone in the boy's downcast eyes.

"That is settled, then. Now let me say what I called you in for. You spoke of being able to illuminate on parchment. Can you restore this old book for me?"

She put into his hand the ancient volume Sir Richard had been reading the day he died. It had lain neglected in a damp nook for years till my lady discovered it, and, sad as were the associations connected with it, she desired to preserve it for the sake of the weird prophecy if nothing else. Paul examined it, and as he turned it to and fro in his hands it opened at the page oftenest read by its late master. His eye kindled as he looked, and with a quick gesture he turned as if toward the light, in truth to hide the flash of triumph that passed across his face. Carefully controlling his voice, he answered in a moment, as he looked up, quite composed, "Yes, my lady, I can retouch the faded colors on these margins and darken the pale ink of the Old English text. I like the work, and will gladly do it if you like."

"Do it, then, but be very careful of the book while in your hands. Provide what is needful, and name your own price for the work," said his mistress.

"Nay, my lady, I am already paid—"

"How so?" she asked, surprised.

Paul had spoken hastily, and for an instant looked embarrassed, but answered with a sudden flush on his dark cheeks, "You have been kind to me, and I am glad to show my gratitude in any way, my lady."

"Let that pass, my boy. Do this little service for me and we will see about the recompense afterward." And with a smile Lady Trevlyn left him to begin his work.

The moment the door closed behind her a total change passed over Paul. He shook his clenched hand after her with a gesture of menace, then tossed up the old book and caught it with an exclamation of delight, as he reopened it at the worn page and reread the inexplicable verse.

"Another proof, another proof! The work goes bravely on, Father Cosmo; and boy as I am, I'll keep my word in spite of everything," he muttered.

"What is that you'll keep, lad?" said a voice behind him.

"I'll keep my word to my lady, and do my best to restore this book, Mrs. Hester," he answered, quickly recovering himself.

"Ah, that's the last book poor Master read. I hid it away, but my lady found it in spite of me," said Hester, with a doleful sigh.

"Did he die suddenly, then?" asked the boy.

"Dear heart, yes; I found him dying in this room with the ink scarce dry on the letter he left for my lady. A mysterious business and a sad one."

"Tell me about it. I like sad stories, and I already feel as if I belonged to the family, a loyal retainer as in the old times. While you dust the books and I rub the mold off this old cover, tell me the tale, please, Mrs. Hester."

She shook her head, but yielded to the persuasive look and tone of the boy, telling the story more fully than she intended, for she loved talking and had come to regard Paul as her own, almost.

"And the letter? What was in it?" asked the boy, as she paused at the catastrophe.

"No one ever knew but my lady."

"She destroyed it, then?"

"I thought so, till a long time afterward, one of the lawyers came pestering me with questions, and made me ask her. She was ill at the time, but answered with a look I shall never forget, 'No, it's not burnt, but no one shall ever see it.' I dared ask no more, but I fancy she has it safe somewhere and if it's ever needed she'll bring it out. It was only some private matters, I fancy."

"And the stranger?"

"Oh, he vanished as oddly as he came, and has never been found. A strange story, lad. Keep silent, and let it rest."

"No fear of my tattling," and the boy smiled curiously to himself as he bent over the book, polishing the brassbound cover.

"What are you doing with that pretty white wax?" asked Lillian the next day, as she came upon Paul in a quiet corner of the garden and found him absorbed in some mysterious occupation.

With a quick gesture he destroyed his work, and, banishing a momentary expression of annoyance, he answered in his accustomed tone as he began to work anew, "I am molding a little deer for you, Miss Lillian. See, here is a rabbit already done, and I'll soon have a stag also."

"It's very pretty! How many nice things you can do, and how kind you are to think of my liking something new. Was this wax what you went to get this morning when you rode away so early?" asked the child.

"Yes, Miss Lillian. I was ordered to exercise your pony and I made him useful as well. Would you like to try this? It's very easy."

Lillian was charmed, and for several days wax modeling was her favorite play. Then she tired of it, and Paul invented a new amusement, smiling his inexplicable smile as he threw away the broken toys of wax.

"You are getting pale and thin, keeping such late hours, Paul. Go to bed, boy, go to bed, and get your sleep early," said Hester a week afterward, with a motherly air, as Paul passed her one morning.

"And how do you know I don't go to bed?" he asked, wheeling about.

"My lady has been restless lately, and I sit up with her till she sleeps. As I go to my room, I see your lamp burning, and last night I got as far as your door, meaning to speak to you, but didn't, thinking you'd take it amiss. But really you are the worse for late hours, child."

"I shall soon finish restoring the book, and then I'll sleep. I hope I don't disturb you. I have to grind my colors, and often make more noise than I mean to."

Paul fixed his eyes sharply on the woman as he spoke, but she seemed unconscious of it, and turned to go on, saying indifferently, "Oh, that's the odd sound, is it? No, it doesn't trouble me, so grind away, and make an end of it as soon as may be."

An anxious fold in the boy's forehead smoothed itself away as he left her, saying to himself with a sigh of relief, "A narrow escape; it's well I keep the door locked."

The boy's light burned no more after that, and Hester was content till a new worry came to trouble her. On her way to her room late one night, she saw a tall shadow flit down one of the side corridors that branched from the main one. For a moment she was startled, but, being a woman of courage, she followed noiselessly, till the shadow seemed to vanish in the gloom of the great hall.

"If the house ever owned a ghost I'd say that's it, but it never did, so I suspect some deviltry. I'll step to Paul. He's not asleep, I dare say. He's a brave and a sensible lad, and with him I'll quietly search the house."

Away she went, more nervous than she would own, and tapped at the boy's door. No one answered, and, seeing that it was ajar, Hester whisked in so hurriedly that her candle went out. With an impatient exclamation at her carelessness she glided to the bed, drew the curtain, and put forth her hand to touch the sleeper. The bed was empty. A disagreeable thrill shot through her, as she assured herself of the fact by groping along the narrow bed. Standing in the shadow of the curtain, she stared about the dusky room, in which objects were visible by the light of a new moon.

"Lord bless me, what is the boy about! I do believe it was him I saw in the—" She got no further in her mental exclamation for the sound of light approaching footsteps neared her. Slipping around the bed she waited in the shadow, and a moment after Paul appeared, looking pale and ghostly, with dark, disheveled hair, wide-open eyes, and a cloak thrown over his shoulders. Without a pause he flung it off, laid himself in bed, and seemed to sleep at once.

"Paul! Paul!" whispered Hester, shaking him, after a pause of astonishment at the whole proceeding.

"Hey, what is it?" And he sat up, looking drowsily about him.

"Come, come, no tricks, boy. What are you doing, trailing about the house at this hour and in such trim?"

"Why, Hester, is it you?" he exclaimed with a laugh, as he shook off her grip and looked up at her in surprise.

"Yes, and well it is me. If it had been any of those silly girls, the house would have been roused by this time. What mischief is afoot that you leave your bed and play ghost in this wild fashion?"

"Leave my bed! Why, my good soul, I haven't stirred, but have been dreaming with all my might these two hours. What do you mean, Hester?"

She told him as she relit her lamp, and stood eyeing him sharply the while. When she finished he was silent a minute, then said, looking half vexed and half ashamed, "I see how it is, and I'm glad you alone have found me out. I walk in my sleep sometimes, Hester, that's the truth. I thought I'd got over it, but it's come back, you see, and I'm sorry for it. Don't be troubled. I never do any mischief or come to any harm. I just take a quiet promenade and march back to bed again. Did I frighten you?"

"Just a trifle, but it's nothing. Poor lad, you'll have to have a bedfellow or be locked up; it's dangerous to go roaming about in this way," said Hester anxiously.

"It won't last long, for I'll get more tired and then I shall sleep sounder. Don't tell anyone, please, else they'll laugh at me, and that's not pleasant. I don't mind your knowing for you seem almost like a mother, and I thank you for it with all my heart."

He held out his hand with the look that was irresistible to Hester. Remembering only that he was a motherless boy, she stroked the curly hair off his forehead, and kissed him, with the thought of her own son warm at her heart.

"Good night, dear. I'll say nothing, but give you something that will ensure quiet sleep hereafter."

With that she left him, but would have been annoyed could she have seen the convulsion of boyish merriment which took possession of him when alone, for he laughed till the tears ran down his cheeks.

Chapter IV. Vanished

"He's a handsome lad, and one any woman might be proud to call her son," said Hester to Bedford, the stately butler, as they lingered at the hall door one autumn morning to watch their young lady's departure on her daily ride.

"You are right, Mrs. Hester, he's a fine lad, and yet he seems above his place, though he does look the very picture of a lady's groom," replied Bedford approvingly.

So he did, as he stood holding the white pony of his little mistress, for the boy gave an air to whatever he wore and looked like a gentleman even in his livery. The dark-blue coat with silver buttons, the silver band about his hat, his white-topped boots and bright spurs, spotless gloves, and tightly drawn belt were all in perfect order, all becoming, and his handsome, dark face caused many a susceptible maid to blush and simper as they passed him. "Gentleman Paul" as the servants called him, was rather lofty and reserved among his mates, but they liked him nonetheless, for Hester had dropped hints of his story and quite a little romance had sprung up about him. He stood leaning against the docile creature, sunk in thought, and quite unconscious of the watchers and whisperers close by. But as Lillian appeared he woke up, attended to his duties like a well-trained groom, and lingered over his task as if he liked it. Down the avenue he rode behind her, but as they turned into a shady lane Lillian beckoned, saying, in the imperious tone habitual to her, "Ride near me. I wish to talk."

Paul obeyed, and amused her with the chat she liked till they reached a hazel copse; here he drew rein, and, leaping down, gathered a handful of ripe nuts for her.

"How nice. Let us rest a minute here, and while I eat a few, please pull some of those flowers for Mamma. She likes a wild nosegay better than any I can bring her from the garden."

Lillian ate her nuts till Paul came to her with a hatful of late flowers and, standing by her, held the impromptu basket while she made up a bouquet to suit her taste.

"You shall have a posy, too; I like you to wear one in your buttonhole as the ladies' grooms do in the Park," said the child, settling a scarlet poppy in the blue coat.

"Thanks, Miss Lillian, I'll wear your colors with all my heart, especially today, for it is my birthday." And Paul looked up at the blooming little face with unusual softness in his keen blue eyes.

"Is it? Why, then, you're seventeen; almost a man, aren't you?"

"Yes, thank heaven," muttered the boy, half to himself.

"I wish I was as old. I shan't be in my teens till autumn. I must give you something, Paul, because I like you very much, and you are always doing kind things for me. What shall it be?" And the child held out her hand with a cordial look and gesture that touched the boy.

With one of the foreign fashions which sometimes appeared when he forgot himself, he kissed the small hand, saying impulsively, "My dear little mistress, I want nothing but your goodwill—and your forgiveness," he added, under his breath.

"You have that already, Paul, and I shall find something to add to it. But what is that?" And she laid hold of a little locket which had slipped into sight as Paul bent forward in his salute.

He thrust it back, coloring so deeply that the child observed it, and exclaimed, with a mischievous laugh, "It is your sweetheart, Paul. I heard Bessy, my maid, tell Hester she was sure you had one because you took no notice of them. Let me see it. Is she pretty?"

"Very pretty," answered the boy, without showing the picture.

"Do you like her very much?" questioned Lillian, getting interested in the little romance.

"Very much," and Paul's black eyelashes fell.

"Would you die for her, as they say in the old songs?" asked the girl, melodramatically.

"Yes, Miss Lillian, or live for her, which is harder."

"Dear me, how very nice it must be to have anyone care for one so much," said the child innocently. "I wonder if anybody ever will for me?"

> "Love comes to all soon or late,
>   And maketh gay or sad;
> For every bird will find its mate,
>   And every lass a lad."

sang Paul, quoting one of Hester's songs, and looking relieved that Lillian's thoughts had strayed from him. But he was mistaken.

"Shall you marry this sweetheart of yours someday?" asked Lillian, turning to him with a curious yet wistful look.

"Perhaps."

"You look as if there was no 'perhaps' about it," said the child, quick to read the kindling of the eye and the change in the voice that accompanied the boy's reply.

"She is very young and I must wait, and while I wait many things may happen to part us."

"Is she a lady?"

"Yes, a wellborn, lovely little lady, and I'll marry her if I live." Paul spoke with a look of decision, and a proud lift of the head that contrasted curiously with the badge of servitude he wore.

Lillian felt this, and asked, with a sudden shyness coming over her, "But you are a gentleman, and so no one will mind even if you are not rich."

"How do you know what I am?" he asked quickly.

"I heard Hester tell the housekeeper that you were not what you seemed, and one day she hoped you'd get your right place again. I asked Mamma about it, and she said she would not let me be with you so much if you were not a fit companion for me. I was not to speak of it, but she means to be your friend and help you by-and-by."

"Does she?"

And the boy laughed an odd, short laugh that jarred on Lillian's ear and made her say reprovingly, "You are proud, I know, but you'll let us help you because we like to do it, and I have no brother to share my money with."

"Would you like one, or a sister?" asked Paul, looking straight into her face with his piercing eyes.

"Yes, indeed! I long for someone to be with me and love me, as Mamma can't."

"Would you be willing to share everything with another person—perhaps have to give them a great many things you like and now have all to yourself?"

"I think I should. I'm selfish, I know, because everyone pets and spoils me, but if I loved a person dearly I'd give up anything to them. Indeed I would, Paul, pray believe me."

She spoke earnestly, and leaned on his shoulder as if to enforce her words. The boy's arm stole around the little figure in the saddle, and a beautiful bright smile broke over his face as he answered warmly, "I do believe it, dear, and it makes me happy to hear you say so. Don't be afraid, I'm your equal, but I'll not forget that you are my little mistress till I can change from groom to gentleman."

He added the last sentence as he withdrew his arm, for Lillian had shrunk a little and blushed with surprise, not anger, at this first breach of respect on the part of her companion. Both were silent for a moment, Paul looking down and Lillian busy with her nosegay. She spoke first, assuming an air of satisfaction as she surveyed her work.

"That will please Mamma, I'm sure, and make her quite forget my naughty prank of yesterday. Do you know I offended her dreadfully by peeping into the gold case she wears on her neck? She was asleep and I was sitting by her. In her sleep she pulled it out and said something about a letter and Papa. I wanted to see Papa's face, for I never did, because the big picture of him is gone from the gallery where the others are, so I peeped into the case when she let it drop and was so disappointed to find nothing but a key."

"A key! What sort of a key?" cried Paul in an eager tone.

"Oh, a little silver one like the key of my piano, or the black cabinet. She woke and was very angry to find me meddling."

"What did it belong to?" asked Paul.

"Her treasure box, she said, but I don't know where or what that is, and I dare not ask any more, for she forbade my speaking to her about it. Poor Mamma! I'm always troubling her in some way or other."

With a penitent sigh, Lillian tied up her flowers and handed them to Paul to carry. As she did so, the change in his face struck her.

"How grim and old you look," she exclaimed. "Have I said anything that troubles you?"

"No, Miss Lillian. I'm only thinking."

"Then I wish you wouldn't think, for you get a great wrinkle in your forehead, your eyes grow almost black, and your mouth looks fierce. You are a very odd person, Paul; one minute as gay as any boy, and the next as grave and stern as a man with a deal of work to do."

"I *have* got a deal of work to do, so no wonder I look old and grim."

"What work, Paul?"

"To make my fortune and win my lady."

When Paul spoke in that tone and wore that look, Lillian felt as if they had changed places, and he was the master and she the servant. She wondered over this in her childish mind, but proud and willful as she was, she liked it, and obeyed him with unusual meekness when he suggested that it was time to return. As he rode silently beside her, she stole covert glances at him from under her wide hat brim, and studied his unconscious face as she had never done before. His lips moved now and then but uttered no audible sound, his black brows were knit, and once his hand went to his breast as if he thought of the little sweetheart whose picture lay there.

He's got a trouble. I wish he'd tell me and let me help him if I can. I'll make him show me that miniature someday, for I'm interested in that girl, thought Lillian with a pensive sigh.

As he held his hand for her little foot in dismounting her at the hall door, Paul seemed to have shaken off his grave mood, for he looked up and smiled at her with his blithest expression. But Lillian appeared to be the thoughtful one now and with an air of dignity, very pretty and becoming, thanked her young squire in a stately manner and swept into the house, looking tall and womanly in her flowing skirts.

Paul laughed as he glanced after her and, flinging himself onto his horse, rode away to the stables at a reckless pace, as if to work off some emotion for which he could find no other vent.

"Here's a letter for you, lad, all the way from some place in Italy. Who do you know there?" said Bedford, as the boy came back.

With a hasty "Thank you," Paul caught the letter and darted away to his own room, there to tear it open and, after reading a single line, to drop into a chair as if he had received a sudden blow. Growing paler and paler he read on, and when the letter fell from his hands he exclaimed, in a tone of despair, "How could he die at such a time!"

For an hour the boy sat thinking intently, with locked door, curtained window, and several papers strewn before him. Letters, memoranda, plans, drawings, and bits of parchment, all of which he took from a small locked portfolio always worn about him. Over these he pored with a face in which hope, despondency, resolve, and regret alternated rapidly. Taking the locket out he examined a ring which lay in one side, and the childish face which smiled on him from the other. His eyes filled as he locked and put it by, saying tenderly, "Dear little heart! I'll not forget or desert her whatever happens. Time must help me, and to time I must leave my work. One more attempt and then I'm off."

"I'll go to bed now, Hester; but while you get my things ready I'll take a turn in the corridor. The air will refresh me."

As she spoke, Lady Trevlyn drew her wrapper about her and paced softly down the long hall lighted only by fitful gleams of moonlight and the ruddy glow of the fire. At the far end was the state chamber, never used now, and never visited except by Hester, who occasionally went in to dust and air it, and my lady, who always passed the anniversary of Sir Richard's death alone there. The gallery was very dark, and she seldom went farther than the last window in her restless walks, but as she now approached she was startled to see a streak of yellow light under the door. She kept the key herself and neither she nor Hester had been there that day. A cold shiver passed over her for, as she looked, the shadow of a foot darkened the light for a moment and vanished as if someone had noiselessly passed. Obeying a sudden impulse, my lady sprang forward and tried to open the door. It was locked, but as her hand turned the silver knob a sound as if a drawer softly closed met her ear. She stooped to the keyhole but it was dark, a key evidently being in the lock. She drew back and flew to her room, snatched the key from her dressing table, and, bidding Hester follow, returned to the hall.

"What is it, my lady?" cried the woman, alarmed at the agitation of her mistress.

"A light, a sound, a shadow in the state chamber. Come quick!" cried Lady Trevlyn, adding, as she pointed to the door, "There, there, the light shines underneath. Do you see it?"

"No, my lady, it's dark," returned Hester.

It was, but never pausing my lady thrust in the key, and to her surprise it turned, the door flew open, and the dim, still room was before them. Hester boldly entered, and while her mistress slowly followed, she searched the room, looking behind the tall screen by the hearth, up the wide chimney, in the great wardrobe, and under the ebony cabinet, where all the relics of Sir Richard were kept. Nothing appeared, not even a mouse, and Hester turned to my lady with an air of relief. But her mistress pointed to the bed shrouded in dark velvet hangings, and whispered breathlessly, "You forgot to look there."

Hester had not forgotten, but in spite of her courage and good sense she shrank a little from looking at the spot where she had last seen her master's dead face. She believed the light and sound to be phantoms of my lady's distempered fancy, and searched merely to satisfy her. The mystery of Sir Richard's death still haunted the minds of all who remembered it, and even Hester felt a superstitious dread of that room. With a nervous laugh she looked under the bed and, drawing back the heavy curtains, said soothingly, "You see, my lady, there's nothing there."

But the words died on her lips, for, as the pale glimmer of the candle pierced the gloom of that funeral couch, both saw a face upon the pillow: a pale face framed in dark hair and beard, with closed eyes and the stony look the dead wear. A loud, long shriek that roused the house broke from Lady Trevlyn as she fell senseless at the bedside, and dropping both curtain and candle Hester caught up her mistress and fled from the haunted room, locking the door behind her.

In a moment a dozen servants were about them, and into their astonished ears Hester poured her story while vainly trying to restore her lady. Great was the dismay and intense the unwillingness of anyone to obey when Hester ordered the men to search the room again, for she was the first to regain her self-possession.

"Where's Paul? He's the heart of a man, boy though he is," she said angrily as the men hung back.

"He's not here. Lord! Maybe it was him a-playing tricks, though it ain't like him," cried Bessy, Lillian's little maid.

"No, it can't be him, for I locked him in myself. He walks in his sleep sometimes, and I was afraid he'd startle my lady. Let him sleep; this would only excite him and set him to marching again. Follow me, Bedford and James, I'm not afraid of ghosts or rogues."

With a face that belied her words Hester led the way to the awful room, and flinging back the curtain resolutely looked in. The bed was empty, but on the pillow was plainly visible the mark of a head and a single scarlet stain, as of blood. At that sight Hester turned pale and caught the butler's arm, whispering with a shudder, "Do you remember the night we put him in his coffin, the drop of blood that fell from his white lips? Sir Richard has been here."

"Good Lord, ma'am, don't say that! We can never rest in our beds if such things are to happen," gasped Bedford, backing to the door.

"It's no use to look, we've found all we shall find so go your ways and tell no one of this," said the woman in a gloomy tone, and, having assured herself that the windows were fast, Hester locked the room and ordered everyone but Bedford and the housekeeper to bed. "Do you sit outside my lady's door till morning," she said to the butler, "and you, Mrs. Price, help me to tend my poor lady, for if I'm not mistaken this night's work will bring on the old trouble."

Morning came, and with it a new alarm; for, though his door was fast locked and no foothold for even a sparrow outside the window, Paul's room was empty, and the boy nowhere to be found.

CHAPTER V. A HERO

FOUR YEARS HAD PASSED, and Lillian was fast blooming into a lovely woman: proud and willful as ever, but very charming, and already a belle in the little world where she still reigned a queen. Owing to her mother's ill health, she was allowed more freedom than is usually permitted to an English girl of her age; and, during the season, often went into company with a friend of Lady Trevlyn's who was chaperoning two young daughters of her own. To the world Lillian seemed a gay, free-hearted girl; and no one, not even her mother, knew how well she remembered and how much she missed the lost Paul. No tidings of him had ever come, and no trace of him was found after his flight. Nothing was missed, he went without his wages, and no reason could be divined for his departure except the foreign letter. Bedford remembered it, but forgot what postmark it bore, for he had only been able to decipher "Italy." My lady made many inquiries and often spoke of him; but when month after month passed and no news came, she gave him up, and on Lillian's account feigned to forget him. Contrary to Hester's fear, she did not seem the worse for the nocturnal fright, but evidently connected the strange visitor with Paul, or, after a day or two of nervous exhaustion, returned to her usual state of health. Hester had her own misgivings, but, being forbidden to allude to the subject, she held her peace, after emphatically declaring that Paul would yet appear to set her mind at rest.

"Lillian, Lillian, I've such news for you! Come and hear a charming little romance, and prepare to see the hero of it!" cried Maud Churchill, rushing into her friend's pretty boudoir one day in the height of the season.

Lillian lay on a couch, rather languid after a ball, and listlessly begged Maud to tell her story, for she was dying to be amused.

"Well, my dear, just listen and you'll be as enthusiastic as I am," cried Maud. And throwing her bonnet on one chair, her parasol on another, and her gloves anywhere, she settled herself on the couch and began: "You remember reading in the papers, some time ago, that fine account of the young man who took part in the Italian revolution and did that heroic thing with the bombshell?"

"Yes, what of him?" asked Lillian, sitting up.

"He is my hero, and we are to see him tonight."

"Go on, go on! Tell all, and tell it quickly," she cried.

"You know the officers were sitting somewhere, holding a council, while the city (I forget the name) was being bombarded, and how a shell came into the midst of them, how they sat paralyzed, expecting it to burst, and how this young man caught it up and ran out with it, risking his own life to save theirs?"

"Yes, yes, I remember!" And Lillian's listless face kindled at the recollection.

"Well, an Englishman who was there was so charmed by the act that, finding the young man was poor and an orphan, he adopted him. Mr. Talbot was old, and lonely, and rich, and when he died, a year after, he left his name and fortune to this Paolo."

"I'm glad, I'm glad!" cried Lillian, clapping her hands with a joyful face. "How romantic and charming it is!"

"Isn't it? But, my dear creature, the most romantic part is to come. Young Talbot served in the war, and then came to England to take possession of his property. It's somewhere down in Kent, a fine place and good income, all his; and he deserves it. Mamma heard a deal about him from Mrs. Langdon, who knew old Talbot and has seen the young man. Of course all the girls are wild to behold him, for he is very handsome and accomplished, and a gentleman by birth. But the dreadful part is that he is already betrothed to a lovely Greek girl, who came over at the same time, and is living in London with a companion; quite elegantly, Mrs. Langdon says, for she called and was charmed. This girl has been seen by some of our gentlemen friends, and they already rave about the 'fair Helene,' for that's her name."

Here Maud was forced to stop for breath, and Lillian had a chance to question her.

"How old is she?"

"About eighteen or nineteen, they say."

"Very pretty?"

"Ravishing, regularly Greek and divine, Fred Raleigh says."

"When is she to be married?"

"Don't know; when Talbot gets settled, I fancy."

"And he? Is he as charming as she?"

"Quite, I'm told. He's just of age, and is, in appearance as in everything else, a hero of romance."

"How came your mother to secure him for tonight?"

"Mrs. Langdon is dying to make a lion of him, and begged to bring him. He is very indifferent on such things and seems intent on his own affairs. Is grave and old for his years, and doesn't seem to care much for pleasure and admiration, as most men would after a youth like his, for he has had a hard time, I believe. For a wonder, he consented to come when Mrs. Langdon asked him, and I flew off at once to tell you and secure you for tonight."

"A thousand thanks. I meant to rest, for Mamma frets about my being so gay; but she won't object to a quiet evening with you. What shall we wear?" And here the conversation branched off on the all-absorbing topic of dress.

When Lillian joined her friend that evening, the hero had already arrived and, stepping into a recess, she waited to catch a glimpse of him. Maud was called away, and she was alone when the crowd about the inner room thinned and permitted young Talbot to be seen. Well for Lillian that no one observed her at that moment, for she grew pale and sank into a chair, exclaiming below her breath, "It is Paul—*my* Paul!"

She recognized him instantly, in spite of increased height, a dark moustache, and martial bearing. It was Paul, older, graver, handsomer, but still "her Paul," as she called him, with a flush of pride and delight as she watched him, and felt that of all there she knew him best and loved him most. For the childish affection still existed, and this discovery added a tinge of romance that made it doubly dangerous as well as doubly pleasant.

Will he know me? she thought, glancing at a mirror which reflected a slender figure with bright hair, white arms, and brilliant eyes; a graceful little head, proudly carried, and a sweet mouth, just then very charming, as it smiled till pearly teeth shone between the ruddy lips.

I'm glad I'm not ugly, and I hope he'll like me, she thought, as she smoothed the golden ripples on her forehead, settled her sash, and shook out the folds of her airy dress in a flutter of girlish excitement. "I'll pretend not to know him, when we meet, and see what he will do," she said, with a wicked sense of power; for being forewarned she was forearmed, and, fearing no betrayal of surprise on her own part, was eager to enjoy any of which he might be guilty.

Leaving her nook, she joined a group of young friends and held herself prepared for the meeting. Presently she saw Maud and Mrs. Langdon approaching, evidently intent on presenting the hero to the heiress.

"Mr. Talbot, Miss Trevlyn," said the lady. And looking up with a well-assumed air of indifference, Lillian returned the gentleman's bow with her eyes fixed full upon his face.

Not a feature of that face changed, and so severely unconscious of any recognition was it that the girl was bewildered. For a moment she fancied she had been mistaken in his identity, and a pang of disappointment troubled her; but as he moved a chair for Maud, she saw on the one ungloved hand a little scar which she remembered well, for he received it in saving her from a dangerous fall. At the sight all the happy past rose before her, and if her telltale eyes had not been averted they would have betrayed her. A sudden flush of maidenly shame dyed her cheek as she remembered that last ride, and the childish confidences then interchanged. This Helen was the little sweetheart whose picture he wore, and now, in spite of all obstacles, he had won both fortune and ladylove. The sound of his voice recalled her thoughts, and glancing up she met the deep eyes fixed on her with the same steady look they used to wear. He had addressed her, but what he said she knew not, beyond a vague idea that it was some slight allusion to the music going on in the next room. With a smile which would serve for an answer to almost any remark, she hastily plunged into conversation with a composure that did her credit in the eyes of her friends, who stood in awe of the young hero, for all were but just out.

"Mr. Talbot hardly needs an introduction here, for his name is well-known among us, though this is perhaps his first visit to England?" she said, flattering herself that this artful speech would entrap him into the reply she wanted.

With a slight frown, as if the allusion to his adventure rather annoyed him, and a smile that puzzled all but Lillian, he answered very simply, "It is not my first visit to this hospitable island. I was here a few years ago, for a short time, and left with regret."

"Then you have old friends here?" And Lillian watched him as she spoke.

"I had. They have doubtless forgotten me now," he said, with a sudden shadow marring the tranquillity of his face.

"Why doubt them? If they were true friends, they will not forget."

The words were uttered impulsively, almost warmly, but Talbot made no response, except a polite inclination and an abrupt change in the conversation.

"That remains to be proved. Do you sing, Miss Trevlyn?"

"A little." And Lillian's tone was both cold and proud.

"A great deal, and very charmingly," added Maud, who took pride in her friend's gifts both of voice and beauty. "Come, dear, there are so few of us you will sing, I know. Mamma desired me to ask you when Edith had done."

To her surprise Lillian complied, and allowed Talbot to lead her to the instrument. Still hoping to win some sign of recognition from him, the girl chose an air he taught her and sang it with a spirit and skill that surprised the listeners who possessed no key to her mood. At the last verse her voice suddenly faltered, but Talbot took up the song and carried her safely through it with his well-tuned voice.

"You know the air then?" she said in a low tone, as a hum of commendation followed the music.

"All Italians sing it, though few do it like yourself," he answered quietly, restoring the fan he had held while standing beside her.

Provoking boy! why won't he know me? thought Lillian. And her tone was almost petulant as she refused to sing again.

Talbot offered his arm and led her to a seat, behind which stood a little statuette of a child holding a fawn by a daisy chain.

"Pretty, isn't it?" she said, as he paused to look at it instead of taking the chair before her. "I used to enjoy modeling tiny deer and hinds in wax, as well as making daisy chains. Is sculpture among the many accomplishments which rumor tells us you possess?"

"No. Those who, like me, have their own fortunes to mold find time for little else," he answered gravely, still examining the marble group.

Lillian broke her fan with an angry flirt, for she was tired of her trial, and wished she had openly greeted him at the beginning; feeling now how pleasant it would have been to sit chatting of old times, while her friends dared hardly address him at all. She was on the point of calling him by his former name, when the remembrance of what he had been arrested the words on her lips. He was proud; would he not dread to have it known that, in his days of adversity, he had been a servant? For if she betrayed her knowledge of his past, she would be forced to tell where and how that knowledge was gained. No, better wait till they met alone, she thought; he would thank her for her delicacy, and she could easily explain her motive. He evidently wished to seem a stranger, for once she caught a gleam of the old, mirthful mischief in his eye, as she glanced up unexpectedly. He did remember her, she was sure, yet was trying her, perhaps, as she tried him. Well, she would stand the test and enjoy the joke by-and-by. With this fancy in her head she assumed a gracious air and chatted away in her most charming style, feeling both gay and excited, so anxious was she to please, and so glad to recover her early friend. A naughty whim seized her as her eye fell on a portfolio of classical engravings which someone had left in disorder on a table near her. Tossing them over she asked his opinion of several, and then handed him one in which Helen of Troy was represented as giving her hand to the irresistible Paris.

"Do you think her worth so much bloodshed, and deserving so much praise?"

she asked, vainly trying to conceal the significant smile that would break loose on her lips and sparkle in her eyes.

Talbot laughed the short, boyish laugh so familiar to her ears, as he glanced from the picture to the arch questioner, and answered in a tone that made her heart beat with a nameless pain and pleasure, so full of suppressed ardor was it:

"Yes! 'All for love or the world well lost' is a saying I heartily agree to. La belle Hélène is my favorite heroine, and I regard Paris as the most enviable of men."

"I should like to see her."

The wish broke from Lillian involuntarily, and she was too much confused to turn it off by any general expression of interest in the classical lady.

"You may sometime," answered Talbot, with an air of amusement; adding, as if to relieve her, "I have a poetical belief that all the lovely women of history or romance will meet, and know, and love each other in some charming hereafter."

"But I'm no heroine and no beauty, so I shall never enter your poetical paradise," said Lillian, with a pretty affectation of regret.

"Some women are beauties without knowing it, and the heroines of romances never given to the world. I think you and Helen will yet meet, Miss Trevlyn."

As he spoke, Mrs. Langdon beckoned, and he left her pondering over his last words, and conscious of a secret satisfaction in his implied promise that she should see his betrothed.

"How do you like him?" whispered Maud, slipping into the empty chair.

"Very well," was the composed reply; for Lillian enjoyed her little mystery too much to spoil it yet.

"What did you say to him? I longed to hear, for you seemed to enjoy yourselves very much, but I didn't like to be a marplot."

Lillian repeated a part of the conversation, and Maud professed to be consumed with jealousy at the impression her friend had evidently made.

"It is folly to try to win the hero, for he is already won, you know," answered Lillian, shutting the cover on the pictured Helen with a sudden motion as if glad to extinguish her.

"Oh dear, no; Mrs. Langdon just told Mamma that she was mistaken about their being engaged; for she asked him and he shook his head, saying Helen was his ward."

"But that is absurd, for he's only a boy himself. It's very odd, isn't it? Never mind, I shall soon know all about it."

"How?" cried Maud, amazed at Lillian's assured manner.

"Wait a day or two, and I'll tell you a romance in return for yours. Your mother beckons to me, so I know Hester has come. Good night. I've had a charming time."

And with this tantalizing adieu, Lillian slipped away. Hester was waiting in the carriage, but as Lillian appeared, Talbot put aside the footman and handed her in, saying very low, in the well-remembered tone:

"Good night, my little mistress."

Chapter VI. Fair Helen

To no one but her mother and Hester did Lillian confide the discovery she had made. None of the former servants but old Bedford remained with them, and till Paul chose to renew the old friendship it was best to remain silent. Great was the surprise and delight of our lady and Hester at the good fortune of their protégé, and many the conjectures as to how he would explain his hasty flight.

"You will go and see him, won't you, Mamma, or at least inquire about him?" said Lillian, eager to assure the wanderer of a welcome, for those few words of his had satisfied her entirely.

"No, dear, it is for him to seek us, and till he does, I shall make no sign. He knows where we are, and if he chooses he can renew the acquaintance so strangely broken off. Be patient, and above all things remember, Lillian, that you are no longer a child," replied my lady, rather disturbed by her daughter's enthusiastic praises of Paul.

"I wish I was, for then I might act as I feel, and not be afraid of shocking the proprieties." And Lillian went to bed to dream of her hero.

For three days she stayed at home, expecting Paul, but he did not come, and she went out for her usual ride in the Park, hoping to meet him. An elderly groom now rode behind her, and she surveyed him with extreme disgust, as she remembered the handsome lad who had once filled that place. Nowhere did Paul appear, but in the Ladies' Mile she passed an elegant brougham in which sat a very lovely girl and a mild old lady.

"That is Talbot's fiancée," said Maud Churchill, who had joined her. "Isn't she beautiful?"

"Not at all—yes, very," was Lillian's somewhat peculiar reply, for jealousy and truth had a conflict just then.

"He's so perfectly absorbed and devoted that I am sure that story is true, so adieu to our hopes," laughed Maud.

"Did you have any? Good-bye, I must go." And Lillian rode home at a pace which caused the stout groom great distress.

"Mamma, I've seen Paul's betrothed!" she cried, running into her mother's boudoir.

"And I have seen Paul himself," replied my lady, with a warning look, for there he stood, with half-extended hand, as if waiting to be acknowledged.

Lillian forgot her embarrassment in her pleasure, and made him an elaborate curtsy, saying, with a half-merry, half-reproachful glance, "Mr. Talbot is welcome in whatever guise he appears."

"I choose to appear as Paul, then, and offer you a seat, Miss Lillian," he said, assuming as much of his boyish manner as he could.

Lillian took it and tried to feel at ease, but the difference between the lad she remembered and the man she now saw was too great to be forgotten.

"Now tell us your adventures, and why you vanished away so mysteriously four years ago," she said, with a touch of the childish imperiousness in her voice, though her frank eyes fell before his.

"I was about to do so when you appeared with news concerning my cousin," he began.

"Your cousin!" exclaimed Lillian.

"Yes, Helen's mother and my own were sisters. Both married Englishmen, both died young, leaving us to care for each other. We were like a brother and sister, and always together till I left her to serve Colonel Daventry. The death of the old priest to whom I entrusted her recalled me to Genoa, for I was then her only guardian. I meant to have taken leave of you, my lady, properly, but the consequences of that foolish trick of mine frightened me away in the most unmannerly fashion."

"Ah, it was you, then, in the state chamber; I always thought so," and Lady Trevlyn drew a long breath of relief.

"Yes, I heard it whispered among the servants that the room was haunted, and I felt a wish to prove the truth of the story and my own courage. Hester locked me in, for fear of my sleepwalking; but I lowered myself by a rope and then climbed in at the closet window of the state chamber. When you came, my lady, I thought it was Hester, and slipped into the bed, meaning to give her a fright in return for her turning the key on me. But when your cry showed me what I had done, I was filled with remorse, and escaped as quickly and quietly as possible. I should have asked pardon before; I do now, most humbly, my lady, for it was sacrilege to play pranks *there.*"

During the first part of his story Paul's manner had been frank and composed, but in telling the latter part, his demeanor underwent a curious change. He fixed his eyes on the ground and spoke as if repeating a lesson, while his color varied, and a half-proud, half-submissive expression replaced the former candid one. Lillian observed this, and it disturbed her, but my lady took it for shame at his boyish freak and received his confession kindly, granting a free pardon and expressing sincere pleasure at his amended fortunes. As he listened, Lillian saw him clench his hand hard and knit his brows, assuming the grim look she had often seen, as if trying to steel himself against some importunate emotion or rebellious thought.

"Yes, half my work is done, and I have a home, thanks to my generous benefactor, and I hope to enjoy it well and wisely," he said in a grave tone, as if the fortune had not yet brought him his heart's desire.

"And when is the other half of the work to be accomplished, Paul? That depends on your cousin, perhaps." And Lady Trevlyn regarded him with a gleam of womanly curiosity in her melancholy eyes.

"It does, but not in the way you fancy, my lady. Whatever Helen may be, she is not my fiancée yet, Miss Lillian." And the shadow lifted as he laughed, looking at the young lady, who was decidedly abashed, in spite of a sense of relief caused by his words.

"I merely accepted the world's report," she said, affecting a nonchalant air.

"The world is a liar, as you will find in time" was his abrupt reply.

"I hope to see this beautiful cousin, Paul. Will she receive us as old friends of yours?"

"Thanks, not yet, my lady. She is still too much a stranger here to enjoy new faces, even kind ones. I have promised perfect rest and freedom for a time, but you shall be the first whom she receives."

Again Lillian detected the secret disquiet which possessed him, and her curiosity was roused. It piqued her that this Helen felt no desire to meet her and chose to seclude herself, as if regardless of the interest and admiration she excited. "I *will* see her in spite of her refusal, for I only caught a glimpse in the Park. Something is wrong, and I'll discover it, for it evidently worries Paul, and perhaps I can help him."

As this purpose sprang up in the warm but willful heart of the girl, she regained her spirits and was her most charming self while the young man stayed. They talked of many things in a pleasant, confidential manner, though when Lillian recalled that hour, she was surprised to find how little Paul had really told them of his past life or future plans. It was agreed among them to say nothing of their former relations, except to old Bedford, who was discretion itself, but to appear to the world as new-made friends—thus avoiding unpleasant and unnecessary explanations which would only excite gossip. My lady asked him to dine, but he had business out of town and declined, taking his leave with a lingering look, which made Lillian steal away to study her face in the mirror and wonder if she looked her best, for in Paul's eyes she had read undisguised admiration.

Lady Trevlyn went to her room to rest, leaving the girl free to ride, drive, or amuse herself as she liked. As if fearing her courage would fail if she delayed, Lillian ordered the carriage, and, bidding Hester mount guard over her, she drove away to St. John's Wood.

"Now, Hester, don't lecture or be prim when I tell you that we are going on a frolic," she began, after getting the old woman into an amiable mood by every winning wile she could devise. "I think you'll like it, and if it's found out I'll take the blame. There is some mystery about Paul's cousin, and I'm going to find it out."

"Bless you, child, how?"

"She lives alone here, is seldom seen, and won't go anywhere or receive anyone. That's not natural in a pretty girl. Paul won't talk about her, and, though he's fond of her, he always looks grave and grim when I ask questions. That's provoking, and I won't hear it. Maud is engaged to Raleigh, you know; well, he confided to her that he and a friend had found out where Helen was, had gone to the next villa, which is empty, and under pretense of looking at it got a peep at the girl in her garden. I'm going to do the same."

"And what am *I* to do?" asked Hester, secretly relishing the prank, for she was dying with curiosity to behold Paul's cousin.

"You are to do the talking with the old woman, and give me a chance to look. Now say you will, and I'll behave myself like an angel in return."

Hester yielded, after a few discreet scruples, and when they reached Laburnum Lodge played her part so well that Lillian soon managed to stray away into one of the upper rooms which overlooked the neighboring garden. Helen was there, and with eager eyes the girl scrutinized her. She was very beautiful, in the classical style; as fair and finely molded as a statue, with magnificent dark hair and eyes, and possessed of that perfect grace which is as effective as beauty. She was alone, and when first seen was bending over a flower which she caressed and seemed to examine with great interest as she stood a long time motionless before it. Then she began to pace slowly around and around the little grass plot, her hands hanging loosely clasped before her, and her eyes fixed on vacancy as if absorbed in thought. But as the first effect of her beauty passed away, Lillian found something peculiar about her. It was not the somewhat foreign dress and ornaments she wore; it was in her face, her movements, and the tone of her voice, for as she walked she sang a low, monotonous song, as if unconsciously. Lillian watched her keenly, marking the aimless motions of the little hands, the apathy of the lovely face, and the mirthless accent of the voice; but most of all the vacant fixture of the great dark eyes. Around and around she went, with an elastic step and a mechanical regularity wearisome to witness.

What is the matter with her? thought Lillian anxiously, as this painful impression increased with every scrutiny of the unconscious girl. So abashed was she that Hester's call was unheard, and Hester was unseen as she came and stood beside her. Both looked a moment, and as they looked an old lady came from the house and led Helen in, still murmuring her monotonous song and moving her hands as if to catch and hold the sunshine.

"Poor dear, poor dear. No wonder Paul turns sad and won't talk of her, and that she don't see anyone," sighed Hester pitifully.

"What is it? I see, but don't understand," whispered Lillian.

"She's an innocent, deary, an idiot, though that's a hard word for a pretty creature like her."

"How terrible! Come away, Hester, and never breathe to anyone what we have seen." And with a shudder and sense of pain and pity lying heavy at her heart, she hurried away, feeling doubly guilty in the discovery of this affliction. The thought of it haunted her continually; the memory of the lonely girl gave her no peace; and a consciousness of deceit burdened her unspeakably, especially in Paul's presence. This lasted for a week, then Lillian resolved to confess, hoping that when he found she knew the truth he would let her share his cross and help to lighten it. Waiting her opportunity, she seized a moment when her mother was absent, and with her usual frankness spoke out impetuously.

"Paul, I've done wrong, and I can have no peace till I am pardoned. I have seen Helen."

"Where, when, and how?" he asked, looking disturbed and yet relieved.

She told him rapidly, and as she ended she looked up at him with her sweet face, so full of pity, shame, and grief it would have been impossible to deny her anything.

"Can you forgive me for discovering this affliction?"

"I think I could forgive you a far greater fault, Lillian," he answered, in a tone that said many things.

"But deceit is so mean, so dishonorable and contemptible, how can you so easily pardon it in me?" she asked, quite overcome by this forgiveness, granted without any reproach.

"Then you would find it hard to pardon such a thing in another?" he said, with the expression that always puzzled her.

"Yes, it would be hard; but in those I loved, I could forgive much for love's sake."

With a sudden gesture he took her hand saying, impulsively, "How little changed you are! Do you remember that last ride of ours nearly five years ago?"

"Yes, Paul," she answered, with averted eyes.

"And what we talked of?"

"A part of that childish gossip I remember well."

"Which part?"

"The pretty little romance you told me." And Lillian looked up now, longing to ask if Helen's childhood had been blighted like her youth.

Paul dropped her hand as if he read her thoughts, and his own hand went involuntarily toward his breast, betraying that the locket still hung there.

"What did I say?" he asked, smiling at her sudden shyness.

"You vowed you'd win and wed your fair little ladylove if you lived."

"And so I will," he cried, with sudden fire in his eyes.

"What, marry her?"

"Aye, that I will."

"Oh Paul, will you tie yourself for life to a—" The word died on her lips, but a gesture of repugnance finished the speech.

"A what?" he demanded, excitedly.

"An innocent, one bereft of reason," stammered Lillian, entirely forgetting herself in her interest for him.

"Of whom do you speak?" asked Paul, looking utterly bewildered.

"Of poor Helen."

"Good heavens, who told you that base lie?" And his voice deepened with indignant pain.

"I saw her, you did not deny her affliction; Hester said so, and I believed it. Have I wronged her, Paul?"

"Yes, cruelly. She is blind, but no idiot, thank God."

There was such earnestness in his voice, such reproach in his words, and such ardor in his eye, that Lillian's pride gave way, and with a broken entreaty for pardon, she covered up her face, weeping the bitterest tears she ever shed. For in that moment, and the sharp pang it brought her, she felt how much she loved Paul and how hard it was to lose him. The childish affection had blossomed into a woman's passion, and in a few short weeks had passed through many phases of jealousy, hope, despair, and self-delusion. The joy she felt on seeing him again, the pride she took in him, the disgust Helen caused her, the relief she had not dared to own even to herself, when she fancied fate had put an insurmountable barrier between Paul and his cousin, the despair at finding it only a fancy, and the anguish of hearing him declare his unshaken purpose to marry his first love—all these conflicting emotions had led to this hard moment, and now self-control deserted her in her need. In spite of her efforts the passionate tears would have their way, though Paul soothed her with assurances of entire forgiveness, promises of Helen's friendship, and every gentle device he could imagine. She commanded herself at last by a strong effort, murmuring eagerly as she shrank from the hand that put back her fallen hair, and the face so full of tender sympathy bending over her:

"I am so grieved and ashamed at what I have said and done. I shall never dare to see Helen. Forgive me, and forget this folly. I'm sad and heavyhearted just now; it's the anniversary of Papa's death, and Mamma always suffers so much at such times that I get nervous."

"It is your birthday also. I remembered it, and ventured to bring a little token in return for the one you gave me long ago. This is a talisman, and tomorrow I will tell you the legend concerning it. Wear it for my sake, and God bless you, dear."

The last words were whispered hurriedly; Lillian saw the glitter of an antique ring, felt the touch of bearded lips on her hand, and Paul was gone.

But as he left the house he set his teeth, exclaiming low to himself, "Yes, tomorrow there shall be an end of this! We must risk everything and abide the consequences now. I'll have no more torment for any of us."

CHAPTER VII. THE SECRET KEY

"Is LADY TREVLYN at home, Bedford?" asked Paul, as he presented himself at an early hour next day, wearing the keen, stern expression which made him look ten years older than he was.

"No, sir, my lady and Miss Lillian went down to the Hall last night."

"No ill news, I hope?" And the young man's eye kindled as if he felt a crisis at hand.

"Not that I heard, sir. Miss Lillian took one of her sudden whims and would have gone alone, if my lady hadn't given in much against her will, this being a time when she is better away from the place."

"Did they leave no message for me?"

"Yes, sir. Will you step in and read the note at your ease. We are in sad confusion, but this room is in order."

Leading the way to Lillian's boudoir, the man presented the note and retired. A few hasty lines from my lady, regretting the necessity of this abrupt departure, yet giving no reason for it, hoping they might meet next season, but making no allusion to seeing him at the Hall, desiring Lillian's thanks and regards, but closing with no hint of Helen, except compliments. Paul smiled as he threw it into the fire, saying to himself, "Poor lady, she thinks she has escaped the danger by flying, and Lillian tries to hide her trouble from me. Tender little heart! I'll comfort it without delay."

He sat looking about the dainty room still full of tokens of her presence. The piano stood open with a song he liked upon the rack; a bit of embroidery, whose progress he had often watched, lay in her basket with the little thimble near it; there was a strew of papers on the writing table, torn notes, scraps of drawing, and ball cards; a pearl-colored glove lay on the floor; and in the grate the faded flowers he had brought two days before. As his eye roved to and fro, he seemed to enjoy some happy dream, broken too soon by the sound of servants shutting up the house. He arose but lingered near the table, as if longing to search for some forgotten hint of himself.

"No, there has been enough lock picking and stealthy work; I'll do no more for her sake. This theft will harm no one and tell no tales." And snatching up the glove, Paul departed.

"Helen, the time has come. Are you ready?" he asked, entering her room an hour later.

"I am ready." And rising, she stretched her hand to him with a proud expression, contrasting painfully with her helpless gesture.

"They have gone to the Hall, and we must follow. It is useless to wait longer; we gain nothing by it, and the claim must stand on such proof as we have, or fall for want of that one link. I am tired of disguise. I want to be myself and enjoy what I have won, unless I lose it all."

"Paul, whatever happens, remember we cling together and share good or evil fortune as we always have done. I am a burden, but I cannot live without you, for you are my world. Do not desert me."

She groped her way to him and clung to his strong arm as if it was her only stay. Paul drew her close, saying wistfully, as he caressed the beautiful sightless face leaning on his shoulder, *"Mia cara,* would it break your heart, if at the last hour I gave up all and let the word remain unspoken? My courage fails me, and in spite of the hard past I would gladly leave them in peace."

"No, no, you shall not give it up!" cried Helen almost fiercely, while the slumbering fire of her southern nature flashed into her face. "You have waited so long, worked so hard, suffered so much, you must not lose your reward. You promised, and you must keep the promise."

"But it is so beautiful, so noble to forgive, and return a blessing for a curse. Let us bury the old feud, and right the old wrong in a new way. Those two are so blameless, it is cruel to visit the sins of the dead on their innocent heads. My lady has suffered enough already, and Lillian is so young, so happy, so unfit to meet a storm like this. Oh, Helen, mercy is more divine than justice."

Something moved Paul deeply, and Helen seemed about to yield, when the name of Lillian wrought a subtle change in her. The color died out of her face, her black eyes burned with a gloomy fire, and her voice was relentless as she answered, while her frail hands held him fast, "I will not let you give it up. We are as innocent as they; we have suffered more; and we deserve our rights, for we have no sin to expiate. Go on, Paul, and forget the sentimental folly that unmans you."

Something in her words seemed to sting or wound him. His face darkened, and he put her away, saying briefly, "Let it be so then. In an hour we must go."

On the evening of the same day, Lady Trevlyn and her daughter sat together in the octagon room at the Hall. Twilight was falling and candles were not yet brought, but a cheery fire blazed in the wide chimney, filling the apartment with a ruddy glow, turning Lillian's bright hair to gold and lending a tinge of color to my lady's pallid cheeks. The girl sat on a low lounging chair before the fire, her head on her hand, her eyes on the red embers, her thoughts—where? My lady lay on her couch, a little in the shadow, regarding her daughter with an anxious air, for over the young face a somber change had passed which filled her with disquiet.

"You are out of spirits, love," she said at last, breaking the long silence, as Lillian gave an unconscious sigh and leaned wearily into the depths of her chair.

"Yes, Mamma, a little."

"What is it? Are you ill?"

"No, Mamma; I think London gaiety is rather too much for me. I'm too young for it, as you often say, and I've found it out."

"Then it is only weariness that makes you so pale and grave, and so bent on coming back here?"

Lillian was the soul of truth, and with a moment's hesitation answered slowly, "Not that alone, Mamma. I'm worried about other things. Don't ask me what, please."

"But I must ask. Tell me, child, what things? Have you seen any one? Had letters, or been annoyed in any way about—anything?"

My lady spoke with sudden energy and rose on her arm, eyeing the girl with unmistakable suspicion and excitement.

"No, Mamma, it's only a foolish trouble of my own," answered Lillian, with a glance of surprise and a shamefaced look as the words reluctantly left her lips.

"Ah, a love trouble, nothing more? Thank God for that!" And my lady sank back as if a load was off her mind. "Tell me all, my darling; there is no confidante like a mother."

"You are very kind, and perhaps you can cure my folly if I tell it, and yet I am ashamed," murmured the girl. Then yielding to an irresistible impulse to ask help and sympathy, she added, in an almost inaudible tone, "I came away to escape from Paul."

"Because he loves you, Lillian?" asked my lady, with a frown and a half smile.

"Because he does *not* love me, Mamma." And the poor girl hid her burning cheeks in her hands, as if overwhelmed with maidenly shame at the implied confession of her own affection.

"My child, how is this? I cannot but be glad that he does *not* love you; yet it fills me with grief to see that this pains you. He is not a mate for you, Lillian. Remember this, and forget the transient regard that has sprung up from that early intimacy of yours."

"He is wellborn, and now my equal in fortune, and oh, so much my superior in all gifts of mind and heart," sighed the girl, still with hidden face, for tears were dropping through her slender fingers.

"It may be, but there is a mystery about him; and I have a vague dislike to him in spite of all that has passed. But, darling, are you sure he does not care for you? I fancied I read a different story in his face, and when you begged to leave town so suddenly, I believed that you had seen this also, and kindly wished to spare him any pain."

"It was to spare myself. Oh, Mamma, he loves Helen, and will marry her although she is blind. He told me this, with a look I could not doubt, and so I came away to hide my sorrow," sobbed poor Lillian in despair.

Lady Trevlyn went to her and, laying the bright head on her motherly bosom, said soothingly as she caressed it, "My little girl, it is too soon for you to know these troubles, and I am punished for yielding to your entreaties for a peep at the gay world. It is now too late to spare you this; you have had your wish and must pay its price, dear. But, Lillian, call pride to aid you, and conquer this fruitless love. It cannot be very deep as yet, for you have known Paul, the man, too short a time to be hopelessly enamored. Remember, there are others, better, braver, more worthy of you; that life is long, and full of pleasure yet untried."

"Have no fears for me, Mamma. I'll not disgrace you or myself by any sentimental folly. I do love Paul, but I can conquer it, and I will. Give me a little time, and you shall see me quite myself again."

Lillian lifted her head with an air of proud resolve that satisfied her mother, and with a grateful kiss stole away to ease her full heart alone. As she disappeared Lady Trevlyn drew a long breath and, clasping her hands with a gesture of thanksgiving, murmured to herself in an accent of relief, "Only a love sorrow! I feared it was some new terror like the old one. Seventeen years of silence, seventeen years of secret dread and remorse for me," she said, pacing the room with tightly locked hands and eyes full of unspeakable anguish. "Oh, Richard, Richard! I forgave you long ago, and surely I have expiated my innocent offense by these years of suffering! For her sake I did it, and for her sake I still keep dumb. God knows I ask nothing for myself but rest and oblivion by your side."

Half an hour later, Paul stood at the hall door. It was ajar, for the family had returned unexpectedly, as was evident from the open doors and empty halls. Entering unseen, he ascended to the room my lady usually occupied. The fire burned low, Lillian's chair was empty, and my lady lay asleep, as if lulled by the sighing winds without and the deep silence that reigned within. Paul stood regarding her with a great pity softening his face as he marked the sunken eyes, pallid cheeks, locks too early gray, and restless lips muttering in dreams.

"I wish I could spare her this," he sighed, stooping to wake her with a word. But he did not speak, for, suddenly clutching the chain about her neck, she seemed to struggle with some invisible foe and beat it off, muttering audibly as she clenched her thin hands on the golden case. Paul leaned and listened as if the first word had turned him to stone, till the paroxysm had passed, and with a heavy sigh my lady sank into a calmer sleep. Then, with a quick glance over his shoulder, Paul skillfully opened the locket, drew out the silver key, replaced it with one from the piano close by, and stole from the house noiselessly as he had entered it.

That night, in the darkest hour before the dawn, a figure went gliding through the shadowy Park to its most solitary corner. Here stood the tomb of the Trevlyns, and here the figure paused. A dull spark of light woke in its hand, there was a clank of bars, the creak of rusty hinges, then light and figure both seemed swallowed up.

Standing in the tomb where the air was close and heavy, the pale glimmer of the lantern showed piles of moldering coffins in the niches, and everywhere lay tokens of decay and death. The man drew his hat lower over his eyes, pulled the muffler closer about his mouth, and surveyed the spot with an undaunted aspect, though the beating of his heart was heard in the deep silence. Nearest the door stood a long casket covered with black velvet and richly decorated with silver ornaments, tarnished now. The Trevlyns had been a stalwart race, and the last sleeper brought there had evidently been of goodly stature, for the modern coffin was as ponderous as the great oaken beds where lay the bones of generations. Lifting the lantern, the intruder brushed the dust from the shield-shaped plate, read the name RICHARD TREVLYN and a date, and, as if satisfied, placed a key in the lock, half-raised the lid, and, averting his head that he might not see the ruin seventeen long years had made, he laid his hand on the dead breast and from the folded shroud drew a mildewed paper. One glance sufficed, the casket was relocked, the door rebarred, the light extinguished, and the man vanished like a ghost in the darkness of the wild October night.

CHAPTER VIII. WHICH?

"A GENTLEMAN, my lady."

Taking a card from the silver salver on which the servant offered it, Lady Trevlyn read, "Paul Talbot," and below the name these penciled words, "I beseech you to see me." Lillian stood beside her and saw the line. Their eyes met, and in the girl's face was such a sudden glow of hope, and love, and longing, that the mother could not doubt or disappoint her wish.

"I will see him," she said.

"Oh, Mamma, how kind you are!" cried the girl with a passionate embrace, adding breathlessly, "He did not ask for me. I cannot see him yet. I'll hide in the alcove, and can appear or run away as I like when we know why he comes."

They were in the library, for, knowing Lillian's fondness for the room which held no dark memories for her, my lady conquered her dislike and often sat there. As she spoke, the girl glided into the deep recess of a bay window and drew the heavy curtains just as Paul's step sounded at the door.

Hiding her agitation with a woman's skill, my lady rose with outstretched hand to welcome him. He bowed but did not take the hand, saying, in a voice of grave respect in which was audible an undertone of strong emotion, "Pardon me, Lady Trevlyn. Hear what I have to say; and then if you offer me your hand, I shall gratefully receive it."

She glanced at him, and saw that he was very pale, that his eye glittered with suppressed excitement, and his whole manner was that of a man who had nerved himself up to the performance of a difficult but intensely interesting task. Fancying these signs of agitation only natural in a young lover coming to woo, my lady smiled, reseated herself, and calmly answered, "I will listen patiently. Speak freely, Paul, and remember I am an old friend."

"I wish I could forget it. Then my task would be easier," he murmured in a voice of mingled regret and resolution, as he leaned on a tall chair opposite and wiped his damp forehead, with a look of such deep compassion that her heart sank with a nameless fear.

"I must tell you a long story, and ask your forgiveness for the offenses I committed against you when a boy. A mistaken sense of duty guided me, and I obeyed it blindly. Now I see my error and regret it," he said earnestly.

"Go on," replied my lady, while the vague dread grew stronger, and she braced her nerves as for some approaching shock. She forgot Lillian, forgot everything but the strange aspect of the man before her, and the words to which she listened like a statue. Still standing pale and steady, Paul spoke rapidly, while his eyes were full of mingled sternness, pity, and remorse.

"Twenty years ago, an English gentleman met a friend in a little Italian town, where he had married a beautiful wife. The wife had a sister as lovely as herself, and the young man, during that brief stay, loved and married her—in a very private manner, lest his father should disinherit him. A few months passed, and the Englishman was called home to take possession of his title and estates, the father being dead. He went alone, promising to send for the wife when all was ready. He told no one of his marriage, meaning to surprise his English friends by producing the lovely woman unexpectedly. He had been in England but a short time when he received a letter from the old priest of the Italian town, saying the cholera had swept through it, carrying off half its inhabitants, his wife and friend among others. This blow prostrated the young man, and when he recovered he hid his grief, shut himself up in his country house, and tried to forget. Accident threw in his way another lovely woman, and he married again. Before the first year was out, the friend whom he supposed was dead appeared, and told him that his wife still lived, and had borne him a child. In the terror and confusion of the plague, the priest had mistaken one sister for the other, as the elder did die."

"Yes, yes, I know; go on!" gasped my lady, with white lips, and eyes that never left the narrator's face.

"This friend had met with misfortune after flying from the doomed village with the surviving sister. They had waited long for letters, had written, and, when no answer came, had been delayed by illness and poverty from reaching England. At this time the child was born, and the friend, urged by the wife and his own interest, came here, learned that Sir Richard was married, and hurried to him in much distress. We can imagine the grief and horror of the unhappy man. In that interview the friend promised to leave all to Sir Richard, to preserve the secret till some means of relief could be found; and with this promise he returned, to guard and comfort the forsaken wife. Sir Richard wrote the truth to Lady Trevlyn, meaning to kill himself, as the only way of escape from the terrible situation between two women, both so beloved, both so innocently wronged. The pistol lay ready, but death came without its aid, and Sir Richard was spared the sin of suicide."

Paul paused for breath, but Lady Trevlyn motioned him to go on, still sitting rigid and white as the marble image near her.

"The friend only lived to reach home and tell the story. It killed the wife, and she died, imploring the old priest to see her child righted and its father's name secured to it. He promised; but he was poor, the child was a frail baby, and he waited. Years passed, and when the child was old enough to ask for its parents and demand its due, the proofs of the marriage were lost, and nothing remained but a ring, a bit of writing, and the name. The priest was very old, had neither friends, money, nor proofs to help him; but I was strong and hopeful, and though a mere boy I resolved to do the work. I made my way to England, to Trevlyn Hall, and by various stratagems (among which, I am ashamed to say, were false keys and feigned sleepwalking) I collected many proofs, but nothing which would satisfy a court, for no one but you knew where Sir Richard's confession was. I searched every nook and corner of the Hall, but in vain, and began to despair, when news of the death of Father Cosmo recalled me to Italy; for Helen was left to my care then. The old man had faithfully recorded the facts and left witnesses to prove the truth of his story; but for four years I never used it, never made any effort to secure the title or estates."

"Why not?" breathed my lady in a faint whisper, as hope suddenly revived.

"Because I was grateful," and for the first time Paul's voice faltered. "I was a stranger, and you took me in. I never could forget that, nor the many kindnesses bestowed upon the friendless boy. This afflicted me, even while I was acting a false part, and when I was away my heart failed me. But Helen gave me no peace; for my sake, she urged me to keep the vow made to that poor mother, and threatened to tell the story herself. Talbot's benefaction left me no excuse for delaying longer, and I came to finish the hardest task I can ever undertake. I feared that a long dispute would follow any appeal to law, and meant to appeal first to you, but fate befriended me, and the last proof was found."

"Found! Where?" cried Lady Trevlyn, springing up aghast.

"In Sir Richard's coffin, where you hid it, not daring to destroy, yet fearing to keep it."

"Who has betrayed me?" And her eye glanced wildly about the room, as if she feared to see some spectral accuser.

"Your own lips, my lady. Last night I came to speak of this. You lay asleep, and in some troubled dream spoke of the paper, safe in its writer's keeping, and your strange treasure here, the key of which you guarded day and night. I divined the truth. Remembering Hester's stories, I took the key from your helpless hand, found the paper on Sir Richard's dead breast, and now demand that you confess your part in this tragedy."

"I do, I do! I confess, I yield, I relinquish everything, and ask pity only for my child."

Lady Trevlyn fell upon her knees before him, with a submissive gesture, but imploring eyes, for, amid the wreck of womanly pride and worldly fortune, the mother's heart still clung to its idol.

"Who should pity her, if not I? God knows I would have spared her this blow if I could; but Helen would not keep silent, and I was driven to finish what I had begun. Tell Lillian this, and do not let her hate me."

As Paul spoke, tenderly, eagerly, the curtain parted, and Lillian appeared, trembling with the excitement of that interview, but conscious of only one emotion as she threw herself into his arms, crying in a tone of passionate delight, "Brother! Brother! Now I may love you!"

Paul held her close, and for a moment forgot everything but the joy of that moment. Lillian spoke first, looking up through tears of tenderness, her little hand laid caressingly against his cheek, as she whispered with sudden bloom in her own, "Now I know why I loved you so well, and now I can see you marry Helen without breaking my heart. Oh, Paul, you are still mine, and I care for nothing else."

"But, Lillian, I am not your brother."

"Then, in heaven's name, who are you?" she cried, tearing herself from his arms.

"Your lover, dear!"

"Who, then, is the heir?" demanded Lady Trevlyn, springing up, as Lillian turned to seek shelter with her mother.

"I am."

Helen spoke, and Helen stood on the threshold of the door, with a hard, haughty look upon her beautiful face.

"You told your story badly, Paul," she said, in a bitter tone. "You forgot me, forgot my affliction, my loneliness, my wrongs, and the natural desire of a child to clear her mother's honor and claim her father's name. I am Sir Richard's eldest daughter. I can prove my birth, and I demand my right with his own words to sustain me."

She paused, but no one spoke; and with a slight tremor in her proud voice, she added, "Paul has done the work; he shall have the reward. I only want my father's name. Title and fortune are nothing to one like me. I coveted and claimed them that I might give them to you, Paul, my one friend, always, so tender and so true."

"I'll have none of it," he answered, almost fiercely. "I have kept my promise, and am free. You chose to claim your own, although I offered all I had to buy your silence. It is yours by right—take it, and enjoy it if you can. I'll have no reward for work like this."

He turned from her with a look that would have stricken her to the heart could she have seen it. She felt it, and it seemed to augment some secret anguish, for she pressed her hands against her bosom with an expression of deep suffering, exclaiming passionately, "Yes, I *will* keep it, since I am to lose all else. I am tired of pity. Power is sweet, and I will use it. Go, Paul, and be happy if you can, with a nameless wife, and the world's compassion or contempt to sting your pride."

"Oh, Lillian, where shall we go? This is no longer our home, but who will receive us now?" cried Lady Trevlyn, in a tone of despair, for her spirit was utterly broken by the thought of the shame and sorrow in store for this beloved and innocent child.

"I will." And Paul's face shone with a love and loyalty they could not doubt. "My lady, you gave me a home when I was homeless; now let me pay my debt. Lillian, I have loved you from the time when, a romantic boy, I wore your little picture in my breast, and vowed to win you if I lived. I dared not speak before, but now, when other hearts may be shut against you, mine stands wide open to welcome you. Come, both. Let me protect and cherish you, and so atone for the sorrow I have brought you."

It was impossible to resist the sincere urgency of his voice, the tender reverence of his manner, as he took the two forlorn yet innocent creatures into the shelter of his strength and love. They clung to him instinctively, feeling that there still remained to them one staunch friend whom adversity could not estrange.

An eloquent silence fell upon the room, broken only by sobs, grateful whispers, and the voiceless vows that lovers plight with eyes, and hands, and tender lips. Helen was forgotten, till Lillian, whose elastic spirit threw off sorrow as a flower sheds the rain, looked up to thank Paul, with smiles as well as tears, and saw the lonely figure in the shadow. Her attitude was full of pathetic significance; she still stood on the threshold, for no one had welcomed her, and in the strange room she knew not where to go; her hands were clasped before her face, as if those sightless eyes had seen the joy she could not share, and at her feet lay the time-stained paper that gave her a barren title, but no love. Had Lillian known how sharp a conflict between passion and pride, jealousy and generosity, was going on in that young heart, she could not have spoken in a tone of truer pity or sincerer goodwill than that in which she softly said, "Poor girl! We must not forget her, for, with all her wealth, she is poor compared to us. We both had one father, and should love each other in spite of this misfortune. Helen, may I call you sister?"

"Not yet. Wait till I deserve it."

As if that sweet voice had kindled an answering spark of nobleness in her own heart, Helen's face changed beautifully, as she tore the paper to shreds, saying in a glad, impetuous tone, while the white flakes fluttered from her hands, "I, too, can be generous. I, too, can forgive. I bury the sad past. See! I yield my claim, I destroy my proofs, I promise eternal silence, and keep 'Paul's cousin' for my only title. Yes, you are happy, for you love one another!" she cried, with a sudden passion of tears. "Oh, forgive me, pity me, and take me in, for I am all alone and in the dark!"

There could be but one reply to an appeal like that, and they gave it, as they welcomed her with words that sealed a household league of mutual secrecy and sacrifice.

They *were* happy, for the world never knew the hidden tie that bound them so faithfully together, never learned how well the old prophecy had been fulfilled, or guessed what a tragedy of life and death the silver key unlocked.

❧ The Skeleton in the Closet

"Louis, to whom does that château belong?" I asked, as we checked our horses under the antique gateway, and my eye, following the sweep of the lawn, caught a glimpse of the mansion embosomed in a blooming paradise of flowers and grand old trees.

"To Mme. Arnheim, the loveliest widow in all France," Louis answered, with a sigh.

"And the cruelest, I fancy, or you would have been master here," I replied, interpreting the sigh aright, for my friend was a frequent captive to the gentle sex.

"Never its master, Gustave—I should always have remained a slave while Mathilde was there," he answered, with a moody glance through the iron gates that seemed to bar him from the heaven of his desire.

"Nay, Louis, come down from the clouds and tell me something of the Circe whose spells have ensnared you; come hither and sit on this little knoll where we have a better view of the château, and while our horses rest, you shall tell the story of your love, as the romances have it." And dismounting as I spoke, I threw myself upon the green sward opposite the flowery lawn that sloped up to the terraces whereon the château stood.

Louis flung himself beside me, saying abruptly, "There is no tale to tell, Gustave. I met Mathilde at the general's a year ago—loved her, of course, and of course without success. I say of course, for I am not the only one that has laid siege to her cold heart, and got frostbitten in the attempt. She is a marble image, beautiful and cold, though there are rare flashes of warmth that win, a softness that enchants, which make her doubly dangerous. She lives yonder with her old duenna, Mlle. D'Aubigny, caring little for the world, and seldom blessing it with her presence. She has made an Eden, but desires no Adam, and is content to dwell year after year solitary in her flowery nook like the English poet's Lady of Shalott."

"And trust me, like that mysterious lady, she, too, will one day see—

"A bow-shot from her bower-eaves,
Riding 'mong the barley-sheaves,
The sunlight dazzling thro' the leaves,

> And flashing on his greaves
>   A bold Sir Lancelot.
> She'll leave her web, and leave her loom,
> She'll make three paces thro' the room,
> She'll see the water-lilies bloom,
> She'll see the helmet and the plume,
>   And follow down to Camelot,"

chanted I, making a free translation of the lines to suit my jest.

"There she is! Look, Gustave, look!" cried Louis, springing to his feet, with an eager gesture toward the lawn.

I looked, almost expecting to behold the shadowy lady of the poet's song, so fully had the beauty of the spot enchanted me. A female figure was passing slowly down the broad steps that led from terrace to terrace into the shaded avenue. Silently I drew Louis into the deep shadow of the gateway, where we could look unperceived.

The slender, white-robed figure came slowly on, pausing now and then to gather a flower, or caress the Italian greyhound tripping daintily beside her. My interest was excited by my friend's words, and I looked eagerly for the beauty he extolled. She *was* beautiful—and when she paused in the shadow of a drooping acacia, and stood looking thoughtfully toward the blue lake shining in the distance, I longed to be an artist, that I might catch and keep the picture.

The sunshine fell upon her through the leaves, turning her hair to gold, touching the soft bloom of her cheek, and rendering more fair the graceful arms half bared by the fresh wind tossing the acacia boughs. A black lace scarf was thrown about her, one end drawn over her blond hair, as the Spanish women wear their veils; a few brilliant flowers filled her hands, and gave coloring to her unornamented dress. But the chief charm of her delicate face was the eyes, so lustrous and dark, so filled with the soft gloom of a patient grief that they touched and won my heart by their mute loveliness.

We stood gazing eagerly, forgetting in our admiration the discourtesy of the act, till a shrill neigh from my horse startled us, and woke Mme. Arnheim from her reverie. She cast a quick glance down the avenue, and turning, was soon lost to us in the shelter of a winding path.

"Come, Louis, come away before we are discovered; it was a rude act, and I am ashamed of it," I cried, drawing him away, though my eye still watched the lover, hoping for another glance.

Louis lingered, saying bitterly, "Gustave, I envy that dog the touch of her hand, the music of her voice, and proud as I am, would follow her like a hound, even though she chid me like one, for I love her as I never loved before, and I have no hope."

Wondering no longer at the passion of my friend, I made no reply to his gloomy words, but turning away, we mounted, and with a lingering look behind, departed silently. Louis returned to Paris; I to my friend General Moreau, at whose hospitable home I was visiting to recruit my health, shattered by long illness.

The general's kind lady, even amid her cares as hostess to a mansion full of friends, found time to seek amusement for her feeble guest, and when I had exhausted her husband's stock of literature, as if prompted by some good angel she proposed a visit to Mme. Arnheim to bespeak for me admission to her well-stored library.

Concealing my delight, I cheerfully accompanied Mme. Moreau, asking sundry questions as we drove along, concerning the fair recluse. There was a slight reserve in Madame's manner as she answered me.

"Mathilde has known much sorrow in her short life, *mon ami,* and seeks to forget the past in the calmness of the present. She seldom visits us except we are alone—then she comes often, for the general regards her with a fatherly affection; and in her society I feel no want of other friends."

"Has she been long a widow?" I asked, impelled by a most unmasculine curiosity to learn yet more.

"Seven years," replied Madame. "Her husband was a German—but I know little of her past life, for she seldom speaks of it, and I have only gathered from the few allusions she has made to it, that she married very young, and knew but little happiness as a wife."

I longed to ask yet more, and though courtesy restrained my tongue, my eyes betrayed me; Mme. Moreau, who had taken the invalid to her motherly heart, could not resist that mute appeal, for, as she drew up the window to shield me from the freshening breeze, she said smilingly:

"Ah, my child, I may repent this visit if I lead you into temptation, for boy as you seem to me, there is a man's heart in this slight frame of yours and a love of beauty shining in these hollow eyes. I cannot satisfy you, Gustave—she came hither but two years ago, and has lived secluded from the world, regardless of many solicitations to quit her solitude and widowhood. Your friend Louis was one of her most earnest suitors, but, like the rest, only procured his own banishment, for Mathilde only desires friends and not lovers. Therefore, let me warn you, if you desire the friendship of this charming woman, beware of love. But see, we have arrived, so bid adieu to ennui for a while at least."

Up the wide steps and over the green terraces we passed into a room whose chief charm was its simplicity; no costly furniture encumbered it, no tasteless decorations marred it; a few rare pictures enriched its walls, and a few graceful statues looked out from flowery nooks. Light draperies swayed to and fro before the open casements, giving brief glimpses of bloom and verdure just without. Leafy shadows flickered on the marble floor, and the blithe notes of birds were the only sounds that broke the sunny silence brooding over the whole scene.

Well as I fancied I remembered Mme. Arnheim, I was struck anew with the serene beauty of her face as she greeted us with cordial courtesy.

A rapt pity seemed to fill the pensive eyes as Madame spoke of my long illness, and her whole manner was full of interest, and a friendly wish to serve that captivated me and made me bless the pallid face that wore so sweet a pity for me.

We visited the library, a fascinating place to me, full of rare old books, and the soft gloom of shade and silence so dear to a student's heart. A few graceful words made me welcome here, and I promised myself many blissful hours in a spot so suited to my taste and fancy.

"Come now to the chapel, where M. Novaire will find another friend whose sweet discourse may have power to beguile some hours of their slow flight," said Mme. Arnheim, as she led the way into a little chapel rich in Gothic arches and stained windows, full of saintly legends that recalled the past.

"Ah, yes, here is indeed a treasure for you, Gustave—I had forgotten this," said Mme. Moreau, as our hostess led me to a fine organ, and with a smile invited me to touch its tempting keys.

With a desire to excel never experienced before, I obeyed, and filled the air with surges of sweet sound that came and went like billows breaking melodiously on the strand. Mme. Arnheim listened with drooping eyes and folded hands; and as I watched her standing in the gloom with one mellow ray of sunlight falling on her golden hair, she seemed to my excited fancy a white-robed spirit with the light of heaven shining on its gentle head.

The beautiful eyes were full of tender dew as they met mine in thanking me, and a certain deference seemed to mark her manner, as if the music I had power to create were a part of myself, and still lingered about me when the organ keys were mute.

Returning toward the château, we found a dainty little feast spread on a rustic table in the shadow of a group of foreign trees. No servants appeared, but Mme. Arnheim served us herself with a cordial ease that rendered doubly sweet the light wines she poured for us, and the nectarines she gathered from the sunny wall.

It was a new and wonderfully winning thing to me to see a creature beautiful and gifted—so free from affectation, so unconscious of self, so childlike, yet so full of all the nameless charms of gracious womanhood. To an imaginative temperament like mine it was doubly dangerous, and I dreaded to depart.

I sat apparently listening to the low dash of the fountain, but eye, ear, and mind were all intent on her; watching the pliant grace of her slender form, listening to the silvery music of her voice, and musing on the changeful beauty of her countenance. As I thus regarded her, my eye was caught by the sole ornament she wore, an ornament so peculiar and so ill-suited to its gentle wearer that my attention was arrested by it.

As she refilled my glass, a bracelet slipped from her arm to her wrist, and in that brief moment I had examined it attentively. It was of steel, delicately wrought, clasped by a golden lock, the tiny key of which hung by a golden chain. A strange expression stirred the sweet composure of her face as she saw the direction of my glance, and with a sudden gesture she thrust the trinket out of sight.

But as her hands moved daintily among the fruit in serving us, the bracelet often fell with a soft clash about her slender wrist, and each time she thrust it back, till her white arm was reddened with the marks of its slight links.

It seemed a most unfitting ornament, and as I watched her closely, I fancied some sad memory was connected with it, for the sight of it seemed painful, and all notice irksome to her. Ah, I little knew to what a fate it fettered her!

As we stood upon the terrace, awaiting the carriage, I turned from the château with its airy balconies without, and its inviting apartments within, to the blooming scene before me, exclaiming with enthusiasm, "This is the loveliest spot in France! A perfect picture of a peaceful, happy home. Ah, madame, many must envy you this tranquil retreat from the cares and sorrows of the world."

Mme. Arnheim's dark eyes wandered over the fair home I admired, and again I saw that strange expression flit across her face, but now more vividly than before. Pain, abhorrence, and despair seemed to sit for an instant on those lovely features; a swift paroxysm of mute anguish seemed to thrill through her whole figure; and I saw the half-hidden hands clenched as if controlling some wild impulse with an iron will. Like a flash it came and went, and with a long, deep sigh she answered slowly, "Do not envy me, for you have all the world before, free to choose a home where fancy leads. This is my world, and is often wearisome for all its loveliness."

There was a mournful cadence in her voice that saddened me, and a black shadow seemed to fall across the sunny landscape as I listened. The carriage came, and when she turned to say adieu, no trace of gloom marred the sweet serenity of her pale countenance.

"Come often and come freely, Monsieur Novaire," she said, adding, with a smile that would have won from me any boon I had the power to bestow, "My books, my organ, and my gardens are most sincerely at your service, and I only claim the right to listen when you fill my little chapel with the melody I love so well."

I could only thank her in words that sounded very poor and cold, remembering the sweetness of her own, and we drove away, leaving her in the shadow of the hall, still smiling her adieu.

Frankly as the favor had been granted, I accepted it, and went often to the château which soon became a "Castle Dangerous," and its fair mistress the one beloved object in the world to me. Day after day I went to muse in the quiet library, or to soothe my restless spirit with the music of the chapel organ. Mme. Arnheim I but seldom saw until I learned the spell which had power to lure her to my longing eyes. At the château she was the stately hostess, always courteous and calm, but when I sat alone in the chapel, filling the air with the plaintive or triumphal melody, I never failed to see a shadow gliding past the open door, or hear the light fall of a step along the echoing aisles, and with an altered mien she came to listen as I spoke to her in the tenderest strains heart could devise or hand execute.

This filled me with a sense of power I exulted in, for, remembering Mme. Moreau's warning words, "If you desire Mathilde's friendship, beware of love," I concealed my growing passion, and only gave it vent in the music that lured her to my side, and spoke to her in accents that never could offend. Slowly the coldness of her manner vanished, and though still chary of her presence, she came at last to treat me as a friend. At rare intervals some sudden interest in the book I read, some softened mood produced by the song I sang, the strain I played, gave me glimpses of a nature so frank and innocent, and a heart so deep and tender, that the hope of winning it seemed vain, and I reproached myself with treachery in accepting thus the hospitalities of her home and the blessing of her friendship, while so strong a love burned like a hidden fire in my breast.

Calmly the days flowed by, and nothing marred my peace till a slight incident filled me with restless doubts and fears. Wandering one day among the gardens, led by the desire of meeting Mathilde, I struck into an unfrequented path which wound homeward round a wing of the château which I had never visited and which I had believed unused. Pausing on the hillside to examine it, my eye fell on an open window opposite the spot where I was standing, and just within it I beheld Mathilde sitting with bent head and averted face. Eager to catch a glimpse of that beloved countenance, I stood motionless, screened by a drooping tree. As I peered further into the shaded room a jealous pang shot through me and my heart stood still, for in the high carved chair beside Mathilde I saw the arm and shoulder of a man. With straining eyes I watched it, and set my teeth fiercely when I saw the arm encircle her graceful neck, while the hand played idly with a tress of sunny hair I would have given worlds to touch. The arm was clothed in the sleeve of a damask robe de chambre, somber yet rich, and the hand seemed delicate and white; its motions were languid and I heard the murmur of a low voice often broken by faint laughter.

I could not move, but stood rooted to the spot till Mathilde dropped the curtain, and a moment after her voice rose soft and sweet, singing to that unknown guest, then I turned and dashed into the wood like one possessed.

From that day my peace was gone, for though Mathilde was unchanged, between us there always seemed to rise the specter of that hidden friend or lover, and I could not banish the jealous fears that tortured me. I knew from Mme. Moreau that Mathilde had no relatives in France, and few friends beside the general and his wife. The unknown was no cousin, no brother then, and I brooded over the mystery in vain. A careless inquiry of a servant if there were any guests at the chateau received a negative reply, given with respectful brevity and a quick, scrutinizing glance—while, as he spoke, down through hall and corridor floated the sound of Mathilde's voice singing in that far-off room.

Once more, and only once, I watched that window, waiting long in vain, but the curtain was thrown back at length, and then I saw Mathilde pacing to and fro with clasped hands and streaming eyes, as if full of some passionate despair; while the low laughter, I remember well, seemed mocking her great sorrow.

She came to the casement and flung it wide, leaning far out, as if to seek consolation in the caressing breath of the balmy air and the soft sighing of the pines. As she stood thus, I saw her strike her fettered arm a cruel blow upon the strong stone balcony enclosing the window—a blow which left it bruised; though she never heeded it, but turned again into the room, as if in answer to some quick command.

I never looked again—for whatever secret sin or sorrow was there concealed, I had no right to know it, for by no look or word did Mathilde ever seek my sympathy or aid; but with a growing paleness on her cheek, a deepening sadness in her eye, she met me with unaltered kindness, and listened when I played as if she found her only solace there.

So the summer passed, and silently the hidden passion that possessed me did its work, till the wan shadow that once mocked me from my mirror was changed into the likeness of an ardent, healthful man, clear of eye, strong of arm, and light of foot. They said it was the fresh air of the hills; I knew it was the healing power of a beloved presence and the magic of an earnest love.

One soft September day, I had wandered with Mathilde into the deep ravine that cleft a green hill not far from the château. We had sat listening to the music of the waterfall as it mingled pleasantly with our conversation, till a sudden peal of thunder warned us home. Shut in by the steep cliffs, the gathering clouds had been unobserved until the tempest was close at hand. We hastily wound our way up from below, and paused a moment to look out upon the wildly beautiful scene.

Standing thus, there came a sudden glare before my eyes, followed by a deafening crash that brought me faint and dizzy to the ground. A flood of rain revived me, and on recovering I was conscious that Mathilde's arms encircled me, and my head was pillowed on her bosom; I felt the rapid beating of her heart, and heard the prayers she was murmuring as she held me thus. Her mantle was thrown about me, as if to shield me from the storm, and shrouded in its silken folds I lay as if in a dream, with no fear of thunderbolt or lightning flash—conscious only of the soft arms enfolding me, the faint perfume of her falling hair, and the face so near my own that every whispered word fell clearly on my ear.

How long I should have remained thus I cannot tell, for warmer drops than rain fell on my cheek and recalled me to myself. Putting aside the frail screen she had placed between me and the sudden danger, I staggered to my feet, unmindful of my dizzy brain and still half-blinded eyes.

"Not dead! Not dead! Thank God for that" was the glad cry that broke from Mathilde's lips, as I stood wild-eyed and pale before her. "O Gustave, are you unscathed by that awful bolt which I thought had murdered you before me?"

I reassured her, and felt that it was now my turn to shelter and protect, for she clung to me trembling and tearful, so changed that the calm, cold Mme. Arnheim of the fair château and the brave, tenderhearted creature on the cliff seemed two different women, but both lovely and beloved.

Swiftly and silently we hurried home, and when I would have quitted her she detained me with gentle force, saying, "You must remain my guest tonight, I cannot suffer you to leave my roof in such a storm as this."

Old Mlle. D'Aubigny bustled to and fro, and after refreshment and repose left us together by the cheerful firelight on the library hearth.

Mathilde sat silent, as if wrapped in thought, her head bent on her hand. I sat and looked at her till I forgot all but my love, and casting prudence to the winds, spoke out fervently and fast.

"Mathilde," I said, "deal frankly with me, and tell me was it *fear* or *love* that stirred this quiet heart of yours, and spoke in words of prayerful tenderness when you believed me dead? Forgive me if I pain you, but remembering that moment of unlooked-for bliss, I can no longer keep the stern silence I have imposed upon myself so long. I have loved you very truly all these months of seeming coldness, have haunted this house not in search of selfish ease, but to be near you, to breathe the air you breathed, to tread the ground you trod, and to sun myself in the light of your beloved presence. I should have been silent still, knowing my unworthiness, but as I lay pillowed on your bosom, through the tumult of the storm, a low voice from your heart seemed to speak to mine, saying 'I love you.' Tell me, dearest Mathilde, did I hear aright?"

An unwonted color dawned upon her cheek, a world of love and longing shone upon me in her glance, while a change as beautiful as it was brief passed over her, leaving in the stately woman's place a tender girl, whose heart looked from her eyes, and made her broken words more full of music than the sweetest song.

"Gustave, you heard aright; it was not fear that spoke." She stretched her hand to me, and clasping it in both my own I bent to kiss it with a lover's ardor—when between my eager lips and that fair hand dropped the *steel bracelet* with a sharp metallic sound.

With a bitter cry, Mathilde tore herself from my hold, and covering up her face shrank away, as if between us there had risen up a barrier visible to her alone.

"Mathilde, what is it? What power has this bauble, to work such a change as this? See! It is off and gone forever; for this hand is mine now, and shall wear no fetter but the golden one I give it," I cried, as kneeling on the cushion at her feet I repossessed myself of her passive hand, and unlocking the hateful bracelet, flung it far away across the room.

Apparently unconscious of my presence, Mathilde sat with such mute anguish and despair in every line of her drooping figure that a keen sense of coming evil held me silent at her feet, waiting some look or word from her.

A sharp struggle must have passed within her, for when she lifted up her face, all light and color had died out, and the whole countenance was full of some stern resolve, that seemed to have chilled its beauty into stone. Silently she motioned me to rise, and with a statelier mien than I had ever seen her wear, she passed down the long room to where the ominous steel bracelet glittered in the light. Silently she raised it, reclasped it on her arm, then with rapid motion rent away the tiny key and flung it into the red embers glowing on the hearth.

A long, shuddering sigh heaved her bosom as it vanished, a sound more eloquent of patient despair than the bitterest tears that ever fell. Coming to my side, she looked into my eyes with such love and pity shining through the pale determination of her face that I would have folded her to my breast, but with a swift gesture of that fettered arm she restrained me, saying slowly as if each word wrung her heart:

"God forgive me that I could forget the solemn duty this frail chain binds me to. Gustave, I never meant to wrong you thus, and will atone for it by giving you the confidence never bestowed on any human being. Come and see the secret anguish of my life, the haunting specter of my home, the stern fate which makes all love a bitter mockery, and leaves me desolate."

Like a shadow she flitted from me, beckoning me to follow. The storm still raged without, but all was bright and still within as we passed through gallery and hall into that distant wing of the château. The radiance of shaded lamps fell on the marble floors—graceful statues gleamed among the flowers, and the air was full of perfume, but I saw no beauty anywhere, for between me and the woman whom I loved an unknown phantom seemed to stand, and its black shadow darkened all the world to me.

Mathilde paused in a silent corridor at length, and looking back at me, whispered imploringly, "Gustave, do not judge me till I have told you all." Then before I could reply, she passed before me into a dimly lighted room, still beckoning me to follow.

Bernhardt, an old servant whom I had seldom seen, rose as she entered, and at a motion from Mathilde bade me be seated. Mechanically I obeyed, for all strength seemed to desert me as I looked upon the scene before me.

On the floor, clothed in the dress I well remembered, sat a man playing with the childish toys that lay around him. The face would have been a young and comely one, were it not for the awful blight which had fallen on it; the vacant gaze of his hollow eyes, the aimless movements of his feeble hands, and the unmeaning words he muttered to himself, all told the fearful loss of that divine gift—reason.

Mathilde pointed to the mournful wreck, saying, with a look of desolation which few human faces wear, "Gustave, am I not a widow?"

Then I knew that I saw the husband of my Mathilde—and he an idiot!

A brief sensation of mingled disgust, despair, and rage possessed me, for I knew how powerless I was to free the heart I coveted from this long slavery; one thought of Mathilde recalled me, one glance into those eyes so full of pain and passion banished every feeling but a tender pity for her cruel lot, and a redoubled love and admiration for the patient strength which had borne this heavy weight of care all those years. I could not speak, I only took that fettered hand and kissed it reverently.

The imbecile (I cannot say husband) rose, when he saw Mathilde, and creeping to her side filled her hands with toys, still smiling that vacant smile, so pitiful to see in eyes that have shone unclouded upon such a wife, still muttering those senseless words so dreadful to hear, from lips that should have spoken with a man's wisdom and a husband's tenderness to her.

My heart ached, as I saw that young, fair woman sit near that wreck of manhood, soothing his restless spirit with the music of her voice, while his wandering hands played with the one ornament she wore, that bracelet whose slight links were so strong a chain to bind her to a bitter duty, so sorrowful a badge of slavery to a proud soul like hers.

Sleep fell suddenly on that poor, wandering mind, and with a few words to old Bernhardt, Mathilde led me back into the quiet room we left.

I sank into a chair, and dropping my head upon my folded arms, sat silent, knowing now what lay before us.

The storm rolled and crashed above our heads, but in the silence of the room, the voice I loved so well spoke softly at my side, as Mathilde told the story of her life.

"Gustave, I was an orphan, and my stern guardian found his ward an irksome charge. He looked about him for some means of relief, and but two appeared, marriage or a convent. I was but sixteen then, blithe of heart, and full of happy dreams; the convent seemed a tomb to me, and any fate a blessed one that saved me from it. I had a friend—heaven forgive her the wrong she did me!—and this friend influenced my guardian's choice, and won for me the husband you have seen. She knew the fearful malady that cursed him even then, but bade him conceal it from my guardian and me. He loved me, and obeyed her, and thus she led me into that dark web of woe where I have struggled all these years.

"I had innocently won a heart that she coveted, and though I did not listen to that lover's suit, he was lost to her, and for that she hated me. I knew nothing of her passion then, and trusted her implicitly. We were in Germany, and I, a stranger in a strange land, followed where she pointed, and so walked smilingly to my doom. Reinhold Arnheim was a gentle but weakhearted man, guided by his cousin Gertrude, my false friend. He loved me with all the ardor of his feeble nature, and I, seeing a free future before me, thought I gave him my heart, when it was but a girlish affection for the man who saved me from the fate I dreaded.

"My guardian's last illness coming suddenly upon him, he desired to see me safe in a husband's home, before he left me forever. I' was married, and he died, believing me a happy wife—I, a child, betrothed one little month.

"Nine years ago, that marriage mockery took place, but to me it seems a lifetime full of pain. Ah! I should have been a happier woman in a nun's narrow cell than a wife worse than widowed, with a secret grief like this!" Mathilde paused, and for a moment nothing broke the silence but the wind, as it swept moaning away across the lake.

"Let me pass lightly over the two years that followed that unhappy bridal," she continued hurriedly. "I was frantic with indignation and dismay when I learned the secret Gertrude's wickedness and Reinhold's weakness had withheld from me. I had no friends to flee to, no home but my husband's, and too proud to proclaim the wrongs for which I knew no redress, I struggled to conceal my anguish, and accept my fate.

"My husband pleaded with me to spare him, the victim of a hereditary curse. I knew he loved me, and pity for his misfortune kept me silent. For years, no one knew the secret of his malady but Gertrude, his physician, Bernhardt, and myself.

"We seemed a happy pair, for Reinhold was truly kind, and I played my part well, proud to show my false friend that her cruel blow had failed to crush me.

"Gustave, tongue can never tell how I suffered—how I prayed for strength and patience; love would have made it easier to bear, but when those years of trial made a woman of the careless girl, and looking into my heart for some affection to sustain me, I found only pity and aversion, then I saw the error I had committed in my ignorance—I never loved him, and this long suffering has been my punishment for that great sin. Heaven grant it may atone!

"Gustave, I tried to be a patient wife—I tried to be a cheerful companion to poor Reinhold in his daily life, a brave comforter in those paroxysms of sharp agony which tortured him in secret—but all in vain. I could not love him, and I came at length to see my future as it stretched before me black and barren.

"Tied for life, to a man whose feeble mind left no hope of comforting companionship in our long pilgrimage, and with whom duty, unsweetened by affection, grew to a loathsome slavery—what wonder that I longed to break away and flee from my prison by the only outlet left to my despair?

"I wavered long, but resolved at length to end the life now grown too burdensome to bear. I wrote a letter to my husband, asking forgiveness for the grief I caused him, and freely pardoning the great wrong he had done me. No reproaches embittered my last words, but tenderly and truthfully I showed him all my heart, and said farewell forever.

"But before I could consummate my sinful purpose, I was seized with what I fondly hoped would prove a mortal illness, and while lying unconscious of all grief and care, Reinhold found and read that letter. He never told me the discovery he had made, but hid the wound and loved me still—never kinder than when he watched beside me with a woman's patient tenderness, as I slowly and reluctantly came back to life and health again.

"Then when he deemed me strong enough to bear the shock, he kissed me fondly one sad day, and going out with dogs and gun, as if to his favorite sport, at nightfall was brought home a ghastly spectacle.

"To all but his old servant it seemed a most unhappy accident, but in the silence of the night, as we watched beside what we believed to be his dying bed, old Bernhardt told me, that from broken words and preparations made in secret, he felt sure his master had gone out that day intending never to return alive—choosing to conceal his real design under the appearance of a sad mischance, that no remorse might poison my returning peace.

"With tears the old man told his fears, and when I learned that Reinhold had read that fatal letter, I could no longer doubt. It was a sad and solemn sight to me—for sitting in the shadow of death, I looked back upon my life, and seeing clearly where I had failed in wifely duty and in Christian patience, I prayerfully devoted my whole future to the atonement of the wrong I had committed against God, my husband, and myself.

"Reinhold lived, but never knew me again, never heard my entreaties for pardon, or my tender assurances of pity and affection—all I could truly offer even then. The grief my desperate resolve had caused him and the shock of that rash act were too much for his weak body and weak brain, and he rose up from that bed of suffering the mournful wreck you see him now.

"Gustave, I have kept my vow, and for seven long years have watched and guarded him most faithfully. I could not bear the pity of those German friends, and after wandering far and wide in search of health for my unhappy husband, I came hither unknown and friendless, bringing my poor husband to a quiet home, where no rude sound could disturb, no strange face make afraid. I was a widow in the saddest sense of that sad word, and as such I resolved henceforward to be known.

"The few who knew of the existence of the shadow you have seen believe him to be my brother, and I have held my peace, making a secret sorrow of my past, rather than confess the weakness and wickedness of those most near to me; I may have erred in this, but wronging no one, I hoped to win a little brightness to my life, to find a brief oblivion of my grief.

"I fled from the world; seeking to satisfy the hunger of my heart with friendship, and believing myself strong to resist temptation, I welcomed you and tasted happiness again, unconscious of love's subtle power, till it was too late to recall the heart you made your own. Gustave, I shunned you, I seemed cold and calm, when longing to reply to the unspoken passion shining in your glance; I felt my unseen fetters growing too heavy to be borne, and my life of seeming peace a mockery whose gloom appalled and tortured me.

"Heaven knows I struggled to be firm, and but for that unguarded moment of today, when death seemed to have bereft me of the one joy I possessed, I should still have the power to see you go unsaddened by a hopeless love, unburdened by a tale of grief like this. O my friend, forgive and pity me! Help me to bear my burden as I should, and patiently accept the fate heaven sends."

We had sat motionless, looking into each other's eyes as the last words fell from Mathilde's lips; but as she ceased and bent her head as if in meek submission, my heart overflowed. I threw myself before her, and striving to express the sympathy that mingled with my love, could only lay my throbbing forehead on her knee, and weep as I had not wept for years.

I felt her light touch on my head, and seemed to gather calmness from its soothing pressure.

"Do not banish me, Mathilde," I said, "let me still be near you with a glance of tenderness, a word of comfort for your cheer. There is a heavy shadow on your home. Let me stay and lighten it with the love that shall be warm and silent as the summer sunshine on your flowers."

But to my prayer there came a resolute reply, though the face that looked into my own was eloquent with love and grief.

"Gustave, we must part at once, for while my husband lives I shall guard his honorable name from the lightest breath. You were my friend, and I welcomed you— you are my lover, and henceforth are banished. Pardon me, and let us part unpledged by any vow. You are free to love whenever you shall weary of the passion that now rules your heart. I am bound by a tie which death alone can sever; till then I wear this fetter, placed here by a husband's hand nine years ago; it is a symbol of my life, a mute monitor of duty, strong and bright as the hope and patience which now come to strengthen me. I have thrown away the key, and its place is here till this arm lies powerless, or is stretched free and fetterless to clasp and hold you mine forever!"

"Give me some charm, some talisman, to keep my spirit brave and cheerful through the separation now before us, and then I will go," I cried, as the chapel clock tolled one, and the last glimmer died upon the hearth.

Mathilde brushed the hair back from my eager face, and gazed long and earnestly into my eyes, then bent and left a kiss upon my forehead, saying, as she rose, "It is a frank, true countenance, Gustave, and I trust the silent pledge it gives me. God keep you, dearest friend, and grant us a little happiness together in the years to come!"

I held her close for one moment, and with a fervent blessing turned to go, but pausing on the threshold, I looked back. The storm had died, and through the black clouds broke the moon with sudden radiance. A silvery beam lit that beloved face, and seemed to lure me back. I started to return, but Mathilde's clear voice cried farewell; and on the arm that waved a last adieu, the steel bracelet glittered like a warning light. Seeing that, I knew there was no return. I went out into the night a better and a happier man for having known the blessedness and pain of love.

Three years went by, but my hidden passion never wavered, never died—and although I wandered far and wide over the earth, I found no spot so beautiful to me as the sunny château in its paradise of flowers, and no joy so deep as the memory of Mathilde.

I never heard from her, for, though I wrote as one friend to another, no reply was returned. I lamented this, but could not doubt the wisdom of her silence, and waited patiently for my recall.

A letter came at length, not to welcome, but to banish me forever. Mathilde had been a widow, and was a wife again. Kindly she told me this, speaking of my love as a boyish passion, of her own as a brief delusion—asking pardon for the pain she feared to give, and wishing for me a happiness like that she had now won.

It almost murdered me, for this hope was my life. Alone in the Far East, I suffered, fought, and conquered, coming out from that sharp conflict with no faith, no hope, no joy, nothing but a secret love and sorrow locked up in my wounded heart to haunt me like a sad ghost, till some spell to banish it was found.

Aimlessly, I journeyed to and fro, till led by the longing to again see familiar faces, I returned to Paris and sought out my old friend Moreau. He had not left the city for his summer home, and desiring to give him a glad surprise, I sprang up the stairs unannounced and entered his saloon.

A lady stood alone in the deep window, gazing thoughtfully upon the busy scene below. I knew the slender figure draped in white, the golden hair, the soft dark eyes, and with a sharp pang at my heart, I recognized Mathilde—more lovely and serene than ever.

She turned, but in the bronzed and bearded man did not recognize the youth she parted from, and with a glance of quiet wonder waited for me to speak. I could not, and in a moment it was needless, for eye spoke to eye, heart yearned to heart, and she remembered. A sudden color flushed her cheek as she leaned toward me with dilated eyes; the knot of Parmese violets upon her bosom rose and fell with her quickened breath, and her whole frame thrilled with eagerness as she cried joyfully, "Gustave! Come back to meet me at last!"

I stirred to meet her, but on the arms outstretched to greet me no steel bracelet glittered, and recollecting all my loss I clasped my hands before my face, crying mournfully, "O Mathilde, how can you welcome me, when such a gulf has parted us forever? How smile upon the friend whose love you have so wronged, whose life you have made so desolate?"

A short silence ensued, and then Mathilde's low voice replied, still tenderly, but full of pain, "Gustave, there is some mystery in this; deal frankly with me, and explain how I have wronged, how made you desolate?"

"Are you not married, and am I not bereft of the one dear gift I coveted? Did not your own hand part us and give the wound that still bleeds in my faithful heart, Mathilde?" I asked, with a glance of keen inquiry.

"Gustave, I never doubted your truth, though years passed, and I received no answer to the words of cheer I sent to comfort your long exile—then why doubt mine? Some idle rumor has deceived you, for I am now free—free to bestow the gift you covet, free to reward your patient love, if it still glows as warmly as mine."

Doubt, fear, and sorrow fled at once; I cared for nothing, remembered nothing, desired nothing, for Mathilde was free to love me still. That was rapture enough for me, and I drank freely of the cup of joy offered, heedless of unanswered doubts, unraveled mysteries and fears.

A single hour lifted me from gloom and desolation to blessedness again, and in the light of that returning confidence and peace all that seemed dark grew clear before our eyes. Mathilde had written often, but not one word from her had reached me, and not one line of mine had gladdened her. The letter telling of her marriage she had never penned, but knew now to whom she owed the wrong; and pale with womanly indignation told me that the enemy who had schemed to rob us of our happiness was Louis my friend.

He had met her again in Paris, and the passion, smothered for a long time, blazed up afresh. He never spoke of it in words lest he should again be banished, but seemed content to be her friend, though it was evident he hoped to win a warmer return in time.

Poor Reinhold died the year we parted, and was laid to rest in the quiet chapel where sunlight and silence brooded over his last sleep. Mathilde had written often to recall me, but when no reply to those fond missives came, she ceased, and waited hopefully for my return. Louis knew of my friendship with Mathilde, and must have guessed our love, for by some secret means he had thus intercepted letters, which would have shortened my long exile, and spared us both much misery and doubt.

More fully to estrange us he had artfully conveyed through other lips the tidings of my falsehood to Mathilde, hoping to destroy her faith in me and in her sorrow play the comforter and win her to himself. But she would not listen to the rumors of my marriage, would not doubt my truth, or accept the friendship of a man who could traduce a friend.

But for that well-counterfeited letter I too had never doubted, never suffered, and my ireful contempt rose fiercely as I listened to these proofs of Louis's treachery and fraud.

He was absent on some sudden journey, and ere he could return I won Mathilde to give me the dear right to make her joys and griefs my own. One soft, spring morning we went quietly away into a neighboring church, and returned one in heart and name forever.

No one but our old friends the general and his wife knew the happy truth, for Mathilde dreaded the gossip of the world, and besought me not to proclaim my happiness till we were safe in our quiet home, and I obeyed, content to know her mine.

The crimson light of evening bathed the tranquil face beside me as we sat together a week after our marriage, full of that content which comes to loving mortals in those midsummer days of life—when suddenly a voice we both remembered roused us from our happy reverie. Mathilde's eye lit, her slender figure rose erect, and as I started with a wrathful exclamation on my lips, she held me fast, saying, in the tones that never failed to sway me to her will, "Let me deal with him, for he is not worthy of your sword, Gustave; let me avenge the wrong he did us, for a woman's pity will wound deeper than your keenest thrust; promise me, dearest Gustave, that you will control yourself for love of me, remembering all the misery you might bring down upon us both!"

She clung to me with such fond entreaty that I promised, and standing at her side endeavored to be calm, though burning with an indignation nothing but the clasp of that soft hand had power to restrain.

Singing a blithe song Louis entered, but with arrested step and half-uttered greeting paused upon the threshold, eyeing us with a glance of fire, and struggling to conceal the swift dismay that drove the color from his cheek, the power from his limbs.

Mathilde did not speak, and with an effort painful to behold, Louis regained composure; for some sudden purpose seemed to give him courage and sent a glance of triumph to his eye, as with a mocking smile he bowed to the stately woman at my side, saying with malicious emphasis, "I come to present my compliments to Mme. Arnheim on my return from Germany, from Frankfort, her old home—and I bear to her the tenderest greetings from our fair friend Mme. Gertrude Steinburg. Will Madame accept as gladly as I offer them?"

"A fit messenger from such a friend?" icily replied Mathilde.

With a quick perception of her meaning, and a warning pressure of my clenched hand, Louis threw himself into a seat, and with an assumption of friendly ease, belied by the pallor of his countenance and the fierce glitter of the eye, continued with feigned sympathy—determined to leave no bitter word unsaid:

"She is a charming woman, and confided much to me that filled me with surprise and grief. What desolation will be carried to the hearts of Madame's many lovers when they learn that she is no lovely widow, but a miserable wife bound to an idiotic husband—how eagerly will they shun the fair château where Madame guards the secret shame and sorrow of her life, and how enviable must be the feelings of my friend when he discovers the deception practiced upon him and the utter hopelessness of his grand passion."

His keen eye was upon me as he spoke, and seeing the conflict which raged within me, mistook it for dismay and fear. A sardonic laugh broke from his lips, and before Mathilde could reply, he said, "I little thought, when listening to the cheerful story Mme. Steinburg told with such grace, how speedy and agreeable a use I should have power to make of it. Believe me, madame, I sympathize with your misfortunes, and admire the art which renders you all ice to one lover, and all fire to another."

Mathilde dropped my hand, and stood with folded arms, lofty pride in her mien, calm pity in her eye, and cool contempt upon her lips, as she replied in clear, cold tones:

"I am not what you think me, sir, and your generous sympathy comes too late. I was a widow; for the husband whose misfortune should have made his name sacred even to you died three years ago—I am a wife, happy in the love doubt could not estrange or time destroy. Your dark designs have failed, and for every year of needless separation we forgive you, since it renders our affection doubly strong, our union doubly blessed. Your absence at Mme. Steinburg's side removed the only barrier that could have kept us still asunder. Let me thank both of those false friends for the one kind deed that crowned our happiness. Gustave has left your punishment to me. See! It is this."

With a gesture of impassioned grace she threw herself upon my breast, and looking out from that fond shelter with a countenance all radiant with love, and pride, and joy, she cried, "Go! We pity you, and from the fullness of our bliss we pardon all."

She had avenged us well, for in the glance my proud eyes met, I read passion, humiliation, and despair, as Louis gazed upon us for a moment, and then vanished, the last cloud that dimmed our sky.

Paris lay behind us, and we stood on the green terrace looking over the fair domain now so full of peace and promise to our eyes.

Remembering the look of hopeless anguish that had stirred the face I loved in that same spot so long ago, I looked down to read its lineaments afresh.

It was there, close beside me, bright with happiness, and beautiful with the returning bloom that banished its former pensive charm. Trust spoke in the clinging touch upon my arm, joy beamed in the blithe smile of her lips, and love sat like a glory in her tender eyes.

She met my glance, and with a sudden impulse folded her hands, saying softly, "The shadow has departed, Gustave, never to return, and I am free at last. May I be truly grateful for my happy lot."

"No, dearest Mathilde, you are a captive still, not to duty, but to love, whose thralldom shall be to you as light as the fetter I now bind you with." And as I spoke I clasped a slender chain of gold upon the fair arm where for nine bitter years lay the weight of that steel bracelet.

❧ The Abbot's Ghost: or, Maurice Treherne's Temptation

A Christmas Story

CHAPTER I. DRAMATIS PERSONAE

"HOW GOES IT, Frank? Down first, as usual."

"The early bird gets the worm, Major."

"Deuced ungallant speech, considering that the lovely Octavia is the worm," and with a significant laugh the major assumed an Englishman's favorite attitude before the fire.

His companion shot a quick glance at him, and an expression of anxiety passed over his face as he replied, with a well-feigned air of indifference, "You are altogether too sharp, Major. I must be on my guard while you are in the house. Any new arrivals? I thought I heard a carriage drive up not long ago."

"It was General Snowdon and his charming wife. Maurice Treherne came while we were out, and I've not seen him yet, poor fellow!"

"Aye, you may well say that; his is a hard case, if what I heard is true. I'm not booked up in the matter, and I should be, lest I make some blunder here, so tell me how things stand, Major. We've a good half hour before dinner. Sir Jasper is never punctual."

"Yes, you've a right to know, if you are going to try your fortune with Octavia."

The major marched through the three drawing rooms to see that no inquisitive servant was eavesdropping, and, finding all deserted, he resumed his place, while young Annon lounged on a couch as he listened with intense interest to the major's story.

"You know it was supposed that old Sir Jasper, being a bachelor, would leave his fortune to his two nephews. But he was an oddity, and as the title *must* go to young Jasper by right, the old man said Maurice should have the money. He was poor, young Jasper rich, and it seemed but just, though Madame Mère was very angry when she learned how the will was made."

"But Maurice didn't get the fortune. How was that?"

"There was some mystery there which I shall discover in time. All went smoothly till that unlucky yachting trip, when the cousins were wrecked. Maurice saved Jasper's life, and almost lost his own in so doing. I fancy he wishes he had, rather than remain the poor cripple he is. Exposure, exertion, and neglect afterward brought on paralysis of the lower limbs, and there he is—a fine, talented, spirited fellow tied to that cursed chair like a decrepit old man."

"How does he bear it?" asked Annon, as the major shook his gray head, with a traitorous huskiness in his last words.

"Like a philosopher or a hero. He is too proud to show his despair at such a sudden end to all his hopes, too generous to complain, for Jasper is desperately cut up about it, and too brave to be daunted by a misfortune which would drive many a man mad."

"Is it true that Sir Jasper, knowing all this, made a new will and left every cent to his namesake?"

"Yes, and there lies the mystery. Not only did he leave it away from poor Maurice, but so tied it up that Jasper cannot transfer it, and at his death it goes to Octavia."

"The old man must have been demented. What in heaven's name did he mean by leaving Maurice helpless and penniless after all his devotion to Jasper? Had he done anything to offend the old party?"

"No one knows; Maurice hasn't the least idea of the cause of this sudden whim, and the old man would give no reason for it. He died soon after, and the instant Jasper came to the title and estate he brought his cousin home, and treats him like a brother. Jasper is a noble fellow, with all his faults, and this act of justice increases my respect for him," said the major heartily.

"What will Maurice do, now that he can't enter the army as he intended?" asked Annon, who now sat erect, so full of interest was he.

"Marry Octavia, and come to his own, I hope."

"An excellent little arrangement, but Miss Treherne may object," said Annon, rising with sudden kindling of the eye.

"I think not, if no one interferes. Pity, with women, is akin to love, and she pities her cousin in the tenderest fashion. No sister could be more devoted, and as Maurice is a handsome, talented fellow, one can easily foresee the end, if, as I said before, no one interferes to disappoint the poor lad again."

"You espouse his cause, I see, and tell me this that I may stand aside. Thanks for the warning, Major; but as Maurice Treherne is a man of unusual power in many ways, I think we are equally matched, in spite of his misfortune. Nay, if anything, he has the advantage of me, for Miss Treherne pities him, and that is a strong ally for my rival. I'll be as generous as I can, but I'll *not* stand aside and relinquish the woman I love without a trial first."

With an air of determination Annon faced the major, whose keen eyes had read the truth which he had but newly confessed to himself. Major Royston smiled as he listened, and said briefly, as steps approached, "Do your best. Maurice will win."

"We shall see," returned Annon between his teeth.

Here their host entered, and the subject of course was dropped. But the major's words rankled in the young man's mind, and would have been doubly bitter had he known that their confidential conversation had been overheard. On either side of the great fireplace was a door leading to a suite of rooms which had been old Sir Jasper's. These apartments had been given to Maurice Treherne, and he had just returned from London, whither he had been to consult a certain famous physician. Entering quietly, he had taken possession of his rooms, and having rested and dressed for dinner, rolled himself into the library, to which led the curtained door on the right. Sitting idly in his light, wheeled chair, ready to enter when his cousin appeared, he had heard the chat of Annon and the major. As he listened, over his usually impassive face passed varying expressions of anger, pain, bitterness, and defiance, and when the young man uttered his almost fierce "We shall see," Treherne smiled a scornful smile and clenched his pale hand with a gesture which proved that a year of suffering had not conquered the man's spirit, though it had crippled his strong body.

A singular face was Maurice Treherne's; well-cut and somewhat haughty features; a fine brow under the dark locks that carelessly streaked it; and remarkably piercing eyes. Slight in figure and wasted by pain, he still retained the grace as native to him as the stern fortitude which enabled him to hide the deep despair of an ambitious nature from every eye, and bear his affliction with a cheerful philosophy more pathetic than the most entire abandonment to grief. Carefully dressed, and with no hint at invalidism but the chair, he bore himself as easily and calmly as if the doom of lifelong helplessness did not hang over him. A single motion of the hand sent him rolling noiselessly to the curtained door, but as he did so, a voice exclaimed behind him, "Wait for me, cousin." And as he turned, a young girl approached, smiling a glad welcome as she took his hand, adding in a tone of soft reproach, "Home again, and not let me know it, till I heard the good news by accident."

"Was it good news, Octavia?" and Maurice looked up at the frank face with a new expression in those penetrating eyes of his. His cousin's open glance never changed as she stroked the hair off his forehead with the caress one often gives a child, and answered eagerly, "The best to me; the house is dull when you are away, for Jasper always becomes absorbed in horses and hounds, and leaves Mamma and me to mope by ourselves. But tell me, Maurice, what they said to you, since you would not write."

"A little hope, with time and patience. Help me to wait, dear, help me to wait."

His tone was infinitely sad, and as he spoke, he leaned his cheek against the kind hand he held, as if to find support and comfort there. The girl's face brightened beautifully, though her eyes filled, for to her alone did he betray his pain, and in her alone did he seek consolation.

"I will, I will with heart and hand! Thank heaven for the hope, and trust me it shall be fulfilled. You look very tired, Maurice. Why go in to dinner with all those people? Let me make you cozy here," she added anxiously.

"Thanks, I'd rather go in, it does me good; and if I stay away, Jasper feels that he must stay with me. I dressed in haste, am I right, little nurse?"

She gave him a comprehensive glance, daintily settled his cravat, brushed back a truant lock, and, with a maternal air that was charming, said, "My boy is always elegant, and I'm proud of him. Now we'll go in." But with her hand on the curtain she paused, saying quickly, as a voice reached her, "Who is that?"

"Frank Annon. Didn't you know he was coming?" Maurice eyed her keenly.

"No, Jasper never told me. Why did he ask him?"

"To please you."

"Me! When he knows I detest the man. No matter, I've got on the color he hates, so he won't annoy me, and Mrs. Snowdon can amuse herself with him. The general has come, you know?"

Treherne smiled, well pleased, for no sign of maiden shame or pleasure did the girl's face betray, and as he watched her while she peeped, he thought with satisfaction, Annon is right, *I* have the advantage, and I'll keep it at all costs.

"Here is Mamma. We must go in," said Octavia, as a stately old lady made her appearance in the drawing room.

The cousins entered together and Annon watched them covertly, while seemingly intent on paying his respects to Madame Mère, as his hostess was called by her family.

"Handsomer than ever," he muttered, as his eye rested on the blooming girl, looking more like a rose than ever in the peach-colored silk which he had once condemned because a rival admired it. She turned to reply to the major, and Annon glanced at Treherne with an irrepressible frown, for sickness had not marred the charm of that peculiar face, so colorless and thin that it seemed cut in marble; but the keen eyes shone with a wonderful brilliancy, and the whole countenance was alive with a power of intellect and will which made the observer involuntarily exclaim, "That man must suffer a daily martyrdom, so crippled and confined; if it last long he will go mad or die."

"General and Mrs. Snowdon," announced the servant, and a sudden pause ensued as everyone looked up to greet the newcomers.

A feeble, white-haired old man entered, leaning on the arm of an indescribably beautiful woman. Not thirty yet, tall and nobly molded, with straight black brows over magnificent eyes; rippling dark hair gathered up in a great knot, and ornamented with a single band of gold. A sweeping dress of wine-colored velvet, set off with a dazzling neck and arms decorated like her stately head with ornaments of Roman gold. At the first glance she seemed a cold, haughty creature, born to dazzle but not to win. A deeper scrutiny detected lines of suffering in that lovely face, and behind the veil of reserve, which pride forced her to wear, appeared the anguish of a strong-willed woman burdened by a heavy cross. No one would dare express pity or offer sympathy, for her whole air repelled it, and in her gloomy eyes sat scorn of herself mingled with defiance of the scorn of others. A strange, almost tragical-looking woman, in spite of beauty, grace, and the cold sweetness of her manner. A faint smile parted her lips as she greeted those about her, and as her husband seated himself beside Lady Treherne, she lifted her head with a long breath, and a singular expression of relief, as if a burden was removed, and for the time being she was free. Sir Jasper was at her side, and as she listened, her eye glanced from face to face.

"Who is with you now?" she asked, in a low, mellow voice that was full of music.

"My sister and my cousin are yonder. You may remember Tavia as a child, she is little more now. Maurice is an invalid, but the finest fellow breathing."

"I understand," and Mrs. Snowdon's eyes softened with a sudden glance of pity for one cousin and admiration for the other, for she knew the facts.

"Major Royston, my father's friend, and Frank Annon, my own. Do you know him?" asked Sir Jasper.

"No."

"Then allow me to make him happy by presenting him, may I?"

"Not now. I'd rather see your cousin."

"Thanks, you are very kind. I'll bring him over."

"Stay, let me go to him," began the lady, with more feeling in face and voice than one would believe her capable of showing.

"Pardon, it will offend him, he will not be pitied, or relinquish any of the duties or privileges of a gentleman which he can possibly perform. He is proud, we can understand the feeling, so let us humor the poor fellow."

Mrs. Snowdon bowed silently, and Sir Jasper called out in his hearty, blunt way, as if nothing was amiss with his cousin, "Maurice, I've an honor for you. Come and receive it."

Divining what it was, Treherne noiselessly crossed the room, and with no sign of self-consciousness or embarrassment, was presented to the handsome woman. Thinking his presence might be a restraint, Sir Jasper went away. The instant his back was turned, a change came over both: an almost grim expression replaced the suavity of Treherne's face, and Mrs. Snowdon's smile faded suddenly, while a deep flush rose to her brow, as her eyes questioned his beseechingly.

"How dared you come?" he asked below his breath.

"The general insisted."

"And you could not change his purpose; poor woman!"

"You will not be pitied, neither will I," and her eyes flashed; then the fire was quenched in tears, and her voice lost all its pride in a pleading tone.

"Forgive me, I longed to see you since your illness, and so I 'dared' to come."

"You shall be gratified; look, quite helpless, crippled for life, perhaps."

The chair was turned from the groups about the fire, and as he spoke, with a bitter laugh Treherne threw back the skin which covered his knees, and showed her the useless limbs once so strong and fleet. She shrank and paled, put out her hand to arrest him, and cried in an indignant whisper, "No, no, not that! You know I never meant such cruel curiosity, such useless pain to both—"

"Be still, someone is coming," he returned inaudibly; adding aloud, as he adjusted the skin and smoothed the rich fur as if speaking of it, "Yes, it is a very fine one, Jasper gave it to me. He spoils me, like a dear, generous-hearted fellow as he is. Ah, Octavia, what can I do for you?"

"Nothing, thank you. I want to recall myself to Mrs. Snowdon's memory, if she will let me."

"No need of that; I never forget happy faces and pretty pictures. Two years ago I saw you at your first ball, and longed to be a girl again."

As she spoke, Mrs. Snowdon pressed the hand shyly offered, and smiled at the spirited face before her, though the shadow in her own eyes deepened as she met the bright glance of the girl.

"How kind you were that night! I remember you let me chatter away about my family, my cousin, and my foolish little affairs with the sweetest patience, and made me very happy by your interest. I was homesick, and Aunt could never bear to hear of those things. It was before your marriage, and all the kinder, for you were the queen of the night, yet had a word for poor little me."

Mrs. Snowdon was pale to the lips, and Maurice impatiently tapped the arm of his chair, while the girl innocently chatted on.

"I am sorry the general is such an invalid; yet I dare say you find great happiness in taking care of him. It is so pleasant to be of use to those we love." And as she spoke, Octavia leaned over her cousin to hand him the glove he had dropped.

The affectionate smile that accompanied the act made the color deepen again in Mrs. Snowdon's cheek, and lit a spark in her softened eyes. Her lips curled and her voice was sweetly sarcastic as she answered, "Yes, it is charming to devote one's life to these dear invalids, and find one's reward in their gratitude. Youth, beauty, health, and happiness are small sacrifices if one wins a little comfort for the poor sufferers."

The girl felt the sarcasm under the soft words and drew back with a troubled face.

Maurice smiled, and glanced from one to the other, saying significantly, "Well for me that my little nurse loves her labor, and finds no sacrifice in it. I am fortunate in my choice."

"I trust it may prove so—" Mrs. Snowdon got no further, for at that moment dinner was announced, and Sir Jasper took her away. Annon approached with him and offered his arm to Miss Treherne, but with an air of surprise, and a little gesture of refusal, she said coldly:

"My cousin always takes me in to dinner. Be good enough to escort the major." And with her hand on the arm of the chair, she walked away with a mischievous glitter in her eyes.

Annon frowned and fell back, saying sharply, "Come, Major, what are you doing there?"

"Making discoveries."

Chapter II. Byplay

A RIGHT SPLENDID old dowager was Lady Treherne, in her black velvet and point lace, as she sat erect and stately on a couch by the drawing-room fire, a couch which no one dare occupy in her absence, or share uninvited. The gentlemen were still over their wine, and the three ladies were alone. My lady never dozed in public, Mrs. Snowdon never gossiped, and Octavia never troubled herself to entertain any guests but those of her own age, so long pauses fell, and conversation languished, till Mrs. Snowdon roamed away into the library. As she disappeared, Lady Treherne beckoned to her daughter, who was idly making chords at the grand piano. Seating herself on the ottoman at her mother's feet, the girl took the still handsome hand in her own and amused herself with examining the old-fashioned jewels that covered it, a pretext for occupying her telltale eyes, as she suspected what was coming.

"My dear, I'm not pleased with you, and I tell you so at once, that you may amend your fault," began Madame Mère in a tender tone, for though a haughty, imperious woman, she idolized her children.

"What have I done, Mamma?" asked the girl.

"Say rather, what have you left undone. You have been very rude to Mr. Annon.

It must not occur again; not only because he is a guest, but because he is your— brother's friend."

My lady hesitated over the word "lover," and changed it, for to her Octavia still seemed a child, and though anxious for the alliance, she forbore to speak openly, lest the girl should turn willful, as she inherited her mother's high spirit.

"I'm sorry, Mamma. But how can I help it, when he teases me so that I detest him?" said Octavia, petulantly.

"How tease, my love?"

"Why, he follows me about like a dog, puts on a sentimental look when I appear; blushes, and beams, and bows at everything I say, if I am polite; frowns and sighs if I'm not; and glowers tragically at every man I speak to, even poor Maurice. Oh, Mamma, what foolish creatures men are!" And the girl laughed blithely, as she looked up for the first time into her mother's face.

My mother smiled, as she stroked the bright head at her knee, but asked quickly, "Why say 'even poor Maurice,' as if it were impossible for anyone to be jealous of him?"

"But isn't it, Mamma? I thought strong, well men regarded him as one set apart and done with, since his sad misfortune."

"Not entirely; while women pity and pet the poor fellow, his comrades will be jealous, absurd as it is."

"No one pets him but me, and I have a right to do it, for he is my cousin," said the girl, feeling a touch of jealousy herself.

"Rose and Blanche Talbot outdo you, my dear, and there is no cousinship to excuse them."

"Then let Frank Annon be jealous of them, and leave me in peace. They promised to come today; I'm afraid something has happened to prevent them." And Octavia gladly seized upon the new subject. But my lady was not to be eluded.

"They said they could not come till after dinner. They will soon arrive. Before they do so, I must say a few words, Tavia, and I beg you to give heed to them. I desire you to be courteous and amiable to Mr. Annon, and before strangers to be less attentive and affectionate to Maurice. You mean it kindly, but it looks ill, and causes disagreeable remarks."

"Who blames me for being devoted to my cousin? Can I ever do enough to repay him for his devotion? Mamma, you forget he saved your son's life."

Indignant tears filled the girl's eyes, and she spoke passionately, forgetting that Mrs. Snowdon was within earshot of her raised voice. With a frown my lady laid her hand on her daughter's lips, saying coldly, "I do not forget, and I religiously discharge my every obligation by every care and comfort it is in my power to bestow. You are young, romantic, and tender-hearted. You think you must give your time and health, must sacrifice your future happiness to this duty. You are wrong, and unless you learn wisdom in season, you will find that you have done harm, not good."

"God forbid! How can I do that? Tell me, and I will be wise in time."

Turning the earnest face up to her own, Lady Treherne whispered anxiously, "Has Maurice ever looked or hinted anything of love during this year he has been with us, and you his constant companion?"

"Never, Mamma; he is too honorable and too unhappy to speak or think of that. I am his little nurse, sister, and friend, no more, nor ever shall be. Do not suspect us, or put such fears into my mind, else all our comfort will be spoiled."

Flushed and eager was the girl, but her clear eyes betrayed no tender confusion as she spoke, and all her thought seemed to be to clear her cousin from the charge of loving her too well. Lady Treherne looked relieved, paused a moment, then said, seriously but gently, "This is well, but, child, I charge you tell me at once, if ever he forgets himself, for this thing cannot be. Once I hoped it might, now it is impossible; remember that he continue a friend and cousin, nothing more. I warn you in time, but if you neglect the warning, Maurice must go. No more of this; recollect my wish regarding Mr. Annon, and let your cousin amuse himself without you in public."

"Mamma, do you wish me to like Frank Annon?"

The abrupt question rather disturbed my lady, but knowing her daughter's frank, impetuous nature, she felt somewhat relieved by this candor, and answered decidedly, "I do. He is your equal in all respects; he loves you, Jasper desires it, I approve, and you, being heart-whole can have no just objection to the alliance."

"Has he spoken to you?"

"No, to your brother."

"You wish this much, Mamma?"

"Very much, my child."

"I will try to please you, then." And stifling a sigh, the girl kissed her mother with unwonted meekness in tone and manner.

"Now I am well pleased. Be happy, my love. No one will urge or distress you. Let matters take their course, and if this hope of ours can be fulfilled, I shall be relieved of the chief care of my life."

A sound of girlish voices here broke on their ears, and springing up, Octavia hurried to meet her friends, exclaiming joyfully, "They have come! they have come!"

Two smiling, blooming girls met her at the door, and, being at an enthusiastic age, they gushed in girlish fashion for several minutes, making a pretty group as they stood in each other's arms, all talking at once, with frequent kisses and little bursts of laughter, as vents for their emotion. Madame Mère welcomed them and then went to join Mrs. Snowdon, leaving the trio to gossip unrestrained.

"My dearest creature, I thought we never should get here, for Papa had a tiresome dinner party, and we were obliged to stay, you know," cried Rose, the lively sister, shaking out the pretty dress and glancing at herself in the mirror as she fluttered about the room like a butterfly.

"We were dying to come, and so charmed when you asked us, for we haven't seen you this age, darling," added Blanche, the pensive one, smoothing her blond curls after a fresh embrace.

"I'm sorry the Ulsters couldn't come to keep Christmas with us, for we have no gentlemen but Jasper, Frank Annon, and the major. Sad, isn't it?" said Octavia, with a look of despair, which caused a fresh peal of laughter.

"One apiece, my dear, it might be worse." And Rose privately decided to appropriate Sir Jasper.

"Where is your cousin?" asked Blanche, with a sigh of sentimental interest.

"He is here, of course. I forget him, but he is not on the flirting list, you know.

We must amuse him, and not expect him to amuse us, though really, all the capital suggestions and plans for merrymaking always come from him."

"He is better, I hope?" asked both sisters with real sympathy, making their young faces womanly and sweet.

"Yes, and has hopes of entire recovery. At least, they tell him so, though Dr. Ashley said there was no chance of it."

"Dear, dear, how sad! Shall we see him, Tavia?"

"Certainly; he is able to be with us now in the evening, and enjoys society as much as ever. But please take no notice of his infirmity, and make no inquiries beyond the usual 'How do you do.' He is sensitive, and hates to be considered an invalid more than ever."

"How charming it must be to take care of him, he is so accomplished and delightful. I quite envy you," said Blanche pensively.

"Sir Jasper told us that the General and Mrs. Snowdon were coming. I hope they will, for I've a most intense curiosity to see her—" began Rose.

"Hush, she is here with Mamma! Why curious? What is the mystery? For you look as if there was one," questioned Octavia under her breath.

The three charming heads bent toward one another as Rose replied in a whisper, "If I knew, I shouldn't be inquisitive. There was a rumor that she married the old general in a fit of pique, and now repents. I asked Mamma once, but she said such matters were not for young girls to hear, and not a word more would she say. *N'importe,* I have wits of my own, and I can satisfy myself. The gentlemen are coming! Am I all right, dear?" And the three glanced at one another with a swift scrutiny that nothing could escape, then grouped themselves prettily, and waited, with a little flutter of expectation in each young heart.

In came the gentlemen, and instantly a new atmosphere seemed to pervade the drawing room, for with the first words uttered, several romances began. Sir Jasper was taken possession of by Rose, Blanche intended to devote herself to Maurice Treherne, but Annon intercepted her, and Octavia was spared any effort at politeness by this unexpected move on the part of her lover.

"He is angry, and wishes to pique me by devoting himself to Blanche. I wish he would, with all my heart, and leave me in peace. Poor Maurice, he expects me, and I long to go to him, but must obey Mamma." And Octavia went to join the group formed by my lady, Mrs. Snowdon, the general, and the major.

The two young couples flirted in different parts of the room, and Treherne sat alone, watching them all with eyes that pierced below the surface, reading the hidden wishes, hopes, and fears that ruled them. A singular expression sat on his face as he turned from Octavia's clear countenance to Mrs. Snowdon's gloomy one. He leaned his head upon his hand and fell into deep thought, for he was passing through one of those fateful moments which come to us all, and which may make or mar a life. Such moments come when least looked for: an unexpected meeting, a peculiar mood, some trivial circumstance, or careless word produces it, and often it is gone before we realize its presence, leaving aftereffects to show us what we have gained or lost. Treherne was conscious that the present hour, and the acts that filled it, possessed unusual interest, and would exert an unusual influence on his life. Before him was the good and evil genius of his nature in the guise of those two women. Edith Snowdon had already tried her power, and accident only had saved him. Octavia, all unconscious as she was, never failed to rouse and stimulate the noblest attributes of mind and heart. A year spent in her society had done much for him, and he loved her with a strange mingling of passion, reverence, and gratitude. He knew why Edith Snowdon came, he felt that the old fascination had not lost its charm, and though fear was unknown to him, he was ill pleased at the sight of the beautiful, dangerous woman. On the other hand, he saw that Lady Treherne desired her daughter to shun him and smile on Annon; he acknowledged that he had no right to win the young creature, crippled and poor as he was, and a pang of jealous pain wrung his heart as he watched her.

Then a sense of power came to him, for helpless, poor, and seemingly an object of pity, he yet felt that he held the honor, peace, and happiness of nearly every person present in his hands. It was a strong temptation to this man, so full of repressed passion and power, so set apart and shut out from the more stirring duties and pleasures of life. A few words from his lips, and the pity all felt for him would be turned to fear, respect, and admiration. Why not utter them, and enjoy all that was possible? He owed the Trehernes nothing; why suffer injustice, dependence, and the compassion that wounds a proud man deepest? Wealth, love, pleasure might be his with a breath. Why not secure them now?

His pale face flushed, his eye kindled, and his thin hand lay clenched like a vise as these thoughts passed rapidly through his mind. A look, a word at that moment would sway him; he felt it, and leaned forward, waiting in secret suspense for the glance, the speech which should decide him for good or ill. Who shall say what subtle instinct caused Octavia to turn and smile at him with a wistful, friendly look that warmed his heart? He met it with an answering glance, which thrilled her strangely, for love, gratitude, and some mysterious intelligence met and mingled in the brilliant yet soft expression which swiftly shone and faded in her face. What it was she could not tell; she only felt that it filled her with an indescribable emotion never experienced before. In an instant it all passed, Lady Treherne spoke to her, and Blanche Talbot addressed Maurice, wondering, as she did so, if the enchanting smile he wore was meant for her.

"Mr. Annon having mercifully set me free, I came to try to cheer your solitude; but you look as if solitude made you happier than society does the rest of us," she said without her usual affectation, for his manner impressed her.

"You are very kind and very welcome. I do find pleasures to beguile my loneliness, which gayer people would not enjoy, and it is well that I can, else I should turn morose and tyrannical, and doom some unfortunate to entertain me all day long." He answered with a gentle courtesy which was his chief attraction to womankind.

"Pray tell me some of your devices. I'm often alone in spirit, if not so in the flesh, for Rose, though a dear girl, is not congenial, and I find no kindred soul."

A humorous glimmer came to Treherne's eyes, as the sentimental damsel beamed a soft sigh and drooped her long lashes effectively. Ignoring the topic of "kindred souls," he answered coldly, "My favorite amusement is studying the people around me. It may be rude, but tied to my corner, I cannot help watching the figures around me, and discovering their little plots and plans. I'm getting very expert, and really surprise myself sometimes by the depth of my researches."

"I can believe it; your eyes look as if they possessed that gift. Pray don't study *me.*" And the girl shrank away with an air of genuine alarm.

Treherne smiled involuntarily, for he had read the secret of that shallow heart long ago, and was too generous to use the knowledge, however flattering it might be to him. In a reassuring tone he said, turning away the keen eyes she feared, "I give you my word I never will, charming as it might be to study the white pages of a maidenly heart. I find plenty of others to read, so rest tranquil, Miss Blanche."

"Who interests you most just now?" asked the girl, coloring with pleasure at his words. "Mrs. Snowdon looks like one who has a romance to be read, if you have the skill."

"I have read it. My lady is my study just now. I thought I knew her well, but of late she puzzles me. Human minds are more full of mysteries than any written book and more changeable than the cloud shapes in the air."

"A fine old lady, but I fear her so intensely I should never dare to try to read her, as you say." Blanche looked toward the object of discussion as she spoke, and added, "Poor Tavia, how forlorn she seems. Let me ask her to join us, may I?"

"With all my heart" was the quick reply.

Blanche glided away but did not return, for my lady kept her as well as her daughter.

"That test satisfies me; well, I submit for a time, but I think I can conquer my aunt yet." And with a patient sigh Treherne turned to observe Mrs. Snowdon.

She now stood by the fire, talking with Sir Jasper, a handsome, reckless, generous-hearted young gentleman, who very plainly showed his great admiration for the lady. When he came, she suddenly woke up from her listless mood and became as brilliantly gay as she had been unmistakably melancholy before. As she chatted, she absently pushed to and fro a small antique urn of bronze on the chimneypiece, and in doing so she more than once gave Treherne a quick, significant glance, which he answered at last by a somewhat haughty nod. Then, as if satisfied, she ceased toying with the ornament and became absorbed in Sir Jasper's gallant badinage.

The instant her son approached Mrs. Snowdon, Madame Mère grew anxious, and leaving Octavia to her friends and lover, she watched Jasper. But her surveillance availed little, for she could neither see nor hear anything amiss, yet could not rid herself of the feeling that some mutual understanding existed between them. When the party broke up for the night, she lingered till all were gone but her son and nephew.

"Well, Madame Ma Mère, what troubles you?" asked Sir Jasper, as she looked anxiously into his face before bestowing her good-night kiss.

"I cannot tell, yet I feel ill at ease. Remember, my son, that you are the pride of my heart, and any sin or shame of yours would kill me. Good night, Maurice." And with a stately bow she swept away.

Lounging with both elbows on the low chimneypiece, Sir Jasper smiled at his mother's fears, and said to his cousin, the instant they were alone, "She is worried about E. S. Odd, isn't it, what instinctive antipathies women take to one another?"

"Why did you ask E. S. here?" demanded Treherne.

"My dear fellow, how could I help it? My mother wanted the general, my father's friend, and of course his wife must be asked also. I couldn't tell my mother that the lady had been a most arrant coquette, to put it mildly, and had married the old man in a pet, because my cousin and I declined to be ruined by her."

"You *could* have told her what mischief she makes wherever she goes, and for Octavia's sake have deferred the general's visit for a time. I warn you, Jasper, harm will come of it."

"To whom, you or me?"

"To both, perhaps, certainly to you. She was disappointed once when she lost us both by wavering between your title and my supposed fortune. She is miserable with the old man, and her only hope is in his death, for he is very feeble. You are free, and doubly attractive now, so beware, or she will entangle you before you know it."

"Thanks, Mentor. I've no fear, and shall merely amuse myself for a week—they stay no longer." And with a careless laugh, Sir Jasper strolled away.

"Much mischief may be done in a week, and this is the beginning of it," muttered Treherne, as he raised himself to look under the bronze vase for the note. It was gone!

CHAPTER III. WHO WAS IT?

WHO HAD TAKEN IT? This question tormented Treherne all that sleepless night. He suspected three persons, for only these had approached the fire after the note was hidden. He had kept his eye on it, he thought, till the stir of breaking up. In that moment it must been removed by the major, Frank Annon, or my lady; Sir Jasper was out of the question, for he never touched an ornament in the drawing room since he had awkwardly demolished a whole *étagère* of costly trifles, to his mother's and sister's great grief. The major evidently suspected something, Annon was jealous, and my lady would be glad of a pretext to remove her daughter from his reach. Trusting to his skill in reading faces, he waited impatiently for morning, resolving to say nothing to anyone but Mrs. Snowdon, and from her merely to inquire what the note contained.

Treherne usually was invisible till lunch, often till dinner; therefore, fearing to excite suspicion by unwonted activity, he did not appear till noon. The mailbag had just been opened, and everyone was busy over their letters, but all looked up to exchange a word with the newcomer, and Octavia impulsively turned to meet him, then checked herself and hid her suddenly crimsoned face behind a newspaper. Treherne's eye took in everything, and saw at once in the unusually late arrival of the mail a pretext for discovering the pilferer of the note.

"All have letters but me, yet I expected one last night. Major, have you got it among yours?" And as he spoke, Treherne fixed his penetrating eyes full on the person he addressed.

With no sign of consciousness, no trace of confusion, the major carefully turned over his pile, and replied in the most natural manner, "Not a trace of it; I wish there was, for nothing annoys me more than any delay or mistake about my letters."

He knows nothing of it, thought Treherne, and turned to Annon, who was deep in a long epistle from some intimate friend, with a talent for imparting news, to judge from the reader's interest.

"Annon, I appeal to you, for I *must* discover who has robbed me of my letter."

"I have but one, read it, if you will, and satisfy yourself" was the brief reply.

"No, thank you. I merely asked in joke; it is doubtless among my lady's. Jasper's letters and mine often get mixed, and my lady takes care of his for him. I think you must have it, Aunt."

Lady Treherne looked up impatiently. "My dear Maurice, what a coil about a letter! We none of us have it, so do not punish us for the sins of your correspondent or the carelessness of the post."

She was not the thief, for she is always intensely polite when she intends to thwart me, thought Treherne, and, apologizing for his rudeness in disturbing them, he rolled himself to his nook in a sunny window and became apparently absorbed in a new magazine.

Mrs. Snowdon was opening the general's letters for him, and, having finished her little task, she roamed away into the library, as if in search of a book. Presently returning with one, she approached Treherne, and, putting it into his hand, said, in her musically distinct voice, "Be so kind as to find for me the passage you spoke of last night. I am curious to see it."

Instantly comprehending her stratagem, he opened it with apparent carelessness, secured the tiny note laid among the leaves, and, selecting a passage at hazard, returned her book and resumed his own. Behind the cover of it he unfolded and read these words:

> *I understand, but do not be anxious; the line I left was merely this—"I must see you alone, tell me when and where." No one can make much of it, and I will discover the thief before dinner. Do nothing, but watch to whom I speak first on entering, when we meet in the evening, and beware of that person.*

Quietly transferring the note to the fire with the wrapper of the magazine, he dismissed the matter from his mind and left Mrs. Snowdon to play detective as she pleased, while he busied himself about his own affairs.

It was a clear, bright December day, and when the young people separated to prepare for a ride, while the general and the major sunned themselves on the terrace, Lady Treherne said to her nephew, "I am going for an airing in the pony carriage. Will you be my escort, Maurice?"

"With pleasure," replied the young man, well knowing what was in store for him.

My lady was unusually taciturn and grave, yet seemed anxious to say something which she found difficult to utter. Treherne saw this, and ended an awkward pause by dashing boldly into the subject which occupied both.

"I think you want to say something to me about Tavie, Aunt. Am I right?"

"Yes."

"Then let me spare you the pain of beginning, and prove my sincerity by openly stating the truth, as far as I am concerned. I love her very dearly, but I am not mad enough to dream of telling her so. I know that it is impossible, and I relinquish my hopes. Trust me. I will keep silent and see her marry Annon without a word of complaint, if you will it. I see by her altered manner that you have spoken to her, and that my little friend and nurse is to be mine no longer. Perhaps you are wise, but if you do this on my account, it is in vain—the mischief is done, and while I live I shall love my cousin. If you do it to spare her, I am dumb, and will go away rather than cause her a care or pain."

"Do you really mean this, Maurice?" And Lady Treherne looked at him with a changed and softened face.

Turning upon her, Treherne showed her a countenance full of suffering and sincerity, of resignation and resolve, as he said earnestly, "I do mean it; prove me in any way you please. I am not a bad fellow, Aunt, and I desire to be better. Since my misfortune I've had time to test many things; myself among others, and in spite of many faults, I do cherish the wish to keep my soul honest and true, even though my body be a wreck. It is easy to say these things, but in spite of temptation, I think I can stand firm, if you trust me."

"My dear boy, I do trust you, and thank you gratefully for this frankness. I never forget that I owe Jasper's life to you, and never expect to repay that debt. Remember this when I seem cold or unkind, and remember also that I say now, had you been spared this affliction, I would gladly have given you my girl. But—"

"But, Aunt, hear one thing," broke in Treherne. "They tell me that any sudden and violent shock of surprise, joy, or sorrow may do for me what they hope time will achieve. I said nothing of this, for it is but a chance; yet, while there is any hope, need I utterly renounce Octavia?"

"It is hard to refuse, and yet I cannot think it wise to build upon a chance so slight. Once let her have you, and both are made unhappy, if the hope fail. No, Maurice, it is better to be generous, and leave her free to make her own happiness elsewhere. Annon loves her, she is heart-whole, and will soon learn to love him, if you are silent. My poor boy, it seems cruel, but I must say it."

"Shall I go away, Aunt?" was all his answer, very firmly uttered, though his lips were white.

"Not yet, only leave them to themselves, and hide your trouble if you can. Yet, if you prefer, you shall go to town, and Benson shall see that you are comfortable. Your health will be a reason, and I will come, or write often, if you are homesick. It shall depend on you, for I want to be just and kind in this hard case. You shall decide."

"Then I will stay. I can hide my love; and to see them together will soon cease to wound me, if Octavia is happy."

"So let it rest then, for a time. You shall miss your companion as little as possible, for I will try to fill her place. Forgive me, Maurice, and pity a mother's solicitude, for these two are the last of many children, and I am a widow now."

Lady Treherne's voice faltered, and if any selfish hope or plan lingered in her nephew's mind, that appeal banished it and touched his better nature. Pressing her hand he said gently, "Dear Aunt, do not lament over me. I am one set apart for afflictions, yet I will not be conquered by them. Let us forget my youth and be friendly counselors together for the good of the two whom we both love. I must say a word about Jasper, and you will not press me to explain more than I can without breaking my promise."

"Thank you, thank you! It is regarding that woman, I know. Tell me all you can; I will not be importunate, but I disliked her the instant I saw her, beautiful and charming as she seems."

"When my cousin and I were in Paris, just before my illness, we met her. She was with her father then, a gay old man who led a life of pleasure, and was no fit guardian for a lovely daughter. She knew our story and, having fascinated both, paused to decide which she would accept: Jasper, for his title, or me, for my fortune. This was before my uncle changed his will, and I believed myself his heir; but, before she made her choice, something (don't ask me what, if you please) occurred to send us from Paris. On our return voyage we were wrecked, and then came my illness, disinheritance, and helplessness. Edith Dubarry heard the story, but rumor reported it falsely, and she believed both of us had lost the fortune. Her father died penniless, and in a moment of despair she married the general, whose wealth surrounds her with the luxury she loves, and whose failing health will soon restore her liberty—"

"And then, Maurice?" interrupted my lady.

"She hopes to win Jasper, I think."

"Never! We must prevent that at all costs. I had rather see him dead before me, than the husband of such a woman. Why is she permitted to visit homes like mine? I should have been told this sooner," exclaimed my lady angrily.

"I should have told you had I known it, and I reproved Jasper for his neglect. Do not be needlessly troubled, Aunt. There is no blemish on Mrs. Snowdon's name, and, as the wife of a brave and honorable man, she is received without question; for beauty, grace, or tact like hers can make their way anywhere. She stays but a week, and I will devote myself to her; this will save Jasper, and, if necessary, convince Tavie of my indifference—" Then he paused to stifle a sigh.

"But yourself, have you no fears for your own peace, Maurice? You must not sacrifice happiness or honor, for me or mine."

"I am safe; I love my cousin, and that is my shield. Whatever happens remember that I tried to serve you, and sincerely endeavored to forget myself."

"God bless you, my son! Let me call you so, and feel that, though I deny you my daughter, I give you heartily a mother's care and affection."

Lady Treherne was as generous as she was proud, and her nephew had conquered her by confidence and submission. He acted no part, yet, even in relinquishing all, he cherished a hope that he might yet win the heart he coveted. Silently they parted, but from that hour a new and closer bond existed between the two, and exerted an unsuspected influence over the whole household.

Maurice waited with some impatience for Mrs. Snowdon's entrance, not only because of his curiosity to see if she had discovered the thief, but because of the part he had taken upon himself to play. He was equal to it, and felt a certain pleasure in it for a threefold reason. It would serve his aunt and cousin, would divert his mind from its own cares, and, perhaps by making Octavia jealous, waken love; for, though he had chosen the right, he was but a man, and moreover a lover.

Mrs. Snowdon was late. She always was, for her toilet was elaborate, and she liked to enjoy its effects upon others. The moment she entered Treherne's eye was on her, and to his intense surprise and annoyance she addressed Octavia, saying blandly, "My dear Miss Treherne, I've been admiring your peacocks. Pray let me see you feed them tomorrow. Miss Talbot says it is a charming sight."

"If you are on the terrace just after lunch, you will find them there, and may feed them yourself, if you like" was the cool, civil reply.

"She looks like a peacock herself in that splendid green and gold dress, doesn't she?" whispered Rose to Sir Jasper, with a wicked laugh.

"Faith, so she does. I wish Tavie's birds had voices like Mrs. Snowdon's; their squalling annoys me intensely."

"I rather like it, for it is honest, and no malice or mischief is hidden behind it. I always distrust those smooth, sweet voices; they are insincere. I like a full, clear tone; sharp, if you please, but decided and true."

"Well said, Octavia. I agree with you, and your own is a perfect sample of the kind you describe." And Treherne smiled as he rolled by to join Mrs. Snowdon, who evidently waited for him, while Octavia turned to her brother to defend her pets.

"Are you sure? How did you discover?" said Maurice, affecting to admire the lady's bouquet, as he paused beside her.

"I suspected it the moment I saw her this morning. She is no actress; and dislike, distrust, and contempt were visible in her face when we met. Till you so cleverly told me my note was lost, I fancied she was disturbed about her brother—or you."

A sudden pause and a keen glance followed the last softly uttered word, but Treherne met it with an inscrutable smile and a quiet "Well, what next?"

"The moment I learned that you did not get the note I was sure she had it, and, knowing that she must have seen me put it there, in spite of her apparent innocence, I quietly asked her for it. This surprised her, this robbed the affair of any mystery, and I finished her perplexity by sending it to the major the moment she returned it to me, as if it had been intended for him. She begged pardon, said her brother was thoughtless, and she watched over him lest he should get into mischief; professed to think I meant the line for him, and behaved like a charming simpleton, as she is."

"Quite a tumult about nothing. Poor little Tavie! You doubtlessly frightened her so that we may safely correspond hereafter."

"You may give me an answer, now and here."

"Very well, meet me on the terrace tomorrow morning; the peacocks will make the meeting natural enough. I usually loiter away an hour or two there, in the sunny part of the day."

"But the girl?"

"I'll send her away."

"You speak as if it would be an easy thing to do."

"It will, both easy and pleasant."

"Now you are mysterious or uncomplimentary. You either care nothing for a tête-à-tête with her, or you will gladly send her out of my way. Which is it?"

"You shall decide. Can I have this?"

She looked at him as he touched a rose with a warning glance, for the flower was both an emblem of love and of silence. Did he mean to hint that he recalled the past, or to warn her that someone was near? She leaned from the shadow of the curtain where she sat, and caught a glimpse of a shadow gliding away.

"Who was it?" she asked, below her breath.

"A Rose," he answered, laughing. Then, as if the danger was over, he said, "How will you account to the major for the message you sent him?"

"Easily, by fabricating some interesting perplexity in which I want sage counsel. He will be flattered, and by seeming to take him into my confidence, I can hoodwink the excellent man to my heart's content, for he annoys me by his odd way of mounting guard over me at all times. Now take me in to dinner, and be your former delightful self."

"That is impossible," he said, yet proved that it was not.

CHAPTER IV. FEEDING THE PEACOCKS

IT WAS INDEED a charming sight, the twelve stately birds perched on the broad stone balustrade, or prancing slowly along the terrace, with the sun gleaming on their green and golden necks and the glories of their gorgeous plumes, widespread, or sweeping like rich trains behind them. In pretty contrast to the splendid creatures was their young mistress, in her simple morning dress and fur-trimmed hood and mantle, as she stood feeding the tame pets from her hand, calling their fanciful names, laughing at their pranks, and heartily enjoying the winter sunshine, the fresh wind, and the girlish pastime. As Treherne slowly approached, he watched her with lover's eyes, and found her very sweet and blithe, and dearer in his sight than ever. She had shunned him carefully all the day before, had parted at night with a hasty handshake, and had not come as usual to bid him good-morning in the library. He had taken no notice of the change as yet, but now, remembering his promise to his aunt, he resolved to let the girl know that he fully understood the relation which henceforth was to exist between them.

"Good morning, cousin. Shall I drive you away, if I take a turn or two here?" he said, in a cheerful tone, but with a half-reproachful glance.

She looked at him an instant, then went to him with extended hand and cheeks rosier than before, while her frank eyes filled, and her voice had a traitorous tremor in it, as she said, impetuously: "I *will* be myself for a moment, in spite of everything. Maurice, don't think me unkind, don't reproach me, or ask my leave to come where I am. There is a reason for the change you see in me; it's not caprice, it is obedience."

"My dear girl, I know it. I meant to speak of it, and show you that I understand. Annon is a good fellow, as worthy of you as any man can be, and I wish you all the happiness you deserve."

"Do you?" And her eyes searched his face keenly.

"Yes; do you doubt it?" And so well did he conceal his love, that neither face, voice, nor manner betrayed a hint of it.

Her eyes fell, a cloud passed over her clear countenance, and she withdrew her hand, as if to caress the hungry bird that gently pecked at the basket she held. As if to change the conversation, she said playfully, "Poor Argus, you have lost your fine feathers, and so all desert you, except kind little Juno, who never forgets her friends. There, take it all, and share between you."

Treherne smiled, and said quickly, "I am a human Argus, and you have been a kind little Juno to me since I lost my plumes. Continue to be so, and you will find me a very faithful friend."

"I will." And as she answered, her old smile came back and her eyes met his again.

"Thanks! Now we shall get on happily. I don't ask or expect the old life—that is impossible. I knew that when lovers came, the friend would fall into the background; and I am content to be second, where I have so long been first. Do not think you neglect me; be happy with your lover, dear, and when you have no pleasanter amusement, come and see old Maurice."

She turned her head away, that he might not see the angry color in her cheeks, the trouble in her eyes, and when she spoke, it was to say petulantly, "I wish Jasper and Mamma would leave me in peace. I hate lovers and want none. If Frank teases, I'll go into a convent and so be rid of him."

Maurice laughed, and turned her face toward himself, saying, in his persuasive voice, "Give him a trial first, to please your mother. It can do no harm and may amuse you. Frank is already lost, and, as you are heart-whole, why not see what you can do for him? I shall have a new study, then, and not miss you so much."

"You are very kind; I'll do my best. I wish Mrs. Snowdon would come, if she is coming; I've an engagement at two, and Frank will look tragical if I'm not ready. He is teaching me billiards, and I really like the game, though I never thought I should."

"That looks well. I hope you'll learn a double lesson, and Annon find a docile pupil in both."

"You are very pale this morning; are you in pain, Maurice?" suddenly asked Octavia, dropping the tone of assumed ease and gaiety under which she had tried to hide her trouble.

"Yes, but it will soon pass. Mrs. Snowdon is coming. I saw her at the hall door a moment ago. I will show her the peacocks, if you want to go. She won't mind the change, I dare say, as you don't like her, and I do."

"No, I am sure of that. It was an arrangement, perhaps? I understand. I will not play Mademoiselle De Trop."

Sudden fire shone in the girl's eyes, sudden contempt curled her lip, and a glance full of meaning went from her cousin to the door, where Mrs. Snowdon appeared, waiting for her maid to bring her some additional wrappings.

"You allude to the note you stole. How came you to play that prank, Tavie?" asked Treherne tranquilly.

"I saw her put it under the urn. I thought it was for Jasper, and I took it," she said boldly.

"Why for Jasper?"

"I remembered his speaking of meeting her long ago, and describing her beauty enthusiastically—and so did you."

"You have a good memory."

"I have for everything concerning those I love. I observed her manner of meeting my brother, his devotion to her, and, when they stood laughing together before the fire, I felt sure that she wished to charm him again."

"Again? Then she did charm him once?" asked Treherne, anxious to know how much Jasper had told his sister.

"He always denied it, and declared that you were the favorite."

"Then why not think the note for me?" he asked.

"I do now" was the sharp answer.

"But she told you it was for the major, and sent it."

"She deceived me; I am not surprised. I am glad Jasper is safe, and I wish you a pleasant tête-à-tête."

Bowing with unwonted dignity, Octavia set down her basket, and walked away in one direction as Mrs. Snowdon approached in another.

"I have done it now," sighed Treherne, turning from the girlish figure to watch the stately creature who came sweeping toward him with noiseless grace.

Brilliancy and splendor became Mrs. Snowdon; she enjoyed luxury, and her beauty made many things becoming which in a plainer woman would have been out of taste, and absurd. She had wrapped herself in a genuine Eastern burnous of scarlet, blue, and gold; the hood drawn over her head framed her fine face in rich hues, and the great gilt tassels shone against her rippling black hair. She wore it with grace, and the barbaric splendor of the garment became her well. The fresh air touched her cheeks with a delicate color; her usually gloomy eyes were brilliant now, and the smile that parted her lips was full of happiness.

"Welcome, Cleopatra!" cried Treherne, with difficulty repressing a laugh, as the peacocks screamed and fled before the rustling amplitude of her drapery.

"I might reply by calling you Thaddeus of Warsaw, for you look very romantic and Polish with your pale, pensive face, and your splendid furs," she answered, as she paused beside him with admiration very visibly expressed in her eyes.

Treherne disliked the look, and rather abruptly said, as he offered her the basket of bread, "I have disposed of my cousin, and offered to do the honors of the peacocks. Here they are—will you feed them?"

"No, thank you—I care nothing for the fowls, as you know; I came to speak to you," she said impatiently.

"I am at your service."

"I wish to ask you a question or two—is it permitted?"

"What man ever refused Mrs. Snowdon a request?"

"Nay, no compliments; from you they are only satirical evasions. I was deceived when abroad, and rashly married that old man. Tell me truly how things stand."

"Jasper has all. I have nothing."

"I am glad of it."

"Many thanks for the hearty speech. You at least speak sincerely," he said bitterly.

"I do. Maurice—I do; let me prove it."

Treherne's chair was close beside the balustrade. Mrs. Snowdon leaned on the carved railing, with her back to the house and her face screened by a tall urn. Looking steadily at him, she said rapidly and low, "You thought I wavered between you and Jasper, when we parted two years ago. I did; but it was not between title and fortune that I hesitated. It was between duty and love. My father, a fond, foolish old man, had set his heart on seeing me a lady. I was his all; my beauty was his delight, and no untitled man was deemed worthy of me. I loved him tenderly. You may doubt this, knowing how selfish, reckless, and vain I am, but I have a heart, and with better training had been a better woman. No matter, it is too late now. Next my father, I loved you. Nay, hear me—I *will* clear myself in your eyes. I mean no wrong to the general. He is kind, indulgent, generous; I respect him—I am grateful, and while he lives, I shall be true to him."

"Then be silent now. Do not recall the past, Edith; let it sleep, for both our sakes," began Treherne; but she checked him imperiously.

"It shall, when I am done. I loved you, Maurice; for, of all the gay, idle, plea-sure-seeking men I saw about me, you were the only one who seemed to have a thought beyond the folly of the hour. Under the seeming frivolity of your life lay something noble, heroic, and true. I felt that you had a purpose, that your present mood was but transitory—a young man's holiday, before the real work of his life began. This attracted, this won me; for even in the brief regard you then gave me, there was an earnestness no other man had shown. I wanted your respect; I longed to earn your love, to share your life, and prove that even in my neglected nature slept the power of canceling a frivolous past by a noble future. Oh, Maurice, had you lingered one week more, I never should have been the miserable thing I am!"

There her voice faltered and failed, for all the bitterness of lost love, peace, and happiness sounded in the pathetic passion of that exclamation. She did not weep, for tears seldom dimmed those tragical eyes of hers; but she wrung her hands in mute despair, and looked down into the frost-blighted gardens below, as if she saw there a true symbol of her own ruined life. Treherne uttered not a word, but set his teeth with an almost fierce glance toward the distant figure of Sir Jasper, who was riding gaily away, like one unburdened by a memory or a care.

Hurriedly Mrs. Snowdon went on, "My father begged and commanded me to choose your cousin. I could not break his heart, and asked for time, hoping to soften him. While I waited, that mysterious affair hurried you from Paris, and then came the wreck, the illness, and the rumor that old Sir Jasper had disinherited both nephews. They told me you were dying, and I became a passive instrument in my father's hands. I promised to recall and accept your cousin, but the old man died before it was done, and then I cared not what became of me.

"General Snowdon was my father's friend; he pitied me; he saw my desolate, destitute state, my despair and helplessness. He comforted, sustained, and saved me. I was grateful; and when he offered me his heart and home, I accepted them. He knew I had no love to give; but as a friend, a daughter, I would gladly serve him, and make his declining years as happy as I could. It was all over, when I heard that you were alive, afflicted, and poor. I longed to come and live for you. My new bonds became heavy fetters then, my wealth oppressed me, and I was doubly wretched—for I dared not tell my trouble, and it nearly drove me mad. I have seen you now; I know that you are happy; I read your cousin's love and see a peaceful life in store for you. This must content me, and I must learn to bear it as I can."

She paused, breathless and pale, and walked rapidly along the terrace, as if to hide or control the agitation that possessed her.

Treherne still sat silent, but his heart leaped within him, as he thought, "She sees that Octavia loves me! A woman's eye is quick to detect love in another, and she asserts what I begin to hope. My cousin's manner just now, her dislike of Annon, her new shyness with me; it may be true, and if it is—Heaven help me—what am I saying! I must not hope, nor wish, nor dream; I must renounce and forget."

He leaned his head upon his hand, and sat so till Mrs. Snowdon rejoined him, pale, but calm and self-possessed. As she drew near, she marked his attitude, the bitter sadness of his face, and hope sprang up within her. Perhaps she was mistaken; perhaps he did not love his cousin; perhaps he still remembered the past, and still regretted the loss of the heart she had just laid bare before him. Her husband was failing, and might die any day. And then, free, rich, beautiful, and young, what might she not become to Treherne, helpless, poor, and ambitious? With all her faults, she was generous, and this picture charmed her fancy, warmed her heart, and comforted her pain.

"Maurice," she said softly, pausing again beside him, "If I mistake you and your hopes, it is because I dare ask nothing for myself; but if ever a time shall come when I have liberty to give or help, ask of me *anything,* and it is gladly yours."

He understood her, pitied her, and, seeing that she found consolation in a distant hope, he let her enjoy it while she might. Gravely, yet gratefully, he spoke, and pressed the hand extended to him with an impulsive gesture.

"Generous as ever, Edith, and impetuously frank. Thank you for your sincerity, your kindness, and the affection you once gave me. I say 'once,' for now duty, truth, and honor bar us from each other. My life must be solitary, yet I shall find work to do, and learn to be content. You owe all devotion to the good old man who loves you, and will not fail him, I am sure. Leave the future and the past, but let us make the present what it may be—a time to forgive and forget, to take heart and begin anew. Christmas is a fitting time for such resolves, and the birth of friendship such as ours may be."

Something in his tone and manner struck her, and, eyeing him with soft wonder, she exclaimed, "How changed you are!"

"Need you tell me that?" And he glanced at his helpless limbs with a bitter yet pathetic look of patience.

"No, no—not so! I mean in mind, not body. Once you were gay and careless, eager and fiery, like Jasper; now you are grave and quiet, or cheerful, and so very kind. Yet, in spite of illness and loss, you seem twice the man you were, and something wins respect, as well as admiration—-and love."

Her dark eyes filled as the last word left her lips, and the beauty of a touched heart shone in her face. Maurice looked up quickly, asking with sudden earnestness, "Do you see it? Then it is true. Yes, I *am* changed, thank God! And she has done it."

"Who?" demanded his companion jealously.

"Octavia. Unconsciously, yet surely, she has done much for me, and this year of seeming loss and misery has been the happiest, most profitable of my life. I have often heard that afflictions were the best teachers, and I believe it now."

Mrs. Snowdon shook her head sadly.

"Not always; they are tormentors to some. But don't preach, Maurice. I am still a sinner, though you incline to sainthood, and I have one question more to ask. What was it that took you and Jasper so suddenly away from Paris?"

"That I can never tell you."

"I shall discover it for myself, then."

"It is impossible."

"Nothing is impossible to a determined woman."

"You can neither wring, surprise, nor bribe this secret from the two persons who hold it. I beg of you to let it rest," said Treherne earnestly.

"I have a clue, and I shall follow it; for I am convinced that something is wrong, and you are—"

"Dear Mrs. Snowdon, are you so charmed with the birds that you forget your fellow-beings, or so charmed with one fellow-being that you forget the birds?"

As the sudden question startled both, Rose Talbot came along the terrace, with hands full of holly and a face full of merry mischief, adding as she vanished, "I shall tell Tavie that feeding the peacocks is such congenial amusement for lovers, she and Mr. Annon had better try it."

"Saucy gypsy!" muttered Treherne.

But Mrs. Snowdon said, with a smile of double meaning, "Many a true word is spoken in jest."

Chapter V. Under the Mistletoe

UNUSUALLY GAY AND CHARMING the three young friends looked, dressed alike in fleecy white with holly wreaths in their hair, as they slowly descended the wide oaken stairway arm in arm. A footman was lighting the hall lamps, for the winter dusk gathered early, and the girls were merrily chatting about the evening's festivity when suddenly a loud, long shriek echoed through the hall. A heavy glass shade fell from the man's hand with a crash, and the young ladies clung to one another aghast, for mortal terror was in the cry, and a dead silence followed it.

"What was it, John?" demanded Octavia, very pale, but steady in a moment.

"I'll go and see, miss." And the man hurried away.

"Where did the dreadful scream come from?" asked Rose, collecting her wits as rapidly as possible.

"Above us somewhere. Oh, let us go down among people; I am frightened to death," whispered Blanche, trembling and faint.

Hurrying into the parlor, they found only Annon and the major, both looking startled, and both staring out of the windows.

"Did you hear it? What could it be? Don't go and leave us!" cried the girls in a breath, as they rushed in.

The gentlemen had heard, couldn't explain the cry, and were quite ready to protect the pretty creatures who clustered about them like frightened fawns. John speedily appeared, looking rather wild, and as eager to tell his tale as they to listen.

"It's Patty, one of the maids, miss, in a fit. She went up to the north gallery to see that the fires was right, for it takes a power of wood to warm the gallery even enough for dancing, as you know, miss. Well, it was dark, for the fires was low and her candle went out as she whisked open the door, being flurried, as the maids always is when they go in there. Halfway down the gallery she says she heard a rustling, and stopped. She's the pluckiest of 'em all, and she called out, 'I see you!' thinking it was some of us trying to fright her. Nothing answered, and she went on a bit, when suddenly the fire flared up one flash, and there right before her was the ghost."

"Don't be foolish, John. Tell us what it was," said Octavia sharply, though her face whitened and her heart sank as the last word passed the man's lips.

"It was a tall, black figger, miss, with a dead-white face and a black hood. She see it plain, and turned to go away, but she hadn't gone a dozen steps when there it was again before her, the same tall, dark thing with the dead-white face looking out from the black hood. It lifted its arm as if to hold her, but she gave a spring and dreadful screech, and ran to Mrs. Benson's room, where she dropped in a fit."

"How absurd to be frightened by the shadows of the figures in armor that stand along the gallery!" said Rose, boldly enough, though she would have declined entering the gallery without a light.

"Nay, I don't wonder, it's a ghostly place at night. How is the poor thing?" asked Blanche, still hanging on the major's arm in her best attitude.

"If Mamma knows nothing of it, tell Mrs. Benson to keep it from her, please. She is not well, and such things annoy her very much," said Octavia, adding as the man turned away, "Did anyone look in the gallery after Patty told her tale?"

"No, miss. I'll go and do it myself; I'm not afraid of man, ghost, or devil, saving your presence, ladies," replied John.

"Where is Sir Jasper?" suddenly asked the major.

"Here I am. What a deuce of a noise someone has been making. It disturbed a capital dream. Why, Tavie, what is it?" And Sir Jasper came out of the library with a sleepy face and tumbled hair.

They told him the story, whereat he laughed heartily, and said the maids were a foolish set to be scared by a shadow. While he still laughed and joked, Mrs. Snowdon entered, looking alarmed, and anxious to know the cause of the confusion.

"How interesting! I never knew you kept a ghost. Tell me all about it, Sir Jasper, and soothe our nerves by satisfying our curiosity," she said in her half-persuasive, half-commanding way, as she seated herself on Lady Treherne's sacred sofa.

"There's not much to tell, except that this place used to be an abbey, in fact as well as in name. An ancestor founded it, and for years the monks led a jolly life here, as one may see, for the cellar is twice as large as the chapel, and much better preserved. But another ancestor, a gay and gallant baron, took a fancy to the site for his castle, and, in spite of prayers, anathemas, and excommunication, he turned the poor fellows out, pulled down the abbey, and built this fine old place. Abbot Boniface, as he left his abbey, uttered a heavy curse on all who should live here, and vowed to haunt us till the last Treherne vanished from the face of the earth. With this amiable threat the old party left Baron Roland to his doom, and died as soon as he could in order to begin his cheerful mission."

"Did he haunt the place?" asked Blanche eagerly.

"Yes, most faithfully from that time to this. Some say many of the monks still glide about the older parts of the abbey, for Roland spared the chapel and the north gallery which joined it to the modern building. Poor fellows, they are welcome, and once a year they shall have a chance to warm their ghostly selves by the great fires always kindled at Christmas in the gallery."

"Mrs. Benson once told me that when the ghost walked, it was a sure sign of a coming death in the family. Is that true?" asked Rose, whose curiosity was excited by the expression of Octavia's face, and a certain uneasiness in Sir Jasper's manner in spite of his merry mood.

"There is a stupid superstition of that sort in the family, but no one except the servants believes it, of course. In times of illness some silly maid or croaking old woman can easily fancy they see a phantom, and, if death comes, they are sure of the ghostly warning. Benson saw it before my father died, and old Roger, the night my uncle was seized with apoplexy. Patty will never be made to believe that this warning does not forebode the death of Maurice or myself, for the gallant spirit leaves the ladies of our house to depart in peace. How does it strike you, Cousin?"

Turning as he spoke, Sir Jasper glanced at Treherne, who had entered while he spoke.

"I am quite skeptical and indifferent to the whole affair, but I agree with Octavia that it is best to say nothing to my aunt if she is ignorant of the matter. Her rooms are a long way off, and perhaps she did not hear the confusion."

"You seem to hear everything; you were not with us when I said that." And Octavia looked up with an air of surprise.

Smiling significantly, Treherne answered, "I hear, see, and understand many things that escape others. Jasper, allow me to advise you to smooth the hair which your sleep has disarranged. Mrs. Snowdon, permit me. This rich velvet catches the least speck." And with his handkerchief he delicately brushed away several streaks of white dust which clung to the lady's skirt.

Sir Jasper turned hastily on his heel and went to remake his toilet; Mrs. Snowdon bit her lip, but thanked Treherne sweetly and begged him to fasten her glove. As he did so, she said softly, "Be more careful next time. Octavia has keen eyes, and the major may prove inconvenient."

"I have no fear that you will," he whispered back, with a malicious glance.

Here the entrance of my lady put an end to the ghostly episode, for it was evident that she knew nothing of it. Octavia slipped away to question John, and learn that no sign of a phantom was to be seen. Treherne devoted himself to Mrs. Snowdon, and the major entertained my lady, while Sir Jasper and the girls chatted apart.

It was Christmas Eve, and a dance in the great gallery was the yearly festival at the abbey. All had been eager for it, but the maid's story seemed to have lessened their enthusiasm, though no one would own it. This annoyed Sir Jasper, and he exerted himself to clear the atmosphere by affecting gaiety he did not feel. The moment the gentlemen came in after dinner he whispered to his mother, who rose, asked the general for his arm, and led the way to the north gallery, whence the sound of music now proceeded. The rest followed in a merry procession, even Treherne, for two footmen carried him up the great stairway, chair and all.

Nothing could look less ghostly now than the haunted gallery. Fires roared up a wide chimney at either end, long rows of figures clad in armor stood on each side, one mailed hand grasping a lance, the other bearing a lighted candle, a device of Sir Jasper's. Narrow windows pierced in the thick walls let in gleams of wintry moonlight; ivy, holly, and evergreen glistened in the ruddy glow of mingled firelight and candle shine. From the arched stone roof hung tattered banners, and in the midst depended a great bunch of mistletoe. Redcushioned seats stood in recessed window nooks, and from behind a high-covered screen of oak sounded the blithe air of Sir Roger de Coverley.

With the utmost gravity and stateliness my lady and the general led off the dance, for, according to the good old fashion, the men and maids in their best array joined the gentlefolk and danced with their betters in a high state of pride and bashfulness. Sir Jasper twirled the old housekeeper till her head spun around and around and her decorous skirts rustled stormily; Mrs. Snowdon captivated the gray-haired butler by her condescension; and John was made a proud man by the hand of his young mistress. The major came out strong among the pretty maids, and Rose danced the footmen out of breath long before the music paused.

The merriment increased from that moment, and when the general surprised my lady by gallantly saluting her as she unconsciously stood under the mistletoe, the applause was immense. Everyone followed the old gentleman's example as fast as opportunities occurred, and the young ladies soon had as fine a color as the house-maids. More dancing, games, songs, and all manner of festival devices filled the evening, yet under cover of the gaiety more than one little scene was enacted that night, and in an hour of seeming frivolity the current of several lives was changed.

By a skillful maneuver Annon led Octavia to an isolated recess, as if to rest after a brisk game, and, taking advantage of the auspicious hour, pleaded his suit. She heard him patiently and, when he paused, said slowly, yet decidedly, and with no sign of maiden hesitation, "Thanks for the honor you do me, but I cannot accept it, for I do not love you. I think I never can."

"Have you tried?" he asked eagerly.

"Yes, indeed I have. I like you as a friend, but no more. I know Mamma desires it, that Jasper hopes for it, and I try to please them, but love will not be forced, so what can I do?" And she smiled in spite of herself at her own blunt simplicity.

"No, but it can be cherished, strengthened, and in time won, with patience and devotion. Let me try, Octavia; it is but fair, unless you have already learned from another the lesson I hope to teach. Is it so?"

"No, I think not. I do not understand myself as yet, I am so young, and this so sudden. Give me time, Frank."

She blushed and fluttered now, looked half angry, half beseeching, and altogether lovely.

"How much time shall I give? It cannot take long to read a heart like yours, dear." And fancying her emotion a propitious omen, he assumed the lover in good earnest.

"Give me time till the New Year. I will answer then, and, meantime, leave me free to study both myself and you. We have known each other long, I own, but, still, this changes everything, and makes you seem another person. Be patient, Frank, and I will try to make my duty a pleasure."

"I will. God bless you for the kind hope, Octavia. It has been mine for years, and if I lose it, it will go hardly with me."

Later in the evening General Snowdon stood examining the antique screen. In many places carved oak was pierced quite through, so that voices were audible from behind it. The musicians had gone down to supper, the young folk were quietly busy at the other end of the hall, and as the old gentleman admired the quaint carving, the sound of his own name caught his ear. The housekeeper and butler still remained, though the other servants had gone, and sitting cosily behind the screen chatted in low tones believing themselves secure.

"It *was* Mrs. Snowdon, Adam, as I'm a living woman, though I wouldn't say it to anyone but you. She and Sir Jasper were here wrapped in cloaks, and up to mischief, I'll be bound. She is a beauty, but I don't envy her, and there'll be trouble in the house if she stays long."

"But how do you know, Mrs. Benson, she was here? Where's your proof, mum?" asked the pompous butler.

"Look at this, and then look at the outlandish trimming of the lady's dress. You men are so dull about such matters you'd never observe these little points. Well, I was here first after Patty, and my light shone on this jet ornament lying near where she saw the spirit. No one has any such tasty trifles but Mrs. Snowdon, and these are all over her gown. If that ain't proof, what is?"

"Well. admitting it, I then say what on earth should she and master be up here for, at such a time?" asked the slow-witted butler.

"Adam, we are old servants of the family, and to you I'll say what tortures shouldn't draw from to another. Master has been wild, as you know, and it's my belief that he loved this lady abroad. There was a talk of some mystery, or misdeed, or misfortune, more than a year ago, and she was in it. I'm loath to say it, but I think Master loves her still, and she him. The general is an old man, she is but young, and so spirited and winsome she can't in reason care for him as for a fine, gallant gentleman like Sir Jasper. There's trouble brewing, Adam, mark my words. There's trouble brewing for the Trehernes."

So low had the voices fallen that the listener could not have caught the words had not his ear been strained to the utmost. He did hear all, and his wasted face flashed with the wrath of a young man, then grew pale and stern as he turned to watch his wife. She stood apart from the others talking to Sir Jasper, who looked unusually handsome and debonair as he fanned her with a devoted air.

Perhaps it is true, thought the old man bitterly. They are well matched, were lovers once, no doubt, and long to be so again. Poor Edith, I was very blind. And with his gray head bowed upon his breast the general stole away, carrying an arrow in his brave old heart.

"Blanche, come here and rest, you will be ill tomorrow; and I promised Mamma to take care of you." With which elder-sisterly command Rose led the girl to an immense old chair, which held them both. "Now listen to me and follow my advice, for I am wise in my generation, though not yet gray. They are all busy, so leave them alone and let me show you what is to be done."

Rose spoke softly, but with great resolution, and nodded her pretty head so energetically that the holly berries came rolling over her white shoulders.

"We are not as rich as we might be, and must establish ourselves as soon and as well as possible. I intend to be Lady Treherne. You can be the Honorable Mrs. Annon, if you give your mind to it."

"My dear child, are you mad?" whispered Blanche.

"Far from it, but you will be if you waste your time on Maurice. He is poor, and a cripple, though very charming, I admit. He loves Tavie, and she will marry him, I am sure. She can't endure Frank, but tries to because my lady commands it. Nothing will come of it, so try your fascinations and comfort the poor man; sympathy now will foster love hereafter."

"Don't talk so here, Rose, someone will hear us," began her sister, but the other broke in briskly.

"No fear, a crowd is the best place for secrets. Now remember what I say, and make your game while the ball is rolling. Other people are careful not to put their plans into words, but I'm no hypocrite, and say plainly what I mean. Bear my sage counsel in mind and act wisely. Now come and begin."

Treherne was sitting alone by one of the great fires, regarding the gay scene with serious air. For him there was neither dancing nor games; he could only roam about catching glimpses of forbidden pleasures, impossible delights, and youthful hopes forever lost to him. Sad but not morose was his face, and to Octavia it was a mute reproach which she could not long resist. Coming up as if to warm herself, she spoke to him in her usually frank and friendly way, and felt her heart beat fast when she saw how swift a change her cordial manner wrought in him.

"How pretty your holly is! Do you remember how we used to go and gather it for festivals like this, when we were happy children?" he asked, looking up at her with eyes full of tender admiration.

"Yes, I remember. Everyone wears it tonight as a badge, but you have none. Let me get you a bit, I like to have you one of us in all things."

She leaned forward to break a green sprig from the branch over the chimney-piece; the strong draft drew in her fleecy skirt, and in an instant she was enveloped in flames.

"Maurice, save me, help me!" cried a voice of fear and agony, and before anyone could reach her, before he himself knew how the deed was done, Treherne had thrown himself from his chair, wrapped the tiger skin tightly about her, and knelt there clasping her in his arms heedless of fire, pain, or the incoherent expressions of love that broke from his lips.

Chapter VI. Miracles

Great was the confusion and alarm which reigned for many minutes, but when the panic subsided two miracles appeared. Octavia was entirely uninjured, and Treherne was standing on his feet, a thing which for months he had not done without crutches. In the excitement of the moment, no one observed the wonder; all were crowding about the girl, who, pale and breathless but now self-possessed, was the first to exclaim, pointing to her cousin, who had drawn himself up, with the help of his chair, and leaned there smiling, with a face full of intense delight.

"Look at Maurice! Oh, Jasper, help him or he'll fall!"

Sir Jasper sprung to his side and put a strong arm about him, while a chorus of wonder, sympathy, and congratulations rose about them.

"Why, lad, what does it mean? Have you been deceiving us all this time?" cried Jasper, as Treherne leaned on him, looking exhausted but truly happy.

"It means that I am not to be a cripple all my life; that they did not deceive me when they said a sudden shock might electrify me with a more potent magnetism than any they could apply. It *has,* and if I am cured I owe it all to you, Octavia."

He stretched his hands to her with a gesture of such passionate gratitude that the girl covered her face to hide its traitorous tenderness, and my lady went to him, saying brokenly, as she embraced him with maternal warmth, "God bless you for this act, Maurice, and reward you with a perfect cure. To you I owe the lives of both my children; how can I thank you as I ought?"

"I dare not tell you yet," he whispered eagerly, then added, "I am growing faint, Aunt. Get me away before I make a scene."

This hint recalled my lady to her usual state of dignified self-possession. Bidding Jasper and the major help Treherne to his room without delay, she begged Rose to comfort her sister, who was sobbing hysterically, and as they all obeyed her, she led her daughter away to her own apartment, for the festivities of the evening were at an end.

At the same time Mrs. Snowdon and Annon bade my lady good-night, as if they also were about to retire, but as they reached the door of the gallery Mrs. Snowdon paused and beckoned Annon back. They were alone now, and, standing before the fire which had so nearly made that Christmas Eve a tragical one, she turned to him with a face full of interest and sympathy as she said, nodding toward the blackened shreds of Octavia's dress, and the scorched tiger skin which still lay at their feet, "That was both a fortunate and an unfortunate little affair, but I fear Maurice's gain will be your loss. Pardon my frankness for Octavia's sake; she is a fine creature, and I long to see her given to one worthy of her. I am a woman to read faces quickly; I know that your suit does not prosper as you would have it, and I desire to help you. May I?"

"Indeed you may, and command any service of me in return. But to what do I owe this unexpected friendliness?" cried Annon, both grateful and surprised.

"To my regard for the young lady, my wish to save her from an unworthy man."

"Do you mean Treherne?" asked Annon, more and more amazed.

"I do. Octavia must not marry a gambler!"

"My dear lady, you labor under some mistake; Treherne is by no means a gambler. I owe him no goodwill, but I cannot hear him slandered."

"You are generous, but I am not mistaken. Can you, on your honor, assure me that Maurice never played?"

Mrs. Snowdon's keen eyes were on him, and he looked embarrassed for a moment, but answered with some hesitation, "Why, no, I cannot say that, but I can assure you that he is not an habitual gambler. All young men of his rank play more or less, especially abroad. It is merely an amusement with most, and among men is not considered dishonorable or dangerous. Ladies think differently, I believe, at least in England."

At the word "abroad," Mrs. Snowdon's face brightened, and she suddenly dropped her eyes, as if afraid of betraying some secret purpose.

"Indeed we do, and well we may, many of us having suffered from this pernicious habit. I have had special cause to dread and condemn it, and the fear that Octavia should in time suffer what I have suffered as a girl urges me to interfere where otherwise I should be dumb. Mr. Annon, there was a rumor that Maurice was forced to quit Paris, owing to some dishonorable practices at the gaming table. Is this true?"

"Nay, don't ask me; upon my soul I cannot tell you. I only know that something was amiss, but what I never learned. Various tales were whispered at the clubs, and Sir Jasper indignantly denied them all. The bravery with which Maurice saved his cousin, and the sad affliction which fell upon him, silenced the gossip, and it was soon forgotten."

Mrs. Snowdon remained silent for a moment, with brows knit in deep thought, while Annon uneasily watched her. Suddenly she glanced over her shoulder, drew nearer, and whispered cautiously, "Did the rumors of which you speak charge him with—" and the last word was breathed into Annon's ear almost inaudibly.

He started, as if some new light broke on him, and stared at the speaker with a troubled face for an instant, saying hastily, "No, but now you remind me that when an affair of that sort was discussed the other day Treherne looked very odd, and rolled himself away, as if it didn't interest him. I can't believe it, and yet it may be something of the kind. That would account for old Sir Jasper's whim, and Treherne's steady denial of any knowledge of the cause. How in heaven's name did you learn this?"

"My woman's wit suggested it, and my woman's will shall confirm or destroy the suspicion. My lady and Octavia evidently know nothing, but they shall if there is any danger of the girl's being won by him."

"You would not tell her!" exclaimed Annon.

"I will, unless you do it" was the firm answer.

"Never! To betray a friend, even to gain the woman I love, is a thing I cannot do; my honor forbids it."

Mrs. Snowdon smiled scornfully.

"Men's code of honor is a strong one, and we poor women suffer from it. Leave this to me; do your best, and if all other means fail, you may be glad to try my device to prevent Maurice from marrying his cousin. Gratitude and pity are strong allies, and if he recovers, his strong will will move heaven and earth to gain her. Good night." And leaving her last words to rankle in Annon's mind, Mrs. Snowdon departed to endure sleepless hours full of tormenting memories, newborn hopes, and alternations of determination and despair.

Treherne's prospect of recovery filled the whole house with delight, for his patient courage and unfailing cheerfulness had endeared him to all. It was no transient amendment, for day by day he steadily gained strength and power, passing rapidly from chair to crutches, from crutches to a cane and a friend's arm, which was always ready for him. Pain returned with returning vitality, but he bore it with a fortitude that touched all who witnessed it. At times motion was torture, yet motion was necessary lest the torpidity should return, and Treherne took his daily exercise with unfailing perseverance, saying with a smile, though great drops stood upon his forehead, "I have something dearer even than health to win. Hold me up, Jasper, and let me stagger on, in spite of everything, till my twelve turns are made."

He remembered Lady Treherne's words, "If you were well, I'd gladly give my girl to you." This inspired him with strength, endurance, and a happiness which could not be concealed. It overflowed in looks, words, and acts; it infected everyone, and made these holidays the blithest the old abbey had seen for many a day.

Annon devoted himself to Octavia, and in spite of her command to be left in peace till the New Year, she was very kind that hope flamed up in his heart, though he saw that something like compassion often shone on him from her frank eyes, and her compliance had no touch of the tender docility which lovers long to see. She still avoided Treherne, but so skillfully that few observed the change but Annon and himself. In public Sir Jasper appeared to worship at the sprightly Rose's shrine, and she fancied her game was prospering well.

But had any one peeped behind the scenes it would have been discovered that during the half hour before dinner, when everyone was in their dressing rooms and the general taking his nap, a pair of ghostly black figures flitted about the haunted gallery, where no servant ventured without orders. The major fancied himself the only one who had made this discovery, for Mrs. Snowdon affected Treherne's society in public, and was assiduous in serving and amusing the "dear convalescent," as she called him. But the general did not sleep; he too watched and waited, longing yet dreading to speak, and hoping that this was but a harmless freak of Edith's, for her caprices were many, and till now he had indulged them freely. This hesitation disgusted the major, who, being a bachelor, knew little of women's ways, and less of their powers of persuasion. The day before New Year he took a sudden resolution, and demanded a private interview with the general.

"I have come on an unpleasant errand, sir," he abruptly began, as the old man received him with an expression which rather daunted the major. "My friendship for Lady Treherne, and my guardianship of her children, makes me jealous of the honor of the family. I fear it is in danger, sir; pardon me for saying it, but your wife is the cause."

"May I trouble you to explain, Major Royston" was all the general's reply, as his old face grew stern and haughty.

"I will, sir, briefly. I happen to know from Jasper that there were love passages between Miss Dubarry and himself a year or more ago in Paris. A whim parted them, and she married. So far no reproach rests upon either, but since she came here it has been evident to others as well as myself that Jasper's affection has revived, and that Mrs. Snowdon does not reject and reprove it as she should. They often meet, and from Jasper's manner I am convinced that mischief is afloat. He is ardent, headstrong, and utterly regardless of the world's opinion in some cases. I have watched them, and what I tell you is true."

"Prove it."

"I will. They meet in the north gallery, wrapped in dark cloaks, and play ghost if anyone comes. I concealed myself behind the screen last evening at dusk, and satisfied myself that my suspicions were correct. I heard little of their conversation, but that little was enough."

"Repeat it, if you please."

"Sir Jasper seemed pleading for some promise which she reluctantly gave, saying, 'While you live I will be true to my word with everyone but him. He will suspect, and it will be useless to keep it from him.'

" 'He will shoot me for this if he knows I am the traitor,' expostulated Jasper.

" 'He shall not know that; I can hoodwink him easily, and serve my purpose also.'

" 'You are mysterious, but I leave all to you and wait for my reward. When shall I have it, Edith?' She laughed, and answered so low I could not hear, for they left the gallery as they spoke. Forgive me, General, for the pain I inflict. You are the only person to whom I have spoken, and you are the only person who can properly and promptly prevent this affair from bringing open shame and scandal on an honorable house. To you I leave it, and will do my part with this infatuated young man if you will withdraw the temptation which will ruin him."

"I will. Thank you, Major. Trust to me, and by tomorrow I will prove that I can act as becomes me."

The grief and misery in the general's face touched the major; he silently wrung his hand and went away, thanking heaven more fervently than ever that no cursed coquette of a woman had it in her power to break his heart.

While this scene was going on above, another was taking place in the library. Treherne sat there alone, thinking happy thoughts evidently, for his eyes shone and his lips smiled as he mused, while watching the splendors of a winter sunset. A soft rustle and the faint scent of violets warned him of Mrs. Snowdon's approach, and a sudden foreboding told him that danger was near. The instant he saw her face his fear was confirmed, for exultation, resolve, and love met and mingled in the expression it wore. Leaning in the window recess, where the red light shone full on her lovely face and queenly figure, she said, softly yet with a ruthless accent below the softness, "Dreaming dreams, Maurice, which will never come to pass, unless I will it. I know your secret, and I shall use it to prevent the fulfillment of the foolish hope you cherish."

"Who told you?" he demanded, with an almost fierce flash of the eye and an angry flush.

"I discovered it, as I warned you I should. My memory is good, I recall the gossip of long ago, I observe the faces, words, and acts of those whom I suspect, and unconscious hints from them give me the truth."

"I doubt it," and Treherne smiled securely.

She stooped and whispered one short sentence into his ear. Whatever it was it caused him to start up with a pale, panic-stricken face and eye her as if she had pronounced his doom.

"Do you doubt it now?" she asked coldly.

"He told you! Even your skill and craft could not discover it alone," he muttered.

"Nay, I told you nothing was impossible to a determined woman. I needed no help, for I knew more than you think."

He sank down again in a despairing attitude and hid his face, saying mournfully, "I might have known you would hunt me down and dash my hopes when they were surest. How will you use this unhappy secret?"

"I will tell Octavia, and make her duty less hard. It will be kind to both of you, for even with her this memory would mar your happiness; and it saves her from the shame and grief of discovering, when too late, that she has given herself to a—"

"Stop!" he cried, in a tone that made her start and pale, as he rose out of his chair white with a stern indignation which awed her for a moment. "You shall not utter that word—you know but half the truth, and if you wrong me or trouble the girl I will turn traitor also, and tell the general the game you are playing with my cousin. You feign to love me as you feigned before, but his title is the bait now as then, and you fancy that by threatening to mar my hopes you will secure my silence, and gain your end."

"Wrong, quite wrong. Jasper is nothing to me; I use *him* as a tool, not you. If I threaten, it is to keep you from Octavia, who cannot forgive the past and love you for yourself, as I have done all these miserable months. You say I know but half the truth. Tell me the whole and I will spare you."

If ever a man was tempted to betray a trust it was Treherne then. A word, and Octavia might be his; silence, and she might be lost; for this woman was in earnest, and possessed the power to ruin his good name forever. The truth leaped to his lips and would have passed them, had not his eye fallen on the portrait of Jasper's father. This man had loved and sheltered the orphan all his life, had made of him a son, and, dying, urged him to guard and serve and save the rebellious youth he left, when most needing a father's care.

"I promised, and I will keep my promise at all costs," sighed Treherne, and with a gesture full of pathetic patience he waved the fair tempter from him, saying steadily, "I will never tell you, though you rob me of that which is dearer than my life. Go and work your will, but remember that when you might have won the deepest gratitude of the man you profess to love, you chose instead to earn his hatred and contempt."

Waiting for no word of hers, he took refuge in his room, and Edith Snowdon sank down upon the couch, struggling with contending emotions of love and jealousy, remorse and despair. How long she sat there she could not tell; an approaching step recalled her to herself, and looking up she saw Octavia. As the girl approached down the long vista of the drawing rooms, her youth and beauty, innocence and candor touched that fairer and more gifted woman with an envy she had never known before. Something in the girl's face struck her instantly: a look of peace and purity, a sweet serenity more winning than loveliness, more impressive than dignity or grace. With a smile on her lips, yet a half-sad, half-tender light in her eyes, and a cluster of pale winter roses in her hand, she came on till she stood before her rival and, offering the flowers, said, in words as simple as sincere, "Dear Mrs. Snowdon, I cannot let the last sun of the old year set on any misdeeds of mine for which I may atone. I have disliked, distrusted, and misjudged you, and now I come to you in all humility to say forgive me."

With the girlish abandon of her impulsive nature Octavia knelt down before the woman who was plotting to destroy her happiness, laid the roses like a little peace offering on her lap, and with eloquently pleading eyes waited for pardon. For a moment Mrs. Snowdon watched her, fancying it a well-acted ruse to disarm a dangerous rival; but in that sweet face there was no art; one glance showed her that. The words smote her to the heart and won her in spite of pride or passion, as she suddenly took the girl into her arms, weeping repentant tears. Neither spoke, but in the silence each felt the barrier which had stood between them vanishing, and each learned to know the other better in that moment than in a year of common life. Octavia rejoiced that the instinct which had prompted her to make this appeal had not misled her, but assured her that behind the veil of coldness, pride, and levity which this woman wore there was a heart aching for sympathy and help and love. Mrs. Snowdon felt her worser self slip from her, leaving all that was true and noble to make her worthy of the test applied. Art she could meet with equal art, but nature conquered her. For spite of her misspent life and faulty character, the germ of virtue, which lives in the worst, was there, only waiting for the fostering sun and dew of love to strengthen it, even though the harvest be a late one.

"Forgive you!" she cried, brokenly. "It is I who should ask forgiveness of you—I who should atone, confess, and repent. Pardon *me*, pity me, love me, for I am more wretched than you know."

"Dear, I do with heart and soul. Believe it, and let me be your friend" was the soft answer.

"God knows I need one!" sighed the poor woman, still holding fast the only creature who had wholly won her. "Child, I am not good, but not so bad that I dare not look in your innocent face and call you friend. I never had one of my own sex. I never knew my mother; and no one ever saw in me the possibility of goodness, truth, and justice but you. Trust and love and help me, Octavia, and I will reward you with a better life, if I can do no more."

"I will, and the new year shall be happier than the old."

"God bless you for that prophecy; may I be worthy of it."

Then as a bell warned them away, the rivals kissed each other tenderly, and parted friends. As Mrs. Snowdon entered her room, she saw her husband sitting with his gray head in his hands, and heard him murmur despairingly to himself, "My life makes her miserable. But for the sin of it I'd die to free her."

"No, live for me, and teach me to be happy in your love." The clear voice startled him, but not so much as the beautiful changed face of the wife who laid the gray head on her bosom, saying tenderly, "My kind and patient husband, you have been deceived. From me you shall know all the truth, and when you have forgiven my faulty past, you shall see how happy I will try to make your future."

Chapter VII. A Ghostly Revel

"Bless me, how dull we all are tonight!" exclaimed Rose, as the younger portion of the party wandered listlessly about the drawing rooms that evening, while my lady and the major played an absorbing game of piquet, and the general dozed peacefully at last.

"It is because Maurice is not here; he always keeps us going, for he is a fellow of infinite resources," replied Sir Jasper, suppressing a yawn.

"Have him out then," said Annon.

"He won't come. The poor lad is blue tonight, in spite of his improvement. Something is amiss, and there is no getting a word from him."

"Sad memories afflict him, perhaps," sighed Blanche.

"Don't be absurd, dear, sad memories are all nonsense; melancholy is always indigestion, and nothing is so sure a cure as fun," said Rose briskly. "I'm going to send in a polite invitation begging him to come and amuse us. He'll accept, I haven't a doubt."

The message was sent, but to Rose's chagrin a polite refusal was returned.

"He *shall* come. Sir Jasper, do you and Mr. Annon go as a deputation from us, and return without him at your peril" was her command.

They went, and while waiting their reappearance the sisters spoke of what all had observed.

"How lovely Mrs. Snowdon looks tonight. I always thought she owed half her charms to her skill in dress, but she never looked so beautiful as in that plain black silk, with those roses in her hair," said Rose.

"What has she done to herself?" replied Blanche. "I see a change, but can't account for it. She and Tavie have made some beautifying discovery, for both look altogether uplifted and angelic all of a sudden."

"Here come the gentlemen, and, as I'm a Talbot, they haven't got him!" cried Rose as the deputation appeared, looking very crestfallen. "Don't come near me," she added, irefully, "you are disloyal cowards, and I doom you to exile till I want you. *I* am infinite in resources as well as this recreant man, and come he shall. Mrs. Snowdon, would you mind asking Mr. Treherne to suggest something to wile away the rest of this evening? We are in despair, and can think of nothing, and you are all-powerful with him."

"I must decline, since he refuses you" was the decided answer, as Mrs. Snowdon moved away.

"Tavie, dear, do go; we *must* have him; he always obeys you, and you would be such a public benefactor, you know."

Without a word Octavia wrote a line and sent it by a servant. Several minutes passed, and the gentlemen began to lay wagers on the success of her trial. "He will not come for me, you may be sure," said Octavia. As the words passed her lips he appeared.

A general laugh greeted him, but, taking no notice of the jests at his expense, he turned to Octavia, saying quietly, "What can I do for you, Cousin?"

His colorless face and weary eyes reproached her for disturbing him, but it was too late for regret, and she answered hastily, "We are in want of some new and amusing occupation to wile away the evening. Can you suggest something appropriate?"

"Why not sit round the hall fire and tell stories, while we wait to see the old year out, as we used to do long ago?" he asked, after a moment's thought.

"I told you so! There it is, just what we want." And Sir Jasper looked triumphant.

"It's capital—let us begin at once. It is after ten now, so we shall not have long to wait," cried Rose, and, taking Sir Jasper's arm, she led the way to the hall.

A great fire always burned there, and in wintertime thick carpets and curtains covered the stone floor and draped the tall windows. Plants blossomed in the warm atmosphere, and chairs and lounges stood about invitingly. The party was soon seated, and Treherne was desired to begin.

"We must have ghost stories, and in order to be properly thrilling and effective, the lights must be put out," said Rose, who sat next him, and spoke first, as usual.

This was soon done, and only a ruddy circle of firelight was left to oppose the rapt gloom that filled the hall, where shadows now seemed to lurk in every corner.

"Don't be very dreadful, or I shall faint away," pleaded Blanche, drawing nearer to Annon, for she had taken her sister's advice, and laid close siege to that gentleman's heart.

"I think your nerves will bear my little tale," replied Treherne. "When I was in India, four years ago, I had a very dear friend in my regiment—a Scotchman; I'm half Scotch myself, you know, and clannish, of course. Gordon was sent up the country on a scouting expedition, and never returned. His men reported that he left them one evening to take a survey, and his horse came home bloody and riderless. We searched, but could not find a trace of him, and I was desperate to discover and avenge his murder. About a month after his disappearance, as I sat in my tent one fearfully hot day, suddenly the canvas door flap was raised and there stood Gordon. I saw him as plainly as I see you, Jasper, and should have sprung to meet him, but something held me back. He was deathly pale, dripping with water, and in his bonny blue eyes was a wild, woeful look that made my blood run cold. I stared dumbly, for it was awful to see my friend so changed and so unearthly. Stretching his arm to me he took my hand, saying solemnly, 'Come!' The touch was like ice; an ominous thrill ran through me; I started up to obey, and he was gone."

"A horrid dream, of course. Is that all?" asked Rose.

With his eyes on the fire and his left hand half extended, Treherne went on as if he had not heard her.

"I thought it was a fancy, and soon recovered myself, for no one had seen or heard anything of Gordon, and my native servant lay just outside my tent. A strange sensation remained in the hand the phantom touched. It was cold, damp, and white. I found it vain to try to forget this apparition; it took strong hold of me; I told Yermid, my man, and he bade me consider it a sign that I was to seek my friend. That night I dreamed I was riding up the country in hot haste; what led me I know not, but I pressed on and on, longing to reach the end. A half-dried river crossed my path, and, riding down the steep bank to ford it, I saw Gordon's body lying in the shallow water looking exactly as the vision looked. I woke in a strange mood, told the story to my commanding officer, and, as nothing was doing just then, easily got leave of absence for a week. Taking Yermid, I set out on my sad quest. I thought it folly, but I could not resist the impulse that drew me on. For seven days I searched, and the strangest part of the story is that all that time I went on exactly as in the dream, seeing what I saw then, and led by the touch of a cold hand on mine. On the seventh day I reached the river, and found my friend's body."

"How horrible! Is it really true?" cried Mrs. Snowdon.

"As true as I am a living man. Nor is that all: this left hand of mine never has been warm since that time. See and feel for yourselves."

He opened both hands, and all satisfied themselves that the left was smaller, paler, and colder than the right.

"Pray someone tell another story to put this out of my mind; it makes me nervous," said Blanche.

"I'll tell one, and you may laugh to quiet your nerves. I want to have mine done with, so that I can enjoy the rest with a free mind." With these words Rose began her tale in the good old fashion.

"Once upon a time, when we were paying a visit to my blessed grandmamma, I saw a ghost in this wise: The dear old lady was ill with a cold and kept her room, leaving us to mope, for it was very dull in the great lonely house. Blanche and I were both homesick, but didn't like to leave till she was better, so we ransacked the library and solaced ourselves with all manner of queer books. One day I found Grandmamma very low and nervous, and evidently with something on her mind. She would say nothing, but the next day was worse, and I insisted on knowing the cause, for the trouble was evidently mental. Charging me to keep it from Blanche, who was, and is, a sad coward, she told me that a spirit had appeared to her two successive nights. 'If it comes a third time, I shall prepare to die,' said the foolish old lady.

" 'No, you won't, for I'll come and stay with you and lay your ghost,' I said. With some difficulty I made her yield, and after Blanche was asleep I slipped away to Grandmamma, with a book and candle for a long watch, as the spirit didn't appear till after midnight. She usually slept with her door unlocked, in case of fire or fright, and her maid was close by. That night I locked the door, telling her that spirits could come through the oak if they chose, and I preferred to have a fair trial. Well, I read and chatted and dozed till dawn and nothing appeared, so I laughed at the whole affair, and the old lady pretended to be convinced that it was all a fancy.

"Next night I slept in my own room, and in the morning was told that not only Grandmamma but Janet had seen the spirit. All in white, with streaming hair, a pale face, and a red streak at the throat. It came and parted the bed-curtains, looking in a moment, and then vanished. Janet had slept with Grandmamma and kept a lamp burning on the chimney, so both saw it.

"I was puzzled, but not frightened; I never am, and I insisted on trying again. The door was left unlocked, as on the previous night, and I lay with Grandmamma, a light burning as before. About two she clutched me as I was dropping off. I looked, and there, peeping in between the dark curtains, was a pale face with long hair all about it, and a red streak at the throat. It was very dim, the light being low, but I saw it, and after one breathless minute sprang up, caught my foot, fell down with a crash, and by the time I was around the bed, not a vestige of the thing appeared. I was angry, and vowed I'd succeed at all hazards, though I'll confess I was just a bit daunted.

"Next time Janet and I sat up in easy chairs, with bright lights burning, and both wide awake with the strongest coffee we could make. As the hour drew near we got nervous, and when the white shape came gliding in Janet hid her face. I didn't, and after one look was on the point of laughing, for the spirit was Blanche walking in her sleep. She wore a coral necklace in those days, and never took it off, and her long hair half hid her face, which had the unnatural, uncanny look somnambulists always wear. I had the sense to keep still and tell Janet what to do, so the poor child went back unwaked, and Grandmamma's spirit never walked again for I took care of that."

"Why did you haunt the old lady?" asked Annon, as the laughter ceased.

"I don't know, unless it was that I wanted to ask leave to go home, and was afraid to do it awake, so tried when asleep. I shall not tell any story, as I was the heroine of this, but will give my turn to you, Mr. Annon," said Blanche, with a soft glance, which was quite thrown away, for the gentleman's eyes were fixed on Octavia, who sat on a low ottoman at Mrs. Snowdon's feet in the full glow of the firelight.

"I've had very small experience in ghosts, and can only recall a little fright I once had when a boy at college. I'd been out to a party, got home tired, couldn't find my matches, and retired in the dark. Toward morning I woke, and glancing up to see if the dim light was dawn or moonshine I was horrified to see a coffin standing at the bed's foot. I rubbed my eyes to be sure I was awake, and looked with all my might. There it was, a long black coffin, and I saw the white plate in the dusk, for the moon was setting and my curtain was not drawn. 'It's some trick of the fellows,' I thought; 'I'll not betray myself, but keep cool.' Easy to say but hard to do, for it suddenly flashed into my mind that I might be in the wrong room. I glanced about, but there were the familiar objects as usual, as far as the indistinct light allowed me to see, and I made sure by feeling on the wall at the bed's head for my watchcase. It was there, and mine beyond a doubt, being peculiar in shape and fabric. Had I been to a college wine party I could have accounted for the vision, but a quiet evening in a grave professor's well-conducted family could produce no ill effects. 'It's an optical illusion, or a prank of my mates; I'll sleep and forget it,' I said, and for a time endeavored to do so, but curiosity overcame my resolve, and soon I peeped again. Judge of my horror when I saw the sharp white outline of a dead face, which seemed to be peeping up from the coffin. It gave me a terrible shock for I was but a lad and had been ill. I hid my face and quaked like a nervous girl, still thinking it some joke and too proud to betray fear lest I should be laughed at. How long I lay there I don't know, but when I looked again the face was farther out and the whole figure seemed rising slowly. The moon was nearly down, I had no lamp, and to be left in the dark with that awesome thing was more than I could bear. Joke or earnest, I must end the panic, and bolting out of my room I roused my neighbor. He told me I was mad or drunk, but lit a lamp and returned with me, to find my horror only a heap of clothes thrown on the table in such a way that, as the moon's pale light shot it, it struck upon my black student's gown, with a white card lying on it, and produced the effect of a coffin and plate. The face was a crumpled handkerchief, and what seemed hair a brown muffler. As the moon sank, these outlines changed and, incredible as it may seem, grew like a face. My friend not having had the fright enjoyed the joke, and 'Coffins' was my sobriquet for a long while."

"You get worse and worse. Sir Jasper, do vary the horrors by a touch of fun, or I shall run away," said Blanche, glancing over her shoulder nervously.

"I'll do my best, and tell a story my uncle used to relate of his young days. I forget the name of the place, but it was some little country town famous among anglers. My uncle often went to fish, and always regretted that a deserted house near the trout stream was not occupied, for the inn was inconveniently distant. Speaking of this one evening as he lounged in the landlady's parlor, he asked why no one took it and let the rooms to strangers in the fishing season. 'For fear of the ghostissess, your honor,' replied the woman, and proceeded to tell him that three distinct spirits haunted the house. In the garret was heard the hum of a wheel and the tap of high-heeled shoes, as the ghostly spinner went to and fro. In a chamber sounded the sharpening of a knife, followed by groans and the drip of blood. The cellar was made awful by a skeleton sitting on a half-buried box and chuckling fiendishly. It seems a miser lived there once, and was believed to have starved his daughter in the garret, keeping her at work till she died. The second spirit was that of the girl's rejected lover, who cut his throat in the chamber, and the third of the miser who was found dead on the money chest he was too feeble to conceal. My uncle laughed at all this, and offered to lay the ghosts if anyone would take the house.

"This offer got abroad, and a crusty old fellow accepted it, hoping to turn a penny. He had a pretty girl, whose love had been thwarted by the old man, and whose lover was going to sea in despair. My uncle knew this and pitied the young people. He had made acquaintance with a wandering artist, and the two agreed to conquer the prejudices against the house by taking rooms there. They did so, and after satisfying themselves regarding the noises, consulted a wise old woman as to the best means of laying the ghosts. She told them if any young girl would pass a night in each haunted room, praying piously the while, that all would be well. Peggy was asked if she would do it, and being a stouthearted lass she consented, for a round sum, to try it. The first night was in the garret, and Peggy, in spite of the prophecies of the village gossips, came out alive, though listeners at the door heard the weird humming and tapping all night long. The next night all went well, and from that time no more sharpening, groaning, or dripping was heard. The third time she bade her friends good-bye and, wrapped in her red cloak, with a lamp and prayer book, went down into the cellar. Alas for pretty Peggy! When day came she was gone, and with her the miser's empty box, though his bones remained to prove how well she had done her work.

"The town was in an uproar, and the old man furious. Some said the devil had flown away with her, others that the bones were hers, and all agreed that henceforth another ghost would haunt the house. My uncle and the artist did their best to comfort the father, who sorely reproached himself for thwarting the girl's love, and declared that if Jack would find her he should have her. But Jack had sailed, and the old man 'was left lamenting.' The house was freed from its unearthly visitors, however, for no ghost appeared; and when my uncle left, old Martin found money and letter informing him that Peggy had spent her first two nights preparing for flight, and on the third had gone away to marry and sail with Jack. The noises had been produced by the artist, who was a ventriloquist, the skeleton had been smuggled from the surgeons, and the whole thing was a conspiracy to help Peggy and accommodate the fishermen."

"It is evident that roguery is hereditary," laughed Rose as the narrator paused.

"I strongly suspect that Sir Jasper the second was the true hero of that story," added Mrs. Snowdon.

"Think what you like, I've done my part, and leave the stage for you, madam."

"I will come last. It is your turn, dear."

As Mrs. Snowdon softly uttered the last word, and Octavia leaned upon her knee with an affectionate glance, Treherne leaned forward to catch a glimpse of the two changed faces, and looked as if bewildered when both smiled at him, as they sat hand in hand while the girl told her story.

"Long ago a famous actress suddenly dropped dead at the close of a splendidly played tragedy. She was carried home, and preparations were made to bury her. The play had gotten up with great care and expense, and a fine actor was the hero. The public demanded a repetition, and an inferior person was engaged to take the dead lady's part. A day's delay had been necessary, but when the night came the house was crowded. They waited both before and behind the curtain for the debut of the new actress, with much curiosity. She stood waiting for her cue, but as it was given, to the amazement of all, the great tragedienne glided upon the stage. Pale as marble, and with a strange fire in her eyes, strange pathos in her voice, strange power in her acting, she went through her part, and at the close vanished as mysteriously as she came. Great was the excitement that night, and intense the astonishment and horror next day when it was whispered abroad that the dead woman never had revived, but had lain in her coffin before the eyes of watchers all the evening, when hundreds fancied they were applauding her at the theater. The mystery never was cleared up, and Paris was divided by two opinions: one that some person marvelously like Madame Z. had personated her for the sake of a sensation; the other that the ghost of the dead actress, unable to free itself from the old duties so full of fascination to an ambitious and successful woman, had played for the last time the part which had made her famous."

"Where did you find that, Tavie? It's very French, and not bad if you invented it," said Sir Jasper.

"I read it in an old book, where it was much better told. Now, Edith, there is just time for your tale."

As the word "Edith" passed her lips, again Treherne started and eyed them both, and again they smiled, as Mrs. Snowdon caressed the smooth cheek leaning on her knee, and looking full at him began the last recital.

"You have been recounting the pranks of imaginary ghosts; let me show you the workings of some real spirits, evil and good, that haunt every heart and home, making its misery or joy. At Christmastime, in a country house, a party of friends met to keep the holidays, and very happily they might have done so had not one person marred the peace of several. Love, jealousy, deceit, and nobleness were the spirits that played their freaks with these people. The person of whom I speak was more haunted than the rest, and much tormented, being willful, proud, and jealous. Heaven help her, she had had no one to exorcise these ghosts for her, and they goaded her to do much harm. Among these friends there were more than one pair of lovers, and much tangling of plots and plans, for hearts are wayward and mysterious things, and cannot love as duty bids or prudence counsels. This woman held the key to all the secrets of the house, and, having a purpose to gain, she used her power selfishly, for a time. To satisfy a doubt, she feigned a fancy for a gentleman who once did her the honor of admiring her, and, to the great scandal of certain sage persons, permitted him to show his regard for her, knowing that it was but a transient amusement on his part as well as upon hers. In the hands of this woman lay a secret which could make or mar the happiness of the best and dearest of the party. The evil spirits which haunted her urged her to mar their peace and gratify a sinful hope. On the other side, honor, justice, and generosity prompted her to make them happy, and while she wavered there came to her a sweet enchantress who, with a word, banished the tormenting ghosts forever, and gave the haunted woman a talisman to keep her free henceforth."

There the earnest voice faltered, and with a sudden impulse Mrs. Snowdon bent her head and kissed the fair forehead which had bent lower and lower as she went on. Each listener understood the truth, lightly veiled in that hasty fable, and each found in it a different meaning. Sir Jasper frowned and bit his lips, Annon glanced anxiously from face to face, Octavia hid hers, and Treherne's flashed with sudden intelligence, while Rose laughed low to herself, enjoying the scene. Blanche, who was getting sleepy, said, with a stifled gape, "That is a very nice, moral little story, but I wish there had been some real ghosts in it."

"There was. Will you come and see them?"

As she put the question, Mrs. Snowdon rose abruptly, wishing to end the seance, and beckoning them to follow glided up the great stairway. All obeyed, wondering what whim possessed her, and quite ready for any jest in store for them.

CHAPTER VIII. JASPER

SHE LED THEM to the north gallery and, pausing at the door, said merrily, "The ghost—or ghosts rather, for there were two—which frightened Patty were Sir Jasper and myself, meeting to discuss certain important matters which concerned Mr. Treherne. If you want to see spirits we will play phantom for you, and convince you of our power."

"Good, let us go and have a ghostly dance, as a proper finale of our revel," answered Rose as they flocked into the long hall.

At that moment the great clock struck twelve, and all paused to bid the old year adieu. Sir Jasper was the first to speak, for, angry with Mrs. Snowdon, yet thankful to her for making a jest to others of what had been earnest to him, he desired to hide his chagrin under a gay manner; and taking Rose around the waist was about to waltz away as she proposed, saying cheerily, " 'Come one and all, and dance the new year in,' " when a cry from Octavia arrested him, and turning he saw her stand, pale and trembling, pointing to the far end of the hall.

Eight narrow Gothic windows pierced either wall of the north gallery. A full moon sent her silvery light strongly in upon the eastern side, making broad bars of brightness across the floor. No fires burned there now, and wherever the moonlight did not fall deep shadows lay. As Octavia cried out, all looked, and all distinctly saw a tall, dark figure moving noiselessly across the second bar of light far down the hall.

"Is it some jest of yours?" asked Sir Jasper of Mrs. Snowdon, as the form vanished in the shadow.

"No, upon my honor, I know nothing of it! I only meant to relieve Octavia's superstitious fears by showing her our pranks" was the whispered reply as Mrs. Snowdon's cheek paled, and she drew nearer to Jasper.

"Who is there?" called Treherne in a commanding tone.

No answer, but a faint, cold breath of air seemed to sigh along the arched roof and die away as the dark figure crossed the third streak of moonlight. A strange awe fell upon them all, and no one spoke, but stood watching for the appearance of the shape. Nearer and nearer it came, with soundless steps, and as it reached the sixth window its outlines were distinctly visible. A tall, wasted figure, all in black, with a rosary hanging from the girdle, and a dark beard half concealing the face.

"The Abbot's ghost, and very well got up," said Annon, trying to laugh but failing decidedly, for again the cold breath swept over them, causing a general shudder.

"Hush!" whispered Treherne, drawing Octavia to his side with a protecting gesture.

Once more the phantom appeared and disappeared, and as they waited for it to cross the last bar of light that lay between it and them, Mrs. Snowdon stepped forward to the edge of the shadow in which they stood, as if to confront the apparition alone. Out of the darkness it came, and in the full radiance of the light it paused. Mrs. Snowdon, being nearest, saw the face first, and uttering a faint cry dropped down upon the stone floor, covering up her eyes. Nothing human ever wore a look like that of the ghastly, hollow-eyed, pale-lipped countenance below the hood. All saw it and held their breath as it slowly raised a shadowy arm and pointed a shriveled finger at Sir Jasper.

"Speak, whatever you are, or I'll quickly prove whether you are man or spirit!" cried Jasper fiercely, stepping forward as if to grasp the extended arm that seemed to menace him alone.

An icy gust swept through the hall, and the phantom slowly receded into the shadow. Jasper sprang after it, but nothing crossed the second stream of light, and nothing remained in the shade. Like one possessed by a sudden fancy he rushed down the gallery to find all fast and empty, and to return looking very strangely. Blanche had fainted away and Annon was bearing her out of the hall. Rose was clinging to Mrs. Snowdon, and Octavia leaned against her cousin, saying in a fervent whisper, "Thank God it did not point at you!"

"Am I then dearer than your brother?" he whispered back.

There was no audible reply, but one little hand involuntarily pressed his, though the other was outstretched toward Jasper, who came up white and startled but firm and quiet. Affecting to make light of it, he said, forcing a smile as he raised Mrs. Snowdon, "It is some stupid joke of the servants. Let us think no more of it. Come, Edith, this is not like your usual self."

"It was nothing human, Jasper; you know it as well as I. Oh, why did I bring you here to meet the warning phantom that haunts your house!"

"Nay, if my time is near the spirit would have found me out wherever I might be. I have no faith in that absurd superstition—I laugh at and defy it. Come down and drink my health in wine from the Abbot's own cellar."

But no one had heart for further gaiety, and, finding Lady Treherne already alarmed by Annon, they were forced to tell her all, and find their own bewilderment deepened by her unalterable belief in the evil omen.

At her command the house was searched, the servants cross-questioned, and every effort made to discover the identity of the apparition. All in vain; the house was as usual, and not a man or maid but turned pale at the idea of entering the gallery at midnight. At my lady's request, all promised to say no more upon the mystery, and separated at last to such sleep as they could enjoy.

Very grave were the faces gathered about the breakfast table next morning, and very anxious the glances cast on Sir Jasper as he came in, late as usual, looking uncommonly blithe and well. Nothing serious ever made a deep impression on his mercurial nature. Treherne had more the air of a doomed man, being very pale and worn, in spite of an occasional gleam of happiness as he looked at Octavia. He haunted Jasper like a shadow all the morning, much to that young gentleman's annoyance, for both his mother and sister hung about him with faces of ill-dissembled anxiety. By afternoon his patience gave out, and he openly rebelled against the tender guard kept over him. Ringing for his horse he said decidedly, "I'm bored to death with the solemnity which pervades the house today, so I'm off for a brisk gallop, before I lose my temper and spirits altogether."

"Come with me in the pony carriage, Jasper. I've not had a drive with you for a long while, and should enjoy it so much," said my lady, detaining him.

"Mrs. Snowdon looks as if she needed air to revive her roses, and the pony carriage is just the thing for her, so I will cheerfully resign my seat to her," he answered laughing, as he forced himself from his mother's hand.

"Take the girls in the clarence. We all want a breath of air, and you are the best whip we know. Be gallant and say yes, dear."

"No, thank you, Tavie, that won't do. Rose and Blanche are both asleep, and you are dying to go and do likewise, after your vigils last night. As a man and a brother I beg you'll do so, and let me ride as I like."

"Suppose you ask Annon to join you—" began Treherne with well-assumed indifference; but Sir Jasper frowned and turned sharply on him, saying, half-petulantly, half-jocosely:

"Upon my life I should think I was a boy or a baby, by the manner in which you mount guard over me today. If you think I'm going to live in daily fear of some mishap, you are all much mistaken. Ghost or no ghost, I shall make merry while I can; a short life and a jolly one has always been my motto, you know, so fare you well till dinnertime."

They watched him gallop down the avenue, and then went their different ways, still burdened with a nameless foreboding. Octavia strolled into the conservatory, thinking to refresh herself with the balmy silence which pervaded the place, but Annon soon joined her full of a lover's hopes and fears.

"Miss Treherne, I have ventured to come for my answer. Is my New Year to be a blissful or a sad one?" he asked eagerly.

"Forgive me if I give you an unwelcome reply, but I must be true, and so regretfully refuse the honor you do me," she said sorrowfully.

"May I ask why?"

"Because I do not love you."

"And you do love your cousin," he cried angrily, pausing to watch her half-averted face.

She turned it fully toward him and answered, with her native sincerity, "Yes, I do, with all my heart, and now my mother will not thwart me, for Maurice has saved my life, and I am free to devote it all to him."

"Happy man, I wish I had been a cripple!" sighed Annon. Then with a manful effort to be just and generous, he added heartily, "Say no more, he deserves you; I want no sacrifice to duty; I yield, and go away, praying heaven to bless you now and always."

He kissed her hand and left her to seek my lady and make his adieus, for no persuasion could keep him. Leaving a note for Sir Jasper, he hurried away, to the great relief of Treherne and the deep regret of Blanche, who, however, lived in hopes of another trial later in the season.

"Here comes Jasper, Mamma, safe and well," cried Octavia an hour or two later, as she joined her mother on the terrace, where my lady had been pacing restlessly to and fro nearly ever since her son rode away.

With a smile of intense relief she waved her handkerchief as he came clattering up the drive, and seeing her he answered with hat and hand. He usually dismounted at the great hall door, but a sudden whim made him ride along the wall that lay below the terrace, for he was a fine horseman, and Mrs. Snowdon was looking from her window. As he approached, the peacocks fled screaming, and one flew up just before the horse's eyes as his master was in the act of dismounting. The spirited creature was startled, sprang partway up the low, broad steps of the terrace, and, being sharply checked, slipped, fell, and man and horse rolled down together.

Never did those who heard it forget the cry that left Lady Treherne's lips as she saw the fall. It brought out both guests and servants, to find Octavia recklessly struggling with the frightened horse, and my lady down upon the stones with her son's bleeding head in her arms.

They bore in the senseless, shattered body, and for hours tried everything that skill and science could devise to save the young man's life. But every effort was in vain, and as the sun set Sir Jasper lay dying. Conscious at last, and able to speak, he looked about him with a troubled glance, and seemed struggling with some desire that overmastered pain and held death at bay.

"I want Maurice," he feebly said, at length.

"Dear lad, I'm here," answered his cousin's voice from a seat in the shadow of the half-drawn curtains.

"Always near when I need you. Many a scrape have you helped me out of, but this is beyond your power," and a faint smile passed over Jasper's lips as the past flitted before his mind. But the smile died, and a groan of pain escaped him as he cried suddenly, "Quick! Let me tell it before it is too late! Maurice never will, but bear the shame all his life that my dead name may be untarnished. Bring Edith; she must hear the truth."

She was soon there, and, lying in his mother's arms, one hand in his cousin's, and one on his sister's bent head, Jasper rapidly told the secret which had burdened him for a year.

"I did it; I forged my uncle's name when I had lost so heavily at play that I dared not tell my mother, or squander more of my own fortune. I deceived Maurice, and let him think the check a genuine one; I made him present it and get the money, and when all went well I fancied I was safe. But my uncle discovered it secretly, said nothing, and, believing Maurice the forger, disinherited him. I never knew this till the old man died, and then it was too late. I confessed to Maurice, and he forgave me. He said, 'I am helpless now, shut out from the world, with nothing to lose or gain, and soon to be forgotten by those who once knew me, so let the suspicion of shame, if any such there be, still cling to me, and do you go your way, rich, happy, honorable, and untouched by any shadow on your fame.' Mother, I let him do it, unconscious as he was that many knew the secret sin and fancied him the doer of it."

"Hush, Jasper, let it pass. I can bear it; I promised your dear father to be your staunch friend through life, and I have only kept my word."

"God knows you have, but now my life ends, and I cannot die till you are cleared. Edith, I told you half the truth, and you would have used it against him had not some angel sent this girl to touch your heart. You have done your part to atone for the past, now let me do mine. Mother, Tavie loves him, he has risked life and honor for me. Repay him generously and give him this."

With feeble touch Sir Jasper tried to lay his sister's hand in Treherne's as he spoke; Mrs. Snowdon helped him, and as my lady bowed her head in silent acquiescence, a joyful smile shone on the dying man's face.

"One more confession, and then I am ready," he said, looking up into the face of the woman whom he had loved with all the power of a shallow nature. "It was a jest to you, Edith, but it was bitter earnest to me, for I loved you, sinful as it was. Ask your husband to forgive me, and tell him it was better I should die than live to mar a good man's peace. Kiss me once, and make him happy for my sake."

She touched his cold lips with remorseful tenderness, and in the same breath registered a vow to obey that dying prayer.

"Tavie dear, Maurice, my brother, God bless you both. Good-bye, Mother. He will be a better son than I have been to you." Then, the reckless spirit of the man surviving to the last, Sir Jasper laughed faintly, as he seemed to beckon some invisible shape, and died saying gaily, "Now, Father Abbot, lead on, I'll follow you."

A year later three weddings were celebrated on the same day and in the same church. Maurice Treherne, a well man, led up his cousin. Frank Annon rewarded Blanche's patient siege by an unconditional surrender, and, to the infinite amusement of Mrs. Grundy, Major Royston publicly confessed himself outgeneraled by merry Rose. The triple wedding feast was celebrated at Treherne Abbey, and no uncanny visitor marred its festivities, for never again was the north gallery haunted by the ghostly Abbot.

❧ Taming a Tartar

CHAPTER I

"DEAR MADEMOISELLE, I assure you it is an arrangement both profitable and agreeable to one, who, like you, desires change of occupation and scene, as well as support. Madame la Princesse is most affable, generous, and to those who please her, quite child-like in her affection."

"But, madame, am I fit for the place? Does it not need accomplishments and graces which I do not possess? There is a wide difference between being a teacher in a *Pensionnat pour Demoiselles* like this and the companion of a princess."

"Ah, hah, my dear, it is nothing. Let not the fear of rank disturb you; these Russians are but savages, and all their money, splendor, and the polish Paris gives them, do not suffice to change the barbarians. You are the superior in breeding as in intelligence, as you will soon discover; and for accomplishments, yours will bear the test anywhere. I grant you Russians have much talent for them, and acquire with marvelous ease, but taste they have not, nor the skill to use these weapons as we use them."

"The princess is an invalid, you say?"

"Yes; but she suffers little, is delicate and needs care, amusement, yet not excitement. You are to chat with her, to read, sing, strive to fill the place of confidante. She sees little society, and her wing of the hotel is quite removed from that of the prince, who is one of the lions just now."

"Is it of him they tell the strange tales of his princely generosity, his fearful temper, childish caprices, and splendid establishment?"

"In truth, yes; Paris is wild for him, as for some magnificent savage beast. Madame la Comtesse Millefleur declared that she never knew whether he would fall at her feet, or annihilate her, so impetuous were his moods. At one moment showing all the complaisance and elegance of a born Parisian, the next terrifying the beholders by some outburst of savage wrath, some betrayal of the Tartar blood that is in him. Ah! it is incredible how such things amaze one."

"Has the princess the same traits? If so, I fancy the situation of companion is not easy to fill."

"No, no, she is not of the same blood. She is a half-sister; her mother was a Frenchwoman; she was educated in France, and lived here till her marriage with Prince Tcherinski. She detests St. Petersburg, adores Paris, and hopes to keep her brother here till the spring, for the fearful climate of the north is death to her delicate lungs. She is a gay, simple, confiding person; a child still in many things, and since her widowhood entirely under the control of this brother, who loves her tenderly, yet is a tyrant to her as to all who approach him."

I smiled as my loquacious friend gave me these hints of my future master and mistress, but in spite of all drawbacks, I liked the prospect, and what would have deterred another, attracted me. I was alone in the world, fond of experiences and adventures, self-reliant and self-possessed; eager for change, and anxious to rub off the rust of five years' servitude in Madame Bayard's Pensionnat. This new occupation pleased me, and but for a slight fear of proving unequal to it, I should have at once accepted madame's proposition. She knew everyone, and through some friend had heard of the princess's wish to find an English lady as companion and teacher, for a whim had seized her to learn English. Madame knew I intended to leave her, my health and spirits being worn by long and arduous duties, and she kindly interested herself to secure the place for me.

"Go then, dear mademoiselle, make a charming toilet and present yourself to the princess without delay, or you lose your opportunity. I have smoothed the way for you; your own address will do the rest, and in one sense, your fortune is made, if all goes well."

I obeyed madame, and when I was ready, took a critical survey of myself, trying to judge of the effect upon others. The long mirror showed me a slender, well-molded figure, and a pale face—not beautiful, but expressive, for the sharply cut, somewhat haughty features betrayed good blood, spirit and strength. Gray eyes, large and lustrous, under straight, dark brows; a firm mouth and chin, proud nose, wide brow, with waves of chestnut hair parted plainly back into heavy coils behind. Five years in Paris had taught me the art of dress, and a good salary permitted me to indulge my taste. Although simply made, I flattered myself that my promenade costume of silk and sable was *en règle,* as well as becoming, and with a smile at myself in the mirror I went my way, wondering if this new plan was to prove the welcome change so long desired.

As the carriage drove into the court-yard of the prince's hotel in the Champs Élysées, and a gorgeous *laquais* carried up my card, my heart beat a little faster than usual, and when I followed the servant in, I felt as if my old life ended suddenly, and one of strange interest had already begun.

The princess was not ready to receive me yet, and I was shown into a splendid *salon* to wait. My entrance was noiseless, and as I took a seat, my eyes fell on the half-drawn curtains which divided the room from another. Two persons were visible, but as neither saw me in the soft gloom of the apartment, I had an opportunity to look as long and curiously as I pleased. The whole scene was as unlike those usually found in a Parisian *salon* as can well be imagined.

Though three o'clock in the afternoon, it was evidently early morning with the gentleman stretched on the ottoman, reading a novel and smoking a Turkish chibouk—for his costume was that of a Russian seigneur in *déshabillé.* A long Caucasian caftan of the finest white sheepskin, a pair of loose black velvet trowsers, bound round the waist by a rich shawl, and Kasan boots of crimson leather, ornamented with golden embroidery on the instep, covered a pair of feet which seemed disproportionately small compared to the unusually tall, athletic figure of the man; so also did the head with a red silk handkerchief bound over the thick black hair. The costume suited the face; swarthy, black-eyed, scarlet-lipped, heavybrowed and beardless, except a thick mustache; serfs wear beards, but Russian nobles never. A strange face, for even in repose the indescribable difference of race was visible; the contour of the head, molding of the features, hue of hair and skin, even the attitude, all betrayed a trace of the savage strength and spirit of one in whose veins flowed the blood of men reared in tents, and born to lead wild lives in a wild land.

This unexpected glance behind the scenes interested me much, and I took note of everything within my ken. The book which the slender brown hand held was evidently a French novel, but when a lap-dog disturbed the reader, it was ordered off in Russian with a sonorous oath, I suspect, and an impatient gesture. On a guéridon, or side-table, stood a velvet *porte-cigare,* a box of sweetmeats, a bottle of Bordeaux, and a tall glass of cold tea, with a slice of lemon floating in it. A musical instrument, something like a mandolin, lay near the ottoman, a piano stood open, with a sword and helmet on it, and sitting in a corner, noiselessly making cigarettes, was a half-grown boy, a serf I fancied, from his dress and the silent, slavish way in which he watched his master.

The princess kept me waiting long, but I was not impatient, and when I was summoned at last I could not resist a backward glance at the brilliant figure I left behind me. The servant's voice had roused him, and, rising to his elbow, he leaned forward to look, with an expression of mingled curiosity and displeasure in the largest, blackest eyes I ever met.

I found the princess, a pale, pretty little woman of not more than twenty, buried in costly furs, though the temperature of her boudoir seemed tropical to me. Most gracious was my reception, and at once all fear vanished, for she was as simple and wanting in dignity as any of my young pupils.

"Ah, Mademoiselle Varna, you come in good time to spare me from the necessity of accepting a lady whom I like not. She is excellent, but too grave; while you reassure me at once by that smile. Sit near me, and let us arrange the affair before my brother comes. You incline to give me your society, I infer from the good Bayard?"

"If Madame la Princesse accepts my services on trial for a time, I much desire to make the attempt, as my former duties have become irksome, and I have a great curiosity to see St. Petersburg."

"Mon Dieu! I trust it will be long before we return to that detestable climate. *Chère* mademoiselle, I entreat you to say nothing of this desire to my brother. He is mad to go back to his wolves, his ice and his barbarous delights; but I cling to Paris, for it is my life. In the spring it is inevitable, and I submit—but not now. If you come to me, I conjure you to aid me in delaying the return, and shall be forever grateful if you help to secure this reprieve for me."

So earnest and beseeching were her looks, her words, and so entirely did she seem to throw herself upon my sympathy and good-will, that I could not but be touched and won, in spite of my surprise. I assured her that I would do my best, but could not flatter myself that any advice of mine would influence the prince.

"You do not know him; but from what Bayard tells me of your skill in controlling wayward wills and hot tempers, I feel sure that you can influence Alexis. In confidence, I tell you what you will soon learn, if you remain: that though the best and tenderest of brothers, the prince is hard to manage, and one must tread cautiously in approaching him. His will is iron; and a decree once uttered is as irrevocable as the laws of the Medes and Persians. He has always claimed entire liberty for himself, entire obedience from every one about him; and my father's early death leaving him the head of our house, confirmed these tyrannical tendencies. To keep him in Paris is my earnest desire, and in order to do so I must seem indifferent, yet make his life so attractive that he will not command our departure."

"One would fancy life could not but be attractive to the prince in the gayest city of the world," I said, as the princess paused for breath.

"He cares little for the polished pleasures which delight a Parisian, and insists on bringing many of his favorite amusements with him. His caprices amuse the world, and are admired, but they annoy me much. At home he wears his Russian costume, orders the horrible dishes he loves, and makes the apartments unendurable with his samovar, chibouk and barbarous ornaments. Abroad he drives his droschky with the Ischvostchik in full St. Petersburg livery, and wears his uniform on all occasions. I say nothing, but I suffer."

It required a strong effort to repress a smile at the princess's pathetic lamentations and the martyr-like airs she assumed. She was infinitely amusing with her languid or vivacious words and attitudes; her girlish frankness and her feeble health interested me, and I resolved to stay even before she asked my decision.

I sat with her an hour, chatting of many things, and feeling more and more at ease as I read the shallow but amiable nature before me. All arrangements were made, and I was about taking my leave when the prince entered unannounced, and so quickly that I had not time to make my escape.

He had made his toilet since I saw him last, and I found it difficult to recognize the picturesque figure on the ottoman in the person who entered wearing the ordinary costume of a well-dressed gentleman. Even the face seemed changed, for a cold, haughty expression replaced the thoughtful look it had worn in repose. A smile softened it as he greeted his sister, but it vanished as he turned to me, with a slight inclination, when she whispered my name and errand, and while she explained he stood regarding me with a look that angered me. Not that it was insolent, but supremely masterful, as if those proud eyes were accustomed to command whomever they looked upon. It annoyed me, and I betrayed my annoyance by a rebellious glance, which made him lift his brows in surprise as a half smile passed over his lips. When his sister paused, he said, in the purest French, and with a slightly imperious accent:

"Mademoiselle is an Englishwoman?"

"My mother was English, my father of Russian parentage, although born in England."

I knew not by what title to address the questioner, so I simplified the matter by using none at all.

"Ah, you are half a Russian, then, and naturally desire to see your country?"

"Yes, I have long wished it," I began, but a soft cough from the princess reminded me that I must check my wish till it was safe to express it.

"We return soon, and it is well that you go willingly. Mademoiselle sets you a charming example, Nadja; I indulge the hope that you will follow it."

As he spoke the princess shot a quick glance at me, and answered, in a careless tone:

"I seldom disappoint your hopes, Alexis; but mademoiselle agrees with me that St. Petersburg at this season is unendurable."

"Has mademoiselle tried it?" was the quiet reply, as the prince fixed his keen eyes full upon me, as if suspecting a plot.

"Not yet, and I have no desire to do so—the report satisfies me," I answered, moving to go.

The prince shrugged his shoulders, touched his sister's cheek, bowed slightly, and left the room as suddenly as he had entered.

The princess chid me playfully for my *maladresse,* begged to see me on the morrow, and graciously dismissed me. As I waited in the great hall a moment for my carriage to drive round, I witnessed a little scene which made a curious impression on me. In a small ante-room, the door of which was ajar, stood the prince, drawing on his gloves, while the lad whom I had seen above was kneeling before him, fastening a pair of fur-lined overshoes. Something was amiss with one clasp, the prince seemed impatient, and after a sharp word in Russian, angrily lifted his foot with a gesture that sent the lad backward with painful violence. I involuntarily uttered an exclamation, the prince turned quickly, and our eyes met. Mine I know were full of indignation and disgust, for I resented the kick more than the poor lad, who, meekly gathering himself up, finished his task without a word, like one used to such rebukes.

The haughtiest surprise was visible in the face of the prince, but no shame; and as I moved away I heard a low laugh, as if my demonstration amused him.

"Laugh if you will, Monsieur le Prince, but remember all your servants are not serfs," I muttered, irefully, as I entered the carriage.

CHAPTER II

ALL WENT SMOOTHLY for a week or two, and I not only found my new home agreeable but altogether luxurious, for the princess had taken a fancy to me and desired to secure me by every means in her power, as she confided to Madame Bayard. I had been in a treadmill so long that any change would have been pleasant, but this life was as charming as anything but entire freedom could be. The very caprices of the princess were agreeable, for they varied what otherwise might have been somewhat monotonous, and her perfect simplicity and frankness soon did away with any shyness of mine. As madame said, rank was nothing after all, and in this case princess was but a name, for many an untitled Parisienne led a gayer and more splendid life than Nadja Tcherinski, shut up in her apartments and dependent upon those about her for happiness. Being younger than myself, and one of the clinging, confiding women who must lean on some one, I soon felt that protective fondness which one cannot help feeling for the weak, the sick, and the unhappy. We read English, embroidered, sung, talked, and drove out together, for the princess received little company and seldom joined the revels which went on in the other wing of the hotel.

The prince came daily to visit his sister, and she always exerted herself to make these brief interviews as agreeable as possible. I was pressed into the service, and sung, played, or talked as the princess signified—finding that, like most Russians of good birth, the prince was very accomplished, particularly in languages and music. But in spite of these gifts and the increasing affability of his manners toward myself, I always felt that under all the French polish was hidden the Tartar wildness, and often saw the savage in his eye while his lips were smiling blandly. I did not like him, but my vanity was gratified by the daily assurances of the princess that I possessed and exerted an unconscious influence over him. It was interesting to match him, and soon exciting to try my will against his in covert ways. I did not fear him as his sister did, because over me he had no control, and being of as proud a spirit as himself, I paid him only the respect due to his rank, not as an inferior, but an equal, for my family was good, and he lacked the real princeliness of nature which commands the reverence of the highest. I think he felt this instinctively, and it angered him; but he betrayed nothing of it in words, and was coolly courteous to the incomprehensible *dame-de-compagnie* of his sister.

My apartments were near the princess's, but I never went to her till summoned, as her hours of rising were uncertain. As I sat one day awaiting the call of Claudine, her maid came to me looking pale and terrified.

"Madame la Princesse waits, mademoiselle, and begs you will pardon this long delay."

"What agitates you?" I asked, for the girl glanced nervously over her shoulder as she spoke, and seemed eager, yet afraid to speak.

"Ah, mademoiselle, the prince has been with her, and so afflicted her, it desolates me to behold her. He is quite mad at times, I think, and terrifies us by his violence. Do not breathe to any one this that I say, and comfort madame if it is possible," and with her finger on her lips the girl hurried away.

I found the princess in tears, but the moment I appeared she dropped her handkerchief to exclaim with a gesture of despair: "We are lost! We are lost! Alexis is bent on returning to Russia and taking me to my death. *Chère* Sybil, what is to be done?"

"Refuse to go, and assert at once your freedom; it is a case which warrants such decision," was my revolutionary advice, though I well knew the princess would as soon think of firing the Tuileries as opposing her brother.

"It is impossible, I am dependent on him, he never would forgive such an act, and I should repent it to my last hour. No, my hope is in you, for you have eloquence, you see my feeble state, and you can plead for me as I cannot plead for myself."

"Dear madame, you deceive yourself. I have no eloquence, no power, and it is scarcely for me to come between you and the prince. I will do my best, but it will be in vain, I think."

"No, you do not fear him, he knows that, and it gives you power; you can talk well, can move and convince; I often see this when you read and converse with him, and I know that he would listen. Ah, for my sake make the attempt, and save me from that dreadful place!" cried the princess imploringly.

"Well, madame, tell me what passed, that I may know how to conduct the matter. Is a time for departure fixed?"

"No, thank heaven; if it were I should despair, for he would never revoke his orders. Something has annoyed him; I fancy a certain lady frowns upon him; but be that as it may, he is eager to be gone, and desired me to prepare to leave Paris. I implored, I wept, I reproached, and caressed, but nothing moved him, and he left me with the look which forebodes a storm."

"May I venture to ask why the prince does not return alone, and permit you to join him in the spring?"

"Because when my poor Feodor died he gave me into my brother's care, and Alexis swore to guard me as his life. I am so frail, so helpless, I need a faithful protector, and but for his fearful temper I should desire no better one than my brother. I owe everything to him, and would gladly obey even in this matter but for my health."

"Surely he thinks of that? He will not endanger your life for a selfish wish?"

"He thinks me fanciful, unreasonably fearful, and that I make this an excuse to have my own way. He is never ill, and knows nothing of my suffering, for I do not annoy him with complaints."

"Do you not think, madame, that if we could once convince him of the reality of the danger he would relent?"

"Perhaps; but how convince him? He will listen to no one."

"Permit me to prove that. If you will allow me to leave you for an hour I fancy I can find a way to convince and touch the prince."

The princess embraced me cordially, bade me go at once, and return soon, to satisfy her curiosity. Leaving her to rest and wonder, I went quietly away to the celebrated physician who at intervals visited the princess, and stating the case to him, begged for a written opinion which, coming from him, would, I knew, have weight with the prince. Dr. Segarde at once complied, and strongly urged the necessity of keeping the princess in Paris some months longer. Armed with this, I hastened back, hopeful and gay.

The day was fine, and wishing to keep my errand private, I had not used the carriage placed at my disposal. As I crossed one of the long corridors, on my way to the princess, I was arrested by howls of pain and the sharp crack of a whip, proceeding from an apartment near by. I paused involuntarily, longing yet fearing to enter and defend poor Mouche, for I recognized his voice. As I stood, the door swung open and the great hound sprang out, to cower behind me, with an imploring look in his almost human eyes. The prince followed, whip in hand, evidently in one of the fits of passion which terrified the household. I had seen many demonstrations of wrath, but never anything like that, for he seemed literally beside himself. Pale as death, with eyes full of savage fire, teeth set, and hair bristling like that of an enraged animal, he stood fiercely glaring at me. My heart fluttered for a moment, then was steady, and feeling no fear, I lifted my eyes to his, freely showing the pity I felt for such utter want of self-control.

It irritated him past endurance, and pointing to the dog, he said, in a sharp, low voice, with a gesture of command:

"Go on, mademoiselle, and leave Mouche to his fate."

"But what has the poor beast done to merit such brutal punishment?" I asked, coolly, remaining where I was.

"It is not for you to ask, but to obey," was the half-breathless answer, for a word of opposition increased his fury.

"Pardon; Mouche takes refuge with me; I cannot betray him to his enemy."

The words were still on my lips, when, with a step, the prince reached me, and towering above me like the incarnation of wrath, cried fiercely, as he lifted his hand menacingly:

"If you thwart me it will be at your peril!"

I saw he was on the point of losing all control of himself, and seizing the uparised arm, I looked him in the eye, saying steadily:

"Monsieur le Prince forgets that in France it is dastardly to strike a woman. Do not disgrace yourself by any Russian brutality."

The whip dropped from his hand, his arm fell, and turning suddenly, he dashed into the room behind him. I was about to make good my retreat, when a strange sound made me glance into the room. The prince had flung himself into a chair, and sat there actually choking with the violence of his passion. His face was purple, his lips pale, and his eyes fixed, as he struggled to unclasp the great sable-lined cloak he wore. As he then looked I was afraid he would have a fit, and never stopping for a second thought, I hurried to him, undid the cloak, loosened his collar, and filling a glass from the *carafe* on the sideboard, held it to his lips. He drank mechanically, sat motionless a moment, then drew a long breath, shivered as if recovering from a swoon, and glanced about him till his eye fell on me. It kindled again, and passing his hand over his forehead as if to collect himself, he said abruptly:

"Why are you here?"

"Because you needed help, and there was no one else to give it," I answered, refilling the glass, and offering it again, for his lips seemed dry.

He took it silently, and as he emptied it at a draught his eye glanced from the whip to me, and a scarlet flush rose to his forehead.

"Did I strike you?" he whispered, with a shame-stricken face.

"If you had we should not have been here."

"And why?" he asked, in quick surprise.

"I think I should have killed you, or myself, after such degradation. Unwomanly, perhaps, but I have a man's sense of honor."

It was an odd speech, but it rose to my lips, and I uttered it impulsively, for my spirit was roused by the insult. It served me better than tears or reproaches, for his eye fell after a furtive glance, in which admiration, shame and pride contended, and forcing a smile, he said, as if to hide his discomposure:

"I have insulted you; if you demand satisfaction I will give it, mademoiselle."

"I do," I said, promptly.

He looked curious, but seemed glad of anything which should divert his thoughts from himself, for with a bow and a half smile, he said quickly:

"Will mademoiselle name the reparation I shall make her? Is it to be pistols or swords?"

"It is pardon for poor Mouche."

His black brow lowered, and the thunderbolt veins on his forehead darkened again with the angry blood, not yet restored to quietude. It cost him an effort to say gravely:

"He has offended me, and cannot be pardoned yet; ask anything for yourself, mademoiselle."

I was bent on having my own way, and making him submit as a penance for his unwomanly menace. Once conquer his will, in no matter how slight a degree, and I had gained a power possessed by no other person. I liked the trial, and would not yield one jot of the advantage I had gained; so I answered, with a smile I had never worn to him before:

"Monsieur le Prince has given his word to grant me satisfaction; surely he will not break it, whatever atonement I demand! Ah, pardon Mouche, and I forget the rest."

I had fine eyes, and knew how to use them; as I spoke I fixed them on the prince with an expression half-imploring, half-commanding, and saw in his face a wish to yield, but pride would not permit it.

"Mademoiselle, I ordered the dog to follow me; he refused, and for that I would have punished him. If I relent before the chastisement is finished I lose my power over him, and the offense will be repeated. Is it not possible to satisfy you without ruining Mouche?"

"Permit one question before I reply. Did you give yourself the trouble of discovering the cause of the dog's unusual disobedience before the whip was used?"

"No; it is enough for me that the brute refused to follow. What cause could there have been for his rebelling?"

"Call him and it will appear."

The prince ordered in the dog; but in vain; Mouche crouched in the corridor with a forlorn air, and answered only by a whine. His master was about to go to him angrily, when, to prevent another scene, I called, and at once the dog came limping to my feet. Stooping, I lifted one paw, and showed the prince a deep and swollen wound, which explained the poor brute's unwillingness to follow his master on the long daily drive. I was surprised at the way in which the prince received the rebuke; I expected a laugh, a careless or a haughty speech, but like a boy he put his arm about the hound, saying almost tenderly:

"Pardon, pardon, my poor Mouche! Who has hurt thee so cruelly? Forgive the whip; thou shalt never feel it again."

Like a noble brute as he was, Mouche felt the change, understood, forgave, and returned to his allegiance at once, lifting himself to lick his master's hand and wag his tail in token of affection. It was a pretty little scene, for the prince laid his face on the smooth head of the dog, and half-whispered his regrets, exactly as a generous-hearted lad would have done to the favorite whom he had wronged in anger. I was glad to see it, childish as it was, for it satisfied me that this household tyrant had a heart, and well pleased with the ending of this stormy interview, I stole noiselessly away, carrying the broken whip with me as a trophy of my victory.

To the princess I said nothing of all this, but cheered her with the doctor's note and somewhat rash prophecies of its success. The prince seldom failed to come morning and evening to inquire for his sister, and as the time drew near for the latter visit we both grew anxious. At the desire of the princess I placed myself at the piano, hoping that "music might soothe the savage breast," and artfully prepare the way for the appeal. One of the prince's whims was to have rooms all over the hotel and one never knew in which he might be. That where I had first seen him was near the suite of the princess, and he often stepped quietly in when we least expected him. This habit annoyed his sister, but she never betrayed it, and always welcomed him, no matter how inopportune his visit might be. As I sat playing I saw the curtains that hung before the door softly drawn aside, and expected the prince to enter, but they fell again and no one appeared. I said nothing, but thundered out the Russian national airs with my utmost skill, till the soft scent of flowers and a touch on my arm made me glance down, to see Mouche holding in his mouth a magnificent bouquet, to which was attached a card bearing my name.

I was pleased, yet not quite satisfied, for in this Frenchy little performance I fancied I saw the prince's desire to spare himself any further humiliation. I did not expect it, but I did wish he had asked pardon of me as well as of the dog, and when among the flowers I found a bracelet shaped like a coiled up golden whip with a jeweled handle, I would have none of it, and giving it to Mouche, bid him take it to his master. The docile creature gravely retired, but not before I had discovered that the wounded foot was carefully bound up, that he wore a new silver collar, and had the air of a dog who had been petted to his heart's content.

The princess from her distant couch had observed but not understood the little pantomime, and begged to be enlightened. I told the story, and was amused at the impression it made upon her, for when I paused she clasped her hands, exclaiming, theatrically:

"*Mon Dieu,* that any one should dare face Alexis in one of his furies! And you had no fear? you opposed him? made him spare Mouche and ask pardon? It is incredible!"

"But I could not see the poor beast half killed, and I never dreamed of harm to myself. Of that there could be no danger, for I am a woman, and the prince a gentleman," I said, curious to know how that part of the story would affect the princess.

"Ah, my dear, those who own serfs see in childhood so much cruelty, they lose that horror of it which we feel. Alexis has seen many women beaten when a boy, and though he forbids it now, the thing does not shock him as it should. When in these mad fits he knows not what he does; he killed a man once, a servant, who angered him, struck him dead with a blow. He suffered much remorse, and for a long time was an angel; but the wild blood cannot be controlled, and he is the victim of his passion. It was like him to send the flowers, but it will mortally offend him that you refuse the bracelet. He always consoles me with some bijou after he has made me weep, and I accept it, for it relieves and calms him."

"Does he not express contrition in words?"

"Never! he is too proud for that. No one dares demand such humiliation, and since he was not taught to ask pardon when a child, one cannot expect to teach the lesson now. I fear he will not come to-night; what think you, Sybil?"

"I think he will not come, but what matter? Our plan can be executed at any time. Delay is what we wish, and this affair may cause him to forget the other."

"Ah, if it would, I should bless Mouche almost as fervently as when he saved Alexis from the wolves."

"Does the prince owe his life to the dog?"

"In truth he does, for in one of his bear hunts at home he lost his way, was beset by the ferocious beasts, and but for the gallant dog would never have been saved. He loves him tenderly, and——"

"Breaks whips over the brave creature's back," I added, rudely enough, quite forgetting etiquette in my indignation.

The princess laughed, saying, with a shrug:

"You English are such stern judges."

Chapter III

I WAS INTENSELY CURIOUS to see how the prince would behave when we met. Politeness is such a national trait in France, where the poorest workman lifts his cap in passing a lady, to the Emperor, who returns the salute of his shabbiest subject, that one soon learns to expect the little courtesies of daily life so scrupulously and gracefully paid by all classes, and to miss them if they are wanting. When he chose, the prince was a perfect Frenchman in this respect, but at times nothing could be more insolently haughty, or entirely oblivious of common civility. Hitherto I had had no personal experience of this, but had observed it toward others, and very unnecessarily angered myself about it. My turn came now; for when he entered his sister's apartment next day, he affected entire unconsciousness of my presence. Not a look, word, or gesture was vouchsafed me, but, half turning his back, he chatted with the princess in an unusually gay and affectionate manner.

After the first indignant impulse to leave the room had passed, I became cool enough to see and enjoy the ludicrous side of the affair. I could not help wondering if it was done for effect, but for the first time since I came I saw the prince in his uniform. I would not look openly, though I longed to do so, for covert glances, as I busied myself with my embroidery, gave me glimpses of a splendid blending of scarlet, white and gold. It would have been impossible for the prince not to have known that this brilliant costume was excessively becoming, and not to have felt a very natural desire to display his handsome figure to advantage. More than once he crossed the room to look from the window, as if impatient for the droschky, then sat himself down at the piano and played stormily for five minutes, marched back to the princess's sofa and teased Bijou the poodle, ending at length by standing erect on the rug and facing the enemy.

Finding I bore my disgrace with equanimity, he was possessed to play the master, and show his displeasure in words as well as by silence. Turning to his sister, he said, in the tone of one who does not deign to issue commands to inferiors:

"You were enjoying some book as I entered, Nadja; desire Mademoiselle Varna to continue—I go in a moment."

"Ma chère, oblige me by finishing the chapter," said the princess, with a significant glance, and I obeyed.

We were reading George Sand's *Consuelo,* or rather the sequel of that wonderful book, and had reached the scenes in which Frederick the Great torments the prima donna before sending her to prison, because she will not submit to his whims. I liked my task, and read with spirit, hoping the prince would enjoy the lesson as much as I did. By skillfully cutting paragraphs here and there, I managed to get in the most apposite and striking of Consuelo's brave and sensible remarks, as well as the tyrant's unjust and ungenerous commands. The prince stood with his eyes fixed upon me. I felt, rather than saw this, for I never lifted my own, but permitted a smile to appear when Frederick threatened her with his cane. The princess speedily forgot everything but the romance, and when I paused, exclaimed, with a laugh:

"Ah, you enjoy that much, Sybil, for, like Consuelo, you would have defied the Great Fritz himself."

"That I would, in spite of a dozen Spondous. Royalty and rank give no one a right to oppress others. A tyrant—even a crowned one—is the most despicable of creatures," I answered, warmly.

"But you will allow that Porporina was very cold and coy, and altogether provoking, in spite of her genius and virtue," said the princess, avoiding the word "tyrant," as the subjects of the czar have a tendency to do.

"She was right, for the humblest mortals should possess their liberty and preserve it at all costs. Golden chains are often heavier than iron ones: is it not so, Mouche?" I asked of the dog, who lay at my feet, vainly trying to rid himself of the new collar which annoyed him.

A sharp "Here, sir!" made him spring to his master, who ordered him to lie down, and put one foot on him to keep him, as he showed signs of deserting again. The prince looked ireful, his black eyes were kindling, and some imperious speech was trembling on his lips, when Claudine entered with the *mal-apropos* question.

"Does Madame la Princesse desire that I begin to make preparations for the journey?"

"Not yet. Go; I will give orders when it is time," replied the princess, giving me a glance, which said, "We must speak now."

"What journey?" demanded the prince, as Claudine vanished precipitately.

"That for which you commanded me to prepare," returned his sister, with a heavy sigh.

"That is well. You consent, then, without more useless delay?" and the prince's face cleared as he spoke.

"If you still desire it, after reading this, I shall submit, Alexis," and giving him the note, his sister waited, with nervous anxiety, for his decision.

As he read I watched him, and saw real concern, surprise, and regret in his face, but when he looked up, it was to ask:

"When did Dr. Segarde give you this, and wherefore?"

"You shall know all, my brother. Mademoiselle sees my sufferings, pities my unhappiness, and is convinced that it is no whim of mine which makes me dread this return. I implore her to say this to you, to plead for me, because, with all your love, you cannot know my state as she does. To this prayer of mine she listens, but with a modesty as great as her goodness, she fears that you may think her officious, overbold, or blinded by regard for me. Therefore she wisely asks for Segarde's opinion, sure that it will touch and influence you. Do not destroy her good opinion, nor disappoint thy Nadja!"

The prince *was* touched, but found it hard to yield, and said, slowly, as he refolded the note, with a glance at me of annoyance not anger:

"So you plot and intrigue against me, ladies! But I have said we shall go, and I never revoke a decree."

"Go!" cried the princess, in a tone of despair.

"Yes, it is inevitable," was the answer, as the prince turned toward the fire, as if to escape importunities and reproaches.

"But when, Alexis—when? Give me still a few weeks of grace!" implored his sister, approaching him in much agitation.

"I give thee till April," replied the prince, in an altered tone.

"But that is spring, the time I pray for! Do you, then, grant my prayer?" exclaimed the princess, pausing in amazement.

"I said we must go, but not *when;* now I fix a time, and give thee yet some weeks of grace. Didst thou think I loved my own pleasure more than thy life, my sister?"

As he turned, with a smile of tender reproach, the princess uttered a cry of joy and threw herself into his arms in a paroxysm of gratitude, delight and affection. I never imagined that the prince could unbend so beautifully and entirely; but as I watched him caress and reassure the frail creature who clung to him, I was surprised to find what a hearty admiration suddenly sprung up within me for "the barbarian," as I often called him to myself. I enjoyed the pretty tableau a moment, and was quietly gliding away, lest I should be *de trop,* when the princess arrested me by exclaiming, as she leaned on her brother's arm, showing a face rosy with satisfaction:

"Chère Sybil, come and thank him for this kindness; you know how ardently I desired the boon, and you must help me to express my gratitude."

"In what language shall I thank Monsieur le Prince for prolonging his sister's life? Your tears, madame, are more eloquent than any words of mine," I replied, veiling the reproach under a tone of respectful meekness.

"She is too proud, this English Consuelo; she will not stoop to confess an obligation even to Alexis Demidoff."

He spoke in a half-playful, half-petulant tone, and hesitated over the last words, as if he would have said "a prince." The haughtiness was quite gone, and something in his expression, attitude and tone touched me. The sacrifice had cost him something, and a little commendation would not hurt him, vain and selfish though he might be. I was grateful for the poor princess's sake, and I did not hesitate to show it, saying with my most cordial smile, and doubtless some of the satisfaction I could not but feel visible in my face:

"I am not too proud to thank you sincerely for this favor to Madame la Princesse, nor to ask pardon for anything by which I may have offended you."

A gratified smile rewarded me as he said, with an air of surprise:

"And yet, mademoiselle desires much to see St. Petersburg?"

"I do, but I can wait, remembering that it is more blessed to give than to receive."

A low bow was the only reply he made, and with a silent caress to his sister he left the room.

"You have not yet seen the droschky; from the window of the ante-room the courtyard is visible; go, mademoiselle, and get a glimpse of St. Petersburg," said the princess, returning to her sofa, weary with the scene.

I went, and looking down, saw the most picturesque equipage I had ever seen. The elegant, coquettish droschky with a pair of splendid black Ukraine horses, harnessed in the Russian fashion, with a network of purple leather profusely ornamented with silver, stood before the grand entrance, and on the seat sat a handsome young man in full Ischvostchik costume. His caftan of fine cloth was slashed at the sides with embroidery; his hat had a velvet band, a silver buckle, and a bunch of rosy ribbons in it; a white-laced neck-cloth, buckskin gloves, hair and beard in perfect order; a brilliant sash and a crimson silk shirt. As I stood wondering if he was a serf, the prince appeared, wrapped in the long gray capote, lined with scarlet, which all military Russians wear, and the brilliant helmet surmounted by a flowing white plume. As he seated himself among the costly furs he glanced up at his sister's windows, where she sometimes stood to see him. His quick eye recognized me, and to my surprise he waved his hand with a gracious smile as the fiery horses whirled him away.

That smile haunted me curiously all day, and more than once I glanced into the courtyard, hoping to see the picturesque droschky again, for, though one cannot live long in Paris without seeing nearly every costume under the sun, and accustomed as I was to such sights, there was something peculiarly charming to me in the martial figure, the brilliant equipage and the wild black horses, as full of untamed grace and power as if but just brought from the steppes of Tartary.

There was a dinner party in the evening, and, anxious to gratify her brother, the princess went down. Usually I enjoyed these free hours, and was never at a loss for occupation or amusement, but on this evening I could settle to nothing till I resolved to indulge an odd whim which possessed me. Arranging palette and brushes, I was soon absorbed in reproducing on a small canvas a likeness of the droschky and its owner. Hour after hour slipped by as the little picture grew, and horses, vehicle, driver and master took shape and color under my touch. I spent much time on the principal figure, but left the face till the last. All was carefully copied from memory, the white tunic, golden cuirass, massive epaulets, and silver sash; the splendid casque with its plume, the gray cloak, and the scarlet trowsers, half-hidden by the high boots of polished leather. At the boots I paused, trying to remember something.

"Did he wear spurs?" I said, half audibly, as I leaned back to survey my work complacently.

"Decidedly yes, mademoiselle," replied a voice, and there stood the prince with a wicked smile on his lips.

I seldom lose my self-possession, and after an involuntary start, was quite myself, though much annoyed at being discovered. Instead of hiding the picture or sitting dumb with embarrassment, I held it up, saying tranquilly:

"Is it not creditable to so bad an artist? I was in doubt about the spurs, but now I can soon finish."

"The horses are wonderful, and the furs perfect. Ivan is too handsome, and this countenance may be said to lack expression."

He pointed to the blank spot where his own face should have been, and eyed me with most exasperating intelligence. But I concealed my chagrin under an innocent air, and answered simply:

"Yes; I wait to find a portrait of the czar before I finish this addition to my little gallery of kings and queens."

"The czar!" ejaculated the prince, with such an astonished expression that I could not restrain a smile, as I touched up the handsome Ivan's beard.

"I have an admiration for the droschky, and that it may be quite complete, I boldly add the czar. It always pleased me to read how freely and fearlessly he rides among his people, unattended, in the gray cloak and helmet."

The prince gave me an odd look, crossed the room, and returning, laid before me an enameled casket, on the lid of which was a portrait of a stout, light-haired, somewhat ordinary, elderly gentleman, saying in a tone which betrayed some pique and much amusement:

"Mademoiselle need not wait to finish her work: behold the czar!"

I was strongly tempted to laugh, and own the truth, but something in the prince's manner restrained me, and after gravely regarding the portrait a moment, I began to copy it. My hand was not steady nor my eye clear, but I recklessly daubed on till the prince, who had stood watching me, said suddenly in a very mild tone:

"I flatter myself that there was some mistake last evening; either Mouche failed to do his errand, or the design of the trinket displeased you. I have endeavored to suit mademoiselle's taste better, and this time I offer it myself."

A white-gloved hand holding an open jewel-case which contained a glittering ring came before my eyes, and I could not retreat. Being stubborn by nature, and ruffled by what had just passed, as well as bent on having my own way in the matter, I instantly decided to refuse all gifts. Retreating slightly from the offering, I pointed to the flowers on the table near me, and said, with an air of grave decision:

"Monsieur le Prince must permit me to decline. I have already received all that it is possible to accept."

"Nay, examine the trifle, mademoiselle, and relent. Why will you not oblige me and be friends, like Mouche?" he said, earnestly.

That allusion to the dog nettled me, and I replied, coldly turning from the importunate hand.

"It was not the silver collar which consoled poor Mouche for the blows. Like him I can forgive, but I cannot so soon forget."

The dainty case closed with a sharp snap, and flinging it on to a table as he passed, the prince left the room without a word.

I was a little frightened at what I had done for a moment, but soon recovered my courage, resolving that since he had made it a test which should yield, *I* would not be the one to do it, for I had right on my side. Nor would I be appeased till he had made the *amende honorable* to me as to the dog. I laughed at the foolish affair, yet could not entirely banish a feeling of anger at the first violence and at the lordly way in which he tried to atone for the insult.

"Let us wait and see how the sultan carries himself to-morrow," I said; "if he become tyrannical, I am free to go, thank heaven; otherwise it is interesting to watch the handsome savage chafe and fret behind the bars of civilized society."

And gathering up my work, I retired to my room to replace the czar's face with that of the prince.

CHAPTER IV

"*CHÈRE AMIE,* you remember I told you that Alexis always gave me some trifle after he had made me weep; behold what a charming gift I find upon my table to-day!" cried the princess, as I joined her next morning.

She held up her slender hand, displaying the ring I had left behind me the night before. I had had but a glimpse of it, but I knew it by the peculiar arrangement of the stones. Before I could say anything the princess ran on, as pleased as a girl with her new bauble:

"I have just discovered the prettiest conceit imaginable. See, the stones spell 'Pardon;' pearl, amethyst, ruby, diamond, opal, and as there is no stone commencing with the last letter, the initial of my name is added in enamel. Is not that divine?"

I examined it, and being a woman, I regretted the loss of the jewels as well as the opportunity of ending the matter, by a kinder reply to this fanciful petition for pardon. While I hesitated to enlighten the princess, for fear of further trouble, the prince entered, and I retreated to my seat at the other end of the room.

"Dear Alexis, I have just discovered your charming souvenir; a thousand thanks," cried his sister, with effusion.

"My souvenir; of what do you speak, Nadja?" he replied, with an air of surprise as he approached.

"Ah, you affect ignorance, but I well know whose hand sends me this, though I find it lying carelessly on my table. Yes, that start is very well done, yet it does not impose upon me. I am charmed with the gift; come, and let me embrace you."

With a very ill grace the "dear Alexis" submitted to the ceremony, and received the thanks of his sister, who expatiated upon the taste and beauty of the ring till he said, impatiently:

"You are very ingenious in your discoveries; I confess I meant it for a charming woman whom I had offended; if you had not accepted it I should have flung it in the fire. Now let it pass, and bid me adieu. I go to pass a week with Bagdonoff."

The princess was, of course, desolated to lose her brother, but resigned herself to the deprivation with calmness, and received his farewell without tears. I thought he meant to ignore me entirely, but to my surprise he approached, and with an expression I had never seen before, said, in a satirical tone:

"Mademoiselle, I leave the princess to your care, with perfect faith in your fidelity. Permit me to hope that you will enjoy my absence," and with a low bow, such as I had seen him give a countess, he departed.

The week lengthened to three before we saw the prince, and I am forced to confess that I did *not* enjoy his absence. So monotonous grew my days that I joyfully welcomed a somewhat romantic little episode in which I was just then called to play a part.

One of my former pupils had a lover. Madame Bayard discovered the awful fact, sent the girl home to her parents, and sternly refused to give the young man her address. He knew me, and in his despair applied to me for help and consolation. But not daring to seek me at the prince's hotel, he sent a note, imploring me to grant him an interview in the Tuileries Garden at a certain hour. I liked Adolph, pitied my amiable ex-pupil, and believing in the sincerity of their love, was glad to aid them.

At the appointed time I met Adolph, and for an hour paced up and down the leafless avenues, listening to his hopes and fears. It was a dull April day, and dusk fell early, but we were so absorbed that neither observed the gathering twilight till an exclamation from my companion made me look up.

"That man is watching us!"

"What man?" I asked, rather startled.

"Ah, he slips away again behind the trees yonder. He has done it twice before as we approached, and when we are past he follows stealthily. Do you see him?"

I glanced into the dusky path which crossed our own, and caught a glimpse of a tall man in a cloak just vanishing.

"You mistake, he does not watch us; why should he? Your own disquiet makes you suspicious, *mon ami*," I said.

"Perhaps so; let him go. Dear mademoiselle, I ask a thousand pardons for detaining you so long. Permit me to call a carriage for you."

I preferred to walk, and refusing Adolph's entreaties to escort me, I went my way along the garden side of the Rue de Rivoli, glad to be free at last. The wind was dying away as the sun set, but as a last freak it blew my veil off and carried it several yards behind me. A gentleman caught and advanced to restore it. As he put it into my hand with a bow, I uttered an exclamation, for it was the prince. He also looked surprised, and greeted me courteously, though with a strong expression of curiosity visible in his face. A cloak hung over his arm, and as my eyes fell upon it, an odd fancy took possession of me, causing me to conceal my pleasure at seeing him, and to assume a cold demeanor, which he observed at once. Vouchsafing no explanation of my late walk, I thanked him for the little service, adjusted my veil, and walked on as if the interview was at an end.

"It is late for mademoiselle to promenade alone; as I am about to return to the hotel, she will permit me to accompany her?"

The prince spoke in his most gracious tone, and walked beside me, casting covert glances at my face as we passed, the lamps now shining all about us. I was angry, and said, with significant emphasis:

"Monsieur le Prince has already sufficiently honored me with his protection. I can dispense with it now."

"Pardon, I do not understand," he began hastily; but I added, pointing to the garment on his arm:

"Pray assume your cloak; it is colder here than in the garden of the Tuileries."

Glancing up as I spoke, I saw him flush and frown, then draw himself up as if to haughtily demand an explanation, but with a sudden impulse, pause, and ask, averting his eyes:

"Why does mademoiselle speak in that accusing tone? Are the gardens forbidden ground to me?"

"Yes; when Monsieur le Prince condescends to play the spy," I boldly replied, adding with a momentary doubt arising in my mind, "Were you not there watching me?"

To my infinite surprise he looked me full in the face, and answered briefly: "I was."

"Adolph was right then—I also; it is well to know one's enemies," I said, as if to myself, and uttered not another word, but walked rapidly on.

Silent also the prince went beside me, till, as we were about to cross the great square, a carriage whirled round the corner, causing me to step hastily back. An old crone, with a great basket on her head, was in imminent danger of being run over, when the prince sprang forward, caught the bit and forced the spirited horses back till the old creature gathered herself up and reached the pave in safety. Then he returned to me as tranquilly as if nothing had occurred.

"Are you hurt?" I asked, forgetting my anger, as he pulled off and threw away the delicate glove, torn and soiled in the brief struggle.

"Thanks—no; but the old woman?"

"She was not injured, and went on her way, never staying to thank you."

"Why should she?" he asked, quietly.

"One likes to see gratitude. Perhaps she is used to such escapes, and so the act surprised her less than it did me."

"Ah! you wonder that I troubled myself about the poor creature, mademoiselle. I never forget that my mother was a woman, and for her sake I respect all women."

I had never heard that tone in his voice, nor seen that look in his face before, as he spoke those simple words. They touched me more than the act, but some tormenting spirit prompted me to say:

"Even when you threaten one of them with a—"

I got no further, for, with a sudden flash that daunted me, the prince cried imploringly, yet commandingly:

"No—no; do not utter the word—do not recall the shameful scene. Be generous, and forget, though you will not forgive."

"Pardon, it was unkind, I never will offend again."

An awkward pause followed, and we went on without a word, till glancing at me as we passed a brilliant lamp, the prince exclaimed:

"Mademoiselle, you are very pale—you are ill, over-wearied; let me call a carriage."

"By no means; it is nothing. In stepping back to avoid the horses, I hurt my ankle; but we are almost at the hotel, and I can reach it perfectly well."

"And you have walked all this distance without a complaint, when every step was painful? *Ma foi!* mademoiselle is brave," he said, with mingled pity, anxiety and admiration in his fine eyes.

"Women early learn to suffer in silence," I answered, rather grimly, for my foot was in agony, and I was afraid I should give out before I reached the hotel.

The prince hastened on before me, unlocked the side-door by which I usually entered, and helping me in, said earnestly:

"There are many steps to climb; let me assist you, or call some one."

"No, no, I will have no scene; many thanks; I can reach my room quite well alone. *Bon soir,* Monsieur le Prince," and turning from his offered arm, I set my teeth and walked steadily up the first seven stairs. But on reaching the little landing, pain overcame pride, and I sank into a chair with a stifled groan. I had heard the door close, and fancied the prince gone, but he was at my side in an instant.

"Mademoiselle, I shall not leave you till you are safely in your apartment. How can I best serve you?"

I pointed to the bell, saying faintly:

"I cannot walk; let Pierre carry me."

"I am stronger and more fit for such burdens. Pardon, it must be so."

And before I could utter a refusal, he folded the cloak about me, raised me gently in his arms, and went pacing quietly along the corridors, regarding me with an air of much sympathy, though in his eyes lurked a gleam of triumph, as he murmured to himself:

"She has a strong will, this brave mademoiselle of ours, but it must bend at last."

That annoyed me more than my mishap, but being helpless, I answered only with a defiant glance and an irrepressible smile at my little adventure. He looked keenly at me with an eager, yet puzzled air, and said, as he grasped me more firmly:

"Inexplicable creature! Pain can conquer her strength, but her spirit defies me still."

I hardly heard him, for as he laid me on the couch in my own little *salon,* I lost consciousness, and when I recovered myself, I was alone with my maid.

"What has happened?" I asked.

"Dear mademoiselle, I know not; the bell rings, I fly, I find you fainting, and I restore you. It is fatigue, alarm, illness, and you ring before your senses leave you," cried Jacobine, removing my cloak and furs.

A sudden pang in my foot recalled me to myself at once, and bidding the girl apply certain remedies, I was soon comfortable. Not a word was said of the prince; he had evidently vanished before the maid came. I was glad of this, for I had no desire to furnish food for gossip among the servants. Sending Jacobine with a message to the princess, I lay recalling the scene and perplexing myself over several trifles which suddenly assumed great importance in my eyes.

My bonnet and gloves were off when the girl found me. Who had removed them? My hair was damp with eau-de-cologne; who had bathed my head? My injured foot lay on a cushion; who placed it there? Did I dream that a tender voice exclaimed, "My little Sybil, my heart, speak to me"? or did the prince really utter such words?

With burning cheeks, and a half-sweet, half-bitter trouble in my heart, I thought of these things, and asked myself what all this was coming to. A woman often asks herself such questions, but seldom answers them, nor did I, preferring to let time drift me where it would.

The amiable princess came herself to inquire for me. I said nothing of her brother, as it was evident that he had said nothing even to her.

"Alexis has returned, *ma chère;* he was with me when Jacobine told me of your accident; he sends his compliments and regrets. He is in charming spirits, and looking finely."

I murmured my thanks, but felt a little guilty at my want of frankness. Why not tell her the prince met and helped me? While debating the point within myself, the princess was rejoicing that my accident would perhaps still longer delay the dreaded journey.

"Let it be a serious injury, my friend; it will permit you to enjoy life here, but not to travel; so suffer sweetly for my sake, and I will repay you with a thousand thanks," she said, pleadingly.

Laughingly I promised, and having ordered every luxury she could imagine, the princess left me with a joyful heart, while I vainly tried to forget the expression of the prince's face as he said low to himself:

"Her spirit defies me still."

CHAPTER V

FOR A WEEK I kept my room and left the princess to fabricate what tales she liked. She came to me every day reporting the preparations for departure were begun, but the day still remained unfixed, although April was half over.

"He waits for you, I am sure; he inquires for you daily, and begins to frown at the delay. To appease him, come down to-morrow, languid, lame, and in a charming dishabille. Amuse him as you used to do, and if anything is said of Russia, express your willingness to go, but deplore your inability to bear the journey now."

Very glad to recover my liberty, I obeyed the princess, and entered her room next day leaning on Jacobine, pale, languid, and in my most becoming morning toilet. The princess was reading novels on her sofa by the fire; the prince, in the brilliant costume in which I first saw him, sat in my chair, busy at my embroidery frame. The odd contrast between the man and his employment struck me so ludicrously that a half laugh escaped me. Both looked up; the prince sprang out of his chair as if about to rush forward, but checked himself, and received me with a silent nod. The princess made a great stir over me, and with some difficulty was persuaded to compose herself at last. Having answered her eager and the prince's polite inquiries, I took up my work, saying, with an irresistible smile as I examined the gentleman's progress:

"My flowers have blossomed in my absence, I see. Does M. le Prince possess all accomplishments?"

"Ah, you smile, but I assure you embroidery is one of the amusements of Russian gentlemen, and they often excel us in it. My brother scorned it till he was disabled with a wound, and when all other devices failed, this became his favorite employment."

As the princess spoke the prince stood in his usual attitude on the rug, eying me with a suspicious look, which annoyed me intensely and destroyed my interesting pallor by an uncontrollable blush. I felt terribly guilty with those piercing black eyes fixed on me, and appeared to be absorbed in a fresh bit of work. The princess chattered on till a salver full of notes and cards was brought in, when she forgot everything else in reading and answering these. The prince approached me then, and seating himself near my sofa, said, with somewhat ironical emphasis on the last two words:

"I congratulate mademoiselle on her recovery, and that her bloom is quite untouched by her *severe sufferings.*"

"The princess in her amiable sympathy doubtlessly exaggerated my pain, but I certainly *have* suffered, though my roses may belie me."

Why my eyes should fill and my lips tremble was a mystery to me, but they did, as I looked up at him with a reproachful face. I spoke the truth. I *had* suffered, not bodily but mental pain, trying to put away forever a tempting hope which suddenly came to trouble me. Astonishment and concern replaced the cold, suspicious expression of the prince's countenance, and his voice was very kind as he asked, with an evident desire to divert my thoughts from myself:

"For what luxurious being do you embroider these splendid slippers of purple and gold, mademoiselle? Or is that an indiscreet question?"

"For my friend Adolph Vernay."

"They are too large, he is but a boy," began the prince, but stopped abruptly, and bit his lip, with a quick glance at me.

Without lifting my eyes I said, coolly:

"M. le Prince appears to have observed this gentleman with much care, to discover that he has a handsome foot and a youthful face."

"Without doubt I should scrutinize any man with whom I saw mademoiselle walking alone in the twilight. As one of my household, I take the liberty of observing your conduct, and for my sister's sake ask of you to pardon this surveillance."

He spoke gravely, but looked unsatisfied, and feeling in a tormenting mood, I mystified him still more by saying, with a bow of assent:

"If M. le Prince knew all, he would see nothing strange in my promenade, nor in the earnestness of that interview. Believe me, I may seem rash, but I shall never forget what is due to the princess while I remain with her."

He pondered over my words a moment with his eyes on my face, and a frown bending his black brows. Suddenly he spoke, hastily, almost roughly:

"I comprehend what mademoiselle would convey. Monsieur Adolph is a lover, and the princess is about to lose her friend."

"Exactly. M. le Prince has guessed the mystery," and I smiled with downcast eyes.

A gilded ornament on the back of the chair against which the prince leaned snapped under his hand as it closed with a strong grip. He flung it away, and said, rapidly, with a jar in his usually musical voice:

"This gentleman will marry, it seems, and mademoiselle, with the charming freedom of an English woman, arranges the affair herself."

"Helps to arrange; Adolph has sense and courage; I leave much to him."

"And when is this interesting event to take place, if one may ask?"

"Next week, if all goes well."

"I infer the princess knows of this?"

"Oh, yes. I told her at once."

"And she consents?"

"Without doubt; what right would she have to object?"

"Ah, I forgot; in truth, none, nor any other. It is incomprehensible! She is to lose you and yet is not in despair."

"It is but for a time. I join her later if she desires it."

"Never, with that man!" and the prince rose with an impetuous gesture, which sent my silks flying.

"What man?" I asked, affecting bewilderment.

"This Adolph, whom you are about to marry."

"M. le Prince quite mistakes; I fancied he knew more of the affair. Permit me to explain."

"Quick, then; what is the mystery? who marries? who goes? who stays?"

So flushed, anxious and excited did he look, that I was satisfied with my test, and set about enlightening him with alacrity. Having told why I met the young man, I added:

"Adolph will demand the hand of Adele from her parents, but if they refuse it, as I fear they will, being prejudiced against him by Madame Bayard, he will effect his purpose in another manner. Though I do not approve of elopements in general, this is a case where it is pardonable, and I heartily wish him success."

While I spoke the prince's brow had cleared, he drew a long breath, reseated himself in the chair before me, and when I paused, said, with one of his sudden smiles and an air of much interest:

"Then you would have this lover boldly carry off his mistress in spite of all obstacles?"

"Yes. I like courage in love as in war, and respect a man who conquers all obstacles."

"Good, it is well said," and with a low laugh the prince sat regarding me in silence for a moment. Then an expression of relief stole over his face as he said, still smiling:

"And it was of this you spoke so earnestly when you fancied I watched you in the gardens?"

"Fancied! nay, M. le Prince has confessed that it was no fancy."

"How if I had not confessed?"

"I should have believed your word till you betrayed yourself, and then—"

I paused there with an uncontrollable gesture of contempt. He eyed me keenly, saying in that half-imperious, half-persuasive voice of his:

"It is well then that I obeyed my first impulse. To speak truth is one of the instincts which these polished Frenchmen have not yet conquered in the 'barbarian,' as they call me."

"I respected you for that truthful 'yes,' more than for anything you ever said or did," I cried, forgetting myself entirely.

"Then, mademoiselle has a little respect for me?"

He leaned his chin upon the arm that lay along the back of his chair, and looked at me with a sudden softening of voice, eye, and manner.

"Can M. le Prince doubt it?" I said, demurely, little guessing what was to follow.

"Does mademoiselle desire to be respected for the same virtue?" he asked.

"More than for any other."

"Then will she give me a truthful answer to the plain question I desire to ask?"

"I will;" and my heart beat rebelliously as I glanced at the handsome face so near me, and just then so dangerously gentle.

"Has not mademoiselle feigned illness for the past week?"

The question took me completely by surprise, but anxious to stand the test, I glanced at the princess, still busy at her writing-table in the distant alcove, and checking the answer which rose to my lips, I said, lowering my voice:

"On one condition will I reply."

"Name it, mademoiselle?"

"That nothing be said to Madame la Princesse of this."

"I give you my word."

"Well, then, I answer, yes;" and I fixed my eyes full on his as I spoke.

His face darkened a shade, but his manner remained unchanged.

"Thanks; now, for the reason of the ruse?"

"To delay a little the journey to Russia."

"Ha, I had not thought of that, imbecile that I am!" he exclaimed with a start.

"What other reason did M. le Prince imagine, if I may question in my turn?"

His usually proud and steady eyes wavered and fell, and he made no answer, but seemed to fall into a reverie, from which he woke presently to ask abruptly:

"What did you mean by saying you were to leave my sister for a time, and rejoin her later?"

"I must trouble you with the relation of a little affair which will probably detain me till after the departure, for but a week now remains of April."

"I listen, mademoiselle."

"Good Madame Bayard is unfortunately the victim of a cruel disease, which menaces her life unless an operation can be successfully performed. The time for this trial is at hand, and I have promised to be with her. If she lives I can safely leave her in a few days; if she dies I must remain till her son can arrive. This sad duty will keep me for a week or two, and I can rejoin madame at any point she may desire."

"But why make this promise? Madame Bayard has friends—why impose this unnecessary sacrifice of time, nerve, and sympathy upon you, mademoiselle?" And the prince knit his brows, as if ill-pleased.

"When I came to Paris long ago a poor, friendless, sorrowful girl, this good woman took me in, and for five years has been a mother to me. I am grateful, and would make any sacrifice to serve her in her hour of need."

I spoke with energy; the frown melted to the smile which always ennobled his face, as the prince replied, in a tone of forgetful acquiescence:

"You are right. I say no more. If you are detained I will leave Vacil to escort you to us. He is true as steel, and will guard you well. When must you go to the poor lady?"

"To-morrow; the princess consents to my wish, and I devote myself to my friend till she needs me no longer. May I ask when you leave Paris?" I could not resist asking.

"On the last day of the month," was the brief reply, as the prince rose, and roamed away with a thoughtful face, leaving me to ponder over many things as I wrought my golden pansies, wondering if I should ever dare to offer the purple velvet slippers to the possessor of a handsomer foot than Adolph.

On the following day I went to Madame Bayard; the operation was performed, but failed, and the poor soul died in my arms, blessing me for my love and care. I sent tidings of the event to the princess, and received a kind reply, saying all was ready, and the day irrevocably fixed.

I passed a busy week; saw my best friend laid to her last rest; arranged such of her affairs as I could, and impatiently awaited the arrival of her son. On the second day of May he came, and I was free.

As soon as possible I hastened to the hotel, expecting to find it deserted. To my surprise, however, I saw lights in the *salon* of the princess, and heard sounds of life everywhere as I went wonderingly toward my own apartments. The windows were open, flowers filled the room with spring odors, and everything wore an air of welcome as if some one waited for me. Some one did, for on the balcony, which ran along the whole front, leaned the prince in the mild, new-fallen twilight, singing softly to himself.

"Not gone!" I exclaimed, in unfeigned surprise.

He turned, smiled, flushed, and said, as he vanished:

"I follow mademoiselle's good example in yielding my wishes to the comfort and pleasure of others."

Chapter VI

THE NEXT DAY we set out, but the dreaded journey proved delightful, for the weather was fine, and the prince in a charming mood. No allusion was made to the unexpected delay, except by the princess, who privately expressed her wonder at my power, and treated me with redoubled confidence and affection. We loitered by the way, and did not reach St. Petersburg till June.

I had expected changes in my life as well as change of scene, but was unprepared for the position which it soon became evident I was to assume. In Paris I had been the companion, now I was treated as a friend and equal by both the prince and princess. They entirely ignored my post, and remembering only that I was by birth a gentlewoman, by a thousand friendly acts made it impossible for me to refuse the relations which they chose to establish between us. I suspect the princess hinted to her intimates that I was a connection of her own, and my name gave color to the statement. Thus I found myself received with respect and interest by the circle in which I now moved, and truly enjoyed the free, gay life, which seemed doubly charming, after years of drudgery.

With this exception there was less alteration in my surroundings than I had imagined, for the upper classes in Russia speak nothing but French; in dress, amusements, and manners, copy French models so carefully that I should often have fancied myself in Paris, but for the glimpses of barbarism, which observing eyes cannot fail to detect, in spite of the splendor which surrounds them. The hotel of the prince was a dream of luxury; his equipages magnificent; his wealth apparently boundless; his friends among the highest in the land. He appeared to unusual advantage at home, and seemed anxious that I should observe this, exerting himself in many ways to impress me with his power, even while he was most affable and devoted.

I could no longer blind myself to the truth, and tried to meet it honestly. The prince loved me, and made no secret of his preference, though not a word had passed his lips. I had felt this since the night he carried me in his arms, but remembering the difference in rank, had taught myself to see in it only the passing caprice of a master for a servant, and as such, to regard it as an insult. Since we came to St. Petersburg the change in his manner seemed to assure me that he sought me as an equal, and desired to do me honor in the eyes of those about us. This soothed my pride and touched my heart, but, alluring as the thought was to my vanity and my ambition, I did not yield to it, feeling that I should not love, and that such an alliance was not the one for me.

Having come to this conclusion, I resolved to abide by it, and did so the more inflexibly as the temptation to falter grew stronger. My calm, cool manner perplexed and irritated the prince, who seemed to grow more passionate as test after test failed to extort any betrayal of regard from me. The princess, absorbed in her own affairs, seemed apparently blind to her brother's infatuation, till I was forced to enlighten her.

July was nearly over, when the prince announced that he was about to visit one of his estates, some versts from the city, and we were to accompany him. I had discovered that Volnoi was a solitary place, that no guests were expected, and that the prince was supreme master of everything and everybody on the estate. This did not suit me, for Madame Yermaloff, an Englishwoman, who had conceived a friendship for me, had filled my head with stories of Russian barbarity, and the entire helplessness of whomsoever dared to thwart or defy a Russian seigneur, especially when on his own domain. I laughed at her gossip, yet it influenced my decision, for of late the prince had looked ireful, and his black eyes had kept vigilant watch over me. I knew that his patience was exhausted, and feared that a stormy scene was in store for me. To avoid all further annoyance, I boldly stated the case to the princess, and decidedly refused to leave St. Petersburg.

To my surprise, she agreed with me; and I discovered, what I had before suspected, that, much as she liked me as a friend, the princess would have preferred her brother to marry one of his own rank. She delicately hinted this, yet, unwilling to give me up entirely, begged me to remain with Madame Yermaloff till she returned, when some new arrangement might be made. I consented, and feeling unequal to a scene with the prince, left his sister to inform him of my decision, and went quietly to my friend, who gladly received me. Next morning the following note from the princess somewhat reassured me:

> MA CHERE SYBIL—*We leave in an hour. Alexis received the news of your flight in a singular manner. I expected to see him half frantic; but no, he smiled, and said, tranquilly: "She fears and flies me; it is a sign of weakness, for which I thank her." I do not understand him; but when we are quiet at Volnoi, I hope to convince him that you are, as always, wise and prudent. Adieu! I embrace you tenderly.*
>
> *N.T.*

A curious sense of disappointment and uneasiness took possession of me on reading this note, and, womanlike, I began to long for that which I had denied myself.

Madame Yermaloff found me a very dull companion, and began to rally me on my preoccupation. I tried to forget, but could not, and often stole out to walk past the prince's hotel, now closed and silent. A week dragged slowly by, and I had begun to think the prince had indeed forgotten me, when I was convinced that he had not in a somewhat alarming manner. Returning one evening from a lonely walk in the Place Michel, with its green English square, I observed a carriage standing near the Palace Galitzin, and listlessly wondered who was about to travel, for the coachman was in his place and a servant stood holding the door open. As I passed I glanced in, but saw nothing, for in the act sudden darkness fell upon me; a cloak was dexterously thrown over me, enveloping my head and arms, and rendering me helpless. Some one lifted me into the carriage, the door closed, and I was driven rapidly away, in spite of my stifled cries and fruitless struggles. At first I was frantic with anger and fear, and rebelled desperately against the strong hold which restrained me. Not a word was spoken, but I felt sure, after the first alarm, that the prince was near me, and this discovery, though it increased my anger, allayed my fear. Being half-suffocated, I suddenly feigned faintness, and lay motionless, as if spent. A careful hand withdrew the thick folds, and as I opened my eyes they met those of the prince fixed on me, full of mingled solicitude and triumph.

"You! Yes; I might have known no one else would dare perpetrate such an outrage!" I cried, breathlessly, and in a tone of intense scorn, though my heart leaped with joy to see him.

He laughed, while his eyes flashed, as he answered, gayly:

"Mademoiselle forgets that she once said she 'liked courage in love as in war, and respected a man who conquered all obstacles.' I remember this, and, when other means fail dare to brave even her anger to gain my object."

"What is that object?" I demanded, as my eyes fell before the ardent glance fixed on me.

"It is to see you at Volnoi, in spite of your cruel refusal."

"I will not go."

And with a sudden gesture I dashed my hand through the window and cried for help with all my strength. In an instant I was pinioned again, and my cries stifled by the cloak, as the prince said, sternly:

"If mademoiselle resists, it will be the worse for her. Submit, and no harm will befall you. Accept the society of one who adores you, and permit yourself to be conquered by one who never yields—except to you," he added, softly, as he held me closer, and put by the cloak again.

"Let me go—I will be quiet," I panted, feeling that it was indeed idle to resist now, yet resolving that he should suffer for this freak.

"You promise to submit—to smile again, and be your charming self?" he said, in the soft tone that was so hard to deny.

"I promise nothing but to be quiet. Release me instantly!" and I tried to undo the clasp of the hand that held me.

"Not till you forgive me and look kind. Nay, struggle if you will, I like it, for till now you have been the master. See, I pardon all your cruelty, and find you more lovely than ever."

As he spoke he bent and kissed me on forehead, lips and cheek with an ardor which wholly daunted me. I did pardon him, for there was real love in his face, and love robbed the act of rudeness in my eyes, for instead of any show of anger or disdain, I hid my face in my hands, weeping the first tears he had ever seen me shed. It tamed him in a moment, for as I sobbed I heard him imploring me to be calm, promising to sin no more, and assuring me that he meant only to carry me to Volnoi as its mistress, whom he loved and honored above all women. Would I forgive his wild act, and let his obedience in all things else atone for this?

I must forgive it; and if he did not mock me by idle offers of obedience, I desired him to release me entirely and leave me to compose myself, if possible.

He instantly withdrew his arm, and seated himself opposite me, looking half contrite, half exultant, as he arranged the cloak about my feet. I shrunk into the corner and dried my tears, feeling unusually weak and womanish, just when I most desired to be strong and stern. Before I could whet my tongue for some rebuke, the prince uttered an exclamation of alarm, and caught my hand. I looked, and saw that it was bleeding from a wound made by the shattered glass.

"Let it bleed," I said, trying to withdraw it. But he held it fast, binding it up with his own handkerchief in the tenderest manner, saying as he finished, with a passionate pressure:

"Give it to me, Sybil, I want it—this little hand—so resolute, yet soft. Let it be mine, and it shall never know labor or wound again. Why do you frown—what parts us?"

"This," and I pointed to the crest embroidered on the corner of the *mouchoir*.

"Is that all?" he asked, bending forward with a keen glance that seemed to read my heart.

"One other trifle," I replied sharply.

"Name it, my princess, and I will annihilate it, as all other obstacles," he said, with the lordly air that became him.

"It is impossible."

"Nothing is impossible to Alexis Demidoff."

"I do not love you."

"In truth, Sybil?" he cried incredulously.

"In truth," I answered steadily.

He eyed me an instant with a gloomy air, then drew a long breath, and set his teeth, exclaiming:

"You are mortal. I shall *make* you love me."

"How, monsieur?" I coldly asked, while my traitorous heart beat fast.

"I shall humble myself before you, shall obey your commands, shall serve you, protect you, love and honor you ardently, faithfully, while I live. Will not such devotion win you?"

"No."

It was a hard word to utter, but I spoke it, looking him full in the eye and seeing with a pang how pale he grew with real despair.

"Is it because you love already, or that you have no heart?" he said slowly.

"I love already." The words escaped me against my will, for the truth would find vent in spite of me. He took it as I meant he should, for his lips whitened, as he asked hoarsely:

"And this man whom you love, is he alive?"

"Yes."

"He knows of this happiness—he returns your love?"

"He loves me; ask no more; I am ill and weary."

A gloomy silence reigned for several minutes, for the prince seemed buried in a bitter reverie, and I was intent on watching him. An involuntary sigh broke from me as I saw the shadow deepen on the handsome face opposite, and thought that my falsehood had changed the color of a life. He looked up at the sound, saw my white, anxious face, and without a word drew from a pocket of the carriage a flask and silver cup, poured me a draught of wine, and offered it, saying gently:

"Am I cruel in my love, Sybil?"

I made no answer, but drank the wine, and asked as I returned the cup:

"Now that you know the truth, must I go to Volnoi? Be kind, and let me return to Madame Yermaloff."

His face darkened and his eyes grew fierce, as he replied, with an aspect of indomitable resolve:

"It is impossible; I have sworn to make you love me, and at Volnoi I will work the miracle. Do you think this knowledge of the truth will deter me? No; I shall teach you to forget this man, whoever he is, and make you happy in my love. You doubt this. Wait a little and see what a real passion can do."

This lover-like pertinacity was dangerous, for it flattered my woman's nature more than any submission could have done. I dared not listen to it, and preferring to see him angry rather than tender, I said provokingly:

"No man ever forced a woman to love him against her will. You will certainly fail, for no one in her senses would give her heart to *you!*"

"And why? Am I hideous?" he asked, with a haughty smile.

"Far from it."

"Am I a fool, mademoiselle?"

"Quite the reverse."

"Am I base?"

" No."

"Have I degraded my name and rank by any act?"

"Never, till to-night, I believe."

He laughed, yet looked uneasy, and demanded imperiously:

"Then, why will no woman love me?"

"Because you have the will of a tyrant, and the temper of a madman."

If I had struck him in the face it would not have startled him as my blunt words did. He flushed scarlet, drew back and regarded me with a half-bewildered air, for never had such a speech been made to him before. Seeing my success, I followed it up by saying gravely:

"The insult of to-night gives me the right to forget the respect I have hitherto paid you, and for once you shall hear the truth as plain as words can make it. Many fear you for these faults, but no one dares tell you of them, and they mar an otherwise fine nature."

I got no further, for to my surprise, the prince said suddenly, with real dignity, though his voice was less firm than before:

"One dares to tell me of them, and I thank her. Will she add to the obligation by teaching me to cure them?" Then he broke out impetuously: "Sybil, you can help me; you possess courage and power to tame my wild temper, my headstrong will. In heaven's name I ask you to do it, that I may be worthy some good woman's love."

He stretched his hands toward me with a gesture full of force and feeling, and his eloquent eyes pleaded for pity. I felt my resolution melting away, and fortified myself by a chilly speech.

"Monsieur le Prince has said that nothing is impossible to him; if he can conquer all obstacles, it were well to begin with these."

"I have begun. Since I knew you my despotic will has bent more than once to yours, and my mad temper has been curbed by the remembrance that you have seen it. Sybil, if I do conquer myself, can you, will you try to love me?"

So earnestly he looked, so humbly he spoke, it was impossible to resist the charm of this new and manlier mood. I gave him my hand, and said, with the smile that always won him:

"I will respect you sincerely, and be your friend; more I cannot promise."

He kissed my hand with a wistful glance, and sighed as he dropped it, saying in a tone of mingled hope and resignation:

"Thanks; respect and friendship from you are dearer than love and confidence from another woman. I know and deplore the faults fostered by education and indulgence, and I will conquer them. Give me time. I swear it will be done."

"I believe it, and I pray for your success."

He averted his face and sat silent for many minutes, as if struggling with some emotion which he was too proud to show. I watched him, conscious of a redoubled interest in this man, who at one moment ruled me like a despot, and at another confessed his faults like a repentant boy.

CHAPTER VII

IN RUSSIA, from the middle of May to the 1st of August, there is no night. It is daylight till eleven, then comes a soft semi-twilight till one, when the sun rises. Through this gathering twilight we drove toward Volnoi. The prince let down the windows, and the summer air blew in refreshingly; the peace of the night soothed my perturbed spirit, and the long silences were fitly broken by some tender word from my companion, who, without approaching nearer, never ceased to regard me with eyes so full of love that, for the first time in my life, I dared not meet them.

It was near midnight when the carriage stopped, and I could discover nothing but a tall white pile in a wilderness of blooming shrubs and trees. Lights shone from many windows, and as the prince led me into a brilliantly lighted *salon*, the princess came smiling to greet me, exclaiming, as she embraced me with affection:

"Welcome, my sister. You see it is in vain to oppose Alexis. We must confess this, and yield gracefully; in truth, I am glad to keep you, *chère amie,* for without you we find life very dull."

"Madame mistakes; I never yield, and am here against my will."

I withdrew myself from her as I spoke, feeling hurt that she had not warned me of her brother's design. They exchanged a few words as I sat apart, trying to look dignified, but dying with sleep. The princess soon came to me, and it was impossible to resist her caressing manner as she begged me to go and rest, leaving all disagreements till the morrow. I submitted, and, with a silent salute to the prince, followed her to an apartment next her own, where I was soon asleep, lulled by the happy thought that I was not forgotten.

The princess was with me early in the morning, and a few moments' conversation proved to me that, so far from her convincing her brother of the folly of his choice, he had entirely won her to his side, and enlisted her sympathies for himself. She pleaded his suit with sisterly skill and eloquence, but I would pledge myself to nothing, feeling a perverse desire to be hardly won, if won at all, and a feminine wish to see my haughty lover thoroughly subdued before I put my happiness into his keeping. I consented to remain for a time, and a servant was sent to Madame Yermaloff with a letter explaining my flight, and telling where to forward a portion of my wardrobe.

Professing herself satisfied for the present, and hopeful for the future, the princess left me to join her brother in the garden, where I saw them talking long and earnestly. It was pleasant to a lonely soul like myself to be so loved and cherished, and when I descended it was impossible to preserve the cold demeanor I had assumed, for all faces greeted me with smiles, all voices welcomed me, and one presence made the strange place seem like home. The prince's behavior was perfect, respectful, devoted and self-controlled; he appeared like a new being, and the whole household seemed to rejoice in the change.

Day after day glided happily away, for Volnoi was a lovely spot, and I saw nothing of the misery hidden in the hearts and homes of the hundred serfs who made the broad domain so beautiful. I seldom saw them, never spoke to them, for I knew no Russ, and in our drives the dull-looking peasantry possessed no interest for me. They never came to the house, and the prince appeared to know nothing of them beyond what his Stavosta, or steward reported. Poor Alexis! he had many hard lessons to learn that year, yet was a better man and master for them all, even the one which nearly cost him his life.

Passing through the hall one day, I came upon a group of servants lingering near the door of the apartment in which the prince gave his orders and transacted business. I observed that the French servants looked alarmed, the Russian ones fierce and threatening, and that Antoine, the valet of the prince, seemed to be eagerly dissuading several of the serfs from entering. As I appeared he exclaimed:

"Hold, he is saved! Mademoiselle will speak for him; she fears nothing, and she pities every one." Then, turning to me, he added, rapidly: "Mademoiselle will pardon us that we implore this favor of her great kindness. Ivan, through some carelessness, has permitted the favorite horse of the prince to injure himself fatally. He has gone in to confess, and we fear for his life, because Monsieur le Prince loved the fine beast well, and will be in a fury at the loss. He killed poor Androvitch for a less offense, and we tremble for Ivan. Will mademoiselle intercede for him? I fear harm to my master if Ivan suffers, for these fellows swear to avenge him."

Without a word I opened the door and entered quietly. Ivan was on his knees, evidently awaiting his doom with dogged submission. A pair of pistols lay on the table, and near it stood the prince, with the dark flush on his face, the terrible fire in his eyes which I had seen before. I saw there was no time to lose, and going to him, looked up into that wrathful countenance, whispering in a warning tone:

"Remember poor Androvitch."

It was like an electric shock; he started, shuddered, and turned pale; covered his face a moment and stood silent, while I saw drops gather on his forehead and his hand clinch itself spasmodically. Suddenly he moved, flung the pistols through the open window, and turning on Ivan, said, with a forceful gesture:

"Go. I pardon you."

The man remained motionless as if bewildered, till I touched him, bidding him thank his master and begone.

"No, it is you I thank, good angel of the house," he muttered, and lifting a fold of my dress to his lips Ivan hurried from the room.

I looked at the prince; he was gravely watching us, but a smile touched his lips as he echoed the man's last words, " 'Good angel of the house'; yes, in truth you are. Ivan is right, he owes me no thanks; and yet it was the hardest thing I ever did to forgive him the loss of my noble Sophron."

"But you did forgive him, and whether he is grateful or not, the victory is yours. A few such victories and the devil is cast out forever."

He seized my hand, exclaiming in a tone of eager delight:

"You believe this? You have faith in me, and rejoice that I conquer this cursed temper, this despotic will?"

"I do; but I still doubt the subjection of the will," I began; he interrupted me by an impetuous—

"Try it; ask anything of me and I will submit."

"Then let me return to St. Petersburg at once, and do not ask to follow."

He had not expected this, it was too much; he hesitated, demanding, anxiously:

"Do you really mean it?"

"Yes."

"You wish to leave me, to banish me now when you are all in all to me?"

"I wish to be free. You have promised to obey; yield your will to mine and let me go."

He turned and walked rapidly through the room, paused a moment at the further end, and coming back, showed me such an altered face that my conscience smote me for the cruel test. He looked at me in silence for an instant, but I showed no sign of relenting, although I saw what few had ever seen, those proud eyes wet with tears. Bending, he passionately kissed my hands, saying, in a broken voice:

"Go, Sybil. I submit."

"Adieu, my friend; I shall not forget," and without venturing another look I left him.

I had hardly reached my chamber and resolved to end the struggle for both of us, when I saw the prince gallop out of the courtyard like one trying to escape from some unfortunate remembrance or care.

"Return soon to me," I cried; "the last test is over and the victory won."

Alas, how little did I foresee what would happen before that return; how little did he dream of the dangers that encompassed him.

A tap at my door roused me as I sat in the twilight an hour later, and Claudine crept in, so pale and agitated that I started up, fearing some mishap to the princess.

"No, she is well and safe, but oh, mademoiselle, a fearful peril hangs over us all. Hush! I will tell you. I have discovered it, and we must save them."

"Save who? what peril? speak quickly."

"Mademoiselle knows that the people on the estate are poor ignorant brutes who hate the Stavosta, and have no way of reaching the prince except through him. He is a hard man; he oppresses them, taxes them heavily unknown to the prince, and they believe my master to be a tyrant. They have borne much, for when we are away the Stavosta rules here, and they suffer frightfully. I have lived long in Russia, and I hear many things whispered that do not reach the ears of my lady. These poor creatures bear long, but at last they rebel, and some fearful affair occurs, as at Bagatai, where the countess, a cruel woman, was one night seized by her serfs, who burned and tortured her to death."

"Good heavens! Claudine, what is this danger which menaces us?"

"I understand Russ, mademoiselle, have quick eyes and ears, and for some days I perceive that all is not well among the people. Ivan is changed; all look dark and threatening but old Vacil. I watch and listen, and discover that they mean to attack the house and murder the prince."

"Mon Dieu! but when?"

"I knew not till to-day. Ivan came to me and said, 'Mademoiselle Varna has saved my life. I am grateful. I wish to serve her. She came here against her will; she desires to go; the prince is away; I will provide a horse to-night at dusk, and she can join her friend Madame Yermaloff, who is at Baron Narod's, only a verst distant. Say this to mademoiselle, and if she agrees, drop a signal from her window. I shall see and understand.' "

"But why think that the attack is to be to-night?"

"Because Ivan was so anxious to remove you. He urged me to persuade you, for the prince is gone, and the moment is propitious. You will go, mademoiselle?"

"No; I shall not leave the princess."

"But you can save us all by going, for at the baron's you can procure help and return to defend us before these savages arrive. Ivan will believe you safe, and you can thwart their plans before the hour comes. Oh, mademoiselle, I conjure you to do this, for we are watched, and you alone will be permitted to escape."

A moment's thought convinced me that this was the only means of help in our power, and my plans were quickly laid. It was useless to wait for the prince, as his return was uncertain; it was unwise to alarm the princess, as she would betray all; the quick-witted Claudine and myself must do the work, and trust to heaven for success. I dropped a handkerchief from my window; a tall figure emerged from the shrubbery, and vanished, whispering:

"In an hour—at the chapel gate."

At the appointed time I was on the spot, and found Ivan holding the well-trained horse I often rode. It was nearly dark—for August brought night—and it was well for me, as my pale face would have betrayed me.

"Mademoiselle has not fear? If she dares not go alone I will guard her," said Ivan, as he mounted me.

"Thanks. I fear nothing. I have a pistol, and it is not far. Liberty is sweet. I will venture much for it."

"I also," muttered Ivan.

He gave me directions as to my route, and watched me ride away, little suspecting my errand.

How I rode that night! My blood tingles again as I recall the wild gallop along the lonely road, the excitement of the hour, and the resolve to save Alexis or die in the attempt. Fortunately I found a large party at the baron's, and electrified them by appearing in their midst, disheveled, breathless and eager with my tale of danger. What passed I scarcely remember, for all was confusion and alarm. I refused to remain, and soon found myself dashing homeward, followed by a gallant troop of five and twenty gentlemen. More time had been lost than I knew, and my heart sunk as a dull glare shone from the direction of Volnoi as we strained up the last hill.

Reaching the top, we saw that one wing was already on fire, and distinguished a black, heaving mass on the lawn by the flickering torchlight. With a shout of wrath the gentlemen spurred to the rescue, but I reached the chapel gate unseen, and entering, flew to find my friends. Claudine saw me and led me to the great saloon, for the lower part of the house was barricaded. Here I found the princess quite insensible, guarded by a flock of terrified French servants, and Antoine and old Vacil endeavoring to screen the prince, who, with reckless courage, exposed himself to the missiles which came crashing against the windows. A red light filled the room, and from without arose a yell from the infuriated mob more terrible than any wild beast's howl.

As I sprang in, crying, "They are here—the baron and his friends—you are safe!" all turned toward me as if every other hope was lost. A sudden lull without, broken by the clash of arms, verified my words, and with one accord we uttered a cry of gratitude. The prince flung up the window to welcome our deliverers; the red glare of the fire made him distinctly visible, and as he leaned out with a ringing shout, a hoarse voice cried menacingly:

"Remember poor Androvitch."

It was Ivan's voice, and as it echoed my words there was the sharp crack of a pistol, and the prince staggered back, exclaiming faintly:

"I forgive him; it is just."

We caught him in our arms, and as Antoine laid him down he looked at me with a world of love and gratitude in those magnificent eyes of his, whispering as the light died out of them:

"Always our good angel. Adieu, Sybil. I submit."

How the night went after that I neither knew nor cared, for my only thought was how to keep life in my lover till help could come. I learned afterward that the sight of such an unexpected force caused a panic among the serfs, who fled or surrendered at once. The fire was extinguished, the poor princess conveyed to bed, and the conquerors departed, leaving a guard behind. Among the gentlemen there fortunately chanced to be a surgeon, who extracted the ball from the prince's side.

I would yield my place to no one, though the baron implored me to spare myself the anguish of the scene. I remained steadfast, supporting the prince till all was over; then, feeling that my strength was beginning to give way, I whispered to the surgeon, that I might take a little comfort away with me:

"He will live? His wound is not fatal?"

The old man shook his head, and turned away, muttering regretfully:

"There is no hope; say farewell, and let him go in peace, my poor child."

The room grew dark before me, but I had strength to draw the white face close to my own, and whisper tenderly:

"Alexis, I love you, and you alone. I confess my cruelty; oh, pardon me, before you die!"

A look, a smile full of the intensest love and joy, shone in the eyes that silently met mine as consciousness deserted me.

One month from that night I sat in that same saloon a happy woman, for on the couch, a shadow of his former self but alive and out of danger, lay the prince, my husband. The wound was not fatal, and love had worked a marvelous cure. While life and death still fought for him, I yielded to his prayer to become his wife, that he might leave me the protection of his name, the rich gift of his rank and fortune. In my remorse I would have granted anything, and when the danger was passed rejoiced that nothing could part us again.

As I sat beside him my eyes wandered from his tranquil face to the garden where the princess sat singing among the flowers, and then passed to the distant village where the wretched serfs drudged their lives away in ignorance and misery. They were mine now, and the weight of this new possession burdened my soul.

"I cannot bear it; this must be changed."

"It shall."

Unconsciously I had spoken aloud, and the prince had answered without asking to know my thoughts.

"What shall be done, Alexis?" I said, smiling, as I caressed the thin hand that lay in mine.

"Whatever you desire. I do not wait to learn the wish, I promise it shall be granted."

"Rash as ever; have you, then, no will of your own?"

"None; you have broken it."

"Good; hear then my wish. Liberate your serfs; it afflicts me as a free-born Englishwoman to own men and women. Let them serve you if they will, but not through force or fear. Can you grant this, my prince?"

"I do; the Stavosta is already gone, and they know I pardon them. What more, Sybil?"

"Come with me to England, that I may show my countrymen the brave barbarian I have tamed."

My eyes were full of happy tears, but the old tormenting spirit prompted the speech. Alexis frowned, then laughed, and answered, with a glimmer of his former imperious pride:

"I might boast that I also had tamed a fiery spirit, but I am humble, and content myself with the knowledge that the proudest woman ever born has promised to love, honor, and—"

"*Not* obey you," I broke in with a kiss.

❧ Doctor Dorn's Revenge

THEY STOOD TOGETHER by the sea, and it was evident the old, old story was being told, for the man's face was full of pale excitement, the girl's half averted from the ardent eyes that strove to read the fateful answer in her own.

"It may be folly to speak when I have so little to offer," he said, with an accent of strong and tender emotion in his voice that went straight to the girl's heart. "It may be folly, and yet if you love as I love we can wait or work together happy in the affection which wealth cannot buy nor poverty destroy. Tell me truly, Evelyn, may I hope?"

She longed to say "yes," for in her heart she knew she loved this man, so rich in youth, comeliness, talent, and ardor, but, alas! so poor in fortune and friends, power and place. He possessed all that wins a woman's eye and heart, nothing that gratifies worldly ambition or the vanity that is satisfied with luxury regardless of love. She was young, proud, and poor, her beauty was her only gift, and she saw in it her only means of attaining the place she coveted. She had no hope but in a wealthy marriage; for this end she lived and wrought, and had almost won it, when Max Dorn appeared, and for the first time her heart rebelled. Something in the manful courage, the patient endurance with which he met and bore, and would in time conquer misfortune, woke her admiration and respect. He was different from those about her, and carried with him the unconscious but sovereign charm of integrity. The love she saw in his eloquent eyes seemed a different passion from the shallow, selfish sentimentality of other men. It seemed to ennoble by its sincerity, to bless by its tenderness, and she found it hard to put it by.

As she listened to his brief appeal, made impressive by the intensity of repressed feeling that trembled in it, she wavered, hesitated, and tried to silence conscience by a false plea of duty. Half turning with the shy glance, the soft flush of maiden love and shame, she said slowly:

"If I answered yes I should wrong both of us, for while you work and I wait that this may be made possible, our youth and strength will be passing away, and when the end is won we shall be old and tired, and even love itself worn out."

"If it be true love it never can wear out," he cried, impetuously; but she shook her delicate head, and a shadow passed across her charming face, paling its bloom and saddening its beauty.

"I know that poets say so, but I have no faith in the belief. Hearts grow gray as well as heads, and love cannot defy time any more than youth can. I've seen it tried and it always fails."

"So young, yet so worldly-wise, so lovely, yet so doubtful of love's dominion," murmured Max, on whom her words fell with a foreboding chill.

"I have felt the bitterness of poverty, and it has made me old before my time," she answered, with the shadow deepening on her face. "I could love you, but I will not." And the red lips closed resolutely as the hard words left them.

"Because I am poor?"

"Because *we* are poor."

For an instant something like contempt shone in his eyes, then pity softened their dark brilliance, and a passionate pain thrilled his voice as he said, with a despairing glance:

"Then I may not hope!"

She could not utter the cruel word "No" that rose to her lips; a sudden impulse ruled her; the better nature she had tried to kill prompted a truer answer, and love, half against her will, replied:

"You may hope—a little longer."

"How long?" he questioned, almost sternly, for even with the joy of hope came a vague disquiet and distrust.

"Till to-morrow."

The tell-tale color flushed into her cheeks as the words escaped her, and she could not meet the keen yet tender eyes that searched her downcast face.

"To-morrow!" he echoed; "that is a short probation, but none the less hard for its brevity if I read your face aright. John Meredith has spoken, and you find money more tempting than love."

Her head dropped on her hands, and for an instant she struggled with an almost irresistible impulse to put her hand in his and show him she was nobler than he believed. But she had been taught to control natural impulses, to bend her will, to yield her freedom to the one aim of her life, and calling it necessity, to become its slave. Something in his look and tone stung her pride and gave her strength to fight against her heart. In one thing he was mistaken; John Meredith had not spoken, but she knew a glance from her would unlock his tongue, for the prize was almost won, and nothing but this sudden secret love had withheld her from seizing the fruit of her long labor and desire. She meant to assure herself of this beyond all doubt, and then, when both fates were possible, to weigh and decide as calmly as she might. To this purpose she clung, and lifting her head with a proud gesture, she said, in the cold, hard tone that jarred upon his ear and made discord in the music of her voice:

"You need not wait until to-morrow. Will you receive your answer now?"

"No; I will be patient, for I know something of temptations like this, and I have faith in the nobility of a woman's heart. Love or leave me as you will, but, Evelyn, if you value your own peace, if you care for the reverence of one who loves you utterly, do not sell yourself, for wealth so bought is worse than the sharpest poverty. A word will put me out of pain; think of this to-day; wear these to remind you of me, as that jewel recalls Meredith; and to-night return my dead roses or give me one yourself."

He put the ruddy cluster in the hand that wore his rival's gift, looked into her face with a world of love and longing in his proud eyes, and left her there alone.

If he had seen her crush the roses on her lips and drench them in passionate tears, if he had heard her breathe his name in tones of tenderest grief and call him back to save her from temptation, he would have turned and spared himself a lifelong loss, and saved her from a sacrifice that doomed her to remorse. She crept into a shadowy nook among the rocks, and searched her self as she had never done before. The desire to be found worthy of him swayed her strongly, and almost conquered the beliefs and purposes of her whole life. An hour passed, and with an expression more beautiful than any ever seen upon her face till now, Evelyn rose to seek and tell her lover that she could not give his flowers back.

As she stood a moment smiling down upon the emblems of love, a voice marred the happiest instant of her life, a single sentence undid the work of that thoughtful hour.

"Meredith will never marry pretty Evelyn."

"And why not?" returned another voice, as careless as that sarcastic one that spoke first.

"He is too wise, and she lacks skill. My faith! with half her beauty I would have conquered a dozen such as he."

"You have a more potent charm than beauty, for wealth will buy any man."

"Not all." And the girl's keen ear detected an undertone of bitterness in the light laugh that followed the words. A woman spoke, and as she listened, Dorn's words, "I know something of such temptations," returned to her with a sudden significance which the next words confirmed.

"Ah, Max will not thaw under your smiles nor be dazzled by the golden baits you offer. Well, my dear, you can find your revenge in watching Evelyn's folly and its dreary consequences, for she will marry him and ruin herself for ever."

"No doubt of that; she hasn't wit enough to see what a splendid career is open to her if she marries Meredith, and she will let a girlish romance rob her of success. That knowledge is an immense comfort to me."

The speakers passed on, leaving Evelyn pale with anger, her eyes keen and hard, her lips smiling scornfully, and her heart full of bitterness. The roses lay at her feet, and the hand that wore the ring was clinched as she watched mother and daughter stroll away, little dreaming that their worldly gossip had roused the girl's worst passions and given her temptation double force.

"She loves Max and pities me—good! I'll let her know that I refused him, and teach her to fear as well as envy me. 'A splendid career'—and she thinks I'll lose it. Wait a day and see if I have not wit enough to know it, and skill enough to secure it. 'Girlish romance' shall not ruin my future; I see its folly, and I thank that woman for showing me how to avoid it. Take comfort while you may, false friend; to-morrow your punishment will begin."

Snatching up the roses, Evelyn returned to the hotel, congratulating herself that she had not spoken hastily and pledged her word to Dorn. Everything seemed to foster the purpose that had wavered for an hour, and even trifles lent their weight to turn the scale in favor of the mercenary choice. As if conscious of the struggle going on within her, Meredith forgot the temporary jealousy of Dorn, that had held him aloof for a time, and was more devoted than before. She drove with him, and leaning in his luxurious barouche, passed Dorn walking through the dust. A momentary pang smote her as his face kindled when he saw her, but she conquered it by whispering to herself, "That woman would rejoice to see me walking there beside him; now I can eclipse her even in so small a thing as this."

As the thought came, her haughty little head rose erect, her eye wandered, well pleased, from splendid horses, liveried servants and emblazoned carriage, to the man who could make them hers, and she smiled on him with a glance that touched the cold heart which she alone had ever warmed.

Later, as she sat among a group of summer friends, listening to their gossip, she covertly watched her two lovers while she stored up the hints, opinions, and criticisms of those about her. Max Dorn had youth, manly beauty and native dignity, but lacked that indescribable something which marks the polished man of fashion, and by dress, manner, speech and attitude betrayed that he was outside the charmed circle as plainly as if a visible barrier rose between him and his rival.

John Meredith, a cold, grave man of forty, bore the mark of patrician birth and breeding in every feature, tone, and act. Not handsome, graceful, or gifted, but simply an aristocrat in pride and position as in purse. Men envied, imitated, and feared him; women courted, flattered, and sighed for him; and whomsoever he married would be, in spite of herself, a queen of society.

As she watched him the girl's purpose strengthened, for on no one did his eye linger as on herself; every mark of his preference raised her in the estimation of her mates, and already was she beginning to feel the intoxicating power which would be wholly hers if she accepted him.

"I will!" she said, within herself. "To-night he will speak and to-morrow my brilliant future shall begin."

As she dressed for the ball that night an exquisite bouquet of exotics was brought her. She knew who sent them, and a glance of gratified vanity went from the flowers to the lovely head they would adorn. In a glass on her toilet bloomed the wild roses, fresh and fragrant as ever. A regretful sigh escaped her as she took them up, saying softly, "I must return them, but he'll soon forget—and so shall I."

A thorn pierced her hand as she spoke, and as if daunted by the omen, she paused an instant while tears of mental, not physical pain, filled her eyes. She wiped the tiny drop of blood from her white palm, and as she did so the flash of the diamond caught her eye. A quick change passed over her, and dashing away the tears, she hid the wound and followed her chaperon, looking blithe and beautiful as ever.

John Meredith did speak that night, and Max Dorn knew it, for his eye never left the little figure with the wild roses half hidden in the lace that stirred with the beating of the girlish heart he coveted. He saw them pass into the moonlit garden, and stood like a sentinel at the gate till a glimmer of white foretold their return. Evelyn's face he could not see, for she averted it, and turned from the crowd as if to seek her room unseen. Meredith's pale features were slightly flushed, and his cold eye shone with unwonted fire, but whether anger or joy wrought the change Dorn could not tell.

Hurrying after Evelyn, he saw her half way up the wide staircase, and softly called her name. No one was near, and pausing, she turned to look down on him. Never had she seemed more lovely, yet never had he found it hard to watch that beloved face before. Without a word he looked up, and stretched his hands to her, as if unconscious of the distance between them. Her rich color faded, her lips trembled, but her eyes did not fall before his own, and her hand went steadily to her breast as in silence, more bitterly significant than words, she dropped the dead roses at his feet.

"Is Doctor Dorn at home?"

The servant glanced from the pale, eager speaker to the elegant carriage he had left, and, though past the hour, admitted him.

A room, perfect in the taste and fitness of its furnishing, and betraying many evidences, not only of the wealth, but the cultivation of its owner, received the new comer, who glanced hastily about him as he advanced toward its occupant, who bent over a desk writing rapidly.

"Doctor Dorn, can you spare me a few moments on a case of life and death?" said the gentleman, in an imploring tone, for the sight of a line of carriages outside, and a crowded anteroom inside, had impressed him with the skill and success of this doctor more deeply than all the tales he had heard of his marvelous powers.

Doctor Dorn glanced at his watch.

"I can give you exactly five minutes."

"Thanks. Then let me as briefly as possible tell you the case. My wife is dying with a tumor in the side. I have tried everything, every physician, and all in vain. I should have applied to you long ago, had not Evelyn positively forbid it."

As the words left his lips both men looked at one another, with the memory of that summer night ten years ago rising freshly before them. John Meredith's cold face flushed with emotion in speaking of his suffering wife to the man who had been his rival. But Max Dorn's pale, impassive countenance never changed a muscle, though a close observer might have seen a momentary gleam of something like satisfaction in his dark eye as he answered in a perfectly business-like tone:

"I have heard of Mrs. Meredith's case from Doctor Savant, and know the particulars. Will you name your wish?"

He knew it already, but he would not spare this man the pang of asking his wife's life at his hands. Meredith moistened his dry lips, and answered slowly:

"They tell me an operation may save her, and she consents. Doctor Savant dares not undertake it, and says no one but you can do it. Can you? Will you?"

"But Mrs. Meredith forbids it."

"She is to be deceived; your name is not to be mentioned; and she is to think Doctor Savant is the man."

A bitter smile touched Dorn's lips, as he replied with significant emphasis:

"I decline to undertake the case at this late stage. Savant will do his best faithfully, and I hope will succeed. Good morning, sir."

Meredith turned proudly away, and Dorn bent over his writing. But at the door the husband paused, for the thought of his lovely young wife dying for want of this man's skill rent his heart and bowed his spirit. With an impulsive gesture he retraced his steps, saying brokenly:

"Doctor Dorn, I beseech you to revoke that answer. Forgive the past, save my Evelyn, and make me your debtor for life. All the honor shall be yours; she will bless you, and I—I will thank you, serve you, love you to my dying day."

Hard and cold as stone was Dorn's face as the other spoke, and for a moment no answer came. Meredith's imploring eyes saw no relenting sign, his outstretched hands fell at his side, and grief, resentment and despair trembled in his voice as he said, solemnly:

"For her sake I humbled myself to plead with you, believing you a nobler man than you have proved yourself. She took your heart, you take her life, for no hand but yours can save her. You might have won our gratitude forever, but you refused."

"I consent." And with a look that went straight to the other's heart, Dorn held out his hand.

Meredith wrung it silently, and the first tears that had wet his eyes for years fell on the generous hand that gave him back his idol's life.

The affair was rapidly arranged, and as no time was to be lost, the following day was fixed. Evelyn was to be kept in ignorance of Dorn's part in the matter, and Doctor Savant was to prepare everything as if he were to be the operator. Dorn was not to appear till she was unconscious, and she was not to be told to whom she owed her life till she was out of danger.

The hour came, and Dorn was shown into the chamber, where on the narrow table Evelyn lay, white and unconscious, as if dead. Savant, and two other physicians, anxious to see the great surgeon at work, stood near; and Meredith hung over the beautiful woman as if it was impossible to yield her up to them. As he entered the room Dorn snatched one hungry glance at the beloved face, and tore his eyes away, saying to the nurse who came to him, "Cover her face."

The woman began to question him, but Meredith understood, and with his own hands laid a delicate handkerchief over the pallid face. Then he withdrew to an alcove, and behind the curtain prayed with heart and soul for the salvation of the one creature whom he loved.

The examination and consultation over, Dorn turned to take up his knife. As he did so one of the physicians whispered to the other, with a sneer:

"See his hand tremble; mine is steadier than that."

"He is as pale as the sheet; it's my opinion that his success is owing to lucky accidents more than to skill or science," returned the other.

In the dead silence of the room, the least whisper was audible. Dorn flushed to the forehead, he set his teeth, nerved his arm, and with a clear, calm eye, and unfaltering hand made the first incision in the white flesh, dearer to him than his own.

It was a strange, nay, an almost awful sight, that luxurious room, and in the full glow of the noonday light that beautiful white figure, with four pale men bending over it, watching with breathless interest the movements of one skillful pair of hands moving among the glittering instruments or delicately tying arteries, severing nerves, and gliding heedfully among vital organs, where a hairs-breadth slip might be death. And looking from behind the curtains, a haggard countenance full of anguish, hope and suspense.

With speechless wonder and admiration the three followed Dorn through the intricacies of this complicated operation, envying the steadiness of his hand, firm as iron, yet delicate as a breath; watching the precision of his strokes, the success of his treatment, and most of all, admiring his entire absorption in the work; his utter forgetfulness of the subject, whose youth and beauty might well unnerve the most skillful hand. No sign of what he suffered during that brief time escaped him; but when all was safely over, and Evelyn lay again in her bed, great drops stood upon his forehead, and as Meredith grasped his hand he found it cold as stone. To the praises of his rivals in science, and the fervent thanks of his rival in love, he returned scarce any answer, and with careful directions to the nurse went away to fall faint and exhausted on his bed, crying with the tearless love and longing of a man, "Oh, my darling, I have saved you only to lose you again!—only to give you up to a fate harder for me to bear than death."

Evelyn lived, and when she learned to whom she owed her life, she covered her face, saying to her hungry heart, "If he had known how utterly weary I was, how empty my life, how remorseful my conscience, he would have let me die."

She had learned long ago the folly of her choice, and pined in her splendid home for Max, and love and poverty again. He had prospered wonderfully, for the energy that was as native to him as his fidelity, led him to labor for ambition's sake when love was denied him. Devoted to his profession, he lived on that alone, and in ten years won a brilliant success. Honor, wealth, position were his now, and any woman might have been proud to share his lot. But none were wooed; and in his distant home he watched over Evelyn unseen, unknown—and loved her still.

She had tasted the full bitterness of her fate, had repented and striven to atone by devoting herself to Meredith, who was unalterable in his passion for her. But his love and her devotion could not bring happiness, and when he died his parting words were, "Now you are free."

She reproached herself for the thrill of joy that came as she listened, and whispered penitently, "Forgive me, I was not worthy of such love." For a year she mourned for him sincerely; but she was young, she loved with a woman's fervor now, and hope would paint a happy future with Max.

He never wrote nor came, and wearying at last, she sent a letter to a friend in that distant city, asking news of Doctor Dorn. The answer brought small comfort, for it told her that an epidemic had broken out, and that the first to volunteer for the most dangerous post was Max Dorn.

In a moment her decision was taken. "I must be near him; I must save him—if it is not too late. He must not sacrifice himself; he would not be so reckless if he knew that any one cared for him."

Telling no one of her purpose, she left her solitary home and went to find her lover, regardless of danger. The city was deserted by all but the wretched poor and the busy middle class, who live by daily labor. She heard from many lips praises, blessings and prayers when she uttered Doctor Dorn's name, but it was not so easy to find him. He was never at home, but lived in hospitals, and the haunts of suffering day and night. She wrote and sent to him. No answer came. She visited his house to find it empty. She grew desperate, and went to seek for him where few dared venture, and here she learned that he had been missing for three days. Her heart stood still, for many dropped, died, and were buried hastily, leaving no name behind them.

Regardless of everything but the desire to find him, dead or living, she plunged into the most infected quarter of the town, and after hours of sights and sounds that haunted her for years, she found him.

In a poor woman's room, nursed as tenderly by her and the child he had saved as if he had been her son, lay Max, dying. He was past help now, unconscious, and out of pain, and as she sat beside him, heart-stricken and despairing, Evelyn received her punishment for the act which wrecked her own life and led his to an end like that.

As if her presence dimly impressed his failing senses, a smile broke over his pallid lips, his hand feebly groped for hers, and those magnificent eyes of his shone unclouded for a moment, as she whispered remorsefully:

"I loved you best; forgive me, Max, and tell me you remember Evelyn."

"You said I might hope a little longer; I'll be patient, dear, and wait."

And with the words he was gone, leaving her twice widowed.

❧ La Jeune; or,
Actress and Woman

"JUST IN TIME for the theatre. You'll come, Ulster?"

"Decidedly not."

"And why?"

"Because I prefer a cigar, a novel, and my bottle of cliquot."

"But every one goes," began Brooke, in a dissatisfied tone.

"True, and for that reason, I keep away."

"You used to be as fond of it as I am."

"At your age I grant it; now, I'm ten years older and wiser. I'm tired of that as of most other pleasures, so go your way, my boy, and leave me in peace."

"Come, Ulster, don't play Timon yet. You are lazy, not used up nor misanthropic, so be obliging, and come like a good fellow."

Fanning away the cloud of smoke from before me, I took a look at my friend, for something in his manner convinced me that he had some particular reason for desiring my company. Arthur Brooke was a handsome young Briton, of four-and-twenty; blue-eyed, tawny-haired, ruddy and robust, with a frank face, cordial smile, and a heart both brave and tender. I loved him like a younger brother, and watched over him during his holiday in gay, delightful, wicked Paris. So far, he had taken his draught of pleasure with the relish of youth, but like a gentleman. Of late, he had turned moody, shunned me once or twice, and when I alluded to the change, affected surprise, assuring me that nothing was amiss. As I looked at him, I was surer than ever that all was not right. He was pale, and anxious lines had come on his smooth forehead; there was an excited glitter in his eyes, though he had scarcely touched wine at dinner; his smile seemed forced, his voice had lost its hearty ring, and his manner was half petulant, half pleading, as he stood undecidedly crushing up his gloves while he spoke.

"Why do you want me to go? Is it on your account, lad?" I asked, in an altered tone.

"Yes."

"Give me a reason, and I will."

He hesitated, colored all over his fair face, then looked me straight in the eyes, and answered steadily.

"I want you to see Mademoiselle Nairne."

"The deuce you do! Why, Brooke, you've not got into a scrape with La Jeune, I hope!" I exclaimed, sitting up, annoyed.

"Far from it, but I love, and mean to marry her if I can," he answered, in a resolute tone.

"Don't say that for heaven's sake. My dear boy, think of your father, your family, your prospects, and don't ruin yourself by such folly," I cried, in real anxiety.

"If you loved as I do, you wouldn't call it folly," he said, excitedly.

"Of course not, but it would be cursed folly nevertheless, and if some friend saved me from it, I should thank him for it when the delusion was over. Love her if you will, but don't marry her, I beg of you."

"That is impossible; she is as good as she is lovely, and will listen to none but honorable vows. Laugh, if you will, it's so, and actress as she is, there's not a purer woman than she in all Paris."

"Bless your innocence, that's not saying much for her. Why, my dear lad, she knows your fortune to a soul and makes her calculations accordingly. She sees that you are a simple, tender-hearted fellow, easy to catch, and not hard to manage when caught. She will marry you for your money, spend it like water, and when tired of the respectabilities, will elope with the first rich lover that comes along. Don't shoot me, I speak for your good; I know the world, and warn you of this woman."

"Do you know her?"

"No, but I know her class; they are all alike, mercenary, treacherous, and shallow."

"You are mistaken this time, Ulster. I know I'm young, easily gulled perhaps, and in no way your equal in such matters, but I'll stake my life that Natalie is not what you say."

"My poor boy, you are far gone, indeed! What can I do to save you?"

"Come and see her," he said, eagerly. "You don't know her, never saw her beauty or talent, yet you judge her, and would have me abide by your unjust decree."

"I'll go; the fever is on you, and you must be helped through the crisis, or you'll wreck your whole life. It always goes hard with your sort."

My indolence was quite conquered by anxiety, and away we went, Brooke armed with a great bouquet, and I mentally cursing his folly in wasting time, money, and the love of his honest heart, on a painted butterfly.

We took a box, and from the intense interest we showed in the piece, both of us might have been taken for ardent admirers of "La Jeune." I had never seen her, though all Paris had been running after her that season, as it was after any novelty from a learned pig to a hero. Having been bored by her praises, and annoyed by urgent entreaties to go, I perversely set my face against her, and affected even more indifference than I really felt. I was tired of such follies, fancied my day was over, and for a year or two had felt no interest in any actress less famous than Ristori or Rachel.

The play was one of those brilliant trifles possible only in Paris; for there, wit without vulgarity is appreciated, and art is so perfect, one forgets the absence of nature. The stage represented a charming boudoir, all mirrors, muslins, flowers and light. A coquettish soubrette was arranging the toilet as she delivered a few words that put the house in good humor, by whetting curiosity and raising a laugh, in the midst of which Madame la Marquise entered, not as most actresses take the stage, but as a pretty woman really would enter her room, going straight to the glass to see if the effect of her costume was quite destroyed by the vicissitudes of a bal-masque. She was beautiful—I could not deny that, but answered Brooke's eager inquiry with a shrug and the cruel words:

"Paint, dress, wine or opium."

He turned his back to me, and I devoted myself to the study of the woman he loved. She looked scarcely twenty, so fresh and brilliant was her face, so beautifully molded her figure, so youthful her charming voice, so elastic her graceful gestures. Petite and piquant, fair hair, dark eyes, a ravishing foot and hand, a dazzling neck and arm, made this rosy, dimpled little creature altogether captivating, even to one as *blasé* as myself. Gay, arch, and full of that indescribable coquetry which is as natural to a pretty woman as her beauty, La Jeune well deserved the sobriquet she had won.

Being a connoisseur in dress, I observed that hers was in perfect taste—a rare thing, for the costume of the Louis Quatorze era is usually overdone on the stage. But this woman had evidently copied some portrait, for everything was in keeping, coiffure, jewels, lace, brocade; and from the tiny patch on her white chin to the diamond buckles in her scarlet-heeled shoes, she was a true French marquise. Even in gesture, gait and accent, she kept up the illusion, causing modern France to be forgotten for the hour, and making that comedy a picture of the past, and winning applause from critics whose praise was tame.

Through the sparkling dialogue, the inimitable by-play, romantic incident and courtly intrigues of the piece, she played admirably, embodying not only the beauty and coquetry, but the wit, *finesse* and brilliancy of the part. I was interested in spite of myself; forgot my anxiety, and found myself applauding more than once. Brooke heard my hearty "Bravo!" and turned with an exultant smile.

"You are conquering your prejudices fast, *mon ami.* Is she not charming?"

"Very. I never questioned her skill as an actress, and readily accord my praise, for she plays capitally. But I'd rather not see her my friend's wife. Just fancy presenting her to your family."

He winced at that as his eye followed mine to the stage, which just then showed the marquise languishing in a great *fauteuil* before her mirror, surrounded by several fops, while her lover, disguised as a *coiffeur,* powdered her hair and dropped *billet doux* into her lap.

Fascinating, fair and frivolous as she was, how could he dream of transplanting her to a decorous English home, where her name alone would raise a storm, if coupled, even in jest, with his. He looked, sighed and sat silent till the curtain fell, then applauded till his gloves were in tatters, threw his bouquet at her feet as she reappeared, and turned to me, saying, with unabated eagerness:

"Now come and see her at home; the woman is more charming than the actress. I am asked to supper, and may bring a friend with me. Come, I beg of you."

To his surprise and satisfaction I consented at once, but did not tell him what had induced me to comply. It was a trifle, but it had weight with me, and hoping still to save my headstrong friend, I went away to sup with La Jeune.

The trifle was this: After one of her best scenes she left the stage, but did not go to her dressing room, as she must re-enter in a moment.

From our box we could command the opposite wings; a chair was placed there for her, and sinking into it, she waved away two or three devoted gentlemen who eagerly approached. They retired, and as if forgetting that she could be overlooked, La Jeune leaned back with a change of countenance that absolutely startled me. All the fire, the gayety, the youth, seemed to die out, leaving a weary, woeful face, the sadder for the contrast between its tragic pathos and the blithe comedy going on before us.

Brooke did not see her; he had seized the moment to sprinkle his flowers, already drooping in the hot air.

I said nothing, but watched that brief aside more eagerly than her best point. It was but an instant. Her cue came, and she swept on to the stage with a ringing laugh, looking the embodiment of joy.

This glimpse of the woman off the stage roused my curiosity, and made me anxious to see more of her.

As we drove away I asked Brooke if he had spoken yet, for I wished to know how to conduct myself in the affair.

"Not in words; my eyes and actions must have told her; but I delayed to speak till you had seen her, for willful as I seem, I value your advice, Ulster."

"Have you spoken of me?"

"Yes; once or twice. Some one asked why you never came with me, and I said you had forsworn theatres."

"How did she take that blunt reply?"

"Rather oddly, I thought, for, looking at me, she said, softly: 'It would be better for you if you followed the example of your mentor.' "

"Art, my child, all art; warn a man against anything, and he'll move heaven and earth to get it. How will you explain this visit of your mentor, who has forsworn theatres?" I said, nettled at having that sage and venerable name applied to me.

"It will be both gallant and truthful to say you came to see her. She bade me bring any friend I liked, and will be flattered at your coming, if you don't put on your haughty airs.

"I'll be amiable on your account. Here we are. Upon my word mademoiselle lodges sumptuously."

As we drove into a courtyard, lights shone in long windows of La Jeune's *appartement,* and the sound of music met us as we passed up the stairs.

Two large, luxurious rooms, brilliantly, yet tastefully decorated and furnished, received us as we stepped in unannounced. Half a dozen persons were scattered about, chatting, laughing and listening to a song from a member of the opera troupe then delighting Paris. Supper was laid in the further room, and while waiting till it was served, every one exerted themselves to amuse their hostess in return for the delight she had given them.

Mademoiselle seemed to have just arrived, for she was still *en costume,* and appeared to have thrown herself into a seat as if wearied with her labors.

The rich hue of the garnet velvet chair relieved her figure admirably, as she leaned back, with a white cloak half concealing her brilliant dress. The powder had shaken from her hair, leaving its gold undimmed as it hung slightly disheveled about her shoulders. She had wiped the rouge from her face, leaving it paler, but none the less lovely, for in resuming her own character, that face had changed entirely. No longer gay, arch, or coquetish, it was thoughtful, keen, and cold. She smiled graciously, received compliments tranquilly, and conversed wittily; but her heart evidently was not there, and she was still playing a part.

I made these observations and received these impressions during the brief pause at the door; then Brooke presented me with much *empressement,* plainly showing that he wished each to produce a favorable effect upon the other.

As my name was spoken a slight smile touched her lips, but her dark eyes scanned my face so gravely, that in spite of myself I paid my compliments with an ill grace.

"It is evident that this is not monsieur's first visit to Paris."

From another person, and in another mood, I should have accepted this speech as a compliment to my accent and manner, but from her I chose to see in it an ironical jest at my unwonted *maladresse,* a feminine return for my long negligence. Anxious to do myself justice, I gave a genuine French shrug and replied, with a satirical smile which belied my flattering words:

"I was about to say no, but I remember to whom I speak, and say yes, for by the magic of mademoiselle, modern Paris vanishes, and for the first time I visit Paris in the time of the Grand Monarque. The illusion was perfect, and like a hundred others, I am at a loss how to show my gratitude."

"That is easily done; madame is hungry; oblige her with a *morceau* of that *paté* and a glass of champagne."

Her mocking tone, the sparkle of her eye, and the wicked smile on her lips, annoyed me more than the unromantic request that made my speech absurd.

I obeyed with feigned devotion, telling Brooke to keep out of the way still longer, as I passed him on my way back. He had withdrawn a little, that I might see and judge for myself, and stood in an alcove near by, affecting to talk with a gentleman in the same sentimental plight as himself.

Mademoiselle ate and drank as if she was really hungry, inviting me to do the same with such hospitable grace that I drew up a little table and continued our *tête-a-tête,* while the others stood or sat about in groups in a pleasantly informal manner.

"My friend is much honored, I perceive. Mademoiselle shows both taste and judgment in her selection, for though young for his years, Brooke is a true gentleman," I said, observing that of all the many bouquets thrown at her feet his was the only one she kept.

"Do you know why I selected this?" she asked, with a quick glance after a slight pause.

"I can easily guess," I replied, with a significant smile.

She glanced over her shoulder, took up the great bouquet, and plunging her dimpled hand into the midst of the flowers, drew out a glittering bracelet, saying, as she offered it to me, with an air of pride that surprised me very much:

"I kept it that I might return this. It may annoy your friend less to take it from you, therefore restore it with my thanks, and tell him I can accept nothing but flowers."

"Nothing, mademoiselle?"

"Nothing, monsieur."

I put my question with emphasis, and as she answered she flashed a look at me that perplexed me, though I thought it a bit of clever acting.

Taking the bracelet, I said, in a tone of feigned regret:

"Must I afflict the poor boy by returning his gift with such a cruel message?"

"If you would be a true friend to him do what I ask, and take him away from Paris."

Her urgent tone struck me even more than this unexpected frankness, and I involuntarily exclaimed:

"Does mademoiselle know what she banishes thus?"

"I know that Sir Richard Brooke would disinherit his only son if that son made a *mésalliance;* I know that I regard Arthur too much to mar his future, and—I banish him."

She spoke rapidly, and laid her hand upon her heart as if to hide its agitation, but her eyes were fixed steadily on mine with an expression which affected me with a curious sense of guilt for my hard judgment of her.

There was a pause, and in that pause I chid myself for letting a pair of lovely eyes ensnare my reason, or an enchanting smile bribe my judgment.

"Mademoiselle understands the perversity of mankind well. It will be impossible to get Arthur away after a command like yours," I said, coldly.

She deliberately examined my face, and a change passed over her own. The earnestness vanished, the soft trouble was replaced by an almost bitter smile, and her voice had a touch of scorn in it as she said, sharply:

"Then Telemachus had better find a truer Mentor."

A gentleman approached; she welcomed him with a genial look, and I retired, feeling more ruffled than I would confess.

As soon as I joined Brooke in the alcove he demanded in English, and with lover-like eagerness:

"What is your opinion of her?"

"Hush; she will overhear you!"

"She speaks no English—she is absorbed—answer freely."

"Well, then, I think her a charming, artful, dangerous woman, and the sooner you leave her the better," I answered, abruptly.

"But, Ulster, don't joke. How artful? Why dangerous? I'll *not* leave her till I've tried my fate," he cried, half angry, half hurt.

I told him our conversation, gave him the jewel, and advised him to disappoint her hopes by departing without another word.

"You think she means to win me by affecting to sacrifice her own heart to my welfare?" he said as I paused.

"Exactly; she did it capitally, but I am not to be duped; and I tell you she will never let so rich a prize escape her unless she has a richer in sight, which I doubt."

"I'll not believe it! You wrong us both; you distrust all women, and insult her by such bare suspicions. You are deceived."

"I *never* am deceived; I read men and women like books, and no character is too mysterious for me to decipher. I tell you, I am right, and I'll prove it if you will keep silent for a few weeks longer."

"How?" demanded Brooke, hotly.

"I'll study this woman, and report my discoveries to you; thus, step by step, I'll convince you that she is all I say, and save you from the folly you are about to commit. Will you agree to this?"

"Yes; but you'll take no unfair advantage, you'll deal justly by us both, and if you fail——."

"I *never fail*—but if such an unheard of thing occurs, I'll own I'm conquered, and pay any penalty you decree."

"Then, I say, done. Prove that I'm a blind fool, and I'll submit to your advice, will forget Natalie and leave Paris."

Grateful for any delay, and already interested in the test, I pledged my word to act fair throughout, and turned to begin my work. Mademoiselle was surrounded by several gentlemen, and seemed to have recovered from her fatigue. Her eyes shone, a brilliant color burned on her cheek, she talked gayly, and mingled her silvery laughter in the peals of merriment her witty sallies produced. As we joined the group, some one was speaking of tragedy, and assuring La Jeune that she would excel in that as in comedy.

"*Mon Dieu,* no; one has tragedy enough off the stage; let us feign gayety in public, and laugh on even though our hearts ache," she answered, with a charming smile.

"Yet I can testify that mademoiselle would act tragedy well if I may judge by the sample I have seen."

I spoke significantly and her eye was instantly upon me, as she exclaimed with visible surprise:

"Seen! where?"

"To-night, as mademoiselle reposed a moment in the wing between the fourth and fifth acts."

She knit her brows, thought an instant, then as if recalling the fact, clapped her hands and broke into that ringing laugh of hers, as she cried:

"Monsieur has penetration! It is true, I was in a tragic mood for the spur of one of my buckles wounded my foot cruelly, and I could not complain. Behold how I suffered," and she showed a spot of scarlet that had stained through silk stocking and satin shoe.

"Great heaven! and does mademoiselle still wear the cruel ornament. Permit me to relieve this charming foot," cried one of the Frenchmen, in a pathetic tone; and going down upon his knee undid the buckle.

I was leaning on the back of her chair just then, and during the little stir said quietly:

"I congratulate mademoiselle, for if the pin-prick can call up such a woeful expression, her rendering of a mighty sorrow would be wonderfully truthful."

"I believe it would."

She looked up at me as she spoke, and in those beautiful eyes I fancied I read something like reproach. For what? Had I touched some secret wound, and was her explanation a skillful feint, as I thought it? Or did she feel with a woman's quick instinct that I was an enemy and set herself to disarm me by her beauty? I inclined to the latter belief, and instantly saw that if I would execute my purpose, I must convince her that I was a friend, an admirer, a lover even. It was evident that simple Brooke had allowed her to perceive that I did not approve his suit; this hurt her pride, and she distrusted me. Deciding to warm gradually, I looked back at her, saying gently, as if replying to that reproachful glance alone:

"I sincerely hope mademoiselle may never be called upon to play a part in any tragedy off the stage, for smiles, not tears, should be the portion of La Jeune."

Her face softened beautifully, and the dark curled lashes fell as if to hide the sudden dew that dimmed her eyes.

"You are kind, I thank you," she murmured, in a tone that touched me, skeptic as I was. "I received much flattery, and value it for what it is worth; but a friendly wish, simple and sincere, is very sweet to me, for even a path strewn with flowers has its thorns."

She spoke as if to herself more than to me, and fancying that sentiment might succeed better than sarcasm, I began one of those speeches that may mean much or little; but in the middle of it detected her in a yawn behind her little hand, and stopped abruptly. She laughed, and with the arch expression that made her face piquante she said with a shake of the head:

"Ah, monsieur, that's but a waste of eloquence. I detect false sympathy in an instant, and betray that I do. Pardon my rudeness, and turn me a charming compliment; that is more in your style."

"Mademoiselle is fatigued; we are unmerciful to leave her no time for rest. Brooke, we should go," I said, repentantly.

"I *am* tired," she answered, with the air of a sleepy child. "*Au revoir,* not adieu, for you will come again."

"If mademoiselle permits," and with that we bowed ourselves away.

For a month I studied La Jeune in ways as skillful as unobtrusive. I made four discoveries, reported them to Brooke, and flattered myself that I should be able to save him from this fascinating, yet dangerous woman.

My first discovery was this. Fearing to rouse suspicion by too suddenly feigning admiration and regard, I began with an occasional call, contenting myself meantime with cultivating the friendship of a gossipy old Frenchman, who lodged in the same house. From him I learned various hints of Natalie, for the old gentleman adored her, and was as garrulous as an old woman. He said there was one room in mademoiselle's suite that none of the servants of the house were allowed to enter.

Several times a week, early in the morning, when her mistress was invisible to every one else, Jocelynd, the maid, admitted a man, who came and went as if anxious to escape observation. He was young, handsome, an Italian, and evidently deeply interested in all concerning Mademoiselle Nairne.

"A lover, without doubt," the old man said. I agreed with him, and Brooke, on learning this, could be with difficulty restrained from demanding an explanation from La Jeune.

My second discovery was made unexpectedly. One night, when she did not play, I went to see her on pretense of finding Brooke, who, I knew, was not there.

Mademoiselle was out, but expected momently, so I went in to wait. I heard her arrive soon after and enter an adjoining room, followed by the maid, who cast a glance into the *salon* as she passed. I stood in the deep window idly looking into the street below, and Jocelynd did not see me, for I heard her say:

"There is no one here, mademoiselle. Pierre was mistaken, and Monsieur Ulster did not wait."

"Thank heaven! I am so fatigued I can see no one to-night. Count this for me. I have been playing for a high stake, but I have won, and Florimond shall profit by my success."

I heard the clink of money, and noiselessly stole away, saying to myself as I went to join Brooke: "She gambles—so much the better."

A week afterward I chanced to be in one of those dark little stores in the Rue Bonaparte, where cigars, cosmetics, perfumery, and drugs are sold. I was standing in the back part of the shop selecting a certain sort of toilet soap which I fancied, when a woman came in, and, beckoning the wife of the shopman aside, handed her a peculiar little flask saying in a low tone:

"The same quantity as usual, madame, but stronger."

The woman nodded, disappeared, and returned; but having left the stopper on the counter, she passed me with the flask uncorked, and I plainly perceived the acrid scent of laudanum. I knew it well, having used it during a nervous illness, and left the shop convinced that La Jeune was an opium-eater, like many of her class, for the woman I had seen was Jocelynd.

The fourth discovery was that some secret anxiety or grief preyed upon mademoiselle, for during that month she altered visibly. Her spirits were variable, her cheek lost its bloom, her form its roundness, and her eyes burned with feverish brilliancy, as if some devouring care preyed upon her life.

I could mark these changes carefully, for I was a frequent and a welcome guest now. By imperceptible degrees I had won my way, and making Brooke my pretext, often led her to speak of him, fancying that topic the one most likely to interest her. Soon I let her see that she had wakened my admiration as an actress, for I was as constant at the theatre as Brooke. Then I, with feigned reluctance, betrayed my susceptibility to her charms as a woman, and by look, sigh, act and word, permitted her to believe that I was one of her most devout adorers.

Upon my life, I sometimes felt as if in truth I was, and half longed to drop my mask and tell her that, with all her faults and follies, I found her more dangerous to my peace than any woman I had ever known. More than once I was tempted to believe that had I been a richer man she would have smiled upon me in spite of Brooke and the unknown Florimond.

As time passed this fancy of mine increased for I observed that with others she was as careless, gay and witty as ever, but with me, especially if we were alone, her manner was subdued, her glance restless, timid and troubled, her voice often agitated or constrained, her whole air that of a woman whose heart is full and pride alone keeps her from letting it overflow.

To Brooke she was uniformly kind, but cold, and often shunned him. At first I believed this only a ruse to lure him to the point, but soon my own penetration, vanity, if you will, led me to think that for a time at least she would hold mercenary motives in check and let the master-passion rule her in spite of interest.

This belief of mine added new excitement to my task, and my undisguisable absorption in it roused Brooke's jealousy, and nothing but a promise to hold his peace till the month was up restrained him from ruining everything, for he refused to accept my discoveries without further proof.

On the last day of the month I went to Natalie at noon, knowing that Arthur would speak that night. I had never been admitted so early before, but sending in an urgent request, it was granted.

I scarcely knew what I meant to say or do, for although my friend and I were freed by mutual consent from the pledge we had given one another, I was hardly ready to fetter myself with a lifelong tie, even to Natalie, whom I no longer disguised from myself that I loved.

I dared make no other offer, for in spite of the gossip and prejudice which always surrounds a young and beautiful actress, I felt that Natalie was innocent, from pride if not from principle, and would be to me a wife or nothing. I loved my freedom well, yet half resolved to lose it for her sake, for in spite of past experiences, I was conscious of a more ardent love at eight-and-thirty than any I had known in my youth.

Natalie came in, looking pale, yet very lovely, for her eyes possessed the soft lustre that follows tears, and on her face there was a look I had never seen before.

She wore a white cashmere *peignoir,* and was wrapt in a soft white mantle. Her hair hung in loose, glittering masses about her face, and her only ornament was a rosary of ebony and gold that hung from her neck.

The room was shaded by heavy curtains, which she did not draw aside, and as she seated herself in the deep velvet chair, her face was much in shadow. I regretted this, for never having seen her by day, except driving, I wished to see and study her when free from the illusion which dress and lamp-light can throw about the plainest woman.

Her hand trembled as I kissed it, her eyes avoided mine, and while I paid my compliments, she listened with drooping lids, a shy smile on her lips, and such a quickly beating heart that the rosary on her bosom stirred visibly. This agitation, coupled with her unusual welcome, banished my last doubt, and before I had decided to betray my passion, the words passed my lips.

As I paused, breathless with the impetuous petition I had made, she looked up with an unmistakable flash of triumph in her eye, an irrepressible accent of joy in her voice, as she answered, with a smile that thrilled my heart:

"Then you love me? You ask my hand? and give your happiness into my keeping?"

"I do."

"You forget what I am—forget that you know nothing of my past; that my heart is a sealed book to you, and that you have seen only the gay, frivolous side I show the world."

"I forget nothing, and glory in your talent as in the fame it wins you. I know you better than you think, for during a month I have studied you deeply, and I read you like an open book. I have discovered faults and follies, mysteries and entanglements, but I can forgive all, forget all, for the sake of this crowning discovery. You love me; I guess it; but I long to hear you confess it, and to know in words that I am blest."

She had questioned eagerly, with her keen eyes full on my face as I replied, but in the act of answering my last speech she rose suddenly as a swift change passed across her face, and in a tone of bitterest contempt, uttered these startling words:

"You say you know me well; you boast that you never are deceived; you believe that you have discovered the secret passions, vices and ambitions of my life; you affirm that I have had a lover, that I gamble, eat opium, and—love you. That last is the blindest blunder of the four, for of all men living, *you* are the one for whom I have the supremest contempt."

I had risen involuntarily when she did, but dropped into my seat as if flung back by the forceful utterance of that last word. I was so entirely taken by surprise that speech, self-possession, and courage deserted me for the moment, and I sat staring at her in dumb amazement. In a voice full of passionate pride, she rapidly continued, with her steady eyes holding me fast by their glittering spell:

"You were wise in your own conceit, and needed humbling. I heard your boast, your plot and pledge, made in this room a month ago, and resolved to teach you a lesson. You flatter yourself you know me thoroughly, yet you have not caught even a glimpse of my true nature, and Arthur's honest instinct has won the day against your worldly wisdom."

"Prove it!" I cried, angrily, for her words, her glance, roused me like insults.

"I will. First let us dispose of the discoveries so honorably made, and used to blast my reputation in a good man's eyes. My lover is an Italian physician, who comes to serve a suffering friend whom I shelter; the laudanum is for the same unhappy invalid. The money I won was honestly *played for*—on the stage, and the secret love you fancied I cherished was not for you—but Arthur."

"Hang the boy; it is a plot between you," I cried, forgetting self-command in my rising wrath.

"Wrong again; he knew nothing of my purpose, never guessed my love till to-day."

"To-day! he has been here already!" I exclaimed, "and you have snared him in spite of my sacrifice. Good! I am right in one thing, the richer prize tempts the mercenary enchantress."

"Still deceived; I have refused him, and no earthly power can change my purpose," she answered, almost solemnly.

"Refused him! and why?" I gasped, feeling more bewildered every moment.

"Because I am married, and—dying."

As the last dread word dropped from her lips, I felt my heart stand still, and I could only mutter hoarsely:

"No! no! it is impossible!"

"It is true; look here and believe it."

With a sudden gesture she swept aside the curtain, gathered back her clustered hair, dropped the shrouding mantle, and turned her face full to the glare of noonday light.

I did believe, for in the wasted figure, no longer disguised with a woman's skill, the pallid face, haggard eyes, and hollow temples, I saw that mysterious something which foreshadows death. It shocked me horribly, and I covered up my eyes without a word, suffering the sharpest pang I had ever known. Through the silence, clear and calm as an accusing angel's, came her voice, saying slowly:

"Judge not lest ye be judged. Let me tell you the truth, that you may see how much you have wronged me. You think me a Frenchwoman, and you believe me to be under five-and-twenty. I am English, and thirty-seven tomorrow."

"English! thirty-seven!" I ejaculated in a tone of utter incredulity.

"I come of a race whom time touches lightly, and till the last five years of my life, sorrow, pain, and care have been strangers to me," she said, in pure English, and with a faint smile on her pale lips. "I am of good family, but misfortune overtook us, and at seventeen I was left an orphan, poor, and nearly friendless. Before trouble could touch me Florimond married and took me away to a luxurious home in Normandy. He was much older than myself, but he has been fond as a father, as faithful, tender and devoted as a lover all these years. I married him from gratitude, not love, yet I have been happy and heart-free till I met Arthur."

Her voice faltered there, and she pressed her hands against her bosom, as if to stifle the heavy sigh that broke from her.

"You love him; you will break the tie that binds you, and marry him?" I said, bitterly, forgetting in my jealous pain that she had refused him.

"Never! See how little you know my true character," she answered, with a touch of indignation in the voice that now was full of a pathetic weariness. "For years my husband cherished me as the apple of his eye; then, through the treachery of others, came ruin, sickness, and a fate worse than death. My poor Florimond is an imbecile, helpless as a child. All faces are strange to him but mine, all voices empty sounds but mine, and all the world a blank except when I am with him. Can I rob him of this one delight—he who left no wish of mine ungratified, who devoted his life to me, and even in this sad eclipse clings to the one love that has escaped the wreck? No, I cannot forget the debt I owe him. I am grateful, and in spite of all temptations, I remain his faithful wife till death."

How beautiful she was as she said that! Never in her most brilliant hour, on stage or in *salon,* had she shone so fair or impressed me with her power as she did now. That was art, this nature. I admired the actress, I adored the woman, and feeling all the wrong I had done her, felt my eyes dim with the first tears they had known for years. She did not see my honest grief; her gaze went beyond me, as if some invisible presence comforted and strengthened her. With every moment that went by I seemed passing further and further from her, as if she dropped me out of her world henceforth, and knew me no more.

"Now you divine why I became an actress, hid my name, my grief, and for his sake smiled, sung, and feigned both youth and gayety, that I might keep him from that. I had lived so long in France that I was half a Frenchwoman; I had played often, and with success, in my own pretty theatre at Villeroy. I was unknown in Paris, for we seldom came hither, and when left alone with Florimond to care for, I decided to try my fortune on the stage. Beginning humbly, I have worked my way up till I dared to play in Paris. Knowing that youth, beauty and talent attract most when surrounded by luxury, gayety and freedom, I hid my cares, my needs, and made my *début* as one unfettered, rich and successful. The bait took; I am flattered, *fêted,* loaded with gifts, lavishly paid, and, for a time, the queen of my small realm. Few guess the heavy heart I bear, or dream that a mortal malady is eating my life away. But I am resigned; for if

I live three months and am able to play on, I shall leave Florimond secure against want, and that is now my only desire."

"Is there no hope, no help for you?" I said, imploringly, finding it impossible to submit to the sad decree which she received so bravely.

"None. I have tried all that skill can do, and tried in vain. It is too late, and the end approaches fast. I do not suffer much, but daily feel less strength, less spirit, and less interest in the world about me. Do not look at me with such despair; it is not hard to die," she answered, softly.

"But for one so beautiful, so beloved, to die alone is terrible," I murmured, brokenly.

"Not alone, thank heaven; one friend remains, tender and true, faithful to the end."

A blissful smile broke over her face as she stretched her arms toward the place her eye had often sought during that interview. If any further punishment was needed, I received it when I saw Arthur gather the frail creature close to his honest heart, reading his reward in the tender, trusting face that turned so gladly from me to him.

It was no place for me, and murmuring some feeble farewell, I crept away, heart-struck and humbled, feeling like one banished from Paradise; for despite the shadow of sorrow, pain and death, love made a heaven for those I left behind.

I quitted Paris the next day, and four months later Brooke returned to England, bringing me the ebony rosary I knew so well, a parting gift from La Jeune, with her pardon and adieu, for Arthur left her and her poor Florimond quiet under the sod at Pere La Chaise.

ೊ Countess Varazoff

Chapter I

"Bonjour, Monsieur Vane. I am consumed with curiosity to learn who the blonde angel is yonder."

"Countess Irma Varazoff," replied the young Englishman, turning to meet the tall Russian who accosted him somewhat imperiously.

Both paused to look after one of the charming little vehicles which fly up and down the Promenade des Anglais at five P.M. in the height of the season at Nice. It was lined with blue silk as daintily as a lady's work-basket, ornamented by a handsome page in the little seat behind, drawn by snow-white ponies in silver-plated harness and blue favors, and driven by a lovely young woman, whose costume of blue velvet and ermine completed the coquettish *tout ensemble*. "Who is she?" asked the Russian as they went on.

"A Polish widow, lately arrived here."

"You mistake, *mon ami;* she is a Russian; Poland no longer exists. You know her, and you will present me, if I ask the favor?"

"Would it be generous to present the conqueror to the conquered?"

"Bah! what have charming women to do with such things; if one admires them they are satisfied," returned the Russian, carelessly.

"Not if the admirer has robbed them of country, friends, and fortune. Some women do not forget," said Vane, ill-pleased.

"They are soon taught that lesson. Is the countess one of these proud rebels?"

"She does me the honor to be my friend, and I cannot offend her by complying with your wish. Indeed it is impossible," and the cool decision of the young Englishman left no hope.

"I ask no more, but permit me to assure you that the word 'impossible' is unknown to me. With thanks for your complaisance I go to salute the beautiful countess."

As he spoke, with an ironical bow, and a significant smile, the Russian passed on, wearing a look which justified the rumor that Prince Czertski never forgot nor forgave a slight.

He was a man of forty, above the usual height, with a martial carriage, a color-less, large-featured face, fierce black eyes, a sensual, yet ruthless mouth, closely cropped black hair, sharp white teeth under a heavy mustache, and delicately gloved hands as small as a woman's. Dressed with an elegant simplicity, and wearing one order at his buttonhole, the prince was a striking figure, even in the brilliant crowd on the promenade.

Both men walked on, a few paces apart, both angry and both ready to annoy each other. The carriage of the countess was seen returning, and both hastened to reach the opening in the blooming hedge which separated promenade from drive, for it was evident that the lady was about to alight. The prince had the advantage and kept it. With no appearance of haste, he emerged from between the roses just as the countess alighted, and in doing so dropped a coral-tipped white parasol. The little page was evidently new to the duties of his place, for he left his mistress to disentangle her train from the step while he held the horses. With the easy gallantry of a foreigner the prince stepped forward and assisted her, taking care to crush the delicate handle of the parasol under his heel. Then affecting to perceive the accident, he caught it up, exclaiming, with well-feigned regret:

"A thousand pardons for my *gaucherie!* Madame will permit me to repair my fault. To what address shall I send this when it is restored?"

"It is nothing; monsieur need not incommode himself," and the countess ex-tended her hand to reclaim her property. At this moment Vane, who had been de-tained by a countrywoman, came up, and the prince, with a triumphant glance, said, in a tone of relief:

"Behold my friend, who is known to madame; he will assure her that I may be trusted with this costly toy."

There was no help for it, and Vane presented him with an ill-grace; this chagrin changed to astonishment, however, for, as he uttered the name of one of Poland's most inveterate enemies, he thought to see the countess betray some sign of emotion; but no, the smile remained unchanged, and her beautiful eyes met tranquilly the glance of undisguised admiration bent upon her.

"I could have believed it of any woman but Irma," he muttered to himself, as the countess walked on, speaking without a shadow of annoyance to the prince, who sauntered beside her wearing his most bland and brilliant smile.

Down the long promenade they went side by side, followed by many eyes and criticised by many tongues. Vane hardly spoke, for the prince absorbed the conversa-tion, and when he chose no one could be more charming. The grace and devotion of his manner to women was doubly flattering from its strong contrast to his brusque and domineering demeanor with his own sex. To most women there was a singular fascination in seeing the fierce eyes soften, the pale, impassive face flush and kindle, and the hard mouth smile as it uttered honeyed compliments or impassioned vows.

Countess Varazoff observed him with furtive glances as if to catch every change of feature, to weigh every word he uttered; and during that careless interview she appeared to be testing the man by some subtle process of her own. Her conclusions were evidently favorable, for her manner became more and more gracious, and when the prince quitted them her fine eyes followed him thoughtfully.

"Have no fears for your parasol; madame, it will return to you with a point lace cover and a jeweled handle; these barbarians love magnificence," said Vane, annoyed by her interest in another.

"You fancy I think of that trifle? One day you will know me better," and the countess turned from him with a sombre smile.

CHAPTER II

ALL THE WORLD was at the consul's *bal masqué* three weeks later, and all the world gossiped about Prince Czertski and the Countess Varazoff.

"My dear creature, she will get him," whispered one dowager to another as they watched the brilliant crowd from the gallery. "His carriage waits at her door by the hour together, her anteroom is supplied by the flowers he sends, and he follows her everywhere like a shadow."

"It is true; he adores her and she permits it, yet my son assures me that not a breath of scandal has touched her name. Another week, they say, will show us one of two miracles, the prince rejected or the lovely Pole the wife of the ugly Russian," returned the other old lady, nodding wisely.

"She is as peculiar as she is beautiful. My friend, Madame Cartozzi, has a maid who formerly lived with the countess, and the girl says she was the saddest creature ever seen—in private, mind you—in public she was then as now all spirit and vivacity. Justine says she often walked her room all night weeping, and the next day would make a splendid toilet and lead the life of a butterfly. It is not wonderful that she mourns her country; but it is mysterious that she smiles on an enemy like the prince."

"He is fabulously rich, my dear, and she must be poor compared to him; he has rank, and hers is nothing but an empty sound now; he has power, and she has not a particle beyond that which her beauty gives her. She will dry her tears and marry him, there is no doubt of that."

"It will be a spectacle, that wedding; and yet I pity her, for they say the prince has the temper of a demon and the pride of Lucifer. She will find herself a slave in golden chains. Apropos of chains, they say she intends to appear to-night as the Genius of Poland, in mourning robes with fettered hands."

"She will scarcely dare to do that with so many Russians and Austrians present," cried the second dowager anxiously.

"She has the courage of a lion if all the tales are true, and for that same reason she will appear before her enemies in the dress I tell you of. See, the prince has stood near the door this half hour waiting for her. I know him by the splendor of his dress. He personates Peter the Great, and does it well, as one may see. But look! she is coming—and yes, she is in black. Great heavens, this grows exciting!" and the two old ladies peered over the balcony with breathless interest.

It *was* the countess, shrouded from head to foot in black crape; her golden hair falling in loose curls upon her shoulders, and her white arms adorned with a light silver chain from wrist to wrist. Never had she looked more beautiful, for through the vail her skin was dazzlingly fair, her eyes shone large and lustrous as stars, her lips were proud and unsmiling, and in her carriage there was a haughty grace which plainly proved that her free spirit was still unsubdued. She leaned upon the arm of a Red Cross Knight, in whom Vane was easily recognizable. As they made their way through the crowd, a murmur followed them, for this was the sensation of the evening. The impressible French and warm-hearted English felt the pathos of the thing, but the Russians and Austrians saw in it only an insult, which irritated them even while they affected to ignore it. The prince knit his heavy brows and swore a Russian oath in his beard as he watched the slender black figure.

"What whim is this?" he muttered. "Why does she annoy me to-night, when I most wished to do her honor and show the world I am about to triumph? Is it a trial of her power over me? or is it merely womanly bravado? We shall see. I shall not yet commit myself."

He kept aloof, but looked and listened carefully as he roamed from group to group. It soon became apparent that something was wrong, for after the first stir of surprise, admiration and conjecture, a scarcely perceptible cloud seemed to over-shadow the company. Frowns, shakes of the head, angry or anxious glances were seen, whispered jests, criticisms, even threats circulated rapidly, and a general impression prevailed that the countess would suffer for her freak. Certain high personages were afraid of offending other high personages by countenancing such an act, and presently a rumor flew about that the beautiful Pole was to be informed of her offense and requested to retire.

"What a mortification that will be," cried one lady to another, as the hint reached her. "If I dared I would warn her, that by retiring at once she might spare herself this disgrace. Surely some friend should tell her she has gone too far. She would be eternally grateful for such a kindness."

"Thanks for the word, madame," said the prince to himself, as he passed the fair speaker with a glance that caused her to maintain for ever after that Prince Czertski had magnificent eyes.

Countess Irma sat in one of the alcoves that opened on the garden, enjoying the fresher air after her slow passage through the saloons. For a moment she was alone, Vane being gone for her mantle. Leaning her head on her hand, she sat looking with absent eyes on the glittering sea below. Her vail was thrown back and the moon-light shone full upon her lovely face, which looked almost stern in its pale immobility. A shadow fell across the light, and turning her head, she saw the prince regarding her with an expression rarely seen upon his face, an expression of pity, touched with some warmer emotion. But his voice was cold and quiet, and his manner distant as he said, glancing over his shoulder to assure himself that they were alone:

"Will madame forgive me if I incur her displeasure by bringing unwelcome news, and believe that I do it in order to spare her the pain of hearing them from less respectful lips?"

"I thank you; pray speak," she answered, with no sign of surprise or interest.

"It is with great reluctance that I obey, but time presses, and I could not resist the impulse which sent me to you in the moment of trouble. Madame's costume has given offense to certain powerful persons, who cannot forgive anything to beauty in misfortune. It is whispered that Madame la Countess will be requested to withdraw, and I hastened to spare her the public insult by suggesting that she leave at once, and do me the honor of accepting my carriage if her own is not in attendance."

She had watched him keenly as he spoke, and in her face he read contempt, defiance, and undaunted courage, but overpowering these strong emotions he saw surprise, gratitude, and something akin to admiration at his act.

"And it is *you* who come to warn and protect me when others fall away?" she said, slowly, looking up at him with the glitter of a tear in her steadfast eyes.

"It is I who venture to prove in act what I have often betrayed by look. Of what use is power if not to protect the weak and innocent?" returned the prince, mildly.

"You are a generous enemy," murmured the countess, evidently touched.

"I am an ardent lover."

"Ah, no; you forget I am an exile, homeless, friendless, countryless, and you—" she paused, with a gesture of her fettered hands more eloquent than words.

"I only remember that you are beautiful, and that *I* love you. Madame, come into the garden for a moment; there we shall be uninterrupted. No breath of air shall chill you. See, the Czar is proud to lend his cloak to cover such shoulders;" and rapidly divesting himself of a short sable-lined pelisse, he laid it about her, and led her away with an air of soft command impossible to resist.

Pacing slowly in the moonlight among the orange-trees and through a wilderness of roses, the prince continued in a tenderer tone, with his hand on the delicate one upon his arm, and his eyes, full of passionate admiration, looking down into her own:

"Madame, others may condemn your act this night and attempt to punish it by banishment; but to me it is a brave deed, and I adore courage even in an—nay, I'll not say enemy; that you can never have the cruelty to be to me. The misfortunes of your country should not be visited too heavily on you, and this harmless tribute to poor Poland should be allowed to pass with pity and respect. You shall not suffer for it, I pledge you my word."

"I do not fear. I have nothing more to lose—but my life, and that is a burden I would willingly lay down."

She spoke bitterly, and a mortal sadness seemed to consume her. For a moment the prince eyed her keenly, then smiled to himself, and said in a lighter tone:

"In making others happy one finds happiness they say; can I not persuade you to try it? We are told to love our enemies; I find it an easy task. Can nothing tempt you to do the same? Madame, you cannot feign ignorance of my passion; I have confessed it in many ways, but never won a sign of hope in return. Ah, let me earn the privilege of protecting you always, as I have the delight of doing now. Put me out of pain, I beseech you," and he bent to read her face.

"I have made no sign, because I have no hope to give. Accept my thanks, and pardon me if I inflict pain where I owe gratitude."

Not a vestige of emotion on her face, the weariness of which piqued him more than the slight emphasis on the word "if." "She doubts me still, or loves Vane," he thought, and glowed with wrath at the idea. Very coldly he bowed, and very proudly he answered:

"Then nothing remains for me but to lead you to a carriage. Our appearance together will quiet the gossips and secure you from further annoyance. I possess power, and for you I do not hesitate to use it."

The last words struck her, she walked in silence a few steps, then looked up with a smile so sudden, so brilliant, that it almost startled him. Leaning more confidingly on his arm, the countess said softly:

"Ah, yes, and you use it so kindly. Pardon my seeming ingratitude, and let me tell you why I refuse the honor you would do me. May I, dare I speak?"

Few men could have refused anything asked in such a voice and accompanied by such a gesture of appeal, such a glance of almost tender longing. The prince yielded to the charm without an effort, and replied impetuously, as he lifted the appealing hand to his lips:

"You may dare anything with me. I am your slave."

"My master, rather. It is I who am the slave, but my fetters are not heavy now." And her eye went from his enamored face to the silver chain which he had involuntarily gathered up as they walked.

"You own it then? You confess that you love me, and permit me to hope?" he cried, seizing both hands in his own.

"I confess my weakness, but I do not yield. I must not, till my work is done, for I have vowed to remain a widow while he suffers."

"He! who?" demanded the prince, fiercely.

"Nay, fear nothing; it is an old man, and no lover," answered the countess, with a laugh that would have sounded unnatural to a less excited listener. Still looking up with the enchanting smile on her lips, the half timid, half tender light in her eyes, and both hands folded on his arm, she continued in a charming tone of confidence which flattered the ruling passion of the prince:

"My friend, that jealousy proves that you love me; I no longer doubt, but will permit the sweet truth to comfort me in the sacrifice I must make. Listen, and help me as only one so powerful, so pitiful can. The old Count Cremlin languishes in an Austrian prison. He was kind to me in my orphaned youth, and I am grateful. He cries to me for help, and I am powerless. He is harmless, feeble, and poor. He desires only to reach England and die free. But he is forgotten, for he has neither friends, influence, or money. You have all; one line of yours secures his liberty, I send him safely to his daughter, and then———"

"Ah! And then, madame?" broke in the prince, pausing to receive the reply.

"And then I thank you," she said, offering both hands with a look that stirred the prince to his heart's core.

"You give me this?" he demanded, while his pale face flushed and his eye kindled as he crushed one of the soft hands in his eager grasp.

"It is not worthy; but place the old count's pardon there, and it is yours."

The words fell slowly from lips that grew white in uttering them, but her eye met his steadily. Something in her manner disquieted him, for the fire of his own love made him quick to feel the lack of it in her.

"She is wily and will escape me; I am on my guard, but will win her at all costs and punish her coldness afterward," he thought, and answered with a smile that chilled her to the heart:

"When my ring is on this hand I place the pardon in it. You agree to this, my charming captive?"

"But why wait? Why keep the old man in his pain till we———?" the word "marry" died on her lips, and her eyes fell, lest she should see the feverish eagerness in them.

"I am right," he thought; "she plays for a precious stake, and must play high if she wins. She tries to dupe me with false tenderness. Good! She shall atone for that by finding that my love and hate go hand-in-hand."

This knowledge added zest to his pursuit and stimulated his purpose to succeed in spite of all obstacles. The cruel mouth still wore a smile, but in the bland voice there was a mocking undertone.

"He shall not wait long, this poor old man; and while I bestir myself to procure his pardon you will make ready for the marriage. It must be soon, for I am recalled, and dare not linger."

"When?" she murmured, in a half audible voice.

"Before the month is out I must be in St. Petersburgh. Come, I have a fancy to make a little bargain with you. I promise to give you this pardon the moment you are mine."

"You do not trust me then?" she said, flashing a look at him.

He laughed, and answered with an air of gallant submission, "I know your fair and fickle sex too well to trust them till they are won; then I am blindly devoted. Shall it be as I say, my Irma!"

"Yes."

The little word cost a heroic effort, but though uttered bravely, she shivered and shrunk from his embrace, and tried to conceal behind her vail the abhorrence and despair written on her face. He felt and saw it all, and set his teeth with a grim smile as he led her on, pale and mute as the statues round them. On re-entering the alcove a mirror confronted her; struck by her own pallor, she steeled herself to meet the curious world, and assuming a gay air, she resolved to play her part well at any cost. A feverish color rose to her cheek, excitement lent her eyes new brilliancy, and the desperation of her heart supplied her with a vivacity that charmed all beholders. Throwing back her vail, she arranged her bright hair with effect, and turning to the prince, she said, with an air of coquetry which he had never seen before:

"Now, my Alexander, I am ready to accompany you in your triumphal march."

"How! you know my name and make it sweet by uttering it in such a tone?" cried the prince, delighted and surprised by the new change.

"I did not know it, but it suits you, and it pleases me to play your captive to-night. God knows I am one," she added low to herself as the prince threw on his cloak again.

"Come, then, let me show them that it is no longer possible to annoy or condemn the countess Varazoff. Now you may defy the world, for in my eyes you are my wife."

With a superb air of protection he laid her hand upon his arm and led her away, listening well pleased to the soft clank of the silver chain she wore.

CHAPTER III

THE FREAK OF the lovely countess was entirely forgotten next day in the excitement caused by the announcement of her approaching marriage with the prince. The fashionable world was enchanted with the romance of the match, and the promised splendors of the wedding, for the prince seemed bent on doing honor to his choice. To the surprise of those who knew her best, Irma threw herself into the affair with an interest entirely foreign to her character. An intense longing for excitement seemed to possess her, and her devotion to the new task left her no time for reflection, except at night. How those hours were spent none knew, but had any watched her narrowly they would have seen with what terrible rapidity she wasted with the devouring anxiety that mastered her.

On the night before the wedding she sent for Vane, and abruptly asked if he would do a service for which she would bless him forever. He eagerly consented, and she added, with an earnestness that haunted him long afterward:

"You are loyal and brave. I need a stanch friend, and I choose you. To-morrow the one gift I value will be the pardon of an old man. I have told you of him and of the price I pay for his liberty. I desire to be sure that I do not pay it in vain; I trust no one but you. I wish to give you the order for his release, and to know that you will see him safe with his children. Will you do this?"

"I will."

"The instant I place the order in your hands, hasten to do your work, and the hour that Count Cremlin lands in England telegraph to me. I may depend on you for speed, secrecy, and fidelity?"

"You may."

"God bless you! Think kindly of me, and when you hear of those who suffered and died for Poland, remember Irma Varazoff."

"Died! suffered! Surely you do not speak of yourself—you, a happy bride?" exclaimed Vane, seized with an ominous misgiving.

"Happy!" she echoed, in a tone of anguish, as she wrung her hands. "Hush! let me tell one living soul why I suffer, and leave one truthful tongue to defend me when I am gone."

"Gone where?"

"We go to St. Petersburgh, you know," she answered, with a shudder, as if the icy winds of the north already chilled her blood. Leaning nearer, with one hand clutching at his sleeve, and her wild eyes on the door, she whispered, "I swore never to forget my country's wrongs, but to avenge them if I could. I am very weak; but one tyrant's heart shall ache, one proud spirit be humbled, and I will free my good old benefactor before I am satisfied. Then I care little what comes. Others suffer and die for their country, I suffer and live. I am ambitious to excel other martyrs, and I shall, for Austrian prisons, Siberia, and the knout itself, are less terrible than life with this man."

"Good God! and yet you marry him?" cried Vane, fearing her mind was touched by past sorrows.

"Yes, and by that bitter sacrifice I pay the great debt of gratitude I owe Count Cremlin, and avenge, as far as I dare, the wrongs he has suffered."

"But how? You will not commit a crime like Corday or——"

"No, I shall not kill him, but I shall rob him of that which he values more than life. Ask me no more. I must be calm for the morrow. When all is over and I give you the precious paper, you shall know more. Now go, my one true friend, pray for me, and serve me faithfully."

He left her, fearing some tragedy that night, but in the morning saw her at the altar calm and fair as the marble image of a bride. The Russian chapel was a brilliant scene that day, and the splendor of the prince's hotel furnished the world with matter for a nine days' gossip. He seemed a proud and happy man, though few guessed the secret thorn that vexed his soul. No one saw the pale bride shrink as the ring went on, no one heard the stern bridegroom whisper "Mine!" as he led her away, and no one dreamed what a strange little scene took place as they stood together in the glittering saloon before a single guest arrived.

"Now the pardon," she said, abruptly, as she turned to him with haggard eyes and outstretched hand.

"You do not trust me then?" he said, echoing her words with a bitter accent, though he smiled on her like an indulgent master.

"I trust where I am trusted. See, my promise is kept; now fulfill your own," and she pointed to the ring on the hand that trembled with impatience.

"Behold it, but before I give it I deserve my reward. Embrace me, my wife."

One hand held the precious paper, the other drew her close as if bent on subduing the rebellious spirit that still unconsciously betrayed itself. One instant she wavered, and her proud eyes defied him; but it was too late for repentance, the prize was not yet won, and with a sudden effort she completed her hard task. As one soft arm encircled his neck the other secured the pardon, and with a kiss as light and cold as a snow-flake she vanished like a white wraith from the room.

Straight to Vane she hurried, for he was waiting, ready to depart when the word came, like a loyal knight as he was.

"Quick!" she cried, "to horse and away! Lose no time, for every hour is an eternity to me till I learn that the old man is safe."

"I am off, and will do your errand if it costs me my life. But you?—what is it? Your lips bleed and you pant like a hunted deer. Who has troubled you?" demanded Vane, still tortured with vague fears for her.

"It is nothing; my lips belied my heart and I struck them. Go, go!" But as she spoke she clung to him as if her last hope would vanish when he went.

Yielding to an uncontrollable impulse, he whispered passionately:

"Irma, let me stay and save you from this fate?"

"No, it is too late; it could never be; I am——" and she breathed the rest into his ear.

"But for that you would have loved me and let me comfort you? Oh, why doubt me, why fear that I should care for this, and so let me lose you?" he cried reproachfully, though his face changed as he listened.

For an instant they stood reading love and despair in each other's woeful eyes, then, as a bell rang loudly, Vane held the beloved creature close, kissed the wounded lips that did not now belie her heart, and tore himself away for ever.

Their honeymoon was waning, and the prince was beginning to believe that he had married a snow-image, not a mortal woman, when the pale statue suddenly woke and warmed. An English letter came, and as she read it the first tears her husband had ever seen her shed flowed freely, while she clasped her hands, murmuring with fervent gratitude:

"He is safe, my debt is paid, and I am free!"

"Who is this who wrings tears from the eyes of my marble princess?" asked Czertski, with a suspicious glance at the letter.

She gave it, and having read, he crushed it, saying, with a glance that would have daunted any other woman:

"You loved this man?"

"I do love him. I gave you my hand according to the bond; my heart was already his. Rest easy, I shall never see him again, and you are my master."

So quietly, so coldly she spoke, that the prince found no words to answer her, but with set teeth, clinched hands, and a face full of the pale wrath more terrible than any violent outbreak, he left her to ponder what punishment was due for such perfidy.

With strange eagerness Irma wrote and dispatched several letters, walked through the apartments that had been a splendid prison to her, and on the threshold of the last turned with a gesture of farewell. She never re-entered them, for when her husband sought her she was gone. Reproach and anger, pain and captivity were over, and he found the beautiful pale statue lying dead in her chamber with this letter in her hand:

"I have kept my promise, and by a month of bitter martyrdom earned my rest. The instant that I am assured of Count Cremlin's safety I break my chain and pass to eternal liberty. In marrying you, Alexander Czertski, I save my beloved benefactor, and return to you as much as I may of the wrong, the shame, and suffering which you dealt out to my countrymen. I am not a countess, a widow, or a gentlewoman, but the child of a serf, freed and tenderly fostered by the old man whom I have saved. To a Russian noble the disgrace of such an alliance as yours is an indelible stain, and knowing this, I married you. There is no cure for such a wound, and your proud heart will writhe under this blemish on the name and honor you hold dearer than life. It cannot be hidden, for the story, told as I alone can tell it, and bearing my name, is already sent abroad to fill the world with pity for me, contempt for you, and obloquy for both. Bequeathing this legacy to you, I escape from you for ever, knowing that I leave one true and tender friend to defend my memory and tell the tragedy of my short life."

❧ The Romance of a Bouquet

As MADEMOISELLE MELANIE'S carriage was about to roll from her door toward the theatre, a hand from without suddenly lowered the window, a bouquet fell upon her lap, and a voice whispered: "Silence *à la mort.*"

Too well accustomed to receiving homage in all manner of eccentric as well as gallant ways, the beautiful actress merely murmured a languid *"Merci,* monsieur," and glanced at the tall, darkly-bearded man in a blouse who bowed and vanished as the carriage moved.

Carelessly examining the gift by the light of the street-lamps, mademoiselle perceived that it was composed of the rarest exotics, and arranged with exquisite skill and taste. A smile touched the lips whose proud and pensive curves so many enthusiasts had admired, and the listless eyes woke with a sudden splendor, as she thrust a dimpled finger and thumb into the fragrant mass, drawing out a folded paper, closely written on two sides.

"*Ciel,* how much he has to say to me! Can he have forgiven my last rebuff, and sacrificed his pride to love? I must restrain my impatience till safely in my box; it is impossible to decipher his *billet-doux* by this fitful light."

Holding the little paper tightly in her hand, mademoiselle fell into a reverie, as she inhaled the odor of the flowers with the air of one who enjoyed such luxuries for their own sake as well as for the giver's.

"If in this note he offers me his hand, how shall I answer him?" she mused, knitting the slender black brows, so like Rachel's. "I do not love him as I might love, and if I marry him, it will be for ambition's sake alone. He is as wild and reckless as a boy, yet brave, and I know well that he can be passionate and tender. I shall have rank, splendor, and, for a time, devotion; then the illusion will fade and I shall be more sorrowfully alone than now. Once his, and I lose my charm; fickle as the wind, he will desert his wife as ready as a mistress, and I shall be forced to console myself with gayety, or do as others do, and turn to lovers for amusement."

For a moment she sat with those wonderful eyes of hers bent darkly on the tiger-skin in which her satin-shod foot lay like a snow-flake. "No!" she suddenly exclaimed, with a proud gesture of her golden-filleted head. "No, I will never stoop to that! As an actress, I have lived without a blemish on the honest name my father left me; I have resisted all temptations to barter it for love, and now I will not sell my peace and freedom for a title. As a girl, I dreamed of finding a man noble and generous, tender and true—a man who would love me faithfully, guard me gallantly, live and die for me devotedly. I have cherished the girl's dream all these years; I'll not relinquish it yet, but still wait and hope, for, brilliant as my life is, flattered, courted, and blest as I seem, my heart is hungry for a pure and loyal love."

The haughty head drooped a little, and two great tears fell upon the flowers, as Melanie, the great favorite of fickle Paris, confessed to herself the secret thorn that made her bed of roses irksome. For a year she had charmed the gay city with the rare and therefore piquant pleasure of admiring a young, lovely, talented and *virtuous* actress. The women, who feared and envied her, insisted that it was all art on her part to entrap a rich lover. The men raved about her, and laid vigorous siege to the beautiful creature, who resisted all attacks with a cool contempt that astonished the gallant gentlemen, while it increased their ardor. The gossips had lately decided that the young Comte de Grammont was to be the happy man, for he was evidently bent on winning the prize, and, it was whispered, would lay his title at the feet of the actress rather than fail.

Melanie wavered between her desire for a protector and a home, and the natural longings of a woman's heart for the genuine love which alone can make home happy or protection a blessing, not a burden. She was not spoiled yet, but stood hesitating where to choose, little dreaming that the events of that night were to decide her fate.

The moment she was safely in her box (for she was not playing that week), she glanced at the note, and turned pale, as she read:

"MADEMOISELLE—*Permit a faithful friend to warn you that Grammont is in danger of arrest for fighting a duel. It is known that he has not left Paris, and it is suspected that he lingers to meet you again. You will be watched by vigilant eyes to-night, but with your wit and courage, you can doubtless devise some way of saving your lover. A friend will be near to help and guard you at all times.* Au revoir.

L'Amour.''

"Great heavens, what is this!" cried Melanie to herself, as she shrunk behind the drapery of her box, and tried to collect her startled thoughts. "Grammont in danger—a duel! was it fought for me? 'A friend always at hand'—who is it who watches over me, who knows my lovers, and will be silent to the death? What can I do? Grammont promised to be here to-night for my last word. He will come at all hazards, for the excitement of the prank and nothing more. He may be disguised. I may not know him, and he may be arrested. *Mon Dieu,* how can I save him?"

She sat a moment with both hands over her eyes, thinking intently. She did not love the reckless young comte, but she could not let him suffer through her, and the generous heart, quick wit, and dauntless spirit of the woman were all alert to warn and save him. Suddenly she caught up the note and examined it; a tiny perfumed sheet, only one-half of which was filled. Tearing off the blank page, she wrote:

"You are in danger. Fly at once. Hope and wait.   M. S."

This she thrust deep into the heart of her bouquet, and, nerving herself to the task, she dressed her face in the enchanting smiles habitual to it, drew aside the curtain, and leaning slightly forward, scanned the crowd below. Grammont was not there, and with a gesture full of coquetry, she unfurled her fan, shading her face, as if annoyed by the lorgnettes persistently upturned the moment she appeared. Drawing a long breath, she leaned back, with her dimpled elbow resting on the velvet cushion in front of the box, and her eyes, under cover of the fan, scrutinizing each new-comer.

"This will be exciting, I fancy. Good: I begin to enjoy it, now the first start is over. When one is dying of ennui, danger becomes agreeable. Some one comes! Can it be Grammont?"

As the words left her lips a tap sounded at the door, and scarcely waiting for reply, the visitor entered. Melanie's heart sank for a moment, and her hand clutched the bouquet, for in Baron Stein she beheld Grammont's most dangerous enemy.

The baron had been one of mademoiselle's most ardent lovers, and though signally unsuccessful, still haunted her, hoping to retrieve the failure which rankled in his heart. Pride as well as passion, revenge as well as regret, possessed him, and in the danger of his happier rival he saw a weapon which he was base enough to use against the woman who had rejected him.

"What happiness to find mademoiselle alone," he exclaimed, with a satirical smile, as he seated himself opposite and surveyed her keenly.

"M. le Baron speaks with the warmth of one who has seldom enjoyed that trifling pleasure," returned Melanie, glancing over her shoulder with an air of surprise which painfully recalled to his memory the fact that she had forbidden him her house. Could he have known that she was thinking, and with secret trepidation, "He suspects, and comes to spy upon me, hoping to discover Grammont," it would have lessened the chagrin which he tried to conceal under a nonchalant air and a careless shrug.

"As mademoiselle is likely to be less occupied with others for a time, I still hope to be recalled, Mademoiselle will find me more useful, though less ornamental than Varnay, Merechall, or— Grammont."

Leaning back in his chair, Stein had spoken with a significant emphasis on certain words, keeping his eye fixed on the lovely face opposite to catch its slightest change. But Melanie was a born actress, and, once on her guard, felt herself his match. Lifting her brows with a pretty air of incredulity, she seemed to dispose of the first part of his threatening speech by a disdainful little gesture, and hoping to lead the conversation from the dangerous direction which Grammont's name seemed about to give it, she said, tranquilly:

"Who is Varnay? The name is familiar, but I forget the man. One sees so many. Recall him to my memory, and amuse me; I find the play dull tonight."

"Who does not when mademoiselle quits the stage?" returned the baron, with an ardent glance, though the satirical smile still lingered on his lips.

"My friend is dangerous to-night; he never compliments with that sneer except when he means mischief," thought Melanie. Shrugging her white shoulders with an air of ennui, she said petulantly:

"Ah! that is so old; have you no newer compliment to offer me? But who is Varnay? I desire to remember him."

"Mademoiselle has but to look below, and in the young man with the rose in his hand behold Varnay," returned the baron, coldly.

As Melanie followed the direction of his eye, her own fell on the figure of a tall, dark-haired man, who seemed leisurely looking for his seat. The moment she recognized him, with an involuntary smile the young man looked up, flushed to the fore-head, and bowed with such marked respect, that several persons turned to see who received such deferential homage. It touched and pleased her, for with a woman's quickness she felt the difference between this salute and those usually bestowed upon her. Others were graceful, gay, familiar, or formal, but in this there was such a happy blending of admiration for the famous actress, and respect for the fair woman, that her cheek flushed with gratified surprise, and her eye lingered with critical interest upon Varnay.

She had seen him often, for he never failed to appear when she played, and night after night his absorbed face met her eyes and silently paid her talent a more grateful tribute than the florid flatteries of other men. She knew his name and rank, for with feminine curiosity she had made inquiries. She had met him in the gay *salons* she frequented, and been attracted by the superior grace, refinement and conversation of the young man. He evidently adored her; yet only by the mute eloquence of his fine eyes did he betray his passion, and she was forced to believe that pride kept him silent. This very reticence charmed her by its novelty, while it piqued her by its persistency.

Vicomte Varnay's name was often on her lips, and Vicomte Varnay's face often in her thoughts. There was a romance about this dumb, reverential love, which was more dangerous than she suspected, and though she found it easier to feign forgetful-ness of the man, her heart beat freer as she saw him, for with his presence a sense of protection came to comfort her.

"So that is he? My faith! a handsome man," she said, with interest, well knowing that her praise would annoy the baron, who was aristocratically ugly.

"Handsomer than Grammont?" asked Stein, as a return shot.

Coolly surveying the young man through her glass, Melanie answered, decidedly:

"In truth I think so, for Varnay looks as if he could be earnest—Grammont never."

"Mademoiselle will soon perceive that her opinion of Grammont is a mistaken one. It is evident that she has not heard the last news of 'Robert le Diable,' as we call him."

"As it is evident that M. le Baron pines to relate some scandal, I take pity on him and give permission, sure that the story will lose none of its point and spirit in the telling."

Obeying an uncontrollable desire to know the worst, Melanie fixed her eyes full on the sardonic face opposite, and braced her nerves to bear whatever shock was in store for her.

"Mademoiselle mistakes again," said Stein, with an injured air, belied by the glitter of his steel-gray eye. "So far from pining to impart bad news to one whom I adore, it deeply afflicts me even to think of it. But rather than leave you to hear it from careless lips, I relate it, with sincerest sympathy."

"A thousand thanks! I wait the blow."

And with a mocking laugh, Melanie settled herself comfortably in her chair, with the bouquet carelessly lying in her silken lap.

"Grammont has fought a duel," abruptly began Stein, evidently expecting to startle her into the betrayal of some secret. But, thanks to the mysterious warning, she was prepared for this, and completely baffled Stein by tranquilly yawning behind her pretty hand as she replied:

"Stale news, *mon ami*. I knew that some time ago."

"But the duel only took place yesterday. Mademoiselle did not return to Paris from her week's tour till this evening, and has seen no one," exclaimed the baron, incautiously betraying his knowledge of her movements.

"True, and yet I know it. Does monsieur think he is the only person who employs spies and receives secret intelligence?" and Melanie gave him a glance which would have daunted many men, so full of contempt and malicious merriment was it.

Concealing his surprise and chagrin under his habitual sneer, he continued, with the keenest relish in the tale he told:

"Then mademoiselle knows the cause of the duel, of course. No? Is it possible! I shall hasten to inform her, though it desolates me to repeat the ungallant truth. It appears that Grammont, on being congratulated upon his approaching marriage with your adorable self, haughtily denied it, and swore that his noble name should never be disgraced by such a—pardon the horrible phrase—*mésalliance*. This occurred at a café, and high words followed, for one of the men called Grammont to account for the insult offered you. Of course the comte refused, was challenged by the fiery gentleman, and wounded him, dangerously it is said. That, however, is false, as I have cause to know." And dropping his eyes with an affectation of reserve, the baron watched covertly the effect of his words.

The indignant color had flushed to her face at first, then faded, leaving her very pale, and with a dangerous fire in her eyes, as she clinched the soft hand lying on the cushioned rail and looked down upon the flowers in her lap. She did not doubt the tale, and it both cut her to the heart and stung her pride, for she had believed Grammont's protestations, and felt sure that love would conquer pride. Now to be discarded publicly with contempt, to know that all Paris was ringing with her name, and that the man who swore to win her had risked his life rather than marry her—this roused all the woman's spirit in her, and tempted her to retaliate with a swift and sure revenge. If Grammont did venture to the theatre that night out of bravado, she would *not* warn him, but leave him to his fate. Nay, why not betray him to the enemy, who sat watching beside her? As the thought came to her, she glanced at Stein. He had raised his glass, and was intently scrutinizing a group of men in one of the stalls opposite. Her eye fell on Varnay, who sat just below, looking up with such a peculiar expression, that it arrested her. Neither love nor admiration now shone in the steady eyes fixed on her, but an intense vigilance; and as she looked on, intelligence shot into them, so expressive, so plain, that it thrilled her with the shock of a sudden intuition. Varnay sent the bouquet and note—Varnay watched over her—and even, as she eyed him, tried to warn her with a gesture and a glance. He raised the rose to his lips, and shot a rapid look at an old man who sat three seats in front of him.

Melanie's eye followed his, and with difficulty recognized Grammont, carefully disguised with gray beard and hair, glasses, and the mufflings of an apparent invalid. One angry glance was all she had time to give, for Stein put down his glass, satisfied that the comte was not in the stall. All this by-play had passed in a moment, and when the baron turned, Varnay was absorbed in the drama, Melanie sitting, with drooping face, half-hidden behind the bouquet. Before he could speak, she asked sharply, "Who fought with Grammont?"

"One of mademoiselle's most devoted lovers; pardon me if I give no name;" and Stein assumed the modest air of one who deserves but declines thanks. Leaning forward, she laid her hand on his arm, saying, with suppressed emotion in eye and voice:

"Was it you? Tell me on your honor as a gentleman. I must know, for the man that did me that grace shall have his reward."

A better man than Stein might have yielded to the temptation of a lie, with that lovely hand on his, that charming face looking into his, flushed and kindled with the passionate beauty of mingled gratitude and indignation, tenderness and pain. Seizing the hand, he kissed it eagerly, exclaiming with well-simulated rapture:

"Ah, this hand can bestow a balm to heal all wounds. Ask me nothing, but give me the reward."

What inexplicable impulse led Melanie to turn and glance at Varnay, as the baron bent to kiss her hand, she never knew; but as she did so, again the vicomte raised the rose to his lips, again he gave the warning look, and, for the first time, she observed his pallor, the negligence of his dress, and that he used his left hand, while the right was concealed in the sleeve of the loose coat he wore. Like a flash of light came the thought:

"He fought for me, he watches over me, and like a generous enemy, would save his rival through me, believing that I love him. Ah, Varnay, you are worth them all."

This discovery, false or true, inspired her with sudden calmness, courage, and a nobler purpose than the one half formed in her resentful mind.

"He sets me a fair example. I'll follow it, and show him that I can forgive the insult he so bravely tried to avenge," she said to herself; and with a change of manner which bewildered the enraptured baron, she withdrew her hand, making a noiseless gesture of applause, as she said, with a tantalizing smile:

"That was well done, *mon ami;* your vocation is the stage. I recommend you to M. Duhamel as an accomplished actor of light comedy."

Falling back with a muttered exclamation, Stein regarded her with an angry stare. But undaunted by his wrath, she added, significantly:

"Your wounds will receive no balm from my hand. I keep it all for my brave Varnay."

The expression of the baron's face as she uttered the name confirmed her conjecture and sent a glow of joy through her frame. Involuntarily she turned to thank the young vicomte with an enchanting smile, and, for the third time, saw the rose lifted, caught the meaning glance of the steadfast eyes, and remembered that Grammont was in danger. This time Stein caught the signal, and was instantly on the alert. His keen eye swept the house, dived into the recesses of opposite boxes, and flashed upon Varnay as if bent upon tearing his secret from him instantly and entirely.

"Mademoiselle found my former compliment distasteful; may I attempt to please her better by prophesying that the public will soon have an opportunity of admiring her talent in tragedy?" he said, with a dangerous glance from Varnay to the beautiful defiant face before him.

"Thanks! Your prophecy may be a true one, for hitherto the world has only seen me in the *role* of an actress. Now I am about to attempt that of a woman; and whether in comedy or tragedy, I assure you, I shall play my part *with my whole heart!*"

She had never looked so lovely as then, for the new hope, the generous purpose, the fearless spirit of the moment, lent brilliancy, grace and power to face and figure, tone and gesture. With a daring glance at Stein, a grateful one at Varnay, and a furtive flash of her scornful, yet warning eyes at Grammont, who now watched her, she dropped her bouquet, as if by accident, from the hand resting on the box front.

It struck Varnay's shoulder, glanced into the narrow aisle, and was about to be appropriated by an antiquated beau, when Varnay stepped forward, snatched it up, and passing rapidly by Grammont, uttered a word without moving his lips, and disappeared, with a bow and a gesture toward Melanie, conveying his intention to restore the bouquet.

"Mon Dieu! what will he do? All is lost if he comes hither with that note among the flowers. Stein will secure it; he sees my game, and will thwart me at all hazards—I have made a horrible mistake; Varnay is *not* in the secret, and will betray everything."

As these agitating fears swept through her mind, Melanie tried vainly to conceal her alarm, for Stein sat watching her, as a cat watches a mouse before she springs. She could not delay or warn Varnay, for it was evident that Stein would not permit her to leave the box; Grammont sat immovable, and another moment might betray him, for the baron had examined the gray-haired gentleman more than once suspiciously.

A tap at the door. Stein sprung to open it, and with a sudden motion secured the bouquet, saying blandly, while a frown gathered on his brow as he turned from one to the other:

"Thanks, Varnay; I was about to descend to secure my prize. Mademoiselle, you promised me a reward. Permit me to keep this, and I am satisfied."

Melanie had fallen back with a stifled cry as he seized the bouquet, feeling powerless to speak; Varnay regarded her with a tranquil smile, and seemed in no wise disconcerted by Stein's words or acts.

"We are ruined!" murmured Melanie, as the baron plucked out the paper with a triumphant glance at her.

"You are saved," whispered Varnay, as he drew nearer, like one obeying an irresistible attraction.

She looked bewildered, for his sang froid amazed her, till the baron's exclamation explained the mystery. Glancing at the morsel of paper, he bit his lip, and turning sharply, held it before her, demanding:

"Did you write this?"

She looked—saw only the last line of her warning, "Hope and wait. M. S.;" and knew that Varnay had torn off the rest, leaving enough to baffle Stein's malice and screen Grammont, if the baron had suspected the presence of the note. The smile she gave Varnay well repaid the quick-witted service he had rendered her, and Stein *was* mystified by the tone in which she answered, coldly:

"Yes, I wrote it."

"And dropped it for—whom?" demanded the baron.

"Vicomte Varnay. Oblige me by restoring to him the little token of my gratitude which I venture to offer."

And Melanie's blush at the mingled truth and falsehood of her speech completed Stein's defeat.

Dropping the bouquet as if it burnt him, he stepped to the door, saying, in ill-dissembled wrath:

"I leave mademoiselle to bestow her own rewards and enjoy the appointed *tête-a-tête* with M. Varnay. Believe me, it will not be a long one." And with a sinister smile he vanished, locking the door behind him, having removed the key to the outside while speaking.

"What shall we do? He is furious, and is capable of any retaliation; arrest, insult, *esclandre!* If I could only pass the door I could escape behind the scenes. Oh, help me, or I am undone!" cried Melanie, losing her self-possession at this last stroke.

"I will! Wrap yourself in your burnous, remain quiet, and you shall be free in a moment. I expected trouble, and came armed at all points, pick-locks as well as pistols. Is Grammont there?"

Speaking rapidly, Varnay stepped to the door and noiselessly did his work, while Melanie, obeying like a child, shrouded herself in her cloak and peeped from behind the curtain.

"He is gone, thank Heaven!" she whispered.

"And so are we," returned Varnay, as the door swung open.

Like a shadow Melanie glided across the lobby, through an obscure door, and threading a labyrinth of dusty passages, came out at the dimly-lighted back entrance of the theatre.

"A carriage? In one instant!"

And before she could put her wish into words, Varnay was gone. Back in a moment, he handed her in, and pausing on the step, asked wistfully, anxiously:

"Home, mademoiselle? Is it safe?"

"Where else can I go?" she cried. "My only friends are poor; I must not endanger them; my lovers vow they will die for me, but not one would risk life or limb in any real danger——-"

"You forget Henri Varnay," broke in the young man, impetuously.

"Dare you help me now? Will you defend me from Stein?" she asked, bending to search his face.

"With my life! Trust me and try me."

"I will. Come in, and while we drive, advise me."

She drew him in, and bidding the man drive toward the Champs Élysées, she said, with a vain attempt at courage:

"Why need I fly? What have I done? and how can Stein molest me? I was needlessly alarmed; let me go home—he dare not follow there."

"Mademoiselle, hear me and then decide," returned Varnay, earnestly. "Grammont has foolishly entangled himself in a court intrigue, and this duel is merely made a pretext to arrest him, for all pranks and follies are forgiven but political ones. He will escape, I hope, for I warned him. But he would see you once more, and I could only trust to the native wit and courage of the gallant comte to save him."

"You speak kindly, and yet you are—enemies." She could not say "rivals."

"Enemies, but also gentlemen, mademoiselle. We do not slander one another behind the back, though we might defy one another to the face," returned Varnay, in a tone which contrasted strongly with Stein's bitter tongue and false speeches.

"As you have done"—began Melanie with grateful emotion, but, as if anxious to shun the subject, Varnay said, as if she had not spoken:

"Under the pretense that you are in Grammont's confidence, and concerned in this intrigue, Stein will arrest you without doubt, and annoy you by every means in his power. He possesses influence, and will use it unscrupulously, hoping through terror, imprisonment and scandal, to win by force what he has failed to win by flattery."

"Yes, it is like him! I have thwarted and defied him, outwitted and openly scorned him—he will never pardon me, unless I buy peace by a sacrifice which nothing shall wring from me. I will leave Paris—but, alas, where can I go? My cousin has gone to England and my old aunt is at Lyons."

"Will mademoiselle permit me to conduct her to a shelter as safe and sacred as a convent? For a little time, if no more; a night at least?—and tomorrow she may depart to Lyons if she will."

The lights of the Place de la Concorde shone full in the carriage and fell on Varnay's face as he leaned toward her with this earnest plea. She regarded it with a searching glance; the handsome countenance was flushed and ardent, but the eyes met hers with the assurance of a truth as loyal as the love they so plainly betrayed. She could not doubt him, and with entire confidence in voice, and eye, and act, she stretched her hand to him, saying, with significant emphasis:

"Take me where you will; I trust you implicitly, remembering that you have promised *silence a la mort.*"

She felt him start as the last words left her lips, and treasured up this new discovery with the others she had made concerning him that night. A short parley with the coachman, and having given some inaudible direction, Varnay resumed his seat, and they rolled rapidly on. The rain fell heavily, a fierce wind blew in gusts, and as they left the city behind them, darkness reigned within and without. One of the long silences which often came was broken by Melanie's silvery voice, saying, in the tone of a wondering child:

"I ask myself why I trust you so entirely—I who have learned to doubt all men—and I can find no answer, unless I may believe that 'the faithful friend' who warned me of Grammont's danger is still near to guard me."

"Henri Varnay and L'Amour are the same, mademoiselle. Pardon me that I interest myself in your affairs, but I could not let you suffer any pain or loss from which I could save you. And I ventured to warn and watch."

"You thought, then, that danger to Grammont would afflict me?" she asked quickly.

"Could I think otherwise, when it is well known that you smile on him as on no other lover?"

The accent of pain in Varnay's voice touched his hearer, who smiled softly in the dark and raised the bouquet to her lips, for she still held it fast, as if to her it was a talisman. With a woman's curiosity all alive, she asked, in a sweetly persuasive tone, that would have lured a man's dearest secret out of his keeping:

"You know that he does not love me, for all Paris has learned what Stein just told me. I mean the duel which Grammont fought, because some one dared believe he would marry me. Who was the man he wounded? Do I know him?"

"No, mademoiselle."

The quiet, almost sad reply daunted her for a moment; then she leaned forward, saying, with a light touch on the wounded arm:

"If I lifted this cloak, should I not find the mark of Grammont's sword on the arm underneath?" No answer, but a rustle as if her companion shrunk a little. "Speak, I beg, I command you; let me know and thank the man who defended my name from insult," she cried with a dangerous tremor in the voice, which she tried to make imperious.

A low laugh broke from the vicomte as he replied with sudden impetuosity:

"Ah, mademoiselle, be merciful; a Varnay never lies, so permit me to be silent, and prove that the only wound I have received is from a woman's eyes;" and in the dark, two hands found and pressed her own in a strong, warm clasp, which made her heart flutter as it had never done before.

Before she could check them, the words, "I do *not* love Grammont," fell from her lips.

"Not love—and yet risk so much to save him!" cried Varnay, eagerly.

"I followed the noble example set me by one whom I must not name. I hated Grammont when Stein told me how false his vows had proved, but I desired to show my friend—I may use that name at least—that I too could forgive an enemy. I know my faults; I desire to cure them, to lead a calmer, better life; and when I believed in Grammont's love, I hoped I might know the peace of a home. That dream is gone; but I still cling to my girlish hope, and daily feel how empty my life is growing."

As she uttered this confession, half warmly, half regretfully, she felt Varnay's lips upon her hand, and Varnay's voice said hurriedly:

"I have had my reward; I pray that the hope may be fulfilled, and if I dared, I would endeavor to make life as blissful to you as this night has rendered it to me, Melanie."

Before she could answer, the carriage stopped, and leaping out, Varnay bore her in his arms up the wet steps, into a large, luxurious room; empty, but so warm and bright and still, it looked a haven of home-peace after the excitement of that stormy evening.

"Where have you brought me?" she asked, glancing about her with a half-pleased expression, that delighted Varnay.

"Home to the love and protection of my mother."

Tears shone in her brilliant eyes as Melanie looked at him doubtingly, wistfully, asking humbly:

"Will she receive an actress?"

"She will welcome the beautiful beloved woman whom her son brings as an honored guest. Here, in the shelter of her roof, I may confess the passion which has possessed me so long, but which I dared not own while I believed you loved another. I do not ask an answer now; let me earn it by longer, worthier services than those of this night. I could not leave you without showing you my heart; give me one smile before I go, and I am satisfied."

"Go! where? must you leave me?" she cried.

"I shall bring my mother to embrace you, and then hurry back to Paris, that my presence may silence the tongue of slander before Stein can set it wagging."

Melanie made no answer, but on her face there shone an eloquent smile as she looked at Varnay, for the light showed her more clearly still the lover she had found in the dark. Pale and wounded, wet and disheveled though he was, to her eyes he seemed the comeliest man she had ever seen, for suddenly she had discovered the hero of her dream, a man generous and noble, tender and true; who had loved her faithfully, guarded her gallantly, and would live and die for her devotedly, if there was any truth in the adoring eyes fixed on her, as he lingered in the presence which made his happiness. Warm and welcome, from the depths of a grateful heart, rose the thought, the resolve: "This man truly loves me, and this man I will truly love."

"What can I do or say to thank you, my faithful friend?" she faltered, ready to grant any boon in the fullness of her gratitude.

"Give me this, and let it bring me again the blessed words, 'Hope and wait.' "

He pointed to the bouquet, broken and faded, but still sweet, and to him most precious, for she had held it close through all the hurry of that hour. She looked lovingly at the frail thing which had played its part in the scenes of that eventful night, she lifted it to her lips, and turning, with a glance, a gesture, which seemed to bestow the giver with the gift, she laid the flowers in her lover's hand.

❧ A Laugh and A Look

CHAPTER I

THERE WAS MUSIC in the Park that night, and I ventured out, for my room was solitary, and my still delicate health made parties distasteful to me. The May night was lovely, with its balmy air, young moon, and the vernal freshness which wakes vague longings even in the least romantic hearts. Leaning against a tree, I listened to the music, watched the wandering groups about me, and dreamed the dreams that young men love. A sudden laugh disturbed my reverie; it was a peculiar laugh, and I involuntarily turned my head to see whose lips uttered it. Just the other side of the tree stood a tall young man, with a slender little woman leaning on his arm. They were talking earnestly, he bending down, she looking up; but I could see neither face distinctly, for the light was dim, his hat-brim hid his features, and hers were concealed by a dark vail. They stood somewhat apart from the crowd, yet evidently fancied they were enjoying the freedom from observation which such a time and place permitted.

"If my husband knew of this, he would be wild," the lady said, in a tone that contrasted strangely with her burst of merriment.

"But, my angel, he must *not* know. So far, you have played your part divinely, but you must guard your voice and eyes, else you'll betray the truth, fine actress as you are. You look at me too much, speak to me with too soft an accent, and your manner at times would inevitably proclaim our secret to the old man if he were not so unsuspicious and obtuse."

"I do my best, but when with you, I forget myself. You must remind me by a look, and show me how to deceive with an innocent face. Ah, me, what madness it all is!"

She drooped her head, and her voice became inaudible as a burst of drums and trumpets broke in on the softer melody of flutes and horns.

"You will surely meet me there in August, Mab?" were the next words that reached my eager ear.

"I will, without fail; you know my poor old dear denies me nothing, and is too busy then to leave town, so we may lay our plans in peace. No one we know will be there, and we can both enjoy our freedom and make it profitable."

"We will, and defy the world. My love, you'll not repent?" asked the man, tenderly.

"Never! with me, as with you, it is 'all for love, or the world well lost.' "

"The steamer sails in September, we must make the most of our time, for I shall be in despair to go without you," said the young man, in an entirely altered tone, when I could hear again.

"Poor Vaughn, he little dreams what's in store for him," and the musical laugh made me shudder, so full of heartless mirth did it sound.

"Privy conspiracy and rebellion suits you, Mab. You've a talent for *finesse,* that quite appalls me sometimes, sinner as I am. Don't you feel remorse when you sit on your husband's knee, and remember that we are about to destroy his peace?"

"A little, Val; but he needs change and excitement; this will give it to him, and he'll soon forget the rest. He'd forgive me the unpardonable sin if I played penitence, for in his eyes the queen can do no wrong. He loves me too much; he never should have married me; I am too young to make him really happy," and a sigh shook the gossamer vail.

"I always thought and said so, you remember, for I meant to have you myself. And so I will, in spite of heaven and earth, an old man's mortgage and a woman's fears."

The fervor of the last sentence sent an odd thrill through me, as I saw the speaker seize the little hand that lay on his arm.

"Don't be absurd, Val; remember where you are. This is no place for that sort of thing," said the lady, glancing hastily about her.

"There's a good deal of it, nevertheless; this is a capital stage for lovers to rehearse on," returned the man, nodding toward several pairs of humble sweethearts near them.

"I'm tired; take me home. It's getting late, and Vaughn will wonder where we are."

"Come and get an ice first. I want something cool, and a sight of your face to set me up for my night's work."

"I hate to think of you in that dreadful place, night after night. When will you give it up, dear Valentine?"

"In another month or two I shall be free; then hey for Paris and Queen Mab!"

The music ceased as they moved on, and in a moment the crowd broke up, streaming away in four directions toward the four great gates.

I meant to follow to see the faces of this pair, for I was in a fever of excitement, and I rushed after them, regardless of the jostlings I both received and gave.

For a time the tall figure of the man served to guide me, but in the crush at the southern gate I lost him, and after chasing several stalwart gentlemen, I hurried to the most fashionable saloon. Here I waited an hour, prowling about or lounging over a cup of coffee, and watching all new comers, till it occurred to me that this mysterious Val and Mab would not desire to be seen together, and had doubtless gone to some less frequented cafe.

Provoked at my own stupidity, I turned toward home, but feeling that I should not sleep, I stepped into the theatre, hoping to quiet myself by a wholesome laugh with the great comedian playing there.

It was a benefit night, and getting interested, I remained till the long performance was over. It was past midnight as I went toward the river, near which my lodgings
were just then, and as I turned a corner, I saw something that made me pause suddenly.

A tall man, wrapped in a curious dark cloak, stood under a lamp, apparently
examining some object in his hand. It looked like a pistol, and the air and the dress
of the man were suspicious. The place was solitary, for the streets were new, and
many of the houses unoccupied. I was still weak and very nervous, and following
an involuntary impulse, I stepped into a dark doorway, hoping he would pass me
unobservantly.

As I stood there, a carriage turned the other corner, and as if he was as anxious
to escape observation as myself, the man threw off his cloak and sprang up the steps
of the door where I was standing.

The suddenness of the meeting startled both. I uttered an exclamation; he
sprang back, and would have fallen, had I not caught his hand. In the drawing of a
breath, he was on his feet, and wrenching himself from my hold, darted away.

I stood a moment to recover myself, and was about to hurry off in an opposite
direction, when a little bright object attracted my attention. I picked it up, and stopping under the light, found it to be a tiny silver imp, curiously wrought and attached
to a broken silver chain, an inch or two long.

I was just going to pocket it, when I was horror-struck to perceive on my hand
the stain of blood. It came from no wound of my own, but evidently from the man
whose hand I had grasped. I stared at it an instant, then dashed home and into bed,
feeling as if I had committed a murder, and the police were on my track.

The imprudence and excitement of that night caused a relapse, and I was a
prisoner for several weeks. When able to care and ask for news, I learned that the
latest sensation had been the assault and robbery of a Mr. Vaughn, one of the richest
and most respected merchants in the city. He had been detained at his counting-room
late one night, and returning with a large sum of money about him, had been stabbed,
robbed, and left for dead by some unseen person.

The offender had been discovered, after much difficulty, and was awaiting his
trial, stoutly denying the act, and refusing to give up the money.

On reading the account in an old paper, the date of the outrage struck me, May
14th. That was the date of my last walk, and my encounter with the bloody-handed
man.

It interested me intensely, but finding that Mr. Vaughn was recovering, and the
offender was taken, I resolved to save myself any further excitement or fatigue, and as
my testimony was now valueless, I held my tongue. I had some curiosity to see the
culprit, for the impression I received from him in the instant we stood face to face,
was of a young and handsome man; blackbearded, pale, and remarkably tall. On
inquiring about the prisoner, however, I learned that he was a short, stout, fair man,
quite the reverse of my mysterious party. After that I let the matter drop, but often
thought of it, and often wondered if the young couple in the Park were in any way
connected with the injured Vaughn, for the two affairs were curiously connected in
my mind from that time forth.

Chapter II

EARLY IN AUGUST I went to the seashore to recruit, choosing a quiet place, once fashionable, but now deserted by all but a few faithful *habitues* who came for health, not gayety. I had lounged through one week, and was beginning to long for some object of interest, when my wish was suddenly granted.

Coming up from the beach one evening, I approached the house from the rear, thinking to shorten the way, and as I passed a room in the wing, I was arrested by the sound of a laugh. I remembered it at once, for it was too peculiar to be forgotten, and I paused with a half-uttered exclamation on my lips. The French windows were open, and a soft gust of wind swayed the muslin drapery far enough aside to show me a lovely young woman, leaning on the shoulder of a man, into whose averted face she was looking with an expression of mingled joy and anxiety. I saw no more, for the curtain fell, and I stole away, longing to hear what that fresh voice was saying.

"What new arrivals are there?" I asked of Mrs. Wayne, a motherly matron, who had expressed an interest in me, because I resembled a son of hers.

"No one but little Mrs. Vaughn and her cousin, Valentine Devon," answered Mrs. Wayne.

"Is she related to the old gentleman who was robbed and wounded last May?"

"Slightly; she is his wife."

"That young creature! why, he is old enough to be her father."

"You know them, then?"

"Not at all; I never saw Mr. Vaughn, and merely caught a glimpse of her just now. She doesn't look as if she came for her health. By Jove, it's August, and the time they planned to meet!"

My incoherent exclamation was caused by a sudden recollection of the words spoken in the Park by the unknown pair; and in a moment I was as excited as before, and actually grateful that fate had thrown them in my way again. So absorbed was I in my discovery, that I stood before Mrs. Wayne, deaf to her surprised inquiry of what I meant by that odd speech. Her curiosity was increased a moment afterward, for, as we still stood in the hall, a voice said, courteously, behind me:

"Will you allow me to pass?"

And, turning abruptly at the sound, I found myself face to face with the tall, darkly-bearded man whose bloody hand had grasped my own. I must have looked even more startled than I felt, for Mrs. Wayne exclaimed:

"Bless me, what is it?"

And the stranger half-paused in passing, as if arrested by my strange expression.

"I beg pardon; it is nothing; a momentary dizziness," I muttered, turning away, quite upset by this sudden rencontre.

There was no doubt of it, for, brief as that glimpse had been, the face I saw that night was clearly impressed upon my memory. The figure, carriage, and expression were the same; the look of wild surprise just seen was a shadow of the startled glance he gave me as he started back when I seized him.

At dinner my eye glanced down the long table and saw the pair at the end, entirely absorbed in each other.

Mrs. Vaughn was younger and lovelier even than I thought, and Devon a fine-looking fellow. No one but Mrs. Wayne knew them, and they seemed to care very little what any one thought, evidently bent on enjoying their freedom.

As we strolled about on the long piazzas, after dinner, Mrs. Wayne kept her promise and introduced me to Devon. While the two ladies chatted, we smoked and discussed meerschaums, as young men have a weakness for doing. I admired his, which was of a peculiar and foreign style, richly carved and ornamented with silver. A tiny cupid sat on the cover to the bowl, and as I examined it, he said, carelessly:

"That is not in keeping with the rest of the ornaments, which are grotesque rather than pretty, you see. Originally there was an imp there—a capital little fellow, but I lost him, and filled his place with that fat cherub."

"Something in this style, perhaps," I said, showing the silver imp that hung from my watchguard, fixing my eyes on his face as I spoke.

"By Jove! that's the image of my Puck! Where did that come from, if I may ask?" he exclaimed, with unfeigned surprise.

"I found it in the street. I dare say it is yours, and I'll return it in a week or two if you care for it," I said, coolly, dropping my guard again.

"Thank you. I do care for it, as my pet pipe is imperfect without it. But I am to sail in ten days for Europe, so if you can spare it I'll gladly replace it with any trinket you fancy," he answered, smiling, yet looking at me with an odd expression.

"You shall have it in time, I assure you," and with a glance still more peculiar than his own, I turned to talk with Mrs. Vaughn. "If this weather holds, you will have a charming voyage," I said, as Mrs. Wayne addressed herself to Devon.

"Voyage! I'm not going abroad," she answered, with well-acted surprise.

"I beg pardon. I fancied it was a party, from something I heard. Your cousin goes alone, then?"

"Alone—unless my husband is persuaded to join him. But that is not probable," and an irrepressible sigh escaped her.

"I hope he is quite recovered from the wounds he received last winter."

As I spoke I fixed my eye on Devon; he did not turn, but I saw his hand close on the meerschaum with such a sudden pressure that the amber mouthpiece snapped.

"Oh, yes; he is entirely himself again, and as devoted to business as ever," answered Mrs. Vaughn, looking from me to her cousin with evident uneasiness.

Mrs. Wayne, with a woman's quick instinct, perceived that something was amiss between us and adroitly changed the conversation. Nothing more was said, but I was satisfied that my suspicions were correct, and not wishing to rouse theirs, I never alluded to the subject, but watched them closely all that week.

They drove, walked, and were much together, and more than once I caught a look, a word, that confirmed my belief in their treachery to the good old man who trusted them.

One evening as I came up the unfrequented path from the beach, I heard Devon passionately declaring that he could not leave her, and Mabel tearfully beseeching him to remember the duty she owed her husband.

"By Jove, it's too bad!" I muttered, much excited. "She wants to do right in spite of her love for this man, and he tempts her. She needs a friend to help her, even against her will, and the struggle that is wearing upon her. Mrs. Wayne is a gossip, so it won't do to ask her advice, for the story would be all over town in a day. No; I'll write to the old man, and let him manage the affair as he likes. It's none of my business, of course, and I shall get into trouble, I dare say; but as fate has mixed me up in the matter, I'll do a man's duty to the injured old party. She don't know that Devon is the ruffian who robbed her husband, but I believe he was, for his looks, his occupation, his bloody hands, and the coincidence of time and place are all against him. I'll inform Mr. Vaughn that I have a clue to the real offender; I'll get him down here privately, and tell him all."

In a fever of virtuous indignation I hurried to my room, and feeling that no time was to be lost, wrote an urgent letter to Mr. Vaughn, begging him to come down by the late train the next night and I would meet him to impart some most important information concerning the robbery and other matters of vital interest.

After the letter was gone and my ardor had somewhat subsided, I began to doubt the wisdom of my act, and to wish it were not past recall. However, I comforted myself by thinking of the wrong and suffering I hoped to spare the old man by what might seem my officious meddling, and soon worked myself into a state of stern complacency at the important part I was playing in this little drama.

My manner must have been peculiar that evening and the next day, for even Mrs. Vaughn observed it, and usually she took no more notice of me than if I had been a child.

Devon looked worried, and both were evidently preparing to leave, though neither spoke of it.

When evening came I stole away to the station, and was rather alarmed to see Mr. Vaughn alight, followed by a person whom I knew to be a policeman without his badge.

The old gentlemen seemed rather excited, and my courage began to fail as the affair approached a climax. Telling him I wished to speak to him in private, the officer was left below, and we went quietly to my room.

There I told him all, and was much amazed at the utter incredulity of the old man. He wouldn't believe a word of it, though I repeated the scene in the Park, the midnight meeting, and showed the little ornament which Devon owned and which proved that he had been abroad that night in a strange dress and with bloody hands.

As I repeated, explained, and expostulated, Mr. Vaughn's faith began to waver. His own memory evidently brought up certain inexplicable and unusual events, words, or acts of the young pair and as he recalled them, his face darkened, his manner changed, and doubt slowly began to creep into his unsuspicious mind.

"Will you come with me and repeat this story before them? You accuse them of heinous offenses; they should have the privilege of clearing themselves. This you owe us all, for, having stirred in the affair, you must help to clear it up."

He said this after a long pause, during which he sat with his hands over his pale face, evidently suffering much in even admitting for an hour any doubt of his young wife.

His unbelief rather nettled me, and feeling sure of my facts, I consented, having a private pique against both Devon and Mrs. Vaughn for the supreme indifference with which they treated me, evidently regarding me as a boy.

I led the way to Mabel's apartments, and, finding my tap unanswered, was about to knock louder, when Mr. Vaughn abruptly opened the door and entered.

A feeling of triumph possessed me, for the scene before us confirmed a part of my charge most conclusively.

Mrs. Vaughn sat on the little balcony in the moonlight, and leaning toward her, with both her hands in his, was Devon, saying, in a low, passionate tone:

"My darling, why pause? The old man's claim can easily be set aside, nay, ought to be, for you love me, and I—"

There he stopped short, sprang to his feet, and stood looking at us in blank surprise.

Mabel hesitated an instant, as if something in our faces daunted her; then came forward with a smile, exclaiming, frankly:

"Why, Vaughn, dear, what a surprise you give me!"

"So I see, and I have still other equally unpleasant surprises for you, madame," he answered, coldly, putting out his hand as if to keep her off, as he eyed her with anger, grief and distrust in his sincere old face.

"I don't understand," she faltered, shrinking back with a bewildered air.

"I do, and fancy we have that young gentleman to thank for this unexpected visit," cried Devon, glancing at me with a significant expression.

"You are right. Speak, if you please, sir," and Mr. Vaughn drew me forward with a decided gesture.

It was a hard task, but there was no help for me, and I blundered through it as briefly as possible.

Judge of my chagrin, amazement, and wrath, when, as my tale ended, the young couple broke into a laugh, and seemed overwhelmed with amusement instead of shame.

Peal after peal rang through the room, while we stood blankly looking from each other to the merry pair, who vainly tried to speak.

As Mabel dropped exhausted into a seat, Devon wiped the tears from his eyes, and with frequent interruptions of mirth, explained the mystery, at least his part of it.

"My dear sir," he cried, ignoring me, "the night you were attacked I was at the Medical College till late, busy in the dissecting-room. You see, we are forbidden to stay after a certain hour, but sometimes, when the students have an interesting subject, they bribe the janitor not to turn off the gas at the usual time, and then stay and work as long as they like. I did it for the first time that night, and being new to the thing, was a trifle nervous when I found myself alone in the great room at midnight, with six or eight dead bodies laid out around me. I worked away till a groan startled me, and, to my horror, one of the bodies began to move under the sheet. In my alarm I cut my hand, dropped my instruments, and made for the door as a ghastly face looked at me from a distant table.

"At that moment the gas went out, and I bolted down-stairs into the street, forgetting my black linen dissecting-gown, my red hands, and the janitor, who, I afterward discovered, was in the joke, got up by some of my mates. I was half way home before I thought of my suspicious appearance; I stopped a minute in a quiet street, meaning to light my pipe and roll up my gown. Hearing some one approach, I stepped into a doorway to escape observation, and there I met that—person, whom I fancied a policeman."

With a scornful glance at me, he turned his back, and Mabel took up the tale.

"Let me explain the part of the silly mystery which most affects me. Vaughn, dear, we were getting up a little play for your birthday, and farewell party for Val—a French play, in which a young wife is tempted to leave her old husband; but she learns his worth, she truly loves him, and she cannot go. I've fancied now and then that you were a little jealous of Val, dear; that you forgot we were brought up like brother and sister and freely show our affection, never dreaming of harm. The conversation this gentleman overheard was half earnest and half quotations from the play. The scenes he has taken the trouble to watch were rehearsals which we came here to have quietly, out of your way. Oh, my dear, kind husband, don't doubt me, don't believe any slander, foolish officious boys may invent. Forgive my little secret, and take me to your heart again!"

It was impossible to doubt that truthful, earnest, loving face, and Mabel was gathered close in her husband's arms.

Devon turned and looked at me. My pitiable mortification and distress touched his heart. He came to me, and frankly offering his hand, said with a hearty laugh:

"My good fellow, I don't bear malice, though, upon my life, you'd got up a nice little tragedy for my benefit. Let me recommend you to curb your romantic tendencies, and busy yourself about something safer and more useful than your neighbors' affairs."

"Well said, Val. It's all right, young man; we'll say no more; and on the whole, I'm not sure I don't thank you for your meddling, since the half hour's heartache you've given me has cured my jealousy forever," said Mr. Vaughn, kindly, as he kissed his young wife.

"You've spoilt my little surprise, but I forgive you, and as your punishment, ask you to come and see the play, in the rehearsals of which you've taken such deep interest," added Mabel, with a half compassionate, half mirthful glance in her beautiful eyes.

I could only stammer my thanks, regrets, and apologies, and retire as speedily as possible.

"You may dismiss the officer who is waiting to take Val in charge," said Mr. Vaughn, as I bowed myself out, and with the sound of a general burst of merriment ringing in my ears, I rushed away, vowing I'd see my fellowmen to the deuce before I'd meddle in their affairs again.

❧ Fatal Follies

"Monsieur le Docteur! Monsieur le Docteur, come at once. Madame de Normande has fainted with fatigue, and we cannot restore her. *Mon Dieu!* it is fortunate that you are here, for Doctor Jumal is leagues away!" cried Madame Bentolet, the hostess of the "Petit Corporal," as she rushed into the room where I sat resting myself after a long stroll.

Throwing away my cigar I followed at once, and in the little parlor below found my new patient. A traveling-carriage stood at the door, with every sign of having been hastily deserted, and on the couch lay a very lovely woman, supported in the arms of a young man, who was hanging over her with an expression of such intense anxiety and tenderness, that I felt assured he was her lover or husband. As I advanced he looked up, showing me a singularly attractive face, full of power and passion, and a strange shadow of melancholy, which even the excitement of the moment could not banish.

The lady was pale as marble, and apparently unconscious, but the moment I examined her I perceived that her attack was not of a dangerous nature. Her hand was warm, her pulse strong, though irregular, and her lips as rosy as a child. Her heart beat rapidly, and as I bent to touch her forehead I saw her eyelids flutter as if about to unclose.

"Speak to her, monsieur; she is recovering," I said, with an odd fancy that the lady was affecting insensibility for some reason or other.

"Leonie, it is I, Louis; speak to me, I implore you," murmured the young man, kissing the pale cheek resting on his shoulder.

A faint color flushed it as if those ardent lips had warmed the snow, and a sigh escaped her, but no word.

"Rest tranquil, madame is conscious, and will soon be herself again. I find no symptoms of exhaustion or suffering."

As I uttered the words my patient opened a pair of soft violet eyes and fixed them on me with a curious expression. In them I fancied I read annoyance, surprise, and reproach; but they passed to that other face, and with a quick, wistful glance fell again, as she said, faintly, "It is nothing. Let us go on."

The instant I said, "Madame is conscious," a change passed over the young man. He started, checked some eager word already on his lips, and gently laying the fair head on the pillow, stepped a little aside, assuming a calm, cool expression, so utterly unlike his former one, that I could not restrain a glance of astonishment.

"A few moments of repose and a glass of wine, will restore madame sufficiently to continue her journey, unless she *is* suffering," I added, as a spasm of pain contracted her white forehead.

"I always suffer, and for me there is no help," she murmured bitterly.

"May I ask madame's malady?"

"My heart—a ceaseless pain there, and no rest," she answered, fixing on me eyes that darkened and dilated with something like despair.

Startled and touched by the sudden energy of her tone, the sad fact she confided to me, I took her hand, and assuming the fatherly air, which my gray hairs and her youth made permissible, I said, gently, "If my experience and skill can serve you, command them freely my child."

She glanced at the card I offered by way of introducing myself, and as she read the name, she half rose, exclaiming eagerly, "Doctor Baptiste Velsor! I have heard of you, of your skill, your success, your benevolence; I searched for you in Paris, but you were gone, and now I find you here. Surely heaven sent you to me." And, to my infinite surprise, she clung to my hand like one in sore need of help. Before I could speak, she asked, in the same eager tone, "You will serve me? I want you very much. Give me a little time at least."

"I am at madame's orders. My holiday is not yet over, and my time is my own."

"Good! Then you can come with us to the chateau, a league distant? You can give me your advice, your help, for in you I have entire confidence. My friends assure me that Doctor Velsor works miracles, and now I will prove it."

I could only smile, and bow, and turning suddenly to the silent gentleman beside me, she asked, with as peculiar a change in her manner as I had marked in his, "You will permit this, Louis? I desire it so much."

He eyed her keenly, and her color faded, leaving her as pale as when I saw her first, but her imploring glance did not fall, and she clasped her hands as if pleading for a great boon. A slight smile softened the firmly cut mouth as he turned to me, with the easy grace of one born to bestow favors, and said, cordially, "If Monsieur le Docteur will pardon us for spoiling his holiday, I shall rejoice in securing his invaluable services for madame, my wife, and Chateau Normande will be honored by so famous a guest."

"You do me too much honor; I am merely a traveler now, and scarcely in fit order to join a gay circle of summer visitors." I began apologetically, for the dress and equipage of the young pair bore the unmistakable stamp of rank and wealth.

"You will see no one; Louis and I are to be there alone—quite alone." And as she spoke an irrepressible shudder passed through Madame Normande's slender frame.

"There is something amiss here, I am interested in this peculiar couple; I am tired of aimless lounging and may do some good, therefore I'll go," I said to myself; and when the young man again urged me, I consented to accompany them at once, and pass a few days in studying the new case so unexpectedly put into my hands.

Madame sat silent behind her vail as we drove toward the chateau, but, as if my presence was a relief to him, my host seemed to shake off his melancholy and exert himself to entertain me.

It was late when we arrived, and pleading fatigue, madame left us to dine alone, begging me, however, to see her before I slept. Chateau Normande was a charming nest of beauty and luxury, a perfect honeymoon home, and old as I was, I enjoyed the romance of the place and its inhabitants. The more I saw of my host, the more interested I became in him, for to my quick eye, it was evident that there was a worm in the bud of this young man's life, prosperous as it seemed. He talked well and wittily on the various subjects that came up, and appeared to enjoy my society, though now and then I detected a slight absence of mind, caught an uneasy, wandering glance, or observed an abrupt pause, as if he listened for some expected sound. No sign of the former melancholy appeared till the conversation fell upon dreams, then I remarked, that as he questioned me or listened intently to the facts I gave him, the same gloomy shadow stole over him which had struck me at first. I tried to change the subject, but he clung to it pertinaciously, till the lateness of the hour reminded me that madame was waiting. As I spoke of this, his manner changed, and with almost startling abrupt-ness he said, arresting me as I rose to leave him, "Have you had experiences in cases of monomania?"

"Many."

"And have you been successful in curing them?"

"Very successful. I have made this a careful study, and take great interest in it."

"Grant me one moment. Have you ever had a case of a person who was pos-sessed to injure the creature most beloved?"

As he breathed the hurried question into my ear, with pale lips and a tragical glance of his fine black eyes, a sudden suspicion of his sanity flashed over me. This was the shadow on his life, this the cause of his young wife's heartache, and the shudder which passed over her as she spoke of their being alone together, and this the secret of their eagerness to secure my services. A sincere pity filled my soul, and laying my hand on his shoulder, I said, earnestly, "My friend, I am an old man, and have kept many secrets in my life. Confide in me, speak freely, and rest assured that your confidence shall be kept sacred. What afflicts you and your lovely wife? Be frank with me, and let me help you."

Tears filled those handsome eyes of his, and for a moment he seemed to struggle with some strong emotion. But second thoughts evidently counselled caution, and controlling himself, he said, gratefully, "Thanks, you are truly kind. We do need help, and I will confide to you all I dare of the sorrow which oppresses me. It wrings my heart to utter the words, but, hoping all things from your skill, I ask you to watch my wife——"

"Your wife!" I interrupted, in surprise. "Is *she* the monomaniac of whom you speak?"

"Hush! Yes, it is she," he whispered, with such an expression of deep pain, of entire conviction, that I relinquished my first suspicion at once. "Listen," he contin-ued, regarding me with the sad composure of one who has nerved himself to a hard task, for my exclamation betrayed my mistake to him, and he forgot reserve in the natural desire to clear himself from the suspicion of unsoundness. "We have been married six months, we love each other, we possess all that should make life blest, and yet we are wretched. I saw Leonie but three or four times before we were married, as the affair was arranged between our families. I was heart free, she was lovely, and I felt sure that happiness would follow our union. I was warned, but paid no heed to the warning; I married her, and my honeymoon was scarcely over when I discovered that, with all her seeming love, my wife desired to destroy me."

"Mon Dieu, how horrible! But are you sure of this? Have you proof? May it not be a mistake, a jealous delusion? My dear Monsieur Normande, what led you to cherish this awful fear?"

Drawing me to a secluded recess, where it was impossible to be overheard, the unhappy young man poured his story into my ear.

"As a physician trusted and honored by many, I confide my secret to your keeping, and as a man of honor I implore you to guard it from the world," he said; and I gave him my hand with the desired promise. "Do you believe in dreams?" was the abrupt question that followed.

"In a measure, as I have told you. But I am not superstitious."

"I am; it runs in our blood, and the dreams of our family have more than once been fatally fulfilled. The week before my wedding I had a dream so vivid that it is still before me, as distinctly as that picture on the wall. I dreamed that I stood in the great *salon* below, and saw advancing toward me the slender figure of a woman clothed in white. Her face was hidden by a vail, under which I caught the gleam of bright hair, but nothing more. In one hand she carried a little casket of ebony and silver, in the other a silver cup like one of those on the table yonder. Gliding up to me, she offered me the cup with an inviting gesture, and I drank. Instantly a horrible pain assailed me, and the figure vanished with a mocking laugh as I fell to the ground, and woke trembling with a strange terror."

"Nightmare, my friend," I began, smiling.

"Listen, there is more," he continued, in the same agitated voice, and glancing behind him with a nervous gesture. "A week after my marriage I dreamed the same dream, more vivid than before, with this difference, that as the phantom vanished it put up its hand, as if to lift the vail, and on that lovely hand I saw the likeness of the wedding ring Leonie wore. A peculiar ring, an heirloom worn by many brides of our house, and never allowed to pass from the family. Observe it when you visit her. Ah, you smile at me and think me a superstitious fool! Wait a little. I told no one of my dreams, but could not forget them, for they haunted me, and disturbed my peace. Just at that time I fancied a change in Leonie. She had begun to love me I felt sure, for I devoted my life to her, and her timidity seemed fast yielding to confidence and affection. She grew sad at times, seemed oppressed with some hidden care or grief; watched me narrowly, shunned me, received my caresses with coldness or tears, and drove me half distracted by her changeful spirits. I bore with it patiently, hoping to win her to a happier mood, but it naturally affected me, and unconsciously our peace was marred by this new and nameless trouble. No entreaties could draw from her a word regarding it, and she turned from me to the gayeties of Paris, as if striving to forget herself and me. This annoyed me, the breach widened, and I was miserable, till a new discovery completed my despair." He paused, went to the table and emptied a glass of wine, wiped his damp forehead, and returning, continued rapidly, "A third time I dreamed the dream, and this time the phantom lifted its vail, showing to me—the face of my wife! A pale, woeful face, full of anguish, remorse, and fear, yet stronger than all other expressions was one of detestation in the eyes she fixed on me, as she offered me the cup, and vanished with the same weird laugh."

"A singular coincidence I allow, but, my friend, remember she was in your thoughts, and by long brooding over this unhappy matter you had, doubtless, excited yourself more than you knew."

"As you will; hear the sequel, and then decide. A few weeks after this third dream Leonie's conduct roused my jealousy, and, fancying that a rival was the cause of her unhappiness, I resolved to learn the truth. One day when she went out alone I searched her room, and, base, dishonorable as it was, I examined her *secrétaire,* thinking letters might be found. In a secret drawer I found something which alarmed me more than any lover's *billet doux.* A little ebony and silver casket, and in it—" here he bent suddenly and breathed into my ear with a look that haunts me still, the one word—"arsenic!"

It startled me, but I concealed my alarm, and answered, gravely, "You are sure it was like the box in the dream, and that its contents *were* poison?"

"I could swear to it, for it was too peculiar to be mistaken, and the dream too deeply impressed upon my memory to be forgotten. If you doubt my word on the latter point, judge for yourself." And producing a little case from his breast, Monsieur Normande laid a few grains of white powder before me. I tested it, and at once pronounced it arsenic. With a groan he replaced the case, and added, "I had seen her turn in confusion from the *secrétaire,* when I entered suddenly one day, and more than once, as I took my favorite draught from her, I saw that her hand trembled and her eye fell before mine. This discovery suggested the dreadful suspicion that she hated me for separating her from some lover, or that she was possessed by that mysterious malady which often afflicts those who seem most blest. Her manner strengthened the latter belief, for all inquiries failed to confirm my fear of a rival. At times her eyes looked fondly on me, and she seemed longing to confess some hidden pain, or doubt, or tenderness. Then again I would surprise a look so dark, so full of reproach, suspicion and anguish, that my heart stood still within me. She evidently suffers, but suffers in silence, and her health is giving way. She has refused medical advice, but consented to come hither for country air and quiet. Her sudden interest in you, amazed me, but your well-known skill and success made me gladly accede to her wish; and now, that I have told you all, I leave the poor child in your hands. For God's sake do something to restore her, or this dreadful life will kill us both!"

As he paused, and leaned his face upon his hands in an uncontrollable paroxysm of grief, a long silence fell upon the room. I broke it by saying cheerfully, as I rose:

"Let me see madame, and hear her confession, then I can act. Believe me, I fancy it is only some womanish pique or whim, some little trouble which you have magnified, and so made yourselves miserable, as young people often do while learning to live happily together."

"But the poison," he cried with a shudder. "I have my idea about that, and will soon prove its truth. Now let me go; leave this sad tangle in my hands, and compose yourself for whatever the end may be."

He wrung my hand, and without a word led me to madame. At her door he paused, to whisper imploringly:

"Be tender with her, Doctor, remember she is so young, and has been mother-less for years."

Reassuring him by a glance, we entered, to find the young lady pacing the room with restless steps, and every sign of feverish impatience. As she paused and watched us approach, I caught, for a single instant, the expression of which her husband spoke. A keen, dark, suspicious look, that made her fair face tragical, and caused me to fear that he was right. Like a flash it vanished, and with a charming smile, she offered her hand, as she welcomed me. As I bowed over it, my eye glanced quickly at the antique ring glittering on the left hand, which played nervously with the ribbons of her *peignoir*. It was too peculiar to be forgotten when once seen, and might well impress one's imagination, even in a dream.

"A thousand pardons for detaining Dr. Velsor so long, but in listening to his interesting travels in Germany, I forgot the flight of time. Now I shall yield him entirely to you, Leonie. Good night, sleep well, *ma amie*."

As he spoke, Normande, who had resumed his cool gentleness of manner, bent, and touched her forehead with his lips, waved his hand to me, as much in warning as adieu, and left the room like one glad to escape. Without a word, madame turned, as if to resume her place in the *fauteuil* beside the fire; but the mirror showed me a face pallid with such mute suffering, that my heart ached for the poor young creature. To put her at ease, and satisfy certain doubts of my own, I talked of her health in a paternal manner, and won from her the frankest replies. She was perfectly well in body, and all her suffering was mental, as I soon satisfied myself. The instant I touched upon that point, she shrunk into herself, and regarded me with a suspicious look, and the hasty question—

"What has Louis told you?"

"Nothing, except that you suffer and will give no reason for your suffering."

"He has no suspicion of the cause then?"

"None, and it afflicts him deeply, that you withhold your confidence from one who loves you so tenderly."

"Loves!" she echoed, with a bitter smile, "yes, he is a model husband, tender, devoted, and patient as an angel. I should be a happy woman, and yet I am utterly miserable."

The words seemed to break from her against her will, for checking the tears that sprung to her eyes, she stretched her hands to me, exclaiming passionately—

"Ah, help me to understand him, to cure him, to make him happy, if that be possible. I love him ardently, and when I married him, I hoped to be all in all to him. But he soon changed, and now there is a barrier between us, that I cannot pass. You deceive yourself, he does *not* love me, he tries to do his duty, but he cannot forget some happier woman."

"I assure, madame, he adores you, and you alone. I know this, for fancying you might have cause for jealousy, with so young and handsome a man, I questioned him, and he rendered it impossible to doubt his love and truth toward you."

I spoke earnestly, feeling sure that my words would heal the breach between the fond and foolish pair; but to my bewilderment, she uttered a cry of despair, and wrung her hands, exclaiming incoherently—

"Then heaven pity me, and help poor Louis! Ah, it is horrible to have my fear confirmed by you. He loves, and yet detests me—he tries to hide the truth from me, but I know it, and my life is ruined."

"What fear, tell me, I entreat you," and I held the hands she was beating distractedly together.

"He is a monomaniac; he loves and loathes me by turns; he is tempted to destroy me, yet cannot nerve his hand to do it, or own the awful truth," she cried.

"Great heavens, what an unhappy mania for self-torture these children possess," I said to myself. "Are both mad? or which is sane! That I must discover at once, or mischief will come of this mysterious mistake."

"Madame, compose yourself, and answer me a few plain questions," I said, authoritatively. "What induces you to think your husband a monomaniac?"

She obeyed like a child, and answered with a sob.

"At first he was all a woman could ask; lover and husband in one, and I was very happy, for I soon learned to love him. Suddenly he changed, grew sad and restless, moody and gay by turns. This increased; he started in his sleep; often walked his room all night; shunned me at times, or watched me with strange scrutiny, as if he feared or suspected something. Then he would relent, be kind and devoted, but never with the former warmth and earnestness. Something burdened and afflicted him, and he would not confide in me. I thought he did not love me, and tried to leave him free from my society, but he haunted me, growing gloomier day by day. Then a dreadful fear possessed me, that he was not himself, for, at times, he frightens me by his violence. As we drove, he suddenly broke a long silence by exclaiming, with a look that made my blood cold—

" 'If it *is* true, I could find it in my heart to kill you, with my own hand!' then seeing my terror, he clasped me in his arms, crying passionately—'Leonie, Leonie, forgive me! I am not worthy of you.' "

"This was the cause of your fainting then?"

"Yes, I am not strong, and it startled me. I was myself again in a moment, but it was so sweet to be the object of his care; to feel his arms about me, his kisses on my cheek, that I feigned unconsciousness till you came. Pardon me, for I love him, and we live like strangers now."

Tears streamed through the fingers of the hands she clasped before her face, and for a moment her sobs were the only sound in the room.

"My child, take heart; your fear is groundless, I will prove this to you. But first tell me truly, do you possess a little casket of ebony and silver?"

She started, dropped her hands, and glanced askance at me, as she said slowly, reluctantly—

"Yes, why ask me that?"

"Do you keep it yonder in a secret drawer of that cabinet?" I added, pointing—

"Yes," and the word fell just audibly from lips as white as ashes now.

"And in it there is—arsenic!"

Colorless, and rigid as a statue she sat, staring at me as if I had read her heart. No answer was needed, I saw the truth in her face, and trying to remove her fear, I added, gently—

"Tell me why it is there, and for whom it is to be used. I think I know, so speak freely."

"How do you know this?" she asked in a shrill whisper.

"Your husband told me."

"Louis! impossible!"

"He was jealous, he searched and found it," I began, but starting to her feet, she cried indignantly, yet with a smile at this proof of love—

"Ah, he suspects, he spies upon me, he hunts out my secrets, and believes that I have given him a rival! I thought he was indifferent, I know him better now. Let him search again, and he will find the casket—empty."

Crossing the room, she flung open the *secrétaire;* tore out the drawer, and, with the ebony box in her hand, turned to me, saying with mingled shame and dignity—

"To you I will confess my folly first. He thought me beautiful, and when my secret trouble lessened my bloom, I feared he would find me ugly, and lose the little love he had for me. My maid told me that arsenic gave one the most dazzling complexion, and I used it. I knew it was dangerous, but for his sake, I would have ventured my life. Now you tell me that he loves me, I fling it away, I forgive him everything, and bless you for the comfort you bring me to-night."

With an impulsive gesture, she was about to throw the box into the fire, but I caught her hand, saying, as I put the dangerous toy in my pocket—

"Let me keep it, dear madame, till I can prove to your husband that he has misjudged you. Sit and listen to the truth, for his confession will complete your happiness."

Then in brief, but earnest words, I told all that Normande had confided to me. She listened breathlessly, and when I paused, exclaimed with a sigh, and a smile of mingled joy and pain—

"Ah, how we have tormented ourselves with these secret follies! My vanity and his superstition, have nearly ruined us. But the dream! that was strange. Will he forget it? will he believe my word, and love me in spite of the veiled phantom that wears my shape?"

"I shall banish these fancies by showing him a living, loving woman, who will bring him only health and happiness in her fair hand. Sleep now, my child, and wake to a new life tomorrow," I answered rising.

With the impulsive gesture of a child, she bent her graceful head and pressed a grateful kiss on my withered hand, as she murmured—

"Surely heaven sent you to me. How shall I thank you as I ought?"

Touched, yet anxious to calm her, I answered playfully:

"Sound my praises as a successful healer of heart complaints. Your cure is decidedly a miracle, madame."

She laughed a happy girlish laugh, that well became her fresh lips, and answered with a pretty blush—

"There was much truth in that seeming falsehood, for my heart *did* ache day and night, and but for you, I think it would have broken soon. You'll not tell Louis all my folly?"

"Nay, I leave that for you, well knowing that the time is near when nothing will be so easy and so sweet as the confession of lover's follies."

"Will that time ever come? It sounds too beautiful to be true," and a strangely wistful look saddened the violet eyes, as they gazed full of love and longing on the miniature of her young husband, which she drew from her bosom.

A foreboding thrill passed over me, and a sudden wish to find Normande took possession of me so strongly, that I hastily made my compliments, and left madame standing in the ruddy circle of the fire-light, smiling down on that inanimate face with a tender beauty in her own, which stamped the little picture on my memory forever.

The salon was empty, and the servant whom I summoned was sure his master had retired. Being anxious to tell my good news, I bade him lead me to M. Normande's apartment. No one answered my tap, and half opening the door, I peeped in. He was not there, but a portrait of madame in her bridal dress, caught, and allured my eye. Stepping across the room, I examined it with interest, and the happy consciousness that, thanks to my exertions, the bloom on that painted cheek would soon be out-rivalled by that upon the living one. A little table stood below the picture, holding a silver salver and cup evidently newly filled with Normande's favorite draught.

"Strange contradictions of the human heart," I mused. "He dreads poison, yet daily empties this cup which might so easily bring him death. He fears, and yet he trusts her. Ah, well, love will work a healing miracle for both."

My old eyes filled at the thought, and pulling out my handkerchief, I dried them, as I stood there, looking up at the lovely image before me. As my host was invisible, I left word with his valet that I would see him early in the morning, and departed to bed.

With the impatience of one who longs to finish a good work, I was early astir. As I went towards Normande's apartment, I met his wife in a charming costume, and with a face as fresh and fair as the roses in her hands.

She greeted me warmly, saying, with an enchanting blush and smile—

"I could wait no longer to ask Louis to forgive me, and am trying to gather courage to go in, and wake him with a wifely kiss."

"You have not seen him then?" I said, hoping that the explanation had been made.

"No, I came up last night to tell him all, soon after you left me, but he was not here, and, as I crept away, he passed me with a strange look, and locked himself in;" and she brushed away a tear that lay glittering on her cheek, like the dew upon her flowers.

"I had not seen him either, therefore he had not learned the truth. Go now and call him, dear madame, he cannot refuse to answer such a summons."

Smiling, she glided to the door and tapped. It was not fastened and swung open; she paused a moment on the threshold, then, softly calling his name, she entered. Knowing that I should be *de trop,* I turned away, but had taken only a step or two, when a cry of mortal fear and anguish rung through the house. With the speed of a young man, I dashed into the room, to find madame senseless on her husband's bosom, as he lay dead and cold upon his bed. The cup stood empty on the table, and beside it the ebony casket, half hidden by a paper bearing these words:

"Leonie, adieu; I will torment you no longer. I heard your voice last night, saying that I should be satisfied, for, when next I found the hidden casket, it should be empty. I *have* found it, for you dropped it as you stole away, before your work was done. I *am* satisfied, and knowing whose hand would have drugged my cup, I add the poison, and drink the draught, preferring death to the misery of life without your love."

As I read it, a great terror fell upon me, for it was *I* who had murdered him. I saw in a flash how the fatal box came there, and what construction he had put upon its presence. In drawing out my handkerchief, the box had fallen noiselessly on the velvet carpet, and I had not missed it. Seeing Leonie stealing away, remembering the broken words which had reached him as she raised her voice, and finding the poison in his room, the old suspicion was terribly confirmed, and in a paroxysm of despair, the unhappy young man destroyed himself, believing his wife mad or false.

I could have torn my grey hair in remorseful grief, for this tragical end to my work. If he had only seen *me,* instead of her, what a different hour that would have been! I went to carry blissful tidings, which would have brightened life, and by a most accursed chance, I left a terrible suspicion which tempted him to death!

He was past help, and all my care was needed for the poor young widow. The awful shock, the sudden fall from the highest joy to the deepest woe, killed her, and the words she uttered the night before, were a prophecy, for she did die of a broken heart. I stayed with her to the end, and when I had seen the young pair laid to their rest, I sorrowfully went my way, comforting myself with the hope that they were happily reunited in a world, where human frailties and follies could never sadden nor separate the hearts that "loved not wisely but too well."

❧ Fate in a Fan

"You have your weapon, Leontine?"

"Yes."

"Use it well to-night, for this person must be finished at once."

"You will show no mercy?"

"None! I hate him, and nothing but his ruin will satisfy me. Remember that."

"I dare not forget."

The low voices ceased, as if the speakers had passed on, and a moment afterward a young man glided noiselessly down the corridor, vanishing in a side-passage which led to the main entrance. His face wore a startled look; his keen eyes shone, and his nervous hand closed like a vice, as he muttered, grimly:

"Weapon! hate! ruin! I knew there was deviltry afloat; tonight I've found a clue, and will follow it up to the death."

A tall, strikingly handsome man, in the brilliant uniform of an Austrian officer, stood in the hall, evidently waiting for someone, as he idly pulled a rose to pieces, humming the refrain of an Italian love-song.

"You disappear and appear like a spirit. Where have you been, Rolande?" he asked, in a gay tone, as the new-comer's touch on his shoulder disturbed his reverie.

"Finding that your *tête-à-tête* with madame's pretty *soubrette* was likely to be prolonged, I strolled away and lost myself among the passages of the hotel. Must you play again tonight, Ulf?"

"I must, or else how recover my losses? I fear to think of them, and see no salvation but in some turn of luck."

The handsome face darkened for a moment, as the Austrian flung away the relics of the rose, and set his heel on them with a petulant gesture.

"This infatuation costs you dear. How will it end, my poor friend?"

"The devil, patron of gamesters, only knows. It can scarcely be worse than it is, and may be better. I cling to that hope, and play on."

"You would not listen to my warnings," began Rolande; but the other broke in:

"I hate presentiments, and would take no warning, even from you, Alcide. Let me go my own way. I cannot in honor stop now. St. Pierre must have his revenge at any cost."

"No fear of that," muttered Rolande, adding, in a lower tone: "One word, and I am dumb. If I can convince you that you have not had fair play, will you quit this dangerous place?"

The young officer opened his blue eyes wide, pulled his blonde mustache thoughtfully for a moment, and knit his brows, as if perplexed. Then his face cleared, and breaking into a boyish laugh, he clapped his friend on the shoulder, saying, blithely:

"You croaking raven! you infected me with your doubts for an instant; but I scorn to harbor them. I'll not let you play the spy for me; nor will I be convinced by any but the most honorable proofs."

"Good! I am satisfied. Come on, we are late, and the old one does not like to wait."

"Ah, you go now with alacrity, though usually I cannot get you up without much coaxing. You are a sphinx to me, Alcide."

"I'll solve my riddles for you soon. *En avant!*" cried Rolande, mounting the stairs, and leading the way to an apartment on the first floor.

If the little tableau which greeted them had been prepared, it certainly had been done with skill, and was very effective. A white-haired, soldierly old man sat in an antique chair placed beside a small green-covered table, and leaning over him, in an attitude of enchanting grace, was his daughter—a slender little creature, shrouded in black lace, with no ornament but tube roses in the bosom. Not beautiful, for the face was pale and thin, the lips almost colorless, and the figure so slight, that even the profuse falls of rich lace could not entirely conceal it. Eyes of wonderful depth and brilliancy, and luxuriant hair of the purest gold, were her only charms, except the grace which marked every gesture, and a voice of peculiar sweetness.

M. St. Pierre's patrician face reminded one of the Frenchmen of the old school—the gallant, pleasure-loving gentlemen, who flashed out their swords at the first breath of insult, who served king or mistress with equal devotion, and rode gayly to the guillotine, with a nosegay at the breast, a laugh on the lips. Whatever his vices, they were concealed under the most perfect manners; and if his life held any secret sin or shame, no trace of it ever appeared in his aristocratic old face, which seldom varied its expression of serene suavity.

As the young men approached, mademoiselle turned to meet them with a shy smile, and her father waved his hand, exclaiming, cordially:

"Ah, I have to thank you for remembering the old man, and sacrificing an hour to give him his one pleasure."

Bergamo, the Austrian, and Rolande, the Frenchman, paid their compliments in nearly the same words, and mademoiselle received them with the same courtesy, yet some indescribable shade of difference was perceptible in her manner. Bergamo kissed her hand, with undisguised devotion; Rolande merely bowed, but the kiss brought no color to her cheek, while the colder salutation made her brilliant eyes fall, the sensitive lips tremble for a second, and though she answered the Austrian's gay flattery with badinage as gay, she evidently listened intently to her countryman's chat with her father.

"Can we not tempt you, M. Rolande?" said the old man, hospitably, when at length they seated themselves about the table.

"Monsieur forgets that I know nothing of the game, and have no gold to lose."

Something in the sharp, cold tone of the young man's voice made St. Pierre cast a quick glance at him. But the dark, grave face was impenetrable, and setting down the sharpness to some natural twinge of shame, at confessing ignorance and poverty, the elder man returned to his cards, and left his guest to amuse himself as he might.

This did not appear a difficult matter, for, as if possessed by some new whim, Rolande seated himself beside mademoiselle, and began to talk. She was evidently well trained, for no sign of emotion was now visible, and the dangerous eyes met his own freely, as she conversed with skill and spirit.

Bergamo, meanwhile, played with the reckless daring of a desperate man, and, as usual, began by winning just enough to whet his appetite and lure him on to large ventures. He fixed his whole mind upon the game, and did not allow his attention to be distracted by the timely chat going on behind him. St. Pierre played with the composure of an accomplished gamester, losing tranquilly, yet expressing naive surprise at his ill luck. Once or twice he glanced at his daughter, as if Rolande's sudden interest amused him, and when the players paused a moment, at the close of the first game, he said, with a persuasive smile:

"Rolande, give us a little music, I beseech you. It disturbs no one, but refreshes all, and you, Leontine, rest, my child; you are too pale to-night."

Both obeyed; mademoiselle leaned back in her chair, and the young man seated himself at the instrument, glad of a moment to collect his thoughts. While he talked, he had watched the girl closely, but discovered nothing to aid him in his search. Now as he played, he continued to watch, yet gained little light on the puzzle which perplexed him. Leontine merely drew out her fan, and languidly observed the game, while listening to the delicious music that filled the room. She sat where she could see Bergamo's cards, yet seemed not to avail herself of the fact, though now and then she gave a smiling reply to his questions.

"Is treachery the weapon?" thought Rolande, playing softly, with his eyes in the mirror, which permitted him to see the group without turning. "No, she makes no signals; St. Pierre never looks at her, she never speaks to him. Her eyes do the mischief. Ulf grows excited now, plays carelessly, and turns often to address her. Poor lad, they will beguile him to his ruin!"

The entrance of a servant with wine and coffee brought a new suspicion to the jealous observer, for Leontine rose at once, dismissed the man, and preparing a cup with care, brought it to Bergamo, herself.

"Ah, is that it? Will she drug him slightly, and let the old villain fleece him before my eyes?" cried Rolande to himself, pausing with a discord.

The Austrian was lifting the fragrant draught to his lips, when his friend's hand arrested him.

"No, Ulf, you must drink nothing to-night; you are not well, and I am to watch over you. Pardon, mademoiselle; do not tempt him."

Rolande's tone was perfectly natural, but Bergamo caught the warning conveyed, and submitted with a good-humored laugh.

"As you will; I regret the loss of nectar brewed by such fair hands; but being under orders, I must obey."

"May he not drink wine?" asked Leontine, following Rolande as he carried the cup away.

"His physician forbids anything after dinner; he is forgetful, but I love my friend, and watch over him with *vigilance.*"

As he slightly emphasized the last word, Rolande glanced at the girl, who averted her eyes, with a peculiar smile. Bent on satisfying his suspicion, the young man added, with the cup still in his hand:

"Will mademoiselle permit me to enjoy the draught so kindly prepared for another."

She bowed carelessly, and the slender hand, that was lifting a glass, never trembled, as Rolande sipped the coffee, with his keen eyes on her face.

"Wrong again," he thought, as she went to carry the wine to her father; "perhaps I have deceived myself; and yet those words, my own forebodings, and the mystery which surrounds the St. Pierres! What weapon *could* the old man have meant?"

As he stood musing, a light object on the dark carpet at his feet caught his attention; absently taking it up, he saw that it was a white lace fan, with a pearl and golden handle, a dainty toy for a fair hand. Before he had time to examine it further, Leontine returned, and the instant she saw it, a curious expression of annoyance came into her face. A careless observer would not have seen it, but Rolande was on the watch, and caught the slight frown at once.

"Thanks, it is mine," she said, extending her hand to reclaim it.

"Pardon, permit me to admire it a moment. I have no sisters, and these coquettish trifles are charming mysteries to me," replied Rolande, with a gallant air, as he unfurled the delicate fan and moved it gently to and fro, affecting to examine it, while he covertly took note of her nervous little laugh, and the faint color which came into her pale cheeks.

His quick eye ran over the fan, hoping to find there some sign of foul play, for he had heard of the Spanish women, who enact both tragedies and comedies with the expressive by-play of their fans. No cabalistic figures anywhere appeared among the light wreaths upon the lace, no mirrors on the pearl framework, no concealed stiletto in the golden handle, to which he gave a shy twist, while praising the filigree which covered it.

"Baffled a third time," muttered Rolande to himself, when he could no longer retain the fan without rudeness, for Leontine stood silently waiting beside him. Just as her fingers closed over it, he saw something which made him regret so soon relinquishing it. As she waited, Leontine had unconsciously laid one hand on the tall coffee-urn, and had not removed it till he gave up the fan, though several of the delicate finger-tips were blistered by the hot silver.

"Nothing but some intense anxiety could have made her forgetful of pain like that. There is some secret about that toy, and I have missed it. I must get back the fan and discover it. First, let me see again how she uses it."

As those thoughts swept through his mind, St. Pierre called to his daughter:

"Leontine, a lump of sugar in my wine." Bland as the voice was, and paternal the smile which accompanied the slight request, the girl started, caught up the crystal basin and glided away, holding the fan tightly in one hand.

Rolande strolled to the window-recess and soon seemed absorbed in the evening papers. Leontine resumed her place by Bergamo, and the game went on. By furtive glances Rolande discovered three things which confirmed his suspicions that all was not right. The Austrian played badly, seeming to have lost his usual skill strangely; he grew pale and silent, his brilliant eyes looked dull and heavy, and the little that he said was neither gay nor sensible. The second discovery was that Leontine fanned herself incessantly, but seemed to take no interest in the game, though her father often addressed some tender remark to her as he played with unusual care. The third was, that the scent of tube roses filled the air, for the spring night was sultry, and a great vase of them stood near the girl.

"Is he drunk with love, overpowered with despair, or oppressed with this heavy perfume?" thought Rolande, eyeing his friend with anxiety and wonder. Rapidly he recalled all the facts concerning their acquaintance with the St. Pierres. The old man had been taken ill in the Tuileries Gardens, the friends had helped him home, seen the daughter, and called the next day to inquire for the father. Rolande had been struck with the loveliness of the girl, who naively owned that she was a stranger in Paris, and devoted herself to her invalid father, who could not bear much society. The lovely eyes, wet with tears, touched the heart of susceptible Bergamo, and finding that his society was agreeable to Monsieur St. Pierre, he fell into the way of frequenting the quiet *salon* to play with the father and admire the daughter. Rolande felt little interest in them, but for his friend's sake made inquiries about them, found that they were unknown except to a few young men, who, attracted by mademoiselle, had lost heavily at play to monsieur. Bergamo's fine fortune was already nearly squandered by the recklessly generous young man, and Rolande, whom poverty had made prudent, tried to restrain him from gambling, his besetting sin. Large sums had St. Pierre won from him, but was not yet satisfied, and the calm looker-on felt that some hidden motive increased the old man's natural rapacity. Alcide set himself to discover this motive, for in spite of St. Pierre's polished manners and perpetual benignity, the acute young man distrusted him from the first. Leontine was evidently a puppet in her father's hands; but, though she obediently smiled on Bergamo, she unconsciously betrayed that she loved his friend. Alcide saw this, and pitied her; but having no heart to give, he tried by cool indifference to quench her timid hopes.

He was roused from his reverie by an exclamation from Ulf, who struck the table with a feeble laugh as he threw down a card, saying, "Another hand like that, and I am finished!"

"You joke, *mon ami;* your princely fortune will sustain the loss of many trifling draughts like mine," replied St. Pierre, dealing with his severest smile and a transient glitter of exultation in his hard eye.

"You play badly; I fancy the odor of these flowers oppresses you; allow me to remove them, mademoiselle, for you also look as if they were too powerful for you."

Rolande placed the great rose on a distant table, and returning, leaned on his friend's chair, troubled and perplexed by the pallor of the girl's face, the strange indifference of Bergamo, and the expression of St. Pierre's inscrutable countenance. Leontine rose at once, saying, with a wan smile:

"I live on odors, but regret my forgetfulness of others;" and casting a glance at her father, she passed into an inner room. Rolande followed her, unobserved, for the old man was intent on the last hand of the game. An uncontrollable impulse led the young man to that inner room, and he lifted the curtain which separated it from the *salon* just in time to see the girl drop her fan, tear the flowers from her bosom, and lean far out at the open window, gasping for air. With a noiseless stride, Alcide clutched the fan before he spoke.

"Mademoiselle is ill; let me call her maid, or bring wine," he said, softly.

She sprang up with a startled look, saw the fan in his hand, and tried to speak, but her white lips made no sound, though her hands were outstretched imploringly.

"No, you are too much overcome; permit me to help you;" and placing her on the couch with gentle force, Rolande moved the fan over her, unmindful of the nervous grasp she laid on his arm.

"One moment; give it back for a moment, I entreat you!" she whispered, eagerly.

"Not till I discover the secret which it holds," he answered, in a low, stern tone.

With a long sigh Leontine's head fell back, and she fainted, looking like one who gave herself up for lost. Shocked, but not turned from his purpose, Alcide sprinkled water on her face, and fanned assiduously, with his eyes fixed on the fragile weapon the strange girl had evidently feared to give up. A strong perfume filled the air, yet no flowers were in the room, for Leontine had flung the tube roses from her bosom into the street—a subtle, penetrating perfume, which made the temples throb after inhaling a few breaths of it, and speedily produced a delicious drowsiness. Rolande lifted the fan to his nostrils and satisfied himself that the fragrance came from it. No aperture was visible, and, impatient at being foiled so long, he struck the handle sharply on a marble console near; the pearl under the filigree was shattered by the blow, and disclosed a slender crystal vial, with a spring stopper, which a touch on some unsuspected ornament would lift. Shutting and pocketing this tiny traitor, Rolande pried into the delicate structure of the fan, discovering that the golden sticks were hollow, and that the hateful perfume rising through them was effectually diffused with every waft of the fan. He was still examining this artful toy when Leontine recovered, saw that her secret was known, and clasping her hands, she whispered, in a tone of despair:

"I will confess all, but oh, save me from my father!"

"Your father!" ejaculated the young man, in astonishment.

"Yes, I dread him more than death. Hush, can he not hear us?" she said, trying to rise, as if to assure herself that no one was listening. Rolande stole to the entrance, peeped beyond the curtain, saw that St. Pierre was absorbed in play, and returned, saying, in a reassuring tone:

"Confide in me, my poor child; I will defend you if you give me all the truth."

"Ah, it is bitter to confess such dishonor, and to *you*," she murmured, hiding her face.

"Regard me as your friend, for I swear to you I will do my best to shield you, if I can also save Ulf," cried Rolande, sitting beside her, and gently taking her thin hand in his.

"So kind! God will reward you, and I shall not long burden any one. The poison is killing me by inches, but I dared not rebel," she answered, glancing at the broken fan with a shudder.

"Speak quickly! is it as I suspect?"

"Yes, that subtle Indian perfume intoxicates and stupefies whoever breathes it. My father learned the secret of it when a soldier in the East. He had the fan made as if for a harmless odor, and forced me to use it with that horrible stuff hidden in it. I sit by his opponents when he plays, and while they fancy it is love, or wine, or the heavily-scented flowers I wear, which excites and bewilders them, my treacherous fan dulls their senses, and my father plunders them."

The poor pale face turned scarlet with shame, as the last words left her lips, and she wrung her hands, as if a proud spirit rebelled against dishonor.

"Ah, and this, then, is the cause of Ulf's strange headaches lately, his watchfulness and alternate lethargy and excitement. Leontine, would you have killed him with this accursed spell?" demanded Rolande.

"No, oh, no! that I could never do. My father hates his family for some old slight or insult, and desires to ruin him, nothing more. It is myself whom I kill," she added, in a broken voice.

"Yourself! how? why? tell me all, I conjure, my poor girl."

"Do you think I can breathe for months, unharmed, a perfume which affects the magnificent health of your friend in a week or two? It is killing me slowly, but surely, and I dare not escape."

"Your father permits this?" cried Rolande, indignantly.

"He is proud and poor; he loves ease and pleasure; I can help to earn them for him; I obey my poor mother's last command, and cling to him through everything."

"There shall be an end to this, and St. Pierre shall restore what he has unfairly won, or be given up to the law," said Rolande, in a tone of decision, which proved to Leontine that the old man would receive no mercy at his hands. She turned her wan face toward him, saying, beseechingly:

"Let *me* suffer, for life is valueless to me, but he finds happiness in it; leave him to enjoy it and repent, if he can."

"Have you always led a life like this?" asked the young man, touched by the misery in her melancholy eyes.

"No; I remember a time when I was happy, but misfortune came, my mother died, and I had no one to cling to but my father."

"Could you not break away, and find friends elsewhere?"

"I tried that lately, but he forbid it; he was very cruel, and threatened to betray my secret," sobbed the girl.

"What secret?"

"I will never tell it!" her lips said, with a passionate resolve; but her eyes told it eloquently, as they sank before Alcide's.

His dark face softened, as he laid his hand on her bowed head, and the tenderest pity lent its music to his voice, as he said, in the friendliest tone:

"Will you put yourself under my old mother's care for a time? She will welcome and befriend you, and so will the little wife whom I am to bring home in a month."

"You are kind, but I have another friend who will take me in when my father deserts me. Think no more of me, but save Bergamo, and deal as kindly as you can with the old man. Hark! they are rising! Go at once; adieu, adieu!"

She caught his hand, kissed it with pathetic humility, and waved him from her with a gesture of farewell. He went just in time to see Ulf drop his head on the table with a groan, as St. Pierre handed him an account of the sums lately lost, saying, with an evil smile:

"It is, of course, unnecessary for me to remind my friend that debts of honor should be promptly paid."

Bergamo sprang up, haggard and desperate, exclaiming, hotly:

"Rest satisfied; you shall be paid to the last franc, though it leaves me a beggar."

"Give yourself no uneasiness, Ulf; *I* shall settle this account;" and Rolande came between them, calm and stern as fate.

"Is it permitted to inquire with what M. Rolande will discharge this trifling sum?" asked St. Pierre, as he pointed to the heavy sum total set down upon the paper, and laughed a soft, sneering laugh.

"With this!" and Alcide displayed the shattered fan.

Bergamo stared wonderingly at it, but St. Pierre's extended hand fell suddenly, and a flash of wrath glittered in his eyes. Only for a moment. He was a consummate actor, and the false smile, the bland tone, the grand air had become second nature. With a slight shrug, he said, quietly:

"Pardon, if I fail to perceive the point of the reply; a woman's bauble cannot pay a man's debts."

"A woman's bauble helped to win that money, and, being fraudulently gained, you will not receive a sou of it, but will restore that already secured, or this frail toy goes to tell its secret to the Préfet of the Police," returned Rolande, with an ominous gesture, as he showed the empty handle.

"Ah, the little traitress betrays her father to her lover, it seems! She has more courage than I thought, and will need it all. You win the game, *mon ami,* and I admire your address; but before I restore the sums you mention, I have a desire to know what is to follow that unusual proceeding?"

St. Pierre had turned white to the lips, and his eyes fell for an instant, and then he was himself again, ready for anything, and wearing the air of a man whom dishonor could not touch or danger daunt.

"For your daughter's sake, I will be silent, if you restore your ill-gotten gains and leave Paris at once. You agree to this, Ulf?" asked Rolande, trying to rouse his friend, who looked from one to the other, as if bewildered.

"Yes, anything, Alcide; I leave it all to you," he said, hastily.

"Good! Then, monsieur, you know my demand and its alternative. Allow me to quote your own words, and remind you that 'debts of honor should be promptly paid.' "

The young man's look and words stung St. Pierre like a blow; but he merely smiled the evil smile, and extended his shapely white hand with a motion which was a menace, as he said, slowly, pointing toward the inner room:

"Has my charming daughter informed her lover of one little fact which may affect his passion? Merely that her mother was not my wife?"

"That fact cannot affect me, except to increase my pity, for I am not the poor girl's lover, but affianced to another. To me the sins of her father far outweigh the misfortunes of her mother," returned Rolande, unmoved.

"I play a losing game and miss my last card; so be it, I am an old soldier. Leontine, my little darling, bring hither the roll of notes from my *secrétaire*."

As he called, in a tone of mocking tenderness, the curtains parted, and his daughter appeared, looking like a ghost risen from its grave at the summons of a master whom it dared not disobey. An awful change had passed over her since Rolande left her, for life, strength, and color seemed gone, and she moved with a feeble gait, extended hands and vacant eyes, like one groping the way through utter darkness. One pale hand held the notes, the other, the tiny vial from the fan, which had slipped, unobserved, from Alcide's pocket as he bent over her.

"Here, father, forgive me, and quit this evil life, as I do. Alcide, take back this proof of my treachery; you may need it; I have left enough."

"It is half gone, the powerful attar! what have you done, poor child?" cried Rolande, supporting her as she would have fallen at his feet.

"I drank it; one drop taken will kill quickly, and there was no other way. Forget me, and be happy with the little wife."

In the act of speaking, her lips grew still, as with one look of hopeless love the poor girl's blighted life ended, and she lay at rest on the only heart that could have redeemed for her the erring past. Bergamo covered up his face, but St. Pierre stood like a man of stone, giving no sign of grief, except the ghostly pallor of his face, and the great drops that shone upon his forehead. As Rolande reverently kissed those pale lips, and laid the lifeless figure tenderly down, the old man flung the money at his feet, and with a superb gesture of defiance and dismissal, moved them from his presence. They went without a word; but, glancing back, saw him bow his white head and gather his dead daughter in his arms, as if he clung despairingly to the frail faithful creature whom he had killed.

❧ Perilous Play

"IF SOMEONE does not propose a new and interesting amusement, I shall die of ennui!" said pretty Belle Daventry, in a tone of despair. "I have read all my books, used up all my Berlin wools, and it's too warm to go to town for more. No one can go sailing yet, as the tide is out; we are all nearly tired to death of cards, croquet, and gossip, so what shall we do to while away this endless afternoon? Dr. Meredith, I command you to invent and propose a new game in five minutes."

"To hear is to obey," replied the young man, who lay in the grass at her feet, as he submissively slapped his forehead, and fell a-thinking with all his might.

Holding up her finger to preserve silence, Belle pulled out her watch and waited with an expectant smile. The rest of the young party, who were indolently scattered about under the elms, drew nearer, and brightened visibly, for Dr. Meredith's inventive powers were well-known, and something refreshingly novel might be expected from him. One gentleman did not stir, but then he lay within earshot, and merely turned his fine eyes from the sea to the group before him. His glance rested a moment on Belle's piquant figure, for she looked very pretty with her bright hair blowing in the wind, one plump white arm extended to keep order, and one little foot, in a distracting slipper, just visible below the voluminous folds of her dress. Then the glance passed to another figure, sitting somewhat apart in a cloud of white muslin, for an airy burnoose floated from head and shoulders, showing only a singularly charming face. Pale and yet brilliant, for the Southern eyes were magnificent, the clear olive cheeks contrasted well with darkest hair; lips like a pomegranate flower, and delicate, straight brows, as mobile as the lips. A cluster of crimson flowers, half falling from the loose black braids, and a golden bracelet of Arabian coins on the slender wrist were the only ornaments she wore, and became her better than the fashionable frippery of her companions. A book lay on her lap, but her eyes, full of a passionate melancholy, were fixed on the sea, which glittered round an island green and flowery as a summer paradise. Rose St. Just was as beautiful as her Spanish mother, but had inherited the pride and reserve of her English father; and this pride was the thorn which repelled lovers from the human flower. Mark Done sighed as he looked, and as if the sigh, low as it was, roused her from her reverie, Rose flashed a quick glance at him, took up her book, and went on reading the legend of "The Lotus Eaters."

"Time is up now, Doctor," cried Belle, pocketing her watch with a flourish.

"Ready to report," answered Meredith, sitting up and producing a little box of tortoiseshell and gold.

"How mysterious! What is it? Let me see, first!" And Belle removed the cover, looking like an inquisitive child. "Only bonbons; how stupid! That won't do, sir. We don't want to be fed with sugarplums. We demand to be amused."

"Eat six of these despised bonbons, and you *will* be amused in a new, delicious, and wonderful manner," said the young doctor, laying half a dozen on a green leaf and offering them to her.

"Why, what are they?" she asked, looking at him askance.

"Hashish; did you never hear of it?"

"Oh, yes; it's that Indian stuff which brings one fantastic visions, isn't it? I've always wanted to see and taste it, and now I will," cried Belle, nibbling at one of the bean-shaped comfits with its green heart.

"I advise you not to try it. People do all sorts of queer things when they take it. I wouldn't for the world," said a prudent young lady warningly, as all examined the box and its contents.

"Six can do no harm, I give you my word. I take twenty before I can enjoy myself, and some people even more. I've tried many experiments, both on the sick and the well, and nothing ever happened amiss, though the demonstrations were immensely interesting," said Meredith, eating his sugarplums with a tranquil air, which was very convincing to others.

"How shall I feel?" asked Belle, beginning on her second comfit.

"A heavenly dreaminess comes over one, in which they move as if on air. Everything is calm and lovely to them: no pain, no care, no fear of anything, and while it lasts one feels like an angel half asleep."

"But if one takes too much, how then?" said a deep voice behind the doctor.

"Hum! Well, that's not so pleasant, unless one likes phantoms, frenzies, and a touch of nightmare, which seems to last a thousand years. Ever try it, Done?" replied Meredith, turning toward the speaker, who was now leaning on his arm and looking interested.

"Never. I'm not a good subject for experiments. Too nervous a temperament to play pranks with."

"I should say ten would be about your number. Less than that seldom affects men. Ladies go off sooner, and don't need so many. Miss St. Just, may I offer you a taste of Elysium? I owe my success to you," said the doctor, approaching her deferentially.

"To me! And how?" she asked, lifting her large eyes with a slight smile.

"I was in the depths of despair when my eye caught the title of your book, and I was saved. For I remembered that I had hashish in my pocket."

"Are you a lotus-eater?" she said, permitting him to lay the six charmed bonbons on the page.

"My faith, no! I use it for my patients. It is very efficacious in nervous disorders, and is getting to be quite a pet remedy with us."

"I do not want to forget the past, but to read the future. Will hashish help me to do that?" asked Rose with an eager look, which made the young man flush, wondering if he bore any part in her hopes of that veiled future.

"Alas, no. I wish it could, for I, too, long to know my fate," he answered, very low, as he looked into the lovely face before him.

The soft glance changed to one of cool indifference and Rose gently brushed the hashish off her book, saying, with a little gesture of dismissal, "Then I have no desire to taste Elysium."

The white morsels dropped into the grass at her feet; but Dr. Meredith let them lie, and turning sharply, went back to sun himself in Belle's smiles.

"I've eaten all mine, and so has Evelyn. Mr. Norton will see goblins, I know, for he has taken quantities. I'm glad of it, for he don't believe in it, and I want to have him convinced by making a spectacle of himself for our amusement," said Belle, in great spirits at the new plan.

"When does the trance come on?" asked Evelyn, a shy girl, already rather alarmed at what she had done.

"About three hours after you take your dose, though the time varies with different people. Your pulse will rise, heart beat quickly, eyes darken and dilate, and an uplifted sensation will pervade you generally. Then these symptoms change, and the bliss begins. I've seen people sit or lie in one position for hours, rapt in a delicious dream, and wake from it as tranquil as if they had not a nerve in their bodies."

"How charming! I'll take some every time I'm worried. Let me see. It's now four, so our trances will come about seven, and we will devote the evening to manifestations," said Belle.

"Come, Done, try it. We are all going in for the fun. Here's your dose," and Meredith tossed him a dozen bonbons, twisted up in a bit of paper.

"No, thank you; I know myself too well to risk it. If you are all going to turn hashish-eaters, you'll need someone to take care of you, so I'll keep sober," tossing the little parcel back.

It fell short, and the doctor, too lazy to pick it up, let it lie, merely saying, with a laugh, "Well, I advise any bashful man to take hashish when he wants to offer his heart to any fair lady, for it will give him the courage of a hero, the eloquence of a poet, and the ardor of an Italian. Remember that, gentlemen, and come to me when the crisis approaches."

"Does it conquer the pride, rouse the pity, and soften the hard hearts of the fair sex?" asked Done.

"I dare say now is your time to settle the fact, for here are two ladies who have imbibed, and in three hours will be in such a seraphic state of mind that 'No' will be an impossibility to them."

"Oh, mercy on us; what *have* we done? If that's the case, I shall shut myself up till my foolish fit is over. Rose, you haven't taken any; I beg you to mount guard over me, and see that I don't disgrace myself by any nonsense. Promise me you will," cried Belle, in half-real, half-feigned alarm at the consequences of her prank.

"I promise," said Rose, and floated down the green path as noiselessly as a white cloud, with a curious smile on her lips.

"Don't tell any of the rest what we have done, but after tea let us go into the grove and compare notes," said Norton, as Done strolled away to the beach, and the voices of approaching friends broke the summer quiet.

At tea, the initiated glanced covertly at one another, and saw, or fancied they saw, the effects of the hashish, in a certain suppressed excitement of manner, and unusually brilliant eyes. Belle laughed often, a silvery ringing laugh, pleasant to hear; but when complimented on her good spirits, she looked distressed, and said she could not help her merriment; Meredith was quite calm, but rather dreamy; Evelyn was pale, and her next neighbor heard her heart beat; Norton talked incessantly, but as he talked uncommonly well, no one suspected anything. Done and Miss St. Just watched the others with interest, and were very quiet, especially Rose, who scarcely spoke, but smiled her sweetest, and looked very lovely.

The moon rose early, and the experimenters slipped away to the grove, leaving the outsiders on the lawn as usual. Some bold spirit asked Rose to sing, and she at once complied, pouring out Spanish airs in a voice that melted the hearts of her audience, so full of fiery sweetness or tragic pathos was it. Done seemed quite carried away, and lay with his face in the grass, to hide the tears that would come; till, afraid of openly disgracing himself, he started up and hurried down to the little wharf, where he sat alone, listening to the music with a countenance which plainly revealed to the stars the passion which possessed him. The sound of loud laughter from the grove, followed by entire silence, caused him to wonder what demonstrations were taking place, and half resolve to go and see. But that enchanting voice held him captive, even when a boat put off mysteriously from a point nearby, and sailed away like a phantom through the twilight.

Half an hour afterward, a white figure came down the path, and Rose's voice broke in on his midsummer night's dream. The moon shone clearly now, and showed him the anxiety in her face as she said hurriedly, "Where is Belle?"

"Gone sailing, I believe."

"How could you let her go? She was not fit to take care of herself!"

"I forgot that."

"So did I, but I promised to watch over her, and I must. Which way did they go?" demanded Rose, wrapping the white mantle about her, and running her eye over the little boats moored below.

"You will follow her?"

"Yes."

"I'll be your guide then. They went toward the lighthouse; it is too far to row; I am at your service. Oh, say yes," cried Done, leaping into his own skiff and offering his hand persuasively.

She hesitated an instant and looked at him. He was always pale, and the moonlight seemed to increase this pallor, but his hat brim hid his eyes, and his voice was very quiet. A loud peal of laughter floated over the water, and as if the sound decided her, she gave him her hand and entered the boat. Done smiled triumphantly as he shook out the sail, which caught the freshening wind, and sent the boat dancing along a path of light.

How lovely it was! All the indescribable allurements of a perfect summer night surrounded them: balmy airs, enchanting moonlight, distant music, and, close at hand, the delicious atmosphere of love, which made itself felt in the eloquent silences that fell between them. Rose seemed to yield to the subtle charm, and leaned back on the cushioned seat with her beautiful head uncovered, her face full of dreamy softness, and her hands lying loosely clasped before her. She seldom spoke, showed no further anxiety for Belle, and soon seemed to forget the object of her search, so absorbed was she in some delicious thought which wrapped her in its peace.

Done sat opposite, flushed now, restless, and excited, for his eyes glittered; the hand on the rudder shook, and his voice sounded intense and passionate, even in the utterance of the simplest words. He talked continually and with unusual brilliancy, for, though a man of many accomplishments, he was too indolent or too fastidious to exert himself, except among his peers. Rose seemed to look without seeing, to listen without hearing, and though she smiled blissfully, the smiles were evidently not for him.

On they sailed, scarcely heeding the bank of black cloud piled up in the horizon, the rising wind or the silence which proved their solitude. Rose moved once or twice, and lifted her hand as if to speak, but sank back mutely, and the hand fell again as if it had not energy enough to enforce her wish. A cloud sweeping over the moon, a distant growl of thunder, and the slight gust that struck the sail seemed to rouse her. Done was singing now like one inspired, his hat at his feet, hair in disorder, and a strangely rapturous expression in his eyes, which were fixed on her. She started, shivered, and seemed to recover herself with an effort.

"Where are they?" she asked, looking vainly for the island heights and the other boat.

"They have gone to the beach, I fancy, but we will follow." As Done leaned forward to speak, she saw his face and shrank back with a sudden flush, for in it she read clearly what she had felt, yet doubted until now. He saw the telltale blush and gesture, and said impetuously, "You know it now; you cannot deceive me longer, or daunt me with your pride! Rose, I love you, and dare tell you so tonight!"

"Not now—not here—I will not listen. Turn back, and be silent, I entreat you, Mr. Done," she said hurriedly.

He laughed a defiant laugh and took her hand in his, which was burning and throbbing with the rapid heat of his pulse.

"No, I *will* have my answer here, and now, and never turn back till you give it; you have been a thorny Rose, and given me many wounds. I'll be paid for my heartache with sweet words, tender looks, and frank confessions of love, for proud as you are, you do love me, and dare not deny it."

Something in his tone terrified her; she snatched her hand away and drew beyond his reach, trying to speak calmly, and to meet coldly the ardent glances of the eyes which were strangely darkened and dilated with uncontrollable emotion.

"You forget yourself. I shall give no answer to an avowal made in such terms. Take me home instantly," she said in a tone of command.

"Confess you love me, Rose."

"Never!"

"Ah! I'll have a kinder answer, or—" Done half rose and put out his hand to grasp and draw her to him, but the cry she uttered seemed to arrest him with a sort of shock. He dropped into his seat, passed his hand over his eyes, and shivered nervously as he muttered in an altered tone, "I meant nothing; it's the moonlight; sit down, I'll control myself—upon my soul I will!"

"If you do not, I shall go overboard. Are you mad, sir?" cried Rose, trembling with indignation.

"Then I shall follow you, for I *am* mad, Rose, with love—hashish!"

His voice sank to a whisper, but the last word thrilled along her nerves, as no sound of fear had ever done before. An instant she regarded him with a look which took in every sign of unnatural excitement, then she clasped her hands with an imploring gesture, saying, in a tone of despair, "Why did I come! How will it end? Oh, Mark, take me home before it is too late!"

"Hush! Be calm; don't thwart me, or I may get wild again. My thoughts are not clear, but I understand you. There, take my knife, and if I forget myself, kill me. Don't go overboard; you are too beautiful to die, my Rose!"

He threw her the slender hunting knife he wore, looked at her a moment with a far-off look, and trimmed the sail like one moving in a dream. Rose took the weapon, wrapped her cloak closely about her, and crouching as far away as possible, kept her eye on him, with a face in which watchful terror contended with some secret trouble and bewilderment more powerful than her fear.

The boat moved round and began to beat up against wind and tide; spray flew from her bow; the sail bent and strained in the gusts that struck it with perilous fitfulness. The moon was nearly hidden by scudding clouds, and one-half the sky was black with the gathering storm. Rose looked from threatening heavens to treacherous sea, and tried to be ready for any danger, but her calm had been sadly broken, and she could not recover it. Done sat motionless, uttering no word of encouragement, though the frequent flaws almost tore the rope from his hand, and the water often dashed over him.

"Are we in any danger?" asked Rose at last, unable to bear the silence, for he looked like a ghostly helmsman seen by the fitful light, pale now, wild-eyed, and speechless.

"Yes, great danger."

"I thought you were a skillful boatman."

"I am when I am myself; now I am rapidly losing the control of my will, and the strange quiet is coming over me. If I had been alone I should have given up sooner, but for your sake I've kept on."

"Can't you work the boat?" asked Rose, terror-struck by the changed tone of his voice, the slow, uncertain movements of his hands.

"No. I see everything through a thick cloud; your voice sounds far away, and my one desire is to lay my head down and sleep."

"Let me steer—I can, I must!" she cried, springing toward him and laying her hand on the rudder.

He smiled and kissed the little hand, saying dreamily, "You could not hold it a minute; sit by me, love; let us turn the boat again, and drift away together—anywhere, anywhere out of the world."

"Oh, heaven, what will become of us!" and Rose wrung her hands in real despair. "Mr. Done—Mark—dear Mark, rouse yourself and listen to me. Turn, as you say, for it is certain death to go on so. Turn, and let us drift down to the lighthouse;

they will hear and help us. Quick, take down the sail, get out the oars, and let us try to reach there before the storm breaks."

As Rose spoke, he obeyed her like a dumb animal; love for her was stronger even than the instinct of self-preservation, and for her sake he fought against the treacherous lethargy which was swiftly overpowering him. The sail was lowered, the boat brought round, and with little help from the ill-pulled oars it drifted rapidly out to sea with the ebbing tide.

As she caught her breath after this dangerous maneuver was accomplished, Rose asked, in a quiet tone she vainly tried to render natural, "How much hashish did you take?"

"All that Meredith threw me. Too much; but I was possessed to do it, so I hid the roll and tried it," he answered, peering at her with a weird laugh.

"Let us talk; our safety lies in keeping awake, and I dare not let you sleep," continued Rose, dashing water on her own hot forehead with a sort of desperation.

"Say you love me; that would wake me from my lost sleep, I think. I have hoped and feared, waited and suffered so long. Be pitiful, and answer, Rose."

"I do; but I should not own it now."

So low was the soft reply he scarcely heard it, but he felt it and made a strong effort to break from the hateful spell that bound him. Leaning forward, he tried to read her face in a ray of moonlight breaking through the clouds; he saw a new and tender warmth in it, for all the pride was gone, and no fear marred the eloquence of those soft, Southern eyes.

"Kiss me, Rose, then I shall believe it. I feel lost in a dream, and you, so changed, so kind, may be only a fair phantom. Kiss me, love, and make it real."

As if swayed by a power more potent than her will, Rose bent to meet his lips. But the ardent pressure seemed to startle her from a momentary oblivion of everything but love. She covered up her face and sank down, as if overwhelmed with shame, sobbing through passionate tears, "Oh, what am I doing? I am mad, for I, too, have taken hashish."

What he answered she never heard, for a rattling peal of thunder drowned his voice, and then the storm broke loose. Rain fell in torrents, the wind blew fiercely, sky and sea were black as ink, and the boat tossed from wave to wave almost at their mercy. Giving herself up for lost, Rose crept to her lover's side and clung there, conscious only that they would bide together through the perils their own folly brought them. Done's excitement was quite gone now; he sat like a statue, shielding the frail creature whom he loved with a smile on his face, which looked awfully emotionless when the lightning gave her glimpses of its white immobility. Drenched, exhausted, and half senseless with danger, fear, and exposure, Rose saw at last a welcome glimmer through the gloom, and roused herself to cry for help.

"Mark, wake and help me! Shout, for God's sake—shout and call them, for we are lost if we drift by!" she cried, lifting his head from his breast, and forcing him to see the brilliant beacons streaming far across the troubled water.

He understood her, and springing up, uttered shout after shout like one demented. Fortunately, the storm had lulled a little; the lighthouse keeper heard and answered. Rose seized the helm, Done the oars, and with one frantic effort guided the boat into quieter waters, where it was met by the keeper, who towed it to the rocky nook which served as harbor.

The moment a strong, steady face met her eyes, and a gruff, cheery voice hailed her, Rose gave way, and was carried up to the house, looking more like a beautiful drowned Ophelia than a living woman.

"Here, Sally, see to the poor thing; she's had a rough time on't. I'll take care of her sweetheart—and a nice job I'll have, I reckon, for if he ain't mad or drunk, he's had a stroke of lightnin', and looks as if he wouldn't get his hearin' in a hurry," said the old man as he housed his unexpected guests and stood staring at Done, who looked about him like one dazed. "You jest turn in yonder and sleep it off, mate. We'll see to the lady, and right up your boat in the morning," the old man added.

"Be kind to Rose. I frightened her. I'll not forget you. Yes, let me sleep and get over this cursed folly as soon as possible," muttered this strange visitor.

Done threw himself down on the rough couch and tried to sleep, but every nerve was overstrained, every pulse beating like a trip-hammer, and everything about him was intensified and exaggerated with awful power. The thundershower seemed a wild hurricane, the quaint room a wilderness peopled with tormenting phantoms, and all the events of his life passed before him in an endless procession, which nearly maddened him. The old man looked weird and gigantic, his own voice sounded shrill and discordant, and the ceaseless murmur of Rose's incoherent wanderings haunted him like parts of a grotesque but dreadful dream.

All night he lay motionless, with staring eyes, feverish lips, and a mind on the rack, for the delicate machinery which had been tampered with revenged the wrong by torturing the foolish experimenter. All night Rose wept and sang, talked and cried for help in a piteous state of nervous excitement, for with her the trance came first, and the after-agitation was increased by the events of the evening. She slept at last, lulled by the old woman's motherly care, and Done was spared one tormenting fear, for he dreaded the consequences of this folly on her, more than upon himself.

As day dawned he rose, haggard and faint, and staggered out. At the door he met the keeper, who stopped him to report that the boat was in order, and a fair day coming. Seeing doubt and perplexity in the old man's eye, Done told him the truth, and added that he was going to the beach for a plunge, hoping by that simple tonic to restore his unstrung nerves.

He came back feeling like himself again, except for a dull headache, and a heavy sense of remorse weighing on his spirits, for he distinctly recollected all the events of the night. The old woman made him eat and drink, and in an hour he felt ready for the homeward trip.

Rose slept late, and when she woke soon recovered herself, for her dose had been a small one. When she had breakfasted and made a hasty toilet, she professed herself anxious to return at once. She dreaded yet longed to see Done, and when the time came armed herself with pride, feeling all a woman's shame at what had passed, and resolving to feign forgetfulness of the incidents of the previous night. Pale and cold as a statue she met him, but the moment he began to say humbly, "Forgive me, Rose," she silenced him with an imperious gesture and the command "Don't speak of it; I only remember that it was very horrible, and wish to forget it all as soon as possible."

"All, Rose?" he asked, significantly.

"Yes, *all*. No one would care to recall the follies of a hashish dream," she answered, turning hastily to hide the scarlet flush that would rise, and the eyes that would fall before his own.

"*I* never can forget, but I will be silent if you bid me."

"I do. Let us go. What will they think at the island? Mr. Done, give me your promise to tell no one, now or ever, that I tried that dangerous experiment. I will guard your secret also." She spoke eagerly and looked up imploringly.

"I promise," and he gave her his hand, holding her own with a wistful glance, till she drew it away and begged him to take her home.

Leaving hearty thanks and a generous token of their gratitude, they sailed away with a fair wind, finding in the freshness of the morning a speedy cure for tired bodies and excited minds. They said little, but it was impossible for Rose to preserve her coldness. The memory of the past night broke down her pride, and Done's tender glances touched her heart. She half hid her face behind her hand, and tried to compose herself for the scene to come, for as she approached the island, she saw Belle and her party waiting for them on the shore.

"Oh, Mr. Done, screen me from their eyes and questions as much as you can! I'm so worn out and nervous, I shall betray myself. You will help me?" And she turned to him with a confiding look, strangely at variance with her usual calm self-possession.

"I'll shield you with my life, if you will tell me why you took the hashish," he said, bent on knowing his fate.

"I hoped it would make me soft and lovable, like other women. I'm tired of being a lonely statue," she faltered, as if the truth was wrung from her by a power stronger than her will.

"And I took it to gain courage to tell my love. Rose, we have been near death together; let us share life together, and neither of us be any more lonely or afraid."

He stretched his hand to her with his heart in his face, and she gave him hers with a look of tender submission, as he said ardently, "Heaven bless hashish, if its dreams end like this!"

❧ Which Wins?

"I TELL YOU, Delmar, it will be as I say. The Viennese Thyra will marry the rich Spaniard, and the Polish Nadine will accept the charming villa at Vichy, and the two hundred thousand francs which the old marquis offers to settle upon her."

"We shall see. It is evident that they are rivals, and cordially hate one another, for it is a race between the two beauties to see which will make the best match. Thyra is the handsomest, without doubt, but Nadine is by far the most bewitching and the most dangerous. I'll wager you any amount you like that she will win."

"Done! I say the blonde Viennese will distance the brunette Pole in spite of her *finesse,* for beauty carries the day in nine cases out of ten. By the way, have you any faith in the stories which begin to be whispered about the Spaniard?"

"No. He roused the ill-will of St. Maur at play, and the latter revenges himself by hinting that the count is an adventurer. He may be, for all I know or care, but the fair Thyra had better make her game without delay if she wishes to become a countess."

"It would be friendly to give her a hint of these reports," said Albany, the young Englishman, to his friend.

"Quite unnecessary. These gay butterflies know how to take care of their own interests with a worldly wisdom which amazes me. Thyra hears all the gossip, for her dear friends would not neglect to tell her anything detrimental to her lover. Say nothing, but stand aside and watch the play; it is almost as interesting as roulette."

"If this Thyra had more life she would be altogether divine, but one cannot fall in love with a statue, however handsome. I should like to see her roused, if it were possible," said Albany, yawning.

"Wait a little, and you will have your wish, if I am not mistaken. Nadine has the temper of a little demon, and will not be outdone without a spirited battle. She will rouse your statue for you if she finds her in the way. Let us go and take an observation of the pretty creatures." And taking his friend's arm, Delmar strolled away.

The persons of whom the young men spoke were two of the fine, charming girls who had exchanged their humble homes for the position of waiters upon the guests at the great "Restauration de Dreher," at the Exposition. Three of these girls had already found, not only admirers but husbands, men of wealth and standing. The fair Hungarian had gained the heart of a gentleman from the Faubourg St. Germain, and had just started on her wedding tour. The pretty Tyrolese married an American nabob, and the stately Belgian had returned to her native city the wife of a rich merchant. But, strange as it seemed, the two loveliest of the five still remained unwon, for, spoilt by adulation, they had grown ambitious, and rejected with scorn offers which their companions accepted gratefully. The spirit of rivalry possessed them, and each was so fearful that the other would outstrip her in the race, that both hesitated long in deciding to which of their many suitors they should give the preference. The spirit which animated these charming girls was not without its effect upon their admirers, who, while they laughed at the ladies' little wiles, caprices and spites, yet watched one another sharply, and contended for the prizes more from emulation than love.

As Delmar, the Frenchman, had said, Thyra was the handsomest, being a stately blonde with magnificent hair, sleepy blue eyes, and the figure of a Juno. She was neither very witty nor wise, but her slow smile was pronounced "divine." The movements of her white arms rendered speech unnecessary, and she had sufficient sense to make the most of her charms, and hold her own against the dashing Pole.

Nadine was a brilliant brunette, with eyes like diamonds, vivid red lips, a slender figure, and a foot that won her more compliments than her witty tongue. She possessed that natural grace which is often more attractive than beauty, and a face so arch, piquant, and bewitching, that few could resist its charm. In her national costume, smiling or frowning with capricious coquetry as she tripped to and fro, affecting to be absorbed in her duties and quite unconscious of the admiring glances which followed the little scarlet boots and vivacious face under the blue and silver cap, she was one of the most striking figures in the great *café*.

As the two young men passed on, a slight female figure, wrapped in a large mantle, slipped out of the flowery recess behind them, and vanished with a stifled laugh into another path.

The *café* was comparatively quiet just then, for all the world was at the Palace of Industry, at the grand distribution of prizes by the emperor. Thyra was reposing after her fatigues, and permitting several of her admirers to amuse her, for she already assumed the airs of a *grande dame*. Not far off Nadine was tormenting the old marquis by affecting sudden coldness and disdain.

"Ah, mademoiselle, if you knew the secret I have just learned you would vouchsafe me a smile," murmured the enamored gentleman, putting down his glass with a sigh.

A careless shrug was all the reply he got for this artful remark.

"Heart of ice! She no longer cares if that big Viennese eclipses her; she yields the palm to the lazy one, and owns herself defeated. I fancied my beautiful Nadine possessed too much pride and spirit for that. Her courage made her beauty all-powerful, but, vanquished, she will no longer charm."

"Will monsieur take another bottle?" coolly inquired the girl, with a demure air, as the old gentleman made a feint of rising.

"If mademoiselle will share it with me, for truly I need some consolation," he returned, reseating himself, well pleased.

Filling a couple of glasses, Nadine fixed her brilliant eyes on him, and answered with a significant smile and a gesture full of coquetry, "I drink to the winners."

"My faith, you do not retreat, then?" cried the marquis, tossing off his champagne with enthusiasm.

"Never!" replied Nadine, clinching her rosy hand, with a flash of the black eyes, that caused the marquis to exult in the success of his words:

"See, then, my angel, the matter is easy; for, armed with my little secret, you may annoy, perhaps defeat the amiable plots of the blondine yonder."

"What is this so important a secret? Tell it, and leave me in peace!" exclaimed Nadine, petulantly.

"It has its price," began the marquis.

"*Chut!* then I will not hear it."

"Little miser! I only ask one kiss of that dimpled hand, one smile of those lips, one friendly glance from the eyes that make my day or night."

"Is it about Thyra?" asked the girl, laughing at the sentimental tone of her ancient lover.

"Yes. And she will be ready to annihilate me when she knows that I have betrayed her."

"How did you discover it?"

"By accident. I felt that she hated thee. I suspected some mystery. I watched, and a judiciously-bestowed napoleon gave me the secret in time to prevent thy downfall at the *bal-masqué,* which I hope to give thee soon."

"Tell me—tell me at once!" cried Nadine, eagerly, for his hints alarmed her.

"You agree, then, to the little bargain?"

"Yes, yes, anything; but first the secret," replied the girl, folding her arms, and placing herself beyond his reach.

"Know, then, that Thyra intends to outshine thee in a dress of great magnificence. She affects to confide in thee, to ask thy advice and admire thy taste, but it is merely to learn thy plans and blind thee to her own."

"She is not going in the costume of La Belle Hélène, then?" asked Nadine, knitting her brows with a menacing frown.

"No, she will appear as a marquise of the time of the *grande monarque.*"

"Ah, the traitress! she knows that you will wear a dress of that period, and she insults me by assuming one like it. Good! Two can play at that little game, and, thanks to you, I shall *not* be eclipsed by that false creature." And Nadine's *méchante* face brightened with malicious merriment.

"I have done well, then, and earned my reward?" murmured the marquis.

"Yes, receive it," was her smiling reply, as she surrendered her hand to him. "Hold, it is enough; tell me more, foolish man, and help me to defeat my enemy," she added, the next minute withdrawing it, red with the ardent pressure he had given it.

"Here is the name of the *modiste* who will prepare the costume; I discovered and preserved it for thee. Order what thou wilt, my little angel, in my name, and outshine this Thyra, or I never will forgive thee."

Nadine's eyes sparkled as they rested on her unconscious rival, and her quick wit suggested a way to return treachery for treachery; but she sighed a quick sigh as the marquis made his offer, for she knew what it meant. She did not love him, but his admiration exalted her in the eyes of others; his lavish gifts enhanced her beauty, his assistance would enable her to defeat Thyra's malice, his protection would lift her above want at once, and his name would ennoble her forever, *if* she could win it. He had never offered it as yet, but as she recalled the words and wager of Albany and Delmar she resolved to delay no longer, but "make her game" at once and throw out her rival's afterward. As these thoughts passed through her mind her vivacious face grew grave and pale, and another heavy sigh escaped her.

"My child, what afflicts you?" cried the marquis, alarmed at the sudden change. "Does my offer offend?"

"No, I thank you; yet I do not accept," returned Nadine, with well-feigned regret.

"And why? What means this sudden coldness? Does not Thyra receive the count's gifts freely?"

"She may, for he loves her."

"Great heavens! and do not I adore thee?"

"Not as he adores Thyra."

"Prove it!" cried the marquis, hotly.

"He gives her all she asks," began the girl, pensively.

"Will I not joyfully give thee anything in the world?"

"I think not."

"Try me!"

But Nadine turned timid all at once, dropped her eyes, blushed, and smiled as she picked his bouquet to pieces with the most captivating little air of embarrassment imaginable.

"Nadine, what will the count give Thyra that I will not give thee?" asked the marquis, tenderly.

"His hand and name," answered the girl, with her softest glance.

"Ah, the devil!" cried her lover, drawing back with a start. "Has he already done this?" he asked, anxiously, after a pause.

"Yes." And Nadine told the lie without hesitation, for on it depended her own fate.

"Then, by all the saints, I will not be outdone by him!" exclaimed the marquis, with the reckless ardor of a young man.

"Wilt thou come to Vichy as my wife, Nadine?" he said, slowly, but with the air of one who had decided.

Then, turning her lovely face, radiant with smiles, upon him, she whispered softly, as she put her hand in his caressingly: "I will make thee very happy there, Gustave."

A week later, on the morning of the day which was to end in the *bal-masqué* given by the gallant old gentlemen in honor of the fair friends, the two girls met in the room set apart for them at the *café*. Both wore an expression of repressed excitement, and both looked unusually gay and blooming. Thyra was remarkably animated, and Nadine's face shone with some secret satisfaction which she could not conceal.

"You are late, my friend," graciously observed Thyra, smoothing her blonde tresses with a plump, white hand.

"I come at my pleasure. They value me too much to complain," replied Nadine, adjusting her dress with the coquettish care of a pretty woman.

"My poor child, you presume upon your charms, but I warn you it is unwise, for these people soon tire of us, and then it fares ill with us unless we have provided for ourselves," said Thyra, in a superior tone.

"Thanks for the advice. I do not trouble myself about the future. I am as yet too young to fear neglect," replied Nadine, with significant emphasis on the word *young,* for her rival was three years her senior, a fact of which she never neglected to remind her.

"Bah! you are too vain, but I pardon it, and when I am madame la comtesse I will not forget you, little one."

Nadine laughed at the superb air of patronage assumed by her friend, and retorted, blandly, "You will then visit me at Vichy? How kind, how condescending."

"You forget that it will be impossible for one of my rank to visit you there. I say nothing of the arrangement, but it will not be *en règle* for me to visit you," said Thyra, with exasperating politeness.

Still Nadine laughed, and slowly pulled off her gloves, as she replied:

"Ah, I had forgotten that a comtesse with a newly-bought title may not, with propriety, visit the wife of a marquis allied to some of the noblest families in France."

"The wife!" echoed Thyra, with a sneer. "You flatter yourself, then, that this old man will marry you? What folly."

"It may be folly to mate my youth with his age, but he is fond and generous, and will soon leave me free to enjoy all that he so gladly lavishes upon me."

"A hundred thousand francs, and dishonor. *Mon Dieu,* I do not envy you," cried Thyra, scornfully.

"He will leave me his whole fortune, his rank and his name; I ask no more."

Thyra laughed shrilly, for something in her rival's imperturbable air annoyed her more than her words.

"When I see proofs of the truth of this absurd story, I will believe it."

"See and believe, then," and Nadine lifted her newly-ungloved left hand with a gesture of triumph, for on the third slender finger shone a wedding ring, guarded by a magnificent diamond *solitaire.*

"Married!" cried Thyra, turning pale with envy and chagrin.

"Married, mademoiselle; but I do not ask your compliments yet, for the fact is not to be made known till this evening. It was my whim to serve here one day longer, a marquise in disguise, and Gustave permits me to have my own way in all things."

There was both gall and wormwood in this speech, for it reminded the hearer that her mock marquise would be entirely eclipsed by the real one, and that her count would *not* permit her to have her own way if she married him, as he was both jealous and tyrannical. For a moment she was speechless with anger and mortification, but she recovered herself with an effort, and forcing a smile, swept a stately curtsey, and saying in a tone of ironical deference:

"I congratulate you, madame, upon your success, and wish you a speedy release from monsieur le marquis."

"Thanks, mademoiselle; I heartily return the compliment, for if you *should* marry the count, I fear you will never live to enjoy your freedom after his death. *Au revoir,* then; we shall meet this evening. I trust your costume is prepared?"

"Quite; and yours?"

"It is ready," and Nadine tripped away with a wicked smile on her lips, leaving her rival to console herself with thoughts of the evening triumph she hoped to win.

So anxious was Thyra to vent her pique, that she arrived at the hotel of the marquis before Nadine, thus losing the satisfaction of making her *entrée* in the presence of her rival. Her costume was charming, for the antique blue and silver brocade set off her fine figure, and the powder in her hair enhanced the bloom of her dazzling complexion. Compliments were profuse, and her spirits rose, for the count was more devoted than ever, and nearer to uttering the long-desired words, she thought.

Just when every one was wondering at her absence, Nadine appeared, and one glance at her assured Thyra that her own reign was over, for the tables had been turned with a vengeance. Nadine wore the costume of a Spanish lady of rank, and wore it with a grace which made it doubly effective. Composed of scarlet, black and gold, the costume was wonderfully becoming, for the rich lace mantilla draped, without concealing, the little figure and lovely face; the little feet were ravishing in slippers which few beside a true Spaniard could have worn, and diamonds as brilliant as her eyes flashed in her dark hair, and shone on wrist and bosom, convincing Thyra beyond a doubt that the infatuated marquis *had* given her a right to his name and fortune. But as the charming Spaniard passed with graceful bows, witty words, and laughing repartees, a general smile appeared on the admiring faces of her friends, for the audacious creature had dressed the little mulatto girl who bore her train, in the same blue and silver brocade, upon which Thyra so prided herself. The point of the joke flashed upon the company at a glance, and they enjoyed it with the zest of Frenchmen.

All eyes followed the rival queens as they met, and all ears were alert to catch the first words which should open the battle. A sudden flush had burned deep on Thyra's fair face, as she saw and understood the insult which Nadine had devised with feminine skill, in return for her own false dealing. But for pride, she could have burst into wrathful tears or vehement reproaches, so intense was her indignation and disgust. The thought of her rival's gratification, in such an open confession of defeat, conquered the first impulse, and gave her courage to control her voice, face, and manner, as the beautiful Spaniard paused before her, saying with a smile that exasperated her almost past endurance:

"Good evening, mademoiselle; you too have changed your mind, regarding your costume. Such caprices are natural, and you are charming in anything. Had I known your plan I could have lent you a magnificent suit, which Gustave's ancestress, a veritable marquise, once wore."

"You are truly amiable, but I am well pleased with the silk which her majesty has approved. Are the pelters the lighter for being made of diamonds," replied Thyra, roused to an unusual degree by the imminence of her peril.

"Infinitely lighter, *ma amie;* the count finds them so attractive on another that he *may* be persuaded to offer similar ones for your acceptance."

The last words were spoken in German, which language the count did not understand. He had followed Nadine with admiring eyes from the moment she entered, and had just offered his arm with a flowery compliment to his "fair country-woman." Thyra set her teeth as Nadine accepted the honor before her face and sailed away, using her fine eyes and glittering face with the grace and effect of a born Spaniard, while the bedizened little mulatto smirked behind her, taking an elfish delight in her own temporary importance, and the success of the plot.

"Behold your wish accomplished; the statue is awake, and the little demon has roused her as I foretold," whispered Delmar to Albany, as he nodded toward the deserted one, to whom excitement had given the only charm her beauty lacked.

"She is magnificent. Go and comfort her till I send the count to complete the cure. He cannot fail to surrender if he sees her now. I began to tremble for my money five minutes ago, but I am sure Thyra will win in spite of Nadine's bold stroke."

The good-natured Englishman executed his manoeuvre successfully, and devoted himself to Nadine, while the count returned to his allegiance, and soon verified Albany's prediction, by surrendering heart, hand, and fortune to the animated statue.

It was a gay and brilliant little ball, such as the pleasure-loving old marquis well knew how to give, and all went smoothly till after supper. Nadine was standing near her husband when a servant handed her a note. Unaccustomed to the etiquette of her new station, she opened and read it without apology. A strange expression passed over her face as the few words it contained met her eyes, and for a moment she seemed about to tear it up. At that instant Albany's laugh reached her, reminded her of the wager, and banished her hesitation like a spell. Turning to the marquis, she showed the note, whispering in a commanding tone, yet with a caressing touch on his arm:

"It is true, but I am to manage the affair, so be silent, my brave old lion, for I will not have you endanger yourself by exciting his anger."

Appeased by the compliment, the marquis submitted, though he assumed his haughtiest mien as the count was seen approaching, with Thyra on his arm, looking more beautiful than ever.

"Good! He has spoken at last, and she is coming to tell me. I know it by the proud air she assumes. Poor thing, I pity her, but my rank demands that I should resent the insult of this man's presence. Restrain yourself, Gustave, a word will finish the affair."

As she spoke of her rank, Nadine laughed so blithely that those near turned to see the cause of her merriment, and both Thyra and the count smiled involuntarily as they paused before her.

"Thanks for the good omen you give us, madame, for we come to ask your congratulations on a union which we trust may prove as happy as your own," began the count, with a courtly air which set somewhat awkwardly upon him.

In an instant such a sudden change came over Nadine that it startled the observers. The brilliant, mobile face seemed to freeze into a mask, expressive of nothing but the most withering contempt; the smile vanished, the dark brows lowered, the lips curled, and the pose of the whole figure added significance to the haughty gesture with which she drew her trailing laces about her, as if there was contamination in the touch of those who stood before her. Entirely ignoring the count, she fixed her eyes on Thyra with a look which chilled her heart, and said, slowly but distinctly:

"Mademoiselle, you told me this morning that your rank would forbid your visiting me at Vichy; permit me to tell you that *my* rank will render it impossible for me to receive you there, or elsewhere."

"I do not comprehend you, madame," stammered Thyra, feeling that some heavier stroke than any she had yet received was in store for her.

"This note, from one in authority, will convince you that the Marquise de la Faille cannot associate with the *fiancée* of a—convict."

As the last word dropped from the girl's lips, the count wheeled sharply round on the marquis, saying between his teeth:

"Monsieur, I look to you to answer this insult."

"Pardon, I can only fight with gentlemen," replied the old man, with all the tranquil hauteur of a patrician.

Pale to the lips with passion the count lifted his hand to strike, but before the blow could fall, Thyra caught his arm and confronted him with a face of such despair that shame quenched wrath and a guilty fear banished the courage of desperation.

"Is it true?" she said, in a tone that pierced all hearts, as she held the note before him, demanding a reply by the eloquence of her eager eyes and grief-stricken mien.

"It is a lie, and I will prove it so!" he answered, defiantly, but as the words passed his lips, his bold eyes fell before her own, a traitorous flush dyed his swarthy cheek, and an involuntary gesture of the left shoulder betrayed that he had felt the fiery torture of the convict's brand.

With a superb gesture of disdain Thyra pointed to the door, uttering the one word "Go!" with a tragic force that would have made her fortune on the stage; and, as if overwhelmed by her scorn, the *ci-devant* count rushed from the room in guilty silence. For an instant no one spoke; then, turning to Nadine, Thyra added, in a tone full of ominous suggestion:

"For this last kindness rest assured, madame, I shall not long remain your debtor. Since I have ceased to be worthy of the honor of your friendship I will at once relieve you of my presence." And with a grand obeisance, full of mock deference, the vanquished queen sailed royally away, leaving the victor but half satisfied at her success.

While waiting for a servant to call her carriage, Thyra paced to and fro along the balcony on which the anteroom opened, trying to assuage the bitterness of her emotions. This balcony ran round the entire wing of the hotel, and, led by an uncontrollable impulse to learn the sentiments of those whom she had quitted, Thyra glided from one open window to another, hearing and seeing enough to nearly madden her. Some laughed and jested at her disappointment, a few pitied, and many condemned her; but nearly all applauded Nadine's success, and admired the skill and courage with which she had won the marquis and defeated the count. Coming at length to a window half-shrouded in flowers, Thyra saw her rival gayly talking with Albany and Delmar. To the wild eyes steadily watching her she had never looked so lovely, and as she listened to the words that followed, Thyra muttered, fiercely:

"I could kill her!"

"But how, in heaven's name, did you discover the man's secret?" asked Albany, rather brusquely, for he had lost his wager.

"I have to thank you, monsieur, for the hint that set me on the trail," replied Nadine, smiling as she glanced up at him with eyes full of merry malice.

"Me! I never spoke to you of my suspicions, or the rumors afloat!" he ejaculated, in surprise.

"The next time you exchange confidences with your friends, choose a safer place than the myrtle alley, near the 'Restauration de Dreher,' " laughed Nadine, with a significance which enlightened both hearers.

"Then you learned our wager and set yourself to win for me? Ah, madame, I am your devoted slave forever, for you have done me a service and proved that I was right in believing that you would outshine and outmanoeuvre this leaden-witted Thyra."

And, as he spoke, Delmar gallantly kissed the pretty hand that wielded the fan.

At that moment a temptation came to the poor girl listening there alone in the dark, and she yielded to it, for this cruel rival had shown her no mercy. One end of Nadine's mantilla had blown out among the leaves that rustled in the wind; some peeping servant had left a half-smoked cigarette on the balcony, and as her eye went from the fiery spark at her feet to the shred of lace that seemed to flutter tauntingly as it unveiled the round arm lying on the cushions just within, Thyra saw a way to avenge her wrongs, and prove herself the victor in spite of all that had passed. It was the work of an instant to lift the smoldering spark and lay it on the filmy fabric, to watch the breeze fan it to a little flame, and the flame steal on unobserved till the mantilla suddenly blazed up like an awful glory about the fair head of its wearer.

A cry of terror, the sudden flight of a burning figure down the long *salon,* an imploring "Gustave! save me, save me!" a rush of many feet, and then a half-senseless creature lying on the breast of the marquis, who had crushed out the fire in his arms.

"Disfigured for life! disfigured for life!" moaned the poor girl, remembering, even in her torture, the deep scars which would mar forever the beauty of the bosom, arms, and face, which a moment ago had been so fair.

"Yes! now love, rank, success, and youth are all poisoned for you, madame la marquise. Now the diamond fetters will grow heavy while you wear them, and liberty possess no charm when they fall off. *I* preserve my beauty and my freedom still, and it is *I* who win at last!"

The exulting voice rose from the darkness without as a beautiful, desperate face flashed before their startled eyes for a second, and then vanished, never to be seen by them again.

🐦 Honor's Fortune

CHAPTER I

SHE STOOD THERE alone, face to face with a great temptation, for she held her fate in her hand. Few girls of seventeen would pause long in deciding between sunshine and shadow. As her eye glanced over the ardent letter of her boy-lover, she contrasted the life that would be hers if she fled with him, and the life she must continue to lead if she refused. On one side, love, wealth, pleasure, freedom; on the other, neglect, poverty, distasteful labor, and the bitterest dependence.

She did not truly love young St. John, but his devotion touched and charmed her; her heart was free, and she believed she could easily learn to love if she became his wife. She hated with all the vehemence of a passionate nature the cousin who grudgingly gave the orphan a home, and made the favor hard to accept by reproaches and injustice.

"I shall do something desperate unless I break away, for this dreadful life will kill me," she muttered, as she glanced about the poor room, and the shabby dress that could not hide her beauty. "Gertrude thinks I have no spirit, and believes I will remain her drudge for ever. She fancies I've neither money, sense, nor courage enough to escape; but I have all three. St. John opens the way, and I'd gladly go if it did not seem wrong to accept his help and marry without love. Poor boy! he is so ardent, and I cannot deny that it is sweet to be loved. There is no other way; I must fly to-night, or wait years, perhaps, for another chance like this."

She stood a moment with her eyes fixed intently on the outer gloom, as if to pierce the future; then a smile broke over her face, and she threw up her hand with a half-triumphant, half-defiant gesture, exclaiming:

"I'll go! Surely with youth, beauty, courage and talent, I can win liberty, and earn the right to enjoy it."

As if afraid her decision might waver, she bestirred herself energetically. A few garments from her scanty wardrobe, and a few little treasures were soon made into a portable parcel. Her plain cloak and bonnet were soon on, and, leaving a note of brief but bitterly ironical thanks for her cousin's kindness, she glided through the silent house out into the autumn night. On the threshold she paused, with a sudden sinking of the heart, for the great world lay before her, unknown, untried, and she was leaving the one refuge she possessed.

As she stood there, a fresh gust blew across the lawn, a brilliant star shone through the flying clouds, and across the silence came the quick tramp of horses' feet, the signal that the hour had come. The free wind, the propitious star, the welcome sound, all cheered her heart, confirmed her courage, and, with a silent gesture, as if she cast off a chain, the girl sprang forward to meet liberty and love.

The carriage waited at the appointed spot, but her lover was not there.

"He was detained by his father's illness, miss; but here's a note saying he'll meet you without fail at Croydon. The night-train gets in at four in the morning, and we shall be there by two, so there is no danger of missing," said the confidential servant, as respectfully as if she was already his mistress.

Away they went, and for an hour Honor enjoyed the excitement and the romance of the flight with all the zest of a girl. But, as the time approached when she should meet her lover, her courage strangely failed, and she almost longed to be safely back in her dreary room. The thought of that hasty marriage daunted her, and she began to frame excuses and delays.

By two o'clock she was quietly settled in a room of the Croydon Hotel to await St. John's arrival. Two hours were hers in which to make or mar her fortune, and, as she paced the luxurious chamber, she was suddenly inspired with a thought that opened a way of escape from both the old bondage and the new.

"How often I have longed to be on my way to London with money in my purse, and no one to control or counsel me? Now my wish is granted, and I should enjoy it heartily but for that poor boy. If I could leave him out I should be entirely content, and——"

There she paused, abruptly, for the new thought came filling her with fresh courage and energy.

"Why not leave him out for a time, at least? Why not go privately away before he comes, leaving word that he shall hear from me soon? London is but fifteen miles away; I have ten pounds in my purse. I remember Madame Paul's address; she loved her little pupil long ago, and will help me now. I have heard more than one person tell Gertrude that my voice would make my fortune; now I'll try it. I'll sing, earn money, repay St. John, and make my peace. Then, if I can love him, I will; if not, he'll soon outlive his boyish passion. Come, this is a good thought; I'll act upon it."

Putting back the curtain, she looked out. A balcony ran along that side of the hotel; steps descended from one end into a small garden; a low wall shut it from the street, and beyond was the sleeping town, the wide common, with London looming dimly in the distance.

"It is possible," muttered Honor, looking and listening keenly. "Nearly an hour before the train is in; by that time I can be lost in the great park yonder, and take an early train on the other side."

Hastily writing a few lines, she left them on the toilet-table, and stole out to essay a second flight.

Gliding like a shadow past the curtained windows looking on the balcony, she crossed the garden unseen, leaped the low wall, and hastened down the deserted street toward the open country. Once in the park she felt safe, and walked rapidly on in the gray dawn, meeting no one but the deer, who eyed her with mild surprise from their lairs among the fern.

When the sun rose, it shone upon her sitting alone on the wide common, with unwonted color on her cheeks, unwonted light in her eyes, unwonted happiness in her heart. A blissful sense of freedom possessed her, and youth's hopeful spirit made all things fair and possible.

"It is too early yet for the seven train. I'll sit here and rest, and try my voice, for no one can see or hear me, and it must be in order for Madame Paul's criticism," she said, smiling, as she glanced about her in all directions, and saw nothing but a few sheep, heard nothing but the larks singing blithely as they went up. With a music as sweet and effortless her own fine voice rang out as she sung her most difficult airs, and rejoiced to find how perfect her execution was.

Very lovely did she look, that young girl, sitting alone on the wild common. Her bonnet lay by her side; the wind lifted her bright hair from her forehead; the sunshine glittered on its gold, and touched the delicate bloom of her cheeks as she sung, with a smile on her lips and a brilliant light in her violet eyes, fixed on the far-off city where her future lay.

As she ended a sparkling canzonet, a soft sound of applause startled her to her feet. Turning like a frightened doe, she faced a man who had noiselessly approached, and seemed to have been listening delightedly, as he leaned on a mossy stone. He swept off his hat with a smile and a bow of half-playful, half-earnest contrition, saying, gently, and with a foreign accent:

"Pardon, mademoiselle. It was impossible to restrain my admiration; though by not doing so I deprive myself of the rest of this charming matinée."

Honor made no answer, but stood regarding him with the grave scrutiny of a child; for, as her alarm vanished, curiosity awoke.

A slender, swarthy man of five-and-twenty, with lustrous, dark eyes, a thin-lipped, scarlet mouth, under a delicate mustache, luxuriant black hair, and the well-cut features of an Arab. Plain as his dress was, it received an air of elegance from its wearer, and the sinewy, brown hand that held his hat was as small as a woman's. Something in the cordial ring of the voice, the frank gaze of the fine eyes, the whole singularly attractive expression of that peculiar face pleased the girl, and won her confidence. With a little sigh of relief she said, in a tone of satisfaction and pleasure:

"I thought it was that boy. Thank heaven it isn't! I'm glad you came———"

"Unhappy boy, to be so shunned, and thrice happy me, to be so welcomed!" broke in the stranger, as she paused with a sudden blush at his smile and her own words.

"I meant I was glad to meet any one who would tell me the way to the station. I haven't been here for years, and forget the place."

"I am going there. May I show you the way, mademoiselle?"

"Thank you, yes—on one condition," she answered, slowly, for, though irresistibly impelled to trust the stranger, she remembered that she was a runaway.

"I agree to anything," he said, still addressing her with the air which a well-bred man assumes toward a pretty child of the fair sex. Honor liked it, for, with all her strength of character, she was as artless as a little girl.

"Please, don't tell any one you met me. Will you promise that? Indeed, you may. I'm doing no harm, and only leaving those who wrong me," she said, earnestly.

"What a heartless boy, to wrong so sweet a sister! Can nothing be done to make him behave?" he answered, laughing.

"Now, you mistake," she cried, hastily, unconsciously betraying that she was no child. "The boy isn't my brother, and he loves me too well to trouble me. Let him be. It is an unkind woman who drives me away. I'm going to an old friend in London, and I go clandestinely, because I will have liberty. Do you blame me?" she asked, with kindling eyes, yet a wistful look that evidently touched him.

"I love freedom too well myself to blame any one for securing it at all costs. Permit me to offer my help, for you are too young, and—pardon me that I say it to your face—too beautiful to travel alone, mademoiselle."

She shook her head impatiently, but gave no sign of gratified vanity, as she fixed her lovely eyes on his in a grave glance of inquiry that would have aroused in any man a sincere desire to win her confidence. He bore that scrutiny successfully, for, with a sudden smile and an impulsive gesture full of grace, she offered her hand, saying, frankly:

"I trust you, sir. I don't know why I do so, but I am sure you will be an honest friend to me."

"I will."

The hearty brevity of his reply was more emphatic and satisfactory than the most eloquent protestations, and the cordial pressure of the hand was a better pledge than any oath.

"Thank you! Now I must go, for the early train will soon pass. Is it far?" she said, rising, with a sudden consciousness that a night of excitement and fatigue was beginning to tell upon her strength.

"Just over the common—you can see the roof of the station in the valley yonder. No, I carry this, and have still an arm to offer you, my tired comrade," he answered, lifting her parcel, and respectfully proffering the much-needed support.

But Honor shyly declined it, and walked on beside him, finding it very pleasant to be traveling in such courteous company. He smiled, but said nothing, till the girl asked, abruptly, as if following her own thoughts:

"Did you really like my singing?"

"I did. You have a wonderful voice."

"Do you think I could sing for money with any chance of success?" she went on, in a pretty, business-like way that would have amused him had he not been too much interested to observe it.

He glanced at the young face beside him, and a shadow passed over his own as he thought how soon its innocent freshness would disappear in such a life.

"I have no doubt of it. But is that necessary?"

"Why, yes, of course it is," she said, opening her eyes at him, as if surprised at the question. "I've nothing in the world but my voice and a little borrowed money. I wish to support myself, and I'll do anything rather than go back, or marry—some one I don't love."

She checked the name on her lips, and looked abashed that she had allowed so much to escape her. The stranger observed this, and made mental notes, but betrayed no especial interest, and replied, kindly:

"You are right; and, if your friend possess the power to help you, both freedom and independence may be yours."

"I'm glad to hear you say that. I'm very hopeful—very ignorant; but I really wish to help myself, and feel that I can if I am only let alone."

She glanced over her shoulder as she spoke, and uttered a low cry of terror, for several men were rapidly approaching.

"It is he!—St. John! Don't let him take me away! I don't love him; I can't marry him; I'll go back and be miserable rather than do that! Oh, help me—I've no friend but you!"

She clung to his arm as she spoke, with the vehemence of mingled fear and resolution.

"No one shall molest you, my child," he said, soothingly. "Tell me how it is, then I can serve you better."

Breathless with the haste she made, and still holding fast to the strong arm of her new friend, Honor poured out her little story as she went, unconscious of the sudden and entire change which passed over her hearer as he listened.

"Rest tranquil, my girl; I shall protect you. See, the station is here, and the train already approaches. Hold fast, and we shall be there in time to escape those persons."

Casting a quick glance behind him, the stranger strode on, half carrying Honor. Just as the train thundered up, they reached the platform, and, with a word to the guard, they sprang into an empty carriage. No other passengers waited at the little station, and they rolled away before the pursuers, if such they were, appeared in sight.

Pale and panting, Honor lay back, quite spent with this last flurry. She dimly wondered at the exulting laugh which broke from her companion as they shot away, and was touched by the gentle care he took of her, trying by every reassuring wile to cheer and restore her. She was soon herself again, and during that brief journey she permitted him to draw from her the story of her past life.

"Papa died long ago, and mamma offended Uncle Hugh by refusing to marry him. He went away to India, and we knew no more of him till two or three years ago he sent word that he was coming home, and the niece who was the best in every way should be his heiress. There is only Cousin Gertrude and myself, and of course he will choose her, for she has written him all sorts of bad reports of me, and tried in every way to win his favor. I don't care much for his money, but I do long for his love, I've had so little since mamma died."

"Why did you not write also, and set the matter straight with the old man?" asked the stranger, as she paused with trembling lips.

"I did, but my letters were not allowed to go. I tried to do well, and live on patiently till uncle came; but Gertrude was so tyrannical and unkind I could not bear it. She is a widow now, and I taught her children, but she wouldn't let them love me, and I was miserable. Then St. John saw me by accident, and loved me. Gertrude refused him, but he managed to write, and so it came about that I ran away. If I only cared for him I should not leave him; but I don't, and every hour makes me surer of it. Am I doing very wrong to disappoint the poor boy?"

"How old is the boy?" asked her companion, knitting his brows, though an amused smile lurked about his mouth.

"Nineteen," she answered, coloring; then she broke into a silvery laugh, and exclaimed, with charming frankness, "I know it must sound very childish and silly, and I dare say I am outraging all the proprieties by running away twice, and telling all my affairs to an utter stranger. But I've been so shut up, I know no more of the world than a child, and I really can't help trusting you, sir, you are so kind."

"Thank you. I'll prove worthy of your confidence, Miss Honor," began the stranger; but the girl exclaimed, abruptly:

"How do you know my name? I didn't tell you."

He bit his lip, his brown cheek flushed a little, and his keen eye seemed to glance over her with a half-scrutinizing, half annoyed expression. Then a quick smile appeared, and with an air of relief he touched the handkerchief that lay in her lap, saying, quietly:

"I read it there."

"What sharp eyes you must have! The words are almost washed out," and the girl gravely examined the corner of the handkerchief.

He smiled, and changed the subject, and beguiled the way so pleasantly that Honor was surprised when the journey ended. The noise and bustle at the Waterloo Station so bewildered her that she gratefully permitted her new friend to take care of her. Placing her in a cab, he gave Madame Paul's address to the man, pressed her hand, and said, emphatically:

"I do not say adieu, because I shall see you again. In any trouble send to me, and remember I am your friend. Here is my address. Be of good courage, little Honor; you will find your fortune soon."

With a smile that seemed to prophesy all good things, he vanished, leaving a card in her hand, bearing the words, "H. Tarifa, St. James Hotel, London."

CHAPTER II

A WEEK LATER a similar card was carried up to Mrs. Gertrude Avon, and threw that lady into a state of joyful excitement.

"News from Uncle Hugh. This is the name of his partner in Calcutta. Perhaps he is coming. How fortunate that Honor has lost all hope of the fortune! Is this H. Tarifa an old man, Annette?" she asked of her maid, who was helping her to give a few effective touches to her dress.

"No, madame—young, and very handsome."

"Ah! the son, doubtless. Give me the wrapper trimmed with Valenciennes, and let down a few more curls. They give a youthful look to my face."

The ten minutes' delay caused by Mrs. Avon's desire to make a coquettish toilet cost her more than she knew; for while he waited, her guest strolled about the room, using his keen eyes to some purpose. A card with these words penciled under St. John's name was one discovery: "She is at Madame P.'s, but will not see me." A portrait of Mrs. Avon caused him to mutter, after a long survey, "Insincere eyes, and a hard mouth. Poor little Honor must have fared ill in the hands of such a woman."

And the prattle of a child playing in the room, whom he questioned, brought out the fact that Honor was much beloved and mourned by her little pupils.

With a soft rustle, a beaming smile, and a white hand hospitably extended, Mrs. Avon glided into the room, paused with well-acted surprise, dropped her fine eyes, and murmured, with charming embarrassment:

"Pardon me. I fancied my dear uncle's partner would be an older man. Nevertheless, permit me to welcome you to England for his sake."

M. Tarifa bowed, and replied, in a cool, calm tone, which made Mrs. Avon look keenly at him:

"I am now the only remaining member of the old firm, my father having retired and your uncle being dead. Excuse my abrupt announcement of the fact; but the letters dispatched before I sailed were evidently lost, therefore I find you unprepared for the sad news."

"Yes," sighed Mrs. Avon, from behind her handkerchief, which she had lifted to hide, not tears, but exultation that the fortune was so near her grasp. "I will not detain you by any selfish grief, for I loved the old man, though we have been parted so long."

"I fear that I have yet another disappointment for you, madame; but perhaps your knowledge of your uncle's whims may have prepared you for any caprice of his. What caused the sudden change of purpose, I cannot tell, unless it was gratitude for a small favor I once did him; but when his will was read, it appeared that his whole fortune was left to me."

"You!" and Mrs. Avon's eyes flashed with irrepressible anger at the downfall of all her hopes.

"To me, with no mention of his nieces, except a wish which I find it somewhat difficult to mention, though far less difficult to obey than I had expected."

Something in the tone of the young man's voice, the smile that touched his lips, and the softened glance of his brilliant southern eyes caused a sudden hope to spring up in the woman's heart. Vailing her sharp disappointment under a half-timid, half-melancholy air, she said, sweetly:

"Believe me, I rejoice at your prosperity, and am sure that you will pardon a mother's regret at the loss which affects her fatherless children. May I ask what my uncle's wish was?"

"That I should share the fortune with one of his lawful heirs by marrying her."

"How cruel of him to hamper his bequest with so hard a condition!" and Mrs. Avon gave him an eloquent look as she spoke.

"Not hard, but every moment growing easier," gallantly replied M. Tarifa. "If you will permit me to make a few inquiries concerning your sister,* I shall be better able to conduct this delicate affair. She is with you, I believe?"

"Alas, no; she eloped a week ago, and is now married, I hope."

"You know nothing of her, then?"

"Nothing, except that she rejected my love and protection, and left me for a wild boy, who will soon desert her, I fear."

---

*Although their precise relationship is not significant to the plot, the sudden mid-story transformation of cousin Gertrude into Honor's sister is a careless authorial lapse.

"If so, you will receive and protect her again?"

"Never! How can I, with my little daughters growing up about me? I pity her; but I must think of them, for I have no one to lean upon, and, though five years a widow, I have not yet learned to bear my solitude with courage."

"I may then regard Miss Honor as no longer worthy a share of your uncle's benefaction?"

"I leave that for you to decide," and Mrs. Avon's scornful face plainly expressed her opinion.

There was a little pause, in which M. Tarifa seemed lost in thought, as he sat looking at the handsome woman before him. She fancied he was embarrassed at the position in which he found himself, and she came to his assistance with an artful question:

"May I ask if this singular desire of the old man is in any way binding upon you, sir?"

"Not in the least; but I desire to show my gratitude by complying with it, if possible. I am anxious to settle in England, to make a home for my father, and find happiness for myself. Being heart-free, and having seen pictures of both nieces, the task seemed full of romance to me, and I came, hoping to prosper in the only means of restitution which it is in my power to make. But as Miss Honor is lost, there is no hope of success, perhaps; at least, I dare not believe so, unless——"

As the last words fell slowly from his lips, Mrs. Avon, colored with soft confusion, dropped her eyes, and tenderly caressing the child leaning on her knee, she murmured, in a low tone:

"It is so very sudden and unexpected—such an embarrassing position—I would do much for my darling. My first marriage was a loveless one, but I have honored my husband's memory by a long widowhood. In time I might find my loneliness too hard to bear. Indeed, I need a friend. Be that to me at least, and ask nothing more as yet!"

As a piece of acting, that speech was perfect, and would have touched any man but the one who heard it. Being forewarned, he was forearmed, and a satirical smile passed across his face as he answered, in a voice to which a softer language than ours lent its music:

"Thank you for that permission. I promised to befriend the old man's niece, and I will. I may come again?" he added, rising.

"Yes," was all she said, but her eyes bade him welcome so eloquently that he could not doubt the sincerity of her invitation.

"And your unhappy sister, is there no way in which I can aid her?" he asked, pausing, with a significant look.

"If she is Mrs. St. John, she will need no help. If she is not, I no longer have a sister. Of course, you are at liberty to do what you will; but remember that you choose between us, for I decline all further friendship, if those reckless children are to be taken up after the disgrace they have brought upon me."

"My dear Mrs. Avon, have no fears. My choice is already made," and kissing her hand in his graceful foreign fashion, M. Tarifa took his leave, wearing an expression of satisfaction which both puzzled and charmed the ambitious widow.

For three weeks the young millionaire came and went, always with some pretext of business to prevent awkwardness in the interviews, which were always very brief, in spite of Mrs. Avon's fascinations.

"He is young," she thought, "and has seen little of women, evidently. This coldness is assumed for my sake. A man with such eyes and voice must be full of fire and tenderness. A little patience and his passion will break out, and then what a magnificent lover he will be! Thank heaven Honor destroyed her chance of winning before he came, for her blue eyes would surely have bewitched him."

One thing struck Mrs. Avon, which was, that at each visit M. Tarifa alluded to her sister; but she fancied that the girl's picture had awakened an interest in the young man's mind, and set herself to efface it as fast as possible by artfully-worded insinuations, accusations, and regrets; all of which were received in grave silence, and with a look of satisfaction which delighted her.

On the fourth week he arrived, radiant with some new happiness, which made him so charming that Mrs. Avon felt that the long-desired moment must be at hand when the lover's ardor was to replace the stranger's natural reserve.

"I have a favor to ask of you—may I say Gertrude?" he began, with a new softness in both face and tone.

"You know you may. What favor, Henri?" and the widow uttered his name with the timid tenderness of a young girl.

"I want you to forgive your sister."

"Never till she is married."

"She is married."

"Who told you that?" and the widow's shyness vanished, as she put the question sharply.

"I saw it done," was the cool reply.

"You! When?—where?—why?"

"Two days ago, at Madame Paul's, and because I felt that the young creature needed a protector."

"And that boy actually married her? Truly, it was the least he could do after the wrong he had done her."

"He felt that, and gladly made the only reparation in his power," replied Tarifa, with a tranquil smile.

"How good you are! That sad affair needed a wise and energetic head to settle it, and in the midst of your own duties you found time to do it. I hope they were truly grateful. I never can thank you for your brotherly care of that headstrong girl;" and Mrs. Avon put both her white hands in his with a tender look.

"They *were* very grateful, and if you will promise to pardon them, I shall consider your debt to me well paid."

"Anything for you, Henri," whispered the widow.

"Thanks! And will you receive them to-morrow for my sake, Gertrude?"

"I will, and gladly forget and forgive the past. Does that satisfy you?"

"Entirely. Now I must leave you; but when I come again receive me with a smile like this, and find that virtue is always its own reward."

Mrs. Avon's toilet was a marvel of taste, and Mrs. Avon's face wore its sweetest smiles as she rose to greet her guests next day, when Tarifa led her lovely sister in to be embraced with well-acted affection and delight.

"Where is the bridegroom? Does he fear to face me? Ah, well he may, after robbing me of my darling; but I have promised to pardon everything, and will keep my word for your sake, Henri," she said, longing to have the scene over, that she might receive the reward.

"Here is the bridegroom, Gerty," and Honor turned to fold both hands tenderly about the arm of Tarifa, who looked the lover to the life now.

"You! It is a lie!" cried Mrs. Avon, in a tone of despair, for his face answered before his lips.

"You told me to choose between you, and I did so. I gave you many opportunities to save your sister, but you rejected them all, to your own loss. I loved her image before I found the fair reality waiting for me on the moor, and when you cast her off, my heart took her in. If the old man wronged her, I have atoned for it by giving her all I possess."

"And she—that imprudent child has won the fortune, after all," gasped Mrs. Avon, as her last hope vanished.

"The only fortune that I covet is here," and Honor leaned her bright head on her husband's breast, thinking only of the generous and tender heart that took her in when most forlorn.

🐛 Mrs. Vane's Charade

"WHAT DO YOU THINK of the bewitching widow?" asked Major Mansfield of his friend, as they stood waiting the summons to dinner.

"She reminds me of a little green viper," replied Douglas, the new-comer.

"The deuce she does! What put such an odd fancy into your head?" cried the major.

"The color of her dress, her gliding gait, her brilliant eyes, and George's evident fascination."

The major put up his glass and took a silent survey of the lady before answering.

Mrs. Vane was pacing up and down the rooms on the arm of George Lennox, the young master of the house. Few little women would have appeared to advantage beside the tall guardsman; but Mrs. Vane moved with a grace and dignity that seemed to add many inches to her fairy-like stature, and make her a fit companion for her martial escort. Everything about her was peculiar and piquant. Her dress was of that vivid, silvery green which is so ravishing when worn by one whose fresh bloom defies all hues. No jewels but an antique chain of gold clasped tight about her slender throat. No ornament but a chaplet of delicate ferns against the rippling chestnut hair, that was drawn back from the face into one great coil behind. A single brilliant flower made her white bosom more dazzling; and glimpses of a marvelously small foot, in a coquetting high-heeled slipper, attracted the eye as she walked with the undulating motion described.

"Upon my life, I see the resemblance, and you have expressed my feelings exactly! I admire the woman's beauty, but I can't fall in love with her to save my soul," said the major, as he dropped his glass.

"She does not care to fascinate you, perhaps."

"Nor George either, for I strongly suspect that you are to be the victim. I shall like to see how you will prosper, for, if rumor does not lie, you have had experiences, and understand womankind."

Though he spoke in a tone of raillery, the major glanced curiously at his companion, for he had never yet discovered why the gay, gallant young fellow who went abroad five years before had returned a cold, calm, haughty man, who bowed at no shrine, and never praised a woman.

The dark, handsome face remained inscrutable, and the only answer Douglas made was a low "Hush! They are here. Present me, and see what comes of it."

Lennox and his fair companion approached, the one bending his tall head to listen ardently, the other looking up with a most tempting face, as she talked rapidly with a charming little accent.

The major presented his friend with *empressement,* for Douglas was the best *parti* of the season, and women seldom failed to greet him graciously, in spite of his well-known coldness. To the major's great surprise, however, Mrs. Vane merely glanced at the gentleman, returned his bow with a slight inclination, and rustled on, as if oblivious that a descendant of the great Scotch earl had been presented to her.

"The game has begun! That slight was artfully executed, and will make more impression than the sweetest smile. Novelty always piques a man," thought the major, watching the sudden fire in the young man's eye as he glanced after the widow.

Here Lady Lennox entered, and their host beckoned Douglas to take Mrs. Vane in to dinner. In spite of his secret reluctance, he could only bow and offer his arm. The lady took it as unconcernedly as if he had been a footman, and gave him her fan and handkerchief to hold, while she gathered up her train, with a careless, "May I trouble you?" as though they had never met before.

Though amazed by her nonchalance, Douglas found something half-amusing, half-captivating in her demeanor; for much as he had been courted and admired, few women were quite at ease with this high-born man, whose manners were so coldly charming, whose heart seemed so invulnerable. It was a new sensation to be treated cavalierly, and cold as he seemed, some old charm touched him again as he felt the soft hand on his arm, saw the dazzle of white shoulders at his side, and inhaled the subtle scent shaken from the gossamer handkerchief he carried.

Not a word was spoken during that short journey, but when they took their places the usual hauteur had melted from his manner, the fire softened to a dreamy warmth in his eyes, and on his swarthy cheek was an unwonted glow.

Bonny Elinor Stuart saw it, and her heart sank, for she loved Douglas, and believed that she had nearly won him from all rivals.

What power had this little woman over him, that, in five minutes, she could change him so?

The girl watched them narrowly, and strained every nerve to catch their words; but they gave her no comfort, for the inexplicable speeches were accompanied by glances that seemed to give significance and weight to the slightest syllable.

"It is evident that you have not heard of your old friend's death, since you offer me no condolence on his loss," began the lady, choosing a singularly inappropriate topic, and emphasizing the words "friend" and "loss" with a sarcastic smile.

"Pardon me if I forgot that you were a widow, and remembered only my own loss."

Douglas glanced at her brilliant costume as he uttered the first sentence, and shot a keen glance at her face as he slowly added the last.

The color flushed to her forehead, but she laughed a scornful laugh, and answered quickly:

"I wear no weeds, because I mourn no loss. If I may believe the gossips, *you* are more faithful to the past."

"Mrs. Vane will find that I *can* comfort myself when I hear her congratulations on my approaching marriage," was the cool reply, though the proud man winced at the stab she had given him.

"Queen Elinor reigns, then, and fair Rosamond vanishes, taking with her the first and freshest love of the king? Ah, well, she should be satisfied and leave time to avenge her, as he surely will, for the rose left a thorn behind that will rankle forever."

As she spoke, Mrs. Vane fixed her brilliant eyes full on her old lover's face, and saw it pale and quiver in spite of the smile he forced to his lips.

"According to the ballad, the king forgot and was happy," he began.

"The new version shows a truer knowledge of human nature, and the story has a different ending," interrupted the lady, with a threatening glance.

"May I know the ending?"

"Not yet."

Douglas had bent forward with an involuntary gesture of anxiety, and the answer had been given in a whisper full of ominous suggestion.

"You have marred my peace once, Celeste; will not that content you?" murmured Douglas, under cover of the hum and stir about them.

"And you mine. That debt is even. If you incur another, rest assured I will be paid. Come, shall we drink to Queen Elinor, or fair Rosamond?"

And she lifted her glass with a look, a smile, that might well bewilder a man of cooler blood than Douglas.

His eye went from the siren beside him to the woman opposite—the woman who loved him, yet tried to hide it with maiden pride. He read the truth now in the mute eloquence of the girl's half averted face, so pale with suppressed suffering that it touched his heart to a tenderness he had never thought to know again. His eye kindled, his head rose haughtily and his voice grew clear and firm as he lifted his glass, looked straight in Mrs. Vane's face, and answered her challenge with a defiant—

"I drink to my Queen Elinor."

Miss Stuart heard the words and crimsoned like a rose with joy; Mrs. Vane drank the toast without a word, but as she replaced her glass its slender stem snapped under the white fingers that held it with a convulsive grasp. Then, as if by mutual consent, each turned to their next neighbor and spoke no more together till dinner ended.

When the gentlemen rejoined the ladies Mrs. Vane sat at the piano singing fitfully to herself. Why did she suddenly break into a tender lovelay, giving it a passionate power that thrilled the listeners to the heart? Douglas had paused beside Elinor, and had just stolen a flower from her bouquet as that magical voice silenced all others and drew all eyes to the fair singer. The words he was about to utter died on his lips, his glance turned from Elinor to his early love, and the stolen flower seemed forgotten, as he unconsciously kept time with it to the song that recalled the blissful past. If Mrs. Vane intended to show him that her power was still strong, she could not have used a more potent spell, for music was the lure that won him long ago, and even now he could not resist its magic. All the familiar melodies were sung again, and as he listened to that voice, so silver-sweet, the present vanished and he was an ardent lover again, far away in sunny France, wooing *la belle Celeste*. How he had loved the girl! what a willing slave he had been, feeling that all favors were overpaid with a smile, a soft word, a touch of the lips that made the music of his life! He lived again that blissful year that was to have ended the wooing with a wedding. He recalled the hopes and dreams, the loving labors and the unbounded faith that made up the happiness of that brief dream; its bitter awakening he dared not remember now, for years had not healed the wound, though he had hidden it well. As if drawn by an irascible attraction, he had unconsciously gone, step by step, from Elinor to the siren who seemed bent on singing his heart away again. Leaning on the instrument, he listened with strange alternations of feeling sweeping across his face, till Mrs. Vane ended with a Spanish air which seemed to touch some chord that would not bear the lightest breath, for, as she began it in the vailed voice of one who sang through tears, Douglas caught her hand with the imploring exclamation:

"Not that, Celeste; I cannot bear it!" and then, as if dismayed at this betrayal, he hurried from the room.

"What is it?" demanded old Lady Lennox, who had been half asleep.

"A little charade got up by Mrs. Vane and Douglas, my lady. Very well acted, but we have not guessed it yet. We wait the third syllable," said the major, promptly.

"Have you had the first?" asked Mrs. Vane, turning to flash a look at him.

"Yes; that ended with a toast. Miss Stuart and I got a clue to the word then. When shall we have the rest?" retorted the major, who had been as keen-eyed as poor Elinor, and espoused her cause.

"To-night;" and with a strange look, Mrs. Vane threw her lace scarf over her head, and went to wander up and down the balcony, leaving the rest to wonder, gossip, and explain.

She had not taken many turns, when a tall shadow fell across the moonlit path, and a low voice said, sternly:

"I must speak to you. Come to the dark corner there. I command it, Celeste."

"Entreat, and I will obey," she observed, in a tone of mingled sadness and defiance.

A pause as if it cost an effort; then Douglas whispered, softly:

"I implore you to come. Does that satisfy you, my lovely tyrant?"

"Yes!" and a little hand took his own prisoner, drawing him away from the lighted windows to a shadowy nook at the end of the long balcony.

Placing herself where a streak of moonlight fell athwart her face, she looked upon him with the most captivating air of confidence, and waited for him to speak.

"Ah! time has not changed you, and you know it; but I warn you that I am not the weak boy you charmed five years ago, although I could not bear that song. Have you no heart, Celeste, that you could sing it here to-night?"

She laughed, and shook her bright head like a willful child; then sighed, and answered in a mournful tone:

"I gave it away five years ago, and never found it again till you came to-day."

"You are sanguine, madame, if you hope to make me believe that you loved, yet left me, so heartlessly, for my richer friend," said Douglas, with a bitter smile.

"I do hope it, for you love me still, and out of your great generosity I know that you can pardon me for that seeming treachery. I was a girl then, half bewildered by my new-found power. You fostered it. You made me a tyrant by your entire devotion. You half frightened me by your passionate love. You should have ruled me, taught me the worth of such a heart as yours, tamed my wild spirit, and made me then what I am now, tender and true—yours wholly, to deal with as you will."

Ah, the art of the woman! appealing to the love of power sure to be strong in such a man; tempting him with dear memories of the past, offering him a tender bond-slave in the woman who had ruled him like a queen, and making of her own humiliation the atonement surest to touch the generous nature which she knew so well. He looked at her as she stood before him with bent head, folded hands, and every line of her lovely figure betraying the soft submission which is the subtlest flattery to man's pride. It touched him in spite of the past treachery, the present hope of a truer love, the sad certainty that this fair, false woman had wasted years of his life, and sued to him now only because of his name and fortune. He knew her well, and yet she tempted him; contempt struggled with desire; beauty appealed to every sense; and a sudden impulse, half fond, half fierce, prompted him to rule over this subject with a tyranny greater than her own had been.

His hand was outstretched to lift up the graceful head, his lips parted to assure his conquest and his eye kindled with the old fire as he thought of recovering the loss he had mourned so long. What saved him from a second and sadder wreck of hope, happiness, and faith? Only a broken flower; for, in his outstretched hand still lay poor Elinor's rose, unconsciously retained, though its leaves were crushed, its beauty gone. He saw it, and something pathetic in its sudden ruin smote upon his heart. It was a thornless rose, and even when he rudely crushed it in careless hand, it gave no wound; only died, and left its perfume as a tender legacy to its destroyer. It was a little thing; but in such moments, when principle and passion struggle to the mastery, a trifle turns the scale, and a life's peace is made or marred even by the falling of rose-leaf.

The girl's innocent face rose before him doubly fair, and her love, so fresh and true, seemed doubly precious by the force of contrast. All that was best and noblest in the man answered the mute appeal of that sweet symbol of silent love, and the glamour of the old delusion passed away forever, consumed by the fire of a genuine passion.

The long silence surprised Mrs. Vane, who had expected a swift answer, a warm welcome, an entire victory. She glanced up with the enchanting smile which should melt the lingering doubt or coldness from her lover's heart—looked up, to find him standing with averted head, and lips pressed to the relics of a rose, as if half forgetful of her presence, wholly regardless of her prayer.

Well for Douglas that he did not see the storm of wrath, despair, and scorn that swept across the woman's face, as she set her teeth, and eyed him with a boding frown. It was gone in an instant, and she rose, erect, pale to the lips, but calm as one who sees his last hope failing, yet utters no lament.

"Edward," she said, and all the tenderest music of her voice was given to the word, "speak to me. Tell me if the bitter blunder made five years ago, and expiated by suffering and remorse that words can never tell, is to be repaired by this late avowal of penitence, submission, and a love grown stronger for delay? I am alone now in the world, poor as when you knew me first, friendless as when you were my only friend, but not what I then was—a gay, shallow girl—oh, no! a woman now, with one hope, one love, one purpose—to be worthy of you."

As the words fell from her lips broken by sobs, she sank at his feet, and lay there in a passion of tears that once would have swept everything before it. Not now; and with the first word he uttered, she knew the day was lost, felt that a power mightier than her own had taken possession of him, and owned with a pang of despair that her spells had failed at last.

"It is too late, Celeste. You killed my faith five years ago. It never can revive again, and without it love is impossible. I think the brief delusion of this hour is but the pale ghost of the passion that died when you deserted me. It has walked for the last time. I see its hollowness, and never can fear it any more, for I have lately found a spell to banish it forever. Let it lie quiet in its grave, and do you atone for the treachery of the past by leaving me to enjoy undisturbed the happiness that comes so late?"

As he spoke, in the calm cold voice that wounded her more deeply than taunts or reproaches, Douglas stretched his hands to her, as if to implore peace and to bestow pardon. As she listened, Mrs. Vane's eyes had been gloomily fixed on the bars of moonlight beyond him, as if looking vainly for help elsewhere when her own guile failed her.

So looking, she had seen a shadow lean from one of the long windows, and linger there, as if its owner watched the pair unseen. It was a woman's shadow, with flowing hair. Elinor's curls betrayed her, and in the drawing of a breath, her rival resolved to deal a parting wound, leaving jealous doubts to poison happy love.

They were too far for the listener to overhear them, but actions speak louder than words; and, as Douglas stretched his hands to her, instead of thrusting them away with scorn, Mrs. Vane threw herself upon his breast, murmuring, half inaudibly:

"I submit. Farewell, Edward, and forever!"

Surprised, yet pitiful, he let her lie there for a moment, feeling a natural regret at parting thus from the woman who had been his first love, and in that moment Mrs. Vane's quick eye saw the shadow throw up its arms with a despairing gesture, and vanish as noiselessly as it came. Then a grim smile touched the wily woman's lips as she turned away, and left her former lover with her face hidden in her hands, like one bowed down by sorrow.

Gliding in at the window, where the shadow had stood, she found herself in the conservatory, and peering into the green gloom which filled the flowery recesses, she soon found the object of her search. Down upon the mossy sward that encircled the fountain lay poor Elinor, struggling with the first great grief of her life.

"I may win yet. Courage, Celeste. A man's moods are many, and a woman may turn each to account, if she be wise," murmured Mrs. Vane, as she approached. Then, with a well-acted start of surprise, she exclaimed:

"Ah, heaven, what is this? Miss Stuart here, alone and in tears?"

"I do not weep!" and the proud girl sprang up, showing a face tearless, but white with the suffering she could not hide.

"Forgive me, but I could not pass without a word. I, too, have known sorrow. Let me comfort you," was the soft reply.

"You!" and the word cut the silence, in a tone sharp with indignant pain. "No, you can say nothing to console me for my loss. Words are useless, and your presence maddens me."

"Loss! dear Miss Stuart. I do not understand. Tell me what you have lost, and let me help you find it," cried Mrs. Vane, with an admirably assumed unconsciousness, which nearly drove the girl distracted.

Leaning toward her tormentor, Elinor fixed her despairing eyes on the lovely face that seemed to have destroyed her peace, and whispered in a tone of anguish:

"I have lost a heart. No, you have stolen it from me. Will you restore it?"

"Never!" and Mrs. Vane feigned innocence no longer. "You have watched us?" she cried, in a tone of scorn that turned the poor girl's white face scarlet with shame. "Ah, you are proud and maidenly-modest, Miss Stuart, yet you stoop to such dishonorable deeds, it seems! Are these the wiles that will win Douglas, think you? You are a child. You know nothing of his nature if you hope to subdue him by such freaks. Spare yourself the shame, mademoiselle, and me the reproaches. You have lost no heart but your own. I have stolen none; only reclaimed that which was all mine once, and has remained true to me in spite of the hard fortune that estranged us."

"He loved you, then—he has hoped and waited all these years, and now—?"

Elinor's voice failed there, but her wild eyes impored the truth.

And, as if reluctantly yielding, Mrs. Vane replied, with the ill-concealed pride and joy of a happy lover:

"Yes, he loved me. We were to have been married. See, I wear the ring now, and only wait for him to put it in its rightful place," said she, unclasping the jeweled locket glittering on her white bosom, and showing a slender wedding-ring, with a smile that made the poor girl shrink and cover up her face. "We were parted by a sad delusion, and while it lasted I married, believing him untrue. But after years of suffering I am free again, and I find that Edward has forgiven but never forgotten me, and waited with a woman's constancy till time restored us to each other."

"Oh, my God! how blind I have been!" moaned Elinor. "I thought he loved me. I gave him all my heart, and now I find it was but a terrible delusion."

"Poor child, I pity you, but thank heaven that you wake before the world discovers the sad infatuation. Conceal your grief. It will soon pass away. A girl's love dies easily; and console yourself with the knowledge that no one knows but Edward and myself—"

"He knows it? He has told you of it? Ah, that is too much!" cried Elinor, stung to the heart.

"Hush, dear. Be calm. Trust to us. We will be discreet, and help you to conceal your little trouble. Yes, Edward could not be blind to your most flattering regard. He confessed to me that his heart was touched with pity; that he almost believed it to be his duty to feign a return; but I came, and he forgot pity in love."

"That explains the kindness which I mistook for tenderness. A girl's love dies easily, you say. Mine ends only with my life. I cannot live to be taunted by happier women with my 'sad infatuation.' Keep my secret, and tell Edward that I thank him for his *pity*."

With a tragic gesture, and a pale face that startled the cold-hearted woman who had driven her half mad, Elinor waved her back and went swiftly out into the shadowy silence of the summer night.

Mrs. Vane stood motionless a moment, then threw up her head with a defiant gesture, and moved away, murmuring with a sarcastic smile:

"Fair Rosamond is not conquered yet, my king."

On re-entering the drawing-room she found Douglas still absent, and permitted young Lennox to resume his devotions, for, with all her seeming innocence and tenderness, Mrs. Vane was worldly to the heart's core, and fearing a failure of her dearest hope, she prudently bethought her of this poorer prize, for her affairs were in a desperate condition, and poverty she dreaded more than death.

As George Lennox leaned over her chair while she affected to be admiring his sketches, she artfully led the conversation to his estate, professing much interest in its beauty, while shrewdly endeavoring to estimate its worth.

"Here is a rough sketch of the park I have been describing. That is the famous oak, and this is the Lady's Pool, so called because a fair ancestress of mine drowned herself there, being crossed in love," said George.

"The pool! is it near?" and Mrs. Vane looked up with a sudden pallor on her blooming face as a foreboding fear came over her.

"Yes; just at the foot of the old garden, in that clump of gloomy firs. We will visit it tomorrow, if you like, and see if we can find any fair ghosts. They say Lady Margaret still walks."

With a shiver Mrs. Vane glanced out into the night, which had grown dark and sultry, and as she looked an awful vision of poor Elinor lying dead in the haunted pool rose so vividly before her, that she could with difficulty restrain herself from rushing out to seek her.

"I never meant to drive her to her death. God forbid! and yet I hate her, for she has ruined my one hope—*perhaps*," and over the last word Mrs. Vane paused with an evil shadow on her face.

"Where is Miss Stuart?" suddenly asked the major, from the window where he had been standing half hidden by the drapery, and watching Mrs. Vane unseen.

"She is tired with her long ride, and slipped away some time ago," said Lady Lennox, looking up from her book.

"I thought I heard her voice in the conservatory just before you came in" and the major turned sharply on Mrs. Vane, for her manner filled him with a vague dread of ill.

"She was not there," and Mrs. Vane looked him straight in the eye.

"Well lied, madame; you have had practice. Pardon me if I go to assure myself," muttered the major, stepping out upon the balcony where more than one love-scene was to be played that night.

The minute seemed hours to Mrs. Vane before he returned, for a guilty fear lay heavy at her heart, and with all her sins, she was a woman still. When at length he entered she looked up quickly, and grew deathly pale as she saw the excitement of the major's face.

"What is it, Mansfield? you look as if your moonlight stroll had woke you up," said Lennox, wondering why the usually brilliant little lady had grown so absent and *distrait* all at once.

"So it has, for I met Douglas roaming about, and he has amused me by telling all sorts of romantic tales."

"Repeat one, I beg; we are awfully dull here tonight, and Mrs. Vane is bored to death, I'm sure."

"Shall I?" asked the major, with a curious look at the lady.

"If you like," replied her lips. "If you dare!" flashed from her eyes.

"I shall be charmed," returned the old soldier roused by the look. "The little story which I found most interesting was of a fine young man who fell madly in love with an actress—a regular little devil, if you will pardon the expression; for she bewitched him entirely, and allowed him to lavish money upon her as if he had been a millionaire instead of a younger son with a small fortune. Well, he was infatuated enough to wish to marry the girl, after she had made him waste a year in wooing her, squander his money recklessly, and anger his father almost to the point of disinheriting him by this foolish passion. But, fortunately, just at that crisis, a richer lover appeared, and mademoiselle, who had no more heart than this marble Venus, coolly turned her back on number one, married the new adorer, and left the poor lad to shoot or drown himself. He wisely did neither, but it spoiled his faith in the sex, made him a woman-hater, and would have darkened his whole life, if a tender-hearted girl had not saved him. Here is the interesting point of the tale, you see, for exactly at this time, the actress, a widow now, having spent her husband's fortune, and worried him into his grave, the gossips say—Mrs. Vane has dropped her fan. Allow me."

And the major restored the remains of the delicate toy which had fallen shattered from her hand.

She took it without a word of thanks, and kept her glittering eyes riveted upon him as he continued with evident satisfaction:

"This lovely but ambitious lady, finding that her old lover had succeeded to his elder brother's princely fortune, felt her regard revive, followed him, and laid siege to the heart which she fancied would surrender at once to its old commander. It did not, however; and, in a fit of wrath at the failure, this sweet soul tried to destroy the happiness of the poor girl who had won her place. With falsehoods, taunts, and every insult which women know how to offer, she drove the innocent creature half wild; for, scarcely knowing what she did, the heart-broken child pushed out into the night to find forgetfulness in—"

"Not death! not the pool! Oh, for the love of heaven, do not tell me that!" cried Mrs. Vane starting up, trembling and terror-stricken, for the major's tone had grown low and solemn, and his stern eyes had never left her traitorous face.

"No, thank God! She sought forgetfulness in death, but found it in her lover's arms; for they met, and in the agitation of that moment, pride, fear, doubt, and despair were all confessed—love consoled them both, and they even forgot the existence of that bad woman in their great happiness."

Mrs. Vane dropped into her seat with a sigh of relief. Then her spirit rose undaunted, and she turned on the major a look that would have silenced a less courageous man, demanding significantly:

"Is that all?"

"I have only to add that, after guessing your charade, I beg to offer you mine. The first syllable you will understand without explanation. The second allow me to illustrate with a little tableaux."

And, stepping to the doorway of a boudoir separated from them only by a curtain, the major drew it, discovering Douglas and Elinor sitting as happy lovers sit, forgetful of all the world in their serene content.

"What the deuce *is* the word?" cried Lennox, quite unconscious of the by-play going on.

"Checkmated!"

▸　　And the major dropped the curtain with an exulting laugh, as Mrs. Vane vanished from the room.

❧ My Mysterious Mademoiselle

AT LYONS I engaged a coupé, laid in a substantial lunch, got out my novels and cigars, and prepared to make myself as comfortable as circumstances permitted; for we should not reach Nice till morning, and a night journey was my especial detestation. Nothing would have induced me to undertake it in mid-winter, but a pathetic letter from my sister, imploring me to come to her, as she was failing fast, and had a precious gift to bestow upon me before she died. This sister had mortally offended our father by marrying a Frenchman. The old man never forgave her, never would see her, and cut her off with a shilling in his will. I had been forbidden to have any communication with her on pain of disinheritance, and had obeyed, for I shared my father's prejudice, and made no attempt to befriend my sister, even when I learned that she was a widow, although my father's death freed me from my promise. For more than fifteen years we had been utterly estranged; but when her pleading letter came to me, my heart softened, and I longed to see her. My conscience reproached me, and, leaving my cozy bachelor establishment in London, I hurried away, hoping to repair the neglect of years by tardy tenderness and care.

My thoughts worried me that night, and the fear of being too late haunted me distressfully. I could neither read, sleep, nor smoke, and soon heartily wished I had taken a seat in a double carriage, where society of some sort would have made the long hours more endurable. As we stopped at a way-station, I was roused from a remorseful reverie by the guard, who put in his head to inquire, with an insinuating shrug and smile:

"Will monsieur permit a lady to enter? The train is very full, and no place remains for her in the first-class. It will be a great kindness if monsieur will take pity on the charming little mademoiselle."

He dropped his voice in uttering the last words, and gave a nod, which plainly expressed his opinion that monsieur would not regret the courtesy. Glad to be relieved from the solitude that oppressed me, I consented at once, and waited with some curiosity to see what sort of companion I was to have for the next few hours.

The first glance satisfied me; but, like a true Englishman, I made no demonstration of interest beyond a bow and a brief reply to the apologies and thanks uttered in a fresh young voice as the new-comer took her seat. A slender girl of sixteen or so, simply dressed in black, with a little hat tied down over golden curls, and a rosy face, lit up by lustrous hazel eyes, at once arch, modest and wistful. A cloak and a plump traveling bag were all her luggage, and quickly arranging them, she drew out a book, sank back in her corner, and appeared to read, as if anxious to render me forgetful of her presence as soon as possible.

I liked that, and resolved to convince her at the first opportunity that I was no English bear, but a gentleman who could be very agreeable when he chose.

The opportunity did not arrive as soon as I hoped, and I began to grow impatient to hear the fresh young voice again. I made a few attempts at conversation, but the little girl seemed timid, for she answered in the briefest words, and fell to reading again, forcing me to content myself with admiring the long curled lashes, the rosy mouth, and the golden hair of this demure demoiselle.

She was evidently afraid of the big, black-bearded gentleman, and would not be drawn out, so I solaced myself by watching her in the windows opposite, which reflected every movement like a mirror.

Presently the book slipped from her hand, the bright eyes grew heavy, the pretty head began to nod, and sleep grew more and more irresistible. Half closing my eyes, I feigned slumber, and was amused at the little girl's evident relief. She peeped at first, then took a good look, then smiled to herself as if well pleased, yawned, and rubbed her eyes like a sleepy child, took off her hat, tied a coquettish rose-colored rigolette over her soft hair, viewed herself in the glass, and laughed a low laugh, so full of merriment, that I found it difficult to keep my countenance. Then, with a roguish glance at me, she put out her hand toward the flask of wine lying on the leaf, with a half-open case of chocolate croquettes, which I had been munching, lifted the flask to her lips, put it hastily down again, took one bon-bon, and, curling herself up like a kitten, seemed to drop asleep at once.

"Poor little thing," I thought to myself, "she is hungry, cold, and tired; she longs for a warm sip, a sugar-plum, and a kind word, I dare say. She is far too young and pretty to be traveling alone. I must take care of her."

In pursuance of which friendly resolve I laid my rug lightly over her, slipped a soft shawl under her head, drew the curtains for warmth, and then repaid myself for these attentions by looking long and freely at the face encircled by the rosy cloud. Prettier than ever when flushed with sleep did it look, and I quite lost myself in the pleasant reverie which came to me while leaning over the young girl, watching the silken lashes lying quietly on the blooming cheeks, listening to her soft breath, touching the yellow curls that strayed over the arm of the seat, and wondering who the charming little person might be. She reminded me of my first sweetheart—a pretty cousin, who had captivated my boyish heart at eighteen, and dealt it a wound it never could forget. At five-and-thirty these little romances sometimes return to one's memory fresher and dearer for the years that have taught us the sweetness of youth—the bitterness of regret. In a sort of waking dream I sat looking at the stranger, who seemed to wear the guise of my first love, till suddenly the great eyes flashed wide open, the girl sprung up, and, clasping her hands, cried, imploringly:

"Ah, monsieur, do not hurt me, for I am helpless. Take my little purse; take all I have, but spare my life for my poor mother's sake!"

"Good heavens, child, do you take me for a robber?" I exclaimed, startled out of my sentimental fancies by this unexpected performance.

"Pardon; I was dreaming; I woke to find you bending over me, and I was frightened," she murmured, eying me timidly.

"That was also a part of your dream. Do I look like a rascal, mademoiselle?" I demanded, anxious to reassure her.

"Indeed, no; you look truly kind, and I trust you. But I am not used to traveling alone; I am anxious and timid, yet now I do not fear. Pardon, monsieur; pray, pardon a poor child who has no friend to protect her."

She put out her hand with an impulsive gesture, as the soft eyes were lifted confidingly to mine, and what could I do but kiss the hand in true French style, and smile back into the eyes with involuntary tenderness, as I replied, with unusual gallantry:

"Not without a friend to protect her, if mademoiselle will permit me the happiness. Rest tranquil, no one shall harm you. Confide in me, and you shall find that we 'cold English' have hearts, and may be trusted."

"Ah, so kind, so pitiful! A thousand thanks; but do not let me disturb monsieur. I will have no more panics, and can only atone for my foolish fancy by remaining quiet, that monsieur may sleep."

"Sleep! Not I; and the best atonement you can make is to join me at supper, and wile away this tedious night with friendly confidences. Shall it be so, mademoiselle?" I asked, assuming a paternal air to reassure her.

"That would be pleasant; for I confess I am hungry, and have nothing with me. I left in such haste I forgot——" She paused suddenly, turned scarlet, and drooped her eyes, as if on the point of betraying some secret.

I took no notice, but began to fancy that my little friend was engaged in some romance which might prove interesting. Opening my traveling-case, I set forth cold chicken, *tartines,* wine, and sweetmeats, and served her as respectfully as if she had been a duchess, instead of what I suspected—a run-away school-girl. My manner put her at her ease, and she chatted away with charming frankness, though now and then she checked some word on her lips, blushed and laughed, and looked so merry and mysterious, that I began to find my school-girl a most captivating companion. The hours flew rapidly now; remorse and anxiety slept; I felt blithe and young again, for my lost love seemed to sit beside me; I forgot my years, and almost fancied myself an ardent lad again.

What mademoiselle thought of me I could only guess; but look, tone and manner betrayed the most flattering confidence. I enjoyed the little adventure without a thought of consequences.

At Toulon we changed cars, and I could not get a coupé, but fortunately found places in a carriage, whose only occupant was a sleepy old woman. As I was about taking my seat, after bringing my companion a cup of hot coffee, she uttered an exclamation, dragged her vail over her face, and shrunk into the corner of our compartment.

"What alarms you?" I asked, anxiously, for her mystery piqued my curiosity.

"Look out and see if a tall young man is not promenading the platform, and looking into every carriage," returned mademoiselle, in good English, for the first time.

I looked out, saw the person described, watched him approach, and observed that he glanced eagerly into each car as he passed.

"He is there, and is about to favor us with an inspection. What are your commands, mademoiselle?" I asked.

"Oh, sir, befriend me; cover me up; say that I am ill; call yourself my father for a moment—I will explain it all. Hush, he is here!" and the girl clung to my arm with a nervous gesture, an imploring look, which I could not resist.

The stranger appeared, entered with a grave bow, seated himself opposite, and glanced from me to the muffled figure at my side. We were off in a moment, and no one spoke, till a little cough behind the vail gave the new-comer a pretext for addressing me.

"Mademoiselle is annoyed by the air; permit me to close the window."

"Madame is an invalid, and will thank you to do so," I replied, taking a malicious satisfaction in disobeying the girl, for the idea of passing as her father disgusted me, and I preferred a more youthful title.

A sly pinch of the arm was all the revenge she could take; and, as I stooped to settle the cloaks about her, I got a glance from the hazel eyes, reproachful, defiant, and merry.

"Ah, she has spirit, this little wandering princess. Let us see what our friend opposite has to do with her," I said to myself, feeling almost jealous of the young man, who was a handsome, resolute-looking fellow, in a sort of uniform.

"Does he understand English, madame, my wife?" I whispered to the girl.

"Not a word," she whispered back, with another charming pinch.

"Good; then tell me all about him. I demand an explanation."

"Not now; not here, wait a little. Can you not trust me, when I confide so much to you?"

"No, I am burning with curiosity, and I deserve some reward for my good behavior. Shall I not have it, *ma amie?*"

"Truly, you do, and I will give you anything by-and-by," she began.

"Anything?" I asked, quickly.

"Yes; I give you my word."

"I shall hold you to your promise. Come, we will make a little bargain. I will blindly obey you till we reach Nice, if you will frankly tell me the cause of all this mystery before we part."

"Done!" cried the girl, with an odd laugh.

"Done!" said I, feeling that I was probably making a fool of myself.

The young man eyed us sharply as we spoke, but said nothing, and, wishing to make the most of my bargain, I pillowed my little wife's head on my shoulder, and talked in whispers, while she nestled in shelter of my arm, and seemed to enjoy the escapade with all the thoughtless *abandon* of a girl. Why she went off into frequent fits of quiet laughter I did not quite understand, for my whispers were decidedly more tender than witty; but I fancied it hysterical, and, having made up my mind that some touching romance was soon to be revealed to me, I prepared myself for it, by playing my part with spirit, finding something very agreeable in my new *rôle* of devoted husband.

The remarks of our neighbors amused us immensely; for, the old lady, on waking, evidently took us for an English couple on a honeymoon trip, and confided her opinion of the "mad English" to the young man, who knit his brows and mused moodily.

To our great satisfaction, both of our companions quitted us at midnight; and the moment the door closed behind them, the girl tore off her vail, threw herself on the seat opposite me, and laughed till the tears rolled down her cheeks.

"Now, mademoiselle, I demand an explanation," I said, seriously, when her merriment subsided.

"You shall have it; but first tell me what do I look like?" and she turned her face toward me with a wicked smile, that puzzled me more than her words.

"Like a very charming young lady who has run way from school or *pension*, either to escape from a lover or to meet one."

"My faith! but that is a compliment to my skill," muttered the girl, as if to herself; then aloud, and soberly, though her eyes still danced with irrepressible mirth: "Monsieur is right in one thing. I have run away from school, but not to meet or fly a lover. Ah, no; I go to find my mother. She is ill; they concealed it from me; I ran away, and would have walked from Lyons to Nice if old Justine had not helped me."

"And this young man—why did you dread him?" I asked, eagerly.

"He is one of the teachers. He goes to find and reclaim me; but, thanks to my disguise, and your kindness, he has not discovered me."

"But why should he reclaim you? Surely, if your mother is ill, you have a right to visit her, and she would desire it."

"Ah, it is a sad story! I can only tell you that we are poor. I am too young yet to help my mother. Two rich aunts placed me in a fine school, and support me till I am eighteen, on condition that my mother does not see me. They hate her, and I would have rejected their charity, but for the thought that soon I can earn my bread and support her. She wished me to go, and I obeyed, though it broke my heart. I study hard. I suffer many trials. I make no complaint; but I hope and wait, and when the time comes I fly to her, and never leave her any more."

What had come to the girl? The words poured from her lips with impetuous force; her eyes flashed; her face glowed; her voice was possessed with strange eloquence, by turns tender, defiant, proud, and pathetic. She clinched her hands, and dashed her little hat at her feet with a vehement gesture when speaking of her aunts. Her eyes shone through indignant tears when alluding to her trials; and, as she said, brokenly, "I fly to her, and never leave her any more," she opened her arms as if to embrace and hold her mother fast.

It moved me strangely; for, instead of a shallow, coquettish school-girl, I found a passionate, resolute creature, ready to do and dare anything for the mother she loved. I resolved to see the end of this adventure, and wished my sister had a child as fond and faithful to comfort and sustain her; but her only son had died a baby, and she was alone, for I had deserted her.

"Have you no friends but these cruel aunts?" I asked, compassionately.

"No, not one. My father is dead, my mother poor and ill, and I am powerless to help her," she answered, with a sob.

"Not quite; remember I am a friend."

As I spoke I offered my hand; but, to my intense surprise, the girl struck it away from her with a passionate motion, saying, almost fiercely:

"No; it is too late—too late! You should have come before."

"My poor child, calm yourself. I *am* indeed a friend; believe it, and let me help you. I can sympathize with your distress, for I, too, go to Nice to find one dear to me. My poor sister, whom I have neglected many years; but now I go to ask pardon, and to serve her with all my heart. Come, then, let us comfort one another, and go hopefully to meet those who love and long for us."

Still another surprise; for, with a face as sweetly penitent as it had been sternly proud before, this strange girl caught my hand in hers, kissed it warmly, and whispered, gratefully:

"I often dreamed of a friend like this, but never thought to find him so. God bless you, my——" She paused there, hid her face an instant, then looked up without a shadow in her eyes, saying more quietly, and with a smile I could not understand:

"What shall I give you to prove my thanks for your kindness to me?"

"When we part, you shall give me an English good-by."

"A kiss on the lips! Fie! monsieur will not demand that of me," cried the girl, whose changeful face was gay again.

"And, why not, since I am old enough to be called your father."

"Ah, that displeased you! Well, you had your revenge; rest content with that, *mon mari*," laughed the girl, retreating to a corner with a rebellious air.

"I shall claim my reward when we part; so resign yourself, mademoiselle. By-the-way, what name has my little friend?"

"I will tell you when I pay my debt. Now let me sleep. I am tired, and so are you. Good-night, Monsieur George Vane," and, leaving me to wonder how she had learned my name, the tormenting creature barricaded herself with cloaks and bags, and seemed to sleep tranquilly.

Tired with the long night, I soon dropped off into a doze, which must have been a long one; for, when I woke, I found myself in the dark.

"Where the deuce are we?" I exclaimed; for the lamp was out, and no sign of dawn visible, though I had seen a ruddy streak when I last looked out.

"In the long tunnel near Nice," answered a voice from the gloom.

"Ah, mademoiselle is awake! Is she not afraid that I may demand payment now?"

"Wait till the light comes, and if you deserve it *then,* you shall have it," and I heard the little gipsy laughing in her corner. The next minute a spark glowed opposite me; the odor of my choice cigarettes filled the air, and the crackle of a bon-bon was heard.

Before I could make up my mind how to punish these freaks, we shot out of the tunnel, and I sat petrified with amazement, for there, opposite me, lounged, not my pretty blonde school-girl, but a handsome black-haired, mischievous lad, in the costume of a pupil of a French military academy; with his little cap rakishly askew, his blue coat buttoned smartly to the chin, his well-booted feet on the seat beside him, and his small hands daintily gloved, this young rascal lay staring at me with such a world of fun in his fine eyes, that I tingled all over with a shock of surprise which almost took my breath away.

"Have a light, uncle?" was the cool remark that broke the long silence.

"Where is the girl?" was all I could say, with a dazed expression.

"There, sir," pointing to the bag, with a smile that made me feel as if I was not yet awake, so like the girl's was it.

"And who the devil are you?" I cried, getting angry all at once.

Standing as straight as an arrow, the boy answered, with a military salute:

"George Vane Vandeleur, at your service, uncle."

"My sister has no children; her boy died years ago, you young villain."

"He tried to, but they wouldn't let him. I'm sorry to contradict you, sir; but I'm your sister's son, and that will prove it."

Much bewildered, I took the letter he handed me, and found it impossible to doubt the boy's word. It was from my sister to her son, telling him that she had written to me, that I had answered kindly, and promised to come to her. She bade the boy visit her if possible, that I might see him, for she could not doubt that I would receive him for her sake, and free him from dependence on the French aunts who made their favors burdensome by reproach and separation.

As I read, I forgave the boy his prank, and longed to give him a hearty welcome; but recollections of my own part in that night's masquerade annoyed me so much that to conceal my chagrin I assumed a stern air, and demanded, coldly:

"Was it necessary to make a girl of yourself in order to visit your mother?"

"Yes, sir," answered the boy, promptly, adding, with the most engaging frankness: "I'll tell you how it was, uncle, and I know you will pardon me, because mamma has often told me of your pranks when a boy, and I made you my hero. See, then, mamma sends me this letter, and I am wild to go, that I may embrace her and see my uncle. But my aunts say, 'No,' and tell them at school that I am to be kept close. Ah, they are strict there; the boys are left no freedom, and my only chance was the one holiday when I go to my aunts. I resolved to run away, and walk to mamma, for nothing shall part us but her will. I had a little money, and I confided my plan to Justine, my old nurse. She is a brave one! She said:

" 'You shall go, but not as a beggar. See, I have money. Take it, my son, and visit your mother like a gentleman.'

"That was grand; but I feared to be caught before I could leave Lyons, so I resolved to disguise myself, and then if they followed I should escape them. Often at school I have played girl-parts, because I am small, and have as yet no beard. So Justine dressed me in the skirt, cloak and hat of her granddaughter. I had the blonde wig I wore on the stage, a little rouge, a soft tone, a modest air, and—*voilà mademoiselle!*"

"Exactly; it was well done, though at times you forgot the 'modest air,' nephew," I said, with as much dignity as suppressed merriment permitted.

"It was impossible to remember it at all times; and you did not seem to like mademoiselle the less for a little coquetry," replied the rogue, with a sly glance out of the handsome eyes that had bewitched me.

"Continue your story, sir. Was the young man we met really a teacher?"

"Yes, uncle; but you so kindly protected me that he could not even suspect your delicate wife."

The boy choked over the last word, and burst into a laugh so irresistibly infectious that I joined him, and lost my dignity for ever.

"George, you are a scapegrace," was the only reproof I had breath enough to make.

"But uncle pardons me, since he gives me my name, and looks at me so kindly that I must embrace him."

And with a demonstrative affection which an English boy would have died rather than betray, my French nephew threw his arms about my neck, and kissed me heartily on both cheeks. I had often ridiculed the fashion, but now I rather liked it, and began to think my prejudice ill-founded, as I listened to the lad's account of the sorrows and hardships they had been called on to suffer since his father died.

"Why was I never told of your existence?" I asked, feeling how much I had lost in my long ignorance of this bright boy, who was already dear to me.

"When I was so ill while a baby, mamma wrote to my grandfather, hoping to touch his heart; but he never answered her, and she wrote no more. If uncle had cared to find his nephew, he might easily have done so; the channel is not very wide."

The reproach in the last words went straight to my heart; but I only said, stroking the curly head:

"Did you never mean to make yourself known to me? When your mother was suffering, could you not try me?"

"I never could beg, even for her, and trusted to the good God, and we were helped. I did mean to make myself known to you when I had done something to be proud of; not before."

I knew where that haughty spirit came from, and was as glad to see it as I was to see how much the boy resembled my once lovely sister.

"How did you know me, George?" I asked, finding pleasure in uttering the familiar name, unspoken since my father died.

"I saw your name on your luggage at Marseilles, and thought you looked like the picture mamma cherishes so tenderly, and I resolved to try and touch your heart before you knew who I was. The guard put me into your coupé, for I bribed him, and then I acted my best; but it was so droll I nearly spoiled it all by some boy's word, or a laugh. My faith, uncle, I did not know the English were so gallant."

"It did not occur to you that I might be acting also, perhaps? I own I was puzzled at first, but I soon made up my mind that you were some little adventuress out on a lark, as we say in England, and I behaved accordingly."

"If all little adventuresses got on as well as I did, I fancy many would go on this lark of yours. A talent for acting runs in the family, that is evident," said the boy.

"Hold your tongue, jackanapes!" sternly. "How old are you, my lad?" mildly.

"Fifteen, sir."

"That young to begin the world, with no friends but two cold-hearted old women!"

"Ah, no, I have the good God and my mother, and now—may I say an uncle who loves me a little, and permits me to love him with all my heart?"

Never mind what answer I made; I have recorded weaknesses enough already, so let that pass, as well as the conversation which left both pair of eyes a little wet, but both pair of hearts very happy.

As the train thundered into the station at Nice, just as the sun rose gloriously over the blue Mediterranean, George whispered to me, with the irrepressible impudence of a mischief-loving boy:

"Uncle, shall I give you 'the English good-by' now?"

"No, my lad; give me a hearty English welcome, and God bless you!" I answered, as we shook hands, manfully, and walked away together, laughing over the adventure with my mysterious mademoiselle.

❧ Betrayed by a Buckle

IT WAS a bitter disappointment, after years of poverty, to find the fortune which I had thought my own suddenly wrested from me by a stranger. I was my uncle's legal heir, for he died childless, as all the world believed, and on hearing of the old man's death, I forgave him his long neglect, and waited eagerly to receive the welcome news of my good fortune. To my dismay, the lawyers wrote me that a daughter had appeared, whose claim could neither be doubted nor set aside; the property was rightfully hers, and I was a poor artist still.

Years ago I had heard of my uncle's marriage, and the birth and death of a little child; he himself died suddenly and left no will, but his last words were:

"Be just—give all to Cecil," and those about him believed that he meant me till this beautiful girl appeared, claiming to be his child, and proving that her name was Cecelia, which gave a new meaning to those last words, uttered with great earnestness and evident distress of mind.

The girl made out her case and won it, for I was too poor to fight against such odds, and all was settled before I could earn enough to leave Italy for home. I resolved to see this unknown cousin before I relinquished all hope, however, for a hint dropped by my old lawyer suggested the possibility of yet winning a share at least of my uncle's handsome fortune.

I was young, comely, accomplished, and the possessor of a good name, to which my talent had already added some honor. Why not woo this bonny cousin, and still be master of the wealth I had been taught to think my own?

The romance of the thing pleased me, and as soon as my engagements permitted I was in England. Desiring to judge for myself, after hearing the dry facts from the lawyers, I went down to the hall, unannounced, meaning to play the unknown artist till satisfied that it was wise to confess the truth.

Armed with a note of introduction from a friend of my uncle's, I presented myself as one desirous of copying a certain fine Titian in the gallery. Miss Stanhope was out, but I was permitted to examine the pictures while awaiting her return. Among the old family portraits was a half-finished one, evidently the young mistress, and I examined it with eagerness.

A very lovely face, yet something marred its beauty. At first I thought it was my own prejudice; but setting aside any natural bitterness of feeling, and regarding it as a work of art alone, I could not escape from the odd fancy that those imperious eyes could flash with a baleful light, that smiling, red mouth might betray with a kiss, and that dimpled hand lead a man to perdition. The warm brown of the luxuriant hair, the smooth curves of the uncovered neck and arms, and the soft, rich coloring of the dress gave a sumptuous and seductive grace to the well-painted picture, the charm of which I felt in spite of myself.

Quite forgetting the Titian, I leaned back in the depths of a luxurious couch, with my eyes fixed on the likeness of my future wife, as I already called my cousin, in the reverie to which I surrendered myself.

A low laugh startled me to my feet, and made me stare in dumb surprise at the apparition before me. The picture seemed to have stepped from its frame, for there in the arched doorway against a background of soft gloom was Miss Stanhope. The same imperious eyes fixed full upon me, the red lips smiling archly, the floating hair, half golden in the streak of light that fell athwart her head and touched the white shoulder, the same dimpled hands, lightly folded, and the same rosy muslins blowing in the wind, that revealed glimpses of the same delicate foot just outlined in the picture.

I was so startled by her abrupt appearance, her strange laughter, and my own contending emotions, that all my wonted composure forsook me, and not one of the smooth speeches prepared for the interview came to my lips.

Bowing silently, I stood like an awkward lout till she completed my confusion by advancing with outstretched hand, saying, in a deliciously cordial tone:

"Welcome, cousin; your little plot was well laid; but a woman is hard to deceive, especially when such a tell-tale face as yours tries to put on a mask."

As she spoke she pointed to a mirror which reflected both my own figure and that of a gay and gallant ancestor, whose handsome face showed the most marked features of our race. I saw the likeness at once, for my mustache, curling hair, and velvet paletot added to the effect most strikingly.

Something in the compliment, as well as her own frank air, restored my self-possession, and, eager to remove all recollection of my *gaucherie,* I joined in her laughter, saying, gayly, as I kissed her hand with the Italian devotion that women like:

"A thousand pardons for attempting to deceive these bright eyes; but the banished prince longed to see the new queen, and so ventured home in disguise."

"I forgive the ruse, because you say *home* in a tone that betrays in you the same solitude that I feel. It is a large, lonely house. There is room enough for both, and as we are the last of our race, why not cease to be strangers and both come home?"

Nothing could have been more sweet and simple than look, voice and manner as she said this. It touched me, and yet the vague feeling of distrust born of my scrutiny of both the painted and living face still lingered in my mind, and robbed my answer of the warmth it should have possessed.

"Miss Stanhope forgets that I have lost my right to take shelter here. But since I have seen her my disappointment is much softened, because for a woman young and beautiful it would be far harder to work for bread than for a man whose bosom friends for years have been poverty and solitude."

She looked at me with a sudden dew in those proud eyes of hers, and for a moment stood silent, with the color varying in her cheeks; then, as if obeying a generous impulse, she smiled, and looking up at me, said, in a tone whose persuasive gentleness was irresistible:

"Cousin Cecil, promise to stay one week, and learn to know me better. I ask it as a favor; and since you possess the Stanhope pride, you shall make me your debtor by finishing this picture. The artist who began it will not return; for his own sake I forbid it."

A disdainful little gesture told the story of the cause of this banishment as plainly as words, and was, perhaps, a warning hint to me. I smiled at it, even while I felt as the fisher might have done when the Lorelei first began to charm him.

"I will stay," I briefly said, and then she asked me about my life in Italy, so pleasantly beguiling confidence after confidence from me, that if I had possessed a secret it would inevitably have passed into her keeping.

I staid, and day after day we sat in the long gallery, surrounded by beauty of all kinds, talking with ever-increasing frankness, while I painted this lovely cousin, who bewildered my senses without touching my heart.

The old lady who played duenna left us free, and little company disturbed the charming solitude that never lost its delight to me.

A whim had seized Cecelia to change the costume in the portrait from modern to ancient, and as the dress of a beautiful ancestress was still preserved, she put it on, enhancing her beauty fourfold by the rich brocades, the antique jewels, and priceless laces of past days.

"This little shoe must have a buckle if it is to be visible, as I beg it may be," I said, as she came rustling in one morning like a *grande dame* of the olden time.

"Bring the steel-bound casket, Adele; we may find something there that will suit this masquerade," said Cecelia to the maid who held her train.

Slipping off the coquettish shoe of white silk with a scarlet heel, she let me amuse myself with trying which of many ornaments would suit it best, while she absently clasped and unclasped the bracelets on her round arm.

"This is in perfect taste, and a picture in itself," I presently exclaimed, holding up the little shoe ornamented with a great buckle of chased silver, set here and there with a diamond, and a true-lover knot formed of a double S in the middle.

"That is one of the very buckles our gallant ancestor wore. You can see them in the picture yonder, and the story goes that they were given him by his lady-love," answered Cecelia, pointing to the portrait of Sir Sidney Stanhope hanging behind us.

This little fact led me to examine the trinkets with interest, and having put it into the silken shoe, I fell to painting it, while my lovely sitter amused me with old legends of our family.

The week had lengthened to three, and I still lingered, for it was evident that my cousin, with a woman's generosity, was willing to make the only reparation in her power. I felt sure that the idea came to her that first day, when, after the long pause, she bade me stay, with varying color and wet eyes betraying pity, interest, and the dawning affection of a lonely heart quick to feel the ties of family. I tried to love her, and grew feverish in my efforts to discover why, in spite of the fascination of her presence, I could not yield my heart wholly to her power. What cause had I to distrust this beautiful and generous girl? None; and yet I did, so much so that I found myself watching her with a curious persistence, as if some subtle instinct warned me to beware.

This habit, and the restlessness which possessed me, led me to roam about the house and grounds by night when all was quiet. My out-of-door life in Italy made this freedom necessary to me, and I indulged my whim so skillfully that no one but the watchdogs suspected it—they knew me, and kept my secret.

One evening twilight overtook me at my easel, and the summons to dinner left Cecelia no time to change her dress. Laughing at the strange contrast between our costumes, I led her to the table, and as I watched the brilliant figure opposite me, I resolved to know my fate that night, and if I had deceived myself, to break away at once from the spell that was increasing daily.

As soon as we were alone again, I led her out along the terrace, and as we paced there, arm-in-arm, I told her my hope and waited for her reply. A strange expression of relief dawned in her face as she looked up at me with eyes full of a tender melancholy.

"I hoped you would tell me this. Do not think it unmaidenly, but believe that I saw no other way of sharing this good fortune with you," she said in a voice curiously calm for such confessions.

"But, dear, I will have no sacrifice for me. If you love me, I accept the rest; otherwise not a penny will I touch," I said, decidedly, for her manner disturbed me.

"*If* I love you!" she cried; "how could I help it when you are all I have in the wide world to keep me from—"

There she caught back some word that trembled on her lips, and threw herself into my arms, weeping passionately.

Annoyed, yet touched, I soothed her, hoping to receive some explanation of this sudden outburst, which seemed more like remorseful grief than happy love. But quickly recovering herself, she murmured, brokenly:

"I have been so alone all my life—exiled from home, I knew not why—kept in ignorance of parents and friends till all were gone—my youth has been so sad that happiness overcomes me."

Here her little maid came to deliver a note; Cecelia stepped into the stream of light which lay across the terrace from the long, open window of the drawing-room, read a few lines that seemed scrawled on a rough bit of paper, told Adele to say she would come to-morrow, and tearing the note to atoms, she rejoined me, saying, carelessly:

"A message from Elspeth, my old nurse, who is ill, and sends for me."

I thought nothing of the note, but why did her heart beat so fast as I drew her to me again? Why were her eyes so absent, her face so full of mingled anger, fear and contempt? and why did she shiver as if, to her, the sultry summer night had suddenly grown cold? But when I asked what troubled her, she shyly said she was agitated by happiness alone, then led me in and sang delightfully till bedtime. As we parted for the night she fixed her eyes on me with a strangely tragic look, and whispered in her sweetest tone:

"Sleep well, Cecil, and be sure I love you."

I went to my room, but did not sleep at all, for my thoughts worried me, and as soon as the house was still I stepped out of my window and roamed away into the park. A storm was gathering, and black clouds swept across the moon, making fitful light and shade; a hot wind blew strongly, and flashes of lightning darted from the gloomy west. The unquiet night suited my mood, and I wandered on, lost in my own thoughts, till a peal of thunder roused me. Looking about for shelter, as I was now a long way from the hall, I saw a steady gleam not far distant, and making my way to the bottom of a wild glen, I found a little hovel half hidden among the trees.

Peering in at the low window before I asked admittance, I saw, by the dim light of one candle, an old crone sitting on the hearth, her withered face turned attentively toward another figure which stood nearer the door—a woman, evidently, though so shrouded in a cloak that age or sex was hard to guess. Her back was turned toward me, her voice fierce and low, her attitude one of command, and the words she uttered so peculiar that they arrested my attention at once.

"If you dare to speak or show yourself till I give you leave, I will silence you in the surest way. I fear nothing, and having played the perilous game so far, I will not be robbed of success when it is dearest, by the threats of a helpless old woman."

"Not so helpless as you think, ungrateful girl; feeble, old, and forgotten as I am, I can undo what I have done by a word, and I will, I swear, if you are not kinder," cried the old woman in a shrill, angry voice. "You promised I should stay with you, should have every care and comfort, and receive a generous share of all you got; but now you keep me here in this unwholesome place, with no one to speak to but half-witted Kate; you never come till I scare you into obedience, and you give me nothing but a paltry pound now and then. You know I'm too lame to escape, and you threaten me if I complain; but hark you, my lady, I set you up and I can pull you down whether you murder me or not, for it's all on paper, safe hidden from you, but sure to come to light if anything goes wrong with me."

As the old woman paused, breathless with her wrath and exultation, the younger stamped her foot with uncontrollable impatience, and clinched the slender white hand that was visible, but her next words were kinder, though bitter contempt lurked in her tone.

"You may trust me, grandmother; I'll not harm you unless you rouse the mad temper which I cannot control. You know why I do not take you home till my own place is secure. You are old, you forget, and babble of things safer untold. Here, it can make no trouble for either of us, but with me, surrounded by curious servants, mischief would come to both. Can you not wait a little longer, and remember that in undoing me you as surely ruin yourself, since you are the greater criminal."

"It would go hard with both of us, but my age would serve me better than your beauty, for I can be humble, but you have the pride of a devil, and death itself could not bend it. I'll wait, but I must have money, my fair share; I like to see and touch it, to make sure of it, for you may deceive me as you do the world, and slip away, leaving me to pay the penalty while you enjoy the pleasure."

"You shall have it as soon as I can get it without exciting suspicion by the demand. An opportunity will soon come, and I will not forget you."

"You mean this marriage?"

"Yes."

"Then you will really do it?"

"I will, for I love him."

"Good! that makes all safe. Now go, child, before the storm breaks, but come often, or I will send for you, and if there is any sign of false play my story goes to this man, and I'll buy my own safety by betraying you."

"Agreed. Good-night," and the shrouded figure was gone like a shadow.

I meant to follow it, led by an uncontrollable impulse, but as I paused to let her gain a safe distance, the movements of the old woman arrested me. Nodding and mumbling with weird intelligence, she lifted one of the flat hearthstones and drew out a packet of papers, over which she seemed to gloat, muttering, as she peered at the scrawled pages:

"I'm old, but I'm wary, and not to be shaken off till I get my share of plunder. She thinks to scare me, but Kate knows where to find my secret if anything goes wrong with me. I've tutored her, and my lady will be outwitted at the last."

Chuckling, the old crone put her treasure back, and, raking up the fire, hobbled away to bed. I waited till her light was out, resolving to secure those papers, for I could not divest myself of the conviction that this secret concerned me. I had not caught a glimpse of the younger woman's face, the voice was unknown, the figure hidden, and the white hand might have belonged to any lady, yet I felt a strong suspicion that this mysterious woman was Cecelia, and this evil-minded beldame was old Elspeth.

The storm broke, but I did not heed it, for my new purpose absorbed me. As soon as all was still I gently forced the low lattice, stepped in, and groping my way to the hearth, stirred the smoldering embers till a little blaze shot up, showing me the flat stone, and glittering also on an object that brought confirmation to my dark suspicions, for there, where the unknown girl had stood, lay the silver buckle. I caught it up, examined it by the dim light, and could not doubt my own eyes; it was Sir Sidney's antique ornament, and that impatient gesture of Cecelia's foot had left it here to betray her. I could readily understand how in her eagerness to slip away she had hastily changed the brocades for a simpler dress, forgetting to remove the shoes. Now I was sure of my right to seize the papers, and having done so stole noiselessly away.

Till dawn the storm raged furiously, and till dawn I sat in my room reading, thinking and resolving, for those badly-written pages showed me that the future I had pictured to myself never could be mine. The charm was broken, the warning instinct justified, and an impassable gulf opened between my cousin and myself. As the sun rose my plan was laid, and making a careful toilet, I tried to remove from my face, also, all trace of that night's experience, but did not entirely succeed, for the glass showed me a pale cheek, eyes full of a gloomy fire, and lips sternly set.

I often breakfasted alone, for Cecelia kept luxurious hours, and we seldom met till noon. That day I waited impatiently in the gallery where we had agreed to have a last sitting. My impatience did me good service, however, for when at last she came my paleness was replaced by a feverish warmth, and the stern lips had been trained to meet her with a smile.

"Good-morning, Cecil," she said, with an enchanting glance and a conscious blush as she gave me her hand.

I did not kiss it as usual, but holding it loosely I examined the soft little fingers outstretched in my palm, wondering as I did so if they could be the same I last night saw so fiercely clinched.

"What is it?" she asked, looking up at me with playful wonder in the eyes now grown so soft.

"Perhaps I was thinking of the ring that should be here," I answered, feeling a curious desire to test the love of this unhappy girl.

"I never thought I should consent to wear even so small a fetter as a wedding-ring, I love my liberty so well; but if you put it on it will not burden me, for you will be a tender and a generous master, Cecil," she answered, turning toward her accustomed seat to hide the emotion she was too proud to show me.

"I have the faults of my race—an unbending will, an unforgiving spirit, and 'the pride of a devil,' so beware, cousin."

She started as I quoted the old woman's phrase and shot a quick glance at me, but I was tranquilly preparing my palette, and she sat down with a relieved, yet weary air.

"Could you be as unmerciful as old Sir Guy, who cursed his only child for deceiving him?" she asked, lifting her eyes to the portrait of a stern-faced cavalier hanging next to debonair Sir Sidney.

"I could, for treachery turns my heart to stone."

I saw a slight shiver pass over her, and leaning her head on her hand she sat silent while I touched up a jewel here, a silken fold there, or added a brighter gold to the beautiful hair. She looked fair, young and tender, but, as I had said, treachery turned my heart to stone, and I did not spare her.

"You are *triste* to-day, sweetheart; let me amuse you as you have often done me by a legend of our family. I lately found it in an old manuscript which I will show you by-and-by."

"Thanks; I like old stories if they are strong and tragic," she answered, with a smile, as she lay back in the great chair in an attitude of luxurious indolence.

"Why, you have forgotten the little shoe; I meant to touch up the brilliant buckle and add a deeper scarlet to the coquettish heel. Shall I bid Adele bring it?" I asked, looking from the black satin slipper to the tranquil face lying on the purple cushion.

"No, it hurt my foot and I threw it away in a pet," she answered, with a little frown.

"Not buckle and all I hope, that is an heirloom."

"I have it safe, but the painted one is so well done I will not have it touched. Let my eyes outshine my jewels, as you gallantly averred they did, and tell your tale while you paint, for I am sadly indolent to-day."

As she added falsehood to falsehood, my heart beat indignantly against the traitorous ornament safely hidden in my breast, but my face did not betray me, and I obeyed her, glancing up from time to time to mark the effect of my words, not that of my work, for I painted with a colorless brush.

"Sir Marmaduke, for whom our uncle was named, I fancy, was a stern man who married late, and treated his wife so ill that she left him, taking with her their little child, for, being a girl, the old man had no love for it. Both the poor things died in a foreign land, and Sidney yonder, the comely nephew, was the lawful heir to the estate. The last words of the old man seemed to express his wish that it should be so, and the nephew was about to claim his own when the daughter reappeared and proved her right to the fortune. You are pale, love—does my dull story weary you?"

"No, it is only the heat. Go on, I listen," and half hiding the tell-tale cheek with her hand, she sat with downcast eyes, and a face that slowly grew a colorless mask with the effort to subdue emotion.

"The old manuscript is not very clear on this point; but I gather that the neglected girl's reported death was only a ruse to shield her from her cruel father. Her claim was accepted, and poor Sidney left to poverty again. Now comes the romance of the tale. He went to see this new-found cousin; she was beautiful and gracious, seemed eager to share her prize, and generously offered the young man a home. This touched and won him. She soon evidently loved him, and in spite of an inward distrust, he *fancied* he returned the passion."

As I slightly emphasized a word here and there in that last sentence, a fiery glow spread over that white face from neck to brow, the haughty eyes flashed full upon me, and the red lips trembled as if passionate words were with difficulty restrained. I saw that my shaft told, and with resentful coolness I went on, still preserving the gay, light tone that made the truth doubly bitter and taunting.

"Take the fan that lies in your lap, dearest; this heat oppresses you. Yes, it was very curious to read how this lover was fascinated in spite of himself, and how he fought against his doubts till he tried to put an end to them by asking the hand extended to him."

The dimpled hand lying on the arm of the chair was clinched suddenly, and I saw again the hand of the cloaked woman in the wood, and smiling to myself at this new confirmation, I continued:

"But here begins the tragedy which you like so well. The cousins were betrothed, and that very night Sidney, who was given to late wanderings, went out to dream lover's dreams, in spite of a gathering storm which drove him for shelter to a little cottage in the wood. Here he overheard a strange conversation between an old creature and a mysterious woman whose face he could not see." (How her eyes glittered as she listened! and what a long breath of relief escaped her at those last words!) "This lively gossip excited Sidney's curiosity, and when the lady vanished, leaving this traitor behind her" (here I produced the buckle), "this bold young man, guided by the mutterings of the crone, found and secured a strange confession of the treachery of both."

Here Cecelia rose erect in her chair, and from that moment her eyes never left my face as she listened, still and colorless as the statue behind her. I think any sign of weakness or remorse would have touched me even then, but she showed none, and her indomitable pride roused mine, making me pitiless. Brush and palette lay idle now, and looking straight at the fair, false face before me, I rapidly ended the story which I had begun in the disguise of an ancient legend.

"It seems that the old woman had been the confidential servant of Sir Marmaduke's wife, and had a grudge of her own against her master. When my lady and the child died, for die they did, as reported, this woman bided her time, artfully securing letters, tokens, and other proofs, to use when the hour came. At Sir Marmaduke's death she put forward her grandchild, the natural daughter of the old man, inheriting both the beauty and the spirit of her race. This girl played her part well; the plot succeeded, and if the sordid nature of the grand dame had not irritated the heiress and kept her in danger of discovery, all would have worked admirably. Half justice, under the guise of generosity, soothed whatever pangs of remorse the girl felt, and as she loved Sidney, she believed that she could expiate the wrong she did him by keeping him happily blind to the treachery of a wife he trusted. A terrible mistake, for when he discovered this deceit, the old distrust turned to contempt, gratitude to wrath, and love to loathing."

"What did he do?" she whispered, with white lips, as an agony of shame, despair, and love looked at me from the tragic eyes.

"Possessing something of the chivalry of his race, he disdained to crush her even by one reproach; but though forced to decline the proposed alliance, he freely offered her safety and a maintenance, never forgetting that, in spite of deceit, and sin, and shame, she was a woman and his cousin."

"Did he think she would accept?" she cried, lifting the head that had sunk lower and lower as I spoke till all the warm-hued hair swept to her feet.

I had risen and looked down at her with an uncontrollable pity softening my stern face. I answered briefly:

"Yes, for where else could she find help but at the hands of her kinsman?"

She sprang up, as if my compassion was more bitter to hear than my contempt, the fiery spirit rebelled against me, and love itself yielded to the pride that ruled her.

"Not even the offer of a favor will I accept from you, for I have a kinder friend to fly to. Take your rightful place, and enjoy it if you can, haunted as it must be by the memory of the stain I have brought upon the name you are so proud of."

She hurried, as if to leave me, but pausing at the easel, cast a sudden look at the smiling image of herself, and as if anxious to leave no trace behind, she caught up my palette-knife, scored the canvas up and down till it hung in strips; then with a laugh which echoed long in my ears she swept slowly down the long gallery, passed through the wide window at the further end to the balcony that overhung the court below, and standing there with the sunshine streaming over her, she looked back at me with an expression which fixed that moment in my memory for ever.

Like a brilliant picture, she stood there with the light full on her shining hair, jeweled arms, rich robes, and stately form, all contrasting sharply with the wild and woeful face looking backward with a mute farewell.

On that instant a terrible foreboding of her purpose flashed over me, and I rushed forward to restrain her; but too late, for with a wave of the white hand she was gone.

Death was the kinder friend to whom she had flown, and when I found her in the courtyard, shattered by that cruel fall, she smiled the old proud smile, and put away the hand that would have lifted her so tenderly.

"Let me die here; I have no other home," she whispered, faintly; then her face softened as she looked up at my pallid face, and feebly trying to fold her hands, she murmured, tenderly:

"Forgive me, for I loved you!"

Those were her last words, and as they passed her lips, I saw nothing but a beautiful dead woman lying at my feet, and Sir Sidney's diamond buckle glittering in the sun, as it fell from my breast to receive a bloody stain which lingers still on that relic of my unhappy cousin.

❧ La Belle Bayadère

Chapter I

THE WHOLE of the immense stage represented a tropical forest, with the skillful fidelity which French artists bring to such work. A wide river, starred with lotus flowers, flowed through the luxuriant jungle; moonlight filled the green gloom with mellow radiance, and unseen music lent enchantment to the delicious solitude. Before the first sound of applause could express the satisfaction of the brilliant audience, stealthy steps seemed to come creeping through the wood, and just when expectation was at its height, a magnificent tiger bounded from the jungle and vanished in its lair. It was a real tiger, and this daring surprise charmed the excitable Parisians by its very danger.

The well-trained beast's *début* was hailed by loud applause, for the chains it wore were invisible, and the wild scene seemed wonderfully real.

"How well it opens! Even you, my *blasé* Philip, will become enthusiastic, I think, as the piece goes on," said beautiful Mrs. Cope, turning toward her husband—a handsome, indolent-looking man, who lounged beside her with an air of supreme indifference to all about him.

"I doubt it, Maud, but if anything could stir me up a trifle it would be these souvenirs of India," he replied, gently yawning behind his hand.

"I thought so, and for that reason persuaded you to come. You want a new sensation, an excitement of some sort, and I promised to give you one. In a few minutes, I suspect, you will own that I have kept my word," and the tender eyes of the young wife turned half-wistfully, half-triumphantly to the dark face of her listless husband.

"I will welcome anything that shall put fire, spice, and interest into my life here in this tame country; but I fancy your idea of excitement, my friend, differs from mine as much as a tiger-hunt does from a flower-show."

Before Mrs. Cope could reply, a sudden change in the music announced the arrival of the hero of the piece. With the barbaric clash of cymbal, drum and horn, the splendors of a mounted guard, and all the pomp of an Eastern satrap, Prince Acbar appeared, reclining on a scarlet and gold howda borne by a white elephant—a slender, swarthy young Indian with magnificent eyes and figure, who looked his part to the life, and played it with spirit, rapidly alternating from the graceful languor to the fiery activity of a true Oriental.

"This is not bad, upon my word," said Cope, lifting his glass to examine the prince as he descended, stepping carelessly on the bowed backs of his kneeling slaves.

"Wait till you see the mate of this splendid creature. My sensation is yet to come," whispered Maud, with a smile.

A wild hunting-song from the guard, and a little necessary by-play, informed the audience that the prince was on a tiger-hunt, and having missed the beast after a long chase, was about to repose. Slaves arranged a luxurious couch of skins beside the river, and then, at an imperious wave of the master's hand, the train vanished, leaving the young man to drop asleep, lulled by the murmur of the stream.

A most effective tableau was produced by the handsome, brilliantly-appareled youth lying on his savage couch in an attitude of graceful abandon, with eyes dreamily fixed on the gleaming water, while behind him from the gloom of the cave glared the tiger's fierce head, stealthily appearing and disappearing as the treacherous brute prepared to spring upon its prey.

A stir of excitement filled the house, and glances of mingled fear and admiration were concentrated upon the daring beast-tamer as he lay tranquilly within reach of the royal tiger; but, as if to whet interest by delay, again the music changed, and a delicious melody entranced the ear.

A light mist floated down the river, and when it lifted, one of the magnified lotus flowers was seen to be unfolding. Leaf by leaf it spread till the last white petal fell, disclosing the "Spirit of the Ganges" nestling in its golden heart.

A diaphanous cloud of illusion revealed a little foot, a snowy arm, and a face of marvelous beauty, framed in waves of darkest hair, out of which shone lustrous eyes, full of a mysterious power.

The great golden showers seemed to surround this charming figure with a soft radiance as she rose, and leaving her flowery bed, danced over the moonlit water like a spirit of the summer night. It was a wonderful piece of art, for the airy grace of the rosy feet, the eloquent gestures of the lovely arms, the languid undulations of the exquisite figure, were beyond the skill of any known danseuse.

No effort was visible, no theatrical tinsel, no hackneyed step or pose marred the illusion, and the "poetry of motion" seemed perfectly illustrated as this strange girl, still half enveloped in the fleecy cloud, hovered to and fro before the entranced spectators.

Floating toward the shore along a path of light, she seemed to smile upon the prince as she sang a canzonet in a voice as full of passionate sweetness as her face was of subtle Southern beauty. In the song was given the key to the piece; the spirit tells her love for the mortal, and promises him the eternal joys of a Hindoo heaven if he is true to her.

As the last note died, the prince awoke from his dream and rushed forward as if to detain the lovely phantom; but like a wraith, she vanished, leaving only the white cloud in his eager arms.

At this instant the tiger leaped, and the young man, rudely startled from his trance, uttered so natural a cry of alarm that many involuntarily echoed it. Then followed the fight which was the *chef-d'oeuvre* of this remarkable beast-tamer.

The well-trained animal played its part so perfectly that women turned pale and men breathed hard as they watched man and monster wrestling together, in such seeming deadly earnest that for a time nothing was visible but a mass of tawny fur, supple brown limbs, savage eyes, and the flash of jeweled robes.

The man came uppermost at last, and clutching the brute by the throat, knelt on its panting breast as he apparently drove his dagger into its vitals with a cry of exultation. A brief struggle, a faint attempt to rend its victor, and the tiger rolled lifeless at the feet of the prince, whom the excited spectators overwhelmed with acclamations.

As the curtain fell, Mrs. Cope drew a long breath of relief, and glanced at her husband to see if he showed any sign of interest yet. She was satisfied—nay, even startled by the entire change which had passed over him.

He sat erect, with wide open eyes, lips apart, and the air of one who had been suddenly surprised out of himself. More than this, his bronzed cheek was pale, his hand clutched the cushioned rail with unconscious vehemence, and he stared at the green curtain before him, as if on its blank surface he saw some figure which absorbed his thoughts.

"What is it, Philip? You look as if you had seen a ghost," whispered his wife, amazed at his appearance.

"I have!" he answered, without stirring.

"Was it the fight that excites you so strangely?"

"I scarcely saw it."

"Then it is the 'Spirit of the Ganges,' and my test succeeds."

"Who is she?" and Cope drew his hand across his face, as to compose his features to their wonted calm.

"I know nothing of her, except that she is the last new sensation. A Spaniard, some one said, and destined to take Paris by storm."

"No Spaniard ever danced like that. I have often tried to describe the Eastern Bayadères—now you have seen one."

"How do you know?"

"No other dancers use the arms more than the feet, or have the art to make each gesture express an emotion. No other women are so lovely, or possess the power of making their beauty felt."

"You speak warmly, and you should know," answered Mrs. Cope, with a troubled look. "This charming creature certainly got herself up wonderfully for the part, and played like a born sprite."

"Better even than you think, for none but a true Hindoo would have remembered the *khol* on the eyelids, the *henna* on the finger-tips, the gauzy *tab* over the bosom, or worn bangles with such ease, and dared attempt to dance with bare feet. Yes, she *is* beautiful, this unknown, who is to enslave all Paris as she has me!"

A strange expression of mingled exultation and melancholy passed over the man's face as he spoke, and turning from his wife, he fell to studying the hitherto neglected playbill, as if eager to gather some intelligence from it.

"What have I done?" cried the poor woman, within herself. "I hoped to amuse him for an hour, and perhaps I have lost him for ever. I tried to banish ennui, and have kindled a flame that may consume my peace. These souvenirs of India recall something more tender than tiger-hunts, and these handsome Indians transport him to the land where, perhaps, the romance of his youth was known."

Here the curtain rose again; but now Cope was the breathless spectator, and his wife, forgetting her interest in the play, watched him keenly, feeling that the test she innocently applied possessed a power she had not suspected.

The scenes which followed were all unusually brilliant, piquant, or daring. La Belle Bayadère danced but three times, yet she created a furore at each appearance, for her beauty, grace and style were too new and striking to fail of impressing the novelty-mad Parisians with the wildest admiration.

Her second dance was in the harem of the prince, who is endeavoring to forget his haunting dream of the "Spirit," in the charms of a bevy of Georgian slaves whom a merchant exhibits. One by one the fair girls sang and danced before him, but all failed to please till Mademoiselle Rahel, the pet danseuse of Paris, executed her most famous *pas* in her best manner. The audience greeted her with enthusiasm, the prince smiled upon her, and the panting beauty was about to accept the royal favor extended to her, when, with startling abruptness, the music broke into a wild strain, and out from the central fountain flashed La Belle Bayadère like a flame of fire.

Scarlet, white and gold was her dress, silver bangles shone on slender wrist and ankle, fire-flies seemed imprisoned in her dusky hair, and she kept time to her winged steps with the clash of cymbals as she danced as no woman had ever danced on that stage before. She seemed another creature from the airy sylph of the moonlight river. All now was fire and force, no leap too daring, no step too intricate, no pose impossible to the agile grace of the lithe figure which darted to and fro like a wandering flame. The vivid coloring, intense vitality, and marvelous skill of the creature electrified actors and audience; all followed her with dazzled eyes, completely carried away by the spirit of that amazing dance. Louder and louder rose the music, faster and faster flew the little feet, wilder and wilder grew the frenzy which seemed to possess the girl, till nothing was visible but a brilliant maze of scarlet drapery, flying hair, and a face inspired by something far more potent than a spirit of rivalry. Then, at the very acme of this enchanting abandon, the music snapped in a broken chord, and with a single ringing clash of the cymbals, the Bayadère paused as if turned to stone, stood for one instant radiant and regal, in an attitude of indescribable grace, and vanished as swiftly as she came.

Before the curtain was fairly down, Cope had darted from the box with a face as full of energy and fire as that of the mimic prince who had watched the beautiful dancer with the pride and ardor of a real lover. Mrs. Cope hid herself behind the curtains of her box, agitated with conflicting hopes and fears, for every moment confirmed her suspicion that she had unwittingly touched some secret sin or sorrow of her husband's past. Not till the last bell rang, after an unusually long pause, did he reappear, flushed, breathless and excited, bringing with him a singular bouquet, formed entirely of cactus-blossoms of the most vivid scarlet, surmounted by their own prickly leaves.

"For whom is that savage-looking nosegay, Philip?" asked Mrs. Cope, as he threw himself into a chair and fixed his eyes eagerly on the ascending curtain.

"Wait and see, madame," he briefly answered in the imperious tone she had often resented for the sake of others, yet never heard addressed to herself before.

She was a proud woman, and his manner wounded her deeply. She set her lips, and her eyes kindled as she said, in a cool, significant tone which arrested his attention in spite of himself:

"I will; and when you fling your thorny gift to the girl, I will offer my roses to her handsome husband."

"Her what?" and Cope turned on her a quick glance full of doubt and dismay.

"I have been told that the young pair are newly married, and fancy it is true, for they play like lovers."

"A jealous woman's fancy," and he looked away with an incredulous shrug.

"Watch and see," she said, echoing his tone if not his words exactly.

"I will!" and Cope's face wore an ominous smile as he turned to follow the handsome Indian through several scenes, in which he and his beasts played stirring parts. Not till the closing act did the charming girl reappear and give an intense interest to a spectacle which one observer watched with an almost fierce scrutiny. As a grand finale the prince is cast into a den of wild beasts by his enemies, to whom he has been treacherously betrayed, and the last scene displayed the faithful lover in a gloomy amphitheatre, surrounded by foes above and savage brutes below. One tiger lay as if already slain by the hero, who waits, wounded but undismayed, the attack of a still more formidable assailant. All the animals were safely held by artfully-hidden chains, except the lion, who was about to destroy the much-enduring prince. He looked a magnificent brute as he stood surveying his victim with thunderous growls, but he was old, toothless, heavily drugged, and his master's all-powerful eye never left him a moment; therefore the danger was slight, great as it appeared. Many shuddered as they looked, and some cried out as the lion crouched before he sprung, but at the instant the dancer bounded over the iron bars which surrounded the mimic amphitheatre, and alighted just between the brute and his prey.

"Great heavens, what courage!" exclaimed the spell-bound audience, as the dauntless creature warily approached the lion, who retreated as she advanced. Half way round the enclosure she paused, and with a rapid gesture flung a golden chain about the royal beast, who dropped submissively at her feet, as if the light fetter possessed an irresistible power. Dancing airily to and fro among the animals, she seemed to cast a spell on all, for one by one they shrunk and cowered before the little red-tipped wand she carried, for the painted toy was as potent in their eyes as the red-hot iron rod their master used to train and conquer them with. As the last leopard fawned at her feet the girl executed a joyful *pas seul* as wonderful as the others had been, and at the end threw herself into the arms of the prince, signifying that the reward was won. A gorgeous transformation scene closed the spectacle with the splendors of a Hindoo paradise, whither the lovers are welcomed by houris to a life of eternal delight.

"She must come now. She dare not refuse to accept our homage," was the universal exclamation as a frantic encore thundered through the house, assuring the unknown danseuse that fame and fortune were awaiting her. "The Spirit of the Ganges" was pronounced a grand success.

She did come, but, as if bent on charming them entirely by her daring freaks, she led the captive lion with her, and while the comely actor gathered up the floral trophies that strewed the stage, she leaned against the stately brute with a nonchalant grace infinitely more effective than the most coquettish smiles or grateful obeisances.

Mrs. Cope forgot to fling her flowers, but Philip, leaning far over the box, cast his exactly at the girl's feet. She glanced up, and the proud weariness of her face flashed into sudden scorn and detestation as her great black eyes rested for an instant on the flushed, dark countenance bent toward her. Then, in the drawing of a breath, she set her foot upon the flowers with a gesture of disdain, and turning, gave her hand to the young Indian, wearing a smile of such tender meaning that few doubted the existence of a real romance behind the mimic one.

As they vanished Cope struck his clinched hand on the cushion before him, exclaiming in a vehement whisper:

"By heavens it *is* she!"

"Who? Oh, Philip, what have I done?" cried his wife, detaining him as he seemed about to go, forgetful of her presence.

He laughed a strange laugh, drew her hand under his arm as if recollecting himself, and said, abruptly:

"You have been trying to rouse me, as you call it, ever since we were married; rest satisfied, you have done it now with a vengeance."

CHAPTER II

FOR SIX WEEKS "The Spirit of the Ganges" was played nightly to packed houses; for six weeks Philip Cope made unavailing efforts to obtain an interview with the lovely danseuse, and for six weary weeks his wife watched him with the jealous vigilance of a proud and loving woman suddenly wakened from a brief dream of confidence and tenderness. She had "roused him with a vengeance," for, from the night when her entreaties had lured him to the theatre, he was an altered man. Brusque and cold, restless and absorbed, he seemed utterly unlike the lover who, with languid devotion, had wooed and won the girl who gladly gave her heart, refusing to believe that he sought her for her fortune, or the husband who for three months had been slowly falling back into the supreme indifference of a man who cared for nothing but his selfish ease. Now Maud began to believe that the elegant ennui was but a mask to cover some secret care, remorse or fear, and this sudden change from perfect indolence to sleepless energy perplexed and afflicted her.

Too proud to demand explanations which had been sternly refused to tender entreaties, she hid her doubts and fears under a calm front, and watched with untiring patience.

Night after night the two sat in their box silent but alert; day after day Philip besieged the dancer with notes and messages beseeching one word with her, and day and night the evil spell which had been cast over both worked its changes unsuspected by all but the subtle mind that gave it birth.

La Belle Bayadère became the rage in Paris, and added to her *éclat* the charm of mystery, for only on the stage was she visible to her adorers. When the curtain fell she vanished with her lover, and the most persistent curiosity could only discover that the Indian troupe lived secluded in a hotel which was reported to be a miracle of

Eastern luxury. Surrounded by her own servants, faithful, silent and brave, the girl was inaccessible, and as she was never seen in public unaccompanied by Indra, the actor, it was in vain to attempt an interview till she willed it.

What Cope suffered in those weeks was but a foretaste of the years to come, and some dim consciousness of this may have given added bitterness to the long suspense, the keen regret, the vivid memories, and the hopeless desires which made that time a torment.

The announcement of the farewell representation of the favorite spectacle brought dismay to Cope and relief to his wife, who had discovered only that Philip had not met the dancer in spite of his unceasing efforts.

On the evening of that day, as Maud went to dress for the theatre, she found a tiny note on her toilet-table containing these words, written in a woman's hand:

"If you desire to know your husband's secret, follow without fear the messenger who will come for you at midnight."

"I will go," she said, with a resolute air, as she hid the billet in her bosom. "If it costs me my life I *will* know what Philip hides from me. Death cannot be worse than this suspense and doubt."

Suspecting whither she would be led, she made a grand toilet, feeling a woman's pride in heightening her beauty for a rival's eyes. As she swept into the *salon* she was joined by her husband, who, for some unknown reason, had made himself a marvel of elegance, and wore a look of triumph that caused the poor woman's heart to stand still with a nameless fear.

"For whom is all this splendor?" he asked, with a careless glance at the lovely wife before him.

"Not for you, Philip. You no longer care for the beauty you once praised. I dress to do honor to La Belle Bayadère," answered Maud, with a keen look.

"I, also," and he gave her back a smile that seemed to defy doubt, reproach and shame.

"Philip, have you nothing to tell me? I can forgive and forget much for your sake. I shall never ask again. Be just, be generous, and do not let a mystery estrange us."

As she spoke with a sudden impulse of tenderness, Maud stretched her hands imploringly toward him, hoping he would spare her from playing the spy by a frank confession. But the glamour of an old love was over him, truth and pity were not in him, and a daring hope had just been kindled which blinded him to right and justice. Hardening his heart, and steeling his face, he met her pathetic appeal with a mocking bow, and said:

"Your interest flatters me; but I have no interesting confidences to bestow. Permit me to button your gloves, for the carriage waits."

But the fingers that performed the little service trembled; as he led her down-stairs, Maud could hear his heart beat rapidly, and his face never lost the pale excitement, which was by turns exultant or intensely anxious.

Neither spoke again during the drive, and through the play an almost unbroken silence reigned in their box, for each was intent on some all-absorbing thought when the stage did not claim their entire attention.

Never had La Belle played more perfectly, and never had a farewell been more enthusiastic than that which she received when she smiled her adieu and was led away by the handsome Indra along a path carpeted with flowers.

"You will go home at once, of course. I have an engagement," said Cope, as he caught up his hat with ill-disguised impatience, and hurried his wife into the carriage.

"Good-night," she said, but he was gone, and she drove on with bitter tears dropping fast upon the hands locked fast together in her lap.

"Madame, it is I," said a low voice near her, and glancing up in alarm, she saw a venerable Indian seated opposite. "Have no fear. I am the messenger, and the time is nearly come," he said, in a reassuring tone; adding, gravely, "do you trust me?"

"Yes," she answered, trembling, yet resolved.

Without a word he leaned out, gave an order, and the carriage rolled rapidly in a new direction.

"Who sends for me?" she asked.

No answer but a finger on the lips, as the old man shook his head and sat motionless.

That night Cope had also received a message, for on his table he had found a single scarlet cactus and three words on a card beside it, "Come at twelve."

"At last—at last!" he had cried, seizing the flower and pressing the well-known signal to his lips. "I knew she would relent, and now nothing shall stand between us if she forgives."

This secret hope agitated him almost beyond control, and when at length free he hurried away to the long-desired interview. No guide was needed; he knew the way but too well, and paced to and fro before the hotel, waiting with fierce impatience for the appointed hour to strike.

As he stood in the courtyard a carriage dashed in, and a vailed lady descended and entered, accompanied by a venerable Indian.

"My Almèe!" murmured Cope, ardently, as he watched the shrouded figures vanish.

Ten minutes later the clocks struck, and he sprang up the steps, fearing no repulse now. Doors opened like magic before him, and he found himself in the long-desired presence of La Belle Bayadère.

Still in the costume she had worn as the "Spirit," the lovely woman looked lovelier than ever, for the flush of some strong emotion was on her cheek, its softness in her eyes, its tender music in her voice.

As Cope impetuously approached, she warned him back, saying, slowly, in the purest French:

"Not yet. I have much to say before I can embrace you. When you have confessed and done penance the reward may come."

"Almèe, forgive me! I will confess anything, do any penance to win my old place back. Say what you will, but do not keep me waiting long, for my patience has been hardly tried, and I am pining for my reward."

A strange smile passed over the girl's mobile features, but she only said:

"I, too, have waited, and now desire my reward. Listen, and tell me if this tale is not true. Two years ago, in India, an English soldier was wounded in a fight among the hills, left for dead by his men, and would have perished had not an old man, a Hindoo, befriended his enemy, taken him home, nursed and saved him. The Englishman feigned gratitude to the father and love to his daughter. They trusted him, and when he tired of them he betrayed the old man to death, and would have made the girl his slave, but she escaped."

"All true—God forgive me! but I did not feign love—I truly loved you, Almèe, and would have married you if it had been safe," broke in Cope, with mingled shame, remorse, and passion struggling in face and voice.

"Let that pass. The girl found a friend, and in time discovered the old lover whom she sought."

"Then, you have come to find me?" cried Cope, bewildered by the keen glitter of her eyes, the soft smile of her lips, and the measured tone of her clear voice.

"Yes, I searched for you through two long years, and found you at last more lost to me than when land and sea divided us."

"Faithful angel! Yes, in a desperate mood I sold myself for a woman's fortune. Till you came I found some pleasure in the bargain, spite of the burden attached, but now it is a worse slavery than the galleys. It has nearly maddened me since I beheld you again, and I'll break loose at once, for it will surely come to that sooner or later."

"You love me still?" asked Almèe, with a sudden tremor in her voice, as Cope paused, breathless and expectant.

"More passionately than ever, for absence has only made you fairer, remorse rendered you dearer, and companionship with a calm, cold Englishwoman shows me how infinitely sweeter is the ardent love, the deathless devotion of my Indian Almèe."

"Will you leave this stately wife, this hard-won wealth, your good name, and honorable place to win me—me, a dancing-girl, who have only my beauty for my dower?" asked the danseuse, bending on him that searching look, while her bosom heaved with the emotions she suppressed.

"I will, and you know it, for the old spirit woke when I saw you; the reckless courage, the wild nature, the fiery heart are all here, hidden so long only to break out stronger than before. Try me. For your sake I will defy the world, and fly to the desert again with my little queen."

Quite carried away by his own untameable desires, Cope threw himself at her feet, and waited her reply without fear. How her eyes shone with sudden fire, and her red lips curled with pride as she watched the man before her, utterly subjugated to her will in spite of all the obstacles that should have restrained him!

In the drawing of a breath her whole air changed, her face was full of the intensest scorn, and her voice startled him by its sharp, stern accent, as she said, with a slow, triumphant smile:

"I am satisfied! For this I have worked and waited; for this I have led you on to break every tie that should bind an honorable man, to sacrifice all hope of future peace, and to find too late that it has been in vain."

"In vain! Oh, Almèe, do not mock me! What stands between us now?" cried Cope, bewildered.

"My husband and your wife."

As the words fell from her lips, she pointed toward two curtained alcoves behind her, and, as if obeying her gesture, the purple draperies parted, showing Indra, splendid in his youth, beauty, and happiness, and Maud, the pale ghost of her former self, while in her eyes burned the quenchless fire of a proud woman's resentment.

In the dead pause that followed, Cope felt to his heart's core the bitter sting of a shame which never could be effaced, owned that Almèe's subtle vengeance had wrecked his life, and followed his wife without a word, when La Belle Bayadère threw herself into Indra's arms, saying, briefly:

"Go! we want no shadow on our happiness."

❧ Bibliography

This chronological listing, prepared by Daniel Shealy, contains all located Alcott thrillers.

"Marion Earle: or, Only an Actress!" *American Union* (ca. July-12 September 1858). Repr. in *New York Atlas* (12 September 1858).

"Pauline's Passion and Punishment," *Frank Leslie's Illustrated Newspaper* (3 and 10 January 1863). Repr. in *Behind a Mask: The Unknown Thrillers of Louisa May Alcott,* ed. Madeleine B. Stern (New York: William Morrow, 1975).

"A Whisper in the Dark," *Frank Leslie's Illustrated Newspaper* (6 and 13 June 1863). Repr. in *A Modern Mephistopheles and A Whisper in the Dark* (Boston: Roberts Brothers, 1889); and in *Plots and Counterplots: More Unknown Thrillers of Louisa May Alcott,* ed. Madeleine B. Stern (New York: William Morrow, 1976).

"A Pair of Eyes; or, Modern Magic," *Frank Leslie's Illustrated Newspaper* (24 and 31 October 1863). Repr. in *A Double Life: Newly Discovered Thrillers of Louisa May Alcott,* ed. Madeleine B. Stern, Joel Myerson, and Daniel Shealy (Boston: Little, Brown, 1988).

"Enigmas," *Frank Leslie's Illustrated Newspaper* (14 and 21 May 1864). Repr. in *Frank Leslie's Ten Cent Monthly* (October 1864) and in *Frank Leslie's Popular Monthly* (April 1876).

"V.V.; or, Plots and Counterplots," *The Flag of Our Union* (4, 11, 18, and 25 February 1865). Repr. as ten-cent novelette by A. M. Barnard (Boston: Thomes & Talbot, ca. 1870); and in *Plots and Counterplots,* ed. Madeleine B. Stern (New York: William Morrow, 1976).

"The Fate of the Forrests," *Frank Leslie's Illustrated Newspaper* (11, 18, and 25 February 1865). Repr. in *A Double Life,* ed. Madeleine B. Stern, Joel Myerson, and Daniel Shealy (Boston: Little, Brown, 1988).

"A Marble Woman: or, The Mysterious Model," *The Flag of Our Union* (20, 27 May and 3, 10 June 1865). Repr. in *Plots and Counterplots,* ed. Madeleine B. Stern (New York: William Morrow, 1976).

"A Double Tragedy. An Actor's Story," *Frank Leslie's Chimney Corner* (3 June 1865). Repr. in *A Double Life,* ed. Madeleine B. Stern, Joel Myerson, and Daniel Shealy (Boston: Little, Brown, 1988).

"Ariel. A Legend of the Lighthouse," *Frank Leslie's Chimney Corner* (8 and 15 July 1865). Repr. in *A Double Life,* ed. Madeleine B. Stern, Joel Myerson, and Daniel Shealy (Boston: Little, Brown, 1988).

"A Nurse's Story," *Frank Leslie's Chimney Corner* (2, 9, 16, 23, 30 December 1865 and 6 January 1866). Repr. in *Freaks of Genius: Unknown Thrillers of Louisa May Alcott,* ed. Daniel Shealy, Madeleine B. Stern, and Joel Myerson (Westport, Conn.: Greenwood, 1991).

"Behind a Mask: or, A Woman's Power," *The Flag of Our Union* (13, 20, 27 October and 3 November 1866). Repr. in *Behind a Mask,* ed. Madeleine B. Stern (New York: William Morrow, 1975).

"The Freak of a Genius," *Frank Leslie's Illustrated Newspaper* (20, 27 October and 3, 10, 17 November 1866). Repr. in *Freaks of Genius,* ed. Daniel Shealy, Madeleine B. Stern. and Joel Myerson (Westport, Conn.: Greenwood, 1991).

"The Mysterious Key, and What It Opened," (Boston: Elliott, Thomes & Talbot, [1867]). No. 50 in *Ten Cent Novelettes* series of *Standard American Authors.* Repr. as No. 382 in *The Leisure Hour Library* (New York: F. M. Lupton, ca. 1900); and in *Behind a Mask,* ed. Madeleine B. Stern (New York: William Morrow, 1975).

"The Skeleton in the Closet," in Perley Parker, *The Foundling* (Boston: Elliott, Thomes & Talbot, [1867]). No. 49 in *Ten Cent Novelettes* series of *Standard American Authors.* Repr. in *Plots and Counterplots,* ed. Madeleine B. Stern (New York: William Morrow, 1976).

"The Abbot's Ghost: or, Maurice Treherne's Temptation," *The Flag of Our Union* (5, 12, 19, and 26 January 1867). Repr. in *Behind a Mask,* ed. Madeleine B. Stern (New York: William Morrow, 1975).

"Hope's Debut," *Frank Leslie's Chimney Corner* (6 April 1867). Repr. in *Louisa May Alcott: Selected Fiction,* ed. Daniel Shealy, Madeleine B. Stern, and Joel Myerson (Boston: Little, Brown, 1991).

"Thrice Tempted," *Frank Leslie's Chimney Corner* (20 July 1867). Repr. in *Louisa May Alcott: Selected Fiction,* ed. Daniel Shealy, Madeleine B. Stern, and Joel Myerson (Boston: Little, Brown, 1991).

"Taming a Tartar," *Frank Leslie's Illustrated Newspaper* (30 November and 7, 14, and 21 December 1867). Repr. in *A Modern Mephistopheles and Taming a Tartar,* ed. Madeleine B. Stern (New York: Praeger, 1987); and in *A Double Life,* ed. Madeleine B. Stern, Joel Myerson, and Daniel Shealy (Boston: Little, Brown, 1988).

"Doctor Dorn's Revenge," *Frank Leslie's Lady's Magazine* (February 1868). Repr. in *From Jo March's Attic: Stories of Intrigue and Suspense,* ed. Madeleine B. Stern and Daniel Shealy (Boston: Northeastern University Press, 1993).

"La Jeune; or, Actress and Woman," *Frank Leslie's Chimney Corner* (18 April 1868). Repr. in *Freaks of Genius,* ed. Daniel Shealy, Madeleine B. Stern, and Joel Myerson (Westport, Conn.: Greenwood, 1991)

"Countess Varazoff," *Frank Leslie's Lady's Magazine* (June 1868). Repr. in *From Jo March's Attic: Stories of Intrigue and Suspense,* ed. Madeleine B. Stern and Daniel Shealy (Boston: Northeastern University Press, 1993).

"The Romance of a Bouquet," *Frank Leslie's Illustrated Newspaper* (27 June 1868). Repr. in *Freaks of Genius,* ed. Daniel Shealy, Madeleine B. Stern, and Joel Myerson (Westport, Conn.: Greenwood, 1991).

"A Laugh and A Look," *Frank Leslie's Chimney Corner* (4 July 1868). Repr. in *Freaks of Genius,* ed. Daniel Shealy, Madeleine B. Stern, and Joel Myerson (Westport, Conn.: Greenwood, 1991).

"Fatal Follies," *Frank Leslie's Lady's Magazine* (September 1868). Repr. in *From Jo March's Attic: Stories of Intrigue and Suspense,* ed. Madeleine B. Stern and Daniel Shealy (Boston: Northeastern University Press, 1993).

"Fate in a Fan," *Frank Leslie's Lady's Magazine* (January 1869). Repr. in *From Jo March's Attic: Stories of Intrigue and Suspense,* ed. Madeleine B. Stern and Daniel Shealy (Boston: Northeastern University Press, 1993).

"Perilous Play," *Frank Leslie's Chimney Corner* (13 February 1869). Repr. in *Frank Leslie's Popular Monthly* (November 1876); and in *Plots and Counterplots,* ed. Madeleine B. Stern (New York: William Morrow, 1976).

"Which Wins?" *Frank Leslie's Lady's Magazine* (March 1869). Repr. in *From Jo March's Attic: Stories of Intrigue and Suspense,* ed. Madeleine B. Stern and Daniel Shealy (Boston: Northeastern University Press, 1993).

"Honor's Fortune," *Frank Leslie's Lady's Magazine* (June 1869). Repr. in *From Jo March's Attic: Stories of Intrigue and Suspense,* ed. Madeleine B. Stern and Daniel Shealy (Boston: Northeastern University Press, 1993).

"Mrs. Vane's Charade," *Frank Leslie's Chimney Corner* (21 August 1869). Repr. in *Freaks of Genius,* ed. Daniel Shealy, Madeleine B. Stern, and Joel Myerson (Westport, Conn.: Greenwood, 1991).

"My Mysterious Mademoiselle," *Frank Leslie's Lady's Magazine* (September 1869). Repr. in *From Jo March's Attic: Stories of Intrigue and Suspense,* ed. Madeleine B. Stern and Daniel Shealy (Boston: Northeastern University Press, 1993).

"Betrayed by a Buckle," *Frank Leslie's Lady's Magazine* (February 1870). Repr. in *From Jo March's Attic: Stories of Intrigue and Suspense,* ed. Madeleine B. Stern and Daniel Shealy (Boston: Northeastern University Press, 1993).

"La Belle Bayadère," *Frank Leslie's Lady's Magazine* (February 1870). Repr. in *From Jo March's Attic: Stories of Intrigue and Suspense,* ed. Madeleine B. Stern and Daniel Shealy (Boston: Northeastern University Press, 1993).

"A Modern Mephistopheles, or The Long Fatal Love Chase," manuscript of a full-length novel written in September 1866; rejected by Elliott, Thomes & Talbot; used by Alcott as a partial source for *A Modern Mephistopheles* (Boston: Roberts Brothers, 1877) and scheduled for publication in 1995. See Introduction to *A Modern Mephistopheles and Taming a Tartar,* ed. Madeleine B. Stern (New York: Praeger, 1987).